TEXAS
James A. Michener

CORGI BOOKS

TEXAS
A CORGI BOOK 0 552 13080 X

Originally published in Great Britain
by Martin Secker & Warburg Limited

PRINTING HISTORY
Secker & Warburg edition published 1985
Corgi edition published 1986
Corgi edition reissued 1987

This book is set in 10/10½pt Ehrhardt

Corgi Books are published by Transworld Publishers
Ltd., 61–63 Uxbridge Road, Ealing, London W5 5SA, in
Australia by Transworld Publishers (Aust.) Pty. Ltd.,
15–23 Helles Avenue, Moorebank, NSW 2170, and in New
Zealand by Transworld Publishers (N.Z.) Ltd., Cnr. Moselle
and Waipareira Avenues, Henderson, Auckland.

Printed and bound in Great Britain by
Cox & Wyman Ltd., Reading, Berks.

This novel is dedicated to three distinguished literary critics:

I have been informed that many books of fiction ... which are unrelated to religion ... go to the Indies [which would include what later became Texas]; since this is bad practice ... I commend you, therefore, from this time henceforth neither to permit nor allow any person at all to take any books of fiction there, but only those relating to the Christian religion and morality ... No other kind is to be allowed.

I, the Queen[1] [of Spain],
4 APRIL 1531

Another damned, thick, square book! Always scribble, scribble, scribble, Eh! Mr. Gibbon?

William Henry, Duke of Gloucester,[2]
to the author of
The Decline and Fall of the Roman Empire,
1781

Third. My will is that my sons receive solid and useful education ... I wish [them] to be early taught an utter contempt for novels ...

Sam Houston,[3]
His Last Will and Testament,
2 APRIL 1863

[1] She issued this order while the King was busy in another country.
[2] He never amounted to much.
[3] He was forced to surrender almost every good job he ever had.

James A. Michener was born in New York in 1907 and grew up in Pennsylvania. After graduating from Swarthmore College, he spent two years studying in Europe. Although he has lectured in social science for many years, been a publisher and served in the U.S. Navy, he is first and foremost a writer. His most famous novels are *Hawaii*, *The Source* and *Centennial*, and he is also the author of what many people consider the finest travel book about Spain, *Iberia*. His most recent novels are *Space* and *Poland*.

Also by James A. Michener

POLAND
THE BRIDGES AT TOKO–RI
THE BRIDGE AT ANDAU
RETURN TO PARADISE
THE FIRES OF SPRING
SPACE
CENTENNIAL
CHESAPEAKE
THE COVENANT
SAYONARA
TALES OF THE SOUTH PACIFIC
RASCALS IN PARADISE (with A. Grove Day)
THE DRIFTERS
HAWAII
THE SOURCE
MICHENER MISCELLANY
IBERIA (Volumes 1 and 2)

and published by Corgi Books

Contents

ACKNOWLEDGEMENTS

Arrangements for my thirty-month research work in Texas were made by then-Governor William Clements, who fulfilled every promise he made and to whom I am grateful. My neighbor Margaret Wilson and my landlord Jack Taylor were helpful in arranging several of the meetings listed. I wish to thank the following for enlightening me on many facets of Texas life and history:

Land: Virginia Madison, Hallie Stillwell and Professor Barton Warnock of Sul Ross University on the Alpine area. Horace Goar on the land formations of East Texas. Clayton Williams on West Texas.

Water: Water, not oil, is the lifeblood of Texas, and the Ogallala Aquifer controls the availability of water for West Texas. During many local inspections of aquifer-fed land, the following were helpful: Dr Idris Traylor of Texas Tech, on the basics; David Underwood of Lubbock and Joe Unfred, on utilization; Derrel Oliver of Muleshoe, on deep wells. Data on rainfall and climatology in general were checked against *Texas Weather*, a new book on the subject by George W. Bomar. Mr Bomar, of the Texas Department of Water Resources, Weather and Climate Section, personally provided data for the rainfall map. David Murrah, Texas Tech, helped with books.

Animals: R. P. Marshall of the King Ranch spent two fine days with me lecturing on the habits of quail, and V. W. Lehman allowed me to read the manuscript of his masterful research study; it is now a beautifully illustrated book and the authoritative work on quail. Sam Lewis of San Angelo, fastest tongue in the West, introduced me to the armadillo, and Don

English, present owner of the historic Appelt Armadillo Farm, allowed me to work with their lively stock. Professor Robin Doughty verified recent scientific data on these controversial little animals. Horace Goar taught me about wild turkeys and took me on a hunt. Bob Ramsey of Hunt showed me how to rattle up a buck and also how to make flint arrowheads in caveman style.

Cotton: Because the cultivation, ginning and utilization of this important fiber would form a leitmotif of the novel, I needed to do intensive work in three different parts of the state. Professors Ray Frisbie and Joe Knox Walker of Texas A&M, on controlling the boll weevil. The Harris Underwood family of Lubbock, on dryland cultivation. Mike McDonald, on preparing cotton for industrial use. Robert Hale of Littlefield, on milling denim.

Ranching: Ranch life is still a salient feature of Texas, and I was privileged to visit some of the best-known or most typical. Mary Lewis Kleburg and Tom Kleburg of the vast King Ranch were repeatedly hospitable. B. K. Johnson of La Pryor was instructive; I attended two of his cattle sales. Bill Blakemore showed me his large spread near Alpine; in the same vicinity D. J. Sibley and his wife, Jane, shared their fairy-tale castle atop a mountain, with the six battlement towers, one for each of the Texas flags. The Presnall Cages of Falfurrias not only let me inspect their ranch but also showed me my first mesquite flooring. At Dripping Springs, the H. C. Carters offered friendship and expertise, and the Hardy Bowmans allowed me to participate in a birthday party at their ranch. Nancy Negley of San Antonio and Las Palomas Ranch arranged a quail and turkey hunt for my instruction, and the Elizio Garcias of Encino showed me one of the oldest ranches in Texas. In Old Mexico, Charlie and Sabela Sellers of Sabinas entertained delightfully. Bill Moody and Violet Jarrett of Del Rio graciously explained their ranches, as did Mac and Eleanor McCollum of Houston. At his ranch near Brownwood, Thomas Cutbirth gave me a fine introduction to old-style barbecuing.

Exotic-game Ranching: I developed a special interest in how

Texas ranchers endeavor to preserve certain forms of wildlife that may be disappearing in other parts of the world. The famous YO Ranch of Kerrville allowed me to prowl its pastures. Veterinarian Dr Stephen Seager of A&M invited me to watch his researches in the field. Thomas Mantzell of Fort Worth had more sable antelope on his ranch than I ever saw in Africa. Lou and Wanda Waters of Utopia had a splendid ranch, and John Mecum, Jr, of Houston invited me to watch the dispersal of his huge exotic-game ranch along the Rio Grande. Dale Priour of Ingram provided technical data.

Longhorns: Charlene and Red McCombs of Johnson City invited me to their ranch for various events and also shared several hours with me on the revival of this historic breed. Jack Montgomery of Yuma, Colorado, read my segment on the Longhorn. Joan and H. C. Carter of Dripping Springs were always helpful, as was Walter Schreiner of the YO Ranch. Don and Linda Wiley of Austin took me to a chain of Longhorn ranches.

Spanish Backgrounds: So much for the land; now for the historical subject matter. On the Spanish heritage San Antonio Mayor Henry Cisneros was most helpful. Victor Neimeyer of the Institute of Latin American Studies at the University of Texas arranged for valuable contacts in Mexico, where Dr Israel Cavazos of Monterrey, and Jesus Alfonso Arreola and Javier Guerra Escandón of Saltillo offered perceptive comments. Countless consultants in both Mexico and Texas offered help of basic understanding, and the fact that I had previously written an entire book on Spanish culture speeded the discussions.

Spanish Mission Life: Dr Felix D. Almaráz, Jr, of San Antonio showed me in detail the great missions of that city. Ben Pingenot of Eagle Pass shared his unrivaled knowledge of San Juan Bautista, the mission which was so important to early settlement in Tejas. Charles Long, the lively curator of the Alamo, was repeatedly helpful in sharing with me his knowledge of that historic mission, and Gilbert R. Cruz, National Parks historian, provided additional highlights. Constant visits to the other monuments of San Antonio were necessary, the restored Governor's Palace being especially instructive.

Early American Settlement: Drew McCoy of Brazoria showed me around that crucial area. Officials of the Star of the Republic Museum at Washington-on-the-Brazos were helpful, as were custodians of other valuable collections, especially Dorman Winfrey of the Texas State Library. For a basic understanding of how the early settlers reacted to the land they were occupying, I am indebted to D. W. Meinig's excellent geographical study *Imperial Texas*. Clifton Caldwell generously presented research material.

The Trace: John S. Mohlenrich of the National Park Service was instructive regarding the history of this important road, which I traveled twice. Ranger-actors who portrayed historical characters at stops en route were much appreciated. Rita Stephens of Natchez told me much about the old days on the Mississippi.

Scottish and Scots-Irish Backgrounds: Myra and Gordon Porter of Carnoustie, Scotland, who own much of the land described in Glen Lyon shepherded me around most of northern Scotland. Ailsa and Alfred Fyffe of Cupar, classmates of mine at St Andrews in 1932, helped and edited the Scottish material.

Three Battles: Anyone writing about the Alamo finds the ground well prepared by two fine books, which do not necessarily coincide in their interpretations: *Thirteen Days to Glory* by Lon Tinkle, and *A Time to Stand* by Walter Lord. I checked with each but obviously did not follow either entirely. I spent many hours inside the Alamo, talking with all the local experts. The Daughters of the Republic of Texas Library staff proved most helpful. For my study of the tragedy at Goliad, I am indebted to Charles Faupel and Mary Jane Plumb, who live in the small town of that name. For basic data of the Battle of San Jacinto, a critical moment in Texas history, I am indebted to Dr Thomas H. Kreneck, in whose care I toured the site, and to J. P. Bryan of Houston. For Sam Houston's conduct prior to the battle, I followed a recent publication of Dr Archie P. McDonald, Stephen F. Austin State University.

Germans: Irma Goeth Guenther, granddaughter of a wonderful diarist who came to Texas from Germany in 1845, was a delightful correspondent. Clifford and Sarah Harle of Fredericksburg went far beyond the demands of hospitality to help, and Ella Gold's memories were sharp and lively. Matthew Gouger of Kerrville showed me significant sites; August Faltin of Comfort was repeatedly helpful, and the writings of Glen E. Lich of Schreiner College were most useful.

Texas Rangers: Gaines de Graffenreid, guiding genius of the Texas Ranger Hall of Fame at Waco was constantly helpful, as was his associate Alva Stem. Former Rangers Alfred Alee and Walter Russel were especially informative, the latter giving me a stout walking stick he had used in his ranging days. H. Joaquin Jackson of Uvalde was informative, and some of my best days in Texas were spent with Clayton McKinney of Alpine. For a review of Texas Ranger activities during the Mexican War, I am indebted to Dr Thomas H. Kreneck, who allowed me to read his manuscript on the subject.

South Carolina: Mary Frampton of Edisto Island was so generous in sharing with me her recollection of Edisto life that she merits special thanks. To Alan Powell of the Charleston Historical Society, I am indebted for an idea which proved most helpful in structuring the novel.

Jefferson: I spent many happy hours in this gracious old town. Mrs Lucille Bullard was my frequent hostess, and I spent a rewarding day with Wyatt Moore of Karnack, the leading authority on the days when Jefferson was in effect a seaport. Numerous Jeffersonians were helpful, especially Mrs Lucille Terry. Professor Fred Tarpley of East Texas State University allowed me to read the manuscript of his book *Jefferson: Riverport of the Southwest*, the best book on this area, and arranged several valuable local contacts.

Slavery: I did much work on this painful subject. Randolph B.

Campbell of North Texas State University allowed me to read his remarkable manuscript on how slavery operated in the Marshall/Jefferson area. It is now a fine book, *A Southern Community in Crisis*. Doris Pemberton of Houston talked to me at different times. Various librarians drew my attention to important studies. Dr James Byrd, Commerce, and Traylor Russell, Mt Pleasant, also offered their insight.

Vicksburg: This great battlefield obviously haunted me. I spent three research trips there, following the experiences of the 2nd Texas Infantry. Katherine C. Garvin provided tour help during one of the trips, and the park staff answered many of my detailed queries.

Frontier Forts: I visited in depth some dozen of these variously preserved sites. At Fort Belknap, Barbara Ledbetter, an enthusiastic local historian, helped. Throughout, Robert Wooster, working toward his PhD in Western military history, provided sensitive guidance. He is writing his own book on the subject. I also had the honor of being thrown out of Fort Davis, a US National Park and perhaps the best restored of the Texas forts. Alas, I never saw it.

Fort Garner-Larkin: To construct this imaginary fort and town, I worked with sites and scholars throughout the entire area. I visited especially all the extant courthouses of that architectural genius James Riely Gordon. At Waxahachie, I met with M. E. Singleton, a man younger than I, whose grandfather, improbable as it seems, fought at San Jacinto.

Oil: Martin Allday of Midland arranged three extensive seminars on Western oilfields, most of which I visited in detail. The following are some of the many who gave generously of their time and knowledge: J. H. Fullinwider, B. J. Pevehouse, Tom Sealy, J. C. Williamson, Ford Chapman, Patsy Yeager, Tom Fowler and Joe Hirman Moore. Don Evans took me on a field trip. John Cox was especially helpful on oil-field financing. Bill Benson of Cheyenne, Wyoming, first put me in touch with the Graham area, about which I would write, and Joe Benson and Ken Andrews explained in detail how oil-field royalties were distributed. In Livingston, Ben Ogletree arranged a unique experience. At three o'clock one morning I stood with him at a drilling site when a well came in. In appreciation of the good luck which he thought I had brought him, he named this substantial field after me.

Religion: I held many separate discussions about the role of religion in Texas, but the most informative was a three-day seminar with the scholars at Abilene Christian University: Professors Ian Fair, Richard Hughes, Bill Humble and R. L. Roberts. Gary McCaleb, public affairs officer at the university, was especially helpful. At a small rural church in McMahan, I heard the unique Sacred Harp Shaped Note singing. William N. Stokes, Jr, allowed me to see his rousing account of how his father was 'churched' for allowing members of his Sunday School class in Vernon to dance.

Football: In Abilene, I also conducted a seminar on the second Texas religion, high school football; Wally Bullington, A. E. Wells, W. L. Lawson, David Bourland and particularly Beverly Ball, who told fascinating stories about the role of girl students and women teachers. George Brazeale, high school expert for the *Austin American-Statesman*, was helpful, but my special debt is to Dave Campbell of Waco, publisher of a spectacularly successful magazine about Texas football. On the university level, Coach Darrell Royal, formerly of the University of Texas, was exemplary in his sharing of knowledge and ideas.

Border Problems: On three occasions I worked with the Border Patrol along the Rio Grande. Officers James J. Fulgham, Dennis L. Cogburn, Clifford Green and William Selzer allowed me to accompany them on patrols in the Laredo district. In El Paso, I worked with Alan E. Eliason, William G. Harrington, Dale Cozart and Raymond Reaves.

Mexican Problems: I was meeting with Isidra Vizcaya Canales, a factory manager in Monterrey, when the peso was devalued. I was serving in Mexico City as an official of the United States Government when relations between the two countries deteriorated. I conducted seminars in various parts of Texas to obtain a wide scatter of opinions. Nowhere did I find unanimity as to what might happen by the year 2010. In Corpus Christi, Dr Hector P. Garcia was most helpful, and in the same city, Tony Bonilla, president of the famous LULAC (League of United Latin American Citizens), was instructive. Yolanda and Mario Ysaguirre of Brownsville were especially gracious and arranged a field trip to Bagdad, and I profited from discussions with Paredes Manzano and Robert Vezzetti of that city.

Texas Business: In the latter chapters of this novel, writing about business and wealth became inescapable. I had the privilege of talking, sometimes at extended length, with the following experts: Trammell Crow, Vester Hughes, John Bucik and Bunker Hunt of Dallas; Gerald Hines, Walter Mischer, Sr, and George Mitchell of Houston; Clayton Williams, Bill Blakemore and John Cox of Midland. David Adickes, an artist friend from the old days in Japan, allowed me to inspect the record of his real estate dabblings, and many others in many locations talked with me about money problems, including John M. Stemmons, Louis Sklar and Larry Budner.

Honky-tonks: I enjoyed interviews with the owners of the two premier honky-tonks in Texas, Sherman Cryer of Gilley's in Pasadena, Texas, and Billy Bob Barnett of Billy Bob's in Fort Worth. Each owner was a novel in himself, each of the dance halls was overwhelming.

Rio Grande Valley: I wanted to represent adequately and honestly the unique Mexican-American world of the Valley and its citrus industry: Professor Julian Sauls of the USDA Citrus Laboratory, Les Whitlock of the Citrus Committee, Professor Dick Hoag of the Texas A&I Citrus Center and Clyde White, president of the Texas Cooperative Exchange. Former Governor Allan Shivers and his wife were especially helpful in inviting me to visit their Sharyland home near Mission, where their manager, Blaine H. Holcomb, gave valuable instruction on the citrus industry.

Miscellaneous Interviews: Robert Nesbitt, Galveston; Hayden and Annie Blake, Corpus Christi; Nelson Franklin and Dean

Cobb, Austin; Ed and Susan Auler, Tow; and Tom Moore, Lajitas. Cactus Prior and John Henry Falk, Austin, provided caustic comments.

Airplane Flights: It is obvious from the above listing that I had to visit all of Texas, not only the easy parts, and in doing so, I was dependent upon generous neighbors who allowed me to use their planes: Trammell Crow and John Blanton of Dallas; Mary Lewis Kleberg of the King Ranch; Walter Mischer, Sr, of Houston; H. C. Carter, Joe Hiram Moore and Howell Finch of Austin, the last-named flying me at very low levels over most of the western oil fields; Bill Blakemore and Robert Holt of Midland; Charles C. Butt of Corpus Christi and Presnall Cage of Falfurrias, who flew me over the sandbanks of Padre Island. I also flew with Clayton Williams on several occasions. He lent me his helicopter for two days of wild exploration in far West Texas, and Bob Macy flew me over the cotton farms of Levelland. When I told Clifford Green of Laredo that I wanted to see the Rio Grande close up from the air, he took me on an extended flight in a one-engine plane along the river at an altitude so low that I had to look almost straight up to see the top of the banks above me.

University of Texas: I enjoyed constant cooperation and scholarly assistance from many faculty members of the university. President Peter Flawn was both understanding and helpful; Dean of Graduate Studies William Livingston swiftly resolved any quandaries; Director Don Carleton of the Barker Texas History Center provided both an office and his constant support; his excellent staff found all the books I needed. Dr Lewis L. Gould, chairman of the History Department, was at all times cooperative, as was Dr L. Tuffly Ellis, director of the Texas State Historical Association, who put me in touch with many valuable contacts throughout the state. Jack McGuire of the Institute of Texan Cultures in San Antonio offered ethnic research material, and Dorman Winfrey, director of the Texas State Library, was continually helpful. John Wheat, an expert in Spanish Studies, gave valuable help when requested. Since the university has eighteen major libraries, with a total of more than five million volumes, it is a great place to work.

Texas Handbook: Any writer on Texas finds himself indebted to the *Texas Handbook*, a unique three-volume encyclopedia. A treasure trove of historical research, it is now undergoing a monumental expansion to six large volumes which will require ten years of work. It will then be indispensable to any serious student of Texas and will have no equal in any other state.

Assistants: John Kings, who had organized my office and helped on research for *Centennial,* proved once more that he is both an editor and an understanding colleague; Robert Wooster and Frank de la Teja, who are studying for their PhDs in Western history and Latin American Studies, respectively, were delightful to work with; Lisa Kaufman was most skillful in word processing and offered cogent comment; her processor was a valued loan from Kenneth Olson, president of Digital Corporation. Debbie Brothers was most adept in coordinating the final revisions. Anders Saustrup, most knowledgeable in the minutiae of Texas history, carefully vetted the manuscript. Melissa helped with the maps, which were drawn by Charles Shaw. In a most generous way, although he lived in San Antonio, T. R. Fehrenbach, author of *LONE STAR: A History of Texas and The Texans*, provided original help and insights when requested. Their interest was remarkable, generous, unprecedented in my experience, and most encouraging to a Northerner like me. Thank you all.

FACT AND FICTION

This novel strives for an honest blend of fiction and historical fact, and the reader is entitled to know which is which.

The Governor's Task Force: The Task Force is wholly fictional, as are all the participants, including the governor. At the end of each chapter the Task Force sessions are imaginary, as are the invited speakers.

I. Land of Many Lands: The three great explorations, and all their incidents, were historical. Only the boy Garcilaço de Garza is fictional. For example, Cárdenas and El Turco were real people.

II. The Mission: Santa Teresa is fictional, but the other five San Antonio missions, which can be visited today, were historical. Of the principal characters, only Juan Leal Goras was real.

III. El Camino Real: Béjar and Saltilla are historical and are accurately reported. All characters are fictional. The Veramendi family of Saltillo and Béjar was real, and very important, but the specific members shown here are fictional.

IV. The Settlers: Only Stephen F. Austin and Sam Houston were historical. Victor Ripperdá is fictional, but his famous uncle was real. The Quimper family is fictional, as is their ferry. Father Clooney and Reverend Harrison are fictional.

V. The Trace: The Macnabs and all other characters are fictional, but the Glencoe Massacre was historical. The De Leóns of Victoria had a real empresario grant.

VI. Three Men, Three Battles: Jim Bowie, Davy Crockett, William Travis, James Fannin, James Bonham, Galba Fuqua, Mirabeau Lamar and Sam Houston on the Texas side were historical, as were Santa Anna, Cós, Urrea and Filisola on the Mexican. Garza, Ripperdá, Campbell, Marr, Quimper, Garner, Harrison and the Macnabs are fictional. Descriptions of the three battles, including the blizzard north of Monclova, strive to depict historical fact. Goliad especially, one of the focal events of Texas history, is accurately portrayed.

VII. The Texians: The Allerkamps are fictional, as is their homeland Grenzler and their ship *Sea Nymph*. The founding of the Texas Rangers was historical, as were their major exploits in this chapter, specifically the expulsion of the Cherokees. Fort Sam Garner is fictional.

VIII. The Ranger: Rangers Macnab, Komax and Garner are fictional. Jack Hays was real. Henery Saxon and Colonel Cobb are fictional. Generals Taylor and Scott were real. Each of the significant actions of the Rangers was historical, but specific sites have sometimes been shifted. The murder of Ranger Allsens was real, as was the retaliation.

IX. Loyalties: Edisto Island, Social Circle and Jefferson are real; the families occupying them are fictional. Events at the siege of Vicksburg are historical, as are the various behaviors of Sam Houston. The cotton trade to Bagdad was historical, as was the now vanished Bagdad. The massacre of the Germans and the hangings along the Red River were historical.

X. The Fort: Fort Sam Garner and its military occupants are fictional. Visiting officers Sherman, Grierson, Miles, Mackenzie and Custer were historical. Chief Matark, Earnshaw Rusk and Emma Larkin are fictional, but each is based upon real prototypes. Quakers did administer the Comanche camps, but Camp Hope is fictional, as is Three Cairns. Rattlesnake Peavine is fictional.

XI. The Frontier: All citizens in Fort Garner are fictional. The architect James Riely Gordon was real, and the famous carvings on his fictional Larkin County Courthouse can be found today on his real courthouse in Waxahachie. The Parmenteer-Bates feud was fictional but it could have been modeled after any of a dozen such protracted affairs. The trail to Dodge City was historical, but R. J. Poteet is fictional. So is Alonzo Betz, but the impact of his barbed wire was historical. The destruction of Indianola happened as described.

XII. The Town: All characters are fictional, including the revivalist Elder Fry, but the church trial of Laurel Cobb is based upon a real incident whose details were provided by a son of the accused. The Larkin oil field is fictional, but its characteristics are accurate for that part of Texas. Ranger Lone Wolf Gonzaullas was real. Details regarding the Fighting Antelopes are fictional but are based upon numerous real teams of the period. Politics as practiced in Bravo and Saldaña County are fictional, but prototypes abound and some still function.

XIII. The Invaders: All characters and incidents are fictional, but the Larkin tornado is based on real and terrifying prototypes.

XIV. Power and Change: All characters and incidents are fictional, except that the summer storm of 1983 was real.

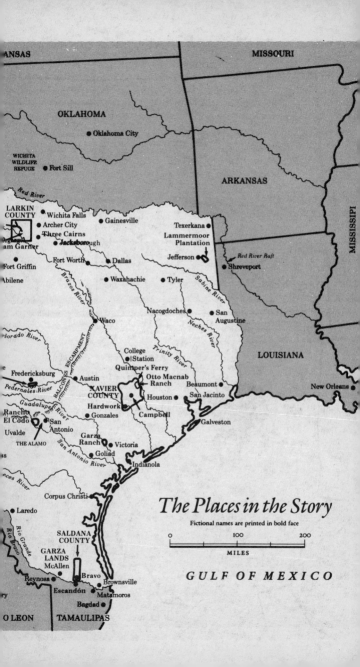

The Places in the Story

Fictional names are printed in bold face

0	100	200

MILES

GULF OF MEXICO

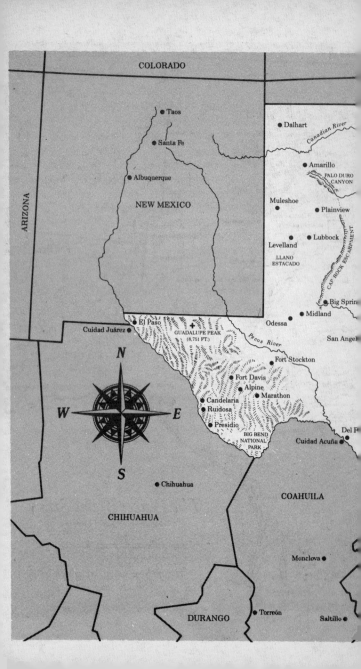

TEXAS

THE GOVERNOR'S TASK FORCE

I was surprised when shortly after New Year's Day of 1983, the Governor of Texas summoned me to his office, because I hadn't been aware that he knew I was in town. I'd been in Austin for some weeks, preparing a series of five lectures I was to deliver at the Lyndon B. Johnson School of Public Affairs at the University of Texas. The rather grandiloquent title, 'Southwest America in the World Society,' had been chosen by local scholars in a desire to broaden student horizons. The university authorities had left me pretty much to myself; I had paid a courtesy call on the president and had consulted two or three times with the dean of graduate studies, but to hear from the governor himself was something quite unexpected.

I was a native son and legal resident of Texas; however, for the past year I'd been working in Geneva on leave from my job at Boulder's well-regarded think tank, the Institute for Cultural Studies, which I headed. While serving in Boulder, I'd learned the truth of the old statement: 'When good Texans die they go to Colorado.'

I was gratified by my return to the university, for I found its students refreshing, even though some of the brightest seemed to come from up North. The best football players, however, enrolled at Texas, and that's what mattered.

I started in a low key with my students, but won their acceptance by stating in a newspaper interview: 'The students at the University of Texas may not be the best scholars in the world, but they're among the bravest. Anyone who crosses Guadalupe, the main drag by the campus, six times a day without police escort, has to be heroic.' I thought people drove crazy when I lectured at Coimbra University in Portugal, but Portuguese drivers are merely in training for the big time in Texas.

3

Confused as to why the governor might want to meet me, I left my guest office in the shadow of the main building. When I got outside I glanced up at its tower; the sight of it always set me thinking about the conflicting messages that it sent. After any university major sports victory, and they came frequently at Texas, it was illuminated gaudily in the school color, burnt orange, but on gray and misty mornings, which came less frequently, I knew that people recalled that horrible August day in 1966 when Charles Whitman, an Eagle Scout, gained a gruesome immortality. After murdering his wife and mother, he filled a footlocker with guns, ammunition and knives and drove to the university. Slaying the receptionist, he took the elevator to the top of the tower, where he unlimbered his arsenal and began shooting at random any students or casual passers-by. In all, he killed sixteen persons before sharp-shooters gunned him down. Saluting the handsome tower, I crossed the bustling campus which had so excited me when I first reported there in 1959. The university now had forty-eight thousand students, with some of the most attractive female students in America, a fact which was confirmed every time I stepped outside my office.

I walked south to Martin Luther King Boulevard and saw before me, six blocks down Congress Avenue, that majestic state capitol which had come into being in so strange a manner and with such curious results. In 1882 the state had been broke, but it lusted for the biggest possible building to adorn the biggest state, so it offered three million acres of seemingly worthless western plains to anyone who would finance the project, and some Illinois investors took the bait. Behaving as if they were honorary Texans, they euchred the government out of an extra fifty thousand acres – and everybody was happy.

How wild the turns of history! The land which the legislature gave the Illinois syndicate did seem worthless, but some comparable West Texas land they gave the university – at about the same time – turned out to be dripping with oil, which made it potentially the richest university in the world.

As soon as I entered the familiar old capitol building with its high dome and nineteenth-century dignity, I was captivated as I had been on that day long ago when I stood in the rotunda with the other children of my grade-school class to honor Sam

4

Houston and the heroes of the Alamo. Today as I passed on my way to the governor's office, a new crop of children listened, eyes aglow.

When I reached the office his secretary, beautiful and leggy, like many Texas women holding such positions of importance, said cheerily: 'So glad to have you with us, Professor. The others are waiting inside.' And with that, she pinned on my left lapel a badge which said 'Dr Travis Barlow, Institute for Cultural Studies.'

'Who are the others?' I asked, and she said: 'The governor will explain.'

She led me to an anteroom decorated with a buffalo head on the wall and two fine Longhorn hides on the floor, but the real attraction was a group of four citizens, chosen with care, apparently, as if to represent the strength and diversity of Texas. Since we were obviously to form a unit of some kind, I tried to fix in memory each face and its accompanying tag.

The first such pair belonged to a tall, thin, droop-shouldered, scowling man whose appearance alone would attract attention regardless of where he sat, but when I saw his tag I understood his real notoriety. He was Ransom Rusk, designated by both *Fortune* and *Forbes* as one of the richest men in Texas, 'net worth probably exceeding one billion.' He was in his late fifties, and from the way in which he withdrew from others, I judged that he was determined to protect both his wealth and his person from would-be intruders. Although he was dressed expensively he was not neat, and this and his permanent frown indicated that he didn't care what others thought of him.

He was talking with a man of completely different cast, a big, easy, florid fellow, also in his fifties, wearing an expensive whipcord suit of the kind favored by ranchers, high-heeled boots, and about his neck a western bolo string tie fastened with a large turquoise gemstone. When I read his tag, Lorenzo Quimper, I had to smile, for he was a legend, the prototypical Texas wheeler-dealer, owner of nine ranches, friend of presidents, dabbler in oil and everything else, and a rabid supporter of his university athletic teams. He was a handsome man, but there was something too expansive about him; if he were your small-town banker, you would not trust him with your money. Seeing me enter, he turned momentarily in my direction, smiling broadly. 'Hiya, good buddy,' he said, offering his hand. 'My name's Quimper. Welcome to the big time.' He returned instantly to his conversation with Rusk, for in his book I was worth three seconds.

The third person I turned to was a tall patrician woman in her late sixties, beautifully dressed, beautifully groomed. She had a no-nonsense mien and looked as if she were accustomed to serving on boards and making important decisions. Her tag said that she was Miss Lorena Cobb, and I recognized her as the daughter and granddaughter of two remarkable United States senators who in the years following the Civil War had made commendable contributions to Texas and the nation. She was one of those standard Texas women, overawed in their twenties by the excessive machismo of their men, but emergent in their fifties as some of the most elegant and powerful females on earth. They formed the backbone of Texas cities, persuading their wealthy husbands and friends to build hospitals and museums, then dominating the society which resulted. Women like her made those of Massachusetts and New York seem downright anemic. But the immediate impression she created was one of agreeableness. I admired her manner, even as she sat there with her hands clasped primly in her lap, for she seemed to be saying, 'Let's get on with it.'

The most interesting of the four was a small-boned man in his late thirties, about five feet five, weighing not over a hundred and fifty, with a smooth olive skin, black hair and a small, neatly trimmed mustache. His tag said 'Professor Effraín Garza, Texas A&M,' and I concluded from the accent mark in his first name that he might be a visiting scholar from Mexico. But if that was true, what was he doing here? I was about to ask questions when the door to the inner office opened and the governor himself came in to greet us. Red-headed, burly, in his middle fifties, he moved with a restrained energy that seemed to warn: 'Let's go. We haven't much time.'

'Hello! Hello! I hope you've all met.' When we indicated that we had not, he stopped and grabbed Rusk by the arm as if the billionaire were, because of his power, entitled to be introduced first: 'You've surely seen this man in the papers. Well, here he is, Ransom Rusk.' The tall man smiled bleakly, and the governor moved on.

'This rascal is the state's unofficial ambassador of good will, Lorenzo Quimper.' Newspapers had dubbed him Lorenzo il Magnifico in recollection of the flamboyant Medici prince, and there was a good deal of the Renaissance condottiere about him: lobbyist, oilman, real estate developer, wrecker of the university, builder of the university, principal cheerleader at any university athletic contest, scourge of liberal Jewish professors from the North, he had been a stormy petrel of Texas life for a generation. Hated by many, loved by others with equal intensity, he was the darling of the rough-diamond element in Texas life, their spokesman and defender. At the university baseball games, which he rarely missed, the irreverent bleachers would rise after the visiting team had batted in the fifth inning, and a tuba, a trombone and a trumpet would play a sustained flourish as a huge sign was draped across the railing: 'All Hail, Lorenzo il Magnifico! The Bottom of the Fifth.' And the leader of the undergraduate gang would hoist an immense whiskey bottle filled with some amber liquid and drain it – to the wild applause of an audience who thus toasted Quimper's remarkable capacity for booze. Now when he smiled at me radiantly, in the way a little boy would, I knew I was going to like him. Curse and even despise him at times, yes, but enjoy him.

At this moment he crossed his legs, allowing us to see the full expanse of his remarkable boots. They were light-gray leather adorned in front by large Lone Stars in silver. Above each star, as if to protect it, spread extended greenish-bronze Longhorns, while along the outer flank of each boot appeared a small Colts revolver made of burnished gold. 'Hey!' Professor Garza cried. 'Are you General Quimper?'

'It's one of my companies.'

'You make terrific boots.'

'We go for the muted understatement,' Quimper said, brushing the right Colts with his fingers. 'We call it "Texas refined."'

'And here is the star of our group,' the governor resumed, 'Miss Lorena Cobb.' He kissed her, whereupon Rusk and Quimper did the same. She held out her hand to Garza and smiled warmly. Then she shook my hand with just a little more

7

reserve, for she was not sure who I was.

'The brains of our group, and I say that enviously,' the governor continued as he reached Garza, 'Professor of Sociology, Texas A&M.'

'Did you hear the one about the meeting of the state library board?' Quimper broke in, gripping Dr Garza by the arm. 'They were doling out funds and this expert from UT said: "Why should we give A&M anything? They already have two books, and one of them isn't even colored yet."' Dr Garza, smiled wanly, like a man who had to suffer much, turned and shook my hand. I was pleased to meet him because unlike Quimper, I had great regard for A&M, in my opinion the top technical school in the Southwest.

Now the governor faced me. 'To head this group of prima donnas, I had to find someone with an international reputation. And here he is, Dr Travis Barlow, who took a distinguished doctorate at Cambridge in England. And you were an undergraduate here at Texas?'

'I was.'

'And you won a Pulitzer Prize for that book you wrote in Colorado?'

'I did.'

'Well, you're to be chairman of this Task Force.'

'Task Force on what?' Rusk asked, and the governor said: 'That's what we're here to talk about. I did not specify your duties because I wanted none of you to decline.'

When we were seated about the big table in his office he said: 'As a main feature of our sesquicentennial, I want you to place before our citizens a comprehensive report on two important questions: "How should our schoolchildren and college students learn about Texas history?" And "What should they learn?"'

'First thing they should learn,' broke in Quimper, 'is that the stupid word *sesquicentennial* means one hundred and fifty.'

'Lorenzo!' the governor retorted. 'All Texans except you speak Latin.'

'I would too, if I'd gotten past third grade,' Quimper said in the mock-illiterate style he sometimes affected.

'Is this to be just another study?' Rusk asked.

'Heavens, no!' the governor moaned, and he pointed to a

8

shelf in the corner of his office where a pile of notebooks rested. 'We've studied Texas education up to our armpits. What I seek now are specific, hard-nosed recommendations.'

'On what?' Rusk asked.

'On how to instill in our children a love for the uniqueness of Texas.'

'Doesn't that sound a little pompous?' Miss Cobb asked, and the governor said: 'On the day you become governor of this great state you realize that it really is unique . . . what a priceless heritage we've been given to protect.' I could hear bugles sounding at the Alamo.

'Como Tejas, no hay otro,' Quimper said with a bow toward Garza. 'There's no place like Texas. I tell that to all my ranch hands.'

'That's the point,' the governor said. 'The six of us know how unique we are, but the hordes drifting down from states like Michigan and Ohio, they don't know. And the equal number flooding in from below the Rio Grande, they don't know, either. If we don't take steps to preserve our heritage, we're going to lose it.'

'What exactly are we to do?' Miss Cobb asked.

'Three things. First, define the essentials of our history, the things that have made us rather more significant than the other states.' Now I could hear the band playing at some remote frontier fort in 1869 when Texas fought off the wild Comanche. 'Second, advise our educational leaders as to how they can safeguard this heritage and carry it forward. Third, I want you to hold your Task Force sessions in various parts of the state – to awaken interest, pose challenges, organize displays of Texas history, and above all, allow everyone with a special interest to have his or her say.'

'We could put together a big television show,' Quimper said enthusiastically, but no one supported him.

'As to housekeeping details,' the governor resumed, 'I have ordered that state funds be made available to pay the salaries of three graduate students to assist you. The three I've chosen happen to be relatives of state senators, but even so, I'm assured they're bright. And they're from different parts of the state. Texas Tech, Texas El Paso, and a very talented young publicity woman from SMU. You have them for the duration,

9

researching the facts, helping to organize the report. You'll also have ample funds for travel and for guest speakers. As I said before, I want you to hold each of your meetings in a different city. So that the whole state participates. And of course you'll have access to books, maps, word processors, and central office space here in the capitol building.'

At this point he stepped back to study us admiringly: 'My Task Force! You know, I served in the navy off Vietnam, and even the words thrill me. A task force, sleek ships speeding through the night. Your mission is extremely important.'

'We may be your Task Force,' Quimper said, 'but I'll bet you don't want us to fire any big guns.'

'Let's go in to lunch,' the governor said, and when we were seated he counseled us: 'Lorenzo was right. No gunfire. Make as few people unhappy as possible. Avoid the adverse headline. But snap this state to attention regarding its history.' Then, pointing his finger at Miss Cobb, he said: 'And people like you are the ones who can do it.'

During the luncheon I noticed two peculiarities. Ransom Rusk seemed to speak only to his equals, Quimper and Miss Cobb, ignoring Garza and me. And everyone said 'Miss Cobb,' except Il Magnifico, who invariably addressed her as Miss Lorena, pronouncing it with a courtly 'Miz', which she seemed to appreciate. After he had done this several times I thought that if I were going to be chairman of the group, I should participate in some of the conversation: 'Lorena's a beautiful name, Miss Cobb,' and she replied with just a touch of restraint: 'It was a cherished song in the War Between the States. Cherished by the Southern troops.'

I detected something else of considerable importance to me personally: Random Rusk and Lorenzo Quimper, as two wealthy Texans accustomed to power, expected to dominate this committee. Everything they said and did betrayed this intention, and while they were not stupid, they were in my opinion reactionary and would, if left alone, draft a right-wing document. I vowed right then that I would prevent that from happening, but how, I did not know, because they were formidable men.

Now the governor, wishing to establish our credentials, addressed each of us in turn: 'Rusk, your people arrived in

Texas when – 1870s? From Pennsylvania? Miss Cobb, your people came from the Carolinas, 1840s, wasn't it? And Quimper, you beat us all, didn't you – 1822 or thereabouts, from Tennessee? Wasn't a Quimper the Hero of San Jacinto?' Lorenzo nodded modestly.

When he came to me, it was obvious he had no knowledge of my ancestry: 'When did your people arrive, Barlow?'

But I had a real surprise for him; I smiled and said 'Moses Barlow. Arrived in Gonzales ... from nowhere known ... 24 February 1836. Three days later he volunteered for the Alamo.'

Startled, the governor leaned back, then reached out to grasp my hands: 'That Barlow? We take great pride in men like him.'

I was eager to hear Professor Garza's credentials, but the charming secretary interrupted: 'Governor, please! The deputation's been waiting twenty minutes.'

After apologies for his abrupt departure, he called back: 'Carry on, Task Force! Let's get the ships in the water.'

We spent about an hour going over basics and I was pleasantly surprised at how knowledgeable these people were. Rusk cut directly to the heart of any problem, as billionaires learn to do, which is why they're billionaires, I suppose. Quimper provided us with a constant and I must say welcome barrage of Texas observations such as: 'He jumped on that one like a duck jumpin' on a June bug,' and, 'They'll be as busy as a cow swatting flies with a bobbed tail.' Like any self-respecting Texan, he was adept in barnyard and ranching similes.

Miss Cobb was, as I had suspected, very bright and well-disciplined, and as always in such circumstances I found myself wondering why she had not married. She was, I learned before the luncheon ended, heiress to the cotton-growing fortune of the two senators, and I was assured by Quimper that 'she could of gone to Washington too, had she wanted to make the fight when Lyndon Johnson pulled that swifty in 1960. He bulldozed a change in Texas election law making it legal for him to run for both the Senate and the vice-presidency on the same day. He won both elections, then surrendered his Senate seat. Neatest trick of his career, because it carried him to the presidency.'

It was she who verbalized our problem: 'We must remind our students and ourselves that Texas is great because it boasts seven different cultural inheritances.'

'Which seven?' Rusk asked.

And now I made an amusing discovery. I had been worrying about the wrong potential dictators, Rusk and Quimper. The real danger was going to be with Miss Cobb, because although she wore the muted gray of a retiring nun, it was really a battleship-gray, and when she spoke it was with steel-like authority.

Standing before the big map in a conference room attached to the governor's office, she lectured us as if we were schoolchildren: 'I'm not speaking about regional differences. Anyone can see that Jefferson up here in the swampy northeast bears little resemblance to El Paso down here in the desert, nearly eight hundred miles away. Such physical differences are easy. Even Northern newcomers can see them. But we miss the whole meaning of Texas if we miss the cultural differences.'

'I asked before, which ones?' Rusk did not suffer vagueness, not even from his friends.

'First, Indian. They flourished here centuries before any of us arrived, but in our wisdom we exterminated them, so their influence has been minimal. Second, Spanish-Mexican, which we try to ignore. Third, those stubborn Kentucky-Tennessee settlers, originally from places like New York and Philadelphia, who built their own little Baptist and Methodist world along the Brazos River. Fourth, we latecomers from the Old South, we built a beautiful plantation life of slaves, cotton and secession. Our influence was strong and lasting, as you can hear when Lorenzo calls me "Miz." Fifth, the great secret of Texas history, the blacks, whose history we mute and whose contributions we deny. Sixth, the free-wheeling cowboy on his horse or in his Chevy pickup driving down the highway with his six-pack and gun rack. And seventh, those wonderful Germans who came here in the last century to escape oppression in Europe. Yes, and I add the Czechs and the other Europeans, too. What a wonderful contribution those groups made.'

Quimper said: 'I'd never have placed the Germans in a major category,' and she replied: 'In the early censuses they accounted for about a third of our immigrant population. My father told me: "Always remember, Lorena, it was the Germans who put us Cobbs in Washington and the Mexicans who kept us there."'

Rusk, who had been studying his fingernails during this recital, said in a deep rumble: 'I don't think the Spanish influence amounted to a hill of beans in this state,' whereupon Professor Garza said sharply: 'Then you don't know the first three hundred years of Texas history,' and Rusk was about to respond when I broke in with a conciliatory statement, but the temporary peace I achieved did not hide the fact that sooner or later we were bound to have a Rusk-Garza confrontation.

The incipient fireworks awakened Quimper's interest: 'Professor Garza, the governor was called away before he finished introducing you. How long you been in Texas?' and Garza replied without changing expression: 'About four hundred and fifty years. One of my ancestors started exploring the area in 1539.'

'I'm astounded.'

'My students are, too.'

This information was so striking that Miss Cobb reached over, and without realizing that she was being condescending, touched Garza's arm as if she were a benign Sunday School teacher and he a promising lad from the other side of the tracks: 'Who was that first Garza?'

The professor, looking at her intrusive hand as if he resented it, decided to ignore her patronizing manner and said, with what I thought was obvious pride: 'An illiterate and penniless muleteer on the Vera Cruz-Mexico run. Born 1525. And since I was born in 1945, more than four hundred years separated us. Now if you allot twenty point six years to a generation, which is not unreasonable, since Garzas usually had sons before the age of twenty-one, that means about twenty-one generations from the original to me.'

Rusk, who had whipped out a pocket calculator, corrected him: 'Twenty point twenty-nine generations,' at which Garza smiled and said: 'There were a lot of early births. But this first Garza didn't marry till he was thirty-three. We counted twenty-one generations.'

'So what's his relation to you?' Quimper asked, and Garza replied: 'My great eighteen-times grandfather.'

As we stared at the handsome young man in the silence that followed, the history of Texas seemed to recede to a shadowy period we had not visualized. But Garza had an additional surprise: 'In his later years our muleteer wrote a few notes about his early adventures . . .'

'You said he was illiterate,' Quimper broke in, and Garza agreed: 'He was. Never learned to write till he was thirty-three.'

'That's the year he married,' Rusk said, still fidgeting with his calculator. 'His wife teach him?'

'They bought themselves a tutor, a learned black slave. From Cuba.'

'You just said they were penniless,' Quimper said, for apparently nothing was going to go unchallenged in this committee, and again Garza agreed: 'He was. And how he got his wife, his money and his learning is quite a story.'

'Does it exist?' Miss Cobb asked, and Garza replied: 'In family tradition and general legend, substantiated by a few solid references in Mexican colonial history.'

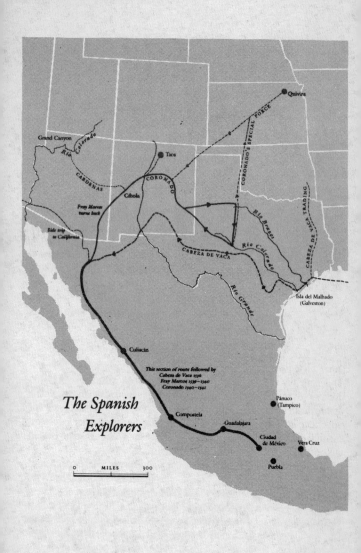

The Spanish
Explorers

Grand Canyon

Rio Colorado

CARDENAS

Fray Marcos
turns back

Side trip
to California

Taos

CORONADO

Cibola

CABEZA DE VACA

Rio Brazos

Rio Colorado

CORONADO'S SPECIAL FORCE

Quivira

CABEZA DE VACA TRADING

Rio Grande

Isla del Malhado
(Galveston)

Culiacán

This section of route followed by
Cabeza de Vaca 1536
Fray Marcos 1539–1540
Coronado 1540–1541

Pánuco
(Tampico)

Compostela

Guadalajara

Ciudad
de México

Vera Cruz

Puebla

0   MILES   300

I

LAND OF MANY LANDS

On a steamy November day in 1535 at the Mexican seaport of Vera Cruz, a sturdy boy led his mules to and from the shore where barges landed supplies from anchored cargo ships. He was Garcilaço, ten years old 'but soon to be eleven,' as he told anyone who cared to listen.

The illegitimate child of an Indian mother and a rebellious Spanish soldier who was executed before the woman gave birth, he was soon abandoned, placed in a home that was run by the local clergy, and then turned over to a rascally muleteer as soon as he was old enough to work. That occurred at age eight, and he had been working ever since.

On this hot morning he had to labor especially hard, for his master had received instructions that the mules must leave immediately for the capital, Mexico City – La Ciudad de México – more than a hundred leagues distant (one league being 2.86 miles), and whenever heavy work was required in a hurry the ill-tempered man rained blows upon the boy.

From his father, Garcilaço had inherited a build somewhat heftier than that of the average Indian; from his mother, the smooth brown skin and the black hair that cut across his forehead in a straight line reaching down almost over his eyes. And from some mysterious source he had acquired a placid disposition and an incurable optimism.

Now, as he loaded his mules with the last of their cargo and headed them toward that long and tedious trip through the lowland jungles, he consoled himself with the thought that soon he would see the majestic volcanoes of the high plateau and shortly thereafter the exciting streets of the capital. As he left the port city he hummed a song he had learned from other muleteers:

> 'Klip-klop! Klip-klop!
> There in the sky
> The great volcanoes of the plain.
> Go, mules! Speed, mules!
> For here come I
> To climb their lovely path again.'

He had memorized a dozen such songs, one for the mules when they were sick, one for dawn over the pyramids, one for a husband and wife tilling their fields of corn. Since he could not read and had no prospect of ever learning, for he was enslaved to his mules, he used his whispered songs as his bible and his dictionary:

> 'Klip-klop! Klip-klop!
> The smoke I see
> Marks where the town hides in the vale.
> Go, mules! Speed, mules!
> Be kind to me,
> And you shall find oats in your pail.'

Each trip up from Vera Cruz was a mixture of drudgery and joy, for although traversing the jungle along poorly kept trails was quite difficult, to travel beside the volcanoes and to see the capital looming in the distance was rewarding, especially since he knew that when he reached it he could count upon a few days of rest and better food. So he kept singing.

On this trip, as he approached the capital, he found his mules competing for road space with unaccustomed hordes of travelers, all going in his direction, and when he asked: 'What happens?' he was told: 'An auto-da-fé tomorrow. A great auto.'

This was exciting news, for it meant that the streets would be crowded, and that vendors of sweetmeats and tips of roasted beef would be hawking their wares. He himself would have no money to buy such luxuries, but he could rely upon convivial participants to provide him with morsels here and there. An auto in Mexico City, in the cool month of November, could be a memorable affair.

A formal auto-da-fé, act-of-faith, as conducted in Spain could be a lavish public display of the spiritual glory and temporal power of the Catholic church in its determination to

18

root out any deviation from the True Faith. It consisted of marching soldiers, military bands, a parade of clerics in four or five differently colored robes, the appearance of the bishop himself riding in a palanquin borne by four Negro slaves, and the final appearance of an executioner leading in chains the apostates who were to be burned that day. But in Mexico in these early years an auto was a much simpler affair; on this occasion, as Garcilaço learned on entering the city, two men were to be executed, but as his informant explained, their cases were quite different.

'The first man, from Puebla, has behaved properly. He's recanted his heretical behavior, pleads to die within the arms of the church and will be mercifully strangled by the executioner just before the flames are lighted.'

'Wise man,' Garcilaço said, for he remembered an occasion when an accused had refused to admit his guilt, and his death had been horrible.

'The other man, from this city, is mad with lust for his own interpretation of God's will. Refuses to recant. Says he'll welcome the flames. He'll get them!'

On the morning of the auto, crowds began to gather along the route the procession would take and, as Garcilaço had foreseen, the streets were crowded with vendors, but the greatest crush came at the public square before the cathedral, where stakes had been erected and dry brush piled beneath the little wooden platforms on which the condemned would stand.

Garcilaço found himself an advantageous spot atop a cask, from which he refused to be nudged by latecomers. Doggedly he held his ground, pushing off whoever threatened and once offering to climb down and fight a young man much bigger than he. When this fellow looked up and saw his opponent's grim determination, hair in eyes, scowl on the brown face, he desisted, left the cask, and elbowed his way to one less vehemently protected.

At noon, with the sun blazing overhead, Indian women sold in wooden cups cool potions of a refreshing drink they made from the sweet limes for which the valleys near the city were famous, and Garcilaço thirsted for his share, but since he had no coins, the women passed him by. However, a Spanish official who had purchased two cupfuls could not finish his second, and sensing the boy's desire, handed him a generous leftover. As Garcilaço gulped the drink while the vendor impatiently tapped her foot, waiting for the return of the cup, the Spaniard asked: 'You're a mestizo?' and Garcilaço, between hurried gulps, said: 'Yes, my father was Spanish.'

'How did he happen to marry . . .?'

'I never knew him. They tell me he was executed . . . before I was born.'

'Why?'

'Drink!' the vendor admonished him, and Garcilaço drained the cup.

'That was good. Thank you, sir.' The man was about to ask further questions when the boy's master ran along the edge of the crowd in the open space where spectators were not allowed.

'There you are!' he shouted when he spotted his helper, and he was about to pull Garcilaço from his cask when the Spanish gentleman gave the older muleteer a hard shove: 'Leave the boy alone.'

The master hesitated a moment, but when he saw the quality of the man who had pushed him and realized that this stranger was probably from Spain and would have a sword ready for instant use if his honor was in any way infringed, he backed away, but from a safe distance he growled at his assistant: 'Bad news! We must deliver our goods to the army in Guadalajara.' Since that city was more than a hundred and forty leagues to the west, Garcilaço knew that the journey would be a continuation of recent hardships, and that was bad enough, but now his master added: 'You must come with me now.'

This Garcilaço did not want to do, for it would mean missing the auto, but his master was insistent, whereupon the Spaniard said in a low, threatening voice: 'You, sir! Begone or I'll have at you,' and off the master went, indicating by his furious stare that he would punish his refractory helper when the auto ended.

'How lucky you are!' the Spaniard said when the man had gone. 'Guadalajara! Best city in Mexico.' And when Garcilaço asked why, the man said: 'From there you can move on to the real west, and along the road catch glimpses of the Pacific Ocean. China! The Isles of Spice!'

He had served as a government official on the western

frontier and said: 'I'd always enjoy going back. You're a lucky fellow.'

Now the real business of the auto began, with functionaries running here and there to ensure proper observances, and in the hush before the procession appeared, the Spaniard tapped Garcilaço on the shoulder and said: 'Your master, he seems a poor sort.'

'He is.'

'Why don't you run away? I did. From a miserable village in Spain where I was nothing. In Mexico, I'm a man of some importance.'

'I'd have nowhere to run,' Garcilaço said, whereupon the man grasped him by the shoulder: 'You have the world to run to, my boy. You could be the new conquistador, the mestizo who will rule this country one day.' He corrected himself: 'Who will help Spain rule it.'

'Look!' Garcilaço cried, and into the square where the kindling waited to be lit came four black slaves carrying the poles of a palanquin on which sat a prelate, dressed in deep purple and wearing an ornate miter, who stared steadfastly ahead. He was Bishop Zumárraga, most powerful churchman in Mexico and personally responsible for the arrest and sentencing of the two heretics who were to be burned. It was obvious from his stern countenance that he was not going to pardon the wretches.

'They deserve to burn,' the Spaniard muttered as the great procession made a circuit of the square, and when the executioner appeared with the condemned, it was this Spaniard who led the jeering.

The ceremony was swift and awesome. Bishop Zumárraga, from beneath his canopy, accepted the repentance of the man who was to be strangled and ignored the contempt of the man who would be burned alive. Soliciting God's approval of the punishments about to be administered, he turned the prisoners over to the secular arm of the government and left the square, followed dutifully by his priests. It would be the soldiers, not the clergy, who would actually light the fires under the heretics.

At dusk, when the flames had died, Garcilaço walked quietly to the compound where his mules waited, aware as never before of the glory of the religion he professed and of the power of

Spain. His mind was confused by a kaleidoscope of images; powerful Bishop Zumárraga's red face as he cried: 'Let the will of God be done'; the soaring chant of the priests as they marched by; imaginary Guadalajara, 'prettier than Mexico City'; and the great Pacific Ocean, 'much more magnificent than what you see at Vera Cruz.'

Most of all he remembered what that unknown Spaniard had said: 'You mestizos can do things. Run away. Accomplish something.' And his own response: 'I'm soon to be eleven,' for he was convinced that when he reached that golden age, things would be better and he would find himself more qualified to reach decisions. With these reassuring thoughts he sang a few verses and went to sleep.

At Guadalajara, which was indeed more attractive than the capital, his master received the unpleasant news that his cargo was needed by the army at Compostela, fifty leagues farther on. He was unhappy, but now Garcilaço was delighted, for the added journey would bring him closer to the Pacific, which he longed to see.

He did not reach the ocean at Compostela, for when he led his mules into that depot new orders awaited: 'Take your goods on to Culiacán, a hundred and forty leagues north. The army waits.' And it was on this leg of the journey that Garcilaço finally saw the Pacific Ocean, that grand, sleeping majesty.

'Oh!' he cried as he gazed westward. 'To sail upon that ocean! To faraway lands!' During the next nights, as he approached the end of his long journey, he could not sleep, for although he had left the ocean, he was aware that it continued to lie just off to the west, and he knew that a daring boy might leave his harsh master, run away, and somehow reach the freedom of the sea.

At Culiacán, the present frontier of the Spanish empire in Mexico, another new order awaited: 'Carry your cargo thirty leagues farther north to our military outpost up there,' and it was on the date Garcilaço had chosen as his birthday that the caravan arrived at that bleak outpost and his Christian zeal was tested, for a soldier came running with astounding news: 'Ghosts!'

Excited at the thought of seeing ghosts in daylight, everyone followed the man to the edge of the settlement, where he kept pointing north and shouting: 'Ghosts! Naked ghosts!'

Down the trail from the mountains, on foot, came four naked men, three white, one black, unlike any Garcilaço had seen before, because they had no bellies. From eating almost nothing for many months, they were perfectly flat from ribs to loins. Not a fingernail's thickness of fat showed anywhere. Their feet had soles as thick as leather; their beards were long, except for the black man, who had none; their hair was matted; but their eyes were clear and defiant, with a look that seemed to challenge: 'We have seen everything and know no fear.'

Garcilaço would always remember the first spoken words: 'What is the month and the year?'

'The twentieth day of March, in the Year of Our Lord 1536,' a soldier replied, whereupon the ghosts fell to marveling, and the one who seemed to be their leader repeated: 'March in '36!' and a look of fierce pride came across his face. 'We've been lost for seven years, and missed our calculations by only two weeks!'

When the soldier asked how this could be, he replied: 'The stars were our calendar, and we were only fourteen days in error.'

Now Garcilaço's master growled: 'What are you saying, you ghosts?' and the leader answered gravely: 'I am Cabeza de Vaca, native of Cádiz, forty-six years of age, and I have been wandering up there, in El Gran Despoblado [The Great Unpopulated],' and he pointed over his shoulder.

Clothes were thrown over the four and they were led with great excitement down to Culiacán, but in the town no one could be found who had ever heard the name Cabeza de Vaca. However, since the man spoke excellent Spanish, his interrogators had to pay attention, and he told the commander: 'I sailed from Sanlúcar de Barrameda at the mouth of the Rio Guadalquivir near Sevilla nine years ago on the seventeenth of June, 1527.'

Still no one could believe him, so a man of knowledge asked: 'On which bank of the river is Sanlúcar,' and he replied without hesitation: 'On the left bank, where they make a fine white wine.'

Another man being sent for, this one said: 'When I served in Cuba, I knew all the sailors who came to New Spain, and there

23

was never a Cabeza de Vaca, and anyway, that's a very foolish name, Head of a Cow.'

'My name is Alvar Núñez,' the ghost said with noble gravity, 'but I prefer the name Cabeza de Vaca, given in honor to my ancestor by the king, whose life he saved. This is my trusted lieutenant Andrés Dorantes, and this is Alonso del Castillo Maldonado, a very brave man, and this,' he said, touching the tall black man with affection, 'is Esteban, a doctor of medicine . . . in some ways.'

The two white men bowed low at their introductions, but the black man just did a little dance on nimble feet, smiling, showing very white teeth.

And that was the beginning of Garcilaço's real life, for these four strangers from another world traveled with him to Mexico City, and on that journey, which took many weeks, the boy heard such wondrous things that he swore to write them down some day, if ever he learned to write.

Garcilaço first experienced the noble quality of Cabeza de Vaca as the result of error on a cold, wet morning as he led his mules south toward the junction town of Compostela. The fault was his, as he admitted later, for he was listening so attentively to any words spoken by the ghosts that he allowed his mules to wander, whereupon his master started belaboring him about the head. He had struck four times when Cabeza de Vaca leaped forward, grabbed his arm, and warned: 'If you strike that lad again, I shall kill you.' From the trembling of his right hand as he restrained himself, both boy and master knew he meant what he said.

When the master retreated, Garcilaço made bold to ask his rescuer: 'Why did you do that for me?' and as they walked together at the head of the column, a little mestizo boy and a grizzled Spanish veteran, the latter told an amazing story: 'I was a slave for long years. I was beaten, and sent into the thorns to collect berries. I was abused. At night I wept from my wounds and the loss of hope. I know what slavery is, and I will not permit that man to treat you like his slave.'

'Did the pirates capture you?' Garcilaço asked, and the Spaniard replied: 'Worse. Savage Indians. Up there.'

Whenever he uttered the words *up there*, and he used them

24

often in his tales, he did so with a mixture of awe and reverence, as if he feared the vast empty spaces but also loved them.

'I sailed from my home in Spain in 1527, when I was thirty-seven. We stopped at Cuba, then explored Florida. We lost our ships, and in boats made principally from the hides of our horses, which we had eaten, we sailed west to join our friends in Mexico, but on the sixth day of November in 1528 we reached an island which we named Malhado [Galveston] where ninety-three of us beached our boat.

'Through cruel bad luck, we lost all our clothes and the boat, too, when we tried to launch it again, and while we were completely naked the hideous north wind which sometimes blows up there struck at us. Within a few days only sixteen of us were left. For the next seven years, under conditions I prefer to forget, I lived stark naked, and on more than a dozen occasions when that terrible north wind howled at me, I thought I would die, and sometimes hoped that I would.'

(No part of Cabeza de Vaca's story is more difficult to believe than this. He certainly said, repeatedly, that he was *desnudo* for seven years, and that word means *naked*. But was he naked in our sense of the word? Yes, with the qualification that his captors must have allowed him a loincloth and perhaps a deerskin to sleep under during the coldest nights.)

When the pair had become firm walking companions Garcilaço asked how he had acquired such an odd name, Head of a Cow, and he explained: 'In the year 1212 the Spanish Christians were fighting the Moors who had occupied our country for centuries, and as usual, we Spaniards were losing. But my grandfather many times back, a peasant named Alhaja, showed King Sancho how a triumph might be achieved by sneaking along an unguarded path and taking the infidel by surprise. To mark this path for the king, my grandfather crept among the Moors and placed the head of a cow at its secret entrance. Before dawn our men ran to the skull, sped along the unknown path, and won a great victory, which freed our part of Spain. That afternoon the king summoned my grandfather and said: "Kneel, peasant Alhaja. Rise, Cabeza de Vaca, gentleman of my realm."'

He then returned to the tale of his own incredible adventures: 'We few Spaniards who survived the shipwreck and the cold were divided into two groups by the Indians who captured us. Most were moved south, but I was left at the north end of the island with an aggravating man named Oviedo. In our previous travels he had shown himself to be the strongest and in many ways the ablest of our group, but in captivity his willpower dissolved. Suddenly he was afraid of everything, and although I begged him each year, from 1529 to 1532, to escape with me, he refused, preferring slavery with the Indians we knew to the risk of worse treatment from others we did not. It became apparent that he was prepared to end his days as a slave, but I was not.'

'You kept hoping?'

'You must always hope. It keeps you alive.'

One part of Cabeza's story the boy found almost unbelievable: 'We lived like this, lad. During the terrible months of winter when useless old men were encouraged to die, we ate only oysters, which were plentiful in the backwaters. During the summer months we ate only blackberries. Best of the year came when we moved inland and gorged on tunas.'

'I love tunas,' Garcilaço interrupted. 'I've eaten them many times when I was hungry. Were yours the same as ours?' Garcilaço asked, and Cabeza said: 'Yes, a cactus flat and round like a dish. And along its edges yellow flowers appear in spring. Then a man's heart leaps with joy, because each flower becomes a prickly fruit, a tuna. When it ripens to a dark red, you peel off the skins, best fruit you ever tasted. We lived on it for months.'

'That's the same,' said Garcilaço, and for a moment he felt that he had been with Cabeza 'up there.'

'In the autumn,' Cabeza continued, 'we ate only nuts of a kind not known in Spain [pecans], a wonderful food. But as the year ended, there was a gap between the end of nuts and the beginning of the oysters.'

'What did you do then?'

'Caught a few fish. Mostly we starved.'

'What did you eat with the oysters and the blackberries?'

'Lad, when I say *we ate only*, I mean just that. While I was a slave, no meat, no fowl, no vegetables, no overlapping the seasons. We ate ourselves sick on whatever we had, maybe a hundred oysters a day . . .' He paused in the middle of the road, recalling those fearful days, then said something which clarified things: 'I would eat nuts until I vomited, and if you placed a bowl before me now, I would once more feel compelled to eat them till I got sick. Because storing their rich oil in our bellies kept us alive through the weeks when there was no food.'

'Which food did you like best?' Garcilaço asked, and he was surprised at the answer: 'The oysters, but not because they were fine eating. When they came, I knew a new year had begun. Stars and oysters, they were my calendar.' Remembering his friend's joy at having his dates confirmed, Garcilaço asked: 'Why was the calendar so important?'

Now Cabeza de Vaca stepped back in amazement: 'Lad, you must always know where you are, in time and space.'

'Why?'

'If your body becomes lost, your soul is lost, and you wither. If we had not fought to keep our calendar and our distances, we would have surrendered, and died.'

'How did you know where you were? You had no maps.'

'Each night as I checked our latitude I would imagine where we would have been on the map of Africa. "Tonight we're the same as Marrakech" or "This night we sleep in Cairo." Lad, I walked clear across the continent, Florida to the Pacific, nearly seven hundred and seventy leagues, and always I knew how far we'd come.' (Florida to Culiacán, straight line east to west, about 1,750 miles; their route, about 2,000.)

'How did you tell, what you call it, latitude?'

'The stars told me how far north we were.'

When they reached Guadalajara, Garcilaço turned his mules toward the capital, and one afternoon the boy said: 'The stars seem to have told you everything,' and Cabeza de Vaca replied: 'They did.'

'Would they tell me, their slave?'

'They come out at night, ready to serve anyone. God brings them up in regular order so that we can know when to plant our crops or when, up there, to move inland for the ripening cactus.' It was during those lovely evenings as they rested that the Spanish explorer taught the little mestizo muleteer lessons he would never forget: how the constellations could be identified, the ways a farmer could use them to determine when to plant his seeds, and how a traveler could verify his location.

With each new concept mastered, Garcilaço found his

27

horizons expanding; he had been eager to see the Pacific, but once he saw it, he knew instinctively that discoveries equally great must wait on its western shore, and he began to dream of China. Now as the Spaniard told him about the wonders lying to the north – within his reach if he walked vigorously in that direction – he wanted to explore those regions too. But most of all he felt a burning desire just to know, to experience, to be a heroic man like Cabeza de Vaca. Garcilaço had stumbled upon one of the greatest treasures a boy can find: a man of dignity whom he would like to emulate.

They had reached a point well east of Guadalajara, in the month of June, when Cabeza de Vaca surprised him by speaking of years when he traveled alone as a trader for a different tribe of Indians. 'But, Señor Cabeza,' the boy said, and the proud Spaniard corrected him: 'My name is Cabeza de Vaca, three words, and I prefer to be so addressed.'

'I am sorry, Señor Cabeza. I meant no offense,' and the great traveler smiled: 'Since you have just turned eleven, as you inform me, you may call me Cabeza. Now, what was your question?'

'Well, if you were a slave, how could you also be free to wander about?' and Cabeza said: 'I left Oviedo, escaped from the dreadful Indians on the island and sought refuge with other kinder souls who live inland.'

'But you were still a slave?' Garcilaço asked, and in reply Cabeza de Vaca related an improbable story.

'After I had shown that I was skilled at trading the seashells my tribe collected in exchange for arrowheads made by other tribes, my Indians encouraged me to travel in search of things they needed, and in this way I went far to the north [Oklahoma], where I saw the remarkable cattle of the Indians, much larger than ours, hairy, with a big hump forward. Sometimes I would see a thousand or ten thousand, so numerous were they, and they provided those Indians with robes to wear, and I also had a chance to taste their meat, which surpassed any roasted in Spain. But you know, lad, men are often imprisoned by chains of their own forging. Living with my kind Indians, I was happy with my freedom, but I could not forget that Oviedo was still a captive. I had to go back.'

'Why?'

'Honor.' He strode ahead in silence, then waited for the boy to overtake him. 'Pitiful though Oviedo was, he remained my only link with civilization.'

Two days later, as they neared the capital, Cabeza's spirits brightened and he spoke with animation: 'In 1532, I finally persuaded Oviedo to escape with me from the island, no mean feat, since the big, hulking man could not swim and I had to coax him through the waves. Once ashore, we learned from passing Indians that three other strangers lived with a tribe to the south, and we were overjoyed, but when these Indians turned ugly, tormenting us with sticks, poor Oviedo grew utterly frightened and begged some women to help him swim back to that horrible island. We never heard of him again, the biggest and strongest of our group. He was afraid of his own destiny.'

This mournful memory silenced Cabeza for the rest of the day, but next morning he was eager to talk again: 'You can imagine how excited I was when I found that those three men were my shipmates. We exchanged stories, learning that of the ninety-three who had landed, only we four and poor Oviedo had survived. Urgently we made plans to escape and walk to Mexico, but our Indian masters became engaged in a great fight over a woman, so we Spaniards were separated for the rest of that year, with never a chance of breaking for freedom.'

'You must have been miserable,' Garcilaço said, and Cabeza replied: 'Yes, miserable, but at tuna-time in 1534 we met again among the cactus plants, and everything was now perfect for our escape, so we four set out . . . no clothes, no food, no maps, no shoes.'

'Señor Cabeza, how could you be so brave?'

He did not answer that day, but on the next he sought the boy, as if he were hungry to share his wild experiences: 'In the first days of our escape we encountered disaster. I, always eager to explore, searched widely for anything edible and became hopelessly lost. And because this was the time of year when the great north winds began to blow, the others had to think of protecting themselves. They left me, and since I was now totally alone, it seemed that I must perish.'

'How did you meet the others again?' Garcilaço asked, and Cabeza allowed pride to creep into his voice. Standing taller, his slim body etched against the sky, he said: 'I determined not to die. Moving in great circles, I quartered the barren land until at last I came upon their tracks, and when I overtook them, they said: "We thought that perhaps you'd been bitten by a snake." I said nothing, but I would never have abandoned one of them had they become lost.'

Dorantes and the other two survivors seldom joined in Cabeza de Vaca's discussions with Garcilaço; they were from one group, Cabeza from another, and by habit they maintained that division. So Garcilaço did not see much of Esteban, but when they did talk, he liked him, for the man's dark face glowed when he spoke of his adventures. Once Garcilaço asked: 'Are you a slave like we get from Africa, or are you a Moor, whatever that is?' and he replied: 'I am many things.'

'You seem to have many names, too.'

The slave laughed: 'You noticed? Dorantes calls me Estevan. Castillo calls me Estevánico. Others called me Estebanico. Cabeza calls me Esteban.'

'What do you call yourself?'

'Doctor of medicine.'

When Garcilaço asked Cabeza about this, the latter chuckled: 'Esteban kept us alive not with his medicine but with his humor. He was a slave, bought and paid for by Dorantes, but on our travels he was free – free to laugh and to be our ambassador to the Indians.'

The amazing thing Cabeza said next explained how these four defenseless men had been able to traverse the vast area later to be called Texas. Indeed, they traveled so widely that they even came into contact with the Teyas, or Tejas, Indians, the Friendly Ones for whom the entire vast area would one day be named: 'When we were in the country of hills, Alonzo del Castillo who is a cultured gentleman from the university town of Salamanca, discovered that he had magical or religious power. Whatever it was, he could cure sick Indians by touching them and assuring them that God in His mercy would make them well. His first patients must have had simple illnesses, for his gentle care cured them, and his fame quickly spread across this desolate land, inspiring Indians to come to him from far distances.'

Cabeza said that many villagers began to travel with the

wonder-workers, sometimes wandering sixty or seventy miles and wailing piteously when they could no longer keep up with the Spaniards. 'Such misguided faith made Castillo afraid that he was trespassing on powers reserved for God and he refused to treat patients who were obviously dying and for whom he could do no good. Not me, for I realized that our power to heal could prove our passport to freedom.

'One morning as we approached a new village, weeping women took me to a man obviously near death. His eyes were upturned. He had no heartbeat. All signs of life were gone. Thinking to make his last moments as easy as possible, I placed him upon a clean mat and prayed to Our Lord to give him peace.

'Late that afternoon the Indian women ran to us, weeping and laughing and cheering, for the dead man had risen from his mat, had walked about and called for food. This caused enormous surprise, and all across the land nothing else was spoken of. In following days Indians came to us from many places, dancing and singing and praising us as true children of the sun.'

Cabeza then said a revealing thing, which at the time Garcilaço could not comprehend: 'When the Indians made a god of me, I behaved like Castillo. I did not want such idolatry, because I knew I was not worthy of it. Any cures I had effected were due to God's intervention, not mine, and I refused to mislead pagan Indians into thinking otherwise. But as captain of our expedition, I needed the assistance our miracles provided, and it was in this cast of mind that we three white men decided that Esteban should be the doctor, since he had no such religious reservations. No man ever accepted promotion with more delight or followed it with finer accomplishment.'

He called for Esteban, who confirmed all that Cabeza had said: 'I started life as a slave in Morocco. I was sold to Dorantes in Spain, and in Cuba and Florida and among the Indians, I was still a slave. I was unhappy, because I knew that with my tricks, I could be a fine doctor.' He smiled at Cabeza as he said this. 'So from the Indians I got myself a pair of rattling gourds, some turkey feathers, woven hair from one of the big humped hides, and announced myself as a healer.'

'He was marvelous,' Cabeza said. 'When we approached a

new village, we allowed him to go first, dancing and leaping and singing Indian songs. Shaking his gourds, shouting incantations, his white teeth flashing, he cured old women and won the hearts of sick children with his radiant smile. Since women loved him, he accumulated a harem of first a dozen, then dozens, and, finally, more than a hundred who trailed him from one camp to the next.'

Esteban affirmed everything and added: 'I liked the women, indeed I did, but I also knew we needed food. So I would not let them come with me unless they brought us real food, not oysters and blackberries. We four lived on my dancing.'

'Would you show me your dance?' Garcilaço asked, and he said: 'I can't do it without my gourds,' so the boy ran to fetch them, but when his master saw him quit his mules, he struck him sharply across the head. When Esteban saw this, he leaped in the air, then rushed at the master to restrain him: 'He is not your slave!' The master glared at the big black man: 'But you are a slave, you damn Moor,' he said, and spat.

As soon as Garcilaço produced the gourds, Esteban forgot his anger, and with a rattle in each hand he began taking short, mincing steps in the dust, at first shuffling rather than dancing, but quickly becoming more agitated. His eyes flashed. His grin widened. His arms flapped wildly, and soon he was leaping in the air, assuming wild and grotesque contortions. Laughing like a joyous spirit, he danced until all the carters in the cavalcade stopped to watch and then applaud. To see Esteban dance was to see the earth smile.

Always when Cabeza spoke of his adventures in the north, he referred in some manner to the look of the land in which an incident had occurred, and it was during such a narration that he happened to use a phrase which determined the character of Garcilaço's subsequent life.

'Señor Cabeza, you speak of the land, but when you do, you describe many different lands,' and the explorer laughed: 'You're an observant little fellow. I enjoy traveling with you.' He said that, yes, he did speak of many different lands; that was the glory of up there.

'Along the coast where I first stayed, there were beautiful sand dunes and marshes filled with birds. Inland, a waving sea of grass with rarely a tree. Farther to the west where we gathered nuts, rolling crests and clusters of oak more beautiful than any I saw in Spain. Then hills, cut through with little rivers, and after them the vast empty plains, flat as tables and sometimes void even of cactus. Finally more hills, the mountains and the desert.'

He closed his eyes, as if he were praying. 'I can see it all, lad. The years were cruel, of that there can be no doubt, but they were also glorious, and if you ever find a chance to go up there,' and here came the words that fired the boy's imagination, 'you too will see the land of many lands.'

As soon as Garcilaço heard that happy phrase, 'the land of many lands,' he was captured by the lure of the north. The Pacific Ocean was forgotten; anyone could build himself a ship and sail on it, Garcilaço thought, but the challenge of those limitless plains, the ferocious winds, the grandeur of an earth that seemed infinite in its variations – these wonders he wanted to see. From this day on he entertained only one vision: to visit that land of many lands.

When Cabeza resumed his narrative about their travels far to the west (into New Mexico, but not as far north as Santa Fe), he said: 'One night while we three white men talked idly with some of Esteban's women, one of them used a phrase which caught my attention: "Fifteen days to the north, the Seven Cities. My mother saw them when she was a girl." That night I could not sleep, because even as a child I had heard vague talk about holy men who had fled Spain and built the fabled Seven Cities of Cíbola. I knew no more of the legend except that these cities held much gold. So very quietly, using signs and the few words we had, I began asking Indian men about the Seven Cities, and they confirmed what the woman had said: "Yes, yes! That one, he saw the Cities." The Indian thus indicated said he had not actually been to the Cities, but he knew a man who had, and this man had spoken of them with awe: "Very big. One, two, three, four, up, up to the sky."

'I asked if he meant that one level of the house stood upon the other, as in Spain, and the man said eagerly: "Yes! My friend said so. Up to the sky!" whereupon I asked if there had been great wealth there, and this question the Indian did not comprehend, for I carried nothing with which to illustrate what I meant, but the Indian liked us so much that he wanted to

33

please, so he talked with his friends, and even though he did not understand my words, he nodded vigorously: "Yes, just as you say."

'"And what is the name of these Seven Cities?" I asked, but the man did not know, nor did anyone, but I believed there was a chance that I had found those cities of sacred legend.' As Cabeza uttered these provocative words he fell silent, and it was then that Garcilaço enlarged his dream to include the finding of those cities clothed in gold.

When Cabeza next talked with Garcilaço he was serious and almost mystical: 'When it happened, after those years of slavery and wandering and storms, it excited us almost to the point of frenzy. One morning Castillo saw, on the neck of an Indian, a little buckle from a swordbelt, and in it was sewed a horseshoe nail. We took it from the Indian and asked what it was. He said it had come from heaven, but when we asked who had brought it, he answered that some men, with beards like ours, had come from heaven to that river; that they rode on animals like very large deer; carried lances and swords; and that they had lanced two Indians.

'As cautiously as possible, we then inquired what had become of those men, and they replied that they had gone to the sea, putting their lances into the water and moving them, and that afterward they saw men on top of the waves heading toward the sunset. We gave God our Lord many thanks for what we had heard, for we had been despairing to ever hear of Christians again.'

During the last days of the journey, Cabeza took an extraordinary interest in Garcilaço, and one morning he cradled the boy's face in his weathered hands and looked deep into his eyes: 'Lad, you were not meant to be a muleteer. But to accomplish anything, you must learn to read and write.' And with an almost furious determination, he taught the lad, as they walked with the mules, the alphabet, and when they stopped to rest he would draw the letters in the ground with a stick.

Cabeza was also eager to share his specific knowledge of the land he had traversed, as if he were afraid that valuable learning might be lost. He described the many Indian tribes, taught Garcilaço some of the phrases they spoke, said that dog was good to eat, and warned of the many dangers the boy would

34

encounter if he ever went up there.

The night before the two parted company, Cabeza grasped Garcilaço's hands and said: 'Lad, if ever the chance arrives, go up there, because that's where fame and fortune will be found – in the fabled Seven Cities of Cíbola.'

On the day after the arrival of the mule team in the capital, it was reloaded and back on the trail to Vera Cruz, so that Garcilaço saw Cabeza no more, but many years later, when he was hauling freight to Guadalajara, an army captain said: 'I knew Cabeza de Vaca in Paraguay. Yes, when he returned to Spain he sought the governorship of Florida, but learned to his great disappointment that this plum had already been awarded his fellow explorer Hernando de Soto, and he had to settle for a miserable post in Paraguay.'

'Did he succeed in that job?' Garcilaço asked, and the man said: 'Oh, no! They nibbled at him, brought infamous charges against him, and I think he left the country in chains. I knew he was in jail for seven years in Spain. My sister-in-law's brother knew him.'

'What happened?' Garcilaço asked, and the captain said: 'I saw him in Africa when I served there. Banished, he was, a man who walked alone, talking with the stars. Years later the emperor came to his senses, brought this honorable man back to court, and paid him a yearly stipend which enabled him to live in relative comfort.'

At age sixty-five, Cabeza de Vaca, the first white man to have journeyed into Texas and across its vast plains, died. Texas, a state which would always honor the brave, had its first true hero.

The miracle of perfect wisdom and sage decision which Garcilaço had expected at age eleven did not materialize; nor at twelve, either. For some days after Cabeza de Vaca's departure the boy wept softly when he went to bed, and for many weeks he recited the alphabet while trudging along with his mules. But one day, when the master caught him looking at the few pages Cabeza had given him, he grabbed them in a rage and tore them up: 'You have no business with learning. Your life is with the mules.' But the master could not take away the boy's knowledge of the stars, and when Orion rose, Garcilaço could see the figure

35

of Cabeza among those brilliant dots of light.

For two long and miserable years he led his mules past the volcanoes, whose charm had fled, and he was supported only by the memory of his brief friendship with Cabeza, foremost of the king's gentlemen, and the hope the latter imparted that day when he took the boy's face in his hands and said: 'Lad, you were not meant to be a muleteer.'

As the hot and sultry summer faded in 1538, Garcilaço, age thirteen, was once more journeying toward Vera Cruz, having accomplished nothing that would release him from his virtual slavery. When the mules reached the outskirts of that teeming seaport where the vessels from Spain waited to be unloaded, he felt sick at heart. All he had achieved was learning the alphabet, but he lacked any prospect of ever owning his own mules.

In this cast of mind he came down the narrow, dirty streets to where the cargo waited, and he was dreaming of Cabeza's clear, open lands up there when he heard a deep-throated cry and felt across his back a blow from a walking stick.

'Watch where your mules go, fellow!' a man called out, and when Garcilaço recovered his senses he saw that the speaker was a friar of more than medium height and well past forty. He spoke with an accent the boy had not heard before, but he was more smiling than angry. When he realized that he had struck a mere lad, he apologized, and for some minutes the two talked in the narrow street.

'I am sorry, boy. Did it hurt?'

'My master gives me worse each day.'

'He must be a cruel man,' and when Garcilaço said that he surely was, the friar became solicitous and asked: 'Are you his son?' Garcilaço replied: 'I never knew my father,' and this became the foundation of their friendship.

He was Fray Marcos, who had recently come to Mexico after service in two lands about which Garcilaço had vaguely heard: Peru, which the friar loved, and Guatemala, which he held in contempt. In Peru he had composed, he claimed, a diatribe against the cruelty with which Spanish conquistadores treated their Indians, and he did not propose to allow such wrong in Mexico. He had arrived only recently and now asked Garcilaço's master if he could accompany the mule train to the capital, from where he would find his way to the great

36

monastery being built at Querétaro, to which he had been assigned. Surly as ever, Garcilaço's master agreed.

As they climbed through the jungles leading to the volcanoes, Garcilaço was impressed by the vigor of the friar's stride; it seemed the mules would tire before Marcos did. His conversation was pleasing, too, for in all he said he displayed enthusiasm: 'Some day a poet will write of our adventures in Peru! Gold everywhere! Majestic mountains! Spanish heroism never before excelled!' He spoke in exclamations, and Garcilaço noticed the way he ended each statement in a rising voice, as if eager to get on to the next wonder. When Marcos saw the great volcanoes he fell silent, captured by awe, and it was some moments before he could speak. When he did, a torrent of words leaped from his lips, and Garcilaço could imagine him back in Peru, reporting on what he had seen in Mexico: 'Such towering volcanoes! So perfect in design!'

It took twenty-nine days to drag the cargo from Vera Cruz to the capital, and during that time Garcilaço told Fray Marcos about his friendship with Cabeza, and when the friar learned that the boy knew his letters, he said: 'You must continue. Learn to read well and you can become a friar, like me, and know a life of adventure.'

When Garcilaço asked him where his home had been, he answered: 'My real name is Marcos de Niza, for I was born in that city which some call Nice. It pertained to Savoy, so I was like you, a nothing, perhaps Savoyard, perhaps French, perhaps Italian. But I fell in with the Spaniards and was saved.'

During the concluding days of the journey he showed Garcilaço his Latin Bible, to see if the boy really could pick out his letters, and the speed with which Garcilaço resumed his mastery of the alphabet, even though he could not understand the words, delighted the friar so much that one evening he went to the master and said: 'I should like to buy the boy.' The ugly man said: 'He's not for sale,' but since he was always eager to swing a good bargain, he added: 'How much would you offer?' So for two pieces of gold brought from Peru, Garcilaço became the responsibility of Fray Marcos, who said as he led him away: 'You shall call me Father, both for my religious position and because I love you and will educate you.'

They had been in Mexico City only two days when a

37

detachment of soldiers came to the monastery where they slept: 'You're both to come with us. Bishop Zumárraga wants to interrogate you.' Garcilaço, remembering the austere figure sitting in his palanquin, started to tremble and then to sweat, for in a swift series of images he could see himself being questioned, condemned, and led to the pyre during some tremendous auto-da-fé. Quaking with fear, he asked the friar: 'What have we done?'

To his surprise, Fray Marcos was completely at ease, even smiling: 'In Peru and in Guatemala, I received many such imperative orders. They usually mean some good thing's about to happen. Let's see what it is this time.'

But when they were marched like prisoners through the streets, Garcilaço kept looking at the passers-by and at the patches of sky as if this were the last time he would see either. However, when they were delivered to Bishop Zumárraga they found a kindly man, dressed in the informal working robes of the Franciscan order, who said, as if he were their uncle: 'Sit down. Take refreshment if you wish. We've important matters to discuss.' With that he rang a small silver bell, whereupon Indian servants appeared, bringing with them a man Garcilaço remembered well and loved. It was Esteban, the Moor.

'I have a new master, Little Muleteer.'

'And I have a new father, Big Dancer.'

'What happens here?' the smiling bishop asked, and he was told that Andrés Dorantes, one of the travelers across El Gran Despoblado who had owned the slave Esteban, had sold him to the viceroy for reasons not clearly understood, while Garcilaço's master had sold him to Fray Marcos for reasons left unexplained.

'So you two know each other?' the bishop asked. 'That's good. You can tell your stories to the viceroy.'

But before they were taken to that austere master of Mexico, Bishop Zumárraga wanted to satisfy himself on one point, and to do this he asked Garcilaço to stand before him and submit to questioning: 'Boy, you traveled with Cabeza de Vaca?'

'I did.'

'And he spoke with you constantly, they tell me.'

'Yes.'

'And did he ever speak of the Seven Cities?' At this point the

38

Moor shot Garcilaço a warning side glance, but to what purpose the boy could not determine, so he answered honestly: 'He spoke of them often.'

Before Zumárraga could question further, Esteban broke in with the start of the great deceit which would engulf many men and color the early history of Texas: 'Excellency, I saw the Seven Cities. They were glorious, and Cabeza de Vaca saw them, too.'

When Garcilaço heard this lie he remembered the honest voice of Cabeza as they had talked on the way to Guadalajara: 'Lad, understand. This Indian woman, she had never seen the cities, her mother claimed that *she* saw them. Nor had the Indian man ever seen them, a friend had reported that *he* had seen them. And certainly none of us Spaniards had come close to seeing them.'

But it was obvious that Bishop Zumárraga wanted to believe that everyone had seen them: 'So Cabeza de Vaca, wily man that he was, kept the secret of their wealth to himself?' As this question was asked, Garcilaço could see Esteban smelling out the situation and identifying what those in authority wanted to hear, so in response to sharp questioning, the Moor divulged these supposed facts: 'The Cities have enormous wealth, the Indians assured us. When I asked about gold and silver, they cried "Yes!" Jewels, cloth, cows twice as big and fat as ours. Cabeza himself saw them, didn't he?' When everyone looked at Garcilaço, the boy had to nod, for this one small part of the statement was true. Cabeza had told him of the large cows with humps over their shoulders.

'Let us speak with the viceroy,' Zumárraga said as he called for his carriage, and off they hurried to meet the man who ruled Mexico.

Few men in history have looked more imperial than Don Antonio de Mendoza, Count of Tendilla, did that day. He was tall and properly lean; his mustache and beard had been neatly trimmed that morning by the barber who visited him each day, and when he looked at his visitors he seemed to regard everyone but the bishop as a peasant. He had sharp eyes which penetrated nonsense and a deep, resounding voice accustomed to command. He was keenly interested in everything relating to New Spain, and even before his visitors were seated he plunged into discussion: 'Tell me, Bishop, what facts do we know about the Seven Cities?' and Zumárraga replied:

'Some say it was in AD 714 when Don Rodrigo of Spain lost his kingdom to the Muhammadans, but others with better cause say it was in 1150, in the reverent Spanish city of Mérida. In either case, seven devout bishops, refusing to obey the infidel Moors who had conquered their city, fled across the ocean, and each bishop established his own powerful city. We've had many reports of the riches those good men accumulated and the wonders they performed, but we've not known exactly where they went. Many have searched for them, and I've even heard it claimed that the Italian Cristóbal Colón was seeking the Seven Cities when he discovered our New World. All we know for certain is that the Seven Cities are grouped together.'

The viceroy pursed his lips, reflecting on what the clergyman had said. Then he asked bluntly: 'Do you believe the Cities exist?'

'Of a certainty.'

'Ah, but do they? Dorantes left a deposition which I read again only yesterday. He said he had met no one, not a single soul, who had actually seen them or known anyone who had.'

For some moments that November day no one spoke, and finally Bishop Zumárraga uttered words which summarized reasonable thought on the matter: 'God never works accidentally. It stands to Holy reason that if He placed Peru far down here, with its golden treasury, and Mexico here in the middle, with its wealth of silver, he must have balanced these two with some great kingdom up here. The Rule of Three, the rule of Christian balance, requires the Seven Cities to be where Cabeza de Vaca's Indians said they were. Excellency, it is our Christian duty to find them, especially since the seven bishops probably converted the area, which means that Christians may be there awaiting union with the Holy Mother Church in Rome.'

'My view exactly!' Fray Marcos cried, with the enthusiasm he always showed, after he, like Esteban, had decided what his superiors wanted to hear, but the viceroy made a more sober comment: 'If we sent a conquistador north to the Seven Cities to bring them back into the fold of the church, who will pay the vast expense? Not the emperor in Madrid. He never risks a maravedí of his own money. I pay, from my own fortune and my wife's, and before I do that I want reasonable assurance of success.'

Suddenly his manner changed, his voice brightened, and he asked: 'What have you heard about this young nobleman Francisco Vásquez de Coronado?' and the bishop said quickly: 'He could lead your expedition. And he could help with the costs.'

'But we must not mount a great expedition – all those men and horses – before the region has been properly scouted.'

'That's why I sought this audience,' Bishop Zumárraga said, and with a bold sweep of his arm he indicated that Marcos, Esteban and Garcilaço were to leave the room.

As soon as only he and Mendoza were together, the bishop said: 'By the greatest good fortune, that friar who just left us is an excellent man with wide experience in the conquest of Peru. I find him a man of prudence and one to be trusted.'

When the viceroy asked if there was aught in the friar's history to be held against him, the bishop replied: 'I would be less than honest with you, Excellency, if I did not also share with you his three weaknesses. First, he has been in Mexico only briefly. Second, he is extremely ambitious, but are not, also, you and I? I cannot hold this a disqualifying fault. Third, he is not a Spaniard, but then, most of our emperor's subjects are Austrians, Lowlanders or Italians. The emperor himself is a German, or, if you wish, an Austrian.'

When the viceroy showed signs of accepting the friar, the bishop seemed eager to disclose even the smallest weakness lest he later be called to account: 'The final point, Excellency, is a delicate one. The boy you saw with him, this Garcilaço, stays by his side constantly, and who he is I cannot say for certain. Some claim he accompanied Marcos from Peru, and these insist that Garcilaço is his son. Others say he was acquired in Guatemala, in which case the boy must have been eight or nine when Marcos got him. Such suppositions are foolish, for we know he was already in Mexico traveling with Cabeza de Vaca. Others, with the better argument, I feel, say that the boy was an alley rat in the sewers of Vera Cruz when Marcos rescued him. You've seen the lad and he seems to show promise.'

'I think we had better question the friar and his boy more closely,' the viceroy said.

Garcilaço would always remember how proud he was of his father that day as the two faced Mendoza and Zumárraga. Marcos wore a voluminous robe made of the heavy fabric favored by the Franciscans, who were often called in the streets of the city 'Christ's little gray chickens,' a phrase he did not find amusing. He was obviously a serious man, and if upon first appearance he had any defect, it was his piercing gaze which revealed him to be a fanatical believer, though what he believed in – the mystery of Christianity or his own destiny – no one could guess.

'Are you a Spaniard?' Mendoza asked bluntly.

'I'm a servant of Christ, and of the emperor, and of you, Viceroy, should you employ me.'

'But you were born in France, they say.'

'No, Excellency. In the city of Nice.'

'So you're a Savoyard?'

'No, Excellency, I'm Spanish. Through service to my church and emperor, I've made myself so.'

'Those are good words, Fray. Now tell me, who exactly is this lad who stands beside you?'

'I was ordered to bring him, Excellency.'

'Indeed you were,' Zumárraga broke in. 'Now explain.'

In the moment of silence which followed this abrupt command, all in the room looked at Garcilaço, and they saw the mystery in the boy. He was one of the first of Mexico's mestizo children, half Spanish, half Indian, that durable breed which even then seemed destined to take over Mexico and remote Spanish territories like the future Texas. In the audience room that day Garcilaço represented the future, a first ripple in the tremendous flood that would one day remake this land.

The boy heard Fray Marcos speaking: 'I have worked in lonely places, Excellencies, and one morning as I stepped off a boat in Vera Cruz, I saw this child here, a lost soul, no parents, no home . . .' He said no more.

'Who were your parents, son?'

Garcilaço shrugged his shoulders, not insolently but in honest ignorance: 'Excellency, here I am, just as I stand.'

For the first time the viceroy smiled. He then turned to Fray Marcos: 'If I gave you Esteban as your guide, could you scout the Seven Cities and then give some would-be conquistador, Coronado for example, instructions as to how to reach them?'

'I would be honored,' Marcos said with no hesitation, and so it was agreed, but after Bishop Zumárraga had taken his charges, and Esteban, from the hall, the viceroy mused:

Who are these strangers who just left my office? Is the friar a faithful Catholic or has he been corrupted by modern ideas? Why should Spain put its trust in such an unknown? And this Esteban, what is he? Dorantes when he sold him assured me he was a Moor. But what's a Moor? The Moors I knew were not black. They were white men bronzed by the sun. Look at him. He's not black. He's brown. And what religion is he, pray tell me that? He was born a Muslim, like all Moors. When did he become a Christian? And how sincerely? And what of the boy? Is he the first of the mestizos who will be seeking power? Spain! Spain! Our emperor is a German. His Spanish mother who should be reigning is insane. And look at me, sending out an untested friar to find the new Peru, and a man of doubtful allegiance to be his guide. Where will it all end?

In order to ensure that at least one verifiable Spaniard participated in this critical venture, Mendoza asked Bishop Zumárraga to nominate as second-in-command a younger friar with impeccable credentials, and the cleric selected a Franciscan in whom he had great faith, Fray Honorato. Mendoza was delighted: 'The Spaniard can keep an eye on the Frenchman, and both can keep an eye on the Moor.'

But this canny safeguard did not work, because when the entourage was only a few days north of Culiacán, Honorato reported a slight indisposition: 'I don't feel well. Nothing, really, but . . .' With remarkable speed Fray Marcos bundled him up and sent him posting back to the capital. He was now in sole charge and intended to stay so.

But there was in the entourage a man just as ambitious as Marcos and even more flamboyant – Esteban, who, since he was the only one who had ever seen the north, now had to be promoted to second-in-command. Younger than Marcos, he matched him in brain power, and was vastly superior in knowledge of terrain and ability to work with Indians. He could speak in signs with many tribes, but more important, he displayed an exuberance which delighted the people of the villages through which the little army passed, and many who saw him shouted greetings, for they still remembered the magician who could heal.

When it came time to depart a village, more women would insist upon accompanying Esteban, so that his harem increased constantly. He had the capacity of being able to keep his many camp followers happy, and at one time nearly a hundred trailed along, singing with him, hunting food for him, and crowding his tent at night.

Fray Marcos was perplexed. He needed Esteban as guide; he resented him as competitor; and he deplored him for his immorality with women; but he could not even begin to know what to do with him. With no fellow friar to consult, all he could do was brood enviously as he watched Esteban preempt more and more of the leadership. It was becoming Esteban's expedition, and the Spanish soldiers recognized this.

'You must do something about the blackamoor,' they warned, but Marcos could not decide what.

However, sixteen days of this rich fol-de-rol was all he could stand, so on Passion Sunday, 23 March 1539, he proposed that Esteban should push on to scout the country through which the larger body of explorers would later pass. Since the black man could neither read nor write, an extraordinary convention was arranged, as Marcos would explain in the report he sent back to Mexico:

I agree with Esteban that if he received any information of a rich, peopled land, he should not go farther, but that he return in person or send me Indians with this signal, which we arranged: that if the thing was of moderate importance, he send me a white cross the size of a hand; if it was something great, he send me a cross of two hands; and if it was something bigger and better than New Spain, he send me a large cross. And so the said Estaban, the black, departed from me on Passion Sunday after dinner, while I stayed on in this settlement.

The plan suited each man for the white was overjoyed to be rid of the difficult Moor, who was equally pleased to be freed of the white, and he set forth in glory, carrying with him a horde which now totaled nearly three hundred singing and dancing Indian followers.

Garcilaço watched him as he left camp marching at the head of his own little brigade, swinging his rattles, leaping in the air now and then, shouting and exuding the joy he felt in serving as the spearhead of a conquering army.

Just before dancing away, he leaped at Garcilaço and cried enthusiastically: 'Little man, we're conquering a continent. You and I will earn great titles and more gold than we can carry.' And into the dusty sunlight he led his happy band.

Four days after Esteban's departure, Indian messengers ran, gasping, into camp, one of them bearing not a small cross, nor a cross of two hands, nor even a large one, but a cross so huge that he could scarcely carry it. To confirm its significance, he said in broken Spanish: 'The Black One, he has reached Indians who have told him of the greatest thing in the world. The cities we seek lie just ahead, and they are far richer than Mexico.' One said that this concentration of wealth was known as the Seven Cities of Cíbola, and when he uttered the words – Las Siete Ciudades de Cíbola – they echoed with romance and cast a spell over all who heard them.

The first thing Fray Marcos did in this moment of wild excitement was to kneel beside the big cross and pray, giving thanks that he would have an opportunity to restore to Christianity the thousands of souls whom the Spaniards would soon encounter. His prayer came from the very roots of his being, for although he did seek fame for himself and power for his king, his first and deepest commitment was to the glory of God – that stray souls now in darkness should be brought back to the light of Jesus Christ. It was a solemn moment, but after he had remained on his knees for some time, worldly ambition took over and he began to think of himself. Drawing Garcilaço down beside him, he whispered: 'It's wonderful that you and I should discover this great thing, for when the settlement is completed, I shall be leader of all the priests and monks, guiding them in the salvation of souls, and you shall command a kingdom, like Cortés and Pizarro.'

Now Fray Marcos began his great deception, for after having traveled less than three leagues to the west, he began to speak as if he had reached the Pacific Ocean, a distance of more than a hundred leagues. Why did he do such a thing?

Hope? He desperately wanted to be recognized as a great explorer and he knew that the Pacific lay somewhere to the west. Anxiety? He carried strict orders to determine how far away the Pacific Ocean lay, so that supplies for the impending conquest might be forwarded by sea, but he was so eager to attend the larger task of finding Cíbola that he refused to be deterred by this lesser side trip to the ocean. Envy? He could not stand to have the former slave Esteban reap all the glory. Mental confusion? He had become so intoxicated with dreams that he ignored the requirement of substantiating them with reality. He dealt with soaring hopes, not facts.

But on Wednesday, 21 May, after evening prayers, those hopes received a harsh rebuff, for as he prepared for bed he heard someone shouting: 'Someone's coming!' and through the shadows he saw a bedraggled Indian, his face and body covered with sweat, stumble toward the camp, weeping and moaning. When Marcos ran to him he wailed a pitiful story, which the scribe later reported in this manner:

'We were one day out of Cíbola, and with due caution Esteban sent ahead a group of messengers bearing a calabash ornamented with cascabels, and two feathers, one white, one red. Something about the calabash infuriated the chief of Cíbola, and he smashed it to the ground, crying: "If you come in to Cíbola, you will be killed."

'When the messengers told this to Esteban, our leader laughed and assured us that this was nothing, and that he had learned from his long travels that when an Indian chief exhibited irritation he proved later to be a good friend. So, ignoring our warnings, he marched boldly to Cíbola, where he was denied entrance and thrown into a house outside the walls.

'All things were taken from him, trade articles and all, and he was allowed no food or drink, and in the morning we who watched saw with horror Esteban running to escape, followed by warriors from the city, and they slew him, and most of those who were with him.'

'Esteban is dead,' the Indians began to wail. 'Esteban's bones lie unburied, unhonored in the sand.' When Garcilaço heard this dreadful news, he wept for his dancing friend, but Marcos comforted him: 'This is but the story of one Indian, and who knows what his motives might be?' However, two days later more messengers from Cíbola arrived, and their news was horrifying:

'Fray Marcos, see our wounds! Of all the warriors who traveled with Esteban to find the Seven Cities, hundreds have been slain, not counting the many women who were with us.'

Marcos and his soldiers now had to admit that Esteban and most of his dancing, riotous followers were dead, and that if they tried to force their way into Cíbola, they, too, would be killed. So they halted where they were, many miles from the golden cities, and in their fear they turned back toward Mexico, and now Marcos concocted a second lie, the really massive one, and reported:

I asked that some of my men should go with me boldly to Cíbola, but I could do nothing with them. In the end, seeing me determined, two chiefs said they would go with me, and I pursued my journey until within sight of Cíbola, which I saw from a hill where I was able to view it. The city is bigger than the city of Mexico, and at times I was tempted to go to it, because I knew that I ventured only my life, which I had offered to God the day I commenced this journey, but at the end I refrained from doing so, considering the danger that if I died, I would not be able to make a report of this country, which to me appears the greatest and best of the discoveries.

Months later, when Garcilaço stood in the reception hall in the capital, listening as Fray Marcos told of these glories to Viceroy Mendoza, he stood silent and ashamed. He knew that his father had never been close to the Pacific Ocean or to the Seven Cities of Cíbola, and as for the claim that Cíbola was grander than Mexico City, that was a preposterous compounding of the lie.

Why did the boy share in this duplicity? Why did he not cry out to Mendoza, 'Viceroy, these are lies! There are no Seven Cities! There is no gold!' He was prevented by three considerations. He loved his father and refused to humiliate him. Also, despite what he had heard from Cabeza's own lips about his exploration of the region, Garcilaço still hoped that the cities of gold and their lost Christians existed. But most important was the matter of personal ambition, for after Marcos had told his infamous lies, the great Mendoza took Garcilaço aside and said: 'Son, you are one half-Indian who has a fine future in this country. Because of your good work on the mission, when General Coronado marches north I want you to accompany him as a guide.'

Like Cabeza de Vaca, like Esteban, like Marcos, and yes, like Viceroy Mendoza himself, the boy was seduced by the vision of what the land of many lands might be, and he kept his mouth shut.

Garcilaço was proud that the official guide for the Coronado expedition was to be his father, but he became apprehensive as to what the soldiers might do when they marched north only to find that the Seven Cities of Gold did not exist. When he asked Marcos about this, the friar airily dismissed such fears: 'The Cities must be there. You heard Bishop Zumárraga prove logically that they had to be.'

Garcilaço shrugged and turned his attention to his own affairs. Only fourteen, but a veteran traveler, he decided to use the great adventure as an opportunity to build foundations of honor and courage which he had seen exemplified so worthily in Cabeza. He endeavored to seem very military when they reported to the western town of Compostela, where the huge expedition was about to be reviewed by Viceroy Mendoza, who had authorized this venture.

First in line was Coronado, a handsome man, lithe, daring and extremely capable; he believed in God and in the destiny of the Spanish race, and he contemplated the conquest of a continent. Also, he could laugh easily, and he enjoyed being

48

with soldiers, parading boldly in the vanguard when on parades like this one, but prudently sending out trained scouts when danger threatened.

Garcilaço's eyes widened when the first elements passed: two hundred and twenty-five horsemen, caballeros they were called, young gentlemen unaccustomed to manual work but eager for battle. 'Look!' the boy called to those about him, for now came a group of horsemen in full armor, some in metal, some in leather. They were a ferocious lot, and Garcilaço heard an official boast: 'Conquerors of Europe, Peru and Mexico! God help the Indian who makes a wrong move in their direction.'

Next came the spiritual representation for this great enterprise: five Franciscan friars, including Fray Marcos, heads high, thirsty to win distant souls to Jesus. How willingly he and his fellows had volunteered to share all dangers; they were indeed Soldiers of Christ.

Behind them marched sixty-seven foot soldiers – some of whom had campaigned triumphantly through the Lowlands and Austria – displaying the sophisticated weapons which had made them famous: harquebuses, those heavy matchlock pieces that threw devastating round balls at least a hundred feet; crossbows made of ash so strong that some had to be cocked by cranks which drew the cord back to firing position; pikes with hideous three-part jagged ends, fine for disemboweling; and all sorts of swords, daggers, stilettos and maces. And when these foot soldiers of Spain concealed their faces behind visored helmets or in jet-black pots with slits for seeing, they struck terror in men's hearts.

More than two hundred personal servants followed, some Indian, some black, and eighty stable hands to tend the horses and see that the six cannon were brought forward in good condition.

Garcilaço enjoyed the end of the procession as much as the beginning, for here came more than a thousand Indian helpers, some in war paint, some with feathers, others with decorated clubs gleaming in the sun, all bowing to the viceroy, who nodded gravely as they passed. The next group caused the boy worry, for he could not comprehend how its members would participate in any battle: several hundred women, Indians and a few Spanish soldiers' wives, wearing beautiful flowers in their hair and bright shawls about their shoulders. Clouds of dust hovered in the air as these women went past. After them came the cows and sheep on which the marchers would feed.

At the rear, so valuable that they could be guarded by Spaniards only, came many horses, wonderful chargers of Spanish and Arab ancestry, bred for the most part in Mexico but with a substantial scattering of steeds imported directly from Spain. As animals of war, they had always created terror among the Indians of Mexico, and Coronado expected them to do so again. These precise figures can be cited because on this day of final review, 22 February 1540, the notary Juan de Cuebas of Compostela made careful record of every Spanish caballero or foot soldier present, noting what mounts and arms he brought, and Garcilaço watched as Cavalry-Captain Don Garcia López de Cárdenas stepped forward to have his property listed: 'Twelve horses, three sets of arms of Castilla, two pairs of cuirasses, a coat of mail.'

Late in arriving for the muster was Infantry-Captain Pablo de Melgosa, a doughty little fellow with a perpetual smile, a great gap between his two big front teeth, hair in his eyes and a nose that had been pushed sideways by several fists. He came dustily into camp leading two small donkeys that could scarcely be seen beneath their load of armament. As soon as he stopped the beasts, he shouted for the notary to come and verify his possessions, and when Cuebas had his quills and papers ready, Melgosa began throwing things at his feet and announcing in a loud voice what they were.

'Two harquebuses, both cast in Flanders. Two crossbows, and note that each is worked by gears. Those two donkeys.'

'We don't list donkeys,' Cuebas said haughtily, resting his quill above the paper.

Ignoring this rebuke, the enthusiastic young captain resumed his listing: 'A gallegán of the best Austrian manufacture. This buckskin jacket, this black pot helmet from Toledo.'

After this minor armory had been recorded, Melgosa began divesting himself of things he carried on his body: 'Two swords, also of Toledo. Dagger. Knife with ivory handle. Two knee pieces, which you can see are of the best steel and leather. Gauntlets with brass fittings across the knuckles. And two stilettos.' Any jovial man so accoutered was bound to become Garcilaço's favorite, and in those first days he became Melgosa's part-time page, hoping to learn honor and the arts of war from him.

Garcilaço divided his time between Fray Marcos and his new hero, Infantry-Captain Melgosa, the walking arsenal, who was a joy to be with, for he was an adventurous, rowdy man who never feared to challenge the presumptions of the cavalry.

'Look at them!' he sneered one night as the unwieldy caravan stumbled to a halt. 'Not a man among these dandies knows how to pack a horse. Ten more days of this and those mounts will be dead.' Each gentleman officer had to transport his personal belongings on his own male horses, while the heavy burdens of the expedition were carried by mares and mules. But even the lighter burdens assigned to the horses could be damaging if improperly stowed, and when Garcilaço watched the caballeros, he saw that Melgosa was right; they were killing the creatures on which they depended.

Melgosa was particularly harsh in his condemnation of Cavalry-Captain Cárdenas: 'He ought to know better. Those are excellent horses he has, the best. And he's destroying them.' Now Garcilaço observed the fiery captain, and he could see that Cárdenas had no regard for his beasts' welfare.

One morning as the cavalry was packing, Garcilaço made bold to address the captain: 'Sir, why don't you distribute your loads more evenly?'

'Why is that your concern?'

'Your best horse is getting deep sores.'

'I leave such matters to the Indian slaves.'

'But they're still your animals. Look, you have five that can no longer serve.'

'Could you do better?' he snapped.

'I could,' and when Cárdenas saw how expertly the young muleteer could pack a beast, and care for it when the pack was unloaded, he appointed Garcilaço to mind his string, and the horses mended so quickly that on one unforgettable morning as the expedition approached the northern limits of civilized Mexico, the gruff captain said: 'You can ride that brown mare,' and thus the boy became a member of the cavalry.

But when foot soldier Melgosa saw him so mounted he

became furious: 'Real men fight on foot. Cavalry is for show.' This was the contemptuous attitude which existed in all armies: the disdain of foot soldiers for the cavalry, and the reverse.

Because Garcilaço was now a horseman, his allegiance transferred to Captain Cárdenas, and the more he studied this hot-tempered man the more he thought he understood the nature of honor. Cárdenas was the junior son of a family bearing an exalted title, and this heritage constantly manifested itself, for he was contemptuous of inferiors, punctilious where his vanity was concerned, and eager to challenge anyone who even appeared to affront him. More than Melgosa, more than Coronado himself, Cárdenas loved the brutality of army life, the forced marches, the sudden forays against lurking enemies, the swordplay at close quarters and the military companionship of the field. Much sterner than Fray Marcos, much more combative than Melgosa (who was content to fire his harquebuses from a distance if that would do the job), Cárdenas became to Garcilaço the ideal Spanish fighting man, supplanting Cabeza de Vaca as his idol.

The army had marched some days when Garcilaço had his first opportunity to see how Spanish caballeros were supposed to behave. He was riding in company with Army-Master Lope de Samaniego, second-in-command, when that gallant warrior, much experienced in Indian fighting, was sent to a village to acquire supplies, and in pursuit of his duty, was struck by a stray arrow which penetrated his eye as he lifted the visor of his helmet. He died immediately, which Garcilaço accepted as something to be expected in warfare, but what happened next amazed him.

Following the orders of Cavalry-Officer Diego López, who now assumed Samaniego's command, Spanish soldiers rounded up as many Indians as they could, and a sergeant passed among them, saying: 'This one looks as if he might have come from that village,' and upon this casual identification the suspect was dragged away and hanged. When a long row of corpses swayed in the breeze, the army left, assured that the Indians of this area at least had learned not to shoot arrows at Spaniards.

The incident was important to Garcilaço in that when the esteemed post of army-master fell vacant, Coronado weighed the matter only a few moments before appointing Cárdenas to fill it, and now the boy tended the twelve horses of the second-in-command, the bravest, wildest fighter of them all.

Shortly thereafter, Garcilaço discovered how his attitudes had changed, for a side expedition to what is now California was arranged under the direction of a real fighting man, Melchor Díaz, who was instructed to intercept a Spanish ship sailing up the coast with supplies for Coronado. Once Garcilaço had dreamed only of adventure on the Pacific, but now that he had a new opportunity to visit that great ocean he turned his back, for he wished to stay with Cárdenas on his quest for honor.

As an advance party now entered upon those vast wastelands in what would later be Arizona, Garcilaço's fears for his father increased, because the boy knew that the friar's gross lies must soon be uncovered. And when horses began to die of exhaustion and men to faint from the burdens they bore, the leaders of the expedition began to glare at Marcos, as if to say 'Monk, where is this paradise you told us of?' And Coronado himself came to the rear, where Marcos had hidden: 'Good Friar, how many days to Cíbola? We perish.' And as Garcilaço tended his horses nearby, he heard Marcos swear: 'Three more days, General. I promise.' And the boy shuddered, for he knew that the friar had not the slightest idea where they were.

But once more luck seemed to rescue Marcos from a crisis, for on 7 July 1540, one hundred and thirty-seven days after departing Compostela, a Spanish horseman riding well ahead wheeled his horse and came galloping back: 'Cíbola! The Seven Cities! Yonder!'

All pressed forward, each wanting to be first among his fellows to see the golden cities, but when a group gained a prominence its members fell silent, and a vast sigh rose from the men as they saw the pitiful scene, a shabby collection of dirty houses, a mud-walled nothing.

'Madre de Dios!' Cárdenas whispered.

Captain Melgosa, standing by the general, muttered: 'I've seen single houses in Castilla that were bigger than this . . . and richer, no doubt.'

Finally Coronado spoke: 'Where is Fray Marcos?' and when the trembling friar was dragged forth, the captain-general asked in a very low voice: 'Good Friar, is this what you saw? Is this your Cíbola covered with turquoise and silver? Are these hovels bigger than in Mexico City?' And before Marcos could respond, the various captains began cursing and shouting: 'Send him back.' 'Get rid of this one.' 'He is a great liar and not to be trusted.'

But it was Cárdenas who voiced the true complaint: 'I do not want this one praying over me, telling me what to do,' and Marcos would have been sent back that night except that he was needed for an important ritual without which the army could not proceed.

It was the Requerimiento (Requisition), issued decades earlier by King Ferdinand himself, who had laid down the basic edict that no Spanish army could attack an Indian settlement until this famous statement of religious principle had been recited 'in a loud, clear voice.'

It was a remarkable document, devised by the religious and civil leaders of Spain during the early years of conquest when thoughtful men struggled with the moral problem of how to deal with pagan Indians. Indeed, conquest itself had been halted for three years until agreement could be reached as to whether Indians were human or not. Finally, after much soul-searching, a statement was prepared and verified by churchmen and lawyers; it offered Indians, who were acknowledged as human, the blessings of Christianity and the protection of the Crown, but only if acceptance was immediate. If the Indians hesitated, as they always did, conversion by the sword was justified.

Since the army was now within the shadow of Cíbola, Coronado summoned Marcos to read the Requerimiento, but when the friar stepped forward to take the parchment, Cárdenas objected strenuously: 'If he reads it, our enterprise will be cursed!' and he seized the document, handing it to another Franciscan, but Coronado intervened: 'Marcos is still the senior, let him proceed.' So the friar took the parchment, held it close to his face, and read aloud. But no Indian in the distant town could possibly have heard the muffled words, much less understood them even had they been audible.

It was just as well, because the Requerimiento was interminably long, with a jumbled theology which would confuse anyone not an ordained priest. It started by explaining how

Adam and Eve launched the human race five thousand years ago and how different nations developed:

> 'Of all these nations God our Lord gave charge to one man, called St Peter, that he should be Lord and Superior of all the men in the world, that all should obey him, and that he should be head of the whole human race ... to judge and govern all Christians, Moors, Jews, Gentiles and all other sects.'

The friar read on, explaining to the distant Indians how St Peter had begun the line of popes who commanded the world, and of how a later pope had asked King Ferdinand and Queen Isabella of Spain for help in ruling certain areas. Then Marcos came to the two parts the soldiers understood: if the Indians immediately accepted the Holy Catholic Faith, great rewards would be forthcoming, but if they subbornly refused:

> 'I certify to you that, with the help of God, we shall forcibly enter your country and shall make war against you in all ways and manners ... we shall take your wives and your children, and shall make slaves of them ... and shall do all the harm and damage that we can ... and the deaths and losses which shall accrue from this will be your fault ...'

Fray Marcos rolled up his parchment, returned it and announced: 'The Requerimiento has been faithfully read. All can testify to that.' The generous offer of peace had been tendered, but there was no response.

'Friar,' Coronado asked, 'are we legally free to attack?' and Marcos replied so that all the captains could hear: 'Jesus Christ commands you to do so!' and battle began.

It was a violent encounter, and Coronado's bright suit of armor flashed in the sun so invitingly that the Indians on the city walls threw down huge chunks of stone that knocked him from his white horse, leaving him defenseless and immobile on the ground.

More rocks came crashing down and would have killed him had not Cárdenas, in an act of spontaneous heroism, thrown himself across the fallen body and absorbed most of the blows.

When Garcilaço saw this valiant act, he dropped down and shielded Coronado's head, and was struck by four rocks which otherwise could have brained the commander.

Bruised, cut in three places so badly that his bloody wounds were apparent to all, Garcilaço listened that night to one of the sweetest sounds a man can hear: praise for having behaved well in battle. 'He was as brave as a tested infantryman,' Melgosa cried, but the moment the boy cherished came when Cárdenas, himself badly wounded, took his hand: 'I could not have saved him without you.' When the boy was alone, he whispered to himself: 'Now I know what honor is.'

With Coronado confined to a litter because of his wounds, Cárdenas assumed command, and his first decision was loudly voiced: 'Fray Marcos must leave this army. He contaminates it.' Melgosa wanted him shot, but Cárdenas said contemptuously: 'Let him go. He carries his punishment with him.'

From his sickbed Coronado accepted this recommendation and added: 'Let the boy go with him, whoever he is,' but now Cárdenas became a defender: 'Captain, this boy helped save your life. And he's no liar, like his so-called father,' so it was agreed that Marcos must go but Garcilaço could stay.

This decision caused the boy much confusion, for he loved Fray Marcos and did not want to leave him in his hour of disgrace. 'I cannot fail him now,' he told Coronado, and the captain-general growled: 'Good. Go with him,' for he saw Garcilaço only as part of Fray Marcos and wished him gone, too.

But Cárdenas and Melgosa were disgusted when they heard of the boy's decision, and they took him aside, with Cárdenas saying bluntly: 'Loyalty is a fine thing, lad, but loyalty to a condemned man must be weighed carefully.'

'It must indeed,' Melgosa agreed. 'Admit it. Your father is a fraud. He's led this great army into deep trouble, and it is proper that he be disgraced. But there are still battles to be fought, and Cárdenas needs you for his horses, and perhaps I may need you. Your duty is here.'

To Garcilaço, honor was much simpler: 'I must stay with Marcos,' and he left the two officers, who called after him that he was being a fool. However, when Garcilaço reached his father, who was packing his mule for the long march back to

Mexico City, Marcos took him in his arms, eyes wet with tears and cried: 'I cannot let you damage your life. Stay with the army you have grown to love.'

'Without you I'd have no army. I'm your son, and I shall stay with you.'

At these words Marcos clasped the boy tightly and sobbed: 'I've ruined everything. Did you hear the curses they heaped on me?' He stood clinging to Garcilaço, then said in a hushed voice, as if he were seeing a vision: 'But the Cities are there. The walls of gold will be found, just as I said.' And with that he shouted: 'Army-Master Cárdenas! Come take your little soldier!' and thrusting the boy away, he started his mournful exile.

Garcilaço was not given time to brood about Fray Marcos' disgrace, for as soon as Coronado recovered from his wounds he dispatched an elite group of twenty-five to make a swift, galloping exploration of lands to the west, and Cárdenas, in command, took the boy along. Now Garcilaço had an opportunity to see what a masterful soldier Cárdenas was, for he anticipated everything: where to find water, how many deer to kill for food, in what safe place to camp. 'I would like to be a soldier like you,' the boy said, and Cárdenas smiled: 'You could never be an officer like me, but you could serve, and honorably.' When Garcilaço asked why he could not attain command, Cárdenas told him truthfully: 'Command is reserved for those born in Spain.' He did not add 'of white parentage,' but he intended the boy to catch that nuance of Spanish life.

Twenty hot and thirsty days later Garcilaço was riding ahead of the file when he stopped, gasped, and held up his hand to warn the others.

'Look!' he whispered, and when Cárdenas drew up he said in reverence: 'Dear Jesus, you have worked a miracle.' And one by one the others moved into line, there at the edge of a tremendous depression, and fell silent. It was a moment of overwhelming discovery, a moment that no one could absorb or summarize in speech.

At their feet opened a canyon so grand, they knew of nothing with which to compare it. A mile deep, mile upon mile across, with a tiny ribbon of river wandering at the bottom, its walls were multicolored, shimmering with gold and red and blue and dancing green. Lovely trees, bent from the wind, adorned its rims and sometimes tried to creep down the sides, their tall crowns like tiny tips of fern, so far away they were. And as the afternoon sun moved across the deep gash of the canyon, it threw weird shadows upon pinnacles far below, and new colors emerged as if some great power were redecorating what was already a masterpiece.

'A miracle!' Cárdenas gasped. 'God has prepared this wonder to show us His power.' They had discovered the Grand Canyon of the Colorado, and Garcilaço felt himself growing inches taller when Army-Master Cárdenas said with affection, as he ruffled the boy's hair: 'Remember, this one found it. Let's christen it El Cañon de Garcilaço.' There was cheering, but in the midst of the celebration the boy looked eastward, for he could not forget that the true adventure still waited there, in what Cabeza had described as the land of many lands.

Cárdenas and his swift-marching men required three months for this trip to the canyon, and when they rejoined the main party they found that it had acquired a stranger, to whom Garcilaço took an instant dislike. This man, in his thirties, was a good-looking Indian whose height, facial tattooing and turban headdress identified him as belonging to some tribe far from Cíbola, perhaps a Pawnee from north and east. He had been captured by the Zuni of Cíbola in a raid years ago and was now a slave, except that he seemed more clever than those who held him. He had a glib manner, a sly, knowing look, and Garcilaço often saw him calculating how to play this white captain off against that Indian chief, and it was clear that he did not propose to stay a slave indefinitely.

He was called El Turco, and nothing else, because the soldiers who found him thought that he looked the way a Turk should, although none had ever seen one and if the boy intuitively disliked El Turco, the Indian reciprocated with intensity, for he saw in Garcilaço the kind of innocent intelligence which might quickly pierce the lies he was about to tell. El Turco had but one ambition, and everything else was subservient to it: trick Coronado into marching toward the empty east, where his army would perish in the desolate wastelands. When confusion was at its peak, he would escape and travel north to his home village of Quivira, whose valleys and running streams he remembered each night of his captivity.

And the tales he told! He started cautiously, for like Fray Marcos, whom he resembled in certain ways, he always wanted to know first what the Spaniards hoped for; then he tailored his reports to please them. For example, after listening closely to every word the soldiers spoke he learned that coins were of extreme value, but he had never seen one. Cautiously he began: 'We have coins, you know.' When pressed as to what form his coins took, he guessed blindly: 'Colored stones,' and then withdrew into his shell as the Spaniards ridiculed him. To demonstrate how foolish he was, the men showed him coins of silver and gold, and in that instant those two metals became part of his arsenal.

To a different group of soldiers he said casually one day, using signs and grunts and a smattering of Spanish words: 'In my land the great chief has a staff made of something that glistens in the sunlight ... yellowish ... very heavy.' He did not at this time mention the word *gold*, nor did he again refer to the chief's staff, but he could almost see his rumors whirling about the camp, so that when Cárdenas came casually by to ask, as if the question were totally unimportant: 'In your land, have you any hard things like this?' as he tapped on his steel sword, the Indian said: 'Oh, yes! But in my tribe only our big chiefs are allowed to own it. Glistens in the sunlight ... yellowish ... very heavy.'

At first Cárdenas affected not to have noticed the description, but later he asked in his offhand way: 'Your big chiefs, do they have much of the ...' He tapped his steel again.

'Much, much!' And both men left it there.

Two members of the army were aware that Cárdenas had been trapped by this clever manipulator: El Turco knew it, and so did Garcilaço. Reporting to his master after the evening meal one night, Garcilaço said: 'Captain, El Turco is a great liar.'

'You should know something about that.'

'I do. My father Marcos lied because he dreamed of doing good. El Turco lies to do something bad.'

'He's told us about gold in his land, and that's what we've come north to find.'

'Captain, he did not tell *us* about gold. We told *him* about it.'

And he tried to explain how El Turco never told them anything but what they had already betrayed as their need or interest. But Cárdenas and the others wanted to believe El Turco, and they did.

El Turco also impressed the Spaniards by making shrewd guesses about the past and future, the kind of clever nonsense any reasonably observant person could make, but when some of them proved true, and the Spaniards asked how he had gained this power of clairvoyance, he said slyly: 'Sometimes the devil comes to visit with me, telling me what will happen.'

When Coronado heard about this he became intensely interested, for he had always suspected that the devil hovered near his army, and since it was essential that the Spaniards know what El Turco was up to, Coronado kept close watch on him. One night, as the general was passing where the prisoner was kept, he heard El Turco talking with the devil, who was hiding in a jug.

'Devil, are you in there?' El Turco whispered, tapping on the jug.

'You know I am. What do you want?'

'Where do you want me to lead them?'

'Take them anywhere but Quivira in the east,' the devil said, 'because if they march there, they'll find all that gold I've collected. They must not have it.'

'Where shall I lead them?'

'To the north. Get them lost in that emptiness.'

'I shall do so, Prince of Evil.'

'If you keep them away from the east, I'll reward you.' And with those clever words El Turco tricked Coronado into going east towards nothingness.

Seeking to have his army in the best possible condition for the march, Coronado decided that if his men had to fight in winter, they would require three hundred sturdy cloaks, which he ordered the villages of the area to provide. When this proved impossible, for there was no surplus, the soldiers went on a rampage, stopping any Indian they encountered and ripping from his shoulders the cloak he was wearing. In this rough way they collected their three hundred, and also the enmity of the owners.

During the confusion, a Spanish cavalryman whose name

was known but never disclosed because of the great guilt that lay upon him, went to a quiet part of one village, summoned an Indian to hold his horse, went inside the pueblo, climbed to an upper room, and raped the man's wife. In order to avert trouble, Coronado ordered all his mounted soldiers to line up with their horses so that the husband could identify the culprit, and since the husband had held the horse for nearly half an hour, he could easily identify it, but the owner denied that he had been in that part of the village and the wronged husband got no satisfaction.

Next day the enraged Indians assaulted the Spaniards in a most effective way. They stole many of their horses and drove them into an enclosed area where the animals had to run in wild circles. Then the Indians, screaming with delight, proceeded to kill them with arrows.

Furious, Coronado summoned Cárdenas, and ordered: 'Surround the village and teach them a lesson.' After Cárdenas had disposed his troops in a circle that enclosed the pueblos, he directed two captains, Melgosa and López, to perform an extremely hazardous action: 'Break into those tall houses where the lower floors are not defended. Fight your way to the roof, and shoot down into the streets.' As Melgosa started toward his assignment he called: 'Little Fighter, come along,' and with no hesitation Garcilaço did.

When they reached the roof, the captains directed the boy to stand near the ladders: 'Push them down if any Indians try to climb up.' And there he stood through a whole day, a night, and most of the next day as his captains fired into the mob below. But without food or water the Spaniards began to tire and might have been forced to surrender had not one of the soldiers below devised a clever tactic: he built a fire on the ground floor of the pueblo, then sprinkled it with water, making a thick smoke. Soon the choking Indians were forced out, making with their forearms a kind of cross and bowing their heads, a most ancient signal for peaceful surrender. It was not binding, however, until the victors also made a cross and bowed their heads, but this Melgosa, López and Garcilaço gladly did. The ugly siege was over.

But Cárdenas, infuriated by the attack on his horses, was so determined to demonstrate the power of the Spanish army that he ordered his other soldiers to surround these men who had honorably surrendered, and then to cut two hundred wooden stakes, each six feet tall, at which the prisoners would be burned alive.

'No!' Garcilaço shouted as dry brush was piled about the first victim. 'We gave our word.'

Cárdenas in his fury would not listen, so Garcilaço appealed to Melgosa and López, who had accepted the truce, but they too refused to support him.

'Master! No!' he pleaded, but Cárdenas was obdurate, his face a red mask of hatred, and the burning started.

The Indian men, seeing five of their comrades screaming at the stakes, decided to die fighting, and grabbing whatever they could reach – clubs, stones, the still-unused stakes – they began a furious assault upon the Spaniards, whereupon Cárdenas bellowed: 'All Spaniards out!' and after Melgosa and López had rushed Garcilaço to safety, soldiers rimmed the area in which the two hundred had been kept and began pouring shot and arrows into it, killing many.

Those who survived now broke free and began running helter-skelter across open land, whereupon Cárdenas and other cavalry officers spurred their horses, shouting and exulting as they cut down the fleeing Indians, other horsemen lancing them with spears until not one man of that entire group was left alive.

Garcilaço was horrified by what had happened, by the faithlessness of his hero Cárdenas, by the cowardice of his other hero Melgosa, who would not defend the truce he had authorized, and most of all by the burning and chasing and stabbing. He was appalled to find that Coronado did nothing. 'We taught them not to offend Spanish honor' was all he would say, and Garcilaço was left to wonder what honor meant. Fray Marcos, he felt certain, would not have permitted such a slaughter had he been in charge of the army's conscience, and from that moment Garcilaço began to see his father in a much kinder light. Because of his enthusiasm, Marcos may have told many lies, but he was a man who had at least known what honor was. Cárdenas did not.

But for a boy of fourteen to pass moral judgment upon adults is a perilous undertaking, for now that Coronado was injured and confused, Garcilaço saw that it was Cárdenas who proved to be the true leader. It was he who supervised the killing of animals for meat to feed his men. Marching across deserts blazing with heat or swirling in storm, it was Cárdenas who buoyed the spirits of the army, and when brief, explosive battles with Indians became unavoidable, his horse was always in the lead. Like his general, he was driven by a lust for gold and fame, those terrible taskmasters, but in discharging his duty like a true soldier, he recaptured Garcilaço's reluctant respect.

But now he did a most unsoldierly thing. He broke his arm, and when it refused to mend and the army set forth to conquer the opulent city of Quivira, he had to stay behind.

On the morning that Coronado started his triumphal march east – toward disaster in the drylands if he persisted – he summoned Garcilaço: 'Son, can you count?'

'Yes, sir. And I know my letters.'

'Good. Start now, and count every step you take. When we strike camp, tell me how many. I'll measure your stride and know how far we've come.'

So the boy walked in dust behind the horses, counting 'Uno, dos, tres, cuatro,' and whenever he reached a thousand he made a mark on a paper the Franciscans had given him. At the end of that first day it showed twenty-three such marks, and when he presented the paper to Coronado, the general thanked him: 'Nearly four leagues. Good for a first day.' And next morning the counting resumed.

After many such days, continuing to count even in his sleep, Garcilaço calculated correctly that considering the distance east from Cíbola, the expedition must have entered the lands traversed by Cabeza de Vaca. He was at last in Tejas, the fabled land of many lands.

What a massive disappointment it was, for Coronado, always obedient to the urging of El Turco, had entered those bleak lands at the headwaters of what would later be called, in Spanish, El Río Colorado de Tejas. Distraught by the lack of any sign of civilization, he then angrily turned north, only to find himself locked in a series of deep canyons of a river of some size, El Río de Los Brazos de Dios, The River of the Arms of God. Here, surrounded by dark cliffs, the Spaniards had to face the fact that they had been led not to gold-encrusted Quivira but into a barren wilderness where they stood a good chance of dying. Sensible men would have abandoned the enterprise right there, but Coronado and his captains were Spanish gentlemen, and a tougher breed was never born. 'We'll go on to the real Quivira,' Coronado said. 'Wherever it is.'

In this extremity, on 26 May 1541, the expedition had been campaigning for more than four hundred and fifty strenuous days without capturing one item of value or finding any kingdom worthy of conquest, so the leaders knew that their venture would be judged by what they accomplished at Quivira, and this powerful obligation made them believe that gold still waited. In a council there in the ravines, Coronado decided that he, with thirty of his ablest horsemen, six sturdy foot soldiers and the Franciscans, would make a last-ditch sortie to the north, relying on the gold they would surely find there to salvage the reputation of his expedition. The bulk of the army would return to familiar territory and there await the triumphant return of the adventurers.

But now the Spaniards were confronted by a quandary best expressed by Captain Melgosa: 'Where in hell is Quivira?' Fortunately, Coronado's group contained two scouts of the Tejas tribe, and they spoke with truth: 'General, Quivira lies there' – and they indicated true north – 'but when you reach it you will find nothing.'

'How can you say that?' Coronado thundered, and they replied: 'Because we have hunted at Quivira. Nothing.' Such discouraging information Coronado refused to accept, so the frenzied search for gold continued.

About this time an extraordinary act of Garcilaço's caused much amusement. Late one summer afternoon, when he saw the northern horizon turn blue and felt the temperature begin to drop, he supposed he was about to experience what Cabeza had so often spoken of with fear and respect. 'It may soon be winter!' he warned the Spaniards, but they laughed: 'Lad, it's July!' However, within the hour a bitter wind was roaring across the empty spaces, and in the midst of this sudden storm, while others were huddling inside their blankets, Garcilaço threw off his clothes to stand naked in the wind.

'What are you doing?' Melgosa shouted from his tent, and when he ran to the boy with his blanket, all Garcilaço could answer was: 'Cabeza told me he lived for seven years attacked by such winds, and he was naked. I wanted to test him.'

'Cabeza de Vaca was a liar. Everyone knows that. Come inside.' When Garcilaço sat crouched by the fire, with the others thinking he had drifted toward insanity, he thought of Cabeza: He must have been a liar, for no man could survive such a norther, yet he did. We know he did.

On a blistering July day in 1541, Coronado and his small band lined up at the southern bank of a miserable arroyo and stared across at Quivira (in what is now Kansas). They saw an indiscriminate collection of low mud huts surrounded by arid fields with few trees and no rich meadowlands. Smoke curled lazily from a few chopped openings in roofs, but there were no chimneys, no doors and no visible furniture. Such men and women as did appear were a scrawny lot, dressed not in expensive furs but in untanned skins. Of pearls and gold and turquoises and silver, there was not a sign. The Spaniards had wandered nearly three thousand miles, squandering two fortunes, Mendoza's and Coronado's, and had found nothing.

Garcilaço noted how the leaders reacted to this final disappointment. Coronado was overcome, unable to comprehend it and powerless to issue new orders. One captain raged, then started to prepare his men for the long homeward journey. Melgosa looked at the supposed city of riches and showed his gapped teeth in a disgusted smile: 'I've seen pigsties in Toledo look better than that.'

It was Melgosa who issued the first order: 'Double the watch on El Turco,' and during the dreadful blazing days the slave who had been the agent of this disaster – but not its cause, for that lay within the cupidity of the captains – sat unconcerned in his chains, humming ancient chants used by his forebears when they knew that all was lost and death was at hand.

Garcilaço himself was anguished by the magnitude of the defeat, even though he had known it was coming and several times he spoke with El Turco: 'Why did you deceive us?'

'You deceived yourselves.'

'But you lied, always you lied about the gold.'

'I never put gold in your hearts. You put it there.'

The dark-skinned man laughed, that easy, ingratiating laugh which had so charmed and blinded the Spaniards: 'As a boy, I had a fine life, chasing buffalo. As a young man, I had two good wives, there by the northern rivers. When we were captured by the Zuñi, the others were treated badly but I protected myself by talking quickly with the leaders in the pueblos. And with the Spaniards, I had my own horse.' He shook his chains, laughing at the rattling noise they made. Then he ridiculed his captors: 'The Spaniards were such fools. It was so easy for me.' And once more he became the insatiable plotter: 'You're an Indian like me. Help me to escape. I know a city to the north. Much gold.'

One night Captain Melgosa said to Garcilaço: 'Come, lad. Work to do,' and he took him into El Turco's tent, where they were joined by a huge butcher from Mexico, one Francisco Martín, who kept his hands behind his back.

'Turco,' Melgosa began, 'each word you've said has been a lie. You led us here to perish.' The Indian smiled. 'And yesterday you tried to persuade the Indians here to massacre us.' Still the great liar showed no remorse, so Melgosa flashed a sign, whereupon Martín brought forward his powerful hands, threw a looped rope about El Turco's neck, and with a twisting stick, drew the noose tighter and tighter until the Indian strangled.

With Martín's help, Garcilaço dug a grave into which the corpse of this infuriating man was thrown. Had he but once told the truth, he could have become a trusted guide. As it was, he deceived everybody, including himself.

Coronado, head bowed and gilded armor discarded because of the sweltering heat, started his shameful retreat, unaware that history would record him as one of the greatest explorers. Under his guidance, Spanish troops had reached far lands: California, Arizona, New Mexico, Texas, Oklahoma, Kansas. His men had described a hundred Indian settlements, worked with and fought with a score of different tribes, and identified the difficulties to be faced by later settlers. But because he did not find treasure, he was judged a failure.

One member of the expedition did find success, although of a temporary nature. One morning a messenger posted north from Mexico with an exciting letter drafted by the emperor, Carlos Quinto, in Madrid:

Captain-General Coronado, Greetings and God's Blessing. You have in your command a Captain of Cavalry, Don Garcia López de Cárdenas of the noble family of that name. Inform the Captain that his brother in Spain who inherited the noble title and all wealth and properties pertaining to it has unfortunately died. Said Captain Cárdenas is to return by fastest route to Madrid, where he will be invested with the title now belonging to him and be handed the substantial properties to which he is entitled. By order of His Majesty the King.

When Infantry-Captain Melgosa heard this news he grinned, spat through his gapped teeth, and told Garcilaço: 'See! It always happens this way. It's cavalry officers who get messages from the emperor.' Then he burst into gusts of laughter, clapping Cárdenas on the back: 'Infuriating! The only man in the whole army who gets any gold is this damned cavalry officer.' And they got drunk on wine Melgosa had saved in expectation of celebrating the capture of Quivira's gold.

How ironic it seemed to Garcilaço that of all who set forth on this glorious expedition, the only one who profited when it ended in disaster was the badly flawed Cárdenas. The rest earned only bitterness.

But the boy need not have envied the apparent good fortune of Cárdenas, for although the army-master was awarded both the title and fortune when he reached Spain, he was then accused of having burned Indians alive. He was in and out of jail for seven years, fined eight-hundred gold ducats and sentenced to serve the king without pay for thirty-three months at the dismal post of Oran in North Africa. But because the king liked him, this was reduced to two-hundred ducats and twelve months' service at the kindlier post of Vélez Málaga, where he prepared for further adventures in new lands.

Coronado's heroic aspirations ended in confusion, for when he issued his reluctant order 'March south!' some sixty of his braver underlings announced that they intended to remain permanently among the pueblos of what would become New Mexico. Coronado flew into a rage to think that they were willing to chance a new life in a new land while he had the doleful task of returning to Mexico to report his failure.

One of the would-be settlers wrote some years later: 'He said we had to go back with him, and he threatened to have us hanged if we refused or said anything more about it.' So the settlement which could have justified the expedition was aborted.

However, three other members of a much different type also asked to remain behind, and they posed a more difficult problem. They were Franciscan friars – Fray Padilla, an ordained priest, and two who had taken only minor orders. In robes already tattered, they came before Coronado to say: 'We will stay here.'

'Why?' the general asked, almost pleading with them to drop their foolishness, and they said: 'Because we must bring Jesus into pagan hearts.'

Officers, common soldiers, even some of the Mexican Indians tried to dissuade them from what appeared to be certain martyrdom, but the advisers were powerless, for God had whispered to the three, and finally Coronado had to give them permission to remain.

One of the minor friars set up his mission near Cíbola, while the other sought to convert the local Indians along the Río Pecos, and they marched off to their extraordinary duties.

As for Fray Padilla, Garcilaço would remember always that final morning when the friar started his long walk back to Quivira, whose Indians he dreamed of bringing into the Holy Faith. He did not go alone or lacking goods, for when Coronado accepted the fact that the friar could not be dissuaded, he provided him with so many people and so much goods that Padilla looked as if he were heading a minor expedition: a Portuguese soldier, two Indian oblate brothers who had taken no orders but whose lives were dedicated to religious service, a mestizo workman, a black translator, a train of mules well laden, a horse, a substantial flock of sheep, a full set of instruments for the Mass, and the six young Quivira Indians who had guided Coronado back from that settlement.

It was a fumbling attempt to Christianize a vast new land, and when Garcilaço, still avid to learn what honor was, watched the little procession depart, he asked himself: 'Why would men volunteer for such a fatal assignment?' But as the words hung in the air he realized that honor included not only physical and moral courage but also a daring commitment to central beliefs, and for a moment he wished that he might one day march in the footsteps of that friar.

As Padilla moved off toward sure death he grew smaller and smaller in the eyes of Garcilaço, but larger and larger in the eyes of God.

Years later a Franciscan gathered reports from all who had known the friar and wrote: 'The Portuguese soldier and the two oblate brothers were traveling with Fray Padilla one day when hostile Indians attacked. Insisting that his friends escape with the only horse, he knelt in prayer and was transfixed by arrows.'

Imperial Spain was neither generous nor understanding with her unsuccessful conquistadores. When Coronado returned with no gold, he was charged with numerous malfeasances and crimes. The great explorer was for many years abused by officials dispatched from Spain with portfolios of charges made by his suspicious king. When Coronado's case ground to a halt, Viceroy Mendoza was similarly charged and harassed. Captain Melgosa received nothing for his many acts of heroism, and the mestizo Garcilaço was treated worst of all.

Even though of the meanest birth, he had striven throughout this long and dangerous expedition to conduct himself according to his understanding of honor. He had been first to sight the deep canyon, but he did not shout: 'See what I have found!' He had saved his commander's life when the stones fell, but he did not cry: 'How brave I am!' And he had fought for two days on the roof, an incident whose aftermath he tried to forgive, because he felt that no man of honor would kill so wantonly.

But at the end of his journey he was dismissed with no pay, no job and no honors, for was judged to be 'merely another Indian.'

He was mustered out in 1542, and lacking funds with which to buy enough animals to work the profitable Vera Cruz–Mexico City route, he had to be content with that portion of El Camino Real, the Royal Road, which ran from Guadalajara to Culiacán, with an occasional side trip delivering mining gear to the new silver mines at Zacatecas. Occasionally he would come upon a cargo destined for Mexico City, and one day in 1558, overworked and disheartened, he was engaged on such a trip when he was accosted on the streets of the capital by a tonsured monk who asked: 'Are you the Garcilaço who once knew Fray Marcos?' When he nodded, the monk said: 'You must come with me,' and he led the way to a small Franciscan monastery, where a very old cleric came unsteadily forward to say in a weak voice: 'My son, why have you not come to me for help?'

It was Fray Marcos, and in succeeding days this frail old man spoke often with Garcilaço, reviewing the evil things that had happened to him and complaining of how his enemies never allowed the world to forget that it had been his misleading information which had tricked Coronado's army into its disasters. 'Son, it's impossible to determine what is truth and what is falsehood. I cannot now remember whether I saw the Seven Cities in reality or in a dream . . . but that's no matter, for I did see them.'

Garcilaço was now a grown man of thirty-three, who worked hard and to whom a crust of bread was either firmly in hand or was not, and he was not disposed to tolerate philosophical niceties: 'You were never on the hill. And if you had been, you couldn't have seen the Cities. Not from where we were.'

'The hill has nothing to do with it. You do not judge a man by whether he climbed a hill or not. I saw the Cities. When I preach about the City of God that awaits us in its glory, do I climb some hill to see it? No, it exists because God wants it to exist. And the Seven Cities of Cíbola exist in the same way. They will be found one day because men like Esteban and me will always seek them.'

At this mention of the dancing black man, Marcos fell to weeping, and after some moments, said softly: 'I was not generous with him, Garcilaço. I deplored his way with women. But in the long view of history, what are a few women, more or less?'

This rhetorical question brought a most unexpected consequence: 'Garcilaço, my son, I have been most eager to find you. I sent that friar to seek you out. When the last viceroy took his Spanish soldiers home with him, one of them left behind a daughter. Ten years old . . . we could find no mother.' He fell to coughing, then said: 'I took her in. She works in our kitchen . . .

María Victoria. But she's getting old enough now that people are beginning to talk, to say ugly things about me – the usual charges you heard when you were her age.' He brought his hands together under his chin and stared at his son: 'It's time that girl found a husband.'

He led the way into the kitchen, where María Victoria, a golden-skinned mestizo girl of fifteen, proved so attractive that Garcilaço asked in honest bewilderment: 'Why should she be interested in me?' and Marcos said: 'Because I've been telling her all these years how brave you were in the north, how you proved yourself to be a man of honor.'

He grasped María Victoria's right hand and placed it in Garcilaço's: 'I give you my daughter.' He kissed them both, then said: 'My children, in this life honor is everything. It is the soul of Spain. Some caballeros have it, most do not. You Indians can earn it too, and if you do, it adorns life.' Tears came to his eyes as he added: 'I've always tried to preserve my honor, and have done nothing of which I am ashamed.'

He himself conducted the wedding ceremony, and shortly thereafter, died. For some years chroniclers, when summarizing his life, belabored the infamous role he had played in lying about Cíbola, but now his scandals have been forgiven and forgotten.

María Victoria and Garcilaço did not forget him, and for good reason. Fray Marcos had been a Franciscan pledged to poverty, but as a prudent man he had always managed to sequester his share of the gold coins which passed his way in either governmental or religious activity. 'It wasn't really stealing, children,' he assured them two days before he died. 'A man of honor never steals, but he can put a few coins aside.'

When Garcilaço asked: 'Where's the gold hidden?' Marcos merely smiled, but some days after the friar's funeral María took her husband to where she used to sleep, and hidden in a wall behind her cot he found a substantial hoard. 'Fray Marcos knew that the father-provincial liked to make surprise visits,' she whispered, 'to make sure his friars kept obedient to their vows of poverty. Father could always guess when the old inspector was coming, and then he gave me his gold to hide.'

The windfall enabled the newlyweds to purchase land, build a house, hire Indians to drive the family mules down to Vera

Cruz, and buy a black tutor from Cuba to educate them. Many years later, when it became customary for well-to-do mestizos to take surnames, the viceroy bestowed *Garza* upon them, and it became a tradition in the family that their progenitor had been a Spanish sailor of that name.

... Task Force

At our organizing meeting in January we had agreed that our young assistants would assume responsibility for inviting to each of our formal sessions some respected scholar who would address us for about forty minutes on whatever aspect of Texas history we might be concentrating upon at that time. Their first offering provided a lucky coincidence.

In conformance with the governor's desire that we hold our meetings in various cities across the state so as to attract maximum attention to our work, our February meeting, which would emphasize Hispanic factors in Texas history, was to be held in Corpus Christi, that beautiful, civilized town on the Gulf. It was appropriate that we meet there, because Corpus was already more than sixty percent Hispanic, with every indication that the percentage would increase.

When I started to make plans as to how we would get there, I learned how convenient it was to work with really rich Texans, for Rusk had three airplanes to whisk him to and from his oil and banking ventures, while Quimper had two for his distant ranches. Since each had a Lear Jet for longer distances and a King Air for shorter, we had our choice, and in this time-saving way we covered much of Texas, for as Quimper told us: 'When you have interests in a nation as big as Texas, stands to reason you got to have planes.'

When we landed at the airport in Corpus, we were met by Dr Plácido Navarro Padilla, an elderly Mexican scholar from the cathedral city of Saltillo, which lay two hundred and sixty miles south of the Rio Grande. During the hectic decade 1824–1833, Saltillo had served as the capital of Coahuila-y-Téjas, so that a natural affinity existed between it and Austin, our present capital.

He was a dapper man, with neatly trimmed gray mustache and silver-rimmed eyeglasses, and had the easy grace which marks so many Spanish scholars. He could disarm those with whom he argued by flashing a congenial smile and an apologetic bow of his head, but in debate he could be fierce. When our staff member from SMU introduced him, she explained: 'Dr Padilla has specialized in Mexican-Texan relations . . .'

'Excuse me,' the doctor interrupted in excellent English. 'My name is Navarro.'

'But it says in our report,' Random Rusk countered, 'that your name is Padilla.'

'That is my mother's name. It comes last, Spanish style. My father's name . . . my name . . . is Navarro.'

'We're proud to have you with us,' Rusk said with an attempt at warmth. 'Proceed.'

'Your Republic of Texas fell under United States rule during the final days of 1845, actual admission coming in 1846. Since this is 1983, you have been American for a hundred and thirty-seven years. But you must remember that Spanish interest in your area started with Alonso Alvarez de Pineda in 1519. Serious settlement started in El Paso in 1581, and Mexican control did not end until 1836, so that you were under Spanish-Mexican hegemony for three hundred and seventeen years. In other words, Texas was Spanish more than twice as long as it has been American, and this must never be forgotten.'

He proceeded with a forceful analysis of the Spanish heritage in Texas, a subject on which he was well qualified, since he had taught it during seven summer sessions as visiting professor at the University of Texas: 'Your land is surveyed in leagues and labors, according to Spanish custom. Many of the laws governing your use of rivers are Spanish in origin. The religion in large parts of your terrain is Roman Catholicism. The names of your towns and counties are often Spanish. Your best architecture is Spanish Colonial, as are many of your rural customs. Texas is indelibly dyed in Hispanic colors, and the inheritance is a good one.'

Rusk, always a defender of Anglo-Saxon superiority, was not prepared to accept this emphasis on things Spanish: 'Suppose we grant that in the beginning your impact was impressive. But it has been the relatively few years of English-speaking domination which have given Texas its character.'

'For the moment it might seem that way,' Dr Navarro conceded, 'but during the passage of centuries cultural influences have a stubborn way of persisting, and I would suppose that with every passing decade the power of your Spanish inheritance will become more evident.'

'Are you equating Mexican with Spanish?'

'I am.'

'Now wait. If I see five hundred Mexicans on Texas streets, Dr Navarro, I see never a hint of Spanish influence, barring their language and religion.'

'What do you see?'

'Indians. You can't find a drop of Spanish blood.'

Dr Navarro smiled disarmingly: 'In odd corners of Mexico you will find people like me. Pure Spanish through unbroken generations.'

I was rather irritated with Rusk because of the surly way in which he heckled our speaker, and I had about concluded that I must rebuke him for his incivility when he smiled bleakly and told Navarro: 'I accept your correction. You've been around here a lot longer than I have.'

It turned out to be a stimulating meeting, for which our young assistants were much relieved. Navarro threw off sparks like a busy grindstone on a frosty morning, especially when he spoke of those first three Spaniards who were associated, if only peripherally, with Texas.

'I understand there's a movement afoot among your historians to play down the importance of Cabeza de Vaca, Fray Marcos and Coronado in the beginnings of Texas, and this I can understand. Cabeza de Vaca never knew he was in Texas; Fray Marcos never came near the place; and if Coronado entered your state, which many doubt, it could only have been in the bleakest part of the Panhandle.

'But our concerns extend far beyond the geographical boundaries of Texas. This state has an imperial significance. Its natural sphere of influence includes all the areas explored by these three men, even those areas in northern Mexico. If we think regionally, we see that every step Cabeza de Vaca, Fray Marcos and Coronado took had implications for Texas and its imperium. These men remain important factors in your history.

'But I am more interested in their psychological reverberations, and here you must indulge me if I wax poetic, for I visualize myself as a poet striving to write the *Odyssey* and the *Lusiads* of Spain in Mexico.

'Cabeza de Vaca established the ideal pattern for a Texan: bold, daring, persistent, observant, optimistic even when disaster hovered. He is the stubborn Texan, the gallant, the unconquered, and I cherish his memory.

'Fray Marcos had an apocalyptic vision of what the Texas imperium might become, and just as he fired the vision of his contemporaries, he ignites ours today. He is the patron saint of the great liars in Texas history, the braggadocios, the adventurers whose tales exceed their adventures. Every Texan land-seeker who assured his wife "The good location for us lies just over that hill," every wildcatter who traced a streambed to the sure oil site, every builder in Houston right now who is convinced he will find tenants for his condominium if only some investor will finance the next six months – they're all descendants of Fray Marcos, the confidence man, and Texas would not be the same without them.

'When I hear the name Coronado, my heart salutes. A great dreamer who in your Texas vernacular "put his money where his mouth was," he risked all and lost all, but in doing so, gained immortality. The history of Texas is filled with his kind, the great gamblers, the men whose eyes were fixed beyond the horizon. Like him they try, they fail, but do not complain. I would like to fail the way Francisco Vásquez de Coronado failed.'

After recommending that we not drop these noble Spaniards from our curriculum, he came to the heart of his challenging talk, which I will abbreviate, using only his words:

'I beg you, as you work at laying the foundations of historical education in Texas, not to fall prey to The Black Legend. This is a historical aberration promulgated by devout Dutch and English Protestants in the sixteenth century. It is a distortion of history, but it has taken root, I am sorry to say, in many quarters of American historical writing. Its main tenets are clearly defined and easily spotted. Do please try to avoid their errors.'

'What are they?' Quimper asked, and Navarro gave a concise summary.

'The Black Legend claims that everything bad which

happened in Spanish history was due to the Spanish Catholic church. The phrase seems to have originated from the black cloth worn by Phillip II and his priests. It claims that insidious popes from Rome dominated Spanish civil government. That priests tyrannized Spanish society. That the Inquisition ran rampant through Spanish society. That Catholic domination caused the end of Spanish culture and inhibited Spanish learning. That priestly domination caused the weakening and decline of Spanish power, both at home and in the colonies.'

In our meetings Ransom Rusk always struggled for clarification of ideas, and now, even though he had a strong bias against Mexicans, he labored to understand the point Navarro was trying to make: 'I was taught in college that Spain was backward because of its religion. Where's the error?'

For the moment, Dr Navarro ignored this interruption, for he wished to nail down an important point: 'So long as The Black Legend muddied only theological waters it could be tolerated, but when it began to influence international relations, it became a menace, for then it claimed that Catholicism, under the baleful guidance of its black-robed priests, sought to undermine and destroy Protestant governments as well as Protestant churches.'

'I've always believed that,' Rusk said, whereupon Navarro looked at him with a forgiving smile: 'I almost believed it, too, when I was a student at Harvard, because that was all they taught. So you can be forgiven, Mr Rusk.'

'Thank you. Now I'd certainly like to hear your whitewash of the situation.'

'That is what I am noted for in Mexican intellectual circles. Whitewashing The Black Legend.'

He proceeded with an insightful analysis of the baleful influence of The Black Legend: 'It obstructed serious American study of Spain's influence because it offered such a ready-made explanation for anything that went wrong. Did Spanish power in Europe and the New World wane? "See? The Black Legend was right!" Did Spain mismanage her colonies in America, much as England mismanaged hers? "The malignant influence of the Catholic church!" Did things go contrary to the way Protestants wanted? "Blame it on The Black Legend."'

Quimper interrupted: 'But Spain did decline. It did fall behind. We all know that.'

Navarro surprised me by agreeing heartily with what Lorenzo had said: 'Of course Spain declined. So has France declined. And certainly England has. But they all declined for the same reasons that the United States will one day decline. The inevitable movement of history, the inescapable consequences of change. Not because either England or Spain was nefarious, or unusually cruel, or blinded by religion.'

This was too much for Rusk's stalwart Baptist heart: 'But damn it all, your Inquisition did burn people!' to which Navarro replied without even pausing for breath: 'Let us say about the same number that English Protestants hanged or burned for being witches. And some fanatics argue that your killings were more reprehensible because they came so late, after a social conscience had been formed.' I seemed to remember that the last auto-da-fé in Mexico occurred in 1815, when the great revolutionary leader Father José María Morelos was condemned by the Inquisition and shot by soldiers. But Navarro's obvious skill at polemics so intimidated me that I remained silent.

But now he changed tactics, becoming even eager to acknowledge each weakness of Spain or her church, and he even conceded that The Black Legend might have contributed some good in that it had driven Spanish historians to a more careful analysis of their culture in their determination to defend it. In the end we respected him for his unrelenting defense of things Spanish.

'You must never let prejudice blind you to the fact that in the years when Spain first explored and took possession of Texas, it was the foremost empire on earth, excelling even China. It dominated the continent of Europe, much of the Americas, trade and the exchange of ideas. It was majestic in its power and glorious in its culture. It controlled far more completely then than either the United States or Russia does today. Its influence permeated what would become the future Texas, and to teach students otherwise would be to turn one's back upon the spiritual history of Texas.'

Just as I began to fear that he was trying to make too strong a case for Spanish and Catholic influence, he broke into a wide, conciliatory smile: 'You must remember one fundamental fact about your great state of Texas. If we date its beginning in 1519 with the Pineda exploration, or 1528 with the marooning of Cabeza de Vaca on Galveston Island, it was about two hundred and fifty years before the first Protestant stepped foot on Texas soil. Of course, Mr Rusk, when the rascal finally appeared his boots made a deep impression.'

He then turned to one of the most difficult problems: 'The glory and the power! You simply must believe that when Coronado ventured into what is now the Texas Panhandle in 1540 he was impelled by two forces of precisely equal importance, spiritual desire to spread Christianity and temporal hunger for gold and the power it would bring. I have read a hundred accounts of those stirring days, and I have done everything possible to discount the bombast and the speeches made for public consumption, but in the end I stand convinced that men like Coronado really did believe they were doing God's work when they proposed to subdue heathen lands in northern New Spain. I can cite a score of instances in which the conquistadores placed the rights of the church above those of the state, and they did so because they saw themselves first as God's servants, discharging His commands. Gold and power the conquistadores did not find in Texas, but they did find human hearts into which they could instill the saving knowledge of Jesus Christ. I have always felt that Texas started as a God-fearing state and that from the first moment it was Christian.'

In a more subdued tone he proceeded to discuss the matter of Spanish power in Texas, and his analyses were refreshingly sophisticated: 'Texas was so far from Mexico City and so infinitely far from Madrid that power was never transmitted effectively. To tell the truth, when I study those two hundred and fifty years of rather futile Spanish dominance I find myself wondering: Why did not Spain send fifty men like Escandón to settle Texas? They'd have altered the entire picture.'

'Who was Escandón?' Quimper asked, and Navarro replied: 'José de Escandón? The wisest and perhaps the best man Spain ever sent to the Río Grande. Arrived in 1747. Please teach your children about him.' He broke into a disarming chuckle. 'Mr Rusk, with five hundred like Escandón we might have worked

78

our way clear to the Canadian border. We came this close' – and he pinched two fingers together – 'to making you speak Spanish.'

The scholarly chuckle turned into a laugh. 'But history and the moral will-power of commanders determine outcomes. It was destined, perhaps from the start, that Texas would not be adequately settled by the Spaniards. The men like Escandón were never forthcoming. They could not be found ... they had no one in Madrid pressing their cause. Spain edged up to the immortal challenge, then turned aside.'

Now our speaker became a true professor: 'I trust that in any published materials for school or college you will, out of respect for your heritage, use proper Spanish spelling. Avoid rude barbarisms like Mexico City. It's La Ciudad de México. It's not the Rio Grande, it's El Río Grande del Norte. And because in Mexican Spanish *j* and *x* are so often interchangeable, please differentiate between Béxar, the original name for what you now call San Antonio, and Béjar, its later name. Same with Texas, then Téjas. And do keep the accents.'

Rusk and Quimper looked aghast at this pedantry and I was afraid they were going to protest, but Professor Garza saved the day: 'Of course, in our scholarly publications we are meticulous in respecting Spanish usage. I'm especially demanding of my students. But in general writing for our newspapers and schools, custom requires Mexico City, the Rio Grande and Bexar. Up here, most accents have vanished.'

'Ah! But I notice from your nameplate that you keep Efraín.'

Garza smiled and said: 'I do that to please my father,' whereupon Navarro asked with an almost childish sweetness: 'Could you not do the same with La Ciudad de México? To honor those of Spanish heritage?' and Garza said: 'Texas honors its Spanish heritage in a thousand ways.'

Navarro bowed politely, then addressed us as a committee: 'When you draft your recommendations you are not required to alter a single item in the American portion of your history. It is sacred. All national histories are. But in the long run, I am convinced that the Spanish heritage of Texas will manifest itself in powerful ways. It will produce results you and I cannot envisage, perhaps a whole new civilization here along the Rio Grande.'

79

Approaching the end of his presentation, he continued: 'Do not, I beg you, teach your children that Spain was a devil. It was merely one more European country trying to do its best. Do not castigate the processes of exploration and settlement available to it as inferior or negative. They were the best that could have happened in the middle of the sixteenth century as Spain started her unfortunate decline.'

Smiling at us in that ingratiating way Spanish-speaking scholars sometimes command, he concluded: 'Some centuries from now, say in 2424, scholars like you and me sitting in Mongolia may argue that in the later years of the twentieth century, North America started its decline. One hopes that those scholars will be generous in their assessment of what you Americans and we Mexicans tried to accomplish.'

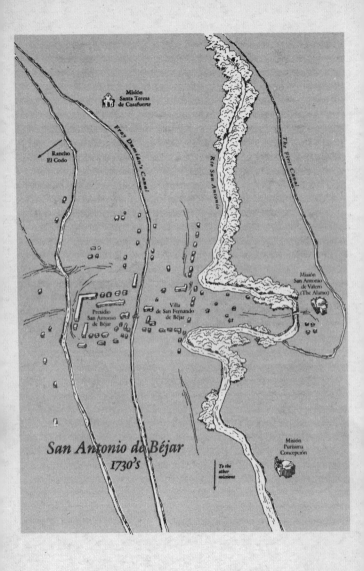

Misión
Santa Teresa
de Casafuerte

Fray Damian's Canal

Rancho
El Codo

Río San Antonio

The First Canal

Misión
San Antonio
de Valero
(The Alamo)

Presidio
San Antonio
de Béjar

Villa
de San Fernando
de Béjar

San Antonio de Béjar
1730's

To the
other
missions

Misión
Purísima
Concepción

II

THE MISSION

When Christianity was about twelve hundred years old, religious leaders sought a tighter structuring of holy orders, and in 1209 the Italian Francis of Assisi started what became the Franciscans, an order of subtle appeal. It stressed celibacy, poverty, profound devotion and a love of humanity. Its members, like all members of the mendicant orders, were known as friars and they did not live in fixed abodes or monasteries; they traveled endlessly, built missions, performed good deeds, and provided examples of humility.

The Franciscans found Mexico a dramatic theater for their operations, and if the Indians of that country escaped formal slavery, it was due in great part to the humanitarian efforts of the Franciscans; if the Indians acquired certain limited blessings of Spanish civilization, it was because brave Franciscans established missions on the remote frontier. They were teachers, hospital attendants, farmers and understanding friends, but primarily they were servants of Jesus Christ.

In 1707 the silver-mining town of Zacatecas, which lay near the center of Mexico, was excited by an announcement that would convert their drowsy rural place into a city of some importance.

'The Franciscans are finally going to build a college here!' ran the rumors. 'We're to be headquarters for all the north.' 'They've started to dig!'

And when men wandered from the central plaza out to the edge of town they saw workmen, Indians mostly, patiently cutting through the rocky earth to provide foundations for a building that would be of surprising size. The gray-clad cleric in charge verified the news: 'It's to stand here . . . just as you see it forming.'

'How many monks?'

'Only friars.'

'But if it's a monastery . . .'

'It's not a monastery, nor is it a proper university like the one in Mexico City.'

'What is it?'

'A teaching center. With some administration on the side.'

The Zacatecans could not comprehend, so he put down his shovel and explained, pointing once more to the north: 'Here we study to prepare ourselves. Up north we do God's work.'

'Then you won't live here?'

'Here while we study. Later wherever God sends us.'

Throughout that first year the many idlers of Zacatecas watched as the Franciscans built the college. More precisely, the friars supervised its building, for the hard work was done either by Indians, who were practically slaves, or by paid mestizo artisans who had worked on similar structures elsewhere in Mexico.

Among the mestizos on the site in 1716, when the interior decoration of the college was in progress, was a skilled worker in wood, Simón Garza, who had been born in the mining town of San Luis Potosí, where his father had followed the family's tradition of carting materials to and from the silver mines. Since the Garzas had had five sons but only twenty mules, Simón, the youngest boy, came too late to inherit any animals. Instead, he apprenticed himself to a carpenter, and after a year of supervising Indians who worked in pits sawing planks from felled trees, he became an expert in fitting together these planks so as to make a solid wall with no chinks. Later, the Franciscans were delighted to find him, and he worked diligently at their building, perfecting his trade.

At age twenty-six Simón was undergoing an experience in this northern town which disturbed and at the same time delighted him. In the past his occupation had kept him on the move and a lack of money had prevented him from paying court to the young women in those towns where he worked, but in Zacatecas he had steady employment, so six nights a week when work was done he found himself in the spacious public square before the cathedral, watching as the young unmarrieds of good family walked about from seven till nine.

They did not walk aimlessly. The men strolled unhurriedly

in a counter-clockwise direction, keeping toward the outside of the tree-lined square, and as they went they looked always toward the center of the square, where, inside the large circle they had formed, walked the young women of the town in a clockwise mode. About every ten minutes a young man would meet head-on, almost eye to eye, a particular young woman, twice in each circuit of the plaza, and in this practical, time-honored Spanish manner the unmarried conducted their courtships. Over a period of three weeks, any young man could pass his preferred young woman more than a hundred times, during which he could notice with the precision of a scholar the degree to which her smiles had softened.

The traditions of this paseo, as it was called, were rigorously observed. Girls of the purest white skin paraded, their mothers protecting them from the advances of any man of lesser standing; these families were the elite of Zacatecas, the peninsulares, born in Spain itself and dreaming always of a return to that splendid land. Almost as exalted were the criollos, of pure Spanish blood but born in Mexico, and these protected their heritage even more carefully, for they realized that they had little chance of ever getting to Spain; their families occupied positions within Mexican society which did not allow the accumulation of enough funds to permit that. Such criollos lived cut off from Spain, especially when their duties sent them to a distant town like Zacatecas, but they were the inheritors and protectors of Spanish civilization, and they never allowed their neighbors to forget it: 'My child is pure Spanish ... eleven generations ... unsullied. We came from Extremadura Province, just like Cortés and Pizzaro ... same family. If you look closely, you'll see she has the Pizzaro eyes.'

Entrance to the paseo was restricted, with Indians being forbidden to participate; Spanish and criollo families did not want to run the risk that their children might strike alliances with the aborigines, no matter how beautiful the girls or manly the young fellows. A few mestizo girls were in the parade, but only as servants who walked well behind their white mistresses, serving as a kind of protecting influence should one of the young men prove too bold. Mestizo men were absolutely excluded, but well-behaved young fellows of good character like Simón Garza were allowed to stand along the periphery and watch.

However, as the sun went down on Sunday nights, the mestizos of Zacatecas held their own paseo in a nearby plaza, and here young people of the most exciting character paraded. Girls with jet-black tresses and delicate olive complexions smiled at young men dressed in freshly laundered trousers and white shirts. Flowers abounded, and occasionally some girl wore about her neck a disk of pure silver, smelted from the ore of the Zacatecan mines. This rural paseo was apt to be far more colorful than the one conducted by the Spaniards.

It might be assumed that Simón Garza, eager for a wife, would participate boldly in this lovely courtship ritual, but he did not. Inordinately shy, he came each Sunday night to this lesser square, watching enviously as young men braver than himself made the rounds and identified the women with whom they might fall in love. Afraid to enter the paseo which he was eligible to join, he spent hours daydreaming about what kind of woman he might ultimately find, and ended by lamenting: I'm growing older and nothing's happening.

One Thursday evening in 1719 when Garza finished work he wandered back to his cramped room, and when he saw the bare walls he was overcome with loneliness: God! I must do something! Splashing water carelessly over his face to wash away the sawdust, he grabbed a crust of bread and some cheese and almost ran to the main plaza, where the young Spaniards and criollos of good breeding were already forming their circles. Trembling, as if he were about to undertake some dangerous adventure, he edged close to where the marchers would pass, maneuvering so that he could view the oncoming girls directly.

During the first three circuits of the parade Simón received only vague impressions of the graceful women as they went by him. They seemed like the sailing ships he had seen at Vera Cruz, proud, beautiful, moving forward, then passing slowly out of sight. But on the fourth round he found himself staring into the face of a mestiza walking sedately behind her mistress. She was somewhat older than the others, and her graceful deportment caused him to gasp. She seemed to be about twenty-two or -three, slightly taller than average and with a mature, gracious smile. When she walked, her long skirts appeared to move of themselves, poetically and barely touching the ground. Her shoulders were heavy-set, as if accustomed to hard work, but her most conspicuous characteristic was the manner in which she leaned forward when strolling, as if prepared to meet life head-on, regardless of its threats.

She was Juana Muñoz, daughter of a farmer whose fields lay to the north of town, and like other such girls, she had worked in various large houses in Zacatecas at whatever jobs were available: maid, cook, governess. Some years back she had been courted intermittently by a soldier, but he had moved on to another post, and now she realized that at twenty-two she was perilously close to an age when chances for marriage would diminish. Therefore, when she became aware that the carpenter from the Franciscan center had begun to notice her, she watched for the moment when she would pass where he stood and sent a carefully orchestrated series of signals, each time a little bolder than before, until he had good reason to think that his intentions were known and reciprocated.

When this subtle communication was repeated on Friday and Saturday at the Spanish paseo, Simón felt with some justification that the time had come for him to make some overt step, but what kind he did not know. A more enterprising man would simply have joined the mestizo paseo on Sunday night, smiled knowingly at the young woman, and when the marching ended, reached for her hand, introduced himself properly, and walked her sedately to where some member of her family waited to take her home. But Simón was not equal to this; he blushed furiously even at the thought, so on Sunday, even though he went to the paseo, he stood mutely at the edge, staring his heart out at the winsome girl but unable to read in her eyes the panic signal: 'Young man, if you wish to speak with me, for God's sake, speak!' When the paseo ended and it looked as if she might come and talk to him, he fled.

On Monday, in considerable confusion, he began seriously to evaluate the friars working at his building and he concluded that Fray Damián, a quiet fellow with a gentle manner, would best understand his plight. So that afternoon he tugged at the friar's sleeve and whispered: 'Could I please speak with you?' and he was relieved when the cleric, only four years older than himself, smiled paternally.

It was a strained consultation, for Simón was ill-qualified to reveal his problem, and through bad luck he had chosen as his confidant the one cleric in Zacatecas least fitted to help. From an early age Fray Damián de Saldaña had known that he would become a servant of God, and his devotion was so concentrated that he passed through puberty hardly realizing that girls existed. He was fully aware that courtship, marriage and parenthood were not for him, and during his assignment at Zacatecas he had not once witnessed the paseo, for he had catalogued it as 'something the others do.' Therefore, he did not understand when Simón said hesitantly: 'At the paseo ... there's a woman ... I want you to speak to her for me. I need a wife, and she seems fine, quite fine.'

'Who is she?'

'You must find out for me.' As soon as Simón uttered these words he was overcome with confusion, and with his hands pressed close to his legs he bowed low and whispered: 'I have reason to think ...'

'Of course I'll help.'

And it was in this way that Fray Damián de Saldaña, thirty-three years old and born in Spain, first went to the Spanish paseo in the great plaza fronting the cathedral of Zacatecas. It was a June evening, not yet summer-hot with a quiet breeze coming in from the uplands. At sunset, when he took his place near the church with the carpenter at his side, a golden glow suffused the town and a pale quarter-moon hung in the starless sky. Flowers, shade trees, fruit trees along the irrigation canals, all prospered in these rich early days of summer, and the loveliest flowers of all were the young women of the town as they casually entered the plaza to begin their promenade.

'Which one is she?' Fray Damián asked, and with the greatest embarrassment, Simón had to reply: 'She hasn't appeared yet. She might not come tonight.' But a short while later he tugged at the friar's arm. 'There she is!' he said with almost boyish delight, but Damián did not hear.

Four places ahead of Garza's mestizo housemaid came three Spanish girls, their insolent swaying and noisy chatter youthful and superior. The girl in the middle position was the housemaid's mistress, an especially attractive lass, with an impish face and long braids, wearing clothes which seemed more perfectly fitted to her fifteen-year-old body than did those of the other girls. She was more frank, too, in greeting the glances of the young men who passed, slowing down so that pleasantries could be exchanged. At such times she almost stopped, so that her friends had to drag her along, slapping her on the back as they might have chastised a wayward child. Then she would giggle, throw her hands over her face, and remove them so quickly that she could still toss a farewell smile at the men.

'Is she not handsome?' Simón asked, but again Damián did not hear, for he was watching with the most intense interest the girl's progress.

She was Benita Liñán, daughter of an official sent from Spain to supervise the agriculture in this part of Mexico. She had been born in Avila, one of the fine walled cities of Castile, and since her family intended returning there as soon as her father's work in New Spain was completed, she had been warned not to express any serious interest in the many young men who sought to woo her, for she was to be married in Spain, but this did not prevent her from flirting with them. Indeed, the older woman who served as her duena, and who watched carefully from the Liñán balcony, sometimes doubted whether she would ever get their headstrong child back to Spain, for Benita showed a strong inclination toward becoming involved here in Mexico.

Fray Damián felt a tugging at his sleeve, and heard: 'That's the one. Walking alone. I think I ought to let her know I'm here.'

'What?' He had forgotten his carpenter's mission.

When Simón explained his plot, that he would arrange to be near the woman when the bell rang, Fray Damián said: 'That's sensible. That's very sensible.' He coughed. 'I'll join you when the bell rings.'

In fact, he moved much earlier in order to gaze more directly at the lively child who had so attracted him, and when he had eased himself unobtrusively into the crowd of watchers, working his way to the front row, he felt his heart thumping whenever she came swinging along, whispering words both to her friends and to the passing young men. He was startled by her beauty, and well he might be, for she was the epitome of all the dark-eyed, laughing women who graced the cathedral towns of Spain, and who gave his homeland so much of its remarkable character.

And then his heart missed a beat, for he realized that Simón's young woman was in the company of his girl, and that in attending to the courtship of his carpenter, he was abetting his own interest: How remarkable! It was almost as if someone had arranged this curious thing.

The bell rang, the paseo ended, and the crowds dispersed, but Fray Damián did not intercept the carpenter's woman and make the introduction, for he was preoccupied with the girl. 'I'm sorry, Simón. I think it'll be much better if we speak to her tomorrow.' And on the next night, after again hovering by the cathedral to watch Benita, he did intercept the woman in whom the carpenter had evidenced such interest: 'I am Fray Damián from the college, and I wish to present Simón Garza.' The carpenter bowed, Juana smiled modestly, and the formalities were honored.

'I am Juana Muñoz, of this parish.'

'And your parents?' Damián asked.

'Farmers, of the parish to the north.'

'I introduce a man of good repute,' Damián said, and then he excused himself and hurried off to see where the saucy girl's duena had taken her, and he saw with uncharacteristic satisfaction that she was being led into the house of a family of some standing. He asked a passer-by whose house it was, and the man said: 'Anselmo Liñán, official from Avila in Spain.'

Even though he was aware that he was becoming enmeshed in a very dangerous game, Fray Damián sought a dozen excuses for being in the plaza during the Spanish paseo: It's as if the gears of a huge grinding machine were working to sort out the persons whom God intended to be married. That poor fellow over there will never find a wife. That lively girl by the cart had better find her husband soon, or she'll be in trouble. And somehow, by God's grace, it works.

He kept a close watch on Benita, whose name he now knew, and was pleased to see that she had formed no attachment of any kind, but he was worried about her flippancy and her predilection for flirting with almost any fellow who happened to catch her eye in the paseo.

He had not yet spoken to the girl, and she was unaware of his presence, but one night an unusually perceptive friend whispered to Benita as they passed under the church towers: 'I think that one is watching you,' and she snapped: 'A priest? Nonsense!' But upon careful inspection of the friar's behavior, she had to conclude that he was watching her, and no others. The idea intrigued her.

In late July, Fray Damián finally had a logical excuse for appearing at the paseo, for his carpenter had asked him to speak formally to the servant girl Juana Muñoz, and Damián added, with grave propriety: 'Your young man Simón would like me to conduct the wedding. Do you agree?'

'I would be honored. My parents will come in from the country.'

So a wedding was announced. It would take place after the turn of the year, and as a gesture of good will toward Garza, Fray Damián sought permission for it to be held in one of the church's chapels. He was directed to consult with Anselmo Liñán, who as a Spanish official helped direct the social affairs of the church, and when details were clarified, Liñán said: 'Fray Damián, the colonel tells me he would like to talk with you about reinforcing the Franciscan presence in the northern areas.'

'I'm ready to go, I assure you.'

'Could you dine with us? This week?'

'Oh, yes!'

Fray Damián was a tall man, very thin, with a sharp nose and beetling eyebrows, who had never paid much attention to his appearance. But on the day of the dinner he tried to make himself presentable. Using much water in an attempt to hold down his unruly hair, he also brushed his sandals and beat out his frock to remove the dust which had accumulated at the building site. Looking somewhat better than usual, he went to the Liñán home, and was delighted to find that Benita, now posing as a demure and well-behaved young lady, would attend the dinner with her mother. His seat was opposite hers, and although he tried his best to avoid her eyes, lest he betray his surging emotions, he could not prevent this from happening. When it did, he blushed so painfully that he was certain everyone at table must see it, but Benita seemed unconcerned, smiling at him as she might have smiled at some elderly uncle whom the family favored.

The talk this evening was mostly about the empty lands north of that river which the Spanish called variously El Río de las Palmas, El Río Bravo, or some other arbitrary name. Lately they had begun to call it El Río Grande del Norte, or simply El Río Grande. 'The problem lies not with the lands themselves,' an enthusiastic lieutenant was saying, 'but the fact that they join us to the French in Louisiana. Mark my words and mark them well, one of these days we'll be at war with the French over those border lands.'

His colonel, an imperious man, smiled condescendingly and said: 'You're a clever lad, Tovar. I received word yesterday that the French have already threatened our settlement at Los Adaes.'

'Why would the French want to invade us?' Liñán asked, but the colonel ignored the question, turning abruptly to Fray Damián: 'Tell me, what plans do you Franciscans have for strengthening the north?' But before Damián could respond, he banged on the table till the glasses rattled: 'Best thing Spain's ever done, the union of the friars at the mission and the army at the presidio.'

'Why do you say that?' Liñán asked.

'Most effective way ever devised for settling and holding a virgin territory. It was originally used as a way of resettling Spain after the defeat of the Moorish invaders, you know.'

'I would have thought bringing in farmers was the telling circumstance,' Liñán argued.

'Men like you will be welcomed in Tejas only when the friar here, and the soldier here' – and he slapped himself on his chest – 'only when we've pacified the place.'

The colonel jabbed a finger at Damián and asked: 'What plans do you Franciscans have for helping your compatriots in the north of Tejas?' and the friar responded: 'We're eager to send men forth tomorrow.'

'I hear the missions you used to have up there accomplished little.'

'Our early missions did falter,' Damián conceded. 'Founded 1690, abandoned 1693. That's why I'd like to explore the north. To find a better site. To do a better job.'

'You'd better take me along,' the colonel joked, 'or those

Indians'll eat you in a minute.'

'It is the salvation of those Indians which will take us north,' Damián said firmly, and as the discussion continued, with a good wine from Andalucía flowing, the three-pronged mission of Spain in the New World was made clear: Fray Damián to Christianize; the colonel to civilize; and Anselmo Liñán, the farmer-businessman, to utilize.

When the discussion reached this level the colonel proved a most sensible man, appreciative of the contributions his two colleagues could make, and willing to concede that he could not operate well without them: 'How do you gentlemen assess the relative contributions of our three arms? I mean, in the problem of settling an area like Tejas?'

To his own surprise Fray Damián was the first to respond, and he did so vigorously: 'The commission we are given by His Majesty the King is so clearly stated that none can confuse it. Spain's responsibility is to save souls, to bring new lands into the embrace of Jesus Christ.'

'That's always said first,' the colonel agreed, 'but let's remember that our fundamental purpose is to find ourselves a new Mexico, a new Peru, and to conquer it and hold it for the empire.'

'In the early stages, yes,' Liñán acquiesced, 'but after the first ten years the goal must be to use the pacified Indians in commerce, as we've done here – to make things, dig ore out of the ground, to farm, if you will, so that Spain can have the profits of trade.'

'You'll produce damned little without an army,' the colonel said, and it was Damián who voiced the sensible approach: 'We serve the king best when we serve Jesus Christ first. But my Franciscans would be powerless in Tejas without the support of you two.'

'You'll have it,' the colonel said. 'As soon as you're ready to move out.'

'I was ready at the age of ten,' Damián said, and this encouraged the other two to ask where his family had lived, and he said: 'In a lovely village named after our family – Saldaña – halfway between Burgos and León in the north of Spain.'

Anselmo Liñán, as the father of a marriageable daughter, was preoccupied with questions of heritage and could not help asking: 'Were you of the nobility?' and when Damián blushed furiously, those at the table concluded that he was not.

But his embarrassment stemmed from a much different cause, which he endeavored to explain as delicately as possible: 'My father had seven sons in a row. I was the fifth. And by country custom dating back a thousand years, he was entitled to the dignified name Hidalgo de Bragueta.' As soon as he uttered these words, the colonel and his lieutenant guffawed, but Don Anselmo blushed as deeply as the friar, and when Benita asked almost petulantly: 'What's he saying, Father?' he hushed her with a stern 'I'll tell you later.'

Hidalgo de Bragueta, a most honorable appellation, could best be translated as *Sir Knight of the Codpiece*, for it proclaimed to the countryside that this prepotent gentleman had sired seven sons in a row without the intrusion or, as Damián's father liked to put it, 'the contamination' of a single daughter.

'You were the fifth son?' Liñán asked, and Damián explained: 'From time long past our family honored the custom of mayorazgo. First son inherited all the land. Second son married a rich daughter of our neighbors. Third and fourth into the army, fifth and sixth into the church. Seventh son? Who knows?'

'Then one could say that you are of the nobility?' Liñán probed. 'Sort of?'

'My grandfather thought he was king, at least of Asturias. My father had more sense.'

'Will you go back to Saldaña?'

'I'm a Franciscan. I roam the world. My home is in heaven.'

At this profession of faith the local Spaniard sighed, for it was understood that every man in Zacatecas who had been born in Spain yearned to return there at the earliest opportunity; they might work diligently in far outposts like this, or along the real frontier in Tejas, but they certainly planned to take their savings back to some Spanish town as soon as practical, even the clergy.

'I have a place at Málaga,' the colonel said. 'A vineyard ... a few oranges. Nothing much, you understand.' Turning to Liñán he asked: 'Where?'

'Avila.' He had to say no more, for his listeners could imagine that fair city perched upon its little hill, the heavy stone walls that enclosed it wandering up and down the slopes.

No one spoke, for everyone in the dining hall loved his or her corner of Spain, that fortunate land which God had created to prove that life on earth could be almost as favorable as life in heaven: Fray Damián could see his father's shepherds bringing in their flocks at night; the colonel could see his silvery city nestled beside the Mediterranean, its streets crowded with revelers at bullfight time; and Liñán could see not only sanctified Avila but also the rich fields that lay beyond her walls.

'To Spain!' the colonel proposed, and the wine was passed, with even young Benita lifting her glass, for she, too, remembered Avila.

'To Tejas!' Fray Damián suggested, and they drank to this also, because the subjugation and settlement of that farthest frontier was their immediate concern; not until it was pacified and producing wealth could they sail back to Spain.

In the nights that followed this dinner Fray Damián began to acknowledge the emotional danger into which he had fallen, but he was powerless to protect himself. He continued to contrive excuses for going to the plaza at sunset so that he might see Benita again, swinging along, joking with her girl friends, trying to escape the surveillance of her duena. Each night she became more haunting, and when he lay on his crude straw-and-hay mattress, he could not sleep, for she appeared in his cell, smiling and biting her lip, as she did so enchantingly when she sensed that older people were watching. When he rolled over and punched his pillow he fell into the habit of whispering her name: 'Benita,' and then looking about in terror lest some wakeful friar had heard.

He realized the wrong he was committing, but he could not drive her from his mind, and when there were marriages to be conducted in the town – mahogany-skinned farmers taking brides with nut-brown complexions – he fell to wondering whether any of these men felt the same emotions as he, and for how long into the marriage. Tormenting visions assailed him as he tried to imagine what marriage was, and he recalled the easy, robust relationship that had existed between his no-nonsense father and his strongly opinionated mother. 'My dowry gave you the fields your peasants plow,' she would shout at her husband, 'and don't you ever forget it.'

Whenever she said this his father would explode in laughter: 'Have you ever seen those damned fields? A crop of rocks.'

'You Saldañas!' She never spelled out what she meant by this, but she did tell her seven sons: 'Remember, you're only half Saldaña. The good half comes from the Bermejos.' His name was really Damián Vicente Ignacio de Saldaña y Bermejo, and he was proud of both halves.

He would die rather than prove false to the vow of chastity he had voluntarily taken, and he could never bring dishonor upon his family name, so he withdrew from any direct contact with Benita Liñán. But neither of these honorable restraints could drive the vision of Benita from his mind, and one night when the anguish was heavy he confessed to himself in his quiet cell: I am a miserable human being. I am as low as a man can fall.

The temptations were exacerbated in 1720 when the time arrived for the carpenter Simón Garza to marry the maid Juana Muñoz, for when Damián saw the couple standing before him he grew faint. Behind the bride stood Benita, and as he began to recite the words of the marriage rite the two women became intermingled, and he believed he was officiating at two marriages: Garza and Juana, himself and Benita.

Clearing his head, he mustered the courage and stumbled through the ceremony, and seeing at last only the two good peasants, he fervently wished them well in their great adventure: 'Simón and Juana, God himself smiles on you this day. Know love with one another. Rear your children in the love and knowledge of Jesus Christ.' And he lowered both his voice and his head, for he acknowledged how unqualified he was to speak on behalf of the Deity.

Fray Damián's infatuation with Benita was solved, or rather alleviated, in a manner which he could never have foreseen. In the autumn of 1721 the young military officer Alvaro de Saldaña arrived at Vera Cruz, through which almost everything coming into Mexico must pass. Five years before, in the town of Saldaña, perched among hills in northern Spain, his practical-minded father had told Alvaro, his seventh son: 'There's no land left for you. Ildefonso will have it all. And I doubt if you would be a proper recruit for the church. What's left but the army?' Using his few remaining connections, Don Vicente had arranged for Alvaro to become an officer and had then pulled strings to have him sent to Mexico, where brother Damián could watch over him. Alvaro was twenty-six, unmarried, afire with ambition, and the bearer of a letter of commendation addressed to a former commander of his father: the estimable viceroy, the Marqués de Valero, considered by many to be the finest man in that office since the days of the great Mendoza, to whom he was distantly related.

The letter begged the viceroy to give consideration to a father's request that Alvaro be permitted to serve in somewhat the same region as Damián, 'it being a distinct honor for one family to provide two such manly sons to the service of our noble King and in a land so far from home.'

When the letter was placed before him, Viceroy Valero regarded it carefully; he had often hunted with the Saldañas; he knew the honorable history of that family; and he had been vaguely aware that one of its sons had been conducting himself favorably as a Franciscan in Zacatecas. But he had an entire country to look after, a job he had performed commendably for nearly six years, and now he rose from his ornate desk to study the large map which dominated so much of his thinking; it showed that impressive network of roads which fanned out across Mexico, binding the various scattered parts together. It was called in its entirety Los Caminos Reales (The Royal Road System), and now Valero inspected the critical segment running from Vera Cruz to Mexico City to San Luis Potosí to Saltillo to the miraculous ford across the Río Grande at San Juan Bautista, then straight through Tejas to a tiny spot at the extreme northeast called Los Adaes. It was a route of conquest, a highway of poetic names, but once the traveler passed Saltillo, it was not a road at all, merely a poorly marked trail through empty land.

Not exactly empty, the viceroy thought. Apache Indians sometimes raid Saltillo, and everywhere in the north they lurk to slaughter my men.

Then he began to laugh, sardonic, bitter chuckles, when he thought of the final destination of El Camino Real: Los Adaes, soon to be the capital, and perched at the farthest edge of the

97

region. Turning away in disgust, he growled, 'Damn the French!'

In three words he had summarized Spanish policy in Tejas: when peace reigned between France and Spain, Tejas could go to hell, not one gold piece would be spent; but when the trouble threatened, Tejas became 'our noble bastion in the north, where heroic Spaniards defend our outpost of empire against the evil plans of the French.' Tejas policy was determined not by the viceroy in Mexico City but by the acts of Frenchmen in Louisiana, and since 1719 their behavior had been ominous.

I'll send young Saldaña to our northern frontier, Valero decided, and when the eager young officer was brought into his presence, he said affably: 'Your father, who fought well for me, asks if you might serve near your brother. I grant his wish. You shall join him in Zacatecas.'

'My father will bless you, sir, as I do now.' When Alvaro reached the mining town he was disturbed to see how much older-looking and leaner his brother had become, but as they talked he found Damián as compelling as ever, for the friar's religious dedication had obviously deepened, causing him to speak with a gravity he had not shown before. The brothers spent two days exchanging information, and they did so enthusiastically, for they had always been friends, sharing secrets they did not share even with their other brothers.

Next morning the colonel told Alvaro: 'The pouch you brought from the viceroy brings a message that you and your brother are to accompany me on a tour of inspection. All of Tejas up to Los Adaes.'

'Excellent!' The young man's enthusiasm was so genuine that the colonel invited him to dinner that night, where he sat facing the provocative daughter of Anselmo Liñán.

The Saldaña brothers formed an interesting pair in the candlelight, Damián in his somber gray habit, Alvaro in his bright uniform, the former thin and moody, the latter robust and smiling. Damián spoke little, nervously; Alvaro, with fluency and confidence: 'The ship that brought us to Vera Cruz was a disgrace, but we had as a fellow passenger a man who could sing like a lark, and he kept us forgetful.' He said also that in the capital the viceroy had explained how important Tejas was and that he, Alvaro, was most eager to see it, to which the colonel replied: 'You'll see enough before we're through.'

As Alvaro continued, Damián became aware, with a mixture of pain and interest, that Benita, seated directly across from his brother, was listening to him with undisguised attention and that whenever he seemed about to stop, she encouraged him with further questions. During the course of the dinner he fairly well presented the outline of his life and his ambitions, with Benita nodding approval.

After dinner she came boldly to Fray Damián and said, in his brother's hearing: 'You must be proud to have Alvaro in your family. We're certainly proud to have him as a visitor.' Given this incentive, Alvaro interrupted: 'Could I take you riding tomorrow?' to which she replied modestly: 'My duena does not ride, but perhaps my father . . .'

The colonel, overhearing the exchange, asked: 'Liñán, is it permissible for me to take these young people for a canter tomorrow?' This posed a difficult problem for Benita's parents, for they still dreamed of seeing their daughter married in Spain, but slowly they were awakening to the fact that families in their modest position usually spent their lives in Mexico, with never enough money saved to enable them to return to the homeland. Therefore, incoming officers of undoubted Spanish blood like this Saldaña were becoming more attractive.

'She can join you,' Liñán said.

No one thought to invite Fray Damián, who spent the hours of their excursion in a grip of a confusion which would engulf him increasingly. He was pleased that his brother had made such a favorable impression on Zacatecas, but he was disturbed that it had to be Benita who translated that favor into action. On the other hand, he realized that she was each day growing closer to that age when she must marry, and since she could never marry him, he was gratified to think that she might choose his brother, for then she would remain within his circle, a part of him, however complex and ill-defined. Now, as he abstractedly placed bricks in a line for the Indian workmen to handle, he awakened to the fact that a tremendous change had overtaken him, as if the normal experiences of a youth which he had avoided were now roaring back in all their tumultuous confusions: 'Dear God! Am I jealous of my brother? Do I wish it was I riding with Benita?' And as he spoke thus to the bricks

99

he was lifting, he visualized the two young people riding ahead of the colonel or falling cleverly behind, and leaning across their horses' necks and kissing.

In the days before the expedition to the north departed, Alvaro and Benita saw a great deal of each other, and often the austere friar was present, watching them as if he were an uncle. And although Alvaro remained unconscious of the meaning of his presence, Benita understood.

On the morning of the departure, 11 December 1721, the colonel produced three fine horses for himself and the Saldaña brothers, but what happened when Fray Damián saw this caused a great commotion, because he said: 'As a Franciscan, I'm forbidden ever to ride a horse.'

The colonel looked at him askance: 'What foolishness have we here?'

'Our vow of poverty. Caballos are for caballeros. Mules and donkeys are for the poor.'

The colonel scoffed at such an idea, but when Damián absolutely refused to accept his horse, the animal was led away and a mule brought forward. It was a criminally inclined beast, one eye lower than the other, one ear cocked, the other flat, and it did not propose to have on its back a friar with a floppy habit, for as soon as Damián tried to mount, it shied away and landed two solid kicks on his right leg.

In no way did this daunt Damián, for looking about, he found a small stick with which he began to hit the mule lightly about the head. The blows did not hurt, but the animal did not like them and drew back in small mincing steps, whereupon Damián danced after him. In time he tamed the animal enough so that he could mount, but the caravan had not even started when the mule leaned forward, planted its two front feet like stone pillars, and tossed Damián over its head.

Again Damián showed no anger; instead, he stood facing the mule, saying: 'I shall have to ride you and you shall have to behave.' At this the mule backed off, and the dancing continued, causing a country poet to begin composing in his head a rather naughty ballad, which would soon be widely recited: 'El Fraile y el Baile' (The Friar and the Dance, or, more colloquially, The Dancing Friar).

At last the mule surrendered, Damián mounted, and the

forward scouts started north. As the main body prepared to follow, with seventeen soldiers and handlers, Benita ran to Alvaro and kissed him. There were gasps from some of the older people, but the colonel approved: 'That's the proper way to send soldiers on a journey.'

'Colonel, bring him back safely! Please bring him back.'

Early December was one of the best times of year in the arid area between Zacatecas and Saltillo, for the intense heat of summer had dissipated. And since this year the fall rains had come late, there was still such a profusion of wildflowers that what would otherwise have been a desert looked like a veritable spring garden. In the invigorating coolness they rode easily, noting the deer on the horizon and the tardy rattlesnake preparing for his winter's hibernation, and often they could see in the distance bands of Indians, who vanished among the gentle hills as the expedition drew near.

Saltillo was a beautiful settlement of stone houses intermixed with low buildings of adobe and a central plaza as charming as any in Mexico. It was so protected on all sides by hills that the colonel said: 'Even a big enemy army would have a difficult time capturing this town if it were properly defended. I'd preempt the high ground and cut the foe to pieces if they tried to come up that valley.'

In Saltillo they witnessed Spain's fundamental attitude toward colonization. This remarkably attractive town contained only two men from the homeland, the commander and the priest, while much rougher Zacatecas had eleven. 'What accounts for this?' Damián asked his brother, and Alvaro offered a shrewd explanation: 'As you say, Saltillo is beautiful, but what is its function? To guard the border in case the French attack. But Zacatecas! Ah! It has those silver mines, and they've got to be protected.'

'Is money everything?' Damián asked, and his brother replied: 'In Madrid, yes.'

One night the Saltillo commander complained: 'We really must have more honest-to-goodness Spaniards. Those born in Mexico can be fine people – my sister's married to one – but they can't be relied upon to preserve the true Spanish culture. And the mestizos they send us?' He spat.

'It's the same in Zacatecas,' the colonel said consolingly. 'Young Saldaña here – the lieutenant, that is – he's the first honest Spaniard we've had assigned there in two years.' He looked approvingly at Alvaro, and then tapped Damián on the shoulder: 'We don't get friars like this one, either, not from the locals they send us.'

'Will the day come,' the Saltillo commander asked, 'when all of Mexico will be governed by mestizos? They'd get their orders from Madrid, of course. They can be very clever, you know. I've had some mestizos on this frontier I'd put up against any of your men from Spain.' He reflected on this, then added: 'But they could never claim to be gentlemen. There's always something missing.'

'I would deplore the day,' the colonel said, tapping a finger as he spoke each word, 'when any part of our empire is governed by locals. We must never allow that to happen.'

'To the north it's already happening,' the commander said. Waving his arm brusquely to indicate all of Tejas, he said: 'You'll find few Spaniards up there, you may be sure.' He summoned an aide: 'Pánfilo, can you think of anyone north of the river who was born in Spain?'

Pánfilo laughed and said: 'There are very few of anything north of the river, regardless of classification. Almost none born in Spain.'

'The missions? Surely, some of our missionaries ...'

'I don't count them,' the aide said.

They dined that night on roast lamb, sweet potatoes, tortillas made fresh from the best corn and a marvelously cool beverage from crushed pomegranate fruit. They toasted the king in Madrid and the viceroy in Mexico City, and when the commander asked if the Saldañas knew any songs from their area in Spain, the brothers offered several with graceful harmony. In response, the two old campaigners offered songs of their own. The formal part of the evening concluded with the opening of a bottle of wine that the commander had been saving for such an occasion.

As the Saldañas walked back under the stars, Alvaro, emboldened by the wine, confided: 'When we return to Zacatecas, I think Benita and I ...' He hesitated. 'I think we shall be married.'

He looked at Damián, expecting congratulations, but his brother had turned his head upward toward the sky to contemplate the heavens. As the friar studied the intricate patterns made by the stars, he imagined the three of them, himself, Benita, Alvaro, existing together in some kind of agreed-upon arrangement. He could not yet envisage what its design might be, but only that it must ensure that he not be deprived of their friendship. 'Father would approve, I know,' he said quietly.

Even the colonel, not a sentimental man, was astounded by the rugged beauty of the trail north from Saltillo, for it penetrated interlocking ranges of mountains that twisted through quiet valleys; these contained no houses or farms, for the Indians in this region could be ferocious. 'This must be the most beautiful empty land in the world,' Alvaro cried, and the colonel replied: 'It's our job to see that it doesn't stay empty.'

The Saldañas received important indoctrination regarding their assignment when they reached the Rio Grande, which had on its south bank a remarkable collection of buildings forming the Franciscan center of San Juan Bautista. It contained three different missions staffed by two friars each; nearby stood a solidly built presidio where the soldiers protecting the area lived. Travelers who stayed at the mission heard from the friars how difficult it was to share a settlement with soldiers who had no love of God or respect for Jesus and who made the work of salvation almost impossible. But those who lodged at the presidio heard whining complaints against the feckless friars who did not work, obeyed no civil law, and converted one dying Indian every two or three years . . . at best.

At the dinner in Zacatecas they had agreed that the Spanish system of settlement was ideal, but when they saw it in actual practice on the frontier, they had to admit that it was painfully disorganized. When soldiers mingled with friars, all kinds of animosities erupted. Soldiers seduced Indian girls in the missions, while the friars carelessly allowed Indians access to restricted areas, where they stole precious supplies needed by the soldiers.

If a friar of outstanding Christian humility governed the mission while a soldier of exemplary character headed the presidio, the system had a chance of functioning, and sometimes it did, but more often a situation developed, like the one in San Juan Bautista, in which overt hostility was avoided but petty antagonisms were inescapable. The colonel, suspecting this, assigned Fray Damián to one of the missions, while he and Alvaro lodged at the presidio, so that the young soldier could experience frontier life at its most typical.

'You'll excuse me, Lieutenant Saldaña, because I know your brother is a friar, and I suppose one of the best,' said the captain in charge of the presidio, 'but these damned friars ...' He shrugged his shoulders as if to say that mere words could not describe their duplicity.

'Anything I should report to Zacatecas?' the colonel asked.

'Nothing, and everything,' the captain said, and with that summation he began listing the malfeasances of the clergy, and a sorry portrait he painted of frontier clericalism, for he charged the friars with theft, willful contravention of the king's ordinance and general insubordination: 'And one particular charge which I do hope you'll mention in your report. By agreement they are obligated to share with us the fruits of their labor – corn, a good goat now and then, a portion of any steer that is slaughtered. And they have green vegetables in their gardens. I know it, I've seen them. But we get none. They use their food to feed their Indians.' The only charge he did not bring against the friars was one which did surface at other posts: 'I must admit, Colonel, that, unsavory as they are, they do not meddle with the Indian women. In their religious duties they're true Christians, anyone would admit that, but in the management of the mission as a part of our system, they're no better than a bunch of lying, lazy thieves.'

At the mission that night charges which did involve Indian women were laid before Fray Damián, with urgent requests that he convey them to the authorities in Zacatecas. 'We cannot prevent those devilish soldiers, whom God has never known, from consorting with our Indian converts. Well, to speak truthfully, they're not really converts, not yet, but we have high hopes. As soon as a girl of that certain age comes to our compound, the soldiers go after her, and before long she's pregnant. At times it seems that our major function on the frontier is the production of mestizo bastards.'

There was one serious complaint which both the friar and the colonel felt must be presented to the authorities, and it was voiced in noninflammatory tones by the friars: 'The order clearly states that we shall have in each mission two friars, which we have provided, and three armed soldiers, which the presidio is to provide. But we never get the soldiers.'

To this justifiable complaint the military officials had solid response: 'We originally placed three soldiers in each mission, as required by the king, but when we did we heard much fault-finding from the friars – "The soldiers did this." "Your soldiers did that." "The soldiers molest the girls." Well, I told them frankly: "If you don't want our soldiers for your work, we can sure as hell use them in ours," so we took them back.'

The colonel suggested that perhaps the presidio could screen its men carefully and find one each for the three missions, but the friars protested: 'That is not what the order provides.' On the night before the expedition departed, the colonel finally put his finger on the sore spot: 'I take my military orders from Mexico City, you know,' and the friars replied: 'And we take our orders from Guadalajara.' It was obvious that the rupture would remain unhealed.

Crossing the Río Grande was physically trivial – water up to the ankle on a stone riverbed as smooth as a table – but emotionally exciting, for now the Spaniards entered a potential battleground: real Apache ready to attack from the west, shadowy Frenchmen lurking in the north. The terrain was inviting to horsemen, great stretches of waving grassland punctuated occasionally by clumps of mesquite bushes, those low, thorny, jagged miniature trees which had always populated the river courses of Tejas but which, in recent years, had begun to invade the grassland wherever the grand balance of nature had been disturbed by the grazing of cattle or the scraping of a hoe. For a friar who hoped to establish there his mission and a presidio, with a town following in due course, this was forbidding land, for it contained little visible water.

But after eight days of such travel, with the crossing of two rivers, the Nueces and the Medina, the Spaniards entered Tejas, where they found sights which gladdened their hearts. A small stream, the San Antonio de Padua, ran with spring-fed water, and on its far bank earlier Franciscans had erected two missions of obvious stability, while on the near bank, a short distance away, a sturdy presidio housed the soldiers guarding the area. Close to the barracks an informal little village consisting of two adobe houses had begun to germinate, and here lived the four mestizo families who endeavored to farm the good fields along the river.

In all ways the settlement was minimal: at the missions, two friars, three soldiers in each and fifty-one Indians, two of whom had converted; in the presidio, a captain, a sergeant and fifty-two soldiers; in the two-hut village, seven adults and three children.

These Franciscan efforts had been named Misión San José and Misión San Antonio de Valero, after the popular saint of Padua and the equally popular viceroy who had authorized its founding. The viceroy carried a formidable appellation: Baltazar Manuel de Zúniga (this could be considered his name) y Guzmán-Sotomayor (his mother's name) y Mendoza y Sarmiento (historic names adhering to his family). And as if this were not sufficient, he was also Marqués de Valero y Duque de Arión (his hereditary titles).

San Antonio de Valero would have been a proper name for this settlement, short and musical, but some busybody remembered that the Marqués de Valero had a renowned half brother, the Duque de Béjar, who had given his life in defense of Christian Budapest during battle with the infidel Turks, and this intruder though it might please the viceroy if the new settlement were named after the hero, so it became San Antonio de Béjar. But as in the case of Méjico and México, local Spanish was cavalier in its interchange of *j* and *x*, so it quickly became San Antonio de Béxar, which the locals promptly abbreviated to Béxar.

Here the internecine struggles which had been so prevalent at the Río Grande missions were avoided, allowing Spanish colonial rule to flourish at its best. Sensible friars at the mission and strong-minded military men in the presidio forced the intricate system to work, riding down any incipient troubles. Into a strange and alien land populated by passive Indians who feared the fierce, untamed Apache to the west, had come a handful of devout Spaniards to build their low-roofed buildings and dig their irrigation ditches.

As soon as Fray Damián saw Béxar he loved it: 'Oh, I would like to work here!' and he asked the colonel: 'Could I not start my mission . . . off to the north, where I wouldn't interfere with San Antonio de Valero? There is so much work to be done.' But the soldier had specific orders: 'Our job is to inspect and protect the real frontier, the area of the Nacogdoches mission,' and so with profound regrets Fray Damián left a place which had excited his imagination and started the long march to the bleak northern extremity of Tejas.

'The journey from Béxar to Los Adaes,' explained a soldier who had fought in Europe's mercenary armies, 'is as long as marching up from Paris, across Flanders, across the Netherlands, and into the Germanies. Tejas is big.'

As they kept bearing to the northeast, the brothers noticed radical changes in the scenery. They started across flat grassland and mesquite, then encountered rolling country with many trees, and next were in a completely different terrain, with trees but also with real prairies suitable for farming. Finally they came to what they thought was best of all, fine woodlands with promising soil: 'Here a man could cut down the trees and make himself a farm that would feed a village.'

As they traveled through this magnificent and almost pristine region, so totally different from the land around Béxar, Damián reflected on an oddity which perplexed him: 'Why is the capital of Tejas so far north? On the borders of Louisiana?' He pondered this, but could find no rational justification: 'By all reason the capital should be at Béxar, for it is central and the source of leadership in Tejas, but since no one at the Council of the Indies in Madrid has ever been to Tejas or seen an accurate map, the capital is kept far to the north, from where it will be almost impossible to provide good government.'

Alvaro offered a clear explanation: 'France. They control Louisiana a few leagues to the east. Our father fought against them three times, and even though we have a kind of peace now, would you like to gamble on what the situation will be next year? Madrid's clever: "Keep the capital on the frontier. Keep your eye on those damned Frenchmen."'

In late January they reached the west bank of the Neches, a stream one could jump, and although military practice required that a military force cross over at dusk so that it would be prepared to march on in the morning, regardless of any change that might have occurred to the river, the western bank was so hospitable that the men had unpacked the mules and pitched camp before the colonel could stop them. That night a winter storm of huge dimension struck, and by morning the Neches was a torrent which raged for seven days, to the colonel's disgust with himself for having ignored a basic rule.

However, since the Saldaña brothers were an enterprising pair, they utilized the forced delay to inspect one of the saddest sights in Tejas, the abandoned ruins of a cluster of missions that had once served the region. They had flourished briefly in the 1690s, giving promise of becoming a focus of some importance, but the hostility of the Indians and the fluctuating attitudes of the nearby French had doomed the effort. Worthy Franciscans had lost their enthusiasm and sometimes their lives in these ruins. Their efforts had marked the high tide of Spain's colonizing effort, and they had failed.

Soldier and friar looked upon the ruins from vastly different perspectives, and it was Alvaro who voiced the no-nonsense interpretation sponsored by the Spanish government in Madrid: 'No cause for grief, Damián. Missions are thrust into locations to establish a foothold, no more. Pacify the Indians, start a community, and when things are stable, invite the civil government to take over. The mission closes, job done. The buildings gradually fall apart. And you friars move along to your next obligation.' He saw the deserted ruins simply as proof that in this instance the procedure had failed.

But Damián saw in the rotting timbers that tragedy of crushed aspirations, the death of plans which once must have seemed so promising, and he could hear the early friars assuring one another: 'We'll establish our mission here, and bring the word of God to the Indians, and watch as families from Spain move in to build a city.' Now only the pines whispered over the graves.

'This could have been a major settlement,' Damián said. 'Families should be living here. Children in the shadow of the church. This is heartbreaking.' He asked his brother to kneel as he said prayers for the departed souls who had struggled so diligently to accomplish so little. For Damián, a mission was not some temporary agency that appeared casually and slipped away when its work was done; it was intended to serve as the everlasting soul of a community, and any abrupt demise was tragic.

When they finally negotiated the swollen Neches, they came upon rude buildings in which new missions were being attempted, but their success seemed doubtful, and as Damián bade these Franciscans goodbye, it was with a sense of futility. Spain was not impressive in these remote corners of its empire.

The ninety-odd miles to Los Adaes were some of the most mournful Alvaro would ever travel, for they proved that the expedition was leaving the Tejas sphere of influence and entering a world in which Spaniards played no significant role. 'It's all wrong, Damián. We should be back in Béxar, building a city.'

The new capital was a pitiful sham, a few wooden buildings at the farthest end of a supply line along which Madrid rarely sent anything usable. Spanish officials confided: 'The French over at Natchitoches arrange things so that we can buy goods smuggled in from the former French capital at Mobile, and for every honest man in the area, there must be a dozen cut-throats who have escaped down the Mississippi River.' The chapel had barely the equipment for a proper Mass, and Damián thought that if this was the best Spain could do with its empire, that empire was doomed.

The captain acting as governor was always sickly, the foul air from the marshes having affected his lungs so that he coughed continuously. After he read the instructions sent to him from Mexico City, he informed Damián: 'You are to come back with settlers and attempt a new mission in these parts,' an assignment which the friar accepted without comment.

'Am I to man the presidio?' Alvaro asked, and the governor tapped the letter: 'No mention of it.' But the colonel interrupted: 'These are good men, Captain. I shall recommend that they work as a team, and I pray that you will second it.' Without giving the suggestion even a moment's study, the weary governor coughed several times, then said: 'Very well. It can do no harm, I should think.'

When the garrison troops were lined up to see the visitors off, Alvaro saw to his disgust that no two men had the same uniform and that most had none. They were a ragtag disgrace to the army, and the governor confided: 'These are my best. The worst run off to New Orleans once they see this place.' And this ineffectual man, governor of all Tejas, wiped his nose on his sleeve.

Joyous news awaited the brothers when they returned to Béxar, for a letter from Benita Liñán informed Alvaro that she was eager to marry him as soon as he returned home. It sounded as if she had wedding plans under way, even though the young officer had not yet spoken to her father, as custom required.

When they reached Zacatecas, Benita told Damián that they wanted him to officiate, and as he was preparing for a day which he knew would bring him confusion, he received good news of his own. The administrator of the district summoned him and his Franciscan superior to headquarters, and told them: 'The new viceroy arrived in Mexico while you were in the north, Fray Damián, and he believes that the French menace has subsided. He doesn't want to build a mission near Los Adaes. But he does command the Franciscans to establish one more strengthening mission at Béxar. And the father-principal and I have decided that you're the one to go. We'll provide you with an escort directly after the wedding.'

Damián, contrasting the fraternity he had experienced at Béxar with the mournful emptiness of the Louisiana border, was delighted with what he held to be a promotion. But when it occurred to him that he might be rejoicing over something which represented a reversal of God's plans for him – perhaps He meant for me to do His work in Los Adaes; perhaps those ruined missions were left along the Neches to inspire me – he felt ashamed of himself for having found joy in a lesser task while escaping the greater to which heaven might have assigned him. This was a real concern, and one which agitated him for some weeks, so that as the wedding approached he found himself beset by doubled turmoil: he was in love with his brother's bride, there could be no other word for it, and he was ashamed of himself for exulting over his escape from un-pleasant or even dangerous duty. He fell into the anguish of self-doubt which would characterize his early years as a missionary: I'm a poor example. I have sin upon me and I cannot cleanse myself. I'm unworthy to be a shepherd and am amazed that God does not strike me.

He was diverted from such self-chastisement when he met the young friar who was to share the duties at the new mission, for Fray Domingo Pacheco, fourteen years younger, was a round-faced, happy, brown-skinned mestizo. His father, a Spanish soldier in charge of a ranch belonging to the viceroy, had been so beset by loneliness that he had taken to wife a comely Indian woman, who had been given the name María and who had raised their son Domingo with songs and slaps, kisses and chastisements.

Fray Domingo looked upon the world as a place of contradiction and insanity which could be managed only with a grin, a shrug of the shoulders and the avoidance of as much unpleasantness as possible, and by unpleasantness he meant work. When assigned a job, he nodded, said it was easy to perform, assured the man in command that it would be done promptly, then worked as little and as slowly as possible, smiling warmly whenever a supervisor stopped by to inspect his progress. With Domingo things were always going well, tomorrow was sure to see the task finished, and for each time an observer saw him frown, he saw him smile a score of times.

He was not a stupid fellow, for in his twenty-two years he had accumulated a world of practical knowledge, so that his instructors at the college were often surprised by the astuteness of his answers and reassured by his obvious devotion to his calling. Though he had been characteristically satisfied with taking only minor orders, he was still a full-fledged friar, and he could perform marriages and baptisms but he could not sing the Mass or engage in certain other restricted rituals. Fray Domingo was a servant of God who believed that with all the sour-faced monks and friars and priests in the world, there must be a place for someone who smiled.

He had what Fray Damián would never attain: an absolute faith in the benevolence of God and a comforting assurance that whatever he, Domingo, did was in accordance with God's will. This supreme confidence came from his mother, who had belonged to a primitive tribe of Indians far south of Oaxaca; this group held women in low regard, and when she first learned of Christianity and the exalted role played by the Virgin Mary, she placed her entire confidence in the new religion. It was a beautiful religion, consoling, rich in its promises and realistic in its earthly performance. If the Spanish conversion of Mexico had accomplished nothing but the reorganization of women's lives, as in the case of María Pacheco, it would have achieved great triumphs, for she accepted the new faith joyously and taught her son to do the same.

Although he shunned work, Domingo was in no way a coward. He knew that the frontier was a dangerous place, for he had seen those plaques shaped like hearts that adorned the walls of the refectory at the college: SACRED TO THE MEMORY OF FRIAR LUÍS GALINDO, MARTYRED AT SANTA FÉ, 1680. There were memorials to the Franciscans who had accompanied Coronado on his expedition and who had remained behind in the wilderness to find their martyrdom, and he had heard of how the missionaries in Tejas, north and south, had had to defend themselves against the very Indians they had been sent to save. But none of this information daunted his resolve to be the finest servant of God ever sent north; he was willing to die, even if he was not willing to work unnecessarily in the years prior to his martyrdom.

'I will be your faithful companion,' he assured Fray Damián, who, in a gesture of gratitude, invited him to participate in the forthcoming nuptials.

The wedding was held in the cathedral, and it seemed that everybody of prominence in Zacatecas and surrounding villages participated in the happy occasion. Women of various hues wept when sprightly Benita Liñán half walked, half danced down the narrow nave to where her future brother-in-law waited to perform the ceremony. Dressed in a fine black habit, he stood very tall as he received the bride, but he did not create an imposing impression, for he trembled and his face grew quite red, as if he had forgotten his lines. When the time came for him to take the hand of the bride and place it in the hand of the groom, he shook so noticeably that those in front feared he might be ill, but he regained control and finished the ceremony in a clear voice, giving a benediction which all who heard it would remember:

'My brother, my sister, may you live within the arms of Jesus Christ, may you create a home which radiates love, may your children prosper in their dedication to God, and may all who see you proclaim: "This is a Christian marriage." Brother Alvaro, sister Benita, this is a day of great joy for me as it is for you, and may the Grace of God descend upon us all who have solemnized this act of Holy Matrimony.'

Damián spent a restless night, rising three times to kneel and pray that his mission in Tejas might reflect in all its operations the will of God. He asked for a blessing upon his companion, that good man Fray Domingo, and he asked special blessings for the couple who were starting their marriage that night, Alvaro and Benita de Saldaña. At the third prayer, when he came to this last name, he dropped his hands from the praying position, allowed his head to fall upon the bed, and wept.

In a thoughtful gesture that gave great pleasure in Mexico City and at the same time ensured financial support in Béxar, the Franciscans decided to name their new mission after the favorite saint of the incoming viceroy, and then add his title so there could be no misunderstanding as to who in heaven and on earth was being honored: Santísima Misión Santa Teresa de Casafuerte. And then, to make clear who in Mexico was running the place, they added: del Colegio de Propaganda Fide de Nuestra Señora de Guadalupe de Zacatecas.

When this grandiose name was first pronounced the mission consisted of some sixty acres of virgin soil containing not even a shed, but it was favorably located on the west bank of the Río San Antonio, about two miles north of Misión San Antonio de Valero, where the Saldaña brothers had once stayed. The new mission had a promising site and nothing more, except grazing rights to some five leagues of range land, twenty-two thousand acres, fifteen miles to the southwest.

To make the place function, the two friars would have to build, with whatever help they could persuade the nearby Indians to lend, all the structures of a substantial establishment. A church would be needed, domiciles for the two friars, quarters for the three soldiers assigned to protect the place, housing for the converted Indians who would live there, and either barns or sheds for the cattle, with several small buildings for the care of such tools as the mission might accumulate. It would require boundless energy to accomplish all this and yet win the watching Indians to Christianity.

In the days when the two friars were getting started they were grudgingly accommodated at Misión San Antonio, which did not welcome their competition and made it clear that this accommodation could not continue indefinitely, so the opening argument at Santa Teresa concerned which building should be erected first. Fray Domingo was all for concentrating on a house for himself and his superior, but Fray Damián believed that their first obligation was to build a church: 'How else can we win the Indians to Christianity?'

'Brother,' Domingo argued persuasively, 'how can we preach to anyone if we ourselves lack a place to sleep?' He punched himself in the belly: 'Feed yourself, sleep well, then worry about the souls of others.'

This advice Fray Damián had to accept, for Fray Domingo refused to work on the church until he had a place in which to live. So with the aid of two Indians he constructed an amazing hut: in front it was composed of rough adobe bricks, unevenly made and haphazardly piled around a big open door. The three other sides were poles stuck upright in the ground, interlaced with grapevines and plastered with mud. The roof was an untidy mixture of logs, thatch, saplings, mud and grass. The whole looked like the lodge of a careless beaver, dragged onto dry land, with projections everywhere and dirt universal. This was the jacal common throughout northern Mexico, and when Fray Damián's mission was finished, it would contain two score of them.

But even after this ramshackle cell-like structure was built, Fray Domingo showed little inclination to do construction work at the church; his strength lay in his ability to talk Indians into becoming members of the mission so that they would do the work. At the end of the first two months, whereas Damián had performed wonders in getting the foundation footings dug and filled with rock, he had not brought in a single Indian, while Fray Domingo, whistling and singing in the fields, had lured more than a dozen into the system. Demanding of them only three or four hours' work a day, 'in the service of the Lord', he had his Indians cut the timbers for the roof of the adobe church in one-tenth the time Fray Damián had been taking.

The first confrontation between the two friars concerned this matter of adobes, for the making of these sun-dried clay bricks was a messy affair, and Fray Domingo flatly refused to step into the mixing trough himself and tread into the muddy clay and straw that bond the bricks together. 'I won't do it, and I can't trust my Indians to do it,' he wailed, so Damián, desperately needing a steady supply of the adobes for his walls, tucked his robes about his middle, kicked off his sandals, and entered the mixing trough, treading the clay and straw until it was ready for pouring into the wooden molds, where it would drain until firm enough to stack in the sun. All this he did himself.

Sometimes at night when he lay exhausted from his arduous labors, he would listen as Fray Domingo explained about the Indians, whose languages he was learning: 'The governor at Chihuahua had one of his scribes make a list of all the Indian tribes in the northern Spanish lands. And how many completely different tribes do you suppose there were? Hundreds of them. And they speak more languages than I could ever learn. Tell me, Damián, how many tribes in the two missions here at Béxar?'

Damián listened drowsily to the recitation: 'Pampopa, Postito, Tacame, a few Borrado, Payaya, Orejone. And remember, Brother, each group has its own interests, its own animosities toward all the others.' Damián did not hear this warning, for he had fallen asleep.

The first significant problem at Santa Teresa arose one day when Domingo rushed over to where Damián was laboring with roof beams: 'Brother! Joyous news! My converts Lucas and María wish to be married in the church, roof or no roof.'

This was a portentous development and the friars knew it, the first visible proof that they were making some headway with the Indians: 'I'm so delighted, Brother Domingo, that you have accomplished this.'

'And he's one of our best workers! He makes our adobes.'

'I shall prepare for the wedding immediately,' Damián said. 'I'll put that big beam in place so that we can have at least part of a roof to stand under,' but as he talked he realized that Domingo had drawn away, almost imperceptibly but definitely away, and when he met with the couple to be married he understood why, for in such Spanish as Domingo had taught them, they said: 'We like this one ... laughing ... to say the prayers.'

Damián's face betrayed no emotion, for he recognized the validity of this request; Domingo had converted them, had shown them the radiance of God's love, had demonstrated the brotherhood of all who lived in Christ. To them he was the shepherd; Damián, the taskmaster. Gravely the disappointed friar bowed to the request of these first converts; as founder of Misión Santa Teresa de Casafuerte, he had aspired to conduct the first marriage, the first baptism, the first prayers for a soul going to heaven, but it was not to be. At the Indian wedding held beneath the protection of the partial roof he had spurred into being, it was laughing, joking, singing Fray Domingo who performed the ceremony and blessed the couple.

The two friars did not allow this first contretemps to disrupt their relationship, for Domingo did not use his personal triumph at the wedding to color in any way his basic subordination to Damián, whom he acknowledged in all things as his superior; and Damián, although hurt, did not seek any petty revenge upon his assistant. The two men remained amiable and friendly, with Damián laboring each day more sturdily, at the building of the church, and Domingo at building good relations with the Indians, who saw his darker skin as proof that he was one of them, partly at least.

But when the tasks of building became more arduous and difficult than even Damián's exceptional energy could manage, he did feel it necessary to draft a careful letter to his superior back in Zacatecas:

Esteemed Father-Guardian. It is my pleasure to inform you that so far affairs at the Misión Santa Teresa de Casafuerte are progressing according to the schedule you proposed and in obedience to God's will. We have baptizèd several Indians of the Orejone and Yuta tribes and arranged Christian marriages for two couples who are now living within God's grace.

Fray Domingo Pacheco accomplishes wonders with his charges and is already talking about establishing a large ranch some leagues to the west. I encourage him in this because he has exceptional skill in working with Indians, who seem to love his friendly ways.

The building of the mission is left largely to me, since Fray Domingo must attend to other matters, and I am afraid that I shall soon fall behind schedule. But you have with you in Zacatecas an excellent carpenter, name of Simón Garza, who is married to the woman Juana Muñoz, and I wonder if you would send him to help me in the building of this mission? I sorely need a carpenter, and Garza is one of the best.

Please give this request your prayerful consideration.

S.S.Q.B.L.M. de V.R.
P.A. Dios G. a V.R.M. Ans.

The formalized signature was to be read: 'Su servidor que besa la mano de Vuestra Reverencia. Pido a Dios guarde a Vuestra Reverencia muchos anos.' (Your servant who kisses the hand of Your Reverence. Pray to God that Your Reverence may have many years.)

The forthrightness of Fray Damián's plea and the double touch of formalized humility at the closing apparently impressed the authorities at Zacatecas, because when the next caravan from Saltillo approached the mission two small horses moved forward, bringing into Tejas a pair of the hardest-working citizens that state would ever know, the carpenter Simón Garza and his wife, Juana.

They were given a corner of the mission compound, in which they built themselves a small jacal, and it was here that Juana had her first child. Her husband worked many hours a day on the mission buildings, and told his wife one night: 'Strange. I was sent here to be an assistant to Fray Damián, but it turns out that he is my assistant.'

'What do you mean?'

'I lay out the work. Where the beams should go and how they should be fastened. But he does all the lifting, the really hard work.'

Garza was correct. Fray Damián, thirty-nine years old, labored like a man possessed: first, dwelling places for his charges, then a dwelling place for the Lord, then a warmer, dryer jacal for Fray Domingo, who worked so diligently among the heathen, then a better barn for the cattle, then a stockade around the entire mission to protect it from the fierce Apache who fought the mission's intrusion, seeing it as an encroachment on their territory; and now his most important project of all, the one that would ensure the prosperity and safety of the fledgling settlement.

Bringing Fray Domingo and Garza together one evening when that day's work was done Damián said: 'We shall never prosper until we bring a little canal from the river, across our fields, where we need water, and directly into our compound, leading it along this depression and out through the part of the wooden fence. Can we do this?'

Garza deferred to Fray Domingo, who disappointed him by saying: 'It would require far too much work and we don't have enough shovels.' When Damián looked at the carpenter, Garza said: 'Domingo's right. Huge effort. And we have only two shovels. But I can make some. For without secure water we can't live.'

So Damián and Garza laid plans for the building of a canal that would eventually run almost a mile, five feet wide and three feet deep, meaning that an immense amount of earth would have to be moved. But like many of the great accomplishments of the world – the building of a pyramid or the digging of a tunnel – it was a measurable job in that one started it, worked for a couple of years, edged it along as best one could, and realized one happy day that it could be finished. The digging of this canal, which would vitalize the mission, was not a gargantuan task that staggered the imagination of those obligated to build it; it was a day-to-day job of moving earth, and the two planners with their Indian helpers attacked it with that understanding.

Garza, forging all the spare bits of metal he could find, and using oak limbs for handles, fashioned two extra shovels, which were converted into badges of honor to be conferred on particular Indians who worked well: 'Juan Diego, you can have a shovel today. Esteban can keep the one he had yesterday. But only if he digs well.'

Invariably Fray Damián assigned himself the most difficult tasks, such as lifting the loosened earth from the trench, but he actually reveled in the hard work, believing that it made him more definitely a servant of God. On Sundays, when all others rested, he rose before dawn, prepared to sing the Mass, cleared his mind of mundane matters and reflected on the majesty of heaven. When the entire community had gathered in the rude church, with soldiers from the presidio often in attendance, he preached his simple message of salvation:

'God willed that a mission be established here, and He did so for three reasons. First, he wanted His word brought to you Indians so that you might gain salvation. Second, He wanted a settlement erected in the wilderness where Christian families could establish themselves, as Corporal Valdez and his Elena have done with His blessing. And third, I think He wanted us to build our canal so that His children could have better gardens and more sheep and a secure fortress against the enemy.

'In all these ambitions we prosper. Fray Domingo's choir never sang more sweetly than it did this morning. The soldiers at the presidio eat better than last year. And soon our canal will deliver water right to the edge of our gardens. Faithful women to whom we owe so much, no longer will you have to haul the water from our wells. It will come gushing right into our furrows and we shall have more beans than we ourselves can eat. Then we can even share our prosperity with Misión Valero.'

In the latter months of 1726 he worked so strenuously on the canal that even when he was dead tired, his bones tingling pleasantly, he would be unable to fall asleep, and one night as he lay awake he recalled a special plea which Fray Domingo had pressed with unusual vigor: 'Fray Damián, you're the master here, no question about that, but I do think that you and I deserve better vestments than they allow us. We're representatives of the church of the King himself, and we should have proper dress in which to conduct prayers. You know that as well as I.'

It was a persuasive argument. If men at the farthest frontier, men on the battle line of civilization, represented the forces of civilization, they should be properly accoutered, which meant that friars who conducted church services ought to have blue robes of decent quality. But a decision to spend the money required for such robes, a considerable sum, could be made only in Madrid, and Damián could think of no reasonable process whereby he might force his petition all the way to the king, and so as he worked he pondered this problem.

Domingo was persistent: 'Damián, I work six days a week out on the ranch we're building so that our Indians can herd our cattle safely, and I don't mind looking like a peasant when I'm building the little jacales my families will stay in . . .' This was a silly petition, and Damián knew it as well as Domingo, for the latter did almost no work at the ranch; he sat astride his mule and directed his Indians to do it, and he was supervising the construction of a small settlement of four jacales in which the shepherds could take shelter when they guarded the remote pasturelands.

Through Domingo's careful husbandry, Santa Teresa had accumulated a herd of more than a thousand long-horned cattle, for which he had paid nothing. 'Any morning four good riders can go out on the range and collect a hundred good bulls and cows, free.' But he had used mission funds to purchase from breeders in Saltillo a starting flock of sheep, a hundred goats and ninety horses, all of which were reproducing well. He had also acquired through ingenious stratagems a mixed complement of donkeys, mules and oxen, so that he was responsible for a substantial investment. It was he who traded the surplus to the army for services only the military could supply, and it was also he who arranged that some of the best horses be herded back to Saltillo and sold for coins which could be spent in Zacatecas for those things like tobacco, chocolate and sugar candies which helped make life bearable. He had a just claim on the Spanish government, for he served it well, and now he wanted a proper blue vestment for Sundays.

Fray Damián could not in clear conscience claim such a garment for himself; he visualized himself as a mere friar obligated to build a mission, and the kind of garment in which he appeared was of no consequence, for he could not believe that Peter or Matthew or Luke had bothered much about his dress when he served Christ. But if he himself lacked pretensions, he realized that other men were differently motivated. He had watched the subtle effect on the Indian Juan Diego when he was allowed to use a shovel – he became a better man when confidence was reposed in him. Domingo was the same; he had resigned himself to secondary orders, but within the limitations of his position, he served well and was entitled to prerequisites. Accordingly, one morning Fray Damián drafted a letter intended for the very highest authorities, whether in Mexico or Spain.

But submitting such a request was not a simple procedure. First, the petition had to be written on stamped paper, printed and distributed by the government; no request or report of any kind could be official unless at its head appeared the stamp of the Spanish government, a system comparable to the one which England would introduce into its colonies facing the Atlantic. Since such paper was jealously guarded and distributed in a niggardly fashion, careless requests rarely surfaced. Fray Damián could get his stamped paper only at the presidio, where the commanding officer had a low opinion of missionaries. For two months the latter refused to issue the paper, but Fray Domingo handled this by quietly suggesting to the commander that if the paper was not immediately forthcoming, there would be no more chickens from the mission farm.

Fray Damián wrote his petition on 21 January 1717:

> Since my faithful assistant Fray Domingo Pacheco of excellent reputation represents the majesty of the Spanish Crown in Tejas, it would be proper for him to have a vestment of blue linen-and wool, highest quality, and I beseech the authorities to allow him to have it. And since I labor constantly to finish the canal upon which the welfare of this mission depends, I ask for three shovels of first-class iron with handles of oak from Spain to match. If the oak cannot be spared, I can fashion handles here, but do prefer Spanish oak, for it is best.

The petition, properly folded, was sent down to San Juan Bautista on 29 January, and there it languished until a courier was sent to Monclova on 25 February. From there it went at a leisurely pace to Saltillo, arriving in mid-March in time to catch a messenger headed for Zacatecas, which it reached on the tenth of April.

The authorities at the Franciscan offices realized that they had no jurisdiction over such a special request, and they had learned through harsh experience not to take such matters into their own hands, not in the Spanish system, so they forwarded the petition to Mexico City, but they were bold enough to add an endorsement: 'These are two good men, so perhaps they might have two vestments, one tall, one short.'

Franciscan headquarters in the capital received the document on 19 May and refused even to study it, referring it to the viceroy's office. This authority kept it on file till the fifteenth of July, when it was forwarded to Vera Cruz for shipment to Spain with a second endorsement: 'Fray Damián de Saldaña is the son of Don Miguel de Saldaña of Saldaña, a man to be trusted.'

A Spanish trading ship sailed from Vera Cruz at the end of July, but it stopped in both Cuba and Española, laying over in the latter port for two months and not sailing for Spain until the third of October. No officials in these two ports were allowed to touch the pouch from Mexico, so Damián's letter was delivered at the port of Sanlúcar at the end of a four-week crossing. From there it was sent to a section of the Council of the Indies holding session in Sevilla, where clerks studied the unusual request for three weeks. It was finally decided what should have been clear at the start, that this was a unique problem which could be solved only by the king, so belatedly a mounted messenger took the letter to Madrid. He arrived on the twenty-ninth of November, and at dawn on the next day the King of Spain eagerly reached for official messages from his dominions in the New World, reading each one meticulously and making upon it such advisory notes as he deemed fit.

In the afternoon he came upon Fray Damián's stamped and endorsed paper: 'A blue habit for Sundays and three iron shovels.'

The king leaned back, rubbed his tired eyes, and tried to visualize Mexico, a part of the empire for the last two centuries. It was difficult, for he was a newcomer to the throne of Spain. When the powerful Austrian Hapsburg line – Charles V, Phillip II and their successors – died out in 1700, the French Bourbons supplied the next king, Phillip V, a boy of seventeen.

Although no member of his royal family had ever visited Mexico, he had seen enough drawings and read enough reports to know fairly accurately what it was like: Mexico City, Oaxaca, Guadalajara and even Zacatecas were familiar locations, but when he tried to picture Tejas, his imagination failed, for it was the loneliest and least important of his frontiers.

'How many Spaniards in Tejas?' he asked the courtiers who brought him his belated lunch.

'Born in Spain, sixteen, maybe twenty. Born in Mexico itself, perhaps two hundred, counting mestizos. Indians, of course.'

'Sixteen Spaniards in the entire territory, and he wants a blue vestment. Notice that he is bold enough to ask for the best linen-and-wool. Who is this man?'

One of the aides looked at the petition and particularly at the endorsement from the viceroy: 'Son of Don Miguel de Saldaña, of the village of Saldaña. He supported you vigorously when Europe wanted to put someone else on our throne.'

'Good man,' the king said, and as he ate, another aide pointed to a peculiarity in the petition: 'Did you notice, Sire, that he asks for the habit not for himself but for his assistant? What he seeks are the shovels.'

The king pushed back his meal, lifted the petition once more, and asked: 'Am I thinking of the same Saldaña? The one who served us so well in Portugal?'

'The same.' Once more the king hesitated: 'Have any of you ever been to Tejas?' No one had, neither in the meeting room nor the entire court, so the king asked: 'Isn't that where they have the buffalo?' and while the courtiers argued whether these great animals – several of which had been imported to Spain for the amazement of the citizenry – inhabited Tejas or Sante Fé, the king impulsively took the petition and not only signed it but even added a notation of his own. The paper was then returned to the Council of the Indies, which endorsed it and started it upon its slow journey back to Sanlúcar, to Cuba, to Mexico City, to Saltillo, to San Juan Bautista and finally to Misión Santa Teresa de Casafuerte. It arrived on 19 July 1728, eighteen months after posting, and with it came a package.

It was so heavy when Fray Damián lifted it in his tired, calloused hands that he cried out thoughtlessly: 'Be praised, Garza. We have our shovels,' forgetting that Fray Domingo, who was eyeing the package jealously, hoped for something much different. And indeed, when he and Garza ripped open the sea-stained crate they found their three shovels, with handles of Spanish oak, best in the world.

'Look!' cried Domingo, and from a corner of a small package inside the larger peeked a swatch of blue cloth, and when he opened his prize with trembling fingers he held up for all to see a most beautiful blue habit with hood and belt and flowing folds. He could not restrain himself from throwing the precious garment about his shoulders, but as he started to parade in the sunlight so that his Indians could applaud, he chanced to look back at the package, and there beneath the first robe lay a second. Stooping to take it in his hands, he allowed its full length to fall free, and he saw that it was a larger robe of much finer cloth than the first, and it was apparent to him that this had been sent by the king as a personal gift to his superior.

'This must be for you,' he said, but Fray Damián pushed it back, and then took the first robe from the shoulders of his assistant: 'This one will do for me.'

'Do you think so?' Domingo asked, and Damián said: 'I'm certain.'

Now that Fray Domingo had appropriated the habit intended for Damián, he took doubled interest in his work, riding out to the ranch southwest of the mission each Monday and working there throughout the week. The Santa Teresa ranch was a reach of unlimited definition, with no roads or fences, nor any houses in which anyone of even the slightest importance would wish to stay. It did contain a rude corral but had no barns or sheds or tool cribs, nothing but an endless expanse of grassland suitable for the untended grazing of cattle. Its effective area was about five leagues, but this meant nothing because if no other owner in the region gained title to adjacent lands, it could just as well have been five hundred.

Its chief asset was that it lay within a sharp turn of the Medina, whence its name, Rancho El Codo (Elbow Ranch). Indeed, the Medina surrounded it on three sides, guaranteeing the cattle all the water they needed.

Within a compound it had four miserable adobe-and-wattle jacales in which the Indian families who tended the cattle lived; two of the hovels were occupied by married men who had brought their wives and children with them, the other two housed unmarried men, and sometimes when Fray Domingo studied the six adults who worked for him he speculated as to why they so willingly submitted themselves to this arduous labor, for neither he nor Fray Damián had the authority to force them to work.

He was pondering this question one August afternoon as the Indians were sweating over the branding of young stock while he rested in the shade. The branding was necessary because the rule from Madrid was stern: 'In settled areas, any cattle unbranded promptly after birth remain the property of the king.' The ranch at El Codo could have twenty thousand cattle if it wanted them, but it had to round them up and brand them, and that work was dusty and dirty and arduous, since each animal had to be wrestled to the ground before the red-hot brand could be applied.

Why do they consent to such toil? Domingo asked himself as he watched the Indians. And for that matter, why does Fray Damián work so hard? And how about me? I could be in Mexico City enjoying myself.

And it occurred to him that he and Damián were much like the Indians: We work because it's the will of God. We build the mission because Jesus Christ wants it. This is honorable work, because my father and mother and the priest in Saltillo told me it was. The Bible says so, too. The Indians obey us because deep inside they know it's right. They're living better lives than their fathers, and they know it.

Wherever he worked with Indians, Fray Domingo organized a choir, and the one at El Codo was among his finest, because three of the men had deep voices, Domingo a lilting tenor, and the fourth Indian man a strong voice which maintained a strict monotone in the middle, never moving up or down no matter how carefully the friar coached him. He was like a cello that could strike only one powerful note around which the other singers had to organize theirs, and when this choir sang on Sundays or in the evenings at prayer, the music glorified the countryside.

It was a tradition of the Franciscans that 'we never discipline the Indians except for their own good,' and Domingo believed that his own rules were just and lenient. If his Indians lagged in their field work, he reproved them. If anyone persisted, he lectured that person severely, and if the error continued, he beat him or her with a leather strap reserved for that use. But as soon as the punishment was administered, he invited the culprit back to the choir, and after a few resentful moments the reproof was forgotten, except by a few who left, never to return.

It was Domingo's love for music which projected Misión Santa Teresa into a storm that nearly destroyed it. An enthusiastic friar newly arrived from the more traditional Franciscan center at Querétaro northwest of Mexico City, took vigorous exception to the fiery dances enjoyed by the Indians of Béxar, for he categorized these exhibitions as 'licentious debauchery of the worst sort, calculated to induce venery and the most debased forms of sexual extravagance.' With written approval from the authorities at Saltillo, who had never seen these dances, he proceeded to stamp them out.

But when he eliminated them at Misión San José, they erupted at Misión San Antonio de Valero, and so on. However, with extraordinary vigor he succeeded for a while in halting them all except for those at Santa Teresa, where Fray Domingo's lyric choir would start a celebration with hymns, move on to Spanish ballads he had taught them, and progress to some lively Indian chants, until they reached the point where all the listeners were stomping their feet and clapping their hands, and even dancing. Sometimes the noise grew so vigorous that the two friars deemed it best to retire.

Fray Damián saw nothing intrinsically evil in such dancing, but the new friar thought differently, and backed by an official paper from the religious authorities in Guadalajara, he marched in to the officer in charge of the presidio at Béxar and demanded that he stop the dancing at Santa Teresa: 'It's an affront to God, who wants it stopped at once.'

The officer had been searching for some excuse to discipline the two friars at Santa Teresa, for he found the senior man, Fray Damián, too aloof, and the junior, Fray Domingo, much too niggardly with the food his Indians grew. So he issued an edict: 'No more dancing at Santa Teresa.'

He expected Fray Domingo, who started his music with proper gravity but allowed it to deteriorate quickly, to object, but to his surprise it was tall, thin Fray Damián who came quietly to the presidio, speaking softly and with obvious deference: 'Captain, the Indians have always danced, and while I admit it sometimes leads to excesses, as the new friar claims, I

126

have found no great wrong in it and much good.'

'But I've issued an order.'

'I think you might want to reconsider your order,' Damián said gently.

'Where Indians are concerned, I never reconsider.'

Damián did not wish to argue, but he did voice an important judgement: 'Captain, when we move in upon the Indians with our missions and our presidios we ask them to surrender a great many things they love, traditions which have kept them strong . . . in a most inhospitable land, I may point out. They've been gracious here in Tejas in making such surrender. Don't ask them to sacrifice everything.'

'But the dances are against the will of God. The new friar said so.'

'I think our laughing Domingo represents the will of God, too.' Before the captain could destroy that specious argument, Damián said. 'I sometimes fear his singing accomplishes more than my prayers.'

'There will be no more dancing.'

'Very well,' Damián said obediently. And when he returned to the mission he waited till his companion returned from the ranch, herding along several steers that were to be slaughtered there.

'The dancing . . .' Damián fumbled.

'What about it?'

'The captain has ordered it stopped.'

'He has no authority . . .'

'He has.'

'The captain is an ass.'

'That we know,' Damián conceded. 'We've known it for better than a year. But he has the civil authority to preserve the peace.'

'Our hearts beat faster . . . with delight. I'll not stop it.'

'You shall. It's my order, too.' And Damián spoke with such unprecedented force that Domingo gasped, and the dancing was halted.

The three soldiers watched very carefully, on orders from the captain, and sometimes the new friar himself stopped by to check on the observance of the edict, and all had to agree that Fray Damián had restored order to the mission.

But one day some weeks later, when gaiety had been stilled in Misión Santa Teresa, the captain and a retinue of soldiers were inspecting the lands west of Béxar to see for themselves how much of the range the mission had expropriated for its cattle, and as they approached the four shacks where the Indian herdsmen lived, they heard much revelry. When they followed the noise they saw that in one of the jacales six Indian adults, three children and a Franciscan friar in a long, dusty habit were dancing in a circle, clapping hands and singing at the top of their voices.

'Look!' shouted a child, and the dancers halted, one by one, and looked toward the outraged captain and his men.

The legal papers were filed next day, a formal complaint signed by the captain of the presidio charging Fray Domingo Pacheco with insubordination, misuse of royal lands, venery and conduct unbecoming a member of the clergy. All the animosity of the presidio versus the mission exploded in this diatribe, and it was expressed so forcefully and in such proper terminology that Mexico City had to respond.

Since ancient Spanish legal tradition provided that members of the clergy could be tried only in courts staffed by fellow clerics, a solemn priest, born in Spain, was dispatched to Béxar, and he started his investigation not by examining the accused friar at Santa Teresa but by moving through the little community and listening to whatever gossip the soldiers and the friars from the other missions wished to reveal. When he was finished he had accumulated enough petty accusations against both friars to charge them with almost anything, and grimly announced: 'Tomorrow I shall examine the culprits.'

When the two friars stood before him they made a poor impression, for they were not the neat, well-shaved clerics he was accustomed to on the streets of Zacatecas; Damián appeared in a faded, dusty blue habit, and Domingo's unkempt beard wandered over his chubby face. Ill-matched – Damián tall, thin and fiery-eyed; Domingo short, fat and marked by a silly grin – they should have stood in silence as he abused them, but to his astonishment, they showed every inclination to defend their actions.

Fray Damián was particularly vigorous in his self-defense: 'I have labored day and night to build this mission ... to make it self-sufficient, to bring Indians into our fold. Some men might have accomplished more, but none could have worked more diligently in the service of our Lord and our king.'

'But you did allow the dancing?' the judge asked.

'I did. I worked my Indians from dawn to dusk, and I thank God that Brother Domingo taught them to sing, for it made them better workers in God's cause.'

'Were you not ordered by the civil authority to stop the dancing?'

'I was. And I did.'

'But was there not continued dancing at the mission's ranch?'

'I'm told there was.'

'And did not your Fray Domingo join in the dancing?'

'I'm told that he did.'

'Are you not responsible for what your friars do?'

Fray Damián considered this probing question for some moments, standing erect, his eyes staring straight ahead, his hands clasped at his chest. It would be both easy and correct for him to claim that what happened at the distant ranch was beyond his control, but to deny his long-time companion would be worse than craven; it would be against the rule of the Franciscans.

'I'm responsible.'

'If I were a vengeful man,' the priest said, 'I would add you to this indictment. You have failed miserably in your duty.'

'I demand that you include me,' Damián said, and he took a step forward.

'Stand where you are!' the inquisitor ordered, his face reddening. But Damián kept moving forward until he reached the desk behind which his judge sat. Once there, he reached for a quill and would have inscribed his name on the indictment had not the priest knocked the quill away and bellowed: 'Soldiers, arrest this man!'

So what had been intended as an orderly hearing ended in a general debacle, for as soon as Fray Domingo saw his protector dragged toward the exit door, he leaped at the guards and began pummeling them. A general melee ensued, in the midst of which the enraged priest shouted: 'Chain them both!'

In a tiny cell behind the presidio, no beds, no water, food only once a day, the two friars remained in manacles for three days, and when released, they had to promise both the priest and the captain that they would henceforth permit no Indian dancing.

They had resumed their now somber duties when a convoy arrived from Saltillo with an unexpected member, a young officer bringing a commission that installed him as the new commander of the Presidio de Béxar and retired the former incumbent.

As Damián came from the mission to greet the officer he saw from a distance that the new man was Alvaro, and ran forward to embrace him: 'Dearest brother! You are needed here.' But before Alvaro could respond, Damián asked: 'How is Benita?'

'Fine. If permission is given, she could be coming here.'

Fired by this hope, and supported by an understanding commander, Fray Damián launched what could be called the golden years of Santa Teresa, for with assistance from the soldiers, the walls of the mission were completed, its canal and, most important, its adobe church; and at the ranch Fray Domingo increased his herds until they taxed the ability of his Indians to control them; and the dancing resumed.

If Fray Domingo had been required to pacify only the relatively amenable Indians at the ranch near Béxar, he would have succeeded, but the Franciscans had had the bad luck to place their missions on land which was more or less claimed by Indians of a much different type.

The Apachería was not a specific land area, nor was it a highly organized brotherhood of tribes. The word represented a mystical concept, *the region and union of the Apache*. The imprecision was twofold: the specific territory was never defined and membership was so elastic that any Apache tribe could be included or excluded, as it preferred. One thing was certain: in recent decades the Apache had come to consider the lands around Béxar as part of their Apachería, and evicting the white intruders became an obligation.

Even so, a kind of truce might have been negotiable – Spaniards to the east, Apache to the west – had not another warrior tribe of Indians invaded the western plains at about this time. The newcomers were the dreaded Comanche, horse Indians from the Rocky Mountain areas, who considered all other humans their enemies. Apache and Comanche, what a sadly mismatched pair; the former somewhat sedentary, the latter constantly roving; the former without many horses, the latter the finest horsemen of the plains; the former a loose confederation of many differing tribes, the latter fearfully concentrated; and both wanting to occupy the same lands.

No Comanche had yet been seen at Béxar; they would not appear in force for nearly fifty years, but their unrelenting pressure on the western reaches of the Apachería meant that the Apache were forced to move eastward, and this brought them into conflict with the Spanish at Béxar. But for the time being, a kind of rude accommodation did exist, as proved by an enthusiastic report on conditions at the mission submitted at this time.

By 1729 an investigative priest from Zacatecas, whose name Espejo fortuitously meant *glass* or, as some said, *spyglass*, visited all parts of Tejas on an inspection tour. After dismal experiences in Nacogdoches and the coastal areas, he reached Béxar in an uncompromising mood, but here he saw how ably the Saldaña brothers cooperated in governing the place:

At the end of September 1729, I came at last to Misión Santa Teresa de Casafuerte del Colegio de Propaganda Fide de Nuestra Senora de Guadalupe de Zacatecas, and all the unpleasantness of preceding days vanished as if God had set down in the wilderness a great shining lantern.

The mission was guarded by two exemplary friars, Damián de Saldaña of good family and superior orders who manages all, and Domingo Pacheco, a mestizo of lower orders who performs wonders with his Indians, of whom 234 Pampopa, Postito and Tacame reside in the mission. About three Indians per year have been formally converted, the rest behaving as Christians but not belonging to the church.

The order of the day reflects the piety of Fray Damián. Church bell at sunrise, when all attend Mass. Copious breakfast for forty-five minutes, then everyone to work on the building projects supervised by Fray Damián, who is an outstanding builder.

Lunch at noon, again well provided, and siesta for all. At two in the afternoon return to work, and at five the church bell again, whereupon the entire population reports to the church to recite the Doctrina Cristiana, which includes: Way of the Cross, Lord's Prayer, Hail Mary, Apostles' Creed, Confiteor, Precepts of the Church, Seven Sacraments, seasonal points of faith, and concluding with the Four Last Things. It is heartening to hear these Indians who only a few years ago followed pagan beliefs about rocks and rivers recite in unison the holy words that mean they are now approaching salvation.

At meals Fray Domingo served us with beef, mutton, cabrito and chickens. He also provided squash, potatoes, watermelons and lentils. From the carefully tended orchard he had all the fruits of the season, including peaches, pears and plums, with dried cherries. In obedience to the strict prohibition issued by our King in order to protect the industries of Spain, the mission grows no grapes or olives, although I believe each would prosper here were they allowed.

Then Father Espejo listed in detail some sixty valuable items owned by the mission, divided into five categories, and samples from which will indicate the material progress Fray Damián had made:

FOR THE WOMEN	FOR THE MEN
1 loom	5 plowshares
3 spinning wheels	7 hoes
4 scissors	5 scythes
17 needles	1 pair tongs
7 candle molds	7 shovels

FOR PROTECTION	FOR THE BUILDERS
3 harquebuses	2 planes
5 pistols	2 iron wedges
20 bullet molds	5 sledgehammers
6 swords	67 iron nails

FOR GOD
2 incense burners
3 small bells
5 sets altar cloths

The report ended with two footnotes, the first displaying pride, the second confusion:

> This mission owns several treasures, a statue of San Antonio de Padua, carved in Zacatecas, and a set of fourteen Stations of the Cross, painted on canvas in Spain. It also has two fine blue habits of linen-and-wool, plus three iron shovels, gifts from His Majesty the King. As to the charge so often voiced that 'the only Indians who ever convert are old people about to die,' I confess that this is justified. Young braves refuse to give up their dancing and other favored abominations, but older warriors as they approach death listen attentively to Fray Damián's preaching. Soldiers at the presidio sneer: 'The friars catch only falling leaves,' but I told them: 'Three souls saved, even in extremis, are still three brands saved from the burning, and you should rejoice in their salvation,' but the soldiers laughed, as young men will.

In his summary paragraphs he delivered his judgment as to this mission, saying in part:

> Santa Teresa de Casafuerte, in its exemplary conduct and its fruitful relationship with its presidio, justifies in unmatched perfection the accepted Spanish theory of governing new provinces: To christianize, to civilize, to utilize. I can foresee only continued blessings for Béxar, and as soon as I return to Zacatecas, I shall recommend to the Council of the Indies that civilian settlers from Spain be brought here to establish the city which shall complement this fine venture.

In a separate memorandum, which he discussed with neither of the Saldañas, Espejo proposed an idea that would bring great happiness to each of the brothers:

> Béxar is now so firmly established, even though its population is minimal, that the time has come when more wives ought to be encouraged to join their husbands at the presidio. This will give the Indians and mestizos a taste of true Spanish civilization, which can only edify them. I therefore propose that Benita Liñán de Saldaña be allowed and

133

encouraged to move with her three sons to Béxar immediately. I know this lady. She is a splendid example of Spanish womanhood at its best and will add honor to the presidio.

The proposal was quickly adopted by the military in Zacatecas, and one morning in December 1729 a soldier posting in from the Río Grande shouted at the gates of the presidio: 'We come bringing great treasure!' and he caused so much excitement that Fray Damián was summoned from his mission labors and was present when a mule train came up to the presidio bearing Benita. When she stepped, dust-covered, from its door Damián gasped, for at twenty-five and the mother of three rambunctious sons, she was far more beautiful than before. Throwing her arms wide, as if to embrace the entire wilderness, she cried: 'I am so glad to be here!'

Brushing aside the soldiers who tried to help with her children, she ran first to her husband, kissing him ardently and displaying their sons. Then she turned, saw Damián waiting beside the wall, and ran to him, throwing her arms about him and kissing him on the cheek: 'Brother Damián, I am honored of God to be allowed to share in your work. These are your nephews.'

The next year was a period of some confusion for Fray Damián: he dined frequently at the presidio, once such an alien and unfriendly place, and there he saw how well Benita had raised her sons; he found many other excuses for visiting, and was invariably heartened by her continued liveliness, though he would never admit even to himself why he kept going there. In his quiet, austere way he was in love, and sometimes when he labored on some new mission structure he felt a deep hunger to see her again, to satisfy himself that she was there, and to appreciate the fact that she was a woman, totally different from himself and wonderful in her unique way. Seeing her, listening to her charming manner with her sons was enough, he thought, and in a subtle act of self-deception he began to convince himself that he visited only to help her with her eldest boy, Ramón, now seven: 'That one, Benita, he'd make a fine priest.'

'How foolish! He's a rowdy little boy who hates to sit still while you say prayers. He has no sense of vocation and little likelihood of ever attaining one.' Damián ignored this sensible assessment and continued visiting the boy, but with no constructive results.

When Alvaro said one day: 'I do not like the idea of your Fray Domingo spending so much time at the ranch,' Damián assured his brother that much good work was being done there with cattle and goats and sheep. But Alvaro's apprehension focused on other matters: 'It's the Apache. They keep moving closer, and sooner or later I fear they'll try to attack the ranch.' Again Damián protested: 'Domingo has the touch of God. He saves souls, and given time, he'll bring peace even to the Apache.'

Alvaro grew quite serious: 'You don't seem to understand. With three walled missions here at Béxar, with this stout presidio, with the armed huts in the village, I'm still afraid the Apache will attack one night. Imagine what they might do at an unprotected ranch.'

'God ordered us to establish that ranch,' Damián said. 'He will protect it.'

'I hope so, because I won't be able to.'

Some days later, when Domingo had returned to the mission, Damián accompanied him to the presidio, where the three leaders consulted, the fat little friar trying to convince Captain Alvaro that life at the ranch was safe: 'Each week the Apache understand a little better what Christianity means, and the salvation it will bring them.'

'Are they living at the ranch? Real converts, I mean?'

'No, but they do come in now and then, and I talk with them.'

Alvaro stood up and saluted: 'You're a brave man, Domingo. Much braver than I, and may God protect you.'

'I dance with them. I sing with them. I pray with them. And that's the pathway to salvation.'

Faithful to his promise, Father Espejo did forward his urgent appeal to the king, begging him to send civilian settlers to Béxar, but before any response was possible, the growing town was tripled in size by an extraordinary event. In early 1731 three faltering missions wasting away in the north were transferred to San Antonio de Béxar, where they joined the three already in operation. Of course, the buildings themselves were not transported; they were so forlorn and storm-shattered they could not have been moved, but the six friars and the best of their Indian helpers made long treks through Tejas, expressing robust satisfaction when they saw the vastly improved site they were to occupy.

How beautiful their names are, Fray Damián thought, as he helped the three new missions select their locations: Nuestra Señora de la Purísima Concepción, San Juan Capistrano, San Francisco de la Espada. Like shining beads on a rosary.

When they were in place – the first two on the eastern bank of the river, like the earliest mission, San Antonio de Valero; the third on the western bank, like Santa Teresa and San José – Damián warned the new friars: 'Your success will depend on two things. Prayers to help you to do better at converting Indians than we've done. And securing an assured water supply for the fields that will feed you and your Indians.'

The incoming friars encouraged Fray Damián to tell them more about bringing water onto their land, and they were so persistent in seeking his advice that he ended by laying out the three additional ditches which would in future years account for much of Béxar's growth. Having shown the newcomers how to survey so as to avoid costly aqueducts unless they were inescapable, he continued to counsel the friars until work actually started, then found himself once more with a shovel, demonstrating how the digging should be done.

Fray Damián was forty-five years old when the new missions started functioning, rather tired and increasingly emaciated in appearance, but he was so eager to help these servants of God get started correctly that he labored on their ditches as if he were a member of their missions, and when at last the precious water began to flow, he felt as if he had helped write a small addition to the Acts of the Apostles.

There was at San Juan Capistrano, the mission which honored a saintly man who had worked among the Bulgarians in much the way that Damián worked with the Indians, a young mestizo friar named Eusebio who, because of his extreme sanctity, had been allowed to take major orders, and he was so awed by this privilege that he honored with extra seriousness each precept of the Franciscans. Particularly, he wore about his waist the long heavily knotted cord that served a double purpose: it was a belt holding the blue habit close to the body, but also a flagellum, a scourge to be applied whenever one felt he was indulging in vainglory. Sometimes when Damián paused in his work, he would see Eusebio walking under the trees, beating himself with his knots and crying, 'Mea culpa, mea culpa.'

One morning as Damián dug in the ditch at one of the new missions he noticed Eusebio sitting on a log, striking himself. 'Really, you're not required to punish yourself that way.'

'I'm vain,' the young friar mumbled. 'Far too proud of the high position to which God has promoted me.' And he struck himself again.

'Stop it! If God did the promoting . . .'

'Are you never vainglorious?'

'I have little to be vain about. At this mission Fray Domingo saves the souls. I dig the ditches.'

'But is your mind never troubled?'

'On the night I was assigned to Béxar, I cried: "I have sin upon me. I'm unworthy to be a shepherd." '

'What changed your mind?'

'Work.'

'But the great battles of faith?'

This last word seemed to animate Damián, for he put down his shovel and climbed from the irrigation ditch to take his place beside the young friar. 'I take great solace from the Epistle of James,' he said, quoting haphazardly as his memory allowed from the startling second chapter which gave Protestant rigorists so much trouble:

'What does it profit if a man say he has faith, but has not works? Can faith save him?

'Faith, if it has not works, is dead, being alone.

'You see then that by works a man is justified, and not by faith only.

'For as the body without the spirit is dead, so faith without works is dead also.'

The young man stared at him, but Damián merely kicked at the earth as he said: 'I know that I am lesser than Domingo, who does the work of God, but I find comfort in doing the work of man. Domingo builds castles in heaven, I build adobe huts here on earth. And I do believe that God sometimes wants both.'

'You never lash yourself?'

'In the morning I am too hopeful that on this day I shall be permitted to accomplish something good. At night I'm too conscious of another failure.'

'Is Domingo really a holy man?'

'He's a good man, and sometimes that's better.'

'His goodness, what does it consist of?'

'He brings happiness to his charges ... wherever he goes.'

'Was he not rebuked for lewd dancing?'

Damián ignored this painful charge, shifting the emphasis: 'From our ranch he attempts to bring peace to the Apache ...'

'I'd be terrified to move anywhere near them.'

'Have you converted any Indians, Eusebio?'

'One. A very old man about to die. He sent his wife running for me, and when I reached him he said with a smile: "Now!" and five minutes later he was dead, still smiling.'

'With your prayers, Eusebio, you saved one man. With his songs and his courage Domingo may save an entire tribe, thousands of Apache living at last in peace ... a glory to the goodness of God.'

'I would be afraid to try,' Eusebio said, rising and whipping himself again, while Fray Damián climbed back into the ditch, determined to help bring water to Misión San Juan Capistrano.

Hernando Cortés had completed his conquest of the Valley of Mexico in 1521, which meant that by 1730 the Spaniards had controlled the country for two hundred and nine years, and while it is true that they had constructed on Indian foundations a chain of glowing cities like Puebla, Oaxaca, Guanajuato, Zacatecas and the charming settlement at Saltillo, they had not accomplished much in remote areas like Tejas. In 1730, Béxar, the leading town, contained a population of some two hundred, Spaniards and Mexicans, only fourteen of which were civilians not associated with either the military or the friars at the missions.

But now the letter which Father Espejo had sent to Spain requesting that true-born Spanish settlers be dispatched to Tejas to build a civilian community reached the king, who had for some years been contemplating just such a solution to his problems in northern Mexico:

> In my opinion we can never secure a frontier province like Tejas until we populate it with trusted men and women of pure Spanish blood, preferably those born in Spain or the Canaries. I advocate sending over a large number of farmers direct from Spain or such persons already in Cuba.

But even though he was an absolute monarch with exceptional powers, he had been unable to move his conservative bureaucracy from their cautious ways, so that the intervening years had seen nothing accomplished in the populating of Tejas. Now, with this new proposal before him, he confronted his ministers and said: 'The time has come. How about those recalcitrants in the Canaries?' And thus he initiated an intricate series of movements which would eventually bring to Tejas its earliest formal colony of civilian settlers.

The Canary Islands lay in the Atlantic Ocean, far removed from Spain and opposite the coastline of Morocco. The islands had been populated centuries earlier by a dark-skinned people from the mainland of Africa, but in time they were conquered by Spain and brought into the bosom of Spanish religion and culture. They were Spaniards, but of a different cast.

The Canaries consisted of seven major islands, none large, and of these, the poorest in material goods but the most stubborn in resisting authority was Lanzarote, the one nearest Africa. By a curious chance it rested on approximately the same parallel of latitude as Béxar (29°/30′), so that in making the move to Tejas, these Canary Islanders would be leaping, as it were, some five thousand eight hundred miles due west to a somewhat comparable climate. The king, in suggesting that the Tejas settlers be drawn from the Canaries, had Lanzarote specifically in mind, for he had recently received a confidential report regarding these unfortunate Islanders:

> I know the people of Lanzarote occupy an island with miserably poor soil, but they have never shown the slightest interest in farming or even in properly tending their scrawny sheep and goats. While we all know that the people of the

Carnaries are generally illiterate, those of Lanzarote are by far the most ignorant. And although our government gives them royal aid, they consistently eat more than they produce. Never have they contributed in any way to the social or economic advancement of our Kingdom and I see no hope for improvement in the future. I recommend that the Crown transplant a number of Lanzarote families to Tejas, where under changed conditions they might under pressure learn to become useful citizens. At least we should give my recommendation a trial.

To this proposal the king gave hearty approval, and steps were taken to deposit a group of Lanzarote families at the doorstep of the Misión Santa Teresa in Béxar.

For the king's command to take effect, his officials had to convince the political leader of Lanzarote that the idea was prudent, and now they were thrown up against one of the wiliest, most contentious, arrogant, conniving and headstrong men of that time.

He was Juan Leal Goras, and according to traditional Spanish custom, he should have been called Leal, his father's name, but he stubbornly insisted that his name was Goras, and so he was known. Now in his fifties, he had five children and one eye, having lost the other in an argument with a mule. Obstinately, he refused to wear a patch over the missing eye and with moisture trickling down his cheek, pointed the gaping hole offensively at anyone with whom he spoke. He was illiterate, a deficiency which did not prevent him from becoming the most litigious man in the Canaries; he initiated lawsuits against everyone – priest, king's official, neighbor with a goat, the sea captain of a little ship plying between the islands – and even when he won, he enjoyed prolonging the hearings in hopes of gaining a mite more advantage.

Even before he and the other fifty-three Islanders boarded the ship that would carry them to Mexico, Goras was shouting suggestions as to how their accommodations might be improved, and when the captain snarled 'Go to hell!' Goras threatened a lawsuit. But on 20 March 1730 the rickety craft set sail, and next morning, after a rough passage, his people landed at Santa Cruz on the main island of Tenerife, where they picked up a few additional emigrants. With inadequate food supplies, they then sailed for Cuba, a difficult crossing of forty-five days of heat and seasickness. At one point the captain, driven almost crazy by the torrent of suggestions from Goras, cried: 'Put that man in chains!' And the would-be admiral crossed the Atlantic bound to two huge grinding stones intended for the first grain mill in Tejas.

The settlers wasted two months in Cuba, then spent ten steamy days sailing to Vera Cruz, where on 19 July a horrendous epidemic of el vómito prostrated most of them and killed several.

They left Vera Cruz joyously on 1 August, headed for the great volcanoes that marked the backbone of Mexico, and they were grateful to reach higher land where el vómito did not flourish, but now they had an equally grave problem.

The two huge millstones were gifts to the Islanders from the king himself: 'The Crown will support you with your every need, clothes, food, utensils, money, until your first crop comes in.' So the stones had sentimental as well as practical value, but they were so large that the oxen drawing them began to die. By the time the Islanders reached the foothills of the volcano at Orizaba, it was obvious that hauling the stupendous things was no longer practical; nevertheless Goras bellowed: 'If the king gave us the stones, we keep them with us.' But when more oxen died, even Goras had to agree that the stones should be abandoned until officials in Vera Cruz could recover them.

After twenty-seven painful days the Islanders entered that majestic valley of Mexico, one of the wonders of the world, guarded by the volcanoes Popocatépetl and Ixtaccíhuatl, garlanded in flowers and protected by one of heaven's bluest skies. There at the center stood the splendid capital itself, with its university, its printing houses, its grand eating places and stately mansions. To see Mexico City after the bucolic simplicity of the Canaries was an adventure in empire, and Goras told his people: 'We'll make Tejas like this, an example to the world,' but a muleteer who had once led his animals to Saltillo warned: 'I doubt it will be the same.'

For almost three months Goras and his Islanders languished in the environs of the great city. A few of them, including his own wife, died; young people contracted marriages; worn-out horses were exchanged at the king's expense, as promised; and some of the Islanders, including Goras, began to think that they should remain in these pleasant surroundings rather than head for Tejas.

But the king's orders were that they must move on to Béxar, and so, on 15 November 1730, they resumed their pilgrimage, reaching Saltillo in mid-December and resting in that lovely town with its salubrious breezes and good food until the end of January 1731.

More people died; children were born; more horses collapsed from exhaustion; and on 7 March the surviving Islanders reached the Medina, some distance east of where Fray Domingo had his profitable ranch. Looking across its narrow waters into Tejas, they were appalled by what they saw: a continuation of the sea of grass, more mesquite, never a hill, not a single habitation, only an occasional wild horse or a strayed cow with enormous horns.

'Oh God!' Goras cried when he saw their new home through his one good eye. 'Is this Tejas?'

He was encouraged, however, by a soldier accompanying the group, who assured him: 'At Béxar, where the missions are, everything is better. They have gardens there and food enough to share.'

On 9 March 1731, Goras led his Islanders to the gates of the Misión Santa Teresa, where they were rapturously greeted by a tall, thin friar: 'Settlers at last. My name is Fray Damián, and everything within this mission is at your service, for God has delivered you safely to this destination.'

The friar embraced Juan Leal and the other men, pressed the women's hands, and fought back tears when he saw the emaciated children. 'Fray Domingo!' he called. 'Do bring these children some sugar squares!' Then he turned to the group and said in a strong, quiet voice: 'Let us kneel and give thanks that your long journey is completed.' As the little congregation knelt inside the mission gates, he prayed, but Goras, counting the days by the system he kept in his mind, did not, for he was thinking: 20 March last year to 9 March this. That's three hundred and fifty-five days, and for this?

If Fray Damián had previously thought he'd known trouble

with his Indians and soldiers, he was forced to come up with a new definition of that word where the Islanders were concerned, because within a few weeks Goras was threatening to bring lawsuits against Damián for failing to provide a suitable place for the Lanzarote people, against Fray Domingo for not carrying out the king's promise that they would be taken care of in these early days, and against Captain Saldaña for malfeasances too numerous to specify. Since none of the Islanders could write, and since he knew the complaints had to be made on the proper stamped paper, he badgered Damián de Saldaña to document the charges against his brother Alvaro de Saldaña, and vice versa. In fact, so many garbled reports reached Zacatecas that the commandant there roared one morning: 'What in hell is going on up there in Béxar?' and he organized an inspection tour which he himself led.

He learned that the major grievance was one that had surfaced in all parts of northern Mexico: Who controlled the water? The six missions, including Fray Damián's, argued with some reason that since they had established irrigation rights on the San Antonio, a limited stream at best, it would be illegal and against the interests of the crown for the Canary Islanders to build their own dam and siphon off an undue share of the river. But Goras argued brilliantly: 'Surely the king did not intend that his loyal servants be brought here and set down in a wilderness with no water.' And he pointed out that the six missions, even with the presidio thrown in, housed fewer Spaniards, real Spaniards, that is, than his new village of San Fernando.

At this, one of the soldiers asked: 'And when have Canary Islanders been considered real Spaniards?' Goras challenged him on the spot: 'A duel. Any weapons you like. Our honor has been abused.'

He was now engaged in five distinct lawsuits, but the Islanders still had no stone houses, no garden plots, no horses and, worst of all, no water. This was an intolerable situation and Fray Damián knew it.

One night after the most acrimonious confrontation, in which the Islanders charged the Saldaña brothers with treason to begin with and thievery and lechery as tempers grew, Damián consulted with Fray Domingo: 'Surely, in the interests of God, we must do something to resolve this bitterness.'

Domingo started to laugh. 'Do you remember, Damián, how we sat here one night, just like this, and you told me in your solemn way: "Domingo, Tejas will never function properly until we import real Spaniards here to establish standards"? Well, now you have your Spaniards. Are you happy about it?'

'I had not expected such Spaniards,' Damián replied, but the two friars decided on their own to take those Christian steps which any man of good conscience would feel forced to take, regardless of what course the presidio or the other missions might follow. 'We must share our water,' Damián said. 'And the richness of our land.'

Before dawn Domingo and three Indians drove out to the ranch with wagons to be filled with produce and spare tools. Cows, goats and sheep were rounded up, and then the men slept for a few hours, but at sunset they started back to where the Canary Islanders needed help.

In the meantime Damián and Garza, working by starlight, traced out a route whereby an irrigation ditch could be led along the crest of hills in such a way that water could be brought from the San Antonio directly onto the fields of the Islanders, avoiding the necessity for a costly aqueduct like the one another of the missions would be required to build. But when Goras saw the run of the proposed ditch, he objected strenuously: 'My fields are over there. The ditch should run here, and if it doesn't, I shall bring a lawsuit to alter it.'

Just as the Saltillo men were sure all problems relating to the Islanders' community had been resolved, Goras, supported by two cronies, marched to the presidio with yet another startling demand: 'We were promised that if we left our secure homes and ventured into this wilderness, we would henceforth be called, because of our bravery, *hidalgos*, with right to the title *Don*. I am to be called Don Juan, he is Don Manuel de Niz, and that one is Don Antonio Rodríguez.'

In Spanish society, the word *hidalgo* carried significant connotations. It was composed of three small words: *hijo-de-algo*, which meant literally *son-of-something* or, by extension, *son-of-someone-important*, and it was impossible for even a minor member of the nobility like Don Alvaro de Saldaña to dream of calling men like Goras and his illiterate peasants *Don*.

144

The soldiers and most of the friars flatly refused to do so, but Goras and his Islanders threatened new lawsuits if they were denied their honorific. Since they had already flooded Guadalajara and Zacatecas with petitions, they fired this one at Mexico City itself, demanding that the commandant draft their protest on his own stamped paper.

This was too much: 'Goras, if you give me any more trouble …'

Before he could complete his threat the one-eyed Islander demanded in a loud, offensive voice: 'And where are those grinding stones the king gave us? I suspect you stole them, and I'm starting a lawsuit to recover them.' The commandant had never heard of the promised grinders, but some months later they were delivered to Saltillo with a specific message from the king that they were to be sent on to his loyal subjects at Béxar, with this added instruction:

> In accordance with promises made on my behalf, all male heads of families who left Lanzarote for this dangerous undertaking are to be known henceforth as hidalgos and are to be addressed as Don.

In this manner the civil settlement of Tejas was launched, with the Canary Islanders becoming aristocratic hildagos at a stroke of the king's pen.

Fray Damián was a saintly man, but he was no saint. No sooner had he championed the Canary Islanders in their demand for an irrigation ditch and helped them start it than he summoned his carpenter Simón Garza and their two best Indians to an emergency meeting: 'Before the Islanders dig their ditch and draw off their water, let us deepen ours, all along the way.'

As the work progressed, he found to his surprise that Simón Garza was frequently absent from the ditch, and Damián began to believe that the carpenter, always so faithful, was scamping his duties. Such unlikely behavior was so agitating that Damián began watching Garza more closely. One morning when the carpenter had sneaked away, Damián followed him to the larger of the two mission barns, where he expected to find him sleeping while the others worked. Entering quietly by the main door, he adjusted his eyes to the darkness and moved to where a shaft of sunlight illuminated a cleared corner, and there Damián saw what amounted to a miracle, a true miracle brought down to earth and given form.

Working in secret, Garza had hewn and bonded together three oaken planks, scraping and smoothing one side of the resulting board until it was quite even. From the long board thus created, he had sawed off seven large squares of wood and had begun to bond three other oak boards together to form a second long board from which he could saw off seven more squares.

Suspended from a nail above his work space hung a painting, done in Spain, of one of the fourteen Stations of the Cross, those panels displayed in all churches showing scenes of Christ struggling through the streets of Jerusalem on the way to His crucifixion. Garza had taken this sample from the mission church; below it on a kind of horizontal easel rested one of his first seven squares. With such tools as he had been able to improvise, Simón had nearly completed his carving of the Third Station, in which the solitary figure of Christ falls to the cobbled pavement of the Via Dolorosa, weighed down by the heavy cross he must bear. Below the figure rose from the wood the words JESUS CAE POR PRIMERA VEZ (Jesus falls for the first time).

With an innate appreciation of what oak could represent and of the mystery of Christ's Passion, this unlettered carpenter was creating a masterpiece, for the figure of Christ seemed not only to rise living from the oaken surface but also to proclaim its religious significance.

And there was the mystery! The Christ that Garza had carved was indeed living, but not in any realistic way. If, for artistic purpose, the arm holding the cross required lengthening, he carved it so, and if the head needed to be cocked at an impossible angle, he cocked it. Indeed, as he studied that painting in the darkness of the barn he had intuitively corrected each wrong thing; he had held to the good basics and discarded all that was meretricious. Simón's Third Station was not Indian art or primitive art or any other kind of art capable of being designated by an adjective; it was art itself, simple and pure, and Fray Damián could only gape in awed respect.

146

Bowing his head in reverence, he could visualize the fourteen completed carvings on the walls of his church, and he knew that they must become the chief treasure of Béxar.

Humbly he faced his carpenter and said: 'Surely God is working through you, Simón, to give us this miracle. Henceforth I shall dig your ditches and you shall complete your carvings in this barn.'

In many ways the year 1733 represented the apex at Misión Santa Teresa, for the peaceful Indians near Béxar had learned to live within the compound and to listen to sermons even though they showed no inclination toward becoming Christians. At the ranch Fray Domingo had achieved great success with his cattle and a limited one with his Apache; indeed, he had two of them singing in his informal choir on those occasions when they wandered by the corrals to inspect the Spanish horses they hoped to steal on their next night raid.

Relations between the mission and the presidio, always a measure of how things were progressing, had never been better; the Saldaña brothers had seen to that. Surprisingly, the religious contacts with Zacatecas and the governmental with Mexico City were also unruffled. It was a time of peace, especially with the French to the north, and Fray Damián could have been forgiven had he taken pride in his custodianship of the most important mission in Tejas.

He did not. His innate self-depreciation prevented him from accepting praise for what he deemed his ordinary duty, and on some days he almost castigated himself for not achieving more of God's work. However, his relationships with his brother and sister-in-law had never been better, for these three sensible adults – Damián, aged forty-seven; Alvaro, thirty-eight; and Benita, twenty-nine – had evolved a routine which produced great satisfaction.

On two or three days each week Damián took his evening meal with his brother's family, bringing with him such produce from the mission farm adjacent to the church as he felt he could spare, plus cuts of meat from the animals that Domingo had brought in from the ranch for slaughter. Benita, on her part, would have her Indian servants bake bread and occasionally a fruit tart, if the mission orchards had provided plums.

The three would bow their heads as Damián asked blessing, and then engage in chatter about the doings in Béxar and Saltillo as the platters of food circulated and the bottle of wine was opened. Whenever a problem of management arose, regarding either the mission or the presidio, the brothers would consult, but often it was Benita who offered the practical and equitable solution.

She had developed into one of those extraordinary women who find in the rearing of a family and the organization of her husband's day-to-day life a key to her own happiness; she had never been overly religious and saw no reason to depend upon the rewards of an afterlife to compensate for disappointments in this. She had been reared by her Spanish parents to believe that the greatest thing that could happen to a woman in Mexico was to marry some incoming Spaniard, make him a good wife, and in later years go first to Spain and then to heaven. In the wilds of Tejas she had begun to doubt whether she would ever return to Spain, and she had long ago decided to leave heaven to God's dispensation.

Sensible as she was, she had always known why Damián wanted to stay close to his brother and why he now brought gifts rather more lavish than conditions warranted. She knew that Damián, thinking of her as his spiritual wife, was joined to her with bonds so powerful that neither imagination nor death could dissolve them, and she felt obligated to him. He was her responsibility, and by her acquiescence she knew she had accepted the pleasant burden of his emotional life. When he was ill, she tended him. When his robe required mending, she sewed it. When he told little jokes about the mission Indians, she laughed. And whenever he appeared at her house or departed, she showed her pleasure at his arrival or her sadness at his going. In Benita he had a wife without the responsibility of one.

Was Alvaro aware of this unusual triangle of which he was a silent part? He never alluded to it. He welcomed his brother with more than brotherly affection and saw no unpleasant consequences from what might have been a dangerous arrangement.

Partly this was because Damián was so helpful, not only with his food contributions but also with his attention to the three

148

Saldaña boys; he played games with them and taught them their letters, and often took them to the mission when Fray Domingo was in attendance so they could learn to sing. Invariably, when he visited their home at the presidio he brought them little presents, sometimes so trivial they could scarcely be called presents, but so thoughtful that they proved his continuing love.

He had always been especially fond of Ramón, a bright, eager lad now eleven and thirsty for knowledge of the world. Damián had long ago surrendered his silly hope that Ramón would one day become a priest: 'That boy would last in a Franciscan college one week, Benita, or maybe one day. Take my advice. Make a pirate of him.'

On Sundays, and high holidays, everything changed, for now the presidio Saldañas entered Damián's world, and they were properly reverent, for no one could live at the edge of the wilderness without speculating upon the nature of the good life, and orderly religion was seen as one of the abiding consolations. When Damián prayed, Alvaro listened, and when his brother preached, the commander followed his arguments. At communion, which carried special weight when one seemed so far from civilization, Alvaro, Benita and their eldest son accepted their wafers solemnly, knowing that by so doing, they were somehow in contact not only with Jesus Christ but with fellow Catholics in Mexico City, Madrid and all other respectable nations of the Earth.

On those occasions when Fray Domingo came in from the ranch to lead his Indian choir, Alvaro sang with them in his strong baritone voice, and at such times the three adult Saldañas often looked at one another, assured that a bond of friendship and love held them together.

They would never see Spain again, none of them, but in Tejas they had discovered the joy of lives decently led and work well done.

On 5 September 1734, a day that would be remembered with horror, a little Indian boy half ran, half staggered up to the gates of Santa Teresa with a story that only a child could tell without retching.

To the ranch belonging to the mission, Apache had come,

scores of them, and with systematic barbarity had burned every building and driven off every animal. The mission Indians who had tried to defend the place had been slain; the children, all nine of them, had been taken captive; and the five women ... The little boy had not the words to describe what had happened to them: 'The Apache undressed them ... then you know ... then they cut them apart.'

Fray Damián clutched at the back of a chair: 'They what?'

'They cut them apart,' and the boy showed how first a finger had been cut away, then another, then a hand and a foot and a breast, until the final rip of the gut, deep and powerful from left to right.

'Mother of God!' Damián cried, and immediately sent Garza to fetch Captain Saldaña, and when the brothers faced the boy, they asked: 'What happened to Fray Domingo?' and now the child burst into tears.

'When they were not looking,' he said in his Yuta dialect, 'I ran to the bushes by the river. I hid there all day, and when night came ... I am sleepy.'

'Of course you are,' Damián said gently, taking the boy onto his lap. 'But what happened to Fray Domingo?'

'Upside down, by the fire. His feet tied to a limb. No clothes on. They built a fire under his head. Each woman puts a stick on the fire to make it blaze, then cuts away a finger or a toe. He screamed ...' The boy shuddered and would say no more.

The Saldaña brothers knew they had to organize an expedition to punish the Apache and, if possible, retrieve the captured children and any young women who might have survived. A force of thirty soldiers, sixteen Spanish and mestizo laymen, two dozen Indians and four friars set out for the Santa Teresa ranch, where the smoldering buildings bespoke the ruin that the Apache had wrought. Not even halting to bury the corpse of Fray Domingo, still hanging from a tree, the infuriated men picked up the trail of the Apache and spurred ahead. For three days they sought to overtake them, but failed; however, just as they were about to turn back in frustration they heard a whimpering in some bushes and found the seven-year-old sister of the boy who had escaped. When it became apparent what indecencies the Apache had visited upon her, several of the fort soldiers began to vomit.

That was the nature of Béxar's endless struggle with the Apache. The familiar Indians of this part of Tejas – the Pampopa, the Postito, the Orejone, the Tacame, the dozens of other tribes – were semi-civilized, like the more amenable Indians the French and the English were meeting along the Mississippi and the Atlantic seaboard; Europeans could reach agreements with Indians like the Mohawk, the Pawnee and the Sioux, for those tribes understood orderly behavior, but the Apaches did not. Their rule was to strike and burn, torture and kill in the cruelest ways imaginable. No persuasion touched them, no enticement tempted them to live harmoniously with anyone else, white or Indian.

They were handsome people physically, lithe, quick, remarkably at home in their environment, and capable of withstanding greatest duress. They could go days without food or water; they could withstand burning heat or sleeted trails; and if they were horribly cruel to their captives, they could themselves accept torture with insolent defiance. They were the scourge of the lower plains, ravaging Tejas and venturing frequently all the way to Saltillo in the south, a city they loved to plunder.

Sometimes they traveled four hundred miles in order to steal an especially fine string of horses, but they liked mules too, for these they slaughtered and ate. But even when there was no prospect of capturing horses, they raided white settlements just for the pleasure of killing people they knew to be their enemies, and when a district held no white people, as most of Tejas did not, they raided the camps of Indians weaker than themselves, slaying them indiscriminately.

When Fray Damián rode back to Rancho El Codo to bury his longtime associate and dear friend, he was well aware of the serious undertaking he was about to launch. Directing Simón Garza to climb the tree and cut the cord that kept the charred remains of Fray Domingo swinging by its ankles, he caught the body as it fell, and staggered with his burden to a proper spot, where a grave was dug. As the body was deposited he uttered a prayer and made a promise:

'Brother Domingo, friend of years and warmth to my heart, you died in an effort which brought joy to God. I promise you that I shall take up the burden that you have put down. I shall not rest until the peace you sought is brought to the Apache and they are safe in the arms of Jesus Christ.'

He proceeded in an orderly manner to fulfill his oath: 'Simón, halt your work on the Stations and carve a fine plaque showing the martyrdom of Domingo, and this we will send to our colleagues in Zacatecas.' To his Indian helpers: 'Cándido, I must leave to you the completion of our ditch, and speed it. Ignacio, I can't ask you to live at the ranch, for that's too dangerous now that the Apache have struck, but you must move through the countryside and rebuild our herds.'

For himself, he must quit the mission walls and move out among the Apache to bring them God's word, but before he could leave he must find someone to guide Misión Santa Teresa temporarily, and he recalled the devout Fray Eusebio who castigated himself so severely. After gaining approval from the head of Eusebio's mission, he installed him, and smiled as the young dreamer lashed himself with his flagellum, crying: 'I am not worthy of such high promotion.'

In the months that followed, Fray Damián was sometimes seen by military expeditions headed north or south from Béxar, and scouts reported back to Captain Alvaro: 'There we were, loneliest stretch we'd ever seen, Béxar two days distant, and out of nowhere comes this gaunt, long-legged friar on a mule. "You must be careful of the Apache at night," he told us. "They'll steal your animals." We asked him where he was going and he said: "To the Apachería."'

And that was where he went, and because he moved alone, on a mule and unarmed, a man approaching fifty, they gave him entry to their camps. When he had learned enough of their language, they talked with him and explained that it was impossible for Indians and white men to live together. They acknowledged that he personally commanded powerful magic, but they also pointed out that they were no longer powerless: 'Those you call the French. Beyond the rivers. They sell us guns. Soon we shoot. Better hunters, you never catch us.'

He was so astonished to find that the French were supplying arms that he told the tribe with whom he had been living and to whom in the evenings he had been preaching: 'I must leave you now and tell my brother at the fort that peace with the Apache must come before everyone has guns.'

They not only let him return to Béxar but they sent a trusted squaw with him, and on the way she confided: 'That other camp. Two days south. They have two of the children taken in the big raid.'

They detoured, and Damián found that what the woman said was true; a boy of ten and a girl of eight were in the tents, and Damián persuaded the Apache to release the latter so that she could return to her people, but the child refused to leave. Her people were dead; she had seen them die; and now she had found other parents in the camp.

'But God wants you to live a decent life, within the church,' Damián argued.

'Leave her alone,' the boy snarled, grabbing her away.

'My son, it is proper that she —'

'Get away.' In some curious fashion the children were blaming the friar for the terrible things that had happened to them, and this Damián could not accept. Reaching for the girl, he drew her to him and with a trembling forefinger traced the scars across her face, put there not in the heat of battle but by Apache braves who tortured their captives, even the children.

'What is your name, Child of Heaven?'

'Let her go!' the boy cried again, and this time he wrenched the girl away, struck her violently, and shoved her along to some older women, who began to beat her.

Regardless of his own safety, Damián lunged toward the little girl to rescue her from such abuse, but he was halted by a tall, powerful Apache warrior whose garb caused the friar to stop in horror. With the hand that had traced the girl's scars, he reached out and touched the man's garment, realizing that it was the robe Fray Domingo had been wearing prior to his horrible death.

Holding on to the robe, he said quietly in Apache: 'This is the garment of my friend. I must have it for his grave.'

The Indian understood and respected the emotion represented: 'Your friend, very brave.'

Still clinging to the robe, Damián said: 'You must let me take it.'

'What will you give me?'

Damián had nothing to offer but his mule, and this the Apache took gladly, for it would make a feast. So Fray Damián de Saldaña returned to his mission, on foot, trailing an Apache woman astride a donkey, and clutching to his bosom the robe in which his dearest friend and companion of many years had approached his martyrdom.

His efforts to bring peace and Christianity to the Apache not only failed, they ended in repeated embarrassment. At the conclusion of his first venture into alien territory, after the Apache woman led him into Béxar, he persuaded Alvaro that the Apache were of sincere intent when they suddenly changed face and discussed the possibility of permanent truce, and he pointed out that with the Indians receiving French guns, it was imperative that a peaceful understanding be reached. So against his better judgement, Captain Saldaña agreed that Damián, with a new mule, should return with the woman and arrange for a plenary between Apache chiefs and presidio soldiers.

Damián, heartened by the possibility that he might be the agent for ending the raids and retaliations, returned to the western lands and persuaded his Apache to send for those who controlled the south. With delight he listened as the newcomers agreed to give his brother's plan a chance: 'We'll go and talk, and if he's like you, a man of bravery, perhaps . . .'

A party of sixteen, led by Damián and the squaw who had made the earlier trip, rode east one March morning in 1736, arriving at Béxar four days later. When the six missions were in sight, Damián and the woman rode on ahead, sounding signals that brought many men to the walls. Captain Alvaro, not at all certain that truce was possible, cautioned his men to remain alert, then nervously admitted the Apache into the presidio.

In sign language the Apache talked incessantly for two days, consuming a vast amount of food as they did, and at dusk on the second day, at a signal from their chief, they suddenly raised a war cry, slew the two guards, and ran outside to join some ninety more of their men who had crept close during the preceding days.

They were a force powerful enough to have assaulted the

presidio itself had they so decided; instead, they drove off more than a hundred and twenty Béxar horses, galloping westward into the shadows, whooping and screaming and firing their French guns in the air.

Fray Damián was so distraught after this debacle, which he had unwittingly engineered, that he fell into a kind of trance, not insensible to those about him but quite unable to talk or act. He lay on his straw paillasse staring at the ceiling, indifferent to food, and from time to time calling out the word *Domingo*, but when attendants hurried to see what he wanted, they found him weeping and unable to speak further.

His health deteriorated rapidly, and it was only the care of Benita, sent to the mission by Alvaro, that saved him. She was a woman of thirty-two now, and as lively in spirit as when Damián had first seen her promenading around the square at Zacatecas. Her eyes still glowed mischievously and her skin remained unblemished, as if time were loath to touch something so flawless. Most surprising of all, under these deplorable circumstances, she still retained a cheerfulness that prevented her from taking troubles too seriously.

'Come now, Damián! We need you in Béxar,' she said teasingly. Disregarding mission rules, she propped open the door to his cell, brought in flowers, and personally cooked nourishing meals for him. When he seemed to revive, with senses clarified so that he could understand what she was saying, she assured him that her husband did not blame him for the disaster with the Apache: 'They're savage brutes, and what could anyone expect?'

'I expected peace,' Damián said.

'No one should have been so easily deceived,' she said.

'Were you?'

She reflected on this for some moments, then said the right thing: 'No, but I love you for being such a dear, good man and I prayed that you might be right.' As soon as she said this she realized that her words stressed the fact that he had been wrong, so she added quickly: 'It's always good to try, Damián. Maybe another time . . .'

As he watched her move about his cell he appreciated anew the miracle that even though he was forbidden by church law to have her for himself, she was nevertheless a part of his being, a mystical wife in another world whose conventions he could not fathom. She was the woman he had loved from the first moment when he saw her laughing with the other girls, and that she should now be so close to him, and mending his broken spirit, was a joy he could share with no one, not even with Jesus Christ in his prayers.

When Damián finally rose from his cot, a most pleasing honor awaited him: Simón Garza had finished his fourteen Stations of the Cross, but their installation had been deferred until Damián could supervise it. Actually, all he did was stand in his adobe church and tell the workmen how to hang the carvings, but when the light fell across them, showing the marvelous detail Garza had achieved with his rude chisels, tears came to his eyes and he fell to his knees and prayed. It seemed that God Himself must have bent down and guided Garza's hand, for Damián could not conceive how an illiterate mestizo carpenter could otherwise have accomplished such a work.

When the carvings were in place, Captain Alvaro, supported by friars from the other missions, told Damián: 'We must have a celebration to dedicate your Stations,' and it was arranged that a cloth covering would be draped over each carving, and that Garza would move from one location to the next, pulling aside the cloth to reveal the beauty beneath. Damián would expound the religious significance while the choir trained by Fray Domingo sang holy verses he had taught them. Fray Eusebio, still protesting that he was not worthy of such high honor, would represent the other missions.

It was the culmination of Damián's custodianship. Indian women filled the rude church with flowers, and as the veils fell away and sunlight illuminated the carvings, Damián thought that Jesus Christ Himself had come to Béxar to relive those tragic, hallowed moments when he moved painfully along the road to Golgotha.

Damián's exultation was short-lived, because when word of the episode with the Apache reached Mexico City, the viceroy cast about for a new governor of Tejas who would bring stricter order to the region. Unfortunately, he had no one available to send, but a conniving assistant who wanted to rid himself of a real incompetent whispered: 'Excellency, why not send

Franquis? He's a Canary Islander and he'll know how to handle things.'

What a sad miscalculation! If one searched the archives to find an example of Spanish colonial policy at its worst, one would surely select Don Carlos Benites Franquis de Lugo, a vain, arrogant, opinionated fop who never displayed a shred of either courage or discernment but who did distinguish himself as one of the most inept and vengeful Spaniards ever to function overseas. In fact, he was too obtuse even to realize that his assignment to Tejas was a demotion, for he boasted to his friends: 'I'm to restore Spanish dignity in an area which has forgotten what discipline means.'

The character of his administration was defined when he reached San Luis Potosí, where he raged at the local garrison for not having fired enough salutes to honor a dignitary of his exalted stripe: 'I am, after all, Governor of Tejas!' At Saltillo he abused the entire establishment because not all the officials were lined up to meet him as he entered town, but he reserved his most ridiculous behavior for San Juan Bautista, a hard-working post with limited amenities. He was so incensed by the lack of spit-and-polish in the presidio that he dismissed everyone on the spot, and then had to hire them back when he learned that no replacements could reach the forlorn outpost in less than a year.

In Tejas he took immediate dislike to the Saldaña brothers, accusing Fray Damián of being tardy in asking Zacatecas for a replacement for Fray Domingo, and of deepening the Santa Teresa ditch without written authority. But his special scorn was reserved for Captain Alvaro, whom he denigrated as follows:

Through arrant cowardice he failed to protect the ranch of Misión Santa Teresa against the Apache, causing the Blessed Fray Domingo, may God smile upon his martyrdom, to lose his life most horribly. Later, acting without reason or military competence, he allowed the very Apache who killed Fray Domingo, may God smile upon his martyrdom . . .'

He became so indignant as he composed this report, he ended by convincing himself that Alvaro was a cowardly incompetent:

'Handcuff the recreant and throw him in jail, being sure that his legs are tightly chained.'

To demonstrate his own heroism, he organized a hastily put-together expedition to subdue the Apache – about fifty Spaniards and their poorly armed helpers against ten thousand scattered Apache – and his troops would have been annihilated had not Simón Garza and two Yuta scouts detected a concentration of warriors hiding in a mountain pass and prevailed upon the governor to beat a disorganized retreat. As it was, the Apache overtook three stragglers and tortured them viciously.

In this sad year of 1736, Tejas saw Spanish occupancy at its worst. Travel between Béxar and the distant capital at Los Adaes was interdicted by the Apache; food was scarce because the irrigation ditches, without Damián's supervision, were not functioning properly; and all else was in disarray because so many of the able administrators languished in jail with chains about their legs.

It was in this ugly setting that Fray Damián proved what a quintessential Spaniard he was; the first responsibility of any man, even before his duty to God, was to protect his own family. Lands for his son, a husband for his daughter, a job for his nephew, an appointment for his brother-in-law – these were the obligations of a Spanish man.

He was so outraged by the arrest of his brother, and so distraught by what might happen to Benita and her three sons, who were, after all, like his own, that he devised a procedure that would have delighted Machiavelli, for he used stamped paper stolen from the presidio on which to press it:

Respected Archbishop Vizarrón. Congratulations on your great success as Viceroy of all Mexico. The King could have chosen no one better fitted for that exalted position, and I stand ready as a humble friar to assist you in all you do.

My brother, Captain Alvaro de Saldaña of the Saldañas of Saldaña, has served bravely on the frontier, and I believe there is a law which states that an officer who has seen active duty in any new territory is entitled to six leagues of Crown lands upon retirement. On behalf of my brother, now occupied with other matters, I beg you to make this award.

There is, a few miles west of here in a bend of the Medina, a stretch of land called Rancho El Codo, once occupied by the ranch of this mission. It has now been abandoned because of Apache raids and is of no practical use to anyone until the Apache are subdued. My brother and his wife, in years to come, can tame this land if you will cede it to them now in reward for the hard work they have completed on the frontier of your dominion.

In composing this seditious letter, Damián was aware of three crimes he was committing: The ranch belongs to the church, and I'm stealing it for my family. I'm drafting letters when Governor Franquis has forbidden anyone to do so. And I'm trying to slip my letters past the officials at San Juan Bautista, who have orders to prevent the entry into Mexico proper of clandestine letters. But then he thought of Benita and her children: I must take the chances.

In one of the other missions he found a Franciscan who was heading back to Zacatecas, and since this friar also hated Franquis, he volunteered to take the risk. The letter reached the archbishop, who was now viceroy, and when he inquired about the reputation of the Saldañas he found it to be exemplary, whereupon he signed a grant awarding former Captain Saldaña more than nine thousand leagues, twenty-five thousand acres, along the Medina.

Later, when he learned of Damián's insubordination, he bore no resentment, for by this time it was evident even to Madrid that Governor Franquis was a horrendous mistake, and he was deposed after little more than a year of his reckless despotism. The unfortunate man had been correct, however, in some of his charges against Damián: he had been so preoccupied with building the mission that he had not attended to the winning of souls, and repeatedly he had left the mission without permission to go wandering through the Apachería. When it became apparent that he was to be removed from Santa Teresa, Damián recommended that Fray Eusebio be given permanent charge of the mission, but Eusebio protested that he was far too humble to warrant such an exalted position. Instead, Zacatecas sent up the trail to Béxar two young friars to assume control at Santa Teresa, one with major orders, to replace Fray

Damián, and one with minor to take over the work done by Fray Domingo.

Damián greeted the two with the warmest brotherhood and even relief, for he knew that his effectiveness had waned. He was fifty-one now, and extremely tired, so that rest in some quiet corner of the Franciscan empire seemed highly desirable, but as the father-principal in Zacatecas had proposed, he would stay on at Santa Teresa until the transition had been smoothly made.

The new friars were enthusiastic young men prepared to repair the situation in Béxar, as they phrased it, and their eagerness to take command provided Damián time to summarize what he had accomplished on the frontier.

'Nothing,' he told Alvaro and Benita. 'I feel my life's been a waste.' When they asked why, he replied: 'Conversions to Jesus? I haven't brought two dozen souls to salvation.'

'That was Domingo's task,' Benita said consolingly.

'But I've done so little.' He felt old, and futile, and superseded.

'Let's look at what you and I have accomplished,' Alvaro proposed, and he recited their litany of constructive deeds: 'We brought order to a region which knew it not,' Alvaro said. 'And we've established regular mail connections with Saltillo.' On he went, naming those simple deeds which taken together represented the quiet triumph of civilization.

But this was not enough for Benita, because she better than either of the brothers thought she knew the cause of Damián's malaise: He sees his life running out, and without a wife or children to represent him when he's gone, he fears it might have been in vain. So she began to tick off his particular achievements: 'You built the irrigation systems, and when Misión Espada needed an aqueduct for its water supply, you showed them how to build one.' Stopping, she formed an arch with her fingers and said: 'Building an arch that will stand is something, believe me.'

She spoke of the compound walls he had erected, of the church, of the houses for the Indians. And then she mentioned the one thing of which she knew he was truly proud: 'You encouraged Simón to finish his Stations of the Cross. Yes, when we three die we shall leave in Béxar an enduring memory.'

When she uttered the word *die*, applying it even to herself,

Damián shuddered, and in the silence that followed he acknowledged for the first time that his mournfulness stemmed from growing awareness of his own approaching death: 'Life is so brief. We should have accomplished so much and we did so little.'

'My three sons!' Benita snapped. 'I call them something. And Alvaro's promotion to colonel, I call that something, too.'

Damián could not accept this reprieve: 'Once we had Santa Teresa firmly planted, I should have gone to Nacogdoches and brought order to the frontier. And after Alvaro established order here, he should have gone on to Los Adaes and done the same there. We do a little and claim it was a lot.'

Benita rose from her chair, walked to where Damián sat, and placed her hand on his shoulder: 'We can be proud of the Béxar we built. It will stand here for a long time . . . a long time.' She bit her lip and pressed Damián's shoulder: 'And you can be proud, Damián. Two hundred years from now, when the work of your mission is long completed, your church of Santa Teresa will stand, and people will applaud it. Yes, I saw that last report of the inspectors from Querétaro: "No mission north of Saltillo, neither in Sonora nor in Tejas, excels what Friar Damián has achieved in Béxar." ' She bent down and kissed him.

Cherishing her touch, he looked up and whispered: 'I suppose it's important that Indians have food if they're to work at Christian duties. And it's very important they have decent houses. And a mission needs walls to keep goodness in and evil out. But I merely built walls. Domingo built souls.'

As the long evening ended he tried to summarize: 'I've one regret I can't erase. I failed to convince Madrid to send us enough real Spanish settlers – farmers who would farm, knitters who would knit.' When he fell silent, Alvaro nodded: 'That was our great failure.'

'I don't discount the Mexican mestizo. All things considered, Simón Garza is one of the best human beings I've ever known, and there must be others like him, but what does the government in Mexico City send us? Rabble, rubbish, and they expect to build a province with such people?'

As he uttered these harsh and true indictments of Spanish policy he did concede that the Council of the Indies had made one serious effort to settle the north, and when he thought of those contentious Canary Islanders calling themselves hidalgos, he had to chuckle: 'They're the best Spaniards we have, and if the king had sent us fifty more boatloads, we could have settled Tejas and conquered Louisiana, too.' He was in this frame of mind one afternoon when the inescapable Juan Leal Goras, his long beard unkempt, appeared at the mission, his devious mind busily at work.

'Fray Damián, I do not come with pleasant news. Your men here at the mission are drawing down more water than we agreed upon, and I'm starting a lawsuit against you before you escape from Tejas.'

'How many suits have you and I had before, Don Juan?'

'Five, and each one essential for the protection of our interests.'

'And how many have you won?'

'None, but that's not the point. Each suit brought to your attention some grievous wrong which you then had the sense to correct.'

'Why didn't you just come and complain without the lawsuits?'

'Because you damned friars will never listen to mere words. But when I start a suit you clean out your ears.' Pushing his face close to Damián's, he added: 'And don't be fooled by the score, five suits, five losses. How could it be otherwise when the judges are all corrupt? All in the pockets of you friars.'

'All the judges?'

'I've conducted lawsuits in all parts of the world . . .'

'You mean the Canaries and Tejas?'

'It's the same the world over. Judges are corrupt.'

'Suppose that when you do engage your suit, Don Juan, that I bring witnesses to prove that you've dug a branch of your canal for which you have no permit? Which was not in our agreement? And I prove that it is you who are breaking the law, not I?'

'That's the kind of argument corrupt judges listen to.'

At this point Don Juan shifted the discussion dramatically: 'Fray Damián, we couldn't have had a better missionary in Béxar than you. Nor a better captain than your brother. I want him to stay on as a civilian. Why don't you stay, too, as our parish priest?'

The suggestion was so improper to make to a Franciscan, whose mission in life was to wander, not to tend a specific church, that Damián remained mute, but it was also flattering, coming as it did from Goras, who pressed on, interpreting the friar's hesitancy as indecision: 'Our whole community wants to have you stay. You're a man we've learned to trust.' Goras could see the friar thinking intensely, but not even his conniving mind could have guessed what Damián was thinking: I could stay here with Alvaro and Benita and watch their sons grow. My home would not be broken.

Slowly and in some confusion he told Goras: 'I'm a Franciscan. I go where God sends me.' And as soon as Goras left, Damián started making his own secret plans to go on a mission which he felt that God had authorized: once more among the Apache, hoping that this time his example of fearlessness and brotherhood would encourage them to consider peace.

One afternoon, when his preparations were almost complete, he went quietly into his little church, and in the quiet shadows he studied once more Simón Garza's Stations of the Cross, contemplating both their beauty and the religious mystery they represented: How fortunate I was to work with men like Simón and Domingo. They made the things I tried to do doubly effective. And how wonderful that I should have done my work in companionship with Jesus Christ. As he looked at Garza's depiction of the crucifixion he could feel the nails in Christ's hands, the thorns digging into His brow: He was such a good man on earth, such a kind man in heaven.

As he prayed before the last Station he noticed that the two young friars now responsible for Santa Teresa had also entered the church, and unaware that Fray Damián was there, they were talking like young enthusiasts.

'I've found this quarry. Rock so soft you cut it with a saw. But when it's sun-dried in place, it hardens like granite. Tufa they call it.'

'With such stones we could replace the adobe. Make this a real church.'

'Better yet, we could replace everything.'

At this Damián gasped, for he could not imagine sacrificing Simón's glorious Stations. The young friars now discovered him, and realizing that he must have heard their plans, were eager to apologize: 'We didn't know you were here. We're so sorry.'

'No, no! I assure you, it's time to build a new church.'

'Do you really approve?'

'Yes!' he cried vehemently. 'Each man builds only for his generation. Everything he does ought to be restudied … improved by those who follow.' He waved his hand deprecatingly. 'I built so poorly. They told me in Zacatecas: "You need build only in wood, for temporary use." ' His voice dropped to a whisper: 'But the heart yearns to build in stone … for eternity.'

As he moved his right arm across the spread of the little church his eyes were directed to the Stations of the Cross, and almost as if he were a parent defending his children, he stepped before the carvings and lifted his arms to cover one of them. 'I would not want you to replace these … do not destroy them, that is.' And his plea was so profound that one of the young friars stooped and kissed his hand.

'We would never have damaged them, Brother Damián. We planned to have them as the heart of our new church.'

'Did you?' he asked in great excitement, and as the two moved about the church, explaining to each other how the roof could be taken off and the walls replaced with minimum confusion, he stayed with them, encouraging them and talking far more than was necessary.

On 21 September 1737, when day and night stood even across the world, Damián left his mission riding a mule, with a donkey in tow. He rode westward toward Rancho El Codo, which Alvaro, Benita and their sons now owned, and here he stopped to utter a long prayer for the soul of Domingo Pacheco as it made its way through purgatory to heaven. He spent his first night at the ranch, and rose refreshed and eager for the serious part of his journey.

Not till three days later did he make contact with any Apache; then he came upon a good-sized band which did not include either the squaw or any of the chiefs who had known him earlier, although there were members who had heard of the decent manner in which he had treated other Apache. They made him as welcome as Apache ever did, but he was aware that some of the younger braves resented him and were advising their fellows against any contact with a Spaniard.

In the two days he spent in the Apachería he found some leaders who were willing to listen when he explained about the advantages of Christianity and an orderly life within the Spanish empire. 'Like me,' he told them, 'you will enjoy the full protection of the King.' He was convinced that the conversion of the Apache was at hand and that God had sent him to be the agent.

But on the third day, in the midst of the most serious explanation of how God and His son Jesus Christ shared responsibilities in heaven, three impatient young braves kicked aside a buffalo skin before which Damián sat, seized him and dragged him to an oak tree, from which they hung him by his thumbs. Then, before the older chiefs could protest, which they showed little inclination to do, the young men stripped the dangling body and began making little cuts across it with their flint scrapers.

They were not deep, just a slash on the arm, or on the leg, but the young men kept darting back and forth, now away from Damián, now toward him, always making another small cut, until his body was red-stained in all its parts.

The young men now called upon the women of the tribe, and with obvious delight the squaws joined them, dancing around and making deeper cuts in parts of the body hitherto untouched. One woman, hair falling across her dark face, evil-smelling, was lifted up to cut at the base of his left thumb, not severing it but nearly so; she and her sisters wanted to see how long it took for the weight of the body to pull the damaged thumb apart, and when this happened, and the body swung sideways, suspended only by the right thumb and twirling in a tight circle, the women shrieked with pleasure, and ran back to stab at the body that now gushed blood from various deep wounds.

Damián, still conscious, for no cuts had yet been made in a vital place, held to his belief that this hideous affair was merely a ritual torture, but now two of the women rushed up and made such deep slashes in the lower part of his stomach that a great shudder ran through all his body, visible to his tormentors.

'He dies! He dies!' they screamed, and this encouraged other women to dance in and stab at him. One was even lifted high enough so that she could cut at his throat, but this terrible pain Damián ignored, for when he stared at her hawklike face he saw not an Apache woman but Benita Liñán. She smiled at him as she had on that first evening in the paseo, and as his blood spurted she leaned forward to cradle him in her arms.

... Task Force

San Antonio! Loveliest city in Texas, Venice of the Drylands, its river runs right through the heart of town, providing a colorful waterway for festive barges and an exotic riverside walk along which one could promenade forever. How glad I was to be coming back to a city I had cherished as a boy, for this had been my family's preferred vacation spot.

I remembered well the Buckhorn Saloon, that relic of the Old West, with its fantastic guns and cattle horns. I sneaked my first beer there, my mother watching from a distance, then teasing when I spat it out. Later, when I returned from Europe to find the Buckhorn moved, I felt as if my youth had officially ended.

San Antonio! Conservative, always lagging behind more daring towns like Houston and Dallas, it had long been the largest city in Texas but had now given way to those two giants. Recently it had stunned the state by electing as mayor a man of Spanish heritage, and in decades to come it might once more become a leading city because of the spectacular development of its Spanish-speaking population.

For our April meeting there our staff had enlisted a Franciscan friar who served in one of the city's famous missions, Friar Clarence Cummings, born in Albany, New York. He was respected as an expert on the five surviving missions that line the river like a string of jewels on a necklace, but even before he appeared he caused animosity in our Task Force.

Rusk complained: 'I didn't join this committee to get a course in Catholic theology,' and Quimper chimed in: 'If this keeps up, next meeting will be a public baptism.'

This was too much for Professor Garza, a wise and prudent Catholic: 'What makes you think the friar will try to proselytize you?' and Rusk growled: 'He better not try!'

In two minutes Friar Clarence won the skeptics over, or at

least neutralized them. He was a tall, good-looking, robust fellow in his late thirties, clad in a brown robe, bare feet in rugged leather sandals. After the briefest introduction he said in no-nonsense style: 'I hope you'll join me in a cell we use as a projection room, because it's important that you see the slides I've prepared,' and when we were seated with our staff in the cell in the Misión San José, he surprised us with the title of his talk: 'Form and Legacy.'

'Now what does that mean?' Quimper asked, and he replied: 'That's what I've come to explain.'

With carefully organized notes accompanying a set of excellent colored slides he had prepared from his own drawings and photographs, he began his talk with a promise: 'I propose to concentrate on two subjects only, the physical form of the Spanish mission in its heyday and its legacy for us today. No theology, no moralizing. We begin with this simple question, which must have preoccupied those in charge at the time: "If your mission is to fulfill its purpose, what form should it take?" '

At that he darkened the cell, and with the heavy stone walls enclosing us, we had little difficulty in imagining ourselves back in 1720: 'This drawing – I studied architecture at Cornell before joining the Franciscans at a rather advanced age – shows the landscape you will have to work with. The wandering river. The loop where the horses pasture. The flat land where your mission will ultimately stand.'

With seven choice slides he showed us the terrain of San Antonio as it must have been in 1717, with no mission visible: 'Since you are Spaniards imbued with the traditions of your homeland, you will insist upon centralization, with civilian settlers and their activities clustered closely together. A main difference between Catholic Spain and Protestant America, I've always thought, is that Spain likes to collect its citizens in villages dominated by the church. There they find mutual protection during the night. During the day, when conditions are safer, they can march out to their distant fields. Americans, fed up with clerical control both in Europe and New England, want their homes and farms as far apart as possible. I grew up in rural New York, with the nearest farm half a mile away, and you cannot imagine my amazement when I first saw the crowded little villages of Spain and Italy, one house abutting the other.

How do they breathe? I thought. And how do they get to their distant fields each morning?'

He warned us not to attribute this spatial difference to social factors: 'The attacks of Apache and Comanche in Texas were just as severe as the attacks of marauding armies in Europe, but the Americans refused to cluster for protection, while the Spaniards did. In San Antonio your civilians will cluster.'

Under his guidance we did imagine ourselves about to build a mission in 1719, and while we were in this frame of mind he flashed onto the screen a majestic slide of the Alamo, that sacred mission, heavily rebuilt, around which the soul of Texas rallies. This time it had been photographed at dusk, with an ominous cloud to the east, and after it had been on the screen for a few moments, Miss Cobb wiped her eyes with a handkerchief, and I noticed that the staff, then even Quimper, and finally Rusk, followed with similar reactions. Here was a photograph that would affect the heart of any Texan who saw it unexpectedly. Within those walls brave men had died defending a principle in which they believed; on those parapets my ancestor, illiterate Moses Barlow, had given his life for a cause with which he had been associated for less than two weeks.

Rapidly, in a series of beautiful slides, the friar now gave us a swift review of the four other surviving missions, those heavy structures with such delicate names: San José y San Miguel, Nuestra Señora de la Purísima Concepción, San Francisco de la Espada and, the one I preferred, San Juan Capistrano.

He showed them in storm, in sunlight, at evening with birds nesting, and at the break of day with a golden sun exploding over their walls. He showed us architectural fragments, and stretches of reconstructed walls, and windows glowing with majesty, and fonts where the friars washed their feet, and after a while we became so much a part of those missions that we were prepared to listen to what he had to say about us.

'Our five San Antonio missions cannot compare in raw beauty with the handsomely preserved and reconstructed missions of California. We have no one superb example of architecture like Santa Barbara, no outstanding summary of mission life like Fray Junípero Serra's San Carlos Borromeo, and the reason is simple. Since the Spanish missionaries in California were not required to face extremely hostile Indians, they did not have to fortify their buildings. They could enjoy the luxury of graceful architecture and widely spaced structures. But our poor friars in Tejas had to build both a church and a fortress to protect it. Most experts agree that if you want to understand mission life, you must come to San Antonio, because our rude buildings, constructed without guile, represent what the mission experience was all about, and now, at the halfway point in my talk, we're going to leave this cell and move out to see the structures themselves.'

To visit the five missions of San Antonio was like walking slowly and with deep passion into the beginnings of Texas history. Each was different. The Alamo had been massively added to; it was really a museum as well as a sacred gathering place, always cluttered with visitors. San José had also been rebuilt, most faithfully, and best represented what mission life had been like within its spacious walls and its little cubicles for Indians. But the mission that clutched at my heart from the time I first saw it as a boy, giving me insight into those early days, was Capistrano, with its simpler lines, its lovely three-part bell tower and especially that long severe wall with the five cemented archways. It spoke to me with such force that even now I fell silent when I saw it.

The Alamo had awed me; San José had delighted me; but Capistrano, when I stood before its simplicity, invited me to become a member of its congregation, concerned about its canal and the gathering of its crops.

As we gazed at this noble relic, Friar Clarence altered the tenor of his talk: 'So much for the past. You've seen what form these missions took, and a very good one it was. But what concerns us now is the legacy of these missions in the life of modern Texas. So as we stand here I want you to focus on the acequia, the little canal that brought water to the mission. It ran over there, we think, and today when Texas needs water so badly that it dreams up all kinds of tricks to find and save it, it's interesting to remember that our first irrigation ditches were dug by the friars of these San Antonio missions. An unusual Franciscan worked here in the 1720s, Fray Damián de Saldaña, born in Spain, who had great skill in laying out irrigation systems. He could be called the Father of Texan Water Conservation, and the work he did back then is as functional as anything we attempt today. I've often thought that the farmers and ranchers and citrus growers who lead water onto their lands should contribute a mite of their profit for a statue to that far-seeing friar.'

'Was he that important?' Rusk asked, and Quimper jumped in: 'Any man who can show Texas how to use its water is a certified Lone Star hero.'

When we returned to the projection room we were eager to hear how Friar Clarence would link the missions to modern Texas: 'If Spain had given us nothing but these five missions, the legacy would have been monumental. Because they had a fine solid form, they stand today as treasures of the first order. So even though they do reach us in damaged or altered state, we can still thank the prudence of our predecessors that they exist at all, because in such buildings the spiritual history of Texas is preserved.'

But whenever he approached such religious matters, he remembered his promise: 'But we're talking about form and function, not theology, and I would like to close with a reminder of how creatively the mission discharged its obligations in the early 1700s and how, its job done, it made itself obsolete by the end of the century. San Juan Capistrano, which seems to have affected our chairman so deeply, is a case in point. Founded near Nacogdoches in 1716, it died there and its functions were moved to a spot near Austin. Dying again, it was brought to San Antonio, where it enjoyed some success. As many as two hundred and fifty Indian residents. Five thousand head of cattle. Its own cotton fields and woolen manufacturing. But by 1793, when it had to be secularized, only a dozen Christianized Indians, less than twenty cattle, and the looms in disrepair.'

'What does *secularize* mean?' Rusk asked, and I was impressed by the manner in which this extremely capable man was always willing to reveal his ignorance when an unusual word was introduced whose exact meaning he wished to learn.

Instead of replying in words, Friar Clarence flashed onto the wall a series of photographs showing the five missions as they had existed at various times in the nineteenth and twentieth centuries, before restoration began. We were shocked at their pitiful condition: walls down, garbage piled high, roofs fallen in, and ruin in each little church. 'Strictly speaking,' Friar Clarence explained, '*to secularize* means *to convert from religious ownership and use to civil*. Like today when an urban congregation finds that its members have moved to the suburbs and it sells the church building to some little-theater group. In Texas the word carried a special meaning, for when the missions finished trying to tame the frontier and Christianize the Indians, in both of which they had limited success, the system had no further utility. So the church turned the missions back to the civil government. Hungry fingers grabbed for the valuable land, but nobody could see any use for the buildings, so they were allowed to fall into ruin or removed for other construction.' On that mournful note the slides concluded.

When the lights came up I saw that he kept his head bowed, and for some moments he remained that way. Then he smiled and said softly: 'How beautiful a concept! And how suddenly it was outmoded.'

'Why?' Miss Cobb asked, and he turned to her: 'I believe that many meritorious ideas are allowed a life span of about thirty years. Liberalism in France flourished briefly before World War II, made its contribution and vanished. Dr Spock's theories of child rearing set a generation free, then collapsed in excess. The Erie Canal in my home state. And the mission concept as applied to Texas. All made great contributions, then perished.'

'Railroads outmoded your Erie Canal after its allotted life,' Miss Cobb said. 'And airplanes killed many railroads and almost all the ocean liners. What killed your missions?'

He reflected on this, then chuckled: 'Texas.'

'Now, what does that mean?' Miss Cobb pursued.

'From its start, any Texas mission was destined for a short life. Distances were so great. The Indians were so intractable. So often, when its work failed in one place, it moved on to some other challenge.'

'If that's true, why do I see five stone buildings?'

'Ah!' he cried, a light burning in his eyes. 'You can never convince a man like the Fray Damián of whom I spoke that what he's doing is temporary. Once he positions that first adobe, he begins to build for eternity.'

'But you say his mission has disappeared?'

'Others killed it, not he. Damián succeeded beyond imagination. His form vanished. Completely destroyed. But the legacy survives.'

As he said this his face assumed a radiance which warmed us: 'I promised you at the beginning: no theology, no moralizing; just form and legacy. But you must have deduced from what I've said that the Texas missions would provide us with only a limited legacy if they were mere architecture. Their grandeur is twofold: art plus the spiritual force which evoked that art. The friars could not have survived in this wilderness without some guiding principle, and it was Christianity. There were drunkards among the friars, and some who chased after Indian girls, and others who had never known vocation, but there were also men of supreme devotion, and upon their efforts the future city of San Antonio and the state of Texas were founded. That is their legacy.'

His words had an astonishing result. 'Friar Clarence,' Rusk said in his deep and rumbling voice, 'you ought to change your name. It doesn't sound appropriate here in a nest of missions.'

'What would you advise?'

'Friar Ignacio. Friar Bernardo. Something Spanish.'

'I suppose we're all stuck with the names we were given. Rusk seems totally inappropriate for a man of your power.'

'What had you in mind?'

'Midas. Croesus. Maybe Carnegie.'

'You gave us a terrific explanation, Friar Clarence. Now tell me, how much would it cost to print your lecture in a book? To be given free to all the schools in Texas?'

I was surprised that a Texas billionaire would concern himself with pennies, but he addressed the problem scientifically, as if it involved great sums: 'Barlow, call a printing house and find out.' When I reported: 'They say that they can give you a black-and-white edition for about sixty cents a copy,' he gave one of his rare smiles, and said: 'That seems reasonable. Friar Clarence, I'd like to print such a book. Give young people the real story of the missions, just as you gave it to us. You're a very solid young man and your ideas merit circulation.'

Friar Clarence said tentatively that he would be honored, but I could see from his hesitation that he expected some catch, and Rusk revealed it: 'Of course, I'd want to eliminate that last part on the religious bit.'

Instantly the young scholar said: 'Then I wouldn't be interested, because obviously you've missed the whole point of my talk. Form and function were the outer manifestations of the mission. The heart and core was the religious conviction, and don't you forget it. Publish a book about missions and ignore their religious base? Oh, no!'

But Rusk was a clever man, and he said something now which absolutely stunned me in its simplicity and moral deviousness: 'I mean a booklet with illustrations – your excellent drawings, your photographs in color.' You could see that Friar Clarence was startled by this new dimension, but you could also see the poison of vanity working in him; Ransom Rusk was the serpent in paradise, tempting not Eve with an apple but a Franciscan friar with an image of a fine book in which his words would be distributed to Texas schools.

Very slowly he said: 'I would like to see that done, Mr Rusk,' and Rusk rose and clapped him on the shoulder, whereupon Friar Clarence added: 'But I would insist upon that last section, for it would be the soul of my book.' And in that simple statement the book became his and not Rusk's.

Now Rusk had to think. He certainly did not want to subsidize Catholic propaganda, and he temporized by asking our staff: 'How much would the cost be elevated if we used color? Maybe sixteen full pages of his best photos and drawings?' The young people consulted on this, recalling projects of a similar nature on which they had been engaged, and they suggested: 'Total cost, about two and a half dollars a copy, but only if you print in large batches.'

'That would be possible. Now, Friar Clarence, here's what I propose. That you and I will agree that Miss Cobb here, a good Protestant, and Professor Garza, an equally good Catholic, will study those last remarks to see if they're acceptable. I mean, not rank proselytizing. Agreed?'

The young friar considered this for some moments, then extended his hand, but as Rusk reached to grasp it, Friar Clarence said to Garza: 'I'll depend on you to see that the vital material stays in,' and Rusk responded as he accepted the hand: 'I'll depend on you, Miss Lorena, to see that the truth of The Black Legend is not completely whitewashed.'

Nueva España y
El Camino Real
1788–1792

*All public roadways in the Spanish Empire
were Caminos Reales, The King's Highway,
but these segments connecting Vera Cruz
and Los Adaes became a principal avenue
of empire.*

Santa Fé

COMANCHERÍA

El Paso del Norte

APACHERÍA

TEJAS

LOUISIANA

Río Sabine

Nacogdoches

Nachitoches

Los Adaes

Río Grande

Río Medina

San Antonio

Chihuahua

El Cíbolo

Río San Antonio

La Bahia

San Juan Bautista

Río Nueces

COAHUILA

Laredo

Monclova

Saltillo

Culiacán

Zacatecas

GOLFO
DE
MEXICO

OCÉANO PACÍFICO

San Luis Potosí

MILES
0   200

Guadalajara

Jalapa

Ciudad de México

Vera Cruz

III

EL CAMINO REAL

Don Ramón de Saldaña, eldest son of Commandant Alvaro and Benita, was sixty-six years of age and sprightly in mind and limb. Often he reflected upon the three great joys in his life and the two inconsolable tragedies.

He was sole owner of the vast Rancho El Codo, twenty-five thousand acres named after an elbow of the Medina, that river which marked the boundary between the two provinces of Coahuila and Tejas. It was a rich and varied parcel, well watered, and stocked with thousands of cattle, sheep and goats. Most important, it bordered a segment of Los Caminos Reales, that system of royal highways which reached out like spokes from Mexico City, the hub of New Spain. This portion reached from Vera Cruz through Mexico City to San Antonio de Béjar, as the town was now called, to the former capital of Tejas at Los Adaes, and its presence along the ranch meant that Don Ramón could sell provisions to the royal troops that patrolled the vital route; Rancho El Codo was an inheritance of which he was justly proud.

He was also inordinately pleased that he had, like his grandfather in Spain, sired seven sons in a row without, as he boasted, 'the contaminating intrusion of a single daughter.' The humorous honorific, Hidalgo de Bragueta, Sir Knight of the Codpiece, was not customarily used in Mexico, but Don Ramón liked to apply it to himself.

His third and chief pride in these declining years of a long frontier life was his granddaughter Trinidad, thirteen years old and as charming a child as could be found in the northern provinces. Petite and dark-haired, she was a lively young lady with a wonderfully free and outgoing nature better suited to a canter over the mesquite range than to an afternoon of sipping hot chocolate with the mission friars, and although she was not a vain girl, preferring at this stage in her life a good horse to a pretty dress, she did like to look trim and paid attention to her appearance.

The thing that strangers noticed most about Trinidad was her curious face, for although it was beautiful, with a flawless light complexion bespeaking her unsullied Spanish blood, her mouth was strangely tilted, creating the impression of a timeless smile. Her lower teeth had grown in most unevenly, preventing her jaws from meeting naturally, and this made the left corner of her mouth dip down while the right turned up. Had her other features been less than perfect, this defect might have marred her looks; instead, it created a kind of additional interest, for when she came up ready to curtsy to a stranger, her unusual mouth seemed to be smiling inquisitively as if to say 'Hello, what have we here?' And when she did speak, a very slight lisp, or unevenness, added to her air of mystery and to her attractiveness.

She was a clever child; her doting grandfather had taught her to read Cervantes, stories from the Bible, and even the less salacious of the romances being published in Mexico City; and a French cleric who had served some years earlier in one of Béjar's five missions had taught her his native language. She also had a marked talent for drawing, and so skillful were her rough sketches of people in the town that everyone who saw them could recognize this pompous priest or that officious occupant of the governor's residence. She was at her best, however, on horseback, for she was at that age when young girls are almost reluctant to face maidenhood and an interest in boys, and seek intuitively to cling to girlhood, lavishing their considerable affection on horses. In Trinidad de Saldaña's case it was one particular horse, a spirited brown gelding called Relampaguito, Little Lightningbolt. She would allow no one to abbreviate this rather long proper name or to give her horse a nickname; he was Relampaguito, a horse of importance, and she cared for him as if he were a much-loved younger brother.

It was Don Ramón's pleasure to ride forth in the early morning with Trinidad at his side, leave the town of Béjar where the Saldañas had their town house, and ride toward the Misión Santa Teresa. From the presidio he would pick up an armed guard and continue on to the edges of his ranch, whose new pastures, acquired from one of the Canary Island families, now reached eastward to those belonging to the mission.

Grandfather and granddaughter rode easily, side by side, admiring the good work begun by Uncle Damián in building this mission and later reveling in the splendid ranch the family had acquired through the energy and the agility of the Saldaña brothers. At such times Trinidad liked to ride on ahead, act as if she were a military scout and call back, 'I see Apache!' Then both grandfather and granddaughter would race their horses toward some spot on the horizon and rein in as if they saw Apache campfires, although once in a while Don Ramón would warn: 'You must never joke about the Apache. At a place like that down there my uncle Damián was martyred and your father killed,' and then the past became painfully real for the little girl.

The great tragedy of Don Ramón's life was that although he had sired seven sons, all had died during his own lifetime; four in service to the king – two in Spain, two in Mexico; one of cholera, which swept the northern provinces periodically, and two tortured and scalped by the Apache. All were dead, and Don Ramón sometimes recalled bitterly the words of that wise ancient who said: 'In peace, sons bury their fathers; in war, fathers bury their sons.' In Tejas it had always been war, threat of war against the French, real war against the Apache, comic war against the pirates who tried to infiltrate from the Caribbean, unending war against nature itself. And what made the slaughter of his sons so difficult to accept was that often the wars in which they engaged were later proved to have been unjustified. His fourth son, Bartolomé, had been slain during a skirmish with the Austrians, and shortly thereafter a solid peace with Austria came into effect. Same with the French. From his earliest days Don Ramón had been taught to fear them, but now all the territories along the Mississippi River which had once been French were Spanish, and to make things even more bewildering, just a few years ago a Paris-born Frenchman living in Natchitoches, had he but lived a little while longer, would actually have served as governor of Tejas.

All his sons dead! Don Ramón, more than most, had witnessed the fearful price paid by those Spaniards who had sought to bring civilization to Tejas: the loneliness of the first missions, the years of unrewarded drudgery in the presidios, the martyrs among the friars, the slain heroes like his sons, the anguish of the governors who tried to rule without funds or adequate police facilities, and the backbreaking efforts of the good women like his late wife who supported their men, making each new house just a little more civilized, just slightly more removed from the roughness of the frontier.

Once when his sorrows seemed almost unbearable, he clasped his granddaughter to him and cried: 'Trinidad, if this forsaken place ever becomes habitable, remember your fathers and your mothers who strove to make it so.' She was ten at the time, and said: 'I have only one mother. I had only one father.' And he swept his arms grandly over the entire town and cried with passion: 'All the good Spaniards here are your fathers and mothers. They have all lived so that you might live. And you shall live so that those who come after ... when this is a great city ...' He kissed her head. 'They will all be your children, Trinidad, yours and mine and Fray Damián's.'

'Even the Canary Islanders?' she asked, for relations with those proud and arrogant people had never been good.

'Today even they are my brothers,' Don Ramón said, but he had not really intended going that far.

Don Ramón, his granddaughter Trinidad and her mother Engracia, widow of Agustín de Saldaña slain by the Apache, lived in a beautiful rambling adobe-walled house facing the Military Plaza that stretched westward from the still-unfinished church of San Fernando. Passers-by were charmed by the Saldaña home: 'Its walls are always so neatly white-washed, and the seven wooden beams which jut out from the front wall are always hung with pots of flowers or with golden gourds or strings of corn and chilies drying in the sun. Don Ramón's house looks as if happy people live inside.'

Behind this inviting wall hid a nest of eleven interconnected small rooms forming a large horseshoe, the center of which was a lovely patio opening onto an even more beautiful garden where stone benches faced a fountain that gushed cool water whenever Indian servants worked the foot pumps. No one who stepped inside this house or into the garden for even two minutes could deceive himself into thinking that it was a

French house or English, and certainly it wasn't German. This was an evocation of Spain set down in a wilderness of New Spain, and as such it epitomized the ancient Spanish preoccupation with protecting families; stout walls safeguarded them from outside terrors, and a tiny chapel enabled them to hold private religious services. And just as the house protected the family, so the family jealously guarded its prerogatives, prepared to do almost anything, including murder, to defend them. The Saldaña family was fighting to avoid submersion in a sea of mestizo and Indian faces, determined to resist intruders coming down El Camino Real from the new Spanish possession of Louisiana or from the uncivilized Yankee lands farther east and north.

And therein lay the second tragedy in Don Ramón's life, festering, causing him nagging grief: his blood was pure Spanish, nobody could challenge that, but it was of diminished quality because he had not been born in Spain. He was a criollo, not a peninsular; that honored name was reserved for those actually born in the Iberian peninsula. Criollos could have pride; peninsulares had glory.

Since the only chance the Saldañas of Béjar had to reestablish their honor was to marry Trinidad to some gentleman of Spain, this became almost an obsession with Don Ramón, and one afternoon in 1788 he said to Engracia: 'Each day our little girl looks more like a woman. Please tell me how we can find her a suitable husband . . . a real Spaniard . . . from Spain.'

Engracia Sarmiento de Saldaña, having been born in central Spain to a minor branch of the notable Sarmiento family and brought to Mexico, where her father served as governor of a province to the south, appreciated the wisdom of getting the Mexican Saldañas back into the mainstream of Spanish life: 'I never forget, Don Ramón, that your father Alvaro and your saintly uncle Damián, may God bless his soul in heaven, were true-born Spaniards. You, unfortunately, were not, through no fault of your own or your father's.'

Don Ramón took no offense at this sharp reminder of his deficiency; he was always ready to lament, even in public, that he was not a peninsular, and he had witnessed too many instances in which families of distinction from the best parts of Spain had slowly deteriorated in Mexico: 'You've seen what happens, Engracia. They come here as proud peninsulares, and first they allow their sons and daughters to marry locals. Good families and all that, but born like me here in Mexico. With that relaxation to begin with, it isn't long before someone marries a mestizo. I've seen it a dozen times. Beautiful girls. Some sing like angels, sew well, keep a good house, tend their babies. But they *are* half Indian. And look what happens to *their* children. Look at young Alençon. He finally did it, married an Indian girl.' He sighed at the incalculable loss. 'The famous Alençón blood, lost in a desert of Indian adobes.'

'Is there any way we could send Trinidad to Spain?' her mother asked.

'If Ignacio or Lorenzo had survived when they went to Spain ... but they died. I suppose we have family, somewhere. How about the Sarmientos?'

'My family would be very contemptuous of any girl born in Mexico ...' She said this without rancor or self-pity, but the manner in which her voice trailed off betrayed the enormous damage she had incurred by marrying a criollo.

'I knew our former governor. Not well, but I did know him.'

'You know what he said when he sailed home. "May the Indian dust of this forsaken land never dirty my boots again." I doubt that he would welcome her.'

'I've been thinking, Engracia, that perhaps you and I ought to travel down to Mexico City. If we started next year in February, Trinidad would be fourteen. She's an extremely attractive girl, you know that. Her quizzical little smile, it tears my heart, and there must be many young officers from Spain ...'

'I would travel a great distance, Father, to find my daughter a proper husband.'

'Let me speak to Veramendi about it.'

And so the serious discussions started, with Don Ramón walking sedately the three blocks that separated the Béjar residences of these two leading families.

On Calle Soledad, for many years the only real street in town, the Béjar branch of the powerful Veramendis of Saltillo owned two elegant many-roomed houses, facing a common patio which was itself a work of art: seven old trees for shade and graveled walks graced with statues carved by Indian workmen who had copied Italian engravings of religious figures. Half a dozen niches in the adobe walls contained flowerpots holding vines whose creeping ends flowed down across the wall, forming beautiful patterns when the sun shone through them.

In the larger house lived the head of the local Veramendis, an austere man who kept to himself, supervising the education of his many children. His very able son Juan Martín, now ten, could already speak three languages – Spanish, French and English – because the wise old man could foresee that these latter tongues were bound to become important in Tejas.

Don Ramón did not go to the big house, but to the smaller one in which lived his good friend Don Lázaro Veramendi, of the lesser branch, who had granddaughters of his own and therefore the same problems as the Saldañas.

'Good day, dear friend!' Don Ramón called out as he entered the patio and saw Veramendi reading under one of the gnarled trees. 'I remember the day the tree was planted ... how many years ago?'

The two men, each approaching seventy, discussed the origin of this garden and agreed that it must have been planted either just before or just after the arrival of the Canary Islanders, sixty years earlier. 'Those were exciting days,' Don Lázaro said.

'And so are these. Do you feel the changes that overtake us?'

'I do.' He was about to specify what changes concerned him when two of his granddaughters, girls of eleven and fourteen, ran onto the patio from one door of their home, past the flower beds and through a door of the larger house. As they ran the two old men studied their untrammeled movement.

'It's them I've been thinking of,' Don Ramón said, and when Veramendi looked up in surprise, Saldaña added: 'I mean all the girls of our families. Our Trinidad especially. Where will she find a husband?' Before Don Lázaro could respond, he clarified his remark. 'I mean, of course, a respectable Spanish husband? Where?

Veramendi, proud of his family's distinctions, astonished his friend by saying judiciously: 'I no longer worry about that, Don Ramón. We're Spanish, yes, and proud to be, but neither you nor I was born in Spain, and we do well in Béjar. I think our children will do the same.'

'But maintaining the Spanish blood, things Spanish, a sense of Castile and Aragon – how can we ensure that if our granddaughters . . .'

'They'll marry as events dictate, and do you know one thing, Don Ramón? I doubt if any of them will ever see Spain. This is the new land. This is our homeland now.'

'Wouldn't you prefer . . . ? How many granddaughters have you – four, five?'

'I have six, thanks to God's bounty,' Veramendi said, 'and five of them will need husbands. María's to be a nun, by the grace of the Virgin, so we need only five young men.'

'And you'll be just as happy if they've been born in Mexico?'

'I was born in Mexico and I yield to no man . . .'

'I mean, wouldn't you be just a bit prouder – more secure, I mean – if your girls were married to men born in Spain? Men with honest Spanish roots?'

Don Lázaro clapped his hands and laughed at his friend: 'You have roots in Spain – the town of Saldaña, if my memory serves me. And what the devil good has it ever done you?'

Don Ramón pondered this difficult question a long time, his brow deeply wrinkled. But then a benign smile appeared: 'I often think of those dark centuries when Spain writhed under the heel of Muhammadanism. There was every reason for my ancestors to marry with the infidels. Power, money, an appointment at the Moorish court. But they protected their Spanish blood with their lives. No Moors in our family. No Jews. We starved, lived in caves, and in the end we triumphed.'

'Do you feel about mestizos the way your ancestors felt about Moors?'

'I do. To be the carrier of pure Spanish blood fortifies the spirit. On that awful day when messengers galloped in to inform my father that his brother, Fray Damián, had been tortured to death by the Apache, our family found courage in the fact that we were Spaniards, untouched by Mexico, and that as Spaniards we have to behave in a certain way . . . to preserve our honor.'

'So what did your Spanish father do?'

'He handed me a gun, although I was barely fifteen, called for volunteers, and set forth to punish the Apache. We killed sixty-seven.'

'And what did that prove? Forty years later the Lipan Apache were still there, and they killed two of your sons not ten miles from where they killed your uncle.'

'Finally we drove them back. In the end, Spain always conquers.'

'So in their place we got the Comanche, and they're worse.'

Don Ramón fell silent, put his left thumbnail against his teeth and studied this amazing Veramendi, who had from boyhood been so willing to accept Béjar as it was, never cursing the Indians, never brawling with the Canary Islanders, never arguing with the friars about the allocation of river water to the irrigation ditches. He had always whistled a lot, and now he whistled easily as if any problems really worth serious worry lay far in the distance.

'Don Lázaro, I don't think you'd worry even if one of your granddaughters married a mestizo!'

Veramendi pondered this, and said: 'It seems highly likely, what with the dilution of our Spanish blood, that two or three of my girls might have to find their husbands among the locals.' When Saldaña gasped, Veramendi added an interesting speculation: 'Let's be perfectly reasonable, Don Ramón. The Spanish army doesn't send many peninsulares to Mexico any more, only a scattering of officers now and then, and damned few of them ever get north to this little town. We don't even get any peninsular priests any more. Saltillo's no better. I looked last time I was down there. And in Mexico City the grand families pick off the young Spaniards as soon as they arrive from Vera Cruz. So true Spaniards are gone. No hope at all.

'That leaves young men like you and me as we were half a century ago. Spanish, but born in Mexico. And there's a limited number of us, believe me. I saw it in Saltillo. So what does that leave our granddaughters, yours and mine? It leaves a crop of fine young men half Spanish, half Indian, and you have some of the best on your own ranch.'

Saldaña was shocked: 'Would you allow a mestizo ranch hand to marry one of your granddaughters?'

Veramendi, not willing to confess that he had been preparing himself for just such an eventuality, changed the conversation dramatically: 'Do you want to know what I really think, old friend?' When Don Ramón said: 'I'm afraid to listen, the way you've been raving,' the old man said firmly: 'I suspect that you and I are looking in the wrong direction. Right now we face south, looking always at Mexico City, from where God in his merciful bounty sends us all the good things we enjoy. Right now we look south along El Camino Real as our blessed lifeline. Dear friend, let's face realities. Let's change our position and look north. The good things of this life henceforth will not come up El Camino Real, they will come down it – from Louisiana, or from Los Estados Unidos.'

When Don Ramón failed to respond, his friend said, as he gazed north: 'So what I really suppose is that my granddaughters will marry Frenchmen posing as Spaniards. Or even worse, one of those rough norteamericanos.'

'But aren't all americanos Protestants?'

'Men can change, especially where a beautiful girl's involved ... and free land.' Again Don Ramón was flabbergasted, whereupon Don Lázaro clapped him on the knee: 'Since your little Trinidad is about the prettiest in town, you may find yourself completely surprised at whom she marries.'

At last Don Ramón found his voice: 'By God, Don Lázaro, you sound as if you wouldn't even stop at Indians.'

'I don't want them for these girls,' Don Lázaro snapped instantly, 'because the Indians are not yet civilized. But the granddaughters of these girls, they might be very proud to marry the type of Indian who's going to come along.'

'When I was a boy, if the viceroy heard a Spaniard utter such a statement ... off to the dungeons at San Juan de Ulúa.'

At this, Veramendi leaped from the stone bench, danced about the garden, and chuckled with delight. Then he took a position staring down at Saldaña and reminded him of a few important facts:

'Two years ago I was sent by our viceroy to New Orleans to help our Spanish Governor Miró bring that French city into our system, and I never worked with a better man. Judicious, far-seeing, patriotic. I wish we had a governor like that in Tejas. He preached constantly to those below him that our new province of Louisiana was to be a haven for people of all kinds, French in the majority, norteamericanos next in number, Spaniards of the better sort ruling fairly and running the businesses, with many, many blacks and Indians doing the work. All nations and yes, unwisely, all religions. Governor Miró accepted everyone as his brother.

'Well, you can guess that his liberal attitude toward religion got him into immediate trouble, because officials in Mexico supported the Inquisition, which is a fine institution, if properly run. But Madrid sent out a wild-eyed, savage-spirited Spanish priest named Father Sadella to head our Inquisition. Yes, Father Sadella came out to New Orleans to establish religious courts, religious jails and religious gibbets from which he was going to hang every damned Protestant or free-thinker like me and maybe even Governor Miró himself. And when Louisiana was sanctified he was going to hang all the Protestants in Tejas. He had lists of names.

'He was a terrifying man, Don Ramón, and had he come down here, in due course you would have found yourself entangled in his webs. For what? I don't know, but he would have found something you had done or hadn't done. He was tall and very thin and had deep-set eyes which darted from side to side as if he constantly expected a dagger. Imagine, jails and gibbets established in Tejas!

'Governor Miró assembled eight of us he could trust and asked us bluntly: "What can we do to save ourselves from this dreadful man?" and I said: "Murder him, tonight," but Miró warned against such action: "If we did that, Madrid would have to respond, and all of us would be hanged." A Spanish officer from Valencia, a pious man I believe, for I saw him always in church, made the best proposal: "Let us arrest him right now, and throw him onto the *Princesa Luisa*, which is ready to sail, and then hope that the ship sinks." A very wise priest born in Mexico City added the good touch: "We'll march him aboard at ten in the morning with the whole town at the docks to jeer at him and laugh. We'll make a holiday of it as if all Louisiana approved what we're doing. And that will draw Father Sadella's ugly teeth."

'So we had a festival, even the firing of a cannon. I arranged for that. And that's how we saved Tejas from the leg irons and gallows of the Holy Inquisition.'

Don Ramón studied his knuckles, which had grown taut as the

tale unfolded. 'Why do you tell me something for which you could still be thrown in jail?'

'Because it represents the new truth, as I see it. Mexico City would never have dared oppose the Inquisition. New Orleans did. Down El Camino Real, from our new holdings in Louisiana, will come new interpretations of old customs. And along the same road, from Los Estados Unidos, will come new ways of doing things, a new sense of government, and lusty, energetic young men who will marry our girls.'

'Will you permit that?'

'Who can stop it?'

'Is the old Spain dead?'

'It's been dead for fifty years. I could have built a great city here. All it needed was two thousand Spaniards of the better sort ruling fairly, supervising things and running their businesses. But they were never forthcoming. Spain had its chance, but passed it by.'

The two men, debris from a flood of empire which had receded with terrible swiftness, sat gloomily for some minutes, seeing in imagination the royal road along which the promised help should have come but never did. Then, as if by malignant design, a bugle sounded from the presidio and the army contingent marched out for one of its weekly parades, seeking to prove that Spain still had the power to defend its farthest outpost.

Two aspects of the march impressed them when they went to the gate to watch: the slovenliness of the drill and the incredibility of the uniforms. Only the two officers, Captain Moncado and Lieutenant Marcelino, were properly outfitted. In gold trousers and smartly polished boots they made a stiff and handsome pair, very military in appearance except that Marcelino had no proper hat. He marched bareheaded, which made him seem two feet shorter than his commander and somewhat ridiculous.

The enlisted complement for Béjar was ninety-four, but of these, only sixty-four had bothered to show up, and of those, only two groups of three each wore uniforms, but no one outfit was complete. The front rank wore fine blue uniforms, but here again hats were missing. The second group, marching immediately behind, wore green uniforms that had been popular thirty years earlier; this time only one hat was missing.

The eight men in the next two ranks also had uniforms, each one completely different, and behind them came twenty men dressed in either leather jackets or army trousers, but never both. And whichever half they did have was preposterously patched with cloth of another match.

The next ranks wore no uniforms at all, only the floppy white garments of the countryside, and of these men half had no shoes; they marched barefoot. Unbelievably, the last fifteen in the parade had no hats, no shirts, no shoes; they marched in trousers only and these of every possible length and style.

At the front, Captain Moncado and Lieutenant Marcelino moved smartly and in step as if they were on duty in Spain, as did the six enlisted men who had matching uniforms. But the rest straggled along, kicking dust, out of step, neither neat nor erect, for all the world more like field hands returning to town at the end of a wearing day than soldiers representing Spanish dominion overseas.

Two-thirds of the troops had guns, but of every imaginable make and age; surely if the poorest dozen were fired, they could not be reloaded in less than ten minutes. Some of the remaining men carried lances, shields or swords, and many had no formal weapon whatever except a club hacked from some tree. And this was the military might which was supposed to protect Béjar and its six missions, safeguard the roads, and defend the outlying farms from the skilled attacks of some four thousand Comanche, those dreaded horse Indians from the north who had captured a few Spanish steeds, bred them, and galloped south to lay waste all Spanish settlements. This was the grandeur of Spain in the year 1788.

Don Ramón, remembering how meticulous his father had been about maintaining the dignity of Spain when he occupied the Béjar presidio, stalked over to the ramshackle building after the parade ended to rebuke Lieutenant Marcelino: 'You could at least wear a proper hat.'

'The government provides us with no hats,' the young man snapped. 'We get damned little of anything, really.'

'If you had any self-respect, you'd buy your own.'

'We're supposed to, but we get no money.'

'And your men! Shocking. Can't you discipline them?'

'If I say one unkind word, make one threat, they desert.'

'You should be ashamed of yourself, young man,' and from that day Don Ramón avoided the presidio and its unruly complement, for he remembered when Spain was Spain.

When Veramendi learned of his friend's unfortunate run-in with the military, he said: 'Old friend, you aren't going to like this, but the two thousand real men who never arrived didn't have to be notable Spaniards like your ancestors and mine. They could very nicely have been Canary Islanders, if they'd had the courage of that fellow who gave your father and uncle so much trouble.' He whistled for one of his granddaughters, and when the girl Amalia appeared, a saucy child of fourteen with bright eyes and big white teeth, he asked her to fetch a book from his desk. As she disappeared Don Ramón asked: 'Would you really let her marry a mestizo?' and Veramendi said with a smile: 'Who else will be left?'

When the girl returned, Don Lázaro caught her by the hand: 'Stay! I want you to hear this. I want you to hear how you should speak to little men who assume authority.' Then, turning to Saldaña, he explained: 'This is a copy of the letter which our famous Canary Islander, Juan Leal Goras, sent to the viceroy in Mexico City, demanding, not begging, for some additional right he was entitled to. Listen to how he begins his respectful plea:

'Juan Leal Goras, Español y Colonizador a las Ordenes de Su Majestad, Quien Dios Protege, en Su Presidio de San Antonio de Béxar y Villa de San Fernando, Provinica de Tejas también llamada Nuevas Filipinas, y Señor Regidor de esta Villa. Agricultor.'

Slapping his granddaughter lovingly on the shoulder, he said: 'That's the kind of man we need in Tejas. Give your full credentials, like some dignitary, then sign yourself "Farmer".' When the girl laughed, not understanding the force of what her grandfather was saying, he drew her to him, kissed her, and said: 'And that's the kind of man I want you to marry, Amalia. Someone with spunk.'

When Trinidad learned that she would be traveling to Mexico

City she wanted to kiss her mother and her grandfather for their generosity, but she was so overcome by love that she stood in the white-walled room where they took chocolate in the afternoons and lowered her head for fear she might cry. Then a most winsome smile took possession of her curiously tilted mouth, and she gave a childlike leap in the air and shouted: 'Olé! How wonderful!'

She maintained this level of excitement for several days as the great trip was planned. Since it was over a thousand miles to the capital, any citizen of Béjar would be fortunate to make the journey once in a lifetime. Trinidad, supposing that she would see the grand city once and no more, packed her two trunks with the greatest of care.

Béjar at this time was not large, less than two thousand inhabitants, but since the old capital of Los Adaes had been abandoned, it had become the principal Spanish establishment north of Monclova. And because of a startling change in viceregal administration, it now had additional responsibility. A vast collection of provinces, including California, New Mexico and Tejas in the north, along with six huge provinces like Coahuila and Sonora to the south, had been united to form the Provincias Internas with their capital at Chihuahua, but since this city was five hundred miles to the west and connected only by Indian trails to Béjar, most local decisions had to be made in the Tejas capital. For extended periods, Béjar was left on its own.

The town was in a fine setting. Four waterways now ran in parallel courses from north to south, lending color and charm with their shade trees: to the east, the original canal servicing the missions; next, the lively San Antonio; to the west, the irrigation ditch that Fray Damián had laid out for the Canary Islanders in 1732; and farther to the west, a little creek whose water serviced expanding agricultural fields. These waterways created four clearly defined available land areas, and by 1788 each was beginning to fill up with the houses of permanent settlers.

Well to the east, on the far side of the river, stood the unfinished buildings of the dying mission that would one day be named the Alamo, and around it clustered a few mean houses occupied by Indians. On the west bank, within the big loop where the horses pastured, stood eleven well-constructed houses belonging to leading mestizos, and along the rest of the river rose twenty-six other houses of a mixed population. The finest area was that between the westernmost irrigation ditches, and on it stood fifty-four homes clustered about the center of the town; the Saldañas and the Veramendis lived here. West of all the ditches were the scattered homes of farmers.

The carefully recorded census showed: Spaniards (peninsular and criollo) 862; mestizos 203; Indians 505; other colored (Indian-Black, oriental) 275; Blacks (all slaves) 37; total 1,882. These citizens performed a rich assortment of duties: ten merchants, each with his own shop; ten tailors; six shoemakers; four river fishermen; four carpenters; two blacksmiths; one barber and one digger of sewers. Lawyers: none.

There were also more than six hundred Indians living in or near the six missions, but the fortunes of these once-valuable institutions had begun to decline so badly that there was talk of closing them down; indeed, a Father Ybarra had recently been sent north to report on that advisability. He was working now on his recommendations, and since he was a gloomy, unpleasant man, the citizens assumed that his document would be, too.

The town was dominated by the presidio, with its ninety-four military misfits, and the large church started in 1738 by the Canary Islanders. Age had softened this building into an object of some beauty, if one appreciated the harsh desert style adopted by its Franciscan architects.

Trinidad loved Béjar and made each of its corners her own, begging her mother to take her first to some site across the river, then to the lovely missions to the south. The best part of town, she thought, was the two plazas facing the church: a smaller one to the east toward the river, a larger to the west toward the hill country beyond. In these plazas she and her friends had whiled away many hours of childhood. But lately Trinidad enjoyed even more the family journeys to what she called 'our family's mission,' Santa Teresa, where the handsome carvings by Simón Garza depicted the Stations of the Cross. She preferred the one in which Santa Verónica wiped Christ's face with her cloth, and the other in which the man stooped to help Jesus carry his cross, for these showed the kindness of humanity; the others showed only aspects of its brutality. The jamming down upon Christ's head of the crown of thorns made her feel the thorns piercing her own forehead, while the actual crucifixion was too painful to contemplate.

After one of these journeys, she asked her grandfather about the carvings: 'Is it true that the man who made them was an Indian?'

'Half Indian. His Spanish blood enabled him to be an artist.'

'Is it true that he was the grandfather, or something like that, of Domingo, who works at the ranch?'

'How do you know Domingo?'

'We played together. I taught him to read. He taught me to ride.'

'You stay away from Domingo.'

'Why?'

'Because I tell you to.'

That night Don Ramón had only a broken sleep, for he was tormented by visions of his granddaughter marrying some savage Indian from the mountains of Mexico, and he knew he must prevent this. Early next morning, before the women were up, he called for his best horse, but before he could leave for the ranch, Trinidad, who had heard the clatter of hooves, bounded into the stables in her nightdress.

'Where are you going?' she called.

'Where you're not welcome. Go back to bed,' and before she could protest, for he had always allowed her to accompany him on his travels, he had spurred his horse and headed for the gates of the presidio. There he rounded up a company of armed men to protect him, and together they rode westward over the plains in the early morning sun.

He rode for several hours, until he came to the cluster of buildings from where his men worked the vast, unfenced ranch of El Codo with its thousands of cattle that fed the little town of Béjar. There was a house for the Garza family, whose men had been supervisors for decades, a barn for storing feed, three different sets of corrals, a line of low shacks for the Indians and a good stable for the horses. There was also a large lean-to under which the awkward carts with their creaking solid wheels were kept. It was a handsome assembly of adobe buildings,

191

none pretentious and all well fitted to the terrain in the Spanish manner. Don Ramón was proud of this ranch and not pleased with the job he had to do on reaching it, but he was so determined to protect his granddaughter from the kind of talk Don Lázaro Veramendi had been engaging in that his mind was firm, and as soon as he saw Domingo's father he began.

'Teodoro, you and your family have worked so well for us . . .'

'Only our duty, señor.'

'We want to reward you.'

'You already have, many times.'

'In 1749, when I helped the great Escandón explore the valley of the Río Grande, he liked my work so much that he awarded me four leagues of land along the river.'

'That could be good land, señor, from what the soldiers say.'

'I'm going to give you that land, Teodoro. We'll never make good use of it, I fear.'

'Señor, I wouldn't want to leave El Codo . . .'

'You must,' Don Ramón said firmly. 'You've earned our gratitude.'

'Magdalena might not wish to travel.'

'Wives do what their husbands say, so let's hear no more about it. You have the four leagues. I've brought the papers, signed by Viceroy Güemes.' From his saddlebag he produced the valuable parchment authorized by King Fernando VI, signed by the viceroy and notarized by the current governor of Nuevo Santander, Melchor Vidal de Lorca. The nearly eighteen thousand acres were worth at that time about one cent an acre; in years to come, six thousand dollars an acre, and after that, much more, for they lay on the rich north bank of the Río Grande, where, according to legend, a walking stick fifty years old would flower and grow fruit if stuck in the loam and watered.

When Garza rode with Don Ramón to the ranch house, he informed his wife Magdalena of the extraordinary proposal, and although neither he nor she could read, he showed her the impressive document heavy with wax seals. They discussed the offer for several minutes while Don Ramón inspected his shoes, his fingernails and his knuckles; then they came to stand before him, holding hands, and Magdalena, delighted to get land, any land, said: 'Don Ramón, we kiss the soles of your shoes. Land of our own after these many years. God will bless you, and we will too. Teodoro and I will go down to the river and take the land' – and here she tapped the precious parchment – 'but because we love you and your family, we'll leave our son Domingo here to care for the ranch, as before.'

'No, no!' Don Ramón said. 'Your son must go with you!'

Now Teodoro began to argue that in simple fairness they must leave Domingo behind, but when this was said a second time, Don Ramón became angry: 'He will go with you. To build the corrals, the barns.'

So it was settled, and Don Ramón slept at the ranch for three nights until the Garzas were packed and lesser hands instructed as to the care of the cattle. He gave the departing family four good horses, a fine bull, six cows and the loan of seven armed men to protect the exodus as it crossed the hundred leagues of Indian lands separating it from the place where the Río Grande approached the Gulf of Mexico. As they pulled away from El Codo, Don Ramón rode with them for several hours to make sure that they were really on their way; then he embraced Teodoro and his wife, wished them luck in their new home, and shook hands formally with Domingo, seventeen years old, handsome, clever, honest. 'You're a good lad, son. Build your own ranch, and make it prosper.' He reined in his horse, told the armed men protecting him to wait, and watched as the little caravan headed toward the southern horizon. By this time next month they'll reach the place, he thought. Rich land, plenty of water, even some trees, as I recall. Escandón advised me to choose my land on the south side of the river. When I said I liked the look of the north, he said: 'It's yours, if you think something can be done with it.' And now it's Garza's. He reflected on this for many minutes, finally muttering to himself: 'Their son could make his fortune on good land like that. That's why I chose it, for its richness.' As he recalled the capable youth he had sent into exile, other thoughts surged into his mind, but he repressed them, for he did not wish to consider such possibilities: He's a mestizo. He has his own place, and it's not here.

Signaling to his escort, he headed back to town.

* * *

The cumbersome entourage which Don Ramón assembled in February 1789 for the long trip to Mexico City would be able to cover about four leagues a day (roughly ten and a half miles), and since the distance was about four hundred leagues, the trip would require a good hundred-odd days of unrelieved travel, plus time for repairs, for rest on Sundays, when Doña Engracia refused to allow the horses to be worked, for the forced halts at swollen rivers, and for much-needed recuperation periods in the provincial cities like Saltillo. The journey would thus require about half a year, then a six-month visit in the capital, plus another half year for the return. No family initiated a trip like this without prayers and solemn adieus, for everyone knew that sickness or flood or the Apache and bandits who prowled the lonely stretches might take the lives of all. When the Saldañas bade farewell to the Veramendis, there were tears aplenty, especially when the dear friends Trinidad and Amalia embraced.

The Saldañas knew that the bleakest part of the journey came at the start, for once they crossed their own river, the Medina, they left Tejas and entered upon those empty, barren plains reaching down to the Río Grande; it was proper, they thought, that these wastes not be a part of Tejas, for they were El Despoblado, totally unoccupied, and could best be understood as the desert which constituted the northern part of Coahuila.

The Saldañas would traverse almost three hundred miles of this desert before they reached partial civilization at Monclova and real settlement at the entrancing city of Saltillo, so they wrapped damp cloths about their nostrils and lips to keep out the dust and plunged into the forbidding lands. After nineteen wearing days they reached the Río Grande and the excellent hospitality of the missions at San Juan Bautista, where they lingered for two weeks. The friars were glad to welcome them, for they brought news of Tejas, and the Saldañas were pleased to stay because the missions had fresh vegetables.

Almost regretfully Trinidad bade the friars farewell, and now started the dangerous part of the journey, eighteen days across the desolate, exposed stretch to Monclova, for it was here that the Apache often struck, wiping out whole convoys. Eleven mounted soldiers accompanied the travelers, for the Saldañas were personages and risks could not be taken. Day after day the wagon in which Engracia de Saldaña rode creaked over the forlorn pathway, this royal road, with never a house to be seen nor even a wandering shepherd. Once Don Ramón told his granddaughter: 'When they ask in the plaza at Béjar "Why aren't there more settlers here?" this is the reason,' and with a sweep of his arm he indicated that terrifying emptiness, that mix of sand and stunted trees and washed gullies down which torrents cascaded when the rains came, pinning travelers inside their tents for days at a time.

South of Monclova everything became more interesting, for now the Saldañas entered one of the most enchanting areas in all of Mexico: beautiful barren fields sweeping upward to become graceful hills, then low mountains and, finally, crests of considerable size. El Camino Real now became truly royal, providing grand vistas and magnificent enfolding mountains, so that one had the impression of piercing into the very heart of the hills. Repeatedly Don Ramón halted the troop to say: 'I remember this spot when I was a boy. Captain Alvaro, my father of blessed memory, brought me and my brothers here and we took our meal by that waterfall. How long ago it seems.' He told Trinidad that she, too, must remember this spot: 'Let's see. You were fourteen last month. If you marry at sixteen, as a girl should ... babies ... then the babies marry ... and they have babies.' He stopped to count. 'You could be traveling down this road in 1843 with your own grandchildren. And when you do, halt here and have your merienda and lift a cup to me, as I now do to my father, may God rest his soul.'

It was from such conversations that Trinidad had acquired for a child so young an unusual sense of the passing of time. She perceived that a human being was born into a certain bundle of years, and that it did not matter whether she liked those years or not; they were her years and she must live her life within them. If they turned out to be good years, fine. If they were bad, so be it, for they were the years in which she must find her husband and have her children and perhaps take her grandchildren to a merienda in the mountains like this, at spots where her grandfather and his father had enjoyed their rest stops and the tumbling waters.

When the picnic ended she ran to Don Ramón and kissed him, and he said: 'There will be even better moments than this,

Trinidad, you mark your old grandfather's words.'

The first of them came in the gracious town of Saltillo, for here Trinidad saw her first community of any size, and she was awed by its magnificence: 'It is so big! There are so many shops! A person could find anything in the world here!'

For the first two eye-opening days she savored Saltillo, especially the new church, so large and so majestic, its ornate façade exquisitely adorned with intricate carving and crowned by a beautiful shell above the entrance. To the right rose a stern tower topped by three tiers of pillars, behind which hid a carillon that echoed long after the last peal was struck. It is overwhelming, like God Himself, Trinidad thought. One side of Him is all gentleness and beauty. The other is almost frightening, so big, so powerful. But the more she studied this uncompromising structure the more she accepted both halves.

Four times she returned in daylight hours, captivated by its mystery, and when Don Ramón teased her for wasting her time, she explained: 'I've never seen anything so grand before. In Tejas . . .' He went to a store and purchased pen and paper for her, and with these she sketched the church, rather effectively, Don Ramón told Engracia, and he pleased Trinidad by asking solemnly if she would sign it for him, and she did: '*Trinidad de Saldaña, Dibujado en Saltillo, 16 de Mayo de 1789.*'

It was not until the evening of the third day that Trinidad discovered another wonder of a city, for then her elders took her to the church plaza, where she saw for the first time not the aimless wandering about of young people in a rural village like Béjar, but the formal Spanish paseo of a major town like Saltillo. She and her family reached the plaza when the paseo was in full swing, and for some minutes she watched, openmouthed, as handsome young men and alluring girls swung past, talking always to someone of their own sex, pretending to be indifferent to the other. Finally she brought her clasped hands up to her lips and sighed: 'Mother, this is so beautiful!.'

It was, and there Trinidad stayed till the last promenaders left the plaza. She had seen something which touched on the rhythms of life, its uncertainties, its mysteries. She could not get to sleep that night, for in her mind rose the awkward towers of the church and in their timeless shadow walked the young people of Saltillo, pursuing their unstated passions in the ancient Spanish way.

It was obvious to Engracia that on the next night her daughter was going to plead for permission to join the paseo, and this posed a problem, which she took to her father-in-law: 'I'm certainly too old to parade with her holding my hand. And she knows no one with whom she can walk.'

'Let her walk alone.'

'Never.'

'I seem to remember girls walking alone, when I was younger.'

'Not girls of good family.'

Don Ramón, recognizing that he must assume responsibility in the matter, went to the manager of the inn at which they were stopping, and said forthrightly: 'Don Ignacio, our fourteen-year-old granddaughter wants to join the paseo. Do you know a girl of impeccable family with whom she could walk?'

'I have a granddaughter, excellent family, her mother born in Spain.'

'Don Ignacio, I would be honored.'

'To the contrary. We've all heard of your martyred uncle, Fray Damián. The honor would fall upon our family.'

So it was arranged that Trinidad would make the paseo with fifteen-year-old Dorotéa Galíndez. When the evening bells rang, the nervous girls asked their elders how they looked, and Don Ramón replied: 'If I were twins, I'd fall in love with each of you.' Then, nodding very low to Dorotéa, he added: 'If there's a cavalier out there tonight, he'll ride away with you.'

Señoras Saldaña and Galíndez waited about an hour before taking their daughters to the plaza, for they wished to introduce them into the parade unostentatiously, but as soon as the two girls entered the plaza the young men meeting them in the paseo grew attentive, and for the first time in her life Trinidad realized that she had more than an ordinary appearance. Her warm smile and uncalculated approach so tantalized the passing young men that one young fellow said to the friend with whom he was walking: 'That's the kind of face you remember at midnight when you can't get to sleep.' Dorotéa, a year older, warned Trinidad that girls must never look directly at boys; they must appear to be engrossed in each other. Dorotéa played this game to perfection, finding in the country girl from Tejas a person of unlimited curiosity, and the two chattered happily as the young men passed. But Trinidad was not interested in games; she was noticing attractive young men for the first time in her life, and she was bewitched, her pretty face turned brazenly toward them, her unforgettable smile greeting them with joy.

That night Dorotéa told her mother about Trinidad's forward behavior, and Señora Galíndez spoke to Engracia: 'You must warn your pretty daughter against an unbecoming boldness.' So the next afternoon Trinidad's mother and grandfather explained that it was most unladylike for a young woman to demonstrate too much interest in young men. 'You are to smile, of course,' Don Ramón said, 'but only to yourself. That adds mystery.' Inviting Engracia to walk the narrow room with him, he explained: 'Your mother is Dorotéa. I'm you.' And he minced along, talking with great animation to Engracia, who smiled back at him. 'This is how proper girls make the paseo,' and on he pranced.

'You look so funny!' Trinidad cried.

Don Ramón stopped, and reprimanded her: 'If a girl of good family like you smiles openly at young men, it's very forward. And if you actually encourage them, you're brazen, as Señora Galíndez warned.'

'She's a busybody.'

'Without her approval you cannot walk with her daughter,' Engracia said, and when Trinidad started to reply, her mother pressed a hand against her lips. 'Child, remember that three days from now we go on to San Luis Potosí. Dorotéa stays here, and if her reputation is damaged by some foolish thing you do, she suffers, not you.' She cuffed her daughter lightly on the ear and said: 'Now you behave yourself.'

Trinidad did behave herself for the first half of that night's paseo, but as the girls rounded a corner by the church steps Dorotéa gasped 'Oh!' and Trinidad looked forward. Then she, too, gasped.

Joining the men's circle in an easy, indifferent manner came the most engaging young man either girl had ever seen. He would have been spectacular even had his face not been so pleasing, for he was an outstanding blond among all the dark-haired Saltillo youths, and so graceful that he seemed to move without his feet actually touching the ground. He was one of those fortunate men who would always be slim, and he would retain that air of youthful excitement, that devastating smile, those bright eyes filled with wonder. Age would not wither him nor years increase his girth. He was now nineteen, a mere five feet five inches tall, weighing not more than a hundred and forty pounds, and so he would remain.

When the young man came abreast, Trinidad threw caution away and smiled directly at him. To her dismay, she realized that he was smiling at Dorotéa, and she at him.

Although Señorita Dorotéa Galíndez had been a very proper young lady when none of the passing men interested her particularly, she became a very skilled young temptress when someone as intriguing as this newcomer came her way. She now lost all interest in Trinidad, and since she would encounter the stranger twice in each complete turn of the circle, as soon as she completed one pass she began preparing for the next, so that although the young man would be meeting many girls in his round, he would meet none more obviously affected nor more eager to make his acquaintance than Dorotéa. She saw to that.

So the enchanted evening progressed, one of the most compelling and confusing that Trinidad would ever know: the beauty of Saltillo, the grandeur of the new church, moonlight filling the plaza, the smell of flowers, this handsome stranger, but most of all, watching a determined young man of nineteen who was making his own plans to entrap her. Trinidad was by no means watching this as one detached; she wished desperately that the young fellow had saved his smiles for her, and the more often she saw him the more she liked him, but she was sensible enough to know that Dorotéa had stepped in before her, so she contented herself with watching Dorotéa's skill.

Bells sounded in the dark tower. Annoyed pigeons flew over the plaza briefly and returned to their roost above the bells. A watchman started his rounds, nodding to the citizens as they made their way home. The flowers of Saltillo dozed and Trinidad de Saldaña, agitated as never before, clasped her grandfather's hand with unwonted emotion and whispered as he led her back to the inn: 'Saltillo is so wonderful, Grandfather, and Tejas seems so bleak.'

Dorotéa, up betimes and asking a thousand questions, had

much to report when the Saldañas came down for eleven o'clock chocolate: 'He's French. He comes from New Orleans. His family owns large vineyards in France, but his father manufactures mining things and ships them to Vera Cruz for the capital.'

'What's he doing in Saltillo?' Don Ramón asked, and Dorotéa said brightly: 'Oh, he's looking to see if we have any mines in places like Béjar and Monclova.' Then she winked at Trinidad: 'And he's going to San Luis Potosí to see if he can sell a marvelous new machine to the people there. His name is René-Claude d'Ambreuze. He speaks fine Spanish, and he's stopping at the other inn.'

'So he's in business?' Don Ramón asked, and Trinidad's heart almost stopped, for she immediately visualized this godlike young man joining their party for the three hundred miles to the mining capital, and before anyone could speak further she saw herself and René-Claude – what a heavenly name! – cantering across the high plains of Mexico, she in the lead, he avidly in pursuit.

'He'll be here soon,' she heard Dorotéa say, at which Engracia asked sternly: 'You didn't speak to him? Without an introduction?'

'No,' Dorotéa said pertly, arranging her dress. 'I told his innkeeper to suggest that he stop by.'

'My dear child,' Engracia protested, 'that was indeed forward. It was even brazen.'

'Look!' And down the narrow street that joined the two inns came the young Frenchman, threading his way through the rubble that had collected overnight, sunlight on his pale hair, that smile on his lips.

'Is this the inn of Señor Galíndez?' he asked, his slight accent betraying the fact that he was not Spanish. He had barely asked the question when he saw Dorotéa; recognizing her, he bowed low and said with great charm and no sense of extravagance: 'The young princess I saw last night.'

Trinidad noticed all this and also that he stood to attention, waiting to be asked properly to join their party. Don Ramón rose, brought his heels together, and bowed like the grandee he was: 'Young sir, my family and I would be most honored if you would sit with us and tell us what's happening in that strange city of New Orleans.'

The young man bowed with equal gravity and said in a voice so low that Trinidad could barely hear: 'I am René-Claude d'Ambreuze, and I would be most honored to join you and your two daughters.'

'I'm of the Galíndez family,' Dorotéa said boldly as he took his seat beside her. 'These are the Saldañas of Béjar in Tejas. And this is my dear friend Trinidad de Saldaña.'

René-Claude scarcely acknowledged the introduction, for little Trinidad seemed quite youthful compared to the dazzling Dorotéa. 'I passed through Béjar some weeks ago. Very small. But this Saltillo! Ah, this is a little Paris.'

'Have you been to Paris?' Trinidad found herself blurting out.

'I was born in Paris.'

'Oh, what is it like?' For the first time young d'Ambreuze looked directly at Trinidad, saw her brilliant eyes, her strangely formed mouth, and thought what a pleasing sister she'd make.

'I know little of Paris,' he said honestly. 'They took me away when I was a child.' Then, turning as was proper to Don Ramón, he said: 'New Orleans, on the other hand! Ah! Queen of the Mississippi!'

'Is the Mississippi really so big?' Trinidad asked.

He turned once more to face her inquisitive eyes: 'Saltillo could be tossed between its banks and we'd all be lost.'

It was a splendid day in that spring of 1789, with René-Claude paying great attention to Don Ramón, much courtesy to Señora Engracia, and distinct respect to the Galíndez elders; he had been well reared by loving aunts and governesses, and he showed it. At four-thirty in the afternoon he took lunch, Mexican style, with the Saldañas, again sitting with Dorotéa, and at eight in the evening he helped Engracia escort the two girls to the paseo, where he saluted them graciously each time he passed.

On the next day two things happened to disturb Trinidad: through unladylike questioning she learned that whereas the Saldañas were going to leave Saltillo three days hence, René-Claude's business interests would hold him here for two more weeks, which meant that she would be leaving the young Frenchman entirely to Dorotéa. And swinging around a corner of the inn late that afternoon, she came upon him and Dorotéa eagerly kissing and clinging to each other. They did not see her, and she drew back, flushed and trembling, as if she herself had participated in this embrace. While she did not begrudge Dorotéa her good fortune, she was chagrined that she had not been the girl in René-Claude's arms.

When she joined her grandfather for lunch, which was served at five, she found that her mother was staying in bed to rest for the next leg of the journey. Alone with Don Ramón, she felt immeasurably old, as if she were coeval with him, and she spoke in that way: 'I doubt that New Orleans will ever be a Spanish city.'

'It is now, silly girl.'

'But I mean truly. French ways, they seem to be very strong wherever the French go.'

'Now, what do you know about French ways, young lady?'

She did not say so, but she felt that she knew an enormous amount, really, an enormous amount. Then she heard her grandfather speaking.

'I've always thought that God placed Spain where He did to keep things organized.' Don Ramón arranged dishes and rolls to represent Europe. 'Lesser nations all around her. Portugal here, and what a sorry land that is. France up here, a bunch of troublemakers. England over here, accch!' The harsh guttural showed what he thought of England. 'And down here the despicable Moors, enemies of God and man.' In the center of this maelstrom of failed nations and infidels he placed a bright orange: 'Spain: God's bastion of reason, and stability, and all the things that represent goodness in this life.'

'Then why has England grown so strong?' Trinidad asked like a philosopher. 'From what we hear, that is?'

'God is preparing them for a fall. They strayed from the true religion, and it's impossible that Protestants should ever triumph. That's why Los Estados del Norte ...'

The table now became North America: 'Up here the French used to be, but they could never govern themselves, as we've seen in New Orleans. Over here godless americanos, who are doomed.'

'They won their freedom from England,' Trinidad said.

'With French help. Two godless nations fighting it out. And

here . . .' Now the orange became Tejas: 'In the middle of this mess, Tejas, Spanish to the core, God's bastion, just as in Europe.' He patted the orange, reveling in its security, and said, 'God arranges these things according to His grand design. Believe me, Trinidad, Tejas is not where it is by accident. And you're not in Tejas by accident. Your destiny is to rear Spanish sons who will build there cities much finer than New Orleans.'

But three days south of Saltillo, during the long ride to Potosí, even Don Ramón had to wonder whether God did not sometimes forget His assignment in Tejas, for the Saldaña caravan, traveling with three other families heading for the capital, came upon a detachment of soldiers marching north, bringing with them the latest gang of conscripts destined for duty in Béjar. And what a sickening lot they were.

'My God!' Don Ramón cried. 'You're not taking them to Tejas?'

'We are,' the commander of the troops said. 'I chain them only when we stop at night.'

And well he might! For he had in his charge a sweeping of Mexican jails: a group of seven who were spared hanging if they would serve in the north, sixteen younger men whose families had abandoned them shortly after birth, and a score who had proven themselves to be worthless workers. Behind them trailed a scruffy collection of women, young and old, whose lives were somehow entangled with those of the prisoners. They were indeed prisoners, and to call them settlers or soldiers was preposterous.

'You're turning them loose in Tejas?' Don Ramón cried in disbelief.

'No great worry. Two-thirds of them will run away and get back to the capital before I do.'

Don Ramón studied the sorry detachment and whispered a suggestion to the commander: 'Couldn't you march them into a swamp? Or just shoot them?'

The commander chuckled: 'The really bad ones we send to Yucatán. These are what we call the hopefuls.'

Don Ramón had to laugh, but the experience fortified his resolve to find for his granddaughter a respectable Spanish husband.

On the nineteenth day after their departure from Saltillo two of the soldiers bringing up the rear galloped forward. 'Party overtaking us from the rear,' one reported.

Everyone turned around, and saw that the soldiers were right; a column of some kind was approaching at a worrisome speed, and a hasty consultation took place. The commander asked: 'Am I right? No unit is supposed to be on this road?'

'None that we know of, sir.'

'Comanche?'

'I think so.'

Men instinctively fingered their guns.

'Women to the front! Immediately!' The captain hesitated: 'I mean to the rear, as we face them.'

The approaching column, which appeared to be some fifteen or sixteen Indians, must have seen the soldiers halt and take up defensive positions, but on they came, and as the dust rose, Don Ramón, his white hair unprotected by any hat, rode back to take position in front of the women: 'You are not to cry or panic. You are not to run. I will hold them off.' He saluted his two women, but the effect of his words was lost when Trinidad cried joyously: 'It's René-Claude!' And deftly she spurred her horse and dashed out to meet the Frenchman, whose party had left Saltillo almost two weeks later than the Saldañas but had been able, by means of long rides each day, to overtake them.

It was a lively meeting there in the great empty upland of Mexico, with blue mountains in the distance and spring flowers covering the swales. Soldiers from both groups swapped stories, and the two other merchants who had been invited by young d'Ambreuze to join his entourage talked with Don Ramón about conditions in both Coahuila and Tejas.

But the two who reveled most in the fortunate meeting were Trinidad and René-Claude, for without the distracting presence of Dorotéa Galíndez, the young Frenchman was free to discover what a delightful young woman Trinidad was. They rode their horses ahead of the line, or off to one side, chattering easily and endlessly. One morning Trinidad thought: Today I wish he would try to kiss me, and when they were off toward the mountains he did just that. She encouraged him at first, then pushed him away and said: 'I saw you kissing Dorotéa,' and he explained: 'Sometimes that happens, but this is forever.'

'Did you enjoy kissing her?' she asked, and he said: 'Of

course, but it was your funny little smile I saw at night when I was alone.'

'You may kiss me,' she said, leaning across her horse's neck.

When they were in the presence of the elders they had to be more circumspect; then they sat and talked, and one evening Trinidad asked him to explain his name.

'Many French boys have two names, like mine. And the little *d'* is your *de*. Means the same, the place where your family came from, an honorable designation.' He tried to teach her how to pronounce his last name with a French twirl, and when her tongue could not master it he accused her of being dull-witted.

'How about you?' And she mimicked him by saying *Trinidad* the way he did, with heavy accent on the last syllable as if it really were *dod*, rhyming with *nod*. 'It's not that way at all,' she protested. 'It's *dthodth*. Soft . . . a whispering song.'

Now it was he whose tongue became twisted, but at last, with her gentle coaching, he mastered this beautiful name: '*Tree-nee-dthodth*! It really is a song!' And so they continued, two young people in love, finding music in each other's names, respect for each other's traditions.

In fact, the pair became so open in their affection that Don Ramón told Engracia: 'Well or sick, you must go out and act as dueña for your child.' Then, in some confusion but with his jaw set, he ordered Trinidad to get into the wagon and sit with Engracia while he rode ahead to talk with the young Frenchman.

'There is always the matter of honor, young man. Surely you will agree to that?'

D'Ambreuze, bewildered that Trinidad had left him and that Don Ramón had taken her place, mumbled something about men always being beholden to the demands of honor: 'Duels, and things like that.' He spoke as if he certainly did not expect to be challenged to a duel.

'I mean,' Don Ramón said, turning sideways on his horse, 'those ancient rules which have always governed the behavior of gentlemen.'

'Oh, that! Yes. Women first into the carriage. Men to hold the horses lest they bolt. Oh, yes!' He spoke with such enthusiasm that one might have thought he was Europe's champion of the ancient rules, that he would lay down his life in furtherance of them.

'I mean the subtler kind, young man.'

'Well ...' René-Claude's voice trailed off, for now he was really bewildered.

'It has always been a rule among gentlemen, rigorously observed by all who presume to call themselves that ...' Now Don Ramón hesitated. 'Are you a gentleman?' Before René-Claude could respond, he added: 'I mean, your father *is* in trade, isn't he?' He spat out the words distastefully.

The young man drew to attention: 'The d'Ambreuze family own large vineyards near Beaune, and do you know where Beaune is? Burgundy, its own principality. No one owns large vineyards there unless they're gentlemen. Nobility, really.'

'But in New Orleans, your father is in trade?'

'My father's an inventor. He devises machines used in mines. I'm a gentleman, so educated and trained, as were my great-grandfather before me and his great-grandfather before him. But more important, I'm a Burgundian.'

'Well, yes,' Don Ramón said, shifting his weight to bring his face closer to d'Ambreuze. 'What I mean, there's a rule among gentlemen that no one can come into another man's castle and seduce his daughter. Not while the visitor is a guest in the castle.'

D'Ambreuze said nothing, for now he knew the burden of the old man's warning. By joining the Saldaña party without an invitation, he had assumed the role of guest whether he intended so or not, and he was bound by the most ancient code not to take advantage of the daughter of the house, not while he was in this privileged position. In the fluid life of San Luis Potosí or on the wide avenues of the capital he might feel free to seduce her, if his charms and stratagems prevailed, but not while he was a guest in the home, as it were, of Don Ramón.

'It would never have occurred to me to take advantage,' he said.

'It occurred to me,' Don Ramón replied. 'Now shall we stop for our morning rest?'

It was this unnecessary halt which made up the minds of the two guest merchants: 'We do not like to say this, but this dallying ... these picnics ... we're wasting valuable time. Our soldiers too, they want to move ahead.'

'We shall. I've been inconsiderate of you gentlemen, and I'm sorry.' Forthwith he announced to the group resting by the side of the road – a rather good highway now, since it had been in use two centuries longer than the miserable roads in Tejas – that he and his company must, reluctantly, forge ahead. He went to Trinidad, and taking her by the hands, he drew her to him and embraced her in front of the others, then bowed low as if wearing a plumed hat in the old days: 'Mademoiselle, we shall meet again in Potosí, or Mexico, or New Orleans, but wherever it is, it will be heaven.' Saluting Don Ramón and the soldiers who would be staying with the slower party, he went to the head of his column and led his entourage across the beautiful spaces of upland Mexico.

Days later, as the Saldañas approached Potosí, Trinidad rode with her grandfather and confided: 'I shall pray tonight that René-Claude's negotiations have kept him here longer than he intended.'

'I doubt, dearest child, that you could ever marry a Frenchman. They're not dependable. I've never believed that they're serious Catholics.' He poured forth a century of Spanish apprehensions about their northern neighbors, ending with a prophetic warning: 'I even doubt that New Orleans will remain Spanish till the end of the century.'

'What possibly could happen?' Trinidad asked. 'René-Claude himself told me they have no armies in America.'

'With the French something always happens. Do not count on young d'Ambreuze.'

'Don't you like him?'

'Too much,' her grandfather confessed. 'And I see that you like him too much, also. Be careful, Trinidad. He comes with the wind. He goes with the sunrise.'

But his granddaughter's ardent hopes were realized. By one device and another, René-Claude had managed to linger on in the mining town, attending to business which he did not have and wasting so much time that his two companions had proceeded to Mexico City without him.

Each day he had watched El Camino Real for signs of travelers coming down from the north, and on a bright July day two men, traveling without military guard, rode into town with the exciting news that Don Ramón Saldaña from the distant town of Béjar in Tejas would be arriving, if his current slow speed held, on the morrow.

Upon receipt of this news René-Claude saddled his horse, hired three companions, and rode north to escort the travelers properly. Trinidad had supposed that this might happen, for she had paid the two men to seek out the young Frenchman and inform him of her coming. She was therefore at the head of her column when she spied the four horsemen, and without waiting for confirmation she dashed ahead, waved vigorously when she saw René-Claude, and brought her horse close to his so that she could kiss him.

When the two groups met formally, Don Ramón said brusquely: 'I had hoped you were in Mexico City.'

'I should be, but I had to see you and your daughter again.'

'Let us not deter you. You've made your welcome. You will show us to our inn, I feel sure, and then you will hurry on.'

'That I shall do, Don Ramón, but first I must speak seriously with you.'

'That can wait till we've cleaned up,' he said, and he would speak no more until he had seen his women properly ensconced in their quarters at the inn. It was a place of thick walls and many rooms, in one of which the two men met over drinks of cool pomegranate juice.

'Don Ramón, I seek permission to pay serious court to your granddaughter.'

'She's not fifteen.'

'She will be when you've returned to Béjar and I stop by to claim her.'

'What are your prospects?'

'The best, Don Ramón, as you will find when you inquire about me in the capital. I am a younger son, it's true, and my older brothers have the vineyards. But I've done well in New Orleans. And in Saltillo. And Potosí. And I'm sure I'll do even better in the capital. For that you need have no concern.'

'In Saltillo you seemed quite enamored of the innkeeper's daughter.'

'In spring the birds inspect many trees before they build their nests.'

'They do, they do,' Don Ramón said, recalling his own casual courtships. But then he spoke forcefully: 'I'm a Spaniard, and

I'm taking my granddaughter to the capital so that she can meet Spaniards. French and Spanish, it's never been any good.'

'You've had Frenchmen as your kings.'

'And that's been worst of all!'

There in Potosí the battle lines were drawn: it was obvious that the young Frenchman would continue to pay ardent suit to Trinidad, while the old Spaniard would do all he could to keep the young lovers separated, or at least under close surveillance. Don Ramón, accepting the challenge, said: 'I doubt that a granddaughter of mine would ever want to marry a Frenchman.'

'With all respect, Don Ramón, I disagree.'

'I doubt that I could ever give my consent.' But he liked the young man's spirit and did not try to prevent him from taking rooms at the same inn.

Now began a clever game of cat and mouse, with the Frenchman testing every gambit to place himself alone with Trinidad, and her grandfather using his talents to outwit him. Alas, Don Ramón's own grandchild sided with the enemy, exchanging surreptitious messages of love and stolen kisses. But with Engracia's determined help, Saldaña did succeed in protecting his child's honor.

After four days of this he suggested bluntly that d'Ambreuze move on: 'Your business waits,' and to his surprise the brash young fellow said, 'It does indeed. But I also shall wait . . . in the capital.' And he was off, this time without escort, for south of Potosí, El Camino Real became a major road in the silver trade, and soldiers guarded it on a permanent basis.

Two weeks later the Saldañas started their own hundred-and-twenty-league trip south, which they took at a pace more leisurely than before, so that it was early August before they entered upon that splendid final plateau on which stood the marvel of the New World.

If Trinidad had been impressed by Saltillo as a major center, she was dumbfounded by the capital, for it exceeded even the stories that soldiers had recited during the long journey. The cathedral was three times the size of the lovely church in Saltillo, the plaza fifteen or twenty times larger, and if the shops in the northern town had been lavish, the ones in Mexico City were true cornucopias, crowded with elegant wares from all over Europe: brocades and silks and intricately woven cottons and hammered gold for women; guns and silver-handled swords and burnished leatherware from Toledo and fine suitings for the men.

What made the capital even more exciting was that on the second morning René-Claude appeared at the Saldañas' inn, prepared to escort Trinidad and her mother to various parts of the metropolis: the bullring, where masters from Spain performed; the concert halls, where fine singers from all over Europe entertained; and those unique taverns which started serving delectable dinners at eleven o'clock at night. Here Trinidad could listen to the wandering Negro poets recite impudent impromptu verses cataloguing the scandals of the day. Standing before her table one night the best of the black poets cried with obvious joy:

> 'Little girl with the laughing smile,
> Please stay among us for a while.
> Mexico is criminal, it's true,
> That's why we need a pretty little . . .
> That's why we need a witty little . . .
> That's why we need a lovely little girl like you.'

The poetry wasn't very good, but it was delivered with great enthusiasm and considerable boldness. To Don Ramón, the poet declaimed:

> 'While you spend money wildly in the city,
> The clerks back home are checking on your books.
> They scratch their heads and say "The pity:
> These figures prove that you're the chief of crooks." '

At this sally the crowded tavern applauded, and other diners pointed their fingers at Don Ramón and chided him for being a thief. He was required to nod and smile and tip the insulting poet handsomely, for if he failed to do any of these things, the black man would remain there shouting really damaging verses. However, on this occasion the minstrel achieved his greatest success with the lines he launched at René-Claude:

* * *

210

'My fine young lad with eyes of blue,
I see you come from France.
But our police are on to you,
So do not take a chance.

'For if you try to steal our girl
This entire town will rise
And knock your head into a whirl
And boot you to the skies.

'Take my advice, young man of France,
Forget the old man's threats.
Lead forth your lady to the dance
And you will cash your bets.'

With this he threw his arms wide, reached down and kissed
Trinidad, embraced René-Claude, and after gathering coins
from the latter, danced his way through the restaurant, a figure
of whirling grace, black as the night and free to exercise
privileges no one else in that room would have dared. At the exit
he leaped, turned in midair, and threw the entire assembly
kisses with his long, agile fingers.

There was nothing in Tejas like this black poet, nor was there
anything like the grandeur of Mexico City or its university
more than two centuries old, and as Trinidad came to know the
metropolis in which she would remain for half a year, she also
came to understand something of Spain's glory. She knew now
why her grandfather was so proud of his heritage and wanted
her to share it with a Spanish husband who might even take her
back to the homeland. One night, after they had attended one of
the city's dozen theaters for a program of one-act plays and
singing, she confided: 'It seems so old and so learned and the
buildings so important ... It's not at all like our poor Tejas,'
and Don Ramón said: 'Spain itself is even better.'

But his search for a Spanish son-in-law was not going well,
and he was relieved when d'Ambreuze announced that he must
go down to Vera Cruz to supervise the arrival of mining
equipment from France, but was appalled when the young man
suggested that the Saldañas accompany him, for it would be a
distance of some seventy leagues through fever-ridden jungle.
However, Trinidad made such an outcry about wishing to visit

Puebla, one of the most gracious cities in the entire Spanish empire, that he did agree to lead his family that far. There, in what was called the City of the Angels, with the great volcanoes looming over the myriad churches – three hundred and sixty-five in outlying Cholula alone – they said farewell to d'Ambreuze. Don Ramón saluted him, Engracia allowed him to kiss her, and Trinidad clung to him as the horses were brought up for the dangerous journey down to where the ships from Europe arrived almost every week.

Back in the capital, Don Ramón made serious inquiry concerning d'Ambreuze, and learned from officials who had served in both Spain and New Orleans that he did indeed come from an excellent family and that his people in Louisiana had been among the first to accept Spanish rule back in the 1760s.

One diplomat said: 'We had to hang a dozen French leaders, you know. They were stubborn, would accept nothing Spanish, so we strung them up. But the d'Ambreuze clan were different. Good Frenchmen. Good Catholics. And now they're good Spaniards. There's been talk that René-Claude's father, or perhaps René-Claude himself, in due course, might be our Spanish governor in New Orleans. So the young man is not a nobody, of that you can be sure, Don Ramón.'

Over the weeks Saldaña pondered his problem, and one afternoon when Trinidad was out with friends visiting the architectural masterpieces of the capital, he said to her mother: 'By sixteen our precious little lady ought to be married. I'm afraid my dream of Spain was fruitless. I have the sad feeling that our good friend Veramendi was correct when he predicted that the real power would be coming down El Camino Real from the north and not up from the south.'

'Are you saying . . . ?'

'I'm saying that when I study the decline of Spain in the New World, our young French friend begins to look better every day.'

'Oh dear.' Engracia was not prepared for a French son-in-law, nor for the French to have a foothold of any kind in Mexico, especially Tejas. 'In the old days things were so much simpler.'

When d'Ambreuze returned from Vera Cruz, bronzed and temporarily underweight because of fever, so that he seemed almost a wraith, he insisted that everyone accompany him on an expedition to the ruins of some pyramids north of the city. A field trip involving many horses and servants was arranged, and when the Saldañas stood at the base of the major pyramid, its sides encrusted with growing trees and small shrubs, they marveled at the building talents of the ancients. For the first time Don Ramón contemplated the fact that before the Spanish came to Mexico, Indians of great ability must have lived here, capable of building edifices ten times more grand than anything yet seen in Tejas. It was a disturbing thought to a man who had always scorned Indians, but the impact of the pyramids was even greater on Trinidad, for she could not believe that these wonders looming out of the wasteland could have been built by the ancestors of the Indians she had known, and a most strange thought occurred to her, which she shared with her parents: 'They must have been different Indians from the ones we see. That Indian maiden who married the Spanish soldier Garza, she must have been quite different.' And when she returned to the city she began looking into the faces of the Indians, staring at them impolitely, trying to find in them any indication of the master-builders who had constructed those pyramids.

When the Saldañas returned to the capital from this excursion, Don Ramón slumped in a chair and told Engracia: 'I don't think we're going to find a proper husband for Trinidad.'

'Not here,' she agreed. 'It looks as if Spain has already surrendered Mexico. She's surely not sending any young officers here.'

Therefore, Don Ramón did not immediately reject René-Claude's impertinent suggestion that he accompany the Saldaña expedition back to Béjar, but something the young man said alerted the old man to the fact that the young couple were rather more deeply in love than he had anticipated: 'I had planned to sail back to France, report to my uncles, and return to my job in New Orleans.'

'Why did you change your plans?'

'I wrote my uncles that I had found in Mexico the girl I wanted to marry, and that I would seek to go home your way.'

'You may join us,' Don Ramón conceded, without enthusiasm, but the young man realized that to win Trinidad, he must please her grandfather, so he said brightly: 'In Vera Cruz a man at the port told me to ask when I next saw you . . .' And here he took out a worn slip of paper: 'Are you really an Hidalgo de Bragueta?'

Don Ramón straightened up as if he were about to salute the king: 'I am indeed.' Then he chuckled: 'Self-appointed, you might say.'

'And what is it? The banker wouldn't tell me.'

'It means that the king himself would have granted me the right to use the title Don, if I lived in Spain.'

'For what?'

'For siring seven sons in a row. No daughters.' But as soon as he said this he added: 'I did have seven sons, and all died, but not one of them gave me the extreme joy my granddaughter does.'

D'Ambreuze rose, stood at attention, and said: 'Don Ramón, I salute you, and I hope that I shall be allowed to give you seven greatgrandchildren.'

But Ramón de Saldaña was no fool, and he knew well that young men often woo young girls with faithless promises, then leave them in despair, and both he and Engracia began telling Trinidad, when they had her alone, of that endless chain of tragedies in which unsuspecting girls were betrayed: 'There was the Escobár girl in Zacatecas when I was young. This high official of the court in Madrid came out to try a case of thievery from the silver mines . . .' It mattered not who was doing the preaching, the histories were all the same: 'Shortly after my father took command at the presidio in Béjar . . . I was just a boy, and I remember this girl Eufemia, sent up from Potosí to stay with her brother, who was our lieutenant, while she had her baby. It was a baby boy, and after Uncle Damián christened him, with her brother attending . . . Well, the lieutenant asked for leave. My father granted it and three months later the young man returned to Béjar with the simple announcement "I killed him," and we were all happy that his honor and that of his sister had been restored.'

In conjunction with his moralizing stories Don Ramón kept a severe watch upon his granddaughter, and this was effective in San Luis Potosí and during the long march north of there. But now, as the young people approached Saltillo, a magical city even if one were not in love, it was obvious that the lovers had reached a point of commitment; they were determined to marry and they wanted that mutual promise publicly announced, so Don Ramón watched with extra diligence.

As they entered the city and Trinidad saw once more the plaza where she had met René-Claude, a frightening thought overtook her, for she remembered that it had been Doroféa Galíndez whom he had kissed in Saltillo, and she wondered what might happen when the two met again. But when they reached the inn she heard Doroféa's hearty cry: 'My dearest friend, Trinidad! Meet my husband!' So that danger dissolved.

It had been a long day's ride, this final stage to Saltillo, and at midnight Don Ramón was truly fatigued; he slept so soundly that he did not hear Trinidad slip down the tiled hall and out through a window where D'Ambreuze was waiting. They walked back to the plaza where they had met and saw two beggars, their clothes in tatters, sleeping in a doorway. They saw the verger swing shut the gates of the church and wend his way home. They heard the nightwatchman, who would query them if he found them in the streets, and then they discovered an alleyway leading to a sheltered garden, and when they were under the trees René-Claude put cupped hands to his mouth as if he were going to shout. Instead he whispered: 'Don Ramón, heaven is my witness that we are not in your castle!' Then he told Trinidad: 'I am free to make you my wife,' and there they sealed their love.

One day south of Béjar, when Don Ramón had about decided that he must soon discuss with René-Claude the size of Trinidad's dowry, most of the soldiers galloped ahead to inform the town of the Saldañas' return, and while the reduced caravan was in the process of fording the Medina prior to reentering Tejas, the Apache struck. There were more than two dozen warriors, and Trinidad would have been carried off had not Don Ramón defended her valiantly, but the Apache, having seen how young she was, stopped fighting the soldiers and tried again to capture her, for she would be a prize among the campfires.

But now René-Claude, only twenty years old, galloped directly at them, drove them back, and took three arrows through his chest. His horse ran blindly on, taking him closer to the Indians, who sought to take him alive for the protracted tortures they enjoyed, but with his dying strength he struck at them until they had to cut his throat to subdue him.

When the Saldañas brought Trinidad to their house in the church plaza, she passed into a kind of coma, unwilling to believe that her chivalric, loving young man had somehow vanished from the earth, as dead as those shadowy figures who had built the pyramids, and she remained in this condition for several days. Fray Ildefonso from Santa Teresa came to talk with her, but she stared right past him and would say nothing. Finally, on the fifth day, he shook her and said sternly, 'Each morning the rooster crows, and you've lost five of his days. Now get up and get dressed.' And he stayed right there in the low-ceilinged room until she left her bed.

When her mother's nourishing meals had restored her strength she ventured into the plaza, but seeing the church at one end and a bed of flowers beside the governor's residence at the other, she imagined that she was back in Saltillo, and sorrow overcame her and she fled back to her room, where she would have returned to her bed had not Fray Ildefonso given strict orders that this must not be permitted.

So she walked like a forlorn ghost through the beautiful rooms of her home and gradually regained control of herself. René-Claude was dead, and a large part of her heart was dead, too. But Fray Ildefonso's sagacious counsel helped her to see her inescapable situation: 'You're fifteen years old. Four times that many years lie ahead, and you must use them wisely. God intended you to be the guiding spirit of a Christian household, the mother of children who will help build His world. That is your proud destiny, and you must work toward it. Sew, cook for the poor, help at the mission.'

It was repugnant to contemplate the full resumption of life after so grievous a loss, and the idea that she should in the future encounter someone whom she might want to marry was inconceivable, but her commonsense affirmed Ildefonso's basic counsel that she must reintroduce herself into the mainstream of life. Few girls of fifteen in northern Mexico had ever seen so clearly the grand design of life, so she squared her shoulders and prepared to take her place within it.

What appealed to her most, after her profound experience at the pyramids, was to work at Misión Santa Teresa, for there she could help the Indian mothers care for their babies. But the new priest in town, this Father Ybarra, who had come north to see if the missions should be closed down, absolutely forbade her to step foot inside Santa Teresa: 'This place is not for women. If God had intended you to enter these precincts, he would have made women friars.'

When Fray Ildefonso explained that this poor child of God needed such work in order to protect her sanity, Father Ybarra, a member of the secular clergy who had never liked Franciscans to begin with, told the gentle friar to mind his own business, and within a week Fray Ildefonso was on his way back to the college in Zacatecas. In his absence Father Ybarra was even harsher with Trinidad: 'Stay where you belong. Pray. Strive to regain God's grace.'

Such orders Trinidad refused to obey, and with obvious distaste Father Ybarra watched her moving about the village as if she were a married woman, and for no specific reason he conceived a great dislike for this girl with the twisted mouth who always seemed to be smirking sardonically at what he said. In church on Wednesdays and Sundays he tried not to look at her, for he was obsessed with the idea that she was somehow allied with the devil. When one of the Saldaña servants informed him that in Saltillo on the way north 'some funny business happened on several nights when the young one slipped past the sleeping Don Ramón,' he began to watch her closely, hoping that she was pregnant. He practiced the anathema he would hurl at her from his pulpit when her shame was known – *hussy, slut, harlot* and *wanton* featured heavily – and he was disappointed when it became obvious that she was not with child.

As he went about his duties, those assigned him by the viceroy, who had long suspected that expenses of the northern missions were unjustified when compared with the meager results they produced, he also developed an intense hatred for Misión Santa Teresa, whose saintly founder Fray Damián he saw as a charlatan: 'Got himself killed by the Apache ... in their camp ... fooling around with their women, no doubt.' He convinced himself, because of his extreme dislike for Trinidad,

217

that he must somehow unmask the chicanery of her great-uncle Damián, and he spent much of his energy trying to do just that.

He also convinced himself that Trinidad herself, a loose girl with an irreverent attitude, would come to no good, and several times he considered excommunicating her until she showed proper humility, but he was afraid to do so because of the importance of the Saldañas and their obvious friendship with the Veramendis.

He was in the plaza one morning, watching attentively as Trinidad left her house to meddle in some improper affair or other, when he saw her run across the square and throw her arms about Amalia Veramendi, Don Lázaro's daughter, as if they were old friends. The girls talked animatedly for some minutes, then walked off arm in arm. He wondered what secrets they had.

It was easily explained. Since the day of the Apache attack Trinidad had been unable to mention René-Claude's name, but desperately she had wanted to, and perhaps it was this cruel blockage that had driven her into a depression; now, with a sympathetic young woman about her own age available and interested, she was at last free to talk: 'You can't imagine, Amalia, how wonderful he was.' This was an unfortunate beginning, because Amalia looked sideways at her friend and thought: You'd be amazed at what I can imagine.

Trinidad, unaware of the envy she was creating, burbled on: 'Grandfather did everything possible to humiliate him . . . drive him away . . . said no child of his would ever marry a damned Frenchman. René-Claude just smiled, gave Grandfather all the courtesies, and melted him the way the sun melts snow in the Alps.'

Amalia, suspecting that her friend had enjoyed experiences denied her, wanted to explore more deeply, but refrained. With feigned girlish modesty she asked, 'Was it . . . well, is loving a man . . . do you have to surrender as much as it seems?'

'Not with René-Claude. He said we would be equals. And he behaved that way. Of course, he'd take care of the money and make all the big decisions, and maybe we'd live in Saltillo or maybe New Orleans. He'd decide that. But he asked me always what I wanted, which horse I preferred.'

The girls, each so eager to confide, still shied away from

218

honest questions and answers. 'Is loving a man,' Amalia began, 'well, is it . . . does it . . . ?'

This should have encouraged Trinidad to speak her feelings. Instead, she reflected, smiled at Amalia, and said: 'It's all right.'

'This new priest, Father Ybarra. He condemns it. He seems very afraid of love.'

'Father Ybarra is a fool.' It was unfortunate that Trinidad said this, even to her trusted friend, because although Amalia was of the same opinion, when she criticized Ybarra to others she repeated not her own judgment but Trinidad's and when word of this reached the priest's ears, his mind became set: he would settle with the Saldañas, important though they might be.

Things were in this state when a lone stranger came down El Camino Real from the north. No soldier protected him, no Indian guides, no companions. Just a tall spare man in his late twenties, with a head of heavy dark hair, a tooth missing in front, and an apparent willingness to challenge the world. He announced himself as Mordecai Marr, trader out of Mobile with important connections in New Orleans. He led a horse that had gone lame two days out and three overburdened mules laden with goods of considerable value which he proposed trading from Béjar, or perhaps from the new capital at Chihuahua if a decent road could be routed to that distant city.

Before he had located a place to stay, and there was only a pitiful half-inn run by some Canary Islanders, he asked for the residence of Don Ramón Saldaña, and when this was pointed out he walked directly there, tied his horse to a tree and allowed his mules to stand free. Banging on the door in a most un-Spanish way, he demanded of black Natán, who opened it: 'Yo deseo ver Don Ramón de Saldaña. Yo tengo letras para él.' He spoke painstaking Spanish but with a barbarous accent, and used the word *letras* instead of the proper *cartas*.

When Don Ramón appeared, it was obvious that Mr Marr expected to be invited in, for he placed his foot against the door so that it could not be closed against him. 'I have letters to you from the d'Ambreuze family in New Orleans. They heard I was coming.'

Don Ramón was not a man to be forced into extending an

invitation, and especially not to anyone like this bold americano, so he spread himself sideways, as it were, until he occupied the entire doorway, then said graciously: 'I am pleased to accept a communication from the distinguished family I had expected to be allied with mine.' He took the letters and was about to shut the door when Marr grabbed his left sleeve.

'Is it true what they said? The Frenchman was killed by Apache?'

'Yes.'

'I saw them trailing me, two days ago, so I laid low and shot two of them. It's good to carry two guns . . . loaded.'

He made another move to enter the house, but this time Don Ramón pressed the door shut and left him standing in the street.

After the most careful calculation, Don Ramón decided against showing his granddaughter the letters, for he felt they would only exacerbate her already tense emotions, but when he read them a second time and felt the warmth revealed in them, the obvious sincerity of a family that had gone to great lengths to have them translated into good Spanish by some official in New Orleans, he felt obliged to share them with her. So, though fearful that such reawakening of her interest in d'Ambreuze throw her again into depression, he decided to give them to her when she arrived home, but Trinidad did not *arrive* home in the ordinary sense of the word; she roared home like a child of eight at the end of a successful game, shouting: 'Grandfather! Amalia told me that letters from René-Claude have arrived!'

Don Ramón did not know what to say, for he had too many things he wanted to say: 'Your Amalia is a busybody.'

'The man stopped there first, asking about rooms and saying he had letters from René-Claude.'

'From his family.'

'It's all the same,' and she jumped up and down, hands out, begging for the letters.

'Stop that! You're a young woman now, not a child. And besides, the letters are for me, not you.'

'It's all the same,' she repeated, and she meant it. René-Claude and his parents, she and hers, all were united by love, so that a letter from his father was indeed a letter from René-

Claude to her.

When she sensed that her grandfather was prepared to surrender the letters her boisterousness stopped; she moved away from him and began to weep, her lovable little face doubly distorted, and in total desolation of spirit she fell dejectedly onto a heavy wooden settee. 'Oh, Grandfather, I loved him so much. Life is so empty when I think of what it could have been.'

Her grandfather sat down beside her, placing his arms about her trembling shoulders: 'I've lost seven sons and a loving wife. I know how terrible pain can be.' They sat there for some time, each unable to speak further; then, with a tightening of her shoulders which Don Ramón could feel, she asked, as if she were a child again: 'May I see the letters, Grandfather, please?'

'Of course,' he said gently, and before she began to read them he rose and wandered into another room.

She had the same reactions that he had had, for the d'Ambreuze parents had written with such obvious pride in their son and such hopes that he had found a good wife that she felt as if they were standing there in the flower-filled room, on the dark-red tiles, and after a long while she sought her grandfather and returned the letters: 'You and I lost a good second family. I'll write in your office.'

'Write what?'

'I want to send them our love. Tell them what good people you and my mother are.' Her voice shook, but she finished her thought: 'They must want to hear as much as I did.' And she wrote a long detailed letter, telling them first of her experiences with their son in Saltillo, which she described lovingly so that they might hear the bells and see the movement of people in the plaza, and ending with what René-Claude's business companions had reported about his strong reputation. It was her hope that the letter conveyed a sense of Béjar and Saltillo and the Spanish family of which their son had been for a brief few weeks a member.

Later, when she went to see Amalia, a year older and two inches taller, she felt as if she, Trinidad, were the more mature, and she spoke like some adult addressing an eager child. 'I'm so glad you told me about the letters. Because I think perhaps Grandfather was going to hide them from me. Afraid they might upset me.' She laughed nervously.

'Can you still see him? I mean . . . in your mind?'

He's standing behind every corner. I expect to see him in your kitchen when we go in.'

'Will you always feel that way?'

'Forever.'

'But you'll marry, won't you?'

'Grandfather says I'll have to. When he dies I'll own the house, the ranch.' She became very serious and asked Amalia to sit with her under the trees in the Veramendi garden. 'I've been thinking about becoming a nun.'

'That would be wonderful! A bride of Christ!'

'And I have a very serious disposition toward it, really I do.'

'You would be wonderful as a nun, and some day, with your brains, Mother Superior Trinidad.'

Later, when things had gone terribly wrong, Trinidad would remember this conversation and particularly this sentence. Amalia had said 'with your brains,' and her tone had betrayed how envious she had become of her good friend.

Even now, perplexed by this change in Amalia, Trinidad went to her mother to discuss it, and Doña Engracia sat her down beside the silent fountain and clarified the situation: 'Don't you see? She's jealous of you. You've been to Mexico City, and she hasn't. You've known a fine young man, and she hasn't. You read many books, and this makes her fear that you're more clever. And I suppose, Trinidad, that she thinks you're prettier.'

'But that's all suppose,' the bewildered girl protested. 'Why would that make her change?'

'Because that's the way of the world,' her mother replied. 'You be careful what you tell that young lady.'

But Trinidad had to confide in someone, and in subsequent meetings with Amalia she returned to the possibility of becoming a nun, and she would picture the entire progression from novice to head of some great religious establishment in Spain, or maybe Peru. 'But the other night when I was thinking quite seriously about this, it occurred to me that to become a nun, I would have to gain approval from Father Ybarra, or from someone like him . . .'

Both girls shuddered, and Amalia said: 'Father Ybarra drives people away from religion. Who could ask his approval for anything?' When the dour priest heard this comment repeated he attributed it to Trinidad, and his antipathy toward her deepened.

On several occasions the two young women pondered why the church would promote such a vain, self-centered man to a position of power, and Trinidad drew the sensible conclusion: 'I suppose all towns get some man like Father Ybarra, sooner or later. The only good thing about him is, he's finishing his report on the missions and will soon be leaving.' She kicked the dust. 'Good riddance, too.'

Now Amalia opened the important topic: 'I was home when he arrived.'

'Father Ybarra?'

'No. The americano. I didn't actually open the door when he knocked, but I could have, and there he was.'

'What did he look like?'

'I'd never seen an americano, of course.'

'Nor I.'

'But he was just what we'd been told. He was taller than usual. White. No mestizo. Lot of matted hair on his head. Blue-eyed. A tooth missing in front. A deep voice. To tell you the truth, Trinidad, he was really rather frightening.'

'How did you speak to him? I mean, if he didn't know Spanish?'

'Oh, but he did! He spoke it hesitatingly and very slowly, like a little boy just learning big words.' Amalia went on: 'He smelled. Yes, like a horse after a hard ride in the sun, and he must have known it because he asked Don Lázaro where he might find lodging and a bath.'

'Where is he now?'

'You know the Canary Islanders beyond the plaza, that nice family with the large house? Grandfather sent him over there, and I believe they took him in.'

The two young women left the Veramendi garden, casually walked south to the big church past the Saldaña house and the low, handsome governor's palace, and there on the western edge of town they studied from a safe distance the adobe house of one of the capable Canary Island families, but they could detect no sign of the stranger.

223

Two days later, however, Trinidad and her grandfather were surprised to see that Mr Marr had somehow got hold of a small building on the opposite side of the plaza, right in the shadow of the church. 'What does he intend doing there?' citizens asked. 'Is this to be a store?'

No, it was a warehouse for the holding of his trade goods prior to shipment onward to Saltillo or distant Chihuahua, but when the goods were stowed and the people of Béjar learned about their excellent quality, they began to pester the americano for a right to buy, and slowly, almost surreptitiously, he sold a copper kettle here, a swatch of fine cloth there, until he was operating a kind of informal shop.

'I wonder if he has a permit?' Don Ramón asked as he observed operations from across the plaza, and apparently others had raised the same question, for when the quasi-store had been in operation only four days, the captain from the presidio and the town's judge appeared at the warehouse to inquire as to Mr Marr's papers.

Without hesitation he produced them, documents signed in both New Orleans and Mexico City granting Mordecai Marr the right to trade in the provinces of Tejas and Coahuila. 'We'll take these and study them,' the judge said, but with a quick motion Mr Marr recovered his papers and said: 'These do not leave my possession.' The fact that he spoke slowly and in a deep voice intensified the gravity of his declaration, and the visitors acceded.

But he was not rude, for as soon as he was satisfied that the papers would remain with him he became almost subservient, asking the good captain and the respected judge whether they would consider taking to their ladies a trivial sample of his wares as thanks for the courtesies their husbands had extended. And he cut off generous lengths of cloth from his best bolt.

When the men had their gifts under their arms and were out on the plaza, he followed them and asked almost conspiratorially, as if they were his business partners: 'Where do you think I might find a house to buy in your town? It's so very pleasant, I need go no farther.'

They thought there might be one available at the far end of the plaza, and with that, they exchanged the most cordial goodbyes, but the two officials did not return to their places of business; they walked across the plaza and knocked on the door of Don Ramón de Saldaña, an elder in such matters, and asked him to send his slave Natán to fetch Don Lázaro de Veramendi, and when the four were assembled in Don Ramón's most pleasant garden, Trinidad, passing to and fro with drinks and sweetmeats, overheard bits of the discussion.

'His papers said he came from Philadelphia. What do we know about Philadelphia?' The four men had considerable if sometimes garbled knowledge on most topics likely to be discussed, for all could read, and their pooled information was that Philadelphia was reported to be the largest city in the new nation to the north. It had been the principal site of the recent revolution against England. It had an excellent seaport, but not directly on the sea. And it had once been the capital but had lost that distinction to New York, another fine seaport but also not on the sea.

'In fact, what do we know about Los Estados Unidos, which seem to be pressing so hard upon us?' They knew that there were thirteen states, maybe more in recent years; one man said he was almost certain that there was also a new state called Kentucky. Another claimed to have special information: 'I've been told that they're Protestants, with many states forbidding Catholics to enter.' One good thing about Los Estados Unidos, some years back, when they were still English, they had fought France and won, but that was in Canada. It was a trading nation, but already showing signs of belligerence. The four men deemed it quite probable that sooner or later Spain would have to teach the americanos a military lesson.

'And most important of all, what do we know about this Mr Marr?' He was a big man who had just shown in the matter of the papers his willingness to fight. He spoke Spanish, but in a way that indicated he had learned it in a hurry, as if he wished to use it for some specific purpose. He was armed. He had come down El Camino Real by himself, a daring feat, and he seemed to be in good funds, as witnessed by the gifts he had just made. But he was not a pleasant man, on this all four agreed.

'He is our first breath of Los Estados Unidos,' the judge said, 'and not a reassuring one.'

'I think we must conclude he is a spy,' the captain said.

'For what? To what purpose?' Don Ramón asked.

'For the general intelligence that all armies need,' the captain replied. 'Else, why was he spying out all the streets of our town?'

'He was looking for a place to lodge,' Don Lázaro explained, and it was strange that though the two older men were willing to accept the newcomer, the two younger ones were prepared to throw him out of town. The difference was that the older men had fought their battles long ago and were now free to agitate for new ones, assured that they would not have to do the fighting, while the younger men knew that if trouble came in this stranger's wake, they would be the ones to bear the brunt.

'I think,' said the judge, 'that we have a very dangerous man amongst us,' and he was about to propose certain protective steps when Father Ybarra burst into the room, flushed and obviously distressed at not having been summoned to a meeting of such importance.

'Why was I not told?' he demanded, and after Trinidad had brought him a glass of wine, which he took contemptuously, he added: 'At a meeting like this I must be represented. After all, it is I who shall be reporting to the viceroy on affairs up here.'

'We met by accident,' the captain lied. 'The judge and I were inspecting his papers, as our duty required, and we assembled quite by chance.'

'What papers has he?'

'Impeccable. Authorized by Mexico City to trade in our province. Customs duties properly paid.'

'How could they be?' Ybarra snapped. 'He came in overland.'

'Nacogdoches,' the judge replied almost wearily, and in that moment the four original members of this meeting combined against the priest in defending the American. For half a year they had watched Ybarra and had recognized him as one of those petty, officious tyrants, adrift in all lands and in all religions, who assumed mantles of superiority in whatever affairs they touched. He was an impossible man, and if he opposed the American, they had to support the stranger.

'Will he become Catholic?' Ybarra asked. 'The law says he would.'

'If he wants land, I suppose he must,' the judge said evasively. 'But as a mere trader ... I'm not sure how the law stands on that.'

'But surely he must become a Spanish citizen,' Ybarra pressed.

'I'm not sure on that either. Did his papers refer to that, Captain?'

'They said nothing specific.'

'You know what I think?' the priest asked. 'I think he's a spy, sent down by the americanos to see where they can attack us.'

The judge looked at the captain, who said slyly: 'We think you're right. We must all watch him . . . very carefully.'

Father Ybarra, thinking that he had the support of these officials, gloated: 'The minute he applies for land, he falls within my reach. Because we do not grant land rights to non-Catholics, is that not right?'

'Absolutely correct,' the judge said, but then he added: 'We have the law, but it's easily evaded.'

'How?'

'Foreign men marry our women and acquire their land.'

'A man like Marr will never settle down,' the priest said. 'No matter how much he wants land.'

How wrong he was! Within a week Mr Marr was asking in his slow, patient Spanish: 'If the government allowed me to buy my shop, will it also allow me to buy land?' and he confided to five different customers at his informal store how highly he regarded the Béjar district, and as the months passed, Béjar began to accept him as pretty much the man he said he was: 'I did well in Philadelphia. Never much money, but always had a job. Never married, but I liked an Irish girl, except that my parents weren't prepared to welcome a Catholic into the family. That and other things, they drove us apart. I tried Pittsburgh and then Kentucky and then down the river to New Orleans. And then I heard of Texas, as we call it up north.'

'How did you lose your tooth?'

'I never allow a man to call me Mordy more than once. But if you travel long enough, you're bound to meet somebody bigger than you are.' He grinned at his questioner, showing the gaping hole, and said, 'But I won a lot more fights than I lost.'

And always he came back to the question of land: 'A man travels as much as I have . . .'

'How old are you?'

'My papers say twenty-eight. I guess that's about right. One thing's for certain, I'm old enough to want to settle down.'

'Why Béjar?'

The man who asked this probing question one afternoon when the store was empty, except for him and Marr, had traveled a good deal in the army and by ship to Cuba, and he knew precisely the value of his town, as he explained to the americano: 'You know, this isn't Vera Cruz, where the ships come in each week. This isn't Zacatecas, with its silver mines. And it certainly isn't Saltillo ... Why don't you go on to that town if your papers say you can? There's action and beautiful girls and real shops down there.'

'I've never been to Saltillo, which must be a fine town from what you say. But it's a far piece down the road, and I doubt it will ever have much contact with America. But Béjar! I tell you, when trade starts with the north, which it must, this town will grow like a mushroom in morning dew. I want to be here when that happens.'

'How soon can it happen?'

'Next year if cities like New Orleans prosper. Fifty years if things lag.'

'And you want to own land when it does happen?'

'I do.'

This questioner, a Canary Islander with all the tough shrewdness and character of that group, began taking Mr Marr about the countryside, explaining who owned what: 'As far as you can see and then twice that, Gertrudis Rodríguez.' On another journey, which covered two days with camping out at night: 'This great holding, Rivas family, one of the best.' The man later remembered that at this point Marr asked: 'Is that the Rivas with the two pretty daughters?' It was.

But the trip which Marr seemed to appreciate most was one that took them along the wandering Medina: 'Pérez ranch here, Ruiz up here, Navarro at the turn.' And then on the second day he was told: 'Here in the big bend of the river, Rancho El Codo. The Saldañas. It once belonged to the Misión Santa Teresa, but somehow it got transferred to the family of the mission's saintly founder.'

'How many leagues?'

'Vast. Who has counted?'

'The Veramendis. Where's their ranch?'

'Bigger than any of these, but down in Saltillo, owned by a different branch of the family.'

They spent that night at El Codo, where the lack of supervision once provided by the Garza family was painfully obvious; Don Ramón had moved in other families, but all they seemed to do was build stronger walls to protect themselves against possible Comanche attacks, and that very night, toward four in the morning when a moon just past full threw a brilliant light, the Indians did strike, about thirty of them. They did not try to attack the biggest of the adobe houses, in which the travelers were sleeping along with the family, but they did surround a smaller house, where they killed two mestizo men and one of the wives, and galloped away with the other wife and two of her little girls.

The camp was in futile uproar when Mordecai Marr shouted for order: 'I want your best horses. All your guns. Juan here will ride with me. Who else?'

He apportioned the guns sensibly; some to the people who would stay behind in case the Comanche tried to attack again while the posse was gone, but most to the five who would ride with him. One man, terribly frightened by the disaster, tried to dissuade Marr from chasing the Indians, but the big American growled: 'We'll catch and kill them and bring back those young ones.'

And he did just that. After a bold two-day run far to the west, he doubled back and took the Comanche by surprise as they came carelessly over a hill with their captives. After an opening fusillade that killed several Indians, Marr grabbed another gun and shot several more. Then, disregarding his own safety in the confusion that resulted and using his gun like a club, he dashed to the two children, dragged them to safety behind a hillock, and returned to the battle, which the Comanche were abandoning.

The other five white men had taken one Indian, and when Marr learned from the weeping children that their mother had been tortured and slain soon after their capture, he went berserk and leaped upon the Comanche, bore him to the ground, and smashed his head with a large rock. He kept pounding at the man's chest until Juan and the other men pulled him away from the bloody mess.

'Come back!' he screamed into the emptiness, his hands dripping. 'Come back any time, you goddamn savages!' With great solicitation he started consoling the little girls, but when he saw their bruises and learned what they had suffered, he burst into tears and had to move away.

Word of his heroic rescue sped through Béjar prior to his return, carried by a workman from the ranch who said nothing to diminish the bravery of this American who had been willing to fight the whole Comanche nation. Marr's rescue of the two children was marveled at, for only rarely did a captive of the Comanche ever return to civilized life; they were either kept in perpetual slavery or hacked to pieces over a slow fire. Dread of the Comanche permeated Béjar, and for good reason, for there had never been enemies like these fearful creatures of the western plains, and any man brave enough to chase them down, his six against thirty, and rip away their captives too, was indeed a hero.

People crowded his warehouse and helped him unpack when a fresh convoy of mules arrived from New Orleans with treble the goods he had had before. He stood beside his bales and recounted his exploit: 'I was a damned fool, understand that, I'd never do it again, of that you can be sure. I went crazy, I suppose. The woman and her children ... And I could never have done it without Juan and the others. What shots those men were.'

'But you did it!' admiring women said.

'Once, but never again.'

The people of Béjar did not believe this, because on several occasions Mr Marr gave clear proof of his hot temper. One day a stranger from Saltillo protested that the price of cloth was too high, and Marr patiently tried to explain that he had to import his goods by land from New Orleans rather than by ship via Vera Cruz. When the buyer pointed out that the distance from Vera Cruz to Béjar was much longer, Marr politely agreed: 'Longer, yes. But from Vera Cruz you have organized roads. From New Orleans, mostly trails.'

'Even so ...'

At this point, Mr Marr, according to people who were there, lifted the Saltillo man by his ears, dragged him to the door, the

American's face getting redder each moment, and tossed him out into the plaza, bellowing in an echoing voice: 'Then buy your damned cloth in Vera Cruz.'

Unwisely, the stranger reached for his knife, whereupon Marr leaped upon him, knocked the knife away, and pummeled him until the captain of the presidio ran up to halt the fray. After that, people did not argue with nice-mannered Mr Marr about prices.

After Trinidad had listened to three or four similar examples of Marr's mercurial behavior, she concluded that he was nothing but an American bully, and she decided to have nothing to do with him. Next morning when he crossed the plaza to speak with her, she rebuffed him. But that afternoon Amelia came running to the Saldaña house with news that led her to change her mind: 'Have you heard about the wonderful thing Mr Marr's doing?' And when Trinidad went to his warehouse she found on the counter a small wooden box with his hand-lettered sign: POR LAS NIÑAS HUÉERFANAS. In it were three silver pieces, his own contribution to the two children orphaned by the Comanche. Soon he would have a substantial number of coins, which he intended giving to the Canary Island family that had assumed care of the little girls, who were slowly recovering.

It was because of this sign that Trinidad found occasion to speak with the American, for later when she returned to add her contribution she noticed that someone, not the one who made the sign, had changed the word *por* to *para*. Both words meant *for*, but in specialized contexts and to use one where the other was appropriate was almost humorous. When she commented on the editorial change, he laughed: '*Para* and *por*, *ser* and *estar*. No foreigner can ever learn the difference.'

She was impressed that he understood the difficulty and spent some time trying to explain the inexplicable, how *ser* and *estar* both meant exactly *to be*, but, again, in minutely specialized applications. She said: 'It's very complicated. *Yo soy* means that I am, that I exist. *Yo estoy* means that I am somewhere.' And he said: 'I solve it easily. I use *ser* on three days of the week, *estar* on the other three, so I'm always half right.' And she asked: 'What about the seventh day?' And he said: 'Like God, on the seventh day I rest. I use neither.'

Instinctively she was repelled by this big, rough man with the missing tooth, for she was finding him to be just what Don Ramón had predicted the americanos would be: arrogant and uncivilized, Protestant and menacing. But he was also intriguing, so despite her apprehensions she began to stop by his warehouse to chat, and one day she startled her grandfather with an extraordinary bit of information: 'Mr Marr is becoming a Catholic.'

Yes, he had gone to Father Ybarra and said with proper humility: 'I wish to convert,' and the priest, eager to bring such a spectacular man into the church, forgot his earlier animosity and started giving religious instruction. It was a case of the brutal converting the brute, and one Sunday at service the dour priest was able to announce, while pointing with satisfaction to where Marr sat: 'Today the last unbeliever in our town has joined the Holy Church, and we welcome him. Jesus Christ is pleased this day, Don Mordecai.' And from that time on he was no longer referred to as Mister, but as Don.

On Monday morning after his conversion was solemnized, Don Mordecai visited the local government offices and started turning over four maps of the area while asking numerous questions of the custodian: 'Who owns this stretch of land?' 'On this map it refers to Rancho de Las Hermanas. Who are the sisters?' 'Who is this man Rivas?' On another day he spread four maps on the floor and pointed to an anomaly: 'The map of 1752 spells our town Véxar. Menchacha's map of 1764 called it Béxar. This map of 1779 calls it Véjar. And the one three years ago calls it Béjar. What is our name?'

The clerk noticed with both pride and confusion that Don Mordecai was now calling it 'our town,' as if his conversion to Catholicism had also conferred citizenship: 'You can spell it however you please, but it's always something soft and beautiful.'

Marr said he did not think of Béjar as soft and beautiful, but the clerk assured him: 'You will when you've found yourself a plot, built your own house, taken a wife, and settled down with us.'

'All those things I should like to do,' Marr said, and by nightfall every one of the Spanish citizens knew what he had said, as did many of the Indians.

But Marr soon found that it was not a simple matter for a foreigner to acquire land in a frontier province, and his attempts to do so met with frustration. Either none of the good land was for sale, or he found himself ineligible to buy any of the marginal fields. Returning to the maps, he identified hundreds of thousands of acres of unclaimed land, but invariably some constraint prevented him from acquiring any. It was the same with purchasing a house in Béjar itself. There were none for sale, even though half a dozen changed hands while he watched.

It was then, in the summer of 1792, that he seriously analyzed his situation: Spain is finished in this part of the world. Within ten years Louisiana will break away. Then Mexico will break away, too. But an independent Mexico will never be strong enough to hold Tejas. And when Tejas breaks loose, everything will be in confusion.

He pondered how he could profitably fish in these troubled waters, and was guided by the folk wisdom his grandfather had often recited: 'Mordecai, I seen it so clear in England. Them as had land, had money. Them as didn't, didn't.' At the conclusion of this silent session, Mordecai summarized his strategy: I'll settle in Béjar, find me a wife, and grab hold of some land.

Before noon next morning he began paying serious attention to Trinidad de Saldaña, for the maps showed that the vast acreage her grandfather owned at El Codo stood right where El Camino Real turned to approach Béjar. Any further road leading to the west toward Chihuahua would have to cross the established camino on this land, and he could foresee settlements there and the exchange of goods and the development of real farms, not just empty land called loosely a ranch, with no fences, few buildings and very little control.

The old man can't live forever, he told himself as he studied the ranch from a hillock to the east. When he dies, it goes to his granddaughter, and a man could do lots worse than her.

He began intercepting her when she crossed the plaza, or speaking to her when she sat under the trees with her friend Amalia. He took great effort to obtain invitations to dinners where she and her grandfather were to be, and when Engracia de Saldaña died of the fever that raged north of the Río Grande

– 'virulent, pulmonary and strangling,' the doctor called it – he paid a formal visit to the house across the plaza with a large package of sweetmeats imported from New Orleans as his contribution to the funeral feast. He spoke with Trinidad for some minutes, consoling her for her grievous loss: 'I liked to see Doña Engracia crossing the plaza, for then I knew happiness was on the way.'

Trinidad, caught up in her new lamentations, perceived nothing of Don Mordecai's plan to acquire her land through his quiet courtship, but Don Ramón smelled him out in a minute, and now began the protracted, painful duel between the elderly Spaniard and the brash American newcomer.

'I don't want you to speak any further with Marr,' Don Ramón warned his granddaughter. 'The man does not have decent intentions.'

If Trinidad had accepted her grandfather's accurate assessment, much trouble would have been avoided, but she was beginning to stare down the corridor of years and see only loneliness ahead. The man she loved was dead. Her mother was dead. Her grandfather was obviously failing, and when he died, she would have to manage El Codo by herself. So although she was not actively seeking a potential husband, she was aware that Mordecai Marr was a vigorous fellow who could solve many of her problems. Her next defense of Marr revealed her increasingly muddled thinking, for she cited the opinion of a man she detested: 'But Father Ybarra has welcomed him into the community.'

'A worse recommendation a man could not have. Stay clear of them both.'

Trinidad certainly had no desire to engage in any close friendship with the americano, but she did recognize him as a man of character, and he certainly represented a vitality which was lacking in her life and in the life of this town. She did not like Marr, but she was stirred by what he represented, and when she compared his stern and unmistakable masculinity with the rather colorless character of the few unmarried Spanish and mestizo men in the region, she had to prefer Marr.

She had not yet begun to consider him as a possible husband, especially since her emotions were now dominated by her grief over the death of her mother, but she was neither surprised nor displeased when one day he caught her in a passageway where none could see and kissed her rather vigorously.

'I'm sorry,' he said immediately, 'please forgive me.' Before she could respond, he kissed her again, forcefully. When she recalled the scene later, she had to compare the delicate, almost unfolding caresses of René-Claude with the elemental love-making of this americano, and although she much preferred the former and was grateful that her first experience had been so reassuring, she did sometimes suspect that it had been the courtship of children, whereas Marr's more assertive approach was that of a mature man for a rapidly maturing woman. In other words, she did not automatically reject his advances, for she sensed without putting her thoughts into specific words that it was understandable for him to come along when he did and how he did.

There was, however, among the soldiers assigned to the presidio that young lieutenant whom Don Ramón had rebuked for sloppiness some years before. He was named Marcelino, born of a distinguished Spanish father and a Mexican woman who was one eighth mestizo, and that eighth dated far back, so that of the young man's sixteen great-great-grandparents, only one had been Indian, and only five of the remainder had been born in Mexico. He was about as Spanish as one could be in the Mexico of this time, but by no stretch of generosity could he be *called* either Spanish or peninsular. At best he could try to pass as criollo.

In both the presidio and in Father Ybarra's headquarters there was a ridiculous list of names, compiled by clerks with nothing better to do, which purported to designate the particular mix of blood for any citizen in the Spanish dominion. This extraordinary list, which no sensible person took seriously, contained eighty-five different categories, for narrow-minded men deemed it important to indicate precisely what percentage of the four major strains each citizen contained: Spanish, Indian, Negro, Chinese, the latter having slipped into Mexico via the Acapulco-Manila trading galleons that crossed the Pacific each year. Also, it was important to know the father's derivation and the mother's; in the samples given here from the preposterous list, the father, of course, comes first:

235

peninsular (gachupín)	Spanish-Spanish, both parents born in Spain
criollo	Spanish-Spanish, but of lower status because
(Español)	at least one parent born in Mexico
limpio (clean) de origen	both parents probably Spanish, but cannot prove it
mestizo	Spanish-Indian
mulato	Spanish-Negro
coyote	mulatto-Indian
calpamulato	Indian-mulatto
zambo grifo	mulatto-Negro
galfarro	Negro-mulatto
zambaigo	Indian-Chinese
cambujo	Chinese-Indian

In this way the purity of the Spanish race was protected and the infiltrations of lesser strains identified, and many of the designations carried derogatory overtones to demonstrate what the superior groups really thought of such mixing:

lobo (wolf)	Indian and Negro
zambo (lascivious monkey)	Negro and Indian

Marcelino carried the designation *limpio de origen*, meaning that he was almost acceptable, but to Don Ramón he was not acceptable, for the latter, with each passing year, took more seriously the responsibility of finding for his granddaughter a husband of proper category.

Therefore, when the attractive young officer began paying court to Trinidad, Don Ramón moved to protect his grand-daughter, unaware that Marr, the americano, posed a much more serious threat. After the lieutenant had thrust himself three times upon the Saldañas, obviously enamored of the household's young lady, Don Ramón stifled his pride and went to the presidio, which he had been avoiding.

'Lieutenant, you've become a credit to the army.'

'I try to be.'

'Of that incredible rabble you brought here two years ago,

236

half ran away, one committed murder, and three raped the little Indian girls in the mission.'

'A sorry lot. Not a credit to Spain at all.'

'That's what I've been thinking of these days, Lieutenant. Spain. I want my granddaughter to marry a man of Spain.'

'I am a man of Spain. For many generations.'

'Not exactly.'

Marcelino, who had always been aware of his classification and was not disturbed by it, laughed easily, and this irritated Don Ramón: 'I'd prefer if you did not present yourself at our house or sit in church staring at Trinidad.'

'Don Ramón, when a man has a very pretty granddaughter, all men stare at her.'

'You're to stop.'

'As you command, sir,' the arrogant young fellow said with a low bow, 'but if I were you, I'd worry far more about an americano suitor than one like me.'

Saldaña reached out to grasp the insolent officer, but the latter merely pushed his hand away, and the interview ended dismally, with Don Ramón embarrassed and Lieutenant Marcelino disgusted with such frontier snobbery. But that afternoon the old man returned: 'Is what you said true, young man? Is the americano paying serious court to my girl, behind my back?'

At the very moment that Don Ramón was asking this question, feeling that as his granddaughter's guardian, he was obligated to know the answer, Trinidad, now lacking a mother or a proper dueña, was slipping across the plaza and into Marr's warehouse. With the door barred, she and the americano were talking in a far corner when he suddenly grabbed her. She tried to scream, but he silenced her with furious kisses, and when she tried to break away, he forcefully prevented her escape. Soon she was upon the floor with him on top of her, but after moments of enormous confusion she stopped struggling and lay in awful turmoil as he made wild love.

When it ended she was appalled by its force, by Marr's uncontrollable passion, and could not comprehend her own inability to fight back; she had submitted against her will, of that she was certain, yet she could not believe that she had stumbled into such a confusing situation without anticipating

237

its outcome.

In the days that followed she and Marr tried, each in separate ways, to reach some understanding regarding the assault and its consequences. He decided, during long lonely walks beside the river, that he must brave Don Ramón's objections and propose to Trinidad, winning himself a good wife and a splendid spread of land. He could foresee years of happiness and wealth in Béjar, and as a man of twenty-eight the time to begin his enjoyment of them was now. As for Trinidad, he liked her and felt sure he could have a good life with her. He failed completely to realize that his violent behavior might have alienated her, but he did tell himself: When we meet, I'll offer an apology, if it looks like she wants one.

Trinidad faced problems that were more complex, for in addition to the big ranch at El Codo, she would, at her grandfather's death, inherit all plots of land in town belonging to the Saldañas, and she wondered whether any young woman of seventeen could handle such responsibilities. She was aware that stalwart women among the Canary Islanders had operated businesses when their husbands died, and she supposed that she could do as well as they, but none of them had had entire ranches to control, and most of them had had sons to help.

She had great respect for the Canary Islanders, who amusingly called themselves Don This and Don That, as if they were real gentry, and she would have been happy had she found some young Islander of promise, but she had not. She liked the young lieutenant at the presidio, but her grandfather had already told her of their quarrel and his dismissal of the man.

That left Mordecai Marr, who had so much to commend him in the way of valor, daring, imaginativeness and masculine ardor, but just as much to condemn him: vile temper, harsh manners, a lack of sensitivity, and the fact that he was an americano of uncertain lineage and unproved character. However, his willingness to convert to the true religion was in his favor, and his obvious love of land made her think that he would be a good custodian of her properties.

Some days later she returned to the warehouse, and when Marr interpreted this as a signal that she had not been unhappy with his behavior, she told him sternly: 'You behaved like an animal, Señor Marr, and I'll have no more of that.' Honestly surprised by her reaction, he promised: 'I'll never offend you. Believe me, a man who wanders about like me ... he doesn't learn how to act with girls.' And this time when they made love he was a different man, even displaying tenderness when they parted.

These bewildering experiences made her hungry to talk with someone, and since no member of her family was available, she turned once again to Amalia Veramendi, in whose garden they conversed.

'Would you ever consider marrying an americano?' Trinidad asked. 'Don Mordecai is attractive. And he works hard.'

'Have you been visiting with him?'

'Well, he has kissed me.'

'What's he like? How does he compare with your Frenchman?'

'They're very different, Amalia.' She hesitated: 'But I suppose all men are different.'

'Do you think he'll stay here ... permanently, I mean?'

'Oh, yes!' Trinidad said with confidence. 'He wants to buy his own land and settle. He said so.'

'I heard him tell Father he might move his headquarters to Saltillo.'

'He did?' Trinidad was startled by this information, for Marr had never spoken to her of such a possibility.

'Well, he discussed the possibility of buying some of our land in Saltillo. Our relatives must have three thousand leagues down there.'

'Did your father say he'd sell?'

'The Veramendis never sell.' Amalia laughed apologetically when she uttered these pretentious words, for she was not an arrogant girl. 'Would *you* marry an americano?' she asked.

'I wanted to marry a Frenchman.'

'I'm afraid, Trinidad. I really am. I don't mean about husbands. I mean about everything.'

'What's happening?'

'My dear grandfather talks so much about the death of Spain. The loss of all things good and gentle.'

Trinidad looked up at the trees, and then, as if relieved to escape from talking honestly about Mordecai Marr, she spoke not about her confusion but Spain's: 'I know what he means.

When we went south on our wonderful expedition to the capital, we met a file of prisoners marching north, some of them in chains ... and where were they going? Right here to Béjar. To serve as soldiers, if you will. Dreadful men, to be the new leaders of Tejas. It was sickening to see them. It's sickening to learn how they behaved when they got here. I had a clear vision that this was the end of Spain. Don Mordecai says it can't hold on another twenty years.'

'He'd better be careful what he says.'

'Oh, he didn't mean that americanos would come down. He meant that the people of Mexico would throw the Spaniards out.'

'He'd better be just as careful about that.'

And then Trinidad returned to the real problem: 'You didn't answer my question. Would you marry an americano?'

'No! I wouldn't be allowed, for one thing. And for another, I wouldn't want to.'

The problem the young women were discussing became academic when Don Mordecai, accompanied by Father Ybarra, came formally to the Saldaña house on the plaza and asked Don Ramón for permission to marry his granddaughter Trinidad. To the old man's amazement, Marr presented him with translations into Spanish of three documents from Philadelphia signed by clergymen and a judge, testifying to the good character of Mordecai Marr and to the fine reputation of his family.

Don Ramón left the two men in the large entrance salon and sought his granddaughter, smiling at her bleakly and confessing: 'It's not what I wanted, and I'm sure it's not what you wanted, but ...'

'There could be only one René-Claude,' Trinidad whispered.

'We should have accepted that Lieutenant Marcelino,' the old man said, 'but I drove him off.' He shook his head and stared at his granddaughter, prepared to terminate this loveless match if she spoke, but she did not.

'Do you accept him?' he asked, and she nodded.

There was no formal announcement of the proposed wedding, but rumors quickly spread through Béjar and even out to the ranch, so that when Don Mordecai rode there with two soldiers to inspect his future holdings he was greeted with congratulations and a jug of strong wine, which he shared with the Mexican and Indian families who would soon be working for him. The ranch men talked about needed improvements and Marr assured them that work would soon start. It was a happy meeting, with much discussion of Indians: 'Don Mordecai, we think that when you rode out and killed the Comanche and took back the children, you scared them away. We've seen none.'

'We'll make this ranch safe, and keep it safe,' he promised.

In all parts of Béjar he delivered the same message: 'We shall build permanently. We shall make this town important.' To the amazement of the townsfolk, he initiated trade with Zacatecas, and what was more important, went to the area capital at Chihuahua over a trail that could scarcely be called a road: 'Béjar will be the major point for trade to the west. Within our lifetime this will be the center of a new empire, the empire of trade.'

But when the town was satisfied that it had obtained in Don Mordecai a new resident with powerful vision and great managerial capacity, it was shattered by the announcement that he was not, after all, going to marry Trinidad de Saldaña, but Amalia Veramendi!

Yes, the more powerful family had approached him with the tempting proposal that if he married their daughter, the couple would be dowered with some forty thousand acres of the choicest land around Saltillo. Banns for the marriage were posted on the church door; congratulations flowed; and because his proposed marriage to Trinidad had remained only an informal arrangement, the community forgave Don Mordecai his impetuous behavior.

Trinidad learned of the astonishing news from the casual conversation of a maid: 'I promised the Veramendi cooks that I would help them bake goods for the wedding.'

'And who's getting married over there?' Trinidad asked, and the maid replied: 'Amalia, to Don Mordecai.'

Trinidad did not weep; she did not even become angry. She walked quietly into her garden and leaned against a tree, endeavoring to understand the various facets of Don Mordecai's behavior; his arrogant arrival, his brutal love-making; his honest attempt to make amends; his obvious hunger for land; the temptation of the Veramendi lands. And she concluded that she'd had the misfortune to encounter a new type of man, with no morals and no honor. Bewildered and deeply hurt, she went to her grandfather and asked him quietly to ascertain the facts, and it was he who became violently angry, and when he returned he was grim-faced: 'The scoundrel has proposed to Amalia and been accepted. I told them frankly of his earlier interest in you, and assured them that if . . .' He could not finish, for he was trembling with an icy rage.

He remained in this torment for two days, then realized what the honor of his family required. Striding across the plaza in the shadow of the church, he banged his way into Marr's warehouse, slapped him stingingly across the face, and challenged him to a duel.

He then reported to the presidio and asked young Lieutenant Marcelino to serve as his second, and the officer said stiffly: 'Duels are illegal, as you know. But I cannot refuse, Don Ramón, for you have been dealt a great blow, and I shall be proud to act as your second.'

Marcelino found the captain of the presidio, José Moncado, and together they went to Marr's: 'Sir, you have been challenged by a gentleman of distinction. He is an old man with a trembling hand. To duel with him would be an outrage. Please, please, go to him and apologize.'

'Nothing of the sort,' Marr said in a slow careful Spanish. 'He's done little but insult me since I came here, and I want to finish with him.'

'It would be murder for an excellent shot like you to accept this old man's challenge.'

'His insults started on the first day . . . when he barred his door . . . refused me entrance.'

'You insist?'

'I do. Amalia's brother will be my second.'

The two men then went across the plaza to dissuade Don Ramón from his folly, and they pointed out the dreadful danger he faced: 'Several times the americano has proved what an expert shot he is. You must withdraw your challenge.'

Don Ramón looked at his visitors as if he were an innocent child being reproved for something he did not understand and

242

which he had not done: 'He has dishonored my granddaughter. What else can I do?'

'But at the Comanche fight, he never missed.'

'What has that to do with me? I fire. He fires. It's a matter of honor.'

When they found that they could not deter him, they enlisted the support of Don Lázaro, a curious choice, since he was grandfather to the Veramendi girl whose acceptance of Marr had caused this trouble; he tried, however, to be persuasive: 'My dear old friend, he will kill you for certain.'

'Not if I kill him first.'

'You can scarcely lift a heavy pistol, let alone fire it.'

'I'll hold it in two hands. It's a matter of honor.'

Don Lázaro considered this for a moment and agreed. 'You have no choice, that is true. May God protect you.' Then he said: 'I had nothing to do with Amalia's agreement to marry him. My son did that. I was ready for an americano, but not this one,' and with that he bowed to Don Ramón and returned home.

So on a June morning in 1792, two parties left town and walked to a slight rise overlooking the river south of town, where three of the missions lay like a string of pearls. A level space was marked off, a line drawn, and starting places for the duelists indicated. Captain Moncado said stiffly: 'I shall count to fifteen. At each count, you will take a pace away. As soon as I cry "Fifteen" you may turn and fire.' Then he changed the tone of his voice and asked passionately: 'Gentlemen, will you reconsider? There is no justification for this duel.' When neither contestant spoke, he said with near-disgust: 'So be it. I shall start counting.'

With each numeral sounding in the crisp morning air, the two men, so pathetically ill-matched – a Spanish gentleman at the end of his days protecting his conception of honor, an American invader with his own rough ideas of justice – moved apart.

'Fourteen!' Moncado shouted. 'Show mercy!'

But Marr, who had anticipated this wild shot and who had postponed firing until it took place, drew steady aim, kept his pistol motionless, and fired a bullet straight into the old man's heart.

When the burial of Don Ramón had been solemnized, by a friar from Santa Teresa and not by Father Ybarra, the heavy consequences of the duel began to emerge, for it was now that the priest saw fit to announce the results of his investigations into ancient malfeasances at Misión Teresa. Had Marr proceeded with his proposed marriage to Trinidad, Ybarra would have buried his accusations out of deference to his prize convert, but with Marr marrying the Veramendi girl, the priest felt free to indulge his vengeance upon a young woman he disdained:

Even the most cursory inquiries at San Antonio de Béjar would satisfy a judge that the so-called saint Fray Damián de Saldaña, founder of Misión Santa Teresa, committed acts of the gravest impropriety in tricking the then viceroy into approving a devious plan whereby Damián's brother, Captain Alvaro de Saldaña of the presidio, obtained possession of lands pertaining to the mission. Some, commenting on the trickery whereby this exchange took place, call it ordinary family protection; others call it more accurately plain theft.

I recommend that even though Misión Santa Teresa may soon be secularized and its possessions redistributed as the court in Madrid decides, it is imperative that lands stolen from it be returned immediately, so that a just disposition of them can be made. I recommend that the ranch known as El Codo in the bend of the Medina west of Béjar be taken from the Saldaña family and restored to its rightful owner, Misión Santa Teresa.

When the order approving this reached Béjar, Captain Moncado sorrowfully and Father Ybarra joyfully served notice on Trinidad that she must surrender the twenty-five thousand choice acres, along with any buildings situated on them and all cattle grazing there. She would be left the house in town and the few plots of land scattered about Béjar, but nothing more.

With her customary nobility, she acquiesced, without showing any rancor toward Father Ybarra, who had persecuted her in so many ways; on the Sunday following her dispossession she even went to church for solace, enduring one of his last sermons prior to his return to the capital. He used as his text the parable of the faithful servant, pointing out how Fray Damián had proved faithless to his trust, whereas he, Ybarra, had come north as a faithful servant to rectify that wrong.

When he was gone, Trinidad discovered that although the court trials and paper work relating to the formal transfer of El Codo would take years, the friars at Misión Teresa retained possession only four days before turning it over to the Veramendis, who gave it to their daughter Amalia as a wedding present. This, when added to Rancho San Marcos, which adjoined it and which was also given to the newlyweds, meant that Don Mordecai, in town barely two years, now controlled forty-three thousand acres; ten miles along the river, seven miles wide.

The happy couple saw Trinidad occasionally, and when they did a miracle of human behavior occurred: they forgave her. As often happens when a crime of grave dimension has been perpetrated, the guilty made a great show of forgiving the innocent, so that when the Mordecai Marrs met Trinidad in the narrow streets or in the plaza, they smiled generously. One afternoon Amalia actually came to visit, a young, gracious, condescending matron, and she explained that since Mordecai had obtained land near Béjar, he now saw no necessity to move on to Saltillo, which had been his original intention when he learned that the Veramendis had huge estates there: 'We shall be very happy here in Béjar, I'm sure. Mordecai's trade with Chihuahua increases monthly.'

These social scandals of Béjar were forgotten when the Comanche went on another rampage. After slaying scores of isolated countrymen to the west they tried to overrun El Codo, but its fortifications held. So they raged on to Béjar itself, mounting such a furious assault that all men and women, and even children, had to be mustered by Captain Moncado to hold them off.

They struck the town with fury, breaking down barricades, killing many but failing to reach the houses about the central plaza. Repulsed by the bravery of Moncado and his stout right arm, Mordecai Marr, who fired four different guns as fast as women could reload them, the Comanche turned abruptly, struck at unprotected Misión Santa Teresa, and overwhelmed

245

it. Two young friars there were pierced with a score of arrows. The older domesticated Indians were slain by fierce stabs and slashes; the younger were kept alive for prolonged torture, the children to serve as slaves. Infuriated by the resistance, the Comanche set all buildings ablaze, battered down the wooden doors of the stone church, and took savage, howling delight in throwing upon the fire Simón Garza's great carvings of the Fourteen Stations.

In flames the patient work of Fray Damián disappeared. The Indian houses so carefully built by Fray Domingo in 1723 vanished; the barns where the cows had given birth and the cribs in which the feed had been stored, the school where children had learned to sing, and the cell in which Damián had prayed for guidance – none survived the rage of the Comanche.

Loss of the northernmost mission caused Father Ybarra to speed his report on the remaining five, and in his careful recommendations to Zacatecas, Mexico City and Madrid, he summarized the criticisms of Spain's mission effort:

> In advising you to halt the operations of the Franciscans in Béjar and throughout the rest of Tejas, with the two exceptions already noted, I act in pain and sorrow, but the facts can support no other conclusion.
>
> The first important mission of which I have knowledge was San Francisco de los Tejas in the Nacogdoches region, established in 1690. Others so numerous that I cannot name them followed, including the six at Béjar starting in 1718. At the end of a hundred years of concentrated and costly attempts to Christianize the Indians, I find after a most careful count that Tejas contains exactly four hundred and seventeen Christian Indians, and not one of them is an Apache or a Comanche. Captain Moncado at the presidio in Béjar estimates that it requires three and one half soldiers to protect each Indian convert, yet the converts perform no tasks beneficial to the general society.
>
> I am most suspicious of the conversions that do occur. Most of the converts are old women who have lived lives of great licentiousness and deem it prudent to have their sins remitted before they die. The young, the hardy and those

who could do strong work for Jesus are little touched by the missions; as a matter of fact, if we secularized them all immediately, the young Indians might well be inclined to join our established churches at one-tenth the cost and ten times the results.

I do not speak disparagingly of the friars who attempted to do God's work in these remote and depressing areas. Those serving now are exemplary Christians, and some have striven mightily, but they have accomplished little. I am told that in the earliest days, when the missions first opened, results were better, but the numbers of Indians converted to the True Religion were always minimal, and to continue this fruitless effort would be financially and religiously unjustified.

Close the missions. Send the friars back to Zacatecas, where they can do some good. Use the emptied buildings as fortresses in time of siege. Sell the mission ranches with their cattle to local men who can make better use of them. And do it now.

What Father Ybarra overlooked in his harsh and overall accurate summary of the mission experience in Tejas – so much bleaker than that in California and New Mexico – was the civilizing effect of men like Fray Damián and especially Fray Domingo in the 1720s and 1730s, when they lit brave candles in the wilderness, demonstrated Spain's sincere interest in the souls of its Indians, and helped establish little centers of safety and learning capable of maturing into fine towns and cities.

Also, the Franciscans did succeed in civilizing the smaller Indian tribes that clustered about the missions, but their failure to domesticate first the fierce Apache and then the terrible Comanche, now the dominant tribe, created the impression that they had failed in all. This was unfortunate, an historic misinterpretation which implanted in Tejas lore the fiction that 'nothing can be done with the Indian.' Father Ybarra's 1792 report summarized what many Spaniards had concluded, and this legend grew and festered until Tejas, once an area teeming with Indians of many tribes, some most civilized, became Texas, a state with almost no Indians, for it preferred to operate under the slogan attributed to a Northern general serving in Texas: 'The only good Indian is a dead Indian.' In due course,

247

the Indians of Texas would be either expelled or dead.

But the greatest injustice in Father Ybarra's judgment on the missions was that he did not take into account the nature of God or the workings of His will. God had not come to Tejas in white robes attended by choirs of angels; He came as a toilworn Franciscan friar, a confused captain trying to do his best in some remote presidio; He came as a mestizo woman lugging two bawling babies who would grow into stalwart men; He came sweating Himself over the vast amount of work to be done before the place could be called civilized; and God knew, if Father Ybarra did not, that fat Fray Domingo who danced at sunset in what his detractors called 'a near state of tipsiness and shouting at the top of his voice' was closer to heaven than Ybarra would ever be.

After the destruction of Santa Teresa, Trinidad spent two agonizing weeks surveying her deplorable situation, but could reach no sensible conclusions. She felt such confusion that during the third week she kept entirely to herself in the beautiful house with the low-ceilinged rooms, tended only by Natán. She applied these hours to an unemotional evaluation of all that had happened to her since she first began to confide in her dear friend Amalia Veramendi. Through the shadows of her darkened room passed ghosts of the two dead men she had loved so dearly, René-Claude and Don Ramón, and images of the two living ones she despised, Don Mordecai and Father Ybarra, and she had to conclude that not only had those two men abused her, but that Amalia had betrayed her. Despite constant review, she could not find herself at fault. She had responded as any spirited young woman would to the courtship of René-Claude, and even though the Galíndez and Saldaña families had rebuked her for unladylike enthusiasm in the Saltillo paseo, she could not think of a single action she would reverse. She had loved him; she still loved him; and she would continue to do so until she died.

Her relations with Don Mordecai were more difficult to evaluate, for she had actively speculated about her need for a husband, and although she had not sought Marr out or overtly encouraged him, she had wanted to know what kind of man he was, and even what kind of husband he might prove to be. What else could I have done? she asked herself in the darkness of her room. That Marr turned out to be unprincipled was her bad luck, not her fault.

Gradually, as sensitive young women had done throughout history, she tried to construct a realistic portrait of herself: I've done no wrong. I regret nothing. And I will not allow them to submerge me in some swamp.

But her normal courage did not solve her personal problems. As she moved about her little town she could feel disapproval directed toward her, but she bit her lip and grappled with specifics: The loss of El Codo? Of course our saintly Fray Damián was less than honest when he maneuvered its transfer to his brother. Away it goes.

Once she had conceded this, she no longer grieved about this loss, but she did realize that she must leave Béjar, though to go where, she did not know. That decision she would postpone until she resolved a matter that was perplexing many thoughtful Mexicans these days. Summoning Natán, she told him: 'It would be painful for me to hold another human being in bondage,' and with exquisite attention to legal detail she gave him his freedom. She also took care of an old Indian nurse, then left funds to the church for perpetual novenas for the soul of Don Ramón. As she delivered the silver she looked up at a crucifix, and without kneeling she stared into the eyes of Christ and whispered: 'You died to save me, and Don Ramón died to protect my honor. I will strive to be worthy of your love.'

Consoled but still uncertain as to what she must do, she returned to her garden and sat alone, allowing tears to flow: 'I'm lost. Oh God, I am so alone.' Then slowly, from some deep reservoir, an idea began to germinate, and with her eyes still wet, she moved inside to find pen and paper, and drafted a letter:

Esteemed Domingo Garza,

I write from the dark valley of the human soul. A beautiful Frenchman who was to marry me was slain by Comanche. My mother has died. A strong americano I was to marry has married another, then killed my grandfather in a duel. The ranch at which you worked has been taken from us. Misión Santa Teresa, where your great-grandfather carved those wonderful Stations, has been burned and his work lost.

In these tragic days I remember when my grandfather made me learn my letters and I taught you, and I remember how your grandfather taught you to ride, and you taught me. I remember how you were always kind and thoughtful, and how you obeyed the harsh rules my grandfather sometimes laid down. I remember you as a young man of goodness, and now I pray with tears welling from my eyes that in your goodness, and if you are free to do so, you will come and rescue me from the terror in which I live.

San Antonio de Béjar
Provincia de Tejas
1792
TRINIDAD DE SALDAÑA

She posted the letter to the growing town of Laredo, from where it would go downriver to the settlements established by the great Escandón in the 1740s, and in time to the lands once held by the Saldañas. There it would be delivered to Domingo Garza, son of the couple that now owned these lands on the north bank of the river.

It would require, Trinidad judged, about three months for the letter to reach Domingo and three months more before she could receive a reply. In the meantime she moved about the paths of Béjar as if she intended remaining there the rest of her life, heiress no more, sought after no more. She attended church; she asked about new laws at the presidio; she watched as Amalia and her husband reinforced their foothold in the community. She never spoke against them to the acquaintances she met, and she counseled with no one.

At the end of two months and two weeks she was startled by an importunate banging on her door, and when she opened it she found standing before her, his clothes covered with dust from his long ride, Domingo Garza. When he faced her and saw once more that twisted smile and those luminous eyes, he was transfixed, unable to move, for he was a mestizo and she was a daughter of Spain, but as he hesitated she looked directly into his eyes and whispered: 'You have saved me,' and thus set free, he swept her into his arms and buried his head against her neck to hide the tears he could not control.

He stayed in Béjar one week, visiting the burned mission and riding out to see the ranch which he had once supposed he would some day manage for the Saldañas, as his ancestors had done for so long. Later, when Don Mordecai heard that he was in town, he sought him out to make a generous offer: 'You know the ranch. I need a manager I can trust. I'll give you a good job and a good wage.' Then he added with a sly wink: 'And if in due course you should care to marry the Saldaña girl . . .'

Domingo said promptly: 'Now that's a good idea. I need a job.'

So the two men, protected by troops from the presidio, rode out to the ranch, and when they arrived they dismissed the soldiers, telling them to wait within the walled area. Without dismounting, they moved about the ranch, with Marr explaining what Domingo's duties would be, and when they were far from the others, with Marr pointing to a fence that Domingo would have to mend, Domingo drew back, leaned forward from his left stirrup, and landed a mighty blow on Marr's chin that toppled him clean out of his saddle.

With never a sound, Domingo leaped onto the prostrate Marr and began hammering him as hard as he could with both fists.

Bigger and stronger, Marr was not defenseless, but overwhelmed by Garza's sudden move, he could not easily apply his superior force. When Marr struggled to his feet, lashing out with his powerful arms, Garza danced and dodged, landing such severe blows that before long the American was winded and sorely hurt.

But still he defended himself, and when Garza saw that his opponent was tiring, he smashed in with a series of wild punches, kicks, jabs and belts, until Marr fell to the ground. As he lay there, clearly defeated, Garza did not grant him the honors of war. Not at all. With his first outcry in the battle he leaped upon the fallen man and smashed him so furiously about the face that blood spurted; the remaining big front tooth popped out, and Don Mordecai fainted.

Wiping his hands on the grass, Domingo tied Marr's horse to his own, then rode slowly back to where the soldiers waited. 'You'd better go out and find him,' he said. Surrendering Marr's horse to them, he started the long ride back to Béjar, asking for no protection.

He arrived at sunset, well speckled with blood, and before the moon was up he and Trinidad de Saldaña, protected by four riders he had hired, were on their way to Laredo, but they had barely left town when she cried: 'Oh! I must go back!' He feared she was reconsidering her decision, but when they reached the beautiful old house on the plaza, all she wanted was that sketch she had made of the church at Saltillo, which Don Ramón had framed. It was one of the memories of her past life which she would never surrender. She moved on, a mature woman of seventeen, granddaughter of a man of honor who had proved with his life that he was entitled to that claim. He had made himself an Hidalgo de Bragueta, siring seven sons in a row without, as he said, 'the contaminating intrusion of a single daughter.' Yet before he marched into the morning darkness to fight his final duel he had embraced his granddaughter, telling her: 'You are the best son I ever had.'

Across the bleak and dusty wasteland she walks, hoping to spare her splendid horse and oldest friend, Relampaguito. She fords the Medina, that stream which had defined her family's ranch, then the Atascosa of the meager water, then the Nueces, on whose bloody banks her grandsons will die, striving to protect it. Still on foot, she crosses the Nueces Strip, which entire armies will contest in future years, and finally she reaches those fertile fields along the Río Grande, where citrus and murder and big families and corruption and untold wealth will flourish.

From her womb will spring nine Garzas, like her, prolific, until it would seem that she had populated the entire river valley. Some Garzas will go to the Congress of the United States, others to distinguished service in the Mexican army to face their cousins fighting against them in the American. A few will become agricultural millionaires; many will die unremembered paupers; but in each generation some Garza men will exhibit the courage shown by Domingo when he rode alone through Comanche country to claim his bride and punish her betrayer; and with reassuring frequency some Garza will display that quizzical half-smile which had distinguished the founder of her family, Trinidad de Saldaña. And like her, she will be memorable and much loved by men.

... Task Force

A week before the June meeting in El Paso the three members of our staff asked to see me privately: 'Dr Barlow, you're playing this too low key. We think you should take command of the formal sessions, knock some heads together, keep Rusk from running everything, with Quimper's help.'

I sat for some moments, contemplating their unhappiness, then asked: 'Have you ever heard of the principle which guides many of our best organizations? *Primus inter pares?*' Apparently no one had, so I interpreted: '*First among equals*, the best possible definition of a chairman.'

'What's it mean?' the young man from Texas Tech asked, and I said: 'The chairman must never think he's the hottest thing on the block. Banging the gavel and all that,' and the young woman from SMU warned: 'You'd better do some gavel banging or those tigers are going to eat you up.'

I assured her that when the time came to write our report, Professor Garza and I would form a dependable team in defense of liberal proposals, while Rusk and Quimper, as announced conservatives, should be expected to oppose: 'That'll leave Miss Cobb with the swing vote, and remember, her ancestors were liberal senators. If our ideas are any good, she'll side with us.'

'You work on that principle,' the young woman said, 'you're going to lose every contest. Those three old-timers will hang together in defense of old principles. They're tough.'

'The governor appointed them for that very reason. And if they weren't tough, I wouldn't want them.'

The young people also warned that Professor Garza's talents were not being properly utilized, and the young man from El Paso said: 'If I was in his place and Lorenzo Quimper made one more joke about Texas A&M, I'd quit. Just quit.' But I said: 'That goes with the territory. You stay around Garza long enough, you'll find he needs no protection.'

And when we met to plan for the meeting, Il Magnifico started right out with his latest joke: 'You hear the one about the Aggie who . . .' and Garza, after winking at me, moved directly up to him, made a tight fist of his right hand, and shoved it two inches from Quimper's nose.

'You know what that is, Lorenzo?' and when Quimper said he did not, Garza explained: 'It's an Aggie-joke stopper,' and Rusk asked: 'How's it work?' and Garza said: 'It moves forcefully against the nose, and Aggie jokes stop.'

For just a moment, Quimper turned pale, but then he saw me laughing and swiftly recovered. Like a big, friendly teddy bear he embraced Garza, assuring him: 'Some of my best friends are Aggies.' The young woman from SMU watched this, and whispered: 'See! I told you measures were needed,' and I whispered back: 'Garza took them.'

The staff informed us that they were finding the chore of locating a speaker for the June meeting so difficult that they suggested we postpone it till July. The problem was: Why has an apparently insurmountable animosity traditionally existed between long-time Spanish-speaking residents and English-speaking newcomers?

This was a topic fraught with danger, both historical and current, and although the staff had already located several scholars well qualified to lead our discussion, they all happened to be native speakers of Spanish, and to this both Rusk and Quimper objected. 'I do not care to listen to any more apologists for Spain and the Catholic church,' Rusk said firmly, and before I could defend our past meetings, Quimper jumped in: 'Texas is a Protestant state. At least, the people who run it are Protestants, and we don't need any further indoctrination to the contrary.'

This was too unfair to let pass, and since it reflected on my leadership, I had to intervene: 'Gentlemen, could we have had more ecumenical speakers than Dr Navarro and Friar Clarence? Did they not anticipate the very points you're making? I hear no misrepresentation or proselytizing. And I'm sure that if –'

Rusk cut me down: 'Barlow, just a minute. Didn't I give those men the respect due them? Didn't I take steps to have the friar's talk published? I think that Quimper, Miss Cobb and I have behaved damned well, and now we say: "No more apologists. Let's hear some straight facts." '

When I looked to Miss Cobb for support, she disappointed me: 'The men are right, Travis. We must have a quite different kind of speaker for our meeting in El Paso.'

I didn't know what to do. Every scholar I knew who was qualified to guide us through the tricky mazes of our topic was either from Mexico or someone who was an apologist for Spanish history, and it looked as if we'd reached an impasse. But then Dr Garza saved the day.

'There's this excellent older man at Michigan State. A Dr Carver, if I have his name right.'

'What does he specialize in?' Rusk asked, for he obviously was not going to allow me to make this important choice.

'That's the interesting part. I've heard him speak. Excellent. And his field is French-English turmoil in Canada, with special emphasis on Quebec Province.'

'Is he a Catholic camp-follower?' Quimper broke in.

'His religion I don't know. But I heard him give a paper at a conference at Arizona State and again at San Diego State. I did not know him personally, which is why I can't remember his exact name. But everyone had the feeling that he was one of the best.'

When our staff had an opportunity to check him out they found that his name was Carter, that his field was minority relations in Canada, and that he had also begun in recent years to specialize in problems along the Mexico-United States border from San Diego to Brownsville.

'What's his religion?' Rusk asked, and when a staff member said: 'Jehovah's Witness,' he replied: 'Jesus Christ!'

For the El Paso meeting Quimper drove from his ranch into Austin, where Rusk's jet picked us up for the short flight to Love Field in Dallas. There Rusk himself climbed aboard, and as soon as we were airborne I reassured my fellow members: 'I've checked Carter out, read some of his papers, and he's just what we've been searching for.' Before either man could respond, I added: 'We must have a couple of clowns on our staff. Carter's a Baptist.'

By the time we landed at El Paso – after a flight longer than from New York to Cincinnati – Rusk and Quimper were in a relaxed mood, and in the long and pleasant evening prior to our meeting they invited us all, including the staff, across the Rio Grande to a festival meal in Ciudad Juárez. But before the waiter could take our order Rusk stared at the three staff members and growled: 'Which one of you comedians told me that tomorrow's speaker was a Jehovah's Witness?' When the girl from SMU said: 'I did,' and Rusk asked: 'Why?' she said: 'Because you were making such a fuss about it.'

Rusk pointed his finger at her: 'He'd better be good, or you're fired,' and she replied: 'If this is the condemned woman's last meal, it'll be the best,' and she ordered extravagantly, at Rusk's expense.

Her position was secure, as we quickly realized when we met our speaker next morning on what must be one of the more distinctive of the American campuses – early Tibetan architecture – with one of the more unfortunate names. UTEP (University of Texas at El Paso). Herman Carter, in his sixties, was the kind of scholar young Ph.D. students aspire to be: knowledgeable, with a constantly growing reputation and an increasing interest in the world as he grew older. He seemed at first to have no sense of humor, and certainly the three publications he distributed to us revealed none, but when pressed on some vital point he was apt to come up with just the right witticism to relax tensions. He produced one Ph.D. student every three years, and saw to it that she or he found a good position, for anyone he trained was employable.

'You could have assigned me no topic more difficult than the one you did, but also none more significant to your purpose. Let's see what generalizations we can establish before the discussion begins, because it would be painful to waste your time and mine in belaboring the obvious.' With that excellent preamble, to which we assented, he launched into his subject, drawing heavily upon his experiences in Quebec, in Belgium and in Cyprus, each of which was engaged in internecine struggles.

'It would not be easy to find two groups of people less qualified by history and temperament to share a land like Texas in the early 1800s than the old Spanish-Mexican to the south and the new Kentucky-Tennessee man to the north. God reached deep into His grab bag when He asked those two dynamite caps to share the land between San Antonio and Louisiana. The older group was Catholic, of Spanish descent, family oriented, careless about on-the-spot administration, town oriented, ranchers if they could afford the land and the cattle, obedient to authority up to the moment of revolution, and extremely proud, punctilious as well. The intruding group was Protestant, British, individually oriented, insistent upon good local administration, farmers with a positive passion for the soil, suspicious of cities, disrespectful of any national authority, especially religious, but just as eager for a duel as any hidalgo. Dear God, what an unlikely mix!'

For an entire day this elderly man threw off ideas like a summer electrical storm over the prairie: sharp flashes of lightning followed by distant and impressive thunder. He had no personal involvement in what was happening along our Rio Grande or along the desert borders between Arizona and California, so he could speak freely and allow his imagination to roam; but he did have an acute concern about the demographics of the Mexican-American confrontation and was vitally involved in the guessing game as to what was going to happen.

At one point I had to break in: 'Dr Carter, you speak as if our problem is nothing but the Quebec-Canada problem clad in serape and sombrero,' and he said: 'Precisely. When cultures are in conflict, certain inevitables result.' I must indicate some of the specific ideas and challenges he asked us to consider as observable in Texas.

Knives versus guns: 'You so often find in Texas newspapers a story which appalls white society. Some agitated Mexican immigrant has found life intolerable and has grabbed his knife to carve up five or six of his friends, sometimes even including his wife. Horror! Indignation! But the same paper will carry a story about some decent white anglo who has shot the same number of people when drunk, and this is condoned because of the stress the man was under or because he was such a good fellow when sober.'

Music: 'I'm distraught when I live along your border to realize that whereas Mexico and her sister nations have produced some of the most wonderful, joyous songs in the world, things like "Guadalajara," "Cu-cu-ru-cu-cu," "La Bamba," and "La Golondrina," your popular music stations play only the most cacophonous noise. This gap is so wide, it can apparently never be bridged.'

Games: 'The difference between a poetic bullfight and a brutal American-style football game is so vast that words cannot resolve the difference. And it's symbolic, I think, that each culture looks with real distaste at the brutality of the other. I've heard sensible anglo women along the border inveigh against the savagery of the bullfight, but make no comment about their own young men who are killed each autumn playing football or about the scores who become paraplegics for the rest of their lives. I don't particularly like bullfighting, but I sometimes think that it's better to kill a bull than to maim a man . . . especially a young man.'

Toward the end of an exciting day he threw at us, as if we were performers in a circus having to catch the Indian clubs he tossed through the air, three ideas of such fresh and startling dimension that they became subjects for repeated discussion in the months to come. In this respect he carried out one of the best functions a learned man can perform: he stirred up the minds of his listeners, who could if they wished reject his conclusions but who still had to grapple with his data, hoping to form generalizations of their own.

A name: 'One of the tragedies of Texas history has been a failure to devise an acceptable name for citizens of Mexican heritage who have lived in the state much longer than newcomers of Anglo-Saxon heritage. We call these distinguished men and women *Mexicans*, ignoring their centuries-old citizenship on our soil, their education and their often superior moral condition and manners. But we also call the illiterate peon from Chihuahua who crawled across the dry river bed last night a *Mexican*, and the tragedy of it is that we do not differentiate between the two. The most ancient citizens are grouped indiscriminately with the most recent infiltrators, and everyone suffers. One day in California, I asked my Hispanic students: "What do you want to be called?" and they said: "Persons of Spanish name and heritage." How could you fit that into a newspaper story? What we seek is a single word which is short and without adverse coloring. *Chicano* is liked by some, deplored by others. It won't work. Many younger students prefer the contentious *La Raza*. Too militaristic. In fact, nothing works, and Texas is stuck with an abominable situation. It uses old words to stigmatize new situations, a classic example of how society so often fails to produce words which define the real problems of our society. We need a verbal invention which acknowledges the grandeur of the Mexican contribution, but we can't find one.'

At this point he stopped, looked at Profesor Garza, and asked: 'How do you like being called a Mexican, after the centuries your family has been in Texas?'

'I don't like it, especially when the person doing the categorizing is some newcomer from Detroit. Appropriates the name *Texan*. Then castigates me as a foreigner.'

'You see any solution?'

'None. It's as you say, a cultural crime that cannot be corrected.'

'What do you call yourself?'

'A Texan of Spanish heritage.'

'That's a hell of a name. By the way, how far do you have to go back to find unmixed Spanish blood in your family?'

'Twenty-one generations, a Spanish soldier in Vera Cruz.'

'So you really are Mexican?'

'Except that in 1792 a wonderful woman of pure Spanish blood married into the family and had nine children.'

'In Texas?'

'Where else.'

Now Miss Cobb surprised us: 'Professor Carter, when you referred to your Mexican students in California you called them Hispanics,' and he asked: 'I did?' and she said: 'You certainly did.'

He laughed and said: 'That may be the solution. Garza, what do you think?' and Efraín said: 'I've never found it offensive,' and we agreed unanimously that our report would use that term.

Government: 'A salient fact about Texas, and one often forgotten, is that in 1824 the Mexican government provided one of the best constitutions our hemisphere has seen. Had this been put into effect, honestly and with respect for its provisions, Mexico and Texas would have enjoyed one of the world's good governments, and separation would not have become necessary. But there's the overpowering difference. Mexicans had the intelligence and mental agility to form a splendid document, one of the best. But they never began to have the managerial ability to implement it. So separatism became inescapable, because American settlers, no matter where they went – Oregon, Utah, California – insisted upon a stable government. Today when I read that Constitution of

1824, I could cry. So noble a document to have so ignoble an end. It could have saved Texas for the Mexicans, but no one could be found to operate it.'

The future: 'Because the people of the Spanish-speaking nations to the south have such a high birth rate ... Did you know that Mexico's population in 1920 was a mere fourteen million and now it's seventy, with no upper limit in sight? And the explosion in Central America is even more startling. Same situation in Canada, the French outbreed the British at a relentless rate. "The Victory of the Crib," they call it. Well, we must suppose that this will continue into the indefinite future, and if it does, we must also expect to see an unconquerable movement of Spanish-speaking people up from the south and the eventual Hispanicization of California, Arizona, New Mexico, Colorado, Texas and no doubt Florida. Let me tell you exactly what I envisage for Texas. I think that along the Rio Grande there is already developing a kind of ipso facto third nation, reaching from Monterrey and Chihuahua in the south to San Antonio and Albuquerque in the north. I'm not sure that this new nation will require any modification in governmental forms. It could still be Mexico and the United States. But the interchange of people, language, money, jobs, education, traditions, food habits, religion and entertainment will be complete and free. And it will be untrammeled because no one will be able to halt it.'

He stopped, rose from his chair, and walked to a window from which he could see much of El Paso, that bustling city, but even more of Ciudad Juárez, that larger city on the other bank of the river. From Juárez rose a huge cloud of dust thrown off by one of the Mexican cement plants, and the winds were such that the heavy dust fell not upon Juárez but upon El Paso.

'The course of history cannot be stopped at will,' Carter said. 'Last night as I understand, you passed freely into Mexico and freely out. I believe it will always be that way.' Then he offered his final judgment. Turning away from the window, he hummed a few notes of 'La Adelita' and said: 'The ultimate mix could be a very good one. The soft beauty of Saltillo and the hard integrity of Kentucky. A new world along a new kind of frontier.'

IV

THE SETTLERS

On a wintry day in 1823 a tall beefy wanderer with a bland, open face like a rising sun stood with his scrawny wife, pudgy eleven-year-old son and three mongrel hunting dogs at the edge of a rain-filled bayou in the western reaches of the new state of Louisiana. A straggler from Tennessee, who had fled to avoid bankruptcy and jail, he was not pleased with what faced him.

'Don't mind the water, we can wade through it. Done so many times on our exploration. But I do worry about this next stretch between here and Texas.'

'We'll get through,' his red-headed wife mumbled. Reaching for her rather unpleasant son, she warned: 'You're to stay close, Yancey. Help us load the guns if they attack.'

The three were dressed in buckskin garments, laboriously cut and sewn by the mother, who appeared to be responsible for all vital decisions while her pompous husband thrashed about deciding issues which never seemed to matter. The conspicuous thing about the family was the incredible amount of gear each member carried: guns, an ax, pots, extra articles of clothing and bundles of dried food. From every angle of their bodies useful items protruded, so that they looked like three porcupines waddling through the woods; they were so impeded that they could cover only about nine miles a day when better-organized travelers would have completed fifteen. 'We'll head due west,' the father said as if he were a general, 'make the shortest transit possible, and be safe in Texas before they know we're about.'

His introduction of words like *exploration* and *transit* betrayed the fact that he had at some earlier time known life within a respectable Tennessee family, but a love of petty gambling and a positive addiction to idleness had led to a sad decline in his fortunes. His fall had not been spectacular, just a slow erosion of holdings and a series of disastrous lawsuits over land titles. When his family lost interest in his welfare because of his marriage to the daughter of a shiftless frontiersman, he had no recourse but to leave home, a man with no land, no prospects, and very little hope of improving his lot.

'Will there be Indians ahead?' the boy asked.

'Worse. Renegades. White men turned sour.'

This man, thirty-three years old, had decided in the fall of 1822 that his condition in Gallatin, Tennessee, was so deplorable that he could escape only by taking to the road: Nashville to Memphis to Little Rock to the southwest corner of the Arkansas Territory. He and his family had struggled to reach the banks of the Red River, which he had followed into Louisiana. There they had cut west toward the Mexican frontier state of Tejas, known along the Mississippi as Texas, refuge for any American who wanted to start his life over in a new and burgeoning area.

But to reach this reported paradise from Louisiana entailed great risk, for when travelers came to these final bayous separating the civilization of New Orleans and its outriders from the wilderness of Texas, they faced, as the Jubal Quimpers did now, about thirty miles of one of the most dangerous territories in the Americas. 'Listen,' they were told, 'and listen close! In the old days they called it the Neutral Ground, meanin' it didn't belong to neither Louisiana nor Texas. They hoped that settin' it up like that, they'd be able to avoid conflict between Americans and Spaniards. But what did they attract? Pirates, murderers, smugglers, women who deserted their families, runaway slaves who stabbed their masters, forgers. Finally they gave it to Louisiana, but it's still scum of the earth. Hell hides in that Strip acrost the water.'

'I don't want to go,' Yancey said, but his mother caught him by the arm and moved him toward the bayou: 'We were pushed out of Tennessee. Got nothin' left but Texas.' Then, touching a sack she had protected since starting their exodus: 'We get this corn planted before May, or we starve.'

Jubal was about to plunge into the muddy water when a voice from the east halted him: 'Hey there! Tejas, mebbe?'

The family turned to see a remarkable sight, a roundish, white-haired, ruddy-faced Irishman in the habit of a Catholic priest, holding his hat in his left hand and puffing heavily as he anxiously endeavoured to catch up, for like the others, he was frightened of the Strip.

When he overtook the Quimpers they saw that he carried very little baggage: a small knapsack made from untanned deerskin, a simple bedroll of sorts and a battered book, apparently a Spanish Bible, for its spine carried in faded gold lettering the words *Santa Biblia*. From its ragged leaves protruded ends and bits of paper, for it served as his file. 'I am Father Clooney' – puff-puff – 'of County Clare' – gasp-gasp – 'servant of God and the government of Mexico.' He uttered the first syllable of his name and of his native county in a beautiful Irish singsong, which made his round face break into radiant smiles as he proudly said the words.

'I'm Jubal Quimper, Methodist, Gallatin, Tennessee, on my way to Texas, and what are you doin' in these parts?'

The priest told a most improbable yarn: 'When the wine was red, I told my bishop in Ireland to go to the devil, and before firing me he advised: "Francis Xavier Clooney, you may think that your bishop should go to eternal damnation but you must never express it." I could find no assignment in Ireland. Bishops have evil memories.

'So I emigrated to New Orleans and could find no parish there. Bishops have long arms. When the Spanish government, some years back, announced that they wanted priests to serve in Tejas, few Spaniards being willing to work there, I sailed to Mexico and volunteered. I was about to take charge of all Tejas north of San Antonio, when the Mexicans threw the Spaniards out, and me job was gone again. The new rulers in Mexico City told me: "We're sending our own people to Tejas. We need no strangers." So back I sailed to New Orleans. But they soon found that Mexican priests were just as reluctant to move into Tejas as Spaniards had been. So back they came running: "Father Clooney, we need you!" '

'Did you learn Spanish?' Quimper asked, and the priest, still puffing from his run, said: 'Some. I can conduct prayers . . . in Latin . . . much like Spanish. And you?'

'You wander through these parts, you pick up words here and there. Did you say you're an official of the Mexican government?'

'In north Tejas, I'll be the Catholic church. I'm to conduct the baptisms, the marriages, the conversions.'

'Conversions?'

'Yes! You told me you were Methodist, a respectable religion I'm sure, but not the right one. Unless you convert to my religion, you'll get no land in Tejas and you may even be thrown out.'

'I can't believe that,' Quimper said, but it was his wife who made the stronger statement: 'We'll stay Methodists.'

'Then go no farther,' the priest said, and from his ragged Bible he produced a paper, printed in Mexico City and delivered to the Mexican consul in New Orleans, which laid down the rules. Spreading it in the rain, he and Quimper, with their fractured Spanish, deciphered the explicit law:

> No immigrant will be allowed to take residence in Tejas or acquire land there unless he brings with him documents proving that he is of law-abiding character. And if he is not already a member of the Roman Catholic Church, he must convert.

Quimper showed the document to his wife, and then asked Father Clooney how the law could be evaded, if one was of reasonably good character but not a Catholic.

'Impossible,' the priest said. 'And I'm surprised you'd ask me such a question, since I'm sent here to uphold the law.'

'What can I do?' Quimper asked, his big, undisciplined body betraying his agitation.

'You can become a good Catholic, like the law stipulates.' Father Clooney had a singing vocabulary acquired in the Catholic schools of Ireland and was always introducing words like *stipulate* into his conversation. 'I'm being sent into Tejas to convert men just like you, Quimper, so that you can legally take up your league-and-a-labor.'

'What's that?'

'The Mexican government is considering a new law. Every Catholic immigrant will get free land. Much more if he's married.' Consulting his document again, he said: 'A league is four thousand four hundred and twenty-eight American acres, a labor is a hundred seventy-seven. The rule is that you get a labor of free land if you intend to farm it, plus an entire league if you run cattle.' He coughed, folded the document, returned it to his Bible, and wiped the rain from his round face: 'If I were you, I'd claim I intended running cattle.'

'We have no cattle.'

'We have no sunshine,' said Father Clooney, 'but we expect to have some soon.'

'I must become a Catholic?'

'There's no other way.'

'And you can make me one?'

'That's me duty. That's why I'm here.'

'What do I do?' Lest he seem too eager to reject his inherited religion, Quimper added: 'I'm a good Methodist, you understand, but I must have land.'

'You kneel, and your wife and your son kneel, and I ask you a few simple questions.'

The three Quimpers moved apart, the big, fleshy father of weak character, the thin, tense wife of tremendous moral force, and the flabby son who understood little and cared less and who now said: 'This paper says just what he said it did.'

'I will not accept land on such terms,' Mattie Quimper said, and from the stern tone of her voice Jubal realized that once more he was going to have difficulty with his headstrong wife: 'You take the oath, or you go back to Tennessee. I'm bound for Texas.'

'I will swear to no such blasphemy,' she said, and since nothing he could say persuaded her otherwise, it looked as if the Quimpers would end their escape to Texas at this bleak frontier.

But now Father Clooney exercised that gentle logic for which he had been famous among his friends in Ireland. He did not have a superior mind, no one ever claimed that, but a friend at the seminary once said: 'He's highly flexible. Finds solutions which you and I would never discover.' Brushing Jubal aside, he took Mattie by the arm and asked in that sweet voice: 'Me daughter, it's land you crave, is it not?' When she nodded, he continued: 'They told me in Mexico there were parcels along certain rivers in Tejas which exceeded that of Jerusalem or

267

Ireland. Now, me girl, if you want to share in that land . . .' He stopped, smiled, and shrugged his shoulders.

'Must I?' she asked, and he replied: 'You must.' She then asked: 'But does swearin' mean I give up my own religion?' and he said, smiling at her benignly: 'Well, yes and no,' and she said: 'I believe you, Father,' and she allowed him to lead her back to her family.

So the three Quimpers knelt in the Louisiana mud, their faces turned west towards Texas. It was a solemn moment both for them and for the priest, for they were formally rejecting a religion which had nurtured them and he was performing his first official act as an agent of his new government. All were nervous as he whispered through the pattering rain, probing at his converts with a series of significant questions: 'Do you accept the Body of Christ? Do you acknowledge in your hearts that the Holy Roman Catholic church is the ordination of Jesus Christ Himself? Do you accept without reservation the supremacy of our Worldly Father, the Pope? Are you willing to announce yourselves publicly as members of the Roman Catholic church?'

When the three supplicants replied in whispers more muted than his own, Father Clooney administered the oath, but young Yancey noticed something that the white-haired priest could not see: his mother, holding her hands behind her back, kept her fingers crossed. His father did not, and as soon as the final blessing was given, making them good Catholics, Jubal leaped to his feet and said: 'Now, can we have this in writin'?' and gladly Father Clooney drew from his untidy Bible a printed document which he now filled in, attesting to the fact that Jubal Quimper *et uxor et filius* were good Catholics.

But this did not satisfy Quimper: 'You must write down that we're entitled to our league-and-a-labor.'

'I have no authority to issue such a statement,' Father Clooney said, whereupon Jubal grabbed the certificate and was about to shred it: 'Then I'm not a convert.'

'Wait!' the priest said. 'Is it so important to you?' and Quimper replied: 'I'm willin' to abide by the laws of any land I live in. But I demand that my new country put in writin' its promises to me.'

'My words would carry little weight,' Father Clooney

protested, but Quimper said: 'I've found that words on documents carry terrifyin' weight. I'm here in this swamp because of words on documents. And I want your words on this one.' So the priest rummaged through his bedroll until he found a pen and a vial of ink.

The paper he signed still exists in the archives of Texas. It is rain-spotted and not legally binding but its import is unquestioned, and was the foundation of everything good that was to happen to the Quimpers in Texas:

> This document testifies to the legal conversion into the true Holy Roman Catholic Church of Jubal Quimper, his wife Mattie and their son, Yancey, aged eleven. By the laws of Mexico this entitles them to take up free and without hinder a league-and-a-labor of the best land, as he may identify it.

The paper was signed boldly by Father Clooney, formerly of Ballyclooney, County Clare, now an ecclesiastical representative of the Mexican government. Since these were his first conversions in his new assignment, he carefully dated the paper '3 January 1823, Provincia de Tejas, Mexico,' and when Quimper pointed out that they were not yet in Texas, Clooney said with that elasticity which would always characterize him: 'In spirit we are. So let's make speedy tracks to take up our inheritance.'

Father Clooney, who had watched many struggling people trying to survive in a harsh world, was always concerned with the physical welfare of those he counseled, and now he gave the Quimpers solid advice: 'You've got to buy a mule. You can't lug all that gear into Texas.' But Jubal asked: 'Who can afford a mule?' and Clooney replied: 'We'll find a way.'

It was providential for both the Quimpers and the priest that they had joined forces at the bayou, for the transit of the Neutral Ground where law did not prevail proved more dangerous than even Jubal had anticipated. 'I want all guns to be loaded,' Quimper said as they entered the Strip, and when Father Clooney warned: 'The powder may get wet if we load now,' Jubal said: 'That's the risk we take.'

They were less than six miles inside the area when three

Kentucky ruffians, fugitives from murder charges, accosted them and demanded tribute. When Father Clooney refused to surrender the few dollars and Spanish coins he had collected, they threatened to kill him as a conniving priest: 'We don't want your kind in Texas.' And they might have slain the four travelers had not one of the robbers dropped dead with a bullet through his head.

Mattie Quimper, off to one side, had listened to the threats and had quietly reached for her husband's gun. Holding her breath to steady her arm, biting her lip to still her nerves, she had aimed not at the biggest Kentuckian's chest but at his head, and when he dropped, she threw Father Clooney one gun and her husband another, and these two men happened to fire at the same survivor, killing him too. The third renegade escaped through the brush, and for the next two days the four immigrants kept a round-the-clock watch lest the escapee return with others to seek revenge.

As they were about to leave the Strip they came upon a small settlement perched on the left bank of the Sabine River, the boundary line between American Louisiana and Mexican Tejas, and here they were accosted by an extraordinary man, sour of face, lean of body and profane of speech: 'Ran me out of xxxxx Alabama, printin' xxxxx dollar bills better'n the xxxxx gov'mint. Now, if you have any xxxxx Spanish coins, I can earn you a tidy xxxxx profit.'

He had been a blacksmith by trade and might have made a good living almost anywhere in America, or Texas, had he applied himself to his calling, but he had an insatiable habit of manipulating coinage, and now he offered his services to the Quimpers: 'What I do, I take a Spanish coin, pure silver, and I smash it so fartin' flat and in such a clever way' – into even a simple statement like that he was able to introduce three horrendous expletives – 'that I can cut it into quarters.'

'Everybody does that,' Quimper said, and he was right, for coinage was so scarce throughout America that the fracturing of dollars into four quarters or sometimes even eight bits was common.

'Of course ever'body does it,' the forger acknowledged. 'But they cut a dollar into four quarters. I cut mine into five.'

And he did. Taking a Spanish coin provided by the priest, he hammered it in such a way that in the end, with the identifying marks preserved, he produced five pieces. Quimper was afraid to risk his own money in this criminal activity, but Father Clooney approved the inventiveness, and from his voluminous robes produced a handful of coins, which the forger quickly cut into fives, keeping for himself one-tenth of the gain.

As the priest was pocketing his profit, a dirty, ill-kempt boy of nine or ten ran up, shouting: 'Black Abe done killed his woman!' and everyone ran to see what new tragedy had struck an area accustomed to disaster.

Black Abe, a white man from Missouri with an infamous reputation even among his evil companions, had tired of his woman's nagging and had stabbed her many times with a long knife. When the priest reached her she was still breathing, but the flow of blood was so copious that she obviously could not survive. 'Do you seek peace with your Maker?' Clooney asked softly. 'No filthy papist touches me!' she managed to whisper, and with that farewell to an ugly world she died, whereupon Father Clooney knelt by her bed and pleaded with God to accept the soul of this bewildered woman.

The sanctity and emotion of the scene was broken by shrill yelling from outside, where the young boy who had brought the message to the forger's shop had taken a severe dislike to Yancey Quimper, much older and heavier than he. For no good reason but with lethal skill the little ragamuffin was belaboring Yancey, bringing blood to the nose and blackening to the eyes.

'Stop it!' young Quimper pleaded, and when his assailant continued pummeling him, he dropped to the ground, protecting his face with his hands. He had assumed, from having watched grown men fight in Tennessee, that when he fell to earth the fight would end, but in the Neutral Strip such a fall merely encouraged the attacker to finish off the job, and now, to the approving yells of the watchers, the fierce little tiger kicked at Yancey's head, then leaped upon him, boxing him about the ears with both fists.

'Finish him!' some of the men shouted, and the boy might have done so had not Father Clooney come out from the house where the dead woman lay. Striding into the middle of the cheering men, he drove off the boy and raised Yancey to his feet, brushing away the dirt and helping to stop the tears.

Deprived of this amusement, the men roiled about for some minutes, after which one of them cried: 'You can't do nothin' with Black Abe. Let's hang him.' So a posse was organized and Abe was soon apprehended trying to escape through the canebrakes.

Dragged back to the informal village on the Sabine, he was reminded of his many crimes and castigated for having slain one of the few women in the area: 'Abe, you gonna die. You want a prayer from this here priest passin' through?' When Abe said that he did, Father Clooney stepped to the tree from which the rope dangled: 'Son, despite your wicked ways, the Lord Jesus Christ intercedes for you at the throne of God. Your repentance is marked. Your immortal soul is saved and you shall die in peace and in the perpetual love of Jesus Christ.'

When the rope was hauled up by four big men, one of them the smith, and Black Abe's kicking stopped, Clooney said: 'I pronounce him dead. Bury him.' As an afterthought he said: 'Bury her too. Side by side, as they lived in this turbulent vale of tears.'

That night the Quimpers observed for the first time that their priest, in times of stress, as after this hanging, would search about for alcohol in which to drown his emotional insecurities. Tippling at first, he would progress quickly to real gulps, and when he was comfortably drunk he would wander among whatever groups were sharing the whiskey, introducing himself with a benign smile: 'Me name's Father Clooney of Ballyclooney on Clooney Bay in County Clare, servant of God and the government of Mexico.' He would sing the words, continuing for about an hour, after which he would calmly lie on the floor wherever he was and fall asleep. When morning broke, the four immigrants were so eager to enter Texas that the priest prevailed upon the forger, who operated a small ferry, to load them into his water-logged craft and pole them across the muddy Sabine. As they reached the midpoint Jubal happened to say the name of the river, whereupon the forger proved that he'd had a fair education: 'Ever' newcomer says it like you just did. *Say-bine*, no accent, rhymes with *wine*. Ancient Greek. Us locals call it *Suh-bean*, heavy accent last syllable, rhymes with *queen*.'

He deposited them on the slippery western bank just as a true deluge broke, inundating everything and especially the unprotected ferry, whose profane operator cursed God, the storm and the crazy Catholic priest who had lured him into this predicament.

Father Clooney paid no attention to either outburst. Shepherding his new flock as if they were a thousand devout souls passionately addicted to his church, he asked them to kneel in the storm, and with water cascading down their faces and soaking their bodies in a kind of heavenly baptism, the Quimpers entered Tejas, and when Jubal rose he proclaimed rather sententiously: 'We wanted to come. God brought us acrost the Strip. And now we enter our inheritance.'

Mattie did not immediately rise from her kneeling; fingering the mud, she delivered an important judgment: 'This earth can grow things. Let's find our land and get the seed in.'

'We have time,' her amiable husband assured her, but she said: 'Even in paradise, if we miss the growin' season, we run into trouble,' and it was she who led the way south.

Father Clooney, now fifty-eight and engaged in what would surely be his final assignment, felt himself fortunate to have found the Quimpers, whom he discussed with God in his prayers: The boy's not much. He needs Your help. The mother could build Rome in a week, and I hope You'll bless her. Did You see her gun down that bandit and then throw me the other rifle? The father? Now there You have a problem. Big, likable, in some ways younger than his son. But he's a good shot and he does keep us in food. Tighten him up a bit.

Together the ill-assorted troop headed south and west into Mexican Tejas toward the new Stephen Austin colony earmarked for American settlers. As they went they lived off the land, and now Quimper was delighted to have Father Clooney as a hunting companion, for as a boy in Ireland the priest had learned the mystique of firearms and enjoyed the ritual of stalking almost as much as the satisfaction of bringing home game. Clooney was a voracious eater, almost a glutton, so he felt a vested interest in killing a deer or a bear with regularity, and he was good at butchering, so that during their journey the Quimpers and their spiritual leader fared well.

Mattie did not entirely trust this Irish priest who claimed he worked for the Mexican government, but she was growing grateful to him for the work he did in their caravan. Always he was first to volunteer for any task, something her husband never did except where hunting or eating was concerned; she must make the fire, and do the cooking, and form the lead bullets, and tend the clothing, and at times seem to carry everything but the guns. With the arrival of this smiling priest always eager to help if food was in the offing, she had a chance to breathe and to be a woman rather than a beast of burden. In fact, after their fifth day together, she found herself liking him, but her stern Protestantism prevented her from showing it.

Two of his weaknesses disturbed her. The Methodist clergymen she had known stormed against drink and gambling, but Clooney engaged in both, for while she labored at cooking or sewing, he and Jubal would play at cards, using awkward pebbles as counters. The betting would become quite furious, and she would hear Clooney cry: 'Aha, Quimper! You tried to hide that ace, and now you'll eat it.'

One night when they were well into Texas, the two men sat playing cards as Mattie inspected the precious corn seed to see if the two wads of smelly plug tobacco were still keeping away the weevils which would otherwise infest it. Clooney, seeing the colorful, easily handled kernels, cried: 'I say, Mattie. Lend us a handful for our game.' She demurred, for to her the corn was sacred, the agency of all that was to follow, but in the end Jubal supported the priest: 'Come on, Matt! We'll guard the corn with our lives. Aren't we using it like money?'

So now the two noisy gamblers fought for kernels of corn, and the competition could not have been more keen had they been using Spanish pieces, but at the close of each session there stood Mattie, reaching out to reclaim and count her corn, which she put safely back into the canvas bag, with the tobacco.

When they were some thirty miles inside Texas they came to their first settlement, a fragile collection of houses on Ayish Bayou, and the comparison of this bayou with the one they had known in Louisiana was so favorable that Jubal had to comment: 'This here is civilization. A man could choose his land right here and be happy.'

The citizens at Ayish Bayou were so proud of their settlement that they suggested to the Quimpers: 'Stay here.

This land was made for farmers.' But their real joy came when they learned that Father Clooney was a properly ordained priest, for they had seen no clergyman for many years, and early on the first morning a family that had moved down from Kentucky approached him with a compelling problem. Their daughter, seven months pregnant, and her young man, a farmer also skilled in building log houses, had entered into a bond two years before, which they now presented to the priest as they were by honor required to do. Clooney had heard of such agreements and had been instructed in how to handle them, but he had not yet seen one, and he inspected the paper with a solemnity which the Quimpers had not previously observed:

Know all men by these presents, that with the public knowledge of this community the maid Rachel King and the bachelor Harry Burdine do undertake to live together as Man and Wife without benefit of clergy, there being none in these parts. We hold them to be truly married in the Eyes of God, and on their part they undertake a solemn pact to marry legally as soon as a Priest of the Holy Roman Catholic Church shall pass this way. In furtherance of this Vow they promise to pay a fine of $10,000 each if they fail to present themselves to said Priest at first opportunity.

We do this thing, all of us, because we are lost in the wilderness without church or clergy but secure in the knowledge that Jesus Christ Himself knew marriage to be a Holy Communion blessed by God Himself. Rachel and Harry are duly married, and promise they will confirm when the Priest passes by.

'This is a precious document,' Father Clooney said as he returned it to the couple. 'If the others will join in a circle, we shall ask God's blessing on this marriage.' So the Quimpers and all from the Bayou who were available formed a tight circle about the priest and the young couple, and in the simplest words the Irishman conducted a wedding and then gave a blessing. Recovering the paper for a moment, he scratched upon it the notation: 'Rachel and Harry were duly and properly married on 10 January 1823 at Ayish Bayou, Provincia de

Tejas. Father Francis X. Clooney, cleric of the Mexican Government.'

As he was about to hand back the certificate, Jubal stopped him: 'Write that the couple, as good Catholics, are now entitled to their league-and-a-labor.'

'We already have it,' Harry Burdine said, but Quimper told him: 'It's good to have it in writin'.' And Father Clooney made the notation.

At the wedding feast – real bread made from hoarded flour and real whiskey made from corn, with venison and bear abundant – four couples asked Father Clooney if he would convert them to his religion and give them certificates of proof, and Quimper noted the offhand manner in which the priest did this. 'It's as if he took the marriage seriously,' he told his wife, 'and the conversions as a kind of necessary joke.'

'Priests don't make jokes,' Mattie protested.

'I think this one does. He knows we're doing this just to get some land, and he doesn't mind. But a marriage ... that's forever, whether it's Catholic or whatever.'

This speculation ended when citizens of the Bayou warned the newcomers as to what confronted them in their new homeland: 'Have all your papers in order when you get to Nacogdoches. You, too, Father. Because in Nacogdoches they're very strict.'

The way this difficult Indian name was pronounced reminded the Quimpers that they were now in a new country, for the sister town in Louisiana, Natchitoches, had been pronounced French style, NAK-uh-tush, while only a few miles to the west its sister town was called in the Spanish manner Na-ku-DOE-chess, and whenever the locals uttered it they betrayed the fear and respect in which they held it. One old Mexican who had lived most of his life along the Bayou, explained why: 'Long ago we had a big, important settlement across the Sabine in Louisiana. Los Adaes it was called, capital of all Texas. So one day what happens? This Barón de Ripperdá from Spain arrives, finds that the people at Los Adaes were tradin' with the French in New Orleans, and why not? There were no Spaniards in the area to trade with. And he becomes so angry that he finished Los Adaes. Just wiped it out. Five hundred settlers were given five days to gather all their goods and march down to San Antonio, four hundred miles through forest and over swollen streams. They pleaded with him. No avail. Off they had to go, and one in three died on the way. Starvation ... Indians ... fever.'

The old man rocked back and forth, then pointed at Father Clooney: 'The priests did nothin' to help. Everyone was afraid of Barón de Ripperdá. And do you know what? Tell them what, Christopher.'

Christopher, a talkative farmer who ran a meager general store and lodging house, was quick to share bad news: 'When you reach Nacogdoches, who do you suppose you'll find in charge? The nephew of Barón de Ripperdá. Same kind of man. Same kind of ideas. Says he wants to shut down Ayish Bayou the way his uncle closed down Los Adaes.' He spat.

'Yes,' the old Mexican resumed, 'you'll find this new Ripperdá in control, and just as mean.'

'You're still here,' Quimper said, and the old man explained: 'The expulsion happened fifty years ago, and when we reached this spot my father knew his family couldn't complete the journey. We'd all die. So he broke away. Wife ... three children ... me just ten weeks old. And he said; "Barón de Ripperdá can go to hell." Father built us a log cabin – you can see it acrost that little stream – and there he raised corn and children and added rooms to the cabin.'

'What you must do with this new Ripperdá,' the settlers advised, 'is agree with everything he says.'

'He won't issue you any land, of course,' one of the women warned. 'He refused to honor promises or contracts. Says we American Protestants are creeping in to steal Texas.'

'I have papers,' Quimper said. 'I'm a good Catholic.'

Several people laughed: 'We're all good Catholics. We're all entitled by law. But Ripperdá gives us no land.'

'You seem to have yours.'

'We've been here a while. Most of us came during the worst days of the Neutral Ground. Just crept in, as Ripperdá says.'

'How do you get title?'

'We don't. What we do is hope that Ripperdá dies ... or goes away ... or somebody shoots him.'

When the four travelers reached Nacogdoches they found two surprises: the little settlement was a real town with a store

and a lodging house, and to Father Clooney, Victor Ripperdá
was not at all as he had been described by the dissidents at
Ayish Bayou. When the priest reported to him, he found a
young man, thin as the noontime shadow of a reed, with a small
mustache and a winning smile that displayed teeth of extreme
whiteness. He was polite, deferential to any visitor, and
meticulous where governmental detail was involved: 'You must
understand from the start, I'm not the alcalde. I'm an army
major guarding the frontier while the real alcalde is absent.'
Almost distastefully he handed Clooney an order issued by that
vanished official: 'Behold your alcalde!'

Sittazins of Nakadochy. I shal be abbsint sevvin weaks. You
must obbay Majer Riperdee til I git bak.
Sined,

James Dill, yore alcaldy.

'He's one of your norteamericanos,' Ripperdá explained. 'From
Pennsylvania.'

'How did he become alcalde of an important post?' Clooney
asked, and Ripperdá laughed: 'How did an Irishman become
our priest?' He then offered Clooney a drink and asked: 'What
did they tell you about me when you entered Tejas?'

Clooney did not want to reply, but when Ripperdá insisted,
he said: 'They spoke of your uncle ... the expulsion.'

Ripperdá shrugged: 'What lies they tell in their cabins. You
know, he had little to do with that sad affair. The Marqués de
Rubí, he made the decision, told my uncle to enforce it.'

'Did five hundred leave? Did a hundred die?'

'Yes, and my uncle did everything possible to help the
survivors regain their old homes. He was a gentleman.'

Waving his hand before his face as if to expunge recollections
of the tragedy, he said: 'Father Clooney, we're so glad to see
you. We haven't had a priest for some time, so you come to a
land which hungers for your care!'

'I'm proud to have so large a parish ... so important a
parish.'

'Sit down, please. Manuel, fetch us more wine. Now tell me,
how did an Irishman who speaks such halting Spanish become

priest of this vast area?'

Father Clooney took a copious draft of wine, savored it, wiped his forehead with the back of his hand, and smiled at his new superior: 'Francis X. Clooney, of Clooney Bay in County Clare, Ireland. I told my bishop to go to hell –'

'You never did!'

'And he told me where I could go. New Orleans. Your Mexican consul found me there, hired me to work in Tejas. Told me to report to you and bring Christianity to this wilderness.'

'You must not tell me to go to hell,' Ripperdá said with an easy laugh.

'I have learned that superiors have powers which . . .' He stopped. 'If I did, where would you send me?'

Without hesitation Ripperdá said: 'Yucatán. That's where we send our bad boys . . . and our bad priests. It's a dreadful place.'

'I'm here to help, as you command,' Clooney said, but Ripperdá corrected him: 'I'm your superior, yes. But years may pass without my seeing you,' and he pointed to a rude map of what the Mexican government assumed Tejas to be, and Father Clooney's territory extended from the Red River in the north almost to San Antonio in the south, a distance of more than 400 wilderness miles, and at least 100 miles from east to west, a staggering total of 40,000 square miles.

'In Ireland, I had a parish of three villages. Of a Sunday I could walk from one to the other.'

'There you'll have a parish bigger than all of Ireland.'

'My word, I do wish me old bishop could hear you say that.'

'To walk this one will take six or seven years. Marriages, baptisms, burials, they all await you.'

The serious official leaned back, stared at the priest and said frankly: 'I would have expected a younger man,' and Clooney replied: 'I have spent my life preparing to do some great work. Tejas is it.'

'Now to those hapless three you brought with you?' Ripperdá said and Clooney corrected him: 'Quimper is the best hunter I've ever seen. Tennessee man.'

At the mention of this state, Ripperdá groaned: 'Tennessee and Kentucky, they'll be the ruin of Tejas. Mind, I prophesied

279

this. Up there they must teach boys to be animals.'

And when the Quimpers appeared before him, documents in hand, he refused to look at the papers or issue them land: 'You have no claim. I have no authority. I advise you in your own best interests, go home.'

'But the law says – '

'My instructions tell me what the law is.'

In their six meetings with Ripperdá he never once claimed that he was the law. Meticulous in his observation of the proprieties, he referred always to some mystical body of law promulgated in Mexico City, just as his famous uncle had depended upon laws passed in Madrid for the closing down of the ancient capital across the Sabine. 'This is not my action,' the baron had protested in 1773. 'It's the king, in Madrid, who views your town as useless. It's the king who has proclaimed: "Close down that wasteful place."'

Victor Ripperdá had no baronial title to protect him, and no king in Madrid to offer him a job when his tour on the Mexican frontier ended; he had to rely upon the good will of the administrators in Mexico City, whose whims were many. He had learned that if in a post like Nacogdoches he did nothing, made no specific decisions, he could not find himself in trouble, so prudently he refused to issue land titles, build a church for the new priest, or authorize the settlement of any of the Americans who were beginning to stream across the Sabine. Mexico's frontier policy, as Americans in Tejas saw it, was 'Do nothing, and nothing bad can happen to you. Make one mistake, and you may be shot.'

This was not a fair assessment. When American settlers probed west they were supported by stable government in Washington and the state capitals. They were backed by a growing economy. They faced Indians who more often than not could be reasoned with. They were pushed along by a constantly growing population of Englishmen, Scots and Germans eager to test themselves against the wilderness. And most important, they carried with them ideas of education, freedom and self-government ideally suited to the establishment of new governments in new areas.

Mexico had an opposite experience, especially in Tejas, where it faced the most intractable Indians in the Americas. It had to rely upon an inadequate number of Hispanic settlers, with no fresh replacements streaming in. Its productive base was limited and its military disorganized by constant rebellion. The preoccupation of Mexicans was, properly, the founding of a stable government, and in their search they experimented repeatedly with imperialism, republicanism and liberal democracy, leaving them little energy for the development of distant territories.

Most important of all, whereas Spanish culture had proved itself capable, in both Aztec Mexico and Inca Peru, of overthrowing established civilizations centered upon cities, it was not well adapted to the settling of vast open spaces. Its religion was communal rather than individual; its educational theories did not apply to the frontier; and the preference of its people for the small, clustered settlement rather than the remote farm proved ill-suited to Tejas.

Individual Mexicans like Victor Ripperdá were as capable as any Americans, and if their Tejas had consisted of well-defined settlements waiting to be taken over, they would have succeeded, as they did at Santa Fé, but to throw such men into an empty wilderness without adequate support was imprudent, as the Quimper family was discovering.

Despite the fact that their papers were in order, they were forced to remain in Nacogdoches for tedious weeks, pestering Ripperdá to make up his mind about their land, but he found it expedient to ignore them, to delay making any decision regarding their immigration, and when in desperation they begged him at least to tell them what their prospects were, he laughed: 'Me? I have no control over immigration policy. The law says one thing, my superiors say another. Who am I to cut that Gordian knot?'

No appeal, no steady decline in the family's funds could move this slim, dapper official, and it became apparent to the Quimpers, especially Mattie, who despised the man, that he was capable of keeping them in suspension not just for weeks, but for months or years: 'Gettin' a decision out of him? Impossible,' and she began agitating for the family to move south toward San Antonio, where some official might be met who would make decisions.

Her husband warned that if they left Nacogdoches without

permission, Ripperdá might dispatch his militia to overtake them, and then they would languish in jail, as many American trespassers did.

Mattie was all for taking the risk; she yearned to get her seeds planted in land which she could call her own, and she pestered her husband to make the move, but he was afraid. The situation became more complicated one morning when young Yancey came running with exciting news: 'Many Americans! Coming from the Bayou!' And when his parents ran out they saw that a substantial contingent of immigrants had arrived from the Neutral Ground, quite different from the customary stragglers who kept drifting in, to Ripperdá's disgust; these men and women had legal documents attaching them to the settlement plans of a man from Missouri whose name the Quimpers already knew but whose reputation for honest dealing they could not yet assess.

'The empresario Stephen F. Austin has called for us,' the spokesman of the group said. 'He has title to vast lands along the Brazos River, and he offers a league-and-a-labor to every family of good reputation.'

'Do you buy the land?' Quimper asked, and the man said: 'No. Surveyor's fee only, if I understand correctly.'

Jubal showed the man his own papers, especially the form signed by Father Clooney proving that the Quimpers were good Catholics and as such were entitled to their land. The newcomer said: 'It's not like the papers we have, an authorization from Austin, but I'm sure it would be acknowledged if you wanted to come along with us.'

As soon as this suggestion – it was not a promise – was made, the Quimpers unanimously sought to join the Austin group, but when they applied to Ripperdá for permission to leave Nacogdoches, he balked: 'Stephen F. Austin I'm aware of. He has empresario rights. His people are free to move south. But you have no rights.' And he was adamant. The Quimpers could not leave the north to acquire land, nor could they obtain other land in the north. It was infuriating, but it was standard Mexican procedure.

When the new contingent of settlers started south, the Quimpers grew desperate, and Mattie wanted to join the procession whether she was entitled to do so or not, but her husband was afraid to take the risk, and the three immigrants watched with longing as the caravan moved on.

The next days were painful, with Mattie even suggesting that they shoot Ripperdá and get going; her husband hid the three guns and went for the last time to see the administrator. For years he would remember that meeting: Ripperdá wore a new outfit imported from New Orleans, fawn-gray in color, neatly stitched, with new boots to match. He wore one small medal bestowed by a previous administration, and an ingratiating smile: 'My dear friend Quimper, I would gladly help you if it lay in my power to do so.' Whenever he said something like this he twisted the left side of his mustache, then raised his hands in a gesture of helplessness. 'But I am powerless, as you know.' He would issue no permissions, make no promises. In fact, he would do nothing at all, and as Jubal's fury rose, Ripperdá's benign calm increased, but as the two men faced each other, Quimper suddenly realized: If we leave for the south, he won't do anything, either. He will never do anything about anything.

That night he told his wife and son: 'Gather what things we have. At dawn we head south.'

Before the sun was risen the three Quimpers were once again laden like oxen, with additional acquisitions from Nacogdoches – among them a stout hoe jutting out from Mattie's back – and they were about to sneak away when Father Clooney, awake for his prayers, heard their commotion and ran to intercept them: 'Dear children! You must not attempt this.'

'Ripperdá won't have the courage to stop us. You know that.'

'But I was thinking of the long trail ahead. You cannot travel it bearing such heavy burdens,' and while they protested in whispers that they must reach their destination in time to plant their corn, he left abruptly, but soon came back with a gift he had purchased to help these good people on their way . . . if they ever gained permission to go.

It was a handcart such as peasants throughout the world used for pilgrimages: two tall wheels shod in iron, a large bed with sides, a canvas cover to guard against rain, two stubby handles with which to guide it. As the priest pushed it forward he praised the wheels: 'Big ones pass easily over bumps. Little ones move faster, but they do catch.'

Mattie, who carried most of the family gear, appreciated

what such a cart would mean, and with a glance of thanks, went to it ceremoniously, depositing on its oaken bed her new hoe, her cache of food, her sewing kit, her hand-shovel and a dozen other items, some surprisingly heavy. But her sack of corn seed she kept tied to her waist.

When the cart had accepted comfortably the family gear, Father Clooney said: 'Now we must add the things that will make life more bearable,' and he left them again, returning with more gifts, items he knew they would need: another ax, a strong hammer, a hatchet, another spade, a big crosscut saw, more salt. 'And you'd better take this auger to bore holes for the legs of your stools.'

But by the time all these things were stowed, the sun was well up, and Father Clooney warned his new Catholics: 'If you start now, Ripperdá will surely know, and he'll have to arrest you.'

'But we must go!' Mattie cried, and he said: 'So you shall. For I must move along the rivers to perform marriages and baptisms, and I'm asking for you as my guide and hunter. To provide me with food and protection. I have reason to think that Ripperdá will approve, because otherwise he'll have to send soldiers, and he wouldn't like to do that.'

So the morning escape was delayed, but by noon, after Father Clooney had met with Commandant Ripperdá and it was agreed that the Quimpers would accompany him on his journey, they started off. As they left Nacogdoches, Victor Ripperdá bade them goodbye with such warm smiles that one might have thought he had arranged the expedition: 'Go, and may God speed you in your great work,' to which Mattie Quimper retorted under her breath: 'Stay, and may the devil take you on his next visit.'

The excursion was a joyful experience, for it was March, and the air was warming and the forests of Texas were threatening to break into leaf. The rivers ran with new vigor, and birds and flowers returned in abundance.

To Father Clooney, who recognized this as his last abode on earth, each day was a new delight, and constantly he said to the others: 'Imagine having a parish like this! Forty miles to the next cottage, with warmth and love awaiting you when you arrive.' He never doubted, not even when he found himself surrounded by Methodists, that when he sat down at dusk he would be greeted with respect and in time with affection.

At lonely cabins he performed weddings and baptisms, usually on the same day. He went to the most forsaken graves, a pile of stone, no more, and said prayers with those who had lost babies and grandfathers. He blessed people. He converted those whose claim to land would otherwise be denied, and he ate voraciously of whatever food the people offered: 'My father always told me, eat beef while you still have teeth. For a long time you'll drink nothin' but broth.'

Few clergymen have ever reported to a new assignment with more abounding love and gratitude than Francis X. Clooney, this exile from Ballyclooney: God has given me a second chance, and I will show my thanks.

To Mattie the trip was equally exciting. Landless in Tennessee, the daughter of a wretched man who had to crop on shares without ever receiving his legal allowance, she had married Jubal Quimper because he did have land, and she had watched helplessly as men more clever than he stole that land with spurious documentation and protracted lawsuits. Landless once more, she had traveled across Tennessee and through Arkansas, seeing people far less able than she enjoying fields and farms and stretches of their own forest, and always before her, as she trudged along, glowed a vision of land which she and her family would one day own: Ever' damned thing we do on it will make it better and our children will make it better still.

'Land hunger' it would be called in later years when scholars tried to explain why so many people like Mattie poured into Texas, and no better description could be fashioned. She was tired, dead tired of being pushed around, and when she picked up that rifle in the Neutral Ground and killed the renegade, she felt that she was protecting her right to acquire land when she crossed over into Texas. The vacillations in Nacogdoches had driven her to such desperation that she might indeed have slain Ripperdá had not her husband restrained her, and now to be freed of those restraints, to be on the way to great expanses of empty land – this was an exploration toward paradise, and she knew it.

Despite the relief the handcart provided from beastlike burdens, Mattie still did most of the work about the nightly camps: she cooked, she laundered in the rivers, she looked after the priest when rain soaked him and he ran the risk of a cold, she molded the bullets and saved the deerskins for later tanning. She hoarded her supply of salt, dispensing it in niggardly fashion when her husband brought in a portion of some bear he had slain, for then she knew that her crew would eat well. But most important of all she kept the fires burning when they sputtered, hauling in the fallen timbers herself.

For Jubal the long trip was merely an extended hunting party: deer, an occasional turkey, pigeon, wild pig or bear. One day he came rushing back to the camp, shouting like an excited boy: 'Mattie! Mattie! What I seen off to the west!' And at her feet he threw a huge chunk of meat and an animal's tongue five times larger than a deer's.

'What is it?' she asked, and he said: 'I went further than ordinary, that's why I didn't get back last night. Far to the west, I saw this movement, huge, like a movin' carpet. Know what it was? Buffalo. Yep, out there we got buffalo.'

'What are they like?' she asked, and he said simply: 'Mattie, they're so big! So much hair. And they come in such endless numbers!'

On some days when he was certain where Father Clooney and the others were headed so that they could be easily overtaken, he would trek to the west, sit on some mound, and watch the herds moving slowly across an open space where the forest ended and the plains began, and he would wonder if the great beasts could be domesticated: They'd make wonderful cows! They must give milk, else how could they feed their young? But I wouldn't want that bull over there to come chargin' at me. When he killed one and cut off only the most succulent parts, leaving the rest to rot, he often mused: We never ate so well. No potatoes or flour, but meat like no man ever saw before.

He would have been content for the trip to continue endlessly, for he had never before enjoyed such hunting, but when Mattie warned him that their supplies of powder and lead were perilously low, he realized that they must soon strike civilization or find themselves in trouble, and he began to ask at lonely cabins along the ancient forest trail: 'How far to Austin's colony?' and invariably the settlers spoke well of the empresario: 'You can trust that one. He charges for his land, but it's worth it. May move down myself one of these days.'

'He charges? I thought all you paid was the surveyor.'

'Yes, you pay him, but it ain't much. Then you also pay Austin, maybe twelve and a half cents an acre, maybe twenty-five, I've heered both.'

Quimper stopped, calculating in his head: How much was a league-and-a-labor? Nearly five thousand acres. Even at twelve and a half cents, that would be . . . Jesus Christ! It was then that he developed his suspicions about Stephen F. Austin: He's nothin' but a Tennessee banker moved south.

He asked Father Clooney about this startling development, and the priest said: 'As I understand it, the way they told me in New Orleans when they gave me the parish, Austin's the only man the Mexican government trusts. He's the only one the American settlers trust. When you get your land from him you get a clear, sound title. Otherwise, real trouble.'

Quimper would confide in no one, not even his wife, how much money he was bringing, but Father Clooney gained the impression that he had enough to pay for his acreage if he so desired but that it galled him to think that he must do so. 'Jubal, if payin' out a little money ensures a proper beginnin', pay it. You'll be happier and so will your woman.'

'It don't matter about Mattie, she'll do what I tell her.'

'Jubal, that woman dreams of havin' her own land. Why else would she work so hard? Get it for her in the right way.'

For Yancey Quimper, eleven years old, growing shrewder each day, the trip was a kind of grand awakening: 'You told me we would be traveling the Camino Real. Don't look very royal to me.' He was a whining kind of boy, noticing everything and complaining about it: 'They ought to build some bridges like we saw in Arkansas.' He also thought the scattered settlers should build better cabins: 'If they fitted the logs closer, the wind wouldn't blow through.'

Astutely he analyzed the elders he was traveling with: Pop don't like work. But everybody seems to like him. When the men play cards at night, they all like Pop. Father Clooney likes whiskey too much. And Mom bites her lip to keep from givin' them both hell. He grew to think of his mother as a workhorse, not masculine like the two men, but not feminine either, and

287

then one day as they approached a well-built cabin by a stream and Mattie saw from a distance a woman in a neat dress, Yancey watched as his mother withdrew from the convoy and stepped behind some bushes, where she slipped out of her dirty buckskins, washed herself in the stream, and then unpacked the gray-blue woolen dress she had brought from Tennessee. When she rejoined the men, her hair drawn neatly behind her ears and fastened with a cord, she appeared as a tall, handsome woman in her early thirties, and for the first time her son realized that under different circumstances she could have been beautiful.

When they reached the cabin, she assumed command of the travelers, introducing her husband and the priest, and when the settlers, a family named Seaver, wanted their two children baptized in order to protect their inheritance, she arranged the informal ceremony, even though it had to be Catholic. Father Clooney performed graciously, assuring the Seavers that they were bringing their children into the family of God and praising them for the loving care they had obviously bestowed upon their offspring. Yancey noticed, during the prayer, that upon any likely occasion Father Clooney spoke of love, and one morning he asked about this, and was told gently: 'Son, we're forced by circumstances to lead harsh and sometimes cruel lives. We're driven from our villages. We live in exile along El Camino Real. We lose our health, and sanity seems not to abide with us. What really is left?' At this point Yancey realized the old fellow was describing his own condition. 'The love that God bestows upon us,' Clooney said. 'And the love that we share with one another, that's all we have.'

'Who do you love?' Yancey asked, and the priest replied in dreamlike sentences: 'I love the bishop who sent me into this exile, because it was his duty to do so. I love Victor Ripperdá, who treated us so poorly because he bears great burdens. I love the Seavers, who watch over their children in this wilderness. And I love you Quimpers for the bold way in which you face life.'

After the Quimpers and Father Clooney crossed the Trinity River, they followed its right bank eastward for some days until they intercepted a minor but well-defined road leading to the old Spanish mission complex at La Baha, later to be known by its more famous name of Goliad. Had they remained on El Camino Real they would have reached San Antonio; this new road would carry them southwest into the empresario lands of Stephen Austin.

At the spot where the Goliad Road crossed the Trinity River they came to a small settlement, and in its cabins were six couples who had married without the sanctification of clergy. They warmly welcomed the arrival of Father Clooney, whose prayers and written certificates would regularize their unions. Yancey, unaware of the insecurities which could gnaw at families in the wilderness, could not appreciate the joy with which the couples greeted the priest: 'Why are they so excited about getting a piece of paper?' His mother tried to explain that not only was legal possession of land involved but also a secure place within society, but he asked: 'They have their cabins. They have their guns. What more do they need?' and his mother explained: 'No man or woman is ever safe until they have their land. So they can pass it along to their children.' He said: 'But with all this empty land, anybody can have anything,' and she warned: 'You can have it for a while, as long as it's still empty. But when people start pressin' in, the sheriff comes around some day and asks: "Where's your paper . . . provin' that this land is yours?" and on that day, if you don't have the paper, other men can move in and take your land away.' She said this solemnly, and added: 'That's what happened to your father in Tennessee. He had made the land his, done everything, but he had no papers, so they took it away.'

Demanding that her son sit down and pay full attention, she said: 'It's the duty of a man to find his land, take possession, and protect it. Because without land, a man ain't nothin'.' And from such admonitions young Yancey began to erect the emotional framework which would structure his life: Get land, like Mom says. Be a good fellow, like Pop.

His attention was diverted by the festive preparations under way for the celebration of the six marriages, and he accompanied his father and three villagers on a hunting expedition to secure meat for the barbecues that would follow the ceremonies. They went far afield, shot two buffalo, six deer and two wild pigs, providing enough food for days of gorging, but Jubal wished to do more: 'You got any turkeys around here?' and when the men said that some roosted in the dead trees along the Trinity, he told them: 'Carry the meat back to the cabins. Yancey and me, we're goin' to get ourself a couple of turkeys.'

This was a dangerous boast, and Jubal knew it, for the shooting of a wild turkey demanded great skill and patience; killing a buffalo was ten times easier. He began his sortie by heading for the river, then trailing along it in search of the kind of exposed tree in which the great birds liked to roost at sunset. The moon was not going to rise till about midnight, and its help would be needed if he was going to see the turkeys perched on the bare limbs. 'Why don't we shoot them in daylight?' Yancey asked, and his father said: 'Nothin' in this world harder to shoot on the ground than a turkey. They got nine extra senses and a bell which rings if an enemy steps close: "Trouble out there!" I've shot me many a turkey, but never on the ground.'

When they found a promising tree, with signs beneath it indicating that birds might have roosted, they took a position from which they would be able to see the turkeys in silhouette, and as they waited for the birds to arrive, Yancey asked: 'Is what Mom says true? Do you have to have land?' and Jubal replied: 'Your mother's very strong-minded on some things, and usually she's right. But on this I'm beginnin' to have doubts. A man needs a woman. He needs children. He needs faith in God. But often he don't need a settled cabin and a hunk of land to which he's tied. He can do very well just movin' about.'

'Do you want land?'

Jubal considered this, sucked his teeth, and said: 'For your mother? Yes. To put her heart at ease. For me? No.' Without endeavouring to explain this decision, he added: 'In Tennessee I had a bad time. I wish I had nothin' to do with documents and lawyers and courts. I'm a better man than any of them, Yancey, and you're to be the same.'

He was not at ease about his son, for he detected in the lad a lack of firm character. Yancey had not mastered the gun. He could not track an animal. And at the slightest inconvenience he tended to whimper, as he was doing now: 'Why do we have to stay here in the dark?'

'Listen! That's turkeys comin' in to roost.' And in the darkness the watchers could hear the movement of heavy wings as the huge birds, barely able to fly, made massive efforts to lift themselves high enough in the air to glide onto the waiting limbs.

'When the moon moves behind them, we get turkeys.' He instructed his son how to pass him the gun when the firing began: 'There'll be time for two shots. We must make them count. So as soon as I fire the first gun, hand me the other, like this. No other way but this: push . . . slap . . . stand back.' After they had practiced several times while the turkeys made soft noises in the tree, he said: 'I think you have it right, Yance.'

There came a moment of great beauty when the moon first edged above the horizon, bathing the river bottom in a radiant light, and even Jubal gasped when he saw the silhouettes of turkeys perched in the farthest trees: 'All day they root about the ground for food. All night they sleep in trees. Waitin' for us, Yance.'

Finally the moon was right, and Jubal whispered: 'No better time than now.' Checking to be sure his son was properly positioned, he took careful aim with his first gun, held his breath, and fired its precious bullet at the big birds. Almost before the sound could be heard, a turkey dropped from the tree, and with a speed that startled his son, Jubal reached for his second gun. But the noise and the unexpected speed startled the boy, who did not deliver as promised. There was confusion and enough delay to allow the turkeys time to scatter, so that when Jubal finally did bring his gun into position the trees were bare.

For a moment Jubal was tempted to berate his son for the maladroit way he had allowed the birds to escape, but he restrained himself, for this incident, coming after many others like it, merely confirmed Jubal's suspicion that his son was never going to be a hunter. He could be something else, for he was intelligent, but the hard, stony character that made a reliable hunter was lacking.

The marriage ceremony for the seven couples – another having come many miles to join the festivities – was both a triumph and a disaster, for the food which the hunters had provided enabled the women to build a feast that would be long remembered, and with a very good fiddler on hand, the dancing would be lively and prolonged. The social success of the affair was assured; it was the spiritual that provided the trouble, because on the afternoon of the day when the weddings were to be solemnized at dusk, with the baptisms of the couples' children to follow, one of the men grew chicken-hearted: 'Hell, I been livin' with Emily for six years, always knowin', that if things went wrong ... ppphhhttt ... no trouble. Now she's tyin' a knot about my neck – no, thank you.' And off he went into the woods.

It was the general opinion that Lafe Harcomb had merely suffered an attack of gun-shy and that within a day his friends could lure him back to the ceremony, so the weddings were postponed, and the men were correct in their guess, because about noon on the next day Lafe came straggling back to town: 'She ain't half bad, my woman. We been through a lot together. Flood ... attacks by them Karankawas raidin' north. I doubt I could do much better.'

So the multiple ceremony was rescheduled for that afternoon, but now a more serious problem arose, and it was the women who circulated the distressing news: 'Father Clooney is too drunk to officiate.' When the men investigated, they found that after the preceding day's disappointment, Father Clooney had found a rather large jug of whiskey. He was immobilized, unable to speak coherently, and just as belligerent as when he had told his bishop to go to the devil.

Since the Quimpers were more or less in charge of the priest, the settlers looked to them for a solution, but they had none. 'He's blind drunk, quite unable to stand, let alone conduct a weddin',' Mattie told the women. 'He's in there singin' old songs and he's wet his drawers.'

For a second time the wedding had to be postponed, and the couples converged on the Quimpers: 'Get him sober and keep him sober till tomorrow mornin'. Husbands runnin' away. Priests dead drunk. Let's get this thing finished.' So a watch was set over Father Clooney, and slowly through the night the tremendous cargo of alcohol he had absorbed drained from his system, and at dawn Mattie assured the others: 'I think he'll be able to stand up after breakfast.'

But during the night a much different problem surfaced at this crossroads, for a tall, acidulous man who introduced himself as Joel Job Harrison came to the cabin where the

Quimpers were tending their drunken priest and said in conspiratorial tones: 'I suppose you know. I'm sure they must have told you.'

'What?' Mattie asked.

Harrison glanced about, then stared contemptuously at the inert priest: 'I'm a Methodist minister. I do what I can to keep the true faith alive in this papist land.'

'Doesn't the government . . .?'

'It must never know. I work in secret . . . to keep the true faith alive.'

'And if they catch you?'

'All the people in these cabins, they all support me.'

'Then why don't *you* marry them?'

'I have. Secretly, at night.'

'Why do they marry a second time with the priest?'

'To ensure their land.' Bitterly, without compassion, he looked down at the prostrate Catholic: 'Look at him! God's vicar! Guide to lost souls, and himself more lost than any.'

Jubal said: 'What's going to happen to you if . . . I mean in the years ahead?'

Reverend Harrison, for he was indeed an ordained Methodist missionary, looked about the cabin, drew close to the older Quimpers, and said: 'Surely, Texas will soon be flooded with trustworthy Protestants. When that happens, we'll break away from Mexico. What will happen to me in the years ahead? I'll build a strong church in a free Texas.'

'You could be shot for such talk,' Jubal said, drawing away.

'Jesus was crucified for His talk, but everything He said came to pass.'

'What do you expect of us?' Mattie asked, and the tall man said: 'Food when I pass your way. Help when I organize meetings in your region.' Again he looked down at the unconscious priest: 'There lies the enemy. As helpless as the Mexico he represents.' And like a ghost he vanished.

On the third try, the seven marriages were solemnized in accordance with Mexican law; Father Clooney was unsteady on his feet and somewhat cotton-mouthed in his speech, but after the vows were exchanged and the paper-marriages brought into the family of the Lord, he surprised the audience by bending his head back and sending to heaven a prayer that might have come from all their hearts:

'Almighty Father, we are Your smallest children. We have no cathedral here in the wilderness. We have no choir to sing Your praises, no trumpets to proclaim Your glory. We are drunk when we should be sober, and we run away when we should stand firm. But we do our best. We join hands in love and have children to bless us. We help the poor and care for the infirm. We pay our lawful taxes.

'God in heaven, we beseech You to look after us. We are not a mighty force and there are no generals or cardinals among us. But we occupy the frontier and establish new footholds for Your law, and in our humility we ask for Your blessing. Amen.'

On the third day south along the Goliad Road, Yancey had a chance to see what his family and Father Clooney meant when they spoke of love, for when they approached a cabin on the western side of the road a bedraggled young woman so weak she could scarcely stand called to them: 'We are dying. We've had no food for days.' And when they entered the cabin they found that it was so.

'My man, a deep fever. He cannot move.' There on the hut's lone cot lay a man near death, shaking with fever, and in a corner, his two daughters, three and five, huddled like skeletons.

'I cannot leave and hunt,' the woman said, and as she saw Mattie, another wife in the wilderness, she ran to her, fell into her arms, and collapsed weeping. Then, slipping from Mattie's grasp, she fell to the floor.

Yancey was astonished by the speed with which his parents and the priest responded to this cry for help: Father Clooney took charge of the children and started feeding them from his store; Mattie prepared a palliasse on the floor and placed the wife upon it, whispering as she did: 'It's goin' to be all right. Your children are bein' fed.'

Jubal said crisply: 'Son, fetch the rifles!' They hunted all morning, killing enough game to feed the family for weeks, then they butchered the best parts and dragged them back to the cabin, where they camped for nine days until the health of the family was restored. As soon as the husband was strong enough to sit up, Jubal and the priest engaged him in gambling for Mattie's corn, and the lonely cabin was filled with jollity as the women did the work and Yancey looked on.

'You can make do, now,' Jubal assured the family. 'We'll kill a couple more deer or somethin', and things'll be all right.'

As they prepared to leave, Mattie asked: 'Have you papers stating that the land is yours?' and when they replied yes, she told them: 'Half the battle's won. You'll surely be all right.'

When they had the cart loaded, the man showed them a trick which would make its progress even more expeditious, for he drove one of his precious iron nails deep into the wood at the front, forcing the nail back upon itself to form a loop through which he passed a rope: 'One pushes from behind, one pulls from the front,' and automatically Mattie fitted herself into the rope and prepared to start pulling, but before she did so the settlers offered advice which they thought might prove vital: 'As you move into Austin's land, keep careful watch for the Karankawas,' and Mattie asked: 'What are they?' and they explained: 'Big Indians, powerful. They live along the Gulf but they been raidin' north. Taller than those we see around here. And they eat people.'

'But that's impossible!' Father Clooney protested, whereupon the wife said sharply: 'It may be impossible in Ireland, but not here. The Kronks, they do eat people.'

'Not in my parish!' Rumpling through his papers, he found a report, and said, almost like a protesting little boy: 'They told me the Indians would be found only along the seacoast.'

'That was last year. But so many white people movin' in, they've had to come inland. We heard they ate a family on the Brazos.'

'I'll put a stop to that,' Clooney said, and the woman warned: 'You'd make a tidy morsel, Father.'

They had been on their way only two days, heading for the Brazos River, when Yancey saw an alligator, huge and menacing, lurking on the bank of a small stream. Its ugly jaws, locked but with teeth showing, seemed capable of biting a man in half; its bumpy hide glistened menacingly in the sun.

'Shoot him!' the boy shouted, but his father said: 'Let him go. If you don't bother him, he don't bother you.' And with a well-aimed stone he nicked the alligator's tail, so that the beast snapped his jaws and disappeared into the muddy water.

One morning Jubal said: 'More trees ever' day. Must be approachin' the Brazos,' and other signs appeared, confirming their nearness to that spinal column of Texas. But Mattie, always alert to messages from their proposed home, saw more ominous signs: 'Someone's out there. Behind the trees. Followin' us.'

Her husband said deprecatingly: 'Nothin' out there, Matt, old girl,' and on they plodded.

But Mattie was not satisfied, so on her own she left the trail to inspect the trees, and when she reached them she found herself suddenly facing nine or ten of the tallest, fiercest Indians in North America. They were immense, powerful of arm and leg, and she knew they were the cannibals. They were supposed to be on the seacoast, but here they were, in the forest.

Before they could grab her, she uttered a wild scream: 'Kronks!' and as the echo ricocheted through the trees, she started running to rejoin her men.

'Over here!' Jubal yelled as he and Father Clooney sprinted with their guns to a smaller grove of oaks which he hoped they could defend. For one pitiful moment young Yancey stood riveted by fright; then, urged by a shout from the priest, he found courage and ran to the trees, arriving there at the same time as his terrified mother.

Wisely, Jubal formed his three helpers in a circle about the the base of a tall oak, from where they fended off the Indians with carefully aimed shots. Yancey reloaded for his father, and Mattie was supposed to do the same for Father Clooney, but after the first round of shots she yelled at the priest: 'Load for yourself!' and she began firing on her own, hitting one of the Karankawas in the leg.

Realizing that the white travelers were going to keep on fighting, the huge Indians fired their two dilapidated muskets a few more times, missing even the oak tree, then withdrew, dragging their wounded companions behind them. 'My God, they were big!' Jubal cried as they disappeared. 'If we'd had only one gun, they'd have killed us all.' Turning to his wife, he kissed her: 'You know how to use a gun, old girl.'

Now came the glorious days! With moccasins, alligators and

giant Karankawas safely passed, the travelers approached the outer limits of the Austin Colony, and as they neared the left bank of the Brazos they saw land that compared favorably with any in the world. Slight rolling hills created lovely valleys and gentle glades. Little streams wandered aimlessly, providing scenes so inviting that Father Clooney cried several times: 'Build your cabin here!' but always Mattie pushed ahead, for she had in mind a picture of the land she wanted, and it featured spacious meadowlands beside a big river, not some picturesque refuge close to a little stream.

Each mile down the Goliad Road brought new surprises, but the miraculously placed clumps of oak trees on the otherwise open land pleased Mattie most: tall and straight, the fifteen or twenty oaks would be arranged in rude circles that resembled Greek temples, with a carpet of grass beneath the lower branches and reaching across many yards to where the next group of oaks stood. The result was a kind of majestic park, stretching forever, and when they had traveled through such splendid regions for two days Father Clooney said: 'We've come to a paradise right here on earth. You can build your home anywhere and live like kings.' And Mattie nodded.

She was also relieved to detect in her son a slight change for the better, because on two occasions the boy had halted the procession to stand in wonder before some miracle of nature, and she thought as she watched him: Any boy who appreciates growin' things ain't all weakness.

The first amazement was a tree called *bodark*, a wonderful, thorny thing which would produce enormous orange-like fruit of thick skin and of absolutely no use to men or their cattle. The proper name, of course, was *bois-d'arc*, later to be known as Osage orange, and what made this particular tree memorable was that on its branches devoid of leaves clustered not less than forty huge round balls of green plant life with no detectable means of sustenance. 'Mistletoe?' Jubal asked, but when Yancey pulled down a cluster for study, the family saw that it was merely a leafy parasite.

The second encounter was more dramatic, for as the family turned a corner in the rude footpath they came face to face with a large live oak from whose many branches tumbled a cascade of the most beautiful gray-green tracery, a delicate vine whose lacy tips drooped nearly to the ground. 'Spanish moss,' Mattie said. 'Heard about it but never seen it.' Yancey, encountering this lovely wonder for the first time, stood silent.

Jubal had to be concerned with more practical matters, for one morning while Mattie and the priest were admiring the varied landscape, he chanced to see at some distance from the trail a sight which caused his heart to skip several beats: 'My God! It's a bee tree!' And when he dragged Yancey to the half-dead tree Jubal thumped the hollow part of the tree with practised knuckles. 'Crammed with honey!' he assured his son. 'With this tree we could feed a village.'

But when he started to show Yancey how to protect his head with his shirt, his belly exposed, the boy began to whimper: 'I don't want to be stung by no bees,' and he ran back to the others, whining: 'Pop wants me to stick my hand in a bee tree.'

Father Clooney, excited by the prospect of finding honey, took the Quimpers' two blankets, ran to the tree and, wrapping himself and Jubal in as much protection as possible, proceeded to break off dead limbs to provide entrance to the tree, and when they had done this they found, as Jubal had expected, the edges of a hoard so rich that it would have supplied a family of three for half a year.

Battling the bees that attacked any naked spot they could find, the two men used oak leaves on which to pile the rich comb they were extracting, and when they had accumulated all they could carry, they started back to the road, with bees following in savage assault. Laughing and running with hands loaded, the two ignored the stings they were receiving and reached Mattie, who slapped away the bees and provided pots in which the seeping comb could be stored.

'Any land that has bee trees is goin' to be a fine place to settle,' Jubal said, and as the days passed he found, to his delight, that in this region such trees abounded. But as they approached what seemed to be the bottom land of some river, they discovered another bounty which promised equal pleasure: very tall trees up which climbed thick vines reaching to the very crown. 'Those look like muscadine vines,' Jubal cried excitedly. 'We had them in Tennessee. Great for jam, better for wine.'

'That's nice to hear,' Father Clooney said, but on that same day they came to other trees, not so tall but holding vines twice as thick and ominous. 'These must be mustangs!' Jubal said. 'I've heard about them. Skin so thick you can't bite it, and if you try, it'll burn your mouth out. But the fruit inside? Delicious. Sweet and acid at the same time. They could make fine jelly.'

'But could they make good wine?' Clooney asked, and when Quimper said they couldn't, the priest said: 'We'll stay with the muscadines.'

And then, as they reached the left bank of the Brazos, thirty feet higher than the bed of the river, they saw on the opposite bank something which gave Mattie such reassurance that she wanted to plant her seeds immediately. 'Look!' she shouted to the others, and when they did they saw soft fields of wild oats and rye, sown by no one, harvested never, just the bounty of the earth and a promise that if here one planted wheat and corn and nurtured it, crops would grow abundantly. In late March this grain, which had ripened the summer before, had been well beaten down by rain or fed upon by birds, but even so, there remained a remembrance of the oats and the rye, wild and tough and scant, but veritable food. Mattie looked at the priest, then at the grain, and said: 'Father, give us a prayer of thanksgivin'. This is land we can use.'

The three men were willing to halt where they were, for this was satisfactory, but Mattie clung to her vision of the perfect site, and forcefully she led the way to a rise from which they could look across the Brazos to land of wondrous beauty: groves of oak trees, swinging paths through rich grass, open areas for the building of homes, and reassuring calm of a blue sky overhead. 'That's what we want,' Mattie said.

But how to get the cart across the river? Each of the men had suggestions: 'Swim across and leave the cart here.' Or 'Cut two logs, wedge them under the wheels, and float it across.' Even Yancey chimed in: 'Cut grapevines and we'll pull it across.' Mattie listened respectfully to each proposal, and rejected them all: 'We'll build a raft, and after it has carried us across, we'll use it as a ferry for others who come this way.' And she would accept no alternative.

With the tools acquired in Nacogdoches the two men and Yancey felled enough trees to form a substantial platform in the muddy water, and when Mattie bound the logs together with long lengths of vine, the cart was gingerly wheeled upon it, and cheers sounded when the raft held firm. With a long pole Mattie shoved the raft and its precious cargo into the middle of the river and across to the other bank.

As soon as the raft touched land she rushed ashore, dropped her bag of seed, and began pacing off the dimensions of her proposed cabin, and when she stood where the door would be, she spread her arms and cried: 'This is it.'

She had chosen a superior site, for here the wandering river formed a large S. At the first turn the current had eaten away the bank, leaving a huge red cliff thirty-two feet high, and then, as if bouncing back from that effort, it had done the same a little farther along but on the opposite shore, so that when Mattie stood on the spot she had selected for her home, she could see a most pleasing domain: the two red cliffs, the tangled woodland along the river, clusters of oaks on the higher ground, deer watching from a distance, soft hills adding movement, and over all, the bluest sky any of them had ever seen. 'We'll build the cabin here,' she said, whereupon her husband broke into rude laughter: 'Build it here and swim to safety when the floods come.'

He took her to a grove of oaks that towered more than thirty feet above the stream below, and stood with his hands on his hips, staring at the trees: 'Don't you see nothin'?' When she asked what she was supposed to see, he pointed to a mass of grass and driftwood caught in the branches ten feet above her head. 'What is that?' she asked, and he said: 'Can't you see? That's where the flood came last time.'

And when she looked more closely, both at the trees on her side of the Brazos and those opposite, she saw that along a line as clearly defined as if some giant had drawn it with his pen, remnants of a great flood were visible; at that tumultuous time the water had stood more than forty feet higher than it did now, and when she moved back to study other trees on the upland plain, she realized that the river must have been two or three miles wide. The awesome size appalled her, and she asked: 'When did this happen?' and her husband said: 'Last year. Ten years ago. You can't tell by the flotsam, because it's dead. But do you doubt it happened?'

'I do not,' she said, and forthwith she moved inland, studying the trees and their trapped refuse, until she reached a high mound to which no flood had crept: 'This will be safe.' And while the men watched, she moved beyond the mound to an open space, where she began to grub the ground with her hoe. When it was well broken, she took from her canvas bag handfuls of corn. 'The place is right,' she said. 'The moon is right and the soil is right. I've come a long, long way for this blessed moment.' Inspecting each kernel to be sure the tobacco had kept it weevil-free, she planted her first crop, and only when each grain had been safely embedded in the rich soil did she look for a place to sleep.

The time had now come for Father Clooney to continue his pastoral way down the Brazos to those settlements whose spiritual life he would be supervising, but before he departed he felt he must help the Quimpers erect their cabin. And now he asked: 'How will you inform Stephen Austin that you've settled on his land?'

'When you see him, you must tell him what land we've taken. I'll write a letter askin' that surveyors be sent.' And when the three adults had calculated roughly what a league-and-a-labor would be – 4,605 acres, or about 2.5 miles long on a side – the men began cutting stakes to indicate their corners, but as soon as the riverside square was determined, Mattie quietly began to move the stakes in order to form a long, slim fronting on the river. 'This gives us a lot more land along the water.'

Satisfied with her little kingdom, she now began to plan her house, but she had not gone far when Jubal interrupted: 'Stop where you are! We're not cuttin' logs for no big cabin. That can come later.'

'What are we doin'?' Mattie asked, and Jubal pointed to the mound that had attracted her to this site: 'We're goin' to dig us a deep hole in the face of that mound, build us a log front out here, and short side walls to close off the rooms.'

'A cave-house?' Mattie cried. 'Not for me!'

'Matt, old girl. Us men got to do the cuttin' of them trees, and doin' it this way . . . Figure it out. Only one wall and two halves instead of four walls. Half a roof instead of a whole one.'

'But we'll be livin' in a cave,' she protested, and her husband

301

said: 'Many do. And I promise you this, once I find the time, I'll cut the rest of the logs and build you a real house.'

But it took him and Father Clooney so much time and effort to cut and notch two big logs for the base of the front wall that they simplified their plan. They used the two finished logs as corner posts, sunk deep into the ground and strong braced, and joined them together by a palisade made of saplings dug into the earth side by side.

'Now we tie all together,' Jubal said as the outside portion of the cave-house was formed. 'Yancey, Mattie, start tearin' down grapevines!' And when these were dragged in abundance to the site, everyone worked at weaving them through the saplings, which were then plastered with a heavy red clay dredged from the bottom of the river, forming a solid wall.

The roof they wove of heavier vines, covering it with sod so that grass would grow and keep it impervious. When all was done, Jubal said: 'We got us a house half in the air, half in the cave. Warm in winter, cool in summer,' but Mattie added: 'And dark all the time. And filled with smoke.'

'Don't you worry, Matt, you'll have better one day.' So the Quimpers moved into their house, with its dirt floor, hastily carpentered benches and stools, two wooden beds, a trestle table, and pegs on which to hang things. It was not what Mattie had wanted, but as she stepped inside she muttered to herself: 'We'll get out of this cave. We'll have a house with proper sides. I don't know when or how, but this ain't a proper home.'

Father Clooney, admiring the handiwork in which he had shared so vigorously, said: 'I think I should bless this home,' and he gathered the Quimpers for a prayer:

'We have come to Texas seeking freedom and a better life. May this house which we have built with our own hands be a perpetual center of love. May the fields prosper. May the animals multiply. And may the owners find that joy which the Israelites found in their new home. Amen.'

As soon as the Irishman departed, carrying in his pocket Jubal Quimper's claim for the land where the Goliad Road intersected the Brazos River, Jubal launched the project that would provide a meager and uncertain income in the new land; he started felling trees with which their raft could be enlarged, and after weeks of the most painful labor, for his hands grew raw, he had himself a serviceable ferry for lifting travelers back and forth across the Brazos. 'Quimper's Ferry' it was called, and as such it would find an honorable place in Texas history, for across it would move men of distinction, and their cattle, and their armies.

But what most travelers remembered about Quimper's Ferry was not the husband's ferry but the hospitality which the wife dispatched, for she ran a kind of inn or stopping place, and hundreds who straggled down the Goliad Road would testify in their memoirs that the difficult travel from the Sabine River to the Brazos almost discouraged them:

> We was attacked by Indians and threatened by panthers in the woods, and our food was low and we seen alligators, and one man died from rattlesnake, and we would of turned back, sick in spirit, but then we come to Quimper's Ferry on the Brazos and Mrs Quimper welcomed us to her cave-house, and we didn't have no money at the time to pay her but she said no mind, and she fed us and give the children honey for their bread. And it was in those days we first thought Texas might be a decent place to settle.

In the autumn of that first difficult year Jubal discovered just how rewarding a place this was, for as he tramped the woods he came upon a tallish tree with fine green leaves and some husks about its trunk, carryovers from the preceding fall: 'This is a nut tree! Look up there!' And scattered profusely through the heavy branches he saw clusters of long, plump nuts in a profusion he had not seen in Tennessee.

They were pecans, still protected by a greenish husk, and in the colder days that followed he saw that the husks curled back toward the stem which attached them to the tree. Reaching up to pick one, he inadvertently shook the tree, whereupon a waterfall of nuts fell about his shoulders as the pecan tree willingly divested itself of that year's crop.

In great excitement he gathered the unexpected harvest, stuffing his clothes with the rich food and running toward the hut, shouting: 'Matt, old girl! God sent us food for the winter!'

Just as Cabeza de Vaca in 1529 had survived autumn and early winter only on pecans, so the Quimpers, nearly three hundred years later, relished the same remarkable bounty.

Now the pattern of Quimper living became clear. On bright autumn days Jubal and Yancey would search out the pecan trees, shake the branches and garner the fallen nuts so rich in foodstuff. Hauling them home like conquering heros who had risked much to catch their prey, they would toss the nuts toward where Mattie waited. 'Matt, old girl! We did it again!' Jubal would shout, and then retire, highly pleased with himself, while his wife built a fire, heated water and dipped the pecans to soften the shell and moisten the nutmeat to make it easier to extract.

While her husband watched approvingly, she cracked the shells, sharpened a fine-pointed stick and made Yancey use it to dig out the meats, which she dried on a flat stone beside the fire. When he had extracted huge quantities, warned constantly by Jubal: 'Don't break them, Yancey,' Mattie prepared her hoard in one of three ways: 'Folks like 'em just toasted, or better if we can find a smidgen of salt, or best of all, if I coat 'em in honey real thick with just a touch of salt.'

Often when travelers stopped, the men would gorge on handfuls of Mattie's pecans as they played cards, almost fighting for the toasted nuts if they were the honeyed version. Jubal always explained the trouble he'd had in finding the trees, watching them through the ripening seasons and dragging home the garnered hoard. 'Yancey breaks a lot of the halves,' he apologized. 'It's a pity, but Mattie's real good at toastin' them and addin' the honey.' The Quimpers were proving that properly handled, this nut provided one of the world's complete sources of food. Yancey was not fond of pecans: 'Too much work. Now, if a family had slaves to do the pickin', that would be somethin'.'

Management of the ferry was arranged slowly and without conscious decision. Jubal had built it, and in the early days had operated it, not effectively – he did nothing effective but hunt, play cards and find pecans – but with enough skill to earn a few coins. However, when more travelers began coming their way, he found himself occupied with gathering meat during the day and gaming with the visitors at night, which meant that he was often too busy to man the ferry: 'Mattie, old girl, I hear a stranger callin'. Can you go fetch him?'

So she would interrupt whatever she was doing, go down the steep incline to where the ferry waited, and with increasing ability, pole it across the Brazos to pick up the traveler. In time she began to think of it as her ferry and to resent it if either her husband or her son, each stronger than she, interfered with her operation, for from it she accumulated small sums of money which she set aside to speed the day when she could have a real house.

The Quimpers had occupied their dwelling about seven months when the owner of their land, Stephen Austin, came up the Brazos to regularize their holding, and as soon as they saw him they liked him. He was an intense smallish man in his late twenties, with a sharp face and gentle eyes. He spoke softly, was greatly interested in the progress of the ferry, and amused by the way the Quimpers had marked out their land. When he saw their corner stakes he burst into laughter: 'You rascals! Stretching your land along the river, preempting the good frontage! Don't you know the law of all nations?'

'What are you talkin' about?' Quimper asked, almost belligerently. He was four years older than Austin and much heftier.

Austin laughed and clapped him on the shoulder. 'Let's have a drink,' he said, and when Mattie came with a weak but sweet wine they had made from their muscadines, he explained: 'From the time of Hammurabi, in all orderly societies, governments have told their people: "Sure you want land. But at the river the frontage on the water can be only a small percentage of the depth of the field. You cannot own a long, narrow strip which prevents others from reaching the river."'

'What percentage?' Jubal asked, and he said: 'The customary Spanish grant along the Rio Grande has been nine-thirteenths of a mile facing the river, eleven to thirteen miles back from the river.'

'Outrageous!' Mattie exploded. 'That's a sliver, not a field.'

'I agree,' Austin said. 'Up here we allow a square,' and using a stick in the dust, he sketched a more legal claim.

He was also amused to find that the Quimpers had staked out a rather large chunk of land on the opposite side of the Brazos, where their ferry landed, and he told them: 'My father taught me to oppose that. "No man shall own both sides of a river." If Mexico City ever lets us have our own legislature, I'll sponsor a law saying so.'

'Our ferry has to land somewhere.'

'But you can't own both sides of the river. That would tempt you, in time of trouble, to close down the river.'

'What can we do?'

'Keep your dock over there. Keep your road up to higher ground. And even build a small warehouse, if you wish. I'll certify to the Mexican government it was necessary ... for public convenience.'

Austin stayed with them for two weeks, paying liberally for his lodging, and in this time they had an opportunity to assess his character: he was straightforward, pedantic, stern in protection of what he viewed as his rights, and a loyal Mexican citizen: 'I have surrendered all thoughts of ever returning to the United States. We have an honorable government in Tejas, and under its protection we can live in dignity and security.'

They did not learn then, or ever, whether Austin was a true convert to Catholicism or not; some travelers insisted that he had been a stout Catholic back in Missouri, others that they knew people there who had seen him attending a Protestant church. It was definite that he had claimed Catholic member-ship when seeking permission to assume the huge grant which his father had acquired shortly before his death, and certainly the Mexican government considered him a loyal Catholic.

This interpretation was strengthened when Austin spoke highly of Father Clooney: 'When sober, he's a devout man of God, and we're lucky to have him in our colony.'

But the religious problem became more complicated in the early months of 1824 when Joel Job Harrison came south from his cabin on the Trinity to organize his clandestine Methodist services. He took lodging with the Quimpers and convened his first study group at their makeshift inn, a gathering of nine families who had converted in order to get land, but whose secret sympathies were still strongly Protestant. At their first meeting up north, Quimper had not liked Harrison, for he had recognized the tall, angular man as the kind of fanatic who plunged his friends into trouble, and the man's frenzied words had strengthened this adverse impression. But now when he saw Harrison engaged in his pastoral work and watched the compassion with which the Methodist greeted these lonely souls along the frontier, he had to admit that the gawky preacher was a man of God, as simple and honorable in his way as Father Clooney was in his, and as eloquent:

> 'It is our holy mission here in the remote woods of Texas to keep alive the sacred fire of Protestant vision. Surely it is the destiny of this great land of Texas to be like the rest of the United States, a haven of Protestant decency and security. We are Methodists and it is our duty to preserve our faith and keep it strong for those who follow. How shameful they will see us to have been if we allow our sacred faith, the noblest possession a man can have, to wither. Friends, I implore you, be of stout heart and soon we shall see our churches flourish openly in this wilderness. We are the beginners, the sowers of seed, the keepers of the sacred flame.'

He made the simple act of gathering for quiet worship away from the watchful eyes of the Mexican authorities an affirmation of religious and political principle, and he implied that any who did not participate were morally defunct and not worthy of the exalted name of Protestant or Texan, for he identified one with the other. He was incapable of believing that a real Texan could be a Catholic, and although he never preached his treason openly, he also doubted that a Texan could be a true citizen of Mexico.

When Quimper asked him about this, Harrison explained: 'I'm sure that what you say is true. Of course Austin pays homage to Mexico. He must. Otherwise he loses his land. And I'm sure he wants the public to consider him a Catholic, for this confirms his ownership. But in his heart, what is he? I'll give you my right hand, up to the elbow, if Austin is not an American patriot waiting to take Texas into the Union, and a loyal Protestant just waiting to open our churches in this colony and in the rest of Texas.'

The two men left it there, with Harrison convinced that the Quimpers were still faithful Methodists prepared to summon their fellow religionists to prayer sessions whenever he had an opportunity to visit his Brazos territory. 'I suppose in my heart I'll always be a Methodist,' Jubal told his wife when Harrison returned north, 'but I don't like worshipin' in secret, especially when it could get us into trouble.' One evening as the pair sat and watched deer graze beneath the far oaks, Jubal asked: 'Mattie, do you consider yourself a Mexican citizen?' She pondered this, then said: 'I never considered myself a Tennessee citizen. I get up in the morning, do my work, and go to bed.'

'But could you be a Mexican? Are you goin' to learn Spanish?'

'Enough people come through here speakin' it, I'll have to.'

'Well, are you a Catholic?'

She evaded a direct answer: 'Two of the best men I've met are Father Clooney and Reverend Harrison. I like them both.'

'But you have to choose sides.'

'Why?' And she displayed no interest in which side he had chosen.

The question of Mexican citizenship became more pressing when a guest reached the ferry to stay at the cave-house while trying to round up extra mules to drove overland to New Orleans. In halting English he gave his name as Benito Garza, said he was eighteen years old and a native of the little town of Bravo down on the Río Grande: 'I cross river' – he called it *reevair* – 'and catch the mule. You know what it is, the mule? Father a jackass, mother a horse. The mule all gunpowder and fury. But I, I tame the mule – '

'We know all about mules in Tennessee,' Jubal interrupted. 'But you're not going to take those seventeen mules all the way to New Orleans? Alone?'

'Oh, no! At the Trinity, I meet Mister Ford. He got fifty mules, sixty, from San Antonio. We take them together.'

The Quimpers liked Garza, for the young man was so enthusiastic that his ebullience became infectious: 'Mr Ford, fine man. He give me money, I get him mules in Mexico. Maybe I buy four, five more right here?'

The Quimpers knew of no farmers in the vicinity who might have bred mules, but they promised young Garza to watch his while he scouted the river, and on the next day the irrepressible young man reappeared with four good animals: 'I always find them somewhere.'

During the young muleteer's last night at the inn, Mattie could not control her curiosity: 'Your mother? What's she think about such a trip? To New Orleans?'

'She's dead. But I go on trail first time, twelve years old.'

'Twelve?'

'She tell me: "You got to learn when you young."'

'Where's your home?'

'Río Grande. Lots of land. Lots of children, too. Brothers get land. I get mules.'

Despite her inclination to be impartial in most things, she could not help comparing this adventurous Mexican with her timorous son: 'Weren't you afraid? Twelve years old?'

'No,' he said brightly. 'Men all alike, Mexican, Texican. You quick, you got a little money, is all right.'

'What was your mother like?' Mattie asked as she passed her salted pecans.

'Most beautiful girl in San Antonio. Everybody said so. Frenchman wanted to marry her. American, too. But she walk to Río Grande to marry my father. Nine children. Wonderful love story.'

'And what will you do?'

'Make much money, New Orleans. Then help my sisters find husbands.'

When the young fellow headed up the trail with his twenty-one mules, Jubal said: 'He's the best visitor we've had since Father Clooney left.' Then he added: 'I think I'll learn Spanish, serious.' When he caught the rhythm of that beautiful language, probably the easiest on earth for a stranger to learn, he told his wife: 'When I had to argue with that Ripperdá at Nacogdoches, I wanted nothin' to do with Mexicans. But now that I see this land, and a fine young man like Garza, I'm beginnin' to think that Mexico is where we'll spend our years.' She replied: 'Texas, Tennessee, they all seem the same. Catholic, Protestant, likewise.'

'But you said you respected Reverend Harrison?'

'I respect Father Clooney, but that don't make me a Catholic.'

At times Jubal could not understand his thin, secretive wife. Her indifference to some things mystified him. She could work interminably without complaint. She ran the ferry, and certainly it was she who kept the inn functioning. But she always came back to her two obsessions: 'Jubal, I won't live in this cave-house much longer,' and, 'Jubal, we got to get hold of that land on the other end of the ferry.'

To the first demand her husband temporized: 'As soon as we get ahead, I'll build you a real house,' and to the second he reasoned: 'You heard Austin say you can't control land on both sides of the river,' and she asked bluntly: 'Does Austin need to know?' and sometimes when the ferry was waiting on the far side of the river, Jubal would see his wife marching about the land, driving stakes to mark what she wanted.

She was doing this one day when the Karankawas struck, and only by rushing down to the river and jumping onto the raft as it slid away from the shore did she escape being killed. The Indians raged along the bank, then disappeared into the wood on that side, rampaging far toward isolated cabins, where they killed the inhabitants.

The response was powerful. A contingent of thirty well-armed men marched down to the new headquarters settlement of San Felipe, where they joined with settlers from the coast in a ten-day campaign against the Kronks. When the Brazos River men straggled back to the ferry, they told Mattie wondrous tales about their battles: 'We overtook them in their camp. Ten of us up here. Ten over here. Ten makin' the attack. Cross-fired them till they had to accept a truce.'

'Was Yancey in the fight?' Mattie asked.

'No, he watched the horses.'

'Not right for a boy to be killin' folks.'

'He better kill Indians or they're gonna kill him.'

There was a strange outcome to this inconclusive battle. One morning when Mattie had guided the ferry to the far bank, depositing two travelers headed for Nacogdoches, she heard a rustling in the woods and saw to her horror that a very tall Karankawa was hiding there, armed with an old-fashioned gun. Unable to reach the ferry as before, she reached for some stick with which to defend herself, but the big Indian put down his weapon and came forward with hands outstretched. Because Mattie had always been willing to accept as her brother any honest man she encountered, she felt no hesitancy in dropping her stick and holding forth her hands, and thus began a strange friendship with a brave the Quimpers called The Kronk.

He lived in a self-made hut beside the inn, and when he had learned a few words of English he explained, with the help of vigorous signs, that the men of his family had led the sortie against the Brazos cabins and had been practically eliminated in the retaliation: 'Sun goes down. Karankawas no more.' He spoke with great sorrow of the deplorable time in which he lived: 'White man too strong. He break us.' He made a snapping sound with his fingers, like twigs being shattered. He was capable of real grief, as when he spoke of his women slain in the last battle: 'Babies, they best. Always hope, babies grow.' He liked Yancey, who was terrified of him, and longed to teach the boy those things fathers teach their sons, but young Quimper drew away, and one night Mattie was appalled when her son said: 'If a new battle starts, the men will kill Kronk for sure.'

When Mattie upbraided him for the insensitivity she perceived, Yancey replied: 'He's an Indian, ain't he?' and the conversation ended.

The Kronk was so helpful around the cave-house that Jubal said one morning: 'Mattie, I think that with Kronk's help we might could build you a set of real outside walls for this dugout,' but she snapped: 'I don't want no improvements. I want a real house with four walls around,' and he laughed: 'We ain't that ambitious.'

With great effort Jubal, The Kronk and Yancey chopped out some stout lengths to substitute for the vertical poles that had framed their cabin, and slowly, finishing one side after another, they inserted the heavy logs, converting their flimsy-walled cave-house into a sturdy one. Travelers familiar with the former stopping place congratulated them on the improvement, but invariably the Quimpers confessed: 'We couldn't of done it without The Kronk.'

Strangers who had often been required to fight the Indians were sometimes startled to find a real Karankawa living at the ferry, but those who settled in the area grew accustomed to the bronzed giant with the flashing white teeth. They often found him sitting with Mattie, talking in his strange way with words which only she seemed to understand. She was not afraid to ask him anything, and one afternoon she said bluntly: 'Why did you

Kronks eat people?' and he explained with grunts and gestures and the few words he knew that it was not done from hunger but as a ritual, confirming victory in battle or as a source of valor, as when warriors ate the heart, liver and tongue of a gallant adversary.

'But you did eat them?' she asked and he replied: 'Good. Like turkey.'

He became a kind of unpaid servant at the inn, but in return for his help he did receive food and such clothing as he wanted and the Quimpers were able to provide. His chief contribution was as a hunter, and under Jubal's tutelage he learned to be as parsimonious with his powder and lead as Quimper himself. With a fine hunter like The Kronk available, Jubal no longer took Yancey with him, for the boy was useless in the field. The Kronk was a skilled shot, and with his gun, which his tribe had purchased from French traders in the early years of the century, he could knock down a buffalo or trail a deer almost as well as Jubal himself. As a pair they were formidable, and travelers grew accustomed to having copious helpings of meat when they visited Quimper's inn.

Once when he returned with three slain deer, Mattie asked: 'Why do you shoot so many deer? So few turkey?' And he explained: 'Deer easy, turkey damn hard.' When she asked the difference, he said: 'Kronk sneak up, deer see. They think, "Is Kronk or tree stump?" and they stand there, I shoot. But when Kronk sneak up on turkey, leader cry, "By God, Kronk comin'!" and off they go. Kronk never see 'em again.'

Often in the long months of that first year before Mattie's corn had ripened or the crops matured, meat was all they had had. Months would pass without flour for the making of bread; salt was scarce; vegetables did not yet exist; and men would say: 'Last night I dreamed of fresh bread, covered with butter and sprinkled with salt. God, how I hate venison.' But when they had Jubal's honey to flavor the great chunks of roasted meat, the frontiersmen stopped complaining. 'It's uncanny how Jubal can smell out a honey tree three miles away,' they said, but others said: 'He's just as good at trackin' bear. When Mattie smokes it properly, you cain't tell it from Pennsylvania bacon.' But what Jubal really enjoyed was stalking the wild turkey, for as he told the others: 'Salt or no salt, bread or no bread, that

312

bird is delicious.'

Once a wandering Irishman named Mulrooney brought the Quimpers a bundle containing real flour, about three pounds, which he had acquired at great cost from an incoming vessel at the mouth of the Brazos: 'Could you make me some bread? I'm starvin' for bread.'

Mattie said that she could, if he'd let her keep some slices: 'Because I'm starvin' for bread, too.' But when he saw that she was preparing to mix a dough using most of his flour, he protested: 'No, ma'am! No!' And he told her that in backwoods Tejas they used half flour, half acorn, and he proceeded to take Yancey with him to gather the latter.

'No, not that kind,' Mulrooney said. 'Them's red oaks. Very high in tannic acid. Burn your gut.' What he sought were the fat, beautiful acorns of the live oak, a variety whose nuts were reassuringly deficient in tannin. The numerous but tiny acorns of the post oak he ignored completely: 'Waste of time. Not enough meat.'

When he and Yancey had a bag full of the rich-looking nuts, he peeled them and asked for a bucket of scalding water, in which he boiled them for three hours: 'We're drivin' out the acid. Now, when that's done, we boil them again for three hours in very salty water. Sweetens 'em up.'

The two boilings took most of a day, but that night he spread the blanched acorns before the fire so that they might be crushed and pulverized at dawn. When this was done he had a fine white flour almost indistinguishable from the bought variety, and from this mix Mattie made her bread.

'By God, that's good!' Mulrooney exclaimed when his first piece was smeared with honey. 'You know, Miss Mattie, you and me could make a fortune with this here bread,' and the Quimpers agreed that it was palatable. It was more than that. 'It's damned good,' Jubal said, and he told Mattie: 'Remember how he did it. Stay away from them red oaks.'

On a summer day in 1824, as Mattie poled her ferry across the Brazos, she saw well to the west a phenomenon which did not startle her but which did attract her attention. As she explained later: 'I thought nothin' of it, at first. Dark clouds along the horizon, but after a while I realized they were darker than any I'd seen before. And they didn't move like an ordinary storm. Just hung there, like a distant curtain.'

While the darkness intensified without any visible motion, she deposited her passenger on the far shore: 'Mister, somethin' strange. I'd watch for cover.'

'What do you think it is?' the man asked, and she said: 'I don't rightly know, but some place back there is catchin' rain. And if they're gettin' it now, we'll get it soon.'

When she returned to her own side of the river she called for Jubal, but he was off tracking honey bees, so she spent a few minutes outside, studying the storm: 'Yancey! Come here and see this cloud.'

When the boy stood with her, she repeated: 'Somebody upriver's catchin' a lot of rain,' and soon thereafter Jubal came running home with news that the river was rising.

For most of that long summer day the tremendous black clouds remained motionless along the northwestern horizon, depositing enormous quantities of rain, so that as dusk approached, the Brazos showed a sullen rise of nearly a foot. Jubal said: 'If it starts to rain here, Mattie, that river could really run wild.'

When the first drops did come splattering down, just at nightfall, Mattie told her men: 'I think I'll stay with the ferry ... in case,' and by the time she poled it across the river to the more protected anchoring place on the opposite shore, the rain was falling not in drops but in torrents, and she realized that it was bound to lift the river level so drastically that she would have to remain there through the night and away from the turbulent center of the rampaging river. She was drenched. Hair, eyes, clothes, hands, all were soaked in the lashing rain. From time to time as she poled away from the uncontrolled flood she became aware that great trees, uprooted from the northwest, were moving down the current, and these she must avoid.

Will the cabin survive? she asked herself toward dawn when it became apparent that this was to be a historic flood, far in excess of any whose remnants Jubal had pointed out to her on that first day. 'Pray God it doesn't reach our hill.'

In its outer reaches, of course, the great flood was not a swift-moving body of water; it was a quiet intrusion, sometimes hardly moving at all, but remorselessly it submerged everything; only at the center of the riverbed did the waters form a foaming, rampaging, irresistible torrent. Fifty miles to the south, where the distance between the Brazos and the Colorado

narrowed to a corridor, the flood became so tremendous that the back waters from the two rivers actually joined in a great sweeping ocean. At Quimper's Ferry the flood rose so high, it drove Mattie three miles inland before she managed to tie her craft to the branches of an oak whose trunk was seven feet under water.

There she remained for two cold days until she saw that the waters were beginning to recede, whereupon she poled across fields to where the ferry was customarily tied, and as the water swiftly dropped, she crossed the Brazos and brought her craft home. 'We thought you were dead,' her husband said matter-of-factly as she climbed up to her rain-soaked cabin, and she told him: 'I thought I was, too, but God helped with the pole.' She looked at their undamaged home, then kissed her husband: 'Thank God, Jubal, you made us build up here.'

Yancey broke in: 'When the flood came three feet up the wall we thought we was done. But The Kronk led Pop and me to that grove of oaks and tied ourself in a tree.' Jubal hushed him: 'We was all lucky. And for that we can thank God. I wish Father Clooney was here to lead us in prayer.' And for the next hundred years people along the Brazos would remember it as 'the year the Brazos ran wild' or 'the year the rivers joined. Mattie recalled it as 'the year I lost my corn.'

The Quimpers were less lucky with another event caused by the flood, and this too would be remembered. The excessive waters disturbed many animals, causing them to venture into new areas and adopt new habits, and one of those most seriously displaced was a huge rattlesnake eight feet three inches long from the tip of his rattle and as big around as a small tree. He was really a monstrous creature, with a head as big as a soup plate and fangs so huge and powerful, they could discharge a dreadful injection. Veteran of many struggles, master of the sudden ambush, he had subdued baby pigs and fawns and rabbits and a multitude of rats and mice. His traditional home had been sixteen miles up the Brazos in a rocky ledge that gave him excellent protection and a steady supply of victims, but the floods had dislodged him and sent him tumbling down the river along with deer and alligators and javelinas. During the height of the flood each animal was so preoccupied with its own salvation that it ignored friends and enemies alike, but as the waters receded, each resumed its habits, and the snake found itself far downstream, lodged in unfamiliar rocks and with a most uncertain food supply.

The rattler now had to be more venturesome than usual, and began foraging far from its crevice. Sometimes it went down close to the river, exploring the rocks there, and on other days it slithered inland, watching always to be sure that it had adequate cover to protect it from the blazing sun whose unimpeded heat would kill it. Mice, rabbits, squirrels, birds – the great reptile devoured them all, stunning them first with sharp jabs of its fangs, then swallowing them slowly and constricting its belly muscles to break down the bones and digest the food.

The rattler was a fearsome beast, made more so by frontier legend, most of it spurious: 'It cain't strike at you elsen it's coiled. Needs the springin' power of its coils. Then it can reach out twice its length.' Coiled, it could strike with remarkable accuracy; uncoiled, less so, and never more than half its length. This monster could strike four feet, a menacing distance.

'The snake, he cain't never strike you elsen he warns you first with a shake of his rattles. "God's recompense," we call it.' Most of the time when hunting small animals it struck with no warning, but often at the approach of a man or a large animal, it activated its rattles furiously to scare away the intruder.

'A rattler is thrifty, carries just enough venom to kill a man.' Later experts would demonstrate that whereas twenty-five milligrams would kill a child, and one hundred a man, a grown rattler could deliver two hundred fifty milligrams, enough to kill two men, while a really big snake could inject a thousand milligrams in one shot.

'One drop of rattlesnake venom in your bloodstream, you're dead.' Many frontiersmen had been struck by medium-sized rattlers and survived, but to be injected with a full charge of venom by a snake as large as this one would be fatal.

'No man ain't never been struck by a full-sized rattler and lived.' A rattler carried only a limited supply of venom in its sacs, and if it had recently discharged this in killing some animal, it could strike its next victim with the full force of its fangs and inflict only a small wound that would quickly heal. Certain boastful men had survived as a result of this phenomenon.

This great beast at Quimper's Ferry, longer than any hitherto seen along the Brazos, did not seek contact with human beings; it did its best to avoid them, but if any threatened the quiet of its domain, it could strike with terrifying force. It would not have come into contact with the Quimpers had not Yancey gone probing along the farther bank, not doing any serious work or accomplishing much, but merely poking into holes with a stick to see what might be happening. As he approached where the snake lay hidden, he heard but did not recognize the warning rattle. Thinking it to be a bird or some noisy insect, he probed further, and found himself staring at the huge coiled snake not ten feet away.

'Mom!' he screamed, and Mattie, working at the ferry, grabbed the gun she kept aboard for protection against wandering Karankawas, and ran to help, but when she reached Yancey she found him immobilized, pointing at the coiled snake whose rattles echoed. 'Do something!' he pleaded.

Infuriated by his craven behavior and terrified of the snake, she pushed her son aside, and with her heart beating at a rate which must soon cause her to faint, she raised the gun. Not firing blindly, because she knew she had only one chance, she took aim as the snake prepared for its deadly thrust, and pulled the trigger. She felt the shock against her shoulder; she felt the snake brush against her knee; and she fainted.

Yancey, seeing only that the rattler had struck at his mother and that she had fallen, concluded that the snake had killed her, despite the gun blast, and ran screaming up the river to the ferry landing: 'Pop! A big rattler killed Mom.'

Jubal and The Kronk waded and swam across the Brazos and ran trembling to where Mattie still lay beside the dreadful snake, and when they saw her they supposed that each had killed the other: 'Snake hit her just as she pulled the trigger. Oh Jesus!' But then the Indian saw her right hand twitch, and when he stepped gingerly past the snake and lifted her head, he saw that she was still breathing. Inspecting her throat and face, he called: 'No dead. Scared. Scared.'

Jubal and Yancey, taking over from the Indian, satisfied themselves that Mattie was indeed alive, and with a love they had not shown before, they carried her upriver to the ferry, where they placed her tenderly aboard, but before they pushed off, The Kronk ran up carrying the enormous snake, whose head had been blown apart. 'We keep,' he said, and the men knew that he intended eating at least part of the fearful enemy out of respect and envy for the courage it had shown.

When Jubal tanned the skin he stretched it to maximum length, extending the accordionlike scales until he had an awesome object that climbed the entire wall of the cabin and back four feet along the ceiling, ten feet, five inches in majestic length. Recovering the skull from The Kronk, he attached it so that it appeared to be striking at the diners seated below, and strangers seeing it for the first time said: 'They warn't never a snake that big,' but Jubal said proudly: 'Finger them rattlers yourselves. They're real, and my little wife's the one who killed it.'

Whenever Mattie looked at the fearful object she thought not of her own heroism in battling the monster but of her son's behavior. She never spoke of this to the boy's father, and certainly not to the boy himself, but she did often recall her own father's stern admonition to his children when they were living in a Tennessee hovel and subsisting on beans with an occasional slab of pork: 'You don't have to fight the world, and you don't have to be the bravest in the village, but by God, if you're my kids, you got to do what's right when you face danger. I don't care if the other man is twice your size. Go at his throat.' Mattie had gone at the great serpent's throat; her son had not.

Mattie kept her small collection of coins gained from running the ferry in the canvas bag which had once protected her corn, and one morning when she felt satisfied that she had saved enough, she asked a farmer who was heading downriver to the rude store at Austin's headquarters at San Felipe to perform a commission for her; two months later a man on horseback arrived bearing a small keg of nails and a long package. It was a pit saw with two big handles, and when it was assembled she told her husband: 'We'll rip us some planks and build us a real house. I'll live underground no more.'

The Kronk was essential to her plans, for she needed his strength to dig a pit deep enough for a man to stand in: 'And now cut the tallest, thickest tree trunk you can move to the pit.' And when it was hauled across the pit, she climbed down with instructions to her men: 'I'll do the dirty work. You do the strong.'

Grasping the lower handle, she pushed the saw up, while one of the men standing astride the log topside pulled it into cutting position. Then the men bore down while Mattie pulled, and in this laborious way, with sawdust in her face day after day, she supervised the cutting of the planks needed for her house. She never complained, for she kept before her the vision of the home that was to be, and when she felt she had enough planks, she climbed out of her pit, dragooned two travelers to stay as helpers, and started building her house.

At various places in Texas she had seen the type of house she wanted; it had come west from South Carolina and Georgia and provided an excellent device for surviving in a hot or humid climate. 'It's called a dog-run,' Mattie explained to The Kronk, who did much of the heavy work. 'We build a little square house here. Leave seventeen feet open space, then build another, same size, over here.'

'Why here?' the Indian asked, and she said: 'One house sleeping. One house living,' and he said: 'Work too damn much.'

Then she explained that the two squares would not remain separated: 'Up there, one long roof over everything. Down here, one long porch, end to end.'

'In between, what?' The Kronk asked, and she said: 'Place for cool breezes. Place for dogs to run in the day, sleep at night.' He then wanted to know what the porch was for, and she said: 'Work done, we watch sunset. Travelers come, they sleep on porch,' and he said approvingly: 'Damn good.'

When it was completed, with liberal use of improvised wattle-and-vine walls that would serve until more planks could be cut, Mattie waited till Reverend Harrison came by on his way to Stephen Austin's headquarters: 'Will you bless this house, Reverend?' He did, praying that the Quimpers would enjoy years of happiness and prosperity in it, but some weeks later, when Harrison was returning from his talk with Austin, he appeared at the door of the house unannounced, to find Jubal and two travelers playing cards and swigging from a jug of muscadine wine. Mattie saw the flare of disgust that crossed his face as he said: 'Do you allow gaming in a house I dedicated to the Lord?'

'I do,' she said. 'Jesus drank wine.'

Coming close to pronouncing anathema upon her, he cried: 'You and your husband and all of them stand in danger of being rejected of God. Gaming and drinking, they'll be the ruin of Texas.'

Jubal had always known it was bound to happen, and now it was upon him: Reverend Harrison and Father Clooney had arrived at the same time, and some kind of ugly confrontation seemed inescapable.

The Protestant clergyman came first, on a surreptitious round of Methodist prayer meetings at which he delivered agitating news about events in Mexico City, the capital of the country: 'They threw out the Spanish, as we know. But before long they invited that fool Iturbide to make himself emperor, and what American would want to live under the dictates of an emperor?'

A man who had traveled in Mexico said dryly: 'They shot him last year,' but this did not alter Harrison's diatribe: 'Each day men like Iturbide remain in control, the yoke of Rome is fastened ever more tightly about our necks. Each day we do not resist, we become more surely the vassals of the Pope, and I can feel in my bones the constant loss of freedom we're undergoing. We're in peril, and we must bind ourselves ever closer or we shall lose our freedom, our church and our understanding of God.'

Night after night he conducted his frenzied meetings, until he had many of the farmers almost prepared to take up arms to defend their rights, and he was equally persuasive with women, for he spoke eloquently of what would happen if their children never learned the beneficent lessons of Protestantism: 'Do you want your daughters to become nuns, locked away in some convent, the prey of priests, never to know the blessings of a true Christian home?' He also frightened them with graphic descriptions of what it meant to worship regularly in the

320

Catholic mode, and he nailed down his preaching with a plea which came from the heart: 'The Protestant church is the true church of Jesus Christ. He called it forth. He ordained us to do His great work on earth. And we must remain faithful to His precepts.'

He was effective because his listeners, hungry for moral guidance, always knew where he stood. He was for the New Testament, morality and Methodism; he was against Rome, alcohol, sexual indulgence, dancing and any kind of irreverence. But in this summer of 1825 he added a bold new dimension to his preaching: 'I cannot believe that the good Christians who came to Texas from Kentucky and Tennessee will long continue under the tyranny of Mexico and Rome.' And once he said this, he realized its implications: 'When that joyous day comes, we'll join the United States.' He justified this treasonous behavior as 'faith plus patriotism.'

He was conducting a secret meeting for elders at the Quimpers' inn late one afternoon, with some twenty farmers surrounding him, when a watcher, posted to detect any approach of Mexican soldiers, ran in: 'Father Clooney comin' on his mule.' And when the conspirators peered out they saw the familiar figure of the Irish priest, older now and thinner, riding up to the porch.

They had no opportunity to disperse before he dismounted, brushed the dust from his black vestments, and entered. One glance at the unusual number of guests and the tall minister who commanded them satisfied him as to what was happening, but he affected not to know. Greeting Reverend Harrison warmly, as if he were no more than some farmer he had met on the Trinity, he smiled at the others he had known before and said to the strangers: 'I don't believe I know you. Father Clooney, of Ballyclooney, County Clare in Ireland, appointed by the Mexican government to be vicar of this parish.'

Having put the conspirators at ease, he then offended their leaders by asking Mattie Quimper: 'Could a perishing pilgrim have a wee nip?' and when she provided one, Reverend Harrison glared at the disgraceful cup as if he wished to turn its contents into vitriol.

Father Clooney was filled with news acquired at the assembly of the Catholic clergy recently convened in San

Antonio, and although his personal recollections of that meeting were not altogether pleasant, he was eager to share the substantial news which came from it. His unhappiness stemmed from the way he had been treated – as an interloping Irishman who spoke abominable Spanish – by the more austere Spanish priests who had been trained in Spain and the older Mexican fathers with their education in Mexico City and Querétaro. They had scorned him as a village nothing, a cactus-priest of the bayous, not really one of them and not to be trusted. They had heard of his excessive drinking and of his casual approach to conversion, and many suspected that he was a secret agent sent by the American government to prepare the way for a Yankee takeover. But since none of them would have dreamed of moving one step north from San Antonio or of serving in wilderness areas like the banks of the Trinity, they were content to let this renegade Irishman do their pastoral work for them. His latest experience with these arrogant superiors had not been pleasant but it had been instructive, and now he gushed forth the resounding news:

'As you've surely heard, there was a wonderful revolution in Mexico last year. Emperor Iturbide was overthrown by a group of sterling patriots, and the old viciousness has been cleansed away. A new Mexico, a new life for all of us.

'The hero of the change is a most splendid man, devout, loyal, brave. General Antonio López de Santa Anna. You'll hear much of him in the glorious days ahead, for he brings freedom and distinction to the word *patriot*.

'But the excelling news is that Santa Anna and his associates have given us a new constitution, and I promise you that in Mexican history the date 1824 will become as famous as 1776 is in your America. Because the Constitution of 1824 is a noble document, assuring us the freedoms we've sought. It gives Coahuila-y-Tejas its own state government. It protects us. It guarantees a permanent republic. And it erases all memories of Emperor Iturbide and his follies. What a glorious day for Mexico!'

His listeners soon caught the infection of his enthusiasm, for if what he said about the new constitution was true, most frictions

322

with the central government would be eliminated, and Tejas, under its own regional government, would have a chance to forge ahead. But Reverend Harrison had a pertinent question: 'What does the new rule say about religion?' and Father Clooney answered forthrightly: 'It says that the official religion of Mexico must forever be Roman Catholicism.'

'And will the official church be supported by our tax money?' Harrison asked, and again the round-faced priest gave a straight answer: 'The church will be supported, as before, by the public treasury.'

'If that is so, men who love freedom must oppose your new constitution.'

It was now dusk, and in the crowded dog-run two men of radically opposing views faced each other: Reverend Harrison, tall, austere, dreaming always of a greater Texas, and touched by God but unable because of the law to stand forth as the minister he was; and Father Clooney, the sometimes wavering Roman Catholic priest who was not wholly accepted by his own church but who stumbled along, fortified by his love of Jesus Christ and his compassion for souls wandering in the Tejas wilderness.

They were ill-matched. Harrison had more vigor and a much deeper conviction that what he was doing represented the drift of history and the will of Jesus Christ; Father Clooney was older, wiser, better educated, and fortified by a church that had existed for eighteen hundred years. One important characteristic was shared in common: both clerics aspired to do what was best for Texas, which they saw as one of the brightest hopes in North America or in the world.

Very carefully the priest asked Harrison: 'You say you cannot accept this excellent new law?'

'Not if it makes me pay for the support of a religion I cannot trust.'

Clooney did not flinch at this harsh dismissal: 'Reverend Harrison? Yes, I've known since the day you started holding these secret meetings who you were and what your interests were. Have I tried to interrupt your preaching? Have I put the soldiers to arresting you, which by law I should have done? Have you and I not survived amiably, and are we not friends this evening? If we trusted each other under that bad old constitution, surely we can do so under this good new one.'

Harrison and some of his people were stunned by the fact that Father Clooney had knowledge of their affairs, for they realized that they were subject to arrest, and one man asked: 'What are you going to do, now that you know?' and Clooney replied: 'Nothing. I would much rather have in Catholic Tejas people who were good Methodists than rascals who were poor Catholics and poor everything else. Friends' – and here his voice broke – 'we are striving to build in Tejas a new society, a strong one, a decent one. We cannot accomplish this if we are at each other's throat. And you cannot find the security you yearn for if you reject this new constitution.'

His urgent words struck a deep chord in Jubal Quimper's heart: 'If the new law gives us everything we want except religious freedom, I say let's accept it, because in the long run the press of people moving into Tejas will make it Protestant.' Unwisely he looked at Father Clooney, expecting the priest to confirm this probability, but this the old man could not do: 'The new law says that Mexico is a Catholic nation. Up here, at the edge of government, it doesn't seem that way. But from San Antonio south, you will travel many days before you find a Protestant. Of course Mexico is Catholic, and of course it must remain so. But the good Catholics of that nation will continue to govern Tejas much as they do now. You will enjoy respect and the ordinary freedoms.'

'I do not believe it,' Reverend Harrison snapped. 'Mark my words, we shall see Mexican troops along this river, coming here to enforce Catholicism and to put down Christianity.'

'What a terrible error in words!' Father Clooney said instantly. 'No religion monopolizes Christianity.'

'Catholicism tries to,' Harrison snapped, and the meeting ended. Many participants, in later years when some of the issues thus raised had been settled, wrote accounts of this famous confrontation, and one almost illiterate farmer summarized it best:

We had met at Queemper's Ferry to pray and bad luck trayled us, for Father Cloony the papist found us out and threttened to arrest us for our unlawful prayrs. Rev Harison debated with him and we went home hopeful for the days

324

ahed becaws the new laws of Mexico sounded good, but feerful of the yeers ahed becaws we beleeved that Rev Harison was right and that Texas would soon have to fite for her verry existance.

Promulgation of the reassuring Constitution of 1824 had a curious aftermath. Hopeful newcomers like Jubal Quimper were now encouraged to think of themselves as Mexicans, citizens of a liberal democracy not unlike that in the United States, and they began to refer to themselves as Texicans, a fortunate verbal invention. 'Stands to reason,' Jubal told Mattie, 'if they're Mexicans south of the Río Grande, we ought to be Texicans north of it.' And it was by this strong, musical name that they knew themselves.

Bathed in euphoria, the Texicans forgot Reverend Harrison's prediction that they would soon be fighting for their existence, but in 1825 that prophecy came true. The enemy, however, was not Mexico. The remaining Karankawas decided they had no chance of living as they had in the past unless they exterminated the white men who had intruded upon their historic territory. Intent upon defending themselves, they launched a series of raids so savage, so cruel in their extermination of lonely cabins and unprotected women that the settlers had no alternative but to fight back. 'Kill them now, or perish later!' was the mood at San Felipe as the settlers prepared for what they prayed would be the final battle.

One group of volunteers assembled at Quimper's Ferry, then marched south, where it would join men gathering along the coast. Since boys above the age of ten were expected to join the expedition with their own guns, Yancey, now aged thirteen, reported, and as the avengers approached the coast he felt his excitement mounting, for he was eager to perform well. But when they had sneaked close to one Karankawa settlement – a cluster of movable ba-acks, or tepees – and the time came for battle action, he froze as he had when confronted by the rattlesnake, and while those about him decimated this first contingent of Indians with a surprise volley, then exterminated them in the wild follow-up, he stood transfixed at the bloody killing.

'We wiped them out!' the volunteers shouted as scouts

advised them where to head in order to trap the next group of Kronks. Two men who had seen Yancey's craven behavior walked with him, offering advice: 'When the firin' starts, don't listen to the noise and never look at the Indians as human bein's. You're shootin' squirrels, that's all. You've shot squirrels, ain't you?' When Yancey said he had not, the men said: 'Well, you're goin' to shoot somethin' much better than squirrels tomorrow. You keep with us. We'll show you.'

That night the Quimper's Ferry people were overtaken by a late contingent from the Trinity, and foremost in that group was Reverend Harrison, who conducted services in the darkness, assuring the avengers that they were doing God's work in removing the Indian menace from this part of Texas: 'We shall always face an Indian enemy, wherever we move in Texas. And we shall enjoy no peace till we exterminate him.' When two men from the ferry region who had not known the minister before asked: 'You think the battle against them will go on forever?' he replied: 'The fight for goodness never ceases. Our grandchildren will be fighting Indians.'

On the next day, at about noon, the last great battle against the Karankawas took place, and these proud Indians, for centuries the lords of the three rivers and the scourge of those lesser tribes who tried to infiltrate, realized that their sunset was upon them, and they fought with terrible valor, one brave driving alone at the heart of the white army, coming on and on until he arrived at the mouth of the guns with only a broken stave in his hand.

'Urrk! Arrgh!' he shouted in meaningless syllables, trying to grasp with his bare hand the rifle barrels whose fiery discharges tore him apart.

In terrible struggle the mighty Karankawas died. Braves . . . old men . . . women . . . little girls . . . boys defying the rifles. A notable tribe endeavoured to protect its homeland, and failed. Toward evening a pitiful remnant fighting on the far edge of the encounter rallied under the leadership of two heroic warriors to break through the encircling ranks of white men. Signaling to other survivors, women and children alike, these few started a long retreat south toward refuge across the Río Grande, and after harrowing days without food or water they vanished, except for a few stragglers, from the soil of Texas, to be known no more except in fabled stories about 'them Kronks who ate people.'

They went in sorrow and defeat, the first of more than four-score Indian tribes who would be banished from Texas until the triumphant whites could boast: 'We ain't got no Indians in Texas. We couldn't abide 'em.' Sister American states would devise ways whereby the Indian and the white man could live together – not wholesome ways, nor sensible – but the citizens of Texas could not. The antipathies were too strong.

Yancey did not distinguish himself in this final battle, for, as before, the sound of gunfire immobilized him, and he could only watch as the struggle evolved. At one point in the battle a Karankawa dashed right past him, not fifteen feet away, and one of Yancey's counselors bellowed: 'Fire, goddamit, fire!' But Yancey was unable to do so.

However, on the way home, when he marched with other men, he began to talk about his heroics among the Karankawas, so that by the time he reached the ferry he had convinced himself that he had behaved with more than average bravery, and when he was close to the family dog-run he told his companions: 'You know, there's a Kronk who moves about here, now and then,' and this so excited the victorious Texicans that when they suddenly saw before them The Kronk, they unhesitatingly slew him, the last Karankawa the Brazos would ever see.

Mattie was appalled by this gratuitous slaughter, but when she confronted the killers, they said honestly: 'Yance never told us he was tame,' and she deduced the criminal part her son had played in this assassination. She did not chastise him for this terrible act, but on succeeding days as she sat on her porch at dusk, exhausted by the multiple tasks she was required to perform while Jubal was out hunting meat or searching for honey trees, she realized how severe her loss was in the death of The Kronk. He had been a member of the family, their custodian, their watchman, the one who stepped forward when there was work to do, the one with whom she talked when the men were away and she faced long days of work. Painfully, this savage Indian had made the transition to civilization, and in the end that civilization had destroyed him for no reason except that he was an Indian.

327

On the third evening, when she appreciated most clearly the dreadful loss she had sustained, and the reasons for it, she began to weep, not for The Kronk, whose days of confusion were over, but for all those who ventured into a strange land or encountered strange responsibilities, and the sorrow of civilization was almost more than she could bear. She wanted no more of war, no more of argument between Catholic and Protestant, no more confrontation between Mexico and the American states. She wanted only to operate her ferry, run her inn, feed the traveler, and save enough money to buy a new dress at the store in San Felipe or perhaps some extra forks and spoons.

But most of all, she prayed in her desolation that her son would somehow or other grow into manhood, with the capacity to meet a man's obligations.

No American settlers since the Revolution of 1776 had faced the nagging moral problems encountered by those citizens of the republic who moved into Texas in the period of 1820–1835. And none faced the confusions with more vacillating reactions than Jubal Quimper.

Even those later settlers who would cross an entire continent to build new homes in California or Oregon would have the reassurance that, in moving from one part of the United States to another, they would carry their religion, their language and their customary law with them. But when people like the Quimpers emigrated to Texas they surrendered such assurances, placing themselves under the constraints of a new religion, a new language and a much different system of law.

Facing these complexities, Mattie and Jubal followed one simple rule: 'Whatever Stephen F. Austin decides is probably right.' Like many others, they revered the strange little man, forgiving him his arbitrary manner. Mattie especially realized that there was a good deal wrong with Austin: Why has he never married? Is he afraid of women? And why does he stare at you with those fixed eyes, like a hawk? All he can think of is his colony.

But despite his faults, and they were many, she saw him as the reliable guide, and and whenever he stopped at her inn during his travels throughout the colony, she nodded approval to what he told the visitors who dropped by to talk politics with him: 'Gentlemen, Tejas will not only live under this new Mexican Constitution of 1824; it will prosper.'

'Aren't there weaknesses in it?' a farmer asked, and Austin snapped: 'There are weaknesses in every document drawn by the human mind. Our new law has certain peculiarities reflecting Mexican custom, but they will not impinge upon our freedom. Tejas is to be a Catholic state, but we've seen how easily we live under that constraint. And, yes, priests and soldiers will be tried in courts manned only by their own people, but that's always been the case and we haven't suffered.'

'Are you satisfied,' a settler from Alabama asked bluntly, 'to live under Mexican law for the rest of your life?' and Austin answered: 'I am.'

Jubal Quimper, usually agreeing with whoever spoke to him last, grasped Austin's hands and said: 'Mr Austin, I'll stand beside you as a Mexican citizen . . . permanent.'

But some days after Austin departed with this pledge of allegiance from the people at Quimper's Ferry, a copy of the new constitution arrived and the man from Alabama who had interrogated Austin rushed to the inn, waving the paper in the air: 'Good God! Listen to what this document says!' And he asked Quimper to read the offending passage: 'With the adoption of this constitution, slavery is forbidden throughout Tejas, and six months from this date, even the importation of slaves already on their way to Tejas will be outlawed.'

Neighbors quickly gathered, and thus began one of the insoluble contradictions of Texas history: of a hundred families like the Quimpers, not more than fifteen owned slaves, which meant that the vast majority could have had no financial interest in preserving slavery, yet most of those without slaves defended the institution and seemed ready to battle Saltillo to preserve it.

Jubal and Mattie were representative: 'We never had no slaves in Tennessee and didn't know many people who did. Lord knows, we don't have any to share our work here in Texas. But it stands to reason, it says right in the Bible that the sons of Ham shall be hewers of wood and drawers of water, and that's the way it's got to be.'

Mattie, who befriended everyone, even Karankawas, was especially strong in her condemnation of the proposed law: 'Niggers ain't really human. I don't yearn to own none, but

329

those good folks who bring 'em here ought to be protected in their property.'

This question so agitated the settlers that a delegation of three planters, led by Jubal Quimper, went resolutely down to Austin's headquarters and told him bluntly: 'Our liberties must be preserved.' And with that simple statement arose the tantalizing ethical issue which would plague Texas for decades, because good-hearted men like Jubal Quimper honestly believed that their freedom could be ensured only by the right to enslave others.

Austin, perceiving the moral wrong in this position, laid bare his honest feelings: 'Gentlemen, I tell you frankly that I oppose slavery with every fiber of my body, now and forever. I condemn it four times. It's bad for society in general. It's bad for commerce. And bad for both master and slave. Never have I departed from this belief and never shall I. The wise men in Saltillo who framed our constitution knew what they were doing, and they did it well. Slavery should be outlawed.'

There could have been no statement of principle more unequivocal than that, and it persuaded Quimper, who spoke for the others: 'You're right, Stephen. What we need is a whole new state. No masters. No slaves.'

But no sooner had Quimper renewed his support than an extraordinary reversal occurred, for that night Austin began to review the problem, not according to his personal convictions but according to his role as leader of a tentative colony not yet securely based, and the more he studied reality the more convinced he became that Tejas had little chance of survival if it failed to attract hundreds or even thousands of established Southern gentlemen who would bring with them prosperity and culture. In an open meeting next morning he attacked the philosophical problem first.

'Gentlemen, order, order. I do not derogate the great states of Kentucky and Tennessee from which many of our finest settlers have come, nor do I speak against any man standing here. But I have become painfully aware that our colony can progress only if we attract in large numbers families of wealth, high cultural attainment and sound moral training from our educated Southern states like Virginia, Carolina, Georgia, Alabama and Mississippi. When they join us with their books, their wealth and their long experience in trade, they will make Tejas a state of which we shall be proud.'

There was a long silence while the inescapable truth of what he had said was judged, and then Quimper cried: 'You're right, Stephen. We need schoolteachers and men who know the Bible.'

While many nodded and some whispered, Austin waited, almost afraid to point out the consequences of what he had just said, but finally he summoned courage and spoke: 'Such men will not join us if they cannot bring their slaves. What white man could grow sugar cane in our steaming river bottoms? What white man from Alabama could toil under our blazing sun chopping cotton? Then pick it? Then haul it to the gin? Only Negroes can do such work, and slavery seems to be the pattern ordained by God for handling them. It is clear that Tejas must have slavery or perish.'

So Jubal Quimper, in a committee of seven, only one of whom owned slaves, helped Austin draft an appeal to the state government in Saltillo and the national government in Mexico City, explaining that whereas the abolishment of slavery was unquestionably right for the rest of the nation, it was not appropriate, at this time, in a frontier region like Tejas: 'We cannot work our fields without slaves, and we cannot populate our empty spaces unless men of property from the Southern states of America are permitted to bring their slaves with them.' Austin, a man who hated slavery, had become its champion.

During the trip back home Quimper reviewed the sudden shifts of their leader: 'First he was stern morality: "Slavery must be abolished." Then he was all for the South: "They must be allowed to bring in their slaves." I wonder where he really stands? Matter of fact, I wonder where I stand.'

This moral confusion on the part of Austin and his adherents would continue, for when Austin concocted a dream for enticing thousands of German and Swiss settlers, he became an ardent opponent of slavery, in deference to their known dislike for keeping anyone in bondage:

'The possibility of such a country as Tejas being overrun by a slave population almost makes me weep. Slavery is an injustice and a demoralizing agent in society. When I started

331

this colony I was forced to tolerate it for a while, because I had to draw upon the slave states for my emigrants. But slavery is now most positively prohibited by our Mexican constitution and I hope it may always be so, for it is a curse of the curses and one of the worst reproaches of civilized man.'

But later he would be forced once more to consider the realities of settlement, and again he would reverse himself completely:

'I used to oppose slavery, but during the last six months I have had to restudy the matter and now conclude that Texas *must* be a slave country. Circumstances and unavoidable necessity compel it. It is the wish of the people, and I shall do all I can, prudently, in favor of it. I will do so.'

Quimper, listening to this speech, noticed that Austin had dropped the Spanish *Tejas* in favor of the English *Texas*, indicating serious doubt that his colony could long remain with Mexico, which he also now pronounced in the American fashion. Never again would his friends hear him use the Spanish names which he had tried so faithfully to defend but which he now abandoned forever.

Jubal's attention to such heady political matters was diverted in late 1828 by an exciting letter from his former lawyer in Gallatin, Tennessee:

Jubal, I send you great news! Your persecutor, Hammond Carver, was killed in a duel, and this legally terminates his case against you. I have ascertained from his survivors that they have no intention of resurrecting the suit, and they have acknowledged in writing that the contested land is yours, along with all the buildings on it. You find yourself not a rich man but one with ample fields and some money, which you can claim only by coming here in person. Do so immediately, for you and Mattie have many friends in these parts who are eager to see you resume your life among them.

This heaven-sent opportunity to escape the tensions of a frontier Texas made Jubal realize how much he longed for the stability of a settled Tennessee, and he was ready to depart immediately: 'Mattie! We're free to go home!'

She deflated his enthusiasm by saying with bulldog stubbornness: 'I have no wish to see Tennessee again,' and he began placing before her all the reasons why they should return to the pleasant life that they could now have in Gallatin: 'Arthur says we won't be really rich, but we'll have enough to buy us a couple of slaves. You won't have to worry about the ferry, and we won't have strangers traipsin' into our home. More important, we can have real walls and windows.'

He threw at her an impressive summary of the differences between civilized Tennessee and barbarian Texas, but in the end she countered with an incontestable reply: 'I like it here.' And in fragmentary comments she let him and Yancey know how deeply Texas had infected her: 'Nothin' I saw in Tennessee is better than that clump of oak trees in the meadow.' During another debate she said: 'I like the Brazos, the way it rises and falls, like it had a will of its own.' On a different day she said: 'My heart beats faster when a stranger comes to the door at night, needin' food – and we have it.' And finally: 'Like a rock gatherin' moss, I've allowed Texas to grow over me, and I admire the feel.'

Guarding each word, she said: 'You and Yancey can go back and settle the claim, and if you're so minded, you can stay. I'll give you your freedom, in the courts if you wish, but this is now my home and I expect to end my days runnin' my ferry.'

The force of her statement made Jubal pause. Twice he started to speak but could find no words, then abruptly he turned away and went to walk beneath the oak trees that Mattie loved so deeply, and as he tried to see their new home through her eyes he began to appreciate why she loved Texas and was so unwilling to leave it. After more than an hour of walking along the Brazos he returned to his wife and took her in his arms: 'Mattie, old girl, if this is your home, it'll be mine, too. I could never leave you, because I know how often it was you held me upright.'

She cherished his embrace but did not wish to impede him: 'If your heart's set on Tennessee . . .'

'Hush! I'll go back, sell the land, and buy some lumber in New Orleans. I'm goin' to build you a proper house.' With this commitment, from which he would never deviate, Jubal Quimper became a Texican.

That day Mattie, with a song trembling on her lips, started to pack the goods her two men would require for their long trip, but her work was interrupted by Yancey, who came whispering: 'I don't want to go. Indians and that Strip and all,' and she could guess that what really held him back was his memory of that fistfight with the smaller boy. What will happen to him? she asked herself. A boy who refuses a journey up the Mississippi?

She had finished packing when a cloud of dust appeared from the south; Benito Garza was on his way to New Orleans with another convoy of mules for the American army. He was twenty-two now, a slim, neat fellow with a small mustache, an ingratiating smile and a fair command of English: 'This time I take the mules myself. I do not need guide or trader from San Antonio.'

He had brought with him a Mexican boy, no more than fourteen, and a large remuda of some three dozen mules, which he hoped to augment as he moved north: 'I like to buy any mules you might have, Señor Quimper?' When Jubal said he had none, Garza asked: 'Is it true, señor? You're going to Tennessee?'

'I must.'

'A town on the Mississippi?'

'It's a state. Like Coahuila-y-Tejas.'

'But it is on the Mississippi?' When Quimper nodded, the ebullient young man slapped himself on the knee and cried: 'Then you must come with us! Save time, save money. Catch a steamboat up the river!' And he worked his arms like the pistons of a river boat, spouting imaginary steam with his mouth and sounding a whistle. Mattie was enthusiastic about such a plan and tried to persuade her son, now sixteen, to go along: 'You can help manage the mules, and you'll see the steamboat,' but he still refused to go, not wishing to take such risks.

The two men left in October and wandered up the Goliad Road with some fifty mules, adding to them at the Trinity and then keeping to the southernmost route along the Gulf till they crossed the Sabine into Louisiana. There they found tolerable roads leading to New Orleans, where Jubal stayed in Mexican lodgings with his two companions. He told Garza as the latter dickered with the American authorities over the prices of his mules: 'Benito, I'd enjoy travelin' with you some time again. You know how to move about.' And Garza said: 'You'd be welcome. I need to practice English if so many of you are coming to Tejas.'

'You must. Because I'm tellin' you ... I'm warnin' you, really, Texas won't be Mexican forever.'

'I think it will be,' Garza said, and when they were back in their mean quarters he asked Quimper: 'How long, señor, have you been in Tejas?' and Quimper thought a moment, then said: 'Six years,' and Garza laughed: 'Señor! And you're telling me who is to run Tejas! My people explored Tejas three hundred years ago.'

Quimper considered this, then said with no rancor: 'Amigo, that may have ensured you a foothold in what you call Tejas. But in the Texas that's comin' you better speak like an American and think like one, or you're goin' to be homeless,' and the young man snapped: 'Garzas will be living here when you've run back to Tennessee.'

The only thing about Garza that Quimper did not like was this quickness at resenting whatever the young man interpreted as an insult to his Hispanic heritage: 'If you're goin' to live in a white man's state, Benito, you mustn't be so touchy.'

'But I am a white man, and Tejas is my state.' Quimper let the matter drop, for he no longer tried to understand how the Hispanic mind worked.

When Quimper left the Mississippi riverboat at Memphis and started overland to Nashville, he experienced several moments of solemn discovery: Tennessee is so cramped compared to Texas ... A man can hardly breathe, hemmed in by all these trees. He did enjoy the snug little towns and the orderly plantations manned by slaves, but repeatedly he caught himself longing for the Brazos and great, open freedom of Texas: I'll sell the land and get back home.

He spent his first two weeks in Nashville listening to talk about those events which had occurred since his hasty departure in 1822: 'We got ourself a great new governor, Sam Houston, him as fought with Andy Jackson against the Indians

335

at Horseshoe Bend. Strong man, strong ideas, outstandin' patriot. Goin' to be President of the United States one of these days.'

Wherever he moved he heard good reports of Houston: 'Big man, you know. Brave, too. Lived among the Indians. Speaks their language, I'm told. Taller than that post, I'd judge.'

'How did he become governor?'

'Oh, he was a military hero! General Jackson thought very highly of him, and that helped him get elected to the Congress, in Washington. How many terms did he serve, Jake? Three?'

'Two,' Jake said. 'Could of been elected permanent, or senator, either. But we wanted him for governor, and with Andy Jackson's help, we got him.'

Quimper had no opportunity to see Houston in Nashville, for men explained that the governor had business to the east: 'You know, he's standin' for reelection this year. Foolish for anyone to run against him, most popular man in the state.'

By the time Quimper left Nashville for the short trip to Gallatin he had heard so much about Houston that he said, on his last night in town: 'He's the kind of man we could use in Texas,' but his fellow diners dismissed the idea: 'His home's in Tennessee. Hell, he *is* Tennessee.'

When Quimper arrived in his old hometown of Gallatin he heard only one topic of conversation: 'Little Eliza Allen of our town! She's goin' to marry the governor! Tomorrow!' Since the Allens were among the leading citizens in Gallatin, Jubal did not know them socially, but he was pleased to think that if the wedding was public, he would have a chance to see and perhaps even meet Sam Houston.

The celebrations took place on 11 January 1829, and they were a sumptuous affair, for not often did a small town like Gallatin find one of its daughters marrying the governor of a state, a man certain to be reelected, and after a term or two in the federal Senate, perhaps be elected to the presidency. Several score of guests rode out from Nashville and others came long distances from the eastern part of the state, where Houston had once lived. He was a rising star with whom politicians of all stripes wished to be associated, and when Quimper saw him, a giant of a man, and holding on to his arm a delicate little woman dressed in white with just a touch of pink in her ribbons, he was awed: He looks like a governor! He looks like a Texican! I was right when I said we could use him.

When the wedding was solemnized in high form, Quimper found himself thinking: Not much like the mass unions that Father Clooney celebrates, and he felt a longing for that simpler life: I know what Mattie meant. I couldn't live here in Gallatin after that free life on the rivers.

But such thoughts were expelled that night when, at about ten, the men of the town were nicely inebriated and someone shouted: 'Let's give the governor and his lady a real shivaree!' Nearly a hundred drunks assembled outside the tavern with horns and drums and washboards and bugles and tin pots. Led by one of Eliza's cousins, the crowd surged along the streets, gathering recruits, until it reached the small house in which the governor and Eliza were spending their first night together.

There a noise was generated which had not been matched since the explosion of a powder depot some years before. Horns blared, men bellowed, drums were banged, and the night was made raucous with a serenade whose tradition dated back two thousand years. A marriage was being launched, and the community wished to mark this mystical occasion not only with prayers but also with riotous celebration, and when two men came up with a barrel of whiskey on wheels, the noise really began.

It was a shivaree honoring a great and much-loved man, a man of dignity and power, and all who shattered the night did so in hopes that somehow their destiny would be matched to his. But it was also a serenade to a gentlewoman whom the town loved, and after a while the men started a chant:

'Eliza! Eliza! The world's fairest flower.
Eliza! Eliza! Pray come to my bower.'

It was well after two in the morning before the barrel was empty and the tin pots beaten beyond recognition. Then off to their beds straggled the celebrants, except those who returned to the taverns, banging on the doors and demanding admittance. Quimper, remaining in the streets through the night, judged that he had never participated in a better shivaree and he doubted that anyone else had, either.

337

A few days later, Jubal found an opportunity to talk with Houston: 'Governor, I've cast my lot with Texas, and I can see that you're the kind of man we need down there. To pull things together before we join the Union.'

Houston, afraid that this might be a trap seducing him into some impropriety, said easily: 'Now, sir, I can tell you that I've always thought well of that part of Mexico. In 18 and 22 I applied for a land grant down there. Can't remember whether I ever received the papers or not, but I know it's a splendid territory.'

'You have a dazzlin' future, Governor, Texas or wherever.'

The big man appreciated such flattery and accepted it gracefully: 'My future's twofold. To build a proper house for my wife and to get reelected governor of this great state. That's enough to keep me busy.'

The next day Quimper was startled to see Governor Houston striding through town in his favorite costume: Indian garb, sandals, buckskin britches, with a bright red shawl draped about his shoulders. 'What's he doing?' Jubal asked a bystander, and the man snorted: 'Keep watchin'. You'll see wonders.' And on subsequent days Houston appeared in three radically different costumes, none appropriate to his high office. Finally Jubal had to comment: 'Governor, you seem to like unusual dress,' to which Houston replied: 'I dress like the land, different seasons, different colors.'

And then, on the sixteenth of April in that first year of marriage, Gallatin and all of Tennessee was stunned by the news that the delicate and lovely Eliza Allen Houston had for some mysterious reason never to be revealed left the governor's bed and board, telling her family that she could never return.

'Impossible!' the men in the taverns cried, while their wives at home met secretly to explore in hushed conversation the devastating possibilities. That Eliza's abrupt behavior must have had some dark, sexual cause, there could be no doubt, and since specifically what it had been would never be disclosed, speculation was not only invited but also inventive.

The scandal was intensified when the governor announced that he must, out of respect to his constituency, refuse to stand for reelection, and when his friends implored him not to take such drastic action, he shocked them completely by resigning the balance of the term to which he was already entitled. While they fumed, he boarded a steamer and sailed into lonely exile among the Indians he had known previously. Rarely in American history had a man who had risen so high fallen so low.

His precipitate departure raised far more questions than it answered, for in the silence surrounding the case his partisans launched an explanation, totally unauthorized, which cleared his name. But this could be circulated only at the expense of Eliza Allen, whose irate family had no intention of allowing her to shoulder the blame for this destruction of Houston's career, so in self-defense the male members of the Allen family engineered a solution unique in American political life.

They nominated a panel of twelve sober citizens of impeccable repute to hold a series of public meetings, the more salacious details kept private, to apportion blame in this affair. At the conclusion a vote would be taken and a determination made as to whether Eliza Allen, of Gallatin, was or was not guilty in even the slightest degree in the scandalous affair of Governor Sam Houston.

When eleven solons had been selected – military heroes, lawyers, clergymen, bankers – one Leonidas Allen, a relative of the abused wife, suggested: 'I'm glad to see this fellow Quimper back among us. He's become a man of sober judgement, reputation restored by the courts. I'd like to see him stay here. Let's signify our acceptance by inviting him to serve on our jury.' No member of the committee listened to the evidence with closer attention than Quimper, and when the time came for the first crucial vote, he experienced no uncertainty. The question was clearly stated: 'Was Eliza Allen, at the time of her marriage to Governor Houston, a virgin?' The vote was eleven-to-one affirmative, and as soon as the man who voted nay was known, one of the colonels challenged him to a duel on the grounds that he had impugned the reputation of a gentlewoman, but the voter justified himself by explaining that he was a lawyer from Virginia who felt that the question as stated could not be answered, since substantive evidence had not been provided. The colonel accepted the apology; the challenge was withdrawn; and the ashen-faced Virginian, aware of how close he had come to being shot, begged permission to alter his vote to affirmative, and when the balloting was announced, Eliza was unanimously found to have been a virgin.

Each of the other possible charges against her was analyzed similarly, and in vote after vote the correctness of her behavior was sustained. When the final tally was made, it was clear that Eliza's reputation had been not only cleared but also burnished; by the twelve ablest men in Gallatin she was found to have been immaculate in both behavior and spirit.

At the conclusion of the investigation two members of the panel composed a stirring document in which Eliza's purity was extolled and the governor's lack of it deplored; it covered all the debatable points and indicated the jury's vote on each, and it ended with an exhortation to the journals of Tennessee and surrounding states that they give the fullest possible coverage to the voting. But the Virginia lawyer, already frightened by what might have happened as a consequence of that first vote, now advised the committee that whereas the report accurately summarized their debate, and while its decisions were irrefutable, it might be wise to delay publication until the jury could be sure that Sam Houston had left the state.

After prudent delay the report was circulated, and interested newspapers did publish it, but by then Houston was lost in the wilds of Arkansas, living among his beloved Indians and remaining drunk most of the time. A traveler told Quimper: 'Shortly after Houston arrived in Arkansas, I saw him drunk in a saloon, where a local braggart challenged him to a duel. I was standin' with Houston when he accepted. Asked me to be his second, so in the mornin' haze, lengths were stepped off. The two duelists, obviously unsteady, marched, turned, aimed and fired. Nobody got hit for the good reason that me and the other man's second, realizin' that our men were drunk and without any sensible basis for a duel, had loaded the pistols with blanks.'

While Jubal was still chuckling over this portrait of the former governor, he was confronted by a great temptation. Leonidas Allen, the man who had sponsored his membership on the Houston jury, invited him twice to dinner in the Allens' spacious mansion, and only the most attractive Southern hospitality prevailed, but on a third visit Leonidas took Jubal aside and said in a low voice: 'Surely you've noticed that my older sister, Clara, is quite taken with you.'

Jubal had not noticed, but when he returned to the company

340

of the ladies he could not avoid Clara's ardent glances. As he left the mansion, Leonidas whispered: 'We would be most honored, Clara and me, that is, if you'd dine with us tomorrow.'

'Sir, I'm married. I have a wife in Texas.'

'Things can always be arranged.'

He spent a feverish night, for with the funds he had received from the settlement, plus those which would accrue to him if he married Miss Clara, who was not at all repulsive, he could own one of the Gallatin mansions. Also, he could hear Mattie saying: 'I'll give you your freedom.' But as he tossed on his straw mattress he thought of the Brazos, and Stephen Austin trying to build a state, and of Texas reaching empty to the horizon, and of Mattie poling her ferry.

Early next morning he went to a bank, arranged for his new wealth to be posted to a New Orleans agent against whom he could draw when he returned home, and headed for the Mississippi without bidding either Leonidas or Clara farewell.

When his boat put in to an Arkansas levee, one of the hands cried: 'There comes Sam Houston. Meets us every trip.' And up the gangway came the former governor, already drunk but looking to the steamboat's bar for replenishment. Jubal, fearing that Houston might have learned about the jury report, hid among the passengers but stayed close enough to hear Houston haranguing the travelers: 'Let's all get off the boat and head cross country to Oregon. I'm goin' there as soon as practical.' When Houston was safely off the boat and lying immobile beside some cotton bales, Jubal said to a passenger: 'Look at him! Governor of a state! We don't need his kind in Texas.'

New Orleans, Nachitoches in Louisiana, Nacogdoches in Texas, El Camino Real and south along the banks of the Trinity to the Goliad Road, this was the pathway of empire, except that other things besides immigrants traveled it. This autumn, cholera made the journey too, meeting up with Jubal Quimper just before he reached the village on the Trinity in which Reverend Harrison hid and from which he conducted his forbidden prayer meetings.

The two men were glad to see each other, and Harrison sat fascinated as Jubal reported upon the doings in Tennessee; it was Harrison's opinion, delivered from afar, that Governor

Houston, a giant of a man, as Quimper reported, must have outraged his gentle wife in some grotesque sexual manner. 'Your jury rendered the judgment he deserved. You did the work of the Lord.'

On the second day of the visit, Quimper fell into a fit of such violent shaking that the preacher cried: 'Dear God, Jubal, you must have the plague!' And as soon as these dire words were spoken they were flashed throughout the small community, and the minister's house was quarantined.

It was a useless gesture, because by that night four other cases of extreme ague had been identified, and by morning it was clear that the Trinity River had received from some mysterious source, perhaps from Jubal Quimper himself via New Orleans, its latest attack of this dread disease. Called alternately *the plague*, or *cholera*, or *the vomiting shakes*, or simply *the fever*, it assaulted the human body so furiously and with such total destruction that the victim rarely survived three full days, and that was the case with Quimper.

Reverend Harrison, ignoring the pleas of his secret parishioners that he dissociate himself from the stricken man, said: 'If Jesus Christ could medicine the lepers, I can medicine Quimper,' and he remained with Jubal, cooling his fevered face with damp towels until convulsive seizures showed that death was imminent.

'Beloved brother in Christ, Jesus awaits thee in heaven. May the merciful God stay this plague and may the earth be made whole again.' In the last minutes he bathed the dying man's face once more, praying frantically, as if to finish his beseeching before his friend died: 'Dear God, take into Your bosom this traveler. On earth he tried to do Your bidding. In heaven he will grace Your throne.'

When Quimper died, Harrison closed the eyelids and arranged the sweat-drenched bedclothes. Then he left his house, but others in the village were afraid to move near him.

Quimper's clothes had to be burned, of course, but a few durable possessions like coins remained, and these the minister gathered, proposing to carry them the sixty miles to Quimper's Ferry, for he felt that it would be improper for Mattie to learn of her husband's sudden death from strangers. He was delayed, however, by the necessity of burying four others who had fallen to the plague, and when this was finished he wondered whether it was proper for him to move into another community, lest he carry the cholera with him.

Waiting six days, he concluded that he was not going to be stricken, so down the Goliad Road he went on his mission of compassion. As he neared the ferry he wondered how he should speak to Mattie, for her husband had been far too young to die, but even when he stood at the pole that carried the flag travelers were instructed by a signboard to raise if they wanted the ferry to fetch them, he was undecided. He heard young Yancey shouting: 'Mom! The ferry!' and he wondered why this growing boy did not himself come across to get him, but since Yancey did not, Mattie appeared, wiping her hands on her apron and heading for the heavy pole.

With the skill acquired from many crossings, she brought the raft to its landing and shouted: 'Welcome, Pastor! Jubal will be coming home any time now.'

When he climbed into the ferry he sat silent for so long that Mattie asked abruptly: 'What is it, Reverend? Bad news?' and he said simply: 'Jubal died. Cholera.'

She did not interrupt her poling. Pushing the heavy post into the bottom mud, she walked along the edge of her craft, shoving the ferry forward, then dragging the pole in the water as she strode forward to push once more. Working and keeping her eyes upon the swirling water, she said nothing till she brought her craft home safely to its resting place. Then, helping the minister to negotiate the steep bank, she said: 'Father Clooney's here. Six weddings set for this afternoon.'

They walked to the dog-run, where the priest was sitting in the shade at the far end of the porch. 'Hello, Reverend,' he said, and Harrison replied: 'I bring heavy news. Jubal ... the plague.'

Father Clooney had helped bury many plague victims, but never could he adjust to the incredible swiftness with which this terrible malady struck, and to have it take a man to whom he, Clooney, was so much indebted was a burden trebly heavy.

'Let us not tell the others,' he suggested. 'It's their wedding.' So the three agreed that not even Yancey would be told until after the ceremony.

'I'll move along,' Harrison said. 'I couldn't attend the

343

weddings.'

'You could if you wished,' Father Clooney said. He wanted to add, so that Harrison would join, that such wedding were formalities demanded by the Mexican government, but he could not frame the words. No wedding was a formality, not any, not under any conceivable circumstances.

Harrison, unwilling to participate in or bear witness to such an improper mixture of politics and faith, moved sullenly away, but Clooney, on the other hand, became more excited and devout as the holy moments approached. Taking a nip now and then to encourage himself, he was feeling at the height of his power by the time the six couples had gathered, and he surprised them by saying with deep solemnity: 'Let us gather at the river,' and he led them to a plateau adorned by oak trees where the couples could look down forty feet to the Brazos as it carried mud to the sea. He had not chosen this spot by accident, for when the farmers stood with their brides and their children, he cried in a kind of chant:

'When storms strike far inland, that little stream down there can rise in fury and sweep across this land which seems so safe up here. Forty feet of sudden turbulence, and who can believe that? It will be the same with your marriages, an unexpected storm can overwhelm you, and who would believe that?

'Wise men and women, when they enter into marriage, do so with some religious blessing, with God's most precious sanction, for they know they need that extra help. If the families of the Brazos did not protect their homes up here, the stormy river would sweep them away. And if you do not call upon God to consecrate your marriages, they too can be swept away.

'In this solemn moment when you start your new lives I give you the balm of God's love. I anoint you. I bless you. I give you the gentle kiss of Jesus. Above all, I give you protection against the great storms of life. In life and in death . . .'

Here he chanced to look across the fields to the house so recently struck by untimely death, and his throat began to close

344

up and his eyes to fill with tears. He lost track of what he was saying and almost began to blubber, so great was his anguish over the fate of Mattie Quimper, and he became so incoherent that the wiser men among the grooms winked at one another: 'The old man's drunk again.'

He wasn't, not then, but when he returned to sit with Mattie on the porch, endeavoring to console her, he did start to drink heavily, so that when Reverend Harrison returned, eligible to rejoin them now that the Romish ceremony was ended, Clooney was ready to embrace him as a brother: 'Harrison, we must both give consolation to this good Christian woman.'

As evening approached he became quite drunk, and at one point he said to Harrison, as if he had never seen him before: 'Me name's Father Clooney, of Ballyclooney on Clooney Bay, in County Clare,' but when the stiff Protestant ignored him, he realized his foolishness and said hastily: 'You're Reverend Harrison! You and I must look after Yancey now. He'll need a father,' and he began calling: 'Yancey, Yancey!' When there was no answer, he looked hazily at Harrison, lay down upon the porch, and passed easily into a deep sleep that would last through the night.

'God blessed me in one thing,' Mattie said as darkness fell. 'He allowed me to know four good men. You. That one down there. Stephen Austin. And Jubal. Many women never know none.'

Harrison said boldly: 'You must take a new husband, Mattie. You'll need help to run the inn and the ferry.'

At this moment, on the far shore, a late traveler hallooed: 'Can you fetch me? I have no food, no blankets.'

She left the porch, went down to the Brazos, and poled sturdily across the narrow river to where the pilgrim waited. When the boat was loaded she shoved off, and in the moonlight brought him to the warmth of her inn.

... Task Force

We experienced the first open break in our Task Force when we met in October 1983 to plan our impending meeting in Tyler, where the topic was to be 'Religion in Texas.' We found it difficult to agree upon an appropriate speaker, for although none of us had strong convictions regarding specific theologies, and certainly we did not want to intrude on clerical matters, we were aware that sectarianism had played a recurrent role in forming Texas attitudes. But we did not know whom to invite, and because there were differences among us we postponed our meeting till November.

The blowup involved not religion but the successful American invasion of the little Caribbean island of Grenada. Rusk and Quimper, as gung-ho Texans, applauded the action. 'We should of done it years ago,' Quimper said. 'And since we have a running start, let's move on to Nicaragua and Cuba.'

Miss Cobb, descendant of Democratic senators, voiced a much different view: 'President Reagan, having seen how much the invasion of the Falklands helped Maggie Thatcher win reelection in Great Britain, is pulling the same trick in the United States.'

'And succeeding,' Rusk snapped, and she agreed: 'He is. Brilliantly. If the election were held tomorrow, he'd win in a landslide. America does love its successful little wars, but tires quickly of its big unsuccessful ones.'

'That's communist talk,' Rusk said, and Quimper agreed: 'If you got strength, you got to show it, or they don't believe you have it.'

Dr Garza tried to slow down the animosities by advancing a more sober theory: 'America must proceed very carefully. In every Latin country there's latent memory of Marines invading at will. If we run rampant in the Caribbean, we'll engender a profound revulsion. We must go slow.'

Rusk spoke like a letter-to-the-editor of a Texas newspaper when he said: 'We shouldn't give a damn what they think about us. We should discipline Cuba, right now. And if Nicaragua is in the Cuban camp, we should knock it out too. We've had enough liberal shilly-shallying.'

'Do you want to nuke Nicaragua?' Miss Cobb asked, and Rusk replied: 'If necessary,' to which Garza asked: 'And risk Armageddon?'

With the battle lines thus firmly drawn – Rusk and Quimper versus Cobb and Garza – the members looked to me, and I could not escape revealing my opinion: 'I side with the popular opinion in Texas. I believe the invasion of Grenada was justified. I think it forestalled Cuban action. And I'm sure it's reelected Ronald Reagan.'

Miss Cobb was disappointed with me: 'Do you know how big Grenada is? Smaller than the tiniest Texas county. Does America gain glory by subduing such a target?'

'Wake Island was lots smaller,' I retorted quickly, 'and we gained a lot of glory there. You excise a cancer when it's small, or you lose a life.'

Garza groaned at this forced analogy, and there would have been further debate had not our staff insisted that we reach a decision concerning the program for our meeting on religion, so we turned from one heated battleground to another.

Dr Garza suggested a professor from a Catholic college in New Mexico, believing that this would provide continuity from the very first days to the present, but Quimper objected vigorously, and with reason: 'I thought we settled that at our El Paso meeting. No more Catholics. Texas is a Protestant state whose moral attitudes were determined by Protestants.'

'You're right,' Garza conceded with no rancor. 'I was just trying to advance the interests of my boys.'

'Don't blame you,' Rusk interrupted. 'But now I want to advance the interests of my boys. My grandparents were Quaker and Baptist. Very few Quakers in Texas, thank God, because the two religions –'

'What two religions?' Miss Cobb interrupted.

'Quaker and Texas, they don't mix. I recommend we invite a Baptist minister.'

'Now wait, Rance,' Quimper protested. 'Texas was settled primarily by Methodists. And I'd like to hear an honest Methodist interpretation.' After the two men wrestled over this without reaching a solution, Rusk asked: 'Lorena, what are you?' and Miss Cobb said: 'What the Southern gentlefolk always were, Episcopalian, but in Texas we've carried little weight.'

The four now turned to me, and Quimper asked: 'Barlow, you've never said what religion you are,' and I replied: 'Home Lutheran,' and they all asked: 'What's that?' and I explained: 'When I taught school in a small town in the Panhandle the board was very nosy about their teachers' religion, and my crusty old principal told me: "Tell 'em you're a Home

347

Lutheran. Very devout, but you conduct your services in the privacy of your home." I did, and got away with it.'

Rusk took me up on this: 'Since we can't agree among the four of us, and since Texas has almost no Home Lutherans, whom would you suggest?'

After making a chain of phone calls I came up with an almost perfect solution, and at our November meeting in Tyler, where a few late roses were still in bloom, I presented him, a tall, thin man in his fifties, wise of countenance and witty of eye. He looked like a clergyman, even in mufti, for you could see that he had been trained to speak in a certain way and to enforce his words with effective gestures. What was equally important to our purpose, for he was to outline a weighty and sometimes contentious topic, he had a sense of humor.

I allowed him to introduce himself, which he did gracefully: 'I'm an ordained minister, professor in the Bible department, Abilene Christian College. The Roman numerals after my name indicate how many generations of my family have served in Texas. I'm Joel Job Harrison VI.' He asked our forbearance as he explained the religious history of his family, for he said that if we understood it, we would better appreciate the religious tempests which had from time to time swept Texas:

'The first Joel Job Harrison came to the Trinity River in the early 1820s, as a secret Methodist circuit rider sent down to infiltrate Catholic Mexico. Devout religionists in Kentucky gave him explicit instructions: "Combat the papists." He seems to have been a violent defender of his faith, conducting secret meetings up and down the rivers, and as you know, he helped ignite the sparks that led to open warefare against Santa Anna. Faithful to his own preachings, he led one of the critical charges at San Jacinto, then roamed across Texas during the republic, building the Methodist churches that had not been permitted under Mexican rule. He was not a likable man, if we can believe the diarists of that time, for some of them dismiss him with contempt. But he was a warrior, and Texas Methodism owes him many debts.

'Joel Job III was one of those titanic clergymen who sweep across Texas from time to time. Reading his Bible one day, he made the discovery that projected him into endless battles against the Baptists, the Presbyterians and all other infidel sects. It was a curious thing. He came to believe that whereas John the Baptist had clearly baptized Jesus Christ in the Jordan River by a process which could only be called total immersion, so that there was Biblical justification for the rite as performed by the Baptists, there was no holy obligation to keep on using it, and he began to preach strong and beautifully reasoned sermons against the Baptists, and especially against the sect called the Campbellites.

'Well, the Baptists weren't going to sit by and allow this to happen, so they threw three of their ablest men against him, one after another, and great public debates were held across North Texas. A tent would be raised or a building rented, and J. J. Harrison III, in heavy black suit and red string tie, his white hair flowing, would take on the current Baptist champion. For five successive days they would debate each afternoon, two o'clock to five, and thousands would lean forward to catch their words. Joel Job III had a majestic voice, a gift for scorn and an unrelenting sense for the theological jugular; both he and his adversary believed they were fighting for immortal souls. Their debates became famous, and the men were fondly referred to as "our peerless ecclesiastical pugilists." You can find in old bookstores printed versions of their battles: "The Harrison-Brand Debates," "The Harrison-Cleaver Debates" or "The Famous Harrison-Harper Debates." Harrison's name always came first because he was the more famous arguer and the one who attracted the crowds, but he confessed in a letter to a fellow Methodist clergyman:

'I always felt that I had defended Our Cause ably, but I rarely felt that I had won, because those Baptists threw against me some of the most tenacious debaters I had ever faced. They were men of learning, devotion and infinite skill in the nasty tricks of argument.

'Lanning Harper was the ablest man I ever battled, and in our four series in 1890 to 1893, I fear that he bested me on several occasions. Looking back on those days, I think of him as a Lion of Judah and I would not care to face him again tomorrow. He had a wry sense of humor, and several times, after we had lambasted each other on Monday, Tuesday and

Wednesday, we would unite on Thursday against the Presbyterians, whose doctrine of fatal predestination we simply could not comprehend, and it was Harper who introduced the doggerel which summarized our contempt. I can still hear the audiences laughing when he recited:

"We are the sweet selected few,
    The rest of you be damned;
There's room enough in hell for you,
    We don't want heaven crammed."

He was smiling as he finished these lines, but abruptly he turned grave, for now he must share with us a somber incident in his family history, one which produced both anguish and theological glory:

'Throughout the lives of I, II and III, my ancestors were aware, vaguely at times, of a powerful, primitive force gathering strength on the horizon. It centred upon a man named Alexander Campbell, born a good Presbyterian in County Antrim, Ireland, in 1788. The birth of a child forced Campbell to decide what he thought about baptism, and the more he studied the Bible the more convinced he became that Presbyterians were out of step with the New Testament when they merely sprinkled a baby and called that baptism, while the Baptists were correct to insist upon total immersion. To the scandal of his time, he left the Presbyterians with loud renunciation and became a Baptist.

'He didn't stay long, for although he granted that his new church was right on baptism, he found it wrong on almost everything else. He especially rejected the vainglorious church structure it had erected to govern what in Christ's day had been free, individual churches, each master of its own destiny. Fulminating against synods, regional associations and presbyteries, he was extremely harsh on professional clergymen who set themselves above ordinary laymen. "Protestant priests," he called them scornfully. In every aspect of religious life Campbell yearned to get back to the simplicity of that first glorious century of the Christian era.

'His theories swept across the American South like a

350

firestorm, with converts announcing themselves as Campbellites. And from what established churches did these converts come? From the Methodists and Baptists. The infection grew malignant, with entire congregations quitting the known churches and moving en masse into Campbell's arms.

'Well, Joel Job III as a faithful Methodist realized that something must be done to stanch this hemorrhaging, so during the great debates, after lambasting the Presbyterians on Thursday, he and his Baptist adversary would unite on Friday to excoriate the Campbellites, who did not like that pejorative name. They called themselves the Churches in Christ, for they believed that they preserved the simplicity that Jesus would have approved. I have several pamphlets which preserve Joel Job's attacks on the Campbellites, and they are rather sulphurous. Again and again he warned: "Do not lure good Methodists into your infamous trap." '

Our speaker paused to reflect upon those tempestuous days, then squared his shoulders and revealed an astonishing fact: 'In 1894 the religious world of Texas was shocked when this tower of Methodism, this peerless debater, went into seclusion, studied his Bible, and emerged with a startling revelation: "I can no longer support the Methodist church as it now exists. I am departing from it to become a minister in the Church of Christ." This was trebly scandalous, since he was in effect joining forces with his ancient foes, the Campbellites, against whom he had so furiously inveighed.'

Harrison shook his head, even now startled by his ancestor's apostasy, but then he smiled like a little boy: 'I warned you that we took religion seriously, and as you might expect, in his new reincarnation Joel Job III became a conservative terror. Apparently he hungered for a simpler, stabler form of worship, so before six months had passed he found himself joyously in the middle of the great fight which tore his new religion apart.

'You may smile when I tell you what four innovations he fought against. Missionary societies and organizations, because they were not specifically designated in the Bible. Sunday School, because he could find no justification in the Bible.

Rebaptism of Baptists, Methodists and Presbyterians who wanted to join the new church: "If one baptism was good enough for John and Jesus, it's good enough for Farmer Jones of Waco." And his most violent hatred: instrumental music inside the church, for he could not find it mentioned as such in the New Testament. He particularly despised organs, which he felt to be an Italian–French contamination and therefore probably Catholic.

'Have you ever read an account of what happened when he learned that members of his own congregation had collected funds for the purchase of an organ? He found that they had got the money by conducting an entertainment of singing at which punch was served. The punch contained no alcohol, but when he shouted about it from his pulpit you'd have thought it was hundred-and-fifty-proof rum.

'When the organ was brought within the church, he threatened to burn the place down, and was halted only by the liberals, who threw eggs at him while newspaper reporters watched.'

Our speaker shivered, recalling the shock of those fevered days, but soon the inevitable smile returned: 'As you probably know, I am myself Church of Christ and happy with the way my ecclesiastical life has developed. Believe me, I burn no churches.'

'Would you object,' Rusk asked, 'if I called you a modern-day Campbellite?' and he replied: 'Yes, I would. My church is much bigger in concept than the doctrine of one man. Why not just call me a Christian?'

He waved his hands as if to brush away the great schism of which Joel Job III had been so conspicuous a part. 'With his son, J.J. IV, our family got involved in Prohibition, which racked Texas politics. He stormed the state with his old Methodist evangelism resurgent. He gloried in hauling onto his stage mothers and children made destitute by the drunkenness of their men, and if some sad bank teller absconded with three thousand dollars, he trumpeted the case in forty counties, proving that alcohol had done the man in. He smashed his way into saloons, offered to wrestle peddlers of booze, and harried Texas into voting for Prohibition. On the day it became national law he cried at a great mass meeting in Dallas: "The

352

soul of America has been saved."

'Now he stepped forward as a watchdog of enforcement, riding with sheriffs as they raided speakeasies and testifying in court repeatedly. Those favoring the free movement of contraband up from Mexico or down from Oklahoma said of my grandfather: "Nothing wrong with Joel Job IV that a couple of cold beers wouldn't fix," but he attained his greatest fame, and I think power, in the election of 1928 when he opposed the candidacy of Al Smith, partly because Smith was Catholic but even more because Al favored demon rum.

'When Smith was nominated in Houston my grandfather shouted from a dozen pulpits: "Darkest day in Texas history. Defames the sacred memory of the Alamo." And from that moment on he toured the state relentlessly, preaching against Smith and the Democrats who proposed to lead the nation astray. Like all Harrisons, Number IV was a Democrat, but Al Smith was more than he could stomach, and after the votes were counted, the Republican National Committee sent him a telegram of gratitude for having moved Texas into their column: "You have done a masterful job for Texas and the entire nation." Grandfather believed this, and one of my earliest memories is watching as he took this telegram from his portfolio to let me read it. Tears streamed down his face as he said: "In 1928 we fought the good fight. But in 1932 the forces of evil struck back." He was speaking of repeal. He died believing that America was sliding to perdition because of its tolerance of drink.'

Quimper, a heavy drinker, interrupted: 'But Reverend Harrison, didn't you recently lead the fight against alcohol? In those three western counties which held a referendum on saloons?'

'I did, and I'm proud to say we kept those counties dry. I consider alcohol an abiding evil.'

'Thank you,' Quimper said, bowing as if to a debating adversary.

Then Harrison said: 'I share these things with you to remind you that in Texas, we take religion seriously. It can even be, as I shall demonstrate in a moment, a matter of life and death.' He then launched into his formal paper, which I shall summarize in his words:

353

'Except during the republic, when secularism ran rampant, religion has always been a major force in Texas life, and often *the* major force. No state in the Union pays greater deference to religion or supports it more vigorously. The founding fathers were unequivocal. Stephen F. Austin sought for his colony only devout Christians. Even a somewhat suspect hero like William Travis of Alamo fame, who dealt in slaves and deserted his family, could in 1835 write to the leaders of his church:

> We are very destitute of religious instruction in this extensive fine country ... About five educated and talented young preachers would find employment in Texas, and no doubt would produce much good in this benighted land. Texas is composed of the shrewdest and most intelligent population of any new country on earth, therefore a preacher to do good must be respectable and talented. Remember Texas.

'Texas became a state partly because loyal Protestants from the North and South refused to accept Catholicism or any other established church as the state religion, and much of the animosity anglos in the new nation of Texas felt toward their Mexican citizens along the border stemmed from the fact that those loyal Catholics adhered to customs which were morally offensive to the puritanic Protestant majority in the northern parts of the state. Even today you less traditionally devout members of this Task Force cannot comprehend how embittered we Protestants can become when we hear that churches along the border permit the drinking of alcohol and the gambling of Bingo on church property. We cannot understand such profanation.

'The religious impulse influences Texas life at every level and in the most unexpected ways. To this day it keeps most stores closed on Sunday. It determined that Texas would lead the nation in the fight for Prohibition. It dominates school boards. It accounts for great universities like Southern Methodist, which Joel Job III helped found, and Texas Christian and Abilene Christian, which J. J. V was so instrumental in financing. In today's world it explains why so many radio and television stations allocate much of their time to media ministers, who collect more funds from Texas listeners than from any other state.

'Indeed, if one studied only the outward manifestations of religion, one would be justified in concluding that Texas is now and always has been the most Christian of nations, and it is understandable that many Texans, and perhaps most, believe this to be the case. We love our churches and defend them vociferously.

'But if one steps back dispassionately and assesses with a cold eye the actual conditions in Texas, one must wonder how deep this religious conviction runs. You are more likely to be murdered in Odessa than in any other city in the nation. It and Grand Forks, North Dakota, are of comparable size, but Odessa produces twenty-nine point eight murders per thousand; Grand Forks, one. Dallas gunmen shoot more police officers in a year than do the citizens of Philadelphia, Detroit, San Diego, Phoenix, Baltimore, St Louis, San Francisco and Boston combined. Such amazing figures can be explained only by some inherent Texas differential. Our state officials go regularly to jail for blatant offenses which do not occur with such frequency in states like Iowa and South Dakota. Each autumn three or four Texas high schools watch their football teams forfeit all their games because they broke the rules, knowingly. Deaths on Texas highways from drunk driving are shattering in their regularity.

'And one has to be amused at the famous bass-fishing contest held at the Lake O' The Pines near Jefferson. Total prize money, one hundred and five thousand dollars. Created an open scandal because Texas sportsmen were caught fastening onto their hooks twelve-pound frozen bass flown down from Minnesota, allowing them to thaw in the warm water, then reeling them in with delighted cries: "Hey! Look what I caught!" When this was detected, other contestants hired scuba divers to swim to the bottom with live bass from Wisconsin to fix to their lines. Solution? Give every fisherman a lie-detector test. When sixty percent of the winners failed, loyal Texans cried: "Understandable. They were all from Oklahoma."

'Historically, Texas Christians, good church members all, have been loath to face up to the moral problems of their time. Joel Job I was a stout defender of slavery, and both Harrison II and III leaped into Confederate uniform during the War

355

Between the States to serve as chaplains, for they believed that slavery was ordained by God and must be prolonged. Harrison IV, who led the fight against drink and Al Smith, also led the fight for the revival of the Ku Klux Klan and preached two notable sermons explaining why it was doing God's work in Texas.'

At this point he coughed, rather nervously I thought, and fumbled among his papers for a small document, whose nature I could not determine from where I sat, before continuing: 'Nothing exemplifies better the complexities of the moral order in Texas than this well-edited little publication: *The Blue Book for Visitors, Tourists and Those Seeking a Good Time While in San Antonio, Texas, 1911–1912*. It defines the red-light district, Via Dolorosa to Matamoras, and lists the more luxurious houses of prostitution therein. Lillian Revere seems to have run an attractive place at 514 Matamoras Street – Old Phone:1357, New Phone:1888, Private Phone:2056. To get there, her advertisement said, you took the San Fernando streetcar, got off at South Pecos and Matamoras, and there you were. The book divides the women into three classes – twenty-two As, twenty Bs, sixty-two Cs – and gives addresses and phone numbers. It also lists thirty-three cabdrivers who could be trusted. Among the names, several attract attention. Beatrice Benedict, Class A, apparently ran three houses, but how she did this is not explained. One of the Class B girls was named El Toro, one of the Class Cs was Japanese. One of the cabdrivers was John Ashton (English Jack). And on page seventeen is something I rather liked, the complete baseball schedule for San Antonio's games in the Texas League.'

Reverend Harrison told us that he had often pondered these apparent contradictions and had decided that they did not really represent moral confusion: 'The Texan who guns down his neighbor does not visualize himself as committing a crime. He is merely settling an argument within the accepted Texas tradition. The Texas billionaire who has three wives, three households and three families of children at the same time cannot conceive of himself as doing anything wrong. He is merely perpetuating the free life of the frontier, and he sees himself as being a better Texan for so doing. With no apologies he supports his church, helping to finance its attack on immorality and loose living.

'Every example of social disorganization which the Northern critic might cite in an attack upon Texas can be explained away by the Texan apologist with the statement: "But that's the way we've always done it in Texas." If any item of behavior is accepted by the majority, then it becomes part of the Texas theology, serving as its own justification. The good people who publish *The Blue Book* were satisfied that they were providing a constructive service.

'In no instance is this more clearly demonstrated than in the case of wetbacks along the Rio Grande. For generations, Texas planters, first in cotton then in citrus, utilized those people under living conditions which were appalling at best and tragic at worst. Good church members who sent their sons and daughters to SMU or TCU and saw nothing wrong in treating their Mexican workers worse than they did their animals, and their justification was: "They're better off here than they would be back in Saltillo."

'In the early 1900s the fiery Baptist minister John Franklyn Norris led a noisy crusade against horse racing, gambling and alcohol. Distressed by the perfidy of women, he launched fevered sermons against short skirts, bobbed hair and dancing. But his fiercest ire was reserved for any professors at Baylor, the Baptist university, who veered even one inch from what he felt was the literal truth of the Bible, and he succeeded in getting several fired. Idolized by Texans as their revealed prophet, he startled some of his weak-kneed supporters in 1926 by winning an argument with a gentleman and winning it by the simple expedient of whipping out a revolver and shooting the man dead with three well-placed bullets. The jury found him innocent on the grounds, I suppose, that he was a member of the cloth, and therefore incapable of doing wrong.

'How tragic these Texas religious debates could become was illustrated in the case of W. C. Brann, the Voltaire of Waco, who in the 1890s published a famous muckraking journal, *The Iconoclast*, which delighted in castigating Baptists for their spiritual and moral deficiencies. Unable to bear his gibes, which circulated about the world, religious fanatics took stern measures: once they thrashed him in public; then they kidnaped him; they came close to lynching him; and finally they killed him with a shot in the back, "right where the suspenders crossed," and later they desecrated his grave.

'The contradictions have survived into our time, for recently Brother Lester Roloff, another powerful evangelist, ran children's homes in the Corpus Christi area which broke every rule in the book, yet the state excused him on the grounds that he was a God-fearing clergyman and therefore exempt from normal restraints.'

'What should we, in fairness, say in our report?' Miss Cobb asked, and Joel Job VI was prompt in his response: 'That Texas really is a state which honors religion far more than most. Basic to everything we do is a reverence for religion, but we insist upon constructing our own theology.'

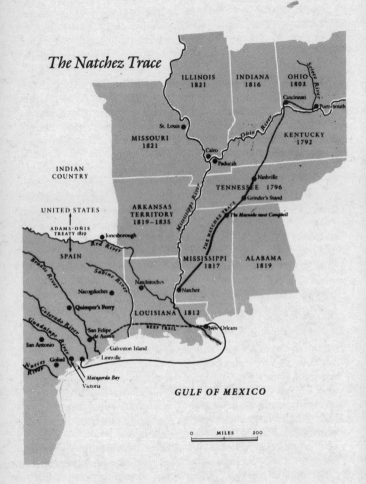

The Natchez Trace

ILLINOIS
1821

INDIANA
1816

OHIO
1803

Cincinnati

Portsmouth

Scioto River

St. Louis

MISSOURI
1821

Ohio River

KENTUCKY
1792

Cairo

Paducah

INDIAN
COUNTRY

Nashville

TENNESSEE 1796

Grinder's Stand

The Meriwether meet Campbell

UNITED STATES

ADAMS-OÑIS
TREATY 1819

Jonesborough

Red River

ARKANSAS
TERRITORY
1819–1835

Mississippi River

The Natchez Trace

SPAIN

Sabine River

Natchitoches

MISSISSIPPI
1817

ALABAMA
1819

Brazos River

Nacogdoches

Quimper's Ferry

Natchez

Colorado River

San Felipe
de Austin

LOUISIANA 1812

BEEF TRAIL

New Orleans

Guadalupe River

San Antonio

Galveston Island

Nueces River

Goliad

Linnville

Matagorda Bay

Victoria

GULF OF MEXICO

0   MILES   200

V

THE TRACE

If the various national groups that settled in Texas, and there were more than twenty – Germans, Czechs, Poles, Wends – the one which gave the area its basic character came from Ireland. They arrived in great numbers, filtering down the famed Natchez Trace from Pennsylvania, Ohio, Kentucky and Tennessee.

They were a resolute, courageous, self-driven, arrogant lot. Often surprisingly well educated, the vast majority had been raised as Presbyterians, although many in recent years had become Methodists or Baptists. To appreciate their unique qualities, it will be instructive to follow one stubborn fellow as he makes his way slowly, accidentally, towards Texas.

To do this it will be necessary to jump backward in time to the blustery winter of 1802 and to a long beautiful glen that ran west to east at the center of Scotland. At its far end, Glen Lyon was marked by a small mountain-girt loch, from which tumbled a sparkling river that bred trout and provided water for the sturdy Highland cattle grazing along its banks.

On the shore of the loch, so positioned that a man could survey the protecting mountains and also see any enemies who might be climbing the glen, stood a dwelling low and dark, of but three rooms. Its foundation was of solid boulders; its sides were of heavy half-worked stone; and its thatch-and-turf roof was held down by a network of thick leather ropes from whose ends dangled large rocks to offset the lifting power of the winds which often howled down the mountains.

This dwelling, Dunessan by name, was occupied by the family of a redoubtable man in his seventies whose forebears generations earlier had fled into the remote fastness of Glen Lyon after being harried and driven from their ancestral lands. A stubborn clan, they had persistently backed the wrong side in wars and had paid the penalty.

The old man was Macnab of Dunessan, patriarchal head of the local branch of the Macnabs, one of the most contentious clans in Scotland. He was a big man, veteran of a dozen Highland battles, and he looked especially formidable when clad in the crimson-green-red tartan of the Macnabs, with dirk and claymore at the ready. He wore white mutton-chop whiskers and a Highland bonnet, and always seemed ready to take up arms for some new battlefield, but recently an old bullet wound in his left leg had begun to impede him, forcing him to stay close to his house, from which he still roared orders to his kinsmen.

On this morning he was in a gentler mood, for he rested with his grandson Finlay on a wooden bench outside the door, trying to catch whatever heat the winter sun provided. 'Have you ever wondered,' he asked the boy, 'why we Macnabs always cling to the Macdonalds and guard against the treacherous Campbells?'

'Glencoe,' the lad said promptly.

'But why Glencoe?'

When the boy, only ten years old, displayed an imperfect understanding of that tragic name, the old man drew him closer: 'In the long run of human history no event surpasses the villainy of the Campbells at Glencoe.' And he proceeded to summarize that Highland horror in which the Campbells, seeking to curry favor with an English king, insinuated themselves into the good graces of the rebellious Macdonalds. Appearing suddenly in the remote and gloomy fastness of Glencoe, they passed themselves off as friendly travelers, but after more than a week of feasting and singing and wooing the Macdonald lassies, the Campbells, in dead of night, fell upon their hosts and slaughtered them.

'It wasn't the killing, mind you,' the old man said, his hands trembling with rage as he recalled this ancient wrong. 'Our glens have seen murder before. It was the perfidy. To sup with a man for ten days in a row, and on the eleventh, when your own belly is filled with his bread, to slay him in the dead of night, befouling his own home . . .'

'Why didn't the Macdonalds fight back?' young Finlay asked.

'Those trapped in their own homes had no chance. But those

clans outside who pertain to the Macdonalds have never stopped seeking revenge.' Taking his grandson's hands, he said solemnly: 'Laddie, wherever, whenever you meet a Campbell, expect treachery. Never forget that your father died fighting them.'

The next two years in Glen Lyon were marked by the arrival of a tall, gawky man who intended to bring piety and learning to this embattled area.

He was Ninian Gow, Master of Arts from the University of St Andrews in eastern Scotland and ordained as a minister in the Presbyterian church founded by John Knox. He was deep-visaged and had large dark hairs which grew out from his Adam's apple and moved in the air when he preached; he was incontestably a man of God and a fearless champion of decency. He loved his church and had made great sacrifices to serve it, but he loved mankind more. His two abiding convictions were that Scotland could not be truly saved until its young people, boys and girls alike, learned to read, and that it was doomed unless it combated the evils of popery.

'The Campbells are Catholics, you know,' he roared during his first sermon in the glen. 'The glorious Reformation which brought us the true religion, Presbyterianism, in its moral grandeur, never reached the blighted glens in which the craven Campbells lurked. They remained unconverted, as they do to this day, ensnared in the web of popery.' At this point he halted in his sermon and stared out at the small gathering of Macnabs and Macdonalds, asking finally in a hushed voice: 'Is it any wonder that they saw no evil in worming their way into the affections of the Macdonalds and then slaughtering them?'

Silence filled the tiny kirk, broken only by Gow's deep voice crying: 'Let us pray.' This was an ominous invitation, for a prayer by Ninian Gow was apt to last a good twenty minutes, and on those sulphurous Sundays when he paid full attention to the papist menace, it could consume twice that time.

He had not been in Glen Lyon long when he began to recognize that Finlay Macnab, grandson of the clan's patriarch, had unusual prospects, and when he consulted the local dominie he was pleased to hear: 'The lad masters his numbers quickly and learns to read more ably than others older than himself.' The teacher said that Finlay had also acquired a fine, open style of lettering, and this obviously pleased him, for he said: 'Clear handwriting is proof of a clear conscience.'

When Ninian Gow made his first report to old Macnab on the boy's progress, he broached the subject of the University of St Andrews as a likely target for the lad's ambitions. Finlay's grandfather had never considered sending his grandson to college, but he had such a high regard for the good sense of the new minister that after he heard him out, he said he would think about it, then asked: 'And where is this St Andrews?'

That simple question was all Master Gow needed: 'It lies on the coast of Fife, an old city of gray stone hard by the Northern Sea. It is marked by ancient ruins and fine new college buildings. It's the foundation of Presbyterianism in Scotland, and it is not by accident that its once Catholic cathedral is now in ruins. God struck it down. And along its hallowed streets, set deep within the cobbled stones, stand memorials to the founders of our religion whom the papists burnt to death for refusing to abjure their new Presbyterianism.'

'It sounds like a holy place,' said Macnab, and his wife nodded silent agreement.

'It's more!' the minister said, revealing a hitherto hidden side of his character. 'For a small town it has an unusual number of taverns, twenty-three in all, it's said, where the scholars gather after their studies, and of course it has the gowf.'

'The what?' Macnab asked.

'The gowf. A links of fair green stretching beside the sea. A wee ball stuffed with feathers. Three clubs to smash it with, and four happy hours in the windy sunlight.'

'Surely it's not a game you're speaking of?' the dour Highlander asked.

'Aye, the grandest game of them all. All the scholars at St Andrews play at the gowf, I more than most.'

'Do you still play?' Macnab asked.

'Aye, that I do. We have no links, that's true, but I have my clubs and I brought with me three wee balls, and in the evening I like to hit them far and away down the meadows, making believe that I am once more at St Andrews, studying the Bible at St Mary's College and playing along the links at the seaside.'

On many occasions he returned to the subject of St Andrews

and the feasibility of young Macnab's reporting there for schooling, but finally the old man told him why he opposed the idea: 'I have no mind to seeing a grandson of mine take up the ministry.'

'Oh sir! Only a few who attend St Andrews elect the ministry. It's for everyone. The merchant. The Laird. The man who sends his ships to Holland.'

'But what would a grandson of mine profit from such a place if he was to come back to this glen and live as I have lived?'

'The learning, man, think of the learning!' And he spoke with such reverence for the simple act of knowing that Macnab began to consider this curious possibility: that a son of the glen could attend the university and become a better man for having done so, regardless of what occupation he followed thereafter.

The practicability of such a move became so challenging to Macnab that one afternoon he walked down to the kirk and asked the minister: 'Tell me one thing. What boy in a crofter's glen needs Latin?' and Gow said softly: 'The boy who is destined to leave the crofter's glen.'

The answer was so perceptive that after supper Macnab held a quiet discussion with his wife and their clever grandson. 'Would you like to go to St Andrews, as the minister says?' he asked the boy, and Finlay replied: 'I'm good at books. First in Euclid and Cicero.'

'To what purpose?' the old warrior asked in real perplexity.

'I don't know,' Finlay said honestly. 'I like to play about with figures and words.'

'What say you, Mhairi?' Macnab asked his wife.

'I have always thought he was a lad of promise.'

'That means he would make a good drover.'

'I would,' Finlay said eagerly. 'I could drove the cattle to Falkirk for the Tryst this year.'

'You?' the old man asked in wonder, for he had not perceived his grandson as ready for such responsibility. 'How old are you, lad?'

'Twelve.'

'At twelve I had not left the glen,' the chieftain said.

'But you had fought the Campbells . . . three times,' his wife reminded him.

'So you would like to go to the college?' the old man asked.

'I am so minded.'

As the summer progressed, Macnab ruefully conceded that he would never again trudge over the far hills to Falkirk, and that it was time for his grandson to do so: 'Besides, there will be older friends to help when it comes time to bargain with those clever buyers from the south,' and once this big question was settled, the old man agreed that Finlay should keep some of the money from the cattle sale and proceed to the University of St Andrews. By July all was settled, and Ninian Gow was writing letters to a friend of his in the old gray city:

> I am sending you a fine wee laddie, Finlay Macnab of Glen Lyon, age thirteen when he arrives. Take him under your wing and tutor him for the University, which he should be ready to enter at age fourteen. He has completed Euclid, is knowledgeable in Sallust and is capable in all ways.
>
> NINIAN GOW
>
> Post scriptum: I am converting heathen Highlanders into good Christians at such a rate that John Knox must be smiling.

The last half of July and all of August were spent in preparing Finlay for the arduous task of droving his cattle to the great market at Falkirk, nearly eighty long miles to the southeast over steep mountain crests and down beautiful glens. The boy practiced with Rob, the deerhound-collie who would do most of the work; whistled signals would direct the dog to round up strays and keep the herd moving forward, but at times it would seem as if the dog was directing the boy and not the other way around, so quick and intelligent was this remarkable animal.

Meanwhile, the boy's grandmother had been gathering the things she must supply: the strong cheese, the beef strips dried in the sun, the oatcakes hardened on the windowsill, and particularly the great kilt in which her grandson would live for many weeks. It was not one of those townsman's kilts, little more than a pleated skirt tied at the waist; this was a Highlander's fighting-droving kilt, a huge spread of patterned fabric – crimson-green-red for the Macnabs – which covered the body from head to heel, with much left over to form a cape in case of storms.

When his grandmother had it trimmed to her taste, she threw it on the ground, spread it out, and commanded her grandson: 'Lie down.' And when he placed himself prone upon it, so that it reached from his ankles to well beyond his head, she showed him how to roll about and dress himself in it, not rising to his knees until it was properly fitted, and then to a full standing position so that he could fasten the overage about his waist, to be unwound when needed. A Scots Highlander dressed in such a kilt carried twenty pounds of tartan, a kind of ambulatory tent, which kept him safe in all weathers.

When he stood before her, wrapped in this cloak of honor, she thought: What a handsome lad he is, with the flashing blue eyes of his clan. And his youthful eyes did have that fire, for in the eighth and ninth centuries the Vikings of Norway had guided their longships to the fjords of western Scotland, raiding and ravishing, and many Highlanders carried the strain of those heroic days: stalwart bodies, placid dispositions until aroused, and always, scintillating eyes like those of the Macnabs.

'You're ready,' his grandmother said.

Toward the end of August the first drovers appeared in the glen, and all stopped by the home of Macnab of Dunessan to exchange greetings and information. They were from the Outer Islands mostly, men from Lewis and Harris and the Uists who had shipped their cattle by boat across the Minch to the Isle of Skye, and then through the perilous open fjord which separated Skye from the mainland. Any drover from the Outer Isles who reached Glen Lyon with his herd intact was already a hero.

These Islanders were an uncouth band, speaking Gaelic with just enough words of mainland Scots to enable them to function. Short, dark, somber in mien and rude in manner, they terrified the normal mainland Scot, who said: 'Two Skye men passing through a glen are worse than three floods or four thunderstorms. And a Uist man is worsen.' They stole cattle, robbed cottages, terrorized daughters, and left scars wherever they touched. They were the scourge of Scotland, the Island drovers who knew not God.

But in Glen Lyon they met their match, for the various Macnabs, long inured to battle, were themselves some of the most polished cattle thieves in Scottish history. It was said of the present Macnab, that sanctimonious, churchgoing scoundrel, that 'he loves animals so tenderly that he feels it his responsibility to take into his care any strays that wander his way.' Many a Skye drover entering Glen Lyon with one hundred and twenty-one animals departed with only one hundred and eighteen, and it was frequently remarked at how good a cowman Macnab was, since his own herd increased so steadily.

'A good dog and a quick eye make the drover,' Macnab often said, and he had both, plus an ingredient he did not specify: he was fearless in the prosecution of his trade and took great risks in augmenting his herd. On the cattle trails he had lived with two dirks hidden in the folds of his kilt, and he had never been afraid to use them. He now quietly handed a pair to his grandson, with the admonition: 'If you ever touch your dirk in a fight, be prepared to use it all the way.'

He would be placing eighty-one head of cattle in his grandson's care, perhaps more if things went well before departure, and since it would have been idiotic to trust so much of value to so young a lad, even though he was a husky fellow well able to care for himself, he was sending along a helper, Macnab of Corrie, who, with his two dogs, had made the trip many times before. They would be twelve days on the trail, up hill and down, and they would expect to deliver to Falkirk Tryst a full eighty-one head, plus such others as they might casually acquire en route.

In the meantime, Ninian Gow instructed young Finlay as to what he must do when the cattle had been delivered and sold: 'You are to leave Falkirk and walk directly to Dunfermline, keeping your money well hidden in your kilt without mentioning it to anyone. From Dunfermline, head straight to Glenrothes and then to Cupar, from which it will be an easy walk to St Andrews and the university, where you will inquire for Eoghann McRae, with whom you will live and who will tutor you for entrance to the university. Above all, lad, be prudent, for this is your entry into the world of learning. Make it a good one.'

That was the miracle of Scotland. From the most impoverished hovels, from the farthest glen, dedicated ministers and schoolteachers identified boys of promise and goaded them into getting an education at the universities in Aberdeen,

Glasgow, Edinburgh and, above all, St Andrews, those centers of learning whose scholars down through the centuries have done so much to alter and improve the English-speaking world. Unable to find employment in Scotland, they emigrated to London and Dublin and New York. They made Canada and Jamaica and Pennsylvania civilized places in which to live; they started colleges in America and universities in Canada. A thousand enterprises in England would have failed without the assistance of the bright lads from Glen Lyon and the Moor of Rannoch and lone shielings on Skye. They would govern India and South Africa and New Hampshire, and wherever they went they would leave schools and hospitals and libraries, for they were the seeds of greatness and of civilization.

There was no sensible reason in the world why a grandson of Macnab of Dunessan, drover and cattle thief extraordinary, should aspire to St Andrews to study Latin, except that for two thousand years the men who governed the world, making it in each century just a little better, had known Latin. And from the moment Gow had first seen young Finlay he had suspected that here was a lad with the potential to become such an individual.

At about this time various women in the glen remarked that the minister had come to them begging for curious ingredients: 'He asked for raisins. Wanted to know who had currants. Was especially eager for some orange peel, and who has such in Glen Lyon?' He borrowed also, with no promise ever to pay back, spices, flour, suet, a dozen eggs, a healthy dram of whisky and two pounds of butter. When all was assembled he went to a young Widow Macnab whose husband had recently died fighting the Campbells and asked her help in sewing a heavy cloth bag, and when this was done he sought permission to use her kitchen: 'But first we must find some treacle, for without treacle it would be nothing.' Then he was ready.

'In my home near the Grampian Hills we called it a clootie dumplin', a dumpling made within a cloth,' and when the ingredients were properly mixed and spiced, he and the widow stuffed them into this cloth, sewed it up, and pitched it into a pot of boiling water, where it seethed for six hours, no less. When it was done, heavy as stone, Ninian Gow told her: 'My mother boiled me one when I set out for college. It will keep twelve days, maybe sixteen, and give the parting lad a kiss of love as he eats each morsel.'

Finlay celebrated his thirteenth birthday at the end of August. Next morning he rose early, eager to head south with his eighty-four cattle, his grandfather having acquired by usual means three additional head. While Rob barked at his heels, his grandmother, with tears in her eyes, gave him his bundle of dried beef, his grandfather handed him a stout walking stave, and Reverend Gow appeared with a heavy gift which he described as a clootie dumplin': 'Eat it sparingly, lad. It should keep you in good health to St Andrews.' And the dominie, a man who always stood at the edge of poverty, offered the only present he could afford: a notebook he had used in his schooling from which a third of the pages had been torn.

'Keep healthy, lad,' his grandmother called, for she might not see her grandson again for a dozen years.

'Keep mindful, son,' his grandfather shouted, tapping his own waist where his dirks were kept.

'Keep honest,' the minister said.

'Keep to your books,' was the dominie's admonition, and the boy was on his way.

His route was eastward down Glen Lyon, a marvelously quiet beginning with hills lining the way, but he was soon joined by a rough Skye man coming across the hills from the dark Moor of Rannoch to the north. Finlay, afraid there might be trouble, drew close to Macnab of Corrie, then said boldly to the Skye man: 'These are the cattle of Macnab of Dunessan,' and when the Skye man finally led his cattle off on their own route, he left behind, unknowingly, a fine animal that Finlay had taken under his protection. His herd was now eighty-five.

At midpoint in the glen Macnab of Corrie said: 'It's best we go boldly over the hills,' so they forded the little stream that defined the glen, their cattle lowing in protest, and climbed steeply into what Corrie warned was dangerous ground: 'This is Campbell country, and when a man droves cattle across such land he does so at his peril, for Campbells will sweep down at any moment and steal half his herd.'

This theft and countertheft among the Highland clans was not judged in the harsh manner it would have been in England, where misappropriation of another man's horse or cow could mean a hanging. Highlanders stole each other's cattle in a kind of game, a test of gallantry and intelligence, with always the chance that one clan might rise up in desperation and launch a general slaughter – not of the other clan's cattle but of the clan itself. It was heroic competition, and none were more cruel at it than the Campbells, or more sly and self-protective than the Macnabs. There was a saying among the drovers from Skye: 'To avoid the Macnabs in Glen Lyon takes twenty more miles, but it could save you twenty animals.'

When the Macnabs dropped down to beautiful Loch Tay they traveled eastward along its northern shore for many miles, then entered with considerable nervousness the narrow glens leading to Campbell lands, and after they had reached a spot where it was necessary to bring the cattle into an orderly ring for the night's rest, both Finlay and Corrie felt uneasy. They slept fitfully while their three dogs watched the cattle, and as they had feared, at dawn a loud, ferocious man challenged them: 'This is Campbell land, and who might you be, trespassin' upon it?'

Finlay was about to say proudly that these were cattle of Macnab of Dunessan, but Corrie, mindful of the fact that the Macnabs had always sided with the Macdonalds in wars with the Campbells, said deceitfully: 'We drove for Menzies of that Ilk.'

'A good man,' the Campbell henchman grunted, 'but the fee for passing here is two of your beasts,' and when Finlay started to protest, he growled: 'No beasts, no passage.'

Corrie, sweatingly eager to maintain peace, said quickly: 'I'll find you two,' but the Campbell said: 'I'll do the pickin',' and he sorted out two of the best.

When the huge guardian started to leave with the animals, Finlay was so outraged that he reached for his dirks, and although he was only a lad and pitifully smaller than the Campbell, he would have tried to stab him from behind had not Corrie restrained him: 'Laddie, sheath your dirks. There's a better way.' And the big man departed, not realizing how close he had been to death.

The two Macnabs made as if they were leaving the glen, but that night, in the silvery glow that passed for darkness in these high summer latitudes, Corrie, Finlay and the dog Rob circled back to where the Campbell cattle rested, and there, with the subtlest whispers, Corrie instructed the boy as to what his dog must do: 'Send him to the far end. Tell him to fetch us three. But make no noise.'

To one not acquainted with the Highland sheepdog, it might seem preposterous to expect Rob to understand such a thieving mission, but the dog was an enthusiastic conspirator and something of a thief himself, so quietly he ran to the grazing beasts, separated five, then turned two loose when Finlay whistled softly in the darkness.

Edging the cattle southward to where his master waited, Rob delivered them without a sound to the boy, who swiftly joined them to the Macnab herd and even more swiftly spirited the whole group out of the Campbell domain.

When all were safe, Corrie, not a demonstrative man, leaped in the air, and in the light of the newly risen moon, grasped Finlay's hands and cried: 'The Campbells stole two of ours but we rescued three of theirs!'

To celebrate, Finlay cut open his clootie dumplin', and he had never before tasted anything so good as this grainy mixture of wheat, fruit, spices and honey, nor had he ever before feasted with such mixed emotions: to have outsmarted a Campbell, to have watched his dog steal the cattle so skillfully, and now to eat in remembrance of his kind minister and mentor Ninian Gow . . . This was a day not to be forgotten, and at its close, when he and Corrie spread their tartans on the bare earth, when Rob and his two helping dogs circled the Glen Lyon cattle, he somehow passed from boyhood to young manhood. With his claymore at his belt and his herd now augmented to eighty-six, he felt ready for the great Falkirk Tryst. He had become an accomplished drover on the route and he would become an equally accomplished trader when the throng of English buyers pressed down upon him, seeking to stampede him into an early sale to their advantage, not his.

But he could not sleep. This day had been too eventful, especially that dreadful moment when he thought he might have to leap at the Campbell with his dirk. As the August night waned and the stars wheeled overhead, Rob became aware that his master was uneasy, so the dog left the care of the cattle to the other two dogs and came to lie with Finlay, and when dawn broke they were still lying there, both asleep, both exhausted from the previous day's excitement.

Why had Falkirk been chosen, years ago, as the center for this great cattle exchange? No one knew, except that Scottish drovers had learned that this was about as far south as their animals could travel without beginning to lose weight, and the English buyers knew that this was about as far north as they cared to adventure into a land that was, in their opinion, still uncivilized. Falkirk formed a reasonable compromise, and a happy one, for in this year 1805, with peace in the land and the great Scottish rebellions of 1715 and 1745 only memories, a horde of wanderers not directly associated with the cattle trade had pitched their tents along the edges of the cattle field, and there they offered revelry of a wild and often bawdy nature.

There were mountebanks from Lowland Scotland, magicians from England, actors and singers from Edinburgh, women who cooked warm and delightful dishes and their husbands or companions who sold tots of whisky under the trees. It was a travelin' carnival, policed by dour watchmen who sprang into action only when some Highlander threatened to cut out the gizzard of the Englishman with whom he had been trading: 'Now, now, laddies! Stop that foolishness!' And often the drover, the Englishman and the constable, friends again, would repair to one of the trees and get seasonably drunk.

Falkirk Tryst lasted about two weeks, during which the cautious Highlanders tried every trick known to their ancestors, a canny lot to begin with, to lure the Lowlanders into paying a more than favorable price for the cattle, while the Lowlanders hesitated, delayed, and even threatened to leave Falkirk altogether, trying to scare the drovers into sacrificing their beasts at a loss lest they fail to find a buyer.

The two Macnabs had improved their chances considerably by the traditional Glen Lyon process of stealing unwatched cattle from their neighbors, and now their herd numbered ninety-one, and since every beast added to their original lot had been a choice animal, they now had a rather fine selection to offer, and Finlay intended making the most of it.

Seven different English buyers had sought to frighten him into disposing of his animals cheaply, and at the close of the second day Corrie warned: 'Laddie, you know we canna take these beasties home wi' us,' and he replied with a mature wisdom which startled the older man: 'Aye, and these buyers cannot come so far and return home empty-handed.'

As Corrie watched his young charge he discovered that the boy had a positive affinity for sharp dealing. He actually enjoyed the danger of holding his cattle back despite the risk of being left with no buyers. He relished contact with the shrewd English experts, and although he did not himself drink whisky at the trees, he found pleasure in joining the men who did. But what surprised Corrie most, this young fellow of his stood wide-eyed when the dancing girls with their many petticoats pranced about.

'Come away from there,' the caretaker warned, but Finlay remained, enchanted by the pirouetting.

Now the Tryst became a thrilling test of wills, and on each of those first seven nights Finlay and Corrie sat beside their valuable herd, arguing and eating a little more of that delicious clootie dumplin', until the once-plump cloth bag became as wrinkled as a hag, and on the eighth night, when the dumplin' disappeared altogether, Macnab of Corrie said: 'Laddie, I think tomorrow we must sell,' and at last Finlay agreed.

The seven potential buyers had dwindled to three, and the one who needed the cattle most noticed that whereas the herd had contained ninety-one beasts at the start of the Tryst, it now numbered ninety-four, and they were choice. Said the would-be buyer to the helper who would drove his purchases south: 'I've always liked doing business with Macnabs. They care for their cattle.'

'And for other people's,' his drover said admiringly.

A deal was struck, and with some regret Finlay watched his precious animals herded south; they had been fine cattle and on the trail they had behaved themselves and grown plump on the good Highland grasses. But now came the painful moment when the Falkirk Tryst drew toward a close. Tents were taken down and the music stopped. Mountebanks joked no more and the dancing ceased. Macnab of Corrie showed Finlay how to tie his coins into a corner of his kilt, then said: 'I shall take my two dogs and move westward toward Argyll, for I have business in Glen Orchy. You trend eastward toward St Andrews, and Rob

374

can fend for himself. He's able.'

So the older Macnab left, with a heavy weight of coins sewn into a corner of his kilt, and his dogs went with him. Now young Finlay was left with a mournful task which certain drovers had been performing at the closing of the Falkirk Tryst for decades. He led Rob to the northern edge of the fairgrounds, and there he tied about his neck a small cloth bag into which had been placed the notation: 'This is Rob belonging to Macnab of Dunessan in Glen Lyon. Cost of his food guaranteed. Finlay Macnab of Glen Lyon.'

When the bag was secured, Finlay felt his throat choking up, so for some moments he looked away, but then he moved close to the faithful dog and talked with him: 'Rob, I may never see you again. You were the best, the very best of all.'

He could speak no more, so he knelt with his dog, embracing him, and finally he patted him lovingly and said: 'Rob, go home!'

Obediently, the red-brown dog left his master and started on the long, long journey back to the head of Glen Lyon. He would be nine days on the trail, and would from time to time come pleadingly to some inn or crofter's cottage, where he would be fed, for the note about his neck assured the owner of that place that next year when the Macnab cattle came south to Falkirk, honest pay for the dog's feed would be delivered.

Rob had gone about a quarter mile on this remarkable journey when he stopped for one last look at his young master, and it was only with the sternest discipline that dog and boy refrained from dashing madly toward each other, but the time for parting had come, and each looked with love at the other and went his way.

It was self-reliant lads like this who walked over the hills from all parts of Scotland to the ancient Kingdom of Fife where, at the eastern edge beside the North Sea, the premier university of Scotland stood. Glasgow's was bigger, Edinburgh's more notable, Aberdeen's the most scholarly, but St Andrews was the peer, the heart and soul of both Scottish history and the Presbyterian faith. It was a noble university, gray and quiet in outward appearance, vital and throbbing with intellectual intensity. Sometimes it seemed as if the preachers of half the

Protestant world had come from this devoted town by the bitterly cold sea, where the warmth of theological disputation often compensated for the rawness of the climate.

During his thirteenth year Finlay Macnab studied with Eoghann McRae, the tutor to whom Ninian Gow had recommended him; he lived with this penurious man and shared his meager table, at which, after the so-called meals had ended, he would pore over his Greek, his moral philosophy and his figures. But in the early mornings, when he and his tutor took their walk before breakfast, he would observe the glory of St Andrews, for in obedience to a very ancient tradition, its students wore bright red gowns, never black until they had acquired degrees, so that the town seemed filled with brightly moving flowers, hurrying this way and that, a blaze of red gowns darting into doorways.

At age fourteen, Finlay was incorporated to the Leonardine College of the university, and the principal of the college asked the young man to meet with him: 'Macnab, I've good reports of your seriousness. I do hope you'll be studying for the ministry.'

'I have no call to the pulpit,' Finlay said honestly.

'Then avoid it, by all means. But make yourself a scholar.'

'With help, I shall,' Finlay said.

During his entire stay at the university he would not see his grandparents or his dog or the lovely shadows of Glen Lyon. He continued to live with his first tutor and to share the miserable meals, but now he was entitled to wear the famous red gown and cherish this badge of scholarly fellowship.

But at the beginning of his third year a totally unexpected transformation took place, as he explained to his tutor: 'I find I am not suited for the higher learning.'

'You're a true scholar.'

'I no longer like the university. My mind runs to the moors – to action, to trading cattle at the Falkirk Tryst.'

'I must summon the medics. You're sick.'

He was not. His mind was clear and it was delivering a masterful image of the kind of man he was intended to be: one who acted, one who dared to take risks, one who loved the hurly-burly of the Tryst. Firmly he told his tutor: 'I am ill-fitted to be a scholar. I shall go home.'

At this moment of confusion he was visited by a man he had

not expected to see again, Ninian Gow, who had been summoned back to the university to occupy a chair of some importance. Unaware of the agitation which had beset his young friend, he resumed conversation as if no change had taken place: 'Well, Finlay, what shall you do, now that you're on your way to becoming a verified scholar?'

'The world has gone topsy-turvy, Master Gow.'

'What could you mean?' the new professor asked, and in a burst of words Finlay revealed recent developments. Gow, sensitive to such matters, allowed the torrent to flood along, then said quietly: 'God has instituted this confusion because He has extraordinary plans for you.'

'What?'

'He wants you to do His work in Ireland.'

'I know nothing of Ireland.'

'God wants you to remain here at St Andrews three more years, make yourself into a devout clergyman, then sail across the Irish Sea and save that benighted country.'

'That I cannot do.' At age seventeen, Finlay was a well-organized, stubborn-minded young man, able beyond his years and of firm conviction. He was devout, convinced that John Knox had been correct in leading the way to Protestantism, and totally satisfied that Presbyterianism was the Lord's chosen instrument for the salvation of the human race, especially the Scottish. But he did not want to become a clergyman, for substantial reasons which he now revealed: 'I could never be a saintly man. When one of the Campbells took away two of my cattle, I wanted to kill him. And would have, had I not been stopped.'

'Campbells deserve punishment,' Gow said, 'but not killing.'

'And when I walk through the shops, I like to to stare at the pretty girls.'

'Clergymen do the same. They marry.'

'But I have not the inner calling.'

Gow studied this solemn declaration for some moments, then said with that generosity of spirit which would make him a notable professor, next at Glasgow and finally at Oxford: 'God summons us in different ways. He doesn't require you to become one of his ministers, or even to finish university. Come with me, and remind yourself as to what service is.'

They walked to that sacred spot where Patrick Hamilton, born a Catholic but inspired by the reform teachings of John Knox, had been burned at the stake by the local Catholics: 'Finlay, he refused to recant even when they piled more faggots at his feet. He was an enemy of popery, and so must you be.'

And beside the reddish stones which marked where Hamilton had died, Gow told of Ireland's problems: 'We have planted, successfully I'm sure, a mustard seed in the northern counties. Trusted Scotsmen by the score cross the Irish Sea to protect the land we've won and to advance Presbyterianism against the onslaughts of popery.'

'What could I do?' Finlay asked, and Gow said: 'There is a need for husbandment, for fine merchants, for anyone who will help strengthen Protestant roots in that ill-fated land.'

'That's the kind of work I'd be fitted for,' Finlay said, and some days later, when Gow brought him the news that a Scottish landowner in Northern Ireland, a trusted Presbyterian, was seeking a man who understood cattle and horses to serve as factor on his estates, Finlay volunteered for the job. After submitting glowing testificates penned by Gow, by his long-time tutor McRae and by the principal of St Andrews, he received from across the Irish Sea the exciting news that he had been selected.

When he bade farewell to Professor Gow, he said apologetically: 'My life was changed at Falkirk Tryst. I discovered that I belong with the sweating merchants, the mountebanks.' When Gow indicated that he understood, the young man added: 'And the swirling petticoats of the dancing girls.'

'When a man once has the Latin, he can never be completely lost. God will find you proper work to do.'

With little regret, Finlay Macnab laid aside forever the good red gown of St Andrews, unmatched in all the universities of the world, and set forth like many another Scottish young man before him to walk across Scotland and say farewell to the lone cottage at the head of his glen, but when he reached it he found it occupied by a different set of Macnabs, for his grandparents were recently dead, and even his dog Rob was missing.

'Did you ever know a dog named Rob?' Finlay asked, and when the new Macnab said no, he stood mournfully by the rough-walled cottage, tested the ropes that kept the thatched roof intact, and lamented the passage of the simple glories he had known here and would know no more. Adjusting his kilt, he started for that exquisite chain of western glens which would take him down to Glasgow, where he would be looking for a boat to Ireland.

As he began the journey that would ultimately lead him to Texas, Finlay was eighteen, of average height, weighing eleven stone four. He came from a line of men who had defended their rights in battle; he was himself a skilled cattle thief, a good man with the claymore, and one who loved the conviviality of his fellows. He had three fundamental characteristics which determined his behavior: he was a fierce Protestant whose ancestors had defended this religion with their lives; he had a stubborn sense of honor which lay quiescent when respected but flared into the wildest self-defense when insulted or transgressed; and he had a passionate love of freedom, which his people in the glen had sustained against Campbells and the English kings. Everything he had experienced – the lessons of Greek and Roman history, the accounts of his own clan, the records of his Scottish church, the works of the great philosophers – had instilled in him an almost fanatical dedication to liberty, which he would not surrender easily.

He was, in short, one of the finest young men his world was then producing, and there were other freedom-seekers like him arising in France, in England and in Germany. But the most able pool of emigrating talent was developing within that intrusive Presbyterian enclave in Northern Ireland, where, in obedience to the thrust of history, many young people were trending toward Texas without ever realizing they were headed that way. When they arrived, they would prove a most difficult group to discipline, especially when the center of political control lay far distant in Mexico City, manned by persons of a different culture contemptuous of their aspirations.

Finlay's employer in Ireland was a big, rugged man with the reassuring Scottish name of Angus MacGregor, whose ancestors had received assistance from the Crown in London in putting together halfway between the towns of Lurgan and Portadown, southwest of Belfast, a tremendous holding of spacious fields reaching all the way to Loch Neagh. It was on this estate that Finlay entered upon his duties: 'Young man, you're to make my herds prosper, trade my horses profitably, and keep the damned papists in line.'

When the first MacGregor had come as a stranger to these lands, the population had been ninety-two percent Catholic; by the time he died, it was down to half. When the present MacGregor inherited, his occupying farmers were about forty percent Catholic, and now they were no more than eighteen percent. In this orderly, irresistible manner the lush green fields of Northern Ireland were being rescued from popery, and after Finlay Macnab had been factor for a while, he could boast: 'All my drovers are now trusted men from Scotland, loyal Highlanders who speak our tongue.'

These invaders became known as the 'Scots-Irish,' which signified that in heritage, religion and firmness of character they were Scots, while in terrain and culture they were Irish. It was a powerful mix, this blending of two disparate Celtic strains, and they might more properly have been called Celts, for that is what they were: dreamers, wild talkers, men of dour concentration when needed, and great colonizers.

The free-living local Celts exerted a powerful negative influence on young Finlay, for they taught him the pleasures of good Irish whiskey and the joy of teasing the local lassies, two occupations which delighted him but which also plunged him into serious trouble. One morning, after being unable to remember how the preceding night had ended, he looked at himself ruefully and mumbled: 'I've made a far journey from St Andrews,' and he was pleased that Professor Gow could not see him now.

In 1810, at the age of eighteen, he found himself involved in two situations from which there could be only one escape. He had fallen in love with the daughter of a Lurgan squire, and he coveted the jet-black mare of a Portadown butcher. The squire would not surrender his daughter to a lad who seemed bent on becoming a rascal, and the butcher would not sell his mare to a young fellow unable to pay a decent price. Young Finlay resolved the dilemma neatly: he stole both the girl and the mare, and after placing the former astride the latter, he led a merry chase over the fields and roads of Northern Ireland. In the end he abandoned both the girl and the mare, who were restored to their rightful owners, while he, always a jump ahead of his pursuers, made his way secretly to Dublin, where he caught a freight boat to Bristol in England, on the safe side of the Irish Sea.

Unable to find work, he resorted to his traditional occupation of cattle stealing, only to discover that in England this had never been a game. When he returned to his lodgings one evening with a fine cow, his landlord whispered: 'They're after you, Finlay, and if they catch you, it's the gibbet.' Finlay suspected that this might be an evil trick whereby the landlord hoped to get the cow for nothing, but he hid in a grove of trees just in case the constables really did come, and when he saw three of them snooping about he scurried down lanes and through alleyways till he reached the Bristol docks. Leaping aboard the first ship available, he found himself, by ironic chance, headed for America's most Catholic city, Baltimore.

In 1812, at the age of twenty, he arrived in America just in time to become involved in the war starting that year, but after trying to decide whether he was an American patriot or a British partisan, he concluded that he was neither and offered himself to both sides, providing each with horses, cows, pigs, sheep and goats.

By 1820, when he was well established in Baltimore, whose German citizens liked to do business with him, his careless dalliance with Berthe Keller, daughter of a Munich baker, obligated him to marry much sooner than he had intended. Berthe was a hefty blonde young woman he would never normally have chosen, but when his father-in-law died in 1824, Macnab found himself proprietor of a flourishing bakery, which he quickly enlarged into a ships' chandlery of impressive dimensions.

He liked working on the beautiful Baltimore waterfront and was on his way to becoming a man of some importance, with a stodgy wife and three flaxen-haired children, when the inherited Macnab tendency surfaced, for in 1827 he was detected in a most nefarious transaction involving cattle owned by neighboring Germans. With no alternative but a term in jail, he decided to leave town.

When his complaining wife, disgusted with his irresponsible behavior, refused to accompany him on his flight, he was rather relieved, for she had proved an irritable woman and he was glad to be shed of her. Leaving his two daughters with their mother, he kept his son, Otto, slipped out of Baltimore before the enraged cattle owners could pounce upon him, and headed for the National Road leading west.

They were nearly eighty miles out of Baltimore, approaching Hagerstown, when young Otto gained his first insight into the nature of this trip, and indeed his first childish glimpse into the structure of life itself. Although not yet six, he was a precocious lad who suspected that he and his father were leaving his mother for good, and this caused pain. He knew that where his father was involved, his mother had been a bossy woman, but with Otto she had been a loving protector, standing always as his principal support, and he missed her. Often in the morning he expected to see her coming toward him with a bowl of porridge, or at night with hot sausages.

He was so confused in his loneliness that sometimes he wanted to cry, but his stern heritage – half dour Scot, half stubborn German – plus a warning look from his father forced him to bite his lip and march resolutely ahead. But at dusk, when he crawled beneath his blanket, he did not try to hide the fact that he was miserable.

But he felt no uncertainty about traveling with his father, and even though he did not fully understand why Finlay had fled Baltimore in such a hurry, he was sure that no blame fell on his father. A perplexed little boy, he stepped forth boldly each morning as they probed into the wilderness.

One evening as they plodded along the ill-kept road, trying to decide where to spread their thin blankets for the night, Otto saw through the growing darkness a light that shone from the window of some cabin situated well off the road, and the little hut seemed so established, so different from the wandering life he was leading that an overwhelming hunger assailed him.

'Poppa, let's stop here!'
'No, we'll find a valley before real darkness.'
'But, Poppa, the light!'
'On ahead.'
They kept to the road, this stubborn father and his son nearing six, and it was then that the little boy fixed in his mind

the image which would live with him for the rest of his life: a cabin secure in the wilderness, a light shining from the window, refuge from the lonely, shadow-filled road. And it was also then, because of the way in which his father urged him to move on, that he first suspected that he would not be allowed to share in that forbidden warmth, at least never for long. And whenever afterward he saw such lights at night his heart hesitated, for he knew what they symbolized.

Twenty-five miles west of Hagerstown the Macnabs had to make a crucial decision, for there a path deviated to the north, heading over the hills to Pittsburgh, an enticing target.

'Is it true?' Finlay asked a traveler as they stood at the junction. 'Do boats with steam engines leave Pittsburgh and run all the way to New Orleans?'

'They do,' the stranger assured him. 'But you'd be wise to beware of them.'

'Why?'

'For three solid reasons,' he said. 'They're very expensive and would eat up your savings. They're very dangerous, for they blow up constantly. And the criminals who sail them will steal what money you have left, cut your throat, and toss you overboard. Stay clear of those boats at Pittsburgh.'

Finlay accepted this advice, but the more young Otto thought about the mysterious boats of steam that wandered down a thousand miles of river, the more obsessed he became with them, and he pestered his father: 'Let's go to Pittsburgh. Let's take a boat. I'm tired of walking.' And when Finlay reminded him of the dangers the traveler had pointed out, Otto said pleadingly: 'But you would know how to fight those bad men.'

'There's the money, too. We'll need all we have when we get to Cincinnati.'

With a melancholy the boy would never forget, the Macnabs rejected the steamboats and continued their way to Morgantown and on to Parkersburg, where at last they would join the Ohio River, along whose grassy banks they would walk the last three hundred miles to Cincinnati.

Otto was a thin, wiry lad who looked as if he might not grow into a tall or robust man. But he displayed, even at this untested age, a cool efficiency and a stubborn determination. He intended one day to sail down the river aboard a steam vessel, and as he walked he remained constantly aware that off to his right, somewhere, lay the great river, and he could imagine himself breaking away from his father, heading north and finding it. He was satisfied that if he ever did so, some boat would see him, stop, and pick him off the bank.

He was lost in such romantic thoughts one morning, when he let out a gasp which seemed to come from deep within, as if his heart had been touched: 'Oh, Poppa!'

For there, in full majesty, rode the Ohio River, highway of the nation, bringer of good things to alien parts. Much bigger than he had imagined, more sinisterly dark, in its motion it bespoke its power and the fact that anyone who ventured upon it would be carried to strange and magnificent places like Cincinnati, Louisville and Paducah.

'Poppa, look!'

From the opposite shore a small craft had set out, obviously intending to cross to where the Macnabs waited, and Finlay told his son: 'That's a ferry. It'll come to our side and carry us across.'

'We ride on it?' the boy cried with delight, and when another traveler said: 'We sure do, sonny,' Otto kept his eyes riveted to this reassuring sight.

But as he waited for the little ferry to cross the river, he became aware that something of magnitude was approaching from the right, and just in time he turned to catch the majestic approach of a large river steamer. Belching smoke, its great paddles churning the water, it was a thrilling sight. Well-to-do passengers lined its two tiers, their fine clothes enhancing its magnificence.

It was the *Climax* out of Paducah, one of that grand, adventurous fleet which had started under the imaginative command of Nicholas Roosevelt in 1811 to bring steam navigation to the network of great rivers which bound the central areas of America together. 'Oh, Poppa!' Otto cried as the lovely boat passed, for he had seen his first riverboat and it had captured him.

On the ferry they crossed into Ohio, then followed country roads along the right bank of the river as it wound its way from

Parkersburg through the empty wastes of southernmost Ohio and on to Portsmouth, where the Scioto River joins the Ohio. It was a journey of compelling beauty; the vistas changed constantly; at night solitary lights glowed on the opposite shore, indicating where some adventurous soul from settled Virginia had decided to test the wilderness in Kentucky.

Deer accompanied the travelers; and one evening a small bear approached their sleeping place when Finlay was absent, gathering sticks for a fire. Otto, who had never faced such an adversary before, hesitated for one frightened moment. Then, realizing instinctively that he must protect their belongings, he grabbed the nearest piece of wood and made right for the beast. Thrashing about with his little club, he bewildered the bear, but not for long. With a sweep of its paw the animal pushed the boy away, nudging him into a thicket.

Astonished at the insolence of the beast, Otto first shook his head, then glared at the animal. With a grunt to give him courage, he fought his way out of the brush, uttered a furious yell, and charged back at the little bear, who was now rummaging among the Macnab possessions.

Otto was prepared to do battle by himself, but his father, hearing the commotion, hurried back: 'Otto, no!'

The warning was ineffective, for Otto was outraged by the brusque treatment the bear had handed him and was determined to drive the creature away, but before he could resume his assault, Finlay rushed up and with a much larger stick belabored the animal, who growled, studied his adversaries, and rumbled off.

Trembling, Finlay sat with his son beside the river, and there they remained as the long twilight waned. 'You were very brave,' Finlay said. 'I'm proud of you.'

'He was stealing our food.'

'Never tangle with a bear.'

'But it was only a little one.'

'A bear's a bear, son. Don't ever tangle with one.'

'But you did, Poppa.'

Finlay could think of a dozen appropriate, fatherly warnings: 'Yes, but I'm a grown man.' Or, 'You were lucky it was a little bear.' Or, 'If you have to fight a bear, don't use a stick. Get a gun.' He stifled such admonition, for he believed his son's

385

action had been proper. Once allow a boy to run away from a serious challenge, he could continue to do so through life.

Softly he said, as if Otto were his own age: 'You were right, son. If you start to do something, keep going and finish the job.'

They followed the good road along the Ohio right in to Cincinnati, a growing town of more than twenty thousand where a few resolute Germans were already establishing firms to serve the various needs of the steamboats plying up and down the river. Three ferries crossed the river to service the citizens in Kentucky, and after several exciting days Otto told his father: 'This is better than Baltimore.'

In many ways the little boy talked and acted like a grown man; as frontier boys did, he was skipping a whole decade of his growing up; he was already a mature young fellow who had walked six hundred miles through the wilderness and fought his bear. He knew what loneliness was, and how a great river served people.

Because of his waterfront experience in Baltimore, Finlay had no trouble finding a job with a German merchant who needed his expertise in buying cattle and hogs for the river traffic, and in pursuit of this work, he often visited the glamorous steamboats that docked at Cincinnati. Aboard these craft he heard for the first time about the real wonders of the river: 'New Orleans! Finest city in America! Them Creole girls. Them great eatin' houses.'

At the age of seven Otto began running errands for his father, learning the names of the steamboats and their home ports, and in doing so, he fell under the spell of a river town much different from New Orleans. He first heard of it from a tall bearded boatman with a poetic touch: 'Tell you what, sonny, when you ship down the Mississip, as you surely will, the place you want to see is not New Orleans. The real spot is Natchez-under-the-Hill.'

'That's a funny name.'

'It's a golden name, like out of one of the Greek fables, like maybe the gods put it there to test men.'

He spoke with such music and strength that Otto leaned forward to catch his words, and as the man continued he became not an ordinary roustabout but a chronicler: 'To make things flower perfect, the gods built Natchez-atop-the-Hill, with gleaming white houses and pillared porches and a score of slaves to keep things clean. That's rich-folks country, and river folks like you and me, we ain't allowed up there. For us the gods built Natchez-under-the-Hill, about the finest little spot in America.'

Aware that he had caught Otto's attention, he moved his hands in ominous gestures to indicate knives and daggers and pistols and gallows-rope: 'A man don't watch out, they knife him. At night you hear screams, somebody's bein' murdered. You hear a splash! There goes a corpse into the Mississip. Men walk bent over, they're smugglers. In the saloons you can get Tennessee whiskey, rots your gut, or a bullet, ends your gut. And there are girls, and dancin' through the night.'

Otto missed not a word of this report, but the riverman would have been astounded had he known the impact his words were having on this flaxen-haired lad. But in succeeding days, when Otto heard more about Under-the-Hill, and when he had time to weigh exactly what had been said, discarding the poetry, he was wise enough, even as a boy, to conclude that the lower Natchez was a sorry place frequented by men and women of a low degree. He could not have explained why he was reaching this conclusion, or what it signified, but he was developing a powerful rejection of goings-on; he was becoming a youthful conservative, in the best sense of that word, who deplored gambling, knifing, girls who danced all night ... and general irresponsibility. He opposed them all.

His father was also hearing a new word, one that would exert an equal influence on his life. Because Cincinnati specialized in butchering hogs, it was known as Porkopolis, and one of Finlay's duties was to provision riverboats with ham, bacon and sausage. One day after Finlay had loaded a boat bound for New Orleans with seventy salted carcasses, the satisfied captain paid him, then uttered a name Finlay had not heard before: 'We find ourselves with extra cargo space, Macnab. Could you scurry about and find us some bolts of cloth? Doesn't have to be fancy stuff, because it'll be trans-shipped to Texas.'

'Where's that?'

'Surely you've heard of Texas? Garden spot of the continent.'

'Where is it?'

'Part of Mexico now, but not for long.'

'What do you mean?'

'Texas is the ass end of Mexico, which don't give a damn for it. Each trip I make down the Mississippi, I carry men from Kentucky and Tennessee who's goin' to Texas. Stands to reason that with their long rifles, they ain't gonna be Mexicans for very long. They's gonna bring Texas into the Union, and the sooner the better, I say.'

'Why do people go there?' Finlay asked.

'To get rich! You plant cotton, it explodes in your face. You plant corn, you get two crops a year. Cows have twins in Texas, it's the law. And you get a league-and-a-labor, that's why.'

'What are they?'

'A league is four thousand four hundred and twenty-eight acres of pastureland, you get it free for cattle. A labor is hundred and seventy-seven acres of better land you get for farming, also free.'

'I can't believe it.'

'You get it the minute you step acrost the border and say – What's your name? Finlay Macnab? When you step up and say "Here I am, Finlay Macnab" you get all those acres of the best land in America.'

'You said it was Mexico.'

'It'll soon be America, you can count on that.'

Macnab asked so many questions about Texas that he became known along the waterfront as a prospective settler, and one day a Mr Clendenning invited him to lunch aboard one of the steamboats docked at the wharves. 'Can I bring my son?' Finlay asked. 'He dreams about steamboats.'

'To be sure,' Clendenning said expansively, and when they were seated in the spacious dining salon with its gold and silver ornamentation, the stranger told Otto: 'This is how we live on the great boats, sonny.'

'Do you live here?'

'Up and down.'

'You live on the river?'

'For the time being.'

'How long?'

'Until I've visited all the ports of call.' He now explained to Finlay that he was the traveling representative of the Texas

Land and Improvement Company, headquartered in Boston, and his pleasant task was to sell future immigrants to Texas the best bargain this weary old world had ever seen. Pushing away the dinner plates, he spread an interesting series of documents on the table and said: 'This is scrip, authorized by the Mexican government and fully backed by the Texas Land and Improvement Company of Boston, Massachusetts. Each unit of scrip you buy entitles you to one acre of the choicest land in North America. Buy yourself three or four thousand units, and you're set for life.'

'Did you say *buy*?'

'Yes. You deliver this scrip to the Mexican officials, and presto – they invite you to go out and survey your three or four thousand acres.'

'I was told I would get a league-and-a-labor free, something like four thousand acres.'

'No, no! You're *entitled* to the league-and-a-labor, and it's there waiting for you. But you have to bring the scrip to prove your legality. My firm vouches for you, says you're of good character, and you get the land.'

Macnab felt deflated. For some days now he had been visualizing his four thousand acres of choice land, his for the asking, and now to find that he must buy something in order to qualify was disheartening. He supposed the cost per acre would be something like a dollar or two, and so large a debt he would not be able to manage: 'How much is this scrip?'

'Five cents an acre.' Clendenning, noticing the relief in his prospect's face, said heartily: 'That's what I said. That's what I meant. Five cents an acre, just to make it legal.' While Finlay was congratulating himself on such a bargain, Clendenning added encouragingly: 'So what our more responsible customers do, they put up one thousand dollars and get title to twenty thousand acres. Then they are really in business.'

'Can I get so much?'

'Dear friend! Mexico wants you to come. They want you to settle their vast empty spaces. You can have forty thousand acres if you wish, but I've been recommending only twenty. More manageable.'

'Have you been there? Have you seen the land?'

'Macnab, do you know the passage in the Holy Book, "A

land flowing with milk and honey"? Some day we'll find that a man from Texas wrote the Bible, for that describes the land precisely. One day I was walking beside the Trinity River – marvelous stream – and what did I see? A shattered old tree whose insides were filled with honey bees, millions of them. There was enough honey in there to feed a regiment. And right beside that tree one of the sturdiest cows ever you saw, aching to give milk. A land flowing with honey and milk, just like the Bible says.'

'How many acres would you go for, if you were me?'

The salesman did not answer. Instead, he turned to Otto, and with a benign look suffusing his face, said: 'I would think only of my son. If I could get twenty thousand acres securely in my hand, and improve it, when I died I would leave this lad' – and here he stroked Otto's head – 'a fortune of incalculable wealth.' In the pause which followed this sensible advice, he smiled at Otto, then added: 'Can you imagine your son at age twenty, with his bride at his side, taking command of a farm of twenty thousand acres? The cattle? The fields of corn? The faithful slaves working the cotton? And you sitting on the porch, surveying it all like a proud patriarch in the Old Testament?'

Mr Clendenning did not press Macnab to make a decision that day, but as the three left the boat Finlay did furnish a useful bit of information: 'I could handle the thousand dollars, if your company guaranteed that I'd get the land.'

'Guarantee?' Clendenning cried as if his integrity had been impugned. 'Look at these guarantees! These ironclad papers.' He made no attempt to close the deal, but when the boat sailed next day for New Orleans, he did leave behind a set of handsomely printed papers which specifically ensured the legality of any sale which might develop.

Being a cautious Scot, Finlay carried them next morning to the office of a German lawyer with whom his employer did business to seek an opinion, but before the lawyer, a man with a high collar and long-tailed coat, would give it he handed Finlay a card on which was printed:

ALL A LAWYER HAS TO SELL
IS HIS TIME AND HIS JUDGMENT

'How much?'

'Two dollars.'

'Good.'

The lawyer studied the documents left by the representative of the Texas Land and Improvement Company, then shrewdly pointed out: 'This is a Boston company presuming to do business in Mexico. I find nothing that binds the Mexican government to honor the promises made here. I'd be very reluctant to hand my good money over to such an agent, with so little to back his claims.'

'I wondered.'

'How much is he charging for the land?'

'Five cents an acre.'

The lawyer was dumbfounded, and showed it. Land touching Cincinnati was selling for two hundred dollars an acre, and he had during the past week supervised the sale of some four hundred acres. Five cents was meaningless.

'How many acres . . .?'

'Twenty thousand,' Finlay said.

Again the lawyer gasped: 'I can't imagine such a piece of land.' Taking a pen, he multiplied some figures and said: 'One thousand dollars. I could find you some wonderful land here, out in the country to be sure. But one thousand dollars is a lot of money.'

'Twenty thousand acres is a lot of land.'

'And Texas is nowhere.' The lawyer rose and placed his arm about Macnab's shoulder: 'It's Mexico, remember, and from what we hear up here, that's a most unstable country. It's not like Prussia, even England . . . and God knows it's not like the United States.'

'They tell me it soon will be part of us.'

'But you do not buy land on such a fragile expectation. Very dangerous, Macnab. Now, if you seek a farm, I know some excellent ones, but if you want full value for the two dollars you paid me, take my advice and buy several plots I know which abut on the river. Growth there is unavoidable.' He even quit his office to show Finlay the land he had in mind, and it was a splendid pair of lots that fronted on the river, so for some days Finlay's dreams deserted Texas and focused upon a chandler's shop on the Ohio.

He never saw Mr Clendenning again, but toward the end of January 1829, another salesman from the Boston firm came ashore from an upriver boat, and where Clendenning had been persuasive, this man was brutally forceful: 'Macnab, the land's selling like icicles in hell. You'd better grab your twenty thousand.'

'I've heard bad reports about the influx of criminals. Men who've been there say it's a madhouse.'

'One or two men fleeing their wives, a handful escaping unjust debts, and that's about it. I'd judge Texas to be one of the most moral states in Christendom.'

When Finlay demurred, the salesman grew angry, a tactic which worked along the frontier, where men appreciated harsh opinions firmly stated: 'Damn it all, Macnab, if you're so lily-livered, write to Stephen Austin hisself and ask him,' and he wrote out for Finlay directions as to how to address the founder of the American settlements in Texas. That night Macnab drafted his letter:

Bell's Tavern
Cincinnati, Ohio
27 January 1829

Dear Mr Austin,

My son Otto, aged seven, and I are contemplating a permanent remove to Texas and feel great solicitude about the nature of the population which will inhabit your country. We have been informed that you permit no one to settle within the limits of your colony unless able to produce vouchers of good moral character. This we can do, from Ireland of the north, from Baltimore and from this town, and we should like to live among other settlers of equal repute.

We are, however, much disturbed by rumors current here that only the worst venture into Texas and that our prisons are filled with persons of low character who swear that as soon as they are turned out they will head for Texas, for they say that it is a territory in which a man with ideas and courage

392

can make a go of it, by which they mean that criminals thrive in your colony.

My son and I are part of a responsible crowd gathered here willing to try our fortune in Texas, and we are awaiting the return of a Mr Kane who left us last September to explore your country. If he gives a good report, we shall want to join you, but in a letter from the east bank of the Sabine River dispatched in October he warned us: 'Tomorrow I shall cross over into Texas. Pray for me, because I am told that no man is safe west of the Sabine.' What are the facts?

We are also apprehensive about becoming citizens of Mexico, for we hear that it is a country ruled by brigands who have a revolution twice a year. Again, Sir, we are desirous of true information.

> Respectfully yours,
> Finlay Macnab
> Presbyterian

Remembering the lawyer's warning that the scrip carried no guarantee that Mexico was bound to honor it, Finlay wanted to ask Austin for clarification, but the salesman protested: 'You wouldn't want to worry an important man with a trivial matter like that!' So the question was not posed.

In the weeks following the posting of this letter Macnab interrogated many travelers regarding Texas and received conflicting reports. Said a Georgia man: 'A noble land. More salubrious than either Alabama or Mississippi. Ideal for the propagation of slaves, and high-spirited. I've never had a regretful thought since establishing my plantation there.'

But an Arkansas woman who had fled the colony for the civilization of Cincinnati groaned: 'Texas no more! They call where me and my man lived a town. No stores, no schools, no church with a steeple, and no cloth for sewin'. My old man and me had a race to see who could get out the fastest, and I won.' But then came a response from Stephen Austin himself:

San Felipe de Austin,
Coahuila-y-Tejas
20 April 1829

Dear Mr Macnab,

Your letter of 27 January reached me yesterday and I now put aside all other occupations to answer the sensible enquiries you make relative to this country.

You express an understandable solicitude as to the kind of settler who will inhabit Texas. In 1823 when I returned from Mexico City to proceed with settlement of my colony, I found that certain criminals had infiltrated and I immediately adopted measures to drive them away.

I forced them to cross back over the Sabine River, but from sanctuary in Louisiana they conducted raids into Texas, and what was worse, they lied about our colony, circulating every species of falsehood their ingenuity could invent. They were joined by others of their kind who had come to the Sabine, hoping to invade our colony, and there they sit in their bitterness, circulating lies about us.

I can assure you, Mr Macnab, that the citizens of Texas are just as responsible and law-abiding as those of New Orleans or Cincinnati, and that ruffians will never be allowed in this colony. The settlers already here are greatly superior to those of any new country or frontier that I have ever seen and would lose nothing in comparison with those of any southern or western state. They are, in my judgement, the best men and women who have ever settled a frontier.

You say you are apprehensive about living under the Government of Mexico. Let me assure you that the policy which Mexico has uniformly pursued toward us has been that of a kind, liberal and indulgent parent. Favors and privileges have been showered upon us to such an extent that some among us have doubted their reality, so generous have they been. The present ruler of Mexico is a man to be trusted, and the Constitution of 1824, under which he rules, is just and liberal, and in no way inferior to the constitutions of your various states. I can foresee no possible trouble that you might have with the Government of Mexico, which is now stable and far-sighted, and of which I am proud to be a citizen.

The minor disturbances which do sometimes arise down in Mexico never affect us here. We stay clear and have nothing to do with them. All that is required in Texas is to work hard and maintain harmony among ourselves. This is a gentle, law-abiding, Christian society and we would be most pleased to have you join us.

STEPHEN F. AUSTIN

When Macnab received these warm assurances he surrendered all doubts about Texas, telling his son: 'It may have a few rascals, but so did Ireland, and I can name several in this town.' He began to collect all debts owed him and to set aside those few and precious things he and his son would carry with them to Texas, but now two problems arose. Austin's letter had been so reassuring that Finlay, despite being a cautious Scot, had buried his uneasiness about the validity of scrip; he was eager to buy some, but found no one at hand to sell him any. And he had developed a real fear of riverboats. Four different steamboats, which he himself had provisioned, had blown up, with heavy loss of life, and he became apprehensive lest the one he chose for passage to Texas become the fifth.

Otto, of course, was eager to board anything that floated, and each day he kept his father informed as to what boats were at the wharf. When one sailed south without the Macnabs, Otto would list its replacement: '*Climax* left, but *River Queen* tied up.' To Macnab's surprise, this particular newcomer brought him an urgent letter:

Finlay Macnab
Bell's Tavern

I shall be in Cincinnati shortly. Make no move till I arrive.

Cabot Wellington
Texas Land and Improvement
Boston, Massachusetts

Now Macnab had to consider seriously his passage to New Orleans, and as he was talking with experienced men at the tavern, one chanced to mention as an alternative to boats: 'Have you ever thought of walkin' down to Nashville and pickin' up the Natchez Trace?'

'What's that?' Finlay asked, and several men crowded in, eager to explain. They said that in old times, before the advent of steam, carpenters along the Ohio used to build huge floating houses-on-rafts on which traders drifted down the rivers, sometimes all the way from Pittsburgh to New Orleans, but often terminating at Natchez-under-the-Hill, where they sold their rafts as house lumber, transferring their goods to real boats that conveyed them in orderly fashion to New Orleans.

'How did they get back without their rafts?' Finlay asked, and the men pointed to a surly-looking fellow who was drinking alone.

'Ask him.'

One of the men accompanied Macnab to the table where the lone man sat and asked: 'You a Kaintuck?'

'I am.'

'Can we join you?'

'No charge for chairs, I reckon.'

The go-between explained: 'Any man who goes downriver on a raft and comes back is known as a Kaintuck. Doesn't mean he's from Kaintucky. Where you from?'

'Kaintucky.'

'Tell my friend here how you came back from Natchez.'

'Walked.'

'All the way back from Natchez?'

'Yep, and my partner, he's still walkin'. On his way to Pittsburgh.'

'Is it difficult?'

The Kaintuck launched into a vivid description of the Natchez Trace: 'Murderers, cut-throats every foot of the way, robbers, horse thieves.' He stopped abruptly and broke into a raucous laugh. 'I'm talkin' about thirty years ago. Today? Much better.'

'How many days to Natchez?'

The Kaintuck ignored this question: 'If you knowed your history, which you bein' a Scotchman you probably don't . . .'

'How do you know I'm a Scot?'

'Because I heerd you. And if'n you knowed American history, you'd know that the great Meriwether Lewis, his as went to Oregon, he was murdered comin' home on the Trace.'

'Do travelers still use it?'

'They do.'

'Is the road still open?'

'It ain't a road. I been tryin' to tell you that, but you won't listen. It's what its name says, a clear-cut trace through the wilderness.'

'But it's still open?'

'If'n it could ever be called open. Four hundred and eighty miles through swamp and forest. Never a store, never a town, a few shacks run by half-breed Indians who cut your throat when you're sleepin'.'

'Could I walk it? With a seven-year-old boy?'

'My mother walked it with two babies,' the Kaintuck said, 'down and up. But maybe you ain't the man she was.'

Other travelers who had journeyed up the Trace gave such confirming reports that Macnab had pretty well decided to follow that land route, when a chance conversation with a loquacious Pittsburgh boatman just back from Natchez raised an ugly question that cast a shadow upon the entire Texas adventure.

The conversation started favorably: 'It's grand, driftin' down the rivers, walkin' home along the Trace.'

'How many miles can you make a day?' Finlay asked during a leisurely meal at the tavern.

'Driftin' downstream, sixty miles in twenty-four hours, not allowin' time lost when hung up on sandbars, which is a lot. Walkin' back, sixteen miles a day, week after week.' Then he added something which Finlay found attractive: 'Some men can make twenty, steady, but I often like to lie under the trees . . . in daylight, so I can watch the birds and the squirrels.'

'They told me murderers prowl the Trace.'

'That ended twenty years ago. But let's be honest. I do hide my money carefully – four different spots so I can give up a small part if I meet up with a hold-up man.' With a deft move of his right hand he produced an imaginary purse from his left breast. 'And I do feel safer if I travel with others through the lonely parts.'

'I wish I could have you as my partner,' Finlay said.

'I won't be walkin' the Trace no more. But if you're set on headin' for Texas, that's the cheap way to go, and you bein' a Scotchman . . .'

'We call it Scotsman.'

'Of course, when you get there, you'll be givin' up a lot more than your money.'

'What do you mean?'

The boatman looked soberly at Macnab and said: 'You're a

397

Presbyterian? I suppose you know that before you can get land in Texas you have to swear to the Mexican officials that you're a true Catholic.'

'What?'

'And your son will have to be baptized in the Catholic faith.'

'I never heard . . .'

'My brothers and me, we was thinkin' of Texas, but we're Methodists, and when we heard about that religion business . . . no, no.'

'You give me dismal news,' said Macnab. 'I'm not sure I should risk going to Texas.'

Things were in this delicate condition when a suave and stately gentleman alighted from the Pittsburgh boat, announcing that he was Cabot Wellington from Boston, looking for a Texas traveler named Finlay Macnab. He was what was known in the trade as 'the finisher,' the relentless man who came in only after the advance men had softened up the prospect.

As soon as he saw Macnab he cried enthusiastically: 'Dear friend! I bring you your passport to riches,' and he betrayed no disappointment when Finlay drew back, refused to accept any papers, and asked bluntly: 'What's this about converting to popery?'

Grandly, and with a condescending smile, Wellington said: 'Many ask about that rumor, and there's no better way to explain than to consult with a settler who already owns an estate in Texas,' and he whistled for a raw-boned, prearranged fellow of forty, who sidled up and allowed that he owned one of the best estancias in Texas.

'What's an estancia?'

'Fancy Mexican word for farm . . . real big farm. I was born, bred a Baptist. Virginia man. So when I gets to Texas, I ain't hankerin' to turn my coat, not me. Trick's simple. Don't let no Mexican priest convert you, because if they do, it's for keeps. But they's five or six Irish priests. Yep, imported direct from Ireland, through New Orleans. They never seen Mexico City or none of that.'

'What are they doing in Texas?' Finlay asked, for he had grown suddenly afraid, knowing that there were not in this world any Catholic priests more devout and stern than the

Irish. He wanted no Irish priest converting him, because that really would be forever.

'Stands to reason, the Mexican government, they cain't persuade any real Mexican priests to travel all the way to Texas. Those hanker after the fleshpots of the big city. So the only priests they can get to work in land s'far away are Irishmen who cain't make no livin' in Ireland, and who cain't speak a word of Spanish neither, if'n you ask me.'

'Aren't they real fanatics?'

'No! No! There's this big, jolly, whiskey-guzzlin' priest called Clooney, goes about on a mule, settlement to settlement, convertin' Protestants by the hundreds, free and easy, with him knowin' it ain't serious just as well as we know it ain't.'

'Did he convert you?'

'Yep. Father Clooney's the name, and a fairer man never lived. You let him sprinkle a little holy water over you, hand in your scrip, which Mr Wellington here will give you, and you get your league-and-a-labor.'

'Is that right?' Macnab asked.

'It is indeed,' Wellington said, and the Texas man added: 'The scrip solves ever'thin', and the day after you get your land you can revert to bein' a Baptist again. I did.'

'I'm Presbyterian.'

'My mother was a Presbyterian,' Wellington cried with real enthusiasm, and the deal was settled. Finlay Macnab and his son were entitled to twenty thousand acres of the choicest land in Texas, purchased at the ridiculous price of five cents an acre.

Otto was delighted when he learned that a firm decision had been reached. A dream long cherished was about to become reality: 'And we'll go by steamboat!' But, he grew apprehensive when Finlay reviewed the perils of such a river trip: 'You know, Otto, the steamers often blow up. Pirates attack from Cave-in-rock.' But when Otto said: 'Maybe we better walk down,' his father said: 'Robbers infest that route. Meriwether Lewis got murdered,' and the boy summarized their situation: 'Getting to Texas isn't easy.

But now Finlay devised a stratagem which would be useful regardless of which route they adopted. They assembled with many furtive moves a pair of homespun trousers for the boy, just a little too large; same for Finlay; long lengths of cloth identical with that used in the trousers; hats for both; cloth identical with the hats; a pair of long, heavy needles, very costly; and most important of all, their total savings were converted from paper and small coins into gold.

When all these items had been smuggled into Bell's Tavern, Finlay placed his son at the door to prevent intrusion, and began sewing. In the lining of the hats, in the waists of the pants and down the seams of the legs, he sewed his new material, embedding as he went, here and there, the gold coins he had acquired. When he finished, the Macnabs were going to be walking mines, as he demonstrated when Otto's pants and hat were finished: 'Try them on.'

Otto did not like the hat, for he had rarely worn one, and he could scarcely sit down because the coins made the pants far too stiff, but Finlay made him take the pants off, threw them on the floor, and jumped on them repeatedly: 'Now try them!' And the pants were manageable.

The Macnabs now doctored Finlay's garments until they, too, were gold-laden, and then they joined in solemn compact: 'When we reach the Trace we will never mention, not even to each other, where our gold pieces are till we get safe to Texas. Tell nobody ... nobody.' But Otto had to break the promise immediately, for he said: 'One piece hurts my bottom,' and this, of course, had to be corrected.

They were an attractive pair of emigrants as they crossed the ferry into Kentucky and started the three-hundred-mile hike to Nashville. Finlay was thirty-seven, medium height, blue-eyed, trim of carriage and sharp of mind. He'd had a solid book education in Scotland and a wealth of practical experience in the United States; he also had that engaging quality which would attract the eye of any unmarried woman looking for a good husband, and his easy manner acquired from working with Irishmen in the old country and with river folk in this made him an amusing addition to any group. Having outgrown those earlier acts of impulsive immaturity that had forced him to flee both Ireland and Baltimore, he now gave the appearance of a man who could work hard and earn his family a decent living, for he was very protective of his son. He was, in brief, the kind of man a nation hopes to get when it throws open its doors to immigrants, and he was typical of many who were beginning to swarm toward Texas.

His seven-year-old son was even more good-looking, with his blond hair peeping from beneath his new cap, his quick step and his thin face that looked almost sallow, for the sun seemed not to affect it. He wore heavy shoes, new homespun pants that came an inch below his knee, a thick woolen shirt and a manly kerchief about his neck. When strangers were with the pair for any length of time they were apt to remark: 'The father has a quick mind. But the lad, he's quiet, always seems to be thinking about something else.'

This was an accurate description of Otto. The confusion caused by his abrupt separation from his mother, the long walk to Cincinnati when he was first seeing the world, the loneliness at night, the fight with the bear, the constant departure of the steamboats he loved, leaving him always on the wharf, the catches of conversation about murders and explosions and sudden hangings – these unchildlike experiences, assaulting him so constantly, had aged him far beyond his years. Save only for the experiences of puberty, he was really a steely-eyed young man better prepared in some ways for the Natchez Trace than his more ebullient father.

But they were both hardened to the road by the time they completed their first two hundred and eighty miles and approached the bustling city of Nashville. There Finlay made a characteristically bold decision: 'What we'll do, Otto, is buy us as many cattle as we can handle, and we'll drove them to Natchez, put them on the boat to New Orleans, and sell them at a huge profit when we get to Texas.' Once this grandiose plan was voiced, no counsel from the experienced travelers in Nashville could dissuade him, and when stockmen pointed out that it was four hundred and eighty miles to Natchez, a right far piece for a man to drove cattle, he snapped: 'Shucks, when I was a boy I herded cattle clean across Scotland.' When he had left, with his thirty head of good stock, one of the sellers said: 'He'll find that Tennessee ain't Scotland.'

They would need a dog to help them, and Finlay knew they could never find a dog like Rob who could herd cattle better than a man, but they could find themselves some mongrel who would nip at the heels of strays. Since one dog would be about as good as another, Finlay left the selection to his son, and the boy identified a collie-sized female with the kind of face any boy would love. Her name was Betsy and she was owned by a family with three sons, each of whom had pets galore. When Otto asked, in his quiet voice, his blue eyes shining, what she would cost, the mother cried, almost with relief: 'Take her!' but two of the boys bellowed that she was their dog, whereupon their mother said: 'All right. Five cents.' And for this amount the deal was concluded.

Betsy had a reddish coat, a pointed nose and a set of the swiftest legs in Tennessee, but she also had a devious, calculating mind and was prone to stop and study whenever a command was given, judging whether Finlay really meant what he was saying. If she detected even the slightest hesitation, she ignored him and went her way, but if he shouted 'Damnit, Betsy!' she leaped into action. She was, in certain important ways, brighter than either of the Macnabs and she intended to train them, rather than the other way around.

The one weakness in her plan was that she quickly grew to love Otto, for he would play with her, test her running, wrestle with her, and keep her close to him when they slept on the ground at night. He also fed her, meagerly at times, but no matter how hungry she became between the food stands run by the half-breed Indians or between the deer shot by Finlay, she always sensed that she was getting her fair share of the food; if her stomach was growling with emptiness, so was Otto's.

With their cattle they could make only eight or nine miles a day, but at least they did not have to worry about pasture for their herd, for the Trace provided ample grass. Slowly, slowly they edged their way toward Texas.

Some eighty miles into the Trace they came upon the first of the notable stands, those extremely rude taverns which sometimes had food and sometimes did not, depending on whether the surrounding Indians had brought in their crops. This one was the infamous Grinder's that the Kaintuck in Cincinnati had warned about, a rough cabinlike affair containing two rooms, in one of which travelers could sleep on the floor, and a spacious porch covered by a sloping roof, where overflow travelers also slept on bare boards.

This time the stand had food, and when the broth and meat and potatoes had passed around, the men began to talk of Meriwether Lewis' tragic death twenty years earlier in 1809. 'Mark my words,' a Tennessee man said when the owners of the stand were out of the room, 'someone in this house shot him in the back, and I have a mind who done it.' He looked ominously at the door.

'You seem to forget,' another expert said, 'that he was killed not inside the stand, but outside,' and this evoked such heated discussion that the owners were summoned: 'Was Lewis killed in here or out there?'

'Out there,' a woman said, irritated by the constant bickering over this ancient crime. 'You know that my uncle was tried in court, all legal like, and not a word was proved agin' him. Clean as a baby's breath.'

When the owners were back at work in their part of the house, one man said firmly: 'My uncle knowed the coroner, and the coroner said: "Meriwether Lewis was killed inside the house, because the back of his head was blowed off and his throat was cut."'

Young Otto was repelled by this talk of murder, rejecting it as one more aspect of the rowdy life he did not wish to lead, and he was about to go outside and play with Betsy when the innkeeper said sternly: 'Time for bed!' But when Otto started to call Betsy inside to sleep with him, one of the men growled: 'We don't allow no damned fleabags in here,' so Otto and Betsy, curled together, slept on the porch.

In the morning they had covered about a quarter of a mile when Otto let out a yell. Still unaccustomed to wearing a hat, he had left his at Grinder's, in the sleeping room, with that passel of dangerous men, so without waiting for his father, he and Betsy dashed back and burst into the stand: 'Forgot my hat.' It was on the floor beside a Virginia man, and when Otto reached for it, the man lifted it and found it suspiciously heavy. Hefting it quietly in his left hand so that others could not see, he guessed the cause of its weight.

He made no comment, but before turning the hat over to Otto he accompanied the boy to the porch, where he said in very low tones: 'Excellent idea, but you would be prudent if you kept it close to you.' And he bowed as if delivering a legal opinion to a fellow citizen.

It was not easy walking the Trace. When rains persisted, freshets formed, and what had been easily negotiable gullies became roaring torrents. Then the travelers would have to camp for three or four idle days until the rains and the rivers subsided. Six men might be waiting on the south bank, heading for Nashville, and three on the north, destined for Natchez, and they would call back and forth, but they could not cross. Each year some impatient souls would try, and their bodies would be found far downstream, if found at all.

Now, in the late summer of 1829, the Macnabs with their dog Betsy and their thirty cows were pinned down on the Natchez Trace by a rampaging stream, and it was in this frustrating but not dangerous position that they met their second Kaintuck. He was a huge man, well over six feet, with bright red hair and massive shoulders; he was traveling alone and seemed indifferent to danger, for even though it must have been obvious that he was coming home carrying the profit from his trip, bandits had learned not to molest the Kaintucks, who observed one governing rule: 'If'n he makes one suspicious move, shoot him.'

This Kaintuck, bearded, scowling and irritable, was on his way north to pick up another boat in Cincinnati or Pittsburgh, and the impassable flood infuriated him.

'What the hell you doin' with them cattle?' were the first words he hurled across the treacherous stream.

'Taking them to Texas!' Finlay shouted back.

'You're a goddamned fool to try it.' That ended that conversation, for Finlay had no desire to defend his operation to a stranger. But as night was settling, the Kaintuck bellowed: 'What's the name of your dog, son?'

'Betsy.'

'That's a damned good name and she looks to be a damned good dog.'

'She is. She helps us.'

'I'll wager you need her, with all them cows.'

'We couldn't move without her.'

'I'll bet you're a big help, too.'

'I try to be.'

That was the beginning of Otto Macnab's fascination with the Kaintuck. During the two tedious days that followed, with the Macnabs only about eighteen feet from the huge man, Otto and he conversed on many subjects.

'Study this stream, son. Looks like a man could jump acrost it, and they say they's a man in Natchez that could. Big nigger with legs like oak trees. But don't never try it, son. Because one slip and they pick your bones up ten miles downstream.'

'Where do you live?' Otto's high voice shouted across the leaping wavelets.

'Goddamnedest place you ever seen. A real hog wallow.'

'Why are you going there?'

'Because it's home.'

'That sounds dumb.'

'It is dumb, but it's home.'

'How's your fire?'

'A fire's always in trouble. With wet sticks, particular.'

'Ours is all right.'

'That's because you ain't dumb, and I am.'

The two talked as if they were equals, which in a way they were, for the big man had ended his education at the level Otto was beginning his, and the more they talked the more they liked each other. The Kaintuck shouted that he'd had a wife, and a pretty good one, but she had died in childbirth: 'You know what that means, son?'

Otto may have been wise beyond his years, but there were certain important things he did not know, and now he faced one of them. Biting his lip and staring at the Kaintuck, he said: 'I think so.'

'Well, ask your father.'

'You tell me.'

'That ain't my prerogative.'

'What's a prerogative?'

'Right, son. Some things is right, some ain't. Ask your father.'

When Otto did he received a totally evasive answer, and it occurred to him that the Kaintuck would not have answered that way, but he sensed that he was caught in a mystery that was not going to be unraveled there by the pounding flood.

On late afternoon of the third day it became apparent that the flood was going to subside during the night and that passage would then be possible, but before it got dark the Kaintuck launched one more conversation.

'What's your name, mister?'

'Macnab, Finlay – and the boy's Otto.'

'That's Scottish, no?'

'You're the first person I've met who didn't call me Scotch.' No comment. 'What's your name?'

'Zave.'

'Zave!' Otto cried. 'What kind of name is that?'

'Best in the world. Named after one of the great saints. Francis Xavier.'

A hush fell over the subsiding stream, and after a long while Macnab asked: 'Is it that you're papist?'

'Aye, but I never force it.'

Macnab said no more. He felt uncomfortable sharing the wilderness with a papist, the more so because when he reached Texas there was bound to be unpleasantness over the matter of forced conversion, fraudulent though Father Clooney's were said to be. He had seen enough of the Protestantism-papism fight in Ireland and he wished for none in the forests of Mississippi.

But as the darkness lowered and shadows crept from the trees like black panthers come to steal the cattle, the Kaintuck spoke again: 'Macnab, you need help with them cattle.' No comment. 'Else you'll never get them to Natchez.' No comment. 'And I was wonderin' if maybe when the creek lowers ... and we cross ...'

'What?' It was a child's voice, trembling with excitement.

'I was wonderin' if maybe we could form partners.'

'Oh, Poppa!' The boy gave a wild cry of delight and started to dance about, then grasped his father's hands: 'Oh, it would be so ...' The boy could not frame his thoughts, and added lamely: 'It would be so welcome.'

'How about it, Macnab?'

'Poppa, Poppa, yes!' For three wet days Otto had watched the big man across the swollen stream and each new thing he saw increased his attachment to the wild Kaintuck. He was strong. He had violent manners when necessary. He could laugh and make jokes at himself. And obviously he had grown to like Otto.

'Where you really from, Zave?' The voice was adult and suspicious.

'Like I said, small town in Kaintucky. Piss-poor place.'

'You mind to settle in Texas?'

'From what you and the boy said, might as well.'

A world of meaning was carried in this brief, elliptical sentence: the conclusions of a man without a home, without prospects, without any visible or sensible direction in his life. If what Macnab said about the glories of Texas and the twenty thousand acres of choice land was true, what better?

Now, across the muddy waters, the Kaintuck pleaded: 'I ain't got no home, really. I ain't got nothin' much but down the river, up the river, and if you really got all that land, I could be mighty useful.' No comment. 'Besides, Mr Macnab, you ain't goin' to get them cattle to Natchez with just the boy to help.'

'Please, Poppa, please.'

'What's your full name, Zave?'

'Francis Xavier Campbell.'

Good God! In the middle of the Mississippi wilderness a traitorous Campbell from the Moor of Rannoch had tracked down a Macnab of Glen Lyon, and as in the ancient days, plotted his murder. 'Campbell is a forbidden name,' Finlay Macnab cried in the darkness. 'Ever since Glencoe.'

'I know Glencoe,' the voice from the other side said, 'but that was a long time ago. I am Campbell from Hopkinsville, not from Glencoe, and I seek to join with you.'

'Please!' came the boy's voice but in the night Finlay warned his son about the infamous behavior of the Campbells at Glencoe: 'I can hear my grandfather's voice: "Wherever, whenever you meet a Campbell, expect treachery." Across that stream waits a Campbell.' And through the long dark hours Finlay kept watch on his ancestral enemy, as if the dreadful crime at Glencoe had marked with blood-guilt every Campbell who would come along thereafter.

At dawn, as Finlay expected, big Zave Campbell gathered his muddy possessions, stepped down into the receding stream, and came directly toward the two Macnabs. Finlay, preparing to fight if necessary, shouted: 'Come no more!'

But Otto, seeing in Zave a needed companion, cried: 'We

407

want your help!' and in that fragile moment he settled the argument, for he ran and leaped into Campbell's arms.

'Come with us, Zave!' he cried, and from then on, it was four who went down the Trace: Finlay Macnab in command; Otto watching and listening; Zave Campbell, with a home at last; and the dog Betsy, terrified of the big man's commands. Under his tutelage she became twice the shepherd's companion she had been before, for when he told her to 'Git!' she got.

From their meeting at the flood they faced two hundred miles to Natchez, and often as they walked – ten miles a day now – Zave complained: 'Hell, I walked up this whole distance and now I'm walkin' down.'

'You asked to come,' Finlay growled, and each day during the first ten he kept close watch on Campbell, waiting for the sign that would betray the intended treachery. As the eleventh day waned he began to perspire so heavily that Otto asked: 'Are you sick, Poppa?' and he replied: 'I sure am. Don't you remember that it was on the eleventh night at Glencoe that the Campbells cut the throats of the Macdonalds?' Otto said: 'Last time you told me they shot them,' and Finlay snapped: 'What difference?'

When the sun set, Finlay refused to go to sleep, satisfied that once he closed his eyes this Campbell would cut his throat; instead, he sat against a tree, rifle across his knees, and when Otto rolled over at midnight and opened his eyes, there his father waited. They both looked a few feet away to where Zave snored easily, and when the boy arose at dawn nothing had changed.

Campbell was never told of the night-long vigil, but on the twelfth day Finlay astonished everyone by blurting out: 'Zave, nobody herds cattle better than you. When we reach Texas and get our land, you can have your share. You earned it.'

'You can build your barn right next to ours,' Otto said.

'You any idea how big twenty thousand acres is, son?' With a twig as chalk and a sandy bank as blackboard, Zave lined it out: 'Six hundred forty acres to a square mile. Six-forty into twenty thousand, that's thirty-five, thirty-six more or less square miles. That means six miles to a side. So my barn ain't goin' to be very close to your barn.'

That day he showed Otto just how far six miles was going to

be: 'Remember this little stream, way back here. I'll reckon the miles as we drive the cattle, but you keep in mind how far away this stream is,' and as they walked off the miles the boy gained his first sense of how vast things in Texas were going to be. He had thought of his future home as a kind of farm; the way Zave explained it, the place would be an empire.

Zave then took in hand Otto's real education: 'I'm surprised you cain't shoot proper. I was your age, I could hit me a sparrow.' Using his own long rifle, he taught the boy the tricks of hunting, especially the art of rapid loading: 'Cain't never tell when that second shot, fired prompt, is goin' to turn the trick.' He drilled Otto in firing accurately, then reloading at finger-numbing speed: 'You got to do it in rhythm, like a dance. And always in the same order. Prop your gun. Right hand, grab the wadding. Left hand, take the ramrod from its place, jam it down the muzzle, tamp down the wadding. Left hand again, ball from the pouch, slide it in. Right hand, take the percussion cap and fix it. Both hands, fire!'

When Otto began dropping birds and squirrels out of trees and reloading instantly for the next shot, Zave was ecstatic: 'Macnab! I think we got us a real man on our hands.'

The hunting experience that Otto would remember longest, however, came early one morning when he was following a squirrel as it leaped through the trees. From the north came a soft whirring sound which increased until it was a dull persistent thunder, and when he looked up he saw coming toward him more birds than he had ever imagined; the sky was dark with them, and as they came in always-increasing numbers, the morning sun was blanketed and a kind of twilight fell over the earth. All morning they came, a flock so great it must have covered entire counties and even large parts of states, an incredible flight of birds.

'Passenger pigeons,' Zave said. 'Always have flown that way, always will.' Once when the birds were low overhead he fired a musket at them, and they flew in such packed formation that he brought down eleven, and the eating was good.

On they went, two Macnabs, a Campbell and a dog, droving cattle through lonely and forlorn land as their ancestors had done two centuries before in the Highlands of Scotland, and at last they came to Natchez, that French-Spanish-English-

American town of great beauty perched high on its hill above the Mississippi, with its squalid row of half a dozen mean streets down on the flats, where the great boats docked, where the saloons never closed, where boatmen from Kentucky and Tennessee lost in an hour what they had slaved for months to earn.

As they drove their cattle along the main streets, lined with expensive and glamorous houses, Otto knew instinctively that he and his companions were not intended to stop there; threatening stares of passers-by in costly clothes told him that, but he was not prepared for what he found when Finlay and Zave herded their cattle down the steep streets leading to the waterfront. Now they passed into an entirely different world – of sweating black porters, shouting women, steamboats with their engines banked being warped into position, side by side, and bands of musicians playing music endlessly. Natchez-under-the-Hill was its own town of several thousand, and here the commerce of the great river basins – Ohio, Missouri, Mississippi – came temporarily to rest in huge warehouses that groaned with the produce of America.

It was an exciting place, a steaming hodge-podge of black and white, of Virginian and New Yorker, of buyer and seller, of slave and free, and many a man who now owned one of the big white-pillared houses on the hill, with many servants proclaiming his wealth, had started buying fish and timber on the wharfs.

But it was also a frightening place, with knives flashing in the dark, and Zave Campbell showed young Otto the spot where one of the greatest knife fighters of them all, Jim Bowie of Tennessee, had demonstrated his ferocious skill. 'Bowie had this fierce knife and he allowed hisse'f to be tied to a log, and his enemy, he was lashed down too, and there they fought it out, slashin' and duckin', and Bowie cut his man to shreds.'

'What did he do then?'

'He asked his brother Rezin to make him an even bigger knife. Foot and a half long, with a heavy guard protectin' the handle from the blade.'

'Why did he do that?'

'He said: "When you're strapped to a log, you cain't have a knife that's too long."'

'Can I see him? Where is he now?'

'Who knows? They run him out of Tennessee.'

When it came time to arrange for the cattle to move south toward New Orleans, Macnab discovered two painful truths: the cost of taking them by steamboat was prohibitive, and he had wasted his energies bringing them down from Nashville. 'Man,' he was told, 'we find all the cattle we need in New Orleans. They bring 'em in from everywhere.' And when Finlay pointed out that he intended to take them on to Texas, the speaker guffawed: 'Hector, come here and tell the man!'

Hector was a dumpy fellow in his forties. He had been to Texas and proposed to return as soon as the two boilers for his sawmill reached Natchez from Pittsburgh, where they had been bolted together and caulked. 'Cattle to Texas?' he said. 'That's the craziest thing I ever heerd of. Cattle run free all over Texas, millions of 'em. I hire two Mexicans to keep the damned things off'n my place.'

'Are you telling the truth?'

'Come here, Buster.' The sawmill man called everyone Buster, and when he had Finlay seated on one of the pilings of a wharf he explained: 'Cattle been breedin' free in Texas since the Creation, or as some say, since the Spaniards arrove. Cattle everywhere. Big ... huge horns ... best eatin' beef God ever made, and, Buster, strike me dead if they ain't all free. You just go out with your lasso ...'

'What's a lasso?'

'Mexican-style rope. You form it in a loop, and you won't believe me when I tell you what a tricky hand can do with that loop.'

'It's hard to believe what you say.'

'Texas is different, Buster, and you got to accept it on faith. If you carry them cattle on to Texas, all you can do is give 'em away. You sure as hell cain't sell 'em.'

'What should I do?'

'I'd sell 'em right here. As beef.'

'They won't bring what I paid for them in Nashville.' He spat. 'And all that trouble on the Trace.'

The sawmill man clapped him on the shoulder: 'Buster, sometimes plans go sour. They promised me, solemn, that my

411

boilers would be here six months ago. I'm still waitin' and I'm still payin' for my room, such as it is.'

Macnab and Campbell spent five days trying to reach the best deal on the cattle, and Otto was surprised one afternoon to hear them telling a prospective customer that they had thirty-three head to sell, for he knew that his father had left Nashville with thirty and had sold two to stands along the Trace that needed beef. There should be twenty-eight for sale, but what he did not know was that it was physically and morally impossible for a Macnab or a Campbell to pass through territory containing cattle without enlarging his herd. By practices going back five hundred years, they had acquired an additional five head.

In the end they had to sell at a severe loss, but the transaction was not without its benefits, because the buyer was a man who ran a repair shop for steamboats, a kind of inland ships' chandlery, and when through casual conversation he discovered how experienced Finlay was in such matters, he pressed him to accept a job serving the big riverboats. At first Findlay demurred, so the man said: 'Help me and I'll double the price I offered for your beef.'

This was too gratifying for a trader like Macnab to refuse, for as he explained to Campbell: 'We make a neat profit on the animals, and we can save money for our start in Texas.' He went back to the man and said: 'I'll take the job, but you must employ my friend Campbell, too. He's a mighty worker.'

'I've seen Campbell on other trips. He eats big and works little.' He would not hire the big Kaintuck, but Macnab did find Zave a job sweeping out a saloon, and when the three settled in to Natchez-under-the-Hill as if it had always been their home, Texas grew farther away.

The only problem was Otto. He was eight now, not much taller than before, and the long tradition of the Macnabs required him to get started on his education, but schools were not a major feature of Under-the-Hill. There were some on the upper level, but it was difficult to get to them, and when Finlay inquired, he was told quite bluntly: 'We do not look kindly upon boys from Under.'

There was, however, a woman on the lower level, now married to a roustabout, who had once taught school in the rowdy town of Paducah when it was still called Pekin, and she said that she could teach Otto reading, writing and numbers up to the rule of three. She was a mournful lady, spending much of each class telling the boy of her more fortunate days in Memphis, where her father sold furniture and coffins, but she developed a real liking for the lad and gave him a rather better education than he might have received in the more fashionable classrooms of the upper level.

It was curious, Otto thought, that the two towns were so separate; a person could live his entire life in one, it seemed, without ever venturing into the other. Under-the-Hill was the bigger, the more flourishing and also much the wilder, but just as he had discovered on the long walk through Maryland that civilization could consist of a cabin in the wilderness throwing light and comfort into the darkness, so now he knew where the good life lay in Natchez: it thrived in those big, clean, white houses atop the hill, and whenever they had the chance, he and Zave would climb the steep streets and walk aimlessly beneath the arching trees, looking at the mansions.

'You ain't to think, son, that everybody in there is happy,' Zave cautioned, and he showed Otto two especially fine houses from which a boy and a girl, desperately and hopelessly in love, had come to Under-the-Hill to commit suicide. And he also knew which big one had contained the man who had run away to Pittsburgh, abandoning his wife and two daughters.

'My father ran –'

'Don't tell me about it!' Campbell thundered, and Otto pondered these complexities.

The year 1830 passed, with Finlay earning substantial wages on the waterfront and with Zave Campbell promoted to bartender, where he could steal from both his boss and his patrons. The trio was prospering financially, but Otto was not advancing in much else, for he had mastered about as much learning as the Paducah woman could dispense and was beginning to lose interest. Also, he was reaching the age when circumstances might throw him in with the rowdy urchins who pestered ship captains when their boats were tied up, and Otto himself worried about this, because everything he had so far observed inclined him toward an orderly life away from the excesses of Under-the-Hill. In that whirlpool even children witnessed

413

murders and shanghaiings and young women committing suicide and endless brawls, and he had no taste for such a life. At age nine he had become more than cautious; he was a little Scots-German conservative set so firmly in his ways that they would probably last a lifetime.

One aspect of life Under-the-Hill he could not adjust to: the presence of so many women. It occurred to him as he looked back upon his travels that he and Finlay, and even Campbell, had always moved where there were no women; on the trails, along the waterfront, in the stands of the Trace, it had been a man's world. Even in settled Cincinnati when they talked with people who had been in Texas, they had met only one woman, the Arkansas lady who had fled.

But now they were surrounded by young women and he perceived that even tough men like his father and Zave sometimes wanted to be with them, those very pretty girls with only first names, and although he did not understand fully, he knew it must be all right. What irritated him, though, was that the girls sometimes showed as much interest in him as they did in Zave and his father, pampering him and petting him and offering to cut his hair. They were, he realized, doing this so as to impress Finlay and Zave that they were the motherly type, and he grew quite sick of the attention.

But his irritation was forgotten whenever Zave and one of the young women from the saloon took him down to the waterfront, with rifles to shoot at objects floating down the Mississippi. Then he liked it if Zave's girl cheered when he hit a bottle and Zave did not, or when with two quick shots made possible by adroit reloading he shattered two bottles.

'You're a little sharpshooter,' a girl said one day as she kissed him, and this he did not protest.

That night he was startled when he overheard his father proposing to a new arrival from Pennsylvania that the man purchase his Texas scrip: 'Partner, I'll sell you this for half what I paid, and you can see the figures right here. Twenty thousand acres, one thousand good American dollars.' The newcomer said he would think it over, carefully, for his heart was set on Texas, and he visualized the twenty thousand acres in terms of the ultra-rich farmland of Lancaster County. He might never find such a bargain again.

Otto was distraught by his father's proposal, and he discussed it with both his teacher and Zave, and they, too, were appalled. The Paducah woman went boldly to Macnab and said: 'You have a treasure in your son Otto. Don't waste him in this sewer.'

'You're doing well here. I'm doing well.'

'I have no choice. You do.'

'A hundred men have started Under-the-Hill and moved up. And I'm to be the hundred and first. You watch.'

'And what in hell will you have if you do move up? Take your kid to Texas and make him a man. And take that worthless Campbell with you.'

Zave was even more insistent: 'Finlay, I'm workin' here only to save money to get to Texas. This is the cesspool of the world. I just been waitin' for you to say the word.'

'You've got a good job, Zave. I got a good job.'

'And Otto, he's got nothin'. He should be on a horse, on open land . . . and so should you and me.'

One night, after work, Finlay broached the subject with his son. They were living in one room over Zave's saloon, where the accumulation of eighteen rootless months lay scattered about. 'I think, Otto, that in another year we'll have enough money to buy a house on top. A hardware store, or maybe a general one like we had in Baltimore, with a good German bakery.'

'People on top ain't always happy,' Otto said. 'Sometimes they do terrible things.'

'Where'd you hear that?'

'Zave told me. He showed me where.'

'What would you like to do?'

Almost defensively the boy drew Betsy to him, cradling her head in his lap, for he was afraid to expose his true longings, but under his father's pressuring he blurted out like the little boy he still was: 'I'd like to get aboard one of those steamboats, and stay aboard when the whistle blows, and just sail and sail, and then maybe have a horse on a great big farm where me and Betsy can run forever.'

Next morning the man from Pennsylvania came to Macnab's shop and said he'd take the scrip, but Finlay said quietly: 'Yesterday it was for sale. Today it ain't. My son wants it.'

415

He never looked back. After giving his employer notice and receiving from him an unexpected bonus, he told Campbell to quit his job at the saloon, paid the teacher more than she expected, and bought three passages on the New Orleans steamer *Clara Murphy*, which would be putting in to Natchez on Thursday morning, 25 August 1831, on its way south from St Louis.

Otto was elated that his long-delayed dream of steaming down the river was at last coming true, and while Finlay and Campbell slept amidst the deck cargo, he and Betsy walked back and forth, surveying the mystery of this great river. It was a trip into wonderland, and he never tired of watching strange happenings along the shore: slaves shifting bales of cotton, mules dragging a damaged boat ashore, freshly cut timbers piled sky-high. That morning, still unwilling to sleep lest he miss some dramatic scene, he imagined himself as captain maneuvering the *Clara Murphy* past treacherous sandbars, docking her at a plantation wharf where white women carrying umbrellas to protect them from the sun strolled aboard. Twice he chanted with the sweating black crew as they worked the boat, and he tried to hide his pleasure when they called him 'our little riverman.' He was prepared, at the end of that first glorious day, to be a Mississippi man for the remainder of his life.

On this trip he saw the richness of Louisiana, for it seemed that all the wealth of the state was crowded along the shores of the river, and he perceived that families acquired fine homes with vast lawns only when they owned many slaves. Not once on this long, revealing trip did it occur to him that the slaves might have rights of their own or that their condition in 1831 could be temporary. They were black, different in all respects, and obligated to serve their masters.

New Orleans was totally different from Cincinnati and Natchez. It exuded both prosperity and pleasure and had a relaxed spirit the other towns lacked. It was obviously very old, with strong French and Spanish accents bespeaking earlier settlers, and the mighty levees, raised high to keep the Mississippi out of the streets and homes, awed and impressed Otto. Also, there was a bustle about the city which delighted the boy, and he perceived that whereas the waterfront of Natchez had been unhealthy and unclean, that of New Orleans was vibrant and almost self-policing, as if the excesses tolerated in Under-the-Hill would be forbidden here.

And there was burgeoning commercial activity. In one afternoon of casual exploration among the shippers his father was offered two jobs, but Finlay had learned from his Natchez experience not to take them lest he become entangled permanently in something he intended to engage in only temporarily. 'Very well,' one trader with a French name said expansively. 'You're the boss. But when you get to Texas and start your plantation, remember me. Louis Ferry, New Orleans. I'll buy your mules, your cotton, your timber.'

'Do all those come from Texas?'

'Look at my yards. I get three parts from Louisiana, seven parts from Texas.'

'How do I get my produce here?'

'Ships run all the time, but they're expensive. Best way is with mules, herd them up and drove them in. Takes time but it costs nothing.'

'You keep speaking about mules. Don't you accept horses?'

'Rich people buy horses, now and then. U.S. Army buys mules all the time.'

He wrote out his name and address for Macnab, and added: 'I've got a better idea. Put together a big herd of mules, bring them in for a good profit, and then stay with me as my manager of the Texas trade.'

'Where would I find the money to get the mules?'

Ferry broke into laughter: 'Man, in Texas the horses run wild. Mustangs they call them. Thousands, thousands, you just go out and rope them and they're yours.'

'Yes, but where do I get the mules?'

'Man, you buy yourself a strong jackass, throw him in with the mares, and let him work himself to death.'

'What happens to the male horses?'

'You drive them to New Orleans. I can always use a few.' When Finlay looked dubious, Ferry cried: 'You ever see a Texas mustang? I got a yard full over here and wish I had a hundred more.' He led Macnab to a corral, where for the first time Finlay saw the powerful little horses of the Texas range, much smaller than he had expected, much finer-looking than he had supposed a small horse could be.

'They run wild?' He studied them carefully, exercising his eye trained among the great horses of Ireland, then said: 'They told me in Natchez that cattle run wild too.'

Ferry clapped him vigorously on the shoulder: 'In Texas everything runs wild. You just reach out and grab.'

'Why aren't you in Texas?'

'Because it's a wilderness. Not a decent place to eat in the whole damned province. And besides, it's a Mexican wilderness, and who wants to live in a country that can't govern itself?'

'Some Americans seem to like it.'

'Right! Right! And if I was that kind of American, I might like it too.'

'What kind of American are you speaking of?'

'An American like you. Energy, courage, stars in your eyes ... and willingness to live alone. Because, man, Texas is empty. Just wild cattle and untamed horses.'

As he said this, the young man who had brought the mustangs to New Orleans appeared in the corral, and as soon as Otto saw him, he was captivated, for the herdsman was the first Mexican he had met. He was in his mid-twenties, whip-thin, dark-skinned, and clad in the distinctive uniform of the range: tight blue pants marked by a tiny white stripe, bandanna, big hat, boots and spurs. To Otto he looked the way a Texan should.

'Show them how you ride,' Ferry ordered, and with just a slight flare of resentment at being spoken to as if he were a peasant, the young man flicked the brim of his hat almost insolently, but then smiled warmly at Otto: 'Is the young man good with the horse?'

'I can ride,' Otto said, and the young Mexican whistled to one of his assistants: 'Manuel, tráenos dos caballos buenos!'

From a hitching rail near the corral, Manuel untied two horses already saddled, and deftly the young man lifted himself onto the larger one, indicating that Otto should mount his, which the boy did rather clumsily.

The Mexican then began to canter about the stable area, shouting to Otto: 'Follow me!' and a delightful comedy ensued, for the Mexican rode with skill, swinging and swaying with the motion of his horse like a practiced professional, while the boy tried energetically to keep up, slipping and sliding and nearly falling from his mount. But he did hold on, grabbing his horse's mane when necessary.

Ferry, Finlay and Campbell applauded the exhibition, whereupon the Mexican rider broke loose from Otto's comical trailing to perform a series of beautiful feats, ending with a full gallop at Campbell, bringing his steed to a halt a few inches from the Kaintuck's toes.

'The boy could learn to ride,' he said as he dismounted, and when Otto came up awkwardly, the Mexican helped him dismount and asked: 'Son, you want to ride back to Texas with me? And help me bring another remuda up for Don Louis?'

'Oh!' Otto cried with enthusiasm. 'That would be wonderful!'

'Who is this young horseman?' the senior Macnab asked, and as the rider continued talking with Otto, Ferry said: 'Young Mexican from Victoria. South Texas. Absolutely trustworthy. What he says he'll do he does.'

'He brought you all these animals?'

'He did.'

'Where did he get them?'

'In this business you never ask.'

'What's your name, young fellow?' Macnab asked.

'Garza,' the rider said, smiling. 'Benito Garza.' He pronounced each syllable carefully, drawing it out in the Mexican way: 'Beh-nee-to Gartsah,' with exaggerated accent on the *nee* and *Gar*. Having introduced himself verbally, he did so symbolically with another flick of his finger against the brim of his big hat, and with that, he disappeared into the stables.

At the inn where they were staying prior to arranging passage to their new lands, the Macnabs and Campbell met two authentic residents of Texas, well-educated plantation owners who had come to New Orleans to arrange for the sale of their products on a regular basis. After they had reached an understanding with Louis Ferry, whom they lauded as the best man in the business, they chatted about aspects of their new home:

'We have great men in Texas, equal of any in Massachusetts or Virginia. We plan to erect a notable state with all the

419

advantages of South Carolina or Georgia. There's a spaciousness to our view. We can see clear to the Pacific Ocean. And a nobility to our minds, because we're determined to build a new society . . .

'Everything is of a vast dimension and we need men with vast potential to help us achieve what we've planned. Weaklings will be erased, by the climate and the distance if by nothing else, but the strong will find themselves growing even stronger. Any young man of promise who doesn't catch the first boat to Texas is an idiot . . .'

When Finlay raised several questions about things that disturbed him, the two men laughed them off: 'The Frenchman said the food was inedible? He's right. Abominable. But it can only get better. The Arkansas woman fled because of loneliness? She was surely right. My nearest neighbor is forty miles away, and I don't want him any closer because then he'd be on my land.'

But when Finlay voiced serious doubts about the instability of the Mexican government, he noticed that the men became evasive, and he was about to find out whether they favored the ultimate incorporation of Texas into the American Union when the men changed the subject dramatically. The leader, spreading his hands on the table, asked energetically: 'And where do you propose settling?'

'I was about to ask your advice.'

'Nacogdoches up here. Victoria down here. Both places wonderful for an energetic man, which I take you to be. But any reasonable place in between is just as good.'

'Where are you?'

'I'm down here at the mouth of the Brazos River. My brother-in-law, he's up here at Nacogdoches.'

'Where should I go?'

'Wherever the ship deposits you. Landing in Texas is not easy. Sometimes the ship can make one spot, sometimes another. How much land you taking up?'

'I've bought myself twenty thousand acres.'

One of the men whistled: 'That's a mighty spread. How'd you hook it?' •

Proudly Macnab opened his papers, showing the men his

authority for the occupation of twenty thousand acres, as approved by the Mexican government, in any likely area. The men studied the papers, then looked at each other and said nothing. Pushing the documents back to Macnab, they changed the subject to shipping.

'What you must do is catch a steamboat that goes to the mouth of the Mississippi. A sailing ship will be waiting there to carry you to Texas.'

'Why don't the steamboats go all the way?'

'They've tried it. Too many wrecks. It's never easy to enter Texas.'

'Where should I head for?'

'We told you. Wherever the ship lands you. It's all good.'

When Finlay was back in his room he pondered the suspicious manner in which the men had reacted to his papers, and he began to worry that his documents might be faulty, so well after midnight he ascertained where the men were sleeping and went to their room, knocking loudly until one of the men opened the door. 'I apologize, but this is terribly important to me. Is something wrong with my papers?'

'No, no! They're in good shape.' The man tried to close the door, but Finlay kept it open.

'They're not, and I saw it clearly in your eyes when you looked at them. You must tell me.'

There was no light in the room, but the man propped open the door and invited Macnab to sit on his bed while he sat on the bed of his brother-in-law. Painfully, hesitantly, they told Macnab the truth: 'Your papers are a fraud. We see it all the time.'

'You mean . . .'

'No standing at all in Mexico. Land isn't given out that way. That traveler in the next room without a single sheet of paper has as good a chance as you of getting land in Texas.'

'How can such a thing be allowed?'

'Two different countries. Your fake company is in the United States. The land is in Mexico.'

'My God! A thousand dollars!' In anguish Macnab leaped from the bed.

'Completely lost,' the man said. But when Macnab groaned, the men both spoke in rushes of encouraging words.

'I didn't mean that everything is lost.'

'You can still get land, excellent land, but never twenty thousand acres.'

'You get it free . . . absolutely free.'

After this burst of warm reassurance, one of the men pressed Finlay to sit back down, then patiently helped as his brother-in-law explained the situation:

'You land in Texas wherever the ship drops you, and you establish contact with the Mexican officials. Being Scotch, I suppose you're Protestant, so you volunteer to convert to Catholicism. We're both Catholics, legally, but we're really Baptists. Conversion entitles you to one thousand acres of land, maybe a little more because of your son. The big fellow with you, he can get the same.

'If you're lucky enough to be unmarried and can find a Mexican girl to marry, you could very well get yourself a league-and-a-labor, and that's a lot of land. Or you could buy land from someone like the two of us who already has his league-and-labor . . . I have three, he has two. We have none for sale, but it goes for about twenty cents an acre and it can be very good land. Maybe fifty cents for bottomland along the river, and I'd advise you to get some of that. Or you can apply to one of the great empresarios who already have legal title to enormous reaches of land, and you can get that for almost nothing, and sometimes for nothing at all, because they want settlers.

'I got mine in three different ways. Mexican government gave me some. I bought some. And Stephen Austin, as fine a man as you'll ever meet, he was so anxious to get settlers on his properties that he gave me a large plot. Originally one bit here, one bit up here and one bit way down there. But I traded even till I had them side by side, and now I have fifteen thousand acres for a little over two thousand dollars. You can do the same.'

The man on the bed asked in the darkness: 'Are you married, Macnab?' and after the slightest hesitation Finlay replied: 'No.' They were pleased at this information, for it meant that if all else failed, he could marry a Mexican woman and get a quadruple portion.

'Why do they make it so complicated?' he asked.

'With Mexicans, nothing is ever allowed to be simple.'

A rickety old steamboat carried thirty American adults, nine children and twenty-two slaves down the tortuously winding Mississippi south of New Orleans. Passengers marveled as they crept past beautiful moss-hung plantations of the lesser sort, for as a deckhand explained: 'If'n they got money, they has a plantation above New Orleans, not below.' Here the air hung heavy and insects droned in the heat as travelers prayed for some vagrant breeze to slip in from the Gulf of Mexico. Entire sections of land became swamps inhabited only by birds and alligators, swamps interminable, until at last the steamboat reached the strangest termination of any of the world's major rivers: a bewildering morass of passes seeking the Gulf, of blind alleys leading only to more swampland. Often it was impossible to determine whether the area ahead was fresh-water river, or salt-water Gulf, or firm land, or simply more weed-grown swamp.

'How can he tell his way?' Otto asked one of the deckhands.

'By smell.'

The answer was not entirely frivolous, for as the great river died, the smell of the vast, free Gulf intruded, and soon Otto himself could detect the larger body of water.

As soon as the vessel waiting in the Gulf became aware of the approaching steamer, its captain fired a small cannon to signify that all was in readiness, and Otto, seeing for the first time an ocean-going craft, shouted: 'There she is!' These last days had been a journey through a primeval wonderland, more challenging by far than that along the river to the north of New Orleans, and to see the sloop *Carthaginian* waiting motionless at the end of the passage was like seeing a light in the forest.

As they threw ropes to the steamer, sailors shouted the good news: 'We sail for Galveston!' and travelers who had hoped to make that important landing cheered. Fare to Texas would be twenty-one dollars total, five paid to the steamboat, sixteen to the sail-borne sloop. But no transfer from one craft to another was ever made easily, no matter how gentle the sea, and now when the steamboat dipped slightly, the sloop lifted, and contrariwise. Shins were barked and baggage imperiled, but finally the adults were safe aboard the vessel, the children could be handed across, and the slaves were able to follow. The returning steamboat, having picked up passengers for New Orleans, blew its whistle three times in farewell. The emigrants cheered. And the trip across the Gulf was begun, with the passengers having only the slightest comprehension of their destination.

'We're making for Galveston,' an officer explained, 'but if the weather's bad, we may have to put in at Matagorda Bay.'

Galveston was some four hundred miles, almost due west, and since there was a sharp breeze from the southeast, the ship could make four knots, or about one hundred and ten land miles a day. 'The trip won't require more than four days,' the officer assured the passengers, 'and I doubt that it will be rough.'

Otto loved the swaying of the ship, and whereas some of the passengers experienced a slight seasickness, he roamed everywhere and ate large quantities of everything. It was a holiday for him, but some of the travelers were agitated by the uncertainty of destination: 'We hoped to put in at Matagorda. Our people are there.'

'You can walk from Galveston to Matagorda,' a sailor said easily, as if the trip were a matter of hours.

'Why can't we go direct to Matagorda?'

'Because on this passage, we never know. I don't even know if'n we'll be able to land in Galveston.'

'What kind of ship is this?' one man growled.

'It ain't the ship. It's Texas,' and the sailor outlined the problem:

'Texas is a great land, I'm sure. It's got ever'thin' a man might want – free land, free cattle, beautiful rivers, and mountains too, I hear, in the west. But one thing it ain't got is a safe harbor. None.

'It has fine big bays, best in the world. Galveston, Matagorda, Corpus, Laguna Madre. I been in 'em all, and they ain't none better. Only one thing wrong with 'em. No way you can get into 'em. God made Hisse'f these perfect bays, then guarded them with strings of sandbars, half-assed islands, marshes, and ever' other kind of impediment you

424

could imagine.

'This is maybe the most dangerous coastline in the whole damned world. Look at the wrecks we'll see when we try to get into one of them bays. Wrecks everywhere. First steamboat tried it, wrecked. Next steamboat, went aground, and you'll see it rottin' there if'n we're driven to Matagorda. The coast of Texas is hell in salt water.'

The weather remained good, the sloop did make for Galveston, and the same sailor came back with one bit of comforting news: 'Maybe I overdone it. This is a mighty tough coast, as you'll see, but one worry we don't have. They ain't no beetlin' rocks stacked ashore. And they ain't none hidin' submerged to rip out your bottom. Anythin' you hit is soft sand.' But he returned a few minutes later with a correction: 'Of course, most of the wrecks you'll see did just that. They hit soft sand, held fast, and then turned over.' Otto noticed that he never said what happened to the passengers.

But as the *Carthaginian* neared Galveston toward the close of the fourth day, a strong northerly wind blew out from shore, creating such large waves that as the sun sank, the captain had to announce: 'Waves get that high, takes them days to subside.'

'Can't we push through?' asked a man whose home ashore was almost visible.

'Look at the last ship that tried,' the captain replied, and off to starboard, rocking back and forth in the grasping sands, a sailing ship of some size was slowly being broken to pieces. On her stern Otto read: SKYLARK NEW ORLEANS.

'It'll have to be Matagorda Bay,' the captain said, and only a few daring souls whose hearts had been set on Galveston demurred, for the others realized that any attempt to land there would be suicidal.

That night, as the ship made its way southwest through calmer seas to the alternate landing, Otto remained topside, running with his dog along the deserted decks, while his father and Zave Campbell remained below at their evening meal. When they were finished, the two men pushed back their plates and lingered in a corner of the cabin, piecing together a rough assessment of their fellow passengers: 'Twenty-three families, but only seven wives. What happened to the other sixteen? Did

425

they all die, except ours?'

Not at all. The twenty-three men represented a true cross-section of those coming into Texas at this time. Seven were married and with their wives along; four were legitimate widowers eager to launch new lives; three had never been married and looked forward to finding women in Texas, American or Mexican no matter. The nine wandering men like Macnab had left wives either abandoned permanently or clinging to some vague promise: 'If things work out well, I'll send for you and the kids.' Few were likely to do so.

Curiously, four of these iron-souled wife-deserters had, like Macnab, brought their sons along – one man from Kentucky with two – but none had brought daughters, and few would ever see them again. These were powerful, stubborn men, cutting themselves loose from society.

'On one thing I seem to have been dead wrong,' Macnab confided. 'I wrote to Austin asking if most of the newcomers were criminals escaping jail back east. From what I can judge, there isn't a criminal in the lot.'

'I wouldn't trust my money with that tall fellow from Tennessee,' Campbell said.

Macnab was correct in his guess, Campbell wrong in his. Among these men there was not one criminal, not one who had had to leave Connecticut or Kentucky under even a minor cloud. They may have been men who had failed emotionally with their wives and families, but they had not otherwise failed as citizens. The popular canard that everyone who headed for the wild freedom of Texas did so because the sheriff was in pursuit was disproved, at least by this sampling.

In fact, among the twenty-three, there were not even any who had suffered a major financial loss that might have propelled them outward from their society. Most of them had actually prospered back home, and this had enabled them to leave their abandoned wives in rather gratifying security: 'You can have the store and the fields, Emma. I'll not be needin' them.'

Macnab chuckled when he thought of his own case, and Campbell asked: 'What you laughin' about?'

'Leaving Baltimore. I didn't steal their damned cattle.'

'Nobody here said you did.'

'I just sold them. They got a fair profit.'

When Macnab thought of his wife, Berthe, and her sniveling brothers he considered himself luckier than most to have escaped, and he would never have conceded that he had in any way been forced out of Maryland: 'Tell you the truth, Zave, I left her a lot better off than when I met her. She and the girls will have no trouble.'

Campbell summarized it well: 'We ain't fleein' *from* nothin'. We're fleein' *toward* freedom.' And Macnab added: 'Those two over there, who stay together all the time. I'd say they were fleeing toward life itself.'

'They escapin' hangin'?' Zave asked, and Macnab explained: 'Their doctors warned them: "You stay in this city two more years, you'll be dead of tuberculosis. Go to Texas. Let your lungs heal themselves in that good, dry air." '

Now the two men tried to tot up the educational background of the passengers, and they found out that of the twenty-three men, twenty-one could read and write, and of these, fourteen had completed academy or high school and had some knowledge of Latin, Euclid and world history. Probing further, Macnab came up with some even more surprising information: 'Did you know, Zave, that six of those men over there have been to colleges like Yale and Transylvania? I know that those two by the door studied law, they said so, and that short fellow who talks so much has a law degree from Virginia.' What the amateur investigators could not know was that five of the immigrants had been to Europe, three of them knew the principles of banking, and one was a medical doctor with service in the United States Navy. Texas was getting prime citizens.

Two other things Macnab and Campbell could not know that autumn day in 1831: four passengers were keeping journals – two men, two women – which would in later years prove invaluable; and of the men, eighteen would soon be serving in battles of one kind or another against Mexico, and of these, seven would become senior officers.

On the most important question of all – the possibility of revolution against Mexico – the two men had no opinion whatever. Few members of this group openly espoused such action; some had vague expectations that Texas would

427

eventually, by means not yet determined, free herself from Mexican control, but they certainly did not come expecting to incite rebellion, as would their successors in 1835 and 1836. This sample of immigrants came primarily in search of free land and a fresh beginning. For example, Macnab and Campbell entered Texas honestly, without the slightest intention of causing trouble. However, like the Quimpers before them, once they settled, they would find it impossible to accept the systems of government, law and society which their new homeland, Mexico, was painfully trying to establish.

As the two men concluded their assessment, Macnab said: 'I do believe you're the only Catholic in the group,' to which Zave replied: 'From what I hear, you'll all be joinin' me within the week. If you want land.'

There was another factor which differentiated the group, as Campbell pointed out: 'Northern, against slavery but quiet about it, maybe nine. Southern, for slavery and ready to fight if you speak against it, maybe fourteen.'

Macnab volunteered two final guesses: 'Every man who can read, save you and me, Zave, has brought his quota of books, and all but one seems to be fond of strong drink.' The abstemious one was Campbell, who explained in a loud voice: 'I used to love it too much. But once you've been a bartender, you know the dangers. And if I got started again, I'd be as bad as an Irishman.' The cabin laughed at this, for all could appreciate its relevance: of this contingent of thirty adults, all but Campbell had reached America after family affiliation with the Protestants of Northern Ireland.

They were Scots-Irish, the whole cantankerous bundle of them, with all the turbulent, wonderful capabilities that the name implied.

Following these ruminations, Macnab went on deck to be with his son as Otto peered into the darkness, hoping for a glimpse of the long sand finger which delineated Matagorda Bay. He had been there only a few moments when a commotion erupted in the cabin, and when voices rose and oaths reverberated, he hurried back to find a gentleman from Alabama shouting: 'Why can't Mexico ever do anything right? Why didn't they tell us?'

'Now, now, Templeton! The solution is an easy one.'

428

'Not if they propose to deprive me of my property.'

'It says that, to be sure, but . . .'

'Why weren't we told?' the Alabama man shouted, and Finlay wondered what could threaten him half as much as the danger which hung over the Macnabs: the loss of their entire investment.

'What you do, Templeton, is what we've all done.'

'But why weren't we warned?'

'In a new land, you learn one thing at a time. Now you're learning that Mexican law absolutely forbids slavery and outlaws the importation of any slave.'

'Damned good law,' a man from the North growled, but softly enough so that Templeton did not hear. That outraged gentleman asked: 'If niggers are outlawed, how are you bringing yours in?'

'By the simple tactic we all use to import our property,' the conciliator said, and he spread upon the cabin table a set of papers, carefully drawn, which both amazed and delighted the man from Alabama: 'Capital! Can I do this?'

'We've all done it,' and the Southerners had. Bowing to the irrevocable law that banned slavery throughout Mexico on pain of severe punishment – and Mexico was one of the first nations to enact such a law – the Southerners had devised a foolproof tactic, and Mr Templeton now put it into effect. Carefully copying the documents laid before him, he penned seven forms replete with legal language, then summoned his seven slaves, but the captain of the sloop warned: 'We allow no niggers in the cabin,' so he went on deck, where he collected his slaves, handed each in turn a pen, and commanded him or her to make a mark signifying acceptance of the terms spelled out in the paper:

Being a free man/woman, of my own free will and determination I do hereby indenture myself to Mr Owen Templeton, formerly of Tarsus, Alabama, for a term of ninety-and-nine years, and do further promise to obey his stipulations on the terms hereby agreed to and for the wages set between us until such time as my indenture is discharged. Obijah, male 27 years, scar on left shoulder, his mark, 16 October 1831.

Each of the Templeton slaves stepped forward and bound himself or herself for this term of ninety-nine years, the period settled upon decades earlier when a Mississippi judge handed down the opinion that if an indenture ran for more than that period, it would be unreasonable.

The passengers slept fitfully that night, and long before daybreak, Otto was back on watch. As black shaded into gray, and gray into a pale rose, the boy peered intently toward the west, and before the others were awake he started shouting: 'Land! Land!' Then everyone, free and slave alike, hurried to the railing to see their new homeland looming out of the morning mists, and they were struck silent by the sight before them.

The *Carthaginian* had made landfall opposite a finger of land no more than fifteen inches above the surface of the water and of no useful purpose whatever. There was not a single dwelling, not a tree, not a rock, not a person, not an animal. It was covered with low grass that sometimes moved softly in the breeze, but the grass, which had to fight salt air, was not nutritious, so none of the famed wild cattle of Texas roamed it. Desolate, windblown, inhospitable, the great sandbars of Texas served only to keep ships from shore and would-be settlers from their homes.

The land was flat, not piled in interesting dunes as on other shorelines of the world, and beyond it the great bays it enclosed were also flat, not etched in leaping waves, and beyond the bays, when the eye could see so far, the mainland itself was utterly flat, with never a tree or a rise or a real hill visible anywhere. It was a land of sheer emptiness and as forbidding as any which had ever rebuffed a group of incoming settlers.

'Look!' Mr Templeton of Alabama cried. 'A bird!' And all eyes turned to watch this precious creature, this one proof that life could be sustained in Texas, as it flew from north to south along the vast sandbar. Otto, stunned by the terrible loneliness of his new home, watched the bird for a long time, and it was he who first sighted the tree.

Far down on another sandbar, its crown almost blending with the sea, rose one solitary tree. Of the millions of seeds which through the generations had fallen on this desolate spot, this one seed had attached itself to some brief accumulation of nourishing soil and had survived, withstanding wind and storm as if it wished to be a hopeful signal to those like the Macnabs and their friends who would later approach by sea. There was no entrance into the bay where the tree stood, and no passage anywhere in its vicinity, but the tree was more appreciated that morning than a lighthouse, and the immigrants watched it with relief and affection, for it was the only familiar sight to welcome them to their land of freedom.

The *Carthaginian* spent most of that day working its way through the perilous entrance to Matagorda, and as predicted, the passengers saw two more wrecks, not big schooners shattered on rocks as they would have been at Hatteras or Cape Cod, but small sailing ships first trapped in sand, then turned over on their beam ends by succeeding waves, immobilized and knocked to pieces by the sea.

In late afternoon the sloop was safely inside the reef, with passengers cheering the cleverness of their captain, but now many hours of sailing to the west still lay before them, for the bay was vast. It was next morning before land was finally reached at the new town of Linnville, where Mexican port authorities waited. Linnville consisted of three wooden shacks, hastily thrown together, with chinks big enough for a hand to reach through.

One of the houses served as a store, but its surly proprietor, an American down on his luck, could offer only strips of sunbaked beef, two flitches of bacon, some rope, some nails and a jar of sugar candies. Indeed, he was much more interested in buying things from the newcomers than in selling to them, and he had ample funds for his purchases, Spanish coins principally.

Mexican authorities occupied the other two houses, and they were even more surly than the storekeeper. A Mexican law passed the previous year had banned all immigration from the United States, for the danger of unlimited influx was appreciated. But because of his enthusiastic adherence to Mexico, Stephen Austin had been exempted; he was permitted to bring in a few selected settlers, so grudgingly the customs officers had admitted the white arrivals but turned away the blacks. Then agitated Southerners cried: 'They're not slaves! They're free

431

men, indentured for a few years.' And when Stephen Austin himself supported this interpretation, they were accepted.

Each newcomer was asked if he had been born a Catholic, and since the greater part had reached America via Northern Ireland, only Zave Campbell could claim right of entry, which was quickly promised: 'The alcalde in Victoria will give you papers.' The Protestants must report to the same official: 'He'll arrange for the Catholic padres to supervise your conversions.'

When Finlay handed these Linnville officials the beautiful sheets of embossed paper that testified to his ownership of land, they guffawed, for during the past two years they had seen many such worthless certificates: 'Nada, señor, nada.' And other Mexicans crowded about the table to laugh and assure the yanqui that his paper really was nothing: 'Es nada, señor. Es absolutamente nada.' One of the officials was about to tear it up, but Macnab rescued it, thinking to proffer it in Victoria as proof of his honest intentions.

Otto enjoyed the tedious walk to Victoria, but no one else did; he marked the soft variations in the flat wasteland: 'Look how that shrub stays protected behind the little rise of sand!' He was delighted by the way deer traveled parallel to the immigrants, always at a safe distance, and twice he saw wild horses, those small mustangs that could run with such impetuosity. On instructions from his father, he kept constant watch for that first line of trees which would mark where men could live and farm, but none appeared. 'This is awful flat,' he said. 'And lonely. Is all of Texas . . . ?' He did not finish his question, for his father was obviously distressed by this terrible bleakness, this endless sea of softly waving grass. 'And now look at that storm!'

Big Zave, staring at the ominous black clouds sweeping in from the west, growled: 'So this is the land of milk and honey they told us about. I don't even see one bee, let alone a cow.'

'Otto!' Finlay called out. 'Cover yourself with a blanket. We're to be soaked.'

Across that endless, unrelieved grassland came a tumultuous rainstorm, immense sheets of dark and splashing water which drenched them until the two men groaned, but Otto, keeping his eyes to the ground, saw that hiding beneath the grass were hundreds upon hundreds of lovely autumn flowers: blue, white, golden yellow, fiery orange, the brightest red. 'Look!' he cried, and the men bent down to inspect the watery garden he had discovered. Soon the storm passed overhead, allowing the sun to reappear above the western horizon. When the travelers wiped the water from their faces they saw, hanging in the eastern sky, a perfect rainbow, a grand multicolored arc which they could almost reach out and touch.

'Look!' Otto cried. 'We're going to walk right into it.'

Upon a bed of flowers, with the sky about them, they walked into the Texas they had dreamed of, until even Zave was awed by the beauty: 'Maybe the Mexicans don't welcome us, Otto, but the land sure does.'

In Victoria the Macnabs learned two things: 'This town and everything as far as you can travel ... it all belongs to the de Leóns. Spanish only spoken here. So you become full Mexican or you perish.' The other bit of knowledge disturbed Finlay equally: 'Señor Macnab, I speak little English, believe me. If you convert with our two Mexican priests ... long walk to the mission, many times, many questions. Very severe,' and the speaker pounded his fist into his hand. Then he smiled: 'But at Quimper's Ferry ... maybe you catch Father Clooney if he's out of jail. He make you Catholic. Very nice ... very sweet man.'

Mexican officials quickly satisfied Macnab that his scrip was worthless, but they displayed none of the harshness he had encountered in the first office at the shore. 'Señor Macnab,' said an officer who spoke English elegantly, 'we want American settlers. That is, if you build your house at least ten leagues inland from the sea. Especially we want fine lads like your son. So you are welcome to apply in the regular fashion, but only if you've converted to our faith. Then you pay only a modest amount for your land. Stamped paper, two dollars. My commissioner's fee, seventeen dollars. The empresario's fee, about twenty-five. And the surveyor's fee, which cannot exceed one hundred and fifty dollars. We want you, but only on our terms.'

Ironically, Zave Campbell received entitlement to his land within half an hour of registering, for he had cleverly brought with him testimonials from two Catholic priests, one who had been doing missionary work among the derelicts of

433

Under-the-Hill, one a cleric in New Orleans well regarded by the Mexican authorities. Zave did not receive a specific allocation; he would be free to choose that later, but he did now possess an impressive document which permitted him to choose his quarter-league, about a thousand acres, from whatever lands in de León's tract had not already been bespoken.

The problem now arose as to where Zave should claim his land, but Macnab prevailed upon him to delay the selection until he, Finlay, could get to Quimper's Ferry and make himself eligible through conversion; then they could choose together. Campbell, however, was hungry for his entitlement and would have designated it as soon as he could find a surveyor, except that he discovered an alluring technicality: 'Finlay, did you hear what they said at the alcalde's? I have my quarter-league, but I can have a whole league-and-a-labor if I find me a Mexican wife. Nearly five thousand acres. You go to Quimper's. I'll look around here.'

'For land?'

'No, for a wife.'

So the Macnabs, with their dog Betsy, moved northeast through land that began to look as if it might be tillable, and the more they saw of the terrain the more eager they became to get their share. Now there was a slight roll to the prairies, a differentiation between this good area and that; there were trees, too, not noble ones like those in Ohio, but real trees nevertheless. Wild horses they saw frequently, and on two occasions they spotted large herds of cattle, lean, rangy beasts with enormous horns, waiting, it seemed, for someone to claim them. It was a rich, varied Texas they saw on this trip, and no part was stranger than the bottomlands bordering some insignificant stream where towering canebrakes, a wild growth much like sugarcane but worthless, grew in such tangled profusion that earlier travelers had been required to hack tunnels through them.

To enter such a dark passageway, with the path scarcely wide enough for one to move, and to see the cane tops meeting in an archway far above the head was tedious for Finlay, delightful for Otto: 'It's a dungeon, Poppa! We're going to meet the dragon, like the King of Crete.'

434

Freed at last of the brakes, they intercepted the Brazos River some miles downstream from Quimper's Ferry, and even this far inland the stream gave the impression of being navigable for another hundred miles, but when Finlay looked more closely he saw it to be clogged with sunken trees and jagged stumps that prohibited vessels. Seeking always to instruct his son in the necessary arts, he asked: 'How wide is the river?' and Otto guessed: 'Maybe three hundred feet.'

'No, I mean exactly how wide,' and to the boy's delight he explained: 'All a surveyor needs is three trees, A, B and C. A is that one on the far bank which you can't get to, B is here on this bank. Now find C along there that makes a right angle with B and an angle of forty-five degrees with A.' Next he showed his son how, by folding a piece of paper, he could accurately determine each angle.

When this disposition was laid out, he revealed the secret: 'Then all you do is step off the distance from B to C on this bank, and you have the exact distance from B across the river to A.' He encouraged his son to measure the distance, and Otto said: 'Four hundred and twenty-nine feet. That's a big river.'

'And not too deep at this point.'

The essence of this vast land was beginning to seep into their souls, as it did with almost all who stayed long enough to savor it, and that night Otto reported to his father: 'When I was little I wanted to be a boatman on the Mississippi. Now I want to live in Texas.'

'So do I,' his father said, and that night they slept with deep contentment.

They were wakened in the morning by loud barking from Betsy, who was nipping at the heels of a brash young man heading upriver with two bundles slung across his back. The first contained clothing, the second the awkward tools of a blacksmith, and it seemed likely that these parcels represented a lifetime's accumulation.

He said: 'Isaac Yarrow, renegade from North Carolina, with a brief halt in Tennessee.'

When Finlay asked: 'Where are you going?' the young man spat and growled: 'Got thrown out of San Felipe de Austin . . .'

'Isn't that the capital of these parts?'

'It is, and a sorrier spot God never made. Thirty-nine

houses, six criminals to a house. Each house hidin' someone wanted for embezzlement, armed robbery, seduction or murder. The alcalde drifted into town smellin' distinctly of tar and feathers, and the esteemed sheriff still has four different wives in four different states, none dismissed by divorce.'

This evaluation was so contrary to the one Macnab had made in the *Carthaginian* that he had to protest: 'The immigrants we sailed with weren't like that, not at all.'

'You saw the goods. I saw the bads.'

'You're telling the truth?'

'Texas is a magnet for criminals.'

'If it's that bad, what did you have to do to get thrown out?'

Yarrow leaned against a live oak and scratched his head: 'They brought seven counts agin' me. Mostly I was too outspoken and too blasphemous.'

'Where you heading?'

'Seems like anyone with spirit who comes to Texas moves on to somewheres else. Missouri, Arkansas, Me, I'm headin' for California. Man can live decent there.'

'I thought men could live decent in Texas,' Finlay said, and Yarrow growled: 'If you want to kiss ass. I never cared for that.'

They joined forces for the short journey to Quimper's Ferry, and when they sighted the sturdy dog-run which served as the inn, Yarrow grew rhapsodic: 'Now, if all people in Texas was like Mattie Quimper, this place would be a hard-workin' paradise.' When Finlay asked who Mattie was, Yarrow said: 'If she was twenty years younger, I'd marry her.'

'But what's she do?'

'She runs the ferry. She runs the inn. And she befriends people like me who've been kicked out of other places.'

As they approached the inn, Yarrow bellowed: 'Hey, Mattie!' and to the porch of the dog-run came a gray-haired woman in her forties, lean and worn from incessant labor. As she peered to see who was shouting, a young man of nineteen joined her, but remained slightly behind, as if seeking the protection of her petticoats.

'Good God, it's Isaac!' the woman called, and with a spry leap from the porch on which two travelers were asleep in their blankets, she ran to the blacksmith and kissed him. 'They tell me you've been in trouble down to San Felipe.'

436

'Got run out of town. They said, "You've got twenty-four hours to git," and I shouted back, "I'll live to see grass growin' in your goddamned streets."'

'Sshhh,' Mattie whispered. 'We got clergy inside.'

'Father Clooney?' Yarrow cried with obvious enthusiasm. 'Did he get out of jail?'

'No, sad to say,' Mattie reported. 'They sent officers from Saltillo to arrest him. Charged him with bein' too partial to the norteamericanos.'

'How long's he been in chains?'

'They didn't chain him. Not after the first month. But he's been in jail a year. Miracle he ain't dead.'

'So who is the God-shouter in there?'

'Reverend Harrison.'

Yarrow spat: 'That sanctimonious . . .'

With a quick swipe of her hand, Mattie slapped the blacksmith on the cheek: 'You shut up! Reverend Harrison has come down to see if I'll marry him.'

Yarrow caught Mattie in his arms and gave her a little waltz, feet off the ground. 'Mattie, old girl! You don't have to waste yourself on that Psalm-singer. I'll stay here and run the ferry for you.'

'Weren't you run out of the whole Austin grant?' she asked, and Yarrow replied: 'I was. But I'd stay here and protect you from Reverend Harrison.' He spoke the name with such disgust that the two Macnabs supposed the clergyman to be an ogre, but when he walked out the door onto the porch, gingerly avoiding the sleeping men, they were surprised by his commanding appearance.

'Isaac!' he said with unfeigned cordiality. 'What evil are you up to now?'

'You'll be gratified to learn that your prophecy came true. They ran me out of San Felipe.'

'High time,' Harrison said, stepping down and throwing his right arm about Yarrow in a brotherly embrace. 'We welcome you here, but we're going to watch you . . . most carefully.'

'I'm on my way to California. Just stopped off to warn Mattie Quimper not to marry you.'

Harrison laughed: 'Bad men flee to Texas. Always have. And the worst move on to California. Always will.'

Mattie, who continued her work as if the marriage under discussion involved someone fifty miles away, invited Yarrow and the Macnabs into the inn for breakfast, and when eggs, bear strips and pecans were on the table she asked Harrison if he would say grace, and the tall, forbidding man asked the others to bow their heads while he raised his face toward heaven: 'Almighty Father, watch over Thy renegade son Isaac as he heads for California. And welcome to Thy bosom the strangers who join us this day. Protect Mattie who does Thy work so endlessly, and speed the day when Thy true religion can be preached openly in these parts. Amen.'

When heads were raised, he placed his hand on young Otto's arm and said: 'They haven't told me your name.'

'Otto, and this is my father, Finlay Macnab of Baltimore.'

'Someone has taught you manners, young man.' Then he smiled at Finlay, asking: 'What brings you to these parts?' and Macnab said: 'Freedom.'

'You'll be welcomed here. What church?'

'Presbyterian. Many generations in Scotland and Ireland.'

'One of God's chosen religions,' Harrison said. 'Here we're all Methodists.'

'Not me,' Yarrow interrupted, at which Harrison warned: 'God has His eye on you, Isaac, and so do I.'

'What's this about a marriage?' the blacksmith asked, and Harrison said, blushing: 'I had not supposed that so delicate a matter would be discussed publicly,' and Yarrow replied: 'If a lovely lady like Mattie Quimper has to be protected from a lecherous old clergyman like you, Harrison, it should become public.'

'She needs a man to help her,' Harrison said with real tenderness as he watched Mattie moving about the kitchen. Smoothing down her apron, she lifted a flat metal slab from the fire and brought to the table her latest batch of salt-and-honey pecans, which she placed before Otto.

'Let 'em cool. Then eat up,' she said. She offered Finlay some and invited Yarrow to sample them, but she took pains to see that when the slab came to rest, it was before Reverend Harrison.

'Now tell me,' she said, 'what brings you to the Ferry, Mr Macnab?'

438

Finlay was too embarrassed to reveal his secret, especially since a Methodist minister looked on, but Mattie could guess: 'You hoped that Father Clooney would be here, didn't you? You want to convert so you can obtain land?'

At this blunt disclosure of his plans, Finlay began to stammer, but he was saved by his son, who said openly: 'Zave Campbell, he's already Catholic, with papers from two different priests proving it, and he got his land right away. And if he can find a Mexican lady to marry, he'll get four times as much.'

To the surprise of the two Macnabs and Yarrow, but not to Mattie, for she now knew Reverend Harrison well and favorably, the austere Methodist said: 'Have no embarrassment, Macnab. It's an immoral law and to obtain your land it's quite forgivable to subvert it. Swear allegiance to the Pope but remain Presbyterian in your heart.'

'Is that your counsel?' Macnab asked, and Harrison said: 'I give it constantly. And do you know why? Because within five years at the most, Texas is going to break away from Mexico. And we can all worship as God wants us to, in His churches.'

Yarrow interrupted: 'You're convinced God is a Methodist?' and Harrison shot back: 'He certainly isn't a papist.' When Yarrow said: 'New Testament says he is,' Harrison growled: 'That's your interpretation.'

Then he changed his tenor completely: 'Isaac, return to San Felipe. Make peace with the officials. Because when war comes we'll need men like you.'

'I gave Texas its chance. And it rejected me. I'm for California.'

The newcomers spent three enjoyable days at Quimper's talking about the future, teasing Reverend Harrison about his courtship, and stuffing themselves with Mattie's good food. Harrison was certain that revolution of some kind was inevitable; Yarrow doubted that weaklings like Stephen Austin would ever muster courage for such an act; and Finlay Macnab was startled by the frankness of the speculation: 'I thought everyone agreed that Texas was to remain Mexican. Austin said so in his letter to me,' and he produced that document.

When Yarrow finished reading it he said: 'The epistle of a weakling,' and when Harrison took the letter he said: 'He's masking his true beliefs.'

As talk turned to other matters, Yarrow said boldly: 'Harrison, why do you insist that Mattie needs your help when she has this fine son who could run things better than you ever would?' and Harrison replied: 'She'll be in real trouble if she relies on that one.'

Yarrow and Macnab had been studying young Yancey, and the more they saw of him the more they agreed that the flabby lad needed some strong influence to force him into Texas ways. 'He's just not Texican,' Yarrow said. 'He'd get along fine in Virginia, or even better in Massachusetts, where they don't have such high standards for manliness. But in this climate I fear for him.'

What the two men disliked about Yancey was the latter's unwillingness, or inability, to take charge of the inn and the ferry. 'No woman should be doin' the work Mattie does,' Yarrow said, and one afternoon he grudgingly told Harrison: 'It could be a proper move, Reverend, if you was to marry her. How old are you?'

'I'm a year older than she is. Lost my wife to the cholera.'

'In principle I still oppose the marriage,' Yarrow said, 'but in practice . . .'

'How old are you?' Harrison asked, not belligerently, and Isaac replied: 'Very old in the ways of the world, and I can see through you. What you want is that ferry. You know it's a gold mine.'

'What I want,' Harrison said, 'is a free Texas. Stay and help us win it.'

But Yarrow, one of the best men to immigrate to Texas during these turbulent years, had seen enough of it. The good men like Austin lacked courage and the bad ones, like the fugitive murderers and embezzlers at San Felipe, lacked judgment. He could see no hope for the colony but he did foresee a kind of permanent tension between Mexico and the United States. He concluded that the best chance for a man of inventiveness and daring lay in California, so on a bright morning in January he bade the residents at Quimper's farewell, shouldered his two packs, and headed west. That afternoon, when all were still lamenting his absence, Yancey Quimper shouted from the porch where he was resting: 'Mom! Here he is!' and the Macnabs assumed it was Yarrow, changing his mind.

440

Instead it was a bent old man, Father Clooney, now sixty-seven but looking much older because of his stay in the Mexican prison. 'Good God!' Mattie cried as she ran to him. 'What did they do to you?' He was limping so badly that he had to be helped by two young priests, who explained: 'The new governor pardoned him. He was supposed to find refuge in Zacatecas with the Franciscans, but he insisted on coming back to his old parish, and here he is.'

'Will you stay with him?' Mattie asked as she helped him onto the porch.

'No, we've been assigned to Nacogdoches, and in the morning we move on.'

The three clerics slept that night on the porch; Mattie offered Father Clooney a bed, but he said: 'I'll stay with me lads this last night,' and in the morning he blessed them as they started for the remotest outpost of the Mexican empire: 'You'll like it up there, lads. Good people and souls to be saved.' As they departed he stood with Mattie, watching as Finlay Macnab poled the ferry across the Brazos: 'How wonderful it must be for them, Mattie. To be young, facing a new world, and knowing there's chapels to be built and pagans to be saved.'

He was not at the inn three days – painful days of recuperation from his travail – before couples started arriving to have their informal marriages solemnized, and now Reverend Harrison felt it obligatory to withdraw. 'No need,' Father Clooney said, 'I'm sure they'd appreciate your blessing too,' but Harrison was worried more for the old man than for himself: 'You speak kindly to a Methodist, and the Mexicans'll throw you back in jail.'

'I think they'll let me run my course,' Clooney said as he wearily prepared for the weddings.

He was a tired old man now, worn out by the pace of life. He had seen enough of frontier living – especially the hideous wars with Indians when each side tried to demonstrate its superior claim to savagery, and the petty rebellions, with fifteen Mexicans dead and sixteen Americans – to know that man was a frail creature who lived on this earth but briefly, and rarely well. A good horse, a reliable woman, sons to protect the old age, and enough to eat, that was the best man could hope for, and if perchance he heard far echoes of God and Jesus, never seen but surely there, so much the better. 'Life,' he told Mattie one evening, 'is a whole lot better if you have reassurances.'

He liked a good steak, cooked over embers, and he was especially fond of white bread smeared with butter, but flour was so rare in Texas that he had sometimes gone for a whole year without tasting bread: 'A hunk of meat, two Mexican flapjacks made of corn, and now and then a beer, that's my penance for having left those fine cooks in Ireland.' Having lived in four different lands – Ireland, England and Louisiana, briefly, and Mexico – it was his measured judgement that Texas cooking was the worst in the world: 'But I eat enough of it to keep me belly fat, and I do believe that when I die the table set in heaven will be a mite bit better.'

He rose at dawn on the wedding day to take breakfast with Mattie, who asked him: 'Should I marry Reverend Harrison?' and he advised her: 'If ever a woman sees a reasonably good man, take him.' She then asked if he considered Harrison a good man, and he said: 'He's a man of God, but also a man of revolution. Does one destroy the other? I don't know.' She asked if he thought the revolution which Harrison preached would materialize, and he said: 'A year in jail knocks desire for revolution out of a man.'

Then suddenly he dropped his weary head on the table, and for a moment she thought he was weeping, but when he lifted his face he was smiling: 'I'm so ashamed, Mattie. I'm covered with disgrace.'

'Why? Jail is forgivable when you go there for the reasons you did.'

'Oh, jail has nothin' to do with it. But recently I've caught myself thinkin' "I hope it all hangs together for the rest of my life, then to hell with it." What a shameful surrender.' He studied her across the rough wooden breakfast table, then confessed: 'Harrison is the voice of the future. I'm the past.' Now tears did come to his eyes, and he did not try to hide them: 'In Ireland, I wrecked my parish. Here, I converted never an Indian. In Mexico, I wound up in jail. And the years have fled so swiftly.'

Mattie rose and went about her duties, leaving him there, and after a while he went onto the porch, where he supervised the placement of the rude altar from which he would preach to the seven couples. When this was completed he returned to the doorway, looked in at Mattie, and said, his face beaming with love for the old days: 'Matt, old girl! I do wish your husband and The Kronk were here this day. I miss them.'

Marriage, to Father Clooney, remained the most sacred of rites, but when the ceremony was over he did enjoy a bit of celebration and was especially appreciative if it involved some warming spirits. That evening the dancing, the fiddle-playing and the shouting were lively, but next morning Clooney was up early, showing no signs of excessive wear.

'Now, who are the ones who seek conversion in order to grab a wee bit of land?' he asked as the day began, and when four families, including Macnab and his son, were lined upon the porch, he proceeded mechanically to make them technical Catholics. But if he took such political conversion lightly, Finlay could not, for when he stood next in line and realized that he must soon take a solemn oath abjuring John Knox's religion for which his Highland ancestors had died rather than surrender it to the Pope, his knees began to tremble, his throat went dry, and a crazed look came into his eye. He recalled those great battles in Northern Ireland between the Presbyterians and the papists, the centuries of struggle of which he had been a part, and he found himself powerless to move forward.

Father Clooney had seen these symptoms before, always in people who had come to Texas via Northern Ireland, and in his compassion he made it easy for Finlay and Otto to step aside. That day the Macnabs were not converted, the shock was simply too great, but that night Clooney talked with both father and son, for he insisted that Otto be present:

'I know well the torment you feel. I've seen it before, and I respect you for your integrity. I can tell you only two things. My religion is one of the sweetest, gentlest in the world, a consolation and a redemption. I've loved it for nearly seventy years, and when I die within its embrace I shall know no fear, for God has been with me always.

'The Mexican government, in its wisdom, said that you cannot have land unless you convert to the religion it sponsors. This is a clear law, not unreasonable, and not

443

unfairly administered. So if you want land, you Macnabs, you must convert this day, for tomorrow I may be gone.

'Let me tell you this, my sons, to own land is a good thing, and if you find it in your hearts to join my church, you may discover, like many before you, that it's a worthy home, one which assures you much benevolence.'

The old man did not go on to finish his statement, the implied part about what would happen if the Macnabs did *not* find their new religion congenial, and he certainly did not say that so far as he was concerned, once they got their land they were free to revert to Presbyterianism, but his entire manner implied that such was his belief.

So Finlay and Otto became Catholics, trembling with fear lest they be struck dead for the blasphemy they were committing, but Father Clooney blessed them just the same and smiled at the heavy perspiration on Finlay's forehead.

That night Father Clooney slept on the porch as usual, but he was uneasy, and long after midnight he roused Finlay and sat with him by the flickering fire: 'My son, we must do something about getting you land.'

'I've converted.'

'That may not be enough. Authorities have grown suspicious of Austin. They're inspecting every grant he makes.'

'What should I do?'

'Forget Austin. Go back to Victoria and ask the de Leóns for an assignment in their grant.'

'Will they give it?'

'I know that family well. One of the best. I'll write them a letter recommending you.'

'I'd appreciate that. I'll get it in the morning.'

To Macnab's surprise, Father Clooney reached and grasped his hand as if he were responsible for his new convert's welfare: 'No, we'd better do it now.' And taking paper from the same old Bible with which he had converted the Quimpers years before, he drafted a warm note to the de Leóns, beseeching them to award land to his trusted friend Macnab. Handing Finlay the paper, he returned unsteadily to the porch.

Sometime after dawn, as was her custom, Mattie went to him with a cup of broth, but when she tried to waken him he did not respond. For several terrifying moments she kept prodding him with her foot, refusing to believe that he was dead. Then his left arm fell lifeless onto the boards of the porch and she could no longer ignore the evidence.

She did not cry out nor did she call for help. She merely looked down at the body of a man she had first suspected, then grown to love, a faithful shepherd whose flock had been so widely scattered that he had worn himself out tending it. As if his death had also terminated a portion of her life, she gave no further thought to the proposed marriage with Reverend Harrison. After the funeral, which the Methodist conducted with a glowing tribute to his one-time adversary, she sent him north, where he married a much younger widow, who helped him fan the fires of rebellion.

Otto observed this tangled behavior of his elders – Isaac Yarrow's bitter dismissal of Texas, Reverend Harrison's erratic courtship, the willful return of Father Clooney to a parish in turmoil, the curious behavior of Yancey, ten years older than himself and therefore an adult in his eyes, and the almost inhuman drive of Mattie – without understanding many of the actions or any of their motivations. But as the Macnabs were preparing to quit the inn and move south with their letter to the de Leóns in Victoria, an event occurred which he comprehended perfectly.

From the opposite side of the Brazos, at eleven one bright morning, a loud halloo came ringing through the air, and Otto ran to see what traveler was coming south. To his delight, it was Benito Garza, the muleteer he had known in New Orleans, so without alerting Mattie he dashed to the beached ferry, jumped in and started poling across the river, shouting as he did: 'Benito! It's me! Otto Macnab!' And as he neared the far shore Garza, standing with his two helpers, recognized the boy and shouted back: 'The little horseman! Hooray!' and the two assistants added their 'Olés!'

The three traders piled into the ferry, and Otto proudly escorted them across the river and up to the inn, where he called loudly: 'Mattie! Strangers!' but when she came to the porch she deflated the boy: 'Garza! We've been friends for years.'

It was a lively reunion but also an emotional one, for after the

445

noise and embraces Garza almost shyly handed Mattie a present, and when she opened it to the applause of all, she found a bolt of English cloth and a simple dress made in France. They were the first such gifts she had ever received, and for a long time she was silent, then she said in a flat tone: 'You carried them a long way, Benito.'

Now everyone spoke at once, and Garza learned of Yarrow's exile, Father Clooney's death and the Macnabs' conversion. He wanted to know where Zave Campbell had located his land, and Finlay explained: 'He hasn't exactly chosen it yet, but he favors a stretch along the Guadalupe,' and Garza approved: 'Any land washed by a river is good.'

It was Otto who spoke the words that mattered: 'Fact is, he's not looking for land. He's looking for a wife.'

As Otto was talking, Benito was holding Mattie's French dress against her spare form, but the boy's words so startled him that he dropped the dress, left Mattie, and took Otto by the arm: 'What did you say?'

'He's not really looking for his land.'

'The other part. Is he looking for a wife?'

'Yes. He gets four times as much land if he finds one.'

It was then that Benito Garza's maneuvering began. Sitting at the rough table and addressing all those in the kitchen, including two travelers who were eating, he said: 'We were nine children and the family had only one ranch along the Rio Grande. No chance for me to inherit the land, so I brought my two youngest sisters with me to Victoria. I'm head of the family. With some difficulty I found the oldest one, María, a husband, José Mardones, but he didn't last long.'

'Did he run away?' Mattie asked, and he replied: 'No. He was shot. Stealing horses . . . from a norteamericano.'

Otto interrupted: 'You told me in New Orleans that horses ran free.'

'Trained horses are different,' Garza said. Then he addressed Finlay: 'So this wonderful woman, only thirty-one, still has no husband, and if Señor Campbell . . .'

'How about your younger sister?' Mattie asked, and he replied: 'Josefina? She's only twenty-six. She can wait. Always get your oldest sister married first.'

This perplexed Otto: 'But if they're older than you, why

don't they find their own husbands?' and Garza replied with dignity: 'In a Mexican family it's the father's obligation. And I am their father, so to speak.'

Now Garza became zealous for an immediate return to Victoria: 'We've got to reach Campbell before he makes a serious mistake,' so before the Macnabs were really ready to depart, Garza applied constant pressure for them to hurry: 'Everything is better for a norteamericano in Texas if he has a reliable Mexican wife. Suppose he wants land? Suppose he gets into trouble with the alcalde? Or if the priests act up?'

'He may already have found a wife.'

'I hope not! He would be throwing himself away if he didn't take María. I promise you, Señor Macnab, this woman is exceptional. A man finds a wife like her once in a hundred years.'

In the morning the Macnabs looked in surprise as Garza bent low over Mattie's hands, kissing each in turn, and even Otto could see that the Mexican herdsman loved this rough woman who ran the ferry, and they treated him with more respect as they moved south toward Victoria. There Garza hurried ahead, shouting as he entered the town: 'Señor Campbell!' He located the big Kaintuck some distance to the north, tenting under a big oak on the banks of the Guadalupe, and his greeting was fervid: 'What fine land you've chosen! Have you found a wife?'

When Zave said 'No,' Garza gave an immense sigh, slumped to the earth beside Campbell, and said softly: 'Señor, I liked you from the minute I saw you in New Orleans. I could see then that you have character. Now let us all go back to Victoria so that Señor Finlay can present the papers given him by Father Clooney and claim his land.' He did not mention his sisters.

The De Leóns accepted the recommendation of the revered priest, and after lamenting his death, they said: 'We welcome you to Victoria. Choose your land wisely.' And it was then that Garza said almost casually: 'Since we're all here, why don't we go see my sisters?' but he could not help adding: 'Señor Campbell, I give you my word, you're going to like María.'

He led the way to a two-room adobe shack he had built near the central plaza, and as he approached it he started shouting: 'María! I bring new friends!' and to the rough wooden doorway came an ample woman with a big warm face. When her dark eyes looked at the newcomers and her mouth broke into a smile

447

of welcome, Otto knew immediately that he had found a replacement for his Baltimore mother, and as the days passed in her benign presence this feeling deepened, for María Garza Mardones was one of those women who embraced the world. Her laugh sounded like a deep-throated bell; she was patient with the follies of men; and she adored children, chickens, colts and hard work.

The closing weeks of 1831 were memorable, because the Americans and the Garzas moved out to Campbell's land and started building a dog-run. The three men chopped trees for the timbers while the two Garza women and Otto mixed mud and straw to make adobes. Since each person worked as if the resulting cabin was to be his or her own, the floor plan could be spacious, with the open runway a full eighteen feet wide, and each of the two halves larger than the ones at Quimper's Ferry.

At the end of the first week the Macnabs were surprised to see that Campbell was driving stakes to outline a third room on the north. 'What's that for?' Finlay asked, and Zave said: 'You and Otto. Till you get your own land and your own house.'

Otto, who had fallen in love with María, considered this an admirable decision, for he expected his friend Zave to marry the Mexican woman, and he was further pleased on Wednesday of the second week when Zave started driving even more stakes for a fourth room, also on the north but well separated from the one intended for the Macnabs.

'What's that one for?' Otto asked, and Zave said: 'Benito and his sister Josefina. They're to be livin' with us, too.'

'Are you marrying María?' Otto asked, and when Zave answered: 'Yep, I cain't pass over a woman who can really work,' the boy rushed to the stalwart Mexican woman and began kissing her.

So before the first room of the dog-run was even well started, Zave had planned what amounted to a frontier mansion, and that was the beginning of the good times at Zave Campbell's. What gave this particular house a touch of extra charm was its position near a solitary live oak festooned with Spanish moss, which meant that the tree provided both decoration and some protection against the sun. Also, a traditional long, low porch joined the two halves on the south side, but in this instance it also swung around to enclose the western end; at close of day the occupants could rest there and watch the sun disappear beyond the river.

María, once her marriage to Campbell was solemnized, showed great affection for Otto, and since she had reason to believe that she could have no children of her own, and the boy was so appreciative of anything she did for him, she considered him her son, and for his part he adopted Mexican ways, learning not only the language but also the handling of cattle. Under Benito's skilled tutelage he improved the shooting skills Zave Campbell had taught him on the Trace.

But it was in horseback riding that he appreciated Benito most, for Garza was both patient and firm in teaching him the basics, and soon he had Otto galloping at the head of the file when the Mexican hands rode forth to round up mustangs. With Benito's help he broke one for himself, a high-spirited little beast with a tawny coat and an obstinate spirit. 'What shall I call him?' he asked Benito, and that excellent horseman said: 'Chico. He'll learn he's Chico real fast.'

For a boy of ten, there was a beautiful world to be explored. It was spring, and the fields along the Gaudalupe were studded with fascinating trees: the wild persimmon, the thorned huisache, the delicate pecans. There were the taller trees, too, that he had missed in those desolate flats by the sea: the post oaks, the cottonwoods, the ash, and always that persistent half tree, half shrub which fascinated him with its gnarled branches and sharp thorns, the mesquite. Sometimes as he wandered among his trees he would come upon a wild boar tusking the earth, or fawns grazing, or the silent slither of a copperhead, the noisy warning of a rattler.

Each evening, when he returned home, he found that María had prepared some new treat, for she was a most ingenious woman, capable of transforming the poorest materials into something delicious, and he grew to love the tortillas she made so patiently, kneeling before the stone metate as she beat the boiled corn into the gray-white mixture she later baked on the flat rocks.

But he liked especially the peasant dish she made with whatever bits of meat her lodgers might provide: bear, buffalo, venison, possum, goat, beef, all were alike to her. Collecting a few onions from her garden and red chili peppers that grew

449

wild, she followed an unbroken ritual, which she explained to Otto in her flowing Spanish: 'You must have two pans. Brown the meat in this one so it looks good. In this one put a lot of bear grease, the chopped chilies, the onions and a bit of garlic if you can find it.' She was generous in the amount of grease she used, because she wanted the final dish to be golden brown in color and with lots of nourishment for her hard-working men.

When the two pans were properly heated on the coals and a rich smell was pervading the kitchen, she took from a treasured hoard imported from Monterrey or Saltillo small samples of two valuable spices, oregano and comino, and after measuring out the proper portions in a pot, she mixed in all the other ingredients with a flourish, stirred well, then placed the pot back on the coals. She would never allow any beans to be added to her dish. 'No true Mexican puts beans in chili.' The result, after hours of careful cooking, was a rich, spicy, aromatic meat dish whose principal flavor was a marvelous mix of red-hot chili and oregano.

But she never served it alone. In the evening before she made this chili con carne she threw into a pot a large helping of beans, any kind available, and these she soaked overnight. She refused ever to cook a bean until it had been soaked. 'I think God would strike me dead if I just threw beans in cold water and cooked them,' she told Otto. 'They must be soaked.' She also insisted upon sieving them three times through her fingers: 'To sort out the little rocks. Many a person has lost a tooth biting into rocks, but not in my beans.'

She rose early in the morning, simmered her soaked beans for two hours, then boiled them for two more. When they were well done, she mashed them, added a little oil and fried onions, then fried them lightly in a pan. 'Now they're ready to eat with chili,' she told Otto, but she was most careful to see that the two dishes never mixed. Each was to be respected for its own uniqueness.

With such food and affection Otto had never been happier, but one aspect of his life along the Guadalupe did cause him worry.

He was a true Macnab, descendant of a clan that had stolen cattle for a thousand years, and he had seen how his father and his dear friend Zave had gathered strays during their trip along the Natchez Trace, but his developing sense of right and wrong had warned him that such behavior was criminal, and he was pleased when his father dropped the habit. Now he watched as Campbell instructed Benito in the tricks of bringing into his care any cattle or horses that did not have a specific home, and some that did.

Otto went to his father, pointing out that in Texas men burned marks on the flanks of their animals to prove ownership, and he had seen in Zave's fields animals with several different brands. Finlay dismissed his fears: 'All Campbells are like that.'

Worry of a more subtle kind was caused by Benito, now twenty-six, for slowly the boy of ten was beginning to realize that his Mexican friend had a violent and often vicious temper. Benito would pummel any Mexican workman who displeased him; often Otto saw that he wanted to punch Zave too, but was afraid; then his neck muscles would tremble and he would turn away and spit. In training mustangs he was needlessly cruel, and when Otto protested, he laughed: 'Horses and women need to be beaten. Then they become the best.' Otto, who had cringed when drunken men had thrashed their easy Under-the-Hill women, asked if María's Mexican husband had ever beaten her, and Benito snapped: 'Plenty, and she deserved it.'

Statements like that bewildered the boy, for he had witnessed Benito's ardor in furthering his sisters' interests, and he remembered his thoughtfulness in bringing Mattie Quimper those presents: Sometimes I don't understand him. It's like he has a dark side.

María had other concerns, for when she was satisfied that her home in the dog-run was secure, and that her norteamericano husband was a good man, she began her campaign to find equal stability for her sister Josefina. Whenever the men complimented her cooking, she told them. 'Josefina did it,' even though Otto knew she hadn't. Any fine sewing was done by Josefina, and occasionally María would say to Finlay: 'This one, she's a good girl, believe me.' When Josefina smiled, María would ask: 'See that lovely crooked smile she has? It came from our mother, Trinidad de Saldana, a refined lady from San Antonio.'

Despite this constant advocacy, Macnab showed no interest, until one noon, when the stew was extra good, thanks to

451

Josefina, María said in Spanish: 'Don Finlay, did it ever occur to you that if you married Josefina, you could get a whole league-and-a-labor next to ours?' Macnab said nothing, but he did sit straighter. 'And when Xavier and I die' – she pronounced the name Hah-vee-EHR – 'who would get our land but Otto?' Now Macnab was all attention. 'Don Finlay, can you imagine your son coming into possession of two leagues and more?'

On this day Finlay made no response, but often during the next month, while María continued to stress her sister's abilities, he thought of the good land along the river to the west which Josefina would enable him to claim, and she became increasingly attractive. One afternoon he rode in to Victoria to talk with Martín de León, who held rights to this huge tract of land, an entitlement from the government in Mexico City in 1824, and without identifying Josefina, he asked whether a converted Catholic would also be ceded a league-and-a-labor if he married a Mexican woman.

'Of a certainty,' de León assured him in Spanish. Then de León said in good English: 'But it would be good if you would caution your friend Xavier about fooling with other people's horses. Tempers can grow very short in Tejas.'

Finlay did speak to Campbell, but not about cattle rustling. He asked: 'Zave, what would you think if I married Josefina? And claimed on the league next to yours?'

The big man rocked back and forth for some time, staring at the prairie, which could be seen from his porch: 'Your wife dead?'

'Divorced.'

'Legal?'

'Yep.'

'Marry her. Land is land.' But later, when Macnab was off tending cattle, Zave asked Otto: 'What happened to your mother in Baltimore?' and the boy replied in some confusion, for his memory of his mother was clouded: 'Things happened, and we left.'

'Was there a judge?' Zave asked.

'There was a lot of yelling,' the boy replied, and Zave said: 'I bet there was.'

The big man never mentioned the matter again, but when

Finlay suggested going back to Quimper's Ferry for the wedding, Zave said. 'More better we use the priest from the mission at Goliad.'

'Why?'

'I hear the new priest serving Quimper's is very strict. Lots of questions. Maybe even letters to Baltimore.'

'You mean the priest at Goliad . . . he'd be less rigorous?'

'He's always in a hurry. Better we use him,' and Zave was so insistent that in the end he and María, Finlay and Josefina, Benito and Otto rode their horses over to Goliad, where the ceremony was performed. When the priest asked in Spanish whether any man had reasons to oppose this marriage or knew of any impediment to forbid it, both Zave and Otto looked straight ahead.

As soon as the newly married couple returned home, Finlay hurried to Victoria and laid claim to his league-and-a-labor. He received it promptly, with one hundred and sixty acres as a bonus for his son.

With full encouragement from María and Zave, the Macnabs delayed building their own house; they stayed on with the Campbells, adding an improvised room to match Benito's, thus increasing the value of their holdings.

Under Benito's tutelage, Zave was becoming an expert in breeding mules and herding wild longhorned cattle; María and Josefina made some of the best food in the area; Otto helped everyone; and Finlay specialized in marketing the various goods they were producing. They also offered the dog-run to the transient public as a kind of inn, one dollar a night, four dollars by the week. Guests slept in a third lean-to which Zave and Benito built, and the rambling affair became one of the better stopping places in that part of Texas, with respectable meals provided by the wives, plus occasional treats that Finlay acquired through sharp trading with ships putting into Matagorda, or from caravans of merchants hauling their goods overland from Mexican cities south of the Rio Grande.

The informal inn had both a good reputation and a bad one. Travelers said: 'No better hospitality than what these women provide at Campbell's. But Zave is exceptionally sharp. Got to keep your eye on him.' Travelers as far away as Nacogdoches and Béxar said this of the posada west of Victoria.

It was Finlay who made the proposal that since mules and cattle were prospering at the plantation, as it was called by travelers from Georgia and Alabama, why did not he and Otto, enlisting Benito as their guide and two of his relatives as helpers, take a herd to New Orleans, where Louis Ferry had promised to buy them at a good price? 'Victoria to the Sabine, maybe two hundred and fifty miles. Sabine to New Orleans, about the same,' estimated a man who had traveled it, whereupon Finlay said: 'We drove cattle lots farther than that on the Trace,' but Zave corrected him: 'Trace is four hundred and eighty. I walked every step, three round trips.'

When it was agreed that such a drive was practical, Finlay hurried down to Matagorda Bay and posted an inquiry to Mr Ferry, and in a surprisingly short time, less than four weeks, had an answer:

Bring all the mules and longhorns you can manage. Also some good horses. Market even better than when you were here a year ago.

Louis Ferry

With this encouragement, Macnab assembled a herd of forty longhorns, thirty-one mules and two dozen mustangs broken to the saddle, and with a double supply of horses for himself and his helpers he set forth, and quickly he found himself on the famous Beef Trail.

Since those early days when Benito Garza had pioneered a trail to New Orleans for his mules, so many Texas drovers had followed in his steps that a well-defined path had taken shape. The Beef Trail flourished half a century earlier than the better-known trails like the Chisholm, which cattle followed on their way to the Kansas railheads, and in its day it provided Texas frontiersmen with a chance to earn hard cash.

Otto had been on the trail only a few days when he realized that his journey down the Natchez Trace had been, in comparison, merely a pleasant excursion. For one thing, the Texas rivers were infinitely more difficult to cross, because their banks could be steep and their currents swift after a rain. Food was scarcer and more poorly prepared, if that was possible, and above all, there was the constant threat that

454

Indians might hear of the movement of so many horses and try to steal their share on the first moonlit night. Finally, the roads and trails in Texas were not yet as clearly marked as the Natchez Trace, which had been used by white men for a long time when the Macnabs traversed it.

But without question, the Beef Trail, rugged though it was, offered more delights to young Otto than anything in Kentucky or Tennessee. This was true wilderness, with birds and animals he had never seen before, with bayous lined by moss-covered trees, with a daring Mexican rider like Benito to search out the trail, and with always the sense of a new country to be explored in whatever direction one might care to go. Also, as Otto confided to his father at the end of a long day: 'It's a lot more fun to ride than to walk.'

Already skilled as a horseman, he now acquired from Benito those extra tricks that would make him a true expert, but Garza was powerless to make him proficient with the lariat: 'Damnit! I know you're not stupid,' he would shout in Spanish. 'You can ride. You can shoot. Surely you can learn to throw a rope.'

But Otto could not. His hands were small and his arms short, and when he tried to twirl the stiff and heavy rope about his head in great circles, he not only got it tangled but he nearly succeeded in strangling himself.

'Damnit, Otto, no! You're supposed to throw it over the mustang's neck, not your own.'

It was hopeless. Despite his sweating determination, the young Scots-Irish-German-American boy could not do what the Mexicans did so effortlessly, and sometimes he would sit astride some huge horse watching in awe as the three men competed in roping; they were superb. But if they wanted to race with Otto, they found him now able to ride as effectively as they, swaying with the horse or leaning far over the neck of his mustang until he became one with his steed, flying over the empty land.

And if the four dismounted and took their guns to hunt for food, or merely to compete at targets, young Otto proved superior. He was a superb marksman: cool, hard-eyed, even of hand and steady of wrist. 'Eres un verdadero tejano,' Benito said approvingly one day, but then he added: 'Of course, if you want to rope cattle, you must hire a real mexicano.'

One evening as he and Benito rode in, tired and dusty from chasing one of the few buffalo left in those parts, Otto washed down his horse, but then stayed with it, saying to himself: I'll never forget this day. I'll never have a friend better than Benito. Nor a mother better than María. Nor a dog better than Betsy. Where's Baltimore? It seems so far away. I'm half Texican, half Mexican. Driven by a sense of wild joy, he leaped back onto his horse and galloped across the countryside. He was an Indian chasing buffalo, a Tennesseeman shooting a deer, a Mexican about to rope a longhorn. When he returned to camp he saw Garza and realized how much he owed him. Riding up to the Mexican, he dismounted, grasped his hand, and said: 'You are my friend.'

Few lads of Otto's age would understand Texas as thoroughly as he. By the time they crossed the Sabine river into Louisiana he had been pretty well across the face of settled Texas, save for the Nacogdoches quarter; he knew most of the ferries where boats could be relied upon, most of the river crossings that could be negotiated on foot. He had stopped in most of the semi-formal inns, and his knowledge of horses, cattle and the Spanish language would make him an invaluable ranch hand, or owner when he had acquired enough money to start for himself.

New Orleans had a magical effect on Finlay Macnab, for the excitement of selling his animals, the bantering of the buyers and the good fellowship of the stockyards reminded him of those faraway days at the Falkirk Tryst when he discovered the kind of person he was, and he hoped that here his son might have the same kind of awakening: 'When I wasn't much older than you I drove my grandfather's cattle to a great fair ... and sold them, too. That was the beginning of my real life. This could be the same for you. Study New Orleans. Learn how men do things.'

Otto's instruction took a rewarding turn when Mr Ferry, pleased by the good condition of their cattle and mules, came by their hotel to invite them to dinner at one of the fine French eating places. As an afterthought he tossed a handful of coins toward the three Mexicans: 'Get yourselves something.' Otto did not linger to see the bitterness with which Benito scorned the coins, letting them fall to the floor, or the furious manner in which he forbade his helpers to pick them up. 'Let the maids have them,' he stormed.

When Otto saw the luxurious dining-room with its high ceilings and glittering lights, he said enthusiastically: 'This must be awful expensive,' and Ferry laughed: 'On the profit I'll make from your animals, I can afford it. I ship your mules to Uncle Sam's army and sell your beef to the riverboats and restaurants like this. Young man, tonight you'll feast upon one of your own longhorns.'

Otto was old enough to relish good food, and hungry enough after the frontier fare of Texas to appreciate a varied menu. In fact, he considered New Orleans to be about six levels better than Cincinnati and said so, to Mr Ferry's approval. But as he gorged on the excellent food he could not help picturing Benito Garza eating in some grubby hole, and he winced as he recalled the niggardly manner in which Mr Ferry had thrown the coins.

Two days later, while walking the streets, Otto came upon an auction house where consignments of slaves from Virginia and the Carolinas were being sold, and he followed the auction with great interest, trying to guess which of two or three competing bidders would stay the course and win this lot or that. When he heard that one would-be purchaser intended taking his slaves, if he succeeded in buying any, to Texas, he approached the man and warned him: 'You know, mister, that slaves are not allowed in Texas.'

This news so startled both the buyer and the men near him that a vigorous discussion occurred, marked by a ridiculous lack of expert opinion, until in the end Otto had to inform the men of the situation. They refused to believe such a mere boy, but an elderly man well versed on the question came to Otto's defense and stated firmly that Mexican law forbade slavery and the importation of slaves.

'Then, by God, we'll change the law!' one hothead shouted, and this brought cheers.

'In five years Texas will be American!' More cheers.

'I'll march to Texas and so will a hundred brave lads like me,' another cried, but when this display ended, the would-be purchaser still did not know how to proceed, and Otto quietly explained ninety-nine-year indentures, and the man was delighted: 'What a thoroughly sensible solution!' And

457

forthwith he bid high on six different lots.

Mr Ferry introduced Macnab to the convenience of letters-of-credit and suggested that he might like to avail himself of one, but Finlay, having been burned by the skilled salesmen of the Texas Land and Improvement Company, did not propose to be hornswoggled again, and said so.

Ferry laughed at his fears but at the same time recognized his prudence: 'Goodness! I don't mean a letter-of-credit on me. I might skedaddle at any moment. No, I mean a letter on the firmest bank in the South,' and he took Finlay to the offices of the famous Louisiana and Southern States banking house, where the manager said he would be honored to accommodate any client of Mr Ferry's.

On the spur of the moment Finlay did a most uncharacteristic thing. He was so encouraged by the success of his droving operation, and so titillated at sitting in the offices of a major bank, with every prospect of sitting there more often in the future, that he decided it would be only decent to share his good fortune with his daughters back in Baltimore, and he asked the New Orleans banker if he could convey half his funds to a bank in Baltimore for the account of the Misses Macnab.

'Easiest thing in the world, Mr Macnab. It can be done at once.'

So it was arranged, and Macnab felt pleased with himself because of his generosity. He then asked how his and Zave's funds could best be handled: 'I'd rather not carry them on my person, seeing that pickpockets infest the steamers.'

'Easiest thing in the world,' the banker repeated. 'Leave your money on deposit with us, earn a tidy interest, and when either you or Campbell requires a load of timber for building a new house, inform me by ship mail, and your good friend Mr Ferry will have it on board the next vessel to Galveston Bay.'

'It won't do us much good at Galveston, seeing as we live near Matagorda.' The banker chuckled and said that one of these days he must get down to Texas, for he was convinced it was bound to be a major trading center of the American Union.

'It's owned by Mexico, you know,' Macnab said.

'At the moment,' the banker said, and wherever Finlay moved in New Orleans he found this same attitude toward Texas, as if the Louisiana men sensed that their western neighbor must soon become a part of the United States.

The closing days of their visit were marred by the discovery that Benito Garza and his two relatives had quit the expedition; for three days the Macnabs tried to find them, learning only that Benito, cursing Ferry, had summoned his two cousins and ridden back to Texas. There was much castigation of the Mexicans, but when the Macnabs were alone, Otto said: 'Remember when Mr Ferry threw the money at them? As if they weren't good enough to eat with us? I don't blame Benito for getting mad.'

When the Macnabs returned to Victoria, Finlay sought out Benito and said: 'I'm sorry for the way Mr Ferry treated you,' and Garza snarled: 'Gringos. What can you expect?'

Since most of the Macnab horses had been taken to New Orleans, Zave had replaced them, but Otto noticed that several bore strange brands, and later two of De León's men took the boy aside and warned him: 'Your friend Señor Campbell, he better watch out. The anglos in this area are fed up with his thieving ways, and something bad will happen to him if he does not mend them.' When Otto, refusing to hear ill of his friend, protested that maybe it was Benito Garza who took horses with other brands, the men said: 'We're watching him, too.'

Otto felt it necessary to warn his father, and Finlay took it seriously, but when he confronted Zave, the big Kaintuck turned the tables by upbraiding him for not having brought home Zave's share of the profits: 'Somehow you made a deal with Ferry that does you good but not me.' When Macnab tried to explain what a deposit in a bank meant, and how it drew interest, the stubborn redhead could not follow and loudly accused his friend of chicanery.

This so irritated Macnab, who understood the facts but could not explain them over Zave's shouting, that in anger he informed Campbell that he and Otto would build their own house. 'Good riddance!' Zave yelled, but Otto cried that he would not permit this, for he had grown to love big, compassionate María and could not visualize life without her. Josefina was equally good, quite a wonderful mother, but María had come first and he saw her as the architect of his good fortunes. When he flatly refused to part from her, the shouting

459

stopped and the breach was healed.

Thus began a perplexity which would haunt him all his life, and haunt Texas; he loved Mexicans like María and instinctively respected their values, so vastly different from his own. He saw that such Mexicans led an easy, singsong life, in harmony with the birds and the rising sun, while Texicans like his father lived a tense one in which cattle had to be counted and delivered on time. María followed the easy traditions of Catholicism, in which saints and the Virgin Mary were as real as the people who lived on the next hacienda; he would always be a Presbyterian, with that religion's harsh commands and unforgiving penalties. She sang, but he brooded; even at age eleven he brooded. To her the family was everything; to him it had proved only a shadowy remembrance. She could forgive a fellow Mexican like her brother Benito his misdemeanors; Otto could forgive no one.

And there his ambivalence deepened. He saw that American immigrants often conceded that María's way of life had commendable aspects; certainly it was more relaxed and in many ways gentler and more humane, as in its care for elderly members of a family; but often some relative like Benito performed an act which should not have been tolerated. Otto heard Mexican men accused of being shifty, unreliable, sycophantic when controlled by others, cruel when they were masters, so that what were deemed María's virtues became flaws when Benito displayed them. For example, Otto had seen Benito excuse his fellow Mexicans for the grossest misbehavior and even encourage it if it helped them gain an advantage over some anglo. Otto heard his own father charge: 'Mexican men can never settle upon one course of action and follow it for a generation; even the slightest mishap diverts them. So revolution is always around the corner.' Reluctantly, the Macnabs concluded that Benito Garza, specifically, was not a very nice person, and they concluded that the chances for his living in harmony with the immigrating Americans was not great.

Otto was not yet mature enough to understand that the incoming settlers demanded that Benito behave like an American, while he and his fellow Mexicans, occupants of Texas for a century, expected the Texicans to behave like Mexicans. It was an impasse that would never be resolved, but Otto was old enough to perceive the most fundamental contradiction of all. He, like Texas itself, needed the Mexicans and often loved them, but he did not always like them.

Several months after the Macnabs returned home, a much more serious problem evolved from Finlay's impulsive generosity in the New Orleans bank, because when the Baltimore bank informed Mrs Berthe Macnab that a substantial sum of money had been forwarded to her daughters by their father in Texas, she interpreted this as a signal of reconciliation. She was tired of living alone, and like scores of other abandoned wives in the settled states, she convinced herself that her husband in Texas needed her. With a vigor and determination that astonished her Baltimore friends, she arranged for a sea voyage to New Orleans and a Gulf trip to Victoria.

Consequently, one autumn day in 1833 a horseman rode out to the Campbell posada when the men were away, bringing news that 'A lady calling herself Mrs Macnab, she's landed at Linnville, and she wants us to bring her here.' Very quietly Otto closed the door so that Josefina would not hear, then asked: 'What does she want?' and the messenger said: 'She told me she has come to join her husband.' When Otto said nothing, the man asked, with a jerk of his thumb toward the room in which Josefina was singing: 'And what about that one?'

Otto considered this carefully, and slowly two reactions began to form. With his real mother at hand, and not in distant Baltimore, he recovered a most positive image of her: it was daybreak and she was bringing him a bowl of hot porridge rich with butter, cream and sugar. She had been a kind mother and he remembered how he had grieved when forced to leave her. But her shadowy portrait was erased by the thought of María, the wonderful Mexican woman whom he had adopted and whom he loved so dearly and in a different way. Desperately he wanted to protect her and her sister from sorrow of any kind.

Accordingly, without saying a word to anyone, he took his horse and accompanied the messenger back to Victoria, where he intercepted his unwelcome mother at the general store, to which she had been delivered. To his amazement he found that his two sisters, striking blondes in their late teens, had accompanied her, and that disoriented him. But he barged ahead, and when his mother sought to embrace him, he held back. 'You must go home,' he said.

'This is to be our home, Otto. We were wrong when we sent you and Father away.'

'You didn't send us. We went.'

This brought sniffles, and she groped for her handkerchief, but Otto was not moved: 'You must go back, because there's no place for you here.'

'You and your father need me, Otto. The girls and I have come all this way to help.'

'Texas is a different place,' the boy said.

'I know. We were warned on the boat.'

'You won't like Texas.' His harshness now brought tears to his sisters, and when he saw these attractive girls weeping he grew ashamed of himself.

'Take them out to the farm,' one of the men in the shabby store said, and when Otto asked: 'How can I?' the man said: 'She has to know sooner or later.' Mrs Macnab asked: 'Know what?' and the man replied: 'Lady, you'll find out soon enough.'

The only wagon in Victoria was procured, and Otto, aware that disaster loomed, was determined to avoid involvement with these unwelcome relatives. Riding in front of the procession like a page leading ladies to a castle, he refused to talk with them, and when the entourage approached the dog-run, he rode ahead, shouting: 'Hey, Poppa!'

Finlay and Zave were home now, and when they heard Otto crying as if for help, they hurried to the spacious porch, and there they stood when Otto delivered the three women. Uncertain as to how he should explain the situation, and confused about using the word 'mother,' he said simply: 'They're here.'

Berthe Macnab burst into tears as she ran toward her husband, and the two girls stood shyly by, as embarrassed as their brother. Macnab was flabbergasted, and it was left to Campbell to extend grudging civilities: 'Madam and you gals, sit down,' and he brought forward three chairs, but he made no motion to invite them inside. However, María, hearing the commotion, came to the door, whereupon Zave said hurriedly: 'My wife, María.' There were muffled acknowledgements, with

462

Zave whispering to his wife in Spanish: 'Dios! La esposa de Finlay,' at which María, thinking only of her sister, screamed: 'Quién es esta?' And then the morning began to fall apart, because Josefina, perplexed by the noise, hurried onto the porch, whereupon Otto ran to her, threw his arms about her, and cried: 'This is my mother now.'

It took Berthe and the girls some moments to comprehend that Josefina Garza was legally married to their father, or perhaps not so legally, because Berthe warned Macnab that she was prepared to throw him into jail, and so on. Zave did his best to placate her, pointing out that Baltimore was a long way from Texas and that oftentimes a man who was starting a new life, as many Americans in Texas were doing, broke all ties with his former life to begin afresh.

'I suppose you have a wife back . . . where?'

'Kaintucky, ma'am.'

'And is your wife waiting there for you?'

'As a matter of fact, she is.' Macnab and his son gasped, for Campbell had told them across that flooded stream on the Trace that his wife had died. Together they stared at this big fellow about whom they knew so little, and instinctively Otto went to stand with him, for if Zave was in trouble, the boy must help protect him. Then María, who knew enough English to understand this last conversation, also went to stand with him, and Campbell placed his arm about her: 'Now this one is my wife, and properly married.'

Then Josefina moved to support Finlay, and the two couples, with their mutual son Otto between them, presented a solid phalanx against the women from Baltimore; it was the emerging frontier against the established city.

'I'll have you all thrown in jail!' Berthe exploded, but Campbell told her: 'You'll have to build a big jail, considering all the men like us in Texas.'

Macnab took no part in this uproar; he had fled Berthe once and was determined not to allow her to complicate his life a second time. His attractive daughters he wished well, as proved by the fact that he had sent them half his profits, but he did not want them in Texas. He was happy with Josefina Garza, and he knew that Berthe, if confined to the house he intended building, would be able to stand the isolation and the brooding loneliness

463

for about one week. Yet he could not even tell her to go back home, but Campbell finally did, pointing out that there was simply no place they could stay in his house and that Finlay had no house of his own, and gradually he eased the three visitors toward their wagon. When both Finlay and Otto refused to accompany them to Victoria and then down to Linnville, where they could catch the next boat back to New Orleans, Zave volunteered to go.

Humiliated, and terrified by the emptiness of Texas, the women started their retreat, while Otto, leaning against the oak tree, watched dispassionately. In confusion he stood looking at his Baltimore family, then turned on his heel and ran back to where María waited on the porch.

When the women reached Victoria, Berthe demanded to see the Catholic priest, intending to charge both Macnab and Campbell with bigamy, but there was of course no priest in attendance and Goliad was twenty-five miles away. The Mexican authorities would not concern themselves with a civil brawl, and especially not when the complainant was an anglo and the women who would be hurt were good Mexicans. In Victoria, Berthe accomplished nothing, but in one of Linnville's three houses, where they waited for the boat to New Orleans, she was approached by an American farmer who had studied the trio these last two days and who asked if he might marry the older daughter.

'I suppose you already have a wife in Kentucky,' Berthe said harshly.

'No, ma'am. I come from Mississippi, and I'm single.'

'I suppose you brought your slaves with you.'

'No, ma'am. Men like me, we can't afford slaves.' When she did not respond to his major question, he turned to the daughter and said: 'Ma'am, you're beautiful. Would you consider marryin' me?' and the women collapsed in tears.

Zave Campbell stayed with the Macnab women until the next sailing vessel arrived, and to his astonishment the ship this time was an improved steamboat that negotiated the entrance to Matagorda Bay as easily as if the pass were ten miles wide: 'Bless my sainted aunt! Civilization comes to Texas!'

But while he was celebrating in Linnville, a posse of white

settlers located near Victoria visited the Campbell dog-run and demanded from Macnab a payment of nine dollars, claiming that among the horses he had driven to New Orleans were several bearing their brands, clearly placed on the flanks of the animals.

Finlay explained truthfully that the animals, cows and mules alike, had been delivered to him by Campbell and Benito Garza, and this seemed to satisfy the men, because one said: 'That's what we thought,' so after the nine dollars were handed over, they rode off, apparently content.

When Otto asked what this visit had meant, his father explained that in frontier communities where policemen and judges could not yet enforce the law, men felt they had to provide their own enforcement, serving as police and judge and sometimes executioner. He pointed out that Otto had now experienced three radically different communities: 'In Cincinnati you had judges and jails, the way things ought to be. In Under-the-Hill you had nothing, and you didn't like it. Here in Victoria we want law, but we don't know how to get it.'

'We have an alcalde.'

'Mexican law doesn't count, because the richest man can always buy the judge.'

'Will there be American law?'

'There will have to be.'

When Otto was alone, herding longhorns, he recalled the predictions of the businessmen in New Orleans; they had foreseen a day when United States law would operate in Texas, but he could not guess how this might come about.

On the day of Zave's return he told María and Josefina about his farewell to the Macnab women: 'They was weepin' and the mother said some real ugly things. She said both him and me ought to be in jail.' Pointing to Otto, he added: 'She said you would end in hell sure, associatin' with men like your daddy and me.'

On the following day, 10 November 1833, Zave rode south to intercept a caravan of merchants from beyond the Rio Grande, hoping to convince them to sell their wares to him rather than to the two storekeepers in Victoria. He told the Macnabs that he would surely be home by nightfall of the next day, but he wasn't; however, this occasioned no worry, since men on this frontier were accustomed to sleeping on the road when necessary, and their women knew it.

On the evening of the eleventh, as the Macnabs prepared for bed, they were startled by a warning cry from Josefina: 'The sky is falling!' And when they ran onto the porch they witnessed a spectacle of awesome beauty, the passage of the earth through a stupendous shower of meteors.

Every year, toward the middle of November, the earth picks its way through the Leonid Meteors, with observers marveling at the lovely fireworks. Every thirty-three years, for some arcane reason, the display is so magnificent that even lay watchers record it. And through the centuries an occasional passage becomes so striking that it is judged to be unique, observers having forgotten the reports of previous such visitations. One of these miraculous passages happened over Texas in 1833, when some thirty-five thousand flaming meteors an hour were seen.

'Look!' Otto shouted. 'It's light enough to read my book!' And for two hours the family watched the spectacular display, unaware that the extraordinary illumination, which made all of southern America about as bright as day, was creating havoc for a friend.

Next morning, right before dawn, as Finlay was getting out of bed, he and Josefina heard a series of suspicious noises, then the squeaking of a door as if someone had opened it, and he was starting to investigate when a piercing scream came from some animal or human, he could not tell which. Dashing into the yard, he found Otto beneath the oak tree, holding aloft the heavy legs of Zave Campbell, who had been hanged from one of the lower branches.

'Poppa! Help!'

Before Finlay could reach the dangling man, stout María had already leaped from the porch and was helping Otto hold him aloft, but she could see that her husband's face was already growing purplish: 'Señor Finlay! Ayúdeme!'

Finlay was unable to loosen the rope that was strangling his partner, and while he was fumbling with the knot about Zave's neck, Otto ran coolly into the house, grabbed a bird gun, and took steady aim at the rope. With the explosion of the gun, Campbell fell, carrying María and Finlay with him to the ground.

Otto was first to pull apart the knot about the neck, and slowly the purple in the hanged man's face began to subside, until at last he was able to whisper: 'Thank you, son.'

That evening was long remembered as 'the night stars fell on Texas,' but in the Victoria district it was 'the night they tried to hang Zave Campbell.'

'Darned things glowed like lanterns,' he said when his windpipe healed. 'Threw a light on me just as I was herdin' the Weavers' steers.' To Otto he said sullenly: 'Don't never steal cows in Texas, boy. Down here they play by different rules.'

... Task Force

The only time in two years we failed to produce full attendance at our Task Force meetings was at our November session in Amarillo. Ransom Rusk felt obligated to fly with a group of Texas sportsmen to their annual safari in Africa, this time to the vast Okavango Swamp in Botswana, and he apologized for deserting us: 'This junket was scheduled three years ago. Maybe I'll get me a trophy for my Africa Room. I'll leave my proxy with Lorenzo.'

I regretted his absence, for his impressive credentials and ponderous manner gave solid underpinning whenever we started questioning our visiting experts; it's extraordinary how a short question from a billionaire seems more penetrating than a long one from an assistant professor. Also, Rusk added necessary coloring to the portrait of Texas which we hoped to present to the public, because Quimper, dressing like a television Texan and speaking like one, often lent our sessions an air of levity that might mislead the unwary into thinking we were a bunch of good ol' boys. It was salutary to let them see that Rusk's more sober competence was also part of the real Texas.

When our staff informed me that the subject for our Amarillo meeting was to be *Anomie in Texas* by Professor Helen Smeadon of Texas Tech in Lubbock, I told them: 'I don't know what that word means and I'll bet none of the others do, either.' After phone calls confirmed this, I asked the young people to formulate a definition, which they circulated prior to the meeting:

anomie (Fr.) or anomy (Eng.). A precise sociological term popularized by the French scholar Emile Durkheim. 1. Collapse of the guiding social structures governing a specific society. 2. State of alienation experienced by a class or an individual resulting from such collapse. 3. Severe personal disorganization resulting in antisocial behavior. [Greek *anomia* = lawlessness < *anomos* = lawless: a — without + *nomos* law.]

Characterized by a feeling of rootlessness and a contempt for others who do obey the social laws. Commonly witnessed 1. in time of radical change; 2. during movement from one society to another; 3. as a result of death in one's family or divorce; 4. following severe or disorienting physical or mental illness. A common cause of movement to frontier societies or a result of such movement. Ultimate manifestation: suicide.

It looked to me as if this was going to be a handful to discuss, and as we flew low in our approach to Amarillo, I was not at all satisfied that our meeting would be a success. However, when I looked down at the amazingly flat terrain and the little roads that cut across the countryside for fifty miles without taking a turn, my mind wandered to other subjects. 'What's the weather going to be down there?' I asked the pilot, and he turned back to tell me: 'Like those three men lost in the Arctic. Howling wind, thermometer way down, dogs howling, and one fellow says: "Thank God for one thing. We ain't in Amarillo on a bad day."'

I loved this lonely part of Texas, so harsh, so unrelenting, where a windmill dominates the sky like one of the Alps in Switzerland. The Panhandle was a powerful place to visit if distances didn't scare you, and I subscribed to the city's motto: 'Hospitality capital of Texas. Weather cold, hearts warm.'

It was so bitterly cold when we landed that my fears about the meeting revived, but when we met Dr Smeadon, who was waiting for us in a cozy meeting room decorated with hot buttered rum, I concluded right away: This woman knows what she's doing. In her forties, tallish, forthright and with a sense of humor, she replied to my questions: 'Undergraduate work at SMU, graduate degrees at Chicago and Stanford, post-doctorate at the Sorbonne, where I specialized in the analysis of anomie with Raymond Aron.'

She barged right in. 'Anyone who seeks to get a grasp on the spiritual history of Texas is obligated to state which of the following four characterizations of our founding American immigrants he supports: "Were the newcomers (one) criminals fleeing justice, or (two) rascals fleeing the bill collector, or (three) average men who were merely restless, or (four) superior individuals tired of the evasions of society back east or overseas and lured by a vision of a better world they might achieve?"'

Rarely had I heard the options stated so clearly, and her subsequent analysis challenged us to sort out our prejudices: 'If we search the historical record, particularly the diaries, we find support for almost anything we care to believe. Who can forget the report of Victor Ripperdá from Nacogdoches to his superiors in Mexico City in 1824:

> I have now served in this forsaken place for three years and in that time have watched a steady stream of Americans sneaking in to steal our frontier. If you scoured the gutters of Europe, you could not find a worse collection of undesirables and troublemakers. Half who creep across the Neutral Ground seem to be fleeing the hangman's noose for murder. The other half have stolen money from their employers. Many were outright pirates with Jean Lafitte, who now ravages the coast of Yucatán, and others fought alongside Philip Nolan when he tried to steal Tejas and was shot by our troops.
>
> The attempt by the United States to fill our countryside with its discarded criminals would be amusing were it not so dangerous. If such rabble continue to pour in, there can be only trouble.

'That's a pretty savage condemnation of our forebears, but we must temper it with the firsthand observations of the good Father Clooney of County Clare, who knew Ripperdá and who must have observed the same immigrants upon whom the Mexican official based his harsh judgments:

469

I admit that during those rainy days when we crossed the infamous Neutral Ground, I was apprehensive about the kind of people who would be forming my massive parish, for I was forced to officiate at several hangings. But when I came to know the real settlers along the three rivers, I concluded that they provided just about the same proportion of rascals as I had found in Ireland, and rather fewer than I had seen in New Orleans. They were a rowdy lot, but so was I when a lad, and if they liked their whiskey, so did I.

Forgetting the occasional shooting and the few who abandoned their responsibilities, I remember them as kind-hearted, generous, quick to defend their rights, and eager to marry, respect their wives, and raise their children as Christians. I was happy to serve amongst them and have bright hopes for the land they are building.

'The judgment that the settlers were average was made rather effectively by Mattie Quimper in the brief summary she left of her days at the ferry bearing her name:

Very few tried to use the ferry without paying, and when they did, others forced them to pay up, not me, because they said it was unfair to rob a woman. I offered bed and board to hundreds stopping at our inn, and apart from an occasional murder or a shooting after too much drink, I saw no misbehavior. If a wandering man had no money he slept free, and ate, too, but if he could afford it he paid, and few cheated me. Times were hard, but they were good, and I never saw much difference between the Mexican government and the Texican. They were both fairly decent.

'And I'm sure you remember Finlay Macnab's moving summary in which he tells of assessing his fellow ship passengers in October 1831 and finding them to be stable citizens with above-average education? There were no criminals among the thirty adults and none who had been forced by the law to quit their homes back east. Remember with what respect he spoke of them and how pleased he was to be a member of such a group. He did, we must admit, point out two

470

weaknesses; several had abandoned their families back home, and quite a few favored heavy drink. But on the whole, they justified Stephen Austin's boast in his letter to Macnab in 1829:

> I can assure you, Mr Macnab, that the citizens of Texas are just as responsible and law-abiding as those of New Orleans or Cincinnati, and that ruffians will never be allowed in this colony.'

With that, Dr Smeadon clasped her hands under her chin and stared at us: 'How shall we resolve these four contradictory statements?'

She spent about twenty minutes parading before us other passages from contemporary documents, some supporting the view that all Texas settlers were criminals, others depicting an orderly society in which newcomers found refuge and encouragement to rebuild their lives. At the end of her recital we were in a jumble, and Lorenzo Quimper said so: 'What do we do, toss a coin?'

'No,' Dr Smeadon said, 'we look for a construct.'

'A what?'

'A theory which will explain the contradictions, resolve the differences.'

'That would have to be some theory! Jean Lafitte and Father Clooney in one bundle!'

'But that's exactly where they belong, where all of us belong, in one big bundle.'

She then launched into her main thesis, and as she developed it we began to acquire another vision of the Texas we loved. We neither defended it nor condemned. We merely looked at it through somewhat clearer glasses.

'The construct that clears away many of the seeming contradictions is *anomie*, and I'm pleased that members of your staff provided the definition they did. It's quite accurate. Anomie is the emotional state of mind we are apt to fall into when we are wrenched away from familiar surroundings and thrown into perplexing new ones. The two key words for me are *disorientation* at first, followed by *alienation* if it continues long enough.

471

'I assure you, Mr Quimper, I have no opinion whatever as to whether our great-great-grandfathers were criminals or rowdies or gentlemen scholars. All I'm concerned with is: "How did they behave? What did they actually do?" And when I study that restricted body of information I must conclude that most of them experienced anomie.'

'Stands to reason, doesn't it?' she asked. 'They were torn from settled homes. They surrendered the assured positions they had enjoyed in the pecking order. And they found themselves tossed topsy-turvy into a new environment they couldn't control.'

'Wouldn't they rejoice in their new freedom?' Quimper asked. 'I would.'

'At first you would, I'm sure. So would I. But then doubts would begin to seep in. You find that what looks like firm ground really isn't. Values begin to shift, and what was secure back east is found to be in flux. *Disorientation* is the word, and once it starts, its effect can be cumulative and catastrophic.'

When we started to argue about our susceptibility to such disorientation, Dr Smeadon asked Quimper if he would mind being a guinea pig, and he said 'Shoot!' so she asked him to stand, and as he smiled down at us she began to dissect him: 'The attractive thing about you, Mr Quimper, is that you wear so forthrightly the badges of your position in our Texas society. Your big hat there on the table. Your attractive bolo tie. Your neat rancher's whipcords. Your very nice boots – you make them, don't you? And your Cadillac parked in some driveway and an oil well somewhere. They define you. They give you assurance that you're part of the team, and a not inconsiderable part.' She laughed, then asked: 'You're proud of being a Texan aren't you?' and he snapped: 'I sure am.'

Now she became serious: 'Mr Quimper, please be seated, and I thank you for your help. But how would you feel if you were suddenly transported, let's say to New Hampshire, which is a very fine state but which respects none of your visible symbols. Its people don't cotton to Cadillacs and oil wells, and its children would laugh at you if you wore a bolo.' She moved closer to him: 'How would you react, Mr Quimper, if all your securities were suddenly dissolved?'

She smiled at him, a generous, warm smile of

472

encouragement. 'From what I hear, you're a strong-minded man, Mr Quimper, and I'm sure you'd fight back. Get the confusing signals sorted out. Establish new bases for self-esteem. And fairly soon, I would suppose, you'd be back on a track.'

Suddenly her manner changed completely. Very gravely she said: 'Look at the conclusion in the definition the young people gave us: The ultimate manifestation of anomie: suicide. Have you ever reflected on the large number of leading Texas citizens, in the early days, who committed suicide? Anson Jones, last-time President of the Republic of Texas, a suicide. Thomas Rusk, United States Senator from Texas and perhaps the ablest man of his time, a possible candidate for President of the United States, suicide. And what perplexes, Manuel de Mier y Terán, the ablest Mexican official ever sent north, he too committed suicide.

'What can that possibly mean?' Miss Cobb asked, and the reply was short: 'That Texas was a fluid situation which attracted people who were prone to anomie, and that in their continuing disorganization they killed themselves.'

She proceeded with additional material which startled us: 'Look at the number of our Texas heroes who abandoned their wives back home. Sam Houston did it twice. That pretty little thing in Gallatin, Tennessee, his splendid Indian wife in Arkansas. Davy Crockett walked out the door one day without even saying goodbye, if we can believe the legend. William Travis did worse in Alabama, and I would not care to know how many others defending the Alamo had fled their wives without the formality of divorce. The Finlay Macnab who had such a favorable opinion of his fellow passengers was a standard case – left his wife and daughters in Baltimore, but brought his son with him.'

After she had poleaxed us with a score of such instances, she chuckled: 'Did you know that one of the first laws passed by the new nation of Texas in 1836 forgave bigamy if the immigrating male, like this Macnab, could claim long separation from his legal wife back east, or mail that had not been delivered, or unavoidable confusion or almost any other claim, no matter how fragile? The law assumed that a de facto divorce had occurred and that the Texas wife was legally married, with the

473

children bearing no taint of bastardy. The law was necessary because in some areas a fourth of the husbands could have been charged with bigamy.'

After allowing this to sink in, she asked: 'What do you make of it, this irresponsible behavior, this wild resort to dueling, this sudden murder in the streets, this refusal of juries to find men guilty, and withal, this insistence that Texas was a religious state observing the highest moral principles?'

After we had paraded our ignorance and our determination to protect the reputation of our state, she said calmly: 'The best explanation, I think, is that the original situation in Texas – with the Neutral Ground more or less inviting disorganization – and the inability of the Mexican government to find consistency, and the protracted uncertainty over whether Texas would join the American Union created a fertile ground for the development of anomie. It became inescapable, a way of life whose lingering effects are with us still.'

After discussion, during which we rejected many of her ideas, she said: 'You people know your own minds, and that's good, that's Texan. But I want to crank in several additional ideas before you set yourselves in concrete. Oregon was settled at about the same time as Texas, but its citizens developed none of the Texan neuroses.'

'Ah!' Quimper cried. 'But Oregon never had the Mexican indecision. Its forerunners were decent, law-abiding Englishmen.'

'But California did have exactly the same background as Texas, and it didn't develop like us.'

'False analogy,' Garza said. 'For a hundred years California experienced orderly Spanish and Mexican governments. Definitions were understood.'

'A very good point, Mr Garza. Maybe that was the difference.'

'You're missing the real difference,' Quimper said. 'California didn't have to battle Apache and Comanche.'

'But that the two states developed quite individually, you must admit.'

'And thank God for that,' Garza said. 'Who would want to live in Los Angeles?'

'Or San Francisco?' Quimper asked. 'All those gays?'

'About the same percentage as in Texas, I would suppose,' Dr Smeadon said.

'You say that out in Lubbock, you're gonna be fired,' Quimper warned, and she said: 'I was thinking of Houston,' at which Quimper said: 'Houston don't count.'

'My next point is that even after joining the Union, Texas continued to enjoy special freedoms denied her sister states. She had the right to separate into five states, any time she wished. Public lands, which other states had to cede to the federal government, she retained. And in many things she went her own way. I'm not sure that these were constructive experiences. I'm not sure at all.'

'What do you mean?' Quimper thundered. 'They're the backbone of this state.'

'And one of the base causes of its neuroticism.'

'Are you saying that we're a bunch of neurotics?'

'I'm certainly neurotic,' Dr Smeadon said. 'And I've just demonstrated that you would be if you were moved to New Hampshire, and if we talked long enough, I'm fairly sure I'd find that even Miss Cobb would be – on certain tender subjects, like Texas patriotism.'

'I never voted for Lyndon Johnson,' Quimper said, 'but I had to respect him that night at the Petroleum Club in Dallas when he told us: "I love three things. God, Texas and the United States." And if there hadn't been a couple of ministers and priests in the audience, I'm sure he'd've changed the order.'

Dr Smeadon nodded, as if she agreed. 'The lasting effect of the Texas version of anomie is that it has encouraged the state and its citizens to believe they're different. This was really the end of the road – for Spaniards, for Mexican officials and churchmen, for Americans. When you reached Nebraska in those heady years, you plunged on to Oregon. When you reached Kentucky, you forged ahead to Missouri. But when you reached Texas, you stayed put. Except for the real crazies like Isaac Yarrow who stumbled on to California.

'I like the Texas mix. The dreamers, the petty criminals. The God-driven ministers, the real-estate connivers. And my heart goes out to the women like Mattie Quimper, who kept the ferries running.' She said nothing for some moments, thinking

475

of her predecessors who lived in sod huts, and bore a dozen children, and died at thirty-nine, but did not commit suicide. 'I mourn for the strong men who were driven to self-destruction by complexities they could not understand. Texas has always been a neurotic place, a breeding ground for anomie. But it's the neuroticism of activity, of daring, and I hope it never changes, even though the cost can sometimes be so tragic.'

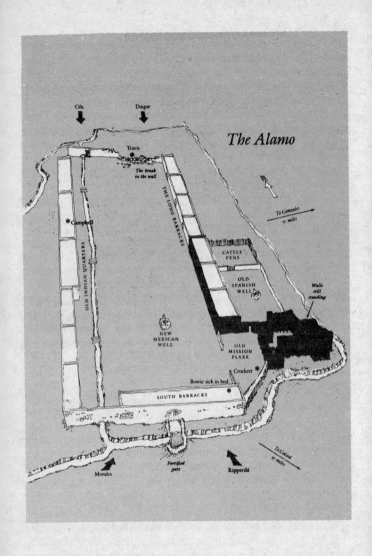

Cós   Duque

The Alamo

Travis

The break in the wall

THE LONG BARRACKS

* Campbell

OLD INDIAN QUARTERS

To Gonzalez
70 miles

CATTLE PENS

OLD SPANISH WELL

Walls still standing

NEW MEXICAN WELL

OLD MISSION PLAZA

Crockett *

Bowie sick in bed *

SOUTH BARRACKS

To Goliad
95 miles

Morales   Fortified gate   Ripperdá

VI

THREE MEN, THREE BATTLES

War forces men to make moral choices, and the stronger the man, the more difficult it can be for him to make the right choice.

Thus, when the great General Santa Anna marched north from Saltillo on the morning of 26 January 1836, determined to discipline the rebellious district of Tejas once and for all, he goaded three men to reach decisions on problems they had been contemplating for some time. Finlay Macnab and Zave Campbell, both married to cherished Mexican women, suffered immediate crises of loyalty, which each would resolve in his own arbitrary way.

But he never made that concession without immediately stating a major impediment: 'Those damned texicanos are so arrogant. Men come here from Tennessee and Kentucky, live on our land for two months, and start telling us mexicanos how to behave. Don't they know that this is our land? Has been for three hundred years. If they had decent manners we would share our land with them.'

In fairness he had to grant certain facts: 'Zave Campbell? No better man ever came to Tejas. Same goes for Finlay Macnab. And I'd be happy if Otto were my son. If all texicanos were like them and all mexicanos like me, we could build a tremendous state in Tejas, and it could be either a part of Mexico or a free nation of its own.'

But insurmountable obstacles intruded: 'Campbell and Macnab are all right, and so is Mattie Quimper. But the others? Impossible. They despise our religion. They laugh at how we act. They even mock our language, imitating the way we sing the last words of a sentence, as if we wanted the melody of our idea to linger in the air. What makes me bitter, they treat our women with contempt, unwilling to recognize the difference

479

between a whore and a gentlewoman. If they insist on ridiculing everything we stand for, how can they hope to share our land with us?'

Because he was an intelligent man, widely traveled, he had to admit a fact which most Mexicans living in Tejas refused to face: 'There seems to be an inevitability about these texicanos.'

Especially tormenting were the problems which perplexed Benito Garza, their unmarried brother-in-law, who faced a decision of the gravest import: To what nation do I owe my allegiance?

As a loyal Mexican he argued with himself, using the Spanish phrases in which he formed his deepest thoughts: 'I love Mexico. My heart beat faster when that fine Constitution of 1824 was announced, because I saw that it made possible a free state in Tejas, one that would enjoy honest freedoms. And I was proud when Santa Anna assumed control of my country, for he promised fine changes.'

But as a young man he had always been generous in welcoming American immigrants, for he recognized that vast changes were afoot and that perhaps even the basic governance of Tejas might have to be altered: 'I like northerners. I greeted them warmly when they arrived. I saw that we needed their vitality to fill our empty spaces, and I proved my good will by marrying my two sisters to yanquis. And when I am able to overlook the wrongs they do us mexicanos I can imagine a new state in which we live together as equal partners.' To his amazement, he was even willing to concede: 'If things go well, we might build in Tejas a new nation, half-texicano, half-mexicano.'

And now his conclusion: 'The only power that can save Tejas from being overwhelmed by the norteamericanos is Santa Anna. Forget that he destroyed the Constitution of 1824. Maybe his way of governing is best. One thing I'm sure of. He'll discipline those damned texicanos. So if he needs me, I'll have to fight on his side.' The moral and political struggle between an old Mexico and a new Tejas under a new form of government had been resolved. Benito Garza committed himself to fighting for the old, and so long as he lived he would never reconsider.

Underlying these complaints, some of them trivial, was a

deeper concern which intensified them all: Garza was a Mexican patriot who loved his beautiful, chaotic country and cherished the Spanish heritage from which his revered mother had sprung. He often thought of Mexico and Trinidad de Saldaña as one entity, an object of enormous dignity and worthy of devotion. To see this glorious world of Spain and Mexico smothered by Kentucky and Tennessee barbarism was so repugnant that he must defend the old values.

On 4 January, while Santa Anna was leading his men toward Saltillo, Benito made his final appearance in the market town of Victoria, where he talked quietly with the mexicanos he felt he could trust. Angel Guerra said frankly: 'When Santa Anna tore up the Constitution of 1824 and made it impossible for us to govern ourselves . . . that day I said "To hell with Santa Anna." I'm fighting with the Texicans.' A surprising number of sensible mexicanos said the same; Santa Anna's dictatorial policies had alienated them.

But certain thoughtful men, and among them leaders of the community like Elizondo Aldama, said: 'If the Texicans assume power, there can never be a decent role for us mexicanos. We'll always be third class, objects of contempt.'

'What are you going to do?' Garza asked guardedly.

'I'm certainly not going out to fight in Santa Anna's army, the way he treats his men, but I shall stay here within my walls and pray for his victory.' Many confided the same.

But a reassuring group took Benito aside. 'We know you're going to join Santa Anna. He'll teach those yanqui invaders. Tell him that when he finishes with Béjar and marches over here, and he'll find hundreds of us eager to help.' Garza judged that the majority of the Victoria mexicanos felt that way.

He also found two young men who were burning to join the oncoming army, and to them he said solemnly: 'I'm riding to Béjar tomorrow at sunrise. Join me two miles west of the Macnab Place, where the road forms.'

It was now midafternoon and Garza rode casually about Victoria, bidding farewell to a town he had grown to love. He was a striking figure, somewhat large for a mexicano, with light-brown skin, neatly trimmed mustache, dark hair across his forehead, an easy seat in his expensive saddle, and that twisted, ingratiating smile which he had inherited from his mother, the well-regarded Trinidad de Saldaña who had once ruled vast holdings along the Rio Grande. At certain turns of the rough streets he felt a pang of regret that he should be proposing to enter a war which might have disastrous consequences for Victoria and those citizens who were electing to side with the Texicans, but he knew it to be inevitable: Texicans and mexicanos cannot live side by side. As soon as he thought this he realized its impropriety: We live side by side right now, nowhere closer than in the Campbell dog-run. But we can't rule side by side. We cannot be treated justly by men who hold us in contempt. Santa Anna is right. Clean house. Shoot the tough old-timers . . . start new.

He shook his head in perplexity, for he had to appreciate the fallacy of what he had just thought. It was not the longtime Texicans who were the firebrands leading the rebellion; most of Austin's famous Old Three Hundred, the earliest anglo settlers, were content to remain mexicano citizens. It was men who had been in Tejas less than two years, less than a year, less, by God, than six weeks, who screamed for war. And now, Garza thought grimly, they're going to get it. He was prepared to annihilate all of them.

But when he reached the Campbell home and saw for the last time his three trusted friends, he had to leave the kitchen where his sisters María and Josefina were preparing supper, lest his confusion betray the harsh action he was about to take. In the darkening twilight he walked disconsolately along the banks of the Guadalupe, and under the oak tree from which Campbell had been hanged he thought of how much he loved these daring men, how he had trusted and worked with them, helping them build their homes and teaching their boy in the ways of his new land. He wondered if he should warn them of the danger that was about to engulf them, and he decided that to do so might endanger his own plans, but as they sat at supper he did suddenly blurt out: 'I think we are all in great danger. I think Santa Anna will sweep through Béjar and be here in Victoria within the month. Be careful, I beg you.'

Macnab said later: 'I guessed that night he was going to fight with Santa Anna.' When another Texican asked: 'Why didn't you stop him?' Finlay said: 'I was worried about my decision, not his.'

At dawn on 5 January, while the two mexicanos waited for Benito at the fork of the road, young Otto, who had suspected what was up, lingered far behind in the darkness to watch the three conspirators ride off. Desperately he wanted to bid his friend Godspeed but was afraid to do so. Unknown to Garza, Otto waved farewell to his Mexican friend as the sun rose over Victoria.

The three mexicanos rode speedily to Béjar, a hundred-odd miles to the northwest, where they found great confusion. Sketchy word had reached town that General Santa Anna was marching toward Tejas with an army of thousands, and Texican military men, or what passed for such, had already begun to survey the only defensible structure in Béjar, the Alamo, as the ruins of the old mission on the east side of the river were called. Since this was obviously to be the keystone of the Texican defense, Garza inspected it as carefully as he could without arousing the suspicions of the rough-clad men who patrolled it.

He saw that it was a spacious place running north and south, with sturdy adobe walls enclosing a central area large enough to house hundreds of cattle and thousands of men. Ancient buildings lined the inside of some of the walls; clearly, the place could be taken by determined assault, but if Tennessee and Kentucky men manned the walls with their powerful rifles, the cost could be sizable.

Still, Garza thought, 'I'd rather be outside with two thousand trying to get in than inside with a hundred and fifty trying to keep them out.' He had made a cautious census of the Texicans but had arrived at a figure slightly too high; the Alamo contained only one hundred and forty-two fighting men.

At the southeast corner of the compound stood the mission church, a crumbling two-story building without a roof. Its walls were of stone and rather formidable. Anyone inside would be momentarily safe, but it could not be termed a fort and would probably play only a minor role in the siege. The ruined church was, in its way, impressive, a falling relic of those better days when Spanish friars had brought Christ and sanity to Tejas; it had been secularized in 1793, forty-three years earlier, and had from time to time been savagely abused by various army units stationed within.

One last thing Garza noticed as he completed his survey. Outside every wall of the old mission there was ample open ground, which would influence the flow of battle in two ways: the besieging army could maneuver and choose its spot for major attack; but the same open ground would enable the defenders to take unimpeded aim at any troops trying to assault the walls. Calculating the comparative advantages, Garza concluded: A determined assault will finish off the Alamo within three or four days.

Leaving the makeshift fortress on 13 January, he crossed the river, entered the town itself and checked the streets to see if any Texicans were stationed there. The Veramendi residence did contain one important Texican, Mordecai Marr, now seventy-two, but since his wife, Amalia, had converted him into a virtual mexicano, he posed no danger. At the former Saldaña house on the plaza, there were no signs of anglos. And the unfinished San Fernando Church looked down impassively on the quiet scene and tolled its bells at regular intervals.

At dusk on the same day Garza said farewell to Béjar. He rode past Rancho El Codo, once owned by the Saldañas, later by the Veramendis, now by the Marrs, and pressed on to San Juan Bautista, now called Presidio del Rio Grande, from there to Monclova, and on toward Saltillo.

He did not reach this delightful little city because on the morning of 27 January 1836 he reined in his horse and stood in his stirrups to view a sight which thrilled him – marching north, raising clouds of dust, came the outriders of Santa Anna's army: Dear God, they've come to rescue us from those damned norteamericanos.

Spurring his horse, he galloped forward to meet the oncoming saviors, and when he drew within hailing distance he shouted: 'I must see General Santa Anna . . . at once.'

'Who are you?' a subaltern asked.

'A loyal mexicano, with information of great importance.'

He displayed such authority that he was led directly to the general, and saw for the first time El Salvador de México, the great Santa Anna. An imposing man of forty-two, tall, trim, dark-complexioned and with very black hair that sometimes drooped over his forehead, Santa Anna dressed himself, even on a march such as this, in uniforms of the most extravagant nature, with a flood of medals cascading down his chest. As a reward for his rape of Zacatecas, Major-General Santa Anna had promoted himself to the rank of general-in-chief and taken the exalted title Benemérito en Grado Heróico, and there was gutter rumor that when he succeeded in subduing the Texicans, he was to name himself Benemérito Universal y Perpetuo.

This was the able, vainglorious, vengeful commander before whom Benito Garza bowed on the road north of Saltillo: 'Excellency, all Tejas is overjoyed to see you coming to our salvation.'

'I thank you. What is your name?'

'Benito Garza, of Victoria.'

'And how are things there?'

'The norteamericanos hold us in contempt. The mexicanos pray for your victory.'

'Their prayers will be answered,' he said, and from the resolute manner in which he spoke, Garza was convinced that they would be.

Who was this charismatic leader in whom all Mexicans seemed to place such hope? Born in 1794 in the Vera Cruz district, he had at age eighteen proved himself to be a man of extreme personal bravery, exhibited in many battles, but also one capable of adapting to almost any situation, as proved by the fact that he would ascend to the presidency of Mexico on eleven different occasions. Four times, at the height of one crisis or another, Mexico would send him into what was intended to be lifelong exile, and three times he would storm back to resume his leadership. The fourth time he tried, he failed.

There is no one in United States history remotely comparable, nor, for that matter, in any other country. He liked to call himself the Napoleon of the West, but Napoleon returned to power only once, and then for a scant hundred days; Santa Anna returned ten times.

It seemed that whenever he resumed power his actions carried special significance for Texicans, and two incidents in his remarkable career were especially relevant. In the hot summer of 1813, when he was nineteen, he had the bad luck to participate in the battle at the Medina River, which took place near San Antonio de Béjar, along the boundary between the Mexican territories of Coahuila and Tejas. Mexican dissidents aided by American adventurers had launched a minor revolution, which Spain's colonial government decided to crush with a harshness that would forever halt subversion north of the Rio Grande.

In the battle, Santa Anna helped spring a trap on the unsuspecting Americans, enabling his general to win a resounding victory, but it was what happened next that made the battle significant, for General Arredondo gave one simple order: 'Exterminate them!' A slaughter followed, with young Santa Anna participating in the execution at point-blank range of more than a hundred prisoners and the running down of many others.

He also helped cram more than two hundred captives into an improvised jail in San Antonio; by morning eighteen had suffocated. Most of the survivors were dragged into the town plaza and shot. But Arredondo's contemptuous treatment of the civilians surprised even Santa Anna. Any who were even suspected of supporting the insurgents were also summarily shot, and when the executions were completed he authorized his troops to loot and rape in the streets. To reinforce his disdain of the populace, the general ordered the leading matrons of the city to report to a detention area, where for eighteen days they were forced to do the laundry of the victorious invaders and cook their food.

This crushing victory, and Santa Anna's resulting promotion, must, however, be judged an unfortunate affair for him. The ease with which the triumph came and the harshness which followed encouraged him to believe that the way to handle insurgents was to beat them convincingly in battle, then execute the men and humiliate the women. Now, twenty-three years later, faced with another insurgency in Tejas, he was not only prepared to duplicate those punishments but also eager to do so, for he could be extremely cruel and unforgiving when he judged it necessary to be so.

Perhaps Mexico required a ruthless leader like Santa Anna, for these were turbulent years. During one period when the United States had only one President – Andrew Jackson, who helped bind his nation together – unlucky Mexico staggered through sixteen different incumbencies, the hideous penalty paid by many former Spanish colonies that seized their freedom without obtaining with it any coherent theory of responsible government.

But whenever Santa Anna resumed his leadership things seemed to be better ... for a while – then he would do some outrageous thing and the government would collapse again. During one return to power, having taken back the presidency on a pompously announced program of reform, he assured the electorate that he was a liberal who would reform the church, discipline the army, and grant each of the constituent states a substantial degree of self-government. As we have seen, Texicans rejoiced in this promise of a constructive freedom under which they could populate and improve their frontier regions.

But in 1834 he had startled everyone, and perhaps even himself, by announcing: 'I now realize that I am really a conservative, and as such, I offer the nation a clear three-point program which will save it from its current turbulence. We must replace federalism with a supreme central government, with the individual states having few powers and no legislatures. The traditional role of the church in national affairs must be restored. And the ancient privileges by which priests and army officers were excused from the rules of common law must be restored.' Reviving the battle cry of 'Religión y Fueros' (Religion and the Rights of Priests and Army Officers), he scuttled the liberal Constitution of 1824 and converted Mexico into a conservative dictatorship – and many citizens applauded. 'At last we have a strong man in control. He should be made our leader for life.'

Now came the move which struck terror into the hearts of Texicans who had hoped for better, more orderly days. The rich silver state of Zacatecas, refusing to surrender its hard-won rights to Santa Anna's central dictatorship, launched a kind of rebellion in defense of its privileges, and this was exactly the kind of challenge Santa Anna loved, for it enabled him to don his general's bemedaled uniform, mount his white horse, and ride into battle.

Leading a large army up to the walls of Zacatecas, he then ripped a page from Napoleon's book, swung around the town, and attacked from the rear. At the same time he ordered several of his best officers to leave his ranks in apparent defection, sneak into the city, and proclaim themselves defenders of the Constitution of 1824, and mortal enemies of Santa Anna. As trained soldiers, they expected to be given command of Zacatecan troops, whom they would direct into certain slaughter when the fighting began.

On 11 May 1835, with this combination of valor and deceit, Santa Anna won a devastating victory, but it was what happened next that boded ill for Tejas, for he turned his men loose in one of the ghastly rampages of Mexican history. During the terror some two thousand five hundred women and children and men who had not participated in the battle were slain. Foreign families became special targets, with English and American husbands bayoneted and their wives stripped naked and coursed through the streets. Rape and pillage continued for two days, until the once-fair city was a burning, screaming ruin.

Zacatecas had been ravaged because it refused to change its loyalty as quickly as Santa Anna had changed his, and word went out: 'If Tejas continues to oppose the central government and tries to cling to its old constitution, it can expect like punishment.' And in the dying days of 1835, backed by an immense army, aided by good generals and strong artillery, Generalisimo Santa Anna marched north, determined to humiliate once more the recalcitrant Texicans. All who opposed him would be slain.

On 13 February 1836 this remorseless general, accompanied by a cadre of senior officers, rode ahead to the Rio Grande and were snug inside San Juan Bautista while the main body of the troops, accompanied by Benito Garza, lagged far behind, marching on foot across that exposed and dangerous wasteland between Monclova and the river. Santa Anna, always looking ahead to the next battle and disregarding the comfort of his troops, had no cause to worry about his straggling men because the day had started with the temperature near sixty and the sun so hot that many soldiers removed their jackets and marched in shirts only, and sometimes not even that.

But this was the region just south of that in which Cabeza de Vaca had experienced the dreaded blue norther, and such a storm now hit men who had never experienced the phenomenon. At its first warning blast they hastily redonned their shirts and jackets.

Rapidly the temperature dropped to fifty, then forty, then to an appalling thirty. Men began to slow their pace, hugging themselves to keep warm, and mules started to wander in confusion. By midafternoon a wild snowstorm was sweeping across the unfettered flatlands of Tejas and northern Coahuila, and at dusk men and animals began to freeze.

All night the dreadful storm continued, throwing twelve to fourteen inches of snow upon men who had never felt its icy fingers before. They began to stumble, and many collapsed; then the snow covered them and they became inert white mounds along the route, as if in their final moments they had pulled fleecy blankets over their dying bodies.

Worst hit was a horde of pitiful Indians from Yucatán marching under the command of General Víctor de Ripperdá, governor of that tropical district and former official in charge of the frontier post at Nacogdoches. His troops, hundreds of them with no shoes, no blankets, no warm clothing of any kind, simply fell down and died. Sometimes Garza, who rode up and down the files, would find eight or nine huddled together in a hopeless mass, clutching one another for warmth; after they all perished, the covering snow formed a rounded hump, a kind of natural mausoleum. When more fortunate Indians from colder climates, those with shoes and blankets, spotted such a mound, they dug inside, stripped the dead bodies of whatever cloth remained, and wrapped their own faces against the storm.

At the rear, Garza came upon soldaderas and their children suffering terribly, but like the Yucatecs they huddled in groups, and although many died, the stronger survived. It was shocking for those soldiers who formed the rear guard to stumble upon the frozen bodies of children abandoned in the snow.

Mules, oxen and horses struggled in the blinding storm, collapsing in huge snowdrifts that quickly buried them. When the norther subsided, and the surviving men and mules were counted, General Ripperdá found that his army had suffered a tremendous loss. Santa Anna, warm inside mission walls, must have known this, but neither then nor after did he refer to it, for he realized that when many soldiers are required to march over a great distance in unfavorable weather, somebody is apt to die. That was one of the chances of war, unpleasant but acceptable.

And from the practical point of view, Ripperdá's experience in the Monclova blizzard may have been salutary, for it rid him of many largely useless Yucatecs, toughened up the line, and enabled one young lieutenant who dreamed of impending glory to assure his fellow officers: 'If we can survive that blizzard, we have little to fear from the rebels in Tejas. It'll be Zacatecas all over again.'

When Benito Garza rode north of the Rio Grande towards Tejas with Santa Anna, he had an opportunity to see why the mexicano troops, officers and enlisted men alike, loved this dynamic man. He obviously thrived on campaign conditions and could hardly wait, Benito thought, to launch the attack. 'Forward, forward!' was his constant command to himself and his troops.

The dictator was going to be forty-two years old the next day, 21 February, and he would spend it in the saddle a few miles south of his ultimate target, the Alamo. The passing years had treated him well, and he looked, if the truth were voiced – and he liked it to be voiced – a good deal like one of Napoleon's marshals, Ney or Soult, or even like the emperor himself.

On this campaign he had brought along none of his mistresses, and Garza heard him complain to General Cós: 'How can a gentleman celebrate his birthday alone?' So on Santa Anna's natal day Cós ordered salutes to be fired and a ration of wine issued for celebration. The troops were now approaching the Medina, where Santa Anna had known his first great victory, with many, many more anglo rebels in the field then than there would be now. The general wanted to leave El Camino Real briefly and veer eastward toward the old battle site, but when this was done and the steep banks of the river reached, no one could locate exactly the scene of the battle, and Santa Anna was mildly displeased.

On the day after his birthday, Santa Anna moved his troops to within sight of the tall tower of San Fernando Church, just across the river from the Alamo, and there he made camp early. Scouts rode in to inform him of conditions in the town, and everything he heard was reassuring: 'No reinforcements and none on the way. Colonel Fannin and his large detachment bottled up at Goliad and he refuses to move to Béjar. Still no more than a hundred and fifty men, but they do have some cannon. And the entire town, General, is eager to welcome you.'

'Are there any mexicanos fighting with them?' This problem of loyalty irritated him.

'Captain Juan Seguín has taken arms against you. Says he will fight for the Constitution of 1824.'

'Do any support him?'

'He led nine others into the Alamo. We have their names. Abamillo, Badillo, Espalier . . .' He continued to read from the grubby paper, nine names in all.

'They're to be hanged. Not shot. Hanged.' Even as he gave this order one of the mexicanos slipped out of the Alamo, but the other nine were determined to oppose the dictator with their lives, in defense of a new Texas which would later have little use for their kind.

Garza rode with the general as he entered the town in the lead, disregarding the possibility of isolated sniper fire from some misguided rebel. No doubt about it, this man was brave. Turning back to face Garza, he gave a short command: 'I want the flag I showed you last night to be flown immediately.' And now they reached the heart of Béjar, with Garza pointing out the church.

'Can its tower be seen at the Alamo?' the general asked.

'Unquestionably.'

'Fly the flag.'

So Benito Garza climbed the quivering tower stairs, accompanied by two dragoons, and when they reached the highest practical point he unfurled the big flag made from cloth which Santa Anna had brought north for this specific purpose.

The rude flag was very large, perhaps twelve feet long and proportionately wide, but despite its size, it carried no symbol of any kind. Its message was its color, a bold, sullen blood-red over all.

As the flag unfurled, a breeze caught it and spread it majestically in the sky. Those who saw it and understood its military meaning gasped, for this was the flag of No Surrender, No Clemency. The soldiers who fought against it knew that

491

they must either kill or be killed, because no prisoners would be taken.

When Garza descended from the bell tower, an orderly informed him that the general wanted his assistance in translating an important document into English.

The two men went to a house located in the smaller plaza between the church and the bridge leading across the river to the Alamo. Here Santa Anna outlined the rules for this and all subsequent battles in the district of Tejas. They were, as he carefully pointed out, in strict conformance with international law and with the recently promulgated rules of the new dictatorship:

> Every Mexican who has fought with the rebels or in any way supported them is to be hanged, and I want no protracted trials. Just hang them for treason. Every American colonist who has taken arms against us, to be shot, and again, no trials. Those who supported the rebels but did not take arms, to be expelled forever from Mexican soil. All American immigrants, regardless of their sympathies, to be moved at least a hundred miles south of the Rio Grande, whether they can bring their household goods or not. Absolutely no further immigration of any kind from the American states into Tejas or any other part of Mexico. The people of Tejas to repay every peso of expense incurred on this expedition to discipline.

> Now this is very important and is to be stressed in any pronouncement we make. Any foreigner in Tejas who is arrested while in the possession of arms of any kind is to be judged a pirate and treated accordingly. Finally, the flag up there tells it better than I can. Once the battle begins, if the enemy has not previously surrendered, no prisoners will be taken. Make this extremely clear. No prisoners are to be taken. They are to be shot on the battlefield where we capture them.

Shortly thereafter a white flag of truce showed at the Alamo and a parley took place on the little bridge crossing the river; here the final terms were spelled out to the Americans, in their own language. But they were, as Garza noted when he delivered them, somewhat softened: 'If you surrender unconditionally, right now, lay down your arms and take a pledge never to appear in Tejas again, your lives and property will be spared.' Garza, hoping that actual battle could be avoided and the invaders peaceably expelled, prayed that the norteamericanos would accept these surprisingly generous terms, but when the emissary returned to the Alamo the answer from there was delivered in the form of a cannon shot, whose roar reverberated across the main plaza. Santa Anna had his answer.

He did not lose his temper. Coolly summoning his generals, he said: 'We'll not throw our entire force against that silly fortress. We'll save it for later punishment of the entire state.'

'How do you propose knocking them out of their position?' General Cós asked, indicating the Alamo.

'Siege. We'll strangle them, bombard them with cannon, and shoot them down when they collapse.'

'With your permission, Excellency,' General Ripperdá said. 'I had a long experience with norteamericanos when I served at Nacogdoches. Those scoundrels will not collapse.'

'Your norteamericanos did not face Santa Anna.'

So the siege began, and no prisoners were to be taken alive. The customs of war as observed by civilized nations justified such terms for treasonous rebellion against a sovereign state, and that is exactly what the Texican rebels were engaged in.

The sad fracture which threatened to destroy this lovely area was reflected in the names used by its people. Mexicanos called it the town of Béjar in Tejas; Texicans, San Antonio in Texas – and between them no compromise seemed possible.

The unfurling of the great red flag produced unexpected consequences in one San Antonio household. At the northern end of Soledad Street, in the old Veramendi place, Mordecai Marr and his mexicana wife, Amalia, saw the flag lazily fluttering in the breeze and realized for the first time that this was to be a battle to the death. They had hoped that differences between the central government in Mexico and the provincial one in Tejas could be peacefully resolved, but now men had to make decisions.

This was particularly difficult for the Marrs. To begin with, they were citizens of Mexico, of that there could be no doubt.

493

She came from the grandest family in the region, with notable ties to the Veramendis of Saltillo, and her husband had embraced Mexican citizenship back in 1792 when he married her and came into possession of the vast ranch at El Codo. Not once in succeeding years had he even contemplated trying to regain his American citizenship, and in recent years when minor troubles flared he had been a pacifying agent, assuring American newcomers that the things they disliked could be easily corrected.

But since the New Year, two events had altered the family thinking. From a Zacatecan refugee connected to the Veramendis they heard harrowing reports of Santa Anna's treatment of that city, and this had made them wonder whether such a leader could retain the good will of his Tejas citizens. More confusing, they learned that inside the Alamo, among the handful of men preparing to defend it, was their respected relative Jim Bowie of Kentucky.

Back in 1831 this colorful outsider had married Ursula Veramendi, the winsome belle of the family. At first the respectable mexicano families of Saltillo and San Antonio predicted only bad consequences from such a union, but Bowie surprised them by becoming an ardent Catholic, a devoted husband and a fine father to his and Ursula's children. Even the local priest had said: 'The Jim Bowie marriage is one of the most reassuring in Tejas. Who would have expected it?'

The Marrs had deemed it imprudent to visit Jim inside the Alamo, for they certainly did not share his determination to resist Santa Anna. Also, when in 1833 the lovely Ursula and her two children died of cholera, Bowie's essential ties with the Veramendi family were broken and the Marrs had not seen him since that tragedy. 'He goes his way,' Mordecai said to the oldtimers, 'and we go ours. But we respect him, always have.'

So there it stood on the afternoon when the flag signaled, and the longer Mordecai contemplated this dreadful twist of events, the more perturbed he became. He ate no supper. Pacing back and forth in the study that he had come to love as the heart of his home, he thought of the curious forces which had brought him to this unlikely spot. He did not love the United States, and he actively disliked most of the immigrants he met. Nor did he love Tejas, but he still loved the freedom, the bigness of the land he had elected for his home, and he did not want to lose that. The men in the Alamo represented a striving to keep that freedom, while the men who had unfurled the flag of death could represent only repression.

It was half after nine when he walked soberly into the big room where Amalia was busy with her needlework, and when he came upon her as she sat with the flickering light behind her lovely head, he saw her as if for the first time. How happy they had been! He'd been on the verge of marrying the Saldaña girl when Amalia Veramendi moved in to sweep him off his feet with her love, her wit, and her promises of a vast ranch if he married her. Never had he regretted the decision, although he did sometimes wonder what had happened to the Saldaña girl, whose first name he could not now remember.

'Amalia, I'm going to join Jim Bowie.'

'I will go with you.' She said this so simply, her needlework in her lap, that he was overcome by her courage, but when he started to say that if she changed her mind – 'What other choice could I have?' she interrupted, rising and kissing him. 'We've had a wonderful life, Mordecai, because we always did everything together. Let's not change now.'

They spent less than an hour getting a few things together, and it was well before midnight when they left the Veramendi home and walked quietly down dark Soledad Street to the church square. There they turned left, walked through the small area subtended by the loop in the river, and approached the little footbridge leading to the Alamo. Santa Anna's guards stopped them, of course, but when Amalia told the officer: 'I'm the Veramendi woman, my family owns that house over there,' they let her and Mordecai pass.

Once across the bridge, the proud couple turned left, their white hair shining in the moonlight, and without provoking any action on the part of the remaining guards, walked purposefully toward the old mission. When they were in hailing distance, an American patrolling the walls shouted at them, and Mordecai called back: 'Veramendis, we come to see Jim Bowie.' They could hear conversation inside and then see the cautious opening of the gate.

Quickly they slipped through, saw the huge area inside the walls and a rather small room to the right, where Jim Bowie lay prostrate from a sudden attack of the fever. Amalia, hurrying to his bed, whispered: 'Jim, Mordecai is here. We've come to be with you.' And the sick man reached out to grasp their hands.

The Marrs found the Alamo dominated by four remarkable men. Two were wild frontier heroes: Jim Bowie, in command of the volunteers, and Davy Crockett. The other two were cool, well-educated gentlemen: Colonel William Travis, commander of the regular troops, and James Bonham, a quiet man with a personal courage matched by few and surpassed by none. The original homes of these four epitomized much of the Texas history: the two frontiersmen were from Tennessee, of course, while the gentlemen were from South Carolina. On the character of these four would depend the defense of the Alamo.

Next morning, while Señora Marr comforted the despondent Bowie, her husband explored the arena in which they would do battle. The huge walled-in area astounded him: 'We could move all the people of Béjar in here and they'd fill only a corner.' But as he walked about, surveying the walls and calculating their ability to withstand Mexican cannon fire, he learned the nature of this siege, for Santa Anna's artillery began their morning bombardment. After taking refuge under a shed, Marr watched while large cannonballs came drifting in over the walls, landed in the middle of the open area, and rolled harmlessly along until they came to rest against some obstruction, hurting no one, destroying nothing.

Since the Mexican gunners seemed never to vary the position, aim or elevation of their cannon, the balls invariably landed in the same harmless spot, and when Marr realized this, he snorted: 'We can hold out a month against that stuff.'

While he was reaching this conclusion, Colonel Travis was working in a small room, as far from the barrage as possible, composing with a scratchy pen a letter that would be remembered in Texas history. Staring at the red flag, he knew that unless reinforcements arrived quickly he and his men were doomed, but instead of surrendering, he threw his gauntlet into the face of the world:

To the People of Texas and All Americans in the World – Fellow Citizens and Compatriots:

I am besieged by a thousand or more of the Mexicans under Santa Anna ... The enemy has demanded a surrender at discretion, otherwise, the garrison are to be put to the sword, if the fort is taken. I have answered the demand with a cannon shot, and our flag still waves proudly from the walls. *I shall never surrender or retreat* ... I call on you in the name of Liberty, or patriotism and everything dear to the American character, to come to our aid, with all dispatch ... If this call is neglected, I am determined to sustain myself as long as possible and die like a soldier who never forgets what is due his honor and that of his country.

VICTORY OR DEATH

William Barret Travis

Substantial help was available in the countryside: at Goliad, some miles to the southeast, there was an organized branch of the army, and at Gonzales, due east, a random collection of untrained patriots. If these forces marched swiftly to the Alamo, it might be saved.

When Zave Campbell heard that Santa Anna was marching north with thousands of troops, his first thought was a practical one: I better get some cattle up to New Orleans. He therefore made hurried plans to get a herd together, but he was temporarily forestalled by the sudden disappearance of Garza and by the fact that Finlay Macnab, also apprehensive about the approach of Santa Anna, would not allow Otto to leave home at this critical time. Despite these two drawbacks, Zave felt that if he could but get to Gonzales and talk to the locals, he could enlist the help he needed there. Accordingly, he scurried about, grabbing items that would prove useful on the long drive and issuing last-minute instructions to María.

'With me gone, you can help the Macnabs, if they need it.'

'Take care of yourself, Xavier.'

In days to come he would try to recall this scene, this parting with a woman he had grown to love late in his life, but he would be unable to do so. There was no significant speech, no meaningful farewell and no commitment one way or another. He had left home often before, and he had never taken much account of parting then, nor did he now.

'Goodbye, old lady. Ten cuidado.' And he was gone, thinking only briefly of how stalwart a woman she was. He knew he'd been damned lucky to find her. Her brother? Ah, that was another matter. With Benito and his hot temper, one never knew. Probably heading south right now to join up with Santa Anna. Well, that was his business and it did not affect María. In this life all men, it seemed, had trouble with their in-laws.

With that succinct summary of his family affairs as of 12 February 1836, he followed the Guadalupe upstream for two full days and part of a third, after which he entered the little town of Gonzales, only to find it so involved with plans for war that any prospect of collecting cattle vanished. One rancher who could have supplied hundreds reported: 'All my hands have quit. You ask me, they're on their way to fight for Santy Anny.'

The Gonzales men took this seriously, and for good reason. Only the previous October the Mexican government had sent soldiers to Gonzales to repossess a cannon loaned to the town; the thinking had been that with agitation spreading throughout Tejas for the establishment of a self-governing state divorced from Coahuila, it was prudent to confiscate any weapons which might be used against government troops.

To the amazement of the Mexican officers, the men of Gonzales had refused to surrender their cannon; instead, they used the thing to lob cannonballs at the troops, then unfurled an insulting flag showing a rude drawing of the cannon and the inscription, neatly lettered: COME AND TAKE IT.

The whole affair was absurd, really, because the so-called cannon was a midget affair so small that two men could drag it along, but it did throw a much larger ball than a rifle, so it was technically a cannon, and the men, exhilarated by their defeat of the Mexican army – one trooper killed – began referring to their brief skirmish as 'The Lexington of the Texican Revolution.' If Santa Anna really was on his way to Tejas, one of his first and most brutal stops would be at Gonzales.

Campbell, irritated by this interruption of his plans, moved from one former customer to another, pleading with them to assign him the cattle he needed for his drive to New Orleans, but they were preoccupied. Disgusted, he stopped on the following morning at the store of the Widow Fuqua to pass the time in idle conversation.

'How did a Jew get to a town like this?'

'We travel to all parts. Always have.'

'Where did you come from?'

'All parts.'

'You any idea how I might get my cattle together?' Mrs Fuqua had no suggestions, for as she reminded Zave, all the Mexicans had fled.

At this moment the shopkeeper's young son, Galba, entered, and Zave asked: 'How old are you, son?' and the lad replied: 'Sixteen.'

'How'd you like to help me herd a string of cattle to New Orleans?' The prospect of such an excursion delighted the boy, small for his age but much like Otto in his apparent ability, and he responded enthusiastically: 'If Mother allows.'

When Mrs Fuqua nodded, Zave said: 'I'll take care of your son, but first we got to gather our herd.'

'That can be done,' the boy said, and on the spot he outlined a plan whereby he and two friends, one of them a lad his own age named Johnny Gaston, could collect the longhorns as effectively as any Mexicans: 'We can ride and rope.' Permission was granted by the owners, who were glad to see their stock moved out of the way of an incoming danger, and by Tuesday, the twenty-third, it began to look as if Campbell would succeed in getting his drove on the road before the beginning of March.

But on Wednesday about noon two dusty horsemen galloped in from the west with a written plea from the American commander in the Alamo:

> The enemy in large force is in sight. We want men and provisions. Send them to us. We have 150 men and are determined to defend the Alamo to the last. Give us assistance.

Now all talk of cattle vanished. Men spoke only of what could be done to aid their imperiled fellows trapped in San Antonio, and many wild proposals involving no risk were made, but suddenly the aching truth was voiced: 'We have got to march a relief force into the Alamo.'

On Thursday the discussion resumed, and now all listened

intently as the messengers honestly laid forth the situation:

'Santa Anna has nearly two thousand men there already, with more marching in daily. We have no more than a hundred and fifty. But think of the men we do have. Jim Bowie, Davy Crockett, this young wild man William Travis. With your help they can win.

'Men of Gonzales, if you do not support us now, the Alamo will fall, Santa Anna will march to your town and destroy it. Upon you depends the freedom of Texas. And you know that on the freedom of Texas depends the freedom of the United States. You must act now.'

These ringing words evoked a flurry of patriotism throughout the town, and women began assembling supplies should their men decide to march; but the decision could be reached only painfully, for the men of Gonzales were intelligent enough to know that odds against them of 2,000-to-150 were perilous. It was clearly understood that anyone who entered the Alamo within the next few days stood a very good chance of dying there, and almost no chance whatever of holding the fortress indefinitely against the overwhelming power of the enemy. On these harsh terms the debate began.

One man asked: 'Did not General Houston advise Texas to abandon the Alamo? Knock down the walls and let the Mexicans have it?'

'He did,' a messenger snapped. His knee had been badly wrenched during an intrepid scout he had made on the oncoming Mexican forces as they approached San Antonio, and he was impatient with these thoughtful, careful men: If I can risk my life on that damned horse, not a hundred yards from the whole Mexican army, why can't they see the crisis at the Alamo? Controlling his temper, he said: 'General Houston did order the place abandoned, but it is always the man on the spot who must make the final decision, and Travis, after weighing everything, decided to dig in and fight. Now you must make your decision.'

On Friday, 26 February, the men of Gonzales were beginning to think that maybe they should organize a relief party and march to the support of the men in the Alamo, and by noon the momentum to join that party became an emotional bonfire which engulfed the town. Twenty men signified their willingness, then another five, then still another five, then the richest man in town, Thomas R. Miller, whose young wife had recently run off with a more attractive fellow. By nightfall, thirty-one men had volunteered to lay down their lives, if necessary, in defense of freedom, and among them were two of the boys on whom Zave Campbell had been depending to gather his cattle: Galba Fuqua and Johnny Gaston, brother of the young girl who had run away from Miller.

Zave Campbell, idled through no fault of his own, did not jump to volunteer; this was not his war; as the husband of a wonderful Mexican woman, who became more precious the more he thought of her, he bore no general animosity toward Mexicans; and as a man who had been damned near hanged by loud-mouthed Texicans, he felt no responsibility to them. But with nothing better to do, he did watch from the sidelines as they formed in their final muster, and a more disorganized group of would-be heroes he had never seen. Short boys and gangling men, lads who had never shaved and oldsters with wandering beards, they were all dressed differently, with not a single item of true military dress in the lot. If they wore hats, they were big and floppy; their shoes were shapeless and worn; their homespun trousers were of a dozen different sizes, lengths and thicknesses. A few wore bandoleers; a few had improvised knapsacks; two had bayonets on their long rifles; but each seemed to have a long-bladed knife and three had a pair.

When the roll call was completed, the newly elected officer announced: 'We march at noon tomorrow,' and that night Zave found it difficult to sleep. He felt no urge to choose sides between the Texicans who had rebuffed him and the Mexicans he loved, but he had to respect the courage of these rude countrymen who felt obligated to defend their freedoms. So as the long night waned, he felt himself drawn ever closer to the patriots.

He spent Saturday morning watching odd corners of the town where volunteers bade farewell to their families, and as he saw these emotional scenes he became so confused that when the line formed for the march to the Alamo, he quietly joined at the rear.

In the entire history of Texas there would be none braver than these thirty-two men from Gonzales, for each man in this heroic file could say to himself, between thundering heartbeats: I know I'm marching to almost certain death, and I know it's insane, but I prize freedom above life itself.

Finlay Macnab, an orderly man of forty-four, was downright disgusted at the chaos into which Tejas had fallen even before Santa Anna fired his first gun. As he explained with some bitterness to Otto: 'It's a damned disgrace. We have an army of maybe two thousand men, but our shaky government has appointed four supreme commanders. And each one holds a commission which confirms that he is superior to the other three.'

Macnab was correct. A wavering revolutionary government, unsure whether it wanted statehood within Mexico, jointure with the United States, or a free nation of its own, had appointed Sam Houston, vainglorious but demonstrably able, as commander in chief of the army on the basis of his militia rank years ago in Tennessee. But they had also designated Colonel James Fannin, a West Point man but not a graduate, as commander of the regular army contingent and subsidiary to no one. Rump forces within the government had given still another command to Dr James Grant, born in Scotland and since 1825 owner of an enormous ranch west of Saltillo; a volatile man much hated in northern Mexico, he had served in the governing body of Coahuila-y-Tejas until Santa Anna prorogued it and now sought revenge.

The fourth contestant for top honors was an irascible Virginia-Alabama-Illinois schoolteacher and greengrocer with military delusions; at a time of crisis in 1835 he had assumed command of a privateering force that had captured the Alamo from General Cós and sent him kiting back to Mexico under pledge never to return under arms. Commander in Chief Frank W. Johnson had his own plans for subduing Mexico; in executing them with total ineptness he would lose his entire force save four, but he himself would escape and live another forty-eight years, during which he would write a five-volume history of the times he had seen and the heroisms he had performed.

There was, of course, a fifth commander, almost insanely jealous of the other four and possibly more gifted as a military leader than any of them: Colonel William Travis, who still held on to the Alamo in gross disobedience to orders from General Houston that he abandon it and blow it up.

These five warring commanders led forces totaling only two thousand troops. All Santa Anna had to do was knock them off, one by one, and this he was in the process of accomplishing.

'It's insane,' Macnab said to his son as they chopped wood on their farm along the Guadalupe. 'A man would be crazy to get himself involved in such nonsense.' Consequently, he was not moved when on 8 January, Colonel Fannin sent a horseman through the countryside with an urgent call for volunteers to help him defend the eastern lands around Victoria.

So the Macnabs refused to attend the big organizing effort at which more than a hundred late arrivals with a Georgia Battalion whooped and cheered as they joined the Fannin crusade. A lively group of Irish immigrants who had recently taken up land in the nearby Irish colonies made even more noise when they enlisted, and equally valued were four well-trained Polish engineers who reported from the scattered Polish settlers in the area. Just as their countryman Thaddeus Kosciuszko had built most of General Washington's fortifications during the Revolution, they would assume responsibility for perfecting Fannin's defenses.

Macnab, listening to reports of how successful the meeting had been, had reason to hope that in this command, at least, things would move forward intelligently, and he concluded that he and his son could leave the prosecution of this war to the enthusiasts. He was startled when he learned that this odd assortment of would-be soldiers had moved practically into his backyard, fortifying themselves noisily in the abandoned presidio at Goliad, less than thirty miles from the Macnab farm. He could no longer escape the fact that the war had encroached upon him.

Even so, he remained reluctant to associate himself with what he feared would be a disastrous experience, and he was in this confused, gloomy frame of mind when, on 18 February, a twenty-nine-year-old man of the most compelling honesty galloped unattended into nearby Goliad with urgent news. He was Lieutenant James Bonham, a lawyer from South Carolina, whose heroic longings had been ignited by reports of what the Texas patriots were attempting. Like so many others whose names would soon glorify Texas history, he had arrived only recently in the territory – less than three months before – but his cool enthusiasm was so respected that he was quickly made an officer, whereupon he volunteered for service in the Alamo. Now, as danger threatened that bastion, he had at incredible risk broken through the enemy cordon and ridden eastward for help, and the men at Goliad listened in deepening apprehension as he informed them of the facts about the Alamo:

'Our side has a hundred and fifty men. Santa Anna has nearly two thousand already, with more on the way. The odds sound impossible, but with the kind of heroes we have – I mean the determination, the steady fire they're capable of – I believe we can hold the fort till the rest of Texas mobilizes.

'What we need now is for every fighting man in this part of Texas to rush to the Alamo. Strengthen our perimeters! Give us help! Start to march now! The freedom of Texas and the whole United States lies in the balance! Help us!'

Colonel Fannin, listening attentively to the plea, assured Bonham that 'he would think it over,' whereupon the impetuous young lieutenant saluted, trying to hide his anger at this vacillation, and spurred his horse onward to Victoria. There he assembled the local farmers, to whom he delivered his message with such dramatic force that young Otto Macnab blurted out: 'Where are you going next?' and Bonham said without hesitation: 'Back to the Alamo.'

'Can I go with you?'

The South Carolinian looked down at the boy and said: 'Take your father to Goliad. March with Colonel Fannin and his men. They're going to reinforce us.'

'Will you go back alone?' Otto said.

'I came alone.'

He said this so simply, so sweetly, as if he were talking to a woman about strolling through a park, that Otto was enthralled. This was the kind of man he longed to be with, and he watched with tumultuous agitation as the former lawyer turned westward toward his elected station in the Alamo. He had fought his way out of that fortress and now he was prepared to fight his way back in.

As he disappeared, Otto asked his father: 'If things are so bad, why does he go back in?' and Finlay replied: 'I doubt he considered any other possibility.'

That night neither Macnab could sleep. Otto's head was filled with images of galloping horses, challenges at dusk, guns blazing, and a lone man leaping his horse across obstacles. His father's visions were more controlled and much more sober; he saw a beleaguered Texas, chaotically led, staggering and fumbling its way toward liberty, and he saw the irresistible logic of Bonham's plea: 'Unite with us! Help us! Give us the time we need till Texas mobilizes.'

All night these words rang in his ears, growing more forceful with each reiteration, until, toward dawn, he rose and walked alone beside the river that he had grown to love. It was peaceful now, a beautiful river, home of birds and haven for thirsty animals, and it had become a real home for him. Looking up to the branches of the trees that stood along its bank, he could see debris from the last terrible flood, many feet above his head. Texas is in flood, he told himself as the sun rose, and no one can predict where the debris will finally rest.

At breakfast he told Josefina: 'Otto and I better get ready to leave.' When she asked: 'For what?' he told her in Spanish: 'We must go to Goliad.'

'To fight against my people?'

'Your people are fighting against us.'

She sat down, with her apron brought to her face as if to hide tears, and said sorrowfully: 'I think maybe so,' but what it was she truly thought, she did not confide.

She was further distressed when Otto left, obviously to say farewell to María Campbell, whom he loved first and strongest, but at noon, when that boy returned, she and Finlay had all things packed, and the two Macnabs headed southwest for the presidio at Goliad.

On Leap Year's Day, General Santa Anna's equerry came to Benito Garza and said: 'I want you to find some soldier, about thirty years old, who could look like a priest.'

505

'Why?'

'Do as you're told.'

So Garza wandered among the troops looking for someone who might resemble a priest if properly garbed, and by chance he came upon a real priest serving the troops, a Father Palacio, whom he took to the adjutant.

To Garza's surprise, the officer was infuriated, and although he tried to mask his rage while the priest was present, as soon as the clergyman departed he slapped Garza across the face and shouted: 'Do as you're told, damn you.' Benito was so astounded by this insulting treatment that he resumed his search in anger and finally found a rather fat fellow who looked as if he might play the drunken friar in a barracks-room comedy put on by locals.

Leading him like a child to the equerry, Garza said hopefully: 'I think this one will do,' and to his relief the officer said: 'So do I. Now find him the clothes.'

'What clothes?' Benito asked, and again the equerry started to slap him, but this time Benito grabbed the man's wrist, twisting it savagely as he whispered in a shaking voice: 'You do that again, I kill you.'

The young officer, stunned that a man he took to be a peasant should behave so, reached forward as if to strike Garza, but when he saw Benito's flaring nostrils and grim eyes, he drew back. In a chastened voice he said: 'We need some priest's clothes.' This proved a more difficult task, but after more than an hour spent searching, Benito came upon an old woman in the main plaza who said that a priest who had once boarded in her house had died. She found remnants of his habit, and when it was fitted to the fat soldier he did indeed look like a priest.

Garza knocked on the equerry's door, and when the officer saw the *soi-disant* priest he was delighted: 'Just what we need!' And he hurried both Garza and the priest down Soledad Street to the Veramendi house, where, in the old courtyard with the fountain playing, a wedding party had assembled.

Benito met the bride, a lively, attractive girl of nineteen whose mother had succeeded in protecting her from half a dozen officers who had tried to capture her: 'She marries, this one, and that's the only way.' Refusing even colonels any access to her daughter, she had proclaimed repeatedly that she and her mother before her were ladies of high quality and rigorous morals, and that she intended keeping her daughter that way. In the end, apparently, some officer had surrendered and proposed marriage, but it was clear to Garza and to the equerry at least, that the wedding was to be a cynical charade performed by a fake priest.

Benito was indignant at this, for the woman and her daughter were respectable mexicanas, and here the mexicano army was treating them with the same contempt the Texicans did. He had expected better from Santa Anna's men. The general himself had repeatedly expressed to Garza his respect for the locals, assuring him that once the norteamericanos were evicted, men like Garza would assume command and make Tejas a rich and leading province within the mexicano system. Benito thought it a good thing that Santa Anna did not know of this burlesque, for he was sure the general would have halted it.

But at this moment cheers erupted and all heads turned admiringly to greet the lucky bridegroom, who marched sedately from the interior of the palace, bestowing nods and smiles on all. It was Santa Anna himself, solidly married in Xalapa, with numerous children and with at least seven mistresses in the capital. As the tedious siege had worn on, day after day, he felt he needed amusement and had found it in the person of this lively lass who seemed to reciprocate his feelings, but her mother had imposed such a rigorous regime, never allowing her daughter a moment to herself, that in disgust Santa Anna had proposed marriage, an honorable gesture which threw the mother into paroxysms of joy.

'I could tell you were a perfect gentleman,' she assured him, and he indulged her when she wanted to make the wedding a gala affair, but he had put his foot down when she proposed to invite the entire mexicano population of Béjar to the ceremony – 'To relieve the boredom of the fighting,' she had said – because he feared that some civilian would be aware that he was already married and would condemn this mock wedding as a fake.

As he stepped into the center of the crowd he bowed low before the fatuous mother, kissed her hand reverently, and said: 'This is the happiest day of my life,' and she responded: 'With me the same.'

And so the preposterous wedding party formed, there in the lovely Veramendi gardens where Jim Bowie had often sat with his beloved Ursula, and the bogus priest was moved forward, mumbling some lines and fumbling with a Bible, and the fat fellow, who really did look the part, pronounced the handsome couple man and wife. When he added: 'You may now kiss the bride,' Santa Anna swept the willing young lady into his arms and carried her into the adobe palace, where the marriage was consummated within minutes.

For many tumultuous hours the newlyweds stayed in their room, uttering squeals and chuckles that seeped out into the hallways, where the adoring mother relished each echo, and then late in the afternoon of Tuesday, 1 March, the general appeared in the garden, his uniform pressed by his new mother-in-law, to issue a rapid chain of commands.

Protected by a convoy of soldiers who could be spared from the siege, his bride was to be taken immediately south to San Luis Potosí, where she was to be given every consideration; he had reason to hope that she was pregnant, and if so, he wanted the child to be treated at least as generously as his other bastards. His mother-in-law was to be given the best house in Béjar and a pension, and to be kept as far removed from him as possible.

Now he plunged vigorously into preparations for bringing the siege to a rousing conclusion. Summoning his aides, he learned from them the gratifying news that through late arrivals his army had now grown to twenty-four hundred effectives: 'Excellent. They have a hundred and fifty. Our superiority, sixteen-to-one.'

'Excuse me, Excellency. While you were' – the colonel hesitated – 'resting, about thirty additional rebels slipped into the mission. We believe they now have about a hundred and eighty.'

'Fools,' Santa Anna muttered. 'Fighting to commit suicide.' Recalculating his figures, he came up with the accurate discrepancy: 'Thirteen of us to every rebel.' It was obvious that he could charge the walls head-on if he was willing to waste the manpower.

When it became evident that the siege was not going to force the rebels to surrender in the near future, since they had all the beef they needed and more than enough water for their two wells, Santa Anna summoned General Ripperdá and said graciously: 'You were right. We'll have to storm the walls.' But before issuing the final order, which could entail the loss of perhaps a thousand of his men, he wanted to see for himself the exact state of preparations at the Alamo, so on March fourth he asked his brother-in-law General Cós and three scouts including Garza to take a long ride with him around the former mission. As they crossed the little bridge leading to the east side of the river, Benito cautioned the dictator: 'Excellency, do not ride carelessly. Remember, those men in there have what they call Kentucky rifles.'

'Every army thinks it has superior weapons.'

'But these are superior.'

'Son, I fought these rebels at Medina in 1813. They possessed nothing to fear, not even personal bravery. We fired at them and they ran.'

'Excellency, have you ever seen a Kentucky rifle in action?' When Santa Anna said 'No,' Benito told him: 'This is one. I bought it from a Kentucky man himself. How far do you think it can fire with accuracy?'

Santa Anna, always interested in firearms, said authoritatively: 'Our muskets, in good condition, ninety yards, maybe a hundred.'

'More like sixty,' Cós said.

'See that tree?' Garza asked. 'With the paper under it. Maybe some bottles. How far?'

The officers agreed that it might be as much as two hundred and fifty yards. 'Watch,' Benito said, and with careful aim he sped a bullet right into the collection of trash, throwing paper and bits of glass high in the air.

'Incredible,' Santa Anna said, drawing away from the still-distant Alamo.

'And remember, Excellency. The norteamericanos established a rule in their two wars against the British: "Always fire for the gold."'

'And what does that mean?'

'My frontier friends told me. "Never fire aimlessly. Never fire at the common soldier. Always aim at the gold decoration of the officer." Today you are wearing your gold medals,

509

Excellency.'

Prudently, the little party moved to a distance of about three hundred yards, where, with a map, they circled the huge grounds of the Alamo, and as they rode from south to north the three scouts relayed to Santa Anna the information they had accumulated:

'The fortified main gate at the south will be impossible to breach. This long west wall is only adobe, but it's very thick. Rooms inside. You can see the patrol already on the roof. This north wall slopes at an angle and is not very stout. Difficult to climb, but our cannon could breach it, for certain.

'Here on the east, a very stout wall, don't try to force it. Those big square things are cattle pens, and the garden with one of the wells. Barracks there for the soldiers. If you try to break in here, you have to penetrate two sets of walls.

'And now the chapel of the old mission. No roof, but extremely thick walls. I doubt they will waste much time defending this, because even if we did break through, we wouldn't be anywhere. But that stretch which connects the chapel to the main south wall could prove to be their weak spot and our big opportunity.

'Look! It has no wall of any kind. Only a ditch in front, wooden palisades of a sort, mostly brush I think. It will be defended, of course, and they may put their best rifles there, but it can be breached.'

At the conclusion of this tour, which took nearly an hour, Santa Anna told Cós: 'We will attack with great force from the north and knock a hole in that exposed wall with no houses behind it. But we will also attack with maximum clamor the palisade and hope to divert their forces.'

'The church?' an officer asked, referring to the roofless chapel. 'What of that, Excellency?'

'Attack it in force, but not seriously. Just enough to keep the defenders pinned down at a meaningless spot.'

Now the deployments were made: 'We'll attack from all sides at four o'clock Sunday morning. We should have the place by sunrise.' He wheeled his beautiful horse, turned back to take one last look at the Alamo, and said: 'Remember, no prisoners.'

From the church tower the red flag of death underscored that decision. When the Macnabs arrived at Goliad toward dusk on Saturday, 20 February, they found affairs in much greater confusion than even Finlay had anticipated. He had assumed that Colonel Fannin, in response to Lieutenant Bonham's plea, would have his men preparing to make a dash into the Alamo; instead, he learned that the two other supreme commanders, Grant the malodorous Scotsman and Johnson the wild-eyed Illinois greengrocer, had marched off on their own in the fatuous belief that with only sixty-odd untrained volunteers they could capture the important Mexican port of Matamoros near the mouth of the Rio Grande. Even their own scouts reported that General Urrea, one of the ablest Mexican leaders, had assembled more than a thousand well-armed veterans there.

'What kind of madness is that?' Finlay asked after he and his son had been assigned places to sleep inside the presidio walls.

'It gets worse,' an embittered member of the Georgia Battalion groused. 'We should be on our way to the Alamo right now. But look at him.'

And for the first time Finlay Macnab, a man whose frontier experiences had converted a somewhat aimless character into one of surprising fortitude, witnessed at close quarters the confusion and lack of decisiveness which characterized Colonel Fannin. Thirty-two years old and disappointed because of his failure to graduate from West Point with a commission in the regular United States Army, he had become a slave trader for a while, then an eager drifter looking for something to turn up. He was an adventurer, inordinately ambitious, now in Texas looking for promotion to general, and reluctant to throw his forces into the Alamo, not because of cowardice or fear of death, but rather because if he were to do so, he would lose his command and be forced to serve under the despised amateur Colonel Travis.

On his visit to Goliad, Lieutenant Bonham had pleaded with all the considerable moral force he could muster for Fannin to march to the relief of the Alamo. Fannin had given an equivocal answer: he would go, he would not go, he would consider it. Six days later, on the twenty-third, he was still weighing alternatives after Santa Anna had surrounded the Alamo, so that reinforcements would now encounter serious trouble if they tried to enter.

Macnab wondered if valiant troops, ready for battle, had ever been led by an officer so pusillanimous: I wish we could light a fire under him, to see if he'd jump. Otto, listening to the complaints of the Georgia and Irish units, decided: If either Father or Uncle Zave was leading, we'd be on our way to San Antonio now. Then, eyes blazing, he thought: And if Lieutenant Bonham had anything to do with it, we'd already be there.

Fannin allowed the most contradictory rumors to agitate his men: 'We're marching to Gonzales!' 'No, it's to Victoria to unite with reinforcements coming by sea.' 'No, that would be a retreat, and I heard Colonel Fannin swear on a stack of Bibles "I will never retreat!" ' 'We march to San Antonio tomorrow to do what we can!'

The ridiculous truth was that Fannin had given each of these orders, within the space of days, and had then countermanded each one. However, on 25 February he finally made up his mind: 'Tomorrow at dawn we march to help defend the Alamo.'

On the morning of Friday the twenty-sixth, Finlay and Otto joined the three hundred and twenty soldiers from the Goliad presidio, and the hearts of all beat a little quicker at the realization that they were at last marching to the Alamo. Colonel Fannin, astride a chestnut stallion, rode to the head of his troops, raised his sword and cried: 'On to destiny!'

But his expedition had progressed only two hundred yards when one of the major supply wagons broke down, and by the time it was repaired, other wagons that had taken the lead failed to negotiate a river crossing, so that total confusion resulted. Noon found the column stalled, and the afternoon wasted away without any significant movement. As day faded into night Macnab realized that in these fourteen hours the expeditionary force had covered less than a quarter of a mile.

At dawn on the twenty-seventh Colonel Fannin awakened to the ugly fact that he faced a seventy-mile march to the next replenishment depot, without sufficient food to sustain his troops. Having relied upon a swift dash to the first depot, he had not bothered to bring along emergency supplies. When Macnab heard that Fannin was going to ask his men to vote as to whether they wanted to move ahead to the Alamo or return to the safety of the presidio and regroup, he was outraged. 'A commander doesn't ask for a vote,' he told the Georgians and Irishmen near him. 'He senses in his gut what must be done and he does it.' But then an Irishman with a wizened, knowing face said: 'He's taking the loss of that first wagon as an omen. "Don't go on!" a little voice is surely whispering to him.'

'My God!' a Georgia man asked in disgust, 'are we bein' led by omens?'

'In this army we are,' the Irishman said, but he was wrong, for Fannin was collecting his commissioned officers to ascertain how they interpreted not the omens but the hard facts:

'Gentlemen, we face a most serious situation. We have, as you well know, inadequate provisions for a long march and no reasonable means of increasing them. We have faulty transport and no way of finding better. Our artillery pieces seem too heavy to drag over riverbeds. And what seems most important to me ... by leaving the presidio without proper garrison, we tempt the enemy to sneak in and take it. What do you recommend that we do?'

In the face of such a pessimistic review, the vote was unanimous: Return to Goliad, bolster the fortifications, and defy the enemy from inside the walls: 'The Alamo? Nothing can be done from this end to support it.'

So the expedition stumbled back to its launching spot, retreated within the safety of its walls, and began a crash program with two objectives: Build the walls so strong that they would be impregnable. Slaughter so many oxen and dry the meat so carefully that the men would never again be short of rations.

Finlay Macnab warned his son: 'When a commander loses his nerve, disasters can happen.'

'What shall we do?' Otto asked.

'Nothing.' Then, afraid that his son might be as disoriented as Fannin, he asked: 'Why? Did you want to leave?'

Otto could not explain in words, but the more he witnessed the ineptitude inside the presidio, the more he longed to serve with someone of honorable purpose like James Bonham. He was sure that Bonham would have quickly handled the perplexities that immobilized Fannin, and in the meantime he, Otto, would keep his rifle clean and await the battle he knew to be inevitable.

Just about this time an event occurred inside the Alamo which would have given Otto reassurance. James Bonham, surveying the situation with Colonel Travis and Davy Crockett, concluded that he must ride once again through the countryside in a last appeal to Fannin at Goliad and to the scattered farmers in the east for aid. Crockett, hearing his decision, said: 'You were lucky last time, threading your way out and back in. This time?'

As if he knew no care in the world, the Carolina gentleman half saluted Travis, smiled at Davy, and mounted the mare that had served him so well before. Darting suddenly from the north wall of the Alamo, he spurred his mount and galloped directly through the Mexican lines. Before the startled besiegers could prevent it, he had broken free and was on his way back to Goliad to make one final, desperate plea for help.

Like the demon rider in an ancient ballad, Bonham rode through the night, and on the twenty-eighth, reined in at the Goliad presidio, where the men cheered him lustily, for they knew what heroism his mere appearance at that spot so distant from the Alamo entailed.

Bonham's arrival did not impress Colonel Fannin, for it reopened questions long since resolved. There would be no rescue operation conducted from Goliad, and patiently he explained why: 'Distance too great, transport too chancy, cannon too heavy, food and water too uncertain.' On and on he went, reciting the best arguments in the world against any desperate lunge to the northwest, and as Bonham listened he had to concede that everything Fannin said was true, and relevant. Any cautious commander would hold back, as he was doing, but any brave commander would correct the disadvantages and forge ahead.

By the middle of the next afternoon Bonham had argued so persuasively that he was within minutes of persuading Fannin to act, when one of those freak accidents which so often determines history occurred. Bumptious Colonel Johnson, who had been trying to invade Mexico with a handful of heroes, stumbled in to the presidio with a harrowing story: 'We were surrounded by Mexicans. Chopped to pieces. Only four others survived.'

'From your entire force?' Fannin asked, his hands shaking.

'And Dr Grant, he seems to be lost.'

'My God!' Fannin cried, for this meant that the two inept leaders had lost a large part of his total force, and Bonham saw that it was futile to pressure this confused man any further. His will was gone and he had best be left alone, but when he looked at Johnson he had to think: His army lost. All but five killed. Yet he comes back alive to report. How?

Aware that he had wasted precious hours listening to such men demean themselves, Bonham saluted his unworthy superiors and told them that he must get on with his duty. 'And what is that?' Fannin asked.

'Return to the Alamo. Colonel Travis deserves a reply.'

'But the place is surrounded. You said so.'

'I got out. I'll get back in.'

'Stay here with us. Help us defend Goliad.'

Bonham looked at the two men with whom he would not care to defend anything, then at the walls they had been reinforcing. He said nothing, but thought: Fannin will pin himself into another Alamo, and three weeks from now he will be sending out cries for help.

Turning his back on the two futile commanders, confused incompetents lusting for power but incapable of the action by which it is earned, Bonham, the medieval knight resurrected for service in modern Texas, rode off toward duty. He carried with him no promises of aid, no hope for rescue, only the mournful confirmation that Texas was in mortal danger.

When Zave Campbell and the thirty-one Gonzales men broke through Mexican lines and entered the Alamo at three in the morning of Tuesday, 1 March, they found a legendary man who, even though confined to his cot with a fever, gave them hope.

He was Jim Bowie, forty-one years old and revered as the best knife-fighter on the entire frontier. He was a big red-headed man of enormous energy, and had the wishes of the men who were to do the fighting been consulted, he would have been

515

their commander during the siege. Unluckily, on the day Santa
Anna's men took their positions ringing the Alamo, Bowie, who
had been ill for some time, was laid low by a raging fever
somewhat like the one that had killed his wife, Ursula
Veramendi, and when Zave went to report he found Bowie in
bed.

Bowie said: 'Glad to have you.'

'You look pale,' Zave said. 'Like maybe Santy Anny hit you
with something.'

Bowie said wanly: 'And you look like your neck's on crooked.
Like maybe somebody tried to hang you.'

'Necks don't straighten easy,' Zave confessed, and the two
old frontiersmen discussed the places and people they had
known, especially in and around Natchez.

'Is it true you used to rassle alligators?' Zave asked.

'Still do, if one comes after me,' Bowie said, laughing. 'Man
never knows when a gator is gonna come after him.'

Zave would never see this once-powerful man standing
upright, but he was impressed by the sheer sense of force that
Bowie exuded, even from his cot. When the sick man learned
that Campbell had also married a mexicana, he said: 'There's
another fellow in here like us,' and when he sent for Mordecai
Marr, these three Texicans shared memories of the joys they
had known with their Mexican wives. 'The others think we
married peasants,' Bowie said. 'You should've heard my wife
order me about. She was twice as smart as me.'

The three men fell silent, for at the far end of the barracks in
which Bowie's cot stood they saw Amalia Marr moving about,
assisting the women and children who had chosen to stay in the
Alamo with their men, and the graceful way she held her head,
the poetry of her motion as she worked delighted them, for
Bowie and Campbell could see in her a portrait of their own
wives. It was then that Bowie exclaimed with deep emotion:
'Dammit, Campbell! It would have been a lot better for Texas if
every unmarried man who wandered down here from Kentucky and Tennessee, or from Georgia and Alabama, for that
matter . . . if he had been forced to take himself a Mexican wife.
Maybe we could have bridged the gap.'

'What gap?' Zave asked.

'Americanos, mexicanos. We're bound to share this land for

the next two hundred years. If we'd got started right . . .'

'They tell me that this guide Deaf Smith, best of the lot, they say he has a Mexican wife.'

'I think he does,' Bowie said. 'I wish he was in here to help us.'

'The men all feel they'd have a better chance of holdin' this place if you was leadin'.'

'Now stop that. Stop it right now. Travis will prove a damned good fighting man.'

'But the men tell me,' Marr said, 'that you were supposed to be in command.'

Jim Bowie, the most belligerent man in the Alamo, sighed: 'It hasn't been a neat affair. Seems like nothin' in Texas is ever neat. We were supposed to share a joint command. Travis in charge of the army men, me in charge of the volunteers.'

'That's what I'm sayin'. Us volunteers want to fight under your orders,'

Bowie's voice hardened with exasperation: 'How in hell can I command if I can't stand? You tell me that.' With the generosity of spirit which marked him he growled: 'I'm perfectly willing to give the leadership to Travis,' and while neither Zave nor Marr believed him, they had to respect him for his soldierly deportment.

The man all the newcomers wanted to meet was Davy Crockett, the former congressman from Tennessee. Tall, clean-shaven, and with a head somewhat larger than normal, he was a famous raconteur whose disreputable stories narrated in dialect often made him look ridiculous: 'They was me and this bear and an Injun. Now that bear was grindin' his teeth, just waitin' to git at me. And the Injun was reaching for his arrers to shoot one through me.'

'And what were you doin'?' someone was supposed to ask, at which Davy would reply: 'I be 'shamed to tell you, 'cept that later I had to do some washin'.'

He was irrepressible, and after conducting a survey of the situation within the Alamo, he had insisted upon defending the palisaded weak spot, where the danger would be greatest: 'I want sixteen good men here with all the rifles we can muster, and them Mexicans better beware.' When Zave saw the frailness of the palisade and the grim look of the men from

Kentucky and Tennessee who would have to defend it, he whispered to Galba Fuqua: 'There's bound to be one hell of a fight here.'

Whenever Zave could not locate Galba, for whom he felt great responsibility, he would look to see where Davy Crockett was holding forth, and there the boy would be, listening intently as the wild frontiersman spun his yarns but fully aware that Crockett's mocking manner masked a character of profound determination. The boy had no way of assessing how strong a man Jim Bowie might have been if healthy, but he knew that Davy was one of the most powerful men he had ever seen. 'You killed more'n a hundred bears?'

'Most dangerous animal I ever met was that Tennessee Democrat Andrew Jackson. He'd cut a man's throat for sixpence.'

'But did you kill forty-seven bears in one month?' Galba asked.

'I sure did. Forty-seven bears, forty-six bullets.'

'How was that?'

'Two of the bears was misbehavin',' and he winked at the boy.

One morning Galba was standing guard with him atop the fort at the southwestern end of the mission. Crockett was dressed as usual – coonskin cap, deerskin jacket with Indian beads, buckskin trousers – and beside him he had two long rifles. 'You see that Mexican over there across the river?' he said to Galba. 'Tracin' marks in the dust? You see that other man behind him? As soon as I fire, slap the other gun into my hand.'

The two men were so far distant that Galba believed it impossible for Crockett to reach them, but he watched as the expert leveled his gun, firmed it against the edge of the rampart, and with breathless care pulled back his trigger finger. Poof! Not much of a crackle, for this was a good tight gun, but down went the man in front.

'Quick!' Davy whispered, as if the other man could hear, and before the latter could seek refuge, a second bullet sped across the river, dipped under the trees on the far side, and splatted into its target.

Insolently, Crockett rose from behind the protective wall, pushed back his coonskin cap, and reloaded his two rifles, daring Santa Anna's men to fire at him with their outdated smooth-bore English muskets that could not carry half that distance.

'How far was that?' Galba asked, as if the dead men had been squirrels.

Crockett said with equal indifference: 'Maybe two hundred and fifty yards,' but quickly added: 'You know, you couldn't do it at that range, not unless you could prop your gun.'

'Could I fight with you, at the palisade?'

Crockett said: 'It's gonna be easy to hold that spot, what with the men I got. A good shot like you, you're needed wherever Travis puts you.'

That night Galba Fuqua lost his heart all over again to Davy Crockett, for the famous bear-hunter astounded everyone by producing a fiddle that he'd brought into the Alamo with him, and for two hours he entertained the fighters with scraping squeals of mountain music so ingratiating that even Zave Campbell danced in the moonlight.

When Colonel Travis was assigning the Gonzales men to their defensive positions, Zave volunteered for one of the more exposed locations. He chose that long western wall, knowing it would be vulnerable if the Mexican foot soldiers were brave enough to bring their scaling ladders there. To Fuqua, who volunteered to stand with him, he said: 'What we must do, Galb, is run back and forth and change our positions. Confuse 'em.'

'Will there be lots of them?'

'Lots.' And he pointed out to the boy where the danger spots would be: 'That gully gives them protection. They'll come up from there and hit us about here. We'll be waitin'. Now keep your eye on those trees – not many of them, but they'll interrupt our fire. They're sure to come at us from those trees. So you're to guard this point, and never allow them to place even one ladder.'

'What am I to do?'

'The minute they place a ladder, you run there with this forked pole and push it down.'

The boy looked at the trees, saw the pitiful distance that separated them from the wall, and for the first time since he left Gonzales, realized that within a few days men were going to be killed, in great number: 'Will many be killed, Mr Campbell?'

'Lots,' Zave said. Then, appreciating the boy's fear, he took Galba by the hand and said: 'That's what a battle is, son. The killing of men.'

'Does the red flag over there mean no surrender?'

'It's them or us, son. Come battle day, it's purely them or us.'

At first Campbell had not liked Colonel Travis, whom he saw as an austere man with a lawyer's finicky attitude toward duty and no sense of humor: 'He talks too big, Galb.' The boy repeated what he had heard many of the men say: 'Bowie ought to be our commander,' but out of respect for the sick man's wishes Zave quieted such talk: 'Travis is our leader now. Bowie said so. And you better do what he says.'

By Wednesday, 2 March, Campbell was developing a much different opinion of Travis: 'He knows what he's doing. He knows how to defend a position. And look how he puts his finger on the weak spots.' Zave liked especially the manner in which Travis disposed his men, never carelessly, never arbitrarily, but always with an eye on firepower.

'You know, Galb, he has every weak man down there caring for the cattle and things. All the good men are up here on the ramparts.'

'You count me a good man?'

'I sure do, and so does Travis.'

But not even after Zave had granted Travis every concession did he like the man the way he admired Bowie and Crockett: 'It's the way he's always tidyin' up his clothes, Galb. When a man does that, he's apt to be prissy. Damnit, Travis ought to be commandin' a cavalry post in Carolina and attendin' afternoon teas with the ladies. He may be a fightin' man, but he sure as hell ain't a frontiersman.'

'You prefer the way Bowie dresses?'

'I sure do,' but as he said this he saw Travis standing atop the fortress corner at the north, surveying the land across which the Mexican attack would come, and his slim figure, so taut, so tense, seemed so extraordinarily military that even Zave had to confess: 'He knows what he's doing, that one.' And when Travis next inspected the rooftops, Zave saluted.

On Thursday, 3 March, at about a quarter to eleven, Colonel Travis and everyone within hearing of Galba Fuqua's voice was startled to hear the lad cry: 'Man's comin' on horseback!' And when they looked toward the sun high in the sky they did indeed see a lone horseman making a wild effort to cut directly through the heart of the enemy lines.

'It's Bonham!' men began to shout. 'Go it, Bonham!'

They did more than shout. Two men limbered up a field piece and tossed cannon shells at Mexican soldiers, who were trying to catch the fleeting messenger, while others grabbed their rifles to pick off individual men who sought to attack them.

'Zave!' Fuqua shouted, proudly aware that his warning cry had helped this incredibly brave rider by alerting the riflemen on the walls. 'He's going to make it!'

'Break open those gates!' Travis shouted, and men eagerly leaped to do so, just in time to bring the dodging, darting Bonham into the protection of the Alamo. Twice out to safety, twice back to his post of duty, he had ridden alone and had four times penetrated heavy enemy concentrations.

His message was brief and terrifying: 'Colonel Fannin refuses to leave Goliad. Gonzales has no more men to send us. No relief is on the way. You already have all the men you'll ever have. There'll be no more.'

Friday, 4 March, was a solemn day within the Alamo, for additional Mexican reinforcements streamed north from the Rio Grande to increase Santa Anna's superiority, so that even the most hopeful Texicans had to confront the fact that within a few hours the mighty attack would begin, and it could have only one outcome.

Each of the doomed men spent this fateful day as his personality dictated: Jim Bowie almost wept at his inability to rise from his cot and help; Davy Crockett entertained his men at the palisade with outrageous stories of his confrontations with his Tennessee constituents and especially with President Andrew Jackson, whom he despised: 'All show and bluster. Calls hisself a friend of the common man, but the only people he really befriends are the rich. If we had a real man in the White House, we'd have three thousand American troops in this building right now, and God knows how many cannon.' He refused to allow any talk of odds or dangers or the likelihood of annihilation. He was in another tight spot and he would as always do his best.

James Bonham was exhausted and reflective. He could not understand Fannin; he simply could not understand. 'Obviously,' he told Travis, 'he could have marched here fifteen days ago. I broke through yesterday and so could he, with all the men he had. I fear a great disaster is going to overtake that poor man.' He slept most of the afternoon.

Zave Campbell, as a good Scotsman, had sought out a kinsman, John McGregor, who he found had brought with him into the Alamo a set of fine bagpipes. So later in the afternoon Campbell, Fuqua and McGregor gathered in the northwest corner of the big field, and there McGregor marched back and forth as if he were in some royal castle on the Firth of Tay, piping the stirring reels and strathspeys of his youth.

Then, without announcement, he switched to a most enchanting tune, not military at all, and when Campbell said: 'I don't know that one,' the piper exclaimed 'We call it "The Flooers of Embry," which means "The Flowers of Edinburgh." A grand tune.' He played this sad, sweet music for some time, then once more without warning he altered his music; with head tilted back as if he were looking for omens in the sky, he offered the near-empty field one of the grand compositions of Scotland, and now Campbell knew well what it was, the great 'McCrimmon's Lament,' that historic threnody for brave men dead in battle, and as he marched back and forth, men in various parts of the Alamo seemed to sense that he was playing some notable piece of music for them, and they began to appear from odd corners.

But this haunting moment lasted only briefly, for Davy Crockett bellowed from the palisade: 'Damn that stuff! Fetch me my fiddle!' And when this was done he took it and ran the length of the field to meet with McGregor, and for about half an hour as day waned the two men gave a wild and raucous concert of wailing pipes and screeching fiddle, and for a rowdy while the hundred and eighty-three men in the Alamo forgot their predicament.

Ominously, on Saturday, 5 March, the daily bombardment by the Mexicans – thirteen days of barrage without killing one Texican – ceased, and Marr predicted to those about him: 'Santa Anna's redeploying his troops. Tomorrow he'll come at us.'

Colonel Travis, reaching the same conclusion, experienced an overpowering sense of doom, and as he realistically surveyed the situation of his troops and the few women and children who had remained with them in the Alamo, he realized that to hope for any further miracles was futile. His aides reported: 'Santa Anna's army increases daily. He's moving up his big guns. The final attack cannot be delayed much longer.'

Everything Travis saw confirmed this gloom. No matter how he disposed his men along the walls, there were empty spaces which the enemy would be sure to spot. And his ammunition was limited. Unlimited was the willingness of his men to fight, but as their leader, he felt obliged to give each man one last chance to escape the certain death which faced them all. That afternoon he assembled his force near the plaza leading to the chapel, and there, with the women and children listening and even Jim Bowie on his cot, which had been hauled into the open, he told them the facts: 'The red flag still flies, and Santa Anna means it. No prisoners. His army is fifteen times ours, and he now has cannon, too. I suspect the attack will come tomorrow – that's Sunday, isn't it? I want to offer every man here one last chance to retire if he would wish to.'

What happened next would be forever debated; some, basing their accounts on those of certain women who escaped the carnage, say that Travis drew a line in the sand with the tip of his sword and indicated that those wishing to take their chances fighting beside him step over it; others laugh at the suggestion of such flamboyance but grant that he may have indicated some kind of line as he scuffed his left foot across the plaza. At any rate, he certainly warned his men that death was imminent and gave them a choice of either staying and fighting a hopeless battle with him or kiting over the wall to such escape as each man could maneuver for himself.

First over the line was white-haired Mordecai Marr, who mumbled to the two who followed: 'I'm American and Mexican, loyal to both, but it seems like the first one wins.' Jim Bowie, without question, asked that his cot be moved to where his one-time adversary was standing, and Travis welcomed him. Davy Crockett shuffled over, and of course James Bonham moved to accept the death which he had known three weeks ago to be inevitable. Zave Campbell looked down at Galba Fuqua, shrugged his shoulders, and said unheroically: 'We've come this far, Galb. So you want to go all the way?' Without hesitation the boy took Zave's hand as they joined the patriots.

When Travis made his remarkable and moving speech, one hundred and eighty-two men and boys faced him. Of that number, all but one crossed to die with him. The one man who did not – and his reasoning for preferring shameful life to heroic death was startling to the men who heard him voice it – was Louis Rose, fifty-one years old, born in France and entitled to wear the Legion of Honor as a distinguished veteran of Napoleon's campaigns in the kingdom of Naples and Russia. He had come to Texas as early as 1826, when he changed his first name to Moses, believing it to sound more American. At first he had served as a day laborer in Nacogdoches, then as a teamster, and finally as a self-trained butcher. Loving the soldier's life, as soon as trouble threatened he mortgaged all his holdings and went off to join the fighting at San Antonio, where he had helped defeat General Cós in 1835.

Rose was by far the most experienced soldier in the group, and it pained Jim Bowie to see such a man reluctant to stay for the fight. Forcing himself upright in his cot, Bowie chided the Frenchman: 'You seem unwilling to die with us, Mose.'

'I came to America to live a new life, not to die needlessly,' the old campaigner said. 'Only fools and amateurs would try to defend this place.'

Davy Crockett said with a touch of levity: 'Mose, you may as well die with us, because you'll never get through them Mexican lines.'

'I speak Spanish,' Rose said, and he bundled up his clothes, climbed the wall to the very spot where Galba Fuqua would stand guard, and hesitated for a moment as if reconsidering. Looking back at his friends, he half nodded, then turned and abruptly leaped to the ground, where he quickly lost himself among the trees.

At three-thirty in the cold morning of Sunday, 6 March, Galba Fuqua reached over and nudged his friend Zave Campbell as they stood watch atop the long barracks: 'I think they're coming.'

Zave rubbed his eyes and peered into the darkness, seeing for himself that there was much movement among the trees to the west: 'I think you're right, Galb. Hey, where you goin'?'

'I gotta pee.'

'You stay here.'

'But I gotta pee.'

'So do I. When men face danger, like a fistfight or a hurricane or a battle like this . . . they often have to pee. Even the bravest. I do too. But up where I'm needed, not down there.'

So the man and the boy urinated against the adobes which they were about to defend, and as they finished, Zave said something that would encourage the boy mightily in the frenzied hours ahead: 'Galb, it's gonna be a tough fight, that's sure. If you see me showin' any signs of cowardice . . .'

'You could never be a coward, Mr Campbell.'

'No man ever knows. So if I start to show signs, you kick me in the ankle. You don't have to say anything. Just kick me in the ankle and we'll know what it means.'

The boy considered this, then said in a trembling voice: 'I see shadows moving, Mr Campbell.' A hush, then: 'Oh! They're coming.'

Then, in the darkness of the night, seven Mexican buglers, each marching with his own contingent, started sounding one of the most powerful calls ever heard on the world's battlefields. It was not a piercing command to charge, nor a stirring cry to enhance courage. It was the 'Degüello,' an ancient Moorish plea to an enemy to surrender. Its name meant 'The Beheading,' and once it sounded, its meaning was stark and clear: If you do not surrender immediately, we shall behead you, everyone.

Across the empty fields of Béjar it came, over the walls and into the Alamo, this wild lament, this recollection of home, of people loved, of the gentler scenes of peace. Through the vast spaces of the Alamo it echoed, this frightful promise that within hours everyone inside the walls would be slain.

Nine times the 'Degüello' was repeated, a terrible tattoo bringing the small, white-clad Indian troops ever closer to the walls. 'Don't waste your bullets,' Campbell told Galba. 'They'll be close soon enough.'

Santa Anna had assigned tasks skillfully. 'Cós, you command our best troops. Hit the northwest wall. General Duque, smash

525

the northeast. That's where I'm sure we can break through. Ripperdá, you have the ones we can send forth in floods. Knock down the palisade. Morales, hit the main gate, but when they concentrate to defend it, slide off to your left. You'll find a weak spot. The rest of you, scaling-ladders against that long west wall. They can't protect all of it.'

During the first minutes of battle the four generals with the important assignments made little progress, for they were attacking major positions, but the nondescript troops trying to scale the west wall became a real threat. Campbell now yelled: 'Galb, we must run back and forth, like we agreed.' And these two, with the assistance of three Tennessee men, threw down one ladder after another.

At the point of great danger, the north wall, General Cós, who had sworn in writing never to return to Tejas under arms, gained one crushing success, although at the time he did not know it: some of his men, firing a blind fusillade, luckily hit a brave Texican who was defending the northern gun batteries. This man took a shot through the heart, pitching backward into the dusty yard. The dead man was Colonel William Travis, whose iron will had kept his men in the Alamo.

The grinding assault came at the palisade, where Davy Crockett had lined up his Tennessee sharpshooters, with Mordecai Marr and twelve Kentucky men in support. These tough veterans laid down a continuous rifle fire, but the pressure against them was unyielding, because General Ripperdá had an unlimited supply of barefoot Yucatán Indians whom he proposed to use as human battering rams.

When Benito Garza first heard his assignment – 'You'll lead the third wave' – he found it difficult to accept, for he knew how perilous such an attack would be, but when he watched the first wave move out and get mowed down, every man, by that unrelenting fire from the palisade, he lost all fear and began to shout to the second wave: 'Take that line of sticks! Damnit, rush them!' And when this wave lost more than eighty percent of its numbers, he could hardly wait to lead his charge.

Ripperdá, cold and stiff as ever, moved always closer to the palisade, ignoring both the whistling bullets and the appalling loss of his Indians: 'Garza, you'll succeed. Drive right at the center.' And he watched with impassive approval as Benito leaped forward, bringing his horde behind him. On this bloody Sunday, Texican and Mexican alike showed what courage was.

At the west wall, Campbell mustered a brilliant defense, running back and forth, firing his four rifles with devastating effect and reloading as he ran. 'We knocked them back!' Galba Fuqua shouted to his mentor, who called back: 'Use your pole! Keep pushin' them ladders down!' And so the first hour ended with no Mexican having attained the top of the wall. It was now nearing six, and Santa Anna's bold boast to be inside the walls by sunrise had failed. Now he threw in fresh troops, who came at the weakened walls with a roar and the popping of guns. The lack of range was no longer important, for the guns were discharged at a distance of thirty feet, and often with telling effect as brave Texicans began toppling backward like their commander.

By six the remaining Texicans numbered only slightly over a hundred, and still those irrepressible Indians and mestizos came at them, little men of giant courage, for they climbed barehanded up the walls or placed their ladders and held them in the face of withering gunfire while those behind them scrambled to the top, to be greeted by swinging gun butts in the face.

But on they came, hundreds of them, thousands it seemed, and for every six of them slain, a Texican fell off the wall, a bullet through his head or a knife through his breast.

At the southern end, Colonel Morales led his troops in a vain assault on the main gate, but as the Texicans cheered his repulse, he slid easily along to the western end of that wall and surprised its defenders with a bayonet attack. The Mexicans swarmed on and gained a major advantage, for they were now inside the walls.

At almost the same moment, Generals Cós and Duque applied maximum pressure at a weak point in the north wall, and there another breach was made. Before the irresistible white-clads could storm into the central area, Benito Garza and his Yucatán troops engulfed the palisade, overrunning old Mordecai Marr, who continued trying to reload even when on his knees. Three bayonets ended his adventurous life.

At this moment Zave Campbell, still atop the roof and still pushing away ladders, uttered a terrible cry of pain, not for himself but for his much-loved companion of these past days, Galba Fuqua, who had taken a pair of bullets right through his upper and lower jaws, blowing away a part of his brave young face.

Zave saw the lad put his hand to his head, then blanch and almost faint when he found what had happened. 'Galb, go down to where the women are. Get help.' With great force he lifted the boy from the post he had defended so valiantly and dropped him to the ground, watching him as he trailed blood across the yard.

Now he fought with deadly vigor, slashing, killing. Once he waited like a cat till two men climbed the ladder at the spot left vacant by Fuqua, then dashed forth like a tiger, swinging one of his guns like a madman and crushing skulls. He was about to return to his own spot, where Mexicans were close to controlling the wall, when he saw Galba climb back into the wall, to resume his duty. When Zave saw the bloody mess he began to vomit, and for some moments he was immobilized, whereupon the boy kicked him and moved the remnant of his face as if he were saying: 'Courage, old man! Don't play the coward now.'

With an anguished roar, speaking for them both, Zave shouted at the climbing myrmidons: 'Come ahead, you bastards,' and he saw with horror how they did come, eight of them, and how they leaped upon Galba Fuqua, and stabbed him a score of times, tossing his body like a sheaf of threshed wheat to the floor below.

Now it was Zave Campbell, with his four rifles no longer of use except as clubs, who rushed at the twenty who stormed the rooftop. Swinging and cursing and lashing out with his two knives, he held them at bay for some moments, sending three more to their deaths.

But not even he could restrain the overwhelming force of this assault, for while he was defending himself against assailants in front, three others crept upon him from behind, and one stabbed at him with such terrible force that the point of the bayonet reached out four inches from his breast. He was so astonished to see it that he gasped, reached down to pull it away with his bare hand, and took nine other stabs simultaneously. Giving a wild bellow of rage, he grabbed for his tormentors, and died draped across the wall he had defended with such valor.

Not three minutes later, James Bonham, hero of heroes, tried to hold off six attackers at the mission chapel, but was overpowered. He died taking several of the enemy with him.

Now all was confusion, and by six-thirty in the morning triumphant bugle calls echoed across the big field as Santa Anna's victorious troops searched every corner of the Alamo's defenses for any remaining Texicans. Whenever they found one they obeyed their general's stern command: 'No prisoners.' Men who had fought bravely until all hope was gone endeavored to surrender, but were either gunned down or pierced by bayonets. There were no prisoners, not among the men, although Amalia Marr and the other women who were inside the walls were spared.

Jim Bowie in his cot was bayoneted.

Long after the terrible victory, when men were trying to sort out details of what had happened to the 182 Texicans, a Mexican officer claimed that the last of the famous defenders to survive was Davy Crockett: 'He hid under a pile of women's clothes and begged and pleaded and wept when we trapped him. Said he would do anything if we spared him, but we shot him in contempt.' Unlikely, that.

Who were these heroes who died defending the Alamo? From what terrain did they come and upon what traditions had they been reared to make them willing to give their lives for the freedom of a territory to which they had so recently come?

Ten were born in England, twelve in Northern Ireland, three in Scotland, two in Germany, and one each in Wales and Denmark. Those born in the United States were thirty-one from Tennessee, fourteen from Kentucky, five from Alabama, four from Mississippi, five from Georgia, thirteen from the Carolinas, eleven from Virginia, twelve from Pennsylvania, and a scattering of others from Vermont, Louisiana, Missouri, New York, New Jersey, Ohio, Massachusetts and Illinois. Of the heroic congregation, only six had been born in Texas itself. Their names: Abamillo, Badillo, Espalier, Esparza, Fuentes, Nava – Mexicans all. Juan Seguín, who was in the Alamo when the siege began, we shall see shortly.

By seven that Sunday morning the battle was over, as complete a victory as any general could have hoped for. The Tejas rebellion was crushed almost before it was fairly launched, and Santa Anna, joyous in his triumph, gave one last order: 'Burn them all.' And the pyre was lit, and all but one were burned. By special dispensation of General Cós, the body of Gregorio Esparza was released to his brother for burial.

Into an unmarked grave, unhonored and spat upon, were thrown the ashes of the Alamo heroes, but even before the acrid fumes from the fire died away, men in various parts of the world were beginning to utter the name with reverence, and anger, and hope, and determination. 'The Alamo!' screamed newspapers throughout America. 'The Alamo!' whispered men to their wives as they prepared to leave for greater battles in the future. And in the weeks ahead, when men from all parts of Texas and the United States began to muster to avenge this savagery, they voiced a threat, a blood-oath that would bind them together: 'Remember the Alamo!'

From the heroism of these ordinary men, from their unmarked grave rose an echo of immortality. By their deaths, the living were morally obligated to finish what they had begun. From their skeletons, burned to ashes, the backbone of a new nation would be formed.

Where was General Sam Houston, the hero of Texas history, when such events were taking place? As one of many would-be commanders-in-chief, he had tried desperately to bring order to the defense of Texas, and he had failed. 'Abandon the Alamo and blow it up,' he had counseled Travis, who had disobeyed him for his own heroic reasons. 'Abandon Goliad and blow it up,' he had ordered Colonel Fannin weeks ago, and again he had been ignored. Like Achilles before Troy, he sulked, this time among his beloved Cherokees, whom he visited to help them regularize their relations with the United States and especially with the Texas that was now arising.

If the present leaders of the emerging nation were proving themselves to be a gang of inept fools, so be it. He would do his job with the Indians and return when the real fighting men were willing to listen, to retreat in orderly fashion, to suck Santa Anna ever deeper into perilous terrain, and to save all energy for one titanic effort against the Mexicans, whose supply lines would grow longer and longer and always more difficult to defend against those backwoods tactics which had proved so disastrous to British hopes in years gone by.

Sam Houston became an American version of the Roman Fabius Maximus, derisively nicknamed *Cunctator*, the Dawdler, who in 217 B.C. avoided defeat by the Carthaginian Hannibal through a series of skillful retreats that wore down the enemy. Houston devised a masterly plan which would enable him to do the same with Santa Anna, who had a vastly superior army, good cannon, able generals, and everything in his favor except time and distance. These two lesser advantages, he thought, could defeat the Mexican dictator.

Houston was in Gonzales when he learned that the Alamo had fallen. The morning and evening guns, which had reassured distant listeners that the mission remained in Texican hands, had fallen silent, so he was not surprised when a woman Santa Anna had released for the sole purpose of spreading her tale of terror reached Gonzales with the awful news that all the Texicans, including the thirty-two from Gonzales, were dead.

Then began the great retreat, the Runaway Scrape, in which civilians fled before the onrushing Mexicans. Towns were abandoned and set to the torch by their inhabitants. Cattle were herded north and east, then left to fend for themselves at river crossings. Hamlets were left bare. Nothing seemed able to halt the victorious dictator.

To Sam Houston, retreating like the others, one thing became essential: Colonel Fannin must get his men out of that trap in Goliad. He must bring his forces north to unite with ours. The safety of all Texas depends upon his actions now.

When Finlay Macnab learned of Colonel Fannin's latest mismanagement he did not despair, though he was appalled to think that an officer with formal training could be so incompetent. Not only had Fannin ignored General Houston's urgent plea to abandon the indefensible presidio, but he was also dividing into smaller groups what few forces he did have, sending badly needed troops on a wild-goose chase to defend some willful civilians who should have left the area long before.

After heated discussion with other concerned volunteers, Macnab sought a meeting with the colonel to protest. Taking Otto along so that the boy could better understand the situation in which they were involved, he reported to the corner of the presidio grounds where Fannin had his tent. 'Sir –' he began, but he had uttered only that word when Fannin interrupted.

'Name and district?'

'Finlay Macnab, Victoria. My son, Otto.'

The colonel acknowledged the pair, then said: 'You have something to say?'

'You see, sir, we live near Victoria, and we understand that General Houston wants us to retreat – in an orderly fashion, of course – and if we go to Victoria ...'

'We retreat nowhere,' Fannin snapped.

'But if the Alamo has already fallen ... It was a make-believe fortress like this ...'

Macnab had used an unfortunate word. 'Make-believe!' Fannin cried. 'Look at those walls. I've strengthened every one of them. I've had seven hundred cattle slaughtered and their meat dried in the sun. We can withstand a siege of weeks, months, till the rest of Texas mobilizes.'

'Colonel ...'

The interview was ended. Fannin rose angrily, stalked out of his own tent, and left the Macnabs standing there.

Back in their own corner of the large compound, Finlay told his son: 'You must remember, Colonel Fannin is a West Point man. He has his own special definition of honor, of propriety. Men with their own definitions always mean trouble for other men.'

'Are we in trouble?'

'Deep. Santa Anna could be here at any minute. He's only ninety-five miles away.'

'And he could break down our walls too?'

'With enough men, he can do anything.'

'What should we do?'

'Like Houston says. Retreat now and fight later.'

Finlay delivered this prudent opinion on Tuesday, 15 March, and he was disgusted on subsequent days to see that instead of preparing for an orderly evacuation, Fannin was assigning his men tasks, adding to the fortifications and storing

532

the dried meat of the slaughtered steers. It was as if, having the fort and the food, he felt obligated to use both, but a member of the Georgia Battalion had a simpler explanation: 'He refuses to join any movement which might mean the loss of his command. He will not serve under another man.'

The remainder of that week was spent in total confusion, then, belatedly, Fannin accepted the fact that he really must retreat; however, even then he could not act decisively. Instead of marshaling a calculated withdrawal with firm, quick decisions about what to take and what not, he vacillated miserably, telling the men first: 'We'll not try to haul those big cannon,' then snapping: 'We've got to take every one of our cannon. We can't let Santa Anna get them.'

The danger was not really from Santa Anna in the west, for he was resting with his victorious troops in Béjar, but from a much different kind of Mexican general, a soft-spoken, humanitarian professional named José de Urrea, who came thundering up from the south, sweeping before him all the American filibusters who had been harassing the Mexicans in that region. It soon became apparent that General Urrea, with a vastly superior force, could overrun Goliad at any time he wished.

'We should have left this place two weeks ago,' Macnab lamented as he watched with dismay the chaos that engulfed the men about him. 'Why doesn't someone establish order?' he asked with Scottish impatience at such sheer folly, but no one did.

At last, on Friday afternoon, 18 March, Colonel Fannin reached a decision, which he announced boldly: 'We start our withdrawal to Victoria tomorrow at dawn. Since it will be a speedy retreat, we shall not try to take our cannon with us.'

'Thank God, he's made up his mind,' Macnab told Otto, and all that day father and son moved about the presidio checking to be sure that everyone had his rifle in good condition and an adequate supply of ammunition.

'Why are you doing this?' a Georgia man asked, and Finlay replied: 'Because I don't see any of the officers doing it.'

'What do you know about military affairs?'

'Nothing. But I have common sense.'

That night he drew upon his fragmentary knowledge: 'Otto,

I read once that retreat is more difficult than marching ahead. The book said you need speed and discipline.'

'Will we have them?' Otto asked, for although he was only a boy he had seen enough of the disorganization at Goliad to make him suspicious of any leadership that Colonel Fannin might provide.

'Son, at military tactics Fannin may be first-rate. It's in the management of his army ...'

'I don't think he knows how to do anything,' Otto said, and through the night they continued to check armament.

At dawn on Saturday the two were ready to serve as scouts, leading Colonel Fannin across land they knew well, sure that by nightfall they could bring the troops to safety in Victoria, only twenty-five miles away. But as they were about to move out, Fannin decided that, after all, he had better take his cannon with him, and during the time consumed in making this radical change, for teams of oxen had to be assembled to draw the heavy pieces, he had a further idea: 'Burn all that piled-up meat. So the Mexicans can't get it.' And through the wasted morning men stacked timbers, set them ablaze, and tossed onto the resulting fire the choice meat from some seven hundred steers.

'This place never smelled so good,' an Irishman shouted, and while the soldiers waited impatiently, another Irishman started playing a mouth organ, and men danced reels.

On a day when speed was essential, for other scouts had reported Urrea on his way to Goliad, the march finally began. 'At last!' Macnab sighed as they set forth, satisfied that the men were at least well-armed and prepared for battle even if overtaken from the rear, as they might well be after such a long delay.

But the farce was not over. When the troops were less than a mile from the presidio a lieutenant, checking the supply train that had been given to him to command well after the march started, found to his horror that all food supplies were gone. In this enthusiasm for destroying huge stacks of beef to prevent them from falling into enemy hands, the men had burned the entire lot. A file of three hundred and sixty men was marching into the hot empty plain east of Goliad with nothing to eat except what the occasional foot soldier had sequestered in his knapsack, if he had one.

When news of this disastrous oversight spread through the ranks, a much more serious one was discovered: no one had thought to bring water, either, so that the big, patient oxen on which the movement of the cannon depended began to weaken from lack of it.

When the Macnabs heard of these incredible blunders, the sort boys would not have made when planning an overnight camping, Otto made a simple suggestion: 'Someone ought to shoot him.'

'Hush!' his father warned, clamping his hand firmly over his son's mouth. 'That's treason, and Fannin would hang you in a minute.'

When his mouth was freed, Otto said grimly: 'Fannin has rules for everyone but himself.'

Foodless, waterless, this shambles of a retreat was struggling across the plain when two rear scouts dashed up: 'General Urrea, with many men and three cannon, will overtake you before sunset.'

When Fannin heard this his face went white, and now Macnab felt that he must intervene, for it was apparent that the colonel had lost all sense of control and needed guidance: 'Sir, I know this land. My farm lies just ahead. You cannot allow yourself to be trapped in this open field. You must, you really must, turn quickly to the left and head for those trees along the river.'

'I never divide my army,' Fannin said doggedly, remembering something he had read in a military manual.

'But, sir! I know these Georgia men, these Tennessee sharpshooters. You turn them loose in those woods, with water available, they'll hold back the whole Mexican army.'

'I do not respond to panic,' Fannin said resolutely, and now, although protection was easily available after a double-time march of less than two miles toward the scrub oak, the mesquite and the river, this obstinate man insisted upon keeping his men on the route he had planned for them, a dusty, waterless path on which his oxen had begun to collapse and his soldiers to gag from thirst.

Finally, when the surviving oxen were no longer able to haul the big, useless cannon, Colonel Fannin had to order a halt. It came in one of the bleakest stretches of the route, an area which provided no protection of any kind – no trees, no water, no gully to serve as a ready-made trench, no soft soil to encourage the digging of real trenches. Fannin brought his men to rest less than a mile from all kinds of safety, and here, with no protection, he formed them into a hollow square such as the Romans had used two thousand years earlier, with wagons as occasional breastworks and the precious cannon at each corner. Meticulously, he ordered that the sides of the square run true to the compass headings, with north facing the river a short distance away, with east facing Victoria, to which they should be marching, and west facing the presidio they had recently abandoned.

It was neat, military – and fatal.

Fannin had three hundred and sixty men, Urrea well over a thousand, and as soon as the unequal battle started, it was clear that the Mexican must triumph. However, Colonel Fannin and his West Point training proved a formidable adversary, for he deployed his men well, gave them encouragement, and conducted himself like a real leader.

But because the Mexicans fought a battle of swift movement, Fannin could not bring his cannon to bear upon them, and by the time the Mexican lines had formed, the only Texicans who knew how to work the cannon were wounded and the big guns stood useless. As night fell it was obvious to the trapped men inside the Roman square that on Sunday, General Urrea could overwhelm them at any time he wished.

It was a horrible night, with the wounded crying for water and the unwounded watching the encircling lights as the Mexicans moved ever closer. At three an ox that had been hit in the shoulder began bellowing so loudly that Otto went to the poor beast and shot it. Others in the doomed square, thinking that the Mexicans were upon them, began to fire wildly, but Colonel Fannin silenced them: 'Save your bullets. We'll need them tomorrow.'

By dawn on Sunday, Urrea had brought up his heavy cannon, with ample horse and oxen power to move them where they would be most effective, and now, with the norteamericanos spread neatly out before him and with not even a surface ripple on the flat to protect them, he fired at will, raking the entire camp with a deadly barrage of canister and grape. The exposed rebels, with no food or water to sustain them, had no chance of escape. Twelve hundred fresh Mexicans faced the three hundred or so exhausted survivors.

In the first three explosions of the cannon, fragments of metal ripped through the camp, killing and maiming. The next three were worse, for the Mexican gunners now had exact range, and before the next salvo could be fired, several junior officers consulted with their men and reported to Fannin: 'No hope with those cannon raking us. You must surrender.' But now the confused leader became heroic: 'Never! We'll fight to the death!' Then he lost control and watched impotently as his officers raised the white flag.

To Macnab's relief, the Mexicans responded quickly with a white flag of their own, signifying that a truce existed, and shortly thereafter Colonel Fannin marched erect and trim to meet Urrea, accompanied by Finlay Macnab as his interpreter. The two commanders settled upon the exact terms of surrender, and a disastrous adventure, mismanaged from the start, collapsed in a disastrous finish.

Macnab, when he reported back to the men inside the square, was quite specific as to the arrangements that had been reached:

'Colonel Fannin demanded that our troops receive all the honors of war. Lay down our arms, officers to keep theirs. Surrender with full right to leave the country. No executions. No reprisals.

'General Urrea did not exactly accept these terms, at least not in writing, but he did agree to an amiable surrender with our rights protected, and a Lieutenant-Colonel Holsinger, acting for Urrea, told me personally: "Well, sir! In ten days, home and liberty." When others on Urrea's staff told us the same, and many heard the promises, we were much relieved, I can tell you.

'General Urrea himself was less specific about the actual terms, but he was quite eager to provide us with water and food and care for our wounded. To me he seemed both a perfect gentleman and a soldier who knew what he was doing.

537

'I did the translating up to the point where Urrea and Fannin drew apart to sign a paper of some kind. What was in it, I don't know. Formal terms and all that, but as we marched out the Mexicans saluted us and Holsinger said again: "Well, gentlemen, in ten days, liberty and home." '

Less than an hour after the surrender, the men who had marched out of the presidio only the day before now marched back in, and when the Macnabs were once more within those familiar walls, Finlay told the boy to kneel beside him. 'Almighty God, we thank Thee for having rescued us from what could have been a great tragedy. Teach us to be humble. Teach us to be grateful. From the bottom of our hearts, we thank Thee.'

He then sat Otto down beside the embers of the burned meat and lectured him on the duties of a man: 'You've seen what indecision and confusion can do. I don't charge Fannin with cowardice, because in battle you saw that he was brave. But in this life, son, you must carefully make up your mind as to the right road, and then march down it. If a wall of water forty feet high comes at you, hold your nose, kick to stay afloat, and when the water recedes, get on with your job. Promise me, Otto, that you'll be a man of determination.'

'I'll try.'

In an unusual display of emotion his father embraced him. 'I was proud of you, son, the way you helped me check the rifles the night before we started our retreat. You and I did our jobs. We did the best we could. It was the others . . .'

He would condemn no one specifically, but he sat silent for a long time trying to understand how this debacle had been permitted, but in the end he said simply: 'We were lucky to escape. Now let's get back to work.'

'Since we're so close to our farm, do you think they'll let us walk home?'

'I'm sure they will,' Finlay said, for that would be the sensible thing to do, and since he was himself a sensible man, he expected others to behave in the same way.

Benito Garza, like many historians in later years, found no fault with General Santa Anna's harsh conduct at the Alamo; a band of uninvited guests on Mexican territory had raised a rebellion, which, according to explicit Mexican law, made them pirates and subject to the death penalty. Most of the dead had been killed in combat, and those few who were shot or sabered after the end of fighting had been killed in the immediate aftermath of that battle, while tempers on both sides were still hot. There had been no atrocities. No women or children had been slain. It had been a clean fight and the mexicanos had won.

True, Garza had experienced one bad moment when on Santa Anna's orders he inspected the ruins of the Alamo to ensure that men like Travis, Crockett and Bowie were dead, for as he turned one of the bodies over with the toe of his boot, he looked down to see his brother-in-law Xavier Campbell's glassy eyes staring up at him.

'Dios mío! How did he get in here?'

No one could give him an answer, for the women who had been inside the Alamo were too frightened to speak much sense, nor would they have known his history had they been able to report.

'Men!' Garza had shouted. 'Let's bury this one.' But the scene was too confused for individualized action and Campbell's body, like the rest, was thrown into a huge pile for burning.

Later, as Benito tried to sort things out, he concluded: 'Well, if he insisted on fighting against his own nation, he deserved what he got.' But this did not alleviate his feeling of sorrow over his sister Matia's loss of her second husband. Of the adult Texicans he knew, Benito had liked Campbell the best, but his conviction of superiority had led him astray, and now he, like the other arrogant intruders, was dead.

Benito had curious and sometimes conflicting reactions to the great victory at Béjar: I'm glad that the norteamericanos received a stiff lesson. They deserved it. I want to see them kicked out of Tejas. But having thus exulted over the victory, he had a less inflammatory reaction: I could have lived with Xavier Campbell. He treated my sister with dignity. I can still live with the Macnabs. They're decent. Perhaps if we have a mexicano government with mexicanos in charge, there'll be a place for a few norteamericanos. They would be very helpful in our trade with New Orleans. Or in running stores in Victoria based on the

New Orleans warehouses. Or maybe even banking in Victoria with New Orleans funds.

So from the sixth of March, when the Alamo fell, to the twenty-first, when news reached Santa Anna of the surrender of the Goliad garrison, Benito Garza luxuriated in the glow of victory, planning what he would do when this mexicano army with its three or four columns had cleared Tejas of the norteamericanos. But with the arrival of the sweating, dusty rider from Goliad, things changed dramatically, for Garza was in a house near San Fernando Church when he heard Santa Anna give the order: 'I told Urrea specifically. No prisoners. No surrender. Remind him . . . order him to shoot them all.'

Garza, as an expert on life in Tejas and a man who had educated himself by reading about Napoleon and other generals, felt obligated to remonstrate against such a brutal, such an unwarranted order, and there in command head-quarters, with no one else present, a vital dialogue began:

GARZA: Excellency, may I respectfully suggest that you do not send Urrea that order.

SANTA ANNA: Why not? My decree of 30 December 1835 clearly states that any foreigner taking arms against the government of Mexico is to be treated like a pirate and shot.

GARZA: But to shoot so many . . . more than three hundred, maybe four hundred. This will be taken poorly in Los Estados Unidos. It will incur lasting enmity.

SANTA ANNA (*with great animation*): Now, there you're wrong, Garza. Remember what happened at Tampico? Just last December? A gang of norteamericanos tried to invade, coming down from New Orleans. We defeated them and shot twenty-eight of them as pirates. Everybody warned me: 'The people of New Orleans will rise up.' Nobody made a move. They realized the dead men were pirates. They deserved to be shot, and I shot them.

GARZA: But I'm worried, Excellency, that this Alamo thing might be differently interpreted. It didn't happen in Tampico. It happened here, and norteamericanos interpret Béjar and Tejas differently from the way they do Tampico.

SANTA ANNA: Again you're wrong. Our great victory here, and Urrea's in Goliad, will show them that Tejas really is an indivisible part of Mexico. That they no longer have any interest in it. They never did.

GARZA: They think they did, and that's what counts. Look at what the messenger said about the men at Goliad who are to be shot if your order prevails. Men from Georgia. From New Orleans. And Louisville. Irishmen. Poles. This is not a collection of random volunteers, like the Alamo.

SANTA ANNA (*very persuasively, his voice low and controlled*): The more reason they must be punished, and openly. See that the order to Urrea goes out promptly.

GARZA: Excellency, I must protest. I must.

SANTA ANNA: Are you a loyal mexicano? Or a damned norteamericano?

GARZA: I hope to be your governor of Tejas one of these days.

SANTA ANNA (*laughing*): And so you shall be, or someone like you. Because from now on, Tejas is forever mexicano.

GARZA: So I speak as a future governor ... if things go well.

SANTA ANNA: I'm sure they will. With Béjar and Goliad in our hands, with our men in control of the coast, with the norteamericanos burning down their own towns – all we have to do is pin this Sam Houston down somewhere and finish him off. Clean our Nacogdoches and never again allow a norteamericano to live west of the Sabine.

GARZA: A large order, Excellency.

SANTA ANNA: It's almost done. (*Then, snapping his fingers*): I'll make you my district governor at Nacogdoches. You can guard our frontier.

GARZA: It is Nacogdoches, Excellency, that I'm worried about. Béjar and Goliad have fallen. Suppose you overtake Houston somewhere on the banks of the Brazos and wipe him out. Don't you see that this drags you all the way to the Louisiana border, and as you approach there, it's going to be like a spring? You compress it and compress it, and always it grows more powerful until ... poof! It blows you apart.

SANTA ANNA: What do you mean?

GARZA: I mean simply this. That you can annihilate the Alamo in fair battle, and that's acceptable. And you can defeat Fannin at Goliad, and that's acceptable. But if you shoot the Goliad prisoners, and then march north, every man in Kentucky and Tennessee and Alabama and Mississippi is going to rally to the cause, so that when you reach the Sabine you will

541

face the whole Estados Unidos.

SANTA ANNA: If the norteamericanos give me any more trouble, I may march all the way to ashington. The execution of the prisoners, that is a risk we must take. It's a risk I'm willing to take, because I feel sure that when they see the irresistible force of our armies – and remember, Garza, I'll have eight thousand shortly and they'll have trouble mustering one thousand . . .

GARZA: Their thousand will be led by Sam Houston, and he's no Fannin.

SANTA ANNA: I know little about him. What kind of man is he?

GARZA: Most of us have never seen him.

SANTA ANNA: What have you heard?

GARZA: He's drunk most of the time, but very clear-eyed when sober. He fought with their President Jackson against the Indians, but he also loves the Indians and is just in his treatment of mexicanos. The norteamericanos I know find him unfathomable.

SANTA ANNA: Nothing but a frontier gallant.

GARZA: But if you proceed with the execution of the Goliad prisoners, Excellency, you place a terrible weapon in the hands of this Houston.

SANTA ANNA: What weapon?

GARZA: Revenge. Excellency, the norteamericanos may forget the Alamo in time. It was a fair fight and they lost. But they could never forget a massacre at Goliad. They will fight us every inch of the way. They'll cut our supply lines, and our lines will be very long.

SANTA ANNA: Damnit, you sound like a yanqui.

GARZA: I want to be governor of a state that can be governed. If we make a just settlement now, bring men like Houston into a decent companionship . . .

SANTA ANNA (slowly and with careful reasoning): I have them by the throat, Garza. With reinforcements arriving every day, I have a chance to wipe them out. Another Zacatecas. Another Tampico. Teach them a terrible lesson, pacify them, and go back to governing Mexico as it should be governed. (A long pause.) So the execution of the prisoners at Goliad must be seen as part of a grand design. All pieces fall into place if you look at it that way.

GARZA (*pleading*): Excellency, there's one thing I haven't told you ... haven't told anyone. But when you sent me into the Alamo to verify the bodies – Crockett and those – the first body I could name was that of my sister's husband, Xavier Campbell, a good Catholic from Scotland ...

SANTA ANNA: Scotland, England, Ireland, Wales ... why do men from such places come to fight against us? What business have they in Mexico? (*Then, gently*): I am sorry for your sister. I shall send her a present, give her some land when this is over.

GARZA: My point is, Excellency, that at the spot where this dead Xavier Campbell defended lay nine dead Mexicanos. When you cross the Brazos you will stand face to face with a thousand Xavier Campbells.

SANTA ANNA (*as if he had not heard*): So I want you, personally, to start riding right now with my message to General Urrea. Every prisoner he has must be shot. And if you do not report to me that this has been done, you will be shot.

So early on Thursday, 24 March, Benito Garza rode hard to Goliad in the company of three soldiers guiding extra mounts; he carried an order he did not want to deliver and one which he certainly did not want to see obeyed. Knowing something of General Urrea, he hoped that this strong-minded professional would refuse to obey Santa Anna and would set the prisoners free. But when he reached the stout walls of the presidio, with its four hundred and seven norteamericano prisoners, including those taken from other areas, he found that General Urrea, anticipating such an order, had generated an excuse to go south, leaving the presidio and its prisoners in the hands of a weak Colonel José Nicolás de la Portilla.

Portilla's hands trembled when he opened the dispatch, and his face paled when he read the blunt command: 'Immediate execution of every perfidious foreigner.'

He received these cruel instructions at about seven o'clock in the evening and spent the next hours in great anguish, because Urrea on departing had given him very specific orders of quite a different character: 'Treat the prisoners with consideration, especially their leader Colonel Fannin, and protect them in every way so long as they remain in your custody.'

So there it was: 'Shoot them all' or 'Protect them until

they're set free.' Through the night he juggled these orders, and toward dawn he concluded that whereas his immediate superior, General Urrea, knew what was the military thing to do under the circumstances, his ultimate superior, General Santa Anna, knew what was best for the nation and was also in a position to punish any subordinate who disobeyed his written order.

About half an hour before dawn on Palm Sunday, 27 March, Colonel Portilla rose, dressed in his finest uniform, and marched to the commissary, where he summoned his juniors officers and told them, 'We're to shoot them all. I said all.'

A great commotion engulfed the presidio, with grim-lipped captains and lieutenants running here and there, and Lieutenant Colonel Juan José Holsinger still reassuring the Texicans: 'We're marching you to the boats. Home free.' He believed what he was saying, because as a German known for his sympathies toward the prisoners, he had not been trusted with the truth.

The prisoners, delighted at the prospect of being freed, were formed into three groups, with Finlay Macnab and his fourteen-year-old son Otto among the Georgia Battalion that would march along the San Antonio River. 'Can we be allowed to drop out when we pass our home?' Macnab asked Holsinger, who replied jovially. 'Yes, yes. That's entirely reasonable.'

But just then Otto shouted: 'It's Benito!' and his cry attracted the attention of Santa Anna's messenger of death, and when Garza saw that the Macnabs, part of his family, were among the unknowing doomed, he moved away lest they detect his anguish.

'Benito!' the boy cried, and Holsinger, seeing this, turned to Garza and told him: 'Friends of yours,' so Benito had to speak with them.

'We're going home at last,' Otto cried, as he reached out to greet his friend.

'Yes,' Garza said. 'You must stay close to me as we march out.'

'I want to,' Otto said, and his father added: 'Holsinger said we could drop out when we reached our home. Will you be joining us, to help your sister?'

'Yes. Yes.'

544

'Campbell was killed, wasn't he? A messenger from Gonzales said that he . . .'

'He died.'

'Were they all killed?'

'Yes, yes,' and in shame he moved away.

Now the condemned norteamericanos were told to form three separate columns and to move toward the main gate. They would march about half a mile, each in a different direction, and then they would be halted, each file out of sight of the others but not out of hearing.

They were well on their way when a male nurse ran into the large room where about forty men wounded the week before lay on cots, Colonel Fannin among them with a leg wound which had nearly killed him. 'Drag them all into the yard. They're to be shot,' the nurse cried hysterically. And slowly, laboriously, the cots were dragged into the sunlight, where the men who had been saved from death now lay dumbly awaiting it. Colonel Fannin, from his cot, begged his men to act bravely.

Soon Mexican soldiers began moving from cot to cot, jamming pistols against the heads of the men and blowing their brains out. Finally only Fannin was left.

West Point to the end, he never flinched, and assuming that his captors were gentlemen, like himself, he made the kind of statement officers were supposed to make in a situation like this: 'Sir, I give you my watch and my money, with only two requests. Please do not shoot me in the face. Please see that I am decently buried with the honors of war.'

When the blindfold was over his eyes the officer who had accepted the watch asked: 'Bueno?' and Fannin replied: 'It is well placed.' He was then shot right through the face and his body was tossed on the pile with the others to be burned, with the charred remains left for the coyotes and the vultures.

These intimate details are known because just before the executions started, a compassionate Mexican officer, knowing that General Urrea's wounded needed medical care, moved quietly among the Texicans, selecting men who had proved helpful in caring for the sick. To each he whispered: 'Move toward the corner. Hide.' His personal courage in disobeying Santa Anna's cruel orders meant that some two dozen Texicans survived, and it was they who in later years reported the atrocity which was now about to unfold.

The marching columns – three hundred and seventy men in all – could not know what had happened to the wounded prisoners, and the Georgia Battalion containing the Macnabs was well on its way to the river, with some of the men singing, when it was ordered to halt. At this moment Benito Garza, who was with the troops, grabbed Otto by the left shoulder, whirled him about, pointed to the nearby woods, and said one word: 'Run!'

The boy, bewildered, did not move, so Garza gave him a strong shove and muttered again: 'Run!'

'My father!'

'Run!' Garza shouted, and this both spurred the boy into action and alerted a wiry Mexican lieutenant with a sword, who saw what was happening. He was about to chase after Otto when the morning's work began, which temporarily delayed him.

When the group of some hundred and twenty prisoners halted, the Mexican soldiers wheeled about, formed two lines, enclosing the Texicans, and upon command began to shoot each prisoner in the head. But when the captives realized the terrible thing that was happening, many started to fight their captors with bare fists so that a general melee developed, with much aimless firing.

Otto, from his place among the trees, saw men from Tennessee grab the guns of their slayers and defend themselves with the butts until some Mexican shot them through the back of the head. Other men, wounded in the first fusillades, lay helplessly on the ground, looking up as soldiers came, pointed pistols directly in their faces, and blew their heads apart. He watched with horror as his father broke loose and started to run across the fields toward where he was hiding, and Finlay might have escaped had not three officers on horseback galloped after him, stabbing him in the back with their lances and cheering as he stumbled blindly about, the lances projecting from his back. Forming a circle about him with their horses, they fired at him six times, and rode off.

Desperately Otto wanted to run out to help his father, but common sense told him that Finlay was dead, so he retreated farther into the woods, and it was good that he did because the

546

officer who had seen him escape now came after him on foot, armed with sword and knife and pistol, to finish him off, but the sight of this great peril gave Otto new-found strength. Grasping for anything, he wrenched loose a stout oak branch, and with a power that frightened him, stripped off the twigs. He now had a heavy weapon with which to defend himself.

The officer, seeing the boy apparently defenseless, moved easily through the woods, brandishing his sword, and when he reached Otto he gave a mighty flash with his right arm, bringing the point of the sword directly athwart Otto's neck, but the boy swerved, taking a deep cut from left ear to chin. So impassioned was he that he did not feel the cut or the flow of blood, but he fell to the ground as if mortally wounded, then jammed his oak branch between the officer's legs. With a sudden twist, he threw the fellow down, grabbed his knife as it fell loose, and with three terrible stabs he stuck the man in the chest, in the gut, and deep in the neck.

He had not time to assess his victory, because two other soldiers had heard the noise of the struggle and now closed in upon him. At first, as he ran for the river, he was so protected by trees that they could not use their rifles, but when he broke for the banks they had a clear shot at him and one bullet tore into his left shoulder, but did not shatter the bone.

Disregarding this second wound as he had the first, he dashed to the edge of the steep bank – it was almost a cliff – and without thinking of hidden rocks or invisible tree stumps he leaped into the water, submerged, and swam underwater for the opposite shore.

This was a mistake, for it allowed the two soldiers to spot him when he surfaced, but before they could take proper aim, he was underwater again, swimming this time for the very bank on which they stood. When he surfaced this time, right under them, they were too surprised to shoot so down he went again, with them firing at his wake, and when signs of blood bubbled up, they assumed that they had killed him.

He had not moved. He had stayed right below them, holding his breath until he feared his lungs might burst, and this time when he edged his nose above the water and then his eyes, he found that they had left.

He remained in the river till late afternoon, allowing the water to cleanse his two wounds, and satisfying himself with probing fingers that the damage was not too serious. He was, however, losing a lot of blood, so at about five in the afternoon he climbed out on the far bank, turned his back on the scene of the massacre, and made his way eastward toward the Guadalupe, which would lead him home.

That night, resting under a tree, his left cheek and left shoulder throbbing with pain, he lost consciousness, and lay there bleeding. Toward morning he roused himself and continued his struggle toward safety, reaching the Guadalupe about sunset. Again he fell unconscious, but when he came to he saw that the bleeding had stopped.

Before dawn he was on his way again, further weakened by a rising fever. Alternately staggering forward and falling to his knees from dizziness, he reached a point along the river from which he could see the Campbell dog-run, and the realization that he was so close to salvation overwhelmed him. All the strength left his body and he fell, face down, and even when he heard a barking and felt a warm tongue licking his face and knew it was Betsy, he could not move.

María, hearing the dog's excited barking, came to her porch. For some minutes she could not see the body lying on the ground, but when Betsy ignored her whistle, she knew that something unusual must have happened, and in this way she found her adopted son.

This was the morning of Wednesday, 30 March, and Otto remained in a feverish coma till the next Sunday. Periodically he revived enough to learn that María was aware of her husband's death in the Alamo, and he told her that his father was dead, too, at Goliad.

In one moment of lucidity he realized that Josefina was in the room, commiserating with her sister, two Mexican women bereft of their anglo husbands.

Mostly, however, he spent these feverish days under the care of stout María, and as he began to mend he felt her warmth rescuing him, her love embracing him, and once he muttered: 'You're like an angel with big hands.' She told him that she had cut the bullet from his shoulder: 'No damage. No danger.' She said that he would always have a scar across his left cheek: 'No damage, no danger.' She fed him the food she had always prepared for her ailing men – refried beans, goat meat well shredded, tortillas, goat's milk with a brown-sugar candy – and he regained his strength.

On Sunday, 10 April, exactly two weeks after his near-death at Goliad, Otto Macnab walked to his own home, fetched two of his father's older rifles, and came back to the Campbell place to pick up one of Xavier's guns and a pair of knives.

'Where are you going?' María asked, her eyes filled with tears.

'To join Sam Houston.'

'To fight against my people again?'

'We've got to settle this.'

'Settle!' María wailed. 'What can you settle? Xavier is dead. Finlay dead. And God knows where my brother Benito is.'

'He's all right. He was with General Urrea.'

'He was fighting against you and Campbell?'

'He saved my life.' And then a vision of that struggle under the trees returned and a thought of striking significance revealed itself. 'María, the officer who almost killed me, he saw it was Benito who saved me. If he had lived, I know he would have reported Benito and maybe had him shot. I saw the look in his face when I started to run.'

'Where is he now? Is he a danger to my brother?'

'I killed him.'

No more was said. The two Garza women had absorbed as much anguish as anyone can accept before the mind rebels; young Otto had seen things which could drive a mind to madness. Mexicana women and American boy, the three were caught in terrible currents, frightening dislocations, and no one had the capacity or the courage to untangle them. The two women knew that they had loved their norteamericano men and they appreciated how kind, how just, how loving they had been, but these same men had taken arms against legitimate mexicano power and had paid for their error with their lives.

Otto knew beyond question that members of the Garza family had twice saved his life; once, Benito on the killing ground; and more recently, María when he was near to death. He owed these wonderful people a debt he could never repay, but now he must join General Houston.

With three rifles, two knives, a pistol and a nondescript collection of clothes, he started for the decisive battle which he knew could not be avoided. Betsy insisted on following him, but when they came to the ford by which he would cross the Guadalupe he told her sternly: 'Go home.' After he waded into the water, he stopped, turned to face the obedient dog, and cried: 'Take care of María!' And for some time Betsy watched him as he marched east.

When Benito Garza rejoined General Anna's staff, he was both surprised and relieved to discover how little adverse effect the Goliad massacre had had upon the reputation of the dictator. Oh, there had been some grumbling among the general population, and several of Santa Anna's European officers had confided: 'I'd not have done it that way,' but since there was no open protest, Benito supposed that the matter would soon be forgotten.

What he did not know was the American journals were already blazoning the story of the Alamo with inflammatory exhortations and that mass meetings were being convened in several states demanding military intervention on behalf of the slain heroes. Nor could he anticipate that these same journals would shortly be characterizing the Goliad massacre as 'three hundred and forty-two individual cases of unjustified murder,' which was the only appropriate way of describing it.

Garza had a remarkably clear perception of the military situation, which he discussed with General Ripperdá, in whose regiment he was again serving: 'We have about seven thousand soldiers either north of the Rio Grande or near it. General Houston can't have more than eight hundred, and I doubt he can ever get them to stay behind him very long. They come and go. I've seen them – farmers, ranchers, men with small shops.'

'But we, too, have a serious problem,' Ripperdá pointed out. 'We do have those seven thousand, but we don't seem able to gather them in one place. Urrea in Matagorda. Sesma bringing his thousand up from Thompson's Ferry. Another batch at Goliad. Right now Santa Anna has less than a thousand under his immediate command.'

'But a thousand of our troops can always defeat eight

hundred of theirs.'

'Certainly,' Ripperdá agreed. 'But I'd feel safer if the margin was what it ought to be. Seven hundred of them, seven thousand of us.'

'Well, isn't that Santa Anna's job? Postpone fighting until we assemble our superiority?'

Garza was confident that the supreme commander would do just that, and now as the mexicanos left Béjar and started the long march to the east, he was gratified to see that various units were catching up, while others were sending messages that they, too, would soon report.

So although he had been repelled by Santa Anna's needless brutality at Goliad, Garza still respected his generalship, for the man had an uncanny sense of what was going to happen next and a conviction that he would be clever enough to bend this occurrence to his advantage. 'An angel hovers above my left shoulder,' the general had said once, and this was proving true, for when the army approached Gonzales with a superiority less than satisfactory – so that if a battle could not be avoided, it might be more risky than desired – they found that the Texicans had set fire to the town and abandoned it.

'See, they run away from us!' Santa Anna gloated. 'But we'll catch them.' And that night amid the smoking embers he sent a series of short, clear dispatches ordering other generals to join him for a swift crossing of the Colorado and a forced march to see if they might trap Houston before he escaped over the Brazos. Once the rebels were forced to stand and fight, Santa Anna was sure his legions would crush them totally.

'We'll hang Houston and so many of his criminal supporters that oak trees will look as if they bore fruit,' he told Garza, who, contrary to what he had argued only a few weeks before, now believed it might be possible to exterminate all the troublesome norteamericanos and establish in Tejas a true mexicano province under benign leadership from Santa Anna in Mexico City, and he continued to see himself as governor.

But as they marched out of Gonzales an old man and his wife, both mexicanos, shouted at Santa Anna astride his white horse: 'Murderer' – and the word hung ominously in the air, clouding and contaminating the high hopes with which the army moved toward battle.

*   *   *

When it seemed that Santa Anna, forging ahead to conquer all of rebellious Tejas, was about to trap the fleeing Houston and his entire ragtag of defenders, one of those romantic miracles occurred which still convince Texans that God is on their side. In 1830 the New York investor John Jacob Astor had authorized the building of a steamboat to be used in the fur trade on the Missouri River. Called the *Yellow Stone*, it entered service in 1831, but ill fortune seemed to haunt the vessel as it tried to dodge the sunken niggerheads of the Missouri.

After less than a year's operation on that river, the *Yellow Stone* was asked to try its luck on the Mississippi, with no better results, but in 1833 the doughty little boat steamed up the Missouri all the way to the mouth of its namesake, the Yellowstone River in far North Dakota. However, that was its last run on its intended river, for soon thereafter it turned up as a grubby freight carrier in New Orleans.

On the last day of 1835, when Santa Anna was already marching north, the *Yellow Stone* left the safety of New Orleans and chugged its way to Tejas, bringing with it the New Orleans Grays, volunteers who were eager to help the rebellious state gain its independence. Having arrived in Tejas, it remained there, and it was picking its way up the tight and shallow waters of the Brazos when Sam Houston's confused army approached, needing all the help it could get.

Miraculously – there is no other word for it – the peripatetic little boat was waiting there when Houston needed it most, and it edged its nose into the western bank so that it could transport all of Houston's men to temporary safety on the eastern shore. By the time Santa Anna reached that area, the boat was gone and Houston's army, such as it was, remained intact.

While this was happening, events of a less satisfactory nature were occurring upstream on the Brazos. Houston's spies had informed him that Victor de Ripperdá, ablest of Santa Anna's generals, was speeding north to intercept the main Texas army from the west, and it was imperative that he be slowed down. Considering the problem with what maps he had, Houston concluded that Ripperdá would make a dash for Quimper's Ferry, hoping to find it functioning.

'That ferry must be destroyed,' Houston said, and two dozen

volunteers hurried upstream, realizing that if they reached Quimper's after the Mexican troops had crossed, it was the Texicans who would probably be destroyed. The average age of the adventurers was twenty-two, their average time within the boundaries of Texas, three months and three days. They came from eleven different states and two foreign countries, and if ever a group of untrained men was willing to fight for the abstract ideal of freedom, it was this disorganized mob.

By forced marches, the contingent reached Quimper's Ferry the day before General Ripperdá's troops would begin streaming in from the south. The men ran to the riverbank, saw that the ferry was on the other shore, and sent two men swimming across to fetch it, but when Mattie Quimper saw what was afoot, she ran down from the inn to confront the men: 'It's my ferry. I know what to do with it.' The men, thinking that she was refusing to destroy it, said: 'Madam, we got orders. This ferry can't fall into the hands of the Mexicans,' and she said: 'It won't.'

With the help of the two soldiers, she poled the ferry to the opposite bank, and when the expedition gathered about her, she grabbed an ax and went back down the slope to where she had tied the crude ferry and began to chop it to pieces, thus demolishing the precious craft that had served her so long. When the watching soldiers saw what she was doing, they ran down the banks and helped her with the destruction.

Slowly the muddy waters separated the logs and turned the superstructure over: 'Better come off, ma'am. She's fallin' apart.'

The ferry did not sink in the sense of disappearing in a rush; slowly the logs settled into the mud along the bank. 'Push that stuff into midstream!' a captain called, and when this was done, railings which had once enclosed the deck remained visible, drifting slowly downstream, useful to no one.

Mattie made no comment as it disappeared; it had been a good ferry, improved and enlarged over the years, and many hundreds of travelers had blessed it. But it had to be destroyed and she expressed no sorrow at its going.

But she was now on the opposite bank of the river from her home. 'I must go back,' she told the soldiers, but when they reported this to the captain, he told her: 'Stay with us. The Mexicans will burn everything over there.' She could not

553

accept this advice and made as if to swim back, whereupon he called to some of his men: 'Fetch the little boat and take her across.' When this was done, she stood on the bank and watched silently as the Texicans marched away, taking her son Yancey with them: I hope they know how to fight. I hope Yancey behaves well.

Left on her side of the Brazos, with all other homes abandoned, all neighbors fled, she spent a lonely night pondering what to do, and looking about her deserted inn, she had visions of those who had inhabited this refuge: her husband, Jubal, with his hunting dogs; the giant Kronk; Father Clooney; Joel Job Harrison, whom she had nearly married; the Jewish peddler who had come this way; the hungry settlers gorging on her honeyed pecans; the almost saintly Stephen Austin, so small, so determined. They had been a motley but noble group, battling the wilderness, and she could not bear to see this precious place fall into enemy hands.

Slowly, and with unflagging determination, she gathered branches of trees and shards of wood, placing them where the wind would catch at them and speed the flames she intended to ignite. When the sun was well up, and the sounds of the marching enemy could be heard to the south, she went from pile to pile, lighting each with brands, and when the inn was well ablaze, with fire eating at the logs which Jubal and Father Clooney first and then The Kronk had cut so carefully, she left what had been first her cave-house and then her dog-run and watched it burn.

It was only partly consumed when the first Mexican troops arrived, followed soon by General Ripperdá and his staff. Infuriated by the sight of a lone woman burning her house to deprive them of its comforts, this officer loudly directed his men to secure the ferry that his spies had assured him would be here, and when soldiers shouted: 'Colonel, it's gone, seems to be sunk, some pieces floating in the river,' he swore and turned his horse aside to view the damage for himself.

Ripperdá, an officer who honored the great traditions of the Spanish army in which so many of his ancestors had served, was not responsible for an ugly incident that occurred at this time. Some of his soldiers, intoxicated by their victories at the Alamo and Goliad, had begun to assume that the conquest of the rest of

554

Tejas was going to be a triumphal affair. 'One more battle, we go home!' was the cry, and now when they saw themselves frustrated by this lone woman they grew enraged, and three men rushed her.

'No!' Benito Garza shouted when he came upon the scene. 'I know her!'

Too late. Three soldiers stabbed at Mattie with their bayonets. She made no outcry. Clutching her throat as blood welled up, she tried valiantly to remain upright beside her burning home, but at last she fell, face down, upon the land she had loved so deeply.

Mattie's prayer that her son would perform honorably as a member of Houston's force bore quick and reassuring results, for when Yancey, now twenty-four, found himself in the company of men his own age he pulled himself together, suppressed his childish petulance, and began acting like a solid, ordinary farmhand forced into military life. He grumbled at the long marches, groused about the miserable food, and fraternized warmly with the other soldiers. What was most surprising, in view of his poor performances in the battles against the Karankawas, he could appear quite belligerent, especially when in the presence of the younger men, and he was always prepared to advise anyone on how to conduct the war.

He was a robust young fellow, with a big confident face and a voice that soared above the babble. He was never reluctant to step forward when dangerous work had to be done, but he did tend to delay his move until someone else had been clearly nominated. He liked especially to instruct the younger troops as to how they must conduct themselves when the Mexicans struck. He had become, in short, a typical Texican patriot, with his long gun, his bowie knife, and his determination to repel Santa Anna.

One April day, as he was explaining strategy to attentive listeners, he suddenly stopped, stared down the road, and cried: 'My God! What is it? A human porcupine!'

For up the dusty trail came a fourteen-year-old boy, blood-red scar across his left cheek, lugging a collection of weapons whose ends stuck out like the disorderly quills of a hedgehog. As the boy came closer, Yancey saw that it was his one-time friend Otto Macnab, who was not in camp ten minutes before he discovered that he was facing a new Yancey Quimper, matured and self-confident, who asked in a condescending way: 'Where do you come from, son?'

'Goliad, and I come to fight.'

'Goliad!' Yancey shouted to those behind him. 'He says he was at Goliad.'

Soon Otto was surrounded by admirers who wanted to know what had happened at the presidio, how he had got that scar across his face, and what it was like fighting the Mexican regulars.

'They know which end of a gun fires,' Otto assured them.

'How's your father allowed you to join us?'

'He was killed at Goliad. Stabbed in the back after he surrendered.' He said this so matter-of-factly, but with such terrible commitment, his blue eyes hard in the river sunlight, that the men said no more.

Later, the men who had questioned him about Goliad regathered to confirm what a sorry affair Houston's march to the east had been, and from the babble of whining voices he collected these offerings:

'Always he runs away ...'

'He's afraid to fight. Alamo and Goliad, they terrified him.'

'He's running to the north, hopin' to escape into Louisiana.'

'We could of licked Santa Anna three times over if we'd stood and fought.'

'He's a coward, and until we get rid of him, we accomplish nothin'.'

Harshest in his criticism was Quimper: 'General Houston has a Gulf of Mexico jellyfish for his backbone. Look at us, achin' for a fight. Eatin' our hearts out to revenge the Alamo and Goliad. And all he does is run away.'

'Maybe he has a plan,' Otto suggested, for from his observation of Colonel Fannin he had learned that commanders oftentimes had plans they did not confide to their troops, and sometimes those plans didn't work.

'Read this, Little Porcupine,' Quimper cried, and he grabbed from a Mississippi man standing nearby a dispatch received some days before. 'Watson here stole a copy, and it tells the whole story.' It was from the man elected president of the interim government and it did indeed lay forth the problem:

To General Sam Houston. Sir: The enemy are laughing you to scorn. You must fight them. You must retreat no farther. The country expects you to fight. The salvation of the country depends on your doing so.

David G. Burnet, President

The letter, as severe a rebuke as a field commander could have received, gave Otto a sick feeling: We're back at Goliad with a general who doesn't know what he's doing. Everything is falling apart.

But toward dusk a commotion along the river forestalled any demand for a new leader, because a gang of sweating men driving sixteen oxen appeared from the east, bellowing the information that they were bringing treasure into camp. Everyone ran to greet them, even General Houston, erect and dignified despite the pressures that assailed him.

Otto, coming slowly to the realization that he would never again see either his father or Zave Campbell, felt the need of someone older to cling to, and kept close to Quimper. Together they watched the oxen drag into camp two handsome cannon, gifts from the people of Cincinnati.

'Did you know, Yancey, I used to live in that town?' Otto said.

'You did?'

'Yep, sold pork to the riverboats.'

A soldier supervising the placement of the cannon said: 'Took three months for them to come down the Mississippi. Slipped past customs in New Orleans listed as "two pieces of hollow ware."'

'Where'd they get the name Twin Sisters?' Yancey asked, and one of the soldiers explained: 'They were christened off'n the port of Galveston by the lovely twin daughters of a doctor who came on the same boat, and they'll blow the balls off'n Santy Anny.'

The men, with so little to cheer during the past weeks, saw the cannon as proof that someone in the States cared, and they insisted that the two be fired right now, to which Houston agreed, and there in the wilderness, with no sensible target

557

before them, the Texicans loaded both, tamped the charges, and blazed away at the tops of distant oak trees. When a scatter of leaves proved that the guns could fire effectively, the men cheered.

Some days later, while helping to drag the cannon along muddy country roads, Otto had a chance to observe how the most trivial accident could sometimes determine the course of history. At this time the sweating Texicans did not know whether they would soon head north to Nacogdoches, surrendering all of central Texas to Santa Anna's fury, or east toward the Gulf of Mexico, hoping to engage the Mexicans on some favorable battleground. General Houston refused to divulge his plans, and many thought he had none. They said: 'He's markin' time, hopin' that somethin' favorable will save us.'

Now came the first accident. One of the wheels of Otto's cannon fell deep into a muddy rut, and when Houston rode by and saw the delay he growled: 'Get some oxen and drag that thing free.'

'We have no oxen,' the captain in charge of the big guns reported, and Houston said: 'Get some.'

A detail consisting of the captain, Otto and another enlisted man went searching the countryside, and soon came upon a strong-minded, brassy-voiced farm wife named Mrs Pamela Mann, who wore men's clothing and was armed with two large pistols.

'We must borrow four of your oxen,' the officer explained courteously.

'You cain't have them,' she snarled.

'We must have them.'

'You touch them oxen, I blow out the seat of your pants.'

'Mrs Mann,' the officer said, 'the future of the Texas Republic depends upon moving our cannon to face Santa Anna, and to do that we must have your oxen.'

'To hell with the Texas Republic. What's it ever done for me?'

The officer dropped his voice and beseeched so earnestly that she had to listen, and after some moments she delivered a curious judgment: 'Tell you what, if'n your general is marchin' east with his cannon to fight Santy Anny, he cain't have my beasts. They'd get kilt. But if'n he's marching north to safety in

Nacogdoches, he can borry 'em.'

'He's marching north!' the captain said quickly, whereupon the other enlisted man, who could be seen only by Macnab, drew his thumb across his throat, indicating that if Houston did march north, he would face rebellion.

So the four oxen were taken away and yoked to the mired cannon, but as the army resumed its forward march the vital question of where they were going was left unsettled. Desiring to be sure that the wheel on Otto's cannon had not been damaged by the hole into which it had fallen, Houston was to the rear when his lead troops approached a crossroads. If they marched to the left, they would retreat to Nacogdoches; straight ahead, they would have to encounter Santa Anna.

The men on the point, not knowing what to do, drifted into a grassy area between the two roads, intending to wait there until General Houston came up to give an order. And then the second accident took place, for at the head of the next group to arrive was a brassy young fellow from Alabama, and he cried to a farmer standing nearby: 'Which way to Harrisburg and Santy Anny?' and the farmer shouted back: 'That right-hand road will carry you to Harrisburg just as straight as a compass.'

'This way!' the Alabaman cried, and by the time General Houston reached the crossroads the forefront of the Texican army was well on its way to battle. For just a moment Houston stopped, studied the terrain, and shrugged his shoulders. Then he also took the road to Harrisburg. A decision of major consequence to Texas, and perhaps to the United States, had been reached: the Texas patriots would seek out Santa Anna and give him battle.

As Otto struggled with the cannon which had kept Houston from his position of command, Yancey Quimper drifted back and whispered: 'If us fellows in front hadn't of made the choice for him, sure as hell Old Shiftless would of skedaddled off to Nacogdoches.' But the officer who had commandeered the mules said: 'Houston always intended taking this road. We talked about it.'

Otto and his borrowed oxen had dragged the cannon less than a mile when Mrs Mann rode furiously up to General Houston, her eyes blazing, her free hand close to the pistol on her left hip: 'General, yore men told me a damn lie. They said

559

my oxen would be safe on the Nacogdoches road. Sir, I want 'em back.'

'You can't have them, ma'am,' Houston said. 'Our cannon need them.'

'I don't care a damn for your cannon. I want my oxen,' and she jumped down, whipped out a big knife, and began cutting loose her beasts. Houston was so astonished that he was speechless, and before he could issue any orders, she was riding off with her animals.

Otto's captain cried: 'Come with me! We'll get them back!' But when the captain and Otto overtook Mrs Mann, she astonished them by leaping from her horse, landing on the captain's back, and thrashing him with her fists as he lay on the ground. When he called for Otto to assist, she poked a gun into the boy's face and cried: 'Make one move, son, and you ain't got no head.' Standing in the mud, she held off the captain, mounted her horse, and resumed her homeward march with her beasts.

When Otto returned to his cannon with no animals to drag it into battle, the younger soldiers taunted him: 'Skeered of a woman!' and, 'You stole her oxen brave enough, but you couldn't keep 'em.' Otto said nothing, but his fists tightened and his blue eyes grew hard. If I'm ever in command of anything, he swore to himself, shameful things like this will not happen.

On the morning of Tuesday, 19 April, General Houston's Fabian tactics came to fruition, because Santa Anna, chasing him wildly, had imprudently taken his entire available force onto a boggy peninsula formed by the San Jacint River, where he could neither retreat nor receive reinforcements except over a narrow bridge. He assumed he was safe because he could not envision Houston seeking battle there, or winning if he did.

But Houston had a daring plan. Assembling as many of his nine hundred-odd troops as he could at the bank of a bayou, he told them in fighting sentences: 'The battle we have sought is upon us. The army will cross and we will meet the enemy. Some of us may be killed, and must be killed. But, men, remember the Alamo! The Alamo!'

Yancey, delighted with the prospect of battle at last, gripped Otto's arm and said prophetically: 'After a speech like that, Little Porcupine, our boys will take damned few prisoners.'

All that day the volunteers worked to get across the bayou and onto that stretch of land from which Santa Anna could not escape. 'How brilliant,' exulted a man from Connecticut. 'We have only nine hundred, true, but Santa Anna hasn't seven thousand. We've tricked him into facing us with less than a thousand. By God, we have a chance of winning.'

On the afternoon of the twentieth the two armies were still moving into position, but any actual engagement seemed unlikely. A detachment of mounted Texicans did make a gallant effort to capture a Mexican cannon that had been giving them trouble, but the Mexicans anticipated the move and gave a solid account of themselves. In fact, when the main body of the Texicans withdrew, three of their horsemen were left isolated – Secretary of War Thomas Rusk, an officer and a private – and a detachment of Mexican cavalry was about to capture all three when a most unlikely hero swung into action.

Infantry Private Mirabeau Buonaparte Lamar, riding a borrowed horse, was a minor poet-politician from Georgia who had arrived in Texas only a few weeks earlier, after both the Alamo and Goliad had fallen, but he was a man of such vision, such patriotism, that he almost leaped into the fight for Texas freedom. Now, with the enemy all about him, he performed heriocally and, by his superb horsemanship and daring, saved both Rusk and another man. Texicans and Mexicans alike cheered as the Georgian, a rather small man, outwitted the Mexicans and brought his two charges to safety. That night many asked: 'Who is this fellow with the French names?' but he did nothing to parade his valor.

On the morning of the twenty-first, General Houston slept late, for the hardships of the march and the exacerbations of command had exhausted him. His men, disgusted by his apparent indifference, renewed talk of deposing him, and they were further distressed to hear about midmorning that General Cós had joined Santa Anna with an additional four hundred-odd fresh troops. By this lucky stroke the Mexicans restored their clear superiority, some fourteen hundred of them to about nine hundred Texicans.

Heroic veterans of the frontier appeared not to be daunted by the disproportionate numbers, but shortly after dawn a grizzled scout named Erastus Smith, deaf from birth and famed throughout Texas as Deaf Smith, a man of strong opinion who never apologized for his black brother-in-law, saw to it that no more reinforcements could reach Santa Anna. Summoning five of his fellow scouts and the boy Macnab, he crept back along the route the Texicans had taken to get onto the peninsula and chopped away the only bridge. When the timbers were down he directed Otto and one of the men to set them afire, and as the smoke rose high in the windless air he led his party safely back. Now Houston and Santa Anna were entrapped; they must fight, with the Mexicans superior in numbers, and each general knew that the resulting battle, which would start next day at dawn, would determine the future history of this part of the world.

Relishing their day of rest, the weary Texicans moved idly about their camp, testing their guns and tending their horses, but at noon General Houston surprised everyone by convening a council of war. Otto and Yancey were assigned guard duty outside the headquarters tent, and there they overheard much heated argument and the taking of votes whose purpose they could not determine, but they did hear General Houston say what others who were near the tent would testify later that he never said: 'Well, the vote is clear. No battle today.'

At this, Quimper uttered a barnyard obscenity such as the Macnabs had never used: 'Shit! When does he intend to fight?'

At that moment a captain rushed into the tent to report with such enthusiasm that Macnab and Quimper could clearly catch every word: 'General, we've consulted the companies, one by one, and they vote unanimously for battle today,' at which Houston snarled: 'All right, fight and be damned.' But again there would be witnesses who swore that it was Houston who made all the decisions, and courageously.

There was one conversation which the eavesdroppers did not hear. Juan Seguín, the mexicano who had chosen to fight on the side of the Texicans, was the only man who would experience both the Alamo and San Jacinto; he had escaped the former tragedy because Colonel Travis sent him from the mission with a plea for aid. Now, in midafternoon on the fields of San

Jacinto, he was consulted by General Houston, who asked: 'Seguín, what will Santa Anna and his men be doing over there?' and Seguín replied: 'Siesta, what else?' Then Houston asked: 'If we were to attack at four this afternoon, where would the sun be?' and Seguín replied: 'Standing low in the heavens behind us and directly in their eyes.'

'Would they be confused?' Houston asked, and Seguín said: 'They'd be blinded.'

It was then that Sam Houston Cunctator ended what his subordinates had called 'running away' and made one of the crucial decisions of Texas history: 'Find the buglers. We attack.'

The Battle of San Jacinto cannot be understood in ordinary military terms; the statistics are too incredible. However, if the fortunes of several typical participants, Mexican and Texican, are followed, rational explanation may result.

Benito Garza had greeted General Cós enthusiastically that morning when the latter arrived in camp, not with four hundred troops as expected, but with a full five hundred. Garza was somewhat disappointed to learn that they were not tested veterans from the Goliad victory but a mass of untried recruits, many of them without shoes or regular equipment.

Seeing that they were exhausted from forced marches, he suggested to Santa Anna that they be granted an immediate siesta, even though it was still morning, and this was agreed to. Said Santa Anna: 'If they sleep well today, they'll fight well tomorrow,' and Garza went off to arrange quarters for the men.

Santa Anna himself did not sleep. Taking a small dose of his favorite narcotic, opium, he called for Garza and told him: 'See if she's out there,' and Benito went to a nearby farmhouse where a beautiful young mulatto slave girl named Emily from the Morgan plantation was being kept, and she was delighted at the prospect of spending yet another siesta with the general.

Garza delivered her to Santa Anna's tent at three-fifteen, and by ten minutes of four the entertainment she had been hired to provide was well under way.

General Victor Ripperdá, perhaps the ablest Mexican leader on the field that day, was a stiff, rigorous disciplinarian who saw no need to wear medals to display his courage. He had devoted his spare time at posts like Nacogdoches and Yucatán to the study of military principles, and one thing he had learned was that generals must anticipate the unexpected. 'One of the best ways to do this,' he had told Garza at two that afternoon, 'is to be sure you have your picket lines in place.'

To check, Ripperdá had foregone the siesta taken by others and was inspecting the entire front, gazing across the empty space toward where General Houston's troops were apparently taking their rest. He realized that when those battle-ready norteamericanos marched forth the next morning, they would be formidable: 'We'll win, of course, but it won't be easy.'

But when he reached the positions farthest forward, he was appalled to find that Santa Anna had not posted advance scouts to give warning if, for some inexplicable reason, the Texicans should decide to attack that afternoon. Such a move was unlikely, but he knew that any army within sight of the enemy ought to have its picket lines at top readiness. Santa Anna had none.

In dismay, and with some apprehension, Ripperdá moved back from where the lines should have been to consult with junior officers at the artillery batteries, and to his horror he found that none were present. Indeed, most batteries had only a scattering of untrained enlisted men who would be unable to operate the big guns if the enemy approached. When he asked where the officers were, the men said: 'Siesta.'

No longer walking but in an agitated run he dashed toward headquarters, shouting: 'Garza! We've got to see Santa Anna! Now!'

Benito, emerging from his tent without a shirt, warned: 'You musn't go in there, General. He's with the girl.'

'To hell with the girl!' Ripperdá shouted. 'Come along!' But just as they reached the dictator's tent they were startled by a savage interruption: cannon fire from the west. Barelegged, Santa Anna rushed out, crying: 'What's happening?' and Ripperdá told him: 'The enemy are attacking.'

Santa Anna, with Emily Morgan cowering naked behind him, looked westward, where he saw in astonishment that the Texicans, marching stolidly forward as if on parade, were within fifteen yards of his still-unformed lines. Not a shot had yet been fired except the cannonade from the two unexpected guns which the Texicans had somehow got hold of.

'Cós!' Santa Anna shouted. 'Where in hell is Cós?'

'Excellency,' a pale-faced aide cried as he dashed up, his eyes still grainy with sleep, 'run for your life. All is lost.'

Even now the Texican foot soldiers had not begun to fire, but another aide dashed up: 'Excellency! They're upon us!' And the Mexican staff officers stared in awe as the bold Texicans, led by Sam Houston astride his white horse with sword aloft, came resolutely forward, no gun firing, across that forward line where the pickets should have been. On they came, and when they were practically inside the Mexican lines, Houston lowered his sword, a military band began playing an old love song, and the slaughter began.

Grabbing his pants, Santa Anna took one terrified look at the carnage about to engulf his sleeping army, and fled.

On the Texican side the three representative participants had at one time known one another at Quimper's Ferry: Otto Macnab, Yancey Quimper and a tall, grim Old Testament prophet who marched resolutely into a battle he had long predicted.

He was Reverend Joel Job Harrison, the Methodist clergyman who had secretly served his flock against the day when righteous revolution would strike down the Mexican oppressors and allow the true faith to flourish. He advanced on the left flank, one of the oldest men in action that day and one of the fiercest. Quietly, insistently, he assured the younger men around him: 'Today you're doing the work of the Lord. Let nothing stop you,' and when in dreadful silence his contingent entered the Mexican lines, it was he who uttered the first cry: 'At them!' and started his long arms flailing. He did not fire the very old gun he carried, he used it like a club, and whenever the men of this flank threatened to waver, it was he who urged them on. He was unstoppable, and his men tore completely through the Mexican lines, creating a havoc which spread to other segments.

In the center Otto Macnab had volunteered, just before the battle began, to test the open ground, nearly a mile of it, and with the aid of a young fighter from Mississippi named Martin Ascot he crept forward, and to his relief he and Martin found no scouts at all, and Martin, who had studied law before coming to

Texas, whispered like a young professor: 'I do believe they've forgotten to post their forward pickets!'

So he and Otto began almost running toward the Mexican lines, and where there should have been a score of guardians they found nothing, until at last Otto stood straight up and signaled boldly that it was safe for the main line to come ahead.

With what terrible determination they came! Nobody cheered. Nobody fired his rifle. The cavalry did not engage in showy display. They just came forward, guns and knives at the ready, while a make-up band played softly a sentimental song the Texans loved:

Will you come to the bower I have shaded for you?
Our bed shall be roses all spangled with dew.
There under the bower on roses you'll lie
With a blush on your cheek but a smile in your eye!

It was perhaps symbolic of national attitudes that Santa Anna's men had marched on the Alamo to the 'Degüello,' that song of death and hatred, while the Texicans marched to their Armageddon singing a love song. But the aftermaths of the two songs would be similar.

'Hold your fire!' officers ordered as the main army caught up with Otto and Martin, and the men obeyed. Hearts pounding, and unable to believe that the Mexicans would allow them to come so close, the avengers moved on, and at this moment Otto looked about for his friend Yancey Quimper, because he wanted to fight this battle alongside someone he could depend upon, but Quimper was not in the front line, where Otto had expected he would be. He was not in the second line, either. In fact, he trailed far behind with two men who had game legs. At the time, Otto thought little of his absence.

At four sharp the Twin Sisters fired, and one set of cannon balls ricocheted through the main Mexican cannon emplacement, knocking several men off their feet. Surging forward, Otto and Ascot, with the center of the Texican line, engulfed that position and silenced the guns.

Now Otto and his new friend Martin were only eight feet – actual feet – from the Mexican lines, and before them they saw chaos: men fleeing, guns cast aside, officers missing. For just a moment Otto paused in disbelief, then coldly started firing, killing his first man with a bullet through the back. Swiftly, with practiced fingers, he reloaded and shot another. With his third bullet he hit a Mexican in the back of the neck and did not even stop to see if the man toppled over, which he did.

Fire – reload – fire – reload – fire!

Otto was seven minutes into the enemy lines before a single bullet was fired at him, and that one so wildly aimed that it posed no threat. At the end of the tenth minute of this fantastic charge, one Texican had been killed by a stray bullet, more than three hundred Mexicans had been slain, but the real horror was yet to come.

For two good reasons Otto had not been able to locate Yancey Quimper. First, the big fellow had been assigned to the extreme right flank, where Colonel Mirabeau Lamar's cavalry were supposed to wreak havoc in Santa Anna's headquarters. Second, the horsemen performed so swiftly and valiantly that Yancey and other foot soldiers who marched in their support had difficulty keeping up. The exciting prospect of an easy victory should have stifled any fears Quimper may have suffered, but when he realized he was about to enter enemy lines, where hand-to-hand fighting was under way, he froze.

Despite every desire to move forward and acquit himself well, he could not make his feet obey; he remained rigid while others rush past, shouting encouragement each to the other.

Finally he saw a Texican with a limp, and although the man was not seriously hurt, Yancey hurried to him, trying to convince both the man and himself: 'That's a terrible cut! Let me help!' The man wanted to break away the rejoin the battle, but Yancey held him, dragged him to the ground, and pretended to tend the wound.

When the fight for the main lines had been won, Yancey regained his courage and roared ahead to participate in the climax, but now he saw an affair that was truly horrible; he grew violently sick and had to turn away. Soon he was back on the ground, crouching, his face ashen, his voice whispering mechanically: 'Charge them, men! Go after them!'

What had sickened him might have nauseated anyone. At the far end of the McCormick farm, on whose broad fields this battle occurred, there stood a body of water called Peggy's Lake; it was actually a swamp, and to its supposed sanctuary had fled the remnants of Santa Anna's army; there, knee-deep in water, the Mexican survivors, with wild gestures, tried to surrender. But the enraged Texicans – shouting 'Remember the Alamo! Remember Goliad!' – waded into the swamp after them, and using rifle butts like clubs, began to shatter their skulls.

'Me no Alamo! Me no Goliad!' pleaded Mexicans who had participated in neither massacre, but no Texican would listen. Men sorely embittered by the earlier battles pressed on, killing any dark-skinned soldier who floundered in the swamp, but especially remorseless were the men who had lost friends or relatives at Goliad, for they were avenging angels, killing even some of the soldaderas trapped in the bog.

This battle, so crucial in history, lasted only eighteen minutes. The Texicans, marching against prepared positions, lost two men, killed; the Mexicans, more than six hundred – but each side had others who were mortally wounded.

Otto Macnab, exhausted from swinging his gun butt and wielding his knife, looked for Yancey to share in the glory, but again he could not find him – in the swamp, nor at the line of battle, nor in the Mexican camp. Yancey had assigned himself the rear-echelon job of guarding some captured stores, and there he was when Otto found him, cheering his fellow men on, telling them how brave they were to have faced such odds.

Otto, looking about for General Houston, was told by a Kentucky man: 'Lordy, he did fight! First horse shot out from under him, I give him mine, and on he goes, right into the guns. This horse killed, too. Shot out from between his knees, his own leg shattered, but on he goes. I like to find the son-of-a-bitch said Houston was afraid to fight.'

But Otto was near the badly wounded general when a large group of Mexican soldiers who had managed to surrender were being marched to their confinement, and Houston, seeing them through the pain which assailed him as he lay immobile, supposed them to be General Filisola bringing up a thousand reinforcements. 'All is lost! All is lost!' Houston cried. 'Have I a friend in this world? Colonel Wharton, I am wounded, I am wounded. Have I a friend in this world?'

'General,' Wharton said, 'you have many friends. What you see are our prisoners.'

When the doctors cut away Houston's right boot, blood welled over the top, and they saw for themselves how seriously he had been wounded at the start of the battle.

How had Benito Garza and his general, Victor de Ripperdá, conducted themselves during this collapse of mexicano morale? Fighting side by side, always endeavouring to stabilize their crumbling lines, they tried vainly to rally their troops. When they saw the center about to collapse, they rushed there, much too late, and escaped death from the Texicans' relentless fire only by shifting to where Colonel Lamar's cavalry were creating havoc.

Doing whatever they could to stanch the hemorrhaging of the mexicano effort, they shouted, implored, and even shot one officer who was abandoning his post, but they accomplished nothing. Finally, when Lamar's cavalry came at them, they were parted. Garza was driven into the swamp, where he sought to surrender. Ripperdá ran to the southern perimeter, where he found protection among some trees, whence he made a courageous journey on foot to intercept General Urrea's army, which would arrive at San Jacinto eager for battle, but two days late.

In the aftermath, strange things happened. General Santa Anna, running through shoulder-high weeds attended only by an aide, came upon an abandoned shack on the McCormick plantation in which he found some old clothes which he put on over his uniform. Fearing that the presence of an obvious attendant might reveal his rank, he set out by himself to hide in bushes until daylight, when he hoped to escape across the shallow streams that enclosed the battlefield.

Otto Macnab, veteran now of the Mexican horrors at Goliad and the American retaliation at San Jacinto, tried to erase both from his mind. They had not happened. He had not participated in either; he had killed no one. At dusk, exhausted, he lay down and slept as if he were a boy back in María Campbell's dog-run.

Martin Ascot, his battlefield friend, did not sleep; seated by a fire, he produced the pen and paper he always kept with him and wrote one of the most reliable accounts of this amazing battle:

San Jacinto River Republic of Texas 21 June 1836

Reverend Father,

Yet once again do I take pen in hand, by way of writing you a few lines to inform you that with God's help I survived the mighty battle, hoping you will inform Miss Betsy Belle of same.

In my last letter I told you of the heroic but doomed stand of our men at the Alamo; by now you will also have heard from the New Orleans papers about the shameless massacre at Goliad.

You would have been ashamed, Sir, of what happened next. Our Texican army, defeated twice at the Alamo and Goliad, started a shameful retreat, allowing General Santa Anna to pillage and burn the entire countryside. One town after another went up in flames and we did nothing to stop it, until we sometimes felt that all Texas was ablaze.

I was convinced that when General Santa Anna caught up with us he was going to whip us badly. But I was wrong. With extraordinary skill General Houston led us into a spot surrounded by water, forcing General Santa Anna to engage in battle at an unpromising spot and well before the rest of the Mexican army could catch up.

Then came the immortal battle! At four o'clock in the afternoon of this day, the Mexicans were resting in their tents, convinced that we would not dare attack until the next day, if ever, for they had 1400 trained men and we had few more than 800 irregulars. But I can tell you, sir, that we marched confidently into battle. We felt that God was on our side. We felt that terrible wrongs must be avenged. And we felt that the future history of this part of the world depended upon our behavior.

On our flank the musicians played *Yankee Doodle*, which inspired us no end. The band had but two members, a Czech named Fred with his fife and a nigger boy named Dick with his drum. They played lustily and were very brave. I carried that good Kentucky gun you gave me when I left and during the sixteen minutes of battle I was able to fire it six times, for as you know, it was never easy to reload. Young Otto Macnab, who fought at my side, had lost his father at Goliad, and in his fury he was able to fire at least twenty times. Like a little machine of vengeance he stalked forward, loading and firing, and with each shot he muttered 'Remember Goliad' or 'This one for Goliad.' We were now so close to the Mexicans that we might have reached out and shaken hands with them, and when they saw us stop reloading and move forward with our rifle butts, they became terrified and started running toward a swamp at their rear.

General Houston galloped up and cried 'Do not kill any more. Take them prisoner.' But when he was gone a Methodist minister name of Harrison who was fighting in the swamp with us, a real old man, must of been near fifty, shouted to Otto and me 'Boys, you know how to take prisoners! With the butt of your gun over their heads and your knife at their throats.'

All us Texicans were now in the swamp, clubbing the Mexicans over the head and causing them to drown, hundreds of them. On the third smack I broke your fine gun, but I think I can get it fixed, so I took my hunting knife and started cutting throats. Otto would club a man, knock him sideways, and I would grab him by the hair and finish him off, and we must have handled a dozen this way, for Otto was a fierce fighter. But late in the battle when I grabbed a Mexican on my own and was about to cut his throat from behind, Otto gave a great cry 'No! No!' and when I put my knife to the man's throat, Otto clubbed me over the head with his gun.

When I revived, very sore in the head I can tell you, there was Otto standing over me with his gun. The Mexican, a man with dark skin and a mustache, was hiding behind him. Otto told me that the Mexican was Benito Garza and that he had saved Otto's life at Goliad. I had the strange feeling that this Garza was looking at me as if he were a rattlesnake, seething inside with hatred which must some day spit forth.

At the end of that last paragraph I fell asleep, and I'm sure you can understand why, but I awoke this morning to a magnificent piece of news. One of our men, name of Yancey Quimper, by a feat of arms which he says was extraordinary, has captured Santa Anna, and we have him now in a tent being guarded by seven. Otto and I and all the men around wanted to kill Santa Anna, and we were downright angry when General Houston treated him like an honorable foe, giving him better food than we're getting. I was one of a committee of six who met with Houston and told him 'We want to hang that man,' but he reasoned with us and said 'Our battle is only half won. Bigger ones may lie ahead, and I plan to use Santa Anna as our principal cannon.'

My friend Otto would not accept this, and when he told General Houston what he himself had seen at Goliad and how his own father had been run down like a coyote, tears came to General Houston's eyes and with his forefinger he traced the scar on Otto's face and asked 'Did you get that at Goliad?' and Otto said 'I did, Sir, killing a man who was trying to kill me,' and Houston said 'It is your badge of honor, son, and mine will be to treat Santa Anna better than he treated us.'

Tonight I am very afraid, Sir, and I hope that you will pray for me, and for Otto and for all the brave Texicans who fought so many with so few, for if the Mexicans assemble their army in this area, they can still overwhelm us.

It is rumored that if I survive the next great battles, I shall be entitled to many acres of the best land in Texas, and this is a country with a potential for greatness. Inform Miss Betsy Belle, if you will, that she should start now to prepare the things she will want to bring to Texas, for Otto tells me that he once traveled along some excellent land on the Brazos River and he will show me how to claim on it. If I live, Sir, I shall post haste to Mississippi and marry Miss Betsy Belle the morning I arrive, and please to inform her of same.

Your loving son in God,
Martin

P.S. Do not tell Mother or Betsy Belle about the knife work in the swamp. They might not understand.

Ascot's report of Quimper's heroism in capturing Santa Anna did not reflect the truth. On the morning after the battle,

Quimper and two buddies, one a young fellow from Kentucky named Sylvester, had quit trying to capture Mexican survivors and were hunting deer for the mess. When they saw six or seven bucks suddenly take flight for no apparent cause, Sylvester, a skilled huntsman, said: 'Somethin' spooked them deer,' and when they investigated, Yancey saw a man huddling on the ground and trying to hide in some bushes, dressed in old clothes.

He was about to shoot him when Sylvester shouted: 'The battle's over, for Christ's sake. Let him live.'

'Get up, you swine!' Yancey shouted, but the quivering man remained on the ground, whimpering. The men dragged their prisoner into camp, and he would have been thrown into the ordinary compound except that sharp-eyed Yancey saw several Mexicans begin to salute.

'Stop that!' one man commanded his fellow prisoners, but it was too late.

'He's a general, by God!' Yancey called, and when the man was shoved forward the Mexicans in the compound began to kiss his hands and call him El Presidente.

'We've got Santy Anny!' Quimper shouted, and he spent the rest of that day parading about the Texican tents, announcing himself as 'the man who captured Santy Anny.'

Otto, who was near General Houston's cot when the Mexican general was brought before him, heard Santa Anna's first words: 'Felicidades, mi General, ha derrotado El Napoleón del Oeste.'

'What did he say?' Houston said.

Otto translated: ' "You have defeated the Napoleon of the West." '

'Tell him to sit down.'

Houston had more difficulty with another visitor, Mrs Peggy McCormick, owner of the farm on which the historic battle had taken place: 'Tell me, who's going to bury all these dead bodies cluttering up my place?'

'We'll bury the Texicans,' Houston replied graciously as he adjusted his throbbing leg.

'How about those hundreds of Mexicans?'

'Why, madam, your land will be famed in history as the spot where the glorious battle was fought.'

573

'To the devil with your glorious victory. Take off your stinking Mexicans.'

'That's Santa Anna's problem.'

She demanded to see the general, and when he was produced she asked him in Spanish: 'And what do you intend doing about all those bodies?' and he replied: 'The fortunes of war, madam. I can do nothing.'

The true miracle of the Battle of San Jacinto transpired some days after it ended, because a greater danger persisted than the one Houston had conquered. The Mexicans had under arms in Tejas some five thousand of their best troops, led by skilled generals: Filisola the Italian, Woll the Frenchman, and Ripperdá from Yucatán, who had joined forces with Urrea, the victor at Goliad. If they coalesced, and they were not far separated, they could drive Houston right to the borders of Louisiana, and annihilate him if they overtook him.

But now Houston's brilliance showed itself, for by the force of his remarkable personality he kept Santa Anna alive, appreciating the fact that if he allowed him to be hanged, as most of the Texicans wished, the man would become an instant martyr, a hero who had to be avenged, just as the martyrs of the Alamo and Goliad had had to be avenged. But if he could be kept alive, a prisoner in humiliating disgrace, his martyrdom would be avoided; also, he would be available to issue orders to the other generals to disband their troops and go home. As dictator of Mexico he would still command their obedience.

So with a skill that Metternich or Talleyrand would have applauded, this Tennessee cardsharp used Santa Anna the way a long-practiced fisherman uses a fly to trap a trout. He coddled him, he flattered him, he even arranged for him to be sent to Washington to interview the President of the United States, but first he obtained from him orders to his generals to go home.

Miraculously, they obeyed. This powerful army, which could have won so many battles, dislodged so many plans, supinely obeyed their imprisoned leader – when the whole tradition of war dictated that they ignore any command issued by a man in the clutches of an enemy – and took their men quietly out of Tejas, which would know that lovely Spanish designation no more. It was now Texas. By the merest thread of chance it had become Texas, and so it would remain.

Of the three men from the Victoria dog-runs, each lost his battle: Campbell in the Alamo, Macnab at Goliad, and Garza in the swamps at San Jacinto. But each contributed to the grandeur upon which the Republic of Texas was founded.

For the living, the fortunes generated by this battle were both mundane and dramatic. Yancey Quimper appropriated the title 'Hero of San Jacinto.' Peggy McCormick, in the years following the war, earned tidy sums from selling the endless battle mementos scattered across her farm, but both Pamela Mann and Juan Seguín ran into trouble.

After the war Mrs Mann moved to the burgeoning town of Houston, where she ran the Mansion House, a disreputable hotel noted for its brawls, duels and repeated police raids, which she handled deftly with her two pistols. However, an especially blatant disregard for the law resulted in a court trial, and she received the death sentence. It was commuted because of her bold behavior during the war.

Seguín started out famously as the mayor of San Antonio, but his tenure was turbulent, and he fled to Mexico. Later he returned as a member of a Mexican invading army that captured San Antonio and held it briefly. A strong opponent to union with the United States, he did his best to make Texas once more a part of Mexico, and died, disappointed, at the age of eighty-three.

Benito Garza, languishing in a prisoner-of-war camp, had to relinquish his dream of ever becoming Gobernador de la Provincia de Tejas; he spent his idle hours brooding over his opposition to the Texicans, an obsession that would intensify and never abate. And Joel Job Harrison acquired the right to conduct Methodist services openly, which he did in the wooden church he built at Quimper's Ferry, where he and his bride waited for the reopening of a ferry to carry travelers back and forth across the Brazos.

Immortality was visited upon the least likely participant in the battle. Emily Morgan, who had diverted General Santa Anna's attention that hot afternoon just before the charge of the Texicans, became celebrated in song as 'The Yellow Rose of Texas' and few who sing it in romantic settings realize that they are serenading the memory of a mulatto slave.

Meteoric was the rise of Mirabeau Buonaparte Lamar: 25 March 1836, return to Texas; 20 April, private foot soldier; 21 April, cavalry colonel; 5 May, Secretary of War in the cabinet of President Sam Houston; 24 June, major general; 25 June, commander-in-chief of the entire Texas army; 5 September, vice-president of the republic. And even greater glories lay ahead.

And Otto Macnab went his quiet but very determined way.

... Task Force

As soon as the staff announced that our December meeting would be held near Houston at the monument marking the Battle of San Jacinto, we members decided that for this important session, no outside authority would be imported. Instead, we would invite the general public to a convocation at which we five would be seated at a table with microphones. Each would offer a brief opening statement regarding the significance of the Texas revolution, after which the visitors would be invited to make such observations as they wished, or pose questions that bothered them.

We anticipated a lively meeting, with perhaps two dozen local history aficionados who would know more about San Jacinto than we did. It was our hope to make them feel that they had shared in decision-making regarding their schools, but when we approached the monument – 'There she stands, five hundred and seventy-one feet high, taller than the Washington one' – we found a line waiting outside and standees crowding the inside. 'What's up?' I asked a guard, and he said: 'The experts you invited are here but so is this mob. They're awaiting to see Ransom Rusk,' and when I asked why, he said: 'They've never seen a real, live billionaire,' but a woman who overheard this corrected him: 'We want to see Lorenzo Quimper and his boots. He's such a dear.'

When the last person had been wedged into the hall and loudspeakers installed for those outside, I opened the session with brief remarks, commending the condition of the monument and reminding visitors that when our meeting ended they would be served punch aboard the battleship *Texas* moored nearby: 'Unique among our great warships, the *Texas* patrolled the coastline during five major landings in World War II. Texans like to participate in major events.'

Miss Cobb started our presentation with a reminder that when Texas patriots defended their rights in 1836, they not only won their own freedom but also set in motion those currents which would, a decade later, secure liberation for New Mexico, Arizona and California: 'The geographical shape of the United States today was ensured by the heroic actions of a few Texicans who resisted General Santa Anna's brutal oppressions on this very field.'

Ransom Rusk told the audience: 'I think we must recognize that even if the Texas revolution had not occurred, states like Arizona and California might have stumbled their way into the Union, because of local conditions. In the case of Texas, it was essential that some kind of stable buffer be established between the anglo-dominated Mississippi River and the Mexican-dominated Rio Grande. During the nineteenth century we provided that buffer, and at times we seemed more like a separate nation mediating between two larger nations than a typical American state like Virginia or Ohio. And I think that Texas will always have that peculiar character. It's a part of the United States, unquestionably, but it has its own personality, something unique and wonderful, which the rest of this nation needs.'

Lorenzo Quimper, recognized by the crowd as a descendant of the Hero of San Jacinto, rather neatly down-played his ancestor's performance while at the same time implying that without the heroic Yancey, the battle would probably have been lost. Starting out with what he called 'my highfalutin' Texan,' he sounded like Pericles delivering his oration on the grandeur of Athens: 'On solemn days like this, when we celebrate our great victory, we must remember the true character of the Texicans who won freedom for us. Five times they faced the Mexican army, and four times they lost by tremendous margins: Alamo, Goliad, Sante Fe and the Mier Expedition, crushing defeats which might have disheartened the bravest. But mixed with those defeats was a resplendent victory, San Jacinto.' Here the audience broke into cheers, which encouraged Lorenzo to relax his speech a bit: 'Us Texans have always had that basic character. We can absorb one defeat

577

after another: drought, financial collapse, heartbreakin' loss in the Civil War, misbehavior of elected officials . . .' At the height of his impassioned oratory he hesitated for just a moment, half smiled, and added: 'Even losin' in football in Oklahoma!' When the crowd stamped and whistled he dropped into pure ranch-hand Texan: 'But us Texans, we always recover. Fact is, we don't never know when we're whupped, which is why we so seldom git whupped.' Il Magnifico was the hit of the show, an authentic voice of Texas.

Efraín Garza took a more sober approach: 'My ancestor fought at San Jacinto, too. In the army of Santa Anna.' Silence. 'So it is highly probable that the early Quimper faced the early Garza that day, perhaps right where we sit. But now we're friends. We're one people.' The crowd cheered and stamped again. 'But as so often happens, the battle settled only part of the problem that had caused it in the first place. It determined, as Miss Cobb has so accurately stated, that a huge corner of Mexico would ultimately become a part of the United States.' More applause. 'But it did not decide how the new addition would be incorporated. What theory of law would prevail? How would my ancestors who had lived here for many generations be received in the Union? And how would their rights be preserved? Some of these questions still wait to be settled.'

These last remarks were not well received by the patriots gathered to honor the Texan victory, because every anglo in the audience, and the audience was ninety-nine percent anglo, believed that the questions Garza raised *had* been settled, so I felt it incumbent upon me as chairman to come to Garza's defense: 'We wanted a Hispanic spokesman on our Task Force, and as you can see, we got a good one.' Two people clapped. 'Every battle has aftermaths, both for the victor and for the loser. Professor Garza has identified some of those which still perplex our state, and now we will accept questions or statements from the audience.'

To my disappointment, the first man to rise was not one of the local experts; he was a belligerent rancher from South Texas, who got us off to a miserable start: 'If Professor Garza don't like how we handled affairs after San Jacinto, why don't he go back to Mexico where he come from?'

I pointed out that since Garza's family had lived in Texas

578

for a much longer time than any other family represented this day, Texas *was* where he came from, but that did not satisfy the protestor: 'If he's Mexican, he accepts the rules we lay down. San Jacinto settled that.'

Eagerly I searched the audience for a more gracious speaker, and my eye lit upon a woman who had written two small books about the San Jacinto area, and she asked: 'If Mexican troops defeated us four times and we defeated them only once, why was San Jacinto so determinative?' and Quimper had a prompt answer: 'Ma'am, quite often it depends on timin' . . . and luck. When we won at San Jacinto, Santa Anna was far from home base and gettin' worried. Psychology, ma'am, sometimes it turns the tables.'

A Houston oil man, friend of Rusk's, had for some years supported scholars working in early Texas history and wanted to know: 'Was this battle as important as you claim?' and Ransom responded: 'I admitted in my opening remarks that great historical currents were already under way which might have carried part of Mexico into our orbit, whether we won her at San Jacinto or not, but the magnitude of those currents and their ultimate significance were intensified by our victory. It caught the imagination of the American people. It showed a light in the darkness. It stimulated the later concept of Manifest Destiny. It made conquest to the Pacific inevitable. Important, Tom? It was far more important than I stated. It was the major gift of Texas to the United States. It awakened patriotism . . . and the idea that we Americans had a duty, a responsibility, to bring democracy to the entire continent.'

Tom persisted: 'I was taught that those things came as a result of the Mexican war in 18 and 46.'

'They did,' Rusk agreed, almost eagerly. 'But remember the irresistible sequence. The Alamo led to San Jacinto. San Jacinto led to a free republic. The free republic led to 1846. And 1846 led to the United States boundaries as we know them today. And never forget, Tom, it all started with a handful of the bravest men this land ever produced, who said at the Alamo: "We will die rather than surrender our freedom."' He paused. 'They said it, Tom, and they did it.' The crowd roared its approval, and Rusk added: 'That may still be our major gift. Courage. Optimism.'

Another woman asked: 'Why do you men always claim it was only men who made the difference?' and Quimper replied: 'Because in battle, ma'am, it's the men who do the job,' but Miss Cobb interrupted: 'That's a cogent question, madam, and in my book our Mr Quimper's other ancestor, Mattie Quimper, who seems to have done most of the work, who kept her family afloat when her husband was away, and who finally destroyed her ferry and burned her inn to keep them from the Mexicans, was a greater Texas hero than her son, Yancey, who captured Santa Anna when the battle had already ended.' Several women applauded, and after acknowledging their support, Miss Cobb resumed: 'Texas has always underrated its women and I suppose it always will. Therefore, we must, when it's appropriate, remind our men, as you have just done, madam, that we, too, helped build this state.'

Quimper leaped to his feet: 'Let me tell you! I'm just as proud of Mattie Quimper as I am of her heroic son Yancey.' The women applauded this generous concession.

After twenty minutes of similar statements, a thoughtful man rose and said: 'I'd like to return to that first question. "What patterns will the anglos and the Mexicans devise for sharing our state?" And I'd like you to answer, Mr Chairman.'

I spent nearly a minute with my hands folded over my chin, for I realized that this meeting would be the first to be widely reported and I did not wish to damage our Task Force before it was well launched. I wanted to say exactly the right thing, so facing the two television cameras, I spoke carefully: 'I could well be the only person in this hall whose ancestor fought in the Alamo. Moses Barlow marched from Gonzales to die there. So I've had to contemplate your question many times, sir, and I've concluded that no heavier cloud threatens our state than our reluctance to define the future relationship between the so-called Mexican and the anglo. This uncertainty keeps us fragmented into unwarranted cells, and I see no solution to this ugly estrangement.

'This morning we've heard two conflicting views. "Critical battles settle everything" or "They settle very little." The truth is that a successful battle can sometimes establish general direction for several decades, but basic, long-term results evolve slowly ... inevitably ... remorselessly. San Jacinto determined that Texas would be ruled in the immediate future by anglos and not Mexicans. But the long-term relationship between the two groups is far from settled.'

'Are you saying that the Mexicans might ultimately take over . . .?'

'Not at all. What I'm saying is that Appomattox determined that the North would establish the rules for our Union . . . for the next hundred years. The North would determine everything, it seemed, and would do so perpetually. But look at the situation today. Where is the power flowing? Always to the South. Where are the seats in Congress coming? To Texas and Florida. Where would you like to live if you were young and active and hopeful? Vermont? Or the Sun Belt?' The audience cheered.

'Battles can be terribly important. Thank God, we won and not Hitler. I'm glad that in the Far East we decided things, not Japan. No man on this earth ever fought a more just war than Chester Nimitz of Texas did in the Pacific in 1943.' This brought more cheers. 'But look at Europe and the Pacific today. The losers in battle are the victors in peace, while the victors seem to be losing. And that's because it is not the climactic battle but the slow, inexorable force of history that determines the future.'

We had discussed these historical truths for some time when a wiry man in his sixties rose, caught my eye, and then made a statement so startling that few who heard it could believe: 'I'm proud to be here today, in the presence of Lorenzo Quimper. My grandfather fought beside Yancey Quimper on this field in 1836.'

'Did you say your grandfather?'

'I did. I'm Norman Robbins, born 1922. My father was Sam Robbins, born in these parts in 1879. His father was Jared Robbins, born in 1820, aged sixteen at the battle.'

'That's right,' a woman who specialized in genealogies called from a back row. 'The two Robbins men married late.'

Suddenly Texas history became very real, and we looked in awe at a man whose family bridged so many great events. How young the state of Texas seemed at that moment! No one in Massachusetts had a grandfather who had fought at Concord Bridge, but Norman Robbins had heard from his father a firsthand account of the launching of Texas.

Miss Cobb snapped us out of our reveries: 'Let's go to the battleship for our punch,' and as we walked across the field we could almost hear the rifles firing, because the fighting seemed so recent.

Rusk, walking with his friend the Houston oilman, said: 'Our state contains hidden powers which manifest themselves in unexpected ways at unexpected times,' and he led us onto the *Texas*.

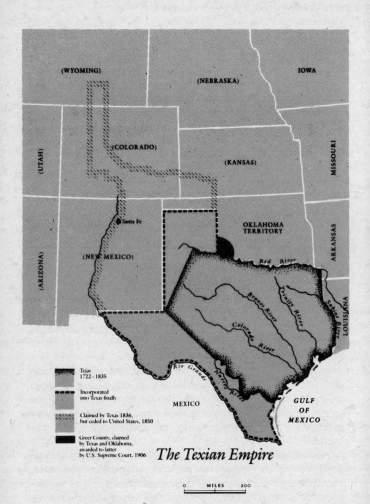

Tejas
1722–1835

Incorporated
into Texas finally

Claimed by Texas 1836,
but ceded to United States, 1850

Greer County, claimed
by Texas and Oklahoma,
awarded to latter
by U.S. Supreme Court, 1906

(WYOMING)

IOWA

(NEBRASKA)

(UTAH)

(COLORADO)

MISSOURI

(KANSAS)

Santa Fe

OKLAHOMA
TERRITORY

ARKANSAS

(ARIZONA)

(NEW MEXICO)

Red River

LOUISIANA

Trinity River

Brazos River

Sabine River

Colorado River

Rio Grande

MEXICO

Nueces River

GULF
OF
MEXICO

The Texian Empire

0   MILES   200

VII

THE TEXIANS

When the sovereign nation of Texas, standing completely alone and allied to no one, inaugurated Sam Houston as its first elected president, Otto Macnab was fourteen. Thus he and the new republic would grow up together, and the major problem of each would be the same – to find a home: Otto, one in which to attain that love and security he had sought since first seeing those lights shining across the Ohio River; Texas, a secure place within the family of nations.

It was a natural affiliation, Otto and Texas, because the two had much in common. Both were self-reliant, both tended to solve problems with the gun, both believed in simple, forward action rather than in philosophical speculation, both were suspicious of Mexicans and despised Indians, and both vaguely wanted to do the right thing. Most important, both entertained lofty aspirations they could not always voice or define. It would be a lively decade as these two matured.

The nation quickly found that conducting a successful revolution was relatively easy compared with organizing a stable society thereafter. Along a hard-drinking frontier it often seemed that the major problem was to find any official who was sober, President Houston being especially addicted to the bottle.

Nevertheless, the fledgling nation made a series of critical decisions which helped establish its permanent character. Fiercely republican and abhorring the dictatorial chaos witnessed while part of Mexico, it decreed that its president would be allowed to serve only three years and then be required to sit out a term before being eligible to run again. Clergymen were forbidden to serve in the legislature, and slavery was not only permitted but protected: 'No free Negro shall reside in Texas

585

'without consent of Congress.'

The basic attitudes of the nation could be summarized in a series of adjectives: individualistic, aggressive, volatile, rural, egalitarian insofar as white Anglo-Saxon Protestants were concerned, and often violent; but the overriding characteristic during these early years would be national poverty. Texas had the bad luck to start its history as a free nation just as financial panic paralyzed the United States and slowed down transactions in Europe. With no solid economy on which to construct a currency and minimal trade on which to levy taxes, the poverty-stricken republic stumbled along, always on the verge of bankruptcy, and since the United States had no paper money or coinage to spare, Texas had to depend upon the most dubious banknotes issued by entities not much more solvent than it was. Currency issued by states like Mississippi and Arkansas circulated at fifty-percent discount, with only the more solid notes of New Orleans and Alabama retaining a value of a hundred cents to the dollar. Mexican money was good, but most prized of all were the notes of Great Britain and France. Even so, the rule among merchants was: 'If you take money in before eleven, pass it along to somebody else before five.'

Of course, Texas did try to float its own paper money, but the result was disastrous: issued at a hundred cents on the dollar, it was immediately discounted to eighty cents, then to sixty cents before it stabilized at about fifty cents. And that was the so-called 'solid dollar backed by collateral.'

But the nation did have one sovereign currency which kept it afloat: millions of acres of unassigned land, and it employed the most ingenious devices for turning this land into cash. It gave free acreage to anyone who had served in its armed forces. It lured residents of the United States with roseate promises. And it hired a firm of New Orleans speculators, Toby and Brother, to print and sell certificates entitling any purchaser to a spacious homestead. The history of Texas in these formative years was an account of how men without money used land to keep afloat.

In the social life of the republic there were subtle changes. People began dropping the name Texican; they became Texians. Spanish accents on some words were eliminated and names simplified, so that the old Béjar became Bexar; Bexar became San Antonio. The Río Grande lost its accent, and all

586

other ríos lost not only their accent but also their Spanish designation; henceforth they would be rivers. The lovely word *arroyo* became *creek*. As if to symbolize the transition from Spanish lyricism to Kentucky realism, poetic family names like Trévino became Trevino for the anglos, and the music was lost.

To facilitate administration, counties had to be established, and in time almost all the heroes participating in the battles were honored by having counties named after them: Austin, Bonham, Bowie, Crockett, Fannin, Houston, Lamar, Rusk, Travis; and all but Travis also had towns named in their honor. To the delight of future schoolchildren, Deaf Smith's county would retain his full name.

The names of certain famous places also became enshrined as counties: Bexar, Goliad, Gonzales and Victoria, with San Jacinto following later. The first-named was awarded an area much larger than many European nations; from Bexar County, in decades to come, well over a hundred normal-sized counties would be carved.

By this lavish display of honors Texas served notice that it took its history seriously and sought to enshrine its nobler moments. Massachusetts and Virginia produced many national leaders, but they did not become the warp and woof of existence as did the heroes of Texas; Pennsylvania had its Valley Forge and New York its Saratoga, but they never became a living part of their region's religion the way the Alamo did in Texas. From the start the new Texians proclaimed, and in a rather loud voice: 'Look at us. We're different.'

Among the counties formed in the first flush of victory was one named after Zave Campbell, whose exploits atop the wall were recited by both Señora Mordecai Marr and Joe, the Negro slave belonging to Colonel Travis, both of whom were spared by Santa Anna. Both told of Zave's Ajax-like defense, but the most telling testimony came from a Mexican captain, who said: 'There was this tall old man whose name was called out as I bore down upon him. "Xavier! Watch out!" someone shouted as I ran him through, and when we counted the dead bodies of our soldiers around his feet, there were nine.'

It was agreed that Xavier County should be established west of the Brazos River, but how the name should be pronounced was not so quickly settled. Older settlers who spoke Spanish

587

wanted to call it Hah-vee-ehr, with accent on the last syllable, but newcomers promptly changed that to Ecks-ah-ver, with accent on the second. Within a few months it was agreed that the county was Za-veer, with a heavy accent on the second syllable, and so it became. Like many of the early counties, and like more than half of those that were to follow, Xavier County had no principal town; there was a miserable crossroads settlement of nine houses called Campbell, and it was designated the county seat, but it would never dominate thinking or become as important as the county it served. A settler rarely said: 'I live in Campbell.' He almost invariably said: 'I live in Xavier County.'

Young Macnab became one of the first new settlers in Xavier. Reluctant to return to Victoria and a Mexican way of life with his adopted mother and aunt, he jumped at the invitation when his companion-in-arms Martin Ascot proposed: 'Let's take our free land side by side, along the river you told me about,' and when this was agreed, the Mississippian said further: 'Otto, let's go to Galveston and meet the ship when Betsy Belle arrives!'

In his battlefield letter to his father he had promised to go to Mississippi to claim her, but the problems of land acquisition had become so demanding and in unforeseen ways so complex that he had sent her an ardent letter: 'I simply cannot leave Texas now. It would be more practical for you to come here, and we shall marry as you step off the steamer.'

So off the two friends went, down the Brazos River in a flat-bottomed scow, then up to the fledgling town of Houston, where they reported to Buffalo bayou for a sailing ship, which carried them across the wide bay to Galveston, the principal settlement in the republic. They were standing on the improvised dock when Betsy Belle's schooner braved the treacherous sandbar that both protected Galveston's harbor and sank unwary ships that could not find the only safe passage.

As soon as Otto saw Betsy Belle in her blue hat with streamers and white dress with ruffles, he knew he was going to like her, for she looked both like a young bride and like the future mother of children. 'You're lucky!' he whispered to Ascot, and he felt even more approval when he stood beside Martin as the Galveston minister intoned the marriage ceremony. When the clergyman, a Methodist with bright eyes, told Martin: 'You may kiss the bride,' Ascot did so, then told Otto: 'You must kiss her, too,' and the fourteen-year-old boy, blushing furiously, did so.

The three partners, for so they termed themselves, spent only two nights in Galveston, for they were eager to locate and take up residence on the land the government was giving them for their service at San Jacinto. Purchasing three horses with funds from the dowry Betsy Belle had brought from Mississippi, they rode the eighty-eight miles back to Xavier County, where Otto identified the land he wanted the partnership to claim, and both he and Martin stepped off the six hundred and forty acres side by side, to which each was entitled, when across the field, riding a very small donkey, came an old comrade who was about to save them from making a serious mistake.

It was Yancey Quimper shouting: 'Wait a minute! Wait a minute!' and when he halted his donkey he gallantly raised Betsy Belle's hand to his lips: 'All Texas is honored to receive such a beauty from Alabama.'

'Mississippi,' Betsy Belle said.

'What are you men doing?'

'Locating our six-forty's,' Ascot replied.

'Six-forty's!' Quimper exploded, and before the day was out he was leading his friends to the county seat at Campbell, where his good friend Judge Phinizy, formerly of the Arkansas bench, would be certifying land entitlements.

During the trip Yancey brought his friends from San Jacinto up to date regarding his fortunes: 'Many people consider me the principal citizen of Xavier County,' but what exactly he did, the travelers could not discern. At twenty-four he was what rural people called 'a fine figure of a man,' tall, rather fleshy and pale of complexion. He seemed to lack strength, as if one or two critical bones had been omitted, but he offset this by a warm, radiant smile that he flashed at anyone he wanted to impress.

He was always dressed in accordance with another ancient truism – 'clothes make the man' – and he had lately purchased a big Mexican hat with a very broad brim. It was precisely sized to match his build, so that when he came picking his way down the dusty streets in Campbell, he proclaimed himself, without speaking, to be 'our leading citizen.'

He had been raised by his Tennessee father to speak rather good English, but after the death of his parents his association with the rude soldiers of the revolution had encouraged him to acquire their informal speech habits, so that now his sentences were colorfully ungrammatical and his words those of the barnyard and ranch. But he spoke with marked effectiveness, often and loud. As a verified hero of the battle in which Texas had won her freedom, he felt himself entitled, and sometimes obligated, to express his opinion on almost everything, but he did so with such an attractive mixture of gravity and wit that he did not offend. He was, in this rural setting, a man of substance.

'For a while after Independence,' he said as they neared Campbell, 'I tried to rebuild the inn at Quimper's Ferry. Impossible to get aholt of any money. Me, a hero in battle, a man with a good reputation, unable to find a cent.'

'What happened to the inn?'

'Charred posts, stickin' out of the ground.'

'Were you able to sell the land?'

'Sell?' Quimper turned sideways on his donkey and told Betsy Belle: 'My mammy gave me one piece of solid advice: "Get aholt of land and never let it go. Burn your house, even burn your Bible, but never let nobody touch your land."'

Judge Leander Phinizy, an unkempt, bearded man with dark sunken eyes that brooded as if they had witnessed all the chicanery the world could provide, had risen to become a major luminary of the Texas bar after a rather devious start. Expelled from William and Mary College in Virginia for 'prolonged, offensive and noisy drunkenness,' he had made his way to Georgia, where such behavior was tolerated. After marrying a local girl whose parents had acreage, he utilized his earlier schooling by reading for law, but before he was accepted by the Georgia bar he became involved in a malodorous land fraud involving widows and found it expedient to take his unquestioned talents farther west. Settling ultimately in the freer air of Arkansas, he announced himself as a lawyer, and when his credentials were requested he stated simply that he had read for law in the offices of 'that notable Georgia jurist Xerxes Noltworthy.' When mail addressed to his supposed mentor produced no reply, Phinizy explained: 'Poor man shot himself. Cancer of the esophagus.'

On the Arkansas frontier he proved himself to be a good lawyer, and after notable success in helping to establish order in rough territories he was promoted to judge, but his probate of certain wills subjected him to unfortunate scrutiny, and he deemed it best to emigrate to Texas. Here at last his deportment was circumspect, and he became, as Quimper had said, 'a shining light of our judicial system.'

Judge Phinizy held court in a one-room, dirt-floored hovel whose only window was a rude hole covered by a piece of calf hide that had been hammered in bear grease until it became remarkably translucent. There were a table and an armchair for the judge, carved by himself, two rickety chairs for plaintiffs, and a large bucket into which the judge shot tobacco juice often and with enviable skill, for it stood some distance from the bench.

Phinizy conducted trials with the aid of a heavy woven-leather riding crop, which he beat furiously against his table when rendering even the simplest decision, and now, as Martin and Otto, as the principals, took the two chairs and Yancey and Betsy Belle stood by the door, Judge Phinizy lashed about with his crop and shouted: 'Goddamnit, is there no courtesy left in the world? Somebody give that beautiful example of Southern womanhood a chair,' and after this was done, the judge explained: 'For jury trials we bring in those two benches.'

Smiling at the claimants, he said: 'You're very fortunate, young men, to have Mr Quimper here to guide you. The Republic of Texas was about to award him the customary six hundred and forty acres which all you heroes get, when he pointed out to the visiting land commissioner that he was entitled to rather more.'

He paused dramatically, and remained silent for so long that Ascot realized that a question was in order, so he asked: 'How much did he get?'

'Well, his dead father should have had a league-and-a-labor from the Mexican government, but the papers were lost in the fire. He himself was assured six hundred and forty acres because of his valiant service at San Jacinto. And under our new constitution he had head rights to his own league-and-a-labor. He gets an additional six-forty for having served six months in the army. That made a total of ten thousand four hundred and ninety acres.'

Admiringly, Martin and Otto turned to nod at Yancey, who held up his hand as if to say 'Wait!' The judge continued: 'Where Mr Quimper showed his brilliance, he asked the commissioner and me: "Isn't the government awarding six hundred and forty acres to the heirs of anyone who died at either the Alamo or Goliad?" The commissioner said: "Yes, but your father was dead before those battles took place," and Mr Quimper explained: "Yes, but my mother wasn't, because she died fighting off Mexican soldiers at her ferry to save General Houston's retreat." So we gave him her award, too. Total? Eleven thousand one hundred and thirty acres.'

Otto gasped, but Martin, who was fascinated by law, asked: 'And what does this mean for us?' and Judge Phinizy said: 'If Mr Quimper is prepared to vouch for Mr Macnab's heroism, I think something can be worked out.'

'He was more than brave,' Yancey intoned. 'Whenever I looked back, there he was, keepin' close.'

'Texas wants to reward its heroes, Mr Macnab ... How old are you?'

Without hesitation Otto said, 'Eighteen.'

'You'll probably get your height in your twenties. Many do.'

With Yancey providing the data, this was the settlement Judge Phinizy approved: 'Otto Macnab, hero of both Goliad and San Jacinto, twelve hundred and eighty acres for your service in the army for the duration of the war, plus six hundred and forty bonus for being at San Jacinto. Then, for your brave father, who died at Goliad, six hundred and forty acres, plus another three hundred and twenty for his service for less than three months in our army. This makes a total, I believe, of two thousand eight hundred and eighty acres. So ordered.' And with a majestic pursing of his lips he arched a magisterial spray of tobacco juice right into the bucket.

Macnab and Ascot were so appreciative of the way Quimper had doubled even Martin's entitlements – 1,280 acres because of extraordinary heroism – that they entered into an agreement. 'Look,' Martin said, 'none of us have much money. Let's work together and rebuild the inn. And then we'll build a house on your land, Otto.'

At this point in the discussion Otto made a significant decision: 'I don't need a house yet.'

'Where would you stay?' Ascot asked, and Otto said: 'I could work for Yancey, maybe,' and Betsy Belle cried: 'Nonsense! You'll live with us.'

In the next weeks the four young Texians did two things: they slaved like beasts of burden to erect at the ferry a shack which could only by the most careless use of words be called an inn, and they laid off the portions of land which the nation had given each of them. Quimper took a strip on the right bank of the Brazos starting from his mother's burned inn and running south; Otto chose his adjacent to that; and Martin stepped off his touching Otto's. When the portions were surveyed and legally transferred, Ascot told his wife one night: 'Come to think of it, Yancey did all the choosing for us,' and she said with a suspicion which had started that first day when he kissed her hand: 'I'm sure he expects Otto and us to clear out some day. Then he'll have it all.'

The work of building was arduous. Not only did everyone, including Betsy Belle, sweat in the summer sun chopping trees and sawing timbers, but at night, often on empty stomachs, they slept on bare ground. Of the many different types of tools they should have had for such a task, they had only three: two axes, a pair of good saws and two hammers, but with these they built a cabin through whose sides the wind and rain would whistle, and when the boxlike structure was what Yancey called 'completed like the finest palace,' they added on the south exposure a long, low porch. Quimper's Ferry was back in business.

With the first hard-earned dollars the foursome collected, Yancey felt he had to go to the national capital, Columbia-on-the-Brazos, to buy the ropes and wires necessary for the reopening of a ferry service: 'Martin, you and Betsy Belle stay here and run the inn. Otto and me, we'll ride down and get the necessaries.'

'When do we start *our* house?'

'First things first. Let's for God's sake get some money around here.' Each of the four realized that from the amount of really strenuous work they had done, they should in an orderly society have earned large sums of cash, but since little was circulating, they ended their labors with nothing. And the first three travelers to halt at the inn before crossing on a pitiful little raft that Otto and Martin had built, had not a cent to pay for their keep. They did have a cow, so a barter was concluded.

When Ascot wanted to know why Judge Phinizy had been so cooperative, Yancey said: 'He don't get paid, either. He's supposed to, but the government's got no money.'

'What's that have to do with it?'

'I give him things to eat. He gives me land.'

On the evening before their departure for the capital, Yancey reported on a discussion he'd had with the judge: 'He told me "That young feller Ascot, he seemed real bright," and when I told him you were, he said "Why don't he read for law?" and I asked where, and he said "I'll teach him if he drops in now and then." I asked him how much, and he said "Nothin'. I could use a cow. And Texas could use a good lawyer," and I asked "How long?" and he said "If he's bright as you claim, he could do it in mebbe six weeks," and I said you'd do it.'

The suggestion was like a rope tossed to a foundering man, for in Mississippi, before the Texas fever caught him, Ascot had been vaguely intending to study law, and his recent strenuous experience in house building had satisfied him that he was better fitted for more cerebral labors. 'When could I start?' he asked eagerly, and Yancey said: 'Right now. He give me these books for you to begin with,' and he delivered two grease-stained books printed in London in the previous century and thumbed by young Virginians who had aspired to the courts: *Blackstone's Commentaries* and *Coke's Institutes*.

Martin, taking the books reverentially, asked: 'What about Betsy Belle?' and Yancey said: 'She can run the inn while you study and we're gone,' and in the morning Martin went to work on Judge Phinizy's lawbooks while Yancey and Otto headed south to obtain equipment for the proposed ferry.

Otto was disappointed in the capital of his new nation, for Columbia had only five houses, one of which was a store-hotel. Government occupied three of the houses: representatives in a two-story frame affair with no caulking to seal the openings; senators in a windowless shack that had been used for storing cattle foodstuffs; the president in another windowless affair of two small rooms, a smoky fireplace and an earthen floor that became a quagmire when water seeped in.

As soon as Yancey saw the presidential mansion his bile began to rise, and he experienced such nausea that he stopped a passer-by to ask: 'Is that where Sam Houston lives?' When the farmer confirmed that this was the home of the President, Quimper asked: 'Is he ever sober?' and the citizen replied: 'As a matter of strict truth, he is never sober before two in the afternoon, and since it's only half past one, you can count on it that he lies in there dead drunk.' The man said that although Houston was a famous drinker, 'best in these parts, past or present,' his average day was orderly: 'Gets drunk every night of the week at seven and raises hell till midnight. Goes to bed about one in the mornin', sleeps till noon, tries to sober up till two. You can't knock him awake when he's drunk, and if the house caught fire, we'd never get him out. That gives him about four good workin' hours each afternoon, and then he does a prodigious amount runnin' the affairs of the nation. When you catch him sober, you have yourself a very good man.'

'Can we leave our affairs in the hands of such a drunk?'

'He handled them pretty well at San Jacinto,' the farmer said, and this incited Quimper: 'He was a coward! Wanted to flee north to Nacogdoches. I led his troops to the fight with Santy Anny. When we got there, he refused to fight, but I moved among the troops and made him start the battle. I say "To hell with Sam Houston." '

'Watch out! Here he comes!' And Yancey stared across the dusty road to the 'executive mansion,' where, in midafternoon sun, the president of the new republic appeared ahead of time. Standing in the low doorway, Houston was forced to stoop while he rubbed his eyes. Then he moved out onto the road, preparing to walk the short distance to where his Congress was in session. He was very tall, very powerful in appearance, and his outrageous dress made him almost a caricature of a frontier leader.

On his head he wore a George Washington tricorn hat from whose left side projected a feather. On his feet he had moccasins made of elk hide, with Indian beads along the high tops. What served as his trousers were of a very thick homespun, no buttons, no belt, simply a huge swath of cloth wrapped about his middle and fastened with a length of rope. But it was his jacket that was most spectacular, for it consisted of a Mexican serape, brightly colored and well fringed, which he swept about his left shoulder so that its far end dragged along the ground. Thus attired, and with a three-day growth of beard, he moved forward to conduct the affairs of state, but when he spotted Quimper he interrupted his unsteady progress and said, without sarcasm: 'Ah-ha! The Hero of San Jacinto!' Yancey, taken by surprise, fumbled for just a moment, then flashed his toothiest smile: 'Good afternoon, sir,' and the President of Texas lurched on, not yet fully recovered from the previous night's bout.

It was on the trip home that Otto began to suspect that whatever Yancey Quimper did had to be inspected closely, because the boy could see that the enthusiastic innkeeper was apt to prove unreliable when his own interests became paramount. From something that Yancey said – 'Gettin' the ferry started is our real job' – he suspected that when the time came to help the Ascots build their house, Yancey would find other obligations to keep him employed.

Otto was wrong. As soon as Yancey reached the inn, shouting to Betsy Belle as he approached, he summoned Martin, who was reading his lawbooks, and cried: 'Look what Otto and me bought for your kitchen!' and to Otto's surprise he produced a small oaken coffee grinder made in France. When Betsy Belle embraced Otto, thanking him for the gift, Yancey winked, indicating that the boy should keep his mouth shut. And next morning it was Yancey who shouted: 'Let's go downriver and build that house.' In the days that followed he labored at least as strenuously as the other two men, and after many tedious days the Ascots had their shack.

Martin's advancement in his other field had been even more spectacular, for on the evening of his third visit to Judge Phinizy, the Arkansas jurist said: 'Martin, I'm sendin' in your papers tomorrow. You're a lawyer.'

'But, Judge . . .'

'Hell, son, you know more law'n I do right now,' and he curved yet another magnificent shot of tobacco juice into the bucket to punctuate his legal decision.

When Martin expressed his gratitude for such assistance, the judge asked for the return of Coke and Blackstone and handed him in exchange the only two books he, Phinizy, had ever purchased with his own money: *Fordyce on Pleading* and *Civil Code of Virginia*: 'I never finished either of 'em, but I have found that the more you know, the better lawyer you'll be.'

Martin's introduction to the law came in two cases involving veterans, and since he appreciated their problems, he was a sympathetic counselor, but he learned quickly that in the tumult of a Texas courtroom good intentions on the part of a man's lawyer or right on the side of a client could mean little.

In his first case he represented a likable young farmer, Axel Vexter, who had fought at San Jacinto and had, with the approval of the Texas government, selected the 640 acres allotted him. He had surveyed the land with the aid of a licensed surveyor and had started erecting a small house when another veteran claimed prior rights. He, too, said he had governmental approval and a proper survey. The case rested, obviously, on the character and witnesses of the two contestants, and with considerable effort Ascot rounded up proof incontrovertible that it was Vexter who had prior rights, but when Phinizy rendered his decision, the land went to the other man, and Vexter's certificate entitling him to 640 acres was available for use elsewhere.

The young veteran was so infuriated by this obvious perversion of justice that he cursed Phinizy in open court, and was thrown in jail for contempt. When Ascot went there to console him, Vexter cursed him too, and threw the certificate in his face. In vain did the young lawyer strive to assure the prisoner that he would soon be released and that other land just as good could be found. Vexter would not listen: 'Take the damned land as your fee. I don't want it.'

This Ascot would not do, and when he told Quimper about the affair, Yancey said: 'Martin! When you have a case before Judge Phinizy, let me know. He owes me so many favors.'

Ascot stared at the innkeeper: 'Do you know what you just said?' and Yancey replied: 'You got to accept Judge Phinizy as he is.'

But when Martin told Yancey about the certificate to land rights which Vexter had rejected, Quimper became quite excited: 'Let me see that!' and when he satisfied himself that it was a legal document assuring the holder of free land, he said: 'I need these. If you have any other clients . . .' He offered Martin ten cents an acre, $6.40, to keep as a fee for services, but Martin would not accept this: 'I want you to hand it to Vexter personally. So he'll know there can be decency in the law.'

But when the time came to count on the few coins that Betsy Belle had been collecting at the inn, Yancey could come up with only $5.10. This certificate entitled the owner to 640 acres of the choicest land in the region of the three rivers, land that would later be of enormous value, but because there was no money in circulation, it could not fetch even ten cents an acre.

'Will he accept five-ten?' Yancey asked, and Martin told him. 'He'll be glad to get anything.' So the two men went to the jail, a chicken-coop affair attached to Judge Phinizy's office, and tendered Vexter the money. When he accepted, gratified by the amount, Yancey said: 'If you know any others who want to sell their rights, send them to Quimper's Ferry.' Then he went to the front of the building and told the judge: 'Let him go. He was at San Jacinto.'

On his second big case Martin Ascot learned the extraordinary legal power of the words Yancey had spoken for this time he was defending, before Judge Phinizy, a farmer of impeccable reputation and deportment who had been grievously defrauded by a rascal named Knobby Horsham, and the case was so transparent that Ascot felt he need not bother his friend Quimper, who appeared to have the judge's ear. Carefully prepared, Ascot appeared on the morning of the trial date only to find that Sam Houston, dressed in Indian garb topped by his serape and with clanging spurs, had asked special dispensation to serve as lawyer for the defendant, despite the fact that he was the president. Judge Phinizy granted the unusual request and the trial began.

In a masterful display, young Ascot deferred to the great Houston, at the same time proving beyond any doubt that Knobby Horsham had behaved despicably. The jury, nine farmers, obviously sided with Martin's client, for some of them had been defrauded by just such rascals as Knobby.

The case really did not need to be submitted to the jury, but Judge Phinizy, in a show of judicial impartiality, asked Sam Houston if he had any witnesses. 'Only one, your Honor.'

Limping to the witness box, his right leg dragging so conspicuously that the jury had to notice, he moved close to his client and looked down upon him as a loving father might, despite the fact that the man was a proved rascal. The audience leaned forward, expecting their voluble president to unlimber a scorching oration, but he uttered only two sentences: 'Knobby, you've heard the serious charges made against you. Where were you on the afternoon of 21 April 1836?'

Knobby looked up like an innocent child and whispered: 'Leadin' the front-line charge at San Jacinto.'

'The defense rests,' Houston said, limping back to his chair.

'Case dismissed,' Judge Phinizy cried.

The next months were the ones that crystallized Otto's character, for he spent them almost equally divided between two contrasting lives, both of which attracted him almost equally. He lived in the rude shack built for the Ascots, which Betsy Belle had converted into a place of warmth and illumination. As finished by the three veterans of San Jacinto, the cabin was little more than a collection of rough-cut logs piled loosely in the form of a large kitchen, a small alcove for the Ascots and a cubbyhole for Otto, but after she finished with making it habitable, it was a snug refuge in the wilderness.

First she took Otto to the river, where they routed out long lengths of soft weeds and pailfuls of mud to caulk the crevices through which wind had been blowing and rain dripping. Then she herself took thin reedlike limbs of trees growing along the Brazos and fashioned them into chairs, four in all, which were both sturdy and comfortable. After what seemed like interminable searching, she procured two iron hooks for the fireplace and three pots to hang upon them. She smoothed out five successive layers of mud to achieve a level, largely dustless floor. And to make the kitchen seem more like a city home, she nailed to its walls two colored lithographs, one sent down the Mississippi from Cincinnati, the other up across the desert from Mexico City. The first showed Andrew Jackson astride a horse at New Orleans; the second, Santa Anna in the battle at Zacatecas. Whenever Yancey Quimper visited the kitchen, he spat at Santa Anna, whereupon Betsy Belle would bang him on the ear.

599

To Otto this kitchen became a university, for here the Ascots introduced him to true learning, Martin speaking of the principles of law, Betsy Belle reviewing the lessons she had mastered at a school in Mississippi. They talked of Napoleon and Charlemagne and Thomas Jefferson, and always they tried to penetrate to those motives which force men and women to behave as they do. Night after night Martin would review cases which he had tried before Judge Phinizy, with Betsy Belle analyzing why this man and that woman had behaved as they had: 'You must have seen she was lying. Surely the judge pointed this out to the jury.' And Martin would explain why it was most unlikely that the judge would have done so.

From such instruction Otto began to formulate his own interpretation of society, and the Ascots might have been surprised had he revealed it. Drawing upon what he had seen at Natchez-under-the-Hill and at Goliad, he discovered that for a man to make a mark in this world, he had better have a tough core of righteousness which he should allow nothing to scar, neither the lure of money nor the pursuit of pride. He had better identify his enemies quickly and beat them down before they had a chance to do the same to him. And it would be best if he kept quiet.

Early in their evening talks around one of Betsy Belle's homemade candles, he decided that he was not fashioned to be a scholar, because the first time Martin handed him a lawbook that explained the topic under discussion, he found that his interest quickly flagged. And whenever Betsy Belle spoke reverently of some romantic tale she had picked up from her study of history, he would dismiss it as imagination. He was a tough-minded little realist, soon to be fifteen, and he would leave the life of letters to others better qualified.

But he never dismissed the essence of what the Ascots were saying. He knew from looking into their excited faces that there was a lower order of life and a higher, and he was instinctively drawn to the latter. In every court case that Martin discussed, he found himself siding with right, and justice, and what Martin sometimes called 'the only sensible thing to do.'

These growing convictions served him in good stead when he worked with Yancey Quimper at the ferry, for there he was a completely different type of person. To begin with, Yancey himself was about as far removed from the Ascots as one could be. For example, when the Ascot cabin needed caulking, Betsy Belle tied up her skirts, went into the Brazos, and dug the clay for it; at the inn when there was work to be done, Yancey always looked about for someone else to do it. He could in a single day find a dozen things for Otto to attend.

The motivations of the inn customers were also quite different from those of the Ascots. Everyone seemed to be conniving for some advantage or trying to acquire land or belongings owned by someone else. Arguments were settled not with carefully marshaled words but with fists or a flashing Bowie knife. Otto was by no means afraid of a fight; he knew from experience that he could control adversaries much bigger than he, but he saw that to engage endlessly in brawling was not productive.

Yet he enjoyed the liveliness of the inn, and despite Quimper's obvious defects in character, he liked being with him, for something was always happening, like the time two toughs from Kentucky stopped on the far side of the Brazos and clamored loudly to be ferried across. 'Go fetch them,' Yancey said, and Otto had gone down the steep bank to where the ferry waited, its two guide ropes attached by rings to the wire that stretched to a big tree on the opposite side. With deft hands he grabbed the forward rope, allowed the current to carry him downstream till the rope was taut, and then pulled sturdily so that the ferry moved forward along the fixed wire.

'What kind of contraption is this?' one of the frontiersmen bellowed as they climbed noisily aboard, and at midstream on the return trip, the man who had spoken grabbed the rope from Otto's hands, while his partner grabbed the stern rope, and pulling in the opposite direction, nearly upset the craft.

'Stop that!' Otto shouted, recovering the rope, but he could do nothing to move the ferry because now both men heaved on the back rope. He was stronger than they and knew better what he was doing, so they did not succeed in taking the ferry away from him in their boisterous game, but they did make orderly progress impossible.

Dropping his rope, Otto whipped from his belt the pistol that Zave Campbell had taught him to use so effectively. Pointing it at the two roisterers, he said quietly: 'Drop that rope.' When they refused, he calmly put a shot between the pair and said: 'Drop it or I'm coming after you.'

The threat was so preposterous, this boy challenging two grown men, that they began to laugh, and if Otto's pistol had had the capacity of a second bullet, he would have blazed away at them. Instead, he leaped forward, knocked one sideways so that he fell into the river and flattened the other.

The pistol shot had aroused men in the inn, and they came streaming down to the bank. A good swimmer, seeing that the first Kentuckian might drown, plunged in to save him, while others waded out to bring the ferry to the bank. When the two travelers were at the bar drinking the watered stuff that Quimper sold as whiskey, one said: 'You got yourself a son who's a tiger,' and Yancey said: 'He ain't my son,' and they said: 'You better adopt him.'

Next morning Yancey tried to do just that: 'Otto, I'm makin' you an offer. You run the ferry, help around the place. I'll give you room and keep, and soon as there's any money, you'll get a share. Meantime, you got yourself a leg up in life.'

'I'll think about that,' Otto said, and he might have accepted, for he knew he needed a home somewhere, and that continued residence with the Ascots was both impractical and unfair. He might have become a river-crossing roustabout had not Martin Ascot been called to the new town of Houston on an important court case. Taking Betsy Belle with him, and inviting Otto to ride along, Martin set out for what was now the capital city of the republic. The three-day ride southeast, across the low, rolling hills between the Brazos and the Trinity, was a reminder of what the new nation might become if it ever stabilized and found enough money to operate, for the fields were rich, the trees grew in attractive clusters, and flowers bloomed everywhere. It was a rougher land, Otto thought, than the terrain he had seen in Ohio, but it was powerful, and he was proud to be a part of it.

The first night out they slept under the stars, but on the second they found a farmhouse where the wife welcomed them and the husband was eager to talk politics: 'As soon as that drunk Houston serves out his term, what we got to do is elect a real fighter like Mirabeau Lamar to the presidency.'

'Who's he want to fight?' Martin asked, and the man said:

'I've heard him twice. He wants to kick the Indians out of Texas. He wants to fight Santy Anny and whip him proper. And he wants us to take Santy Fay.'

'That would be a lot of fighting,' Ascot said, and the farmer replied: 'Us Texians can do a lot.'

The town of Houston was a revelation: first houses built in late 1836, a bustling town of 1,200 by the spring of 1837, capital of the nation in May 1837. When the Ascot party rode in, they found movement everywhere – new stores being built at a frantic rate and eight principal streets, each eight inches deep in mud. Betsy Belle, trying to alight from her horse, felt her left foot sinking into a quagmire, and remounted.

There were no hotels yet, but local citizens, inordinately proud of their metropolis, directed the visitors to a remarkable substitute, and when they were comfortably fitted into the private home of Augustus Allen they heard an extraordinary yarn from Allen himself: 'Yep, my brother and I came down from Syracuse, New York, a few dollars in our pockets, dreams in our hearts. We bought, one way or another,' and here he shrugged his shoulders to indicate the chicaneries he and his brother had engaged in. Losing his train of thought, he asked Martin: 'Do you know how much a hundred Mexican leagues of land is?' Before Ascot could reply, he said: 'That's nearly half a million acres, and that's what we acquired.'

'You have to shoot anybody?' Betsy Belle asked, and he chuckled.

'Well, we set aside the best of our land, here beside Buffalo Bayou with entrance forty miles out there to the Gulf, and we decided to make this the capital of Texas. Yes, we give the government all the land they needed, free. We give churches all they asked for, schools if you wanted to start one. We give away so much damned land you wouldn't believe it, and why do you suppose we done that?'

They learned from Allen's wife that her husband had been a child prodigy in mathematics and a college professor at seventeen, 'the wizard of upper New York, they called him.' And he made no apologies for what he and his brother had done in founding Houston: 'We did it to make money. We give away lots to attract attention, then sell what's left at a good profit. There's no hotel for distinguished visitors like you, so I open my house to all who come, free.' To close the gap between his prodigious learning and the local customers' lack of it, he had adopted Texas speech and sounded sometimes like an illiterate, but on their third night in Houston, the Ascots were invited into the parlor of Allen's house, for he was the treasurer and motivating force.

As an afterthought, Allen had said when extending the invitation: 'Bring the boy, if you wish,' and Otto found himself among the founders and philosophers of his nation. Congress was meeting in Houston that week, so many of the legislators participated in the discussion, and Otto quickly realized that these men were much like his father: serious, sometimes robust in their humor and obviously committed to finding a constructive life. After a satisfying meal cooked by Mrs Allen, she and Betsy modestly retired, as if incapable of understanding the august subjects about to be discussed, while the men listened attentively to two essays: 'The Federalist Papers, Key to the American Democracy' and 'Fielding's *Tom Jones*: A Threat to Public Morals?'

Otto could not fathom either the concepts involved in these discussions or the vigor with which they were pursued, but he was proud when Martin Ascot entered the debate with such forceful comment that in the midst of the proceedings Mirabeau Lamar, president of the society and vice-president of the nation, proposed: 'Gentlemen, our young lawyer from Xavier County has spoken much sense here tonight. I recommend that he be made our corresponding member from Xavier.' The proposal was approved by acclamation, after which Lamar reported: 'At the conclusion of our last meeting several members, including Anson Jones, Thomas Rusk and James Collinsworth, suggested that the topic then debated with such illumination be continued into this meeting, should time permit. Well, time does permit, and I would like our esteemed secretary, David Burnet, to state the question.'

Burnet, an older man who had served briefly as president of the fledgling nation during its formative period, rose, coughed, and read the title of the debate which had so exercised the members: 'Women: Why Have We Had No Female Painters or Musicians?' and when the pros and cons of this question were discussed, often with great heat, even Otto could understand the proceedings. It was conceded by both sides – anti-women, eighty-eight percent, pro-women twelve percent – that females were flighty, inconsistent, unable to pursue a goal over any extended period and apt at any moment to fly off the handle, and that these weaknesses disqualified them for any sustained intellectual or creative work such as the composition of a Mozart symphony or the paintings of the Sistine Chapel, two examples of art with which most of the members seemed to be familiar.

But granted these deficiencies, was the female physique such that it automatically precluded greatness in the arts? The majority decided that it was. Just what these limitations were, Otto could not decipher, for when they orated on this fascinating subject, the members inclined to talk in a code that he could not penetrate. However, several speakers referred with great emotion to 'the sublime work of art which women are capable of, the birth of those children on whom the future of any society must and does rest.' Such statements were always greeted with cheers, but toward the end of the evening Martin Ascot rose and said: 'I have heard much comment about the inability of women to sustain any effort through an extended period. Anyone like me who has lived on the far frontier and seen what a wife can accomplish is astounded by her energy.'

From his seat in front, ex-President Burnet grumbled: 'Ascot, you're so young.' And the meeting ended.

Its effect on Otto was magical. Even he could see that these earnest men, stuck away on a far frontier so different from either Baltimore or Cincinnati, were striving to maintain their interest in the entire world, and especially in those wellsprings of human behavior from which goodness came. He liked these men and their pompous oratory. He was proud of how a younger man like Martin fitted in. And he saw with remarkable clarity that he was intended to be a man like them, and not a man like Yancey Quimper. When he returned to Xavier County he would tell Yancey that he did not want the job at the Ferry. But what he did want, and where he would make his home, he did not know.

If Otto was confused as to where he would find his home, Texas faced an equal quandary. Shortly after the establishment of its government, a plebiscite had been taken, and the citizens produced an irrefutable plurality in favor of joining the United States immediately, and upon any reasonable terms offered, but to their chagrin, the nation to the north rejected the offer. 'We ought to march to Washington!' customers at Quimper's Ferry bellowed, and Yancey predicted: 'We'll see the day when Washington comes beggin' for us. And what will we do then?'

'Spit in her eye!' the belligerents cried, but in his kitchen Martin Ascot provided a more cautious analysis: 'This dreadful panic makes everyone afraid of making bold moves.'

'I think what people are really afraid of is another war with Mexico,' Betsy Belle said, but her husband struck the deeper chord: 'It's slavery. Those damned Northerners will never let us come in as another slave state.' And he was right, because year after year the Northern senators excoriated Texas as a nest of backwardness and slavery, and annexation seemed impossible.

Now the contest for the allegiance of Texas became an international affair, with three nations involved, and with debate in the Ascot kitchen divided three ways. Betsy Belle, who had learned French from a Louisiana slave who had reared her, hoped that France would assume the control she had tried to exercise back in the 1680s when Texas was theoretically French, and from time to time this seemed possible and even likely: 'I should love to see this vast area civilized. We have great affinity with the French.'

Her husband, now a serious student of English law, hoped that Great Britain would take control, and quickly: 'We would fit in so perfectly with English ways of justice, law and government.' He was, as a Southerner, so convinced that entry into the United States was unlikely that he actively sought union with Britain and propagandized any who would listen, especially Otto: 'Can't you see? In states like Virginia and Pennsylvania and Carolina, we were English. It would be proper for us to reunite.' He assured Otto that Texas rights would be protected and even extended in such a reunion.

Quimper's interest centered on Mexico, which was threatening to resume the war. No peace treaty between Mexico and her former colony had ever been promulgated, so that renewal of the war was a real possibility: 'What we ought to do is let those damned Mexicans make a move against us, and then march right down to Mexico City and take over the whole country. They'll never be able to govern it by themselves.' Of course, when Mexico did invade Texas and capture San Antonio, which happened twice, Quimper could not believe that his Texians had allowed this to happen, and became terrified lest Santa Anna come storming back to burn once again the Quimper inn and ferry.

Young Otto, listening to these debates, kept quiet, as usual, but his ideas on foreign affairs were beginning slowly to solidify, and had he been asked for his opinion, he would have said: 'I had enough of foreigners with those Baltimore Germans. I don't want France or England, either one. And I hate the Mexicans for what they did at the Alamo and Goliad.' What did he advocate? He told no one, but he had firm beliefs: We shouldn't march to Mexico City, like Yancey says, although we could do it easy. We should go clear to Panama, and then maybe take Canada, too. He could see no reason why all of North America should not be Texian, except that the eastern seaboard, which was already American, could stay that way. Then, if the United States should some day wish to join Texas, it would be welcome.

The internal affairs of the nation were also maturing, but not always in the direction intended. All observers agreed that Texas could never become a first-class nation unless it developed both a harbor on the Gulf for oceangoing vessels, and steamboats for transit up the three principal rivers, Trinity, Brazos, Colorado. Unfortunately, immense sandbars, tenacious and drifting, blockaded all available harbors, especially Galveston's, so that sometimes two ships out of five would not make the wharves, with lives and cargo alike being lost.

River traffic was even less successful, because here, too, forbidding sandbars menaced any ship that tried to enter from the gulf, and those that did succeed immediately encountered snags, sunken logs and smaller sandbars, and such twists in the course that boats could negotiate the worst corners only with the help of ropes dragged along the shore by sweating passengers who debarked to do the hauling.

Occasionally, some daring vessel would make it as far upriver as Quimper's Ferry, but two that did were trapped by falling water and spent the summer there. Yet it was an unbroken act of faith, all along the rivers, that 'one of these days we'll see scheduled boats putting into that dock.' In the meantime, the loss of shipping was disastrous: *Ocean* sunk at Brazoria; *Clematis* sunk trying to get to Brazoria; *Mustang* sunk at Jones Landing; *Lady Byron* sunk near Richmond; *Creole Queen* and seven others sunk trying to get into the Brazos.

But when this doleful litany was recited at Quimper's Inn, Yancey insisted, with most of the men supporting him: 'When a Texian starts to do something, he does it. We'll have steamboats up here yet.' The same prediction was made along both the Trinity and the Colorado, where losses paralleled those on the Brazos.

Education was also a function of society about which something was going to be done ... one of these days. The nation could not afford to spend what little money it could accumulate on free schools, so there were none, but it did allocate liberal portions of the only currency it did have, land, to schools. Xavier County, for example, was awarded 17,712 of its choicest acres, but no way was found to turn this into cash, so no school was founded.

However, the county did eventually offer some education, for after the children of Xavier had gone some years without schooling, the Reverend Joel Job Harrison, tall and fiery and with a wife who could cook, appeared with handbills announcing his intention to open a school: 'First course: reading, writing, spelling, multiplication tables, $1.50 per month. Second course: arithmetic, grammar, oratory, astronomy, $2.00 a month. Third course: Latin, Greek, algebra, geography, the copperplate, $3.00 a month. Mrs Harrison will accept a few girls and boys in her home, good table, Christian discourse.' To inquiring parents, Reverend Harrison gave these assurances: 'I am an ordained minister, Methodist faith but courteous to all. I am proficient in the subjects offered. And I can promise firm discipline, for I will brook no insolence or insubordination, since I believe I can whip all but the very biggest boys in fistfighting.' He called his one-room school, a reasonably good one, the University of Xavier.

The citizens of Texas sometimes acquired a peculiar insight

into how their nation functioned. When General Felix Huston, no relation to the president, was to be replaced as commander-in-chief of the Texian forces by Albert Sidney Johnston, the former, refusing to cede office to the latter, warned Johnston that if he wanted the command, he would have to duel Huston for it, and when the duel took place, Huston shot Johnston in the behind and held on to his command. Said the enlisted men who witnessed the duel: 'It was a fair fight. If a man wants to lead the Texian army, he better be prepared to fight for the job.'

But always the limiting factor was this strangling lack of currency, and when the distressed nation, swamped in debt, tried to salvage itself by printing two million dollars' worth of 'red-back bills' supported by no collateral except the government's word and faith, citizens evaluated the issue realistically. On the first day it was issued, a dollar bill was worth fifty cents, a few days later, thirty cents, then ten cents and four cents, until it bottomed out at an appalling two cents.

Shocked by this experience, the government sought another solution: 'We'll encourage private firms with good reputations to issue their own currency.'

'Backed by what?' cynics asked, and the government said: 'Their goods. Their mills.'

The experiment was tried, and a relieved Texas watched as this private money system stabilized at about eighty cents on the dollar. One firm whose notes ranked even higher announced that it was backing them with 'every item of our merchandise, our steamer *Claribel*, eighteen nigger slaves and our sawmill.'

In Xavier County, Yancey Quimper planned to print five thousand dollars' worth of bills 'redeemable at the Ferry,' but since he could not specify redeemable in what, the government ordered him to desist, so Xavier continued to suffer.

However, Yancey did find a way to profit from the emergency, for he let it be known that he stood ready to exchange what little cash he had for any land certificates in the possession of San Jacinto veterans, and Otto watched as a shattered chain of young men wandered in with certificates that they sold for two and three cents an acre, and glad they were to receive even those small amounts.

When Otto learned what Yancey was doing with these papers, he was amazed. One day a European gentleman, neither

French nor German but something else, stopped by the inn, behaving as if he had been there before, and he gave Yancey real money for a stack of the certificates. When he was gone, Otto asked: 'What's he do with them?' and Yancey said: 'Peddles them through Europe. Everybody wants to come to Texas.'

'Even when we have no money?' and Yancey said: 'To people who know, Texas is still heaven.'

He was right in this assessment, for despite continuous setbacks, the dogged Texians strove to forge a nation based upon distinct characteristics, and none was more basic than the Texian's ability to absorb temporary setbacks. An impartial observer from either London or Boston, evaluating the new nation during this tempestuous decade, would have predicted failure, for nothing seemed to work, but he would have underestimated the capacity of the Texian to take enormous risks, sustained by the conviction that 'sooner or later, things will work out.'

Thus the Allen brothers could speculate in Houston real estate, hoping that land which they bought at twenty cents an acre would soon be worth two hundred dollars; Reverend Joel Job Harrison could call his cabin-school a university in the honest belief that it would some day become one; and Yancey Quimper could spend his last penny on land certificates, trusting that dreamers in Europe would grab them at inflated prices. Everywhere this faith in the future prevailed.

In the midst of Otto's confusion as to his future, the Texas government circulated through the counties a document which would lead to the creation of one of the cherished symbols of Texas life. It called for volunteers to man a unique corps whose nature could best be explained by stating what it was not.

First, it was not a police force with uniforms, specified duties and restricted terrains of operation. Particularly, it would not be subject to supervision by county authorities.

Second, it was not a branch of the army with highly organized structure and national obligations. The new force would have no distinguishing uniforms, no government-issued arms, no epaulet distinctions, no medals, no drill. Rarely would it perform in battle formation and never would it parade.

Finally, it was not a secret detective agency, working under the command of any district attorney, for even though it would often perform detective functions, its allegiance was to the national government, which insulated it from petty local pressures.

What would this potentially powerful new arm of government be called? During one discussion at the ramshackle capital a proponent had finished making the point that 'the men will not be tied down to any one locality, they will range all over,' and someone suggested: 'Let's call them ranging companies.' And thus were born the famous ranging units – no set duties: 'Just range the countryside and keep order.'

The unit to be enrolled from the counties centering on Xavier would be commanded by Captain Sam Garner, distinguished veteran of San Jacinto, twenty-five years old and as tall and thin as an unclothed scarecrow. His general responsibility would be along the north shore of the Nueces River, and as soon as this was known, the toughest men flocked to his temporary headquarters in Campbell, because to serve along what was called the Nueces Strip was to serve in the wildest, most dangerous and challenging part of the new nation.

The word *Strip* was misleading, for this was not some narrow stretch of land between two settled areas. At its greatest east-to-west reach, it extended some two hundred miles; at its widest north-south, a hundred and sixty. It was best visualized as a healthy wedge of pie, the arc of crust running along the Gulf, the point far to the west along the Rio Grande. It was much larger than many European nations – Belgium, the Netherlands or Switzerland, for example – and also considerably larger than substantial American states like New Hampshire, Vermont or Maryland.

Except for a few meager towns along the north bank of the Rio Grande, it was largely unsettled insofar as permanent ranches were concerned, but it was not unoccupied. for more than a century Mexican herdsmen living south of the river had run their cattle on the Strip, and now cattlemen from the Victoria area in Texas were doing the same. An interesting rule developed: if a Mexican crossed the Rio Grande to work his cattle and picked up a few strays belonging to a Texian, he was a bandit, but any Texian who led a foraging party into Mexico to increase his herd by lifting a few hundred longhorned cattle was considered a prudent citizen.

When Texas gained its independence, delineation of the border between the two countries was imprecise, with Texas claiming that its southern border lay along the Rio Grande, and Mexico arguing that the border followed the Nueces River far to the north, which under Spanish rule certainly had formed the southern border of their Tejas. A bleak, forbidding, unpopulated no man's land existed between the two rivers, and from within it undeclared warfare developed. Mexicans prowling in the Strip would strike north across the Nueces at desolate ranches in the Victoria area; Texians would organize furtive excursions across the Rio Grande.

The Texas government, ignoring the depredations of its own citizens, deplored the behavior of the outlaw Mexicans. As a senator described the situation during an impassioned debate in Houston: 'In organizing furtive thrusts into our territory north of the Nueces, the Mexicans are without shame or honor. A secret crossing of our river, a wild dash to some unprotected Texian hacienda, gunfire, a flaming dog-run, a murdered family, and cattle stampeding as they head south becomes common, after which the invaders scurry to sanctuary in the Strip, from where they laugh at us derisively.' It was this kind of sortie that Captain Garner's ranging company was expected to halt. Among the first group of volunteers was Otto Macnab, age fifteen but more a man than many who stepped forward. Garner, certain the boy was grossly underage, but not knowing by exactly how much, asked: 'Son, how old are you?'

In January 1838, Otto would be sixteen, so he lied and said: 'I'll be eighteen in January.'

'Come back in January,' the lanky man said, and then he instructed the others as to the rules of the new organization: 'Provide your own good horse, a change of clothes, a rifle, a pistol and a Bowie knife.'

'What kind of clothes?'

'Whatever you have. No insignia.'

'Same with the boots?'

'Whatever you have, but they should come mostly to the knee because we'll be hitting mesquite and rattlesnakes.' Believing that he had covered everything, he started to go inside the shed that served as an office; then he stopped: 'We think you should wear a big hat. Keeps the sun out of your eyes in summer, your head warm in winter.' And studying Otto carefully, he added: 'It would make you look taller, too.'

On 2 January 1838 Otto bade the Ascots farewell, placed his two rifles across his saddle and headed south, his big hat bobbing in time with the horse's gait. Before nightfall he was sworn in, smallest man in his unit, a taut little fighting machine with no uniform and no stated commission, eager to help tame the frontiers of Texas.

During the second week in January word reached the capital that the bandit Benito Garza had invaded Texas and raided a ranch north of the Nueces River, killing two Texians. This was precisely the kind of outrage the ranging companies had been organized to punish, so the informal Xavier County unit was assembled by Captain Sam Garner, twenty-six years old, six feet two, a hundred and fifty-eight pounds, flowing mustaches, icicle-straight and icicle-cool, and a very good man at firing his rifle at full gallop. His first assistant was Otto Macnab, the young fellow of indeterminate age. He claimed he was eighteen, but looked twelve because of his beardless chin, his almost-white baby-fine hair, and his slim, unmuscled body. 'This Macnab,' Garner told his superiors, 'impresses me as a chilly hombre. When those blue eyes fix on you, beware!'

The company assembled in the town of Campbell, fifty-two men on their own horses and with their own guns and knives who would ride casually south 'to knock some sense into the Mexicans.' When they neared Victoria, their first important stop, Otto surprised his captain by saying: 'I want to break away. My mother lives on the Guadalupe west of town.'

'We'll all head that way,' Garner said, for he was in no hurry; he had learned that fighting could be depended upon to find him out at the appointed time, no matter where he went or what he did. So the other volunteers followed Otto as he headed for the Garza dog-runs, and all were astonished when Macnab presented to them the two widows, his stepmother Josefina and his adopted mother María, for the women were obviously Mexican.

The men appreciated the hospitality the two women extended and were favorably impressed by their well-kept homes, and what won them over completely was the discovery that María had been married to Xavier Campbell, the hero of the Alamo, after whom their country and their town had been named.

'What was he like?' they wanted to know. 'Where was the tree they hanged him from?' One man, about twenty, just sat munching tortillas and staring at María: 'Were you really married to Campbell?'

'I was,' she said as her plump body moved about the kitchen.

Macnab gave his mother a farewell embrace and then kissed María affectionately. 'That one's a good Mexican,' the staring fellow said, but when they were once more on the road south he asked Captain Garner and Macnab: 'Say, I just thought of something. Isn't this troublemaker Benito Garza – the one we're supposed to catch – isn't he from Victoria somewheres?'

'He's María's brother,' Otto said with no embarrassment.

'What will you do if we catch him?'

'Arrest him.'

'Is he really as clever as they say?'

'He can ride better than you . . . or me. He can shoot better than you . . . or me. And he probably can think better than you . . . or me.'

'Why is he raising so much hell?'

'He's a Mexican,' Otto said. 'He fought with Santa Anna.'

'Didn't we capture him at San Jacinto?'

'We did.'

'Why didn't we shoot him?'

'We don't shoot prisoners.'

At first hearing, this might seem a naïve thing for a member of a ranging company to say, because these troops had already acquired a reputation among the Mexicans of Texas as ruthless killers – Los Tejanos Sangrientes, The Bloody Texians. But upon reflection it wasn't so absurd, because as Captain Garner himself explained to one newcomer: 'We rarely take prisoners,' which meant, of course, that after a fight, there were few left to take alive.

The lethal efficiency of the ranging company was multiplied by a factor of five by a fortunate incident which occurred as the riders were approaching the Nueces River. A supply officer from the Texas army overtook them to distribute the first official issue of weapons the men would receive, and from the first moment the rangers inspected this small piece of armament they sensed that it was going to remake Texas and the West.

It was a revolver, .34 caliber, with a short octagonal barrel of blue-gray steel and a grip that nestled in the hand. It had a revolving cylinder that enabled the user to fire five times without reloading, and was, in every respect, a masterful piece of workmanship. It was made by Sam Colt in some small town in Connecticut, and a salient feature was that any one part of a given revolver could be used interchangeably in any other gun. And for some curious reason never explained, the first users, all Texians, referred to this superlative revolver as 'a Colts' – no apostrophe, just a Colts, as in the sentence 'I whipped out my Colts and drilled him between the eyes.'

Understandably, the Colts became the preferred weapon of the ranging companies, and armed with these revolvers, Captain Garner and his men crossed the Nueces confident that they now had a real chance of cleansing the Strip of Mexicans. But when they rode to the crest of a rise so slight it would have gone unnoticed elsewhere, Otto's mind was attracted to other matters, for as he reined in his horse he stared in wonder at the vast expanse of emptiness that stretched before him – an empire off by itself, brown, sere, populated by rattlesnakes and coyotes. It was his first glimpse of the Strip, and it awed him.

It's like no other part of Texas, he said to himself. And look at that sky. Then he shook his head: I'll bet the traveler who gets lost in there stays lost . . . till the buzzards find him.

As he studied the tremendous land he observed various interesting aspects: Flat as that new billiard table Yancey Quimper put in at the Ferry. Brushland with scrub oak, no tall trees. But I'd hate to ride through that thicket without protection for my legs. Cut to shreds. In these decades the land seemed almost without vegetation, for the ubiquitous mesquite had not yet taken over, but when Otto looked closer he saw the real miracle of the semi-desert as it prepared for spring: Are those flowers?

They were, a multitude of the most gorgeous tiny beauties – gold, red, blue, yellow, purple – forming a dense, matted carpet covering a million acres. It was an incredible display of nature's

615

profligate use of color, so luxuriant and beautiful that although Otto had seen the flowers of Texas before, some of the most varied in the world, he felt he had never beheld anything like the minute blossoms of this exploding garden.

Captain Garner, seeing that his young assistant lagged, rode back and said: 'Immense, eh?' and Otto replied: 'One of those flowers would be beautiful. But a million million of them!' Garner said: 'They stretch two hundred miles,' and Otto said: 'I thought I knew Texas . . .'

'Let's get moving,' Garner said, and as they overtook the others he observed: 'Some say we should let Garza and his local Mexicans have this wilderness. Folks tell me they have a reasonable claim, but I say no. With Texas, you can never predict what value land is going to have. You bring water in here, you got yourself a gold mine.'

'And how do you bring water?'

'That's for somebody else to solve. Our problem is that bastard Garza.'

Wherever the company came upon Texian cattlemen searching for cattle in the Strip, Garner's men heard constant complaint: 'This damned Benito Garza has been raidin' and runnin' off our cattle.' And as the men rode farther south they began to come upon the ruins of isolated settlements which had been razed, leaving not a shack or a longhorn. The missing owners had been either kidnapped into Mexico or shot, and after the company had seen more such scarred remains, its members became decidedly vengeful.

'God help the Mexican I meet,' one of the men said.

One afternoon the company apprehended eight Mexican vaqueros struggling to herd a large number of unbranded cattle toward the Rio Grande, and without asking questions, the Texians initiated a gun battle in which they killed five of the Mexicans. Captain Garner, by merely looking at the bodies, declared them to have been rustlers stealing Texian cattle, but when the interrogation of the three survivors made it clear that the cattle had legally belonged to the Mexicans, who had traditionally used this range, he had to concede that his enthusiastic riders might have shot the wrong men.

'What shall we do with the others?' Otto asked, and Garner weighed this problem for some minutes: 'If we keep them prisoner, a lot of questions will be asked. If we let them go, they'll get other Mexicans excited in Matamoros.'

'Hang 'em,' a rider from Austin County suggested, and it was agreed that this was the most prudent solution, so without further discussion of the legality or propriety of such action, the three trespassers were hanged.

Their leader, before he was strung up, protested vehemently: 'But we were on Mexican soil.'

'It ain't Mexican no longer,' the rope man growled as he kicked at the horse on which the doomed man sat, hands tied behind him. With a startled leap the horse sped off, leaving the Mexican suspended.

Otto did not protest this arbitrary denial of justice, for although he was as firmly as ever dedicated to the preservation of law, he, like the rest of his company, refused to concede that the law was also intended to protect Mexicans.

In succeeding days, the ranging company similarly disciplined sixteen other Mexicans, but uncovered no trace of Benito Garza, who was known to be leading this attempt to control what he and others honestly believed to be Mexican territory. One fiery-minded Mexican shouted: 'Garza will teach you, you bastards!' That hanging did not take place because an infuriated Texian shot the man, even though his hands and legs were tied.

At the end of the tour, Captain Garner spoke encouragingly to his youngest trooper: 'Otto, how many did you get in the battles?' and the boy replied, with some pride, for he had not blazed away indiscriminately like some: 'Four.' Otto Macnab had found his occupation.

When the ranging company disbanded in Xavier, for any assignment was temporary, its members found their nation involved in a presidential election unlike any other that had ever occurred in the Americas. General Sam Houston, forbidden by the constitution from serving two terms in a row, had to relinquish the presidency in December 1838, but members of his Pro-Houston party, as it was called, were determined to elect as his successor some compliant person who would merely hold the office until Sam could reclaim.

Party choice centered upon a distinguished fifty-year-old

617

lawyer from Kentucky, Peter Grayson, who had served the new nation in such crucial posts as attorney general and as negotiator with the United States government in Washington. Grayson's candidacy delighted Martin Ascot, who as a fellow lawyer spoke vigorously in his behalf among the settlers.

Houston's opponents saw Grayson as a colorless functionary totally unfitted for high office, an assessment which anti-Houston partisans were not slow to point out: 'A nincompoop, as bad for Texas as Houston has been. The only man worthy to be our president is Mirabeau Buonaparte Lamar, a proven hero, a man of great intellectual brilliance, and a general who'll know how to handle Indians and Mexicans.'

The campaign had become quite heated, and because of the brilliance and roughhouse vigor with which Houston defended his tenure, his supporters assumed that his man would win.

Otto, as in the days when he had not known with whom he wished to live, was confused by the haranguing, and he confided to Betsy Belle, who was not supposed to have any opinion about the choice of who would lead her nation: 'Betsy, when I listen to Martin, I'm all for Grayson, because Sam Houston saved this nation and I like his ideas. But when I hear Yancey and those others at the inn, I'm for Lamar. I think he has the right approach to Indians and Mexicans.'

'What approach?'

'Shoot them all. No place in this nation for Indians or Mexicans.'

It seemed certain, in early July, that Grayson would win, but on 9 July 1838 the Pro-Houston party received a bitter jolt. Because Grayson was so drab, so without charm on the hustings, so miserable a speaker and so without any reputation for heroics during the great battles of the revolution – which he had side-stepped by one clever trick after another – the Houston people had thought it prudent to keep him out of the country during the critical days of the campaign. As loudmouth Yancey Quimper shouted: 'They're afeerd to let us see how dumb he is. They let Sam Houston do his dirty work for him.'

But even so, Grayson might have won had he not, while hiding out at Bean's Station in Tennessee, fallen into one of the depressions to which he was subject and shot himself through the head.

This stroke of bad luck appalled Ascot and his pro-Houston cohorts, and some wanted to thrash Yancey Quimper when the big fellow chortled throughout Xavier County: 'God's will. He wants no more of Houston or his cronies.'

After a few days of sad confusion, the Pro-Houston party came forward with a much better candidate than the late Grayson. James Collinsworth, an able lawyer from Tennessee, had served Houston in many capacities, currently as the respected chief justice of the Texas Supreme Court. He was a handsome man, a gifted speaker and an able defender of Houston's policies, for he advocated conciliation with Mexico and peace with the Cherokee. After his first successful engagements, Ascot and his friends agreed: 'We got ourselves a better man. Collinsworth will be our new president.'

The chief justice had only two drawbacks. First, he was thirty-two years old, three years shy of the constitutional requirement for president. No one in the Houston camp had bothered to check, and when troublemakers like Quimper bellowed: 'Even if he wins, he cain't serve,' the Houston men replied confidently: 'We'll take care of that when we get to it.' One enthusiast told Otto: 'You see, Collinsworth is already chief justice, so when the question comes before him, he can rule in his own favor.' Otto felt instinctively that there was something wrong with this strategy, and in quest of enlightenment he consulted Ascot.

'In the English-American system,' Martin said, 'any judge must excuse himself from a case in which his own interests are involved. We call that recusation.' He spoke with such clarity and with such obvious devotion to the law that Otto returned night after night to talk with him, and Ascot's little sermons formed Otto's basic attitudes toward law and order: 'Law is one of the noblest of all human preoccupations, for it establishes agreed-upon rules and states them clearly. It protects you and me from the excesses of the mob.' He always spoke to Otto as if the boy were an audience of fifty elders, and this was admirable, since the truths he enunciated were so advanced that they stretched the boy's mind. It was then that Otto developed his conviction that the law ought to defend the weak, erect protective barriers against the mighty, and clarify obscurities and conflicts. As a man who had ridden with the local ranging company and who wanted to ride again, he saw clearly that it would be his obligation to enforce just laws and dispense honest justice, and he vowed to do so. Therefore, he noted a contradiction in what Ascot was saying.

'But if Judge Collinsworth is too young, won't Lamar's people throw him out if we do elect him?' Otto asked, and now Ascot revealed to him the other side of the law: 'One of the beauties of practical law is that it enables men and women to do the things they want to, even if the printed law says otherwise.'

'What do you mean?' the young Ranger asked.

'It's the law's responsibility to find a way.'

'How?'

'To prove that things aren't always quite what they seem.'

'Could you defend Judge Collinsworth? And prove that he has a right to be president, even if he is three years shy?'

'I think I could find a way,' and Otto marveled as the young lawyer began to shift ideas this way and that. 'Yes, I'm sure I could come up with a solution.'

Judge Collinsworth's second impediment was an hilarious one: he was inclined to be drunk four days each week, so drunk that he could not even dress himself, and Yancey's unrelenting gang made a great deal of this, but the pro-Houston forces had an ingenious defense. They did not try to deny the charge; too many citizens had seen Judge Collinsworth stumbling into a tree or falling into a ditch to claim that the anti-Houston forces were defaming him. They did point out, however, that since Texas had prospered rather well under General Houston, who was drunk every morning, it was reasonable to suppose that it would do even better under Collinsworth, who would be drunk all day. As one orator shouted: 'You don't want a president who sticks his nose into everything, every day,' and this argument was so persuasive that it began to look as if the all-day-drunk Collinsworth would succeed the half-day-drunk Houston.

But one day in late July, Judge Collinsworth, while crossing Galveston Bay on a steamer, jumped from the aft end, thus becoming the second opponent of Lamar to escape an election fight by suicide.

Yancey Quimper and his associates were now convinced that God was participating in the election, since He obviously wanted Lamar to put into operation his announced platform against Indians and Mexicans, and they ridiculed the Pro-Houston party's third nominee, a roustabout boat captain from the Eastern Shore of Maryland. Robert Wilson did not have a history; he had a dossier which summarized scandalous behavior in at least seven different states. In Texas he had been a little of everything – land promoter, gambler, sawmill operator, soldier in the 1835 capture of Bexar, senator – but his behavior in the last-named job was so malodorous that he had to be expelled. Promptly reelected by a district that wanted to be represented by just this kind of man, he told his supporters: 'You have reinstalled me as a great man in spite of myself.' He offered himself to the public as 'Honest Bob Wilson, a man who is always as honest as the circumstances of a particular case and the public conditions of the country at the time allow.'

Wilson was such a pathetic candidate that even stalwarts like young Otto Macnab could not stomach him, and when the presidential vote was counted, Lamar had 6,995 to Wilson's 252. The Georgia poet was now president, by a landslide, and yet his inauguration turned out to be a sorry affair.

On 10 December 1838, Mirabeau Lamar was prepared to deliver a ringing inaugural speech outlining his plans for the next three years, and supporters like Yancey Quimper were delighted with the rumors that circulated regarding the doughty little man's plans: 'War against the Indians! War against Mexico! Occupation of Santa Fe! Texas is on the move!'

It was assumed by the Lamar men that President Houston, whose nominees had fared so badly both at their own hands and at the public's, would quietly retire from the office which he had occupied with so little distinction, but he astonished them by appearing on the platform in exactly the kind of dress George Washington had worn at his farewell, even to the powdered wig. Then, grasping the lectern with unsteady hands, he delivered a three-hour blistering defense of his conduct and a warning to his successor not to change policies in midstream. At first the audience grew impatient, then restive, and finally, so rebellious that when the tirade ended, poor Lamar folded his grandiloquent speech and passed it along to an assistant, who read it in a confused monotone.

As soon as Lamar assumed the presidency, things began to

change in Texas, and fire-eaters like Yancey Quimper felt their day had come: 'No more of that Houston nonsense. Now we fight.' To hear Yancey, one would suppose that the Texians were prepared to march to Santa Fe, Mexico City and anywhere else that came to mind. They were also ready to fight the Cherokee in the east and the Comanche in the west. In fact, if one listened to Yancey, there had never been as belligerent a young nation as Texas.

Lamar himself had more sense. As a poet and a well-read Georgia gentleman, he stated frequently that his first priority was education, and he laid the foundations for the little that Texas was to do in this field, for as one of his supporters complained: 'The Texas Congress is always prepared to pay verbal tribute to education but never prepared to vote a penny toward its attainment.' This was a policy established by General Houston, who was wary of books for the general public, and who absolutely despised all works of fiction, advising his friends never to bother with them. Texas would for decades speak well of education but do little about it.

Nevertheless, Lamar kept prodding his people to establish colleges and support free public schools, and many years later, when the state felt it must do something if it wished to maintain its self-respect, it did so in conformance to the ideals promulgated by its poet-president.

Lamar also advocated homestead legislation that would enable Texians to establish their families on public lands, but his greatest contribution was in the world of the spirit, for he expanded Texians' belief that they were a special people, obligated to pursue a special mission. Standing amid the mud-and-dust of Houston at the eastern edge of his nation, he could see westward to a new capital in Austin, to powerful future cities like Lubbock and Amarillo, to Sante Fe, which by right belonged to Texas, and beyond to the Pacific Ocean. And when he proposed such a vision as the guiding light of his administration, he received enthusiastic cheers from men like Yancey Quimper, who believed that one day New Mexico, Arizona and California must fall within the Texas orbit, as well as most of Mexico and what would later become Oklahoma: 'And Mirabeau Lamar is the man to see that it happens.'

But once the visionary aspects of his administration had been stated, the little president launched what might be termed the practical obligations: kill Mexicans, expel Indians and lure New Mexico into the Texas nation. In pursuit of the first goal, Lamar dispatched Captain Garner's ranging company back to the Nueces River, which they crossed on various short expeditions in hopes of catching Benito Garza. They failed, but they did shoot up several groups of Mexicans and would have gone after more had they not been stopped by a surprising development which forced them to withdraw: two messengers from the north rode in to announce that Indians had attacked the republic.

The official messenger was an army officer; his guide was Yancey Quimper, big hat down over his eyes, his voice quivering with rage. 'Them damned Cherokee that Sam Houston said he'd pacified . . .'

'What are they up to?' Garner asked.

'Nacogdoches way . . . Uprising . . . People being kilt.'

It was always difficult to ascertain exactly what truth lay behind anything that Quimper said, but when the officer took over, it was clear that an Indian war was under way and that the government wanted all companies to converge on Nacogdoches for a final assault on the difficult Cherokee. With some regret, the Xavier County men started north.

As they rode, the messenger explained the source of trouble: 'An eastern tribe – doesn't belong to Texas – was moved west by the United States government. They argue that they're a nation too, with the right to make treaties same as England or Spain.'

He said that the Cherokee were led by a notorious warrior, Chief Bowles, known with respect as The Bowl. He was eighty years old and carried into battle a sword given him by Sam Houston; it brought him luck, for he had never been vanquished.

Now Quimper broke in: 'When you were away, President Lamar issued a proper policy for handlin' Indians: "Get out of Texas or get killed."'

The officer laughed: 'He didn't say it that way. His message to Congress was "Eviction or extermination." First we'll try to evict them.'

One of Garner's men said: 'Mexicans and Indians, you can't

tell the difference.' And this verdict represented the consensus, for Yancey Quimper said loudly: 'In Texas they ain't no place for a Cherokee or a Mexican.'

When the riders reached Victoria, Quimper insisted that he accompany Macnab when the latter rode out to visit with Josefina and María, and although Otto took no special notice of this at first, he did later realize that his friend Yancey had a deep interest in the two league-and-a-labor plots owned by the Mexican women.

'Campbell leave any children?' he asked María, and when she said no, he wanted to know how his land was left, and she said firmly: 'It was always my land.' And when he asked: 'What happens to it when you die?' she said forthrightly: 'I have signed it to my brother, Benito.'

'Did Otto's father leave any papers . . . about the land that is?'

'It was never his land. It was always my sister's.'

'Then it would become Otto's, wouldn't it?'

'Whenever he wants it,' Josefina said with a quiet smile at her son, 'but he told me that General Houston gave him land – up north – for fighting in the war. He said he did not need my land.'

When Otto moved aside to speak with his mother, Quimper hectored María: 'Where's your brother now?' and she replied honestly: 'I don't know. He comes, he goes,' at which Yancey said: 'I'll bet he does.' Later, Otto asked María the same question, and she gave the same answer: 'He comes, he goes.'

'Tell him to be careful,' Otto said. When the company approached Xavier County a scout rode up with devastating news: 'War up north has turned full-scale. Cherokee on the rampage, and they tell us Benito Garza's with them.'

This news infuriated Garner: 'We're down south chasing his ghost while he's up there burning our farms.' It was quite clear from what Quimper kept threatening that if Garner's men ever caught Garza, they were going to hang him within the minute, but Otto argued with them: 'That's only what they say. I know Garza, and he's not messing around with Indians.'

Nevertheless, Otto decided to stay close to Quimper when parleys with the Cherokee began, to forestall precipitate action, but this wise precaution proved unnecessary because when the troop finally reached Xavier County, Yancey discovered that he had important business that would keep him there, so Captain Garner's men rode north without him.

They had barely pitched their tents in Cherokee country when Otto was summoned to a night interrogation by the colonel in command, who asked: 'Son, have you ever heard of Julian Pedro Miracle?'

'I have not, sir.'

'Do you know that we shot him about a year ago?'

'No, sir.'

'And have you heard that we found some very incriminating papers on him? That he was attempting to incite the Cherokee to join the Mexicans? To drive us Americans out of Texas?'

'I did not hear this,' Otto said.

'Well, did you know the Manuel Flores we also killed some time ago?'

'I did not, sir.'

'Have you heard what papers we found on Flores?'

'I've heard nothing, sir.' In the tent the officer thrust a translation in English of the terribly damaging report that the dead Mexican spy Flores had written just before the start of the Cherokee uprising, and they directed his attention to one paragraph:

> I have completed plans whereby the Cherokee will launch a major harassment of the norteamericanos to coincide with the army attack of mexicano troops under Generals Filisola, Cós, Urrea and Ripperdá. At the same time our trusted revolutionary Benito Garza of Victoria will set the countryside ablaze, and we shall expel all norteamericanos and regain control of Tejas.

Otto was shaken, and in the dark silence his mind flashed pictures of the Garza he had known: the bright young fellow trying to find husbands for his sisters, the gifted teacher of riding, that moment of terrible truth when he had saved Otto's life at Goliad, and the swamp knifings at San Jacinto when Otto had reciprocated. During all the chases south of the Nueces, Otto had hoped that the Mexican government would see the wisdom of letting Texas have the disputed land. Then peace between Mexico and Texas would be possible, ensuring peace between Benito and himself. Now he saw his dream was futile.

'I am not surprised,' he told the colonel.

'Is this Garza a friend of yours?'

'My father's brother-in-law. I lived with him for three years.'

The officer in charge of the interrogation breathed deeply. 'I'm glad you admitted that, son, because we knew the answer before we asked the question.' And to Otto's amazement an orderly brought into the tent Martin Ascot, who nodded in Otto's direction and smiled in friendly fashion.

'They arrested me this afternoon.'

'You were not arrested,' the officer corrected. 'You were interrogated.'

'And I told them "Of course Macnab knows Garza" and I told them about the incident in the swamp at San Jacinto when you stopped me from killing him. You see, Otto, they had a letter . . .'

'I saw it. The one they captured when they shot . . . what was his name?'

'Flores,' the officer said. 'Manuel Flores. But that is not the letter Ascot speaks of.'

'Someone who knew you in Xavier County – didn't sign his name – sent a letter,' Ascot said, 'which charges you with complicity in this affair.'

The anonymous letter was produced; its ugly charges were ventilated; and Otto had to deny on the Bible that when he stopped at the Zave Campbell dog-run on the return from the Nueces, he had consorted with his renegade brother-in-law Benito Garza.

'Why did you save his life at San Jacinto? If you knew at that time that he was an enemy?' Silence. 'Well, you knew he'd joined Santa Anna, didn't you?' Silence. 'You better speak up, son. You're in trouble.'

Very quietly Martin Ascot, the young lawyer, counseled his neighbor: 'You must tell them what you told me that evening.'

Standing very straight, the youngest and shortest in the tent, Otto recounted his adventures at Goliad, his surrender, the march out from the presidio that Sunday morning, the dreadful execution of his father, his fight in the woods with the Mexican swordsman, the cut across his face, the gunfire of the two foot soldiers. At the conclusion he said: 'I stand here today only because Benito Garza, under risk to himself, helped me to escape.'

The silence in the tent was overpowering. Finally the officer in charge asked: 'Macnab, what would you do tomorrow if you encountered Benito Garza on the battlefield? These papers prove he may be there.'

'I would shoot him,' Otto said.

Next day the battle was brief, and terrible, and heartbreaking. The Cherokee nation, which had been so pathetically abused by the American nation, brought eight hundred braves onto a rolling, wooded plain near the Neches River, where they faced nine hundred well-mounted, well-armed Texians led by men skilled in such fighting.

The Bowl, eighty years old and white-haired, friend of Sam Houston and honorable negotiator with Spain, with Mexico, with the United States government and with the emerging nation of Texas, saw through copious tears that any hope of living in peace with these harsh newcomers to his land was vain. Indian and white man could not coexist in Texas, not ever.

Dressing on the morning of 15 July 1839 in his finest elkskin robes and wrapping about his waist the golden sash General Houston had given him as proof of their perpetual friendship, he girded on the silver-handled sword which Houston had also given him, mounted his best horse, and led his men into a battle he knew he could not win.

All that day Texians and Indians blazed away at each other, and at dusk it was clear to General Johnson and Vice-President Burnet that if equal pressure was applied on the morrow, total victory must be theirs. That night the confident Texians slept well, all except Martin Ascot, who had tormenting doubts. Shaking Otto awake, he asked: 'Why can't we find some kind of arrangement to let them live off to one side?' and Otto gave the answer he had developed while chasing Mexicans along the Nueces: 'Texians and Indians ... impossible.'

'Why?'

'Martin,' Otto said like an old campaigner to a raw recruit, 'go to sleep. We got work tomorrow.'

Next day the fighting was brief, concentrated and brutal.

627

There was a violent chase all the way into another county, where the troops cut The Bowl off from his braves, shot him from his horse and shot him again as he lay on the ground, his white hair caked with blood, his silver-handled sword a trophy to be cheered.

Without their leader, the Cherokee were lost, and well before noon they surrendered. They asked if they could go back and gather their still-unreaped crops, for they had no food, but the victorious Texians said they should just continue north and get the hell out of Texas.

So they went, honorable wanderers who had known many homes since the white men began to press down upon them. East Texas would know its Indians no more.

Mirabeau Lamar's imperial designs suffered humiliating defeats but also enjoyed significant triumphs, proving that although Texas was no supernation, it was more viable than its economic performance might suggest.

The history of his attempt to invade Santa Fe and bring it into the Texas orbit can be told briefly. 14 April 1840: President Lamar drafts a letter to the people of New Mexico telling them of the glories of Texas and warning them that sooner or later, they will have to join up; the letter is ignored by loyal Santa Fe citizens, who are Spanish-speaking and happy under Mexican rule. 19 June 1841: Lamar personally but not governmentally approves of a convoy of twenty-one ox wagons, with military support and a contingent of 321 eager settlers, which sets out to take over the government of New Mexico. 5 August to 17 August, same year: the expedition, having no guides who have ever been to Santa Fe, becomes hopelessly lost and sends out horsemen to see if anyone can identify anything. 12 September same year: the would-be conquerors stagger into a remote Mexican settlement and beg for water and help. 17 September, 1841: the entire expedition surrenders to Mexican troops without having fired a single shot or having been allowed to peddle their promises to a single resident of Santa Fe. 1 October 1841: almost all of the Texians are marched to Mexico City and on to the old fort of Perote in the jungle, where they are thrown into prison. 6 April 1842: most of the Perote prisoners are released, but with bitter memories of their mistreatment.

On the other hand, President Lamar's negotiations with powers other than Mexico and the United States progressed handsomely, and in 1839, France signed a treaty recognizing the independence of the new nation, thus assuring Texas of full international standing. England, too, made overtures, and the future looked bright. As for the United States, Lamar perceived it as the enemy and refused either to initiate or to participate in talks leading to annexation.

Regarding Mexico, he was generously prepared to offer either war or peace, but he was not prepared for what his neighbor to the south actually did. Its troops marched across the Rio Grande and captured San Antonio, but fortunately for Lamar, they withdrew of their own volition.

So Texas was not an unalloyed success, but the valor of its poet-president did encourage it to make certain sensible moves, chief of which was the incredible decision to shift the capital from Houston, on the eastern malarial fringe of the nation, into Austin, at the edge of the salubrious highlands. On the day the governmental party surveyed the site for the new capital, buffalo scampered down what was to become the main street.

The intellectual life of the new nation also flourished, thanks to men like Martin Ascot, who took seriously his duties as Xavier County's corresponding secretary of the Philosophical Society. Otto watched admiringly as his friend spent six nights in a row, hunched over the table in the kitchen, drafting by candlelight his first submission to the society, and although Otto could not know it at the time, the resonant success of this paper was to account for an experience from which Otto would profit.

Corresponding secretaries were obligated to report on the 'scientific, agricultural, historical, political, moral and geographical phenomena of their counties,' so Martin chose for his topic 'The Texas Pecan, Salvator Mundi,' and wrote with such charm that older members said: 'There's a lad to watch!'

He extolled the pecan as a miracle food, a possible source of oil, a tree with unique capabilities and God's particular blessing on the new nation, insofar as native foods were concerned. What was remembered best was the way he harmonized scientific knowledge about its cultivation with his personal reaction to it:

If corn is our nation's primary cereal and the pecan our finest nut, is it not appropriate that the two be blended in some perfect dish? My wife, Betsy Belle, has discovered a way of doing this in a pie which has considerable merit. Using corn flour and bear grease, she bakes a fine crust, in which she pours a cooked mixture of syrup made from the boiled stalk of the corn mixed with the finest ground corn thickening. She sprinkles the top so richly with pecan halves, lightly salted, that nothing else is visible. She then puts everything in a flat iron receptacle with a cover and bakes it for an hour until all ingredients combine in what I do believe is the most tempting pie in the world.

The country's leaders in Houston were so impressed by Martin's report, and their wives so pleased with Betsy Belle's recipe, that President Lamar gave Ascot an assignment which required work in Xavier, travel to the new capital at Austin and the delivery of papers back to Houston, Martin, who had a case scheduled before Judge Phinizy, completed the work but turned it over to Otto to deliver at government expense.

Otto rode to Austin with Martin's papers, got them signed, and was told that he could take the new stagecoach down to Houston. The firm of Starke and Burgess had been awarded the right to operate a stage between the new capital and the old, and to accomplish this, had imported coaches that had seen decades of service in Mississippi and two drivers with almost as much experience in Alabama. Otto would ride to Houston in the Thursday coach driven by Jake Hornblow, who had a wealth of beard, a brazen voice and a sulphurous vocabulary. When the six passengers were assembled, four men, two women, Jake instructed everyone there to sit, then glared at Otto and said: 'You, fetch the pole and rope.'

'Where are they?'

'Damn it to hell, if I have to tell you people everything, like you was babies, we'll never get to Houston.' Asking around the office, a one-room shack with a heavy iron safe, Otto found the gear, and when he delivered it, Jake studied him contemptuously and growled: 'I was goin' to let you have the pole, but you ain't got the weight to give it leverage. Keep the rope.'

It was a scheduled three-day trip, and before it started, Jake assured his passengers, 'If this was July or August, we'd get there in great shape,' but it was late March, in the rainy season, and when they were only a few miles out of Austin, Otto learned what the rope was for, because they came to a place where a swollen stream had overrun the road, turning it into a Texas quagmire.

'All out!' Hornblow bellowed, and when everyone was standing beside the mired coach, he threw Otto the rope and told him to take it to the far side of the huge mudhole, but as Otto started to obey, Jake cursed at him as if he were both idiotic and criminal: 'Goddamnit, you stupid horse's ass. You're supposed to tie one end to the coach.' So back Otto sloshed, with Jake heaping scorn on him as he bent down to tie the hitch: 'If you was in the rangin' company, like they say, the Indians have nothin' to worry about.'

Then, surveying the male passengers as if they were members of a chain gang, he nominated one: 'You, take the pole.' This stout lever was rested upon a pile of rocks with one end thrust under the rear of the wagon, whereupon Jake yelled at the two women passengers: 'Yes, you, goddamnit, lean on the pole with the gentleman.' The other men were expected to go into the mud up to their boot tops and push.

In this way, with the horses straining, Otto pulling, the man and the two ladies prizing the rear with their lever, the others in the mud, and Jake cursing God, the rain, the creek and his lazy companions, the coach worked its way through.

The three-day trip took six days, with the rope-and-pole trick being utilized at least four times each day. The cost was fifteen dollars per passenger, not including food, which was invariably cornbread, greasy bacon and weak coffee, three times a day. When the trip ended, Otto and the other men were so outraged by the treatment they had received from Jake Hornblow that they wanted to thrash him, but when they considered his size, they refrained.

The high regard in which Lawyer Ascot was held was further demonstrated when President Lamar appointed him to head a commission with important duties in San Antonio. He was to have in his entourage a company of Texas soldiers and Captain

631

Garner with three members of his ranging company. Ascot suggested that Macnab be one, and the party set forth in the late winter of 1840.

As they rode, Commissioner Ascot explained the purpose of the meeting: 'At last the Comanche see the folly of their ways. They want a treaty with us. They propose a wide strip where a truce will be permanently observed, so that maybe now the killings will stop.'

'What did they say about the white people they hold captive?' Otto inquired, and Ascot said: 'If a treaty can be arranged, the Comanche promise to surrender every prisoner they now hold, perhaps as many as a hundred.' This was joyous news, if true, for the idea that savages held white women and children was repellent.

Captain Garner offered verification: 'I was assured all prisoners would be released. We wouldn't talk, otherwise.'

'What are we expected to do?' Otto asked, and Garner explained: 'The army's in charge. They'll give the orders. My job is to deliver Mr Ascot to supervise the legal arrangements.'

'But what do we do?' the two other Rangers asked, and Garner snapped: 'Obey orders.'

'Whose orders?' Otto asked, for he did not work well in a confused chain of command.

'The army's orders,' Garner said.

When they got to San Antonio and saw what a handsome town it was, so much more civilized than their frontier settlements and with buildings so far superior, they had moments of real delight. The beer was good, the Mexican dishes were new to many of the soldiers, the winter vegetables were a surprising relief from the drab food many of the men had been eating, and there was an air of levity unknown in the grimmer, less settled parts of Texas. It was as if the men had come into another country, one of ancient charm rather than new rawness.

The job of Garner's three young men was to stand watchful guard at the courthouse in which the important meetings with the Comanche were to be held, and they were attentive to the plans the army officer outlined: 'Don't frighten them when they ride in tomorrow. Try to accept them as neutrals. And for God's sake, make no move toward your guns. Just let them come at us, and pray for the best.' When there was a rumble of apprehension, Garner whispered to his men: 'If trouble starts, give 'em hell.' The Rangers nodded, indicating that they understood.

Macnab and his two companions staked out a corner of the public plaza where they could stand by next morning as the Comanche braves rode in with their prisoners. 'They say there may be as many as a hundred white women and children delivered,' Otto told the Rangers, and one asked Captain Garner if he could be detailed to help these unfortunates, who might be in pitiful condition if frontier tales could be believed, but the captain pointed to a small building in which the women of San Antonio would care for the captives.

'You stay where you're put,' Garner said with unexpected sternness, emphasizing the seriousness of this assignment.

That night an old scout who had prowled the frontier with Deaf Smith told the young army men who the Comanche were:

'They came to Texas late, maybe 1730, not much sooner. Come down across the prairie from Ute Country. Mountain Indians movin' onto the plains. And why? Because they got theyselves horses, that's why. Yep, when them mountain Comanche got aholt of some good Spanish horses, they went wild. Now they could ride a hundred mile for buffalo, two hundred to find and burn a Mexican rancho.

'They took no prisoners, except women and children as slaves. Well, they did keep the eight or ten strongest men alive temporary. Me and Deaf Smith had a pact. "If'n I'm wounded and cain't ride and the Comanche is comin' at me, you got to shoot me, Deaf." And he said "Same with me, Oscar."

'Well, when they hit Texas, about 1730 like I said, they like to tore this place apart. Terrified the other tribes that didn't have horses. You know how the old-timers was scairt of the Apache? The Comanche treated the Apache like they was nursin' babes, that's how they treated the Apache.

'These is the savages that now say they want a treaty with us. You know what I think? I think it's all a trap. Tomorrow in that building and out here on this square somethin' terrible's goin' to happen. With Comanche it always does.'

633

Apparently Captain Garner and his army superiors had the same fear, because about midnight Garner told Macnab: 'Tomorrow may be touch-and-go. If at any time I rush out that door waving this handkerchief, I want you three to dash in, right past me, guns ready. No Comanche is to escape alive ... that is, if they start something.'

There was great excitement that Thursday morning 19 March 1840, when from the west the awesome Comanche rode in, for they were ghostly figures from some gruesome fairy tale. Taller than the Cherokee, thinner, with hollow cheeks and deep-set eyes, they wore battle finery that made them seem even more imposing, and by some trick they kept their horses stepping nervously sideways, as if the animals, too, were aching for a fight.

But there was also the gravest disappointment, for when the troop of about sixty-five neared the entrance to the town, it was obvious that only one captive was being led in, a girl of about fifteen whom someone recognized as Matilda Lockhart, captured two years before. When people saw her pitiful condition, sobs of the most deep and painful grief welled up, and many had to look away as she rode silently past.

The Comanche were led by an elderly wizened chieftain named Muguara, veteran of a hundred raids and killings, but one now apparently desirous of peace. Looking eagerly about, like a scout on the trail, he studied each element that faced him in San Antonio as if to satisfy himself that he was not heading into an ambush, and when he felt that the meeting could proceed, he signaled his women to remain behind, guarded by most of the braves, while he, twelve others and an interpreter dismounted and marched to the council house, almost dragging the mute Lockhart girl with them.

When he brought her into the room where the negotiators waited, with Commissioner Ascot prepared to offer clemency if only peace could be established, the Texian delegation gasped and one man clutched Ascot's arm: 'Jesus Christ! Is that a human being?' It was a fair question, for when Ascot moved forward to give her comfort, she quivered like some tortured animal and looked at him with wild, uncomprehending eyes.

It was with difficulty that Ascot prevented a break right then,

634

but with great fortitude and holding back his own tears, he counseled patience, reminding his negotiators that they were dealing with savages who would have to be tamed by time, and he took the Lockhart girl, who would have been an attractive young woman had she been allowed to grow up on her ranch outside of San Antonio, and delivered her to the women waiting in the adobe house where they had hoped to welcome at least a hundred more. When they saw her, they began to weep, and the Rangers outside heard their cries of rage.

'Let's go in and get them now,' one shouted, but the others calmed him, and the soldiers waited, fingering their guns.

With the dreadful evidence of the Lockhart girl removed from the council house, it was possible to start serious discussion, but first Ascot and his team had to know the whereabouts of the other prisoners. However, when they asked, Chief Muguara lacked the English words for a conciliatory answer: 'Not my prisoners. Other tribes. You pay enough, you get them.' Then he added a most unfortunate phrase: 'How you like that for an answer?'

Even Ascot, who had vowed not to be unnerved by anything the Comanche did or said, blanched: 'Interpreter, tell Chief Muguara that he and his dozen warriors will be our prisoners until he arranges for the other captives to be brought in.'

The interpreter, knowing that such an ultimatum must mean war, shouted the words in a jumble, then bolted through the door, right past Captain Garner, who stood guard, and shouted to the Indians in the plaza: 'War! War!'

Garner, recovering from the shock of having the interpreter knock him aside, waved his handkerchief, at which Macnab and half a dozen others dashed into the council hall, where a general melee had erupted. Otto arrived just in time to see one of Muguara's braves leap upon Ascot and drive a long knife into his heart. The astounded commissioner gasped, and with blood gushing from his mouth, fell dead.

This so enraged Macnab that he began firing coldly at any brave who could be separated from the white men, and the room became a miasma of gunsmoke, screams and death. Macnab and others kept firing with relentless accuracy, and within a few minutes all thirteen of the Comanches inside the hall were dead.

Outside, in obedience to army commands, the soldiers stationed about the plaza killed thirty-five more Comanche before the others fled. Six white men lay dead.

It was a ghastly affair, a ghastly mistake, and it terminated any efforts to bring about peace with the Comanche. Captain Garner and his men saddled up to join the army in pursuit of whatever Comanche tribes might be in the vicinity. They came upon campfires recently abandoned where corpses testified to the fact that the Indians, enraged by their betrayal in the council house, had savagely executed all their white prisoners.

Macnab came upon one site where the rampaging Comanche had assaulted a Texian ranch; two wagons had been placed beside a fire, their tongues projected over the embers. To the tongues, face down, had been lashed the living bodies of the men running the ranch, and the wagons had been adjusted so that the men would slowly burn to death.

'Well,' Otto said, 'Martin met the Comanche.'

That happened in March, and for the next five months the Comanche retreated deep into the plains, tricking the Texians into believing that the massacre had been so devastating, there would be no further raids.

But two days before the August moon, one of the largest bands of Comanche ever gathered for a single raid assembled well west of San Antonio, and under the leadership of skilled chiefs, prepared to spread fire and terror across Texas. Cunningly, they slipped past military outposts, keeping well to the north of Gonzales, and fell with great fury upon the unprotected town of Victoria. They captured the entire town, burning and raping and killing. Corpses were scattered about, and more than two hundred horses were herded off. On they went, down to the little town of Linnville, where Finlay Macnab's Baltimore wife had landed with her two daughters, and here, at the edge of the sea itself, they rampaged unmolested all through the day, burning more, killing more, and stomping in fury at the shore as certain clever townspeople took refuge in boats, standing well out into the bay without food or shelter until the savages departed.

With these two incidents – the shooting of the Indian chieftains during a parley at which they were supposed to be protected by the white man's code of honor, and the burning of Victoria and Linnville – the Texians spoke no more of rapprochement with the Comanche. War of annihilation was seen to be the only recourse, and it would be fought with terrible intensity by both sides. In 1850 the slaughter would be appalling; in 1864, when the whites were engaged in a great civil war of their own, with their men assigned to distant battlefields and unable to protect their homes, the Comanche would ride right into towns and set them ablaze; in 1870, the same; and up to 1874 this terrible war would continue. Along the frontier Deaf Smith's rule prevailed: 'Never let a Comanche capture you. Better you shoot yourself in the head.'

When Otto Macnab heard of the disaster at Victoria he had to assume that his mother's unprotected home, and his aunt María's as well, must have been assaulted, so he sought permission from Captain Garner to ride down to see if the women had survived, and the captain said: 'Sure, but watch out for stray Comanche.'

So Otto rode south from Xavier County, and as he approached Victoria and saw the desolation spread by the Comanche six days before, it became clear that only a miracle could have saved the Garza women.

When he reached the Guadalupe River and started down it toward Victoria he found only burned-out ranches: 'Around the next bend, I'll see it,' and when he made the turn he did. The two houses which had known so much love between Texian and Mexican were gone. The drying corpses of the two women still lay under the hanging oak, where they had fled to escape the lances.

I better bury them, Otto told himself matter-of-factly, but digging in this hard, clayey soil had never been easy, and he had to be satisfied with very shallow graves indeed. But you could call it Christian burial, he thought.

That evening he bunked in one of the houses in Victoria that the Comanche had not burned; the man in charge told him: 'Señor got himself killed out in the street. Señora, she's with the other family.' He said it would be all right if Otto stayed there and he even helped prepare some beans and goat's meat, but Otto could not sleep, and at about nine he told the man: 'I think I better go back and say goodbye.' The man insisted upon joining him, just in case, but Otto said: 'No, it'll be all right. They've gone.'

He rode slowly back to the ruins, giving no consideration as to what he might do when he reached them. The Comanche moon, as it was called in these parts – that bright full moon which encouraged the Indians to raid – was waning, but it would remain a crescent in the sky until morning, enabling him to see once more the landscape he had loved so much when he first came to Texas: the silent Guadalupe, that first important stand of trees after the bleak marshes of the shore, the gently rolling hills that gave the land variation, the oak tree from which Zave . . . Suddenly he became aware that someone else was near the tree.

'Who goes?' he called, readying his pistols.

'Amigo,' came a strong Mexican voice. 'That you, Otto?'

From behind the oak, his own pistols at the draw, came Benito Garza, who had ridden north from the Nueces Strip to pay homage to his sisters. Standing quietly, he pointed with a pistol to the new graves. 'You bury them?' he asked in Spanish.

'I did,' Otto said. Slowly the two men lowered their pistols and moved closer.

'What brought you?' Garza asked, still in Spanish.

'You hear about the big fight at San Antone?'

'Those Comanche can be bastards,' Garza said, still in Spanish.

'Why are you speaking Spanish with me?'

'I don't speak English no more,' he said in English, and after that explanation he used the language no further.

After they had found rude seats on the blackened remnants of a wall, Otto asked: 'If you think the Comanche are such bastards, why did you work with the Cherokee, against us?' Garza was late in replying, so Otto said: 'We found papers on the dead spy Flores . . .'

'Is he dead?'

'On his corpse were these papers, they named you as a principal. We have orders, I suppose you know, to shoot you on sight.'

'Are you going to try?'

'Why side with the Indians? Will you be partners with the Comanche next?'

638

Garza laughed, freely, easily. Punching Otto on the arm, he said: 'You try making friends with the Comanche. Go ahead, try.'

'They sure raised hell here,' Otto said.

'What will you do with your land?' And Garza pointed west toward where the Macnab dog-run had once stood.

'It was never our land, Benito. It always belonged to your sisters.' There was silence for a moment, then Otto reached out with his boot and kicked at some blackened clods: 'It was your sisters' land. And now it's yours.'

'Your government will never let me have it. Me fighting on the side of Santa Anna.' He ignored his later conspiracy with the Indians.

'I'm sure they will,' Otto said. 'We want to forget the battles.'

'You don't want it?'

'I have no use for it. They gave me land up on the Brazos. For bein' a hero, I guess.'

'You norteamericanos got your revenge at San Jacinto.'

'You heard, I guess, Santa Anna went free. Used our good money and rode back to Washington in style. Talked with the American President and all that.'

'You have not heard the last of Santa Anna,' Benito predicted. 'He'll be back.'

'And you'll be with him?'

'The moment he issues his grito.'

'Who will he be fighting?'

'You bastards, who else?'

'And you'll fight with him . . . against us?'

'Certainly.'

Otto pondered this a long time, then said slowly: 'You saved my life. I saved your life. We're even, Benito. Next time we meet as enemies. Draw fast, because I'll kill you.'

Garza laughed easily: 'Little boy, I taught you all you know. I can handle you.'

'But you taught me very well, Benito. Next time . . .'

They parted. No handshake. No farewell words of the affection each felt. Over the graves of the women they had loved they parted, each believing that Mexicans and Texians could never share this land.

When Otto returned to Xavier County he was a forlorn young man, bewildered by the tragedies that had overwhelmed those he loved: good, bountiful María and Josefina, slain; Martin Ascot, most promising lawyer in the nation, killed in San Antonio; Betsy Belle and her infant child adrift.

By the time he reached Xavier he had concluded that it would be improper for him to continue living in the shed at the Ascot place, for although he was five years younger than Betsy, his continued presence could cause comment, and this he would not allow. But when he came to the shack and started to collect his few belongings, Betsy said: 'What in the world are you doing?' and when he explained, she burst into robust laughter: 'People might talk? Otto, I'm trying to run a farm. I'm trying to care for a baby. I need help. I need you.'

Sometimes when he took a side of venison in to Campbell to barter for things like flour and bacon, he was aware that the townspeople did talk in whispers, just as he had expected, but one day the schoolmaster, Reverend Harrison, stopped him as he was passing and said: 'Son, you're doing God's work in succoring the fatherless child. Take Mrs Ascot this basket of food my wife cooked.' When Otto thanked him, he added: 'But, son, if you continue to live there, I do think you ought to marry. It's the only decent way.'

Such advice caused Otto greater confusion than any he had previously known; even the death of his father had been easier to fit into the grand scheme of things, because fathers traditionally died sooner than their sons. And right there, in that simple statement, resided the source of his confusion.

'She's so much older!' He was barely eighteen, Betsy Belle twenty-three, but she was also a mite taller and had always looked upon him as a child. She was a woman wise in the twists and turns of the world, and mature enough to be his mother, a role she had adopted from the start. How vast the difference between them seemed, not only to him but also to her.

So he continued to live in the cramped shack he and Martin had built, and sometimes in the evening after an arduous day of work, he and Betsy would sit and talk about the future, and one night she said: 'You must start looking for a wife, Otto, and I must find a father for my son.' He was staggered by this bold statement, then listened as she ticked off the local girls whom he might reasonably court. She even went so far as to invite one of them to visit, and the three spent a long Sunday afternoon getting acquainted, and it was obvious that the visitor liked Otto, even though she was a mite taller than he. The visit had one salutary outcome: Otto no longer feared that Betsy Belle might be interested in him as a husband.

The presence in Texas of a widow of good character who had a son to raise became widely known quickly, and one morning a fine-looking gentleman from Nacogdoches appeared at the Ascot cabin to introduce himself. He was from Mississippi, he was a widower, he had a farm and a daughter, and he had brought with him two extra horses in hopes that Mrs Ascot would consider riding back with her son and her family goods. He was a pious man, a Baptist, and said: 'I'd not contemplate this, ma'am, unless we was married proper before we started,' and Betsy asked: 'How did you know about me?' and he said: 'Your father,' and he showed her a letter:

> Jared, my beloved daughter Betsy Belle is a widow in Xavier County, Texas. If your sorrow over the death of your Norma has subsided, as God always wants it to, ride down and make Betsy's acquaintance, with my blessing.

At the wedding, held in Reverend Harrison's school, Yancey Quimper served as best man, and when Joel Job asked in his resonant voice: 'Who gives this woman in marriage?' Otto said: 'I do,' and it was on his arm that Betsy Belle approached her new husband.

For some days Otto lived alone in the Ascot cabin, now shorn of its warmth and liveliness, and he spent the time brooding about the inescapable manner in which the world turns, bringing day after night and the passage of months and years. He knew almost nothing about girls or women and had been astounded when one of the Rangers on a night ride in pursuit of bandits told him that 'a woman can have babies only so long, you know, and if she misses her chance, she misses.' He had never spoken to Betsy Belle about this; indeed he had been completely embarrassed that Sunday when she invited the girl to visit, but he now supposed that she had ridden north to

Nacogdoches so soon after the death of her husband because she felt the passing of the years and the limited time she could expect on a frontier like Texas.

'And what of me?' he asked in the darkness.

He was diverted from such mournful speculation by the eruption of another presidential campaign in which the men at Quimper's Ferry were determined to prevent Sam Houston from returning to power. There was much loud talk about emasculating the old drunk, and one evening when Yancey had himself imbibed rather heavily his cronies persuaded him to pen a vitriolic attack upon Houston's morals, courage, thievery, treason and bigamy. When Houston refused even to acknowledge having read the widely publicized assault, Yancey was goaded by his friends into challenging Houston to a duel. Had he been sober, he would not have dared.

Houston handled the Quimper affair with that sense of the ridiculous which characterized so many of his actions. Informed by his partisans that Yancey, now sober, was paralyzed by the anticipation of a duel in which he was likely to be killed, Houston sent him a letter which treated him as a serious opponent. Widely circulated, its ludicrous nature not only delighted Houston's rowdy partisans but also provided serious ammunition for those sober citizens who were determined to end this murderous folly of dueling:

My dear Yancey Quimper,

I have before me your challenge to a duel. My seconds will await yours and we shall fight at the spot and time they elected. Since I am the challenged party, I shall demand horse pistols at five feet.

However, I have been much challenged of late and at present have twenty-two duels scheduled ahead of yours. I calculate that I can fit you in about August of next year. Until then, I am your humble servant,

Sam Houston

Allowing and even encouraging a brief spell of hilarity – 'Horse pistols at five feet, they'd blow each other's guts out' and 'Who can imagine Sam Houston being anybody's humble servant?' – he put a sudden stop to it and began speaking of Quimper as if the latter were an authentic and dangerous duelist. This achieved two purposes: it brought public attention back to the absurdity of dueling, and it created the image of President Houston dealing courageously with a hazardous opponent.

He abetted the rumor: 'I'd be damned lucky to escape that duel with Quimper. He's a killer. At San Jacinto he was a savage, nothing less. Quimper would do me in.'

When Yancey heard this assessment he did not appreciate what Houston was doing; and when no one took the trouble to explain, he actually began to believe that Houston was terrified of him, and as time passed he further convinced himself that had the duel taken place, he would have dropped the big drunk. He could see Houston appearing at dawn, badly inebriated, shooting wildly, then crumpling under the devastating fire of Yancey Quimper.

Free Texas being what it was in those wild days, many citizens were tricked by Houston's game, and in time it was credibly reported that the duel had taken place, that Houston had reported drunk and had fired but missed, and that Quimper, gentleman to the end, had deliberately fired in the air rather than kill a former president of Texas. Yancey was now not only the Hero of San Jacinto but also the Man Who Shamed Sam Houston in the Duel.

With this fresh-minted glory, Yancey felt encouraged to take a step popular with Texians: he awarded himself a military rank, and since he was now famous for two different acts of gallantry, San Jacinto and the duel, he made himself a general, and as soon as he had done so, an amazing transformation occurred. He stood taller. He shaved his ineffectual mustache. He sent away to New Orleans for a uniform with a decided French swagger, and he discarded his big slouch hat in favor of a smaller one with a neat cockade. He also began pronouncing final 'g's as if he had been to military school, and referred often to West Point without actually claiming that he had enrolled there.

When General Quimper learned that his friend Judge Phinizy was scheduled to hold sessions in Victoria County, he left the inn, explaining: 'I have some legal work to clean up.' By paying assiduous attention to all property law passed by the Texas Congress, he had learned that the ten thousand acres of choice land along the Guadalupe River – called the Wharloopey by many Texians – once owned by the dead Garza women was in jeopardy, because their brother Benito, who should have inherited it, had proclaimed himself to be an armed enemy of the nation, and had thus forfeited any right to own land in it.

The case that General Quimper brought in the Victoria court was so complicated and long-drawn that Judge Phinizy had no chance of unraveling it, but when the court was not in session Yancey explained the complexities to him. He also attended court in his new general's uniform, which lent dignity to his claims, and when he encountered any members of the huge Garza clan who were defending their shadowy rights against him, he was immaculately courteous, as if his only interest in the suit was to see justice done and the land distributed equitably.

In a series of decisions so perverse that no sensible man could have explained them, and certainly not Judge Phinizy, who handed them down, General Quimper achieved ownership of all the Garza lands, and then, as a result of additional suits equally intricate, he was awarded a further twenty-two thousand acres, the courts invariably transferring title from indistinct Mexican owners to this very real Hero of the Republic who obviously knew Texas land law better than the judges and certainly better than the original owners.

Thousands of acres which had once been owned by Trinidad de Saldaña were now passing quietly into the hands of enterprising Texians like General Quimper, until in the end more than two million of the best Nueces acres would be so 'verified,' as the Texian judge explained, or 'stolen,' as the owners complained.

The lands did not always pass quietly. When Benito Garza heard of the theft of his acres by Quimper, he led a daylight raid boldly into the outskirts of Victoria, where with the help of sixteen dispossessed men like himself he gunned down a Texian who could be considered a sheriff, so once again the ranging company had to be sent to the Nueces.

When Otto returned, with three more Mexican bandits to his record, he sat alone in the Ascot kitchen, staring at the wall. At any sound he whipped about, hoping it was Betsy Belle returning with her child, and after several such incidents he realized that it was the baby he really missed. How proud he had been to serve as its father when it cried for attention. A wolf howled, and he leaped in frustration: God, I've got to do something.

Thousands of miles from the new nation, in one of the many German principalities, historical events were painfully forging a solution to Otto's problems. The Margravate of Grenzler was in trouble. Not only did economic crisis grip the Rhineland, but a frightening surplus of population inhibited the normal functioning of society. Young people could find no homes and older ones no employment; Germany itself remain divided because no central power had yet arisen strong enough to force consolidation. There was talk that perhaps the sturdy kingdom of Prussia might provide leadership, but only the sanguine could hope for this, because each petty ruler like the posturing Margrave of Grenzler held jealously to his ancestral rights, refusing to accept leadership from anyone more powerful or more intelligent.

In the old days – the 1100s, for example – Grenzler had played such an honourable role in defense of the area, standing like an impregnable rock at the confluence of rivers down which invaders from the east must come if they sought to attack established centers like Cologne and Nuremberg, that its stubborn ruler was given the title Margrave, and although justification for continuance of his august honor had long since vanished, descendants of those ancient heroes clung to it.

On a spring day in 1842, Ludwig Allerkamp, forty years old and the father of four, prepared to leave his bookbinding shop at Burgstrasse 16 in the capital town of Grenz for an interview he dreaded. As if to exacerbate his anxiety, his wife came to the door to remind him of his duties: 'Keep in mind, Ludwig. One, two, three,' and to illustrate her points she ticked off the numbers on her fingers, which she folded back into her palm as she counted.

Ludwig was extremely fond of his wife, Thekla, and he did not interpret her reminders as heckling. No, she was simply bringing to his attention once more the perilous condition into which the Allerkamp family had fallen, so as he strode along the principal street of the town toward the rude castle at the far end

645

where the Margrave himself lived, he lined two of his children before him and kept his eye on them, using them to tick off his duties the way his wife had dropped her fingers.

One, he told himself as he looked at his son Theo, aged twenty, I must insist that he have the right to marry. Two, my daughter – this was Franziska, aged thirteen – must be allowed entry to the school. That took care of his children; he himself was the third obligation: I must have more salary for tending the castle library. I really must. Good God, we're near to starving.

He was not exaggerating. Across the German states and especially in the cold northern areas, a series of unprecedented winters had produced successive crop failures, making food so scarce and costly that families were fortunate if they ate two meals a day, because sometimes they ate none. It seemed as if the entire system had broken down; farmers could not produce enough, and what little food they did bring into town, they could not sell because people had no money. A tedious barter system had developed, much as the peasantry had operated four hundred years earlier, and there was constant grumbling.

'We must be very polite to everyone,' he warned his children. 'Not only to the Margrave but also to the Gräfin, and especially to the bailiff, for who knows, he may be in a position to influence decisions.' He spoke with almost a classical ring to his voice, for he had attended two universities, Jena and Breslau, as had his father and grandfather before him. He had hoped to attain a professorship and was more than qualified, but the present depression had begun just as he finished his studies, so no positions were available. At first he had tried teaching in the town school, but the pay was so miserable that no man could even dream of getting married.

About this time he met Thekla during a walking tour through the countryside west of the capital, and once he saw this woodland sprite, blonde and lively and with a voice like a woodthrush, he knew that they must marry and earn their living as they could. Never had either of them regretted this hasty decision; despite privations, they had enjoyed a good and loving life, and on the meager salary he earned as a bookbinder, plus what he had picked up from doing casual jobs, they had raised their three boys and then grave, beautiful Franziska. It had been worth the struggle, more than worth it, for both husband and wife felt blessed a hundred times, but now they were close to starvation.

As he approached the castle, a stubby stone building whose outer walls dated back to the 1300s, he took a deep breath, surveyed his children's dress, and tugged at the bell cord. After a few moments a bailiff opened the big brass-studded door, and looked down his nose as the intruders entered an anteroom whose walls were made of unfinished rock and whose floor was paved with massive slabs of polished stone.

A door opened, and into the waiting-room came the Gräfin, as she was called in deference to her family position before marriage. She had once been a great lady, but now her sixty-year-old face was painted like a girl's, and she wobbled as she swept forward, faced Franziska, and imperiously extended her right arm.

Franziska did not know what to do, nor did Ludwig, but after a moment of their agonizing indecision the bailiff pinched the girl painfully on the arm and whispered hoarsely so that even the Gräfin could hear: 'You're supposed to kiss the hem of her dress.' This Franziska was most eager to do, but as she bent forward the bailiff pushed her heavily on the shoulder, whispering again: 'Stupid, you must kneel,' and in his roughness he forced the child down onto the stone pavement, from where she grasped the hem of the great lady's gown and brought it to her lips, as all women in Grenzler were obligated to do when presented to this august personage.

But that was not the end of the affair, for when Ludwig saw the burly bailiff smiting his daughter, as it were, he lost his temper, slapped the man's hand away, and said impulsively: 'Do not strike my daughter.'

The Gräfin, who was embarrassed by nothing, saved the day. With a tinkling laugh that drew attractive wrinkles across her heavily powdered face, she said: 'He wasn't striking her. Simply teaching her how to respect her betters.' And she stalked off, to be seen no more.

The bailiff then led them out of the reception hall and into the throne room, a vaulted affair with rock walls and on a dais a heavy chair occupied by an imposing ruler. Margrave Himlar of Grenzler was in his seventies, a big man with a red, puffy face, white hair and bushy muttonchop sideburns; for almost fifty years he had dominated this castle and the surrounding lands. As a youth he had been to Heidelberg, had lived for a while at the court of Bavaria, and had risen to the minor rank of colonel in the army of one petty German state or another. He enjoyed reading and had developed an affinity for the clarity of Schiller, whom he considered vastly superior to Goethe, who tried to encompass too much in his poems. He had dabbled in astronomy and had even purchased a small telescope with which he entertained his guests, for it was just powerful enough to show the moons of Jupiter, a sight which he still considered unbelievable.

He was in some ways an enlightened monarch, but his territory was so small and in recent years so poor that he could accomplish little. He believed that the stringent measures advocated by Prince Metternich had saved Europe from turmoil, and he would have been astounded had one of his subjects told him that Metternich was one of the sorriest forces ever to hit the Continent. Each year that the Austrian's reactionary policies prevailed, principalities like Grenzler fell deeper into despair. There are many things in this world worse than an orderly revolution that turns tables upside-down for a while, for in such violent periods men still eat and marry and think great thoughts and rearrange their prejudices and launch new ventures; and one of the worst alternatives is a deadly hand of repression which inhibits all forward motion and stifles all adventure. Ludwig Allerkamp and his son were about to experience the soured and withered fruit that grew upon the tree cultivated by Metternich.

'Excellency, my son Theo comes before you seeking permission to marry.'

As Ludwig prepared to assure the Margrave that his son had found a proper girl in one of the ruler's subjects, the daughter of a well-regarded family, the Margrave raised his hand to stop discussion, and when there was silence he asked the two questions which at that time ruled Germany: 'Has he a house into which he can take his proposed bride? No? Then he cannot marry.' And when this was settled he asked: 'Has he a job which pays a living wage? No? Then certainly he cannot marry.'

Ignoring the father, the ruler turned to face the son: 'This is a harsh decision I must render, but throughout Germany the rules are the same. No house, no job, no wedding.' Before either of the Allerkamps could protest, he added, in an almost fatherly tone: 'But we can hope that as the years pass, conditions will relax. Maybe you'll find work. Maybe a house will fall vacant. People die, you know. When that happens, come back and I shall gladly grant you permission.'

Now, hurting inside, Ludwig pushed his daughter forward and said pleadingly: 'My wife and I wish that an exception could be made for this child. She should be in school, learning her numbers and music and –'

The Margrave nipped this line of nonsense quickly: 'In this land we do not educate ordinary young women.' He would discuss the matter no further.

So Ludwig, almost crushed by now, launched his third futile plea: 'Excellency, I work long hours in your library, taking charge of accounts, seeking new works for your inspection, rebinding your most valued editions, and many other duties. I do most urgently request a larger salary from you, most urgently.'

Now the Margrave really hardened, because this was an attack on his generosity. In his own mind he had never really needed Allerkamp's assistance and had employed him in one trivial capacity or another merely because he was educated and pleasing to talk with; however, in recent months he had detected in his librarian's comments slight traces of instability.

'If you are unhappy with the terms of your employment, Allerkamp, it can be terminated.'

'Oh, no!' Ludwig cried with obvious terror. 'Oh, please, Excellency!' He groveled, and both he and his children knew he was groveling.

The Margrave seemed to enjoy it, for he pressed on: 'I can think of six young men in this town who would be most happy . . .'

'Please!' Ludwig begged, and the interview ended. But as the bailiff was leading the Allerkamps from the castle, Ludwig suddenly told his children to return home without him, ran back to the throne room, and threw himself upon the mercy of the Margrave: 'Excellency, I beg you, allow us to emigrate.'

As soon as that fearful word *emigrate* was spoken, the

slouching Margrave stiffened, his hands gripped the griffin armrests, and he rose to an impressive standing position. 'Never speak to me of leaving Grenzler. We need you here.'

Ludwig, realizing that once broached, this vital subject had to be pursued logically regardless of how angry the Margrave might become, forged ahead: 'Excellency, I have four children, and only one house to leave one of them when I die. What are my other three to do if they can find nowhere to live, no place to work?'

'God will provide in His own mysterious way.'

'But if you allow us to go to America, as you did Hugo Metzdorf . . .'

'Worst mistake I ever made. We need men like him working here.'

'But if my sons can find no work . . .'

'Allerkamp!' the old man shouted in real irritation over being goaded into revealing his true reasoning. 'Grenzler, and Germany, need your three sons. We could be at war with France tomorrow, or with Russia, or with that unreliable fellow in Vienna. We never know when we shall be attacked.'

'But if my sons can't marry, if they can't work . . .'

'They can do the noblest work allotted man, fight for their homeland.'

'Their country orders them to fight for it but will not allow them to live?'

'Talk like that will get you into grave trouble.'

'But Metzdorf writes from Texas . . .'

The mention of this short, memorable word *Texas* infuriated the Margrave, because there circulated throughout Germany in these years many enthusiastic accounts of travel in the western portions of the United States, with special emphasis on the advantages of settling in Texas. Most impressive was a book which the Margrave had acquired in 1829 for his own library: Gottfried Duden's *Report on a Journey to the Western States of North America*. Even the Margrave had been so excited by its roseate evidence and reasonable arguments that he had in his first flush of enthusiasm committed the error of allowing a dozen of his Grenzler families to emigrate, but when he realized that he was losing valuable manpower, he called a halt.

There was another impetus to emigration, perhaps the most

insidious and long-lasting of all: thousands of young Germans had been beguiled in recent decades by an American book that had enjoyed not only public acceptance but also circulation among the knowing, who read it, savored it, dreamed about it, and discussed it with their friends. It was James Fenimore Cooper's *The Last of the Mohicans*, which extolled the frontier and gave a flashing, exciting portrait of life among the Indians. In a score of cities and a hundred small towns young men referred to themselves as Uncas or Leatherstocking or, especially, Hawkeye. The Cooper novels evoked a powerful dream world, but letters from Germans who were actually living in Texas made that dream such an attractive possibility that thousands of young people in the little states sought to emigrate. When denied official permission, they formed a slow, clandestine movement of escape, peopled by those whose hope of a good life in Germany had been killed by repression and hunger. Quietly, without even informing their rulers or obtaining proper certification, they began drifting toward the port cities of Bremen and Hamburg, dozens at first, then hundreds, and finally, thousands.

It was this seepage of young men who might be needed to fill uniforms that infuriated the princes, and now the Margrave thundered: 'You mentioned the Metzdorf I allowed to emigrate. Let me tell you, Allerkamp, the police are fully aware that he keeps sending seditious letters to someone here in Grenz, and they also know that the letters circulate, exciting people to go to Texas. The police keep a careful record of everyone who reads those letters, and they stand in the gateway to prison. And if you're not careful ...' With this gratuitous advice the Margrave dismissed his librarian, and when Ludwig left the castle he carried with him the harsh realities of life in a German state, which he reviewed as he walked across the causeway over the moat: The Margrave cannot provide his men with homes or jobs, but he clings to them for manpower in case of war. How immoral.

He was pondering this irony when he passed the bookshop of his neighbor Alois Metzdorf, and since they were in related businesses, he stuck his head in the door and asked: 'What's the news?' Something in the way he did this, perhaps the obvious hesitancy of his stopping, alerted Metzdorf: 'What's the matter,

Ludwig?' and although Allerkamp was still in the street, he started to talk. With confidences he would never before have shared with the bookseller, he told of his disastrous meeting with the Margrave, and when he was through, Metzdorf said: 'I have a letter you should read. It comes from my brother Hugo in Texas,' and he pulled the bookbinder into his shop, while a policeman far up the street took note of this latest visitor.

'What an exciting letter!' And when he passed it along, Allerkamp's hands almost trembled as he turned the flimsy pages covered with small, precise gothic script, and his breathing almost stopped as he focused on particular paragraphs which arrested his attention:

No matter what they tell you, Alois, rattlesnakes leave an area which is well tended. I have not seen one in six months. And mosquitoes which are so dreadful along the shore of the sea do not molest us here ...

I assure you that there are a million wild horses to be caught and tamed if one has the patience, but we buy ours from Mexicans, who are superb at this skill ...

Melons, squash, beans, potatoes, cabbages of immense size, rutabagas, beets, celery, onions, radishes, peaches, pears and corn, we have them all in abundance. Venison, beef, mutton, pork we enjoy every week, but fish we do not have as yet ...

We do not bother with a church or the ministrations of a clergyman because we have such strong memories of their having been the agents of the Margrave back home, but we do go to the English minister for our marriages, which should always be entered into with God's blessing. In daily life we are our own priests ...

Land is available in vast quantities, millions of unclaimed acres. It is waiting for you when you come ...

Night after night we go to bed exhausted from hard, manly work. Bohnert who was a poet in Grenzler builds furniture, the best in this area. Hoexter who wanted to be a professor in Germany is a farmer in Texas. Your friend Schmeltzer who trained to be an engineer is a grower of sheep and cattle, and a good one. And I who was to be a professor am a farmer of more than five hundred hectares. How the great wheel of the world changes in its revolutions.

I will tell you one thing, Old Friend. Sometimes at night my heart breaks in longing for Grenz, the good food, the singing, the winter fires, prayer in the church. And if you join us, as I pray you will, your heart will break too in its hunger for the old ways, especially in December and January when there is no snow on the ground. But there is a great consolation. Here you will be free. No Margrave, no thundering minister, no conscripting officer from the regiment. You will be free, and, Alois, that makes all the difference . . .'

Carefully Allerkamp refolded the letter and shoved it back to Metzdorf: 'Powerful statement. He certainly seems to be happy in Texas.'

'Every letter, he begs me to join him. I don't think Hugo would deceive me.'

Allerkamp reached out and tapped the letter: 'So you accept what he says?'

Metzdorf looked about his shop and whispered: 'Every word. My brother would never deceive me.' Ludwig nodded, for the two men wanted to believe that a refuge like Texas existed.

'But,' Allerkamp warned, 'he says nothing reassuring about the Indians.'

'Ah!' Metzdorf cried. 'He said that in his last letter,' and he produced an earlier, well-thumbed epistle in which Hugo had said explicitly:

I know you must be apprehensive about the Red Indians. They have long since left these parts, and I myself in all this time have seen only three or four who came here to trade. They were much like the Poles we saw that day in Grenz, different in speech, different in coloring and appearance, but ordinary men otherwise. I myself have traded with them and thought nothing of it.

After studying this letter, Allerkamp started toward the door, wildly excited by the visions of Texas both epistles had reawakened, but before he could leave, Metzdorf said quietly:

653

'I have this new book from Paris, and I want you to read it.' And he took from a hiding place beneath his counter a small, unimpressive book which had been smuggled across many borders: *Poems* by Heinrich Heine, the Jewish exile. It was not a crime to have a book by this unpleasant man, but copies were confiscated when found and persons who had read them were noted by the police.

Allerkamp, like most Germans of his type – men who had been to university as had their fathers and grandfathers – adhered mainly to the great poetry of Goethe and Schiller, whom they revered, and few had any acquaintance with the renegade Heine, but they had heard rumors that he was an impassioned poet with much to say, so that they were naturally inquisitive as to his message. Also, the fact that he was Jewish lent his poetry an added aura of mystery, for such men knew few Jews and were alternately repelled by them and fascinated.

'Listen to what he says about us:

> "And when I reached St Gotthard Pass
> I could hear Germany snoring,
> Asleep down below in the loving care
> Of her thirty-six rules." '

'Do the police know you have this book?'
 'No, no, but I want you to read it. Heine has a lot to say to us.'
 'Will you try to join your brother in America?'
 Metzdorf made no reply. He simply forced the book into his friend's hands and led him to the door. When Ludwig left the shop he looked up and down the main street, but the policeman was gone.

That evening Ludwig Allerkamp assembled his family and said gravely: 'Franziska, fetch the Bible.'
 The quiet little girl, her two pigtails bobbing beside her ears, went to the bedroom, where she lifted the heavy brassbound Bible and carried it to her father. He opened it to Psalms, from which he read regularly to his brood, and asked each member of the family to place a hand upon the sacred book. This was a curious, meaningful act, for in recent years he had grown increasingly impatient with the church, which sided always

with the government and invariably against the interests of its parishioners. In fact, Ludwig Allerkamp, like most Germans who were contemplating emigration, had begun to drift away from the stern Lutheranism of his youth, for he found the church repressive and unresponsive. Yet still, in any moment of crisis, he turned instinctively to the Bible.

'Swear that you will repeat what we are about to say to no one, absolutely no one.'

Six right hands shared the two pages of Psalms. Six voices took the oath.

'The question before this meeting of the Allerkamp family – shall we, with or without permission, leave Germany and go to Texas?'

No one responded. Each member of the family visualized such evidence as she or he had heard and each weighed the awful consequences of the decision to be made. Thekla the mother recalled the two earlier Metzdorf letters she had read telling of life on the prairie and all that she had heard reassured her that only in some such refuge could her four children find freedom. She was prepared to brave the dangers of the ocean crossing, the mosquitoes and the rattlesnakes, if only she and her offspring could build good new lives, and all negative considerations were abolished, even her fear of Indians. Her eldest son, Theo, who so desperately wanted to marry but who had been sentenced perhaps to perpetual bachelorhood by the stern laws of Germany, was eager to do anything to escape. He would emigrate tomorrow and would say so when invited to speak. Brother Ernst, aged eighteen, had for some years imagined himself to be Uncas, striding through primeval forests, and was most eager to undertake such adventure. Brother Emil, sixteen, was prepared to go anywhere, and the more Indians, pirates and gold-seekers en route the better.

That left Father Ludwig and Franziska, and their preferences were more tentative than those of their kinfolk. Ludwig loved Germany and even though prevented from entering his chosen profession of teaching in some university, he felt a burning desire to stay and witness the unfolding of German history. He felt his homeland to be on the verge of great accomplishments; perhaps a unification of the hundred petty states, perhaps a release from the strictures of

Metternich's oppression, perhaps a bursting forth of the German spirit into brave new worlds of industrial expansion and revitalized universities. He was extremely optimistic where Germany was concerned and foresaw the gradual disappearance of anachronisms like the old Margrave. But he was also cruelly aware that his family must somehow survive the period of transition, and he saw no likelihood of accomplishing this under current circumstances. His persistent fear was that Germany would engage in a revolution which would accomplish nothing but which would surely engulf his three sons, for they were lads of strong opinion and firm character, not likely to remain aloof from such vibrant movement. Hugo Metzdorf's most recent letter from Texas strengthened his resolve to seek refuge there immediately.

Up to now, Franziska had rarely participated in family discussions of any gravity, for she was a carefully nurtured girl who had been taught to sit properly, never intrude on a conversation, and respect the instructions of anyone older than herself. But she had a most lively imagination and a sharp perception of what was occurring about her, and her family would have been surprised at the accuracy with which she assessed their motives and anticipated their actions. Encouraged by her brother Ernst, who wanted to roam with Uncas, she had read *The Last of the Mohicans* and seen pretty quickly that it was largely romantic nonsense; also, several reports in the German press, inspired by rulers who were determined to keep their subjects at home, had told of great dust storms, hurricanes, Indian attacks and the prevalence of rattlesnakes in Texas. Unlike her brothers, she had read books sponsored by the rulers and written by Germans who had emigrated to Texas, only to return home on the first available ship:

Texas is a dreadful place. The food is inedible. The houses have no windows. Paved floors do not exist. A strange disease they call El Vómito kills people within a week of landing. Indians and rattlesnakes prowl behind the barn, if a man is lucky enough to have a barn. Do not come to Texas. I tried it and lasted only one week. How passionately I kissed the deck of the good German vessel that carried me back to Bremen.

She was therefore not at all eager to leap into such an adventure, but when she remembered how her brother Theo had sagged when the Margrave said 'You may not marry,' she could look ahead to the mournful day when it was she standing before the ruler seeking permission to marry some young man of Grenz, only to hear the harsh words 'You may not,' and she knew that her only salvation was emigration to some free land like Texas.

She also recalled how her plea for an education had been denied, and she became angry: 'We should go,' and when her small voice uttered these words a flood of comment was loosened, and the Allerkamp family, aware of all the terrors mental and physical which threatened, decided that as soon as the opportunity presented itself they would quietly slip away from the beloved Margravate of Grenzler, with or without legal permission, and make their way through whatever dangers to the wharf at Bremen, where they would offer themselves as emigrants to a better land.

When the unanimous decision was reached, Ludwig asked them to replace their hands on the Bible, and said: 'On our solemn oath we speak to no one.' And when this was agreed, he told his children: 'I want you to study these poems of Heine again. He's a Jew, and his work is outlawed, but he speaks like a golden trumpet,' and before passing along the book he read from it:

'Time passes on but that château
That old château with its high steeple
It never fades out of my mind
Filled as it was with stupid people.'

'That's what we're exchanging, the stupid château for the free forest.'

'Will you be a bookbinder there?' Franziska asked, and her father said: 'No. They'll have no need of bookbinders in the forest.'

'What will you do?' the girl asked, and before her father could respond, Ernst-Uncas cried: 'He'll shoot deer and make moccasins.'

'We'll certainly have a farm,' Ludwig said. 'But I'll find other work, too.'

'What kind of work?' Franziska asked, and he replied: 'We'll have to see.'

They all agreed later: 'It was a miracle.' And in a way it was a twofold miracle, because the very next day a wanderer from the north came to town and passed along the main street, stopping everyone and asking: 'Do you wish to buy paper which entitles you to free land in Texas?'

In various ways a large supply of scrip issued by the Republic of Texas had found its way to Germany, and each certificate entitled the purchaser to acres of land without further payment. Half the paper for sale consisted of legal documents circulated by Toby and Brother of New Orleans to encourage immigration, and this carried certain complexities regarding surveying and court procedures, but the other half were bounty warrants issued to veterans of the war, and this gave immediate title to three hundred and twenty acres, provided only that an official surveyor could be found to identify and map the land chosen. It was supposed that the surveyor would receive for his services one-third of the land so identified, unless the holder of the scrip wished to pay a fee in cash.

Ludwig Allerkamp, a cautious man, suspected chicanery in such an offering and would have nothing to do with the paper, regardless of which form it took. Some did buy, however, for modest sums, and it was here that the second miracle occurred, because the mayor of the town bought six certificates – four Toby, two soldier bounties – for a modest sum, only to find that the police were taking down the names of all holders: 'Nothing illegal, Mayor, but the Margrave wants to know who's been dabbling with the idea of emigration.'

'Not me!' the mayor lied. 'I have no papers of any kind.' And to make this assurance viable he quickly hurried to the bookshop of Alois Metzdorf, known to be an agitator, to whom he confided in a jumble of whispers: 'These papers ... the police inspectors ... In my position as mayor, you know, there's nothing wrong, you understand ... but in my responsible position as mayor ... Here, you take them, they can do you no harm.'

As soon as the mayor left, Metzdorf slipped out the back

door and ran through alleys to the home of Allerkamp: 'Ludwig, it's providential! I know you want to go to Texas, and someone I can't name just gave me six certificates for land there. I can't emigrate yet, but . . .'

The conspirators stood silent, and slowly Metzdorf pushed the sacred papers into his friend's hands. No one spoke, and then in a rush of gratitude Allerkamp embraced his friend: 'Alois. I'll hold the best fields for you . . . till you come.'

In this way the lands of Axel Vexter, hero of San Jacinto, found an owner.

To help the Allerkamps make decisions, Alois Metzdorf loaned them *A Practical Guide to a Wealthy Life in America*, in which sixteen German families advised newcomers as to how they could strike their fortune in the New World. It advised travelers as to what they must take for areas such as Pennsylvania, 'the most hospitable of the States and the most like Germany'; Missouri, 'the state with the most attractive free land and the greatest opportunity for getting rich'; and Texas, 'the most exciting land, an independent nation now but likely to become a part of the United States.'

'We shall need tools, and medicines, and all the clothes we can carry,' Ludwig said after studying the recommendations.

'Books?' Thekla asked, and here her husband had to make painful choices: 'Our Bible, Goethe, Schiller, the book on agriculture.' By curious choice upon which the family would often comment in later years, he added: 'It'll be a practical land. I'll take along my two mathematics books.' These would prove to be more useful, ultimately, than all the others, but it would be the books of poetry that would echo most strongly and persistently, for they represented the soul of the Germany they were leaving.

When the secret packing was completed and hidden away so that guests could not see, the Allerkamps invited into their home for the last time the members of a singing group with whom they had known so much enjoyment, and when the various families gathered that last Sunday afternoon, the four strong-voiced Allerkamp men led the others in songs that had echoed through the town of Grenz for centuries. Ludwig had a strong baritone and Theo had a clear, ringing, high-voiced

659

tenor, with the two younger boys filling in nicely; others of the group had fine voices too, and the air was rich with music. But Franziska saw that as her mother played the accompaniments tears filled her eyes, and the child knew that she was saying farewell to this splendid piano over which both mother and daughter had studied to diligently. No more would this instrument guide them in song, and the realization that a glorious part of her life was ending was almost too painful to bear.

They sang till midnight, and in some mysterious way, without a word having been spoken, it became apparent to many of the older people that a requiem was being sung. Some profound change was under way; someone was departing; some new force was arriving; some secret aspect of Germany was being modified; but if certain canny men suspected what Allerkamp was up to, they did not reveal it.

Accepting what money they could get from a surreptitious sale of their possessions, they slipped out of town before dawn one Wednesday morning and slowly made their way toward the port of Bremerhaven, negotiating one passport and customs barrier after another. They moved from one petty kingdom to the next, where the rulers of each tried to prevent the entry of refugees from other principalities, lest they become squatters and a financial drain, but Ludwig, by means of cajolery, lies and even small bribes, maneuvered his caravan across half of Germany, coming at last to the busy city of Bremen, some distance from the harbor from which the ships sailed. Here he reported to the offices of the Atlantic and Caribbean Lines, which owned two sailing vessels plying to Texas, the *Poseidon* and the *Sea Nymph*. Captain Langbein, in command of the latter, assured the Allerkamps that they had chosen wisely and that he would personally oversee their pleasant trip across the Atlantic. Since his ship would not be departing for nine days, he directed the family to lodgings utilized by his firm and then extended them the courtesy of his home, where Frau Langbein proved to be a gracious, motherly lady and a superb cook.

'The captain wants me to serve you the best food,' she explained, 'so that you'll get homesick and sail back to Germany some day with him. That way he earns double fares.' She said that she had sailed once with him to Galveston: 'I was seasick, but it passes quickly. I loved the voyage, and would go tomorrow if he'd allow me.'

As guests of the Langbeins the Allerkamps attended two operas in Bremen, Mozart's *Figaros Hochzeit* and Weber's *Der Freischütz*, and the emigrants showed such appreciation of the robust singing that Captain Langbein volunteered advice: 'Take plenty of music with you. It tames the wilderness.'

'We'll have no piano,' Thekla explained, but he was insistent: 'There will be many pianos in Texas. You'll find one. And then you'll be sorry you didn't bring music for it.' This posed a problem, for the family had only the most meager funds, with not a pfennig to spare for luxuries, but as they prowled the back streets, seeking bargains, Thekla came upon used scores of Beethoven and Schubert and a collection of Mozart piano sonatas, and they were so reasonable that she cried: 'I cannot cross the ocean without them.' But when Ludwig approached the owner, even the reduced price was forbidding, and he was about to lead his family from the shop when to his amazement Franziska intruded: 'Sir, we are sailing to a far land and we must have the music.'

The man stooped till his face was level with hers and asked: 'But can you play Mozart?' and she went stiffly to a piano, adjusted the stool, and began to play with youthful skill the Mozart sonata in C major – known as the 'Easy Sonata' – with such grace that he cried: 'Buy the Beethoven and Schubert, and I'll give your little princess the Mozart.'

Next day the Allerkamps sailed for Texas.

It was not till the rickety, swaying *Sea Nymph* reached midocean that Franziska Allerkamp felt well enough to make her first entry in the diary she had acquired in Bremerhaven:

> *Monday 31 October.* This ship is a leaky tub. It is tossed about by every wave. There's not enough water and the food is horrible.
>
> To save his leaky ship, Captain Langbein had all men passengers operate the pumps twenty-four hours a day.
>
> I have thrown up so much that I can no longer be sick. How pitiful man is upon an ocean like this.

Despite the inconvenience of shipboard life, Franziska found ways to care for her appearance, combing and braiding her hair each morning and doing everything possible to present the picture of a well-bred German lass. Her neatness was remarked by many, and several older women, when they were well enough to move about, congratulated Thekla on her daughter's cleanliness: 'And charm, too. She's a fine child.' Since Franziska secretly coveted such approbation, she took extra pains, and inevitably some of the young men began to pay attention, but her mother, obsessed with creating in Franziska a model German girl who could sew, play the piano, cook, and observe what Thekla called 'the niceties,' quickly disciplined the would-be suitors: 'No, she cannot sing with you. And she certainly can't walk the lower decks, either.'

Wednesday 9 November. Grandmother taught me always to be neat and Grandfather warned me many times: 'You must smile at young men, to show them respect and make them feel important, but you must never flirt.' I don't think I would care to marry before twenty-one, because the village girls who did so and who then came in to Grenz were never happy. I could tell from looking at their long faces that they yearned to join our dances in the town square, but with babes at the knee they could not.

Obedient to her mother's standards, she had stopped being a young girl and had already become a poised little woman. As she moved about the upper decks she avoided conversation, preferring to listen to others, but on the rare occasions when she did speak she could be quite firm. Sometimes when she eavesdropped, which was not very ladylike, she picked up bits of information that confused her:

Saturday 10 December. Mother and Father did not think I was listening, but I heard the elders discussing Captain Langbein, whom I like very much. A man who lives in Texas but had business in Germany told them that Captain Langbein has a wife in Texas, as well as the one in Bremen whom I met and liked so much.

I am worried about this and would like to ask Mother whether it could be true, for if it is, Captain Langbein must be a very bad man, which I find hard to believe.

Two days later, as they were approaching Cuba, a storm more violent than any they had known in the European seas overtook them from the east, throwing their pitiful craft about as if it were a cork adrift in a whirlpool. Nearly everyone was wretchedly sick and often too weak to stagger from the cabins, but Franziska, one of the few able to stand, volunteered to clean up the smelly messes.

She had no inclination to feel sorry for herself because Captain Langbein, in obvious distress, called for all men to return to the pumps, and for three perilous days, 21 December through the night of 23 December, she knew that all four of her family's menfolk were toiling in the bowels of the ship, straining at the powerful German pumps, but almost to no avail, for an incredible amount of water continued to stream in through the many cracks, and toward midnight on the twenty-third, Ludwig staggered topside to speak with his wife: 'Thekla, if anything happens, look first for Franziska. The boys and I will have done all we could.'

At about four that morning the frail ship plowed headlong into a huge series of waves which swept a sailor and two passengers overboard. Their screams were heard briefly, then only the howling of the terrible wind. Thekla, in the cabin, was sure the ship must come apart under the dreadful strain, and so was her husband at the pumps. But these towering breakers marked the end of the violence, and by sunrise on 24 December the Caribbean had begun to subside, so that when Christmas Eve approached, a weak sun actually appeared through the clouds.

Sunday 25 December 1842. We had a quiet Christmas. Father took me down into the ship, and when I saw the holes through which the sea came at us, I wondered why we did not sink. I was not afraid during the storm, because I kept busy helping the women with children, but tonight I am terribly afraid. I know this ship cannot last much longer, and I think Father knows it too. And from the look on Captain Langbein's face, he knows it better than any of us.

I no longer care if he has two wives. He was very brave

663

during the storm, always taking the wheel when the waves were worst. When I marry I would want my husband to be much like Captain Langbein, but I would not be happy if he took another wife, too.

When the limping *Sea Nymph*, her backbone almost shattered by the storms, staggered into Matagorda Bay, all hands cheered. But the sudden onset of a howling wind from across the bay prevented them from landing that day:

Monday 2 January 1843. After breakfast this morning we finally landed, and it was lucky that we did, for although we got quite dampened by the heavy spray, no great damage was done. But when almost everyone was ashore, and I was looking inland to see our new home, one of the young men who had been nice to me cried in a loud voice 'Jesus Christ!' And all of us turned to look back at the sea, where our *Sea Nymph* rolled quietly over and sank.

Captain Langbein swam ashore, and when he joined us he said 'For the past two weeks I thought we'd probably sink.' And I asked him what others were afraid to ask, 'Did you think so during the bad storm?' And he said 'I expected to go down any minute, little girl.'

This afternoon some of the women told Mother 'The sinking of that ship was God's curse on the Captain for having two wives,' and I thought about this for a long time. Suppose the ship had sunk six days ago, with all of us passengers lost. Would that still have been God's way to punish one immoral Captain? What about us? I think the ship sank because the company took too great a risk in sending out such a rotten crate.

When the six Allerkamps stood with their luggage on the shore of Matagorda Bay, they had no specific idea of where they would sleep that night, or where they would travel in the days ahead, or where they would locate the land on which they would build their permanent home. If ever the word *immigrant* meant *one who comes into a new country*, it applied to the members of this family.

A man who built handcarts with solid wooden wheels

approached Ludwig: 'You'll have to have one. Three dollars.'

'Have you ever heard of Hugo Metzdorf?'

'All the Germans have. You can trust him. Lives at a place called Hardwork,' and in the sand the wagonbuilder showed them in general how to find their way first to Victoria, forty miles to the west, and from there to Hardwork, ninety miles to the north.

'Everyone,' Ludwig cried, assembling his family and pointing to the sand, 'memorize this map.' And with no aid but that, the Allerkamps loaded their handcart, tied a rope to the front, put Theo at the handles, and set out, with Ludwig hauling on the rope and leading the way.

It was simpler than it sounded, because even in the earlier days when Otto Macnab and his father traversed this route, there was a kind of path to Victoria; now it was a dusty road. From there, another rough-and-ready trail led north, so there was little chance of getting lost. But to walk a hundred and thirty miles with a handcart and sleep on the bare ground in January was not easy. However, in due course the pilgrims reached a slight rise, and there they looked down upon a sight that warmed them. It was a replica of a German village, complete with rough stone houses, a central square, and prosperous fields that stretched out to thick woodland.

'It was worth it!' Ludwig cried as he started down the slope, and Franziska asked: 'Is this where we'll take our land?' and her father said: 'We'll find even better.'

Until they located the land they wanted, they would stop temporarily at Hardwork, but they were surprised to find that earlier German arrivals already owned the locations in town and that in the surrounding countryside, for many miles in every direction, the attractive rolling land was also taken. 'I thought,' Theo said, 'that everything was free.'

It wasn't. Hugo Metzdorf, the acknowledged leader of the community, explained there there were millions of acres to which the Allerkamp certificates could be applied, but they were always 'out there,' meaning to the west. The newcomers were assured, however, that their papers were authentic: 'None better than these four sold by Toby and Brother in New Orleans, and of course your two military ones are best of all.'

Metzdorf, who had done a good deal of land selection, ticked off the situation, indicating each paper as he did, and in the end he whistled: 'Three thousand acres in all! You must have paid a pretty pfennig for these!' When Ludwig nodded, Hugo asked: 'You bring much money with you? No? Well, neither did any of us.' He flexed his right arm: 'That's what does it in Texas.'

He advised the Allerkamps to spend their first two years in Hardwork: 'Fine German woman here lost her husband a year ago. She'll rent you a room. Later on, build yourself a shack, not a house like mine. Then look around you, visit other towns, get yourself a horse and ride west, and wherever you go, study the land.'

'What do we do when we find it?'

'Now you have to have some money, because you must get a surveyor. He lines it out proper and files his papers with the government, and then you get title. But you have to pay the surveyor.'

'If we have no money?'

'Customary rate, he takes one-third of the land.' When Ludwig whistled, Metzdorf said: 'I know it sounds high. In your case, a thousand acres, and at eight cents an acre, that's eighty dollars American, and who in Texas has eighty dollars?'

The widowed woman was actually eager to have the Allerkamps share her half-empty house and to sell them a small plot of land, and in a shorter time than even Metzdorf, an energetic man, could have anticipated, they were at work building not a shack, as he had prudently advised, but a real house – a kitchen and alcoves for beds – and in doing so, they repeated the heroic steps by which all parts of Texas would be settled: sunrise to sunset, work; Sunday, prayers; clothes and furniture made by hand; fields cleared by chopping and plowed by foot-shovels; food, an endless repetition of corn bread, bacon and coffee. But when a family had two energetic elders and four stalwart young people, the outcome was apt to be startling, and in the case of the Allerkamps, it was doubly so. By the end of the second month they had the corner posts of their home in place and all members of the family were learning English from a book they had purchased in Bremen.

Much sooner than they expected they were brought into full citizenship, for in early March a man came to their farm riding one horse and leading another. He was a smallish fellow, and he brought a surprising invitation: 'Name's Otto Macnab, Texas Ranger. Trouble along the Nueces River, and Captain Garner of this county would like to have one of your boys join him in an expedition.'

'Is it that we are obliged to?' Ludwig asked on behalf of his three sons.

'Not an order, but if you're going to live in Texas . . .'

'We have only the guns we need for food. No horse.'

'Captain Garner figured that. He sends this horse. Guns?' He slapped the space behind his saddle, and the Allerkamps saw three rifles, plus the two pistols protruding from Otto's belt.

'Can you speak the truth?' the father asked, and before he could continue, Otto said: 'No, you don't have to come, but this is how we protect places like yours.'

'Against maybe who?'

'Mexicans, Indians . . .'

As soon as he heard the word *Indians*, Ernst Allerkamp, the middle boy reared on James Fenimore Cooper, stepped forward: 'I will go,' and it was agreed.

When Otto turned to untie the trailing horse and hand over one of the guns, he became aware of a girl hiding in the shadows, and his eyes wandered from the men and focused on her. She was a small girl, fourteen or fifteen, with flaxen braids and a shyness which manifested itself in the curious way she stood, half withdrawn from the scene, half participating. He could not bring his eyes back to the men and paid little attention to what they were saying about the Indian war; he was riveted by the girl and drank in every aspect of her attractive appearance: her white stockings, her homemade shoes, her dress with that flowery bit about the hem, her belt encompassing her narrow waist, the way her blouse was beginning to protrude, but most of all, her placid face framed by the two braids of golden hair. It was an image, emerging from shadows, that would live with him forever.

For her part, the girl saw a young man not much older than herself, tow-headed, blue-eyed, clean-faced, revolver in his belt, homespun clothes and very dusty, heavy leather boots square as a box, never a smile, leading a horse by a bridle that hung carelessly from his left arm, a young man who spoke in a low voice and who stared at her as if he had never seen a girl before. From her place in the shadows she could imagine him astride his horse, riding through rolling woodlands that seemed to stretch endlessly west and south. He was capable, of that she felt sure, and she supposed that he could use the pistols and rifles which projected from his saddlebag. He was the new man, the man of Texas, and she was fascinated by him, but as a well-bred daughter of a conservative German family, she kept to the shadows.

Neither the young man nor the girl smiled during that first meeting, nor did they speak, nor did they reveal by any gesture other than those endless glances the impression that each had made on the other, but all during his three-month fight in the Nueces Strip the man could think of little else when he rode silently or slept fitfully. And during those same long days the girl saw horsemen galloping across battlefields, or resting beside rivers, or splashing through fords, and invariably this quiet young fellow with the blue eyes and sand-colored hair was in the lead.

When Ernst Allerkamp returned to Hardwork he found his community in an uproar, because a recent immigrant named Pankratz, from the area near Munich, had arrived in town with his wife and two children, had studied the local economy with more than usual intelligence, and had decided that he could make a real profit on his investment if he bought himself a slave. In a town well to the north he found a strong young black man, and the cost was so minimal that he bought the slaver's wife as well. With them he would grow cotton, for which there was a permanent demand in the markets at New Orleans.

But when Pankratz brought his two slaves to Hardwork the older residents objected not only strenuously but bitterly, with Hugo Metzdorf and Ludwig Allerkamp stating flatly that slavery was not a condition that the freedom-seeking Germans could tolerate. The Allerkamp boys supported their father, and began circulating among the people in town and those in nearby farms, arguing against the introduction of slavery into the community.

'But it's legal,' Pankratz said with stubborn force. 'It's one of the reasons why Texians fought against Santa Anna. He threatened to take away their slaves.'

'It may be legal,' Ludwig conceded, 'but it is not what Germans who flee tyranny should allow in their new villages.'

Pankratz, believing himself immune to such pressure, housed his slaves in a rude shack behind his well-built dog-run, and proceeded to use them, fourteen hours a day, in the planting of a cotton crop.

'You cannot keep human beings in such a hovel,' Hugo Metzdorf protested formally, but Pankratz pointed out that many German settlers, when they first arrived in Texas, had lived in worse.

'Yes,' Metzdorf granted. 'We did. But we did it voluntarily and with the knowledge that we would soon have better, if we applied ourselves. You intend to keep your slaves –'

'Don't tell me what I intend!'

Pankratz was an able man who believed that southern Germans were better educated and more civilized than men like Metzdorf and the Allerkamps, who had come from a ridiculous place like Grenzler, and he rejected this censure, insisting that since the Texas constitution protected slavery, he had every right to utilize his two blacks as he saw fit, so long as he did not punish them in uncivilized ways.

He did, of course, punish them. When they lingered in their work he found it productive to lash them with a leather strap attached to a stout oak handle, not savagely or in any brutish manner, but enough to make them realize that if they abused the freedoms he allowed them, sterner punishment would follow.

When Ludwig first saw his neighbor lash the woman slave across her back and her thinly clad buttocks, he was outraged and went directly to Metzdorf as head of the community. They discussed the matter, with great fury at first and later with controlled bitterness, and the outcome was that one morning when Pankratz had his two slaves in his far fields cultivating the land prior to planting, Ludwig, aided by his Ranger son Ernst, went quietly to the Pankratz place and dismantled the slave shack, hiding its valuable timbers in half a dozen different spots well removed from the farm.

When Pankratz was summoned from the fields by his wife, who had watched the destruction from her kitchen, he stormed about the village threatening lawsuits and bodily damage to his enemies, but when he saw that the entire community was opposed to his remaining there with his slaves, he put a loud curse upon the place, sold his land at a loss to Yancey Quimper and moved to Victoria, where several families owned slaves.

When the ugly affair ended, Ludwig told his children: 'You do not flee from an evil, and then introduce that same evil in your new home.'

The Allerkamps were constantly aware that the land they now had was not to be their permanent home; they had those four precious documents which entitled them to free land in Texas and they intended identifying their homestead and moving to it as soon as practical. But now they entered upon the heartbreak of Texas land ownership: the acres were theirs, no doubt about it, but to secure them, one had to locate a surveyor. Also, the land system was Spanish in origin, using strange units of measurement and customs not known in Grenzler, so that no man merely trained in trigonometry could presume to set himself up as a surveyor; he had first to master the tradition of varas, cordeles and leagues. So a man like Allerkamp might have entitlement to three thousand acres, but five or six years could elapse before he located his land or came into possession of it.

'I am consumed with anger over this system,' Ludwig cried one day, for he saw time wasting, with no permanent house built and his family still not established on their own land. Meanwhile he must earn a living and see to it that his three sons earned theirs. Theo wanted a job that paid a good salary so that he could send money back to Grenzler for the ocean crossing of the young woman he had not been allowed to marry.

'I liked that area on Matagorda Bay, where the *Sea Nymph* landed us,' he told the family as they discussed their problems. 'I asked the men there and they said: "This place has got to become a major seaport. We need young men to help build it." I'm going to try.'

The family could not give him money for his venture, but they did share generously their tools and clothing, and there were tears of regret and apprehension as they bade him farewell at the start of his long walk back to that remembered spot in the Matagorda region; soon it would acquire jetties and wharves and storage warehouses and the melodious name of Indianola. Theo Allerkamp would be well regarded by the German ship captains who put in to Indianola, and to the immigrants they deposited there, for he was a man of integrity, and also a man unusually gifted with a high tenor voice, which he would display effectively in the local singing societies. In quicker time than he now expected, he would be able to send for his bride.

Ernst Allerkamp found his occupation in a curious way. When he helped tear down the Pankratz slave quarters his job was to rip off the shabby roof, and during his trip on the *Sea Nymph* he had worked the pumps so diligently that he had become distressed by any structure that leaked. 'What a miserable roof this must have been,' he told his father, who replied: 'No house can be better than its roof. Thatch on German farms. Tiles in German towns. In Texas, they seem to use cypress shingles. Properly cut and nailed, they could be best of all.'

So Ernst had started studying roofs, and although there were few in Hardwork of thatch, for this part of Texas did not produce the necessary low shrubs, there were some houses whose owners tried to utilize sod roofing; it was too heavy and too subject to moisture penetration. He saw only one house that had half-moon tiles for its roof, and he was most favorably impressed, but these had been hauled north years ago from Saltillo and could not be duplicated in Hardwork.

Some roofs, like that on the slave hut, were disgraceful and almost a waste of time; the best they did was to keep out the sun during the blazing summers. To rain they were small impediment. So the more he studied, the more satisfied he became that his father was right, and he told his family: 'I think I could earn a good living from cypress shakes.' When he explained how simple the required tools were and how easily he could master their use, the Allerkamps agreed that he should make the effort. With saw, frog and mallet to flake off the shingles, he moved about the countryside, searching for cypress trees of proper size and testing junipers also, and as he went he stopped in villages and at crossroads to assure the settlers that he could provide them with the best roofs they had ever known.

The more Ernst worked with his shingles, the more clear it became to his father that what the various German settlements really needed was a sawmill. Always a reflective man, he mused: Civilization in a frontier like this is chronicled twice. The date of the first gristmill, so that the people in the houses can eat. The date of the first sawmill, so that proper houses can be built. But to have a sawmill required the importation of expensive equipment from centers like Cincinnati or New Orleans, and then the diversion of some stream or river to provide the waterpower to turn the great wheels that ran the heavy saws.

The Allerkamps had no money for machinery, but as the months passed they were acquiring a reputation for working hard and honoring their promises, so when in the middle of the first year Ludwig came forward with a proposal, his neighbors listened: 'Our family has no money, but we do have men who can work. If you others band together, send a deposit to Cincinnati, and buy the saws and wheel, my boys and I will dig the millrace and build the housing.'

It was a deal, and while the heavy equipment made its way slowly down the Mississippi, the Allerkamps dug the footing for the sawmill building, erected the stone walls, and set the pits in which the great saws would move slowly up and down, producing the planks with which this section of Texas would be built. When the housing was finished, they turned to the laborious task of digging the millrace along which the water from the nearby stream would run on its way to turning the big wheel that would move the saws.

It was work of such strenuous effort that once Emil joked: 'I wish we had those slaves,' and this callous remark caused his father to assemble his family on Sunday for a sharp lesson in civilization: 'It's only natural for someone doing hard work, like digging a millrace, to wish that he could have slaves to do it while he rested. You spoke sense, Emil, when you said that, but we find in history that if a man does the work himself, he gets treble benefits from it. He does it better. He does it quicker. And in doing it, he amasses capital which enables him to finance additional tasks. We learn by doing.'

The Allerkamp women never idled while their men labored; Thekla and Franziska made all the clothes worn by the family, and although they purchased a little cloth, releasing their hoarded money in a most miserly way, for the most part, they spun cotton and wove their own. Depending on the time of year, they always had something to sell to strangers: extra cloth, eggs, deer and bear meat; they also sewed the ubiquitous sunbonnets that became the mark of the Texas woman, and it seemed to Ludwig that half the women in the area wore sunbonnets made by his wife and daughter.

Ernst had been home several weeks following his duty along the Nueces before Franziska found a way to ask about Otto Macnab without using his name or betraying her interest in him: 'Did you fight alone, Ernst?'

'No, we fought as a company. Captain Garner.'

'Did you pair off, each caring for the other?'

Since Ernst had been striving to forget some of the things he had seen, he found this questioning distressful. Reluctantly he replied: 'If a man fell, we all looked after him.'

'Did your company do well? I mean, were all the men responsible?'

'Dirty work, but we were powerful.'

'Did you have a special companion?'

'No.'

'Did the Rangers from Xavier County perform well?' She used a classical kind of speech, learned from her memorization of Schiller and Goethe, and tried to speak in complete sentences.

'We did. That short fellow you met, Otto Macnab . . .'

The magical name had been spoken, and without changing her expression in any way, with her face still turned to the spinning wheel where the cotton transformed itself into thread, she asked: 'Was he brave?'

'Well now . . .' He was still reluctant to speak.

'What?' she asked softly.

'Brave he was. Blue eyes hard as flint.'

'He sounds very brave.'

'He was. But . . .'

'What?'

Memory of a confusing incident came flooding back, and now he wanted to speak: 'We were patrolling north of the Nueces where the Mexican bandits had been raiding, and we came upon a white woman whose husband had been slain. I think she was out of her mind. Anyway, we left one of the men to take her to Victoria when we rode on. At a gallop we overtook three Mexican men. I thought they were farmers, maybe. They didn't look criminal. But this Otto Macnab rode right up to them and started firing.'

He stopped, and after a while his sister asked very carefully: 'You mean, the three Mexicans had no guns?'

He shook his head and could say no more, leaving his sister with the lonely problem of sorting out what had happened and what it signified.

When the Hardwork sawmill came into operation, civilization in Xavier County took a giant leap forward, because now the heads of families could drive their oxcarts to the mill, load up with beautifully sawn timbers – two hundred produced in the time it took two men to saw one in a hand pit – and build houses of real substance. Some of the most beautiful farmhouses in this part of Texas were built with that first flood of Hardwork timber. The German carpenters did not like the rather sprawled-out and formless dog-run of the Georgia and Carolina settlers; they preferred the compact, well-designed two-story house, with cedar or cypress shingles, neat board siding, stone fireplace and chimney at each end, and a trim small porch to provide protection against rain and sun.

Earlier settlers who had lived in Texas for some years warned the Germans: 'Without the dog-run to provide ventilation, you're going to be very hot in summer,' but the stubborn Germans replied: 'We can stand a little heat in exchange for a beautiful house.' Of course, when the summer of 1844 produced a chain of forty days when the thermometer hovered above the hundred-degree mark, the Germans in their tight, compact houses did suffer, but they made no complaint; they simply lay in bed almost nude, sweated inordinately, and rose in the morning gasping for the fresh air which circulated so easily through the dog-runs. Summer in Texas, they were discovering, could be a blast straight out of hell, untempered by way of passage over snowy mountains or cooling oceans. Said one old-timer: 'Come July, the devil stokes his furnaces real high, opens the draft, sends the flames to Texas so he can set up headquarters here in August and September.'

During this time of intense heat the Germans did have a respite which they enjoyed immensely, for a messenger rode in from the new settlement at a place called Lion Creek with news that there was to be an informal two-day Sängerfest to which all Germans living nearby were invited.

Any German Sängerfest, even a limited one like this, was a glorious affair, with almost every man in the community participating, as soloists if their voices were exceptional, as part of the humming chorus if obviously inadequate, and as an honorable part of the singing group if average. No women were allowed to join in the singing, of course, nor were they permitted to give the talks on such subjects as 'The Historical Plays of Friedrich Schiller' or 'The Metaphysics of Goethe'. But they did provide the food, and that most abundantly, and the younger unmarried women were the principal reason why many of the men attended, for finding a bride in German Texas was a grievous problem for which there seemed to be no solution, other than sending to Germany for one, as Theo down in the Matagorda area had done.

Of a hundred typical German men, at least ninety-seven, and perhaps even ninety-nine, would marry German women: 'It keeps the bloodlines clean. It keeps out the lesser strains.' It was therefore inevitable that when an industrious, attractive girl like Franziska appeared at a Sängerfest, her dress beautifully embroidered by her own hand, her hair in two neat braids with flowers plaited into the ends, she must attract attention and proposals from the hungry young men. Her father treated each approach with dignity, telling the swain that Franziska was too young to be thinking of such things, but his wife gave the young fellows hope that these conditions might change within the year. Franziska herself said nothing, did nothing. She had not at this time ever been kissed by a man, not even by her father or her brothers, and she felt no desire to be so by anyone at the festival.

But if she had never been kissed, and in this respect she resembled many reserved German girls of that time, she did experience a rich emotional life, as revealed in her diary:

I shall hide this book even more carefully after today, because I must confide to it a thrilling event in my life. I do believe I have fallen in love. Since I cannot discuss this with anyone, I cannot be sure, but there is a young man, from

Ireland I think, who stopped by our house and who has all the qualities I would seek in a husband. He is handsome, though smaller than my brothers, and he has the frankest blue eyes. Ernst assures me that he is brave in battle with brigands, and I learned from Herr Metzdorf that he runs a respectable farm. When shall I meet him? And what shall I say to him when we do meet? These questions are important, because I do honestly believe that one day I shall marry him, even if he is a Catholic. What an amazing thing to write!

Her behavior was not exceptional in these years, for the diaries of various German girls would reveal instances in which young women attended Sängerfests year after year, always knowing which of the young men they would ultimately marry, but never would the two young people speak. They would look, and remember, and fifty years later they would confess 'I knew I loved him' or perhaps 'I loved her from that first moment.' Germans could bide their time.

The Sängerfest this year provided two grand days of German singing, German poetry and German food, and not even the heavy rains that came at the close of the second day diminished the ardor of these good people who were keeping alive the traditions of the homeland which had treated them so badly but which still commanded their memories. Indeed, the rain became so heavy that most of the visitors from Hardwork had to lay over an extra day, and when they did set forth for home they found that what had been little streams during the trip to Lion Creek were now surging torrents, so they were forced to waste a fourth day till the floods subsided.

As they neared their house in Hardwork, Hugo Metzdorf, his face ashen, came to greet them, and without speaking, thrust into Ludwig's hand a letter just received from Grenzler. When Ludwig finished reading, he passed it dumbly to his wife, who studied it, then grasped Metzdorf's hand and uttered a low sigh: 'Ach, mein Gott!'

The letter said that the secret police had arrested Alois Metzdorf, charged him with treason and thrown him in jail, where he had hanged himself.

Unable to speak to either Metzdorf or his wife, Ludwig walked unsteadily to a rock, sat down and covered his face, overwhelmed by the tragedy. Alois, the dreamer, the one who had really wanted to come to Texas, the man who had given him the certificates. Ludwig had shaken hands with him on the pledge: 'Alois, I'll hold the best fields for you . . . till you come.' He retched, for a horrible suspicion assailed him: 'Alois Metzdorf would never commit suicide. Visions of freedom kept that man alive. My God! They hanged him in his cell.'

His hands fell to his lap, and when Thekla whispered: 'Ludwig, we must go,' he was unable to move. Stricken by grief over the death of his old friend, he could only sit there and mumble acid verses of Heine. In the depth of his despair, and in his sorrow for the German people, he understood as fully as any man might the meaning of emigration, its terrors, its relief, and the wonder of finding after long struggle a new life in a new land. Had he been invited at that moment to occupy a castle in the Margravate or any other German principality, he would have refused. He was in Texas and he loved every rolling hill, every relentless, heat-filled day.

In a rush of enthusiasm like none he had known before, he decided that the Allerkamps must immediately utilize their certificates, and with the aid of a surveyor, stake out their own farm. To their relief, a man said to be an expert in such matters arrived at this crucial time to inform them that he knew a surveyor who would locate land for them if their papers were in order. When the certificates were presented, he said: 'Everything fine. Your land is on the way.'

When they met the surveyor, a thin small man from Alabama who chewed grass stems, he laid the situation honestly before them. 'We find the land together. We mark it off together. I build three-foot piles of earth and rock at each corner, and then you stand in the middle and dance up and down, shout to the four winds, and fire a gun two or three times to inform the world that this is now your land. For my fee I get one-third, so since you have certificates for six parcels, I'll just take these two and you have yourself two thousand acres, more or less.'

It seemed so simple, with the surveyor assuring them there would be no other costs, that the Allerkamps in family session agreed, and Ludwig said when the deal was closed: 'We'll have our own land. We'll work for ourselves.' They further agreed that they would apply the four certificates they still retained to

677

some choice land in the northern part of Xavier County, not on the Brazos, for that was all taken, but not too far inland. Franziska was quietly excited when she realized that the land her father was speaking of would place her close to where Otto Macnab had his property; they had not yet spoken, but she was decidedly interested in being near him.

Unfortunately, the Alabama surveyor was a scoundrel. Immediately after obtaining possession of the Allerkamp entitlement of a thousand acres, he sold it to another man and was never seen again in that part of Texas. When Ludwig and his son Ernst tried to recover their certificate, the buyer went before Judge Phinizy and proved that he had obtained it not from the Alabama surveyor, because had he received stolen goods he would have to return them, but as a finder's fee from Allerkamp direct, in which case the land pertaining to the certificate was certainly his.

When Ludwig heard this decision, typical of hundreds then being handed down by the Texas courts against immigrants and Mexicans, he was so outraged that he could not for several days even discuss his indignation with his family, but when his fury subsided he assembled them. 'There is much wrong with Texas. The way they treat Indians, the way they own slaves, the way they allow a man like that to steal from everyone. But there is also much that is right; our neighbors represent that goodness. They're still willing to provide us food for the next six months while I study and find our land. I'm going to be a surveyor, and an honest one.'

With that firm decision as a rocklike base, he took out his trigonometry book, associated himself with a man from Mississippi who had mastered Spanish land law, and began the laborious study of varas, cordeles, labors and leagues. 'A vara,' he told his family, 'is exactly thirty-three point thirty-three inches, which means that it's just short of a yard. Texas system, seventeen hundred and sixty yards to the mile. Spanish system, nineteen hundred and one varas to the mile.' He purchased a surveyor's chain of twenty varas and accompanied his tutor on various jobs, during which he learned the rudiments of his new trade. He found that he liked the rough life of tramping across open land; he learned how to shake brush and low shrubs with a warning stick to scare away rattlesnakes; and he enjoyed the closing ceremonies when the new owner stood in the middle of his selection and jumped in the air and shouted to the four winds and fired his gun. At such moments he felt that he had accomplished something: he had helped a man to be free.

On one prolonged survey he was led to a river far to the west, the Pedernales it was called, the River of Flints, and he vowed that when he had his own credentials as a surveyor, he would return to the Pedernales and stake out his claim on the two thousand acres to which he was entitled, paying himself the surveying fee, and then buy as much more as he could afford. He said nothing of this to the man from Mississippi, lest he spread the news that his German helper had found a paradise among the rolling hills and green forests of the west.

For a long period Captain Garner's company of Rangers received no call to duty, because with the Cherokee expelled and the Comanche pushed back from Austin, the only recurring trouble spot was along the Nueces River, and this contested region fell strangely inactive.

'What's your friend Garza doing down there?' Garner asked Otto when they met in Campbell.

'Up to no good, you can be sure of that.'

'Government wants me to make a scout. But it has funds for only three Rangers.'

'I'll go without pay. I go crazy just sitting around.'

'Would you ride down and see if that Allerkamp fellow cares to come along?'

With an enthusiasm which almost betrayed his real purpose, Otto cried: 'Hey, I'd like to do that,' and it was in this way that he saw Franziska for the second time. As before, he remained on his horse, instructing Ernst as to where they would meet, and as he had hoped, the Allerkamp girl stood by the door, watching him intently. She was now a petite, handsome sixteen-year-old young miss whose flaxen hair was wound about her head. Again, neither she nor Otto spoke, but she believed that he was somewhat taller than before and he saw her as infinitely more beautiful.

When Mrs Allerkamp came to the door to ask in heavily broken English: 'Is it that you would like maybe some drink?' he blushed painfully and allowed as how he wouldn't.

679

On the way home he rode in great perplexity, for if he had shied away from Betsy Belle Ascot because she was so distressingly much older than he, all of five years, he was now ashamed of himself for being interested so achingly in a child who was obviously years younger than himself. Desperately he had wanted to accept Mrs Allerkamp's invitation to sit in the kitchen, perhaps with the daughter, whose name he did not even know, but he had been afraid. However, when Ernst joined Captain Garner for the scout, Otto did contrive a tortuous way of discovering his sister's name.

'Franziska,' Ernst said, and there the conversation ended.

At the Nueces they did not find Benito Garza, and for a reason that would have astonished them. Now thirty-nine years old and, like Otto, still unmarried, Garza was far south of the Rio Grande astride a stolen horse and leading two others acquired in the same way. He wore a big, drooping mustache, which had become his trademark: no waxed points, no fanciness, just an ominous growth of hair which gave his face its sinister look.

He rode in bitterness, a man whose world had fallen apart. It galled him to think that because he fought to retain the Nueces Strip for Mexico, he was characterized a bandit and that notices were plastered along the Nueces River: $300 Dead or Alive THE NOTORIOUS BANDIT GARCIA.

'They can't even get my name right,' he grumbled as he continued down the dusty road. He thought of himself as a patriot, never a bandit. When he raided in the Nueces Strip, using ugly tactics in doing so, he saw himself, and justifiably so, as a defender of his land, land which his family had occupied long before even the first dozen anglo families had filtered in to Tejas. In recent months he had even revived his vanished dream of becoming Gobernador de la Provincia de Tejas, and he knew that to achieve it he must, as before, depend upon Santa Anna.

When he came in sight of Mexico City his heart quickened, for here he was to meet his hero, the general, and learn from him when the reconquest and punishment of Tejas was to begin.

But when he entered the capital and reported to military headquarters he learned that Santa Anna, now dictator with powers unprecedented, had as so often before left the government in the hands of others while he loafed on his beloved ranch near Xalapa, and Garza showed his disappointment. 'Damnit,' he complained to headquarters, 'I've ridden all the way from Tejas to learn how my volunteers can serve when the new war begins, and I find the commander-in-chief idling on his ranch.'

A very young colonel, Ignacio Bustamante, related in some way to the politician who served as nominal president in Santa Anna's absence, took him in charge: 'Never speak badly of our president. He has ten thousand ears.'

'I fought for him. I revere him.'

'That's good, because he wants to see you ... at his hacienda.'

As the two officers rode east past the great volcanoes, Bustamante brought Garza up to date on the doings of their general: 'I suppose you know that a long time ago some high-spirited young Mexican officers stole a few pastries from the shop of a French patisserie, and when the French ambassador was unable to collect damages for his countrymen, France imposed a blockade. Yes, a real war with ships bombarding Vera Cruz.

'Well, you know Santa Anna. Let an enemy touch his beloved Vera Cruz, and he's off like a lion. As the French landed, he leaped on his white horse and dashed into town to defend it. As usual, he behaved heroically and had the great good luck to be hit by a French cannonball, which so damaged his left leg that it had to be amputated. Yes, our noble warrior now has only one leg.'

'How does he get about?' Benito asked, and the colonel explained: 'He has four wooden legs that he carries with him in a leather case, one for dress, one for everyday wear, one for battle, and I've been told what the fourth is for but I forget. Each different, each made of different materials. The one for evening wear is very light, made of cork.'

'You said he was lucky to have been hit by the French cannonball? I don't think losing a leg is luck, even if you have four replacements.'

'Oh! You miss the meaning! You'll not listen to our general speak four sentences in a public oration, and he makes them constantly, without hearing an account of how he lost his leg in

681

the service of his nation. He has fifteen clever ways of casually referring to it. Heroic: "I galloped into the very mouth of the French cannon and lost my leg in doing so." Self-pity, with tears: "In a moment of great danger I surrendered my leg to the glory of my country." Challenging: "Do you think that a man who has lost his leg defending his country is afraid of a threat like that?" His missing leg is his passport to glory.'

When they rode past the grim prison at Perote, where various Texian adventurers still languished in dark cells, Colonel Bustamante began pointing at choice fields and saying repeatedly: 'Santa Anna has acquired this ranch,' or 'Santa Anna had this owner shot as a traitor and now the ranch is his.' The dictator owned nearly half a million acres on which roamed more than forty thousand cattle, all obtained at no cost, and Garza, proud of his hero's accomplishments, failed to realize that Santa Anna's stealing of land from peasants was precisely the same as the anglos stealing land from mexicanos in the Nueces Strip. Nor could he know that the total corruption made popular by Santa Anna was going to become a way of life in Mexico, contaminating government for the next century and a half.

Garza was astonished when he met his hero, for Santa Anna was extremely thin, his face poetically gaunt, his heavy head of hair beginning to show gray. He limped pitifully as he came forward to greet his Alamo lieutenant: 'I lost a leg, you know, defending our nation at Vera Cruz.' He was wearing his country-landowner leg, and before Garza could reply, he reached out, clasped him by the shoulder, and said with unfeigned enthusiasm: 'In honor of the great days, my Gobernador de Tejas, let us see the cocks fight,' and he led the way, now springing along, with no perceptible difficulty, to the small circular building in which he conducted his famous cockfights.

He had invited some sportsmen up from Vera Cruz, each with three or four champion birds, and for three loud and dusty hours the great dictator indulged himself with one of the things in life he prized most, the slash-and-flash of the cockfight when two noble birds, trained to the last degree and fitted with three-inch scimitar blades, fought to the death.

Next morning Santa Anna revealed why he had asked Garza

682

to make the long ride to Manga de Clavo, and to Benito's surprise, it did not concern the invasion of Tejas or even the guerilla warfare there; it was an imperial concern which no visitor could have anticipated: 'My dear and trusted friend, I seek a guard of honor for a deed of honor. In response to demands from the people of Mexico, and also its religious leaders, I have consented with some reluctance, for I am essentially a modest man, to have my left leg disinterred, borne to the capital, and buried in a pantheon reserved for heroes.'

'Your leg?' Benito asked.

'Why not?' Santa Anna snapped. 'It gave itself in service to our nation, did it not? What leg has ever meant so much to a nation? Does it not deserve the treatment we give other heroes?'

'It certainly does,' Benito said hurriedly, and he was present when the leg was dug up, placed upon an ornate catafalque, and started on its triumphal journey to the capital.

He and seven other lieutenants, men who had proved their worth in battle, were issued special green-and-gold uniforms and horses with silver-encrusted saddles, and they led the procession, clearing the way through villages where entire populations turned out to honor the great man's leg as it made its way slowly past Perote prison, into Puebla, and beneath the noble volcanoes.

Garza and Bustamante rode ahead into the capital, to alert the city that the leg was coming and to ensure that multitudes lined the avenues when it arrived. Thousands turned out, and at the splendid cathedral in the center of town more than fifty priests of various ranks, including a number of bishops, waited to place the leg in a position of honor below the altar. Here legions of the faithful could come and kneel and say brief prayers.

Two days later, with Santa Anna himself in attendance, entire regiments of cavalry in resplendent uniform, young cadets from the military academy at Chapultepec, a solemn procession of priests and religious dignitaries, the entire civilian cabinet and most of the diplomatic corps marched to the beat of seven military bands, leaving the center of the city and progressing to the historic cemetery of Santa Paula, where a cenotaph had been erected to the dictator's leg.

Prayers were said. Chants were sung. Rifles fired. Santa

Anna wept. The multitude cheered. And soldiers such as Benito Garza stood stiffly at attention while flags were draped over the coffin and the leg was lowered into its new and stately grave.

Garza was still in the capital when a vast revulsion against the pomposity of Santa Anna surfaced, and he watched in horror as a mob tore down a gilded statue of the dictator in the center of the city, rampaged through the streets, and cheered when a crazy-eyed leader shouted: 'Let's get that goddamned leg!' From a safe distance Garza followed the frenzied rabble as it broke down the gates of Santa Paula, destroyed the cenotaph honoring the leg, dug up the bones, and dragged them ignominiously through the very streets where they had a short time before been paraded with such majesty. He was aghast when the bones were separated, some going to one part of the city, some to another, and all of them ending in rubbish piles.

Through back streets he made his way to the palace from which the dictator had ruled with such unchallenged authority, and there he found him packing his wooden legs in their case as he prepared for flight. When Garza informed him of events at the cemetery, the great man sat heavily upon a trunk packed with silver objects and sniffled: 'My leg! The symbol of my honor! They dragged it through the streets!' Then, pulling himself up, he hobbled off to what appeared to be a lifelong exile.

As he disappeared in the dusk, Garza swore an oath: I shall drive every norteamericano out of the Strip. I shall ride and burn and kill, because that land is Mexico's, and I shall hold it until General Santa Anna marches back with a great army to reconquer it. He had to realize, of course, that his one-legged hero was nine parts charlatan, but this deficiency was offset by the fact that it was only Santa Anna who stood any chance of defeating the Texians, and he dreamed of the day when fighting would resume.

By the spring of 1845 the varied assignments given the self-taught surveyor, Ludwig Allerkamp, had enabled him to know more of Texas than most of its other citizens, and since he had an innate curiosity and a love of nature acquired from his ramblings in the woodlands of Germany, he perceived relationships which others did not. He saw, for example, that this central part of Texas consisted of five clearly defined strips, each a minor nation of its own.

Along the Gulf, where his son Theo and his wife now had their store, Texas was a swampy flatland inhabited by mosquitoes of enormous size and birds of great beauty. Summers were intolerably hot and damp, but the remainder of the year could be dazzling in its movement of wildlife and the brilliance of its long sunsets. People brave enough to live here tended to love the loneliness, the vast expanses of marshland and the interplay of sea and shore.

Inland came the treeless flats, enormous stretches of prairie populated by wild horses and unbranded cattle. Low shrubs dominated the sandy soil and a thousand acres represented a small field, indistinguishable from a hundred others reaching farther than the eye could see. This was going to be excellent land, Ludwig believed, for the raising of cattle, and whenever he surveyed a segment he assured the new owners: 'Your land will be of great value one day.'

He appreciated most the third strip, and one in which he lived, that mysterious area in which the land began to form small hillocks, the streams wandered easily down twisting valleys and, most precious of all, trees began to appear, cedars, cypresses and four different kinds of oaks, including a small-leafed variety covered with some dead-looking substance of crepuscular character. When he asked about the sickness which attacked these small-leafed trees, he was told: 'Those are live oaks, and that's Spanish moss.' Very quickly the family came to revere the live oak as one of the great boons in Texas.

When the new capital at Austin had to be surveyed, Allerkamp had an opportunity to see at close hand the fourth strip, one of the marvels of Texas, a sudden uprising of cliffs and rocky prominences called the Balcones, which stretched north to south for more than a hundred miles, delineating the end of the prairies and the beginning of the hill country. Here trees began to show in great variety, flat plains disappeared, and rivers ran through gorges. The Balcones had no great depth; east to west they were rarely more than half a mile wide, but they formed a remarkable feature which could not be missed. As Ludwig told his family when he returned from his assignment: 'It's as if nature wanted to give a signal: "Here begins a new world!" And she laid down this barrier of great rocks and hills.' He told them: 'Austin will become the most beautiful city in Texas because it lies right on the Balcones, land goes up and down, up and down.'

Now the government assigned him the task of inspecting the fifth and most noble strip, those marvelous, quiet lands which lay to the west of the Balcones. With his two sons, Ernst, home from his service with the Rangers, and Emil, he set out to explore the very best part of Texas, the hill country.

As soon as the three Allerkamps left the capital city they found themselves surrounded by low, wooded hills of the most enchanting variety, graced by exquisite valleys hiding streamlets. The scene changed constantly as they moved westward, now opening out into vistas, now closing in so that they could see only short distances ahead. 'These aren't even what they'd call hills in Switzerland,' Ludwig told his sons. 'Around Munich they'd not be dignified with names, but after the flatlands they seem like mountains. In years to come, I'm sure that people who live back there in the flatlands will rush to these hills for the summer breezes,' and the boys could see a score of places they wished the Allerkamps owned for just such relief when the hot winds arrived in July.

Such speculation about possible homesites was not idle, for the Allerkamps still owned four certificates authorizing them to claim free land. The catch, of course, was that it had to be legally surveyed, but since Ludwig was now an authorized surveyor, he could pretty much select exactly what he wanted in this fairyland so rich in hills and tumbling streams.

It was in this frame of mind that the Allerkamp men came one afternoon upon the Pedernales River, which Ludwig had discovered the year before. In those days he had deemed the river remote, but now it seemed to run only a short distance from the capital, and he and his sons began to speculate on its virtues, and after they had surveyed it for about thirty miles, they stopped at a point where a nameless little creek wandered in to join the Pedernales from the north, and without any discussion they agreed that this was the land they had been seeking since fleeing Germany.

Very quietly Ludwig told his sons: 'Let's lay out an area of ten thousand acres.'

'Our scrip allows only two thousand.'

'We'll pay for the extra.'

'How?'

Ludwig stood silent for a moment, his face in the wind. 'I've been saving,' he said, and in the deep lines of his face his sons could see the endless labor and the deprivation he had suffered to earn his family their land.

'Start stacking rocks at our corners,' he said, and when their new farm was delineated the three men stood in the center, fired their guns, threw rocks and twigs into the air, jumped up and down as custom required, and then yelled at the top of their voices: 'It's ours! It's ours!'

Back in Hardwork, Ludwig reported to his women: 'Our farm will have the big Pedernales running along the south for about six miles, and halfway along comes this beautiful little creek from the north ... you couldn't call it anything bigger. One stretch of river cuts through a gorge, real cliffs north and south, and everywhere trees, trees, trees.'

'Is it like Germany?' Thekla asked, and her husband replied: 'Well, almost. The trees are farther apart. The land is rougher. The banks of the river are cluttered with debris from floods. And it might be difficult to build only with stone. You could never claim it was Germany, but it will be very congenial.'

'Will there be fields for us to grow crops?' practical-minded Thekla asked, and when the men assured her that with minimum effort large meadows could be cleared for crops, she said: 'It doesn't sound like Germany, but I'm ready.'

This finicky evaluation of their new home distressed Emil: 'I saw deer and rabbits and skunks and so many different birds, I lost count. We have turkeys in the woods and fish in the river, and I'm sure the soil can grow pears and peaches. Father has claimed a paradise for us, and as soon as the papers are cleared in Austin we ought to sell this place and move immediately.' He caught his mother by the hands and danced with her: 'For the hills are beautiful, Mother! They are beautiful.'

When they contacted Yancey Quimper at the county seat they found him most eager to buy their property in Hardwork, and he also offered, in an embarrassing confrontation with the two Allerkamp seniors, to take their daughter Franziska

687

off their hands. The Allerkamp men, who had begun to worry about the future of their unmarried girl, considered his proposal seriously, for as Ludwig pointed out: 'He is well-to-do. He's respected by Xavier County as the Hero of San Jacinto, and he's certainly no coward, for he forced General Houston to back down from a duel. Of course, he's not a German, but . . .'

Mrs Allerkamp said nothing, but her sons, eager to see their sister married – and to almost anyone – threw reasons at her: 'He's a patriot. He has that profitable ferry. He's strong in debate. And he's . . . well . . . presentable.' When the barrage was at its most intense, Mrs Allerkamp stared at her daughter, aware that this marriage would be highly improper.

Franziska, taking strength from that silent stare, said no. She gave no reason. Drawing her arms close to her side as if protecting herself from an alien world, she shook her head, uttering only one word: 'No.' She did not say it with any undue emphasis or animosity; she simply rejected her fifth serious suitor and went about her work. She was now an expert spinner and a good weaver; she could sew clothes out of the cloth she made and form rough shoes out of the cowhides her brothers provided. She could also embroider seats for chairs and sew patterns on the dresses she made for herself and her mother. Best of all, she was an excellent cook, specializing in heavy meat dishes for the men and cookies for all festive occasions. These she liked to decorate with colored jellies and thumbprint designs, spending hours of an afternoon to make them works of art as well as delights to the taste. She had prevailed upon her brothers to carve a set of hollowed-out stars and crescents and ovals and zigzags out of oak, and with these she cut her cookies, so that when at last she brought a platter of them to the table, they shone with color and danced in lovely forms and patterns. And she always held the platter on the palms of her hands, as if she were a young goddess of the hearth, presenting her offerings to some pagan statue.

Yancey Quimper took his rejection with good spirit, half relieved that he had escaped the bondage that marriage often became in a frontier community. His failure to catch Franziska did not influence his business judgment, and he offered the Allerkamps just enough to encourage them to sell but not so much that he stood to lose. It was a good clean deal, and when it was concluded, with the two Allerkamp women weeping to think that they had lost a home in which they had known stern obligation but also much happiness, Quimper said: 'I'd like to take possession as soon as possible. I have a buyer in mind.'

So in June of 1845 the five Allerkamps loaded all their goods on two ox wagons and set out for the hill country. When they reached Austin they heard exciting news: 'A group of more than a hundred German immigrants stayed in the settlement at Neu Braunfels. But they wanted their own land. They're planning to move into that area you surveyed. Near the Pedernales.'

Many parts of the hill country, that precious segment of Texas, would be German. Its public schools, among the first in Texas, would be German, and the songs sung by the men's choruses at its great festivals would be German, and fathers would teach their daughters the poetry of their homeland, as Ludwig Allerkamp had taught his Franziska the delicate words that summarized their new life:

> 'In that exquisite month of May
> When all the buds were breaking,
> I felt within my bosom
> New life and love awakening.'

So the Allerkamps from Hardwork and the other German families from Neu Braunfels established excellent homes in a settlement they named Fredericksburg, after a Prussian prince, and in quick order they built a struggling community in which English was almost never heard. In time it would become a superior town, with stores, watchmen and a good lodging place run by the Nimitz family; at first there was only one meeting house, but it was unique. Octagonal, it was affectionately called 'The Coffee Grinder,' and was shared amicably by all denominations.

The Allerkamps were delighted to have Fredericksburg only six miles from their farm, and even before the town was well started, Ludwig rode in to talk with the elders, purchasing from them a quarter-acre near the Nimitz farm. When the Fredericksburg people asked: 'Are you going to sell your place out in the country?' he replied: 'Not at all. In here we'll have a resting

689

place for the women,' and this is what it became, a tiny house with only one room and a row of beds. Now the Allerkamp women could come to town on Saturday in the family wagon, while the men rode in on horseback early Sunday.

In this way the Allerkamps obtained two homes, one in the country, one in town, while Otto Macnab still had none. In fact, he was about to surrender the homestead he did have, for with the Ascots gone his only remaining companion was Yancey Quimper, and the more he inspected that man's shady dealings the more convinced he became that Yancey was the kind of devious man with whom he did not care to associate: 'Life in Xavier County is finished for me. I better get going.'

One morning he rode up to the Ferry and surprised Yancey: 'You want to buy my land?' Quimper made no false show of saying: 'Otto, you mustn't leave!' Instead, he jumped at the offer, and men lounging at the bar who overheard the transaction said: 'Otto's bein' smart. He cain't farm it hisself and he ain't got no wife to tend it in his absence, so hell, he might as well pass it on to someone as'll care for it.' Quimper, aware of the young bachelor's determination to be gone from these parts, drove a hard bargain and got the spread for sixteen cents an acre, and before the week passed he had sold it to immigrants from Alabama for a dollar-ten.

When Otto learned of the outrageous profit Quimper made, he merely shrugged, for he had lost interest in the land. Rootless, he drifted about the county seat, accepting the hospitality of Reverend Harrison at the school, but when Captain Garner rode in one morning with the news that Company M was being reactivated for duty with the United States Army at Corpus Christi, Otto quickly volunteered, for he wanted something tangible to do. It was as if he realized that his destiny was not a settled home but the wild, roving life of a Ranger.

During the time when Otto was stumbling about, trying to find a home, the young nation of Texas was doing the same: it was bankrupt, it owed tremendous debts; in Mexico, General Santa Anna, magically restored to power yet again, refused to acknowledge that Texas had ever separated from Mexico, and there was violent talk about launching a real war to recover the

690

lost province; and from Europe, France and England continued their seductive games.

Relations with the United States were as confused as ever, for when Texas had wanted annexation, the States had refused to accept her; and recently, when a worried United States invited her southern neighbor to join lest some other nation snatch her, Texas said no. Something had to be done or the fledgling nation might collapse.

At this juncture a small-town lawyer from the hills of Tennessee, a modest man without cant or pretension, stumbled his way into the White House as America's first 'dark horse,' to the amazement of men much better qualified, such as Daniel Webster, John Calhoun, Henry Clay and Thomas Hart Benton. Future historians and men of prudent judgment when assessing the American presidents would judge this modest but strong-willed man to have been one of our very ablest holders of that office, perhaps Number Six or Seven, behind such unchallenged giants as Washington, Jefferson, Jackson, Lincoln, and especially Roosevelt – Republican partisans nominating the first of that name; Democrats, the second.

It was said of James K. Polk: 'He entered the White House determined to serve one term and accomplish two goals. Having attained these aims, he retired as he promised he would. No President can perform more capably.'

Polk's two aims were simply stated: he wanted to bring Texas into the Union, regardless of the slavery issue or the feelings of Mexico; and he thirsted to extend American territorial sovereignty to the Pacific Ocean, even if that necessitated seizing vast portions of Mexico. To the pursuit of these aims and against venomous opposition, he dedicated his energies and his life itself, for soon after attaining them he died. Quiet, retiring in manner, he was remarkably daring, risking possible war with European powers as he hacked his way to the Pacific and provoking actual war with Mexico when he proclaimed that the Nueces Strip belonged undeniably to the new State of Texas, with the Rio Grande as its southern boundary.

He would bring into the United States more new territory than any other president, including even Thomas Jefferson with his extraordinary Louisiana Purchase. He was the personification of Manifest Destiny, and when he left the White

House the outlines of the continental United States would be set, geographically and emotionally. Every nation, in time of great decision, should have in command a man of common sense like James K. Polk, for such men strengthen the character of a country.

When Polk won the 1844 presidential election on a program of annexation, the outgoing president, in obedience to the will of the nation, rushed through a joint resolution, offering Texas immediate annexation. But now Texas, certainly the slyest potential state ever to dicker with Congress on terms of entry, delayed acceptance of the belated invitation until Washington approved the draft constitution under which the new state would be governed. It was a document which reflected accurately the beliefs and prejudices of the Texians: no bank could be incorporated, never, under any circumstances; married women enjoyed full property rights; no clergyman, regardless of his church affiliation, could ever serve in the legislature. Two provisions enshrined principles to which Texians were committed: on the side of freedom, the governor would serve for only two years and not for more than four out of every six years; on the side of bondage, slavery was enthusiastically permitted. State Senator Yancey Quimper, campaigning for the constitution, shouted that it made Texas a nation within a nation, and when the vote was counted, it stood 4,000 in favor to 200 against.

And then the Texians demonstrated what a canny lot of horse traders they were. They wheedled the American Congress into awarding entry terms more favorable than those enjoyed by any other state, including two unique provisions: Texas and not the federal government would own all public lands, and the state would retain forever the right to divide into five smaller states if that proved attractive, each one to have two senators and a proportionate number of representatives.

But Congress, liberal in all else, issued a stern ultimatum on timing: Texas must accept this final offer before midnight, 29 December 1845, or annexation was killed. This did not faze the Texians, who waited till the last practical moment, the twenty-ninth, before voting acceptance, after which Senator Quimper roared: 'Texas will now lead the United States to greatness.'

Ceremonial transfer of power did not occur until 19 February 1846, when a soldier started to lower the flag as President Anson Jones uttered these words: 'The final act in this great drama is now performed. The Republic of Texas is no more.'

As the beautiful Lone Star fluttered downward, it was caught in the arms of Senator Quimper, who pressed it to his lips while tears streamed from his eyes. The free nation of Texas was no more, but the resonance from its brief, bankrupt, chaotic and often glorious existence would echo in Texas hearts forever.

... Task Force

As I was certifying our year-end expense accounts I uncovered a fascinating bit of trivia. Quimper's legal name was not Lorenzo, but Lawrence, and when I asked about this, he volunteered a revealing explanation: 'It happened one morning like a bolt of lightning. I was a sophomore at UT, forty-five pounds overweight, bad complexion, making no time with the coeds and accomplishing zilch in general. I stared at the mirror and said: "Son, you are not a Lawrence. You're more like a Lorenzo."'

'Where'd you get that name?' I asked, and he said without hesitation: 'Heard it in a movie.'

'About the Medici?'

'Knew nothing about them. This was a thriller and Lorenzo was the villain. Played by Basil Rathbone, I think. Very slim, good at dueling, dynamite with the ladies. That's how I fancied myself.'

'Where did Il Magnifico come from?'

'Girl named Mildred Jones. Freshman history major. Nuts about Italy. She gave me the name. And do you know what? I lost forty pounds. My face cleared up. I became manager of the football team. My entire life salvaged.'

'What happened to Mildred Jones?' I asked, and he said: 'Never married. Teaches history at San Marcos. Each Valentine's Day, I send her two pounds of Godiva chocolates.'

For our February meeting in Abilene, intellectual and religious capital of West Texas, the two young men on our staff, abetted by Rusk and Quimper, said: 'We've had enough outside

693

professors to address us. We want to hear at least one from a real Texan.'

I had no idea what they were talking about, and was further confused when they explained: 'We want to invite this professor from Tulane in New Orleans.'

'But you just said you were fed up with outside professors,' but when they told me his name I had to admit that he was about the finest example of 'a real Texan' extant.

Diamond Jim Braden was a wiry, tense thirty-eight-year-old folk hero from Waco, and his name was doubly identified with Texas virtue. That is to say, he was a former football player. His father, also known as Diamond Jim, had played on those immortal Waco teams of the 1920s when scores were apt to be Waco 119 – Opponents 0.

The first Diamond Jim, much larger than his son, had been a legendary halfback, scoring so many touchdowns that the record books exulted. Volunteering quickly in World War II, he had risen to captain and had led his company through the roughest fighting in Italy, had been repeatedly decorated, and had died just as his battalion was preparing to capture Rome. 'He behaved,' as a Waco editorial said, 'the way we expect our football heroes to behave.'

Now, there is nothing in Texas to which a man can aspire that is held in more reverence than skilled performance on the football field, especially a high school field, and Diamond Jim II, born in 1945 as a happy result of the compassionate leave granted soldiers with older wives, was reared on one simple truth: 'Your father was the best halfback this town ever produced, and he proved it against the Germans.' The second Diamond Jim might have been smaller than his illustrious father, but he had equal grit and determination, if that was possible. He, too, played halfback at Waco High, but fell short of equaling his father's scoring records because competition among the high schools had been equalized. However, he was All-State and he did win a scholarship to the University of Texas, where under Darrell Royal, patron saint of Texas football, he won All-Conference honors and nomination by quite a few national selectors as All-American.

By such performance he had assured his future; insurance companies, banks, oil prospecting consortiums and a score of other businesses sought his services. Because nothing opened the doors of Texas business more effectively than for an older man to be able to say: 'and this is our new star, Diamond Jim Braden, who scored those three touchdowns against Oklahoma.' The young man was required to know nothing about insurance, banking or oil; he did have to know how to dress, how to smile, and how to marry some extremely pretty and wealthy young woman from Dallas, Houston or Midland.

Diamond Jim, however, followed a more individual route, ignoring established precedents except for wanting a beautiful cheerleader as his wife. Selecting early and with great determination a most attractive English major at the university, he had entered the long and tedious course leading to a professorship, which, with the help of his wife, who took a teaching job in Austin, he attained.

As a lad playing football he had been fascinated by the various parts of Texas to which his team traveled, and by the time he was a senior he was a confirmed geographer, even buying with his own funds books on the subject. He grew to love the dramatic manner in which the regions of Texas changed, and once when his team played a title game in Amarillo, he sought permission to stay behind and spend three days exploring the great empty flatness of West Texas, responding to its messages as if he had been afoot in some celebrated area of geographic greatness like the Swiss Alps. As early as age eighteen he could read the messages of the land, and they thrilled him.

At the university, after his athletic advisers had arranged what they called 'a pushover schedule,' he astonished them by enrolling for a geography major. Taking the toughest courses available, he drew down straight As and started compiling a notebook of hand-drawn analyses of Texas land types. His coaches, after their initial shock, supposed that their boy was training to go into the oil business, and with the prudence that marked the behavior of Texas coaches, they arranged for several legendary oilmen to make him offers of employment after graduation.

To their further consternation, he announced that he really wasn't interested in oil. He wanted to be a geographer, and at this critical point two vitally important things happened that altered his life: he had the great good luck to run into Regent Lorenzo Quimper, who said: 'Jim, if you really want to be a geographer, great. We can buy all the oilmen we want from the University of Oklahoma. But if it is geography, be the best. Take your graduate work at this top school in Worcester, Massachusetts. Clark University. They've forgotten more geography up there than anyone down here in Texas ever knew.'

When it was revealed that Diamond Jim lacked the funds to enter such a school, Quimper mysteriously provided a fellowship that enabled the football hero not only to study at Clark but to travel widely on field trips and explorations. There was no discussion as to repayment of the fund, only the admonition: 'If you're gonna do it, son, do it Texas-style.'

Jim's second experience was one which comes to many young people. He read a book that was so strikingly different from anything he had ever read before that it expanded his horizons. *Imperial Texas*, had been written by D. W. Meinig, a cultural geographer from Syracuse University, a far distance from Texas, but it was so ingenious in its observations and provocative in its generalizations that from the moment Jim put it down he knew he wanted to be such a geographer, showing the citizens of his state the subtle ways in which their land determined how they acted and governed themselves.

With his Ph.D. from Clark, Diamond Jim landed an instructorship at Lyndon Johnson's old school, Southwest Texas State at San Marcos. From there he was promoted to an assistant professorship at TCU in Fort Worth, and he was obviously headed for a tenured professorship when he abruptly quit his job, took a lesser one in New Mexico, then one in Oklahoma, and finally a full professorship at Tulane, in New Orleans.

'What the hell are you doin', son?' Quimper asked during one vacation. 'Hopscotchin' about like a giddy girl?'

'I'm trying to learn the borderlands of Texas. When I've learned something, I'll hit you for a job at Austin.'

'I'll be your blockin' back,' Quimper assured him, and it was this remarkable scholar that Rusk and Quimper had invited to address us at Abilene.

Braden's thesis was simple and provocative: 'I have worked

in Old Mexico, New Mexico, Oklahoma and Louisiana, trying to identify the factors which those areas share with Texas, and I must confess that I find very few. Texas is unique beyond what even the most ardent Lone Star patriot realizes, and the difference lies in the marvelous challenge of our land. New Mexico has primarily an arid, beautiful wasteland, but so does Texas. The difference is that we have five or six other terrains to augment our wastelands. Oklahoma has striking plains, and so does Texas, but we also have a wild variation to supplement them. Louisiana has a charming old South terrain, but so does Confederate Texas in the Jefferson area, plus so much more.

'If a settler didn't cotton to one type of Texas land, he could move to some other that suited him better, and his options were almost unlimited. That's fundamental to an understanding of the Texas mind. The land was worthy of being loved. And both Texas women and Texas men grew to love it.'

At this point in his talk he quit his posture of lecturer and sat on the edge of a desk, legs dangling, cowboy boots showing: 'I think your committee is aware that any Texas man who makes it big in anything, first thing he wants is a ranch. If he's an oilman from Houston, he finds his ranch in the hill country back of Austin. If he's from Dallas, he finds it out toward Abilene. And if he's from Abilene, he wants his out toward the Pecas River. And when he finds his Shangri-La, he tends it as lovingly as if it were his mistress.'

Abruptly he pointed at Quimper: 'How many ranches do you have?' and Quimper said quietly but with obvious pride: 'Nine.' He then asked Rusk, who answered: 'Seven.' He was about to continue his interpretation of Texas geography when Miss Cobb said almost petulantly: 'Ask me,' and when he did, she said: 'Three.' Again he was about to proceed, when Professor Garza asked: 'And how about my family? Originally some forty thousand acres along the Rio Grande, and I still have a very small ranch down there, like you say.' Now Braden smiled at Quimper and confessed: 'I have my own little ranch. Near Hardwork, the old German settlement. Mr Quimper made me buy it with my first savings.'

I felt naked. I was the only one in that room without a ranch, but when they teased me about this, as if I were somehow disloyal, I defended myself: 'I've been working outside the state for some years, and I'm not a millionaire.' This did not satisfy Quimper and Rusk, who said that if I was really a Texan at heart, I'd own some small piece of the countryside, no matter where in the world I worked.

Without further interruption, Diamond Jim shot generalizations at us, which our staff recorded as follows: 'Basic to an understanding of how a Texan feels about his land is the fact that for a ten-year period, 1836 to 1845, the Texians had been in command of a free, sovereign republic, and this generated such deep-rooted characteristics that all who subsequently came to live within the boundaries were subtly modified. To be a Texian implied something quite different from what was indicated when a man said "I'm a New Yorker," or "I'm a Georgian." '

'Intensely varied, cruelly harsh, the land of Texas formed a little continent of its own, won by bloody courage, subdued by stubbornness, and maintained by an almost vicious protection of ownership. Men felt about the land of Texas differently from the way men of Massachusetts felt about their land; Texians devised new laws to protect their holdings, harsh customs to ensure that each family's land remained its own. I suppose you know that the homestead of a Texas man cannot be stolen from him in a bankruptcy proceeding brought by some bank.

'Newcomers from states where hunting is popular, like Michigan or Pennsylvania, experience shock when they move to Texas. It comes on the opening day of deer season, for in their home states they are accustomed to hunting pretty much where they wish, and vast areas of state-owned forests are opened to them, but in all of Texas there is no acre of land on which an uninvited hunter can trespass in order to shoot a deer. Land privately owned is sacrosanct. Indeed, in Texas the verb to *trespass* is identical with the verb *to commit suicide*, for it is tacitly understood that any red-blooded Texan is entitled to shoot the trespasser.

'On his piece of land the early Texian demanded freedom. He wanted no regular army to dictate his behavior; he called his Rangers to arms only infrequently, and even then for brief and limited periods; he was never overawed by judges; and he allowed no central bank which might dictate economic policies.

He was willing to act in concert with neighbors if an enemy threatened, but as soon as the danger abated he insisted upon returning to civilian life so that he could resume fighting with his neighbors. Of all the groups which would constitute the final United States, none would surpass the Texan in his devotion to freedom.'

Before sharing with us his next thesis he smiled, for he realized that he was treading where mythology and custom meet, and he wanted to exaggerate to score a point: 'The Texan sanctified his freedom behind a score of unique traditions. Any man whose wife's affections had been tampered with was free to shoot the other man, to the applause of the jury, impounded not to try him but to proclaim his innocence. And, of course, any good-looking woman was free to shoot any man at any time if only her lawyer could prove that love and honor were tangentially involved. Intrusion by the federal, state or county government into a family's basic freedoms was intolerable.

'Of course, this absolute freedom did not apply to blacks, Indians or Mexicans. Unlike the other Southern states, Texas did not provide a cadre of philosophers who agonized over this basic contradiction of freedom for everyone like me, slavery or extermination for anyone different. It was a way of life approved by ninety-seven percent at least of the anglo population, and as such, it would be preserved and augmented. In time labor unions, liberal newspaper editors and free-speaking college professors would be as outlawed as the Cherokee, the Mexican, the black slave imported from Alabama or the Comanche.

'Texas has been from the start and will always remain a frontier. It was a distant frontier for the kings of Spain from Madrid; it was a shadowy frontier for Napoleon ruling from Paris; and it was always a most remote frontier for Mexican presidents and dictators attempting to rule from Mexico City. When Mirabeau Lamar had the courage to move the national capital to Austin, it was on the frontier. When Sam Houston first came to Nacogdoches, the wild frontier lay only a few miles to the west; thirty-nine fortieths of future Texas was then a forbidden wilderness. During most of Texas history a wild frontier was always at hand, and not until 1905 or thereabouts could even half the state be classified as "settled". As late as the

1970s it would sometimes seem as if the frontier ran down the middle of Main Street in Dallas or Houston, and if you want to see the frontier still in existence in the 1980s, go to the little Rio Grande town of Polk in West Texas, where it glares across the river at the lawless Mexican town of Carlota.

'This frontier spirit engrained in Texas a spirit of adventure, a willingness to face whatever challenge came along. It encouraged the young people of Texas to be insolent, daring, self-assured and competent. It led to the imaginative utilization of natural resources and the speedy building of free-wheeling communities of unique and robust charm. The meanest family, the poorest boy in school, could persuade themselves that life was still dominated by the frontier, and that the qualities which had ensured success there were still honored. Texas was the permanent last frontier.

'The penalty for the perpetuation of this legend was a general lawlessness. Fistfights, duels, murders and countrywide insurrections became shockingly common, and when the lynching of black men had begun to fade elsewhere, it still flourished as a form of community entertainment in Texas. Texas cities became murder capitals of the nation and therefore the world, but no one complained excessively and anyone misguided enough to preach that guns should be controlled could never hope to become an elected official. Texas would always remain one of the most violent of the American states and would violently defend its right to behave pretty much as it damn well wished.

'Texans will also be inordinately proud of their history, cognizant of the ways in which it differed from the history of the rest of the states, passionately devoted to the stories of the Alamo and San Jacinto while endeavouring to forget how they had messed up Goliad and the Santa Fe expedition.'

At this point Braden stepped down from the desk and went back to his podium: 'I studied Texas history in Grade Three, again in Grade Seven, took a special course in high school, an advanced course in college, and a regional course in graduate school. I can't tell you much about unimportant countries like Greece, France and ancient Persia, but I sure as hell can tell you about McLennan County, Texas.'

He told us that Texans revered their ancestors as only the

citizens of Virginia and South Carolina could, but Texans did it with a fierceness that would have caused the other two states to be considered pusillanimous. Perhaps it was this constant living within the living past that made Texans different; certainly it made them more patriotic, so that no one could imagine a citizen of Iowa feeling about his state the way a loyal Texan felt about his.

'Despite their appalling record against Mexican armies – five losses, one win – the Texan citizen still believes he is invincible and that one good Texan can whip ten Mexicans, five Japanese, four Indians or three Germans, and they have never been loath to put this theory to the test. In later years it seemed as if Texans were running the entire American military machine, and rarely to its disadvantage. Texans boasted, but they also produced.

'Out of this heady mélange of patriotism, chauvinism and love of land evolved a way of life that Texans cherished and defended, but it produced constant contradictions. Women would spend vast amounts of money to dress better than those of Boston or Philadelphia, but their men would prefer the rough yet independent dress of the frontier. Sam Houston – congressman, governor, senator, president – established the pattern: boots, rough Mexican-style trousers, a wildly colored and embroidered shirt, a Napoleonic jacket, an immense flopping hat, all topped by a huge Mexican serape. Today the wealthy give mammoth parties at which a whole steer is barbecued, and in the early days solitary wanderers into the wilderness, which seemed always to be two miles to the west, knew that they could halt at the meanest shack and be offered bread and maybe some cheese. Titles and prerogatives meant little; courage and robust fellowship, everything.

'Very quickly Texas became a bastion of free economic activity. Speculate on the land. Risk driving seven hundred head of cattle to New Orleans or to the new railhead in Kansas. Take a chance on a wagon convoy of goods across the desert to Chihuahua. Drive the iron spikes of your railroad three hundred miles across the empty plains to El Paso. Fight the bankers. Fight the government, whether in Austin or Washington. Keep out the agitators and the labor leaders and the radicals. Protest like hell against any kind of taxation at all. And any frontier town of six hundred that did not have two or three millionaires wasn't really trying.

'In the arts the new state was unlucky. Because in its first stages it had been of Spanish heritage, it did not have among its original settlers a cadre of men and women accustomed to writing freely; it could not therefore duplicate settlements like Boston, Philadelphia, Williamsburg and Charleston, in which a predominantly English population already trained in a free English culture produced newspapers, books, impressive schools and thriving colleges. Also, Texans were so busy trying to take their frontier that they had little time for culture, and their refusal to support education vigorously, as states like Massachusetts and Ohio did, meant that they lacked a constant infusion of fresh intellectual ideas.

'So, at the end of the nineteenth century and the beginning of the twentieth, when indigenous forms of Texas culture should have been emerging, as such forms did in the rest of America, both the foundation and the desire were lacking, and a notable Texan culture composed of songs and paintings and plays and operas and epic poetry and delightful stories did not come forth.

'But the impulses for great art, if they are legitimate, never die, and in those fallow years Texas was accumulating a legend which will surely explode into expressive statement later on. I'm confident that we'll enjoy a vigorous renaissance about 1995, because legendary storytellers like Esteban the Moor, Yancey Quimper and Panther Komax keep the legends, the icons and the images burnished until the dreaming artists of a later day mature and take them in hand.

'Texans of the Republic found it easy to transfer their loyalties to the United States, which was no surprise, seeing that the vast majority of them had lived much longer in states like Tennessee and Alabama than in Texas. Later, Texans never forgot that they had once operated a free nation of their own, and a surprising number felt that if ever things went wrong in the United States as a whole, they could secede and revert to their own nationhood. In fact, one of the permanent weaknesses of Texas has been one which has not been acknowledged until recently: Texans, even today, look back to the decade of 1836 to 1845 when their ancestors enjoyed national status as "the great old days." As Americans, they feel that they are the elite among nations. As Texans, they know they are the elite among Americans.

'In the summer of 1846, a New Orleans newspaperman, endeavoring to evaluate the characteristics of the new state which now abutted Louisiana's western border, wrote:

"Louisiana and Texas are sisters, and have always been. At many times their heritage was identical, and far more of the supplies that Texas relied upon reached her via New Orleans than through Galveston. Today, the two states should be identical in the manner of Alabama and Mississippi.

"But Louisiana and Texas are not alike and never shall be. An immense gulf has been dug at the Sabine River, separating Texas not only from Louisiana but from all the other states of the Southern Tier, and it can never be bridged. What does the gulf consist of? The great Spanish missions, for one thing. Texas had them. We didn't. The Alamo and San Jacinto separate us, too, because Texas went through those dramatic experiences and we didn't.

"But at its widest extent, and deepest, the chasm consists of something much simpler. For the last ten years Texas has been a free nation. Louisiana never was. And the experience of such freedom, once enjoyed, seeps into a people's soul, never to be eradicated."

The Mexican War
1846–1848

0   MILES   200

VIII

THE RANGER

It was an interlude, a tragicomic interruption which few in Texas sought but which most later accepted as a turning point in their history. At a time when the newly approved state should have been paying attention to the building of governmental process and the sorting out of priorities, it found itself enmeshed in the Mexican War of 1846–1848, a minor affair militarily, a major event diplomatically.

Internally the effect on Texas was minimal; two battles and a disastrous cavalry encounter were fought on its soil, and its men invaded a foreign country, where they gained attention because of their bravery and lack of discipline. More important, men from the other twenty-eight states – Iowa becoming the twenty-ninth in 1846 – served in Texas and sent home harrowing stories of 'bleak empty spaces, drought, Mexicans and rattlesnakes.' Of maximum importance, national newspapers sent to the war reporters, sketchers and a remarkable man named Harry Saxon, who brought with him an unprecedented amount of gear to report upon Texas and the war. Their stories and pictures circulated around the world to launch the legend of Texas.

The American army was not in Texas by accident, nor was it there in response to any specific threat by the Mexican government. Instead, there had been a gradual worsening of relations between the two countries and some curious actions on the part of each. President-elect Polk, having been a prime force in bringing Texas into the Union, was determined to add New Mexico and upper California, so as to round out the continental reach of the United States, and since Mexico was either uninterested in developing these areas, or incapable of doing so, he supposed that the Mexicans might be willing to sell them for a decent price in order to be shed of responsibility. He was aware, of course, that the sudden acquisition of so much new land would force the American government to decide once and for all whether the resulting new states should be slave or free, and that would ignite dormant antipathies between South and North, but on that thorny question he was willing to postpone decision.

Even before Polk had been inaugurated in 1845, the kettle of war was bubbling. The United States Congress authorized annexation; Mexico, feeling insulted, terminated diplomatic relations; and the new president initiated a pair of daring moves. First he ordered a sizable army unit to Corpus Christi on the northern border of the Nueces Strip, and warned its commander to be prepared to strike if events required. Next he dispatched a personal emissary, John Slidell, to Mexico with an offer to buy New Mexico for $5,000,000, California for $25,000,000, and to pay up to $40,000,000 for a more complete package. When the Mexicans rebuffed Slidell for having offended their national honor, Polk saw that the two nations were on what he believed to be an unavoidable collision course. Forthwith he began to prepare for the war which he knew, and even hoped, must come.

In command of the eager troops at Corpus Christi was a crusty general, known for his courage, his stubbornness and his lack of education, who had been sent into Texas with orders to protect the American frontier but not to invade Mexico unless hostile action made this inescapable. Zachary Taylor was an almost perfect choice for the job; his frontier manner made him congenial to the Texans and his dogged, no-frills approach to battle made him an effective opponent to the flamboyant Mexicans. He did, however, face a difficult problem: Where was the Texas frontier he was supposed to protect?

When France controlled the Mississippi, Spain had been agitated over the border between Spanish Tejas and French Louisiana, and after Mexico won her independence she, too, kept careful watch along that border. But neither Spain nor Mexico cared much what the border between Tejas and its neighboring districts to the south was; it was assumed that this inconsequential delineation ran along the Medina and Nueces rivers. So when Tejas broke away in 1836, officials in Mexico honestly believed that these rivers still marked the boundary between new Texas and old Coahuila and Tamaulipas, and that the infamous Nueces Strip was Mexican. But the nation of Texas, and now the United States, had always argued that the boundary lay south at the Rio Grande, but neither had much reliable documentation to prove this. Now, in 1845, the Nueces Strip was as much an area of contention as it had always been.

The site of the troop concentration had not been chosen at random. The village of Corpus Christi with its two hundred citizens lay where the Nueces River entered the Gulf of Mexico, and this put it at the northeastern edge of the Nueces Strip. From here the army would stand in readiness for a leap into Mexico proper whenever events warranted. The soldiers at Corpus came from all parts of the Union and represented the emerging mix of national origins – 24 percent Scots-Irish, 10 percent German, 6 percent English, 3 percent Scots direct, 4 percent other foreign-born, and 53 percent native-born – nicely balanced between infantry, cavalry and artillery, with emphasis on the last.

When President Polk learned that John Slidell's offer to buy most of northern Mexico had been rejected, he judged that relations between the two countries had deteriorated so noticeably that he had better move General Taylor and his army closer to Mexico, so in late March 1846 Taylor leapfrog-ged clear across the Nueces Strip and assumed a position near the mouth of the Rio Grande. He did this knowing that such an invasion of territory claimed by Mexico must provoke reaction, and he was prepared for war, as was President Polk in Washington. If the truth were known, both the general and the president hoped for war.

Old Rough-and-Ready Taylor may have been as slow-witted as his junior officers sometimes thought, and the depths of his ignorance and fumbling were widely known, but when an enemy took a defined position on terrain that had been scouted, Taylor, sixty-two years old and wheezing, knew what to do. The first order he had issued upon leaving Corpus Christi endeared him to his subordinates: 'When we have marched three miles into the desert, I want every camp follower who has attached herself or himself to my army kicked the hell out. If they won't go back to Corpus on their own, put them in irons and march them off with bayonets at their backsides.' And in one grand sweep the hundreds of prostitutes, pimps, gamblers, whiskey peddlers, thieves and petty traders were booted out. Among these disreputables was a large, pompous gentleman who had been making a small fortune by selling a fantastic variety of things to Taylor's army: whiskey, tobacco, socks, hard candy, cigars, big hats to replace the inadequate type provided by the commissary and, some said, the favors of Mexican girls who seemed always to be available wherever he located. As soon as the order went out to rid the army of such trash, a rigidly proper West Pointer from South Carolina, Persifer Cobb, took it upon himself to arrest this man, whose operations he had monitored and whose behavior he deplored. But once he had the unsavory fellow corralled, Cobb found himself involved in a political scandal.

'I am a state senator of Texas,' the prisoner bellowed, 'and a general in the militia!' When Cobb questioned other prisoners, they confirmed the claims: 'He's Senator Yancey Quimper, Hero of San Jacinto, and you're in trouble, Colonel, because he has connections.'

'Damn Texas,' Cobb muttered under his breath. 'Where else would you find a general running a whorehouse?' But when Quimper kept demanding that he be taken to General Taylor, and threatening to have Cobb cashiered from the army 'because of my powerful associations in Washington,' Cobb had to protect himself, and shortly Yancey Quimper was standing before General Taylor.

'Are you indeed a senator?' Taylor asked, and when Quimper replied: 'In charge of military affairs,' Taylor asked: 'And what in hell were you doing among the rabble of my army,' and the senator explained: 'Looking after my land interests here.'

This lie was so offensive to Cobb that without having been invited to speak he blurted out: 'He was running a cheap store, a liquor bar, and worse,' at which Quimper drew himself to attention: 'I was a general in the Texas army, and I demand an apology.'

For one sickening moment Persifer Cobb feared that General Quimper intended joining the Texan volunteers, and his face drained of blood, but General Taylor, a rough old customer who could at times be magnificent, said: 'Get the hell out of here. I suspect you're a fraud.' And Senator-General Yancey Quimper retreated, muttering threats he knew he could not fulfill.

South of the Rio Grande there was a Mexican who had spent a dozen years also longing for such a war, but who now, when it was about to erupt, had ambivalent feelings arising from an event he could never have anticipated. Benito Garza, aged forty, had fallen in love.

When it became apparent that Mexico, in protection of its honor, must oppose any yanqui intrusion into the Nueces Strip, irrevocably the territory of Mexico, Garza had ridden north to assist General Mariano Arista in his defense of Mexican integrity. He was now serving Arista as a superior scout well informed about the area under contention, and in this capacity he was willing to lay down his life.

However, when he moved with Arista to Matamoros, where the Rio Grande enters the Gulf, he found attached to the command a purveyor of salted beef, one José López, who had an attractive daughter bearing a name highly favored by Spanish mothers of a religious bent: María de la Luz, Blessed Mary of the Holy Lights, which children traditionally abbreviated to Lucha. Lucha López was nineteen when Garza met her, a tall, slim young woman of curious beauty and dominant will. Her beauty was unusual in that her features were by no means perfect or strikingly regular; rather, they were strong, powerfully molded, with high cheekbones indicating a pronounced Indian origin. Her hair, which she wore in a long braid, was jet-black, which accentuated her black and piercing eyes.

When Garza first saw her delivering a basket lunch to her father, who had been negotiating with General Arista over the price of beef, he noticed that her dark eyes carried a clear sense of sadness, and he asked her father: 'Why is your daughter so mournful?' and he replied: 'The man she was to marry was killed on the other side of the river, where he kept his cattle.'

'Who killed him?' Benito asked, and the meat-dealer said: 'Tejas Rangers.' He pronounced the hated word in the manner common along the river, *Rinches*.

'When he was on his own soil!'

'Next they'll be shooting us in Matamoros.'

In his long years in the saddle Benito had seen many attractive girls and had idly courted some of them, but his manner of life had prevented him from seriously contemplating marriage. At first when he met this impressive young woman he shied away, because he knew that wars and incursions and revolutions would deter him from being a good husband or even a reasonable one.

But Lucha López was not an easy woman to dismiss, and during a six-week interval before open warfare began, he courted her, at first tentatively, then with growing ardor. Once as he left her reluctantly, he thought: She weaves a web about me, as a spider traps a fly. And I like being trapped.

Their cautious relationship did not follow customary patterns, for on those occasions when they managed to escape her dueña they often discussed military matters. 'Is it true,' she asked one afternoon, 'that General Taylor has ten thousand troops?'

'I've been north twice to see, and I doubt he has ten thousand. But many . . . many.'

'Then war is inevitable?'

'Surely.'

'Will it involve Matamoros?'

'I don't see how you can escape.'

'Can we win?'

Since Benito had been pondering this difficult question for some months, he should have been able to respond quickly, but he did not. Very carefully he said: 'If we had not driven Santa Anna into exile, if he were here instead of languishing in Cuba, we'd have a splendid chance of recapturing Tejas.'

'Is Santa Anna so good a general?'

'He's wonderful at collecting a rabble of men and forging them into a grand army. If only we had him now . . .'

'Father thinks highly of General Arista.'

'And so do I. He'll give a good account of himself . . .' His voice trailed off.

'But he's no Santa Anna?'

'In all the world there's only one Santa Anna. And he wastes away in Cuba.'

'You will fight the norteamericanos?'

'Until I die.'

She kissed him fervently: 'Benito, I feel the same way. "The Colossus of the North" someone called them the other day. They press down upon us. We can never live with them ... never.'

'How did your man die?'

'They came upon him, gathering his cattle. He had taken them across the river in April, as always, and they hanged him in July. No questions, no charges. He was mexicano, and that was enough to hang him.'

The hatred in her voice echoed Garza's own, and in this mutual rage against an oppressor their love deepened. But still Benito shied away from any commitment, when to his astonishment Lucha said: 'In this great battle ... it will last our lifetimes, Benito, I want to share it with you. Marriage, home, a garden in peace, we'll not know them. They're concerns for people like my mother ...'

He placed his fingers across her lips: 'It would have to be marriage, Lucha. I've seen how the norteamericanos ridicule us because of some of our women ... the soldaderas they don't marry. With a respectable woman like you, it must be marriage.'

'I am not a respectable woman,' Lucha said harshly. 'I'm a woman of the new Mexico, the Mexico that's going to be free.'

'And I'm a man of the new Mexico too, the Mexico that's going to demand respect among nations. We marry, or we part now.'

Lucha's parents, respectable citizens of Matamoros with their own good home and land in the country on which López had raised most of the cattle whose meat he sold, strongly opposed the match, for as López pointed out: 'He's forty years old. He could be your father,' and as Señora López warned: 'He's a bandit, a good one, I'll admit, and on our side, but a roving bandit nevertheless. What kind of home life could you expect?'

'What kind of home life will you expect, if the Rinches keep coming over the Rio Grande?' she asked.

When her parents realized that she was stubbornly prepared to accompany Garza, married or not, they were appalled, and now they became strong advocates of immediate marriage, though not necessarily with Garza: 'A girl as pretty as you, you could have any man you wanted. How about that major on General Arista's staff? He keeps making eyes at you.'

'Aren't a major and a bandit pretty much alike?'

'That I wouldn't know,' Señora López granted, 'but this I do know. A soldadera who follows the troops is no better than a puta.'

The impasse among the four troubled Mexicans was resolved in a bizarre way. Within the body of patriotic Mexicans prepared to make extreme sacrifices for their country was a renegade priest, born in Spain, who was known only as Padre Jesús. For some years, in moral desperation and with incredible courage, he had fought for Mexican freedom, a gaunt, determined man, a natural-born ascetic, who wore clerical garb and who opposed corruption and injustice wherever he found them, in the church, in politics, in the army or in the general society.

Padre Jesús no longer bothered to report his comings and goings to his conservative religious superiors, and now, with a threat of war menacing the northern boundaries of his adopted nation, he had come without authorization to the Rio Grande to do what he could to help, and the troops had a deep affection for his efforts.

When Padre Jesús heard of the conflicts within the López family he proposed a simple solution: 'Senora Lõpez, you have a daughter who is a gem of purest category. You are correct in wanting to see her safely married to a safe man. But she is like me, a child of the revolution that must sweep Mexico. It is proper for her to marry Benito Garza, for he is the new Mexican, the honorable man. They will never have a home like yours, a garden and six children. But they will live in the heart of the real Mexico, as I do. Let them marry.'

When the elder López refused to accept this advice, Benito and Lucha faced a dilemma, for ancient Spanish custom, now hardened into a law which Mexico honored, held a female to be her father's ward until the age of twenty-five, and without his consent she could not marry; if she did, the marriage could be annulled or she could be disowned. And when Lucha pleaded for her parents to relent, they cited this law and their opposition stiffened.

But if Padre Jesús was correct in proclaiming Benito a new Mexican, he could have continued that 'I, Jesús, am the new Catholic priest,' for when he learned that Lucha's parents were obdurate, he broke the deadlock simply: 'Come with me to the rallying field,' and here, where irregulars like himself had gathered, a confused rabble of adventurers and patriots prepared to support the formal army when hostilities began, he married this ill-matched pair: the groom, more than twice the age of the bride and a son of revolution and disarray; the bride, a daughter of middle-class respectability who should have married a rich landowner.

Just as the impromptu ceremony concluded a messenger splashed across the Rio Grande: 'Norteamericano soldiers! Not ten miles from the river!' At this exciting news the new husband kissed his wife, then rode hard to General Arista's headquarters, where a team of skilled frontier fighters was assembling. 'Let me ride with them as scout,' Garza pleaded, and the request was granted, for among the troops, regular or irregular, no one was better at operating in the chaparral of the Nueces Strip.

'We must be very quiet, very wily,' he warned the regular cavalry as they crossed the river. 'If, as they say, the norteamericanos have Rinches as their scouts ... they will be watchful.'

The oncoming Americans, more than sixty in noisy numbers, did not have Rangers as scouts, but they were led by two able captains, one a West Point graduate. However, the captains were not cautious men, for their big horses raised clouds of dust and their men engaged in careless chatter, which betrayed their advance.

Garza, slipping silently ahead of the Mexican force, watched the approach of the norteamericanos in disbelief: Where do they think they're going? Why don't they have any scouts out ahead? And after a long inspection: Good God! They don't have any Rinches, none at all!

Unable to believe that the enemy was behaving so unprofessionally, he trailed them for more than half an hour, expecting that at any moment some knowing scout, perhaps even Otto Macnab, would come upon him suddenly from the rear, but in time he satisfied himself that his first impressions were correct: No scouts. No Rinches.

As silently as a rattlesnake slipping through the grass, Garza made his dusty way back to the Mexican cavalry and helped its commander set a trap for the unsuspecting norteamericanos, who were now less than two miles from the river. Placing riders at various points, the Mexican leader kept his formidable lancers, those daring fighters with steel-tipped poles as sharp as needles, in reserve, and in this disposition his men awaited the bumbling arrival of the enemy.

Garza, well forward of the secluded Mexicans, was accompanied by the best of the irregulars, who moved their horses about so that the norteamericanos must detect them, and when this happened, there was a flurry of shots and much galloping, but Benito and his men knew how to avoid that first fierce charge. With great skill they rode this way and that, confusing the norteamericanos and leading them into the well-laid trap.

The battle was harsh and brief. Just as the American cavalry was about to overtake Garza, who fled in apparent terror, he flashed a signal, whereupon General Arista's best lancers swung into action, and before the hard-riding dragoons from Pennsylvania, Ohio and Missouri knew what was happening, they were surrounded and captured, all sixty-three of them.

By lucky accident, sixteen of the intruders were killed or badly wounded; by design, one of the wounded was set free to inform General Taylor of the humiliating loss. He was outraged that troops of his could be so inefficient in the field, but pleased that at last the Mexicans had come across the Rio Grande and actually killed American troops. To President Polk he was able to send the message that those who sought war with Mexico had awaited: 'Today Mexican troops have invaded American soil and killed American troops. Hostilities may now be considered as commenced.' The war with Mexico had begun.

Taylor's army had three weaknesses, and he was now painfully aware of them: his horses, though big and sturdy, were not accustomed to operations in an extreme southern climate like the Strip's; he had few scouts experienced in such terrain; but most important of all, his enlisted men were an untested collection whose officers could only speculate on 'how they will perform in battle.' Therefore, when the state of Texas offered to provide a group of Rangers well versed in chaparral fighting, he faced a dilemma: as a strict disciplinarian, he did not relish accepting a group of unruly Texans into his orderly ranks, but as a general responsible for the safety of a large army in a strange land, he knew he must have sharp eyes out front, and these he lacked. With great reluctance and after a painful delay, he grudgingly announced: 'We must have reliable scouts. We'll take the Texans.'

However, West Point men like Lieutenant Colonel Cobb warned of the dangers: 'The Texans may be fine horsemen, but the word you just used doesn't apply to them.'

'What word?' Taylor growled.

'*Reliable.*'

'They won their independence, didn't they?'

'On their peculiar terms.'

'Damned effective terms they were,' Old Rough-and-Ready snapped. 'Kill Mexicans.' Then he added, in gentler tones: 'Before we took them into the Union they had half the nations of Europe invitin' them to join their empires, didn't they?'

'Granted, but now we're talking about bringing them into the regular army, and frankly, sir, I don't think they'd fit.'

'Why not? If we swear them in and place reliable officers over them, like yourself, Cobb, they'll do fine.'

'But their clothes! They're a rabble.'

'Cobb, haven't you noticed? I often go without a military uniform.'

'Please, sir! Don't encourage the Texans. They think they're still a free nation. They're dickering with us on the terms under which they will provide us with men.'

'They're what?'

'The state government wants to negotiate.'

'What in hell do you mean?' Taylor thundered, and Cobb explained: 'It says it may be willing to let you have two full regiments, but only on its own conditions.' He summarized the limiting conditions under which all volunteers joined the regular army, plus a few galling additions which Texas had added: 'Variable terms of enlistment. Their own rate of pay. It's just as if Prussia were offering us units, on Prussian terms.'

'We'll have none of that!'

'Then you'll have no Texans.'

'You mean that at the end of three months, maybe, they could go home?'

'They'd insist upon it. That's the way they've always served.'

A colonel from Mississippi explained: 'They're farmers. They like to get back home to tend their crops. Of course, they'll come back to the army when the crops are in . . . if they feel like it.'

Cobb added: 'Nor do they wish to wear our uniform. Or use our horses. Or use our rifles. Each Texan feels he knows more about fighting than any man from New York possibly could, and he insists upon doing it his way, dressed in whatever makes him feel comfortable.'

Taylor grew impatient with the wrangling: 'Don't you suppose I know they'll be troublesome?' For some minutes, which he would in months to come remember ruefully, he toyed with the idea of rejecting them as ungovernable, but in the end he growled: 'We'll take the two regiments,' and then he added words which Cobb would also remember with bitterness: 'And since you seem to know so much about them, Persifer, you can serve as my liaison.'

It was under these slippery conditions that thirty-six Rangers of Captain Garner's Company M joined General Taylor's army of regulars, and their arrival caused Persifer Cobb only grief.

In these years the United States army roster listed many soldiers bearing the unusual first name of Persifor, also spelled Persifer, and what accounted for its sudden popularity, or even its genesis, no one could say, but there was General Persifor Smith and Colonel Persifer Carrick and a smattering of Major Persifors This and Captain Persifers That. Ordinary privates bearing the name have not been recorded.

The Persifer Cobb serving under General Taylor came from a noble cotton plantation which comprised most of Edisto Island off the coast of South Carolina. He had been a tense, proper young gentleman of twenty when his father announced: 'Any self-respecting Southern family ought to have a son in the army. Persifer, off to West Point!' In that austere environment he had conducted himself honorably, and upon graduation into the regular service he strove to exemplify in thought and action the best of Southern tradition. He spoke with an excessive drawl and defended in both mess and field the highest traditions of Southern chivalry. But now, on the dusty fields of Texas, he was not a happy man.

The first source of his discomfort was that irritating adjective which preceded his rank. He was a colonel, one of the most proper in the national force, but he was not yet a full colonel; he was only a lieutenant colonel, rightfully convinced that he merited higher rank. The special nature of his displeasure manifested itself in his first letter home to his younger brother, who was overseeing the Edisto plantation during the colonel's absence:

Rio Grande
30 April

Dear Brother Somerset,
General Taylor and his troops are encamped at a new fort on the north bank of this river opposite Matamoros, and we would be well prepared to meet the Mexicans had we not been joined recently by a civilian muster out of Texas, and a more disgraceful, unruly and downright criminal element I have rarely seen. They call themselves Texas Rangers, although I am informed that not more than ten percent have previously served in that informal service. They wear no uniform, no badges of distinction, so that we regular army men cannot separate a captain from a private, and discipline they know not.

General Taylor has made no secret of the fact that he did not want any Texas volunteers, but Texas, as you know, is now a state, having been an independent republic, and since its citizens, having once been members of a free nation, carry an exalted opinion of their own importance, local politicians forced their native sons upon us.

Well, the Texas Rangers are among us, and their presence must give the Mexican generals hope, for a more worthless collection of men one rarely sees. What purely galls us regular army men who have slaved in the colors for years to gain our promotions is that when the Texans come slouching into camp, they, like all volunteers, immediately hold an election, an *election*, mind you, to choose their company

717

officers, and yesterday a Texan with never a day at military school rode into our camp announcing that the state of Texas had appointed him full colonel, and now he brazens his way about camp superior to me. I, a graduate of West Point with twelve years of arduous service behind me in all military specialties and all geographical areas, must take orders from a man who last week was herding cattle and has never heard of Hannibal or Marshal Ney.

I was requested by General Taylor, and of course accepted, to take under my charge the Company M of Rangers who are to serve as my scouts, and it will suffice to describe three of them to you. Captain Garner – *captain*, mind you, who was never lieutenant, just mysteriously captain – is enormously tall, enormously thin, with great flowing mustaches and a leather belt six inches wide. He wears whatever comes to hand, including a jacket which once served the Mexican army, for he says he took it from an officer he shot along the Rio Grande. Taciturn, mean-spirited, grimly silent when reproved, he stalks about like an avenging angel, taking orders from no one and always wanting to lead his men off to some foray under his own direction. In our regular army he would not last through sunset of the first day.

His chosen assistant, a lieutenant perhaps, but without rank, for the Rangers care little about such distinctions, is a slight young man of no more than twenty, although he claims twenty-six. I know him only as Otto, but he is unforgettable: small, not more than a hundred and forty, wiry, blond, silent, and with the brightest blue eyes. He never smiles, just looks right through you, the other men consider him the best Ranger of the lot. What makes him stand out more than anything else is that he wears a garment they call in these parts a duster, a very light coat of linen and cotton which reaches from neck to boot top with only three buttons to fasten it en route. Otto's is a pale white in color and is supposed to keep the dust off during long rides, but when he walks about our camp the duster makes him look like a little lost ghost, for his small feet seem scarcely to move under it as he steps. On his first day in camp I told him, rather sternly: 'We do not wear clothes like that in this camp,' and he replied: 'I do,' and off he waddled, looking so much like a duck that I had no further desire to discipline him.

The third Ranger is like no one you have ever seen on Edisto. He calls himself Panther Komax, because of the panther-pelt hat he wears with the tail hanging over his left ear, and where he comes from no one can tell me, least of all he. When I asked, he said: 'People get finicky if I bust another man over the head with an ax handle and run off with his horse and his wife.' He would put the horse first. He mentions Georgia, Massachusetts and Missouri without actually claiming to have lived in any of them. I think of him mostly as hair, for he has a huge head of it, coal-black, which he grows long, tying it matted behind his ears with a deerskin thong. He wears a beard which almost hides his face, has heavy, menacing eyebrows and long black hairs growing out of the backs of his hands. He is over six feet tall, heavyset, and with the meanest look in his eye I have ever seen. It is appropriate that he should call himself Panther, because he really is an animal. He carries an enormously heavy rifle and a knife with a twelve-inch blade. The Rangers tell me he was a member of that ridiculous Mier Expedition of 1842, when a rabble of Texans invaded Mexico, thinking they could defeat the entire Mexican army. Outnumbered ten to one, they were tricked into surrendering, and the disaster would have been long forgotten except that the Mexican general, Santa Anna, about whom I wrote you when we were in camp in Mississippi, ordered one Texas prisoner in every ten shot, and the decimation was to be determined by drawing beans from a clay pot. White bean, you lived. Black bean, you were shot on the spot. I asked Panther Komax if he had drawn a bean, and he said: 'Yep, white.' I then asked him if he had served time in Perote Prison, an infamous place somewhere deep in Mexico, and he said: 'Yep, killed two guards and escaped.' He is a frightening man, capable of anything, and when I asked him why he wanted to go back into Mexico with us, he said: 'They is certain individuals down there as I would like to meet again.'

These are the men, the untrained ruffians, who are to be my scouts. I have not the slightest hope of disciplining them or converting them into regular army members. I do not look forward to leading such riffraff into Mexico, but just before starting this letter I saw my three chosen Rangers coming at me from a distance, lanky Captain Garner on the left, big, burly Panther Komax on the right, and little-boy Otto in his long, flapping duster in the middle, a head or more shorter than his companions, and as I watched them come at me I thought: God preserve the officer who attempts to lead those fellows, and God preserve doubly any Mexicans they meet, for I have learned an interesting fact from my orderly: 'This kid Otto, his father and uncle was killed by Mexicans, his mother and aunt by the Comanche. He's afraid of nothing. Just starts comin' at you and never stops.'

I am not happy in Texas and shall feel greatly relieved when we finally cross into Mexico.

Your brother,
Persifer

With his reconnaissance and cavalry problems solved, General Taylor was able to deploy his inferior number of troops into excellent arrangement, especially his heavy guns, and at Palo Alto on 8 May 1846 and Resaca de la Palma on the following day, gained victories which sent the Mexicans fleeing in disarray back across the Rio Grande. Persifer Cobb, who was cited in dispatches for his personal bravery, gave most of the credit to his infamous Texans:

Somerset, there can be no glory like the smoke of battle on a hard-won field. General Arista, seeking to cut our supply lines, brought his troops deep into the Nueces Strip, where in a two-day battle involving thousands we taught him a lesson. I was commended for turning the enemy's right flank in a hot and dusty business. Rarely have I known a day of such blazing sun and such constant sweat. It was no parade exercise, and had not our artillery provided a stout performance, we might have lost.

The Mexicans fought with a valor we had not expected, but what amazed me was the skill of my Texans, for I believe that they can, at full gallop, deliver a greater concentration of fire than any other troops in the world. An officer on our staff who knows cavalry history told me: 'I would choose these men above Rupert's Cavaliers, or the best Cossacks, or the Turkish Mamelukes or even the Moss Troopers who used to surge out of the bogs of Scotland to ravage the English towns.'

At the height of the battle yesterday I understood what he meant, for I was riding with this boy Otto at my side, his white duster flying behind, and he was so skilled with his various arms that after we had routed the Mexican cavalry I talked with him. His name is Macnab, which means that he comes of good stock, which counts for something, I think. When we started our run at the enemy he had two rifles, two pistols, two daggers and two revolving pistols of a new make. He told me they were called Colts, of the Texas design, made in Paterson, New Jersey, and he showed me how they came completely apart into three separate pieces: barrel, a revolving cylinder containing five bullets, and stock.

This young fellow could fire ten shots with his two Colts while I fired one with my old-fashioned pistol, and he was so dextrous that he could reload without dismounting and then fire ten more times. When you have twenty such men at your elbow, you can turn any Mexican attack. Tonight I am not displeased with my Texans, except that when you see twenty of them dashing ahead, each on his own, each wearing his own outrageous interpretation of a military uniform, you do wish that they'd had some proper training.

Postscriptum: Macnab, the little killer, just came to me with an astonishing request. He wants to quit the army temporarily, and for what reason do you suppose? To get married! Yes, he told me shyly that he had known his intended for some years, a fine German lass. 'And has she accepted your proposal?' I asked, and he surprised me by saying: 'I haven't spoken to her yet.' I asked if it wasn't risky, riding so far to court a lady when the outcome was uncertain, and he astounded me by confessing: 'I mean, we have never spoken.' 'Not one word?' I asked, and he said: 'Not one.' I asked: 'Then how do you know she'll say yes?' and he replied: 'I know,' but he did not explain how he knew.

Before he left camp I asked if I could rely upon his returning to duty, and he said rather grimly: 'I have several scores to settle with Mexico. I'll be back.' Strange thing,

Somerset, I already miss him, for I have found him to be a man I want at my side when the fighting begins.

One afternoon when the Allerkamps returned from a visit to Fredericksburg, Emil said a surprising thing: 'They told me that one of the Rangers on leave from chasing Mexicans with General Taylor has taken a room at the Nimitz place.'

Mrs Allerkamp happened to be looking at Franziska when this was said, and she noticed that her daughter stiffened, hands pressed close against her dress, and when Ludwig asked: 'What young man?' and Emil said: 'His name is Macnab,' Mrs Allerkamp saw that Franziska blushed furiously, even though, to her mother's knowledge, she had never even spoken to the young man.

The name Macnab caused Ernst, the now-and-then Ranger, to say: 'What a wonderful fighter he is! Nothing scares him!' Now Ludwig spotted his daughter's extremely flushed face and asked her sternly: 'Franziska, what's the matter?'

Sitting very straight, her little body drawn together as if facing an assault, her hands in her lap, Franziska said softly: 'He has come to marry me.'

Her statement created an uproar: 'You've never met the man!' 'How do you know what he's here for?' 'Who ever heard of such an idea?'

But now the great force of character which had been building in this quiet young woman – product of her bravery during the ocean crossing, of her ceaseless work around the farm, of her unwavering love for a young man to whom she had never spoken – manifested itself, and she fended off her entire family: 'He's come to marry me, and I shall marry him.'

This was a challenge which her father could not ignore: 'Have you and he had some arrangement?'

She blushed even more at the suggestion, set her jaw more firmly, and said: 'No. How could we?'

'Then it's true? You've never spoken to him?'

'Never.'

'Then how can you say such a thing? That he's come to marry you?'

'I know and he knows.' She was so resolute that her father gave up, but now her mother took over.

'Isn't he Catholic?'

'He is,' Ernst interrupted. 'But I think he did it only to get land.'

'He's Irish, isn't he?' Thekla asked.

'Yes, but I don't think all Irish have to be Catholic.'

'I think they do,' Mrs Allerkamp said, and she looked fiercely at her wayward daughter.

Ludwig was not satisfied: 'You still say he's come here to marry you?'

'Yes.'

'But how can you possibly know that?'

Now Emil interrupted: 'I heard that someone had taken papers on the land just west of ours.'

'Where did you hear that?' Ludwig snapped. This conversation was becoming too involved for his fatherly tastes.

'Someone, I don't remember who, said that papers from the land office in Austin had been forwarded.'

'Do you think it could have been this Macnab?'

Emil broke in again: 'He'd be a good man to have on our frontier against the Comanche. He knows how to handle them.'

Such talk disturbed Ernst and irritated Ludwig, who rose from the table, stalked out of the kitchen, saddled his horse, and rode in to town, for he was not a man to delay unpleasant obligations.

When he reached the wide and dusty main street of Fredericksburg, he reined in at the Nimitz place, where the family was building an extension to their small house in order to open a formal inn for the convenience of the travelers who would soon be coming this way. There he asked: 'Have you a lodger named Macnab?' Without waiting for permission, Allerkamp strode to the door, pushed it open and stood face-to-face with Otto Macnab.

'Are you Macnab?'

'The same.'

'You the one who rode with Ernst in the Nueces Strip?'

'The same.'

'And you've been with General Taylor at the big battles?'

I have.'

With both men still standing, Ludwig asked: 'Have you come to marry my daughter?'

723

Otto had not intended that his proposal be broached in this abrupt manner; he had been in the vicinity three days, scouting his newly acquired land, satisfying himself that it abutted the Allerkamp acres, and learning to his relief that Franziska was not already married. With his courage increasing daily, he had decided that tomorrow he would let Ernst know he was in the vicinity and perhaps in a day or so he could meet Franziska herself. Speaking to her parents could come the following week. But here stood her father, far ahead of schedule.

'Will you sit down, sir?'

'I will,' Ludwig said fiercely. 'Now tell me, how did you get to know my daughter?'

'I saw her . . . twice . . . when I came to fetch Ernst.'

'What kind of secrets did you have with her?'

'None. We never spoke.'

'And just looking . . . ?'

'Yes, just from looking, and from what Ernst told me.'

'Did he discuss his sister?'

'Never. But he told me of your family, and I decided . . .'

Otto could not continue. Either Mr Allerkamp understood what impels a young man to sell his land and travel so far into a wilderness, or he did not, and if he had forgotten what tremendous pressures of emotion and longing and desire a mere glimpse of a beautiful girl could arouse, there was no sense in talking. Nor could Otto speak of the nights along the Ohio River when he first became aware of what a home was, nor of his intense sense of tragedy when Martin Ascot was killed during the murder of the Comanche, leaving pretty Betsy Belle a widow, nor of the fact, to put it simply, that he was in love and had been for a long time.

Abruptly, Ludwig asked: 'Are you Catholic?'

Firmly, Otto answered: 'I had to be, for my father to get us land.' He winced, then laughed nervously: 'It was useless, because we never got the land.'

'Are you a Catholic now?'

'Who knows?'

'Well, shouldn't all Irishmen be Catholic?'

'I'm not Irish.'

Allerkamp was startled: 'What are you?'

'Scots. My family moved to Ireland years ago, then left.'

'You're a Scotchman?'

'We call it Scotsman. And my mother was German.'

Allerkamp gasped, looked at the young man sitting opposite him, and asked in a low voice: 'What did you just say?'

'I said we call it Scotsman, not Scotchman.'

'I mean the next part.'

'Oh, my mother was German. From Baltimore.'

'What was her name?'

'Berthe.'

'I mean her last name.'

'I don't know. I never knew.'

This Allerkamp could not believe – to have had a German mother and to have forgotten her name, the name that entitled you to membership in the greatest of all races! 'You forgot? You forgot your mother's German name?'

'I never knew it.'

For a moment the two sat facing each other, then Allerkamp rose with a cry of joy and embraced his newfound friend, his son-in-law to be: 'You're German! How wonderful!'

Otto, who had never up to now considered his German ancestry an asset, was not allowed to remain indifferent, because Allerkamp grasped him by the shoulders, gave him a second embrace, and cried: 'Come! We must tell her at once.'

He dragged Otto out of the boardinghouse, obviously intending to ride the six miles out to the farm.

'It's almost dark,' the young man protested, but Ludwig dismissed this sensible objection: 'If she's waited this long for you, she deserves to know.' When Otto said nothing, Allerkamp went on: 'We found her four good husbands – five, counting Quimper – but she'd have none of them.' He said no more as they mounted their horses, then added: 'We could never understand why she refused. She never mentioned your name until tonight. When Emil told us that you were at the Nimitz house.'

'What did she say?' Otto asked as they rode.

'She said "He's come to marry me." She must have known all along.'

The two men followed a rough road out of town, and as the stars appeared, always brighter as if to encourage them, each knew a great joy: Allerkamp realizing that his child had come

725

safe to harbor with a trustworthy German; Macnab accepting the miracle that his strange courtship had come to such splendid fruition.

At eight the moon appeared, waning, but still strong enough to lighten the way, so that the happy travelers rode through the best of Texas in the best of conditions. In the tall branches of one tree a brood of turkeys conversed briefly as they passed, as if they were gossiping about the strange events of this long day, and a coyote moved furtively along with them for a short distance, then cut sharply to the west in search of prey.

They moved through gently rolling hills, with trees sparsely distributed marking the watered valleys. Live oak, post oak, ash and hickory showed their rounded forms against the sky, with cedars standing darker in the background. 'It's not like a proper German forest,' Allerkamp said, 'but it will do.'

'What's different?' Otto asked, and the surveyor, who had mastered all the nuances of his new land, explained: 'There we had real trees. One after another, all joined together. Here each tree stands apart ... jealous of its allotted space.' After reflecting on this for some minutes, he snapped his fingers and said: 'Maybe that's the difference, son. In Germany we were like the trees, all forced to live together wherever the Margrave said. In Texas each of us stands stubbornly apart, each man on his own land.' As they made their way toward the Pedernales, Allerkamp continued his reflections: 'Not a day passes, son, but that I think of Germany – the wine, the singing, the walks in the forest, the peasant food I knew so well, the good talk with Metzdorf at his shop. I long for those things so desperately, my heart could break.' He turned in the saddle to face Otto: 'You know what I don't long for? The tyranny. The false preaching of churchmen. The horrible day when the Margrave told my son Theo he couldn't marry.'

The passionate remembrance of that day which had so altered his life brought tears to his eyes, and after a moment of silence he offered Otto remarkable advice: 'When we get to our home, if suddenly I should cry out "Macnab, you can't have her. You can't marry," kick my backside, grab her, and go where you will – but find freedom.' He was trembling; he allowed his horse to move away from Otto's; then from the darkness that rose up between them he said: 'Freedom is everything. Freedom is the salt of life that makes hard work palatable. Freedom is the only basis for a home, and marriage, and children.'

In some dim way Otto had already discovered the truth of what Allerkamp was saying. He had sensed it when his father railed so bitterly against the ineptitude of Colonel Fannin: 'Damnit, son. If a group of men are fighting for their freedom, they ought to do certain things, instantly, without thinking.' He had perceived it also when his detachment started marching head-on into the Mexican lines at San Jacinto. No sensible men would perform such an extraordinary act unless impelled by a lust for freedom, a determination to be free. And he glimpsed the universal truth of this when he saw the new Allerkamp farm along the Pedernales, for no family would have the courage to move so far from settled areas unless it longed for the freedom which space assured.

'There it is!' Allerkamp said as he pointed to the solid house he and his sons had built. And with a sharp goading of his horse, he rode into the yard before the entrance, shouting: 'Here he comes! Tell Franza that here he comes!'

When the men entered the warm kitchen they found Thekla Allerkamp and her two sons sitting there. Franziska was not visible, for she had gone early to bed, and her absence caused Otto to feel a stab of disappointment. Ludwig, sensing this, shouted: 'Franza! Out of bed! He's come to claim you!'

As Mrs Allerkamp disappeared quietly into the smaller of the two bedrooms, Otto was left standing awkwardly in the middle of the room, twenty-four years old, blond hair, blue eyes, short, less than a hundred and fifty pounds, hands close to his sides and extremely nervous. 'He came, just as she said,' Ludwig told his sons, and he was about to say more when Thekla reappeared, leading her sleepy-eyed daughter into the light of the kitchen.

For a protracted moment the two young people stood there, each looking with delight at the other, but the spell was broken when Ludwig shouted with joy that could not be misunderstood: 'And he's German!'

When questions were asked, with the two lovers still gazing at each other, Ludwig explained his marvelous news: 'He's not Irish at all. And he's not Catholic, not really. He's a good

German. His mother was from Germany, from Baltimore.' Mrs Allerkamp and her sons breathed with relief at this extraordinary news. In order to find Franziska a long-overdue husband, they had been willing to have their unsullied German line diminished by the admission of a non-German man, even a Catholic, and to find that he was of their stock was a reassurance which they had not expected. The bloodlines would remain clean; the admission of lesser strains would be avoided; a good thing was being done and a faulty one had not happened. Otto Macnab was to their satisfaction German, and all was well with the world.

'Kiss her, you dummy!' Ernst cried, pushing his fellow Ranger forward.

'You may kiss her!' Ludwig shouted.

And the first word Otto and Franziska shared was kiss.

After his resounding victories at Palo Alto and Resaca de la Palma, General Taylor could well have thundered across the Rio Grande and chased the demoralized Mexicans all the way to some logical stopping point like San Luis Potosí far to the south, but he was an extremely cautious man who could not visualize penetrating so far into enemy territory without his supply lines in good order. He dawdled away the months of May, June, July and much of August before making a move against the northern Mexico fortress city of Monterrey, and when he finally did start, he had no clear idea of what route to follow.

In his confusion he called upon Captain Garner to take sixteen of his Rangers and a unit of dragoons to explore the long southern route via Linares while regular army scouting parties surveyed the more direct but potentially dangerous route along the Rio Grande. Garner elected to take with him his usual companions: Panther Komax, who had proved himself a terror during the two big battles, and Otto Macnab, now back from Fredericksburg, whom Garner called 'my artillery on the right.'

The Rangers headed due south to explore the possibility of a route through the small town of San Fernando, and since it formed an important launch point for a dash westward to Linares, they anticipated a difficult fight. But when they approached San Fernando, with Macnab and Komax slipping ahead as scouts, they found the place undefended, so the dragoons placed their Negro cook at the head of the column, where, on a fiddle he had brought with him from Alabama, he played a screechy *Yankee Doodle* while the surprised victors marched into the empty town.

In their attack on the next little town, Granada, the Rangers behaved differently, leaving the regular troops ashen-faced. The unimportant little town lay to the west, towards Linares, and was defended by a ragtag rearguard of the regular Mexican army. When these troops satisfied themselves that the norteamericanos seriously outnumbered and outgunned them, they fired a few shots and withdrew, but a handful of village youths decided to protect their settlement.

From atop the roofs of houses they sniped at the invaders, and by ill luck, killed a Ranger named Corley who rode with a good friend named Lucas. When Lucas saw his companion fall from this casual fire, he dashed into the village and began shooting at anyone or anything he saw. His fire was so intense that other Rangers believed him to be in peril, so in they dashed, Komax and Macnab among them, and now the firing became so furious that houses were pocked with bullet holes.

Soon Captain Garner and his men were in the heart of the village, where the killing became so general that a regular from Illinois listened in a state of shock: 'What in hell are they doing in there?'

He could not know that Otto Macnab had been at the massacre at Goliad, or that Panther Komax had one evening been forced at gunpoint to pick a bean from a clay pot and then watch as his friends who picked black were shot, or that Ranger Lucas had just lost his best friend, or that Ranger Tumlinson had seen his father's ranch near the Strip burned to nothing and his father slain by bandits who called themselves Mexican patriots. The Illinois man could not conceive of the general hatred with which most of the Rangers viewed all Mexicans, not appreciate why, now that sniper fire had endangered them, they wanted to punish the little town for every accumulated wrong they thought they had suffered: substantial ones like real murders and burnings, imaginary ones like whispered tales of Mexican barbarities.

When Lieutenant Colonel Cobb read reports of the incident at Granada, he was so shaken by the brutal behavior of his Texans that he conducted personal interviews with all regulars who had information about the slaughter, and when he was satisfied that the evidence was accurate, he marched into General Taylor's tent and demanded that the Rangers be dismissed from the army and sent home.

'That I cannot do,' Taylor said flatly.

'They will destroy your army, sir.'

'How?'

'By their senseless slaughter of Mexicans. They'll ignite the whole countryside against you.'

'That's a risk I must take. I need them as my eyes and ears.'

'You know that they take no prisoners?'

'Santa Anna took none of them prisoner.'

'Are we to descend to Santa Anna's level?'

'Texans are different. They were their own nation. They have their own rules. But remind them that this time they aren't fighting Santa Anna.'

'Respectfully, sir, I see only tragedy ahead. Send them home. Now!'

General Taylor, always mindful of difficult tasks to come, refused, and a month later even Cobb was quite satisfied to have the Texans on the scene, for when the army reached Monterrey everyone saw that the capture of this sizable city, with its numerous forts, gun emplacements and interlocking alleyways that armed civilians could defend, was not going to be easy. East of the city the ground was relatively flat, but it too was guarded by numerous forts, each with its own heavy artillery; and west of the city, on the important road to Saltillo, rose two small mountains, not unduly large but high enough and protected by slopes that looked impossible to scale.

The mountain on the south flank of the road was Federación, topped by a substantial fort; the one to the north was Independencia, topped by a massive, stout-walled, dilapidated building called the Bishop's Palace. To capture Monterrey, these two peaks must be taken; if they were left in Mexican hands, enemy artillery would make retention of the city impossible.

The Texas Rangers, supported by a much larger cadre of the

best regular army troops under General Worth, were assigned to take the two mountains while Taylor took the city itself, and on the night of 19 September amid a downpour the Texans moved in a wide circle to the north, coming down to the Saltillo road, where on the next day they captured that highway. Now all they had to do was climb two mountains in the face of heavy enemy fire and capture a fort on one of them, a stout-walled, defended palace on the other.

On 22 September, a rainy Monday morning, General Worth decided to make the attempt on Federación and its fort. His men spent the first six hours gaining, with much difficulty, positions from which to launch the charge up the final slopes, and at noon all was ready. 'We go,' Captain Garner called with no discernible emotion.

Up the formidable steeps, the Texans went, and whenever they were pinned down by enemy fire, the regular troops, just as brave, surged forward in their sector, but as the miserably hot afternoon unfolded, the wiry Texans had one advantage: they were accustomed to the oppressive heat and the rivers of sweat that poured down their faces.

'Give 'em hell,' Garner called quietly, and on his Rangers went.

Incredibly, they gained the crest of the mountain and diverted so many defenders that the panting regulars soon took their sector too. Without cheers or battle cries, the regular officer in charge simply pointed at the waiting fort, and like an army of remorseless ants attacking a parcel of food, they started across the top of the mountain and literally overwhelmed the fort, not by sheer numbers, but by the terrible firepower and irresistible force they represented.

At three that hot, wet afternoon Federación and its fort were in their hands, but before the Texans could congratulate themselves, Garner pointed north across the chasm that separated them from Independencia and said: 'Tomorrow we take that.'

Without adequate food and with no tents or protection from the intermittent rains, the Rangers passed a short, fitful night, during which Lucas, who had led the slaughter at Granada, asked Otto Macnab: 'Do you think we can climb that one? It looks steeper.'

731

'We'll see.'

'That stone building. Much stouter than the fort.'

'We'll find out.'

'Were you afraid, today? I mean, you're so much younger than me.' When Otto made no reply, Lucas confessed: 'I was scared real bad.'

'Only natural.'

'Tomorrow, can I fight alongside you? I never seen a man fire as fast as you can.'

'I always fight with Panther Komax.'

'I know. But can I sort of trail along?'

'Nobody stopping you.'

At three in the morning, when the rains ceased, the Rangers launched their attack on Independencia, but now the rocky slopes were so steep and slick that it seemed absolutely impossible that they could be scaled. 'Christ, this can't be done,' but then came the quiet voice of Garner, that indomitable man who found handholds where none existed: 'A little more,' and up the struggling men went.

This time they left the regular troops well behind, but close to the top their sector became so steep that each man had to fend for himself, and the regulars moved well ahead over their easier terrain. At this perilous point, with Mexican riflemen shooting down from the rim of their protected hilltop, Otto found himself with Lucas, who was on the verge of exhaustion.

'Breathe deep,' Otto said, and, extending his right leg so that Lucas could grasp it, he pulled the near-fainting man up to the next level. There they rested, unable to catch any breath, but soon Otto pointed to a declivity in the rocks and said: 'Looks easy,' and he led Lucas up a steep incline and onto the crest of the hill.

There a wild fight was in progress, with the regular troops giving an exceptionally strong account of themselves and driving the enemy always backward toward the security of the Bishop's Palace. But now Garner, seeing an advantage while the Mexicans were engaged with the regular troops, gave a wild shout, no longer muted, and rallied his Texans, who with a mighty surge drove at the palace gates. The fighting was intense and terrifying, but with the horrendous firepower of their repeater Colts, the Texans simply shot the Mexican defenders out of their positions.

'Otto!' came a fierce cry from Panther Komax, and together the two men dashed at the gate, blasting a score of Mexicans and forcing their way into the interior. In doing so, they had moved far ahead of their companions, but their experience as Rangers made them confident that others would soon crowd in to support them. Within minutes Garner and six or eight of his best men had joined them inside the walls.

The killing was short and sharp, for the Mexicans had no response to the deadly fire of the Colts. How many died was not immediately determined, but when the fight was almost over, a brave Mexican who had holed himself into a position from which there was no escape fired resolutely at the Texans, and put his last bullet through the guts of Ranger Lucas, who died in prolonged agony.

Macnab, seeing him fall, wheeled about, spotted the trapped Mexican and blasted him with his revolver.

The guardian hills were taken and the fall of Monterrey was assured. The pathway to Saltillo lay open and the culminating battle of the north now became inevitable, for a Mexican adversary much more powerful and competent than pusillanimous General Arista was preparing an army at San Luis Potosí, an army so huge that it might well drive the norteamericanos from the soil of Mexico forever.

Although President Polk and General Taylor started this war, it was Benito Garza who started the fighting with his bold foray across the Rio Grande. But he did not participate in the disaster at Monterrey, where a fortified city protected by superior numbers failed to defend itself. As recognized leader of the irregular forces in the north, he had been summoned south, where he would participate in a bewildering series of events that would alter the progress of the war.

In Havana the exiled dictator Santa Anna, who faced immediate death if he returned to Mexico, had been having clandestine discussions with American officials during which the invasion of Mexico was discussed in candid and sometimes shocking terms. The wily general pointed out that a bumbling old fool like Zachary Taylor was never going to march all the way to Mexico City. 'Frankly,' Santa Anna told his listeners, 'he's incompetent,' and he proceeded to analyze with remarkable insight the other weaknesses of the American position: 'Should you try to land at Vera Cruz and force your way onto the central plateau, all Mexico will rise against you and cut your supply lines, and no army can sustain an invasion over that distance without adequate supplies.'

When the American strategists argued that their troops could live off the land, Santa Anna replied: 'Never! A million patriots will destroy them in the night.'

His arguments were so seductive that President Polk, hoping that a bold move would solve the strategic impasse, launched one of the most extraordinary diplomatic maneuvers in history. 'What we must do,' Polk told his advisers, 'is test this Santa Anna to determine how reliable he will be ... how far we can trust him, that is. Then use him to our advantage.'

'Risky,' an army man warned. 'He's a sly fox.'

'We're just as sly,' Polk assured him, a boast that each man would often remember in later years.

New negotiators sailed to Havana, where they talked frankly with Santa Anna, receiving from him a brazen proposal: 'There is only one sure way to end this war. Have your fleet deposit me at Vera Cruz with half a million dollars, in gold. I will then act as your agent and terminate this unfortunate affair on terms favorable to you and acceptable to Mexico.'

'But will Mexico accept you?'

'When I set foot in Vera Cruz ... I lost my leg in that city, you must remember. The people of Vera Cruz venerate me. I can handle this in a week.'

The American representatives were not fools, and before accepting such a proposal, they investigated it from all angles, but when they talked with silver-tongued Santa Anna, who knew English well enough to smother them with glibness at any difficult juncture, they convinced themselves that here was a noble patriot who wished only to end a disagreeable war on terms favorable to both sides.

A remarkable agreement was drawn up, initialed by everyone: Santa Anna would be given a huge sum in gold, with more to come when the peace treaty was signed; a boat of British registry would be provided at the port of Havana; and Commodore David Conner, commanding the United States

734

Caribbean fleet, would be issued presidential orders directing him to assure Santa Anna's ship safe passage through the American blockade and into the port of Vera Cruz. If necessary, Commodore Conner could sink any Mexican vessels that tried to prevent the return of the hero to his native soil.

At this point Benito Garza received cryptic instructions forwarded secretly from Cuba: 'Report immediately to Vera Cruz and prepare a spectacular reception for a secret arrival.' He was not pleased with these orders, but he was a patriot, prepared to report where his country needed him.

So Benito dropped other responsibilities, including his often-interrupted honeymoon, rode south along back roads where norteamericano patrols would not stumble upon him, reached Potosí, and hurried on to Vera Cruz, where secretly he organized a rabble for one of those demonstrations that flourished regularly in Mexico. He had not the slightest intimation of what was afoot, but he supposed that some general opposed to the present inept government of the country was going to make a pronouncement with a fresh new plan – fifty-third since 1821, counting those which flourished for a single heady afternoon – for saving the country. On the reasonable grounds that anything would be better than what Mexico now had, he supposed that he would support the new grito.

How astonished he was on the morning of 16 August 1846 when the latest hero prepared to save the country arrived not from some inland barracks but from the little British steamer *Arab*, delivered into the harbor by the American fleet itself! Even at that dramatic moment Benito did not guess the identity of the savior, and then to his great joy he saw General Santa Anna, Benemérito de la Patria, come stumping down the gangplank on his best ceremonial leg. Garza needed no prodding to start his wild cheering, but to his dismay hardly anyone watching this charade bothered to join him, and the resuscitated dictator marched into his domain in near-silence. Seven or eight men, led by Garza, shouted: 'Santa Anna! Santa Anna!' but older men and wiser asked quietly: 'What can he be up to this time?'

Soon all knew that Antonio López de Santa Anna was once again Mexico's El Supremo, with powers doubling any he had enjoyed before, and it was rumored that he himself would assume command of all armed forces, north or south. But whether he would fight, as some said, or sell out to the norteamericanos, as others predicted, no one knew.

When Benito and a score of trusted lieutenants met with Santa Anna that night, they asked bluntly: 'Excellency, what are your plans?' and he replied: 'Only one. Crush General Taylor at Saltillo. Drive General Scott back into the sea if he tries to land here in Vera Cruz.'

When the applause ended, Garza asked: 'When do we march north?' and his hero replied: 'When my nation calls me. And she will call.'

President Polk had by this rash action placed on Mexican soil the one leader who had a chance to defeat America's grandiose plans, and what was more astonishing, Polk had also provided the American dollars which could help Santa Anna turn the trick.

When word reached General Taylor that Santa Anna had returned to Mexico as supreme dictator and was assembling a massive army to bring north, the old man faced a series of difficult decisions. It had become apparent to President Polk, a Democrat and a wily one, that General Taylor, a Whig and a blunt one, was receiving in the press a flood of adulation as reward for his victories at Palo Alto, Resaca and Monterrey. With the shrewd insight which characterized Tennessee politicians like Andrew Jackson and Sam Houston, Polk foresaw that Taylor was going to use his military popularity to win the presidency in 1848, and this had to be forestalled, because Polk considered that the general would be a hopeless president.

Making a move that was both politically and militarily astute, Polk forbade Taylor to leave Monterrey lest he become trapped in the vast desert area separating Saltillo and San Luis Potosí. When Taylor's officers received the orders, they immediately spotted the error: 'My God! This keeps us from chasing the defeated Mexicans into Saltillo and crushing them there.'

Persifer Cobb fired off a bitter letter to his brother:

The only good news I can report is that during this enforced

736

idleness we have had the good sense to send all the Texans home. Yes, they're all gone, and I'm a free man at last, one who can sleep well at night. Did you know that at the height of our effort one Texas company of foot soldiers demurred at fighting as infantry, saying that every decent Texan was entitled to his horse? Well, they took a vote. Yes, Somerset, on the eve of battle they took a vote whether to fight or not and it was 318 to 224 in favor of quitting. So they just quit. Can you imagine Hannibal, as he faced the Alps, allowing his soldiers to take a vote as to whether they wished to scale those snowy heights? That clinched matters with General Taylor, who summoned me and said: 'I want no more of your Texans. Send them home.' I wanted to remind him that they were not *my* Texans, but instead I saluted and informed Captain Garner: 'Your Rangers are dismissed. Take them home.' And what do you suppose he did? Stared at me with those icy eyes and said: 'We voted last night to quit when our second three-month enlistments were up. You're not *sending* us home. We're *going* home.' As we watched them ride off, one of my officers muttered: 'I pray that all decent Mexicans are safe in their beds,' because as I've told you, the Texans shoot at anything that moves and take no prisoners.

When one Mexican general surrendered at Monterrey he insisted upon an unusual paragraph in the papers of the agreement: 'I must be accompanied from the city by a strong escort of regular army officers lest I fall into the hands of your Texans.' I led him forth assisted by eleven well-armed officers who had orders to shoot to kill if the Texans tried to attack.

I was sorry, in a way, to lose Otto Macnab, not because I liked him, for he is a steely-eyed killer, but because I wanted to understand how a man so young could have developed so forceful a character. Judging his entire performance with me, I found him an abler tactician than Captain Garner and certainly a more controlled fighter than Panther Komax. But I simply could not understand his savagery. During the incident in Granada, I'm told, it was he who reloaded his four pistols twice, meaning that he may have killed as many as twenty-four Mexicans, none of them well armed. When I asked him about this, he said nothing.

737

Rumor insists that General Taylor will ignore orders and march directly to Saltillo, daring Santa Anna to challenge him. I hope he does, but when I discussed the possibility with his assistants they alarmed me by saying: 'If he does, he'll need your Texans again. He despises them, but he knows he can't move without their scouting.' My God! They may come back!

Otto Macnab, mustered out at Monterrey on 29 September 1846, rode with Garner and Panther to Laredo, then on to San Antonio, where the other two cut east to Xavier County. 'Give them my best,' Otto said in farewell.

From San Antonio he headed north toward the German settlement at Fredericksburg, and as he rode down the side of a hill he saw in the distance the outlines of the rude wooden house that, in his absence, the Allerkamp men had erected for their sister. It was such a surprising object of civilization that those sentiments which had first overcome him when he saw the light gleaming from the cabin surged back, causing him to halt his horse while he gazed at this symbol of what was good in life. The powerful difference was that this was *his* home, *his* light in the wilderness, and he was so overcome by this powerful sensation of love and things civilized that he spurred his horse and raced down the rest of the hill, shouting at the top of his voice: 'Franziska! Franziska!' And when at last he saw her come to the door, wiping her hands on her apron, he thought to himself: This is what we fought for.

He spent most of these days of autumnal peace working slavishly to improve his home. And when he went into Fredericksburg on Saturdays he spent much of his time playing with the neighbors' children and teaching them games, or serving as their four-legged horse, down on his knees, while they galloped about the grass, lashing at his flanks with little twigs. Franziska, watching with pleasure as he gamboled with the children, wished that she could add to his pleasure by informing him that she was pregnant, but for the present this was not to be.

He had once told her, during their long talks when they were getting to know each other after their unusual marriage, that he had been driven to acquire the land at Fredericksburg not only because of his intense love for her, but also because he had so treasured those evenings spent talking with Martin Ascot and Betsy Belle that he had become determined to have a home of his own, 'where people could stop by and talk about what was happening.'

They did not as yet actually have such a home, on their own land, that is, because it had been deemed prudent, in view of Otto's absences as a Ranger, for everyone to delay building a Macnab house on the Macnab holdings. But during this unexpected reprieve from battle they began collecting the field stones and slabs of limestone from which a true Macnab home could one day be built.

If the Germans had the materials, the manpower and the determination to build Otto and Franziska a house, what deterred them? The Comanche. As soon as the Indians learned that the Texans were embroiled in a war with Mexico, with most white fighting men engaged below the Rio Grande, they moved daringly closer to all white settlements, so that there was a constant fear of new massacres, kidnapings and burnings. 'It would be unthinkable to leave our daughter alone on a farm two or three miles away from our protection,' Ludwig explained to Otto when the latter wanted to start building his own home. 'The Comanche are becoming bold and terrible.'

The Germans had acquired extra rifles and were teaching Thekla and Franziska to reload and fire the weapons, and no Allerkamp man ever worked alone in a field. He either worked with another man, or perched his woman on a stump to guard him with a loaded rifle while he labored.

'Ernst is different,' Franziska explained to her husband one night soon after his return as they lay on their straw-mattress bed. 'We didn't want to worry you, but he actually goes out among the Comanche.'

'What?' Otto sat bolt upright.

'Yes, he knows their language now. He talks with them.'

'Why?'

'He's trying to persuade them to make a lasting peace treaty with us Germans. He tells them we're different. That we can be trusted.'

'Good God! Doesn't he know what happened at the San Antonio council house . . . the massacre?'

739

'He tells them that was not our fault. That with us Germans it could never happen.'

'But what about Victoria?' In his confusion, Otto rose from bed and stomped about the little room. 'The Comanche are our enemy. You didn't see my mother ... my aunt. Franza, it was horrible.'

'Ernst says it needn't be that way any longer. Not here. Not with us Germans.'

'I better talk with Ernst,' and despite her protests and the lateness of the hour, he strode over to the other house and roused his brother-in-law, the one who called himself Uncas.

'I know all about the massacres, Otto, and I know how much you loved your two Mexican women. The Comanche are terrible, but the time comes when peace must be reached.'

'With the Comanche, never.'

'What's going on there?' Ludwig's deep voice called, and when the two young men explained they were arguing about the Comanche, he growled: 'Argue outside and let honest people sleep.'

Wrapping themselves in blankets, they went out into the October stillness, and when Ernst saw the huge golden disk of the full moon he said: 'Comanche moon, that's what they call it. It's on bright nights like this they make their attacks,' and the two men looked into the shadows, half expecting to see the savages preparing for an assault on the Allerkamp place.

'Do you honestly think that peace ...?' Before Otto could finish his question, Ernst gripped his arm and said: 'I know that peace is possible with anyone ... anyone. When your battles down there end, won't you have to arrange peace with the Mexicans? Of course. And we must arrange peace with the Comanche.'

In the days that followed, Franziska told her husband about an astonishing frontier drama centering upon a German immigrant whom Otto did not know. Ottfried Hans, Freiherr von Meusebach, was one of those admirable, inquisitive young noblemen whom the European countries occasionally produced. Born in a German duchy, educated in various German universities, he spoke five languages and seemed destined to follow his brother as a major diplomat, when he was dispatched to Texas to bolster the sagging German settlements in the area north of San Antonio. Instantly charmed by the democratic freedoms of his new country, he surrendered the honorific Freiherr, took an American name, and performed notably as John O. Meusebach.

As soon as he had arrived he was visited by Ernst Allerkamp, who assured him: 'I have worked with the Comanche for two years. I know their language. I think I know their hearts. And they have told me: "Peace is possible. But only with you Germans."' Meusebach, listening carefully, said: 'Let us talk further about this,' and when the two men found themselves in harmony on all points, they issued a simple statement: 'We think a lasting treaty of peace with the Comanche is possible.'

Frenzied discussion had followed, Franziska told Otto, with old-time Kentucky settlers warning Meusebach: 'You wasn't here when President Lamar laid down the basic rule for handlin' Indians in Texas. "Eviction or extermination!" Ain't no way white men can live aside Indians, because they ain't human like us.'

'How did Ernst take that?' Otto asked, and she replied: 'Shouted in a public meeting "Peace is possible!" and he volunteered to lead a party out to the Comanche, if anyone was brave enough to follow.'

'Anyone volunteer?'

'Meusebach.'

'The German nobleman?' and Franza said: 'Yes.'

So that was the way things stood at year's end: two young men ready for great adventure, Ernst among the Comanche, Otto back in Mexico if the army called.

The Meusebach expedition into the heart of the Comanchería assembled its gear in mid-January 1847, and when Otto realized that these men really were going to plunge into enemy territory, where the risk of death by torture was great, he insisted upon going along with his multiple weapons, but Ernst said: 'No, this is a peaceful mission,' and Meusebach agreed.

Otto, disgusted by this non-military attempt, warned: 'You'll die staked out before a fire, but don't call for the Rangers. It'll be too late.'

He was considering whether he should, to protect these headstrong Germans, gather a few men like himself and ride discreetly behind the would-be peacemakers, when he heard Franziska call from her kitchen door the single word 'Lieb-chen.' Their affinity through the years of their extraordinary courtship and in the early months of their marriage had become so intuitive that whenever Franza uttered the word *Liebchen* in a certain inflection, her husband knew that she was about to say something of importance.

'What?' he asked, turning his whole attention to her.

She blushed, hesitated, then said in a low voice: 'I'm to have a baby.' She said no more, and he refrained from jumping in the air or embracing her fervently; instead, he bowed to her and she to him, for they were people of silent moments deeply cherished.

But the moment of reverence was broken by the arrival of Panther Komax, who bellowed as he approached the cabin: 'Macnab! General Taylor needs us at Saltillo! Garner's taking down his best men from Company M.'

When the bearlike man saw Franziska, he whisked her up in his arms, threw her in the air, and shouted: 'How did you ever catch this one, Little Nubbin?'

'Put her down!' Otto yelled, and when he saw her safely on the ground he whispered to Komax: 'She's going to have a baby.'

Panther stepped back, surveyed the couple, and clucked his tongue: 'Fräulein Macnab, you are beautiful! Simply beauti-ful!' And he gave her a great hairy kiss which practically covered her face. He was the second man to have kissed her, and she was astonished at his boldness.

'Yes,' he snorted as the Allerkamp women fed him gargan-tuan quantities of food, 'messengers came north with news that Old Rough-and-Ready was bulldogging his way into the heart of Mexico. Without scouts. With disaster every time he moved. After six or seven routs of his dragoons . . .' Here he leaped to his feet and galloped about the place, imitating the American cavalry on their big horses riding fat and dumb right into Mexican ambushes. 'Hell, he knowed he needed us to do his dirty work.'

'Can't you stay the night?' Thekla asked, and he said: 'Nope, we got to join up with Garner and the others at Laredo.'

So packing was done hastily, but when Franziska went out to

put Otto's gear on his waiting horse, she saw his saddle blanket and uttered a cry: 'There's blood on your saddle.' And when Panther went to scratch the discoloration, he confirmed: 'Yep. It's blood.'

'Otto, were you wounded?' Franza asked, her face even paler than before, but Panther dissipated her fears: 'Your little man never gets wounded. He wounds other people,' and the two Rangers explained how they had captured those two little mountains at Monterrey, Federación and Independencia, and how on the latter hill, when they attacked the Bishop's Palace, Ranger Lucas had been killed.

'Me and your husband carried his body down and tied it to Otto's saddle,' Panther said, and when he saw Franziska blanch, he added: 'Hell, ma'am, him and me's been in a dozen fights like that. We never get hurt.'

This mention of death, something the families of Rangers rarely discussed, for they appreciated the perils of their men's rough occupation, spurred Franziska to reveal something she had intended never to tell her husband. Now, taking his hand and leading him away from Panther, she whispered: 'While you were in Mexico, your friend Yancey Quimper rode into Fredericksburg, seeking to buy land, or open a store, or anything. Nobody trusted him, so he left. But he stopped by here and asked me many questions, and ... Otto, he wanted to know ... if you got killed in the war ... if he could come speak with me ... and ...'

She hesitated, for she knew that if she revealed the remainder of that incredible visit, Otto might go storming out and kill Quimper, but the realization of death compelled her to speak: 'He tried to kiss me. I pushed him away and told him to be gone. He stood in the doorway and said: "Remember, Franziska, I wanted to marry you before Otto ever saw you. If anything happens ..."'

Otto said nothing, hands at his side, linen duster about his feet, but his wife added: 'He wants you dead, Otto. Please, please take care of yourself.'

'Time to go!' Komax warned, and the two Rangers, taking extra horses with them and Otto's arsenal of guns, headed south and overtook Garner and the rest of the company at Laredo. From there they splashed across the shallow Rio Grande and

743

started the dangerous passage to Saltillo, where General Taylor would be encamped awaiting the arrival of Santa Anna with the main Mexican army.

'Any danger of Mexican raiding parties?' Otto asked, and Garner replied: 'There's always danger as long as Benito Garza is alive, and especially when Taylor's army hasn't been keeping scouts on the perimeters.'

Each day Otto served with this gangling man he respected his abilities more; Garner was certainly not a compelling figure, and he lacked the fiery oratory of a dashing leader, but in all he did he was completely sensible, a man who seemed to anticipate the flow of battle with an acute awareness of where he and his troops could be used with maximum effect. Panther once said: 'Twenty of us Rangers with Garner at our head is equal to forty. Outen him, we're just twenty.'

Garner demonstrated his professionalism shortly after his contingent completed its furtive crossing of the northern desert on 4 February 1847 and reported to Lieutenant Colonel Cobb, who, as before, would serve as their superior. The fastidious South Carolinian, watching them straggle in, a disjointed file with men and horses in every conceivable condition, winced at the ugly prospect of dealing with them through another campaign, but he did take Captain Garner in to see General Taylor, who proved to be as gruff as ever: 'Bad situation. We know Santa Anna's coming north. But where and when and how many? That we don't know.'

'And it's our job to find out?' Garner asked without bravado.

'That's why I sent for you.' The general hesitated, then decided to be frank: 'I was damned glad to see you go, Garner. Never seen a rowdier group of soldiers. Can't you instill any discipline?' Before the lanky captain could respond, Taylor added: 'And I'm damned glad to have you back.' He wanted to shake Garner's hand or even embrace him in a soldierly way, but instead he said gruffly: 'Everything hangs on the next few days. Find out what they're up to.'

Garner decided to take eight Rangers with him on a protracted scout of the southern approaches to Saltillo, and as his men gathered in that beautiful cathedral square where the Frenchman René-Claude d'Ambreuze had courted Trinidad de Saldaña, he knew their task was a dangerous one, for if discovered on this foray, they might have to fight large forces of Mexican lancers. But the Rangers were skilled in clandestine operations, and if a solitary Ranger was suddenly cut off from his fellows, he would know that he must proceed alone; he could be counted upon to sneak his way back to headquarters with a reliable report of how things stood in the areas he had seen. And if only that one Ranger survived to deliver essential information regarding the forthcoming battle, the scout would be judged a success.

When Garner's men left Saltillo they entered almost immediately upon a terrain that seemed as if it had been carved out of rock by the god of battles for some special Armageddon. It was a narrow defile, lined on the east by mountains so high they could not be scaled; their lower reaches, however, provided a sloping field across which cavalry could charge. The west flank consisted of a deep gully backed by lower hills; here cavalry could not function but foot soldiers could. General Taylor, marching south into the defile, would have to smash head-on into General Santa Anna marching north, and the outcome would depend upon how skillfully each general utilized the sloping hills to the east and those gaping gullies to the west.

'This ain't gonna be easy,' Panther told Otto as they studied the brutal terrain. When Otto made no reply, for none would have been relevant, Panther added: 'But I guess you fight your battles where they happen,' and again Otto said nothing, for he was studying those ominous slopes to the east, wondering how his Rangers would utilize them if an attack by Santa Anna's lancers suddenly developed.

On 20 February 1847, Garner and his men reconnoitered the oncoming Mexican army, and as brave as the Rangers were, they were shaken when they got to the crest of a hill and saw the endless manpower that Santa Anna was bringing north. Panther called back to those still climbing below: 'Damned lines go on forever.'

'Can you spot the camp they'll be using tonight?' Cobb asked, cupping his hands to muffle his voice.

'Off to one side,' Komax replied, lowering his voice too. And then he tossed in a typical Ranger addition: 'We can reach it tonight.'

When the huge fellow clambered down, Garner asked: 'Panther, can you and three men ride ahead and create a diversion? Allow them to chase you back this way without getting caught?'

'Don't mind if I do get caught. We can handle them . . .'

'Panther, you're not to get caught. You're to tease them on. Because me and Macnab, we're gonna go right into the heart of their camp, and we want them to be chasing you, not us.'

Otto displayed not the slightest emotion. He dismounted, took off his white duster, folded it meticulously, and handed it for safekeeping to one of the two Rangers who would not be involved in either foray. This done, he hitched up his trousers, felt for his two Colts, stowed his two old pistols in his saddle, and climbed back on his horse. Together with Garner he started the perilous, tortuous advance to the Mexican lines.

They rode through the scattered advance posts, boldly keeping to their horses. Disguised as Mexicans, with Garner wearing a colorful serape, they rode straight into a position at which they could dismount, tethered their horses, and moved cautiously about, noting strengths and dispositions.

For a day, twenty-six hours, they remained inside enemy lines, one sleeping while the other watched, and in the early part of the night when the Mexicans were careless and talkative, they crept very close to the tents, and it was in the moon-cast shadow of one of these that Macnab saw a Mexican officer bending over to tighten the guy ropes. As he did so, Otto realized that it was Benito Garza, not fifteen yards away.

'Captain,' he whispered. 'That's Garza, I'm sure. I'm going in and kill him.' Garner restrained him: 'Any noise would be fatal.'

'But he's the brains in the Strip.'

'I know who he is,' Garner snapped, 'and I know that any motion now . . .'

Now Macnab experienced agonies of indecision: there was Garza, an enemy he was obligated to kill, almost within touching distance; behind was the American army needing information. It was Garner who solved this dilemma: 'If he's that important to you, Otto, break in and shoot him. You'll not get out alive, but . . . Give me fifteen minutes lead, and I'll be safe.'

'It is that important,' Macnab said.

'So be it,' Garner said, but before he could return to his tethered horse, someone else left the tent to catch a breath of clean night air, and the watchers saw that it was a woman, a young woman of great charm and obvious breeding. She was, it seemed likely, the wife of some officer, and her presence deterred Macnab's plan of bursting in with pistols blazing. Garner grasped him by the arm, as if to pull him away, but then Garza reappeared, and placed his arm about the woman's waist, and kissed her.

Who could the woman be? She seemed no more than twenty, and Garza must be at least forty, but that they were in love there could be no doubt, none whatever.

'Has he a wife?' Garner asked.

'Who knows?' Otto replied, and quietly the two Rangers retreated.

They slept about a hundred yards from their horses, Garner spreading his serape on the ground for both of them, and when the sun was well up, they mounted their steeds, walked them quietly north, saluted sentries as if on an inspection tour, and when they saw a break in the lines, galloped like terrified ghosts, neither shouting nor looking back at the men who were firing the bullets that whistled past their heads.

When they reported to General Taylor, he was awed by their adventure and dismayed by the estimates they gave of Santa Anna's strength. 'We must draw back,' he said. 'If we stay, we're trapped.' He thanked Garner for his daring and turned to do the same for Macnab, but the little Ranger was gone.

'Where is he?' Taylor asked, and Garner pointed to where Otto was retrieving his duster from its custodian. Shaking it out and slapping away any dust, he slipped it about his shoulders and considered himself ready for the impending battle.

Benito Garza, commanding General Santa Anna's scouts, was not informed of the infiltration of the mexicano lines by American spies; the sentries who had fired at Garner and Macnab were afraid to report the sorties lest they be shot for having allowed it to happen.

He remained in his tent with his wife, Lucha López, and with the regular army officers with whom he worked. This was 21

February 1847, a cold, damp day, and because the two armies had moved so near to each other, it was obvious that battle could not be avoided, with visible advantage to the mexicanos. Garza was especially hopeful: 'This time, Lucha, we annihilate them.' He spent the morning making arrangements for her to move far to the rear, to be with the other women who had accompanied their men, but at noon he was alerted by reports from his scouts: 'General Taylor is retreating.'

Kissing Lucha, he rode out to check this surprising development and found that the news was accurate: the Americans were withdrawing, and rather precipitately, but he was not deceived by their tactics: 'They're seeking more favorable ground, and they're right.'

Nevertheless he had reason to be hopeful about this battle, for Santa Anna, blustering across Mexico, a wooden leg in one stirrup, had performed his customary miracle of assembling a huge number of men and forging them into a respectable army. He had at his disposal, of course, a reliable cadre of young, able and dedicated officers like Benito Garza, none better in all the armies of the world, and on them he relied to stiffen the ranks. He was also supported by a fierce patriotism which invariably rallied whenever Spanish, or French, or especially American enemies threatened. But most important, he still retained that tremendous charisma which designated him a true romantic hero and which bound men like Garza to him with unbreakable bonds.

Santa Anna in the saddle again! A thrill ran through the nation. Santa Anna was in command of the army again! Men marched with more vigor, lancers rode with more élan. Santa Anna was heading back to avenge his unlucky defeat at San Jacinto, to repeat his earlier triumphs at the Alamo and Goliad. Tejas would be regained. New Mexico and California would be saved. As the sun set almost every man in the mexicano army believed that on the morrow Santa Anna would celebrate his birthday with another stupendous victory.

He almost did. In fact, he should have, not on the twenty-second, which was more or less a stalemate, with the Americans suffering major casualties and a loss of valuable position, but on the twenty-third, when the three-to-one Mexican superiority in numbers and mobility began to tell.

748

About midmorning the attack along the foothills of the eastern mountains, the attack which Garner and his men had known to be inevitable, began, with a furious charge by several companies of elite lancers supported by rapid-firing dragoons. Ashen-faced, General Taylor observed: 'They're turning our left flank!' Perceiving that if they did, the superb Mexican cavalry would chop up his rear echelons and throw the entire American army into rout, he called for all available men to stanch the blood being let by the lancers, and under his stalwart leadership, a few cavalry and many foot soldiers assembled to halt the surging Mexican horsemen.

Old Rough-and-Ready may have been slow-witted, but he was no fool. Never first-rate in overall strategy when engaging in a special battle, he knew where to throw his strength at critical moments, and now he dug in, a stubborn man fighting his last encounter.

With appalling power and skill the Mexicans hammered at his left flank, but like a wounded bear Taylor growled and gathered power and fought back. At the critical moment, when the battle seemed lost, he called upon a Mississippi gentleman whom he had once despised to save the day. Twelve years before, Colonel Jefferson Davis, then age twenty-seven, had eloped with Taylor's daughter Sarah, completely against the general's wishes. But now Taylor had to swallow his pride and call upon Davis and his Mississippi Rifles to hold off Santa Anna's rampaging cavalry, and with support from the Texas Rangers, Davis led his troops in a gallant charge.

The Rangers were led by Persifer Cobb, braver almost than they, who relished the chance to gallop his horse right at the Mexican lancers and test his skill against theirs. Cobb was supported, he was relieved to note, by Garner and Komax on his left and Otto Macnab on his right, the latter firing pistols like a little arsenal. Together they simply rode down the Mexicans, who had smaller steeds and inferior firepower.

'Watch the lances!' Cobb shouted as he knocked down a lancer about to pierce Macnab, who raised his Colts in a salute as he roared past in pursuit of his own targets.

When General Taylor saw that the day had been saved, he had the grace to say to his son-in-law: 'Colonel Davis, my daughter was a better judge of men than I was.' But none of the

Americans believed this battle to have been a victory, not by any means. Losses were great. Valuable positions had once more been wrested away by superior Mexican numbers and performance. Indeed, as night fell General Taylor had to consider the likelihood that on the morrow he was doomed to suffer a crushing defeat, and with this mournful prospect staring at him, he assembled his officers.

'Can we hold them if they make a dawn attack?' he asked.

'Our men and horses are exhausted.'

'But can they make one last effort?'

'They can always make an effort. But . . .'

Throughout the night the discussions continued, and at one o'clock or thereabouts Taylor suggested that his best Texas scouts be sent out to bring news of exactly when the Mexicans would begin their major attack. Lieutenant Colonel Cobb thought the general had tears in his eyes as he said: 'Give us what you can, Persifer. I knew your uncle Leander. Good man. Good man with horses, that one.'

Despite Captain Garner's urgent suggestion that Cobb remain safe with General Taylor, the South Carolinian insisted upon sharing the scout with his Texans, and they went alarmingly deep into enemy territory. Two o'clock, and only sporadic signs of enemy action. Three o'clock, and still darkest winter night, with Mexican troops huddling to keep warm. Four o'clock, and only that ominous silence. Five · o'clock, and just a faint show of light from a campfire visible here and there.

At six, when dawn would betray their presence, the Rangers were in maximum danger, and Cobb, aware of this, cautioned additional care, but Panther Komax ignored his warnings, rose boldly in his saddle, stared ahead in disbelief, and shouted: 'Jesus Christ!'

When the others rode up, several of them repeated Panther's cry: 'Jesus Christ!'

On the evening after the great battle of Buena Vista, when the Mexicans had stood within six inches or six minutes of an astounding victory, General Santa Anna had convened a meeting of *his* officers, and such is the strangeness of battle that approximately identical questions were being asked.

'Can we crush them in the morning?' the one-legged Napoleon asked.

'Our lancers, all our cavalry, they did what they could this afternoon.'

'Can they repeat?'

Silence. No one dared tell the dictator of Mexico, the commander in chief, the Benemérito de la Patria, El Supremo, that something was impossible, but it was clear even to him that the mexicano cavalry had shot its bolt. It had been a gallant bolt, one of the best, but it was finished.

'The infantry?'

More silence. No other infantry in the world suffered the disadvantages that were the common lot of the peasants who formed the bulk of any Santa Anna army. Conscripted at gunpoint, they marched barefoot, clad only in thin cotton shirts even in the dead of winter – like now. And they bled and shivered and died of dysentery, for their army provided no field hospitals to accompany them and no medicines to soften the dreadful fevers they contracted. Despite these deprivations and the lack of food, they were obedient and brave, and when they started running at an enemy line they usually breached it. Such soldiers had defeated Spaniards, Frenchmen, Americans and other Mexicans, and if ordered on the morrow to attack the weakened American lines, they would do so, until their bodies piled higher than a small tree.

But their officers stood silent, for they knew that because of supply problems, those faithful soldiers shivering in the wintry blast had eaten nothing for nearly thirty hours. They would obey orders and start toward the norteamericano lines tomorrow, that was certain, but they might well collapse before they got there, and not necessarily from enemy gunfire.

To the surprise of everyone in his tent, Santa Anna changed the course of his discussion and said most abruptly: 'We had a great victory today, did we not?'

'Yes, General.'

'And we overran six or seven headquarters positions, did we not?'

'We did.'

'Did we capture many enemy flags?'

'We did. Cortés alone has seven. I saw them.'

'Let Cortés speak for himself.' The gallant lancer was sent for, and Santa Anna asked: 'Did you capture enemy flags?'

'Yes, General, seven.'

'Any other trophies?'

'Many. Many.'

Santa Anna now turned to the one man he knew he could trust in any adversity, a man who had always given straight answers: 'Garza, can we defeat them tomorrow?'

'Unquestionably.'

'Why do you say that, when these others . . .'

'Because I know what's going on over there.' He pointed north, toward Saltillo and the American lines: 'They're holding a meeting like this, and they know they've been defeated.'

'Will they retreat, do you think?'

Now Garza had to pause, for in his careful study of the norteamericanos he had perceived that Zachary Taylor was not the clever kind of general who saw things in big design. He was a man who took a position and held on to it until he was knocked off. 'Retreat?' Garza said slowly. 'Maybe not, but . . .'

Santa Anna had heard enough. On the very threshold of a victory which would have enshrined him in the bosom of Mexico forever, he gave his order: 'Immediately, we march back to Potosí.'

'Excellency!' Garza protested, but the fatal die had been cast.

'Strike camp. Abandon everything not instantly needed, and march. Before dawn.'

When Garza dashed to the tent where his wife was sleeping, he awakened her roughly: 'It's ended, Lucha. Back to Potosí.'

'Oh, no!' she cried, for she saw in the resumed battle a chance of victory for her beliefs.

'It's the end for Santa Anna,' Garza said with great sadness, and when his wife, packing furiously, asked what he meant, he explained prophetically: 'Another norteamericano army will land at Vera Cruz. They'll march to Puebla and surround Mexico City. Defeat, defeat. They'll depose Santa Anna, and then they'll go home, thinking it's all over.' He interrupted Lucha's packing and took her by the hands: 'But for us it will never be over. If they want to steal that land south of the Nueces, they better be prepared to pay in blood.'

It was this flight south at dawn that had so astonished

Panther Komax and his fellow Rangers.

On the day that General Taylor realized he had won the battle of Buena Vista – if one did not inspect the facts too closely – he agreed to let the Texans disband and go home. He explained to Garner that although he appreciated their contributions, 'none more valiant,' he could not endanger the security of his army by allowing them to harass guiltless Mexican citizens and expose the regular army to guerrilla action in retaliation: 'You must leave at once, and try not to arouse the countryside by thoughtless killings as you go.'

In the morning Taylor said goodbye to the Rangers: 'I thank you for your gallant efforts. But before you depart, I want you to hear the summary prepared by Colonel Cobb,' whereupon the South Carolinian, in his trimmest uniform, stepped forward to read a report he had compiled:

'While it is conceded by all that the Texas Rangers have performed satisfactorily all military tasks assigned them, there have unfortunately been certain deficiencies in discipline, the consequences of which I shall now summarize.

'General riots, pitting volunteers against regulars, five. Ordinary courts-martial, one hundred and nineteen. General courts-martial, eleven. Murders, four. Murders of Mexican citizens, eighty-four. Attempted murder, eleven. Insubordination and mutinous acts, sixty-one. Cowardice in the face of the enemy, nine.' (At this, several Rangers cried 'No! No!' – but the charges continued). 'Desertion, seventeen. Discharged by the commanding general because of general worthlessness, nineteen. Discharged because of suspicion of insanity, no other charge appearing to be reasonable, eleven.

'The Ranger known as Panther Komax, who started the riot last night which caused at least six hundred dollars' worth of damage to government property, and who told a superior to go to hell, was subjected last night to a legally convened court-martial whose judgment is hereby delivered: "The Texas Ranger Leroy Komax, known as Panther, shall receive a dishonorable discharge and shall hear 'The Rogue's March.'"'

753

Panther stood rigid, but many Rangers, including Captain Garner, shouted 'No! No!' – for there was no greater disgrace in the armed services than for a man to stand at his final attention as the band started to sound the miserable notes of 'The Rogue's March,' and then to march goosestepping out of the company while some stout sergeant jerked high the seat of his pants.

Four burly sergeants surrounded Panther and brought him to face the band, which launched immediately into that soulful, insulting lament for things gone wrong. As soon as the first notes sounded, a fifth sergeant, bigger than the others, grabbed Panther by the seat and started marching him off the parade ground; never again could such a disgraced man serve with the regular army, and Panther should have gone in silence, accepting his punishment, but at the edge of the field as he was about to be shoved off, he turned and challenged the army of northern Mexico: 'Give me six good Rangers and we'll knock the shit outa your whole force.'

When he was removed, Persifer Cobb returned stiffly to the reading of the citation:

> 'Acts of bravery, unnumbered. Devotion to duty, unparalleled. Patriotism, unquestioned.' (He paused.) 'Rangers of Texas, you are unforgettable.'

With that, both he and General Taylor snapped to attention and saluted.

Often during these hectic days of the Mexican War, Otto worried about what was happening to Ernst Allerkamp on his foray into the Comanchería, and on the way back to Texas he told Komax, who seemed undisturbed by his rude dismissal from military service: 'I'll bet those men who went out among the Indians had it a lot rougher than we did,' and as soon as he reached his home and satisfied himself that Franziska was in good health, he asked: 'And what happened to Ernst?'

In response she rang the bell which the Allerkamp women used for signaling their men – two short, two long for Ernst – and in a moment he came from the fields, delighted to see his brother-in-law. In self-effacing words he summarized a remarkable event:

> 'Three days after you left for Mexico, Herr Meusebach

754

started his expedition for the Comanchería, and I was able to lead him to the principal chiefs. I translated, you know, and we conducted long talks, for the Indians like to go over everything many times.

'But during hours when I wasn't working I made friends with a young Comanche warrior. Blond hair, pale complexion, he was surely a white man. At first he would explain nothing, but when I gave him tobacco he wanted to talk. "My name is Thomas Lyons. I lived near Austin. The Comanche came to our farm and murdered my parents. Took me away with them. I like being an Indian and do not care to go back to Austin, where my brother lives."

'I could understand this; as a boy I wanted to be an Indian. But what shocked me was the answer I got when I asked: "Who is this little Mexican boy who follows you about?" And Thomas Lyons said: "I captured him during one of our raids on the Rio Grande." And when I suggested that I take the boy with me and return him to his parents, Lyons asked: "Why?"'

Ernst fell silent, still disturbed by the fact that Indians, too, had slaves, and after a while Otto asked: 'What happened with the Comanche?' and Ernst explained how Meusebach, with skill and patience, had engineered a compassionate treaty which was to be ratified in Fredericksburg within two weeks.

Otto was alarmed: 'Ernst! The Comanche never honor a treaty!' and in the days that followed, while Ernst rode out to lead the great chiefs of that tribe in for the signing, Otto moved through Fredericksburg, repeating his softly stated warning: 'I'm a Ranger. I've fought Indians and Mexicans alike. They're both no good. No place in Texas for either of them.'

For three days, as Ernst and the chieftains approached from the west, Otto strove to discredit the treaty, and he might have continued had not Franziska intervened: 'Otto, there's a new day. New rules. Ernst is right. It's time for peace.'

Macnab was so startled to hear a woman oppose him, a dutiful German housewife, that he stood agape. He looked at her, small, tense, her hair in braids as if she were still a young girl, and to his own amazement he dropped the argument.

755

Taking her in his arms, he whispered: 'I came home to build us a real house. Our home. If Ernst's treaty makes it possible, I'm all for it.' He kissed her twice, then added: 'But when those Indians come into our town, I'm going to be watching. Very careful.'

On a lovely May morning the Comanche arrived, fearful Indians on sleek ponies. Remembering well the tragedy their brothers had encountered during such a meeting in San Antonio, they insisted upon a safeguard, which Ernst interpreted: 'They will lay down their weapons, all of them, even their daggers, in the middle of the roadway if we Germans will do the same.' Meusebach pleaded with the townsmen to accept these terms, and when, against Otto's advice, the pile was made, two Indian braves and Macnab were assigned to watch it.

Otto had wanted to be inside the hotel to safeguard the meeting, but Meusebach had outsmarted him, so there he sat in the warm May sunlight, guarding the weapons and noticing where his Colts five-shooters lay in case he had to grab them in a hurry. He noticed also that the two braves were marking the location of their weapons in case of crisis: he judged that he could outgrab and outshoot them. Next he studied how, having gunned down the two guardians, he could whip about and aim his fire at the entrance to the Nimitz House to shoot the parleying chiefs if they attempted to join the fray.

But the tragedy of San Antonio was not repeated, because John Meusebach, supported by Ernst Allerkamp, had convinced both the Comanche and the Germans that this little paradise set down among the hills, this land of tumbling fields and flowing streams, this Eden of bluebonnets and Indian paintbrush, was indeed different, and that amidst the gunfire that echoed across Texas, here stood a refuge of sanity.

The treaty was agreed upon. Braves and Germans recovered their weapons. Macnab, as he picked up his revolvers, muttered to himself: 'Be on watch when the next Comanche moon rides the sky.' He wanted peace as much as anyone in Fredericksburg, but he would continue to prepare for war.

At Easter, as he had predicted, the Comanche came sneaking back, and on a night as calm and lovely as the hill country had known, they crept toward the sleeping town.

Otto Macnab, always on guard, saw them first, terrifying

figures on the silvery horizon, and running for his guns he shouted: 'Franza! Quick! Bring the extra powder!' But Ernst stopped him, pointing to the surrounding hills – and there in the brightness of the Easter moon the Indians had lighted signal fires, scores of them on all perimeters, signaling the Germans that in these valleys at last peace prevailed, now and in the future.

Otto was amazed. With Franza beside him, he laid down his guns to watch the fires, but Ernst did not look. Uncas had lowered his head, and he was weeping.

When General Zachary Taylor failed to crush the Mexican army in his questionable victory at Buena Vista, General Winfield Scott was given the job of disembarking at Vera Cruz and finishing the job in the vicinity of Mexico City, but with an army of only ten thousand American troops to subdue millions of Mexicans on their home ground, he was forced to take draconian steps. When guerrillas struck at his supply lines, secretly at night and outside the rules of what he called 'organized warfare,' he issued a startling set of orders, summarized in these words:

> No quarter will be extended to murderers, robbers or any man out of uniform who attacks our convoys. They are equally dangerous to Mexicans, foreigners and American troops, and they shall be exterminated.
>
> But you are to observe certain rules. Your prisoners are not to be put to death without due solemnity. That is, there shall be no killing of prisoners. What you must do is arrest them, hold them momentarily as prisoners, convene a hearing, sentence them on the spot, and then shoot them.

Therefore, the Americans who had protested so vigorously the savage actions of General Santa Anna at the Alamo and Goliad were now going to operate under almost the same rules.

Scott's second action was perhaps the more significant, for in order to have at his command men prepared to act with such severity, he asked the army to call back into service as many Texas Rangers as possible, and in compliance with this summons, Captain Sam Garner, in retirement on his farm, agreed to reassemble his Company M, if he could have with him Otto Macnab and Panther Komax.

Garner had no trouble signing up the Panther: 'I'd rather fight greasers than eat!' But after the captain had spent two days with the Macnabs, he knew that Otto was completely absorbed in his son Hamish and not at all disposed to return to Mexico: 'Look, I got me a son. I want to stay here and help Franziska with the place. You know, Captain Garner, it really is something for a man to have a son. Can you imagine a tiny little hand like that ... he can't even keep it straight ... holding a Colts one of these days?'

Garner was finding it difficult to believe that Otto, deadliest of his Rangers, could be so domesticated, so on the third day at breakfast he turned to Mrs Macnab: 'Franza, I want to take your man with me again,' and she agreed: 'I think he's ready to go now. Be careful. All of you.'

When the company assembled, Otto was surprised to see Panther in the ranks: 'How can you go back after they gave you that "Rogue's March" in Saltillo?' The big man brushed aside such apprehension: 'That was up north, Scott's down south.' And when Otto reminded him that armies keep records, he said: 'They do, that they do. Come peace, they don't want bastards like me. But come war, and Scott has plenty of that, they're glad to have us.'

'Aren't you afraid your record will follow you?' Otto asked, and Panther replied: 'And when Scott sees it, he's gonna shout: "That's just the son-of-a-bitch I want." He may even make me an officer.'

When the warship delivered them to the steaming port of Vera Cruz, the Rangers lining the rail of the tender that brought them ashore let out a wild yell of joy, for awaiting them stood the austere, primly dressed figure of their old commander, Persifer Cobb, breveted to full colonel for his bravery. 'We're back!' Komax shouted exuberantly, and when the South Carolinian realized that this incorrigible was being returned to his command, he blanched. 'Oh, no!' he cried to no one. 'That I will not tolerate!' But when the reunion was completed, Colonel Cobb outlined the Rangers' new mission.

'We're trying to do what no major army in recent history has ever attempted, so far as I know. With only a handful of men, cut off from reinforcements, we're trying to conquer and pacify an entire nation. We're Hernando Cortés in the nineteenth century, and we're in just as much danger.'

He traced the perilous route to the capital: 'Guerrilleros molest every column we send over these hills. Our job is to stop them. To exterminate them. Without quarter.'

Stern disciplinarian that he was, Persifer Cobb took pride in being as strict with himself as with his underlings, so he firmed his jaw and tried once more to bring some sort of order to the Texans. But he failed. Despite orders, the Rangers drank whatever water they pleased, and soon they were stricken with violent cases of dysentery, which immobilized them for about a week; they were too sick to stand, let alone march. And even when the tougher men like Macnab and Komax revived, they found that their captain remained terribly sick, not only with dysentery but also with the more threatening El Vómito.

Practiced hands advised Colonel Cobb to send Garner back to a homeward-bound ship, but the fighting Ranger would not allow this, so on a litter he made the painful progress to the upland town of Jalapa. In that beautiful spot, where the rigors of Vera Cruz vanished amid flowers, beautiful homes and literally acres of fresh fruit and fields full of cattle, Garner recovered, and it was believed later that had he been in full health and therefore better able to command his men, the tragedy at Avila might not have happened, but Colonel Cobb did not agree: 'All Texans are murderers whenever a Mexican is involved, and had Captain Garner been his usual self, I'm sure he would have led the disgraceful affair.'

La Desolación de Avila they called it in the steamy rain forests leading to the altiplano, and it was the result of the daring action of the guerrilla leader Benito Garza, who waited in the jungle until Captain Garner's detachment was well strung out, then struck with fury at the vulnerable midpoint. The sudden attack caught the still-weakened Garner unawares, and before his startled men could protect him, he was impaled by three swords. Summoning all his frail strength, he straightened in the saddle, tried to catch up with his men, then toppled forward over his horse's neck.

His men, seeing him fall, lashed out at any Mexican they

759

could find, and in their blind rage came upon the innocent village of Avila, in which one of Garza's men had taken refuge.

Galloping into the central plaza, they began shooting any Mexicans they saw, whereupon the guerrilla took aim and struck the man riding next to Komax square in the forehead, dropping him like a bird; he did not bleed profusely, but the bullet hole was so conspicuous on his fever-blanched skin that every Ranger who leaped over his dead body could see it.

No person inside the sniper's hiding place survived the Ranger's revenge, not even the three children. Methodically the Texans then swept through the half-dozen adobes that lined the square, and by evil luck Komax and Macnab found themselves dashing from the last house directly at the open door of the village church. Without stopping, they burst into the church, killed three old men who had taken refuge there, and proceeded to wreck the place, scattering holy implements here and there in the roadway outside. As they withdrew, they killed six cows in a final surge of fury.

When a great outcry rose from Avila and surrounding towns, with the bishop himself protesting, Colonel Cobb summoned offending Rangers.

'We were fired on by irregulars,' Komax explained.

'Is that true, Macnab?' Cobb asked.

'From the house with the brown door.'

'Were guerrillas found inside? When you finished, that is?'

'There were,' Macnab said.

'What about the church?' Cobb asked. 'The desecration of the church?'

'Three guerrillas ran in there,' Komax said.

'Did you see them run in?' Cobb asked Macnab.

'I did.'

'And what did you do?' Cobb asked.

'I stood guard in the street. I figured Panther and his men, they could handle it.'

'Did you see the guerrillas? You, yourself?'

'Twice. When they ran in. When they were dead.'

Colonel Cobb turned to the bishop and the other protesters: 'Gentlemen, I'm sure you have copies of General Scott's orders concerning the suppression of guerrillas. They're to be eliminated, for your safety as well as ours.'

'But the children . . .' the bishop pleaded.

'Our men cannot check in advance, at peril to their lives.'

'And the church? The holy vestments, the altar?'

'Major Wells will give you a signed statement attesting to the fact that known guerrillas unfortunately ran into the church and that in pursuit, some minor damage proved unavoidable. There will be compensation.'

Some time later, after the dead Ranger was buried, and the graves of the villagers decked with flowers and the church restored, Cobb asked Komax and Macnab: 'Were there guerrillas in the church?'

'There could of been,' said Panther.

.

Riding with the Rangers was a civilian from New York named Harry Saxon, twenty-two years old, red-headed and encumbered by an extraordinary amount of gear which he protected with a horse pistol. At first Cobb's men thought he must be a medical man, but when Saxon ignored the fallen and trembled whenever he saw blood, they knew that guess was wrong. Finally Komax, catching the newcomer staring at him offensively, roared: 'Son, who in hell are you?'

'Harry Saxon, *New York Dispatch*.'

'Newspaperman?'

'Yep.'

'And what is all that stuff?'

'I'm a photographer.'

'And what in hell is that?'

Patting his gear, he explained: 'I make pictures. They're called daguerreotypes.'

These words were new to the Rangers, who crowded about to see the miracle of photography. Unwittingly, Harry Saxon occupied a unique place in world military history: he was taking the first-ever photographs of an army engaged in battle, and it was the photograph he took this sunny afternoon, with the desolated buildings of Avila in the background, which made him famous and which would last as long as men cherished visual records of their exploits.

This daguerreotype, remarkably clear and evocative, showed the ruined church, a tethered donkey and, in the foreground, two savage, scowling Texas Rangers: a towering Panther

761

Komax, bearded, unkempt, with his coonskin over his left ear; and a small, smooth-faced Otto Macnab, linen duster covering his toes and a hardened stare which warned: 'Don't touch me!' It was a summarizing picture of the newly fledged Texas state at war, seeking revenge for past insults, and to look at its subjects was to share their seething rage.

But it was Saxon's written account of how the victorious Texans entered Mexico City in their crusade of pacification that was of the greater significance to the new state. Unfamiliar with the insolent behavior of Rangers, he could not comprehend what he had witnessed, and when wood-engravers in New York translated his word-pictures into newspaper illustrations, citizens across the nation asked, also in disbelief: 'My God, is that Texas? Have we taken men like that into our Union?'

Hearing that the Texans were about to approach the capital, I left Mexico City and rode east toward the little village of Avila, hoping to intercept them as they came up out of the jungle. I arrived on a fateful morning and had breakfast with their captain, Sam Garner, a scarecrow, gaunt from prolonged dysentery, who told me: 'We teach them that you can't stop a man who knows he's right and keeps coming, especially if he has two Colts .44 and you don't.' An hour later weakened Captain Garner was killed by a Mexican guerrilla.

Deprived of their captain, the Rangers were in an ugly mood when we entered Mexico City this morning, but no one could have guessed how they would express their rage. At the outskirts of the capital a big, hairy Ranger called Panther Komax shouted in a loud voice: 'Men, let's remind these b-----s who's in charge.'

I supposed they were going to gallop in, firing their Colts, but no, they had a true Texan gesture up their sleeves, one that I could never have imagined. What they did was clothe themselves in their most outrageous garments, no two alike, fluff out their beards, stow their Colts so they were always visible, don their big hats, and then take every imaginable position astride their horses, some riding fallen forward as if asleep, others facing sideways and ignoring their horses as they glared at the Mexicans crowding the sides of the streets. Eight or nine, including Panther with red flowers in his hair, sat backwards, facing the tails of their horses and looking very serious as if that was the way they always rode.

No Ranger spoke. They just came into the city, announcing with their brazen behavior that they were now in Mexico City and that the town was under their control. Los Tejanos Sangrientes, the local people who have heard of their exploits call them, and one incident during the entry gave support to this name. A daring pickpocket, believing backward-riding Panther to be asleep, which he feigned to be, deftly reached up and filched the colorful handkerchief that some Rangers wear about their necks. Without making any protest, or even moving unusually, Panther unlimbered his Colts, shot the thief in the back, rode over, leaned way down, recovered his neckerchief, retied it about his throat, and rode on. Believe me, the streets cleared. The Texans were in town.

Colonel Cobb did not write his brother about the dreadful incident of 13 February 1848, nor did Harry Saxon report it to New York, for it was too disgraceful to record; indeed, it was later characterized as one of the least explicable of American military exploits. On that afternoon a gang of knife-wielding thieves caught a Ranger named Adam Allsens alone in an unsavory corner of the city. He apparently did nothing to provoke them, and even when they began to assault him he allowed them to have his neckerchief and his hat, for he realized that he could not fight his way clear from so large a mob. Encouraged by their initial success, they began to stab at him so viciously that he fell to the street, almost dead.

When Otto Macnab and two others came to his rescue, they found him in pitiful shape, one deep cut across his chest having exposed his heart, which beat visibly while they carried his failing body to headquarters. Eighteen or nineteen Rangers watched him die; they actually saw his heart begin to falter and then stop. At supper than night Macnab had to leave the table.

Toward ten the next night, when the streets of the capital were crowded, Panther Komax began quietly circulating among the Rangers, and with no one speaking or making any kind of commitment, men like Macnab, acting individually,

763

started leaving the mess hall. A short time later, Harry Saxon entered the hall and asked: 'Where's everyone?' but no one offered a sensible answer. He therefore reported to Colonel Cobb: 'I think something's amiss. Your men were extremely silent at supper.'

'They feel the loss of Allsens,' Cobb said, offering Saxon both a cigar and a shot of whiskey. The two men were talking amiably about the favorable terms of the peace treaty when Saxon thought he heard distant gunfire.

'Could that be any of your men firing?'

'Certainly not,' Cobb said warily. 'They would not be firing at night.'

At about eleven the firing increased in volume, and now Saxon cried: 'That could come only from Colts!' but Cobb assured him: 'It's that company of Horse Marines, practicing.'

'Why would they practice at night?'

'You never know.'

But now the firing drew so close that any military man would have to know it came from repeating revolvers, and both Cobb and Saxon ran out into the night, but at this point the shooting had stopped.

At breakfast no Ranger said anything about the night firing, but at about midmorning Harry Saxon visited the Mexican police, who showed him the wooden litters on which it was their custom to collect dead bodies found in alleyways at dawn, and on a dozen of them were piled some fifty corpses. When Saxon inquired what had happened, an officer explained: 'The Rangers took their revenge,' and fifty-three bodies were counted out for him – pimps, pickpockets, paid murderers, scoundrels, plain citizens, all shot at random – and some had apparently taken three or four shots right in the face, for the big Colts bullets had blown their heads apart.

All day Saxon tried to piece together what had happened, but no one would tell him that a band of some dozen Rangers, led by Panther Komax, had roamed quietly through the back alleyways of the city, through the slums and the red-light districts, and had carefully executed anyone who even looked as if he might have wielded a knife on Adam Allsens.

In the late afternoon Saxon went to the morgue, where he saw an additional eighty dead Mexicans, and he noticed that in the capital the Rangers were molested no more.

Photographer Harry Saxon took two more daguerreotypes of historic interest. One showed three fighting men, unposed and beautifully positioned against the background of Popocatépetl: Colonel Cobb – stiff, proper in his most imposing uniform – talking with Komax and Macnab, who were dressed like a pair of complete degenerates.

The other picture was more carefully posed, for it had been taken only after sustained negotiation. It depicted the leadership of the Mexican side, General Antonio López de Santa Anna in full regalia with at least eight big medals, accompanied by his guerrilla leader Benito Garza, jungle-thin and glaring behind his huge mustaches. The text that Saxon submitted to accompany his two splendid pictures explained how they were related and summarized the ending of this strange war:

> Your correspondent was privileged to participate in the final stages of the Mexican War. Hearing that General Santa Anna, a major cause of the war and a principal agent of its loss, was being sent into exile in disgrace, I dogged the Mexican headquarters, for an opportunity to capture a picture of this colorful man. I failed.
>
> Returning to the Texas Rangers, whom I had accompanied in their campaign against the guerrillas, I found their leader and two of their most colorful members in deep conversation, and I took a chance that they would remain relatively stationary and allow me to use my camera. They did, but at the same time they talked loud enough for me to hear their conversation, which I report faithfully:
>
> COBB: 'It's true. Santa Anna passes through our lines tomorrow at eight.'
>
> KOMAX: 'Let's shoot him.'
>
> COBB: 'None of that! He has a safe-conduct from General Scott.'
>
> KOMAX: 'Santy Anny is a butcher. Let's give him a taste of butcherin'.'
>
> COBB: 'Macnab, can you reason with this wild man?'
>
> KOMAX: 'You ain't never drawed a bean outen a clay pot. You ain't never seen your father speared down in cold blood,

while he was a honorable prisoner.'

COBB: 'Gentlemen of Texas, we've been through a great deal together . . .'

KOMAX: 'You had me given "The Rogue's March."' '

COBB: 'And I'd do it again tomorrow, but here in the south I've learned what a heroic group of men you are. I have never served with better. I would ride anywhere on earth, up to the face of any cannon . . .' (At this point his voice broke and for almost a minute he stared at the ground.) 'Men, do not sully a splendid reputation. If you assault your defeated enemy . . .' (His voice broke again and, angry at himself, he spoke rapidly.) 'Hell, he's your prisoner. He's unarmed. Do you want to be regarded by all the civilized world as lacking in honor? What are you, anyway, a bunch of miserable bastards? Do you really want to befoul the fair name of Texas? Do you want to stand in shame before the world?'

KOMAX: 'We'll think about that.'

Unable to extract a promise, Cobb drew himself to full height, saluted, and left his men for what I believe was the last time. His final words to Macnab and Komax which I heard as he passed me were: 'Don't be a pair of Texas sons-a-bitches.' He left us, head high, eyes straight ahead, his beautiful uniform without one misplaced seam.

It was a bright morning when General Antonio López de Santa Anna prepared to ride through the gauntlet of American soldiers.

In the open carriage, pulled by four horses and managed by two drivers fore and two uniformed outriders standing aft, the newly wedded general and his child bride would ride, accompanied by Benito Garza and Lucha López. As Garza stepped into the carriage he blurted out: 'Mi General, the heart of Mexico goes with you into exile.'

Hands clasped about his bejeweled sword to mask their trembling, Santa Anna gave the order 'Forward!' – then stared straight ahead. Silently he passed between the double file of Rangers standing less than five feet from him on each side. He glanced at none of them, because he knew that they had sworn to kill him and he could not guess at what signal they would strike.

766

Each Ranger looked hard at him, each conveyed the bitterness of this extraordinary moment, but none looked with more strangled emotions than their liaison-colonel, Persifer Cobb: 'God, let this moment pass. Let them keep their big mouths shut.'

Otto Macnab stared at Santa Anna as if to engrave the Mexican's features on his memory, then, turning his head, stiffened with shock when he saw who was sitting opposite the general. It was Benito Garza, and for a long moment the two old friends, the two perpetual adversaries, looked into each other's eyes – Garza's ebony-black, Macnab's cerulean-blue – and the respect, the hatred and the confusion glowed. Neither man made a gesture of recognition. For some reason the carriage hesitated, and the moment of meeting was agonizingly prolonged.

Then the carriage moved forward again. Each man kept his head turned toward the other until dust intervened. The war had ended.

It was a perplexing war, which few had welcomed except President Polk and the expansionists, and its significance is revealed only when viewed from three aspects.

First, it was an inescapable prolongation of the 1836 Texas revolution. Since Mexican leadership had never accepted the loss of territory resulting from that struggle, and since Mexico had as many superpatriots as Texas, it was inevitable that continued attempts would be made to recapture the lost province. Arrival of United States power put a stop to such plotting.

Second, the war was an application of the new slogan of Manifest Destiny. American patriots had looked at the map and proclaimed almost automatically: 'We must control this continent from the Atlantic to the Pacific.' Texas dreamers could cry: 'We must have everything down to the Isthmus of Panama,' and frenzied New Englanders could and did shout for the annexation of Canada, even launching abortive military campaigns to achieve that worthy purpose. The successful outcome of the Mexican War meant that the Pacific coast was secured, and a good thing, in terms of geography at least, was accomplished.

Third, the war had a powerful psychological effect on the new state of Texas. It was exerted not on Texas itself, for the war really had only a limited influence internally: it was fought primarily by men and officers from the twenty-seven other states in the Union and it served as a training ground for the greater War Between the States of 1861–1865, which lurched ever closer. The names of the younger officers who had fought under Taylor and Scott sound like a roll call to military greatness: Robert E. Lee, Ulysses S. Grant, Braxton Bragg, George Gordon Meade, Albert Sidney Johnston, Jubal Early, William Tecumseh Sherman, P.G.T. Beauregard, Joseph E. Johnson, James Longstreet, George B. McClellan, and the two popular heroes Stonewall Jackson and Fighting Joe Hooker.

It also strengthened the American propensity for electing military heroes to the presidency, four of the American officers in this war attaining that high office – Taylor, Grant, Jefferson Davis, Franklin Pierce – with three others, Scott, Fremont and McClellan, trying. Three Mexican officers also attained the presidency of their nation, including the ineffable Santa Anna, who would be summoned back from exile to lead his country once more.

If the war had little effect in Texas in tangible terms, how was its significance for the state manifested? Thanks to the newspaper stories of reporters like Harry Saxon and the brilliantly colored lithographs of Currier and Ives, the rest of the nation acquired a romantic and often favorable view of their new state. The Texas Ranger became a legendary figure, composed partly of Panther Komax and his undisciplined ways, partly of Otto Macnab and his merciless efficiency. A deluge of lurid penny-thrillers recounted the adventures of Davy Crockett, Jim Bowie and the Texas Rangers. Tall stories were told about life in Texas decades before most people had heard the word *cowboy* or ever a longhorned steer was driven north.

Of course, not every soldier who served in Texas returned home singing its praises. One Pennsylvania volunteer said: 'If I was ordered back to Texas, I'd cut my throat.' A general said later: 'If I owned Hell and Texas, I would rent out Texas and live in Hell.' Perhaps Colonel Persifer Cobb of Edisto Island, South Carolina, said it with deepest feeling: 'I am often haunted by nightmares. I'm back in Texas trying to discipline thirty-six Rangers.'

The war left one indelible heritage: it intensified the animosity that already existed between Texans and Mexicans. The savage behavior of the Rangers in both the Monterrey area and Mexico City established them nationally as Los Tejanos Sangrientes, and along the Rio Grande as Los Rinches.

War often produces unexpected transformations of social life, and this one gave America and Texas each an unusual boon. During negotiations with Santa Anna, that wily gentleman told a group of American businessmen: 'When I was on duty in Yucatán, I came upon a product which I am sure will make one of you rich. It was called chicle.' And thus chewing gum was introduced into the States. Texas received a gift almost as far-reaching, for in one of Harry Saxon's finest daguerreotypes, he caught the birth of a legend. Panther Komax, hairy as ever, is shown with a barefoot Mexican peon kneeling at his feet. The accompanying story read:

I must confess that I posed this picture the morning after the event occurred. When Colonel Cobb and I went out on the night of the great killings in Mexico City we were so late that we discovered nothing, so we returned to quarters, but shortly thereafter I returned to the streets, suspecting that something of moment was occurring, and I came upon the tail end of the slaughter. Komax and his partner Otto Macnab had been shooting anyone in sight, but they ran out of ammunition. Seeing this disreputable peon who looked as if he might have been one of the murderers of Allsens, Macnab was preparing to cut the man's throat when the latter broke loose, fell to the ground, and began grabbing at Komax's boot.

From prolonged use, the boot was in sad repair, and this the groveling man indicated, tugging at it and informing us in some way that he, the peon, was a bootmaker, and that given the proper tools, he could mend that boot. Macnab, who spoke excellent Spanish, put away his knife and interrogated the man. Yes, he carried the universal name Juan Hernández. Yes, he was a bootmaker and a good one.

Yes, he could either mend Komax's boot or make him one much better.

Komax, catching the drift, raised the man to his feet and asked, through Macnab: 'Can you make a boot as good as this?' and Hernández broke into nervous laughter: 'If I made a boot that bad, my mother would beat me.' In this way, on a night of carnage and at the very point of death, my company of Texas Rangers acquired a bootmaker who now marches with us, tending our shoes.

When the Rangers left their transport at Indianola, that thriving harbor on Matagorda Bay, Otto stayed three days with his brother-in-law, Theo Allerkamp; then, on a horse provided by Theo, he started on the long ride to Fredericksburg.

His spirits rose as he neared Austin, where he spent two days verifying title to his acreage at Fredericksburg. With reassuring documents in his pocket he started westward, and for the first time in his life took time to appreciate the miracle of a luxuriant Texas spring, not the ordinary blossoming of trees at Victoria, or the sparse flowers along the Brazos, or that wilderness of minute flowerlets in the Nueces desert, but the unbelievable expanse of two distinct flowers, one a rich blue, the other a reddish gold. Sometimes they covered entire fields: And not little fields, either. Look at them! How many acres?

He was staring at a spread of flowers along the banks of the Colorado River, so many and in such dazzling array that they almost blinded him. Here rose the wonderful bluebonnets of Texas, each stem ending in a sturdy pyramid of delightful blue flowers. Intermixed with them was the only other flower that could make the blue stand out, the Indian paintbrush in burnt orange. Blue and red-orange, what a surprising combination, made even more vibrant by the fact that both flowers bore at their apex a fleck of white, so that the field pulsated with beauty. So vast it was in extent that Otto could scarcely believe that so many flowers, each its own masterpiece, could combine to create a picture of such harmony. 'Red, white and blue,' he murmured. 'What a flag.'

But then he reached the spot where the Pedernales River joined the Colorado, and now he knew he was approaching his destination, and as he climbed a slight rise he was confronted by a field not of forty acres or of eighty, but of limitless extent, and it was solid bluebonnet and paintbrush, a benediction of nature so prodigal that he could only halt and gaze. Then slowly he turned his horse and rode toward home.

Benito Garza also went home, but to a tormented scene. Exhausted from long days of guerrilla warfare, he left Vera Cruz with his wife and three commandeered horses as weary of battle as their riders. Painfully the couple made their way through the jungle and up to the altiplano, where they witnessed the desolation of Avila and the other ruins wrought by the war.

They felt a bleeding sorrow for their country, for wherever they looked they saw the costs of defeat: the punished villages in which they had sometimes hidden; the horribly wounded men striving to master new crutches; children with distended bellies; the ugly penalties paid by those who had obeyed the rash decrees of Santa Anna.

During the first eighteen days of this bleak pilgrimage Benito refused to place the blame upon his hero: 'No! Don't say that, Lucha. Santa Anna had a fine plan, but it fell astray.'

'His plans always fell astray.'

'He'll come back, I promise you. He'll land at Vera Cruz, just as before, except that this time . . .'

At the start of the third week, when the Garzas learned from friends in Mexico City how tremendous the loss of territory was to be – more than half the country turned over to the norteamericanos – he began to admit that his hero had made fearful errors: 'He could have engineered it better. Lose Tejas, yes. But never should he have given up so much more.'

When they reached San Luis Potosí they heard a constant wail of grief, and now the recriminations against Santa Anna became vociferous, for this region contained many who had fought at Buena Vista, and who knew that Santa Anna had fled the battlefield when victory was at hand. As Lucha said: 'That last night María and I crept out on scout while you were meeting with Santa Anna. Secretly, along the shoulder of the hill, we could see that the yanquis were retreating in disarray. But when we returned we were not allowed to report. Women were not welcomed in that tent.'

How tragic the defeat was! The litany of lost lands carried its own sorrow, never to be erased from the mexicano soul: 'Tejas, Nuevo México, Arizona, California, qué lástima, qué dolor!' The names formed a rosary of despair, the heart of Mexico torn away and bleeding.

As the Garzas approached the Rio Grande before turning east toward Matamoros, they paused to look across the river into the still-contested Nueces Strip, and resting in their saddles, they reached brutal conclusions: 'Santa Anna failed us. In the present leadership there is no hope. Mexico will never know peace, and there is no chance of turning back the norteamericanos.' But in the depth of their despair they saw a chance for personal salvation, and Benito, his mustaches dark in the blazing sunlight, phrased their oath: 'The yanquis who try to steal that Strip from us, they'll never know a night of security. Their cattle will never graze in peace. By God, Lucha, they'll pay a terrible price for their arrogance. Promise me you'll never surrender.'

'I promise.'

. . . Task Force

I believe that all of us, older members and youthful staff alike, looked forward with greater eagerness to our April meeting than to any before. It was to be held in Alpine, an authentic frontier town of some six thousand population situated in the heart of rugged ranch country in West Texas. To the south, along the Rio Grande, lies remote Big Bend National Park with its peaks and canyons, an over-grazed semi-desert in 1944, when it was taken into the park system, but now a miraculously recovered primitive wilderness. To the north, rising as if to protect it, are the Guadalupes, tallest mountains in Texas, and Fort Davis, best restored of the old Texas battle stations.

Alpine stands at an altitude of 4,485 feet, blizzardlike in winter, ninety degrees in summer, and its charm lies in its successful preservation of old-time ways. It serves as the seat of Brewster County, an almost unpopulated area about the size of Rhode Island and Connecticut combined, and is surrounded by ranches of staggering size.

'Out here, ma'am,' said the tour driver, 'we never state the size in acres. It's sections. The Baker Ranch you're asking about, it has fifty-five sections, that's better'n thirty-five thousand acres. Middlin' size, I'd say, because it takes a hundred and fifty acres of that barren land to feed one unit . . . A unit, ma'am, is a cow and a calf, with hopefully another calf on the way. So the Bakers, they cain't run but two hundred-odd cows on their ranch, and that's why we classify it middlin'.'

Ransom Rusk had provided the planes to fly us to Alpine, and as we drove from the little airport we saw signs which prepared us for what was to be one of our best sessions: REAL OIL PAINTINGS $3.50 AND UP and THIS MOTEL IS RUN BY HONEST NATIVE-BORN TEXANS.

Our meetings were to be held at Sul Ross University, a handsome collection of red-brick buildings perched on the side of a hill, and there a real surprise awaited us, for we were met by a short, white-haired, sparkling-eyed man in his sixties whose face positively glowed with enthusiasm: 'I'm Professor Mark Berninghaus, Texas history, and we'll pile right into these two ranch wagons.' He would drive the lead car, he said, which the Task Force members would share. Then he introduced us to a young man of imposing build wearing a big Stetson: 'This is Texas Ranger Cletus Macnab, and if you know your frontier history, you'll remember that one of his ancestors was the legendary Ranger Otto Macnab. And another was the equally famous Oscar Macnab, also a Ranger.'

Macnab, a handsome young fellow in a pearl-gray whipcord suit, bowed to us but did not remove his hat. To the girl from SMU who had arranged this session he said: 'Staff'll ride with me,' and to the rest of us he said: 'I've provided maps of the region we'll be traveling,' and with that, we headed south along Route 69 to the twin border towns of Polk on the American side and Carlota on the Mexican. It was a journey of eighty miles through absolutely empty land – not even a filling station – but one which, under the loving tutelage of Professor Berninghaus, provided us with an intimate glimpse of a Texas that few visitors ever get to see.

'I want you to notice the vegetation, and how it changes as we drop down to the Rio Grande, two thousand feet lower in elevation.' Then he began an instruction which was shared by intercom with the staff in the following car: 'Look at the bleakness of land, only one shrub to an area the size of a football field.' When we studied the barren earth we saw at first only a reddish, rocky soil, but as our eyes grew accustomed to the vast empty space and the arching blue sky, cloudless and perfect, we began to see lone bushlike plants clinging to the arid earth. They were dark green and had many narrow leaves that branched out like untended hair, forming beautiful globes: 'Sotol, one of the major plants of our barren plains. Remember how green it is, because later I'll provide you with a surprise.'

Imperceptibly the landscape changed – worsened, in my opinion – until we were in the heart of a real desert, but not the sandy kind featured in Grade B movies: 'We call this the Chihuahuan Desert, eight hundred miles, maybe, north and south, two hundred east to west. And here we have one of its characteristic plants.' He pointed to a remarkable growth, a tall, reedy plant composed of forty or fifty slender whips, each bearing at its tip a cluster of brilliant red flowerlets. The ocotillo, which looked as if it had been thrown together helter-skelter, was appropriate to its bleak surroundings, for only a plant so thin, so conservative of water, could have survived here.

'Look!' Miss Cobb cried as we descended into a protected valley. 'What can that be?' It was an imposing plant of the desert, a low-growing cluster of heavy brownish leaves, quite undistinguished, except that from its middle rose a thick stem high in the air, topped by clusters of beautiful gold-white flowers that seemed to fill the blue sky.

'A special yucca,' Berninghaus said over his intercom. 'But hold your applause till we climb out of this depression. Because then you're going to see what many never see. A forest of yucca . . . many species . . . beautiful.'

I think we watched with a sense of disbelief, for we could not associate this tremendous desert with a beauty as we were accustomed to know it, but as we reached the crest of a small rise we saw spreading off to our right a vision of Texas that would never be erased; it was so different, so grandiose that it seemed to represent the state in its original form before intrusions like Houston and Dallas.

It was a small forest of three kinds of yucca: the noble ones we'd already seen, a more beautiful version called Spanish Dagger, and a veritable tree with a sturdy jagged trunk, a cluster of leaves well above the ground, and a glorious collection of white flowers rising high into the air. The sight was so compelling that several of us in the lead car said: 'Let's stop!' And when we looked back we saw that Ranger Macnab had already done so in order that his young passengers might see these splendid plants.

They had a strange effect on me. I compared them to the delicate garden flowers I'd known when a student in England, and with the carefully cultivated flowers in Geneva. Obviously they were flowers, but big and brutal and self-protective against the rainless wind. Compared to the pansy or the tulip, they were gross; one handful of their heavy blooms at the end of a stalk seemed larger than a garden of English flowers or a bed of Boston blooms. They were frightening in the awkwardness of their limbs, unkempt in the way their trunks shed, and when Miss Cobb insisted upon leaving her ranch wagon to inspect one of the nearer yuccas, she quickly returned, for a rattlesnake lay coiled at its base.

How beautiful they were, those yuccas of the Chihuahuan Desert, how Texan. As we moved past their tremendous forms we carried with us a new understanding of the West, that bleak and barren land which offered so many hidden rewards.

But now we were descending to regions with a much different vegetation, and Berninghaus assured us: 'Flowers that look like flowers. See down there.'

He was pointing to one of the strangest flowers I had ever seen, or rather, to a cluster of some hundred individual flowers congregated into a round cactuslike globe more than four feet in diameter. When I looked closely I saw that each plant forming the globe had powerful thorns that interlocked with those of other plants to make the globe impenetrable. These proved that the thing was a cactus, but the blizzard of delicate purple flowers proved that it was also a luxuriant bouquet. However, the real surprise was to come: 'In the autumn each of these flowers produces a spiny fruit, brilliant in color. When you peel away the skin you find a delicious treat. Tastes like strawberries.'

'What's it called?' one of the students in the rear asked, and Berninghaus said: 'Strawberry cactus.'

And then, at the lower levels, we came upon the plant that

affected me most deeply; I saw it first alongside the road, a low gray woody bush with tiny five-thorned leaves. I took it for a weed, but Berninghaus said: 'Let's stop and inspect it.' He broke off a branch to show that the interior wood was one of the most vivid yellows in nature: 'The Indians prized it for coloring their blankets,' and I supposed that this completed the story, but he continued: 'It's one of our best shrubs, quite precious, really.'

'What's it called?' I asked, and he said: 'Cenizo, but some spell it with a final *a*. Its more effective name, Barometer Bush.'

'Why?'

'If we pass a spot that's had some recent rain, you'll see why,' and before long we came to such a place, and there a stretch of cenizo had burst into soft, gentle gray-purple flowers. They were like miniature lilacs beside some Illinois farmhouse, or dusty asters in a Pennsylvania field; they spoke of home and evening firesides. As I looked down at them, imagining how joyously they must have been greeted by Indians who sought their brilliant dye, I felt as if Texas had somehow reached out to embrace me, to protect me from the barrenness of this western land, and I could understand how Berninghaus had come here from his doctorate at Chicago and decided after one week that this would be his home for life. We would have known only half of Texas had we missed Alpine.

Just as I was beginning to feel sentimental about the plant, Berninghaus threw in one of those obiter dicta which can make travel with a scholar so rewarding: 'This is the flower, of course, which made Zane Grey immortal. But imagine how flat his title would have sounded had he called the plant by its proper Spanish name, *Riders of the Purple Cenizo.*'

Now the talk turned to what Texas seemed to like best: numbers of staggering dimension. 'We're threading along the great Ramsdale Ranch, six hundred thousand acres.' Or, 'Over there, reaching twenty miles, is the Falstaff Ranch, nearly as big as Rhode Island and filled with deer and javelinas and mountain lions.' But when I asked who owned these ranches, I was invariably told: 'Fellow from Houston who struck it big in oil,' and I began to realize that no matter how far one traveled from the oil fields of Texas, the pervasive power of petroleum remained.

When we stopped for cold drinks at Polk, the forlorn American settlement, Ranger Macnab informed us: 'We'll cross into Carlota so you can see what a Mexican border town can sometimes be, but I must in fairness warn you that there'll be other settlements of larger size which are much better. This one is pathetic.'

When we saw it, we agreed. Four times as large as Polk, it was a hundred times more desolate. It was as if the centuries had hesitated, waiting for some revolutionary invasion to burn down the walls. The fabulous wealth of Mexico had not penetrated here, and the streets were mean and forbidding. Adobe houses crumbled and open sewers went untended. Stores were adorned with broken bottles and old cars rusted at the crossroads. The railway station had lost its tiles and the policemen guarding it wore outmoded and tattered uniforms.

Carlota, named in honor of a European empress who had gone mad as her husband tried to govern Mexico, wasted in the blazing sunlight, and we were content to go back across the bridge to Polk. At first sight we had not rated the American town favorably, but now it seemed a beacon of civilization. Ransom Rusk, who had shown in previous meetings that he disapproved of Mexican ways and also of Mexicans living in Texas, said as we left Carlota: 'Now I can understand why they want to slip into the United States. I would if I had to live over there.'

Our town ranch wagons now headed northwest along the Rio Grande, passing an adobe fort long vacated and the dusty town of Presidio, famed for its appalling summer temperatures. Television viewers grew familiar with the refrain: 'Hottest spot in the nation today, Presidio, Texas, 114 degrees Fahrenheit.'

Then we passed through empty land leading to nowhere, and when we paused to drink from our thermos I asked: 'Where are we going now?' The staff members smiled, and Berninghaus said: 'We've a few more surprises for you.'

I could not imagine what this forbidding land could hold as a surprise, but at the end of the paved road, which must have been in one of the loneliest and gloomiest sections of Texas, we came upon a minute village. Ruidosa, with six houses and a crumbling low Spanish mission, the Sacred Heart, built like a fort and now moldering in the desert sun. When I saw it I said

777

over the intercom: 'At our first meeting the governor said we were to probe into every nook and cranny of the state. This is one of the crannies.'

It still retained its roof, though probably not for much longer, and its facade was sturdy, with a wooden entrance that must often have been barricaded when the Apache attacked. It was an honorable relic, testifying to the courage of the missionaries who had stubbornly tried to subdue this part of Texas.

For me the most rewarding segment of the trip now began, for our cars skirted the mission ruins to pick up a trail which appeared on none of our maps. It wound its way due north for eighteen miles along the Rio Grande, so that whenever we looked to our left we saw the mountains of Mexico. Over the intercom we heard our young woman from SMU ask Ranger Macnab: 'Tell us the truth. Does this trail lead anywhere, or is this a kidnaping?' and he replied: 'We're heading for the end of the world.'

When we stopped we found ourselves in the adobe village of Candelaria, where the pretensions of Texas and the United States ended, for this was one of the loneliest and most inaccessible settlements along the southern border, with people living much as they had in the previous century.

But to me it was compelling, a view of Texas that few ever saw, and my heart beat faster when Berninghaus said: 'Imagine, an international border, and from here, for more than a hundred miles, nothing.' But what delighted our staff was the fact that when we strolled down the the Rio Grande, that river with the magical name, it was so narrow and shallow that a tattered rope-and-wire suspension bridge sufficed to cross it. And as we looked a pantalooned workman from Mexico carrying a battered gasoline tin with handles came across its swaying planks to purchase some commodity in Candelaria.

'Behold the commerce of great empires!' Berninghaus cried, and we stood silent, confused by the hugeness of Texas and the meanness of its historic river. I think we were all gratified when Berninghaus explained the anomaly: 'We Americans in New Mexico and Texas take so much water out of the Rio Grande for irrigation that if this little stream were allowed to run toward the Gulf in this condition, it would simply disappear. But at a spot near Presidio, a large Mexican river joins up, the Rio Conchos. So the fabled Rio Grande, which we admire so much downstream, should more accurately be called the Conchos. It's mostly Mexican.'

Then came a clatter from the town, and he said: 'I think they've arrived,' and when we returned to our cars we found that students from Sul Ross had brought a picnic lunch for us, and had spread it on blankets under a tree.

'There will be no speeches,' Berninghaus assured us. 'I wanted you to imagine yourselves as Spanish immigrants coming here to settle, four hundred years ago. I wanted you to see the great empty Texas that they saw.'

On the trip back, following an unmarked trail through mountains and canyons, I noticed that Berninghaus maintained a sharp lookout, and finally he announced: 'If I remember correctly, it's in the next valley that our little cheerleaders climb the hillside,' and when we reached the crest from which we could look across to the opposite hill we saw a bewitching sight, for the entire hill from creek to crest was covered with something I could not identify.

'Look at them, the golden leaves at the bottom, the beautiful green at the top. And tell me what they are if they aren't a gaggle of girl cheerleaders in the stadium on a bright autumn day.'

From a distance, that's what they were, a host of girls in the green-and-gold of their team, scattered at random over a sloping field of some fifty acres, as jaunty a performance as nature provided.

'What are they?' one of the students asked, and Berninghaus said: 'Sotols. Dead leaves golden at the foot, new leaves green at the top. I feel better about life whenever I enter this valley.'

So for sixty miles along a forsaken road we picked our way toward Marfa, one of the choice cattle towns of the West, with a flawless courthouse. There we turned east, and when we reached the outskirts of Alpine, to which most of us now wanted to move, we saw our third sign:

U.N. OUT OF U.S.
U.S. OUT OF TEXAS

779

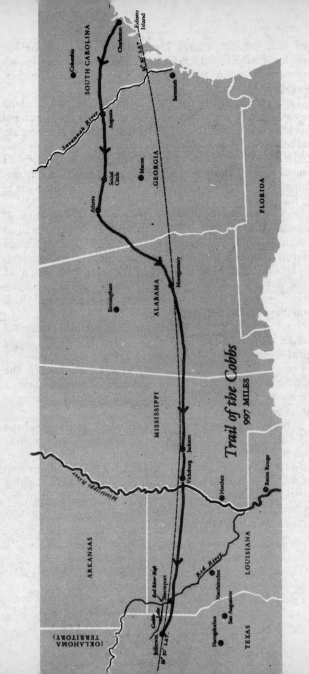

Trail of the Cobbs
997 MILES

IX

LOYALTIES

As soon as it was consonant with his understanding of military honor, Persifer Cobb resigned his commission in Vera Cruz, but when he submitted his papers to General Scott's aide, Brigadier Cavendish of Virginia, the latter tried to dissuade him: 'Colonel Cobb, since the days of Washington we've always had a Cobb among our leaders. We can't let you leave.'

'I will never again accept the humiliation I've had to suffer in this war. Deprived of a rightful command. Sentenced to work with those Texans.'

'Are you aware that we've sent your name up for promotion?'

'Too late.'

'You mean you won't accept it if it comes through?'

Cobb was polite but resolute: 'No, sir.' He thanked Cavendish for his concern and was about to leave when the brigadier pushed back his chair, rose, and took him by the arm: 'Perse, my dear friend . . .'

In the formal discussion it had been 'Colonel Cobb', as was proper, and this sudden switch to the familiar unnerved Persifer, who mumbled 'Yes, sir' with the respect he always accorded superior rank.

'Could we walk, perhaps?'

'Of course, sir.'

In the public park that fronted the sun-blinded Gulf of Campeche the two officers stared for some moments at that bleak fortress out in the bay, San Juan de Ulúa, where Mexican prisoners sentenced in Vera Cruz rotted in their dark dungeons. 'How would you like seven years in there?' Cavendish asked.

'I have much different plans.'

'Then you won't change your mind? You're definitely leaving?'

'I decided that two years ago . . . at least.'

'And I understand your bitterness. But do you understand why we cannot lose you?'

'I can think of no reason.'

'I can.' Very cautiously the Virginian looked about him, as if spies might have been planted even in this Mexican port city. Taking Cobb by the arm, he drew him closer and said in a conspiratorial whisper: 'Many of us are looking ahead.' Then, fearing that Cobb was not alert enough to have caught the signal, he continued: 'We're on a collision course.'

'Meaning?'

'Two irresistible forces – South, North.'

'You think . . .'

'I see it in signs everywhere. I read it in the papers. Even my family hints when they write.'

'Is it that bad?'

'Worse. The North will never stop its aggressive pressure, and if it worsens, as I'm sure it will, we'll have to leave the Union and that means . . .'

Cobb had not interrupted. The brigadier had hesitated because as a loyal officer he was loath to utter the word, so Cobb said it for him: 'War?'

'Inevitable. And that's why it's important to keep in uniform. Because when the moment of decision comes . . .'

Cobb, reluctant to contemplate another war so soon after finishing one he had found so distasteful, tried to end the conversation, but Cavendish, having parted the veil that hid the future, kept it boldly open: 'Each man in uniform will have to decide. Men like me, we'll fight for the South till snow covers Richmond sixty feet deep. Stupid bullies like some we know, they'll stay with the North. I suppose men like Robert Lee will, too, out of some sense of loyalty to West Point. But really able men like Jefferson Davis, Braxton Bragg, Albert Sidney Johnston, they'll give their lives to defend Southern rights. And you must be with us.'

'I'm still sending in my resignation,' Cobb said, and he returned to his quarters, where packing had to be completed before reporting to the waiting ship.

When he stepped ashore at New Orleans, a civilian, and saw the mountain of cotton bales ready for shipment to Liverpool, where world prices were set, he was eager to hurry back to his family plantation on Edisto Island and assume command of its cotton production. Prior to enrolling at the Point he had known a good deal about cotton, for the Cobb plantation had for many decades produced the best in the world: the famed Sea Island, with the longest fibers known and a black, shiny seed which could be easily picked clean even before the invention of the gin.

As soon as he had located a hotel and arranged for his journey northeast, he asked the way to the offices of a journal which his family had read since 1837 and to which cotton growers looked for guidance. When he introduced himself to the editor of *New Orleans Price Current*, a scholar from Mississippi, he was warmly greeted: 'A Cobb from Edisto. Never expected to see one in my office. You are most welcome, sir.'

'I'm returning home after military service and wanted to learn how things are going in the trade.'

'Never worse.'

'Do you mean it?'

The editor slid his yearly report across the desk, and before Cobb had finished the third paragraph he grasped the situation:

The commercial revolution which had prostrated credit in Great Britain, and which subsequently spread to nearly all parts of the Continent of Europe, and to the Indies, put a sudden check to our prosperous course ... A still more severe blow was given by the startling intelligence of a revolution in France, and the overthrow of the monarchy. This movement of the people in favor of popular rights rapidly spread to other countries of Europe, and in the tumultuous state of political affairs, commercial credit was completely overthrown and trade annihilated ...

All this produced a more rapid depreciation in the price of cotton than we remember ever to have witnessed. At Liverpool sales were made at lower rates than were ever before known for American cotton ... Many English mills simply shut down, while others were compelled to resort to part-time working ...

Cobb, feeling his mouth go dry, asked: 'How bad is it?' and the editor handed him the price report for Middling as sold at New

Orleans: 'Here's how bad it is.'

As Cobb took the paper he asked: 'What do you figure it costs to raise and deliver a pound of cotton these days?' and the expert replied: 'With care, seven cents.' When Cobb saw the record he felt dizzy: 3 September 1847, 12⅝¢ and a modest profit; 26 November, after the first flood of bad news, 7½¢, right at the no-profit level; 28 April 1848, when Europe was falling apart, 6¢, which meant a cash loss on each sale.

'Do you see any relief?' Cobb asked, and the editor pointed to his explanatory notes for this dismal year:

... The Royal Bank of Liverpool suspended business.

... Numerous business houses of great antiquity and reputation closed.

... Many contracts with American shippers voided without recourse.

... Forced abdication of King Louis Philippe from throne of France.

... All Europe in worst condition since 1789.

... Angry mobs of Chartists threaten the peace in England.

... Population of Ireland in an unruly mood.

'Surely,' Cobb protested, 'our marvelous victory in Mexico must have affected the market favorably,' but with his ruler the editor pointed to a minor note at the very end of his gloomy report: 'This shows how the rest of the world evaluated your war. "Our own war with Mexico was brought to a successful close by Mexico's cession of California &c. to the U.S."'

'What can be done?' Cobb asked.

'You long-staple Sea Island men, you don't have to worry.' He showed Cobb his summary: South Carolina short staple, 280,671 five-hundred-pound bales, 7 9/16 ¢; they lost a fortune on that. Sea Island long staple, 18,111 bales, much of it from Edisto; price held reasonably firm, 19½¢.

And there was the difference: short staple, eight cents; long staple, nineteen cents, and Edisto grew only the long. Other plantations, of course, would have grown Sea Island had their land permitted, but it did not, and they were condemned to growing the more difficult and less profitable sort.

'Haven't you a brother in Georgia who grows short?' the

editor asked, and Persifer smiled: 'A cousin. My father's brother became insulted over some fancied grievance years ago, about 1822 if I recall, and off he trundled to Georgia, predicting that he'd make a fortune. But of course he couldn't grow Sea Island up in those red hills. He was stuck with short, and he's never done too well with it.'

'Why didn't he return to Edisto?'

'When a Cobb leaves, he leaves.'

'Did you say you were leaving the army?'

'I did.'

'But in case of trouble ...' The editor paused exactly as Brigadier Cavendish had paused.

Cobb, who had refused to consider such a possibility in Vera Cruz, now responded as an honorable soldier would: 'If real trouble threatened the Union, of course I'd report. So would you.' A long silence ensued, and it was obvious that neither man wished to be the one to break it. Then the editor surprised Cobb by switching subject matter dramatically.

'Your cousin in Georgia should study this,' and he shoved a provisional report into Cobb's hands. 'I was going to print it in this year's summary, but I wanted to verify some of the amazing statistics.' And Cobb read:

AVERAGE YIELD PER ACRE (ACTUAL)
OF COTTON CROP IN NINE STATES

Florida	250 pounds
Tennessee	300 pounds
South Carolina	320 pounds
Georgia	500 pounds
Alabama	525 pounds
Louisiana	550 pounds
Mississippi	650 pounds
Arkansas	700 pounds
Texas	750 pounds

'Could these figures be real?' Cobb asked, astonished by that last line. 'We think so,' the editor said, 'but we're going to double certify. If they prove out, we'll print them. So you and your cousin both ought to move to Texas. Looks as if it's to be our major cotton state.'

When Cobb started to ridicule the idea, the editor returned to his gloomy summary, tapping it with his pen: 'The lesson, Cobb, is that cotton prospers, and you and I prosper, when things around the world are kept in order. Why would the French throw out a perfectly good king? Why would the damned Chartists raise trouble in England, along with those idiotic revolutionaries in the Germanies and the Austrian Empire? For that matter, you tell me why the abolitionists are allowed to rant and rave in this country?'

'They'd better not rant and rave in South Carolina.' In swift, inevitable steps Persifer Cobb had progressed from being against any war, to defending the Union in case of trouble, to championing the South.

'The world would be so much better off,' the editor said, 'if only people would remain content with things as they are. Tell me, in Texas did you hear any agitation against slavery?'

'In Texas I heard nothing except the buzz of mosquitoes.'

'I envy you that plantation on Edisto. One of the world's best.'

'I aim to keep it that way.'

Edisto Island was a low-lying paradise formed in the Atlantic Ocean by silt brought down the Edisto River, a meandering stream that wound its way from the higher lands of South Carolina. An irregular pentagon about ten miles long on the ocean side, the island's highest elevation was six feet and its dominant physical characteristic large groves of magnificent oak trees, some deciduous but most live, which were decorated with magnificent pendants of Spanish moss. Its fields were miraculously productive, with soil so soft and even that it could be plowed with a teaspoon.

About fifty white people lived on the island's great plantations, and fifteen hundred black slaves. Except for small family gardens and some acreage of rice, the only crop grown was Sea Island cotton: sown in March, ginned in September, shipped to Liverpool in Edisto ships in January.

Every white family who owned a plantation home on Edisto – handsome affairs, with white pillars supporting the porch – also maintained a grander home along The Battery in Charleston, twenty-four miles away. In that congenial city the spacious life of the Carolina planter unfolded, and Cobb was most eager to renew his acquaintance with it. Both his father and his wife would be in Charleston, and he longed to see them, but he felt it his duty to report first to the plantation, where his brother would be in charge.

He liked Somerset, four years younger than himself, and had felt no qualms about turning the plantation over to him when he enrolled at West Point. His letters from the Mexican War had testified to their continuing rapport – they were more like those of a friend than of an older brother – and he was impatient to see Sett, as the family called him.

He therefore ended his homeward journey at a road junction some twenty miles west of Charleston; here the Cobbs maintained a small shack in which lived an elderly slave whose duty it was to drive members of the family down the long road to the ferry that would carry them across to Edisto. This slave bore the extraordinary name of Diocletian, because an earlier Colonel Cobb had loved Roman history, believing the gentle-folk of the South to be the descendants of Romans. He had named all his house servants after the emperors, except his personal servant-butler-valet, whom he invariably called Suetonius, on the logical grounds that 'Suetonius was respon-sible for all we know about the first Caesars. He wrote the book. So you, Suetonius, damn your hide, are responsible for all the Caesars in this house.' He usually worked it so that he had twelve house servants, which permitted him to make the joke: 'My Suetonius and his Twelve Caesars.'

Diocletian, an artful one-time house slave who knew that his welfare depended upon keeping various masters pacified, created the impression of being deliriously happy at seeing the colonel home from the wars. 'Get dem horses!' he shouted at his sons. 'We gwine carry Gen'ral Cobb to de ferry!' But when he was alone with his aged wife he predicted: 'Ol' Stiff-and-Steady back with his big ideas. Don't look good for Somerset.'

Rapidly a buggy was prepared, and with Cobb holding the reins, he and Diocletian started the pleasant nine-mile ride to the ferry. As they rode, the slave spoke of events on the island, and since he had for some years served as a house servant, he could speak English rather well, but he was basically what was called a Gullah Nigger, and as such, used the lively, imaginative

787

Gullah language, Elizabethan English spiced with African Coast words. Since Cobb had learned it as a boy, he encouraged Diocletian to use it as they talked of familiar things:

'E tief um.'	*He stole it.*
'Ontel um shum.'	*Until I saw her.*
'Wuffuh um sha'ap?'	*Why is she so smart?*
'Hukkuh im farruh ent wot?'	*How come his father isn't worth much?*
'Um lak buckra bittle.'	*He likes white man's food.*
'Bumbye e gwine wedduh pontak Edisto.'	*By-and-by it's going to rain upon Edisto.*

But now, as they passed the interminable wetlands whose lazy waters and wind-blown reeds pleased Cobb, for he had not seen them in five years, Diocletian switched subjects, and as he spoke of Cobb affairs he used English: 'You wife, Miss Tessa Mae, she never better. Sett's wife, Miss Millicent, she not too well, two chir'ns now.'

'Boys, aren't they?'

'Boy 'n' a girl, bofe fine.'

Diocletian said that he himself had 'two gramchir'n, bofe fine.' When the buggy approached the ferry, he began to shout and snap the whip, which he had taken from Persifer, and in this way he roused the boatman, who also gave the impression of being delighted to see the colonel after such a long absence.

'How dem Mexicans?' he wanted to know. 'Dem Mexican womens, dey all dancey-dancey like dey say?'

The three men discussed the war, after which Diocletian bade his master farewell: 'We hopes you bees here long time, Colonel. Dis yere's you home.' In fluent Gullah, Persifer thanked the slave for the pleasant ride and immediately thereafter boarded the ferry, allowing its keeper to pole him across the shallow North Fork of the Edisto River.

Before the little craft landed, slaves on the island side had saddled a horse for the colonel, dispatching one boy on a mule to alert the big house that Persifer was about to appear after his long absence. Down the tree-lined roadway the boy sped, kicking his mule in the sides as he shouted to everyone he met:

'Colonel Cobb, he come home!'

It was about seven miles from the ferry landing to the gracious two-story white house in which Somerset Cobb, as plantation manager, lived with his wife Millicent and their two children, and as the ride ended, it became apparent that the messenger had spread his news effectively, for everyone inside the house, and from outlying work houses too, had crowded beside the long lane leading to the colonnaded porch, prepared to give him the kind of enthusiastic welcome he expected. Ten whites and about fifty blacks stood waving as he and his attendant cantered through the spacious gateway. Modestly but with no excessive show of subservience, the slave slowed his horse and stopped it by the side of the roadway while Persifer rode on ahead, wearing the uniform of his country but with no insignia marks to show that he had once been a colonel.

He stopped and gazed in surprise, for from the porch came someone he had expected to be in the more salubrious climate of Charleston. It was his wife, Tessa Mae, daughter of a leading Carolina family, a slim, self-possessed young woman who rarely said anything thoughtlessly, and for that reason commanded his attention as well as his affection. 'Darling,' he cried. 'How wonderful to see you!' Easily he swung his right leg free of the saddle, leaped to the ground and took her in his arms.

Over her shoulder he saw his brother, a bit heavier now but with the same manly appearance he remembered so well. He was dressed, Persifer was glad to see, in expensive boots from England; trim trousers, made to order by a Charleston tailor; an open-neck shirt, of good French cloth; and a soft beige scarf from Italy, tied loosely about his neck. He was a fine-looking fellow of thirty-one, rather retiring in disposition, who appeared to have managed plantations all his life and intended continuing. Although he was quiet, there was about him none of the softness which so frequently attacked second sons of planter families when they realized they would not inherit the family estate and life goals became indistinct. It was also apparent that he liked his older brother very much, and he now waited for a proper chance to show it.

'Somerset!' the colonel cried, moving on to his brother. 'I've thought of you and this house whenever I sent you a letter.'

'How wonderful they were!' Millicent Cobb interrupted as

789

she moved forward to receive an enthusiastic kiss. 'You should be a novelist, Persifer. I could see your Panther Komax coming at me through the woods.'

'That would be a very bad day for you, Lissa, when that one came at you.'

'Did he wear a panther cap?' the Cobb boy asked, and Persifer said: 'Indeed he did, and he smelled like a panther, too.'

Turning to his wife, he asked, 'And where are our children?' and she replied: 'At school. In Charleston.'

It was quickly agreed that the four older Cobbs would leave at once for Charleston to go to the great house on The Battery, and orders were sent to the plantation ferry – a much different one from the general ferry which Persifer had used to get to the island – to prepare the boat and the rowers for the delightful voyage to that golden city of the southern coast. But now Millicent, who seemed frail in everything but determination, put her foot down: 'We shall not go today. Persifer is tired, whether he realizes it or not, and we can go just as well in the morning.'

However, the brothers felt that servants should be sent ahead in a smaller boat to alert their father of his son's return, and Millicent saw nothing wrong with that: 'I'd have preferred a surprise, and so would Father, I judge. But let it be.'

Talk turned to cotton prices, and Persifer reported what the New Orleans editor had said about how adverse conditions in Europe affected them.

'What the German barons ought to do,' Persifer said, 'is line those agitators up and spread a little canister about.'

'Give them time, they will.'

They both thought it unfair for peasants in Europe and especially in Ireland to be causing disturbances which unsettled the Liverpool market, and Somerset was astounded when his brother informed him of the collapse of Liverpool's Royal Bank: 'Good God! Rioters tearing down a great bank! I was damned pleased, Persifer, when you told us how your Texans handled those rioters in Mexico City. What they need in Europe is about six regiments of Texas Rangers.'

'Please!' the colonel said. 'Don't send them anywhere. Not even to the Ottoman Empire.'

Later in the evening, when the brothers were alone, each realized that he should speak openly of the altered situation on the plantation now that Persifer had resigned his commission, but each was loath to broach this delicate question, so Persifer raised one of more general significance: 'In New Orleans men spoke openly ... well, not directly, but you knew what was on their minds. They spoke of a possible rupture between our oppressors in the North and ourselves. Have you heard any such talk, Sett?'

'There's been constant talk since I can remember. But only by the irresponsibles who seem to flourish in this state and Georgia. Men like you and me, we'd surrender many of our advantages if we broke with the North.'

'Have we any advantages left?'

'Cotton. Every day I live, every experience I have, proves anew that the rest of the world must have our cotton. Cotton is our shield.'

'Even when it can drop from twelve and five-eighths to ...? What price did you say our upland people got? Four cents plus? That's a two-thirds drop in three months.'

'And we'll see it back to twenty cents as soon as peace is regained and the mills resume weaving.' He leaned forward: 'If a man grows Sea Island, he worries far less, and we grow Sea Island.' On that reassuring note the brothers went to bed.

They rose early, walked down to the plantation landing, entered their long, sleek craft, its six slaves already in position, and started one of America's outstanding short voyages. When they left the pier they had a choice of two routes. They could head east and soon enter the Atlantic Ocean, where a rough thirty-mile sail would carry them to Charleston. Or they could head west and enter a fascinating inland passage that would take them to the same destination, except that on this route, protecting islands would hold off the Atlantic swells, making the voyage a sea-breeze delight.

If the brothers had been sailing alone, they would surely have taken the open-sea route for its challenge, but with their wives aboard, they chose the inland passage, moving through vast marshes until they saw above them the headland on which rested the beautiful homes and majestic trees of Charleston.

Now, with the wind gone, they dropped sail, and the slaves,

their back muscles glistening in the sun, leaned on the oars, their voices blending in a soft chantey as they moved the boat toward its docking place near The Battery:

> 'Miss Lucy, don't you bake him no cornbread,
> Don't you feed him like you done feed me.
> Miss Lucy, don't you dare bake him no cornbread
> Till I comes home wid your two possum.'

When they broke out of the narrow channel and into the glorious bay which made Charleston so distinctive, they could see dead ahead the glowering walls of Fort Sumter, unassailable on its rock; and while the sails were being hoisted again, Persifer told his listeners of San Juan de Ulúa, a comparable fortress set in another part of the same great ocean.

With deft moves the black helmsman brought the craft about and landed his four passengers on The Battery, one of the nation's majestic streets. It stood on a hill so low it scarcely merited its name, but so pleasingly high that any house atop it caught a breeze off the sea. The stately house was not positioned like those of any other American street; because a house was taxed according to how much of the precious Battery it took up, the Charleston mansions were not built with the long axis facing the sea, which would have been reasonable, but with the shortest end possible facing east and the longer sides running far back into the town.

'Charleston has always looked sideways at the world,' Persifer said as he saw once more those homes in whose pleasant gardens he had spent the better hours of his youth. There was the Masters mansion, in which he had courted Tessa Mae, and farther along, the Brooks house, where he and Somerset had gone so often to visit Millicent Brooks and her sister, Netty Lou; for almost a year it looked as if the two Cobb boys were going to marry the two Brooks girls, but then Netty Lou met a dashing boy home from Princeton, and Persifer had to settle for the Masters girl. Out on the great plantations and along The Battery it seemed as if a Charleston man did not marry a specific young lady on whom his fancy fell; he married the heiress to some other plantation, some other mansion along the seafront.

The Cobb mansion, which at the present had no girls to

marry off, but which soon would when Somerset's daughter matured, was, from the street, a modest red-brick structure of three stories, with two ordinary-looking windows on each floor but no door for entrance. A stranger to Charleston's ways, seeing this plain facade for the first time, would glean not the slightest indication of the quiet grandeur hidden behind the plain walls. But let him move slightly to the left and enter the beautiful wrought-iron gate, set between two very solid brick pillars, and he would come upon a fairyland of exquisite gardens, elegant marble statues from Italy and brick sidewalks wandering past fountains, all enclosed by the long, sweeping, iron-ornamented porch on the right and the high brick wall on the left.

The wall, about ten feet high, was a thing of extraordinary perfection, for its bricks were laid in charming patterns which teased the eye along its immense expanse, and it was finished at the top in graceful down-dipping curves whose ends rose to finials on which rested small marble urns. On a hot afternoon one could sit on the long porch sipping minted tea and study the variations in the wall as one might study a symphony or a painting.

The porch was the masterwork of this excellent house, for it ran almost thirty yards, was two stories high, and was so delicately proportioned, resting on its stately iron pillars, that it seemed to have floated into position. Wicker chairs, placed about round glass-covered tables, broke the long reach into congenial smaller units that could be comfortably utilized by any number of visitors from one to twenty. Flowers adorned the porch, some planted in beds along its front, some in filigreed iron pots hanging decorously from the posts, but its salient characteristic was its sense of ease, its promise of shade on a hot day, the glimpses it provided of the nearby bay, and its constant invitation to rest.

When the Cobb brothers came through the gate they saw, resting on this porch at one of the smaller enclaves, their father, Maximus Cobb, seventy-two years old, his two canes perched against an unused chair. White-haired, with a prim white goatee but no mustache, he was dressed wholly in white, from his shoes to the expensive white panama resting on a table which also held his mid-morning tea.

He did not rise to meet his sons, for to do so would have necessitated use of his canes, but he did hold out his hands to Persifer, holding on to his older son for some moments with obvious delight and love.

'Suetonius!' he called. 'Come see!' But Suetonius, a slave now in his late sixties and weighted down with dignity, did not appear. In his place came a moderately tall, handsome black man in his early thirties, very dark of skin, with close-cropped hair, flashing eyes and a constant smile that showed extremely white teeth. He was not amused by the life about him, for he was painfully aware of being a slave, but he did prefer easing each day along with a minimum of difficulty, and had found that the simplest way to accomplish this was to smile, no matter what absurdity was thrown at him. Now, although he spoke good English, he used the dialect expected of him: 'Suetonius, he workin' wid de cook.'

'Trajan!' Colonel Cobb cried as soon as he saw the graceful figure appear in the doorway, and the slave, having been forewarned by yesterday's messenger that the young master of the plantation was to arrive, smiled with genuine affection and stepped forward to clasp the extended hand.

Three years younger than Persifer, a year older than Somerset, Trajan had grown up with them, had played with them at wild games along the marshes of Edisto and, at their suggestion, been brought into the Charleston mansion and given a Roman name. He had always liked the boys, finding in them not a single mean streak that the young men of Charleston sometimes displayed in their treatment of blacks, and he had never quailed when one of them became momentarily angry in some game, shouting at him: 'You damned nigger! I'll break your kinky head.' When they had tried, he had fended them off with ease, knocking them about until everyone collapsed with laughter.

Under their tutelage he had dropped his Gullah to acquire proper English, and under his teaching they had learned Gullah, which helped them enormously in dealing with the field hands. He now looked approvingly at the almost emaciated body of his friend Persifer, so debonair in his military uniform, and cried, 'He come home!' These simple words, spoken so obviously from the heart, touched Persifer deeply, and he gripped his slave's hand more tightly.

Maximus Cobb felt, with some reason, that he had only a limited time to spend in any day – for he required long naps – or in the passage of life itself, so with no embarrassment he asked Trajan to tell Suetonius to have the slaves rearrange the porch and move four chairs near his. Then, when the slaves were gone and the two couples faced him, he launched right into the heart of the problem that faced the Cobbs: 'When our ancestors settled Edisto, English law required that family estates be handed intact to the eldest sons. In South Carolina that's no longer the law, but we Cobbs and other families of ancient repute still honor it. Just as my father turned the plantation over to me rather than to Septimus, so that I could perfect the Sea Island cotton which has made it flourish, so now it must go to Persifer, who will make the decisions that will enable it to prosper in the new decades.' He nodded to Persifer, who nodded back, taking at the same time Tessa Mae's hand in his.

'When responsibility was given me,' he said slowly, looking now at Somerset, 'my younger brother Septimus felt that a great wrong had been done, and as you know, he hied himself off to Georgia, a terrible self-banishment. I could never persuade him to return, and there he rotted, in the wilderness.' Tears of regret did not come to his eyes, but he did wipe his lashes, for he knew that tears might come at any moment.

'Somerset, I know this must be a difficult situation for you, because you had reason to suppose that your brother would spend his life in the military. That was not to be. He's home, and the responsibility becomes his. I know you'll accept it gracefully, and I do not want you to scuttle off to Georgia like your uncle Septimus. I beg you to stay and assist your brother in running our very large plantation. He needs your help, and so do I.'

Neither Somerset nor Millicent volunteered any response; from the time they received that letter, more than a year ago, in which Persifer first suggested that at the end of the year he was going to quit the service, they had known that this day of decision would inevitably be upon them, and they had often discussed it quietly between themselves, never letting Tessa Mae or the old man know how deeply concerned they were. They had even gone so far as to send Cousin Reuben in the hill country of Georgia a secret inquiry: 'What is the quality of land in your district? And how difficult is it to grow short staple?' He had replied enthusiastically – which they had to discount, because everything Reuben did was marked with disproportionate enthusiasm – that a man was a darned fool to waste his energy on worn-out Carolina plantations making three hundred pounds an acre when his good fields in Georgia were making five hundred and fifty. He had added a paragraph which bespoke ancient grudges:

A man is stupid, insanely stupid, to believe that he is somehow socially superior if he grows a few pounds of long-staple cotton with its easy black seed while his neighbor in Georgia grows an immense crop of short staple with its difficult green seed. The world of cotton is dominated by the short-staple men, and if you have any sense, you'll become one of us.

But such gnawing decisions were relegated to the shadows that evening when Maximus Cobb entertained the Charleston elite in his home by the sea. Now the big gates at the rear were thrown open: six slaves in blue livery guided the broughams and the phaetons as they deposited the plantation gentry at the long porch; Suetonius, in gorgeous attire suitable for a French palace, greeted each guest by title and name; and Trajan, in a similar garb, led them to the punch table for their beginning glass.

An orchestra played. Couples danced quietly both in the large room and on the porch. Candles in the glittering chandelier from Bohemia and refined whale oil in the lamps along the brocaded walls cast a soft light on the fine faces. Everyone seemed glad to have Persifer back home where he belonged.

The two Cobb boys, as they would always be called while their father lived, passed among the guests, treating each with lavish deference, aware that one day soon they must find husbands and wives for their children from the families here represented. No Cobb within memory had ever married anyone not from Charleston. But if the Cobbs had to be polite to the guests against the day when they would have to seek marriage alliances, so did the guests – especially those with smaller plantations – have to be especially attentive to the Cobbs, for their children would represent the best catches in the 1850s.

The evening was one of the most festive that the Cobb mansion had known in years, and it was capped when Maximus banged on the floor with one of his canes to announce: 'We welcome home our son Persifer, mentioned in dispatches from the various battlefields in Mexico. Tomorrow he resumes stewardship of our plantations, and we wish him well.' Glasses were raised; toasts to Persifer's success were drunk; and in every carriage that pulled out of the circular driveway at midnight, someone asked: 'And what will young Somerset do now?'

Young Somerset was the gentlemanly kind of man who would never challenge his brother's assumption of the Cobb plantations, but he was not allowed to surrender because his wife, Millicent, one of the sagest women in Charleston, would not. Under her coaching, he spent the closing months of 1848 outwardly calm, apparently preoccupied with the job of instructing Persifer in the complexities of the big plantation on Edisto, and inwardly contemplating a score of practical alternatives which Millicent kept placing before him.

'You must see, Sett,' she said with unwavering determination, 'we really have to leave. And I think it ought to be done before this year ends.'

'No, I'd never quit before the next crop is planted. But go we shall.'

They had six sensible choices, which Millicent reviewed whenever they talked, keeping them in strict order of preference: 'First, buy our own plantation near Charleston, but have we the money? Second, take over the Musgrave place, which their old people have suggested from time to time . . . not directly, of course, but they have intimated. Third, manage one of the great plantations, of which there seem to be many, but I wouldn't care for that, and I'm sure you wouldn't either. Fourth, with Persifer leaving the army, you could join, but it could only be in the militia, and you'd have to start so low. Fifth, join your cousin Reuben in Georgia, but that sounds so desolate after you've known Charleston. Sixth, pull up stakes and move to fresh new land, new friends in Mississippi.'

Unemotionally, and always willing to explore even the more distasteful alternatives, they analyzed the positives and negatives of each solution and found themselves on dead center, almost equally doubtful about each of the options. They were hindered in making a decision because they could obtain no clear understanding of how much money they controlled. Sett had a private bank account, of course, but it contained only eight thousand dollars; he had never received a wage and had no land of his own to sell. He had always assumed that when his father died, there would be ample cash to distribute between the two sons, but then again, there might not be, because a great plantation family like the Cobbs often had 'much land, many Nigras, no cash,' as the saying went.

But now another Cobb woman entered the debate, never openly, never betraying her plot to anyone but her husband in the secrecy of the night. It was Tessa Mae, daughter of a family that had prospered only because it adhered tenaciously to one rule: 'Get possession of a good plantation and never borrow money against it.' In the darkness she whispered: 'Persifer, I'm glad you chucked the army. I needed you here at home. We must do everything to make Sett and Lissa get out.'

'I wouldn't do anything . . .'

'Perse, it's them or us. Mark my words, if quiet Sett stays around long enough, he's going to lose that modest charm and become a real bastard.'

'Tessa!'

'Keep applying pressure on him. I'll work on Lissa. But let's get them out of here.'

In early 1849, Millicent saw that any continued co-occupancy of the Cobb plantations was impossible: 'Sett, that Tessa Mae's a wily witch. Three times now she's suggested in various clever ways that we might be moving to Georgia. And mealy-mouthed Persifer, so tall and proper, he throws barbs at you. I'm fed up. I want to hear from your father himself what your financial prospects are, and I want to hear it now.' So, much against her husband's wishes, she marched down to the jetty alone, climbed into the longboat, and had the six slaves take her to The Battery, where she clanged her pretty way through the gates and confronted Maximus as he sat on the porch.

798

'Somerset and I need to know what money arrangements we can expect, Father.'

The old man harrumphed. He had never discussed such matters with women, not even with his wife, one of the Radbourne girls. Now he equivocated: 'Well, with Edisto . . . our income from all that land . . . he has no cause to worry.'

'But if we wanted to purchase a plantation of our own . . .' Millicent said boldly.

'That would be foolish in the extreme, wouldn't it?'

'We don't think so,' she said bluntly.

'Well, I do,' and he would discuss the matter no further. He did invite her to stay for lunch, and though she was strongly disposed to reject the courtesy, because he was a lonely old man hungry for companionship, she did stay, but that was a mistake, for when the slaves were gone from the room she said bluntly: 'Father, you really must explain to Sett and me what our position is going to be . . .'

'When I die?'

'I didn't say that.'

'But you meant it.'

'I did not mean it. I meant that my husband is a grown man of thirty-two and you're treating him like a boy of thirteen.'

'Why do you need to know about money? Haven't you always been cared for?'

In a moment of anger she snapped: 'Because we might want to move to Georgia.' As soon as the words were out she regretted them, for at the reiteration of a name which had given him much grief he seemed to wilt, as if his long-absent brother, now dead, had thrown at him once more the word *Georgia*.

'You would go to Georgia?' He uttered the word as if it represented some leprous site denied the graciousness of Carolina, and Millicent was prepared to retract, but before she could do so, Trajan came in to clear the table, and it was at that moment, seeing this impeccable black man, that she thought: When we go we must take Trajan with us.

Upon her return to the house on Edisto, which they now shared with the Persifer Cobbs, she very quietly told Sett: 'Your father practically dismissed me. Would tell me nothing. On Edisto we're millionaires. On the streets of Charleston we're paupers. Now I want you to find out in exact dollars how much we have.'

When Somerset, as an obedient son, learned that his wife had actually revealed their conversations about going to Georgia, he was aghast, for he appreciated how deeply this must have hurt his father. Still, he had long realized that sooner or later the possibility of such a move must surface, and when Millicent's unemotional review of the situation ended, he concluded that perhaps she had accomplished something desirable in clearing the air. Next day they posted a letter to Cousin Reuben in Georgia, asking him to come down and give advice.

In such speculation, whether family or public, Sett remained so passive that some considered him slow, especially when his wife's opinions were so pertinent, but it was genteel reserve rather than lack of comprehension which prevented him from airing his opinions. So he allowed her to pose the options, Georgia or Mississippi, with her favoring the longer jump west and he the shorter. However, each was willing to adjust to the other's preference.

On a fine summery day in June, when the cotton was well established and hoed, Reuben Cobb and his wife, Petty Prue, each twenty-six years old and brimming with vigor induced by the Georgia uplands, roared into Charleston and pretty well blew the place apart. Reuben was six feet tall, slim and fine-looking like all the Cobb men, but with fiery red hair, which none of the others had. He wore long mustaches, also red, which he liked to twirl when disputing a point in a powerful voice which rode down opposition. At the first big dinner in his honor, given grudgingly by his uncle Maximus, he was out on the porch arguing cotton, when his loud exclamation penetrated the room inside as he boasted, to the disgust of certain gentlemen who specialized in Sea Island: 'Short staple is king. Those Manchester mills can't get enough of it. And whether you're ready to believe it or not, the man who rules short staple is goin' to rule this country.'

The eye of the Georgia hurricane was Petty Prue, the tiny, winsome daughter of a Methodist clergyman who had never planted a row of cotton in his life but who had taught his little girl all she needed to know: 'To get along in this life, you got to please people.' She was five feet one, weighed not over a hundred pounds, and had cultivated such an excessive Southern drawl that she could pronounce even the briefest word in three syllables. With her, *more* became *moe-weh-err*, delivered in a high, lilting voice. She looked directly at anyone who spoke to her, smiling ravishingly at women and men alike, as if each in turn were the prettiest or wittiest in the room. She was a giddy little bird, all gold and silver, who engulfed the normal reticence of Southern decorum in an irresistible enthusiasm which bubbled unceasingly from her pouting lips.

Two women, watching the visiting Cobbs from a corner, observed: 'You can tell they're not from Charleston.' But they were clearly eligible to belong had they wished, for they were charming, volatile and, according to Georgia standards, well bred, and at every critical moment they assured listeners of their undeviating loyalty to the South.

'Our men could sweep the field, if it ever came to a test of arms,' Reuben boomed from his position near the punch bowl. 'Ask Persifer. In the Mexican War hardly a single Northern officer measured up to the best of ours. Don't lecture me about railroad mileage and factories that belch smoke. It's character that counts.'

By the time that first noisy evening ended, the ladies and gentlemen of Charleston were satisfied that the Cobbs of Georgia were not only acceptable but also downright enjoyable: 'Shame he ever left us. We need men like him.' And as for Petty Prue: 'Clearly not gentlefolk, and rather loud, but she has a quality that melts the heart. Let's have them over.'

However, it was on the plantation that the Georgia Cobb revealed his true merit, for Reuben had the rare ability of looking at evidence and quickly reaching sound conclusions, a skill that few men commanded: 'Your soil's failing, Persifer. Per nigger, there's no way you can do well on this plantation.' And when Persifer said that he could always import fertilizer, Reuben said loudly: 'Waste half your profits. At your age, with your skills, you ought to get out of here.'

'And go where?' Persifer asked with obvious disdain. 'Georgia?'

'No. It's doomed, too. Yield per nigger way down.'

'Where then?'

'Texas.'

At the sound of this unfortunate word, Persifer Cobb winced; that any man in his right mind might wish to leave the cultivated paradise of Edisto Island and emigrate to the savage wilderness of Texas was so improbable that it did not even deserve comment. But Sett Cobb, to whom such a proposal had never before been suggested, was intrigued.

Now Reuben took from his pocket a clipping from a Louisiana newspaper, and when Persifer read it, echoes of an earlier discussion began to vibrate: 'I saw these figures at an office in New Orleans.' And there they were: South Carolina, 250 pounds of cotton per acre. Texas, 750.

'And you believe these figures?' Persifer asked, and with almost trembling excitement Reuben replied: 'I've written to the experts. They assure me that for the first years, virgin soil and all that, these results have been proved time and again.'

'But for how long?' Persifer asked, and Reuben replied: 'Long enough to make a fortune. By then you'd be ready to move on to fresh land. Damn, this could be the most exciting adventure in America. Perse, Sett, let's all go west.'

The idea that a Cobb would exchange Edisto for Texas was so repugnant to Persifer that he dismissed it haughtily, but when Reuben and little Petty Prue were alone with the Somerset Cobbs, the discussion continued: 'Sett, Lissa, we must all go to Texas, really. We're used up in Georgia. You're obviously used up in Edisto. We can buy land, the best bottom land, for two dollars an acre. Take our wagons, our niggers, money enough to start a new paradise.' He stopped abruptly and asked: 'Sett, how much hard cash could you scrape together?'

'Now that's difficult to say. I have a few thousand saved but . . .'

'Don't tell me "a few thousand." How much?'

'I have eight thousand, and I suppose Father would want to give me something.'

'Don't count on that. His father gave my father nothin'. But could you take your slaves with you?'

'Lissa and I have about six each, personal. We could surely take them.'

'Hell! Excuse me, ma'am, but I'm talkin' about fifty, sixty.

Surely you could talk your family into at least fifty.'

Obviously he had for some months been reviewing the possibility, for he took from his pocket a carefully tabulated list of things he and Petty Prue could provide for such an expedition, and the Cobbs were amazed at its completeness: 'I'll provide the cotton gin, because it has to be the best. I'll provide the cotton seed, the best Mexican strain, tested on land like we'll find in Texas. I'll take the blacksmith shop.'

'How many wagons are you thinking about?' Somerset asked.

From another pocket Reuben produced a list of wagons, each specified as to size, the numbers of mules or oxen required to draw it, and its order of contents. Thirty-seven were numbered, at which Millicent asked: 'But why the frenzy? You don't have to move. We do.'

And then little Petty Prue, in her high-pitched voice and delightful accent, revealed her real reasons: 'Georgia's changed. Old men makin' new rules. What we seek is a new life where we can invest our money and our energy and build our own paradise.'

Millicent was startled to hear this giddy child speaking so boldly: 'You'd be willing to take such great risks?'

'I want to take them. I'm bored with Georgia.' When she pronounced the word *boe-we-edd* it sounded amusing, but when Millicent saw the hard set of her chin, it wasn't funny at all. Now Petty Prue hammered at Lissa: 'After all, you sent the letter, we didn't. And you sent it because you knew you were finished here. It was one of your best ideas.'

But when the three Cobb families dined together on the second night, some of the things that motivated red-headed Reuben began to surface: 'Another reason I'd like to be in Texas, I'd like to keep my eye on the northern part of the Indian Territory that they're calling Kansas.' The word had never been mentioned before in Edisto, and it sounded strange the way Reuben said it, as if it carried terrible freight: 'Great decisions are going to be made in Kansas, and I want . . .'

'What decisions?' Millicent asked.

'Slavery. If those swine in the North can prevent us from carrying our slaves into open territory like Kansas, they can halt our entire progress.'

'Will Texas remain slave?' Somerset asked, and his cousin cried: 'Without question. They fought Santa Anna because he wanted to end slavery. They know how to protect their rights.'

'I would not care to bet on anything, where Texas is involved,' Persifer said, but Reuben stopped this reasoning bluntly: 'Where are Texans from? Tennessee, a slave state. Alabama, Mississippi, Georgia, all slave. Texas will be there when we need her.'

'Will we need her?' Persifer asked, and a hush fell over the candlelit room. The long silence that followed was broken only by the chirping of crickets in the warm night air, until finally Reuben stated his beliefs: 'I've met a few abolitionists. Sneaked into Georgia. Fine-looking men, but absolutely corrupt at heart, coming here to steal our property. They'll never surrender. But men like us three won't ever surrender, either. There must come a testing.'

'I should think you'd want to be here,' Persifer said, for he had heard that his Georgia cousin was a violent man.

'In Georgia, each good man will count for one. In Texas, he'll count for two.'

'Why do you say that?'

'Because many of the big decisions will be reached there. Control of the West. Control of Kansas. And a role in helping to control the Mississippi. I want to be where I'll count double.'

The men now went onto the porch, where Somerset tried quietly to explain that he believed the real disparity between South and North was not slavery, but the callous way in which the North profited from Southern raw materials and then imposed through Congress excessive tariffs which prevented the South from obtaining the goods it needed from Europe.

Millicent, listening to an argument she had heard before, indicated to Petty Prue that she wanted to pursue further their abbreviated table discussion, so when Tessa Mae took herself to bed, the two younger women sat in the light of a flickering candle and discussed the tremendous matter of moving a civilization west for more than a thousand miles. 'Does it frighten you?' Millicent asked, and Petty Prue said brightly: 'Not a bit. Thousands are going to California all the time. If they can do it, we can easily reach Texas.' She sought for a word and said: 'It'll really be like a great picnic ... that lasts for a hundred days.'

'A hundred days!'

'Yes, Reuben has it all worked out, from Edisto —'

'He seems sure we're going.'

'And so am I.' With never a faltering doubt, the little Georgia woman, in her mid-twenties and already the mother of three, said: 'The time comes, that's all I can say. It's like when a young man of twenty and a young girl of eighteen . . . the time comes, and everything that seemed so tangled falls into place. It's time for you and Sett to get out, and that's that.'

In the days that followed, when it became generally accepted that the Somerset Cobbs were going to withdraw gracefully from any competition for the Edisto plantation, both Persifer and Tessa Mae became wondrously generous. No decision had yet been voiced by their father as to how much money Sett could take with him, but word on that would come in due course; for the present, Persifer said: 'You can take twenty of our Edisto field hands, no question.'

'Trajan belongs on Edisto, really. But I'd want him.'

'Trajan you shall have. I'll explain to Father.'

Millicent nominated nine of the best female house slaves, women who could sew dresses and shirts, and they were surrendered too, with Tessa Mae adding two others that she knew Lissa favored, making thirty-two in all. Persifer, looking far ahead, said: 'Western Alabama and Mississippi, those roads were never solid. You'll need the best wagons,' and he started his wheelwrights and carpenters to mending nine wagons already in existence and building seven new ones, but when the first provisional lists of gear were compiled, it was obvious that Sett would be wise to buy another three in Charleston.

Maximus Cobb made petulant protest over the loss of Trajan, whom he had been breaking in nicely as a house servant, but on this point his sons were adamant, with Persifer leading the fight: 'A Carolina gentleman is entitled to at least one perfect servant. It lends him distinction, and for Sett, Trajan is ideal.' When his father continued to demur, Persifer said: 'They were like brothers,' and to this the old man had to assent.

When the time came that discussion of money could no longer be deferred, Maximus said: 'I'll tell you one thing. If you were going to Georgia, like my brother Septimus, you'd get not a nickel. Not a nickel. But if you're going to Texas, to help preserve our Southern way of life ... to spread goodness and justice ...'

He fumbled with his ivory-headed cane, and tears came to his eyes: 'Why do young people feel they have to leave? What have we ever done to wrong you, Somerset? Tell me, what?'

'The time comes,' Somerset said, and his father seemed to accept this, for he took from his pocket a letter – a copy of one, the original having already been mailed to a New Orleans bank – and before delivering it to his younger son he said, with evident sadness: 'It's my gift to you and Lissa in your new life.' It was a draft for twenty thousand dollars.

On Sunday, the last day of September 1849, the Cobb brothers, their wives and their five children, gathered at the mansion in Charleston, where an Episcopalian minister had been invited to say prayers, after which a fine feast was managed by Suetonius and three of his Caesars: Tiberius, Claudius and Domitian. Trajan was overseeing the four wagons that would leave from Charleston in the morning to meet up with the fifteen others that would be crossing the Edisto ferry and coming up to the main road.

It was a beautiful day, and in the late afternoon the two couples with their children walked along The Battery, looking out to Fort Sumter in the bay. At night singers came from a mansion nearby, and various families who had once thought of allying their children with Somerset's dropped by to say confused farewells, for they were losing prime candidates for future marriage alliances.

At dawn everyone was alert. The four wagons with their borrowed horses were ready for the taxing ride to where the heavier wagons coming directly from Edisto would be waiting. Kisses, tears, embraces and prayers were exchanged, and finally old Maximus waved one of his canes, and the Somerset Cobbs bade farewell to one of the most gracious houses in Carolina and to the best of the offshore islands. G.T.T. (Gone to Texas) could have been painted on their four wagons, for like thousands who preceded them, they had watched their fortunes at home slowly decline.

But it was at dusk on that first day when the true farewells were said, because as the little caravan approached the spot where the ferry road from Edisto joined the main road, the Cobb children riding in the lead wagon shouted back to their parents: 'Oh, Look!' And there ahead, waiting as shadows deepened, stood the other fifteen wagons. Around them clustered not only the slaves who would go with them to Texas but also some hundred others who had trudged up from the island to say goodbye.

There was not much sleeping that night, for groups clustered here and there, exchanging little gifts, whispering in Gullah, and savoring the precious moments of friendships that would be shared no more. For as long as anyone could remember, no Cobb of Edisto had ever separated a slave child from its parents, and none were being separated now – for example, Trajan and his wife were taking their boy Hadrian with them – but inevitably, adult brothers and sisters were seeing each other for the last time, and many others were being separated from their old parents. There was sorrow, but as the night waned, there was also singing, soft hymns chanted in Gullah.

'Oh, I shall never see you again!' a young woman cried to a man she might have married had he stayed on Edisto, and at dawn the caravan of nineteen wagons moved on to Texas, four white people and thirty-two slaves, plus three babes still in arms.

On this second day of October 1849 the plodding trek westward began, with Trajan's wagon in the lead as the mules and oxen shuffled along at their own measured pace. By noontime the drivers had learned how much distance to leave between wagons so that dust did not engulf them. By late afternoon, when the first stop occurred, the line of wagons covered about a mile and a half, and there was much joking among the slaves as the last one pulled in.

As soon as the wagons carrying the Cobbs and their private gear halted, male and female slaves sprang into action, pitching the masters' tents, arranging for baths, and starting the evening meal. On this first night it was a noisy game, with cooks unable to find pots and maids not knowing where the bedding was, but with stern prompting from Trajan, things were straightened out, and the expedition assumed some kind of rational order.

807

It was a hundred and thirty-four miles from Edisto to the South Carolina line opposite the city of Augusta, and Somerset had calculated that the distance could be covered in not more than twelve days, but on Saturday, when they were about halfway across the narrow part of the state, Millicent announced with some finality that she did not intend traveling on Sunday. When he started to protest, he found that all the slaves supported his wife, most vociferously: 'We ain't never work Sundays. Ain't proper.' With Mrs Cobb it was a matter of religion, but with the slaves it was religion-cum-custom, with the latter weighing the heavier: 'Work six days, God says so. Even He work six days. But come seven, no more, neither God nor man.' Trajan was a leader in this rebellion, so at sunset that first Saturday, Sett Cobb ordered the tents pitched securely, for nothing he could say or do was going to change the fact that they would stay beside this rivulet for two nights.

On the second Saturday night the enforced halt irritated him even more, because the caravan had now reached the Carolina shore of the Savannah River, across which the buildings of Augusta could be clearly seen. 'We could get up tomorrow at dawn and be in the city in time for morning prayers,' he argued, but Lissa would not listen: 'The Sabbath is God's holy day, and if we profane it at the start of our trip, what evils will He pour down upon us in the later days?' Sett said that he doubted God was paying much attention to one small group of wagons on the Augusta road, but Millicent prevailed.

They entered Augusta very early on Monday, October fifteenth, and spent the next two days making purchases of things they had discovered they needed. Sett figured that this shopping would please his wife, but when he returned to the wagons at dusk on Tuesday, he found her looking across the river and weeping: 'I shall never see Carolina again. Look at it, Sett, it's the gentlest and loveliest state in the Union.' He remained with her for a long time, staring back at that lovely state in which he had been so happy and of which he was so proud.

The next week was hard work, a slow, slogging progress along the bumpy roads of northern Georgia, and for three solid days, enduring a considerable amount of rain, they pushed their way west through the little towns of Greensboro and Madison, and by Thursday morning, when the sky cleared, Sett was in fine spirits. At breakfast he said: 'Everybody watch closely today and tomorrow. May be a big surprise.'

So the two children rode forward with Trajan, peering ahead like Indian scouts, and about noon they were rewarded by seeing a lone rider, a very large black man, coming toward them on a mule. As he drew closer he began to shout: 'You de Cobbs fum Edisto?' and when Trajan waved his whip enthusiastically, the big man reined in his mule, lifted his arms in the air, and began shouting: 'Halley-loo, I done found you.'

He was Jaxifer, prime hand of the Georgia Cobbs, dispatched along this road to meet the caravan. He had acquired his name in a curious way. Reuben Cobb, seeking to retain a sentimental tie with his cousins on Edisto, had named him Persifer, in honor of the family's soldier-hero, but in Gullah the word had been quickly corrupted to Jaxifer. 'My job, show you de way home,' he explained, and after the wagons fell in behind him, he pranced his mule and shouted: 'Halley-loo, we on our way to Texas!'

He rode with them all day on the twenty-sixth, shouting to everyone they passed: 'Halley-loo, we for Texas!' and that night he told the children, who had by now adopted him, for he was just as vigorous and loud as his master: 'Tomorrow we home. Finest town in Georgia.'

'What's its name?' the children asked, and he replied: 'Social Circle,' and they said: 'That's no name for a town,' and he corrected them: 'It be the name of dis town, and dis town is Queen of Georgia.'

Early on Saturday he led them along the last dusty roads to Social Circle, an attractive village which boasted two cotton gins, warehouses for the storing of finished bales and a beautiful old well right in the middle of the main street. Waiting there, as men and women had waited for many decades to greet their friends, were Reuben and Petty Prue, who provided ladles of cool water for the travelers.

'Our town had another name, once,' Petty Prue explained, 'but since everyone gathered about this pump for local gossip, it became Social Circle.'

After so many days of dusty travel, twenty-seven of them, the Edisto Cobbs were delighted with the five days they stayed over in Social Circle. The main street was lined with nine large houses, each with handsome white pillars supporting fine balconies that opened out from the upper floors, each with flower beds and finely graveled turnarounds for the carriages.

'Somebody's making money here,' Sett cried when at the end of this first parade of tall mansions he saw another six of somewhat smaller size.

'Everybody is . . . for the moment,' Reuben said. 'These men know how to grow cotton, how to work their slaves.'

Sett was especially interested in the cotton gins, for as a grower of Sea Island, he had never worked short-staple and for some years had believed that no one else could, either, so Reuben took him to a gin owned collectively by all the Cobbs of the region, a sturdy wooden building of two stories, with the bottom one mostly open so that slave boys could lead two pairs of horses around and around in a perpetual circle. The horses were harnessed to long wooden arms projecting outward from a central pillar, which revolved slowly but with great force.

The pillar reached well up through the second floor, where its constant turning provided motive power for an Eli Whitney gin of fifty saws. The bolls of filmy white cotton passing these saws had their tenacious green seeds removed, the latter falling down a chute to the ground after wire brushes caught their filaments.

'Not much different from what we do by hand with Sea Island in Carolina,' Somerset muttered while studying the wonderful effectiveness of the gin. As it continued its work, handling the fractious seed so competently, he had a vision of that endless chain of which he had always been a part: the land tilled, the seed sown by slaves, the tender plants chopped to eliminate weeds and weaklings, the bolls gathered, the seeds removed, the bales sent to the rivers, the ships loaded, the cotton delivered to Liverpool, the spun thread delivered to Manchester, the cloth woven, the clothing made, civilization enhanced – and every man in the chain earning a good living from this miraculous fiber. Cotton was surely a king among crops.

The slave, Cobb reflected, lived well under the loving care of kind masters; the planter watched his hands flourish; the owner of the gin extracted his fee; the shipper his, and the Liverpool merchant his pounds and shillings. The weaver seemed to earn most, with the manufacturer of clothes not far behind. 'Wait!' he called to the busy gin as if to correct some misapprehension under which it toiled. 'The one who makes the most is the damned banker who finances it all.' In his many years of supervising the vast fields on Edisto Island, Cobb, unlike Tessa Mae's family, had never once planted with his own or his family's money. Now he thought: It was tradition to use the bank's money. Always they got their share first. He supposed that in Texas it would be the same.

Reuben nudged him: 'Wonderful machine, eh? How simple. How difficult it was to work cotton before it came along.' Rather ruefully he added: 'You know, Sett, we Southerners dreamed about a gin like this for a hundred years. Even worked on crude designs now and then. A damned schoolteacher from Massachusetts comes down here on vacation or something, studies the problem one week, and produces this.' With profound admiration he watched the gin as it ceaselessly picked the fiber from the seed; as long as the boys below kept the horses walking, and the central pole turning on its axis, so long would the miraculous gin do in an hour what a thousand nimble fingers in Virginia once took a month to complete.

'This gin ensures the South's domination,' Reuben said, almost gloatingly. 'The world needs clothing, and it can't afford wool.' Grabbing a handful of lint, he apostrophized it: 'Get along to Galveston, and then to the mills in Lancashire, then as a bolt of cloth on some freighter headed for Australia. The world has to have what you provide, and if the North ever tried to interrupt our cotton trade, all the armies and navies of Europe would spring to our defense.' Patting the gin, he said: 'You are our shield in battle.'

Then he laughed: 'How ironical history can be, Sett. Maybe the greatest invention of mankind, certainly of our South, and the genius who made it earned not a penny.'

'I didn't know that. Of course, gins aren't that important to Sea Island.'

'Whitney lost his patent. Never really got it, because the gin was so vital that everyone moved in and simply copied it. Lawyers, you know.'

As Reuben said these words, his cousin noted that he was

looking at the gin strangely, as if trying to remember each element of its movement so that it could be duplicated in Texas, but this seemed odd, because a good commercial gin could be bought from many sources for less than a hundred dollars. Powered by one of the new steam engines, it might cost a hundred and a half, so that any important cotton plantation could afford its own.

For five days the citizens of Social Circle entertained the emigrants in one big mansion after another, until Millicent cried at one dinner: 'You have certainly proved your right to your name. This is the socialest circle I've ever been in,' and a banker responded with an apt toast: 'To the Cobbs, the first group ever to leave Georgia for Texas without the sheriff chasing them.'

On the morning of Thursday, November first, the Georgia Cobbs moved their wagons into line, and as they did so, Millicent, to her amazement, counted thirty-eight. 'Good heavens, Prue, are you taking everything you own?' she asked, and Prue replied: 'Yes.' So the caravan was formed: Edisto wagons, nineteen, Georgia, thirty-eight; Edisto slaves, thirty-two, Georgia, forty-nine; Edisto whites, four, Georgia, five; plus one Bible from Edisto and certain remarkable items from Georgia.

On Friday, Sett discovered how remarkable the items were, for when one of the wagons mired in the mud, he saw that it contained the metal parts of the disassembled gin which he had been studying only a few days before. He recognized the splashes of yellow color and especially the saw mechanism, which carried in iron letters the name of the manufacturer. Reuben Cobb, on that last night when the banker was extolling his honesty, had been busy stealing one of the town's two gins.

'Oh, it belongs to me, you might say,' he explained. 'It's a Cobb gin, that's for sure, but it belonged to the other Cobbs. They owed me a lot, and they can get another.' However, Sett noticed that despite his bravado, Reuben followed a most circuitous route around Atlanta, keeping a rear lookout posted in case sheriffs tried to recover the gin.

Once when the lead wagon was well and truly mired in the mud of Mississippi, the Edisto Cobbs caught a glimpse of their cousin's darker nature, for after minutes of bellowing at Jaxifer to get the wagon moving, Reuben lost his temper and thrashed the struggling slave with a whip he kept at hand. Seventeen, eighteen times he lashed the big, silent man across the back, and it would have been difficult to guess who was the more appalled by this performance, the Edisto whites or the Edisto blacks, for during his entire stewardship of the island plantation Sett Cobb had never whipped a slave. He had disciplined them and occasionally he threw them into the plantation jail, but never had he whipped one, nor had he allowed his overseers to do so.

Although the whites and blacks may have been equally appalled, it was the latter who suffered in a unique way. You could see it in the way Trajan cringed when the strokes of the whip fell; you could hear it in the gasps of the Edisto women, for this incident in the swamps of Mississippi demonstrated what slavery really meant: when one slave was whipped, all slaves were whipped.

When Trajan, quivering with outrage, sought to move forward to aid Jaxifer, Sett reached out a restraining hand, and without words having been said, Trajan knew that his master was promising: 'We Edisto people will never do it that way.'

It was an ironclad rule of the cotton states, broken only by fools, that one white master never reproved another in the presence of slaves, and Somerset Cobb was especially attentive to this rule, so that when the thrashing ended he felt ashamed of himself for having revealed his feelings to his slave Trajan, and he attempted to assuage his conscience by going quietly to Reuben that evening and saying: 'You were having a hard time with Jaxifer. That wagon was really mired.'

'Sometimes boys like Jaxifer require attention.'

'They really do, Reuben, they really do.' Then he added, almost offhandedly: 'At Edisto we never whipped our niggers.' And he said this with such calm force that Reuben knew that whereas he might beat his own slaves, he must never touch Sett's.

A genteel Southern family traveling anywhere seemed always to have waiting in the next town a cousin or business associate who had left the Carolinas or Georgia some time back. In Vicksburg, that important town guarding the Mississippi

River, the Cobbs visited a delightful pair of spinsters, the Misses Peel, whose parents had left Charleston some forty years earlier to acquire a large plantation bordering the river.

The sisters, unable to find in Vicksburg any suitors of a breeding acceptable to the elder Peels, had languished, as they said amusingly, 'in unwedded bliss.' They were charming ladies, alert, witty and given to naughty observations on their neighbors.

Their gracious home was located on a bluff at the north end of Cherry Street, and so situated that it overlooked the great dark river below. 'The Mississippi isn't the first water you see,' one of the Misses Peel explained. 'That's the Yazoo Diversion. It's a canal that makes our town a riverport. But beyond, out there in the darkness ... when there's a full moon the Mississippi glows like a long chain of pearls.'

'It's good of you to entertain us so lavishly,' Petty Prue exclaimed, 'because when we leave Vicksburg we separate.'

'Oh, dear! You're not parting?'

'Only temporarily. Somerset and Millicent, they're taking a riverboat down to New Orleans and then up the Red River. To make all the arrangements in Texas before Reuben and I get the wagons there overland.'

One of the Peels said with great enthusiasm: 'Millicent, you and Somerset don't have to sail all the way to New Orleans. Twice when I've gone, our big boat has stopped in the middle of the Mississippi while a small boat came out from the Red to take passengers from us. How romantic, I thought, changing ships in midocean, as it were. How I wanted to quit my cabin and join that small boat to see where it might carry me.'

'But, Lissa, you wouldn't want to miss New Orleans,' Petty Prue cried in her high, lyrical voice. 'All those shops.'

'I have little taste for shopping,' Millicent said. 'I'm impatient to reach our new home.'

The Peels now turned to Petty Prue: 'Surely, you're not going to ride those rough wagons across Arkansas when you could sail to Texas in a big riverboat!' But the saucy little Georgian snapped: 'I ride with my husband. Where he goes, I go.' Miss Peel said: 'But the boat would be so comfortable,' and Prue replied: 'After three months of wagons, my backside's made of leather.' And she helped supervise the loading of the wagons Reuben would be taking, placing them just so on the rickety ferries which would carry them across the Mississippi to start them on their way to Texas. She waved goodbye to the Edisto Cobbs: 'We'll overtake you about the first of February. Have our lands selected, because Reuben will want to plant his cotton.'

And so the two families separated, one leading a slow caravan crosscountry to Texas, the other going by swift riverboat down the Mississippi to a romantic halting place in midriver, where a much smaller steamer waited to receive passengers bound for the Red River. When heavy planks were swung to join the two vessels, the four Cobbs, seven of their slaves, two disassembled wagons and six horses were transferred. Then, as whistles blew, the emigrants started one of the more surprising journeys of their lives.

The Red River ship was small; it smelled of cows and horses, and the food was markedly less palatable than that on the larger boat. But the river itself, and the land bordering it, was fascinating, a true frontier wilderness with just enough settlement scattered haphazardly to maintain interest. The Cobb children were delighted by the closeness of the banks and the variation in the plantations. 'These aren't plantations,' their mother said with equal interest in the new land. 'These are farms. White people work here.' She was seeing a new vision of America, one she had not known existed, and she was impressed by its sense of latent power.

'Will we have a farm like these?' the children asked, and she laughed: 'For a year, maybe, yes. But at the end of two years we'll have a plantation just like Edisto. Cousin Reuben will see to that.'

Near Shreveport the Cobbs made their acquaintance with one of the marvels of America, as explained by two red-faced men who were conveying a passel of slaves for public auction in Texas: 'Dead ahead, blockin' things tighter'n a drum, what we call the Great Red River Raft.'

'What could that be?' Somerset asked, and with obvious delight the two men told of this natural miracle: 'First noted by white men in 1805, and what they saw fairly amazed them. Centuries past, huge trees, uprooted by storms, floated downstream and were trapped by bends in our sluggish river.'

The second slaver broke in: 'Happens in all rivers, but in the Red the trees carried so much soil in their matted roots, they provided choice growin' ground for weeds and bushes and even small trees.'

'Like he says, more big fallen trees trapped in the river meant more small trees growin' in the mud. There! Look ahead! A whole river shut down.'

And when the Cobbs looked where he pointed, they saw a major river, one capable of carrying big steamboats, closed off by this impenetrable mass of tree and root and tangle and lovely blooming flowers. 'How far does it reach?' Cobb asked, and the answer astounded him: 'Ah-hah! That first report in 1805 said: "We got a Raft out here eighty miles long. In places, maybe twenty miles wide." So officials in Washington said: "Break it loose," and they tried, for it converted maybe a million acres of good farmland into swamp.'

'Why couldn't they break it up?' Somerset asked, and the men cried gleefully, each trying to convey the story: 'They tried. Army come in here and tried. But for each foot they knock off down here, the Raft grows ten feet up there. Last survey? One hundred and twenty miles long, packed solid, no boat can move.'

'Then why have we come here?' Cobb asked, and the men gave a startling reply: 'Miracles! Bring your children up here and they'll see miracles.'

So the four Cobbs stood beside the slavers as their steamboat headed right for the Red River Raft, and when it seemed that the boat would crash, it veered off to the left to enter a bewildering sequence of twists, turns, openings and sudden vistas of the most enchanting beauty. The boat was picking its way through a jungle fairyland stretching miles in every direction.

The slavers seemed to take as much delight in this mysterious passage as did the Cobbs: 'Nothin' anywhere like it! The Raft backs up so much water that these private little rivers run through the forest. But the best is still ahead.'

They were correct, for as they emerged from the watery forest, a grand lake, mysterious and dark, opened up. 'It's called Caddo,' the men said. 'After a tribe of Indians that once lived along its shores.' The lake had a thousand arms twisting and writing inland, a hundred sudden turns which allowed the boat to keep moving forward when passage seemed blocked. The live oaks that lined this vast swamp especially pleased the older Cobbs, because from all the lower branches hung matted clumps of Spanish moss; Caddo Lake was virtually identical with the swamps of Edisto, and when they consulted a map they saw that the two locations, so far apart, were on almost the same latitude, about 32° 30′.

After intricate maneuvering, the steamer broke out of Caddo Lake, and on 24 January 1850, entered a small cypress-lined creek and blew its whistle as it steamed into the wharf at Jefferson, Texas: population 1,300; distance from Edisto, 997 miles.

When Somerset and Trajan met Reuben Cobb and his wagons a week later in Shreveport, they had exciting news, and Trajan told the other slaves: 'Land almost de same. First class fo' cotton. Carpenters already buildin' us homes.'

Somerset was more specific: 'Reuben, you led us to a treasure,' but before he could say more, his cousin interrupted: 'Sett, I want to talk with you and your boy Trajan,' and Somerset was perplexed, because he could not imagine what might have happened which would involve both him and his slave.

Reuben's words were grave: 'First day west of Vicksburg we come upon this man, his slaves in bad shape. He was in bad shape too, damn him. Begged me to lend him one of our slaves to drive his wagon for the rest of that day. Out of the goodness of my heart, I loaned him Hadrian.'

'Where is my boy?' Trajan cried.

'Gone. The son-of-a-bitch stole him. It was a trick.'

'Gone?' Trajan wailed.

'Yep, stole clean away. But we propose to get him back.' He suggested that he, Jaxifer, Trajan and Somerset mount their horses, arm themselves and fan out to catch that swine, so for two days the Cobbs searched the countryside, looking for the kidnaper, questioning everyone they met.

Somerset had never seen his cousin so furious: 'Damnit, Sett, to steal a boy like that. To take a boy that age away from his father. Trajan, if we catch him . . .'

817

They did not find him, then or ever. When it was clear that they were not going to recover this promising boy worth three hundred dollars, Reuben Cobb's fury increased, and on the night they abandoned the chase both brothers spoke with Trajan. Somerset said, tears moistening his eyes: 'As long as I live, Traje, I'll search for your son. I'll find him for you. I'll find him.' Reuben, clasping the slave by the shoulder, said: 'We got ourselves an orphaned boy, good lad I believe. Not your son's age, but would you consent to care for him? I'd pay you a little somethin'.' But the boy himself, Trajan's son, was never found.

The putting together of the Cobb plantation at Jefferson became an act of high comedy, because whereas Somerset in his first days had found some three thousand acres exactly to his liking, it was settled land with a good portion of the fields already cleared, and it was priced at three dollars and seventy-five cents an acre, which Reuben believed to be excessive. The land lay just south of town and belonged to an enterprising Scotsman named Buchanan, who had accepted four hundred dollars as down payment on the deal.

Reuben, assured that he could find better land for much less, roared into the home of the astonished Buchanan like a wayward tornado, demanding a refund of the four hundred dollars on grounds that the Scotsman was a thief, a perjurer and a scoundrel who had viciously misrepresented both the land and its value. When the startled Scotsman said there was no chance that he would return the money, Reuben warned him that he, Reuben, was a practiced attorney from Georgia, well versed in land law, and that if Buchanan did not hand over the deposit immediately, he was going to find himself in a court of law charged with even worse offenses than those so far enumerated.

The four hundred dollars was returned, whereupon Reuben directed the workmen who had been building the slave shacks on the Buchanan land to tear them down and save the lumber. When asked where the shacks were to be built, Reuben said: 'I'll tell you in three days.'

He now became tireless, rising before dawn in the tiny rooms the family had rented in the home of a Baptist minister, riding back and forth along all the dusty roads so far opened and looking at fields near and distant which might be for sale. At the end of four days he had settled upon three thousand acres a few miles east of town and situated nicely on the north bank of the stream which connected Lake Caddo with Jefferson. The land was owned by a widow who felt that she could not handle it by herself, now that her husband was dead, but realizing that it was favorable land, she wanted three dollars an acre, which again Reuben still considered excessive.

He therefore paid ardent court to the widow, explaining that the best thing for her to do was sell the land, which would require an excessive amount of effort to clear, and hie herself to New Orleans, where she could live in comfort for the rest of her days. When she replied that she had never been in New Orleans and knew nobody there, Reuben assured her: 'I know people of excellent reputation. The day you sell I'll put you on the steamer with your money and letters of introduction, and you'll thank the day you met me.'

When Somerset heard of the negotiations, he said flatly: 'I'll not cheat a widow,' and since he liked the new land very much, acknowledging that Reuben had found better than the first lot, he wanted to pay the asked-for three dollars. But this Reuben would not permit.

'I'll tell you what,' he told the widow. 'If you persuade Mr Adams, who owns the land adjoining yours, to sell it to me for a dollar an acre, I'll give you two twenty-five for yours,' and when Mr Adams demurred, Reuben promised him: 'If you can get me that two thousand acres of bottomland owned by Mr Larson ... obviously floods every year and is worth almost nothing ... if you can get him to sell it to me for twenty cents an acre, I'll give you a dollar twenty-five for yours.'

He now had three owners involved, and wa dickering with a fourth, a Mr Carver, for the purchase of eight hundred acres of the best cleared fields he had ever seen, contiguous to the rest, for a flat three dollars an acre when it was obviously worth at least four.

When the pot was bubbling, with the four owners pondering their parts in the intricate sale, Reuben rode from farm to farm one afternoon, warning each of the people that his offer was good only till noon of the next day, and he came to his quarters that night satisfied that he and Somerset were going to get possession of their land by next nightfall: three thousand of the widow's acres, four thousand of Mr Adams' uncleared acres, two thousand of Mr Larson's useless bottomlands, and eight hundred of Mr Carver's prepared fields. It was a massive deal, one which would exhaust much of the cousins' cash, but he was convinced that this was the way to acquire a major land holding in Texas.

He went to bed pleased with his manipulations, but at four in the morning he sat bolt upright, catching for breath as if someone were strangling him. 'The Raft!' he told his wife, and he ran across the hall to waken Somerset: 'Don't you see, Sett? They're willing to sell because they know the Great Raft is going to be removed.'

'What are you talking about?'

'The Raft! The Raft! The minute it's removed, we lose all the water in our river. No boats will ever get to Jefferson. This land won't be worth fifty cents an acre.'

In real anxiety he threw on his clothes and dashed out to where the Cobb horses were stabled, and calling for Jaxifer, he leaped into the saddle. 'Meet with them,' he shouted back to Somerset. 'Tell them I'll be back in five days. Appendicitis.' When his own lead slave could not be found, he pressed Trajan into sleepy service, and off they went to inspect the Raft.

Somerset was embarrassed to visit with the four sellers, but decided to explain to each that his cousin had been called urgently to Shreveport to handle a large amount of money being forwarded from Georgia, and when the widow who was selling the first parcel asked if it was true that the other Mr Cobb had influential friends in New Orleans, he found himself assuring her: 'He'll take care of your interests, believe me.'

Five days later Reuben returned, tired but happy and fully prepared to go ahead with the four purchases. When Sett asked about the Raft, he said: 'Even God couldn't remove it.' The water at Jefferson seemed guaranteed for all time.

The Cobbs got their nine thousand eight hundred acres for the prices that Reuben had wanted, but even when they had them safely in their possession, he wanted two hundred more to make a round ten thousand, and he uncovered a wispy little fellow who owned four hundred of the most miserable bottomland, underwater twice each year, so he bought the whole batch for ten cents an acre.

The Cobbs were finding that Jefferson, settled by responsible immigrants from the Southern states, was almost indistinguishable from a town of similar size in Alabama or Georgia, but what made it especially attractive was the fact that it combined the best features of each of those states, for this corner of northeast Texas was a flowering paradise. 'No wonder they call it the Italy of America,' Millicent cried one February morning when she saw the stately trees on their new land, the wealth of casual flowers beginning to appear on all the fields.

Reuben, always with an eye to future business, had been enumerating the trees which awaited the ax: 'We have six kinds of oak: live, black, post, water and the two tough types, white and red. I've seen elm, hundreds of good ash, maple, sycamore and two that are going to be damned valuable for shingles and fencing, cypress and red cedar. But I want you all to see a real wonder.'

He led them to a tree they had not known. It grew abundantly but not in height and produced thorns of immense size. 'They call it two ways,' Reuben said, '*bois d'arc* or Osage-orange. You can see a few of last year's oranges up there.'

'Are they palatable?' Millicent asked, and her cousin said: 'Not even for cows. But I want you to look at the wood,' and he sliced off a small branch of the Osage to show the women the bright yellow color, wood and sap alike. 'It's very hard, and what I like about it, if we plant two rows, side by side with the trees of the second row filling in the gaps in the first, within three years we'll have fences that no cattle can penetrate. You're going to see a lot of Osage-orange on Lakeview.'

Reuben had insisted that the name of the plantation be Lakeview, and when Sett objected: 'But there's no lake,' the determined redhead said: 'There will be.'

Even when the Cobb plantation was finished, the cousins would plant only a relatively few acres of cotton; the major part would be held in woods, or used for cattle and hogs. But as soon as that first small stand of cotton was planted, and before their homes were built, Reuben put all the slaves plus six hired men from town with their mules and iron sleds to work digging out to the depth of four feet an immense sunken area immediately adjacent to the river.

'Leave a dike wide enough to keep the water out,' he ordered, and as the depression deepened he worked as strenuously as any of the men, digging deeper and deeper and moving a huge amount of earth to be piled along the rim of the future lake. When everyone was exhausted, he gave the crew two days' rest, then brought them back to finish off the bottom and dig a six-foot channel from the river to the place where the future plantation wharf would be built.

The men dug this channel in an interesting way. The hired hands from town hitched their mules to a heavy iron implement that looked like a very large sharp-edged dustpan, except that it had higher sides and two handles instead of one. When the mules strained forward they dragged this huge pan behind them, so that the man holding the handles could tip the edge forward and slice off a huge wedge of moist earth, which stayed in the scoop as the mules moved faster, dragging it aloft to the sides of the depression.

When the channel was well dug, wide enough to safeguard a boat coming in from Lake Caddo, Reuben announced: 'Now for the fun!' He directed the slaves to pare the top of the dike, which kept out the river, down to the very water's edge. He then dug holes in the remaining walls, filled them with explosives, and warned everyone to stand back. When he detonated the charges, the dike crumbled and waters from the bayou rushed in to fill the man-made lake and the channel leading to where the wharf would stand.

From the side of the slight hill on which the Cobb mansions would one day be erected, the women and children watched with delight as their lake came into being. 'How beautiful!' Petty Prue cried, and Millicent, less openly enthusiastic, agreed. It was a splendid lake, which would be even lovelier when the trees which Reuben proposed planting were established.

The Cobb men were not foolish. They never believed for an instant that two families as distinct as theirs, or two men as radically different as they, could own a plantation in common, and as soon as the purchases of the land were completed they consulted a Jefferson lawyer – there were three to choose from – who drew up a most detailed schedule of who owned what:

'Now, as I understand it, Somerset is to have the initial three thousand acres purchased from the widow, plus four hundred of the very fine acres of the Carver land. Reuben is to have clear title to all the four thousand acres bought from Mr Adams, plus all the bottomlands from whomever.'

'That's my understanding,' Sett said. 'And mine,' agreed Reuben.

'But the entire is to be called Lakeview Plantation?'

The Cobbs looked at each other and nodded: 'That's what we want.'

'Most unusual. Two plantations, one name.'

'Doesn't seem unusual to me,' Reuben said, and the lawyer coughed.

'Now, the lake, and ten acres of land about it, plus access to the river, that's to be held in common, owned by no one specifically, and with each of your two houses to have equal access and equal use, in perpetuity.'

'Agreed.'

'And that also includes any wharf that will be built there, and any cotton gin or storage buildings which might be called warehouses.'

'Agreed,' Reuben said. 'We'll build them with common dollars and have common ownership. But I wish you'd put in there not only the gin but also any other kind of mill we might want to operate.'

'And what kind would that be?' the lawyer asked.

'That's to be seen,' Reuben said.

So before even the wharf was built, or the family houses well started, he was preoccupied, along with Trajan and Jaxifer, in laying out the kind of mill complex he had long visualized. Because no running stream passed through the land, he could not depend on water power, and he did not want to go back to the old-style gin operated by horses walking endlessly in a circle. Instead, he hired three skilled carpenters from the town – one dollar and ten cents a day, with them supplying all tools and nails – and working alongside them, he built a two-story gin building, traditional except that on the ground floor he left only a small open space.

When Trajan warned: 'No horse kin walk there!' he explained: 'Somethin' a lot better'n a horse,' and he had the slaves erect a rock-based platform on which a ten-horsepower steam engine would rest; he would purchase this from Cincinnati, where it seemed that all the good machinery of this period was manufactured.

But the gin was only a part of his plan, for when a heavy leather belt was attached to the revolving spindle of the engine, it activated, on the upper story, a long master spindle from which extended four separate leather belts. There would not be sufficient power to operate all the belts simultaneously, but any two could function. One, of course, led to the gin, and it drew down little power; another returned to the first floor, where it operated the massive press which formed the bales that would be shipped down to New Orleans for movement to Liverpool. It was the third and fourth belts which led to the innovations of which Reuben was so proud, and one might almost say that these accounted for the material growth of Lakeview Plantation.

The third belt carried power to an enlargement of the gin building that housed a gristmill, a massive stone grinder which revolved slowly in a heavy stone basin, producing excellent flour when wheat was introduced between the stones or golden meal when corn was used. The fourth belt powered a sawmill, and it required so much power that it could run only when the press and mill were idle.

Cotton was ginned and pressed less than half the year; the grist mill and sawmill could be utilized at any time, and it was these which determined the plantation's margin of profit. The gin, using less power than any of the other three, provided the great constant in Texas commerce, the lifeblood, but with this assured, the quality of life depended upon what was accomplished additionally. Only a few geniuses like Reuben Cobb realized this interdependence; the great majority of Texans never would – and from generation to generation producers and their bankers would believe in turn: 'Cotton is King. Cattle are King. Oil is King. Electronics are King.' And always they would be deceiving themselves, for it was the creative mix of efforts, plus the ingenuity and hard work of the men and women involved, that was really King.

The four combined mills at Lakeview Plantation constituted an early proof of this truism, and one aspect of the operation was startling: after the buildings were constructed and the machinery installed, Trajan was in charge. He had mastered the technique of mending the leather belts when they tore; he knew how to guard the water supply to the engine; he knew what types of wood to cut for stoking the engine; and he, better even than Reuben, appreciated the subtle interlocking relationships of the four components. The building and its contents had been put together only by the ingenuity of Reuben Cobb, who had learned by studious apprenticeship in Georgia what was needed, but it was managed successfully by Trajan – no last name – who had that subtle feel for machinery which characterized many of the ablest Americans.

The lake had been so judiciously placed that the Reuben Cobbs could build their home on a promontory overlooking it, while the Somerset Cobbs could place another house on their rise and obtain just as good a view. But in the actual construction of the two houses, there was a vast difference.

The cousins had learned from the building of their slave quarters and the dredging of the lake that skilled workmen could be hired in Jefferson for around a dollar a day, and good husbandry advised the Cobbs to pay the fee and use these craftsmen. A good slave shack, caulked to keep out the rain, could be built by these artisans for less than fifty dollars, and an entire house, dog-run style for white folks, could be put up for six hundred dollars. The Somerset Cobbs built such a house, hastily and with no amenities, fully expecting to tear it down and build a better in the years ahead.

Reuben, with a keen sense of his position in Jefferson, did not do this. Instead of the traditional four small rooms at the compass points, he built four surprisingly large rooms, and instead of perching them on piles of stone at each corner, he used slaves and employed townsmen to dig substantial footings, four feet deep, which he filled with stone and rubble and sloppy clay in order to establish a firm, unshakable base. It, too, was a dog-run, but the central breezeway was twenty-six feet wide and the roof was not thrown together; it was most sturdily built and covered with cypress split shingles hewn from Lakeview trees.

To everyone's surprise, Reuben paid little attention to the

porch, accepting one that was both shorter and narrower than his cousin's, so that when the unusual house was finished, several people, including some of the workmen, said in effect: 'Hell of a big breezeway. Itty-bitty porch. It don't match.'

He did not intend it to, for as soon as the plantation began prospering he did three daring things: he boarded up the two open ends of the breezeway, paying great attention to the architectural effect of door-and-window; he built at each far end of the axis a stone chimney, tying the two halves of the house together; and he tore off the inadequate porch and installed instead a magnificent affair supported by six marble Doric columns shipped in segments and at huge expense from New Orleans.

The Redheaded Cobbs, as they were called in the community, now had a mansion which would have graced Charleston or Montgomery. It was clean, and white, and spacious, and the happy combination of the two stone chimneys and the six marble pillars gave it a distinction which could be noticed when one first saw it from the steamboat landing down on the lake. But what pleased Reuben most, when he surveyed the whole, was the developing hedge of Osage-orange that enclosed and protected his grand new home.

When the mansions were livable, Sett, as the steadier of the two Cobbs and the more experienced in managing a sizable plantation, cast up the profit-and-loss figures for their enterprise, and when he displayed them to his partners, the wives declared that with Reuben's sharp purchasing and Sett's good management, the family was on its way to having a very profitable operation:

10,200 acres bought at various prices, total cost	$14,590
81 Carolina and Georgia slaves, less Hadrian stolen, plus 12 additional acquired en route means 92 at $425 per head, fair average	39,100
Cost of equipment for the slaves, plus cattle, hogs and fowl to keep the plantation running, at $62 per slave	5,704

Total investment	$59,394
Counting all slaves, each slave produces .89	
bales of cotton per year times 92	82
Each bale contains 480 pounds times 82	39,360
Each pound sells at 10.8¢	$4,250
$4,250 divided by $59,394 yields yearly profit of	7.11%

'And remember,' cried Reuben when he saw the final figure, 'nine of us Cobbs had a good living from our land. Each year the value of our slaves increases. And I'm convinced cotton will sell for more next year when it reaches Liverpool.'

Cautiously, lest he excite too much euphoria, Sett added: 'We'll soon be showing substantial profit from our mills and gin,' and Petty Prue burbled: 'Hail to Cobbs! Best plantation in Texas.'

While the Cobbs were establishing themselves so securely, Yancey Quimper was taking his own giant steps down in Xavier County, for at the moment back in 1848 when he learned of Captain Sam Garner's death on the uplands of Mexico, he thought: He leaves a widow, damned nice, and two children. With all that land, she's goin' to need assistance.

Actually, Garner had not acquired a great deal of land: six hundred and forty acres because of his services at San Jacinto; some acres that his wife, Rachel, had managed to acquire; and a couple of hundred that he had taken over for a bad debt. Right in the heart of Campbell, the county seat, the Garner lands were worth having.

Keeping a watchful eye on the Widow Garner lest some adventurer sneak in ahead of him, General Quimper waited what was called 'a decent interval' and then swooped in, his colors flying. Actually, in a frontier settlement like Texas where women were scarce, the decent interval for an attractive widow to mourn after the sudden death of her husband was anywhere from three weeks to four months. Men needed wives; wives needed protection; and orphaned children were a positive boon rather than a hindrance.

When Quimper first began speaking to Rachel Garner about her perilous condition, he stressed only her responsibility for the rearing and education of her children, and in this he was not being hypocritical, for he liked the boys. 'These are children worth the most careful attention,' he told her, sounding very much like a clergyman.

But on subsequent visits he began talking about her problems with the eight hundred and forty acres with which she found herself: 'Today they're worth nothing, maybe a dollar an acre. But in the future, Rachel . . .' He now addressed her only as Rachel and always saw to it that one of her children was at his side as he spoke. He dwelt upon the difficulties an unmarried woman would face if she endeavored to manage too much property. He stressed the fact that the land lay half within the town, half out in the country, a division which trebled the complications.

On an April day in 1850, at the time the Cobbs were excavating their lake, he suddenly took Mrs Garner's hands, her children being absent, and gazed at her as if overcome by a totally unexpected passion: 'Rachel, you cannot take care of a farm and two lovely children alone. Allow me to help.'

Everything he had been saying for the past months had made sense, indeed the only common sense she had heard for a long time. A preacher for whom she had little respect had mumbled: 'God always looks after the orphaned child,' but General Quimper had outlined practical courses of action which did not depend upon God's uncertain support, and she was now disposed to listen seriously to his next recommendations.

Having uttered the critical words, he retreated from her kitchen as if overcome with embarrassment and stayed away for two days, but on the third day he returned filled with apologies for his intemperate behavior during his last visit, and with great relief he heard Mrs Garner say: 'No apologies are necessary. You were seized by an honest emotion, and I respect you for it.'

When the proposed marriage was announced, Rachel Garner was visited by an unexpected member of her community, a tall, shaggy, rough individual known unfavorably as Panther Komax, whom her dead husband had once described: 'An animal. Good with a gun, but an animal.'

Panther's message was blunt: 'Don't marry him, Mrs Garner.'

'What are you saying?'

'He does nothin' withouten a plan.'

'What do you mean?'

'He plans to grab your land. He plans to grab ever'thin'.'

'My children need a father.'

'They don't need him.' In the silence that followed, Panther studied the neat kitchen, then said: 'You're doin' all right as it is. Captain Garner would be proud of you.'

At the mention of her husband's name, Rachel frowned, as if Komax had been unfair in bringing into the discussion that fine man, that unquestioned hero, but since Sam had been brought into the room, she said, as if for him to hear: 'Sam would want his children to have a father. He would understand.' Then almost aggressively, she turned on Panther and demanded: 'What has General Quimper ever done to you?' Komax, not wishing to compound a mistake which he now realized he had made, replied: 'Nothin'. I was only comparin' him and your husband. And when I do I get sick to my stomach.'

Actually, Quimper had been doing a great deal to Panther, and as soon as the marriage to Rachel Garner had been safely solemnized, with her children in attendance, the general directed his attention to a business matter which had been concerning him for some time.

Like the rest of Xavier County, he had watched in disbelief when Komax returned from Mexico in 1848 leading a chubby Mexican bootmaker named Juan Hernández, who proceeded to make the best boots the men of the county had ever seen. They were pliable, yet so sturdy that mesquite thorns could not penetrate them, and when three different users reported that rattlesnakes, 'and damned big ones, too, thick as your leg,' had struck the boots without forcing the fangs through the hide, Komax Boots began to be discussed favorably wherever men appreciated good leather.

In fact, Juan's boots became so popular that Panther could not supply all the men who sought them, even when he raised his price to four dollars a pair. Therefore, in December 1849, when hordes of prospectors were pouring through Texas to reach the California gold rush via the overland route through El Paso, Komax was embarrassed by the number of gold-seekers who offered him up to forty dollars for a pair of Juan's boots.

But embarrassment soon gave way to enthusiasm, and Komax told his bootmaker: 'Go down to Matamoros or

Monterrey. Find five or six good cobblers. Bring 'em here, and we'll make a fortune if these California men keep comin'.' But before Juan set out, Komax gripped him by the wrist: 'You promise to come back?' and the Mexican replied in Spanish: 'Amigo, I never lived so well. You are a man to trust.'

Soon Hernández was back in Xavier with five Mexican bootmakers, who, under his and Panther's tutelage, began to turn out boots of such remarkable quality that even when the California gold rush petered out, the demand from Texas men continued to snap up all that Panther could supply.

The price was now fixed at eleven dollars a pair, twelve if Hernández himself decorated the upper part with the Mexican designs he liked. He favored the symbol of his nation, the valiant eagle battling the rattlesnake, but most Texans rejected this: 'Damned vulture eatin' a worm,' they called it, and they asked instead for the Lone Star with crossed pistols. Juan could do either.

But the main advantage of a Komax boot was that it fitted properly, and in this respect it was unique. Up to this time, in both Mexico and Texas, shoemakers had been accustomed to make simply a boot: big, square, solid, but with the same outline for left foot and right. Such boots were so uncomfortable that a buyer sometimes had to wear them for six months before they adjusted to his feet, or vice versa. Juan Hernández changed this by drawing on a piece of paper the exact outlines of a customer's feet, properly differentiated as to right and left, and then shaping boots to fit. Men were apt to sigh when they first put on such boots: 'They fit!'

The lucrative trade which Komax had developed by his simple device of having befriended a weeping bootmaker about to have his neck slit attracted the attention of many Xavier men, who wondered why they had not thought of importing shoemakers from Matamoros, but no one paid closer heed than General Quimper, who said, one afternoon as a new rush of California-bound men clamored for boots: 'This dumb ox has a gold mine.'

It offended Quimper, offended him deeply, to think that a reprehensible man like Komax had stumbled upon such a bonanza, and he felt it his duty to see that the manufacturing operation, as he called it, was brought under honest control. He could think of no one better qualified to exercise such control than himself, for he spoke Spanish, knew men of property who could afford to buy the boots, and obviously was reliable, for he had both land and money.

To accomplish this transfer, General Quimper needed the cooperation of either a judge or a sheriff, and in frontier Texas both were available to a gentleman of good standing, especially if he came from Tennessee or Alabama and had some gold coins in his pocket. Yancey decided upon a three-pronged assault, so one morning Judge Kemper summoned Komax to his chambers: 'Panther, you could go to jail for bringing in those Mexicans.' There was no law forbidding this, for law-abiding Mexicans had always been free to cross the Rio Grande, but the judge's manner was ominous, and it was substantiated by a visit from Sheriff Bodger, who said: 'Us sheriffs in these parts got our eye on you, Panther, and your illegal operations.' The convincing blow, however, fell when six gunmen appeared at the workshop, threatening to shoot everyone in sight if they didn't get the hell out of Texas.

Quimper himself, terrified of a brute like Komax, did not make an appearance till the threats had softened up the wild man. Then he appeared, unctuous and reassuring, to deliver the good news that he could protect Panther and square things with the law by taking the offending Mexicans off his, Panther's, hands. By this simple but effective strategy, General Quimper obtained control of the bootmaking operation, and it must be conceded that once he got it he knew what to do with it. Advertising in both Houston and Austin, he visited the many United States Army forts, peddling his excellent boots to the eager officers, and he established the designation 'General Quimper Boots' as effectively as Samuel Colt had made his name synonymous with good revolvers, or as John B. Stetson would make his with hats. In the great war that was about to erupt, generals and colonels fighting for both the North or the South were apt to wear the heavily ornamented Quimpers, as they were called; but very few enlisted men would have them unless they stole them from the bodies of dead officers. Yancey did not find it comfortable selling to enlisted men.

The Cobbs now had eleven thousand acres, Reuben having

acquired eight hundred more of relatively useless river-bottom swamp, and to run it they had ninety-eight slaves, not all field hands. Since from long experience the owners had learned that one strong field hand could effectively tend only ten acres of cotton and six of corn, this meant that much of their land had to lie idle, and this was just what Reuben had intended: 'Today those bottom acres look like nothin', but time's comin' when they'll be priceless.' When someone asked why, he smiled, for what he had in mind was to dike them in, play farmer's roulette, and make enormous crops when the great floods stayed away, lose everything when they came. 'But even when floods do hit,' he told his cousin, 'we win because they bring down fresh silt from somebody else's place to enrich ours.'

The Cobb cotton fields were like no others in the area, for they were hardly fields at all, merely open spaces between tall trees, so that in early March a slave with a plow could never follow a furrow for very long before being stopped by one of the trees, and when in late March the plants showed their pale-green heads, they did not appear like proper cotton at all but rather like patches of green thrown helter-skelter. However, if the fields lacked neatness, they did carry signs that three years from now they were going to be masterpieces, because each tree which now prevented proper cultivation had been girdled and was dying; in two years it would wither, and in three it could be pushed down and the stump drawn.

Reuben did not propose to be girdled, not by nature, which he battled, nor by Northern abolitionists, who threatened his prosperity and his way of life, and he was more afraid of the latter than the former: 'Nature you can control. If the great flood comes, you hunker down and let it come, then use it later to your advantage.' At Lakeview there were three bottomlands: the low-bottoms, which were underwater much of the time; the middle-bottoms, which presented a reasonable gamble; and what might be called the upper-bottoms, which had been underwater centuries ago when the streams were powerful but which now were relatively secure against flooding. In these rich upper fields the Cobbs had planted their first crops and on them built their homes. Reuben was not worried about the ultimate worth of any of his fields, and since he had reassured himself about the permanence of the Great Raft he was satisfied that his water supply was guaranteed also.

It was his slaves about which he worried, for in a distant land like Texas, where replenishment was not easy, they were of considerable value, and if he should be deprived by Northern guile, he would lose not only his investment in them but also his capacity to work his plantation. The worth of an average adult male slave in Jefferson had increased to $900, a female, to $750, and since he and Sett had brought with them only the best, their investment, forgetting the children, stood at something better than $60,000. Since the value of a good slave seemed to rise steadily, he could anticipate that with natural increase by birth, which he figured at 2.15 percent per year, and the judicious purchase of new slaves from the farmers going out of business, by 1860 he and Sett ought to have no less than a hundred and fifty slaves worth more than $1,000 each. This was property worth protecting.

He was therefore most attentive when a Northern newspaper writer named Elmer Carmody arrived in Jefferson. Carmody told everyone quite frankly what he was up to: 'I'm writing a series of essays on the New South – Alabama, Mississippi, Texas ... We already know about the Old South. But Texas is of powerful concern to Northerners.'

He talked with anyone who would pause, and showed an intelligent interest in all details of plantation life, taking careful note of financial and husbandry details. As he went about in the small town he heard repeatedly of the Cobb brothers, as they were called, for the size and ambition of their plantation excited admiration: 'Mister, they have the best mill in the whole South, Old or New.' Several Jeffersonians volunteered to drive Carmody out to Lakeview, but he preferred to take things easy, and on the fifth day of his stay, Reuben Cobb did indeed drop by to see him.

'We hear you're writin' about us.'

'I propose to.'

'Unfavorable, I suspect?'

Carmody extended his right hand palm down, and rotated it, up and down, to indicate strict impartiality: 'I write as the facts fall, Mr Cobb. And the facts I've been hearing tell me that you and your brother ...'

'Cousin. He's from Carolina. I'm from Georgia.'

'Would I be presuming . . .?'

'To my mind, you're presumin' by even bein' in this town. But if you want to see a plantation at its best, I'd be proud to have you ride back with me.'

Reuben was on horseback, and he naturally assumed that Carmody had a mount, and when the newspaperman confessed that he didn't, Cobb hastily arranged to borrow one from a grocer with whom he did business, and soon the pair were heading out to Lakeview.

'I hear you have more than ten thousand acres. Why were you so willing . . .?'

Carmody rarely had to finish a question, for Cobb had such an acute interest in everything, he could anticipate what data an intelligent man might seek. 'We believe in Texas,' he said, turning sideways. 'We're willing to invest all our savings.'

'What did the land cost you, on the average?'

Cobb was surprised; no Southerner would dream of asking such a question of a plantation owner. Forbidden were: 'How many acres?' 'How many bales?'

Next Carmody asked: 'How many bales do you hope to ship?' And before Cobb could answer, he asked: 'Is it true you have your own wharf?'

By the time they reached Lakeview, Reuben actually liked Carmody, for in his brash twenty-six-year-old way the young man asked probing questions without a shred of guile, doing so in such a rational progression that Reuben wanted to answer, and when the four adult Cobbs met with Carmody, who stayed with them three days, the conversation became extremely pointed, with Reuben asking at the beginning of the first session: 'Are you an abolitionist?' and with Carmody replying: 'I'm nothing. I look, I listen, I report.'

'And what are you goin' to report about us? Here in Texas?'

'That you are the last gasp of profitable slavery.'

'You admit, then, that we do make profits?'

'You do, but not for long. And at a terrible cost to your society.'

Reuben flushed, and there might have been harsh words, for he was a voluble defender of the South and its peculiar traditions, but he also wanted to hear a logical explanation of the Northern point of view, so he restrained himself and asked:

834

'Why do you say our obvious profits exact a terrible cost?' and Carmody launched into a careful analysis:

'Let us suppose two recent immigrants go, one, like you, to Texas, another, also like you, to Iowa – two states that joined the Union at about the same time. You each bring to your new location the same amount of cash, the same amount of intelligence and energy. I'm afraid that the man who goes to Iowa will in the long run have every advantage, and the cruel difference will be that he will not be encumbered by slaves and you will.

'This difference will manifest itself in every aspect of life, but principally in two vital ways, manufacturing of goods and self-government. Let's take manufacturing first. Because the Iowa man has no slaves, he can rely on no ready crop like cotton. He must work in many different fields, and when he does he builds skills. Pretty soon everything he needs to live on is available locally. If he wants a bricklayer, he can hire one. If he wants an engineer, he can ask about the neighborhood, and soon he has produced a diversified society capable of supporting itself by the exchange of money for services.

'The man who comes to Texas with his slaves cannot do that, for he must apply all his own energies and that of his slaves to growing one cash crop, cotton. Now, the profits from cotton can be great. My studies satisfy me that even a poor farmer can produce his crop for seven cents a pound. But with good management you can bring it in for five and three-quarters cents, and then, even if you have to sell at seven, you prosper, and if you can get sixteen, you make a fortune. I know that in many years you do even better. But you must buy more slaves and more land. What happens when the land gives out? Your profits are not invested in the creation of a multiple society. Now and next year and for all the years to come, when you need something, you must send to Cincinnati to find it. You are not producing those useful things upon which a complex organization depends, and down the road a way you're bound to pay a terrible price for this neglect.

'Eight or nine times during my travels I've heard sensible

835

men say: "We may have to go to war, some day, to protect ourselves from the Yankees . . . to protect our sacred way of life." And the speakers have convinced me that they mean it and that their young men are the bravest in the world. But, Mr Cobb, if the North has all the production, all the railroads, all the arsenals, all the shipbuilders, it must in the long run prevail, no matter how gallant your young men prove to be.

'And before you argue me down, let me say that the gravest price you pay for your slave economy is the tardiness it encourages in the building up of government, of education and of the good agencies of societies. You have no public schools because half your population, the Negro half, does not need them. Your friend in Iowa will soon have libraries and publishing houses, and you will not. He will have lively politics, divided between reasonable factions, and you will have only the party dedicated to the preservation of slavery. This is the terrible cost of your peculiar institution. You ought to abandon it tomorrow.'

Each of the four Cobbs had a dozen points on which to debate Carmody's thesis, and he proved responsive to all of them, listening sagely, nodding his head agreeably when they scored and shaking it when they indulged in fantasy, not fact. He really was seeking information, and when he assured them that he was not an abolitionist, they believed him: 'I truly have no preconceptions. I've studied Adam Smith and have learned from him that economy governs a great deal of human effort, and the more deeply I probe into the economy of the South . . .'

'What is this word *economy*?' Petty Prue asked.

'It means everything we do at work and trade. For example, the most interesting thing I've seen at Lakeview, and let me tell you, this is an impressive plantation and you're impressive people . . . No, you guess what's been most interesting.'

The Cobbs guessed that it was their manufactured lake where none had been before, their multipurpose mill, perhaps the girdling of the trees and letting them stand in the midst of the cotton. 'No,' Carmody said, 'it's that slave Trajan. He runs your mill, you know. Gin, press, grist, saw, he does it all. Frankly, he's a better mechanic than any I saw in Iowa. And you must have in these fields around Jefferson . . .' He threw his arms wide to include all this part of Texas. He had become so excited that he lost his line of reasoning; ideas cascaded through his mind with such rapidity that this sometimes happened.

'Tell me,' he said, 'is that Great Raft I saw at Shreveport, is it there forever?' When the Cobbs assured him that it was, he said: 'Remarkable. But then, a great deal in this part of the world is remarkable.'

For two more days he talked with the Cobbs, and on the evening before his departure Reuben said: 'You know so much about us, I'd like to hire you as manager,' and Carmody replied: 'You've almost convinced me that plantation life can work,' and Somerset asked: 'But you leave us still unconvinced?' and he said: 'Yes. This way of life is doomed. Its economy must deteriorate.'

'Now, that's where you're wrong!' Reuben cried, leaping to his feet. 'If we can keep moving our slaves westward, we can maintain the paradise forever.'

Carmody stiffened, visibly, and Petty Prue wished her husband had not spoken so openly, for she knew the young visitor must respond; he was the kind who did: 'Mr Cobb, the nation will not permit you, will never permit you, to carry your slaves even ten miles west of Texas.'

Reuben flushed and his neck muscles grew taut, whereupon Petty Prue said blithely: 'I've prepared a small libation in honor of your departure, Mr Carmody,' and the tempest was avoided, but just before retiring for the night Carmody said something which caused Reuben to fall silent: 'Up on the Red River, I met this Methodist preacher, man named Hutchinson, not a very good preacher, if you ask me, in the pulpit I mean, but a man of profound wisdom. He told me that he's been teaching slaves in that district to read and figure, and he's found that some of them were distinctly clever.'

On the day that Elmer Carmody left Jefferson, Reuben Cobb and two neighbors rode north to the Red River, a distance of only sixty miles to the Indian territory, and there they made quiet inquiry as to the comings and goings of this Methodist minister Hutchinson. When they had him well spotted, they enlisted the aid of several local plantation owners, and in the dark of night they apprehended the lanky, weepy-eyed man and

837

tied him to a tree. Warning him that if he continued preaching insurrection to slaves in the district, they would kill him next time, they then lashed him till he fainted. Leaving him tied to the tree, they returned to their homes.

Just before Christmas 1850, the Cobbs met General Yancey Quimper and were at first impressed by the man's bearing and his obvious patriotism, although they differed as to the amount of support they wished to give him. Reuben, always on the hair trigger where Southern rights were concerned and looking far forward in his defense of slavery, thought that Quimper made a great deal of sense in his opposition to Henry Clay's notorious Compromise of 1850, which restricted the spread of slavery, and he supported Quimper with special vigor when the general objected to the part of the compromise which delineated the boundaries of Texas.

'Look at this map, what they did to us,' Quimper cried as he explained how Congress had stolen immense areas of land from what should have been Texas. 'We won all this territory from Mexico, won it with our guns . . .'

'Is it true that you led the infantry at San Jacinto?' Somerset asked.

'Most powerful sixteen minutes in the history of Texas,' Quimper said. 'In those flaming minutes we won all this land, and now Congress takes it away.'

His map was compelling, for it showed the original Republic of Texas in 1836, bordered on the west by the Rio Grande in such a way that Santa Fe was part of Texas, and there was also a panhandle which stretched all the way into what would later become the states of Colorado and Wyoming, encompassing much of the good land of New Mexico and Oklahoma. 'If we'd of kept this,' Quimper stormed, 'we'd of been one of the major nations of the world.'

Somerset tried to placate him: 'General, you forget that Congress paid us ten million dollars for our rights.'

'No honest Texian would ever sell his birthright for a mess of potatoes.'

'We call ourselves Texans now. The old days are gone.'

'Ah-ha!' Reuben cried. 'Did you hear that, General? First time my cousin used *we* when speakin' of Texas. Always before it was *you*, like he was a visitor here.'

'I feel myself to be part of Texas,' Sett confessed, 'and while I can't see the other states allowing us to hold all that land, especially up in the North, I do think we ought to have had the upper reaches of the Rio Grande as our western boundary.'

'Exactly!' Quimper shouted. 'Then we'd have Santa Fe as a counter-balance to El Paso.' With a broad and generous hand he gave away Colorado and Wyoming, but with hungry fingers he drew Santa Fe back into the Texas orbit.

The cousins were at first charmed by this affable man with the very attractive wife. The general was now thirty-eight years old, fleshy, clean-shaven, and often prophetic when peering into the future: 'Worst mistake Texas ever made, gentlemen, was when we sent Sam Houston to the United States Senate. Hell, he don't represent the interests of true Texans or the future of the South.'

'Wait a minute,' Somerset interrupted. 'I've seen pamphlets in which you and Houston fought side by side in getting Texas into the Union.'

'We did, that we did. Even a habitual drunk can sober up sometimes and do the right thing. But he's a man who cannot be trusted, never could be.'

Reuben said: 'They tell me you had a chance to shoot him in that duel, and that as a gentleman, you shot off to the side.'

'Worst mistake I ever made. Sooner or later, somebody's goin' to have to handle that old drunk.'

When Quimper left Lakeview, the Cobb cousins remained confused because so much of what he said was true, so much of what he did was false, and it was during these days of review that Reuben and Sett began to draw apart in their judgment of the man. Reuben, always thirsting for action, was eager to associate himself with Quimper and was uneasy lest the tall-talker initiate some campaign without including him, but Sett, a cautious judge of men, grew more suspicious of Quimper the more he thought about the man's behavior. In this he was abetted by Millicent, who said simply, when they were alone: 'He's a fraud. Couldn't you see that?'

'I did see it, but I also saw that he makes great sense when he talks about South and North.'

'Easy. Listen to him when he talks, but leave him when he begins to act.'

In 1854, Yancey Quimper rode back to Jefferson with a band of nineteen Southern patriots who were determined to move Kansas into the slave column and he was not only prepared to march them right into that area but also to help them in disciplining any Northerners who might have slipped across the border. He was so excited, so persuasive, that Reuben Cobb rode north with him.

They entered Kansas quietly, in three separate groups, and spent two weeks listening to accounts of Northern perfidy. For fifteen days they did nothing except scout the land and establish escape routes in case a superior Northern force attacked. Of course, at this time there was no Northern force, superior or inferior, but they did come upon a pair of isolated farms occupied by families from Illinois, and these they surrounded and attacked on their last night in the area.

'No killin'!' Quimper ordered as his men crept closer, and his command was obeyed, for the Texans ran at the houses shouting and yelling, and so swift were they in executing Quimper's commands, they had possession of the farms before the occupants could think of gunfire. The families were herded onto a hillside, where they watched as torches were applied to the rude homes they had built with painful effort.

'You go back where you belong,' Quimper warned them. 'Your kind is not welcome here.'

When the vigilantes returned across the Red River, recognized by Congress as the northern boundary of Texas, they learned that Reverend Hutchinson, the Methodist minister who had been punished before because of his incendiary work among slaves, was still up to his old tricks, so Quimper, Cobb and three others rode out to his parsonage and hanged him.

The group then separated, Cobb heading east to Jefferson and Quimper south to Xavier, but each carried a promise from the other: 'When the trouble starts, you can rely on me.'

When Elmer Carmody published his travel book, *Texas Good and Bad*, he could not have foreseen that his carefully considered judgment on two types of Texas community,

English and German, would place the residents of the latter in mortal danger. First, his generalizations about the typical Texas town of that period:

> South of the Brazos, I stopped overnight at the hostelry of one Mr Angeny, from parts unknown. He had four guests that night, but explained to us: 'I ain't got no food in the place, saven some cornbread and lard and sugar.' That's what we ate. He had no blankets, either, and his two beds in which four of us would sleep with all our clothes on for warmth were lice-ridden. He also had no hot water for shaving, no chamberpot for convenience, and very little hay for our horses. Charge $1.50 for man, $.85 for beast.

In this frame of mind Carmody chanced to move west from Austin, which he considered a pitiful excuse for a state capital, 'worst in America, all spittoons and greasy beef,' and in his casual wandering he came upon Fredericksburg, which he extolled:

> It was with these gloomy reflections that I turned a bend in the Pedernales River and came upon the two beautiful stone houses of the Allerkamp family, and immediately I saw them, I realized that I was passing from barbarism into civilization.
>
> The trees were trimmed, as trees should be when they stand about homes. The lawn was green, and flowers were confined to neat beds upon which someone had spent considerable care. The well-designed houses were of stone, with no open spaces for the wind to enter, which I had been accustomed to on my Texas travels. And over everything there was a cloak of neatness, of respectability, of the very best husbandry.

As a practiced writer, Carmody realized that for an outsider to venture into a sensitive area like Texas and offer comment on its way of life was hazardous and bound to excite criticism, but even he did not appreciate how inflammatory it was to compare the Germans so favorably to the barbarians he encountered elsewhere. Especially dangerous were his comments about white cotton growers:

841

I had been assured since entering Texas that the cultivation of cotton could be achieved only with the work of slaves and that no white man could possibly plant and harvest this demanding plant. I saw that the Germans of the Hill Country did very well with cotton. They grow it efficiently, bale it more carefully than others, then watch it bring a marked premium at Galveston, New Orleans and Liverpool. Fredericksburg proves that most of what Texans say about slavery is nonsense.

A writer has certain advantages. He can publish such evaluations, then scurry out of the country, but his words remain behind, generating bitterness, and in the years following the circulation of Carmody's *Texas Good and Bad*, other Texas citizens began to look upon the Germans as aliens who refused to enter the mainstream of Texas life, as cryptic abolitionists, and even as traitors to the fundamental patriotism of the state.

When General Quimper visited the Cobbs, he found them incensed at what Carmody had written about them, but they had not finished voicing their grievances when he interrupted: 'Gentlemen, it isn't only his infringement of your courtesy that should bother you. What can you expect of a writer? It's his praising of the Germans. And particularly what he says about slavery.'

He took the Carmody book and read with emphasis the passage about growing cotton without slaves: 'That's treasonous! The time could come when we might have to teach those Germans a lesson in manners. They invade our land and then try to tell us how to behave. If we catch them tamperin' with our slaves ...'

He had touched upon one of the strangest aspects of Southern life: many slaveholders were convinced that their slaves, at least, were supremely happy in their position of servitude; but at the same time, the owners were desperately afraid of slave uprisings, or of Northerners inciting their slaves; there was a constant tattoo of hangings, beatings and terrible repressions whenever it was suspected that the 'happy' slaves might be surreptitiously preparing a general slaughter. Thus there had been fierce punishments meted out when it looked as if the slaves might rebel at Nacogdoches, and white clergymen had been hanged at the Red River on the mere suspicion that they had been 'tamperin' with our loyal slaves.'

Any serious consideration of punishing the insidious Germans was forgotten in early June of 1856, when word reached Texas of the insane behavior of John Brown and his sons in Kansas.

'They've murdered Southerners!' General Quimper cried as he carried the news from house to house, and before the details could be verified, Quimper and Reuben Cobb were back on the trail to Bleeding Kansas. With the nineteen men who accompanied them, they formed a powerful support for the Southern agents who were trying to ensure that if a plebiscite ever occurred, the vote would favor slavery. Of these twenty-one vigorous defenders of the Southern position, only four owned slaves – Quimper was not one of them – and only thirteen had come into Texas from Southern states, but all were willing to risk their lives in defense of the South. As Quimper himself explained, after a wild skirmish in which four abolitionists were slain: 'You have a strong feelin' that God intended things to be the way they are in the South. And any man can see that the welfare of Texas depends on our standin' shoulder to shoulder with our Southern brothers.'

When Cobb and Quimper reached home with the exciting news of their victories in Kansas – 'Nine abolitionists killed without the loss of a Texan' – they started to try to whip up enthusiasm for some kind of vague action against the Union, but now they ran into the iron-hard character of Sam Houston, who was determined to protect the Union and keep his beloved Texas firmly within its protection.

Quimper, an able man where political savagery was required, led the fight to humiliate the 'old drunk,' as he still called him: 'He sits there in the Senate of the United States and does everything possible to humiliate Texas. Always he votes against our interests. He might as well be an abolitionist.'

His charges were partially true, because in these closing days of his life Sam Houston, now sixty-four, dropped the vacillation which had sometimes clouded his character and came out strongly and heroically in favor of preserving the Union, regardless of the offense to local preferences: 'I support the

Union which has made us great, and if there are any temporary imbalances, they can be corrected.' When pressed, he admitted that he was now and had always been a strong pro-slavery man, but that slavery could be protected and even advanced within the existing structure, and he begged his fellow Texans to protect it in that constitutional manner.

In a time of threatening chaos, he was a constant voice of reason, and when others talked with increasing passion he became more conciliatory, imploring his friends, North and South, to retain the rule of common sense. When he had felt that to preserve the Union he must vote for the Compromise of 1850, because he saw it as the only way to prevent dissolution, he had been denounced as a traitor to the Southern cause, and when he spoke even more forcefully against the shameful surrender of the 1854 Kansas-Nebraska Act, he was vilified.

It was as a consequence of this general disfavor into which Houston had fallen that General Quimper devised a clever manipulation to show Houston and the rest of the state just how deeply Texas now despised its former hero. 'Let's show the old fool we mean business,' Quimper argued. 'Let's elect his replacement in the Senate right now.'

'His term has two more years to run. Such a rebuke has never before been given.'

'We'll do it, and he'll be the laughing stock of the nation.' And forthwith Quimper bullied his fellow Texas state senators into designating Houston's replacement while he was still in office.

But Houston was a fighter, and in 1859 he astounded Quimper and his cronies by announcing that since he was being denied his Senate seat, he would run for the governorship of Texas on a platform of preserving the Union. Aware that sentiment was veering against him on this point, he mounted an intensely personal campaign, crisscrossing the state and applying his unusual powers of persuasion. People swarmed to meet with him, listened, rejected his program but supported him personally. Some felt that the old Indian-lover could solve the Indian problems that agitated the western counties, and when the votes were counted, this man who swam against the tide had won, capping a career unmatched in American history: congressman from Tennessee, twice elected governor of that state, twice president of the Republic of Texas, United States senator, and now governor of the state of Texas. He had known more ups and downs than any other major figure in American politics, for after almost every victory, there had come defeat. Now, with the Union in peril, he would launch a heroic defense of his principle.

It was not going to be easy. General Quimper, encouraged by Houston's foes, dusted off his old anti-Houston pamphlet of 1841, the one written by another hand, and added a salvo of subsequent charges:

> We have known for many years that Houston is a drunk, a bigamist, a liar, a land-office crook, a despoiler of ladies and a coward who avoided battle and an honest duel whenever possible. But did we then know that he was also an enemy of the South, a betrayer of the interests of Texas, a cheap tool in the hands of abolitionists and a stealer of public moneys? That is the real Sam Houston, and he is powerless to deny even one of these charges, because the entire nation, and Texas in particular, knows they are true.

As the crucial presidential election of 1860 approached, Quimper maintained the drumbeat of charges against Houston, and the agony into which the nation was stumbling encouraged people to believe the accusations, so that within months of his surprising victory at the polls, the reputation of Sam Houston had fallen to new depths. He may have sensed that he was heading for the major role in a Greek tragedy of destroyed ambitions, but if he did, he still plunged ahead, his actions showing his belief that the preservation of the Union was more valuable to the world than the salvaging of a local reputation.

From the vantage point of Texas, the presidential election of 1860 can be quickly summarized but not so easily understood. The new Republican party nominated a former congressman from Illinois, Abraham Lincoln, whose very name was anathema to the South; when planters like the Cobbs were forced to speak it, they either spat or cursed.

The Democrats, split over the question of slavery, produced splinter groups that nominated three candidates whose combined popular vote smothered Lincoln, 2,810,501 to a mere

1,866,352. However, the peculiarity of the electoral system gave the Illinois lawyer the victory, 180 to 123, enabling him to become President of a nation already painfully divided on a vital issue, all of his electoral votes coming from the Northern states. In Texas he collected not a single vote, popular or electoral; he was not allowed on the ballot. But the most shocking fact was that in the Southern states, which he must now try to govern, he received less than 100,000 votes in all. Tragedy became inescapable, and men of all parties sensed it.

Everything Sam Houston had wanted to preserve, all the honorable things he had fought for, he had lost. But he was still governor, and from his powerful position he was determined to keep Texas on a sober course. There would be no impetuous acts while he was in control.

But to keep Texas in line he had to contend with hotheads like General Quimper and relative moderates like Reuben Cobb, who had been terrified by the various John Brown raids. As soon as the election results were known they and thousands like them began to shout: 'Immediate secession! Abe Lincoln is not our president!' Houston, ignoring the fact that this cry galvanized the state against him, vigorously opposed secession, reminding his Texans that the Union still stood, still protected freedom as in the past.

When South Carolina, always the incendiary leader, always first to defend its rights regardless of cost, voted to secede on 20 December 1860, Houston fought even more valiantly to prevent his state from following, whereupon Quimper and his fellow secessionists decided to make their own law: 'We'll assemble a convention of elected delegates and let them determine what course Texas shall take.' When it became clear that this revolutionary tactic was going to succeed, Houston bowed to the inevitable and sought to give the action a cloak of legality. Calling for a special session of the legislature, he allowed it and not Quimper's compatriots to summon the convention.

It was a fiery assembly, determined to break away from the Union, and when one fearless delegate tried to persuade his fellows to remain loyal, the gallery hissed, inspiring one of the great statements in Texas history: 'When the rabble hiss, well may patriots tremble.'

A plebiscite was authorized, and when the popular vote was counted, the men of Texas had decided 46,153 to 14,747 to secede, even if this resulted in warfare. The tally provided an interesting insight into Texan attitudes, because only one person in ten owned a slave, but nearly eight in ten of those who voted defended Southern rights, and when the test of battle came, nine in ten would support the war.

When these results were announced, General Quimper felt justified, for they proved that his ancient nemesis, Sam Houston, had been repudiated by the state he was supposed to lead. 'He should resign,' Yancey shouted. 'He has lost our confidence.' As before, Houston ignored such talk, arguing ineffectively with any who would listen: 'Yes, yes, Texas has withdrawn from the Union. But that doesn't mean we have joined the Confederacy.'

'What does it mean?' men like Reuben Cobb demanded, and Houston, not wishing to see Texas take arms against the Union he loved, proposed a pathetic alternative: 'The vote means that Texas is once more a free nation, strong enough to ignore both South and North. Let us now resume control of our own destiny.' But the majority was so hungry for war that his advice was rejected.

Houston, nearing seventy and failing in health, now fought his greatest battle. Still governor of the state, but scorned by all and calumniated by General Quimper, who once again challenged him to a duel, he sat in the governor's mansion in Austin and reflected on what he must do.

The new laws of Texas stated that if he wished to retain office, he must take an oath of allegiance to the Confederacy, and this would have been an easy gesture, except for one constraint: 'I have always been and am now loyal to the Union. My tongue would cleave to my mouth if I took a contrary oath.' He decided that when the test came, if men like Quimper forced him to deny his allegiance to the Union, he would resign.

But before he was forced to act, an escape presented itself. President Lincoln secretly offered to send Federal troops into Texas to assist Houston in retaining his governorship and thus keep Texas within the Union, and this was a most alluring temptation. But Houston could discuss it only with a man who would be honor-bound to respect the secrecy, so he sent for a man he had met only once, Somerset Cobb, the big plantation owner at Jefferson, and when the two men talked in Austin, Houston said: 'In the debate about secession, Cobb, you were a voice of sanity. How do you see things now?'

Cobb had not ridden so far to talk platitudes: 'War is inevitable. The South will fight valiantly, of that you can be sure, but we must lose.'

The two men sat silent, tormented by the problems of loyalty. Houston was loyal to the Union, that splendid concept so ably defended by Andrew Jackson when Houston was a young man learning to master politics. But he was also loyal to Texas, the state he had rescued from burning embers. God, how he loved Texas.

Cobb, for his part, would be forever loyal to the principles upon which he had been weaned in South Carolina, and if his natal state declared war, he must support her. But recent experiences had made him loyal also to Texas, and he saw that her present course was self-defeating. Even so, he must volunteer his services in a cause he knew would lose. Loyalties, how they cascaded upon a man, confusing him and tearing him apart, yet ennobling him as few other human emotions ever did.

'What should I do, Cobb?'

'Can you, in honor, take the oath of allegiance to the Confederacy?'

'No.'

'Then you must resign.'

'And Lincoln's offer of military aid? To keep me in power?'

Now the silence returned, for how could the governor of any state accept outside force to retain office when the people of that state had shown they rejected him and all he stood for? In his question Cobb had touched the vital nerve which activated the best men in these perilous days: Can you, in honor, do thus or so? Men like Cobb and Houston had been raised in that Virginia-Carolina tradition of honor; as boys they had read Sir Walter Scott and imbibed from his dauntless heroes their definitions of honor. They had fought duels to prove their integrity, and when Houston's first wife behaved in a peculiar way, his sense of rectitude prevented him from explaining his position. Now honor demanded that Somerset Cobb respond to the bugle calls, and honor required that Sam Houston refuse

President Lincoln's offer of aid, which could bring only war to Texas. There was not a chance in ten thousand that Cobb would refuse to fight for the South; the odds were the same against Houston's accepting outside aid to hold grimly to a governorship he had already lost.

Twice in one lifetime, as a young man in Tennessee, now as an old man in Texas, Houston faced the moral necessity of surrendering a governorship, and surrendering Texas proved twice as bitter as the earlier debacle. On 15 March those state officials eager to fight on the side of the Confederacy, should war come, revoked their pledge of allegiance to the Federal Union and took in its place an oath to defend the Confederacy.

Sam Houston refused to do this, so he was commanded to appear at high noon on Saturday, 16 March, and pledge allegiance to the new government. That night the old lion read from the Bible, spoke gently with his family, then went aloft to his bedroom, where he stalked the floor all night in his stockinged feet, wrestling with the monumental choices that faced him. When he came down for breakfast, gaunt and worn, he told his wife: 'Margaret, I will never do it.'

As noon approached, he retreated to the cellar of the Capitol building, sat himself firmly in an old chair, took out his knife, and started whittling a hickory limb. From the top of the stairs a messenger from the new government cried three times: 'Sam Houston! Sam Houston! Sam Houston! Come forth and swear allegiance!' Silent, he continued whittling, and thus surrendered the nation-state he had called into being.

Although Houston preferred exile in silence, there was such a public demand that he explain his unpatriotic behavior, he, against his better judgment, agreed to defend himself at an open meeting held in Brenham, a little town due east of Austin, and people gathered from far distances to hear his attempt at justification.

When General Quimper and other staunch Southern partisans learned of the meeting, they were infuriated: 'His views are downright treason!' and a half-dozen rowdies announced that they would shoot Houston the moment he appeared on the platform. Friends urged Houston to cancel the meeting, but to retreat under such circumstances was not his style: 'I shall speak.'

Millicent and Petty Prue rode south to hear the historic address, and were startled at how old Houston looked when he came on stage, six feet four, rumpled hair, his shoulders warmed by the Mexican serape he favored, his eyes sunk, but visible in every feature that old fire, that love of combat.

'Look!' Millicent whispered. 'He sees Quimper,' and indeed he did, for he looked directly at his would-be assassin and nodded.

'See those men!' Petty Prue cried loud enough for others to hear, and all looked to where six of Quimper's followers were moving resolutely toward the stage.

But then Millicent uttered a low 'My God!' – and when Prue looked to where she pointed, she saw that onto the stage had come the two Cobb men, pistols drawn.

'No shooting!' Prue whispered. 'Please God, no shooting.'

'We've gathered here tonight,' Reuben said quietly, 'to hear a great man try to justify his mistakes. Sett and I, we oppose everything he stands for. We deem his actions a disgrace to Texas, but at San Jacinto he saved his state and we propose to let him have his say.'

Some cheered, but it was Somerset who electrified the hall: 'If anyone makes a move to interrupt this meeting, Reuben and I will shoot him dead.' And he pointed his two guns directly at Quimper while his cousin covered the others.

'Let him speak!' people began to shout, and when the noise subsided, the old warrior stepped forward, drew about his shoulders the tattered serape, and said:

'I love the plaudits of my fellow citizens, but will never sacrifice my principles in order to gain public favor or commendation. I heard the hiss of mobs in the streets of Brenham, and friends warned me that my life was in peril if I dared express my honest convictions.'

At this point Quimper and his men started to move forward, but Sett Cobb raised his pistols slightly and whispered: 'Keep back.'

'Never will I exchange our Federal Constitution and our

Union for a Confederate constitution and government whose principle of secession can be only short-lived and must end in revolution and utter ruin.'

This blunt rejection of the Confederacy, to which almost every man in the audience had pledged his loyalty and his life, outraged the listeners, the Cobb brothers included, but the old fighter plowed ahead. Now, however, he threw a sop to the Southerners, for he rattled off that impressive list of great leaders provided by the South:

'Our galaxy of Southern Presidents – Washington, Jefferson, Madison, Monroe, Jackson, Taylor, Tyler and Polk – cemented the bonds of union between all the states which can never be broken. I believe a majority of our Southern people are opposed to secession.' (Loud cries of No! No!) 'But the secession leaders declare that the Confederate government will soon be acknowledged by all foreign nations, and that it can be permanently established without bloodshed.' (Cheers, followed by the thundering voice of prophecy.) 'They might with equal truth declare that the foundations of the great deep blue seas can be broken up without disturbing their surface waters, as to tell us that the best government ever devised for men can be broken up without bloodshed.'

Now he called upon his wide knowledge of war and politics, and like the great seer he was, he hammered home a chain of simple truths: 'Cotton is not King, and European nations will not fight on our side to ensure its delivery.' 'One Southern man, because of his experience with firearms, is not equal to ten Northerners.' 'The civil war which is now at hand will be stubborn and of long duration.' 'The soil of our beloved South will drink deep the precious blood of our sons and brethren.' And then the tremendous closing of a tremendous speech, the mournful cry of an ancient prophet who sees his beloved nation plunging into disaster:

'I cannot, nor will I, close my eyes against the voice of light and reason. The die has been cast by your secession leaders, whom you have permitted to sow and broadcast the seeds of

851

secession, and you must ere long reap the fearful harvest of conspiracy and revolution.'

The crowd was silent. Quimper and his rowdies stood aside to let him pass. The Cobb brothers put down their guns. And Sam Houston left the stage of Texas politics.

What contribution could Texas make to the Confederacy? It was far removed from the fields of battle and possessed no manufactures of significance: if it wanted to arm its men, it had to forage through Mexico to find guns and ammunition.

It had only a sparse population – 420,891 white persons, 182,566 slaves and 355 freed blacks – most of whom lived in communities of less than a thousand. Only two towns, Galveston and San Antonio, had as many as five thousand people.

Nor could the Confederacy look to Texas for large numbers of recruits, since the state was heavily agricultural and required its men on its farms. Also, it offered an insane number of exemptions from military service: Confederate and state officers and their clerks, mail carriers, ferryboat operators, ship pilots, railroad men, professors in colleges and academies, telegraphists, clergymen, miners, teachers of the blind or any kind of teacher with more than twenty students, nurses, lunatic custodians, druggists – one to a store – and operators of woolen factories. Matters were further complicated in that any man chosen for military duty could purchase a substitute and stay home. Also, most Texans wanted to fight as cavalry, and in extension of the rough-and-ready rules of the Mexican War, they wanted to enlist for brief, stipulated periods and then fight only under Texan officers whom they elected.

It was a rule of thumb in all the armies of the world that a civilian population could never be expected to provide more than ten percent of its total population to a draft. Texas, with less than half a million white persons, should at best have provided about fifty thousand soldiers to the Confederacy. Despite all the exemptions, it sent between seventy-five and ninety thousand.

Reuben Cobb, as the operator of a cotton gin, was specifically excused from military service: 'The Confederacy will survive only if its cotton continues to reach European markets, for then we'll bring in the money we need for arms and food.'

But Reuben would have none of this, and on the first day that volunteers were accepted he enrolled, telling his wife: 'Trajan and Jaxifer can run the gin as well as I can,' and off to war he went, never doubting that the two trusted Negroes would keep his plantation prospering.

Cobb was welcomed as a proven fighter, but it was judged that he would be most useful not in the east with General Robert E. Lee, well regarded in Texas for his frontier wars against the Comanche, but as a member of a force defending the Red River approaches to the state. Elected by his troops as their captain, he roamed his command, assuring the safety of the Confederacy in that underpopulated quarter; he would have preferred more active duty and put his name in for either the Mississippi campaign or what General Quimper called 'our attempt to recapture Santa Fe,' but to his disgust he was left where he was.

His post had one advantage: he could at various times ride south to visit Lakeview and his family. His two sons, of course, were in uniform, one with the Texas Brigade, one with fellow Texan Albert Sidney Johnston; and his wife, Petty Prue, was more or less in charge of the plantation, assisted when possible by Cousin Sett. Somerset Cobb, too, could have claimed exemption under a '20-slave owner' rule, but he had quickly volunteered at the first news of Fort Sumter. The government had then decided that he was more needed at home, supervising the movement of cotton that brought the Confederacy wealth when delivered at New Orleans, which remained open at the moment. There brave rivermen sneaked it through the blockade to waiting English and French ships.

'Are we winning?' Sett asked during one of his cousin's unannounced visits.

'You know more than I do.'

'Any trouble along the Red River?'

'A great deal, if the truth were known. We suspect rebellion in that quarter. Watch it closely.' Flicking dust from his handsome General Quimper boots, he asked solicitously: 'How are the women? Is Petty Prue able ...?' His voice drifted, indicating the concern he felt about leaving a woman in charge of a major plantation.

'We give her what help we can.'

'We?'

'Yes, Trajan and I. He really runs things, you know.'

'The mills, yes. But surely he doesn't . . .'

'Reuben, we have to use every hand we have. You know, I'm going off, first chance I get.'

'You're needed here, Sett.'

'I cannot have my son in uniform, my two nephews . . . What do you hear from the boys?'

'John tells me that the Texas Brigade has seen more battle than any unit in the army. Wherever they go, major combat. If it's critical, Lee calls for Hood.'

'He hasn't been wounded . . . or anything?'

'God looks after brave men. I believe that, Sett. If two men march into battle, it's the coward who dies first.' He reflected on this, then asked: 'And how's Millicent?'

'Poorly. But she was never strong, you know. The absence of the boys, mine and yours . . .'

'You mustn't let her grieve. I ordered Petty Prue not to grieve just because she has two sons in service. Fact is, Sett, we should all be celebrating. Lee and men like Jeb Stuart, they're pushing the Yanks about.'

Very carefully Sett asked: 'Do your men, the sensible ones, that is, do they still think we can win this war?'

Reuben leaped to his feet. 'What an awful question! In my own house!' When his temper cooled he said: 'We've got to win. The entire fate of the South . . .'

'But *can* we win?' Sett hammered, and Reuben avoided an answer: 'I'm puttin' in for duty in the east . . . with Lee.' He submitted his papers and was accepted, but he was deterred by an extraordinary adventure into which General Quimper projected him.

When the Texas plebiscite on secession was broken down by counties, it was found that eighteen out of a total of 152, of which 122 were organized, had signified their desire to remain in the Union: seven along the northern border, where Southern traditions had not been able to prevail because of the constant influx of settlers from the North, ten among the German counties in the center of the state, where abolitionism had gained root, and one, Angelina, which stood alone and unexplained; its vote defied logical explanation. Equally dangerous, eleven other counties had come within ten percent of voting for the Union. Texas had not been nearly as unanimous in its support of the South as the Cobbs had predicted.

In the Hill Country, fiery abolitionists were visiting German settlements and trying to inflame the residents with talk about opposing slavery. When they reached Fredericksburg they awakened response in certain families who felt that slavery was an intolerable wrong, but they accomplished little with the Allerkamps or with their daughter, Franziska, whose husband was down along the Nueces pursuing Benito Garza. However, they did enlist the vigorous support of three families, who put them in touch with like-minded Germans to the south.

After a careful evaluation of that area, the abolitionists returned to the Allerkamp settlement with a persuasive proposal: 'We all know that slavery is wrong. We know it debases the man who practices it and the man who suffers it. What we propose is nothing radical. It injures no one. It can raise no opposition among those who support the Confederacy.'

'And what is that?' Ludwig asked, because he had for some time now been seeking just such a solution to his confusion.

'We shall leave Texas for the moment. We shall quit all the wrongdoing, all the killing. And we shall go quietly down into Mexico, hurting no one and seeking refuge there until this senseless war is over.'

On 1 August 1862, sixty-five Germans, including Ludwig Allerkamp and his son Emil, headed west, then south, to escape the war.

General Yancey Quimper, feeling himself responsible for the safety of the Confederacy, whether the threat came from the Red River or from Fredericksburg, had infiltrated into the latter area a spy named Henry Steward, who reported to Quimper:

Fifteen hundred fully armed and rebellious Germans have been meeting secretly at a place in the hills near

Fredericksburg, where not a word of English is spoken, at a secluded spot called Lion Creek. I know that these men are plotting to terrorize towns like Austin and San Antonio, then cross the Rio Grande into Mexico, from where they will sail to New Orleans in hopes of joining the Northern army.'

When Quimper, keeping an eye on Northern sympathizers along the Red River, read this report and visualized a contingent of fifteen hundred effectives joining the Federals, he became determined to thwart them and wanted to leave immediately to engage them in battle before they could reach the Rio Grande. But when he presented the details to Major Reuben Cobb, the latter said: 'This is the word of one spy, and not a reliable one, if what I hear of him is true,' so the dash south was postponed. In further discussion Cobb pointed out several weaknesses in the story: 'How do we know they intend enlisting in the Northern army? What proof have we that they're doing anything but escaping into Mexico?' Three days later the spy Steward was found with his throat cut.

Infuriated by this attack, Cobb became even more eager than Quimper to punish the Germans, and together they rushed south to place themselves under the command of a mercurial Captain Duff, who had been dishonorably discharged in peacetime, but allowed back in war. Duff's ninety-four mounted men sighted the sixty-five Germans fleeing on foot at the banks of the Nueces, a river accustomed to violent deeds, and less than fifty miles from Mexico. 'We must not let them escape,' Quimper whispered to Duff, who replied: 'They ain't goin' to.'

On the night of 9 August 1862, with safety in Mexico near at hand, Ludwig Allerkamp was most uneasy when the men commanding the German escape decided to spend a relaxed evening under the stars rather than forge ahead to the Rio Grande. 'We should get out of Texas immediately,' Ludwig argued, but the commander lulled him with assurances that no Confederate troops would bother them, or even care that they were heading for Mexico.

It was a lovely summer's night graced with fresh-shot turkey, the inevitable choral singing and even several bottles of San Antonio beer used to toast homes in Texas: 'Till we come back in peace.' And of course, when the eating ended there were the inevitable formal discussions which Germans seemed to need; a man from Fredericksburg served as chairman for 'Crushed Hopes in Germany,' and a doctor for 'Health Problems We Will Encounter in Mexico,' but at the conclusion of the discussions Ludwig suggested: 'I think we should post sentries tonight,' and when the others asked why, he responded: 'We are of military age and we are leaving the country. We could be arrested as deserters.' The others laughed at his fears.

General Quimper said as the sun set: 'We were damned lucky to have overtaken them,' but he was grievously disappointed to find that instead of the fifteen hundred Germans his spy had reported, there were fewer than seventy. 'Not many Germans,' Quimper told Duff, 'but they form a dangerous body,' and every precaution was taken to see that none escaped.

The Confederate troops were astonished at how close to the Germans they were able to move without detection, and the contingents that waded across the Nueces to cut off any rush to the south splashed water when two men fell in, but even this did not alert the sleepers.

At three in the morning Ludwig Allerkamp awakened and grew uneasy when Emil did not answer his call. He started to look for him, but before he could find the young man he stumbled into a nest of soldiers, who fired at him indiscriminately; they missed him but killed his son, who had leaped to his feet when the firing started.

Now the shooting became general, and terribly confused, with the Confederate soldiers firing their deadly Sharps directly into the terrified mass of Germans, who tried to establish a defensive line from which to return fire. But soon the discipline and superior firepower of the army men began to take effect, and it became obvious that the Germans could not protect themselves.

Some fell, shot dead; some splashed back across the Nueces and fled north; most stood firm and fought it out against vastly superior odds. Allerkamp, raging because his son had been slain in such a senseless battle, was one who stayed, and in the heat of morning he saw that others he respected were with him too. Cried one: Laszt uns unser Leben so teuer wie möglich

857

verkaufen!' (Let us sell our lives as dearly as we can) and this the man did, blazing away in defense of freedom until he fell.

Three soldiers in gray charged at Allerkamp, stabbing at him with their bayonets and shouting their battle cry 'For Southern Freedom.' When the bloody skirmish ended shortly after dawn, there were nineteen Germans and two Confederates killed in one of the least justified actions of the war.

There were also nine wounded Germans who, seeing no possibility of escape, surrendered. And it was what happened to them that caused the battle at the Nueces to be so bitterly remembered, for while they lay helpless in the morning sunlight, Captain Duff asked Quimper to help him drag them off to one side. When Major Cobb heard about this he cried automatically: 'Oh Jesus!' but he was too late to interfere, for as he ran to halt whatever evil thing was afoot, he heard shots, and when Duff and Quimper returned they were smiling.

'What in hell have you done?' Cobb shouted, and Duff said: 'We don't take prisoners.'

When Cobb checked the battlefield, he found that twenty-eight Germans had been slain and thirty-seven had escaped. Eight would be killed later trying to cross the Rio Grande, nine others were killed elsewhere, one crept back to Fredericksburg, and the rest escaped either into Mexico or California, where, as Quimper had feared, some of them joined the Union army.

On the way back to the Red River, Major Cobb pondered this extraordinary act, and as a partisan of the South he felt obligated to find an excuse, if there was one: If the Germans had escaped into Mexico, certainly they'd have run to New Orleans or Baltimore to fight against us . . . We've instituted a legal draft, and they refused to comply . . . This is war, and they killed some of our good men. But no matter how he rationalized Quimper's actions, he could construct no justification. Damn it all, no gentleman that I know would shoot nine helpless prisoners.

As a result of this self-examination, Cobb made two major decisions. The first was inevitable: I shall no longer place my honor in the hands of Yancey Quimper. He disgusts me. The second, representing his growing maturity, was reported in a letter to his wife:

I've been thinking about honor and battle a good deal recently, and especially those fine talks we had with the Peel people in Vicksburg. I'm fed up with second best. I love the people in Walter Scott's novels and want to conduct myself like them. I made a terrible mistake when I named our plantation Lakeview. Means nothing. From here on, with your permission, it's to be Lammermoor. That sings to the heart.

On the night before they reached the Red River, with Major Cobb encamped as far from General Quimper as he decently could, another soldier embittered by events at the Nueces told him: 'You know, Major, I've heard that Quimper was never a real general, and his behavior at San Jacinto ... he talks so much about it, maybe it wasn't the way he says.' If such rumors were true, Cobb thought, they would explain a lot.

Cobb refused to ride with Quimper when they headed north to duty along the Red River, and he suspected that when they met, there would be a certain tenseness. But the big, flabby fellow was as sickeningly jovial as ever: 'Great to have you back, Reuben. Important work up here.'

Trying to mask his dislike, Cobb temporized: 'Yancey, the way you handled those German prisoners ...' Quimper leaned in to forestall criticism: 'We did all right. But now we're onto something much bigger.'

And on the very next day Cobb was with Quimper when two spies came before them to report:

'Evil elements have slipped down from Arkansas. They've accumulated massive arms and have conspired with Texas citizens to stage a vast uprising. Our slaves are to cooperate when the signal is given and kill all white men in the district, women and children too.'

Cobb, remembering that Quimper's other spy had detected fifteen hundred Germans in motion when there were actually fewer than seventy, was reluctant to accept this new call to frenzy, but when he quietly initiated his own inquiries, he learned to his dismay that there was a plan for insurrection and that nearly a hundred participants were incriminated. So once more he was thrown in with Quimper, whether he wished it or not, and now began one of the startling events of the war, as far as Texas was involved.

The frightened defenders of the Confederacy placed their security in the hands of General Quimper, who, with considerable skill, arranged for a coordinated swoop upon the plotters. This move bagged some seventy conspirators, and there was serious talk of hanging them all. General Quimper loudly supported this decision, but Major Cobb rallied the more sober citizens, who devised a more reasonable procedure. A self-appointed citizens committee, hoping to avoid any criticism of Southern justice through the accidental hanging of the innocent, met and nominated twelve of the best-respected voters of the area, including two doctors and two clergymen, to serve as a court of law – judge, jury, hangman – and these twelve, following rules of evidence and fair play, would try the accused.

It was this laborious process which Quimper wanted to by-pass with his waiting nooses, but men like Cobb insisted upon it, so on the first day of October 1862 the drumhead court convened. Its first batch of prisoners was quickly handled:

'Dr Henry Childs, in accordance with the decision of this Court you will be taken from your place of confinement, on the fourth day of October '62 between the hours of twelve and two o'clock of said day, and hung by the neck until you are dead, and may God have mercy on your soul.'

The executions were held in midafternoon so that townspeople could gather about the hanging tree, a stately elm at the edge of town from whose branches three or sometimes four corpses would dangle. No observers seemed dissatisfied with the hangings, for the victims had been legally judged and the verdicts delivered without rancor. There was, moreover, considerable interest shown in the manner with which each of the condemned met his death, and those who did so in ways deemed proper were afterward applauded.

On and on the fearful litany continued: Ephraim Childs, brother of the above, hanged; A. D. Scott, hanged: 'He viewed calmly the preparations for his execution. And when the last awful moment arrived he jumped heavily from the carriage; and falling near three feet, dislocated his neck. He died without the violent contraction of a single muscle'; M. D. Harper, hanged; I. W. P. Lock, hanged: 'His conduct throughout revealed all the elements of a depraved nature, and he died upon the tree exhibiting that defiance of death that usually seizes hold on the last moments of a depraved, wicked and abandoned heart.' His crime, and that of the others: he had preferred the Union to the South.

After twenty festive hangings had occurred, Major Cobb was sickened by the illegality of such actions, for he had reason to believe that several men clearly innocent had been hanged. He spoke with certain humane men on the jury, advising against any further executions, and his arguments were so persuasive – 'Excess merely brings discredit to our cause' – that the hangings were stopped, and nineteen additional men who would otherwise surely have been executed were to be set free, an act which most citizens approved, for they had wearied of the ringing of the bell that announced the next assembly at the hanging tree. Quimper, however, railed against what he called 'this miscarriage of justice.'

'Hang them all!' he bellowed so repeatedly that the rougher element in town began to take up the cry, and he would have succeeded in organizing a mob to break down the jail had not Cobb and others prevailed upon the men not to stain their just cause by such a reprehensible act. That night, however, someone in the bushes near town – who, was never known – shot two well-regarded citizens, partisans of the Confederacy, and now no arguments could save the men still in jail. Quimper wanted to hang them immediately; Cobb insisted that they be given a legal trial, and they were: fifteen minutes of rushed testimony and the embittered verdict:

'C. A. Jones known as Humpback, James Powers known as Carpenter, Thomas Baker known as Old Man, and nine others tried on the same bill, all found guilty and sentenced to be hung, the evidence having revealed a plot which for its magnitude, infamy, treachery and barbarity is without a parallel in the annals of crime.'

So thirty-nine men guilty only of siding with an unacceptable moral position were hanged; three who had nebulous connections with the Confederate military were tried by court-martial and hanged; two others were shot trying to escape. But this was not a lynching or a case of mob frenzy; it was an instance of the heat of warfare in which men dedicated to one cause could not see any justification in the other. Even in its fury the jury endeavored to maintain some semblance of order, and of the accused men brought before it, twenty-four were found not guilty and set free.

Cobb, a tempestuous man who had always fought his battles openly, was now thoroughly revolted by the hangings, and in a letter to his wife, posted on the last day of the executions, he wrote:

> There was a man in jail who was charged with being a deserter from the Southern army, and a horse thief. When the jury on this day failed to furnish any Northerners to hang, the bloodthirsty men outside took that man from the jail and hanged him.

Two days later Cobb left his post at the Red River without permission, rode south to his plantation, and announced that he was organizing a unit for service with General Lee. Among his first volunteers was his cousin Somerset, who apologized to his ailing wife: 'Lissa, it tears my heart to see you in worsening health, and I know it's my duty to stay with you, but I simply cannot abide in idleness when others die for our cause.' The brothers' first flush of patriotism waned when they learned that they would be serving not in the cavalry with Lee, but in an infantry unit, for as Reuben exploded: 'Any Texan with a shred of dignity would ride to war, not march.' But march they did, to Vicksburg. The hinge of victory in the west would be Vicksburg, and as the Cobbs moved toward it, always striving to join up with their parent regiment already in position at Vicksburg, they could hear their soldiers grousing: 'We still ain't got no horses, and that's a disgrace. And we still ain't got enough rifles, and that's a disaster. And we're bein' led by a Northerner, and that's disgusting.'

Yes, the army which was to defend Vicksburg was

commanded by a Philadelphia Quaker who despite his pacifist religion had attended West Point, where he had acquired a fine reputation. Marrying a Southern belle from Virginia, he considered himself a resident of his bride's family plantation, where he became more Southern than Jefferson Davis. A man of credibility and power, he had not wavered when the great decision of North or South confronted him; he chose the South of his wife's proud family and quickly established himself as one of the abler Confederate generals. Now General John C. Pemberton had a command on which the safety of the South depended, and his men, who had been born in the South, did not approve.

'With all the superb soldiers we have,' Reuben growled, 'why do we have to rely on a Northerner of doubtful loyalty? If Vicksburg falls, the Mississippi falls, and if that river goes, the Confederacy is divided and Texas could fall.' He lowered his voice: 'And if Texas falls, the world falls.'

He was also having trouble with a Texas Ranger assigned to his unit, a Captain Otto Macnab who had reported to the bivouac area with guns and pistols sticking out in all directions. Some men in Cobb's force had Enfields of powerful range, some had the old Sharps that could knock down a house, and a few had old frontier single-shot rifles which their grandfathers had used against Indians.

But there were nearly two dozen in the company who had no armament at all, and Major Cobb fumed about this, dispatching numerous letters to Austin begging for guns. None were available, he was told, and so he moved among his men, trying to find any soldier who had more than one, and of course he came upon Captain Macnab, who had an arsenal, but when he tried to pry guns loose from the former Rang , he ran into real trouble: 'I don't give up my guns to anybody.'

'If I give you an order . . .' Cobb suddenly remembered from Macnab's enlistment papers that he had been a Ranger, and Somerset had warned: 'Reuben, never tangle with a Ranger. My brother Persifer had Rangers in his command and he said they were an army of their own, a law to themselves.'

'They're in my command now,' Major Cobb had replied, 'and Macnab will do what I say.'

'Don't bet on that,' Sett had said, and now when his cousin

tried to take one of Macnab's guns, the red-headed warrior met real opposition.

'Isn't it reasonable,' Cobb began, 'that if you have two rifles and the next man has none . . . ?'

'I know how to use a rifle, maybe he don't.'

There might have been an ugly scene had not Somerset intervened: 'Aren't you the Macnab who served in Mexico with my brother?'

'Colonel Persifer Cobb?' Macnab asked, and when Sett nodded, Macnab said: 'He knew how to fight. I hope he's on our side now,' and Cobb replied: 'No, he's tending our family plantation in Carolina.'

A month before, that statement would have been correct, for Persifer Cobb, like many of the great plantation managers throughout the South, had been asked to stay at home producing stuffs required for the war effort, but as the fortunes of battle began slowly to turn against the South, men like him had literally forced their way to the colors, sometimes riding far distances to enlist, and as a former West Point man, his services were welcomed.

So now three Cobbs of the same generation were in uniform: Colonel Persifer in northern Virginia; Major Reuben in charge of replacement troops for the Second Texans; and Captain Somerset. There were also five Cobb sons from the three families, while at the various plantations the wives of the absent officers endeavored to hold the farms and mills together: Tessa Mae at Edisto, Millicent at Lakeview, and Petty Prue at the newly christened Lammermoor. The Cobbs were at war.

Major Cobb wisely withdrew his attempt at forcing Macnab to surrender one of his guns, but he was gratified when his tough little officer came into camp one day with seven rifles of varied merit which he had scrounged from surrounding farms. 'They'll all fire,' he told Cobb. 'Not saying how straight, but if you get close enough, that don't matter.'

When the contingent crossed over to the east bank of the Mississippi, Major Cobb saw that his Texans would have to fight their way into Vicksburg, for a strong Union detachment was dug in between them and the town. He could have been forgiven had he turned back, but this never occurred to him. Acting as his own scout and probing forward, he identified the

864

difficulties and gathered his men: 'If we make a hurried swing to the east, we can circumvent the Northern troops, then dash back and in to Vicksburg.'

'What protects our left flank if they hear us and attack?' Macnab asked, and Cobb said: 'You do.'

'Give me a couple of dozen good shots and we'll hold them off.'

Through the dark night Otto coached his team, and at two he said: 'Catch some sleep,' but he continued to prowl the terrain over which they would fight. Just before dawn a Galveston volunteer asked: 'If we do get in to Vicksburg, can we hold it, with a general like Pemberton in charge?' and Otto gave him a promise solemnly, as if taking a sacred oath: 'When we set up our lines at Vicksburg, hell itself won't budge us.'

This reckless promise did not apply to the battle next morning at Big Black River, for Grant was moving with such incredible swiftness that he overtook the Confederates before dawn, and launched such a powerful attack that he drove the gray troops right across the deep ravines and back to the gates of Vicksburg.

In previous battles and skirmishes Captain Macnab, now a man of forty-one and extremely battlewise, had not in even the slightest way tried to avoid combat – that would be unthinkable – but he had thoughtfully picked those spots and developing situations at which he could do the most good. However, this battle degenerated into such a hideous mess that plans and prudence alike were swept aside, and he found himself in such a general melee of gray and blue that in desperation he lashed out like a wild man, casting aside his rifles and firing his Colts with such abandon that he himself drove back almost a squad of Yankees. In those moments he was not a soldier, he was an incarnation of battle, and when because of their tremendous superiority the Northern troops began to sweep the banks of a little stream which the Texans were struggling to cross, he shouted to his men: 'Don't let it happen!' When by force of ironlike character he had driven away the Northerners so that his troops could complete their escape he contemptuously remained behind, searching the field the Yankees had just deserted, even though their sharpshooters still commanded it.

'Macnab!' Major Cobb shouted from a distance. 'What in hell are you doing?'

'Looking for my guns.' And when he saw where he had discarded his rifles during the chase, he calmly stooped down, retrieved them, and headed into Vicksburg.

On 19 May, General Grant brought 35,000 Union soldiers before the nine-mile-long defenses of Vicksburg; there he faced 13,000 Confederate troops well dug in, with 7,000 in reserve. The Northern battle plan was staightforward: 'Smash through the defenses, take the town, and deny the Mississippi River to the Confederates. When that happens, Texas will be cut off from the Confederacy and will wither on the vine.' So every Texan fighting at Vicksburg knew that he was really fighting to defend his home state.

As soon as his massive army was in position, Grant ordered a probe of the Confederate lines, and to his surprise, it was thrown back. For the next two days he prepared the most intense artillery bombardment seen in the war so far. It would utilize every piece of ordnance – hundreds of heavy cannon – and it would start at six in the morning.

On the night of the twenty-first he assembled his commanders and issued an order which demonstrated the mechanical strength he proposed to throw against the Southerners: 'Set your watches. At ten sharp, the artillery barrage will cease. And your men will leave their positions, attack up that hill, and overwhelm the enemy.' For the first time in world history, all units along a vast front would set forth at the same moment.

'There's bound to be some ugly skirmishing,' an Illinois captain warned his troops, 'but before noon we should have their lines in our hands. Then an easy march into Vicksburg.'

That last night, as the two armies slept fitfully, General Grant's order of battle was awesome, studded as it was with distinguished names: the 118th Illinois Infantry; the 29th Wisconsin Infantry; the 25th Iowa; the 4th West Virginia; the 5th Minnesota; and then two names that symbolized the fraternal agony of this war: the 7th Missouri, the 22nd Kentucky. Their brothers would be fighting the next day as Confederates: the 1st Missouri, the 8th Kentucky.

To reach the Confederate lines, the Union soldiers had to

sweep down into a pronounced valley, then climb a steep hill and charge into the teeth of cleverly disposed fortifications. These were of three types: the redoubt, a large square earthwork easy to hold if there were enough men; the redan, a triangular projection out from the line to permit concentration of fire upon an attacker; and the smallest of the three, the lunetter, a crescent-shaped earthwork, compact, with steeply sloping sides and not easy to capture.

Tough Louisiana swamp fighters occupied the major redan. Detachments from various parts of the South held the Railroad Redoubt, and the 2nd Texas Sharpshooters, a name recently bestowed because of their great accuracy with rifles, held the key spot in the line, a lunette guarding the main road back to town. Here Major Cobb's replacement detachment finally joined up with their fellow Texans.

During the furious cannonading on the morning of 22 May, Cobb's men took what shelter they could, doing their best to survive until the attack began. 'Why can't our side fire back?' a frightened boy of seventeen asked, and Cobb said bluntly: 'Because they have the cannon and we don't.'

At ten minutes to ten, all the Yankee batteries fired as rapidly as they could, in order to provide their troops with as much last-minute cover as possible. At ten o'clock the fiery monsters fell silent, and in that first awful hush bugles began to sound, first one and then another, echoing back and forth until the valleys facing the redoubts, the redans and the lunettes reverberated with their clear and stirring sounds.

Then came the infantry attack, down slight inclines at first, then across level ground, then straight up the steep flanks protecting the Confederate line. It required about eighteen minutes for the thousand or more blue-clad troops assigned to take the Texas lunette to advance across the open land, and to some who watched the solemn approach from inside the fortification, it seemed as if the Northerners would never reach their goal, as if they would march forever like dream figures across a timeless landscape. But quickly enough for both attacker and defender, the ominous blue line reached the steep flanks, scrambled up, and broke into the lunette, where a wild, confused struggle took place. With rifles, pistols, revolvers, even with bayonets and clubs, the Texas defenders threw back

867

the Union attackers, South and North falling upon each other in bloody fury.

The struggle went on for an incredible number of hours, with the dogged Texans repelling first one assault, then another, then countless others. Each time the Yankees surged forward, up those steep final flanks, they did reach the top, and they did kill defenders, and always they seemed to have victory just within their grasp. 'Follow me!' shouted a lieutenant, waving his blue cap until a Texas rifle ended his charge and his cry and his life.

Otto Macnab kept his men from panic by constantly moving among them with gestures of encouragement – he used few words – and by leaping into the breach whenever a perilous weakness showed. Indeed, he stifled so many nearly fatal assaults that his survival was a miracle.

Well into the afternoon the Yankee assault on the lunette halted, to enable the batteries encased in the hills behind to throw down a savage curtain of fire, hoping thus to dislodge the weakened Texans, but when the cannonade stopped and the men in blue resumed their charge, the indomitable 2nd Texas repelled them yet again.

The slaughter now became obscene, a grotesque expenditure of life, Gray and Blue, on the sloping edges of a lunette which could never quite be taken. Loss came closest at about two-thirty, when a determined captain from Illinois led a charge with such bravery that he carried right into the lunette, with some nine or ten Yankees following, and had even a dozen more succeeded in joining him – and they tried, desperately – the Texans would have been subdued and Grant would have had the one foothold he needed to break the line.

But at this moment, while Macnab was engaged with a mighty assault on his little sector and Reuben Cobb was involved on his, Captain Somerset Cobb, with a courage he had not known he possessed, leaped directly at the Illinois leader and drove a sword clear through his body. The man staggered forward, thinking victory still within his grasp, clutched at the air and fell back, and the crucial charge faded.

But now a young boy, not over fifteen, ran screaming into the lunette from the southern stretch of the trench line: 'Railroad Redoubt's fallin',' and when the Texans looked across the short distance to the big fort on their right, they saw that the messenger was correct. This redoubt, big and loosely constructed, was protected by a much less severe slope than the Texas lunette, and against it the Yankees were having real success. Some were already in the fort and others seemed about to break through. If Northern guns occupied the redoubt, the Texas lunette was doomed.

It took Major Cobb and Captain Macnab about five seconds to see and to appreciate the peril in which the Confederate line stood, and without consultation these two plus some fifty of their men ran like dodging, frightened, low-clinging deer across the open space between the two projections. They arrived just in time to meet the day's most furious battle, Blue and Gray in one tremendous tangle, with the former on the knife edge of victory.

'Stop them!' Major Cobb shouted to the men following him. 'In there!' Macnab never uttered cries in battle; he was always too busy managing his deadly guns, but this time the peril was so great that even he shouted: 'Here!'

He and some fifteen others leaped directly into the foremost Yankee guns, and although several of his men went down in the dreadful fusillade, their sheer weight carried them forward. But as soon as this breach was stabilized, Otto saw that Federal troops were streaming in through a larger break farther on.

'Cobb!' he shouted, and the red-haired major, his cap lost in the battle, swung about to face some new enemy when a musket discharge caught him full in the face, blowing his head apart.

'Men!' Macnab cried, and his high voice was so compelling, so unique among the battle sounds, that his men formed behind him, and in a surge of slashing and firing, repelled the attackers from the wavering line.

Grant had been denied his victory. The Confederate lines had held firm, all the way from the Railroad Redoubt at the south, which Major Cobb and Captain Macnab had saved at the last moment, to the bloodied Stockade Redan at the north. Now the long, cruel siege would begin.

The terror of Vicksburg lay not in those wild charges of that first day, for then men from both sides fought in white heat, and death came so explosively, so suddenly that there was no awareness that it had struck until a companion fell silent amid the roar. The real terror began on that night of 22 May, because in the open space between the two battle lines lay several thousand Union wounded, and for reasons which have never been explained, General Grant decided to leave them there rather than allow the customary battle truce for the removal of the dead and the rescue of the wounded. Perhaps he thought that on the next day the Confederates would be so exhausted that his men could gain an easy triumph, and he did not want to give the enemy any respite. At any rate, he left his dying exposed to the cold night air; but what was worse, he left them there all during the next day, that fiercely hot May morning, that blazing May afternoon.

Now some of the men dying on the dusty field were so close to the lunette that the Texans could hear them pleading for water, and others were so near the Federal lines that Union men could hear their companions' pleas, but all across the vast battlefield the order stood: 'No truce.'

Night brought no release, for now the battle wounds, some of them forty hours old, had grown gangrenous from the day's prolonged heat, and both the pain and the smell were unbearable. It was unspeakable, the agony that came as a result of this hideous decision not to clear the battlefield. 'If I ever see Grant,' a Texan shouted into the night, hoping that some Northern soldier would hear, 'I'll shoot his bloody eyes out.'

At about two in the morning Otto Macnab, who had seen a great deal of war and who knew how men should die, could stand no more. Leaving the lunette, he went out among the dying, and when he found a Northern soldier in the last shrieking pain of gangrenous agony, he shot him, and in doing this he attracted the attention of a Missouri man who was doing the same from his lines. Meeting in the dark shadows, neither soldier entertained even the most fleeting idea of shooting the other.

'That you, Reb?'

'Yank. What unit?'

'Texas. You?'

'Missouri.'

'We have Missouri men on our side. Good fighters.'

'You know a sergeant named O'Callahan?'

'I don't know many.'

'Should you come upon him . . . ?' The man was a schoolteacher.

'I'll tell him.'

'My brother. Good kid.'

When Otto crept back to the lines he went to all parts of the lunette and even back to the Railroad Redoubt, shaking men awake and asking if they'd seen a Missouri man named O'Callahan.

On the morning of 24 May, in response to a plea from the Confederates, General Grant relaxed his inhumane order, a truce was agreed upon, and men from each side moved out upon the battlefield to look at the bodies of those who might have been saved had it come earlier. When the truce ended, the soldiers returned to their respective lines, the war resumed, with General Grant bitterly acknowledging that he was not going to capture Vicksburg by frontal assault. He would have to do so by siege, which he promptly initiated. Not a man, not a scrap of food, not a horse would move in or out, and the last bastion on the Mississippi would fall.

But during the truce soldiers from each side had met with their opponents, and a respect had developed, so that invariably in the quiet evenings the men began to fraternize and sing. The Northern troops refrained from insulting their friends with the *Battle Hymn* while the Southerners rarely sang *Dixie*. Always, in the course of the night, some group of Southerners would begin the song they loved so deeply, and Northerners would fall silent as the winsome harmony began:

> 'We loved each other then, Lorena,
> More than we ever dared to tell;
> And what we might have been, Lorena,
> Had but our lovings prospered well.'

The song had a wonderfully rich sentiment which sounded elegant in the stillness, and some from the North almost chuckled at it, but toward the end, even the most indifferent hushed when a strong high tenor sang solo of death and life hereafter:

> 'There is a future, O thank God,

Of life this is so small a part,
'Tis dust to dust beneath the sod;
But there, up there, 'tis heart to heart.'

Otto did not care for such songs, too much about death, but he did stop his battlefield wandering when Northern troops sang one song he had not known before. *Aura Lee* spoke of love as he recalled it, and sometimes when the singing ended he found himself humming the tune to himself or mumbling the words:

'Aura Lee, Aura Lee,
Maid with golden hair,
Sunshine came along with thee
And swallows in the air.'

He thought of Franziska in those terms. He could see her bringing sunshine and it was not preposterous to think of her as attended by swallows.

In the following weeks, when starvation clamped its iron claws about the innards of the Texans, both Somerset Cobb and Otto Macnab took short, dreamlike excursions: Cobb, into Vicksburg to meet with the Peel sisters he had stayed with while on his way to Texas in 1850; Macnab, out into the battlefield at night to compare situations with O'Callahan of Missouri.

The Peel sisters still had their house at the north end of Cherry Street, but since it was exposed to artillery fire from Federal warships in the Mississippi below, they lived, like so many others, in hillside caves. Lucky for them the caves were available, for their house had already taken two hits, and had they been sleeping upstairs, they would probably have been killed.

Like all the citizens of Vicksburg, the Peel sisters had started out confident that Grant would be forced to withdraw, but as the foodless weeks passed they began to see the inevitability of defeat. However, they would not speak of it.

'You mean that fine young man who traveled with you from Carolina . . . ?'

'From Georgia, ma'am. My cousin.'

'And he was killed on the first day?'

'Most gallantly.'

'I remember his reading to us from *Ivanhoe*.'

'He loved Scott. We named our Texas plantation Lammermoor.'

'That's nice. That's very nice.'

'Miss Emma, I wish to God we had food in the lines to share with you.'

'No, Major. We wish we had food for you.'

Miss Etta Mae said: 'Is my sister right? You're a major now?'

Before he could answer, the cave in which they were meeting was shaken by a violent attack of shellfire from the warships, and as soon as it stopped, a cluster of explosions from the batteries inland rocked the area. 'They hold us in a crossfire,' Miss Emma said. 'It's murderous. Three slaves on this street killed this week.'

The Peel sisters did not leave their cave except for sunlight on quiet days, and even then they never knew when a stray shell from the river or from the battle line might kill them and everyone else in sight. They were wraithlike, each weighing less than a hundred pounds, but they maintained high spirits in order to encourage the soldiers who stopped by to see them.

On the evening of July first, Otto Macnab, suffering from the acute hunger which had attacked him viciously that day, wandered through the battlefield during the customary informal truce, and when he saw how close to the Texan lunette the Yankee sappers had brought their trenches, he gasped. Starting to pace off the tiny distance that would separate the two lines when battle resumed next day, he was interrupted by a voice he was delighted to hear. It was O'Callahan.

'Distance is seven feet, Reb.'

'You could spit into our lunette.'

'Spittin' even a foot with you Rebs is difficult.'

The two men sat side by side on the edge of the fatal trench, and each knew that when it progressed a few feet farther, the Texas position could be blown to hell with dynamite charges.

'You 'bout starved out, Reb?'

'Well, now . . .' The posturing was ended. Macnab could joke about death, and the Union failure to consolidate, but he could no longer joke about starvation. 'One hell of a way to end a battle.'

873

'Only way you left us, you stubborn bastards.'

As they parted for the last time, the Union man looked about swiftly, then moved toward Macnab: 'I could be shot. If they catch you, say you stole it.' And into Otto's pocket he stuffed two pieces of bread and a chunk of Wisconsin cheese.

Back in the lunette, Macnab knew that as a human being and especially as an officer, he ought to share his unexpected treasure with his men, but this he could not do. Surreptitiously he gnawed at a tiny piece of the cheese, and he believed that he had never tasted anything so delicious in his life; he could feel the nourishment racing through his body, as if one organ were shouting to another: 'Food at last! Sweet Jesus, food at last.'

He had slowly, secretly consumed one of the pieces of bread and much of the cheese when an orderly passed by: 'Colonel wants to see you.'

When he reported, his stomach reveling in the food it had found, the colonel, a medical doctor from Connecticut and a Yale graduate but now the defender of a lunette on the Mississippi, said: 'I suppose you've heard about Major Cobb?'

'What?'

'Visiting his two old ladies. Smuggling them food, I suppose. Came out of their cave just in time to meet a Union shell head on.'

'Dead?'

'Left arm blown off. The slave who ran out here said they thought he bled to death.

'May I go in?'

'You're needed here. You're Major Macnab now, and your job is to hold off those sappers at the foot of our lunette.'

'Yes, sir.' All day on the second of July, Macnab devised tricks for rolling giant fused bombs down into the Northern trench only a few feet away, and once when he was successful, blowing up an entire length of the trench and all its occupants, his men crowded around to congratulate him. That was the last major event at the Texas lunette, for that night the soldiers of each side, without orders from General Grant or anyone else, quietly decided that this part of the war was over.

'Pemberton sent Grant a letter,' a Northerner said. 'I spoke with the orderly.'

'I think Pemberton wants to surrender right now,' a Rebel

reported. 'But Grant, he'll want it for a big show on the Fourth of July.'

'For us it ends tonight.'

Otto searched for O'Callahan, but no one had seen him, so, still a professional, he walked to the daring sap which had carried the Union lines so close to his. 'Six more days,' he told a Northern soldier, 'you'd have made it.'

'We'd've made it today, but some clever Graycoat dropped a tornado on us.'

'You know a man named O'Callahan?'

'One of your rolling bombs got him this afternoon.'

'Dead?'

'Probably alive. I saw them drag him away.'

In the distance there was singing, *Aura Lee* from the Northerners, and then, as an act of final Confederate defiance, *The Bonnie Blue Flag*, whispered at first by the defeated Southerners and then bellowed, with many Northerners joining in:

> 'We are a band of brothers
> And native to the soil,
> Fighting for the property
> We won with honest toil.'

Along the Vicksburg line that night there was not one Negro in uniform, on either side. The fight had been about him but never by him. One Confederate trooper, who operated a cotton gin at Nacogdoches, summarized Texan thinking: 'No nigger's ever been born could handle a gun. They'd be useless.'

The month of July 1863 was one of overwhelming sorrow at the Jefferson plantation, for tragedy seemed to strike the Cobbs from all sides. Petty Prue, in the big house at Lammermoor, knew that her husband was dead at Vicksburg and her older son at Gettysburg. Her younger boy was fighting somewhere in Virginia. On some hot mornings she doubted that she could climb out of bed, so oppressive was the day, so oppressive was her life.

But she had a plantation to run, some ninety slaves to keep busy, and cotton to be handled for the Confederacy, so at dawn each day she was up and working just as if her husband were absent for a few weeks and the crop promised to some factor in New Orleans. What perplexed her as the cotton matured in its bolls and the picking began was how to handle the crop when it had been harvested, for the Yankee blockade of all the seaports prevented open shipments of fiber to Liverpool. Cotton was being grown but it was not being moved, and there was always the danger that if the bales accumulated at a spot like Jefferson, so near the border, Union forces might rush in and burn them, and the plantations, and set free the slaves. Now, with the entire Mississippi River in Union hands, the possibility of such a foray grew, and a lone woman like Petty Prue, somewhat flighty in peacetime, faced problems she could scarcely solve.

The dismal news affected Millicent too, for in mid-July word was received via the telegraph to New Orleans that Colonel Persifer Cobb of Edisto, that erect, formal gentleman with his West Point education, had died at Gettysburg. The telegram had ended:

SON JOHN ALSO DIED WILL YOU ALL COME BACK AND SUPERVISE PLANTATION TESSA MAE

Millicent, weakened by the privations of war, was incapable of grappling with the changes contained in this message. Vaguely she remembered that it had been sweet-talking Tessa Mae who had encouraged the expulsion of the Somerset Cobbs from Edisto, and Millicent could not imagine any terms on which they might consent to return. But such selfish considerations vanished when she thought of Tessa Mae's double bereavement and of how distraught she must be trying to manage that vast plantation. During the better part of a morning she wept for the lone widow on Edisto and for all the other widows this war was making.

This led her to thoughts about herself, and her head sagged, for she could not be sure that Somerset was alive. All she knew for certain was that in the final days of Vicksburg a Yankee shell had ripped off his left arm. At first he had been reported dead from loss of blood, but then soldiers from his unit, now in prison camp in Mississippi, had sent word that Major Cobb – 'not the red-headed one' – had been taken in by two elderly

876

women in the town and nursed. 'And you can thank God for that,' a fellow officer wrote, 'because if he had fallen into one of our hospitals or into a Yankee prison camp, he'd be dead.'

Perhaps he was dead. Perhaps her son Reverdy was dead, too. Perhaps the Yankees would invade Texas and set the plantations aflame, as they were doing in other parts of the Confederacy. The possibilities for disaster were so overwhelming that she could not face them, and her health, never good, began to deteriorate badly. As the heat of summer increased she found difficulty in breathing, and on one extremely hot afternoon she felt she must apologize to her energetic cousin: 'Petty Prue, I am not malingering. I want to help but I'm truly sick, and I'm frightened.'

'Stay in bed, Lissa. I'll manage.'

Prue could not have done it alone, but like many women all over Texas who had to manage large holdings while their men were absent, she learned that she could rely on her slaves, especially Jaxifer from Georgia and Trajan from Edisto. With no white master to berate him, and sometimes beat him, Jaxifer assumed a more important role, issuing orders to other slaves and seeing that they were carried out. It was he who kept a small herd of cattle hidden in the brakes, away from government agents who would have impressed them for military use. Occasionally he would butcher one of the precious steers in the dark of night and mysteriously appear in the morning with small portions of beef for all: 'We gots meat.'

Trajan was even more ingenious. He found the honey trees which provided a substitute for sugar. He tracked down a bear now and then, knowing that when smoked, this made bacon almost as tasty as a hog's, but when he first placed it on the table, Millicent whispered: 'One can hardly eat this without salt.' Trajan heard, and although store salt was absolutely unobtainable, he had the clever idea of digging up the soil where meat had been cured in peacetime and boiling it until salt could be skimmed off. It was dirty, but it was good.

His major contribution to Petty Prue was the substitute he devised for coffee: 'Now, this here is parched corn and this is charred okra, you mix them just right, you got ...'

'It tastes ... well ...'

'Well, it ain't coffee, and it don't taste like coffee, but it looks like it.'

Often during that dreadful July, Petty Prue wondered why her slaves did not run away, for with no master to check them they could have, but they stayed, without restraint, to keep the two plantations running. 'It's because,' Prue explained to her neighbors, 'they're happy here. They like being slaves when the master is kind.'

In whispers, when she attended church on Sunday, she asked the older people: 'Do you think the slaves know what Mr Lincoln's done?' The white folk were aware that on the first day of January 1863 he had tried to put into effect his Emancipation Proclamation freeing slaves, and by the most rigid controls the whites in remote areas like Jefferson prevented this news from reaching their slaves, so that men like Jaxifer and Trajan worked on, legally free but actually still slaves.

'Tell them nothin'!' Petty Prue warned Millicent and the two Cobb daughters, and when an elderly white man from the village came to visit and refresh himself with the good food raised at Lammermoor, he gave them reason to keep silent.

'Emancipation Proclamation! Rubbish. The most cynical thing that evil man in the White House ever did.'

'Some day the slaves will have to be freed,' Millicent protested.

'Many would agree with you,' the old man said. 'Economically?' He shrugged his shoulders. 'That young fellow who stayed with you – Carmody, who wrote the book about us. He made some points. But the slaves will never be freed the way Lincoln said.'

'What did the gangling fool say?' Petty Prue asked, for she was willing to believe anything bad about Lincoln, author of so many tragedies.

'It isn't what he said. It's what he didn't say.'

'Tell me, please.'

'Duplicity. Total duplicity. He has freed the slaves in all those parts of the former Union over which he now has no control. And he has not freed them in the areas which he does control.'

'I can't believe it,' Prue snapped.

'You better. Your slaves here in Texas – where his words

don't mean a damn, thank God – are freed. So are they in Carolina and Georgia, and the rest of the Confederacy. But in Maryland, and Kentucky, and Tennessee and even in Louisiana, where the Federals control, they are not freed, because Good Honest Abe does not want to irritate his Northern allies. God damn their souls.'

The four Cobb women had a difficult time digesting this immoral Northern charade, but the old man made it simple: 'Where he can, he won't. And where he can't, he does. Some patriot with good sense ought to shoot him.'

The owners of plantations had extra reason for caution, because once the slaves learned that they were free, they would surely desert and the cotton would rot in the fields. But by extreme caution they continued to keep news of emancipation, fraudulent though it might be, from their slaves, and it was well known that anyone who divulged the information, or even hinted at it, would be hanged.

But now the problem arose as to what to do with this new crop of cotton which could no longer be sent to New Orleans, and Petty Prue, as the one who had to make decisions, pondered this for a long time, and the same old man, a furious patriot, came out from Jefferson to counsel with her.

'If I was younger, ma'am, you can be sure I'd be tryin' to sneak this cotton through the blockade to Liverpool. But I'm not young any more, and no woman by herself could do it.'

'What can I do?'

'Keep your voice down,' the old man said conspiratorially as he led her to the gin, 'but this cotton is the lifeblood of the Confederacy. We have no manufacturing, as your book-writing fellow said. And we have few railroads. But by God we have cotton, and the world needs it.' Picking at the edge of a bale, he fingered the precious fiber he had spent his life producing. 'On this wharf it's worth a cent and three-quarters a pound. Aboard ship to Europe, it's worth a dollar sixty a pound. With Vicksburg gone and Lee thrown back at Gettysburg, we must get it on board some ship somehow.'

'I'll try anything,' Prue said.

The old man looked at the bayou to which boats ought to have been coming, and tears showed in his eyes: 'By water, no hope. Even if you could get it overland to Galveston, the

Yankees would still intercept it when you tried to ship.' Then his eyes brightened with the thrill of old challenges: 'But, ma'am, if you could somehow work your bales far inland and then drop down to the safety of Matamoros in Old Mexico, you'd have a market as big as the world.'

'I do not understand,' Prue said, and the old man explained: 'Abe Lincoln's warships keep us bottled up everywhere. Oh, a few blockade runners slip in and out of the Atlantic ports, but not many. They've tied up Texas, too. For a while Brownsville was kept open, but Abe corked that real quick. So what does that leave us? Matamoros, just over the Rio Grande from Brownsville.'

When he told her that sometimes as many as a hundred ships lay off Matamoros, hungry for cotton, she asked: 'Why doesn't Lincoln sink them?' and he cried: 'That's the arrow that we have in our quiver. What one thing could win the war for us tomorrow?' When she said she didn't know, he explained: 'If England and France jump in on our side to ensure safe delivery of cotton. Lincoln doesn't dare antagonize Europe. So he's got to let English and French ships come to Matamoros and load up.'

Petty Prue walked up and down her wharf, studied the accumulating bales, then snapped her fingers: 'I'm taking ours to Matamoros.'

Once the decision was made, she never looked back. With an energy that would have alarmed her husband, who had known her as a little wren of a woman, she worked almost without sleeping, and her enthusiasm ignited the imaginations of her slaves.

'There are two ways we can go,' she said at the beginning of the discussions with Jaxifer and Trajan. 'We can cut west to Waco, where they're assembling shipments, and sell to the government. Lose half our profit. Or we can drop in a straight line down to Matamoros, and sell our bales for maybe eighty cents a pound.'

The two men listened, then Jaxifer asked: 'You goin' wid us?'

'It's my cotton. My responsibility.'

A plan was devised whereby four extra-stout carts would be loaded, each with five bales of five hundred pounds each. If they could deliver the cotton to the Mexican side, it would bring eight thousand dollars, a gamble worth taking. But one night as she concluded the final plans for the bold journey, she had a frightening doubt, and ordering her carriage to be readied, she had Jaxifer drive her to Jefferson, where she asked the old man one question: 'When we get to the Rio Grande, how do we get the bales across to Mexico?' and he said: 'If cotton is so valuable, they'll work out a way.'

'But they say there's no bridge. No ferry could handle all the bales you speak of.'

'If the world needs cotton, they'll find a way.'

'I'll risk it, then.'

The old man grasped Prue's hands: 'I wish I had a daughter like you,' but this farewell was dampened by the agitated arrival of a horseman from Lammermoor: 'Missy, hurry! Miss Lissa, she sick bad.'

The old man insisted upon accompanying Prue to the plantations, and when they reached the kitchen at Lammermoor they found that Millicent had been working there with the slaves, making jelly and preserving fruit in the last moments before she died. Prue, looking at the scene she had shared so often with her cousin, did not weep or cry out. Slowly she slipped to the polished floor, and there she stared at the uneven patterns, for life had become too complex for her to unravel.

The old man proved to be most valuable, not because of anything he did, for he was frail and nearing his own death, but because of the sensible advice he gave and his shrewd analysis of alternatives: 'Of course you could go with your cotton, Miss Prue, but what happens to the plantations if you do? What makes you think Somerset will ever return, if his wound was as bad as they say? With you gone, Jaxifer gone, Trajan gone, crows will tend cotton on this farm.' Patiently he led her to the only sensible conclusion: 'Would to God I could volunteer to manage your place while you go, but I'm too old.' He fought back tears. 'I won't live to see the end of this war. If I did take charge and died while you were gone, chaos, chaos.'

'What must I do?'

'You have two treasures. These valuable bales. These valuable plantations. Surely, the second is more important than the first.'

'But I'm going to protect both,' she said stubbornly.

'The only way, send your cotton south with Trajan and Jaxifer.'

'Can I trust them?'

'What choice have you? You've got to stay here, with that trustworthy slave Big Matthew. And pray for the best.'

Again, once the decision was reached she did not flinch. Inspecting the four wagons, she was satisfied from what Jaxifer told her that they would withstand the load and the six-hundred-mile trip. She watched as the men loaded each wagon, three bales crossways on the bottom, two perched on top, and satisfied herself that each wagon carried heavy grease for the axles, and when all was ready she asked the old man to deliver to each of the four slaves who would be driving the wagons a copy of a letter he had had the local judge prepare:

Jefferson, Marion County, Texas
21 July 1863

To Whom It May Concern:

This will certify that the bearer of this note, the slave known as TRAJAN, is on official duty for the Confederate government, delivering cotton to Matamoros in Mexico and returning home to his plantation, as above. The government will appreciate any consideration and protection you may give him while he is discharging this important assignment.

Henry Applewhite
Judge of the County Court

To travel six hundred miles to the Rio Grande with the heavily laden wagons was a journey of at least two months, for rivers had to be forded and forests negotiated. Also, the route had to be painstakingly deciphered, with rascals on every hand to belay and betray, especially when the men in charge were slaves. But Trajan was resourceful, forty-seven years old and afraid of very little, and with Jaxifer's help he proposed to deliver this cotton to Mexico and earn his mistress a fine penny for doing it.

They had been on the trail about a week when Trajan saw, joining them from the west, a remarkable sight: two wagons, well loaded with bales but without drivers. 'What can this be?' he asked his fellow drivers in Gullah, and they could not guess,

882

so he left his own wagons and started walking toward the mystery, but as he drew close he heard a child's voice crying: 'Don't you come no closer,' and when he looked up he found himself facing a very big gun in the possession of a very small boy. On the second wagon, with his own gun properly pointed, sat an even smaller boy.

'What you doin'?' Trajan asked, indicating that the boys should put up their guns.

'One more step!' the first boy warned, and Trajan realized that he meant it, so he stopped, held out his empty hands, and asked: 'What you doin', boys?' And after a pause in which the first boy looked back to the second, they confessed that they were taking their family's cotton to Galveston.

'Where's your father?'

'Dead at Vicksburg.'

'You got no uncles?'

'They're at war.'

'Your mother?'

'She's workin' the farm.'

'Galveston is not the best –'

'Don't you take a step. They told me people would try . . .'

And then Trajan saw that the two boys were near to exhaustion, for the one in back had begun to cry, at which his older brother shouted: 'Stop that, damnit. We're bein' held up.' But the younger boy could not stop; these days had been too long and cruel, and now to be accosted by a bunch of slaves who intended cutting throats: 'I want to go home.'

'Course you do. So do I.' And something in the way Trajan spoke softened the heart of the boy in front, and now he, too, began to cry.

'Now, you hold on to your guns, boys. But you got to get some rest,' and hardly had he led the two wagons to his four than the two young fellows were sound asleep. Trajan lifted them onto his wagon, and as they slept, the most powerful and confusing emotions swept over him, for the boys were about the age his son had been when he was stolen. Endlessly he had brooded about his lost son, wondering where Hadrian could be, and now he asked himself: Was he as brave as these two youngsters were in defending their bales of cotton?

When the boys at last awakened, aware that they were at the

mercy of the strange Negroes, Trajan did his best to comfort them, but whenever he tried to explain why they must not go to Galveston, where the Federal ships prowled trying to steal Confederate cotton, they suspected trickery, so always the slave said: 'All right, all right. We'll go as far as we can together. Then you hie off for Galveston and the enemy.'

The oldest boy, Michael, was eleven, and old enough to think that there might be something most suspicious about Trajan and his three companions, especially Jaxifer, who looked very black and ferocious.

Trajan himself had no clearer view of things, for he knew that in delivering cotton to Matamoros, he was aiding the Confederacy, which was determined to keep him a slave forever, and therefore what he was doing was stupid, but he also knew that through the years he had lived in moderate decency with the Cobbs of Edisto, and that they had not changed for the worse in moving to Texas. He suspected that within his lifetime all slaves would be set free, for he had heard through rumors and the surreptitious teaching of Methodist ministers that there were large parts of the nation where blacks were free and where food and clothing and medicine were just about as available as in Texas.

He had known perhaps a dozen slaves who had tried to escape to Mexico; most had been recaptured quickly with the aid of tracking dogs; others had returned of their own will, unable to cross the great expanse that seemed to encircle the little green paradise at Jefferson; and he had seen both groups savagely whipped for their attempt to escape bondage, but he also knew that a handful had either made it to freedom in Mexico or died in the attempt. He had never felt impelled to run away from the Cobbs, for they were about as decent as the system provided, despite Reuben's hot temper at times, but he did know that if the new masters who might be taking over at Lammermoor proved brutal, he would flee.

Why, then, did not he and the other three plan at that moment to get as close to Mexico as practical, take the money for cotton, and run for freedom? They were restrained because all they knew, all they loved, centered on Lammermoor. In Trajan's case there was another factor: he had been given a responsibility, and as a man of honor he must discharge it.

He was considering these conflicts, answers to which could determine his chance for freedom, when he was faced by a more immediate problem. 'We want to go to Galveston,' Michael said one morning as he and his brother faced the four slaves. 'We think you're kidnaping us and stealing our cotton, and we want our guns back.'

'You have them,' Trajan said. 'You've always had them.'

'Then can we go to Galveston?'

'You're going to Galveston. That's always been understood.'

'Where is it?'

Now Trajan asked the boys to sit with him, and as they perched beside the road, he had to confess: 'I don't know where it is. But the first person we meet on this road, we're goin' to ask.'

The boys could not believe that Trajan was telling the truth, and they wanted desperately to draw apart and discuss the trap into which they had fallen with their mother's cotton, but they were afraid to do so lest the slaves kill them right there. So they were overjoyed when they saw coming at them from the south a group of riders, and they were especially relieved to see that they were white.

But when the riders reined in at the lead wagon, they were far less pleased, for the leader was a terrifying man, very tall, covered with hair, dirty, mean-looking, and topped by a Panther pelt which he wore with the tail hanging down the left side of his face. 'Sergeant Komax, Confederate army. On duty with these men to gather all cotton wagons headed for Matamoros and bring them in safely.'

'Which way is Galveston?' Michael asked very politely.

'Don't matter. Ever'body goes to Matamoros. You niggers, what you doin'?'

Very carefully, very politely, Trajan directed Jaxifer to show the paper which the judge had written; he certainly did not propose to show *his* copy lest the soldiers keep it. When Komax had one of his men read the safe-passage to him, he grunted: 'We find a lot of slaves takin' their plantation cotton south. Join up.'

Komax had little trouble convincing Trajan to agree, but when he turned to the two boys he found himself looking into the same cumbersome rifles that had stopped the slave. 'We're goin' to Galveston,' Michael said in his quavering voice, and he was supported by his brother, who cried: 'You come closer, we shoot.'

To Trajan's surprise, the big, hairy man halted immediately and withdrew: 'Do somethin' with them kids!'

'You act as if they's gonna shoot.'

'At their age I'd of shot.'

So once more Trajan had to convince his two charges that going to Galveston was not only impractical but also forbidden. With the gravest foreboding that they might be slain or their cotton taken from them, the boys lowered their guns, but during the rest of this dangerous journey they remained close to Trajan, for Panther Komax terrified them.

By the end of that week three other wagons had fallen in line, and during the week after, four more. The plodding caravan had now passed Victoria and was about to skirt the dangerous port city of Corpus Christi, blockaded by Union ships. By the time Komax was ready to ford the shallow Nueces River, other Confederate scouts had rounded up a dozen or more creaking wagons, and Panther gave stern orders: 'Yonder, the Nueces Strip. We keep together for three reasons. Benito Garza and his bandits might attack. Union troops comin' at us from the sea might attack. And if you fall behind, you will perish for lack of water. Git!'

It was about a hundred and forty miles, in the hottest time of the year. The draft animals sometimes staggered in the blazing heat, and men fared little better, so that even the slaves, who were supposed to be impervious to heat, sweated and groaned. At times there seemed to be not a single living thing on the vast coastal plains, so flat they were, so devoid of pleasant vales and cool streamlets. The drivers wrapped rags across their faces and looked like ghosts gray with dust, but still the dreadful heat assailed them.

Water was rationed, and at the worst of the journey exhausted men and animals simply lay on the ground during the sunlight hours, sweating and jabbing at insects; there was no shade except under the wagons. It seemed stupid to be lying bathed in sweat, but the brief rest enabled the teams to travel through the cooler night. And then the miracle of Texas happened, because wherever in this vast state one traveled, arid and forbidding land finally ended and green pastures appeared. Komax had brought his caravan safely into the valley of the Rio Grande, that fragile paradise where a few industrious farmers were beginning to coax the waters of the river inland to produce the finest fruits and dairy cattle in this part of the world. Rarely were travelers more delighted to find shade and cool water.

At Brownsville the difficulty that Petty Prue had foreseen eventuated. Overland convoys like the one Panther Komax had brought through safely were arriving constantly, and with only one small, overworked ferry available for carrying the bales across the Rio Grande, a swirling confusion developed. Men with the loudest voices and the roughest manners preempted the ferry, and even though Panther was strong in both departments, he had learned that he had little chance of forcing the cotton of these slaves and their two small boys onto that precious craft.

'Why wait?' he said to Trajan. 'You can swim it acrost.'

'Me?'

'Yes,' Panther explained. 'You lug them bales to that river's edge, and then you shoves 'em in and you follow. And you kick your feet like a puppy dog, and pretty soon you're on the other side.'

'Not me!'

'If you don't do it, it ain't gonna get done.' He showed the slaves how to muscle the bales right down to the river, and then he demonstrated how Trajan must jump in after the bale and push it to the far side, but Trajan was terrified.

'Cotton don't float, and Lord knows, I don't float.'

'But it does float. Enough air locked in there, makes it a boat.'

'Water hit cotton, it's ruined.'

'It's packed so tight, water don't penetrate quarter of an inch.' Carefully Panther explained that perfect safety prevailed: 'Cotton floats. You float. Nothin' gets wet but your black hide. You ride back on the empty ferry.'

If Trajan was scared of the water, Jaxifer and the other two were paralyzed, and there seemed no way that the Cobb bales were going to be delivered to the people on the south shore who were eager to pay a fortune to get them. So, cursing all black men in words which ought to have shriveled Trajan's skin but which affected him not at all, for he was not going into that river, Panther shed most of his clothes until he stood a forbidding, hairy ape at the side of the Rio Grande. Instructing the slaves how to get the heavy bale into the water, he swore and plunged in after it, but he had taken only the first few kicks when off to his right he heard a boyish shout: 'It's easy!' and Michael was steering across the first of the many bales he would manage that day.

Swearing a new set of oaths, Komax crawled out of the water, grabbed Trajan by the neck, and thundered: 'If he can do it, you can.' And Trajan, trembling like an aspen edged into the water, kicked, and found that it would require fifty strong men to sink that bale of air-filled cotton.

On the next trip, even the smaller boy, Clem, swam his bale across, but no one, not even Komax with all his profanity, could get Jaxifer and the other slaves into that river.

Returning on the ferry after each trip, Trajan and the boys got their entire cargo across, and then the slave offered the lads a proposition: 'Clem, you the littlest, you swim over to the other shore and mind our cotton. Jaxifer, you stay here. Michael, you and me is gonna earn a fortune.' And they did. Well practiced now in swimming, they invited cautious owners to shove their bales into the water, where they took charge, maneuvering them to the Mexican shore.

They charged for this service, and so jammed were the supply lines that after several dripping days, they had accumulated quite a few dollars and would have been willing to continue the traffic indefinitely, for as Michael said: 'After you been without water in the Strip, this is fun.'

But now problems of a much different nature confronted them, because they must arrange a deal for their cotton and see that it reached some waiting cargo ship off the Mexican shore, and this threw them into the tremendous chaos of Matamoros, which stood twenty-seven miles inland from the Gulf. More than sixty small sailing craft crowded the river, clinging meticulously to the Mexican half, with each owner screaming: 'I'll carry your bales out to the big ships waiting in the Gulf.' And if one did elect one of these boats, greater confusion followed, for when the open sea was reached, the pilot must turn immediately south and take refuge in Mexican waters, where two hundred ships from all the ports of Europe posted seamen on their decks who bellowed: 'We'll take your cotton to Liverpool.' Off to the north, sometimes less than a hundred yards away, hovered warships of the United States Navy, never leaving American waters but always ready to pounce upon any ship laden with cotton that moved even a foot north of the international line.

Day after painful day the comedy was played out. Cargo ships owned by supposedly loyal Northern merchants in New York sailed blithely to some British or French port – or to any neutral port – where they were instantly issued papers by European powers hungry for cotton. Then, as privileged ships of that nation, they sailed to join the fleet waiting at Matamoros, hoping to acquire a load of cotton. In exchange they would give the Confederates shot and shell, muskets and hardware, cloth and food. If the Confederate government could move its cotton into a European ship, it could acquire in exchange almost anything it needed.

But how, in this welter of thievery, chicanery and murder, could a slave like Trajan or two boys like Michael and Clem hope to get their bales from Matamoros to the waiting fleet? There was a way. The Confederate government had assigned a clever, manipulative man to Matamoros, and his job was to collect the cotton ferried or swum across the river and move it overland to the fabricated port of Bagdad – a line of shacks along an open beach – and there turn it over to an even more ingenious Mexican conniver who saw to it that the bales got aboard ship.

The Confederate was big, jovial Yancey Quimper, dressed in full uniform, ideally qualified as an expediter and willing to pay any graft to accomplish his ends; the Mexican was a dapper man in a bright-red uniform laden with medals known as El Capitán. The two connivers were well matched, with Quimper's military rank as spurious as El Capitán's medals, and together they controlled the movement of cotton to the world markets.

The finances of this sleazy operation were interesting; cost of growing, 7¢ a pound; value on an interior Texas plantation, 1¾¢; value delivered on the north bank of the Rio Grande, 22¢; on the south bank, 37¢; delivered by General Quimper to the improvised Mexican seaport of Bagdad, 49¢, of which he pocketed 6¢; delivered to a waiting ship by El Capitán, 89¢, of which he pocketed 7¢; placed on the dock at Liverpool, $1.60, of which the shipowner retained a large portion.

Since thousands of pounds were being moved daily, it was obvious that the two expediters were getting rich, but so were many other patriots who managed to escape battle. There could have been unpleasantness over the fact that the captain was stealing a penny more per pound than the general, but Quimper also had a neat plan working whereby he bought for his own account, and not the government's, five or six bales each day if he could force some unfortunate seller to unload them at bottom price. These bales he disposed of through a special, undocumented arrangement with a Russian ship captain.

One praised men like Major Reuben Cobb for being loyal to his theory of honor, or Sam Houston for being loyal to his theory of government, but it was also possible for a man to be loyal only to himself and to adjust quickly to every whimsical gale which affected his interests. Yancey Quimper saw in the Union effort to strangle the Confederacy a chance to make his fortune; every situation in which decent men exalt noble sentiments is used as a chance to profit by those who look at such sentiments cynically.

One Confederate soldier assigned to help Quimper in his work, a veteran who had fought at Shiloh, summarized it well: 'This is a rich man's war, a poor man's battle.' Quimper, evaluating the same evidence, said: 'When bugles blow, wise men know.'

How had this man of no character and limited talent found himself in so many theaters of the war: at the Kansas preliminaries, at the massacre of the Germans, in charge of the hangings along the Red River, and now supervising operations in the cotton exchange, not to mention months spent tracking down draft evaders hiding in the Big Thicket northeast of Houston? Two reasons: the war was appallingly prolonged, with the nation's best men dying year after hideous year, and this provided time for those left at home to pursue many activities; indeed, a man like Quimper was forced into them. He was in Brownsville because the Confederacy needed him there. Also, when good men like Somerset Cobb and

Otto Macnab were engaged in battle, only the dregs were left to manage scandalous operations like those along the Rio Grande.

It was highly improbable that naïve cotton handlers like Trajan and Michael could bring their bales into Quimper's maelstrom and end up with any money at all, but they had one advantage: Panther Komax had grown to love Texas, and this meant that he hated Abe Lincoln and the North, and if he had brought his convoy so far, he was determined to see that his bales, at least, reached their proper destination. More important in the present situation, he had once watched helplessly as Yancey Quimper stole his bootmaker, Juan Hernández, so when he overheard the general trying to pluck off the cotton of his charges, he suddenly leaped from behind a stack of bales, gun drawn and shouting: 'Quimper! You'll take these bales to your Russian captain, and you'll pay nobody, not even yourself.'

Terrified and sweating, with the gun at his belly, Quimper took the boys and their cotton out to Bagdad, waved away El Capitán with the warning 'This is special,' and concluded a deal which gave the amateurs an honest profit. And Komax and the boys watched from the beach as the Russian ship raised sail and started for Europe.

In Brownsville, Komax arranged for their funds to be transferred by a letter of credit on an English bank: 'So they don't steal them from you on the way home.' The boys did not trust this, fearing that Panther was stealing from them the way General Quimper had tried, but Trajan, who had seen letters of credit at the mill, although he could not read them, assured the boys that Komax was telling the truth: 'The money be waitin' for you when you gits home. Gemmuns do bidness this way.'

But now he had his own problem. From his tireless work swimming the bales across the Rio Grande, he had accumulated more than a hundred dollars, and he knew that if he appeared at the plantation with such funds, he would be accused of having stolen them. So he asked Komax if he, Panther, would write him out a statement explaining that the money really was his. 'I cain't write,' Panther said, but he found one of his men who could, and the precious document was executed:

891

To Who It Concerns:
   This sertificate pruves the Slave Known as Trajan erned $139.40 by swimming cotton acrost the Ruy Grandee. The money is his, duttifully erned, and I sware to said.

Johnson Carver
Confederate Army

Trajan had been so preoccupied with financial arrangements for himself and the boys that he failed to notice a development in his group. Now Jaxifer came to him, no longer the noisy young clown whom Trajan had met on the approach to Social Circle, but a powerful man, mature and thoughtful: 'Micah, he done gone.' And Trajan realized that Micah had found the temptation of freedom in Mexico too powerful to resist, and was no doubt already in Monterrey.

This presented difficult choices for the three remaining Lammermoor slaves, who discussed them, using the deepest Gullah. When such slaves used their fragmentary English they came up with constructions which sounded funny, like *He done gone*, but when they spoke in Gullah they had a complete language for the expression of complete thoughts, and there was nothing amusing about it.

'Why should we three go back to slavery?' Jaxifer asked.

'Micah did no wrong,' Trajan replied evasively. 'If he felt he had to be free . . .'

'How about us?'

'There Mexico is, spit across the river. You'll never be closer.'

'If I go, will you try to stop me?' Jaxifer asked, for it was obvious that the third slave, Oliver, would not make the attempt.

Trajan pondered Jaxifer's question a long time, for it cut to the heart of black-white relations, and also to the core of his own behavior: 'A man wants to be free, that's maybe the biggest thing in life. If you feel it in your heart, Jaxifer, go.'

'How about you?'

'Well, now. No man wants freedom more than I do. I lost my son because people knew they could steal from a slave, no trouble. I lost my wife, worked to death.'

'Then join me.'

'No, I want to be free, more than any of you. But freedom is surely coming in Texas.' He hesitated before making a point which for him weighed most heavily: 'Better to work hard for freedom in a good place like Texas than accept it easy in a place not so good like Mexico.' Before Jaxifer could respond, he added: 'At night I say to myself: "Trajan, you built Lammermoor as much as any Cobbs. It's your place too." I do not want to give up a place I built.'

'But up there you'll always be a slave.'

'Not always.'

'Do you believe that?'

'If I didn't, I would cut my throat.'

Jaxifer asked: 'If I cross the river, will you send soldiers after me?'

'Oh, Jaxifer! How can you ask?'

'Then why don't you come with me?'

Again Trajan thought a long time before answering: 'I promised Miss Prue and the old man – I'd get the cotton south, I'd collect the money, and I'd bring it home.'

'But it went home by the bank, you said so.'

'The money's home, yes. But now I have to go. Jefferson is where I belong.'

At the edge of the Rio Grande, Jaxifer stared in silence at his longtime friends Trajan and Oliver. Then, turning his back upon them, he strode to where bales waited and pushed one into the river. Terrified though he was, he plunged in, grasping a corner of the bale with both arms and kicking his feet frantically as the cotton carried him to freedom.

It was chance, an intervention of fate, which led Panther Komax to get his homebound convoy on the road when he did, because in early November, Federal troops launched a determined invasion that captured Brownsville, thus terminating the Matamoros-Bagdad trade. To prove that they meant business, the troops also ranged inland at isolated spots, attacking any southbound convoys and burning the cotton, or bursting the bales and scattering it across the landscape until snow seemed to be falling on the brushy plains.

One evening such a foraging party came upon Komax and his

893

stragglers. Panther shouted to the slaves and the boys: 'Run! Hide!' but when he and his men turned back to fight off the attackers, a sudden fusillade of Union bullets ended his violent life.

Major Somerset Cobb did not return to Lammermoor until after Lee's surrender at Appomattox. Then, his left arm gone, his weight not more than a hundred and twenty, he came up the Red River from the hospital at New Orleans, with the doctor's benediction: 'God must have saved you, Cobb. We did damned little.'

At Shreveport he was pleased to see that the Great Raft was still in place, and his heart expanded and he felt something close to joy when the limping steamer, one boiler gone, edged into Lake Caddo and he saw once more the knobby cypresses and the Spanish moss hanging in lovely festoons from the live oaks that crowded the shore.

As always, the steamer sounded its whistle as it approached Lammermoor, and he saw with fresh pleasure that slaves aboard the craft were preparing to unload at that wharf called the Ace of Hearts. With pulsating enthusiasm he explained to a first-time passenger: 'Our slaves can't read, you know. We mark shipments Spades or Clubs, showing where parcels go. We're Ace of Hearts.'

The little vessel docked and the pain of return took command. He saw fields rotten with weeds, buildings unpainted. But the mill still stood, and here came Trajan, best slave a man ever had. Cobb leaped ashore, his empty left coat sleeve pinned up, and embraced him.

'It's good to be home, Trajan.'

'Been a long war, master.'

Slowly, for Sett was very tired, they walked up the slope toward his house, and now a small, fearfully thin woman came to greet him. It was Petty Prue, much smaller than he remembered, much more worn by the last years of war than he could have imagined.

Reaching for his one hand, she said: 'It was always stupid to have two plantations here. I've joined them, Sett.'

She had joined not only the land, but also their lives.

* * *

On 23 June 1865 there was great excitement in Jefferson, for a Union captain attended by fourteen soldiers marched in, ordered a bugle to be sounded, and informed the white citizens who assembled: 'I am here to address your former slaves, too. Call them.' Stiffly he waited till the latter were gathered, then signaled for another blast on the bugle. A sergeant shouted 'Silence!' and the fateful words were spoken:

'Citizens of Jefferson! On the nineteenth of June instant, General Gordon Granger of the United States Army issued at his headquarters in Galveston General Orders Number Three. All slaves are free. This involves an absolute equality between former masters and their slaves. The new connection between white and black is that of employer and hired workman.' (Here he turned specifically to the Negroes.) 'You freedmen are advised to stay at your present homes and work for wages. You are informed, and most strongly, that you will not be allowed to collect at military posts and you will not be supported in idleness. You must find work to do, and it would be best if you continue to work for wages at your present jobs.'

The captain stepped back, pleased with the impression he had made, then signaled his sergeant, who cried: 'Former slaves! You are free!'

There was a rustle, more of confusion than of comment.

'Slaves, you are no longer slaves,' the captain said. 'You are as free as I am or . . .' He looked about for some white person, spotted Cobb, and pointed at him: 'As free as this man.'

An old slave in the front rank fell to his knees, raised his hands over his head, and shouted in a feeble voice: 'I lived to see it. Praise God A'mighty, I lived to see it.'

When the reality of what had been announced struck home, there was no wild outcry, no jubilant dancing in the square, and white men were surprised that the former slaves took word of their freedom with such composure. But there were scenes which epitomized that crucial day in Jefferson history. One black woman, obedient to impulses no one could later explain, grabbed her seven-year-old boy and shook him violently, shouting at him: 'You ain't no more slave. Now will you mind?'

And she wept.

Major Cobb had come to the meeting anticipating what might happen, and he moved among his former slaves, assuring them that what the stranger said was true: 'Yes, you're free,' but his attempt at conciliation failed when Big Matthew ran up to him, shook a fist in his face, and shouted: 'Don't work for you no more.' When a laundry woman asked Matthew: 'What I do wid your clothes?' he roared: 'Burn 'em.' And again he shook his fist at Cobb: 'Don't work for you no more. Don't work for your bitch no more.'

Instinctively, Cobb raised his right arm, but a Union soldier prevented any further action.

The meaning of true emancipation – not President Lincoln's false gesture of some years before – was brought home to Lammermoor the next afternoon when amidst the clamor about freedom, Trajan appeared at the mansion, a place he had rarely entered, knocked politely at the door, and asked to see the master. Standing respectfully, he said: 'Major Cobb, you got the plantation under control, I'se leavin'.'

'What?' The statement was like the explosion of a bomb.

'I wants a place of my own. I got no more taste for livin' in slave quarters here at Lammermoor.'

'But you helped build this place. You're part of it.'

'Always I builds for someone else. Now I wants to work for myself.'

Cobb called for his wife, and when Petty Prue heard of the former slave's unexpected announcement, she echoed Sett's reaction: 'Haven't we always treated you decently?'

Trajan would not be sidetracked by any discussion of past conditions. Standing very erect, as he had been taught to do when reporting to a master, he said: 'I come home from Mexico, two years ago, money I earned swimmin' the river.'

When he saw incomprehension on the faces of the Cobbs, he produced the receipt signed by Johnson Carver during those days of high adventure with the two boys. And there in the silent room, when he thought of those daring lads, so like his son, he hung his head and the terrible grief of this war and these tangled years overcame him. He could not present his case, and the Cobbs let him go, thinking that emancipation had unsettled him.

Next day Major Cobb and his wife invited their former slave to meet with them, in the same room, and this time they asked him to sit down. 'Trajan, we suppose that with your money . . . And congratulations on having so much. I know many white families who would –'

Petty Prue, suddenly the more masterful of the Cobbs, broke in: 'Don't spend your money on land. You've been so faithful and we appreciate you so profoundly . . .' She choked and seemed not so masterful after all.

'What we propose,' her husband said, 'is to give you five acres of your own. That land against the oak trees.'

Trajan rose: 'All these years I got my eye on a nice strip of land, edge of Jefferson. Last night I bought it.'

'A slave? Buying land?' The words had slipped away from Petty Prue, who was immediately sorry she had said them.

'I bought it. I paid dollars and I'm leavin' this mornin', and your maid, Pansy, wants to go with me.'

'But Trajan,' Petty Prue cried in real confusion. 'You were so wonderful, helping me. Taking that cotton down to Mexico and coming back home.' She looked at him in near-despair: 'We thought you liked it here.'

Trajan moved to the door, determined not to be swayed by any argument these good people might advance. With tall dignity he told them: 'You can say I was faithful, because I was. And you can say I come back when I could of run away, because I did. And you can say I was respectful, because I liked the way you handled this plantation with the men gone, Miss Prue. I tried to be a good slave, but don't never say I liked it.' And he was gone.

Not long after, Major Cobb and his new bride entered their carriage, old now and needing refurbishing, and rode in to Jefferson, where on the edge of town they found the small cottage for which their former slave Trajan had paid twenty-two dollars and fifty cents, including an acre of land. The spring flowers were fading, but the Cobbs could see where the summer beauties would soon be peeking out.

'We've come to make you a proposition, Trajan.'

'I been expectin' you.'

'How so?' Petty Prue asked, accepting the chair her former

maid Pansy offered. The others would stand, for there was only the one.

'Because you need me. You goin' to need me bad, to run your gin, your mills.'

'You're right,' Cobb said. 'We do need you.'

'We miss you,' Petty Prue said, 'and we trust you.'

'What I'd be willing to do,' Cobb said enthusiastically, 'is buy this house from you. Give you the land I spoke of, and you could –'

'This is my house,' Trajan said. 'Pansy and I, we live here. You want us to work for you, we walk to work. But when work's over, we come back here.' He said this so forcefully that the Cobbs were stunned; they could not imagine that a black man would surrender such an obvious financial advantage in defense of a principle.

There was silence, broken by a practical suggestion from the major: 'We'll give you a mule so that you can ride to the mill.'

'I would like that,' Trajan said. Then he added a suggestion of his own: 'To run the mill right, we ought to have Big Matthew back.'

Cobb noticed Trajan's use of *we*, as if he were once more in charge of things, but the suggestion that Big Matthew be forgiven for his intemperate behavior was too much. 'No,' Cobb said gravely. 'Matthew tried to strike me, and that I cannot forgive.'

'Don't you think he got a lot to forgive?'

Cobb studied this sensible question for some moments, then asked: 'Will he work?'

When Cobb reluctantly agreed to hire the big man, Trajan brought forth a most unexpected request: 'Major Cobb, Miss Prue, I knowed you would be comin' and I knows what you was goin' to propose this mornin'. And I knowed I would accept, because I loves Lammermoor. But I had to jump the gun a little.'

'You borrowed money?'

'No!' He broke into an easy laugh. 'Smart man like me don't throw money around. I still got all but what I paid for the land.'

'What then?'

'Union officers been houndin' us. In a nice way, but they say all us former slaves got to take last names. They come to me yesterday, very forceful. This is the one they give me' – he hesitated – 'at my suggestion, if you ain't mad?'

He presented the Cobbs with a card bearing his new name: TRAJAN COBB, and Petty Prue said: 'We welcome you to freedom.'

... Task Force

The magazine *Washington Insider Post* almost wrecked our two-day May meeting in which we were to discuss the effect on Texas history of Southern immigration from states like Georgia and Alabama. Three days prior to our session the magazine revealed in a long think-piece the secret deliberations of a committee that had been assigned the task of selecting a new director of the Smithsonian Institution. The names of the four finalists were disclosed not in alphabetical order but according to their position in the betting, and the committee was astonished to find my name given last but with the notation 'May be the dark horse. Apparent favorite of the board's intellectuals.'

Before we could open our meeting in Dallas, a pulsating city whose vitality excited me, members of the press wanted to interview me, and when they were through, our own committee took over.

'It's a big job,' I said, but immediately I corrected my phrasing: 'Make that "It would be a big job . . . for whoever gets it."'

'What are your chances?' Rusk asked, cutting as usual to the crucial question.

'You saw the story. Last in line but still fighting.'

'Do you want it?'

'Anyone like me would want it, Ransom. Best job of its kind in the nation. But my chances –'

He cut me off, asked for a phone, and within eight minutes had spoken to his Texas friends serving in Congress, telling them, not asking, to get on the ball and see that I got the appointment. He put in a special call to Jim Wright, the representative from Fort Worth, majority whip in the House, asking him for special help.

Much of our first day was wasted in aimless discussion about the possibility of my going to Washington, but the situation was placed in its proper perspective by the arrival in the late afternoon of a senior editor from the *Insider*, who asked to have cocktails with us and who divulged in the course of our chatting the actual situation: 'I hate to say this, Barlow, but I have reason to believe that the selection committee threw your name in the hopper only to avoid the charge of parochialism. Most of the leading candidates were from the Northern and California establishments and they wanted the news stories to carry at least one Southern or Western name, and you covered both Texas and Colorado. To provide a respectable balance.'

'Wait a minute!' Rusk protested with the automatic defense of Texas which made men like him so abrasive. 'You don't use a Texan for window dressing. Damnit, we'll soon be the most powerful state in the Union –'

'But the University of Texas! A national committee would never –'

Now Quimper broke in to defend the school on whose board of regents he sat: 'Our university takes a back seat to no one.'

'In academic circles it does. That miserable show you people put on some years back, that regent Quimper going around firing everyone he didn't like.'

'That was my father,' Quimper exploded, 'and you're right. Some people condemned him as a meddler. Those who knew him considered him a genius. At any rate, Texas now has two first-class public institutions.'

'Which two?' the visitor asked, and I was astonished by Quimper's answer: 'Texas and A&M.' Often at our meetings he had joked about the latter school, denigrating it horribly, but now he was defending it; the difference was that when he joked, he was doing so to fellow Texans; when an outsider presumed to criticize, he became defensive.

'They're decent schools,' the Washington man conceded. 'Of the second category.'

'What the hell are you sayin'?' Quimper asked, his face growing red and his pronunciation more Texan. 'The university has Stephen Weinberg, Nobel winner, and A&M has just signed up the great Norman Borlaug, also a Nobel winner for his work on grains.'

'Yes,' our visitor conceded, 'but you hire them long after they've done their best work elsewhere. It's doubtful you'll ever produce a Nobel winner of your own.'

'You Washington know-it-alls make me puke,' Quimper said, retiring from the conversation. But the rest of us accepted the challenge, and in a series of short, impassioned statements we defended the intellectual honor of our state.

Miss Cobb was most effective: 'You must remember, young man, that power is flowing into Texas at an astonishing rate. More congressmen with every census. More industry. More of whatever it is that makes America tick. You unfortunate people in the North will be spending the rest of your lives dancing to a Texas tune. You should accustom yourselves to it.'

'There are rules of quality which cannot be evaded,' the editor, a graduate of Amherst and Yale, said. 'Texas will have the raw power, yes, but never the intellectual leadership. You'll always have to depend on the areas and the schools with higher standards.'

'That's the sheerest nonsense I've heard in a long time,' Rusk grumbled. 'In the fields that matter these days, Texas is already preeminent ... and we'll stay that way.'

'What fields?' the Washington man asked, and Ransom ticked them off: 'Petroleum, aviation, silicon chips, population growth.'

'When your oil wells dry up,' the Washington man said, 'you become another Arizona. Colorful, but of little relative significance.'

Rusk leaned back and looked at the young expert: 'Son, of a hundred units of oil in the ground in 1900 – take any well, any field you want – how much do you suppose we've been able to pump out so far? Go ahead, guess, if you're the last word on petroleum.'

'What? Seventy percent taken out, thirty percent still underground?'

'We've taken out twenty percent. The limitations of present techniques prevent us from taking any more. So eighty percent of Texas oil, and that's a monstrous reservoir, is still hiding down there, waiting for some genius to invent a better pump, a better system of bringing it up to where we need it. And you can be sure we'll invent some way of doing just that.'

Now Quimper snapped back: 'And the man who figures it out is gonna get his own Nobel Prize.'

Since the discussion had centered on me originally, I felt obligated to make a contribution: 'I wanted the Smithsonian job. Anyone would. To shepherd the material record of the nation. But in a way, these two men are right. That's a museum job. The past. The great struggles of the future are going to be fought out here in Texas. Even more than in California.'

The young man had excited our minds so thoroughly that Rusk suggested: 'Some of the things you say make a lot of sense. Have dinner with us.'

During the meal the visitor made two points which kept the pot of agitation bubbling: 'Texas will accrue power, that's obvious, but two deficiencies will hold you back. Because you produce no national newspaper like the *New York Times* or the *Washington Post*, you'll not command serious intellectual attention. *Newsweek* losing its Texas editor, that hurts the opportunities of other Texans like Barlow enormously.'

Before either Rusk or Quimper could leap to defend the young man who had left *Newsweek*, the editor made a humorous evaluation which ignited the basic fires of patriotism. 'And because your diet is so very heavy and unimaginative, you'll lose ground to California, which eats so sensibly.'

This was too much for Quimper: 'A good chicken-fried steak smothered in white gravy, or a big slab of barbecue with baked beans and potato salad, that's man's food. That keeps the blood circulatin'.'

'And the cholesterol raging.'

'I wouldn't be surprised,' Quimper said, 'if quiche and endive salad don't destroy California, grantin' it's still there after the earthquake hits.'

As the night wore on, Professor Garza asked seriously: 'So what are the chances that our boy will land the Smithsonian job?' and our visitor said: 'Nonexistent. They'll have to have someone with more prestige, and from a more acceptable locale, but even listing Barlow was a vote of confidence. Twenty more years, if things progress as Miss Cobb suggests, someone from Texas will be acceptable.'

'At that point,' Rusk said firmly, 'we'll be sending our young people to see Washington and New York the way we send them now to see Antwerp and Milan. Interesting historical echoes but no longer in the mainstream.'

When we convened in the morning we found that our staff had provided us with a professor from Texas Christian University, who offered a genteel antidote to the heated argument of the night before: 'I must warn you right at the start that I'm a Georgia woman who did her graduate work at South Carolina, so I'm imbued with things Southern, and the more deeply I dig into our past, the more respect I feel for Southern tradition. So please bear with me as I parade my prejudices.'

She delivered one of those papers that flowed along amiably, making subtle points whose veracity became self-evident as she marshaled her data; if the *Insider* man had dealt with the turbulent future, she led us seductively into a gallant past: 'When I was a student, Southern professors made it a point to avoid what they called "that unfortunate phrase *The Civil War*." They claimed it was never a civil war. They said that implied that in a state like Virginia, half the families sided with the North and took arms to defend that cause, while the other half favored the South and fought for it, with blood from two members of a given family mingling as it ran down some country lane in Virginia. They argued that that did not happen, not even in fractured states like Maryland, Kentucky and Missouri. "No," they said with great emotion, "this was a war between states, Massachusetts versus Alabama. And when those Missourians who did favor the North fought their fellow Missourians who sided with the South, they did so at outside places like Vicksburg and Shiloh, never in Missouri itself." For them it was a war between sovereign states, and in our papers we had to refer to it as such. But now, for historians South and North, it's the Civil War.'

Having instructed us on that important point, she proceeded to the heart of her statement: 'While I find it impossible to describe Texas as a true Southern state, I do not ignore the profound influence that Southern mores have exerted. In 18 and 36, Texas had principally a Northern cast, as installed by people from Connecticut and Ohio who had laid over in Kentucky and Tennessee. But within the next twenty-five years, say to 18 and 61, the influence of the South became overwhelming.'

'The vote on secession,' interrupted Rusk, who was always surprising us with his command of relevant data, 'was more than three-to-one – forty-six thousand to fourteen thousand – in favor of quitting the Union and fighting on the side of the South.'

'Far more important was the cultural domination. The few Texas children who had schoolteachers tended to have Southern ones. Children able to go away to college often went to Southern ones. Books by Southern authors were purchased from Southern stores. Southern newspapers were read.'

Turning to Garza, she said: 'You won't like this, Professor, but recent studies are beginning to suggest that the Texas cowboy derived not primarily from Mexican prototypes, but from the habits of drovers coming in from the Southern states.'

She cited a score of challenging statistics and illustrations showing that the impact of the South on Texas custom was pervasive, but as so often happens in such discussion, three of her almost trivial observations aroused far more interest than those of a graver nature: 'Food! Here the traditions of the South dominated. The Texan's love of okra, for example. One of the world's great vegetables, not native to Texas and unknown in states to the north, but a staple in the South. One could claim that the finest contribution we made to Texas life was the introduction of okra.

'Corn bread the same. Iced tea, which is practically the national drink of Texas, especially with a touch of mint or lemon. And I'm particularly fond, as many Texans are, of dirty rice.'

'What's that?' Garza asked, and the lecturer looked at him as if he were deprived: 'You don't know that gorgeous dish? Rice steamed in bouillon, with chicken giblets and chopped onions and pepper? Professor Garza, you ain't lived!'

Her second point was more serious: 'The most lasting influence may have been the language. The famed Texas drawl is nothing but the Deep South lingo moved west. You never say *business*. It's *bidniss*. And I am very partial to the dropping of the *s* in words like *isn't* and *wasn't*: "Iddn't today glorious and wuddn't yesterday a bore?"'

It was her third assertion which generated most comment: 'I sometimes think that the major importation from the South was a sense of chivalry – a dreamlike attitude toward women. The

904

men coming west really had read their Walter Scott. They did see themselves as avatars of the heroic age. They lived on the qui vive, always ready for a duel if their honor was in any way impugned. They had exaggerated interpretations of loyalty, and were ready to lay down their lives in obedience to those beliefs. Passionately devoted to freedom, they sacrificed all to preserve it. And like champions of old, they were not afraid to defend losing causes.

'Texas today is Carolina of yesterday, and in no aspect of life is this more apparent than in your attitude toward women. You cherished us, honored us, protected us, but you also wanted us to stay to hell in our place. In no state of the Union does a woman enjoy a higher social status than in Texas. She is really revered. But in few states does she enjoy more limited freedoms. If I were, and God should be so generous, nineteen years old, with an eighteen-inch waist, flawless skin and flashing green eyes, I'd rather live in Texas than anywhere else, because I would be appreciated. But if I were the way I actually was at that age, thirty-one-inch waist, rather soggy complexion and an IQ hovering near a hundred and sixty, Texas would not be my chosen residence.'

Quimper took vigorous exception to this: 'No state in the world pays greater deference to women than Texas.'

Our speaker proceeded: 'Texas has its own peculiar set of laws, and they stem directly from the tenets of Southern chivalry. But this also has its drawbacks. Because Texans prize freedom so highly, they refuse to burden themselves with the obligations which other less wealthy states have assumed. In public education, very tardy in establishing schools, very niggardly in paying for them. In public services, except roads, among the least generous in the nation. In health services, care for children, care for the aged, provisions for prisoners, always near the bottom.'

This was too much for Rusk and Quimper, who battled to see who would refute her first; Rusk won: 'But does not Texas stand, when all's considered, as one of the best states in the Union?' and she said: 'Unquestionably.'

Then Quimper asked: 'Wouldn't you rather be working in Texas than in Carolina?' and again she said: 'Of course.'

'Then what's this beef against chivalry? I'm proud of the way

I treat women,' and she said: 'Chivalry is a man's determination of how he should treat women. It's his definition, not hers. I would like to see a somewhat juster determination of the relationship.'

'You ain't gonna like it when you get it,' Quimper warned. 'I got me a dear little daughter, comin' on sixteen. I would like nothin' better for her than to build a good life here in Texas. Maybe a cheerleader at the university. Find herself a good man, maybe a rancher or an oil man out on the firin' line. Ma'am, that's true chivalry. That's Texas.'

'I'm willing to grant that,' the speaker said, 'but I'm trying to make two points. One, the values you've just defended are essentially Southern. Two, it's easier to maintain them, Mr Quimper, if you have nine ranches and nineteen oil wells.'

Il Magnifico startled our visitor by swinging the conversation around to where we had started the night before: 'Did you know, Dr Frobisher, that our boy here, Travis Barlow, is bein' denied a major job up North because he's Texas? Because he ain't from Harvard or Chicago?'

'I find that difficult to believe.'

'It's true. It's what we Texans have to fight against. And much of the stigma comes from the fact that like you said, we adopted all those Southern rules and customs.'

'I suppose that's right,' she said. 'I sometimes see the next fifty years as a protracted effort by the South to reestablish its leadership of the nation. We Carolinians and Virginians aren't powerful enough to do it by ourselves. So we're going to use Texas as our stalking horse. With your strength, your duplicity, we have a chance of winning.'

'Ma'am,' Quimper said, 'you've made a heap of sense this mornin'. You did us great honor in comin' here to share your views with us.' He was growing more Southern by the minute.

'I'll tell you something,' she said to all of us as she gathered her papers. 'I stay here at TCU because I love Texas. I've been invited back to four different schools in Carolina and Georgia. Sometimes I long for that easier life, that civilized custom, but I stay here for one good reason. I want to be where the action is. I love the skyline of Fort Worth ... the noise, the vitality, the wheeling and dealing, the expensive shops, the good restaurants.'

Rusk interrupted this song of praise with a blunt question which any of us might have asked: 'Are you classifying Texas as a Southern state?'

'Definitely not. It has none of the basic characteristics of Mississippi or Virginia.'

'It's Southwestern?'

'No. It lacks the qualities of Arizona and New Mexico.'

'What is it, then?'

'Unique.' Jamming her papers into her briefcase, she smiled: 'When you reach the age of forty-seven, if you have any brains, you awaken to the fact that the race is going to be over much sooner than you thought. So if I have only one life to live, only one dent to make, I want to make it where it counts, in Texas.'

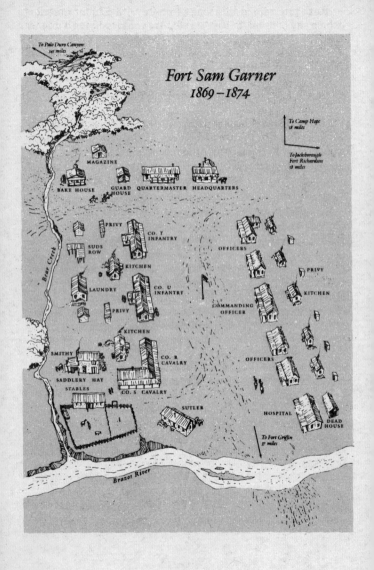

Fort Sam Garner
1869–1874

To Palo Duro Canyon
341 miles

To Camp Hope
18 miles

To Jacksborough
Fort Richardson
18 miles

MAGAZINE

BAKE HOUSE

GUARD
HOUSE

QUARTERMASTER

HEADQUARTERS

PRIVY

SUDS
ROW

CO. T
INFANTRY

OFFICERS

Bear Creek

KITCHEN

LAUNDRY

CO. U
INFANTRY

PRIVY

KITCHEN

PRIVY

COMMANDING
OFFICER

KITCHEN

SMITHY

CO. R
CAVALRY

SADDLERY HAY

OFFICERS

STABLES

CO. S CAVALRY

SUTLER

HOSPITAL

DEAD
HOUSE

To Fort Griffin
9 miles

Brazos River

X

THE FORT

When Ulysses Grant, one of the bloodiest generals in United States history, assumed the presidency in 1869, his fellow officers serving in the West were jubilant: 'Now we can settle with the Indians once and for all!' and they made preparations to do so.

To their astonishment, Grant initiated a thoughtful, humane and revolutionary Peace Policy, which he believed would lure the warring Indians into some kind of harmonious relationship with the white settlers who were increasingly invading their plains. His proposal had several major aspects: instead of allowing the army to govern Indian affairs, the churches of America would be invited to nominate from their congregations men of good will who would move west to the reservations, where they would be in control. Their task would be to win Indian allegiance by kindness, by distributing free food and by setting an example of Christian brotherhood. Funds would be provided from the national treasury to support the new plans. In return, all Indians would be expected to live peacefully on reservations, where they would be taught agriculture and where their children would attend schools that would Christianize them and teach them to wear respectable clothes instead of deerskin and feathers.

When Captain Hermann Wetzel, a veteran of both the Prussian army and the Civil War, and now serving with the 14th Infantry on occupation duty in Texas, read the new orders he threw them on the table: 'The General Grant I knew never signed such garbage,' an opinion shared by most of the army, which saw its freedom to act diminished and its prerogatives shaved. Like Wetzel, many officers were determined to sabotage what they considered General Grant's misguided order.

The religious group most eager to supply civilian personnel for the new system was the one whose principles were most antithetical to army methods, the Quakers of Pennsylvania, one of whose major tenets was pacifism; in this Indian challenge they saw an opportunity to prove that friendly persuasion produced better results than military force. Indeed, they called themselves Friends and their church the Society of Friends. They were a small group, concentrated mainly in Pennsylvania and New Jersey, but they had gained notoriety throughout the South for their vigorous opposition to slavery. Loyal Texans like Reuben Cobb and Yancey Quimper had characterized the Quakers as 'damned fools and troublemakers,' a view generally held throughout the state, for those who had fought against the Indians, especially against the Apache and Comanche, could not imagine how the peace-loving Quakers intended handling them: 'It's gonna be a shambles when Comanche like Chief Matark go up against them Bible-pushers.'

One of the first men to be considered for this challenging task was a young farmer from the tiny village of Buckingham in Bucks County, Pennsylvania. His place of residence reminded people of George Fox, the founder of Quakerism, who had had powerful associations with Buckinghamshire in England. 'Earnshaw's a fine Quaker,' they said of him, so when the letter from President Grant arrived, asking the local Quakers to nominate men qualified for this critical new assignment, the elders naturally thought of Earnshaw Rusk, twenty-seven years old and unmarried: 'It's as if he were designated by God to carry on the good works of our founder, the saintly Fox.' Without alerting Rusk, they sent his name forward.

Rusk gave the impression of being saintly, for he was tall, very thin, diffident in manner and rumpled in appearance, with the detached behavior of some minor Old Testament holy man. Even as a young boy he had seemed gawky and apart, his trousers ending eight inches above his shoetops, his sleeves seven inches from his wrists. His piety evidenced itself before he was nineteen, when in Meeting he was constrained to lecture his elders about what was proper in human behavior; and at twenty he ventured behind Confederate lines in Virginia and North Carolina, seeking to rouse the slaves in those states to demand their freedom. His innocence had protected him, for he had bumbled into three or four really perilous situations, only to find miraculous rescue. Once, south of Richmond, a black family whose members thought him quite irresponsible had hidden him in a cotton gin when a posse came searching for him, and in North Carolina a woman who owned slaves lied to the searchers about to arrest him, then told him when they were gone: 'Go home, young man. You're making a fool of yourself.'

But in the summer of 1865, when everything he had preached had come to pass, he returned to those slaves who had saved his life and to the good woman in Carolina, bringing them food and money contributed by the Philadelphia Quakers, and he had prayed with both the blacks and the whites, assuring them that God had ordained that they save him in 1862 so that he could return now to help them get started in a better life. The Carolina woman, whose farm had been burned by Sherman's rioting men, warned him once more that he was making a fool of himself, but after he had stayed with her for three weeks, helping to clear away the ruins and make space for a new home, she concluded: 'Rusk, you're a living saint, but you're not long for this world.'

The officials appointed by President Grant to receive nominations for the new posts were delighted to hear of a man who seemed to fill every requirement: 'He's vigorous. He has no wife to cause complications and expense. And he will love the Indians as he loved the slaves.'

There was a dissenting vote, for an older man who had made his living in Philadelphia commerce, a harsh testing ground, feared that anyone as naïve as the recommendations showed Earnshaw Rusk to be was bound to have trouble translating his piety into positive action: 'I'm afraid that if we throw this young fellow in a place like Texas, they'll eat him al' e.'

'He won't be going to Texas,' a member of the committee explained. 'He's ticketed for a location in the Indian Territory,' but the other man warned: 'That's pretty close to Texas.'

The committee, eager to announce its first appointment, overrode the businessman's objection and informed President Grant that 'Earnshaw Rusk, well-respected Quaker farmer of Buckingham, Pennsylvania, unmarried and in good health, is recommended for the position of United States Indian Agent at Camp Hope on the north bank of the Red River in the Indian

Territory.' Grant, also quite eager to get his program started, accepted the recommendation. 'We've found the perfect man to tame the Comanche.'

Earnshaw was plowing his fields when a local newspaperman came running to him: 'Rusk! President Grant has appointed you to a major position in the government!' Unprepared for such news, Earnshaw asked to see verification, then stood, with the telegram in his left hand, reins in his right, and looked to heaven: 'Thee has chosen me for a noble task. Help me to discharge it according to Thy will.' But the reporter broke in: 'Says in the telegram that General Grant did the choosing.'

When confirmation reached Buckingham, Rusk felt inspired to address his final First Day Meeting:

'I must demonstrate to the army and to the nation as a whole that our policy of peace and understanding brotherhood is God's elected way for bringing the savage Indian into productive partnership. I deem it my duty to work among the Indians as I worked among the slaves, and I am satisfied the results will be the same.

'If William Penn could bring peace to his Indians, I feel certain I can do the same with the Apache and the Comanche. I seek your prayers.'

A cynical Quaker businessman who had traveled in Texas whispered to the man next to him: 'William Penn would have lasted ten minutes with the Comanche.'

As Rusk spoke his hopeful words in eastern Pennsylvania, the rambling family of Joshua Larkin was preparing to establish rude quarters on a site Larkin had scouted about sixty miles west of the newly established town of Jacksborough, Texas. Army officials stationed at nearby Fort Richardson warned the Larkins as they arrived that they ran serious risks if they ventured so far west, and Captain George Reed, a gloomy man, was downright rude: 'Damnit, Larkin, if you stick your neck way out there, how can we protect you?'

'Six times in Texas we've moved west, always to better land. And six times we heard the same warning. The Waco will get you. The Kiowa will get you. And now you're sayin' "The

Comanche'll get you." ' Larkin, whose lined face seemed a map of the frontier lands he had conquered, poked Reed in the arm: 'We ain't never been as afraid as the army.'

'And you ain't never battled the Indians, the way the army has,' Reed snapped, imitating Larkin's raspy whine.

'That's because we're smarter'n the Indians, and you ain't.'

'You're from Alabama, aren't you?'

'Sure am.'

'I learned twenty years ago, you can never teach an Alabama man anything.'

'That's why we conquered the world.'

'Up to a point,' Reed said, indicating his blue military sleeve.

'You had the big factories, the railroads,' Larkin said without rancor as he prepared his wagons for the final push. 'Any time we start even, we'll whip you Yankees easy.'

'Why you so eager to move west?' an older officer asked, and Joshua replied: 'There's two kinds of Americans in this world. Them as looks east and them as looks west.'

'Meaning?'

'East men look for stores and banks and railroads. They have dollars in their eyes. Us west men look for untamed rivers, deep woods, open prairies. In our eyes we have the sunset. And we'll keep goin' till we stand with our feet in the Pacific, lookin' at that sunset.'

'Aren't you afraid of Indians?' the officer asked, and Joshua replied: 'We Larkins been fightin' redskins fifty years. No reason to stop now.' But as soon as he had uttered this boast, he added: 'As for me, I never killed an Indian, never propose to.'

Next morning the sixteen pioneers departed: Joshua; his two married brothers; the three wives; an unmarried brother, Absalom; and nine children of all ages. 'There they go!' a soldier shouted as the wheels began to turn. 'Israelites pouring into the Land of Canaan.'

They would head slightly northwest along almost unbroken trails until they intersected the Brazos River, the aorta of Texas, coming at them from the left. 'And when we go along it a bit we come to Bear Creek, joinin' from the north. Prettiest little creek you ever saw, and where they touch, that's where we'll call home.'

It was a sixty-mile journey, and since experience enabled

them to make fifteen miles a day, they planned to reach their new home at the end of the fourth day. Joshua kept his brother Absalom riding ahead as scout, and repeatedly the latter galloped back to assure the wagons that on the next rise they would see wonders, and they did, the great opening plains of West Texas, those endless, rimless horizons of waving grass and sky. Rarely did they see a tree, not too often a real hill, and never growing things on which to subsist.

Through various devices the Larkins had obtained title to about six thousand acres of this vast expanse, at a cost of four cents an acre, and they realized that it was no bargain, but it did have, as Joshua had reported after his scout, four advantages: 'Cattle unlimited, wild horses for the ropin', constant water, an open range for as far as a man can throw his eye.'

There was excitement when Absalom rode back to inform his relatives: 'Brazos River ahead! One more day's travel!' He was correct in his guess, and when the Larkins started their trip along its northern bank they felt as if they were once more safe. When they reached the confluence with Bear Creek they stopped on a small rise and surveyed their promised land: 'Ain't nothin' here but what we're goin' to build. All ours.'

They had brought with them a few domesticated cattle, a string of good horses and six wagons containing a bewildering mixture of whatever goods they had been able to amass: cloth and medicines, nails and hammers plus the lumber on which to use them, spare axles and wheels, a few pots, a few forks and two Bibles.

The Larkins were Baptists, Democrats, veterans of the Confederate army, excellent shots and afraid of nothing. The three wives came from three different religions, Baptist, Methodist, Catholic, but all knew 'The Sacred Harp,' that twangy religious music of the South, and now as they prepared to pitch their tents for the first time at their new home, they united in song. Their nine children joined in, and when the lilting hymn ended, Joshua cried: 'Lord, we made it. The rest is in your hands.'

To the three sod houses they were about to build they brought an arsenal of firearms: Sharps, Colts, Enfields, Hawkens, Springfields, and each child above the age of five was trained in their use. They did not anticipate trouble, since, as

Joshua had boasted to Reed, they had edged their way five previous times into lands recently held by Indians and had invariably found ways to neutralize the savages, principally by trading with them, giving them a fair exchange. Of course, when Texas Indian policy had become expulsion or extermination, their bold forebears had helped in the former and applauded the latter. But this generation, probing into a more dangerous section of the state and up against a more dangerous type of Indian, hoped for peace.

They spent two days of hectic action gouging a large sod dugout in which all would sleep at first, and then Joshua turned to the second preoccupation of all Texans: 'The land is ours. The water we got to collect.' And he put all the men and boys, even the tiny lads, to the task of throwing across a gully a rude dam which would impound enough water to form what Alabamans called a pond but Texans a tank. 'With a good tank,' Joshua said, 'we can manage cattle and horses. But now we got to get ourselves some ready cash,' and he divided his work force into two groups: one to rope wild horses and bring in stray cattle that could be sold in Jacksborough, the other to go out onto the plains with their powerful Sharps rifles to kill buffalo. They would be skinned, with the aid of horses that pulled loose the hairy hides and dragged them back to where they could be baled for shipment to markets in the East. The carcasses, of course, they left to rot.

It was miserable work, and as the buffalo began to withdraw westward, travel to the killing grounds became more onerous, but always Joshua spurred his brothers: 'Get horses. Get cattle. Kill the buffalo.'

His strategy was not accidental, for if the Larkins could assemble horses and cattle, they would poss s the basis for a prosperous ranch, and if they could exterminate the buffalo, they would make the plains uninhabitable for the Indians. The Larkin brothers did not want to kill off the Comanche; they wanted to ease them onto reservations north of the Red River, leaving Texas as it was intended to be, freed of Indians.

'Give us three years of peace,' Joshua said at the end of one vigorous stretch, 'and bring soldiers fifty miles west to a new chain of forts, we'll have this land pacified.' He never said that Bear Creek would be their permanent home, for he and one of his brothers had already scouted more than two hundred miles west to where green canyons dug deep in the earth, with plenty of water and even some trees. Given time and persistence, the Larkins were going to own those canyons.

The particular tribe of Comanche led by Chief Matark, a forty-year-old veteran of the plains wars, had for many generations occupied the rolling area west of Bear Creek, and from this sanctuary, had ranged two hundred miles north into Oklahoma lands and five hundred miles south into Mexico. They had ravaged competing tribes of Indians and plundered white settlements, including El Paso and Saltillo. Whole decades would pass without a major defeat, for under Matark's strategies the Comanche eluded pursuit by the enemy, avoided pitched battles, and struck whenever a position stood exposed. They were cruel and crafty enemies, well able to defend themselves and remorseless when an isolated ranch seemed unprotected.

In the autumn of 1869 the bold appearance of the Larkin clan at the confluence of Bear Creek and the Brazos troubled Chief Matark so much that he did an unusual thing: he convened a war council; it was unusual because customarily he made all military decisions himself.

'How many are they?'

'Four grown men, all good with the rifle. Three wives who can also shoot. Nine children, some old enough to use guns.'

'How do they dare move onto our land?'

'They expect the fort they call Richardson to protect them.'

'How far are they from the fort?'

'Their huts stand three days' walk to the west.'

'Three days!' the chief cried. 'In that time we could wipe them out.' But then he grew cautious: 'Could they have an arrangement with the soldiers there? Detachments hiding in the gullies? Waiting for us to attack?'

'No soldier has visited the three sod huts. Never.'

'But could there be a secret? Something we can't see?'

'There is no secret. If we strike now, as we should, the army cannot reach us in two days.'

Matark, not wholly satisfied with the reports of his younger braves, sought counsel from two old men who had seen many battles, and the older of the two, a man with no teeth who stayed alive by willpower, said: 'It is not the army. It is not how many guns they have in the three sod houses. What will destroy us is the way they kill our buffalo.'

Said the second old man: 'With each moon the animals move farther away.'

'And few of them.'

'If they stay at Bear Creek ...'

'And if more come, as they always do ...'

'What shall we do?'

'Now, there we face trouble,' the first old man said. 'If we could only pray that the fort at Jacksborough would be the last ...'

'Always they push the forts closer,' his associate pointed out. 'That's how it always has been. That's how it always will be.'

'Until we are pushed where?' Matark cried in what was for him close to desperation.

The two old men looked at each other, well aware of what must be spoken but each afraid to utter the doleful words. Finally the older spoke: 'We shall be pushed to the sunset death.'

'But not quickly,' Matark said, betraying the tragic strategy he intended following.

'No!' the younger of the two sages cried, happy to hear the courage in his chieftain's voice. 'It will be like the old days, when every hand was raised against us. Kiowa, Apache, Mexican, Texan. We shall strike them all.'

With these fighting words, re-creating the bravery the Comanche had displayed against all enemies, a grand euphoria filled the air and imaginary arrows whistled around the conspirators. The Comanche would strike again. They would strike again and again. They would battle the entire blue-clad army. They would protect their range, they would expel invaders, now and forever.

'We will destroy them!' Matark decreed, and with a mixture of fear and joy the old men ran out to reveal the decision to the braves. They knew that judged by the long years, this strategy must fail, but they also knew that it was a gesture which had to be made. The odds against them were tremendous, for they knew how few in number they were and how powerful that line of Texas forts could be, crammed with blue-clad soldiers. The Comanche could recite the fearful names: Fort Richardson in the north, the new Fort Griffon, Fort McKavett, Fort Concho where the many rivers met, Fort Stockton to the West, Fort Davis, strongest of all beneath the mountains, Fort Bliss at the Rio Grande, and a dozen more.

There were also forts in New Mexico, in Arizona and California, so placed that cavalry troops could strike at Indians from any direction. The old men knew they were doomed, but they also knew that they had no alternative but to defend their rolling plains as they had always defended them. And they were proud that a young chief whom they had helped train was willing to assume the burden. So they moved among the warriors, crying: 'It's to be war!' and they kept their voices strong to mask their fears.

One hundred and nineteen Comanche braves left their camp at the headwaters of the Brazos River and rode in three separate groups, quietly and with sullen determination, toward Bear Creek, and on the morning of the third day, just after dawn on 15 October 1869, they came thundering down upon the three sod huts.

Catching Absalom as he tended his horses, they tomahawked him immediately and made off with about half the animals. They then struck the westernmost of the huts before the occupants could organize its defense, and with total superiority, overwhelmed it, killing the wife and her two children but saving the husband for ritual tortures later.

With the second house they ran into real trouble, for here Micah Larkin and his wife were ready with a full arsenal, with which they held off the attackers for more than an hour. In the end the defenders were helpless; the Indians rode their horses right up to the walls and fired into the openings. Again, the wife was killed with her child but the man was spared for attention later.

At the somewhat larger home of Joshua Larkin the defense was formidable, with father, mother and two children firing guns with deadly result. Nine Indians died while circling this house, until finally Matark himself had to lead a charge which set fire to the grass roof, forcing the occupants out. When Joshua appeared, he was slain instantly, but the wife was captured alive. Of the six children in the hut, three were killed with tomahawk blows to the head, two were lanced, and the girl Emma Larkin, twelve years old, was taken alive to serve as a plaything for the younger braves.

Because the nature of Indian warfare on the Texas range must be understood if the history of Texas is to be appreciated, it must be recorded that during a span of about thirty years dozens of farmers and ranchers and traders were killed each year by the Indians, an awesome total. But it was the manner in which they were killed that enraged the settlers and made any peace with the Indians impossible.

At Bear Creek, two of the youngest children were grabbed by the heels and bashed against rocks, three were hatcheted and three were lanced. Absalom and a brother were tomahawked in what might have been called fair fight, and two of the wives were also slain in the heat of battle. But even the bodies of these four were sought after the slaughter and ceremoniously mutilated, appendages being cut off and sexual organs defiled in savage and repulsive ways.

It was the four living prisoners, three adults and a young girl, who suffered the real terrors of Indian warfare, because the two men were staked out in the embers of their burned homes, and living coals were edged about them while their extremities were painfully hacked off. Their genitals were amputated, dragged across eyes from which the lids had been cut away, and then stuffed into their mouths. Their eyes were then blinded, and slowly they were roasted to death.

The third wife was saved till last, and even the official reports of the massacre, compiled by Captain Reed from Jacksborough, refrained from spelling out in detail what she had suffered, for it was too horrible for him to write.

Not one of the fifteen dead bodies was left whole. Heads were cut off. Arms and legs were chopped into pieces. Breasts were severed. Eyes were gouged out. And not even torsos were entire. From the evidence I saw, I must conclude that four adults were burned alive after the most terrible tortures.

I cannot imagine that a chief as wise as Matark is supposed to be can think that by such actions he can frighten away our legitimate settlers or deter our army from retaliation. When I buried the fifteen bodies I stood beside their common grave and took an oath, which I required the men at Fort Richardson to take with me when I returned last night: 'I will hunt down this savage killer, even though he hides at the ends of the earth. These dead shall be revenged, or I shall die in the attempt.'

But after the oath was taken, a soldier who had kept records of settlers passing through reminded us that the Larkin family had consisted of sixteen members, which meant that one must still be alive, and with the help of my men who assisted at the burial, we reconstructed the family and concluded that a girl named Emma, about twelve years old, was not among the dead. She must be with them, and with God's help we shall win her back.

As he forwarded his report to Department headquarters in San Antonio, which in turn would send it along to Divisional offices in Chicago, the girl Emma was indeed alive. She was in a camp out toward the canyons, where she had already been raped repeatedly by young braves and where jealous women and sportive young men had begun the slow, playful process of burning off her ears and her nose.

The orders initiated by four-star General William Tecumseh Sherman in Washington for Captain George Reed, Company T, 14th Infantry at Fort Richardson near Jacksborough, Texas, were concise:

You will proceed immediately to the spot where Bear Creek joins the Brazos and there establish a fort of the type common in Texas and the Indian Territory. You will take with you two companies of the 14th Infantry and two from the 10th Cavalry, plus such supporting cadre as may be required, not to exceed the authorized complement of 12 officers, 58 non-commissioned officers and 220 privates, 8 musicians and 14 auxiliary personnel (total 312). The fort is to be named, with appropriate ceremony, in honor of the Texas Ranger captain who distinguished himself so heroically at Monterrey, Sam Garner. Your mission is to protect American settlers, to establish working relations with the Indian reservation at

Camp Hope in the Indian Territory, and to capture and punish Chief Matark of the Comanche if he strays into Texas.

At the end of October 1869, Captain Reed, thirty-three years old, crop-headed, clean-shaven, underweight, and the owner of an unblemished military record, led his contingent west. Symbolic of the condition in which he would find himself during the next three decades of his command, his paper allotment of 312 effectives was 66 short, including a Lieutenant Renfro, whose energetic and conniving wife, Daisy, had succeeded in gaining him a third extension of his temporary desk assignment in Washington. Since the conclusion of the Civil War, Renfro had avoided any frontier duty and seemed on his way to avoiding this stint as well.

Several aspects of Fort Sam Garner were noteworthy. First, it was not a *fort* in the accepted sense of that romantic word, for it boasted no encircling walls and provided no secure defense against an enemy. It was instead a collection of some two dozen buildings laid out neatly on a large expanse of open ground. Second, the buildings were not of stone or brick but of timber, adobe, fieldstone or whatever else might be at hand. Third, even these miserable accommodations were not in existence when the 246 effectives arrived on the scene; the enlisted men would have to erect them in haphazard fashion as time passed. Until then the men would live in tents, and since winter was approaching, the men worked diligently, requiring little urging from their officers, because until houses of some sort were slapped together, they were going to freeze at night, regardless of how much they sweated during the day. Fourth, when General Sherman assigned two companies of the 10th Cavalry to the fort, he knew that he was creating permanent trouble for Captain Reed, because the 10th Cavalry was an all-Negro regiment, which meant it would generate not only the customary animosity which existed between foot and horse soldiers, but also the more serious viciousness stemming from the difference in color.

One aspect of the typical Texas fort in 1869 would have surprised the Northern troops who built it had they known the facts. Their wall-less, adobe, unfortified assembly of buildings resembled strikingly the old presidio which the Spanish military had erected in San Antonio a century and a half earlier. Like sensible men, the Spanish and the American soldiers reacted almost identically to similar geographical and logistical problems.

But the outstanding characteristic of the fort was the nature of its officer cadre, as revealed by the roster shown opposite.

One interesting thing to be noted was that none of the officers – and only an occasional black enlisted man – came from the South, because that region had recently been in rebellion, with even its West Point sons like Generals Lee and Davis rejecting their oath to defend the Union: 'You cain't never trust no Southron, and we won't tolerate 'em in our army.' Of the many forts that would protect Texas in these years, none would be manned by Texans.

The presence of a German and an Irishman at Fort Garner was not unusual; thousands of such volunteers had served in the Union forces, usually with distinction, and not infrequently it was these European veterans who formed the backbone of the frontier army. They were belligerent, sticklers for proper drill, and dependable. In Hermann Wetzel and Jim Logan, Fort Garner had two of the best: the former a Prussian disciplinarian in charge of all foot soldiers; the latter a daring, laughing horseman who worked with the black troops.

It was the last column of the roster that showed the heartache of a peacetime fort, because, as can be seen, all the officers except Lieutenant Toomey had enjoyed, during the Great War, a brevet or temporary rank considerably higher than what they now held. A brevet promotion could have been conferred in one of many ways: a new regiment would be formed, requiring colonels and majors, so officers much lower in rank would be temporarily promoted to meet the emergency, it being under-stood that when peace came, they would revert to their lower rank. A senior officer would be killed in battle, and a replacement would be breveted. Often in the heat of battle some extremely brave lieutenant would be breveted to colonel, and he would be addressed as colonel and treated like one, but his real rank would remain lieutenant. Now it was peacetime, and military personnel was savagely reduced – 1,000,516 men in 1865; 37,313 now – and even the slowest-witted officer could

Fort Sam Garner Roster

OFFICER	BORN	WIFE	NATAL STATE	DUTY	PERMANENT OFFICIAL RANK TODAY	TEMPORARY BREVET RANK DURING CIVIL WAR
Reed, George	1836	Louise	Vermont	Co. T, 14th Inf. Fort Commander	Capt.	Brig. Gen.
Minor, Johnny	1839	Nellie	Wisconsin	Co. R, 10th Cav. Senior Cavalry Officer	Capt.	Col.
Wetzel, Hermann	1829	Bertha	Germany	Co. U, 14th Inf. Senior Infantry Officer	Capt.	Col.
Sanders, Tom	1840	Ruth	Maine	Co. T, 14th Inf. Adjutant	1st Lt.	Capt.
Harrison, Tom	1843		Iowa	Co. S, 10th Cav.	1st Lt.	Lt. Col.
Logan, Jim	1844		Ireland	Co. S, 10th Cav.	2nd Lt.	Major
Masters, Andrew	1845		Illinois	Co. U, 14th Inf.	2nd Lt.	Capt.
Toomey, Elmer	1849		Indiana	Co. R, 10th Cav.	2nd Lt.	
Renfro, Lewis	1838	Daisy	Ohio	Co. S, 10th Cav. Detached duty Washington	1st Lt.	Col.
Jaxifer, John	1827		Georgia	Co. R, 10th Cav. First Sergeant	1st Sgt.	1st Sgt.

923

foresee that he was going to remain in his lowered permanent rank for years and years. During the war an able soldier like Reed had almost leaped from second lieutenant to brigadier general, six promotions in heady sequence; he, George Reed, a schoolteacher from Vermont, had actually been a general in charge of a flank attack on Petersburg, and now he was a lowly captain, four demotions downward, with every expectation of remaining indefinitely at that level. During the war the leap from lieutenant to major had required, in his case, five months, for attrition had been great. In peacetime the slow crawl back to major would require at least a quarter of a century, if it was ever attained.

Yet all except young Elmer Toomey could remember when they had been officers of distinguished rank. Johnny Minor had been a full colonel and a good one, but now and for as long as he could see in the future he would be a captain in charge of one company of black troops, and he could not reasonably anticipate higher promotion, not ever. White officers who served with black troops were contaminated, and scorned by their fellow officers; to such men few promotions fell.

However, within the security of these remote forts, it was customary when speaking directly to an officer to award him the highest rank he had held as brevet, so although the adjutant, when reporting in writing to Washington, had to write: 'Captain Reed, Commanding Officer, Fort Garner, wishes to inform . . .' when that same adjutant addressed Reed within the fort he would say: 'General Reed, I wish to report . . .' It was a delicate game, where sensitivities were constantly exposed and where imagined insults rankled for years, and nowhere was it played out with richer variation than on the vast expanses of Texas. Actual duels were forbidden, but they sometimes occurred; what was more likely, some disgruntled first lieutenant who had once been a lieutenant colonel would nurture in secret a grudge against a lieutenant who had been only a brevet major, and on some hate-filled day would find an excuse to bring court-martial charges against him. This then became an affair of honor, dragging on year after year; often each officer would publish a small book giving his *True Account of What Transpired at Richards Crossing*, proving that it was his accuser, not he, who had been craven.

This was Fort Garner in 1869, a collection of makeshift and undistinguished buildings, but each laid out with that compass-point precision which would have prevailed had they been built of marble. Reed had insisted on this, and during the planning he had appeared everywhere with his chalk line, squaring walls and ensuring that buildings of the same character stood in orderly array: 'It may be an unholy mess now, but it won't always be.'

After consultation with Wetzel, who had a keen sense of tactics, he had decided that the fort would be built east of Bear Creek, so that any Indians coming at it from the west would have to attack across that stream or across the Brazos. To safeguard against flooding, he had his men spend two weeks deepening each stream, and then he strengthened the mud dam with which the Larkins had constructed their tank.

Fort Garner would stand fifty-eight miles west of Jacksborough, same distance south of Camp Hope in the Indian Territory. The five officers' buildings, each with detached kitchen and privy, would form the eastern boundary of the long parade ground; the enlisted men's quarters, the western. The northern limit was hemmed in by the service buildings, while the southern was defined by the hospital and the store run by the post sutler.

As if to give protection from the west, where the enemy roamed, the stables were located there as a kind of bulwark, north of which stood one of the curiosities of the western fort, Suds Row, where the hired laundresses, sometimes Mexican, sometimes reformed prostitutes, but most often the wives of enlisted men, washed uniforms six days a week. When the men of Fort Garner were at their home station they were a natty lot, especially the Buffalo Soldiers, as the blacks were called because their knotted hair was supposed to resemble that of the buffalo.

Buffalo Soldier, originally a term of opprobrium, had been adopted by the black cavalrymen as a designation of honor, and one fact about Fort Garner summarized that situation: the effective complement had begun at 246, but because of desertion, conniving to escape difficult duty and slow recruitment it would become only 232; but of the 134 black horsemen assigned to Fort Garner, only two would desert over a period of three years; of the white infantrymen, fourteen had already gone by the end of the first four months. To be a Buffalo Soldier was a sterling attainment. Many of these men had entered Union service in the darkest days of the war and they had served heroically, fighting both the avowed enemy at the South and the insidious one at the North. From the beginning they had known they were not liked and were not wanted, and during peace this dislike was hammered home in a hundred mean and malicious ways.

For example, the parade ground at Fort Garner had been in operation less than a week when Wetzel came to Reed with a serious complaint: 'General, when the troops line up at morning and evening review, the Buffalo Soldiers, as is proper, stand at the south, before their stables. Could you direct Colonel Minor to keep his niggers well removed from my men? We cannot tolerate the smell.'

When Reed broached the subject to Minor, the Wisconsin man showed no animosity, nor did his cavalrymen when he jokingly asked them to muster 'Just a wee bit to the south, so we don't offend anyone.' The cavalrymen knew how desperately they were appreciated when at the height of some offensive against the Indians they appeared at the critical moment to support infantry units pinned down by Indian fire: 'We was there when you needed us and we'll be there next time, too.' It was unpleasant, sometimes, being a Buffalo Soldier, but the work provided moments of great satisfaction, and it was for these that the black troops drilled so strenuously and served with such resilient humor.

A distinctive component of any frontier fort was the group of wives who managed to stay with their hubands, often under the most appalling conditions, and Fort Garner was blessed with two of the finest. The mud huts had scarcely been roofed over when Louise Reed, the commander's wife, and Bertha Wetzel, wife of the senior infantry officer, appeared in a cargo wagon which they had commandeered at Jacksborough. Mrs Reed brought her ten-year-old daughter, who reveled in the ride across the plains, and such household gear as she and Mrs Wetzel could assemble, not only for their own families but for all the others at the fort.

When the two women drove onto the parade grounds, men cheered, for those long associated with the four companies were well acquainted with the contributions such energetic wives made to soldiering, and within two days evidences of improved conditions were seen. Mrs Reed gave a tea at which the eight officers and the four wives were present, and on the next day Mrs Wetzel carried her teapots to Suds Row, where she assured the washerwomen that if they had any problems with the men, they would find support from her. She served them sandwiches and called each by name.

The two women were remarkably similar. Each was a little taller than average, a little thinner. Mrs Reed was from her husband's state of Vermont; Mrs Wetzel had met her German husband when he was stationed at a fort in Minnesota. Each had a strong affiliation with her Protestant church, and each was painfully aware that her husband was probably going to remain in his present rank for as long as he wore the uniform. They were about the same age, too, in their early thirties, and whereas neither could ever have been termed beautiful, each had acquired from years of service that noble patina which comes from dedication to duty and the building of a good home. One enlisted man who had never spoken directly to the commander's wife said: 'The two good days at a new fort: when we put a roof over where we sleep and when Mrs Reed appears.' In the postwar period she had helped make life easier at three different forts as the army moved resolutely west, and although this was the poorest site of the lot, she observed with pleasure that the land was flat and easy to manage and the water supply copious: 'The rest will come in due time.'

One factor at Fort Garner displeased her. Johnny Minor, one of the best leaders of cavalry and a man who already bore a heavy burden because he was required to lead black troops, had a pretty little wife named Nellie, who gave him much trouble. She despised his assignment and humiliated her husband's black cavalrymen by refusing ever to speak to them. To her they did not exist, except when she was talking with the other wives. Then she called the Buffalo Soldiers 'those apes,' and lamented that it was they who prevented Johnny from gaining the promotions he deserved.

Mrs Reed would not tolerate such dissension and halted

Nellie whenever it began, but Mrs Wetzel, so admirable in other respects, shared her husband's deep distrust of colored troops: 'Colonel Wetzel tells me constantly when we talk at night of how irresponsible they are. He says it's bad enough to serve with cavalry ...' At the most inappropriate times she would forcefully proclaim her husband's harsh theories about the cavalry: 'And I mean any cavalry, not just the unfortunate Negroes. The Colonel tells me: "Horses require so much fodder, and this must be carried along in so many wagons that the cavalry winds up doing nothing but riding happily along, guarding its own train. In fight after fight, the poor infantry is far ahead, doing the dirty work, while the cavalry lags behind, bringing up its food."'

Mrs Reed, wife of an infantry officer, believed that most of what Mrs Wetzel said was true: 'The cavalry really is a most wasteful branch,' but she also knew that to keep peace in the fort, this constant barrage of criticism must be silenced, or at least muffled, so she cautioned her friend against blatant disparagement. For some days Mrs Wetzel kept quiet, but she was a Scandinavian, well educated by her parents, who found it impossible to remain silent when she saw error, and one afternoon when most of the officers and all the wives were present, she erupted: 'It's a known fact that during the first days of a campaign against the Indians, the cavalry is most daring, dashing here and there. But we rarely encounter Indians during those first days, and soon the cavalry horses are worn down, so that they can barely keep up with the infantry. And by the end of the second week the horses are so tired, they cannot keep up. On all days after that, the foot soldiers have to make camp early, and sit there waiting for the cavalry to drift in. From the twelfth day on they're really useless, for not only are they exhausted, but they've also used up all their fodder.'

'Why do we bother with them?' young Andrew Masters from Illinois asked, and Mrs Wetzel replied with more insight than she suspected: 'Because generals like to ride horses at Fourth of July parades.'

This was too much for Louise Reed: 'This talk must stop. And it must not be resumed in my house. My husband is commander of a mixed unit, mixed in all ways, and it must remain harmonious.'

The attention of the two senior women was diverted from the deficiencies of the cavalry to the more exciting behavior of young Nellie Minor, who found time heavy on her hands while her husband was off on an extended scout with his black horsemen. On the first afternoon she arranged an uneasy tea for the other wives. On the second she took the Reed daughter on a canter along the Brazos River. And on the third, following the good example set by Mrs Wetzel, she went down to Suds Row to encourage the women there, but she was repelled by the conditions in which they worked and could find nothing in common to talk about.

On the fourth day she saddled one of the horses reserved for wives and planned her informal saunter along Bear Creek in such a way that she had a good chance of encountering the Irishman Jim Logan as he returned from a morning canter to the north. They did meet, well apart from the fort, and they rode for several exhilarating miles back toward Jacksborough. They did not dismount, but each was aware of considerable electricity in the air, for as Nellie observed as they rode side by side: 'It's like the quiet before a summer thunderstorm.' Actually, it was well into the winter of 1870, but she was correct in feeling that great events impended, for not only was her attraction to this dashing Irishman becoming known at the fort, but Comanche to the west were about to become active again.

On this afternoon neither she nor Jim Logan was much concerned about Indians, for when they dipped down behind a small hill to the Larkin tank where no one could see them, she rode very close to him, saying as they moved slowly across the grassy plain: 'You ride extremely well.'

'My father taught me, in Ireland.'

'What's Ireland like?'

'Greener than this.'

'Do you miss it?'

'We starved.'

'Were you brave in the war?'

'I knew how to handle horses, I know how to fight. So they made me a major.'

'I know. Do you mind being a lieutenant now?'

'Wars come and go. I was lucky to have found mine young. But to tell you the truth, Mrs Minor, I don't feel unlucky to be a

929

lieutenant during the long years.' He turned sideways and smiled, a ravishing, honest smile: 'My level even in war was just about captain. I was never meant to be a major, wasn't entitled. But I'm a damned good lieutenant.'

She leaned over and kissed him: 'You're a captivating man, Major, and in my mind you'll always be a major.'

He grasped at her arm, holding her close to him for a protracted kiss, and each knew at that moment that if either made even the slightest motion toward dismounting, there would be a frenzied scene among the sagebrush, but neither made such a move, and gradually they worked their way back toward Bear Creek, along which they rode with feigned unconcern until the fort became barely visible on the far horizon.

'Shouldn't you ride in alone?' Logan suggested, and she agreed that this might be prudent, but before they parted she moved close again, and kissed him even more passionately: 'I long to be with you, Jim,' but he said simply: 'Johnny's my superior, you know.'

So she rode directly to the fort while he made a far swing to the east, coming in much later on the Jacksborough Road, but such maneuvers fooled no one. Fort Garner quickly knew it had a dangerous love affair on its hands, and Mrs Reed did not propose to have some young snippet bored with frontier life imperil her husband's already difficult command. As always, she went directly to the source of potential trouble, or rather, she summoned the source to her quarters.

'Nellie, sit down. It's my duty as an older woman and as the wife of the commander to warn you that you are playing a very dangerous game.'

'But –'

'I seek none of your shabby excuses. Nellie, at the fort in Arkansas you behaved the same way, and you came very close to ruining three careers. I shall not allow you to imperil my husband's command. Stay away from Major Logan.'

'I haven't –'

'Not yet. But you intend to.'

'How can you talk like this? I'm not obligated –'

'You're obligated to conduct yourself properly when you're in my husband's command.' She said this with such accumulated force of character that Nellie blanched.

'I will endanger no one,' she said softly.

'Nellie, can't you find happiness with your husband? He's a splendid man. My husband cherishes him.'

'He works with niggers, and he smells of niggers, and he can never amount to anything.'

Very harshly Mrs Reed said: 'If you believe that, Nellie, you must leave this fort today.' When the sniffling younger woman tried to speak, Mrs Reed silenced her. 'I said *today*.' Her voice rose: 'Pack your things while I stand over you, and leave this fort, because if you stay, you can bring only tragedy.'

'I can't go. I have nowhere to go.' She began to weep.

Mrs Reed did not attempt to console her. Instead, she waited for the tears to halt, and then she asked, flatly but also with obvious compassion: 'So what shall we do?'

'We?'

'Yes, this is as much my problem as yours.'

'I can't go. I have nowhere, I tell you.'

'Then I shall tell you what you must do. Love your husband. Help him as Mrs Wetzel and I help ours. Take pride in his accomplishments, which are many. And stay clear of Jim Logan.'

'Will you tell the others?'

'The others told me.' Now she softened: 'Nellie, I'm always the last woman on the post to know what's happening to the wives in my husband's command. Believe me, I do not look for trouble, I castigate no one. But when trouble is brought to my attention, so blatantly that I cannot . . .' She hesitated, choked, and had to fight back her own tears.

'Nellie, I think we should pray,' and the two officers' wives, there at the remotest outpost of their civilization, knelt and prayed. When they rose Mrs Reed took Nellie's hand and said: 'Who ever promised you that an army officer's life would be pleasant? Believe me, this storm which assails you now will pass.'

'I am torn apart, Mrs Reed.'

'Have you ever sat in a lonely fort, with snow about the door, and watched your child die? That's being torn apart, and even that storm passes.'

'I shall try.'

'And I shall . . .' She wanted to say either 'I shall pray for you' or 'I shall watch you,' but she knew that each was inappropriate and inaccurate. So she did not finish her promise, because what she proposed doing was much more practical. She would ask Captain Reed to keep his young Irish cavalryman absent from the fort as often as possible and on missions of maximum duration.

Among the men on the frontier who followed the establishment of Fort Garner with close attention was a small, scrawny fugitive with watery blue eyes and a somewhat withered left arm; he lurked in Sante Fe, waiting for any good chance that would enable him to slip back into his preferred Texas. His name was Amos Peavine, and his ancestors had prowled the Neutral Ground, that bandits' no-man's-land bordering old Louisiana.

As a young man with a bad arm he had had to be more clever than most and had soon built a reputation throughout east Texas as a holdup man and a ruthless killer. He was so devious, so quick to strike, that men started calling him Rattlesnake, and some, to their quick dismay, tried shooting at him, but he, well aware of his disability, had trained himself so assiduously in the use of guns that it was always he who drew first, fired first, and nodded ceremoniously as his would-be assailant fell.

Frontier gunmen, noticing his affected left hand, assumed that it played no part in his behavior, but they were wrong. Through long practice Rattlesnake Peavine could bring that left arm up across his belt, providing a rocklike platform on which to rest the gun as it was being fired, and the action was so swift and smooth that even close watchers could not detect exactly what had happened.

In those hectic days he began to carry two Colts, and since his left hand was practically useless, he slung them both on his right hip, the only gunman known to do so. He spent about a year, 1863, perfecting holsters for his two guns, and then another, 1864, in shortening the barrels to make the guns easier to swing loose. This made his draw a fraction of a second quicker than that of a challenger. He also invented a clever way of making the trigger more responsive to his right forefinger: he filed down each sear until even a whisper would release it.

Peavine did not notch his guns to keep track of their effectiveness; he was content to be known as 'that little bastard, about a hundred and thirty pounds, who can shoot faster than a rattlesnake strikes, and more deadly.' At nineteen he was an authentic Texas badman.

During the war he had ranged the northern border, siding now with the Union forces, more often with the Confederate, but proving so unreliable to each that in the end both armies were trying to hang him, and it was then that he felt it advisable to quit Texas: 'I got me a passel of enemies in this state. North or South, they don't realize a man is entitled to make a livin'. No future for me here.' What was more persuasive: 'Hell, come peace they hain't much goods movin', a man hadn't got much chance to pick a few bundles off for hisself.'

He had drifted slowly toward Santa Fe on the principle 'A man cain't make it in Texas, he can always succeed in New Mexico,' and after trying vainly to profit from the exposed trade with Mexico, he discovered that the real money was to be made in a trade centuries old and infamously dishonorable. The Plains Indians wanted whiskey and rifles, and generations of disreputable traders had found profitable ways of supplying them. Spaniards had done so in the 1600s, Frenchmen in the 1700s, Mexicans in the first years of the 1800s, and now a wily crew of adventurers from Kentucky, Mississippi and Texas continued the tradition.

Amos Peavine was the most daring of the bunch, for he traded with the most deadly of the tribes. He was a Comanchero, a lawless man who roamed the Comanchería, that vast expanse of wasteland which coincided with the buffalo range. Especially he worked the Texas plains, and when he learned that a new fort was to be established on Bear Creek, he rejoiced, because although it brought more soldiers into the area, which meant a greater chance that he would ultimately be shot, it also brought two developments extremely favorable to him: the Indians under attack would have to have more guns, and the slow military trains crossing the empty plains carrying guns and ammunition would be more open to attack. A really crafty Comanchero stole guns from the army, sold them to the Comanche, then served as tracker for the army when it went out to confront the well-armed Indians. A Comanchero prospered in troubled times, and was adept at devising strategies for keeping them troubled.

While Mrs Reed was lecturing young Mrs Minor on proper behavior at a frontier fort, Rattlesnake Peavine was some two hundred miles to the west, astride a winded old horse and leading a Rocky Mountain burro he had obtained from a Mexican family by the persuasive process of shooting the entire clan in one unbroken fusillade.

He was on a mission fraught with a medley of dangers, and any man who was afraid of nature, Indians or the retaliation of the United States Army would have blanched at what faced him as he probed the empty plains, seeking contact with Chief Matark of the Comanche. Scorpions and snakes awaited him if he was careless when he dismounted; death from dehydration got those who missed their water holes, so infrequent and so hot and alkali-ridden when found. Indian tribes at war with the Comanche would surely kill him if they caught him, and he faced equal danger from Comanche to whom he could not identify himself quickly. And there were always new forts with energetic new commanders eager to take up the chase against any despised Comanchero.

Amos Peavine, threading his way through these encroaching disasters, was a brave man, almost a heroic one, for the forces of evil require just as much strength of will as do the angels of goodness; it is only the force of character that is missing. Peavine had enormous will; he had no character at all, not even a consistently bad one, for, as in the old days of 1861–65, he stood willing to trade with anyone, to betray everyone. Now he had a promising scheme which might produce substantial profits if acted upon swiftly, but before action could take place, he had to find Matark.

He had left New Mexico, haven for Comancheros like himself and other bandits who ravaged Texas, and had entered that refuge known through the West as the Palo Duro Canyon. It was a formidable depression, more than a hundred miles long, dug through solid rock by millions of years of active water, and so lonely and awesome that white men rarely tried to conquer it. Those who did saw sights that were majestic. High walls of colored rock hemmed in valleys of surprising richness, where a man could herd a thousand cattle and be assured that they could feed themselves on the evergreen grasses but not escape from the natural corral which kept them penned.

Cattlemen were not able to try this experiment because the Comanche had reached Palo Duro first and had for more than a hundred years utilized it as their one totally secure hiding place. Within the canyon, at about the center of its east-west reach, rose a pile of reddish rocks known as The Castle, and it was to this traditional meeting spot that Peavine was heading.

He did not ride the well-marked path at the bottom of the canyon, for that would trap him in too dangerously; he kept instead to the less comfortable trail along the south rim, because from here he could look down into the rocky depths and also across to the other side, for the canyon was not extensive in its north-south dimension. And now as he led his complaining burro along the trail from which The Castle should soon be visible, he was satisfied that he had once more negotiated the canyon and brought himself into contact with the Indians he sought. There was, of course, still the possibility that he might encounter some idiot lieutenant from one of the forts, out seeking glory, who had boasted to his troop as he led his cavalry out: 'I shall invade Palo Duro and bring back the scalp of Chief Matark.' Often such a man would utter an extra vow: 'And I'll rescue Emma Larkin,' for she was constantly on the conscience of these soldiers.

Peavine laughed as he thought of the men within the forts: Better they stay home. Come up here, to these walls, they're goin' to get shot. Various expeditions had come to grief at Palo Duro and it seemed likely that more would follow. 'These canyons will be Indian for a long time,' Peavine muttered as he saw the familiar signs which indicated that The Castle was not far off. He was justified in using the plural *canyons* because each small stream that fed the main architecture of this deep cut had gouged out its own smaller canyon, so that at the center, where he now rode, the land became a jumble of lateral cuts, some so deep that they could not be traversed if Peavine kept to the upper plateau.

So, crossing himself as if he were a believing Catholic, he edged his tired horse toward the rim, tugged at the rope guiding his burro, and started down the steep and rocky path to the lower level. He was now at the most dangerous point of his two-hundred-mile expedition, for he rode so close to the wall of the canyon that any rattlesnake, awakening from his winter sleep, could strike him full in the face if it darted forth; also, if either enemy Indians or roving troops were setting a trap, here is where they would spring it. But this time he made his descent peacefully, and when he gained the floor of the canyon he found himself once more in a congenial fairyland which he had known in the past.

Land about The Castle leveled out and produced such a richness of grass, such protection from storms, and had such an equable climate – cool in summer, warm in winter – that it formed a kind of Indian Garden of Eden. Here, within this security, some squaws more adventurous than their sisters even tried growing vegetables from seeds captured on raids against ranches.

Turning a familiar corner, Peavine waved to the scouts he knew would be watching, licked his lips in preparation for the Comanche words he would soon be speaking, and headed his horse toward the Indian encampment. It was an amazing collection of tepees, for in their travels south from their original Rocky Mountain homeland the Comanche had acquired a variety of housing, some with tall cedar poles lifting the buffalo-hide covering high into the air (these were the Cheyenne contribution) and others little more than rounded huts depending not upon long poles but bent branches for their form (a pattern used by the Ute). Most notable were the small, compact tepees built about a minimum of moderately long poles; these were some of the best (a device of the Pawnee). The Comanche, a wandering tribe that had developed only a limited culture of its own, had borrowed types of tepees from everyone. Their fierce courage and their appalling cruelty to any captive they invented themselves.

'I seek Great Chief Matark,' Peavine cried loudly as he entered the haphazard arrangement of tepees, and he repeated the announcement until a group of young braves ran over to surround him, leaving behind the half-naked creature they had been tormenting.

'Is that the Larkin girl?' he asked as the young men came up, and they looked back as if bewildered that anyone should care who the child was. They had already burned off her ears, and her nose would disappear before the summer was out; she was thirteen now, a most pitiful thing, but miraculously she retained enough intelligence to know that the arrival of a white man, any white man, meant that her chance of rescue was by that small degree enhanced.

She took a tentative step toward Peavine, praying that he would take notice of her, but he looked the other way, and two of the young men grabbed stones and threw them at her with great force, shouting as they did so: 'Get back!'

Matark and his four wives occupied a large tepee in the Cheyenne style, its cedar poles emitting a pleasing fragrance. It had a low entrance, requiring the visitor to stoop, but inside it was spacious and festively decorated with elkskin hangings on which had been depicted in various colors the history of this portion of the tribe. Matark himself, tall and brooding, was a striking figure whose command over his men was understandable. Obviously he had a superior intelligence, which he began to display immediately.

'What new thing brings you here?' he asked.

'Word from St Louis.'

'What word?'

'Cavin & Clark, they've been hired to carry guns, many guns and all ammunition, to the new fort at Bear Creek.'

'Oh!' Matark did not try to hide the weight and pleasure he accorded such news. To attack successfully one train of this probable magnitude would supply him with armament for three years. But he was suspicious where white men were involved, and he asked: 'If you know this . . . the guns . . . aren't they already there?'

'The system, Chief. You know the system.' And the plotters had to laugh at the incredible stupidity of the United States Army, which placed men like Captain Reed in remote outposts like Fort Garner, then gave them no authority over responsibility for their supplies. Desk officers in Washington, inordinately jealous of their prerogatives and aware that their jobs were safe only if constantly enhanced, had prevailed upon Congress, at whose elbows they sat while men like Reed battled Indians, to initiate one of the stupidest plans in military history. Every item shipped to Fort Garner was requested not by the man on the scene but by some desk officer two thousand miles away. And when it was authorized, belatedly, another desk officer in another building in Washington decided when and by whom it would be railroaded from the depot in Massachusetts to the warehouse in St Louis, and by what frontier carter it would be finally dispatched to the intended recipient.

Because the desk officer in charge of transportation sought a carrier who charged the least or bribed the most, he usually employed some carter with the least reliable drivers and the least expensive horses, and none was more deficient than Cavin & Clark in St Louis. Cargoes consigned through them sometimes required half a year to cover half a thousand miles, and when they arrived, there would always be shortages due to the C&C drivers' tricky habit of selling off portions to storekeepers en route.

So when Rattlesnake Peavine told Chief Matark that the guns for Fort Garner were being shipped by Cavin & Clark, the Indian knew that anyone who sought to intercept this shipment had plenty of time. There was even the possibility that gunfire from ambush might not be necessary, because it was sometimes possible for a Comanchero to arrange an outright deal with the C&C driver: 'I'll give two hundred dollars for the whole train.'

'Could you buy the guns?' Matark asked.

'They know me too well. I killed two of their drivers.'

'Then we must capture them?'

'I think it's the only way.'

'Will the wagons have an escort?'

'Probably. A new fort. A new commander.'

'And eager young officers,' Matark said. 'Well, I'll send my eager young braves.'

'When I entered the canyon,' Peavine said, 'I saw your young fellows playing with a white girl. Could that be the Larkin girl?'

'Yes.'

'You know, I could earn you a lot of money if you'd let me trade her back to the Texans.'

'I have plans for her,' Matark said. 'And you're right. She'll bring us a lot of money.'

'Then I can't have her?' Before the chief could reply, the wily trader explained: 'Some day I'll have to make peace with the Texans. No more trading. Too old. If I could appear with the Larkin girl, I'd be a hero . . .'

938

Matark looked at him and thought: Yes, and then you'd turn against us. It would be you, the Rattlesnake, who would lead the blue-coats against us. You'd bring them right into this canyon. For one savage moment he considered calling for his braves and killing Peavine right then, but the canny little trader divined his thinking and quickly said: 'You know you need me. To keep getting guns, you need me.'

'I do,' Matark conceded, and a deal was firmed whereby Peavine would get many Mexican pieces of gold if the guns were captured, but when he left Matark's tent he took great care to seek out Emma Larkin, for if she was ever released, he wanted her to testify to the fact that he had tried to be helpful.

He found her huddled in the shade of a tepee, ignored for the moment by her tormentors, and he was appalled by her appearance. She was thin almost to the point of death, her hair and nails filthy. Only knotted nubs remained to show where her ears had been, and her nose was in fearful condition. Looking at her as she trembled by the tepee, he wondered how the Comanche had fallen into the abominable practices they followed with their prisoners, and he recalled having chided Matark about this: 'Why do you burn the ranchers alive? Why cut them to pieces?' and the chief had replied: 'That's our custom.' Peavine then asked: 'Why not just kill them?' and Matark had said: 'To watch an enemy die is good.' Peavine said: 'But why torture them so?' and Matark had explained: 'If enemy dying is good, long-time dying is better.' Peavine had inquired further: 'Does it mean something? Does it add strength to your braves?' and Matark had said with solemn finality: 'It has always been our custom.'

That explained so much, not only regarding the Comanche but all fighting men, and Peavine, reflecting on the customs of his own profession, could hear his father admonishing him: 'Never shoot a man in the back. Never! It hain't tolerated.' It was also not tolerated to kill women unless in the heat of battle or when they were shooting back. Texans, he noticed, bore no grudge if a man shot another with a rifle, even if from ambush at a safe distance, but they deplored the Mexican who killed with a knife, even at close hand when he ran great risk. The gun was manly, the knife was not.

French, German, Russian armies, he had heard, all had their

939

traditions, as iron-clad as the Comanche attitude toward prisoners; he had been told of the Prussian custom of leaving a disgraced officer alone with a loaded revolver, expecting him to blow his brains out – 'Not with me. They got to do the shootin!'

But no rationalization could justify the Comanche treatment of their girl prisoners: 'Why do you let them do such horrible things to the little girls?' he had asked Matark, who had again replied: 'It is our custom.' Peavine had not liked being allied with Indians who behaved so barbarously, but with the plains depleted of other tribes, he had few options, and hiding his disgust, he moved closer to the girl, whereupon a transformation took place.

For when she looked up at him she was no longer a terrified object of torture; she was a fighting little tiger with the same determination to survive that animated him. This child was not going to die easily, regardless of what the Comanche did to her, and for a fleeting moment he wanted to embrace her and carry her with him on the raid against the supply train. His life had taught him to revere persistence, and this child was persisting against terrors which would have deranged even strong adults.

'My name is Amos Peavine,' he said. 'I wish I could help.'

These were the first words in English she had heard since the massacre, and she was obviously pleased that she remembered what they meant: 'I am Emma Larkin.'

'I know. I will tell the others you are alive.'

'You!' a surly brave shouted. 'Get back!' And with a well-directed stone he hit her sharply on the leg. Knowing that if she did not obey instantly, the tortures would resume, she scurried away as if she were a frightened dog, but Peavine, catching a glimpse of her eyes, realized that she was not frightened; she was acting so to be rid of the stone-throwing, and he muttered to himself: 'Some night she'll cut that one's throat. Go it, lass!' With that, he turned to the organizing of the raiding party which would ambush the Cavin & Clark shipment.

When Captain Reed received official notice from the young officer in Washington that his supplies, including needed guns and ammunition, would be arriving sometime in May via Cavin

& Clark, he shuddered, because he knew that if C&C performed as always, the shipment might arrive in May as scheduled, but it also might arrive in September, or perhaps not at all.

'I cannot understand,' he complained to Wetzel, 'how Washington can ignore our negative reports on Cavin & Clark and still use them.'

'Saving money,' the German suggested.

'But it loses money. We proved that in our last report.'

'Men at the desk never believe men in the field.'

Reed said no more to Wetzel, who, in the great Prussian tradition, respected whatever the higher command ordered, but he did seek out his adjutant, Lieutenant Sanders: 'I'm not easy about this Cavin & Clark shipment. What ought we do?'

'We need those supplies. I'd sent a detachment of cavalry to Fort Richardson. Protect the wagons every inch of the way from Jacksborough.'

'We've not been ordered to do so.'

'I'd do it, anyway. Those are our goods, and we need them.'

'Who would you send?'

'Well, the Comanche will probably be reluctant to strike so far behind our lines.'

Reed grew impatient: 'You just said we had to protect the wagons.'

'I'm not afraid of the Comanche. I'm afraid of Cavin & Clark. If we don't watch them, they'll sell the whole consignment.'

The two officers shook their heads in disgust, and Reed spoke first: 'Hell of a situation. We have to fight the Indians. We have to fight Cavin & Clark. And we have to fight Washington. But who to send?'

'With Fort Richardson at the other end, the likelihood of a fight is not great. I'd send young Toomey.' He reflected not on Toomey's ability but on the terrain between the two forts. 'Yes, I'd send Toomey, but I'd also send Sergeant Jaxifer. He knows the lay of the land.'

Sanders, although not a member of the 10th Cavalry, had had ample opportunity to assess the character of Jaxifer, a forty-three-year-old veteran of mounted action. He was a big, very black man, with almost no neck and with forearms that could have wrestled bears. Surprisingly quick on his feet, he leaped into any action that confronted him, and on a horse, was practically unstoppable. He said little, told no one what his antecedents were, and if asked, said New York was his home, even though the roster listed his birthplace accurately as Georgia. He had joined the Union forces in December 1863, after escaping from the Confederacy by swimming the Rio Grande into Mexico, and had attained the impressive rank of first sergeant through a mixture of quick obedience and obvious bravery. When Northern blacks who had never known slavery asked his opinion of the system, he said: 'I had some bad masters, more good. But I run away from both.' The fact that he was now surviving in an army which despised him was proof of his intelligence.

He was harsh with his men: 'This got to be the best unit in the army. You step out of line, I cut your neck off.' Even Wetzel, who had objected to having the black cavalry so close to his white infantry at morning parade and evening retreat, occasionally complimented Jaxifer on the snappy drill his men performed: 'In the Prussian army, a lot more precision, of course, but very good by American standards.' Once Wetzel even placed his hand on Jaxifer's arm as the two stood watching their men drill: 'We have a first-class fort here. We can be proud.'

John Jaxifer was the kind of man one sent to reinforce a junior officer on a scouting expedition, but the importance of the proposed exercise was somewhat diminished when a group of four horsemen arrived from Fort Richardson with head-quarters' plans for the movement of Cavin & Clark wagons: 'General Grierson will send some of our troops to protect it halfway. At Three Cairns you'll take over and bring the train safely in.'

'We had stood ready to pick it up at Jacksborough,' Reed said, but the other men assured him that Grierson was more than happy to extend the courtesy: 'We have some young fellows who need the experience.'

'Likewise,' Reed said, and it was arranged that six days after the Fort Richardson men started west, Second Lieutenant Elmer Toomey, supported by First Sergeant John Jaxifer, would ride toward Three Cairns, those informal piles of rock which had been stacked on the treeless plains to mark the way to

Fort Garner, to pick up the wagon train and bring it safely home.

Chief Matark and Amos Peavine had been kept informed of both the arrival of the C&C train at Jacksborough and the movement of a four-man escort west from Fort Richardson. 'If they join up with the men from Fort Garner coming east to meet them,' Matark warned, 'they might be too strong for us.' But Peavine reassured him: 'The Fort Richardson men will come only halfway, then ride back to Jacksborough. We'll have to fight only the small escort sent out by Fort Garner.'

'If that, where do we attack?'

'During the last half. Then the stronger force at Fort Richardson would have more difficulty sending help.'

Carefully the two plotters analyzed the situation, with Peavine supplying the relevant details concerning army strength: 'Eight wagons, driver and shotgun each, that's sixteen guns right there, but those C&C drivers don't like to fight. Real cowards. The Buffalo Soldiers, they like to fight and think three of them can lick twenty of us.' Any crusty Comanchero like the Rattlesnake liked to use the pronouns *we* and *us* when talking with his Indians. 'Grierson, he'd send four men at most. Reed, this is his first fort as commander. He'll send maybe a dozen. But whereas Grierson would never send an untried man, not on any mission at all, Reed might.'

'More men in the second half?' Matark asked. 'But weaker?'

Before Peavine could respond, a scout rode up, quivering with excitement but also laughing: 'Come see! You must see!' And he led the two men nearly a mile south to where two other scouts were lying on the ground at the edge of a slight rise, below which nestled a small protected tank near which a soldier whose blue jacket lay beside him was twisting on the ground with a young woman who looked as if she might be very pretty indeed. They were making love, and for a long moment the five watchers looked approvingly.

'Shall we kill them?' one of the scouts asked, and each of the other four men thought how astonished these lovers would be if they were interrupted in their raptures by four Comanche and a white man with a withered left arm.

The three braves were ready to make the charge down the

943

slopes of the little vale when Peavine halted them: 'It would alert the fort.'

'But they're so far away.'

'They would be missed. Their bodies would be found.' He spoke harshly: 'It's the wagons we want,' but as the five rode away he had to chuckle: 'Wouldn't they have been surprised?' And he reined in his horse to look again at the lovers sprawled upon the ground in their secluded swale beside the tank.

At the end of May 1870 the eight creaking and complaining wagons left Jacksborough, throwing clouds of dust so high that Comanche scouts well to the north were assured that the convoy was under way. It was attended, the Indians quietly noted, by only seven cavalrymen: four blacks in front, two at the rear, and one white officer riding slowly back and forth to maintain communication. It was not an orderly procession, nor a compact one, because each driver, his own boss and in no way obedient to the army of which he was not a part, chose the track that he thought best, which meant that the line straggled ridiculously.

'I'd keep that line firmed up,' one of the troopers advised the carters, but they snapped: 'You mind your horse, we'll mind our mules.'

'You'll want us soon enough if the Comanche strike.'

'That's what we always hear. If, if . . .'

'Well, damnit, when they do strike, and we've heard rumors out of Santa Fe, I want these wagons in a quick line.'

'They been in line since we left St Louis.'

Grierson's men brought the wagons safely to Three Cairns, and when the watching Indians saw that an orderly transfer of responsibility was being made, they faced a problem: 'If we attack too soon, the Fort Richardson men may gallop back to help. If we attack too late, men from Fort Garner will hear and come out with support.' They were additionally perplexed when the eastern group, pleased with their work on the plains and loath to ride back to dull garrison duty at Jacksborough, stayed with the Fort Garner men till morning of the second day.

'When will they leave?' Matark grumbled, and Peavine had to reply: 'Who knows? Soldiers, who ever knows about those idiots?'

That morning, however, the Fort Richardson men retired, rode a short distance eastward and fired their guns in the air. Some of the shotgun men riding next to the drivers responded, and now Elmer Toomey, a twenty-one-year-old farm boy from Indiana, fresh from West Point, was in command of his first important detachment. He rode at the front, always attentive to the boundless horizon for indication of storms or Indians; at certain periods only a few trees would be visible, and sometimes he would scan the four points of the compass and see none at all.

At such times Sergeant Jaxifer rode slowly back and forth, checking on his ten horsemen but never speaking to or even looking at the sixteen carters, who were disgusted to think that they were being guarded by niggers. One, a surly fellow from West Virginia who would have sold half his cargo in Jacksborough had not one of the cavalrymen kept close watch, protested to Lieutenant Toomey: 'You keep them niggers well shy of me. You ask me, we fought on the wrong side in the Civil War.'

'They're soldiers of the United States Army,' Toomey said stiffly. 'I'm an officer in their company,' and the carter sneered: 'The more shame for you.'

'Attention, you bastard! One more word like that and I'll have you in the guardhouse when we get there.'

The driver, knowing that he could exercise no control over him, laughed: 'Little boy, don't play soldier with me. Now run along and nurse your niggers.'

An hour after dawn on the next day this driver shrieked in terror: 'Comanche! Where in hell's the army?'

Sixteen unreliable carters and eleven enlisted men led by an untested lieutenant were suddenly responsible for holding off more than a hundred Indian braves on terrain that afforded no protection. But they were not powerless, because the black cavalrymen were toughened professionals and their white lieutenant was about to prove that he more than deserved his rank.

'Wagons form!' he shouted, personally leading the tail wagon toward the head of the line and showing the others how to place themselves.

'Sergeant Jaxifer! Keep your men inside the line of wagons!' When carters were slow to obey, he threatened to shoot them, and before the Indians could strike he had his band in the best

945

defensive position possible, but even so, they were not prepared, not even the black veterans, for the fury with which the Comanche struck.

From his command post Matark ordered: 'Circle them! Set them on fire.'

His entire contingent formed a huge circle around the wagons, his braves wheeling counterclockwise, as they preferred, for this enabled them to fire across their steady left arms as they sped. But as the battle waxed, a cadre of fourteen braves bearing lighted brands detached themselves from the circle and dashed boldly at the wagons, trying to throw their flames so as to ignite the canvas covers. Six fell from their saddles, shot dead, but the other eight delivered their fiery brands, which the carters extinguished.

Inside the ring of wagons no orders were issued, for these embattled men required no exhortation. Each was aware of the terrible tortures he was going to undergo if he lost this fight, and each resolved that there would be no surrender. This was a fight to the death, and several wagoners muttered to their friends: 'If they come at us, at the end I mean, shoot me.'

The eight carters who rode shotgun knew how to use their weapons, and the eight drivers, shaking with fear, also fired with determination, with the early result that the Indians were kept some distance from the wagons; eleven now lay dead before the first member of the convoy had been seriously wounded.

Toomey stayed mostly with the panicky drivers, and he was furious when the mean-spirited men began to blame their plight on the fact that black troops had been sent to protect them: 'Damned niggers, don't know nothin'.' One man growled as he fumbled with his gun, which had suffered a minor jam: 'Niggers is no better than Indians. Curse 'em both.' Toomey said nothing, interpreting the ugly expressions as signs of nervous fear, but he did what he could to reassure the civilians: 'My men know how to hold a line. We'll get out of this.'

'Jesus Christ!' One of the carters pointed to the north, where a line of at least forty shouting warriors came in solid phalanx.

'Hold your fire,' Toomey cried, knowing that Jaxifer would have his own men in readiness. He then called for two of the troopers to help him defend the spot at which the oncoming force seemed likely to hit, and there he stood, heels ground into the sandy soil as if he intended never to be budged.

The Comanche were so determined in what they expected to be their final charge that despite heavy losses to the steady fire of the black troops and the trained shotgun men, they simply rode down the defenders at two points, the victorious braves in the lead galloping right through the circle where mules attached to the wagons lay dead.

But they did not stop. They were not given time in which to rampage inside the circle, because whoever tried was either shot or clubbed down by the troops. They had broken the line, as they were determined to do, but they had not disorganized it, and they had lost many in the attempt. They did, however, succeed in taking with them a good portion of the horses, and had not the mules drawing the wagons been left in harness, they too would surely have been stolen. The men of the 10th Cavalry were now on foot.

Toomey was appalled to see his horses go, but he knew that he must not display either fear or consternation lest the civilians panic: 'Sergeant Jaxifer, your men in good shape?'

'Fine, sir.'

Indeed, the cavalry veterans were handling this battle as if it were a parade-ground exercise; they were not impeded by the loss of their horses, for they had learned that in a dozen typical engagements, they would in at least ten be expected to fight on foot. Said critics: 'They ride comfortably to battle. Dismount and become infantry. Why in hell aren't they infantry in the first place?' Such critics were about to receive the best possible answer, but before it manifested itself, the Comanche organized another frontal assault, and this time they directed it specifically at where the surviving drivers stood, for their clever fighters had detected this to be the weak spot of the circle.

Toomey, seeing them come, stood beside the drivers, and once more twisted his heels to dig them in, but when the Indians struck he was powerless to hold them off, and he was tomahawked twice. His head was split open and his left arm, with which he tried vainly to defend himself, was nearly severed.

Jaxifer was now in control, and he was ruggedly determined

947

to save the remnants of this escort, but when he started to tell the carters how they must arrange themselves to be most effective in the charges that he knew would soon come thundering at them, they refused to obey his commands: 'No nigger tells me what to do.'

He did not respond. Instead he said slowly: 'Two carters, one cavalryman. That way we can cover the space better.'

'Don't you touch me, nigger.'

'You must move to that weak spot.'

'I ain't takin' no orders . . .'

Sergeant Jaxifer stopped, smiled: 'Man, we gonna survive this. They ain't gonna ride us down, never. But we got to do it sensible. You been in this one fight. I been in sixteen. I don't lose fights, and I ain't gonna lose this one. Now fill those gaps.'

After thus disposing of the survivors, he threw a blanket over the corpse of his lieutenant, but even as he did so a terrible pain struck at his heart. He knew that as long as he remained in the service, he would be remembered as the black sergeant who had lost his white commander.

During the fight so far, no member defending the wagons had seen Chief Matark, nor could anyone have been aware that a white man was helping direct the fight, but had the defenders been told that such a man was hidden behind the first small hill, they would have guessed that it was Amos Peavine, for the Rattlesnake's reputation had reached all the forts. He was the Comanchero they despised but also feared, and the men of this train would not have been surprised to learn that he was again trying to steal army guns for sale to his Indians.

At nine-thirty that morning Peavine was counseling Matark: 'Wear them down. Send your men in from a different direction each time.'

'How soon will they surrender?'

Peavine did not want to tell the chief that the behavior of the Comanche toward captives made it unlikely that soldiers would ever surrender, or carters either, so he dissembled: 'By noon we'll have the wagons.'

'The next charge, I lead.'

Peavine did not like this at all, for he had often observed that when a great chief died, the problem of succession could

948

become messy, with the friends of the old chief suddenly the enemies of the new, and he did not like to speculate on what might happen to him if, on this lonely plain, Chief Matark perished in a fruitless attack which he, Peavine had recommended and helped organize. It was in his interest to see that Matark lived, so he counseled against participation in the charge: 'You are needed here.'

'I am needed there,' Matark growled, and when the charge began, directed at a spot with three fallen horses, he was in the lead. Again his men ripped right into the circle, and again the stubborn black troops with their fiercely effective gunfire drove them out.

But Matark had seen the diminished strength of the defenders, and now he knew for certain that their officer was dead: 'By noon we take the wagons.' And this would have been a safe prediction except for the cautious behavior of two men who were not yet engaged in the battle at Three Cairns.

Hermann Wetzel never slept well if even one of his soldiers, infantry or cavalry, was absent from any fort to which he was attached, and he had been attached to many. His stubborn German conscience and his love of Prussian order hounded him if any man was not safely accounted for. Furthermore, the absence of Toomey made him most uneasy, for the young lieutenant was untested and operated under two severe disadvantages, which led Wetzel to interrupt his breakfast and hurry over to Reed's quarters.

'It's a short ride in from the Cairns, and Toomey's a good man.'

'But he's cavalry and they never know tactics. And his men are niggers, and they don't know anything.'

'None of that, Colonel.'

'I'm still worried, sir. Very.'

Reed had put down his knife and fork, arranging them meticulously beside his plate: 'I'm concerned too. What do you recommend?'

'I'd send troops out to intercept them. The Comanche have been silent for too long.'

Reed, a man who never flinched from hard decisions, looked directly into the eyes of his German adviser: 'I think you may be right, Colonel.' And as soon as these words were uttered, he leaped from the table, rasping out orders for an immediate formation of the remainder of Company R, 10th Cavalry, to intercept the incoming train. Of the company's authorized strength of eighty troopers, only sixty-eight had been sent to Fort Garner; of these, one had deserted, seventeen were on guard duty or in the hospital, and twelve, including young Toomey, were already at Three Cairns. Thus, only thirty-eight answered the muster call.

He would lead, of course, for whenever there was a likelihood of action he insisted upon being in the vanguard; Wetzel, who disliked serving with the cavalry, would remain in charge at the fort, which he could be depended upon to defend should the Indians strike when the others had been lured away. Isolated forts were sometimes endangered, but not when Captain Wetzel was in command.

Reed wanted to take Jim Logan as cavalry officer, but the Irishman was absent, on a scout, his men said, and when Reed checked quietly, he learned that Mrs Minor was absent too, but for the moment he decided to do nothing about this: 'Colonel Minor, you will be second in command.' And then, with that second sight which had made him an able commander, he added: 'Full campaign issue.' Minor deemed it folly to carry full battle gear on such a trivial excursion, considering the abundance of supplies this involved, but he assumed that Reed wished to test his men, so he said nothing, and within eighteen minutes of having made his decision to intercept his young lieutenant, Reed was headed east with Minor and thirty-eight Buffalo Soldiers.

He posted scouts well in advance, of course, but they could find only remnants of Toomey's march in that direction and no signs whatever of Indian activity. However, one of the ragged older men who served the army, a tracker with one-quarter Indian blood, elected to ride well to the north, from where he returned with ominous news: 'General Reed! One hundred, two hundred Comanche headed east, maybe six days ago.' Now it was clear Chief Matark had made a most daring move.

'Colonel Minor, he's going to attack the wagons between here and Jacksborough.' He was inclined to start immediately at full gallop, but his innate caution directed him to consult his subordinate: 'How could he be trying to trap us, Minor?'

'He could be feinting, then attack the fort.'

'Colonel Wetzel can handle that. How about us?'

'If he tricks us eastward, what gain to him? Moves us closer to the wagons.'

'Bugler!' A muted call, which could be heard only yards away, was sounded and the force of thirty-eight blue-clad troopers spurred their horses into an easy trot. They had gone only a few miles when another scout reported the news which Wetzel had intuitively feared: 'Major battle. Hundreds of Comanche.'

Without halting, Reed shouted his tactics: 'Half left, half right. But the moment we spot where their command is, everyone straight at it. Ignore the wagons.'

When they reached a rise from which they could see the embattled wagons and the Indians assaulting them, Reed ordered his bugler to sound the charge. With Minor and the black cavalrymen at the gallop, they rushed to join the battle.

Reed's men behaved with precision, his group following him in a circle to the north, with Johnny Minor's horsemen riding swiftly to the south, where they picked off several stragglers. At the far end of the circle they joined, then wheeled about to face a main charge of nearly eighty Comanche. It was a mad struggle lasting nearly ten minutes, but in the end the blue-clads were driven back to the wagons, where steady fire from the circle supported them.

It now became a melee, not a battle. Many Indians were killed and five of Reed's men. Minor was badly wounded, taking a bullet through his left hip, but the circle remained intact as the charge of the Indians wavered and then broke. The attack on the Cavin & Clark wagon train at Three Cairns had failed. Thirty-one Indians and nine defenders lay dead, but the fight was over.

When Reed learned that Toomey had died he went to where the body lay, drew aside the blanket, and saluted: 'He died bravely, I'm sure.'

'That he did,' one of the carters said, 'but I'm bringin' charges against them damned niggers. They let us down.'

Reed did not listen, and a few moments later one of the

shotgun men came to him: 'That big sergeant, none braver. He held us together.'

'I'd expect him to,' Reed said.

Reed now faced a series of difficult decisions, which he proceeded to make in rapid-fire order, as if he had long contemplated them. First he had to know his exact strength: 'Sergeant Jaxifer, your condition?'

'Started out with Lieutenant Toomey and ten men. Toomey and three dead, three wounded. Five effectives, including myself, sir.'

Reed turned to Corporal Adams, who had ridden with him: 'Started with you, Colonel Minor and thirty-eight men. Five dead. Minor and three men wounded. Thirty-one effectives, sir.'

Reed studied the situation for less than ten seconds: 'Our immediate job, get this valuable train safely to Fort Garner. Our permanent job, catch Matark before he leaves Texas.'

To the horror of the C&C carters, he assigned the six wounded Buffalo Soldiers and Corporal Adams to escort the train on the remainder of its journey. This, of course, brought wild protestation from the carters, who wanted the entire force to lead them to safety.

Reed listened to their protests for about twenty seconds, then drew his revolver and summoned Adams: 'Corporal, if this man gives you any trouble, shoot him.' He rode to the eight drivers, looking each in the eye: 'Men, you've brought your wagons this far. Finish the job.' To the eight men riding shotgun he said: 'My men couldn't have held them off without your fire. Keep it up.' With an icy smile he tapped one of the loaded wagons: 'If you should need more ammunition . . .' He turned on his heel and paid no further attention as the C&C men organized their wagons for the limping journey to Fort Garner.

His job was to pursue Matark, but with Corporal Adams gone he had only thirty-four men, including himself, to do battle with the much larger Comanche force, but this disparity gave him no trouble, for if he had with him no fellow officer, he did have Sergeant Jaxifer, who was a small army in himself. With such men he could give the retreating Comanche a lot of trouble.

So twenty minutes after the battle at Three Cairns ended, Reed was in foolhardy pursuit of Chief Matark and his many

Comanche, and not one of the black horsemen who followed him was apprehensive about overtaking the Indians or fearful of the outcome if they did: 'They got the men, but we got the guns.'

The chase continued for a day and a half, but when it looked as if the cavalry, with its superior horses and fire power, were about to overtake the Comanche and punish them, another act in the great tragicomedy of the plains unfolded, for when Reed and his men threatened to overtake the Comanche, the latter simply turned north, reached the Red River, swam their horses across, and found sanctuary in Camp Hope, administered by the Pennsylvania Quaker Earnshaw Rusk.

Under the specific terms of General Grant's Peace Policy, the army was free to discipline the Indians as long as they operated in Texas south of the Red River, but the moment they crossed north into Indian Territory the Quakers were in control; specifically, no soldier could touch a Comanche and certainly not fire a gun at him so long as he was north of the river and under the protection of Earnshaw Rusk.

As soon as Reed saw Matark and his men fording the river he knew he was in trouble, but ignoring it and his official directives, he followed them across and with all his men cantered in to Camp Hope, demanding to see the agent. The Indians, now dismounted and almost beatific in their innocence, smiled insolently as he rode past.

'Agent Rusk? I'm Captain Reed from Fort Garner.'

'I've heard the warmest reports of thee, Captain.'

'I've come to arrest Chief Matark of the Comanche.'

'That thee cannot do. Matark and his men are in my charge now, and as the terms –'

'I know the terms, Mr Rusk, but chief Matark has just waylaid a supply train and killed ten American citizens, including eight soldiers under my command.'

'I'm sure there's been a mistake in thy reports,' Rusk said.

'And I'm sure there's not, because I personally counted the bodies.'

'It's thy word against his, Captain Reed, and we all know what thy soldiers think about Indians.'

'Will you surrender Chief Matark to me?'

'I will not.'

'Will you allow me to arrest him, then?'

'I forbid thee to do so.'

'What am I allowed to do?'

'Nothing. Thee controls south of the Red. I control north, and it's my duty to bring these Indians to peaceful ways.'

So the two Americans faced each other, the blue-clad soldier representing the old ways of handling Indians, the homespun Pennsylvanian farmer representing the new. Reed was a Baptist who believed that God was a man of battles, a just judge administering harsh punishments; Rusk, a Quaker who knew that Jesus was a man of compassion who intended all men to be brothers. Reed trusted only army policy: 'Harry the Indians and confine them to reservations'; Rusk believed without qualification that he could persuade Indians to move willingly onto reservations, where the braves would learn agriculture, the women how to sew, and the children how to speak English. Reed interpreted his task as clearing the land for occupation by white ranchers and then protecting them and their cattle from Indian raiders; Rusk saw his as helping both the white newcomer to the land and the original Indian owners to find some reasonable way of sharing the plains. In fact, the only thing upon which the two administrators agreed was that the West should be organized in some sensible way that would permit the greatness of the American nation to manifest itself.

They even looked as dissimilar as two men of about the same age could: Reed was not tall, not heavy. He wore his dark hair closely clipped and affected no mustaches. He stood very erect and spoke sharply. His eyes were piercing and his chin jutting. By force of unusual character he had risen in the Union army from being a conscripted teacher from a small town in Vermont to a generalship in command of an entire brigade of troops. He loved the order of army life and expected to obey and to be obeyed, an attitude which manifested itself in all his actions. He looked always as if ready to step forward and volunteer for the most difficult and dangerous task. By the sheerest accident he had stumbled upon the one career for which he was best suited, and he proposed to follow it with honor as long as he lived.

Earnshaw Rusk was a gangling fellow whose unkempt hair matched his ill-fitting clothes. He had such weak eyes that he disliked looking directly at anyone, and his voice sometimes cracked at the most embarrassing moments, as if he were

954

beginning a song. His Quaker parents had trained him never to press an opinion of his own, for Quakers tended to reach decisions by unspoken consensus rather than through exhibitionist voting; but he had also been told that when he was right 'to forge ahead without let or hindrance.' He had never been sure what those words meant, but he did know from observation that it was fairly difficult to dislodge a believing Quaker from a position morally taken, and he saw no reason why he should be different.

'Agent Rusk,' Reed said as if launching a new problem, 'you and I share a most difficult responsibility.'

'We do.'

'Now you are harboring in your camp –'

'We harbor no one, General. We provide a home for Indians on their way to civilization.'

'This time you're harboring a fiendish killer, Chief Matark of the Comanche.'

'I know Matark. I cannot believe –'

'Have you ever heard of the Bear Creek massacre?'

'I've heard the usual ugly rumors people spread.'

'Have you ever heard of the little girl Emma Larkin?'

'I don't know that name.'

'At Bear Creek, Matark massacred fifteen men, women, and children, and he massacred them most horribly. Would you care to hear the details?'

'I am not interested in soldiers' campfire tales.'

Reed did not hesitate: 'When you and I find the little girl, and we will – believe me, Agent Rusk, we will – we'll see that her ears and her nose have been burned off. We'll find that she's been raped incessantly. She'll probably be pregnant, but we'll find her.'

Rusk blanched: 'I find such stories repulsive.'

'They are,' Reed said, 'but in this case they're real. I found the bodies, hacked apart. I reassembled them as best I could. I buried them.'

'That's a terrible charge for thee to make, on a guess.' And there the struggle intensified, for Rusk's continued use of the Biblical *thee* seemed to be parading his virtue, as if to say: 'I am more Christlike than thee. I am of a higher moral order.' This infuriated army men, for they interpreted his pacifism as the

behavior of a simple-minded man who could scarcely differentiate dawn from dusk.

Reed, having sworn not to lose his temper with this difficult
Quaker, smiled icily. 'I am not guessing, Agent Rusk. I know.'

'Thee is being terribly unfair to Chief Matark.' Impulsively,
for he was a good man striving to protect other good men, he
sent for Matark, and within a few minutes the three protagonists who would compete for Texas rights so desperately faced
one another. Matark appeared as if he had come from a pleasant
hunt, his features in repose, his body at ease. It seemed
doubtful that he had ever committed an act of warfare, let alone
massacre, but Reed noticed that he did stay close to Rusk, as if
he realized that this man was now his appointed protector.

'This is my friend Chief Matark,' Rusk began, and he
expected the two men to shake hands, but Reed refused to
touch the Indian. 'Chief, Captain Reed tells me that thee
attacked supply trains.'

'Lies, lies.'

'He has men out there to prove that thee attacked the train,
black soldiers whose reports we can trust.'

'Must have been Kiowa. No Comanche. None.'

When the interpreter translated these words, Rusk smiled
thinly and held up his hands: 'Thee sees, I was sure it must have
been other Indians. We have great trouble with the Kiowa,
chiefs like Satanta, Satank.'

'Matark's Comanche were nowhere near Three Cairns?'

'No. Never so far south. We hunting Indians, not fighting.
We stay on reservation.'

Reed did not respond to this. Suddenly he asked: 'What have
you done with Emma Larkin?'

Matark stiffened, a fact which Rusk noticed, then said:
'Kiowa killed her people. We rescued her. She safe with us.'

Reed bowed his head, visualizing what *safe* meant in such
situations. Rusk noticed this too, and asked: 'It is true that thee
holds a white child?' and Matark replied: 'For safety. To keep
her from the Kiowa.'

Even Rusk could see the cynicism of this response: any white
child held captive by Indians should be returned to white
protectors, and if the child was a girl, the obligation was
doubled. For the first time since he came west, this

peace-seeking Quaker experienced a grain of doubt about the goodness of his Comanche, but he raised no questions because he honestly believed that Matark was an innocent man vilified by the rough soldiers at Fort Garner. Rusk still did not comprehend the terrible problems faced by white settlers in Texas, and he refused to admit that his Indians ever raided down in Texas and then found sanctuary a few miles to the north in Indian Territory.

Reed and Matark understood each other: with them it was a duel to the death, and if Matark had had just a little more time the other day, he would have captured one of Reed's wagon trains and killed every soldier guarding it; on the other hand, if Reed had been able to keep the Indians south of the Red River for one more day, he would have tried to annihilate them. It was brutal, incessant warfare, and each man wondered at the naïvety of Agent Rusk, who did not comprehend this.

Captain Reed accomplished nothing at Camp Hope except his own humiliation, which he accepted silently, but on his return to Fort Garner he felt he must as a responsible commanding officer broach a subject which threatened to undermine the effectiveness of his troops. He summoned Logan and began cautiously: 'Were you able to speak with Colonel Minor when they brought him in? Very bad knock on the left hip.'

'Two minutes, three minutes. As you would expect, he was smiling.'

'Very good man, Minor. He performed well at the Cairns.'

'You'd expect him to.'

'He'll be a long time mending. Perhaps we should send him home.'

'He wouldn't like that. He asked me to assure you . . .'

Reed had to wonder whether Minor had actually said that, or whether Logan was merely endeavoring to keep Nellie Minor close at hand, and he judged that now was the time to be frank: 'Major, Johnny Minor's going to have a rough time with that hip. He'll need all the support he can muster. From his wife especially.'

'That is sure.'

'I'd take it kindly, Major, and so would Mrs Reed, if you saw less of Minor's wife.'

'Yes, sir.'

No more was said, and Reed told his wife: 'I think the matter of Nellie Minor has been settled,' and Mrs Reed said: 'Thank God. These things can get so out of hand in a lonely fort.'

This one was far from settled, however, because if Major Logan was willing to cease the affair, Nellie Minor was not, and one morning, after dressing her husband's suppurating wound, she mounted a horse and rode far out to the tank, where she had insisted that Jim Logan meet her. They allowed their horses to wander into that glade where the Indians had observed them before the attack on the wagon train, and there they renewed their passionate love. When they lay looking up at the endless blue sky, Logan said: 'The last time. I can't make love to the wife of a wounded comrade.'

'You damned men! You know he cares nothing for me.'

'He did. And now he needs you.'

'Need! Need! That's all I hear. I need things too.'

Mrs Reed, who learned quickly of Nellie's brazen escapade, was not disposed to have this headstrong young woman wreck her husband's command by some act that would be reported to Washington. Fort Garner had already been marked unfavorably because of the loss of men in the attack upon the wagons and because Reed had allowed Matark to reach sanctuary across the river, and one more unfavorable notice might be decisive. She therefore summoned both Nellie and her lover to her rooms in the commander's building, the second on the base to be converted to stone – the hospital invariably being first – and there she presented them with surprising information.

'I have consulted with the surgeon from Fort Richardson, and he at first warned me that Colonel Minor was too weak to be moved. So I had to bide my time and let you two run wild.'

'We have not –' Nellie tried to break into the speech, but Mrs Reed ignored her.

'But now your husband is mending, Mrs Minor, and I am asking that he be taken from here in an ambulance ... tomorrow. And my husband is recommending that when he is recovered he be assigned to desk duty with Lieutenant General Sheridan in Chicago. You will accompany him when he leaves this fort.'

Logan felt that he must protest: 'There is no cause for such dismissal.'

'Mrs Minor is not being dismissed. She is merely accompanying her husband, as a good wife should.'

'But –'

'Especially when he has been wounded in a gallant charge against the Comanche.' She was implacable in her opposition to this adulterous pair and had taken the precaution of informing others, before the meeting took place, that the Minors were being shipped out, and had arranged that the ambulance which would carry them away be brought to the rear of the hospital, where its wheels and fittings were being checked.

So when Johnny Minor's lady and her Irish lover left the commander's quarters, everyone on the base, even the black cavalry privates, knew that they were in disgrace, and since her reputation could degenerate no further, Nellie went boldly to the stables, where she asked one of the cavalrymen to saddle her horse, and upon it she rode toward the tank. Moments later Logan, in disregard of the punishment that must surely be visited upon him, rode after her, and the fort buzzed at his arrogant defiance. Even a laundress who worked sometimes in the hospital as a kind of nurse felt obligated to inform wounded Captain Minor of his wife's intemperate behavior; he ignored the gossip, taking refuge in the fact that very shortly he would be rid of Fort Garner and its complexities, but finding no assurance that when his headstrong wife reached Chicago she would behave any differently.

Before Nellie had reached the tank, Logan had overtaken her, and when he saw the extreme agitation which possessed her, he realized for the first time that their love-making had become considerably more than a mere escapade. It was now something so important in her life that she could not face surrendering it, no matter what cold New England women like Mrs Reed said or what Reed himself might do to protect the integrity of his command.

'I won't go to Chicago. I won't waste my life with that cripple.'

'You'll have to. Can't stay here.'

'I'll leave the ambulance when we reach Jacksborough. Finish with the army, Jim, and join me there.'

'And do what?' This was a compelling question, for he was an

959

Irishman trained only in the care of horses and their utilization in battle. He had not wanted assignment to a regiment of Negro cavalry, but he had accepted because that was the only pattern of life open to him, and now even that frail opportunity was being threatened. 'I can't leave the regiment.'

She sat on the ground beside the gray water and enticed him to join her, and after they had made love, for the last time he swore to himself, she casually reached across to where his belt lay and took from its holster his heavy Colts, pointing its barrel at her head: 'I think it best if I end this nightmare.'

'Nell! Put that down!' He reached out to retrieve his gun, when he saw to his horror that she was now pointing it at him, and with a skill he had not suspected, she was releasing the safety. The last thing he saw was the steel-gray barrel aimed at his forehead and her finger pressing the trigger.

As soon as he fell, she resolutely and with no regrets placed the barrel deep in her mouth, its end jammed against the roof, and pressed the trigger a second time.

Preoccupation with the tragedy ended when a special courier arrived from headquarters in St Louis in response to an urgent appeal from the Governor of Texas. Major Comstock, after revealing his purpose to Reed, asked permission to address the officers: 'Gentlemen, as you've probably heard, the Texas Rangers are being reactivated for the first time since the end of the late war. They're needed because that damned bandit Benito Garza has been chewing up American settlements along the Rio Grande. They need our help.'

Wetzel, as a professional soldier, growled: 'If you listen to the Texans, their Rangers can defeat anybody. Why do they need us?'

Comstock had a reply so convoluted that these professionals gasped in wonder at its fatuity: 'Garza holes up on the Mexican side of the river. The US Army can't touch him. From that sanctuary he makes sorties into the United States, robbing and killing. If we catch him over here, of course we can kill him, but we cannot chase him if he escapes to Mexico. Forbidden by international law. Absolutely forbidden by Washington.'

'Then why are we going?' Wetzel asked.

'To support the Rangers. They can cross the river. Not being legally a part of our forces, they can pursue the bandits in what they're calling "hot pursuit," that is, in the heat of battle.'

Reed broke in: 'So our troops are to protect the American side while the Rangers go after them?'

'Precisely. And that's all you're to do. Because if you invade Mexico to get him, you become bandits, just like him.'

For two hours Comstock reviewed this unusual situation, placing before the restless officers so many ramifications that Wetzel snapped: 'Hell, this sounds like our border with Indian Territory. The Comanche sneak in and kill, then dart back across the border and claim immunity.'

'Exactly, but in Garza's case it's even more complex, because a foreign power is involved.

Now the question became 'whom to send?' – and Reed pointed out that with the deaths of young Toomey at Three Cairns and Logan at the tank, plus the disabling injury to Minor, his staff was pretty well depleted, especially in the cavalry.

'What about this Lieutenant Renfro?'

'Desk duty, Washington. Can't seem to pry him loose.'

'One of those,' Comstock said with disgust, and no more was needed.

Finally, both Reed and Comstock agreed that the ideal man for the assignment was Wetzel, and when this was decided, the courier asked that he meet with Reed and Wetzel alone. As they sat in Reed's stone house the major was blunt: 'Captain Wetzel, I've heard only the highest praise for your military prowess, but this is an assignment fraught with danger. Can you be trusted to take your men right up to the edge of the Rio Grande and keep them there, regardless of provocation, until you catch Garza on our side of the river?'

'Yes, sir.'

'None of this "hot pursuit"?'

'No, sir. Here on this northern border of Texas we learn discipline.'

'Captain Wetzel, on this border you have hundreds of observers to report if you stray. On the southern border you have only yourself to enforce the rules.'

'Sir, I'm an army captain. I'm also a Prussian. I've been trained to obey orders.'

'And you understand those orders?'

'I do. No soldier under my command will step one inch into Mexico.'

'Good. I want it in writing.' And while Reed watched, Comstock took from his papers an order, prepared in St Louis, stating that the officer who endorsed it would allow no excursions into Mexico. The signing was as solemn an undertaking as Wetzel had ever participated in, and when he finished he saluted.

Comstock resumed: 'Now, as to your mounted scouts. They'll have to be black, of course.'

'We'll send Company R,' Reed said, 'but the only officer we can spare is that chinless wonder Asperson they just sent us from West Point.' When Wetzel groaned, Reed added: 'But this big sergeant, Jaxifer, he'll more than make up.'

Next morning reveille sounded at half an hour before dawn, and when the files were mounted and Reed had delivered a farewell address wishing his men well, Major Comstock, astride a black stallion, motioned Wetzel aside and shared with him certain verbal orders which moved this expedition into its proper military framework. He chose his words carefully, for upon them would hang the reputations of many officers: 'General Sheridan commanded me to tell whoever led the troops to the Rio Grande that he must not, repeat not, cross into Mexico.'

'I endorsed that order.'

'But he told me further that this officer would be responsible for the honor of the United States, and that in extremity the officer must follow the highest traditions of the army ... as he interprets them ... on the spot.'

As the sun rose above the buildings of Fort Garner, the two officers saluted.

Wetzel's force consisted of forty-eight infantry plus a truncated company of Buffalo Soldiers, a tough, experienced, well-disciplined group of men. Their path to where Benito Garza was raiding was compass south, then a slight veer toward San Antonio, and another slight jog east toward the small riverfront town of Bravo, where headquarters would be established at Fort Grimm and where contact would be made with the Texas

Rangers.

On the trip south only one problem arose: Wetzel still did not like black soldiers and found it impossible to be congenial with them, but he did try to be fair. However, no matter what decision had to be made, the black troops knew that invariably they got the worst location for their tents, the poorest food and the most grudging amenities. The situation was exacerbated by the poor performance of their young officer, Lieutenant Asperson, scion of an old New England family that had prevailed upon their cousin, a senator from Massachusetts, to get the boy into West Point and, upon graduation, an assignment in some post of importance. The authorities, irritated by such pressures, had assured Senator Asperson that his nephew would 'get one of the finest duty stations,' and had then sent him to Fort Garner, one of the most dangerous.

Armstrong Asperson was an awkward, inept, stoop-shouldered fellow who should have worn a frown to reflect his inability to adjust to the normal world. Instead, regardless of what disaster overtook him, and he was prone to disasters, he grinned vacuously and with a startling show of teeth. Did it rain when his men had no ponchos? He grinned. Did Wetzel give him his daily chewing out? He grinned. After he had been at the fort for about a week he went down to Suds Row for his laundry, and one of the toughest washerwomen summarized him in words which ricocheted about the station: 'They hung the clock on the wall but forgot two of the parts.'

Armstrong Asperson, with two parts missing, was heading for his first battle, and both his colonel and his company were aghast to think that soon they might be fighting alongside this grinning scarecrow. Wetzel treated him with contempt and Jaxifer with condescension. 'What we got to ɔ, men,' he said, 'is stay close to him if anything happens so he don't shoot hisse'f in the foot.'

Jaxifer, whose entire life had been spent protecting himself from the peculiarities of white bosses, found little difficulty in adjusting either to Wetzel's injustices or to Asperson's in-adequacies. Of Wetzel he said: 'Look, men, he infantry and he just don't know nothin' 'bout cavalry. Keep yore mouf shut.' Of Asperson: 'Remember, even General Grant, he have to start somewhere. But I doubt he start as low as Asperson.'

Thanks to Jaxifer's counsel, the long march ended without incident, and during the second day in their quarters at Bravo they met for the first time a Texas Ranger, and they were not impressed. He wore no uniform; in an almost ludicrous manner he carried strapped to his saddle two rifles and four Colts, and nothing about him was army-clean. A small, wiry man in his late forties, he reported to Wetzel's tent wearing a long white linen duster that came to his ankles.

Without saluting, the small, diffident man said: 'You Wetzel? I'm Macnab.'

'You?' Wetzel said in unmasked surprise. 'I thought you'd be much bigger.'

'I look bigger when I'm on a horse,' Macnab said without smiling. 'I'm sure glad to have your help.' And without further amenities he began to draw maps in the sand outside Wetzel's tent.

'It's tough down here,' Macnab said. 'Maybe even tougher than fighting Comanche.'

'Now that would be pretty tough.'

'Problem is, this Benito Garza, I've known him all my life, he's a lot smarter than me, and if you'll permit the expression, maybe a lot smarter than most of your men.'

'I've heard that,' Wetzel said, displaying a professional interest in a military situation. 'How does he operate?'

'Clever as a possum,' Macnab said, and he let his explanation end as the cook beat upon a ring, signaling supper.

While Wetzel smoked his cigar at sunset, Macnab resumed his map drawing: 'Garza waits till something happens on this side of the border. And things do happen.'

'Like hanging Mexican landowners?'

'Mexicans ask for hanging,' Macnab said. 'But when it happens, Garza feels he must retaliate. And he does.'

'In the same region?'

Macnab looked about for a blade of grass, found one, and chewed on it: 'Now there's the problem. Always he confuses us. Four times in a row he strikes within a mile of where some Mexican was hanged. Next time, fifty miles away.'

'How can you anticipate?'

Macnab chewed on his grass, then confessed: 'We can't.' There was a long silence, then as darkness approached from the east, Macnab said quietly: 'Captain Wetzel, let me tell you what's going on now.'

'Proceed.'

'We have good reason to think that Garza has taken command of a ranch, El Solitario, about ten miles south of here. He has forty, fifty men there, and they fan out to execute their revenge up and down the river.'

No one spoke. More than two minutes passed without a word, for each of the three men attending the meeting knew what Macnab was proposing: that he and his Rangers cross the Rio Grande, make a sudden descent upon the hidden ranch, shoot Garza, and rely upon the United States Army to support them as they beat a frantic retreat with forty or fifty well-mounted Mexican riders striving to overtake them.

Still silent, Macnab drew in the sand the location of Bravo, the river, the distant location of Rancho El Solitario, plus the circuitous route to it and the short, frenzied retreat back to the Rio Grande. When everything was in place he said softly: 'It could be done.'

Bluntly, Wetzel scuffed his foot along the escape route: 'You mean, if someone came along here to hold off your pursuers?'

'Couldn't be done otherwise.'

Wetzel leaned back, folded his arms like an irritated German schoolmaster, and said: 'I have the strictest orders forbidding me to step one inch onto Mexican soil.'

'I'm sure you do,' Macnab said quietly. 'But what if my sixteen Rangers came down that road you just scratched out, with fifty Mexicans sure to overtake us before we reached the river?'

'I would have my men lined up on this side of the river, every gun at the ready. Sergeant Gerton and a Gatling gun would be prepared to rake the river if the Mexicans tried to invade this side. And I would pray for you.'

'Would you allow your men to come to the middle of the river to help?'

'Is that the boundary between the two countries?'

'It is.'

'My best gunners would be there.'

Now came the time for a direct question: 'But you wouldn't come into Mexico to help?'

'Absolutely not.'

That ended the consultation, so without showing his disappointment, Macnab rode back to his own camp upriver, and it was unfortunate that he went in that direction because downriver some recent arrivals from Tennessee slew four Mexicans trying to prevent illegal seizure of their ancestral ranch land.

Next morning, about noon, Otto Macnab was back to consult with Wetzel: 'I'm sure Garza will strike within the next three days. But where?'

'Do you think we should scatter our forces?'

'I really don't know. If he starts out now, within three days he could be almost anywhere. Since spies must have informed him of your arrival, he'll hit somewhere near here, to shame you.'

'So we should stay put?'

'I think so.'

Garza, infuriated by the killing of peasants trying to protect land once owned by his mother Trinidad de Saldana, was grimly determined to let the intruders know that this fight was going to be interminable and, as Macnab had predicted, he could do this most effectively by striking close to the new encampment. He allowed five days to lapse, then six, then seven, so that the Rangers and the soldiers would be disoriented. On the night of the eighth day he rode with thirty of his best men across the Rio Grande and devastated two ranches east of Bravo, killing three Texans and escaping to safety before either the Rangers or the soldiers could be alerted.

He took his men on a wide swing back to the safety of El Solitario. This nest of adobe houses was completely surrounded by a high stone-and-adobe wall, which enclosed fruit trees, a well and enough cattle to feed his men for more than a month. It was a frontier ranch, so built as to protect its inhabitants from assaults coming from any direction, but its major asset was that it lay far enough inland from the river to make an attack from Texas unlikely.

Macnab did not think it was impregnable: 'Informers tell us Garza did the job downriver with no more than thirty men, who are now holed up at his ranch with about twenty others. I'm going in there and finish Benito Garza.'

He spoke these words not to Wetzel but to his Rangers, sixteen of them, the youngest only sixteen years old. Then he added: 'I do not order any of you to come with me, but I'm inviting volunteers.' As two men stepped forward he stopped them: 'You know, I've been after Garza for thirty years. I've made it my life's work. I have to go. You don't.'

'I want him too,' a thin, fierce Texan said. 'He killed my brother.'

Every Ranger volunteered, but the boy he turned back: 'No, Sam. It wouldn't be fair.'

'I'm here because he burned our ranch.'

'Well, you stay behind and lead the troops when they come to rescue us.'

'They said they wouldn't do that.'

'That's what they said, but they'll come. Lead them to that fork we saw on our last scout.' When the boy showed his disappointment, Macnab asked: 'You remember where the fork is? We'll be coming there hell-for-leather. Have the soldiers in position to do us some good.'

He took off his duster, folded it neatly, and stowed it. His men placed beside it things they did not care to risk on this adventure, and when everyone was ready, Macnab took out his watch and handed it to the boy, instructing him as to how it should be used. At five that afternoon Captain Macnab and his Rangers forded the Rio Grande, rode north, then cut into heavy mesquite. Through the night they moved cautiously toward Garza's ranch, but at half an hour before sunup they had the bad luck to be spotted by Mexicans living on a smaller ranch. There was some noise and a scattering of chickens, after which a young man shouted: 'Rinches!'

Men started running for their horses, but each was shot before he could mount. There would be no messenger riding forth from this ranch, and to ensure that no woman tried to spread the alarm, all horses in the corral were shot, and Rangers bound the four remaining women and locked them in a room.

It was nearly dawn when Macnab's men reached the high walls of the Garza compound, and now a brief council of war was held, not to devise tactics, for they had been agreed upon days before, but to specify tasks. At a signal, four Rangers

967

crashed through the main gate, paving the way for the rest to follow. There was a blaze of gunfire, and then in the doorway appeared the white-haired figure of Benito Garza, his two pistols drawn, ready for battle.

Macnab, who had anticipated such an appearance, steadied his rifle against a watering trough and for a second recalled that similar moment on the eve of the battle at Buena Vista when through gallantry he had allowed Garza to escape, and he saw also that incredible scene in 1848 when Garza had passed by him within inches during the escape of Santa Anna into exile. 'Not this time, Uncle Benito,' he muttered as Garza started to leave the doorway.

The heavy bullet sped straight to the heart, and the great bandit, protector of his people, lurched forward, expecting to see his ancient enemy in some shadow, but he saw nothing, and toppled to his death.

'Away!' Macnab shouted, and according to plan, three of the Rangers tried to shoot the Mexican horses, but failed. In a wild exit, during which one of the daring Texans was picked off, fifteen Rangers including Macnab made their escape from within the high walls and started their ride of desperation toward the river.

At four o'clock that morning the sixteen-year-old Ranger began looking at Captain Macnab's watch, and at four-thirty he followed instructions. Galloping his horse past the sentries, he pulled up at Captain Wetzel's tent and shouted: 'The Rangers are attacking El Solitario!'

'When?' Wetzel cried as he left his tent with a sheet about his shoulders.

'Right now!'

'Why wasn't I warned?'

'I am warning you. Captain Macnab told me: "Tell him at four-thirty. I don't want him to worry all night." '

'Bugler, sound assembly!' and in the darkness Wetzel mustered his men, ordering them into full battle gear.

'Are we going across to help?' Sergeant Gerton asked, and Wetzel said: 'No.'

At dawn he mounted his black charger and rode about supervising the placement of his troops, putting his best sharpshooters along the American bank of the Rio Grande. He personally directed Gerton and his two men where to place their Gatling gun to command the crossing. He called for volunteers to wade out into the shallow river and point their guns to where the fleeing Rangers would probably appear, and then he rode to where his Buffalo Soldiers were encamped, some distance from the white troops. Almost contemptuously he dismissed Lieutenant Asperson with a curt order: 'Take half your company and guard that other crossing.' Then he rode to where Sergeant Jaxifer waited with ten mounted troopers, and started this crucial conversation:

WETZEL: You know what's happening over here?

JAXIFER: I can guess.

WETZEL: You know my orders?

JAXIFER: Yes, sir.

WETZEL: When those Rangers come galloping to that river, what will you and your men do?

JAXIFER: Wait for orders.

WETZEL: Will you be ready to cross and hold back the Mexicans?

JAXIFER: We ready right now.

WETZEL (*listening for the sound of gunfire to begin*): I've learned respect for you on this trip, Jaxifer. Why do we have so much trouble with our white infantry and so little with your black cavalry?

JAXIFER: Because we black.

WETZEL: What does that mean?

JAXIFER: You white officers never understand.

WETZEL: Tell me.

JAXIFER: In the whole United States ain't nothin' a black man can hope for half as good as bein' in the Buffalo Soldiers. Black men dream of this, they pray, they do almost anything for white men, just to get in the Tenth Cavalry. I'm the biggest black man in Texas, because I'm a sergeant in the Tenth. Colonel Wetzel, I will die rather than lose that job.

WETZEL: Why didn't you tell me this before?

JAXIFER: Because it's our secret. We ain't never before had honor, but we got it now, and we will not risk it.

WETZEL: What does that mean to me this morning?

JAXIFER: Without orders from you, we don't move. With orders, we'll ride to Mexico City or die tryin'.

WETZEL: Everything ready?

JAXIFER: When you sent Asperson away, I kept the best men with me. We all want to be on the far side of that river.

WETZEL: If the Mexicans make one wrong move, I'll lead you.

JAXIFER: We hungry to go.

The two men remained astride their horses, immobilized by the great traditions of their army. Jaxifer desperately wanted to lead his men in a charge to rescue the white fighters; this was the whole purpose of his cavalry and the reason for his being in uniform, but he could not move, even though the Rangers died, unless he had an order. And Captain Wetzel, who had followed soldiering since a boy, in both Germany and America, longed for battle. He loved it, loved the excitement of the chase, the fury of the sudden explosion when armies met. But he had unmistakable orders to refrain unless the United States was invaded.

But then the secret words of Major Comstock echoed: 'The officer will be expected to follow the highest traditions of the army.' That had to mean the rescue of fellow Americans in danger, and for such action he was more than prepared. Spurring his horse toward the river, with Jaxifer following, he turned and said: 'I hope those Mexicans make one mistake, fire one bullet into our territory.'

The tangled reflections of the two impatient soldiers were broken by the appearance of the young Ranger. 'Where are you going?' Wetzel asked and the boy replied: 'To lead the niggers to where the trails meet.'

'Who told you to do that?'

'Captain Macnab. He was sure that when you heard gunfire you'd send them, no matter what your orders said.'

Disgusted by this unprofessional behavior on the part of the Rangers and wishing to rid himself of the boy, Wetzel growled: 'They're down there,' indicating the other crossing, where lanky Lieutenant Asperson sat grinning with a smaller group of Buffalo Soldiers.

* * *

While Wetzel and Jaxifer were agonizing over their

alternatives, Otto Macnab and his Rangers were in full retreat, fighting a rearguard action of desperation, and they might have escaped without help from the hesitant soldiers had not a daring Mexican bandit, accompanied by six others, known of a shortcut to the river. Pounding down its narrow turns, these determined men reached a point on the escape route just before Macnab, and a furious gun battle raged, forcing the Rangers to move downriver from their planned route.

This threw them onto a trail which would bring them to the lesser crossing of the Rio Grande, guarded by the lesser black cavalry, and as the Rangers and their pursuers approached the river, Asperson could hear the sound of gunfire. Excited by the likelihood of his first battle, he started his Buffalo Soldiers toward the river, then stopped them in obedience to the orders he had memorized. The young Ranger, watching with dismay as the rescue operation halted, pulled a clever trick. Throwing a sharp pebble at Asperson's horse, he made the horse rear, and the nervous lieutenant cried in a high voice: 'My God, we're under attack!'

Consulting no one, waiting for no verification, he waved his revolver in the air as if it were a sword, and shouted: 'To the rescue.' For him there was no anxiety, no nagging moral problem. Americans were under attack by foreigners, and by God he was going to do something about it. With a roar, his black troops followed.

During the disorganized charge, in which black cavalrymen passed and repassed their ungainly leader, he did retain enough control to order the bugler to sound 'Charge' so that the beleaguered Rangers would know of their coming. Because of the uneven terrain, the bugle kept slipping from the bugler's lips, but the broken sounds did reach the battle area, giving the Rangers hope and throwing their pursuers into confusion.

Macnab said later: 'The Buffalo Soldiers came roaring out of the mesquite like six different armies. They were a mob, but they were magnificent.'

The confused battle – more like a riot, really – lasted only a few minutes. Not many Mexicans were killed and no Americans, but when it was over, Macnab and Asperson rode like Roman victors down to the Rio Grande, and as they splashed their horses into that shallow, muddy stream, the regular army on the American side went berserk. The advance guard, standing in the river, fired indiscriminately. Sergeant Gerton and his Gatling gun sprayed the empty Mexican shore, the others cheered, and Wetzel looked on in amazement.

By ten that morning he had a telegram started on its way to headquarters:

IN OBEDIENCE HIGHEST TRADITIONS US ARMY 10TH CAVALRY 2ND LT. ASPERSON CAME UNDER ATTACK BY MEXICAN BANDITS. RETALIATED WITH GREAT GALLANTRY. BENITO GARZA DEAD ONE RANGER CASUALTY NO ARMY MANY MEXICAN.

When Sergeant Jaxifer read his men a copy of this precious verification of their victory, one of his troopers said: 'Cain't understand. They tell me Macnab just kill his best friend, but he act like nothin' happened. Look!' And the cavalryman watched as Macnab unfolded his white linen duster, threw it about his shoulders, and started that day's routine.

With Captain Wetzel and Lieutenant Asperson absent on detached duty along the Rio Grande, Fort Garner was hurting for officers, and what made the deficiency most painful was that clever Lewis Renfro still malingered in Washington. In some anger Captain Reed dispatched an urgent appeal to St Louis: 'Fort Garner has acute need services First Lieutenant Lewis Renfro, Brevet Colonel, currently on detached duty Washington.'

In the capital there was a good deal of dickering with Congress before Renfro could be released for active duty, because both he and his wife pulled strings to prevent him from being moved out of his socially pleasing job as liaison with the omnipotent Quartermaster Corps. Mrs Renfro was especially effective in this campaign, for she knew several senators and representatives on the military committees, and she lobbied to keep her husband in the capital: 'Senator, you served during the late war. You know that speeding supplies to the troops, it wins many a battle.' Since she was pretty as well as clever, her arguments were almost irresistible, but when a gruff colonel who had behaved with distinction at both Gettysburg and the Wilderness presented the Congressional committee with the record of Lieutenant Renfro, they had to pay attention: 'Gentlemen, since that day at Appomattox your Lieutenant Renfro has been constantly assigned to battle stations on the frontier, that's a period of seven years, and during that time he has maneuvered detached desk assignments for all but five weeks. Renfro is another fighting man who never fights.'

One senator, who had been impressed by Mrs Renfro's defense of her husband, asked: 'But doesn't he make a crucial contribution here? Assuring your men their supplies?'

The colonel refrained from pointing out that anyone with a fifth-grade education could do as well; instead he made a clever observation: 'Senator! I am not for one minute denigrating Renfro's enviable record in the late war. I am thinking only of his career.'

'What do you mean?'

'Unless he can show on his record proof of command in the field, how can he ever be promoted to the high rank which every fighting man aspires to? If he doesn't include active duty in a position of importance, he can never become a general.'

Such argument made sense to the congressmen with military records, and shortly thereafter Renfro received orders to report at once to his assigned Company S, 10th Cavalry at Fort Sam Garner on the Texas frontier, to serve under the command of Captain George Reed (Brevet Brigadier General).

When Daisy Renfro heard the doleful news she stormed: 'A nigger regiment! It scars a man for life. Lewis, you will not be in that fort six weeks, I promise. We did it before, we can do it again.' And she started immediately the intense campaign to recall her husband to his preferred job in Washington.

Before the Renfros had time to report, two inspection teams visited Fort Garner, for the army feared that something fundamental might be wrong at this lonely command; newspaper stories had begun asking questions which had to be answered.

The first visit came from regimental headquarters at Fort Sill, and it was led by one of the splendid, tragic figures of the Civil War. Benjamin Grierson, a Pennsylvania farm boy, had been serving as an underpaid music teacher in Illinois when the late war started. Distrustful of horses after having been kicked in the face by one, he protested when assigned to a cavalry unit, of which he became the commander. Soon thereafter, finding no one else eligible, the quiet music teacher was summoned for a most difficult and dangerous mission: 'We must prevent the Confederates from moving reinforcements to the defense of Vicksburg. Take your troops as a raiding party. Move behind enemy lines on the east bank of the Mississippi and disrupt communications as much as possible.'

With no fixed headquarters and no reliable supply, the thirty-seven-year-old music teacher ran wild for sixteen days, always on the verge of capture by superior Confederate forces, always on hand at some surprising moment to wreck a train or burn a stores depot. He fought innumerable small battles, fleeing always to some new position from which to make his next assault. At the conclusion of these incredible raids, his men reported: 'Seventeen hundred of us rode six hundred miles behind enemy lines, losing only three killed, nine missing. We killed about a hundred of the enemy, captured and paroled over five hundred, destroyed more than sixty miles of railroad, captured three thousand stands of arms, and took over a thousand mules and horses.'

Grierson had been a military phenomenon, an untrained layman who intuitively understood the most subtle arts of mounted warfare. His men loved him for they knew him to be both lucky and brave, an irresistible combination, and he achieved a much greater success in the backwoods of Mississippi and Louisiana than more notable cavalry commanders like Jeb Stuart did in the East. He was one of the foremost cavalry commanders in American history, and as a consequence he had risen to the rank of brevet general.

But when peace came he faced the unalterable opposition of all West Point officers, who leveled four charges against him: he was a civilian; he was a music teacher; on the Texas frontier he tried to treat Indians as if they were honorable opponents like Frenchmen or Englishmen; and he was soiled by being personally responsible for the black troops of the 10th Cavalry, an unacceptable command with which he would be stuck for twenty-two years.

Grierson was a talented man, a true genius, and he suffered the contempt of his fellow officers without complaint. He did believe that if Indians were treated justly, they could be brought into full citizenship, and he did defend the bravery and competency of his Negro troops, for he knew from frontier reports how well the latter performed under fire. It was headquarters that did not believe; most critically, it was the newspapers in Texas that deplored having Negro troops protecting the Texas frontier. Their attacks were savage: 'We need no niggers here. Give us fifty Rangers and we can clear the plains all the way to California.'

When General Grierson, his brevet rank honored along the frontier, arrived at Fort Garner he was forty-six, still lean, still alert. He was stigmatized immediately by the Prussian Wetzel, back from the Rio Grande, as a man deficient in discipline, one of those weaklings who try to rule by the affection of troops rather than by rigorous command, and Wetzel had watched too many times as such officers came to a bad end. Wetzel, like most of the regulars, held the former music teacher in contempt.

The other officers, especially those in the 10th Cavalry, did not. They knew from personal experience that he was a gallant leader who defended the prerogatives of his men and who led them to one quiet success after another; some actually loved him for the legendary heroics he had performed during the war, but most of the infantry officers and men, who could not believe what this quiet man had accomplished, dismissed him as another eccentric leader of colored troops.

In a tremendously concentrated half-day General Grierson satisfied himself on many points, which he stated in the report he wrote that night:

At the Battle of Three Cairns units of the 10th Cavalry deported themselves according to the highest traditions of the service. 2nd Lt Elmer Toomey directed his men properly and died gallantly at their head. 1st Sgt John Jaxifer assumed command as expected, and defended an exposed position with valor. I can give no credence to charges made by the Calvin & Clark drivers that Sgt Jaxifer was in any way deficient. This battle will shine brightly among the laurels gained by this Regiment.

The death of 2nd Lt Jim Logan, one of our most accomplished horsemen from Ireland, and the scandal attaching thereto, is the kind of tragedy which can overtake

975

any unit of any kind, civilian or military. I treasured Logan as a brave man and I mourn his death. In all respects I find these units of the 10th Cavalry in good condition, battle-ready and well led. Their desertion rate is 1 in 300. Desertion rate of the white troops at the fort, 48 in 100 over a period of four and a half years. I especially commend these enlisted men who serve so faithfully and with such enthusiasm, and I applaud Capt Reed's leadership, finding nothing to censure.

On the next day General Grierson reviewed his troops and then asked Sergeant Jaxifer to lead him out to where Jim Logan and Johnny Minor's wife had died. Jaxifer told his men later: 'General, when he see the spot, and the water, and the birds, he dismounts and stands by the spot weepin'. I stayed clear, but he motion me to dismount, and together we placed some stones. "Two good men," he said a couple of times, meanin' Logan and Minor. He never mention Miss Nellie.'

That night the Reeds held a gala for the visitors, and one of the Mexicans whom the soldiers employed to work the horses appeared with a violin, one of the laundresses beat a tambourine, and there was dancing, and the best food possible purchased from the post sutler, and much conversation about the old days. Even Wetzel relaxed, telling of his unit's exploits at various battles, and it was 'General This' and 'Colonel That' as if the old ranks still pertained, as if the old salary scale were still being paid instead of the miserly pay accorded these heroic veterans: once a lieutenant colonel, now a first lieutenant, $1,500 a year; once a general, now a captain, $1,800 a year.

Grierson was at his best, even joking with dour Hermann Wetzel: 'Your boys over in Prussia are going to conquer all Europe one of these days,' to which Wetzel replied: 'They will certainly conquer France.'

That night Reed could not sleep, and when his wife heard his restless turning she asked why, and he said: 'My mother was an educated woman, you know, and she made us memorize poetry. She taught us that the finest single line comes at the end of Milton's sonnet to his dead wife.'

'I don't know that,' Louise said in the darkness.

'The first thirteen lines tell of how the blind poet dreams that she has come back from the grave to speak with him. "Love, sweetness, goodness in her person shined," that was my mother, too. But then came the fourteenth line, and everything fell apart. Mother said its ten short words were arrows pointed at the heart, showing what blindness meant: "I waked, she fled, and day brought back my night." '

They lay in the darkness for some time, and then the general sighed deeply, making the anguish of his thoughts echo through the room: 'Tonight I was a general once more. Tomorrow the bugles will sound, dawn will break, and I shall be a captain again . . . and forever.'

The second investigating team was completely different. Lieutenant General Philip Sheridan, a marvelously con-centrated Irishman with a bullet head and drooping walrus mustaches – a sort of roundish, ineffectual-looking man until one discovered that every bulge was muscle – rode into the fort with three of his pet colonels, men, he said, of infinite promise. Most powerful was Ranald Mackenzie, a man so intense, said his troops, that 'his eyes could cut rocks'; he was destined to leapfrog his contemporaries and stand at the threshold of commander-in-chief, until his mind snapped, destroyed by syphilis and by the burdens he had placed upon it.

There was Nelson Miles, not a West Point man but something much better: the nephew-by-marriage of both General William Tecumseh Sherman, head of the Army, and Senator John Sherman, the powerful political leader from Ohio; he was an unproved quantity at the threshold of his career, but with his uncles' help he would gain constant promotion, a vain, arrogant, impossible man with only one credit to his name: he was a phenomenally brave officer when leading men into battle.

Most impressive, to men and women alike, was Lieutenant Colonel George Armstrong Custer, nearly six feet tall, never weighing more than a hundred and seventy, and of such elegant bearing that he commanded attention wherever he went. Like the other two, he was thirty-four, but he was totally unlike them in other respects: they wore ordinary military uniforms, well-pressed and tended; he wore custom-tailored trousers and jacket, spats over his General Quimper boots, and a remarkable Russian-type greatcoat cut from a heavy French cloth and with a monstrous cape adorned with Afghanistan caracul fur at the neck, along the front and at the cuffs. His face was cadaverously thin, with romantic hollows under his cheekbones, and he was obviously worried about the gradual retreat of his hair, for like many vain men he twisted and trained it to lie across his forehead and hide the loss. At the neck he wore his hair very long, and since it was naturally wavy, enhanced by his wife's constant attention with hot irons, it added considerably to his appeal. Like most officers of that period, he wore a mustache which he kept so carefully trimmed that it added dignity to a face already as compelling as that of any Roman emperor's.

They were, as both Sherman and Sheridan agreed, three remarkable young colonels, and it was inevitable that one of them would gain supreme command. Mackenzie, perhaps the ablest of the three, would be disqualified because of creeping insanity; Custer would perish because of his inexcusable arrogance at the Little Big Horn; Miles, the political conniver, would prevail. In the military, as in all human endeavour, it can sometimes be the man who merely survives who triumphs, whether his skills warrant it or not.

Sheridan and his three aces needed little time to assess the situation at Fort Garner: 'Second rate in every respect. When a wife misbehaves like Nellie Minor, she should be soldiered out within the day. When an important supply train approaches, it should be protected by more than an untested second lieutenant. And when an Indian marauder like Matark ravages a countryside, he should be caught and hanged. Captain Reed is moderately acceptable, but the only officer present who seems to have an understanding of what a frontier fort should be is Captain Hermann Wetzel, who is hereby commended for his attention to detail.'

No formal rebuke was leveled against Captain Reed, but a kind of sorrow suffused the visit, as if the young colonels regretted that he was not a better man. Colonel Custer went out of his way to applaud Mrs Reed's handling of the Johnny Minor affair, and he spellbound the other wives with his graciousness and warmth of understanding.

When Sheridan led his army away, the fort continued under the aura of the three colonels and there was much discussion as to which one would triumph in the battle for promotion. Wetzel summarized opinions: 'Miles is political, but very strong in the field, a powerful combination. Custer can achieve anything if he attends to details. Mackenzie's the one I'd like to lead me into battle.' The women did not bother with the credentials of the other two colonels: 'Custer is magnificent.' And he was, for he was considerate, charming, persistent, and suffused with that glamor which can only be called *romantic*. Even their husbands could not denigrate him when their wives applauded, for he was unquestionably the most dramatic leader ever to have visited Fort Garner, and his heavy felt spats and fur-trimmed greatcoat would long be remembered.

The fort received a shock when Lewis Renfro arrived with his alert wife, Daisy, for the traditional desk-hog was apt to be an obese, slovenly fellow with little military bearing. Renfro was quite the opposite, a thirty-six-year-old West Point man from a good family in Ohio, tall, erect, ten pounds underweight from daily horsemanship in the parks of Washington, and a man determined to give a good account of himself on the frontier. He would take Minor's place as head of Company S, 10th Cavalry, under the command of Captain Reed, to whom he said unctuously: 'I want you to rely on me as one of the best officers you've ever had. When you give me an order, consider it executed.'

Fawningly eager to create a good impression, he sought out Captain Wetzel and assured him: 'I'll not permit any ridiculous cavalry-infantry unpleasantness, while I command the Buffalo Soldiers. They'll be disciplined.' But that same day he implied quite the opposite to Jaxifer, to whom he told an outright lie concerning his experiences in the war: 'I served with Negro troops on three different occasions. None better. If the infantry give you any trouble, you'll find me on your side all the way.' But despite this trickery in fort politics, whenever an expedition against the Indians was organized he wanted to be in the lead, and from that position he gave a good account of himself.

'He knows how to fight,' Sergeant Jaxifer told his troopers. 'We got a good man this time.'

This was a sensible estimation, because when an energetic foray led by Renfro ran into outriders of the main Comanche force, a bitter running battle ensued, forty Indians on mounts of superior speed against nineteen cavalrymen with superior fire power. Neither side could claim a victory, but Renfro pursued the Indians with such vigor that any Comanche whose horse faltered even slightly was overtaken and shot. Renfro was always in the lead, probably the best single horseman on the field that day, and when the chase was over, the black soldiers were satisfied that they had gained a proficient leader.

In a second foray, when Reed was in command, Renfro accepted his subordinate position graciously and moved his contingent instantly when Reed signaled. He was a good officer, and Reed told Wetzel: 'Had he stayed out here with us instead of hiding in Washington, he could have been one of Sherman's Young Colonels,' and the German agreed that Renfro was first class. 'I think his name must be German,' Wetzel said. 'He carries himself so well.'

But Lewis Renfro had no intention of laboring on the frontier to establish his reputation as the fourth of the Young Colonels. He would perform impeccably with the troops, but he would also pull every string to get back to his desk job in Washington. By-passing established channels, he and his wife bombarded everyone in real command with clever petitions, and were assured: 'As soon as anything interesting happens, back you'll come.' What the incident might be the Renfros could not guess, but their hammering at the doors of preferment became so well known that Mrs Reed felt she had to caution Daisy against her excesses, and in the room where so many had been quietly reprimanded by the general's wife, Daisy now took her place, but she proved to be quite different from her predecessors.

'Do you not see that your actions may be prejudicing your husband's chances?' Louise Reed asked.

'I am improving them. Lewis was born to serve in Washington, and I shall do my best to see that he does so.'

'But he is so capable at the front. He could be one of the great leaders.'

'He's already one of the great leaders, Mrs Reed. He fights in Washington with a skill that not even Sherman and Sheridan could exhibit.'

'But the real fighting is out here, against the Indians.'

'Half of it is,' Daisy replied. 'And I do believe that the more important half, in peacetime, is back with us, fighting the battles in Congress.'

'But look at this fort, Mrs Renfro. Does not the building of an establishment like this mean anything to you? When my husband came here . . . not a post erected, not a wall in place. He built a mud fort, and when the dead-house is finished, it will all be stone. A permanent testimony to the brave men who occupied it.'

Mrs Renfro had to laugh: 'One act of Congress and this fort vanishes. Back to the mesquite. It's in Congress where the peacetime army fights its battles, and Lewis is going back to work with Congress, where he can do some good.'

Mrs Reed had to be blunt: 'Mrs Renfro, you certainly must be aware that your husband's report will be written by my husband. Why are you so daring in disregarding my counsel?'

'I do not disregard it, and I'm sure Lewis doesn't disregard your husband's. What can Captain Reed possibly report except that Lewis was foremost in battle, striking in his courage and immediately responsive to orders?'

'Yes, yes.'

'We both try to be like that. Haven't you seen that if you even hint at an instruction, I comply?'

'But I am now more than hinting that you should stop these letters.'

Now it was Daisy's turn to be obdurate: 'That's quite a different matter, dealing with the welfare of the entire army, not with a single fort. Lewis can aid immensely in getting our army the funds it needs, the support it requires. Of course I shall continue to help him get the post he deserves.'

The interview ended poorly, with battle lines drawn and animosities flaring, but the impasse did not continue long, because the kind of incident which the Renfro adherents in Washington needed to bring their man back home occurred, with an incandescent explosion that not even the most stalwart Renfro supporter could have anticipated.

During the hottest part of the summer of 1874, Renfro, Jaxifer and all the effectives of Company S, forty-seven in number, set forth on the supposed trail of Chief Matark, whose braves had spent that summer ravaging the ranches along the frontier. The Texas government had warned settlers not to venture too far west, and the United States government had explained that protection even from forts like Richardson and Garner could not ensure safety, but the insatiable hunger for land which would always characterize Texans lured the adventurers farther and farther west. Just as the four Larkin brothers had dared the empty plains, claiming their six thousand acres and holding them nicely until the Comanche struck, so now other daring men and women staked out their claims beyond the forts, and during this summer alone, sixty white men, women and children had been slain, usually in a manner so brutal and horrifying as to shock even those Texans who had become accustomed to the barbarisms.

After the annihilation of four ranch families well to the south and west of Fort Garner, Renfro sought permission to make a major sortie, and with innate cleverness he did not ride directly south to where the crimes had occurred, but in a contrary direction, far to the west toward the Palo Duro Canyon and the extreme limits of the Indian Territory, for he reasoned that the triumphant Indians would have sped away from the burning ranches, then taken their time to head for sanctuary.

He was right. He and his men attacked the celebrating Comanche from the north, sweeping down on them in a sudden shattering attack, and because newspapers throughout the nation gave much space to what happened next, it is essential that the exact details be understood.

With Renfro in the lead, the 10th Cavalry launched a major attack, and according to plan, at the height of battle half the troops swung west under Renfro, half to the east under Jaxifer. Renfro and his men performed with signal valor, everyone testified to that, and by tremendous exertion turned the flank of the advancing Comanche, throwing the rest of the Indians into confusion.

When this occurred, Sergeant Jaxifer on the east saw a chance to sweep in and disrupt the Comanche completely, and he did this, but as his men galloped through the Indian ranks he caught sight of what he believed to be a white girl, and the idea flashed through his mind: That must be the Larkin child. Reacting more to instinct than to conscious plan, he wheeled his horse and pursued that group of Indians who held the child. Alone and threatened by dozens of braves, he plunged on, overtook the fleeing Indians, reached out, and miraculously snatched the child from her captors, clubbing with his gun the head of the brave who had been holding her.

Turning once more, he broke through the confused Indians to a point where his astonished black troops could give him coverage, and for some moments a violent struggle ensued, but with the child in his arms, Jaxifer rallied his men until they prevailed. At this moment Renfro galloped up, saw the child, and perceived at once her magical significance. Taking her gently from the sergeant, he held her close and asked: 'You are Emma Larkin?' and she replied, with full knowledge of what her words meant: 'I am.'

Thus the legend was born. Lewis Renfro, in an attack upon the savage Comanche when his men were outnumbered a hundred to forty-nine, had recovered the white child Emma Larkin, whose family had been murdered at Bear Creek in 1869 and who had been captive of the savages for five long years. Stories were written in such a way as to indicate that Renfro's feat was the more astonishing in that he was supported by only Negro troops, whose effectiveness in such warfare was not proved. Apparently it was his heroic persistence that had made the rescue possible.

The story proved wildly popular, with *Harper's* and the New York newspapers sending artists to Texas to depict the battle and the manner of Emma's rescue. Pictures proliferated, but they all faced two difficulties: it was not practical to depict black troops at the scene, so faces were blurred, except for Lieutenant Renfro's, and the fact that little Emma had no nose or ears meant that she could not be depicted either, which meant that Renfro pretty well stole the show. In fact, on two occasions when the press were permitted to see Emma, some of the men vomited, and quite a few of their stories said merely that she had been 'poorly treated by her captors,' and even those two or three reporters who did mention the mutilations did not speak of the rapes. Americans then, as later, wanted their stories heroic but also respectful of the niceties.

More than two dozen detailed interviews spelled out Renfro's heroism and audacity; no one questioned Jaxifer. At one point Emma told a woman reporter the facts, but when this woman searched out Jaxifer, she was frightened by his bigness, his lack of a neck and his thick lips, so his part in the rescue was ignored.

This was the incident that Daisy Renfro needed to get her man back to Washington, and she orchestrated the affair skilfully. She sought a congratulatory telegram from Colonel Custer, and tender stories from other Texas settlers who said they wished that Lieutenant Renfro would rescue their lost children from Matark. Before the month was out, Washington was clamoring for its newest hero to return, and when Daisy and Lewis left Fort Garner they took care to ensure that both Captain and Mrs Reed received credit for the fine manner in which the fort had been administered. Said Renfro to the press: 'You cannot have brave soldiers at a lonely frontier unless you have a fine commander in charge of them. Than Captain Reed there can be no finer.'

When the train pulled out of the station at New Orleans, he told his wife: 'We'll never see Texas again. What a desolate land.'

Emma Larkin, a twelve-year-old captive of the Comanche, had been a kind of holy grail of the plains, with all decent men striving to rescue her, a challenge that would not dissipate even with the passage of years; but Emma Larkin, a seventeen-year-old young woman aged beyond her years, was an embarrassment, and after the first flush of her victorious recapture, no one knew what to do with her.

The women at the fort, of course, had rejoiced at her return, but quickly they realized that there was no place for her in their lives; nor anywhere else, for that matter. For one thing, she had no family, all of her immediate relatives having been exterminated at Bear Creek and possible ones back east having been lost in the normal experiences of immigration. But more important, she was hideously ugly, a frail, stringy girl with almost no bosom and those terrible scars where her ears and nose should have been. Furthermore, she had formed the habit of speaking in a whisper, so that she often seemed like a ghost wandering in from another world. And after a few days of compassion, no one wanted to have her around.

Mrs Reed did take it upon herself to represent the girl's interests in the land court at Jacksborough, for it was clear that

984

Emma must have inherited all the lands once owned by her father and her uncles; rapacious men had tried to obtain squatter's rights on the six thousand acres when no surviving Larkins stepped forward to claim them, but it was apparent that if poor Emma had experienced such tortures, the least society could do was return her patrimony. As always when Texas land was involved, the fight became vicious, and Mrs Reed was advised to withdraw lest she endanger the good community relationship with the fort, and she would have done so had she not obtained unintended support from Earnshaw Rusk, up at Camp Hope.

Rusk now had Matark's fleeing Comanche living peacefully on his grounds, and they had many complaints against Captain Reed and his soldiers: 'This man Renfro, he attacked us when we were hunting buffalo. We were doing nothing but hunting, and his Buffalo Soldiers charged upon us and killed our braves. He also stole one of our women.'

This latter charge, delivered with much excitement and waving of arms, electrified Rusk, for it represented exactly the kind of army behavior that he was determined to stamp out, so on a clear day at the end of summer, 1874, he and two of his Comanche assistants rode the fifty-eight miles south to Fort Garner to lodge an official protest, but before departing he thought it prudent to inform his superiors in the Interior Department of what he was about, lest contrary reports filter in from the fort:

At last I have a fool-proof case against the Army at Fort Garner, and I intend to pursue it vigorously. In August of this year, when my Comanche under the peaceful guidance of Chief Matark, about whom I have written before, were trailing buffalo, they did, I must admit, stray into Texas territory. But they were behaving like the good citizens I have taught them to be when they were fallen upon by Col Renfro and a horde of his cavalrymen. Several braves were slain, and an Indian woman was taken from them.

I hold this to be a gross infraction of the rules which govern this area and I shall go personally to Fort Garner to seek redress for my Indians. I am leaving Camp Hope in the hands of Chief Matark during my absence, which ought not to be prolonged, but I assure thee that I shall speak harshly to the Army.

When the righteous Quaker appeared at Fort Garner, Wetzel wanted to arrest the two Comanche braves, but Rusk made such a howl that Reed had to promise safe passage, as the Peace Policy required. The discussions continued as before, with Rusk insisting upon the peaceful intentions of his Indians, and Reed enumerating the hideous roster of Texas ranches burned and Texas ranchers slain. None of these charges, which seemed so specific to the army men, would Rusk accept as proof of Comanche guilt; instead, he launched vigorous protest against army brutality, and there the debate hung suspended, with each man accusing the other of duplicity and moral blindness.

'Can't you see, Rusk, that your beloved Indians are a gang of murderers who should be shot?'

'Can't thee see, Captain Reed, that thy men are a gang of undisciplined bullies who love to harass my Indians?'

'What about the murders at the seventeen ranches I've listed?'

'What about your men kidnaping one of my Indian women?'

Reed stopped and gaped at the Quaker: 'You don't know who that woman was?'

'Then thee admits the kidnaping?'

Reed almost laughed: 'Everyone in the world knows who she is, but you live a few miles to the north, and you haven't heard? Rusk, are you truly innocent, or are you stupid?'

'I expect to be abused at your hands, but I also expect –'

'Louise!' Reed shouted. 'Ask Bertha Wetzel to bring the girl here.' As might have been expected, Mrs Wetzel, the practical frontier woman, had given the unwanted child a temporary home, and now she grasped Emma's hand and brought her to the commander's office.

Mrs Wetzel entered the room first, with the girl lagging behind, so that Rusk could not see who was coming, but when the pair were well inside, Mrs Wetzel stepped aside and Emma Larkin stood revealed. With the ability she had acquired to suffer anything, she kept her chin high and looked right at Earnshaw Rusk, and when he saw her he gasped. Trying to speak, he could not, and for a long moment these two stared at each other – the near-crazed child of torture and the near-godlike believer in the goodness of man. When the moment passed, Rusk stepped boldly to the girl and put his arms about her: 'Jesus Christ has thee in His heart.' He tried to say more, but he could not, and after a moment most embarrassing to Reed, Mrs Wetzel and even the girl, he bowed his head and quiet tears welled in his eyes.

He was so shaken that he had to sit down, and as he huddled there, his world falling apart, Reed said with less severity than he had intended: 'This is Emma Larkin. Sole survivor of Bear Creek. Prisoner of your Comanche for five years.'

Slowly Rusk regained his feet, staring in anguish first at Reed, then at Mrs Wetzel: 'Is this truly the Larkin child?'

'It is,' Reed said, 'and I want you to hear her story, every word of it, without my presence or Mrs Wetzel's. Come, Bertha,' and he led her away.

'Sit down with me,' Rusk said when they were gone, and in the stonewalled office built with such care under the supervision of Mrs Reed, began the conversation which would change so much along the Red River.

EARNSHAW: Is thee really Emma Larkin?

EMMA (*in her soft whisper*): I am. I remember my family, all fifteen. Do you want me to name them?

EARNSHAW: And thee was present at Bear Creek?

EMMA: This is Bear Creek. This is where it happened. My father and my brothers were killed in our house not far from here.

EARNSHAW: And thee is sure Indians did it?

EMMA: They took me captive, didn't they?

EARNSHAW: But was it Matark?

EMMA: I have lived with Matark for four summers. Matark's sons . . .

EARNSHAW: Thy ears?

EMMA: His sons burned them off, slowly, night after night.

EARNSHAW: That I cannot believe.

EMMA: Look at them.

EARNSHAW: Thy nose?

EMMA: They would take embers from the fire, and dance

987

around me, and then jab the embers against my nose. And when the scab formed . . .

EARNSHAW: Please. (*Fearing for a moment that he was going to be sick, he changed the subject.*) Did they beat thee?

EMMA: Especially the women.

EARNSHAW: The men?

EMMA: They came at night. To sleep with me. (*Such a statement embarrassed Rusk so profoundly that once more he stopped the conversation. He had never kissed a woman and deemed their behavior a great mystery.*)

EARNSHAW: Thee mustn't speak of such things. Thee must forget them.

EMMA: I've tried to. It's you who asked the questions.

EARNSHAW: Did no one ever treat thee kindly?

EMMA (*after a prolonged reflection*): No one. But there was a white man with a lame left arm. They called him Little Brother, because he sold them guns. I think his name was Peavine.

EARNSHAW: He was with them?

EMMA: Often. They told him what they needed and he went back and stole it.

EARNSHAW: Did thee ever hear them call him Rattlesnake?

EMMA: No, but things were always better for me when he came, because he brought guns and other things and for a while they forgot me. (*She weighed her next comment carefully.*) He always took me aside and promised that one day I would be set free. I dreamed about that day, but it never happened.

EARNSHAW: This man? Thee is sure he had a weak left arm?

EMMA: They also called him Little Cripple. (*Since both spoke Comanche, she could report precisely what the Indians had called their Comanchero.*) He never beat me or abused me. One time Chief Matark said, and I heard him say it: "You can sleep with the thing if you wish," but Peavine said: "I do not wish," and that night I was left alone.

EARNSHAW: Did thee ever ride with the Comanche when they came down into Texas?

EMMA: Many times.

EARNSHAW: And did thy Indians burn ranches in Texas?

EMMA: Like here at Bear Creek. Many times.

EARNSHAW: But that was long ago, I'm sure.

EMMA: It was one moon ago, when the black soldiers captured me.

EARNSHAW: Thee was hunting buffalo that time. I know thee was hunting buffalo.

EMMA: We had all the buffalo we needed, north of the river. We came into Texas to burn and kill.

EARNSHAW (*weakly*): Thee means . . . the Comanche planned it that way? Strike south, then run back north?

EMMA: Why not? Those were the rules. You made them, we obeyed them. (*She spoke these sentences in Comanche, which gave them a lilting, arrogant echo which cut so deeply at Rusk's integrity that he shuddered.*)

EARNSHAW: What will they do now?

EMMA: I know nothing. (*She said this with such simplicity, such willingness to throw herself upon the mercy of God, that he was awed.*)

EARNSHAW: Surely thee has friends. Thee must have family.

EMMA: I have no one. I am not like others.

EARNSHAW: Thee can wear thy hair about thy ears, and no one will see.

EMMA: But this?

EARNSHAW: And thee can make thyself a nose. I'm not sure how right now, but I know it can be done. (*He spoke with great force.*) We will make thee a nose. We will make thee friends.

EMMA: Who would want me as a friend? You know I had a baby?

EARNSHAW: Good God! (*He stalked about the room.*) Good God, thee hasn't told anyone, has thee?

EMMA: Nobody asked.

EARNSHAW: Thee had a child?

EMMA: My moon period came. Like the others, I had a child.

EARNSHAW (*totally disoriented*): Thee must not speak of this, not to anyone. (*Then, overcoming his embarrassment, he regained courage.*) Thee means . . . the Indian men? They?

EMMA: I told you they came to my bed at night. One after another. (*At this appalling news, which he had not fully comprehended before, Rusk drew away from the girl, a fact which she noticed and accepted.*) I'm sorry I told you, Mr Rusk.

EARNSHAW: Thee knows my name?

EMMA: We all knew your name. The-Man-Who-Lets-Us-Do-Anything they called you.

EARNSHAW: Why did I never see thee at Camp Hope?

EMMA: They never brought us captives . . .

EARNSHAW: There are others?

EMMA: Each tribe has many. They trade us back and forth.

EARNSHAW: Always children? Always little girls?

EMMA: The men they kill, always. Grown women they keep alive for a while, use them, kill them. The boys they train as young braves. They become Indians. The girls they use, like me.

EARNSHAW: Oh, my God. What have I done?

EMMA: My child was a boy. I do not want him.

EARNSHAW: But if he's thy child?

EMMA: I did not want him then. I do not want him now. I want to forget them all.

EARNSHAW: Does thee know what prayer is?

EMMA: We prayed here at Bear Creek. I prayed that I'd be rescued some day.

EARNSHAW: Will thee pray with me now? (*She dropped to her knees, but Rusk caught her by the arm, the first time he had touched her, and brought her upright.*) I am a Quaker, and we do not feel the necessity of kneeling. We speak to God direct.

So the two casualties of the frontier prayed that God would give bewildered Earnshaw Rusk guidance to rectify the errors he had fostered, and that assistance would be provided Emma Larkin in the fearsome decisions she must make. He ended the prayer with the hope that Emma would find in her heart renewed love for her baby boy, but when the prayer ended, she told him bluntly: 'The child is gone. It is all gone.'

When he returned to Camp Hope, Earnshaw Rusk assembled his Comanche and berated them as never before: 'Thee has lied to me. Thee has crossed the Red River not in the chase of buffalo but to burn and kill. And thee keeps hidden from me other children like Emma Larkin. And such behavior must stop.'

Matark said boldly: 'We will go where we wish. And we will give them the children when they offer enough money.'

'Thee hides the man called Rattlesnake Peavine in thy ranks, and he is wanted for many murders.'

'He is our friend. We will always protect him from the army.'

Astonished by the boldness of the Comanche, Rusk pleaded with them to make an honest peace with the army and refrain from any further raids into Texas: 'Noble Chief Matark, I promise thee that even now it is not too late. If thee and I ride to Fort Garner and enter into solemn promises ...'

'No Indian can trust their promises. They kill our buffalo. They ravage our camps.'

'Up to now, yes. It's been warfare. But warfare always ends, and peace brings consolations.' He was speaking in Comanche, most eloquently, depicting the longed-for solution to the Indian problem, and tears came to his eyes as he pleaded: 'Great Chief Matark, the grandest thing you could give your people, the gift that would make your name sing across the plains ... Peace. A final agreement to stay north of the Red River. An agreement to live a new life here on the vast reservations the Great White Father has promised thee.'

'They are big now,' Matark said with exceptional insight, 'but they will become very small when your people want them back.'

'If we ride south,' Rusk said, imploringly, 'even now we can arrange a peace in which all past raids will be forgiven. Thee will return the stolen children, and thee will live here happily with me.'

'We cannot trust you.'

'Please, please!' the Quaker pleaded. 'Listen to reason. For the love of God and the safety of thy own children, ride with me and let us make peace.'

Matark's response was hideous. Enlisting more than a hundred chanting braves, he led them deep into Texas, where they burned six isolated ranches, killing the men with customary tortures and running off with seven additional children. After they crept back to sanctuary at Camp Hope, he actually boasted in the presence of the agent: 'We taught the Texans a lesson,' and with insulting belligerence he refused to surrender the children, asking Rusk: 'And what are you going to do about it?'

Now a bizarre chain of frontier incidents occurred. To the astonishment of Captain Reed at Fort Garner, Earnshaw Rusk rode south unattended and humiliated himself in the stone-walled headquarters. 'I was deluded. I was lied to. Chief Matark is a dreadful killer who keeps numerous white children in his camps. My way was wrong. I ask thee, Captain Reed, to send thy troops into the Indian Territory and arrest this brutal man.'

'Is this a formal request, Agent Rusk?'

'It is.'

'You know that your superiors at Fort Sill and Washington . . .'

'I know they will be disgusted with me, going against our agreement. But even for a Quaker the time comes when crime must be punished.'

'I will have to have this in writing, Mr Rusk.'

'And thee shall.' Sitting at the general's desk, he penned a formal request for United States troops to invade Camp Hope in the Indian Territory, and there to arrest Chief Matark of the Comanche for crimes innumerable. When he signed this document, which negated a lifetime of religious training and abrogated his promises to President Grant, his hands trembled. But it was done, and then he surprised the soldiers by asking if he could see the girl Emma Larkin, for he had brought her something.

More or less in hiding, she was still living with the Wetzels, who were beginning to see in her a sensitive human being with the merits of courage, forthrightness and a surprising sense of humor as she went about the housework which the German family assigned her. When Mrs Wetzel brought her before Agent Rusk she noticed that the girl actually seemed happy to see him, and he said: 'No, Mrs Wetzel, thee must stay. I need thy help.'

He took from his pocket a carefully carved wooden nose to which were attached two lengths of braided horsehair, and with Emma standing by a window, he placed the nose in the middle of her face and asked Mrs Wetzel to hold it firm while he tied the horsehair braids behind the back of Emma's head.

'Oh!' Mrs Wetzel cried with real joy. 'Now you have a nose!' And she hurried for her mirror, and when the girl saw the transformation that had occurred, she could only look first at Rusk, then at Mrs Wetzel and then back at the mirror. Finally she put the mirror down and took Mrs Wetzel's hands, which she kissed. Then she did the same with Rusk, but as soon as she had done this she grabbed the mirror again and studied herself, and as she did so, Rusk reached out and pulled strands of her hair across the stumps of her ears, and when she saw herself whole again she did not burst into tears of gratitude. She jumped straight up in the air and gave a startling Comanche yell: 'I am Emma Larkin. I am Emma Larkin.'

But she was not allowed to keep her nose, because Mrs Wetzel took it from her and left the room; when she returned she had replaced the horsehair braid with an almost invisible white thread, and now when Emma looked in the mirror that Mrs Wetzel held for her, neither she nor anyone else could detect that it was the thread which held the wooden nose in place, and seeing this perfection and realizing what it meant – an invitation back into life – she wept.

The men at Fort Garner lost little time in mounting a massive attack on Camp Hope, and although other Quaker commissioners at posts in the Indian Territory tried to halt this breach of the Peace Policy, officers waved Agent Rusk's written request at them and plunged ahead. In a series of daring moves they caught Matark and three of his principal supporters. They also captured nine white children, whose stories inflamed the frontier so much that the court in Jacksborough sentenced Matark and his men to hanging.

However, the Quakers were not powerless, and they stormed into federal courts, getting not only injunctions against the hanging but also an agreement whereby Matark and his men would be assigned temporarily to a low-security Texas prison. They were there only a few months when another court set them free, on the theory that they had learned their lesson and would henceforth be reliable citizens. A month after their return to Camp Hope they broke loose and raided savagely along the Texas frontier, burning and torturing as before.

The response from Washington was swift. Gentle-hearted Benjamin Grierson would remain at regimental headquarters in Fort Sill to make way for a real fighting man, Ranald Mackenzie, who was brought in to lead one of five converging columns which would bear down on any Indians found outside their reservations. They would come at Matark and his killers from Texas, New Mexico, Arkansas and the Indian Territory, with Colonel Nelson Miles leading the force opposite to Mackenzie's. These two fiery colonels would form the jaws of a nutcracker in which the enemy would be caught.

When grim-lipped Mackenzie set out after Matark, Reed insisted on leading the three-company detachment from Fort Garner, with Wetzel left behind to defend the place with one company of infantry. As bad luck would have it, the Garner contingent found itself facing the most difficult part of the terrain, that series of smaller canyons which protected Palo Duro on the south, and Jaxifer told his men: 'Seem like we march one mile down into the canyon, then one mile back up to make half a mile forward.' Mackenzie, observing the brutal terrain the Buffalo Soldiers were struggling with, commended them: 'You men are fighting your battle before the battle begins.' Nevertheless he told Jaxifer: 'Hurry them up.'

The excessive heat was a more serious matter, for this was early September when the plains of Texas blazed their hottest; many a newcomer to the state moaned during his first August: 'Well, at least September will soon be here.' But he was remembering September in New Hampshire or New York; when that Texas September struck he shuddered.

In 1874, September was exceptionally hot, with the entire surface of the Panhandle becoming a mirage, dancing insultingly along the horizons. Mesquite trees huddled, scorched by the sun, drawing into their limitless roots what little water they found deep down, and even jackrabbits hid in their burrows. Rattlesnakes appeared briefly, then had to seek shade to protect their body temperature, and those few buffalo that had survived the onslaught of commercial teams wandered aimlessly among the bleached skeletons of their brothers.

It was a huge concentration of Indians that huddled in the various canyons of Palo Duro as a last defense against the approaching army: Kicking Bird and his thousand Kiowa; White Antelope and his many Cheyenne; Matark and his nine hundred Comanche. They did not fight as a combined army; Indian custom would never permit that kind of effective coalition, but they did support one another, and to rout them out of their protective furrows was going to be difficult.

On came the five columns, with Miles and Mackenzie always

supplying the pressure, but as they approached Palo Duro the ordeals of a Texas September began to take a heavy toll, and as water supplies diminished, the men learned the agony of thirst.

When Reed's 10th Cavalry ran completely out of anything to drink, Jaxifer, acting on his own, ordered one of his men to kill a horse so that his troops could at least wet their lips with its blood, and after Reed's infantry, lagging far behind, suffered for two days of staggering thirst, he ordered his men to take their knives and open veins in their arms so that their own blood could sustain them. When some demurred, he showed them how by cutting into his own arm, then offering it to two soldiers while he pumped his fist to make the blood spurt. One of the men fainted.

Texas weather, particularly on the plains, could provide wild variations, and in mid-September, at the height of the heat and the drought, a blue norther swept in, and during one daylight period the thermometer dropped from ninety-nine degrees to thirty-nine. For two days the freezing wind blew, threatening the lives of men who had been sweating their health away, and on the third day torrential rains engulfed the entire area. Now the war became a chase through mud, with the sturdier, slower horses of the cavalry having an advantage.

From all sides the blue-clads began to compress the thousands of Indians, and although the latter, under the expert guidance of chiefs like Matark, succeeded in avoiding pitched battles, they could not escape the punishing effect of the swift cavalry raids, the burning of lodges and the destruction of crops. Their most serious defeat came on a day when they lost only four braves: in drenching rain Mackenzie and Reed found a defile on the face of the canyon wall and with great daring led their cavalry down that steep and almost impassable route. When they reached the canyon floor they found a concentration of Chief Mamanti's Kiowa, Ohamatai's stubborn Comanche and Iron Shirt's Cheyenne. Thundering through the Indian camps, they scattered the enemy and burned all their lodges, but with even more devastating effect, they captured their entire herd of horses and mules, 1,424 in number.

With practiced eye, Mackenzie rode through the animals, selecting about 370 of the best, then gave Reed an extraordinary command: 'Kill the rest.' When Reed relayed this to Jaxifer, the big black man who loved horses and who tended his own as if they were his children, demurred, but Reed said: 'It's an order!' and the black troops carried it out while from a distance the captured Indian chiefs looked on in horror.

Never did Mackenzie's troops, or any from the other four columns, engage the Indians in a pitched battle, but the despair they spread through the Indian camps, with their incessant burning of villages and routing of camps and slaughter of horses, convinced the enemy that sustained resistance was going to be impossible, and it was a Kiowa chief named Woman's Heart who made the first gesture. Assembling thirty-five of his principal braves he told them: 'We can no longer hold them off. Get your families.' The men supposed that they were about to make a gallant last stand. Instead, when the large group was assembled, he told them: 'We shall ride to Camp Hope.'

'To attack it? There'll be soldiers.'

'No. To surrender to the agent there. This day we start for the reservation that will be our home hereafter,' and while women wept and braves stared at the canyon walls which had for so many decades been their protection, Woman's Heart led his Kiowa away.

Soon Stone Calf and Bull Bear of the Cheyenne, accompanied by 820 of their warriors, straggled in to the reservations, as did White Horse and 200 of his Comanche, and Kicking Bird and Lone Wolf with almost 500 of their Kiowa. What gunfire had been unable to accomplish was achieved by remorseless pressure and destruction. The backbone of Indian resistance had been broken by the irresistible courage of the young colonels, Miles and Mackenzie, and their men.

The last Comanche to operate on Texas soil was Chief Matark, and in those final days at the canyons he had with him an extraordinary ally, the old Comanchero Amos Peavine, for the Rattlesnake, always aware that in troubled times he stood a chance to make a dollar, had slipped through the army forces, moving in from New Mexico with three large wagonloads of guns stolen from the depots of Cavin & Clark. The word *stolen*, when so used, covered a horde of possibilities; after investigations were completed, it seemed likely that C&C personnel had *sold* the illegal weapons to Peavine; or, as another investigator suggested: 'The Rattlesnake stole not only the guns but also two C&C drivers who realized that by working with him, they could earn a good deal more than the company paid them.'

At any rate, Rattlesnake Peavine had come down the rocky trails of Palo Duro some two weeks ahead of the army, but once there, with his guns sold and his Mexican gold pieces safely stowed, he realized that this time the encircling force of blue-clads was so powerful, escape was unlikely. He therefore started to build a close friendship with four white girls, thirteen to sixteen, held by Matark's men, and he became extremely kind to them, giving them most of his food allotment and protecting them from the torments of the young braves.

After the first huge defections, Peavine strongly recommended that Matark and his remnant also surrender and find their home on the reservations north of the Red River, but the Comanche spoke for his men when he replied: 'I live on no reservation.'

But the time came when pressure from the north made it imperative that Matark find temporary refuge by moving south, and he did this with such skill that he evaded Colonel Mackenzie's men pressing north. This placed him south of Palo Duro, down where the Panhandle joins the rest of Texas, and here he roamed and pillaged.

The great Indian tribes had once covered the land called Texas, from the Gulf of Mexico to the mountains of the Far West, from the Red River in the north to the Rio Grande in the south, and now they were diminished to this handful of Comanche under Matark and a few Apache who would soon be driven into the arid wastes of Arizona. It would fall to Matark to make the last stand.

Scouts quickly informed Mackenzie that Matark was running wild to the south, so he dispatched Reed and the Fort Garner men to capture the raiders, and as winter approached a great chase developed across the northern plains. Matark and Peavine would strike an exposed ranch, and Reed and Jaxifer would pursue them. Matark would make a long swing to the west, and Reed would cannily move northwest to intercept him in that unexpected quarter, but Peavine would warn his Comanche that this might be Reed's strategy, so they would move off in the opposite direction.

But now the Indians were up against a man of both skill and endurance, and he led battle-hardened cavalry units. Slowly but remorselessly, Reed closed in on these raiding Indians, edging them always closer to the southern rim of Palo Duro, where Mackenzie's superior numbers would annihilate them.

The final battle that Reed envisaged did not occur, for a daring move by Jaxifer cut the Indian force in half, with disastrous consequences for the Comanche. Reed, suddenly aware that his portion of the force faced only a segment of Matark's men, made a frenzied attack at four in the morning, encircling Matark's camp, killing many of its inhabitants, and taking the great chief captive.

At the same time, Jaxifer invested the other half, and although many escaped his net, he did capture some three dozen, including Peavine and the four white girls he was protecting. With tears of joy, the Rattlesnake told his captors of how he had been a peaceful rancher in the vicinity of Fort Griffin and of how Matark's men, damn them, had overrun the place and taken his four granddaughters captive, and while the cavalrymen were celebrating and giving the girls attention, he made his quiet escape with three of their best horses.

When Reed learned that Jaxifer had also been successful, he dispatched a scout to inform Mackenzie of his unqualified success, including the rescue of the four white girls, but it was not till after the horsemen had ridden north that he began interrogating his black troops about the details of their splendid victory, and heard about the elderly white man who had delivered the girls.

'You mean,' he asked with a sick feeling, 'that the old man had a withered left arm?'

'Yes, he did.'

Knowing what his next answer would be, he asked the girls: 'Did the old man bring guns for the Indians?' and when they said that he had, but that he had also been extremely protective of them, he asked: 'Did the Indians call him Little Cripple?' and when they nodded, he jumped up and began kicking a saddle.

'Good God! Sergeant Jaxifer, you had Rattlesnake Peavine in your hands and you let him go!' And right there the Fort Garner detachment, all hundred of them, and the four girls entered into a compact: 'We need tell no one about Amos Peavine. Girls, he saved your lives, didn't he? So keep quiet about him. Men, do you want the rest of the army laughing at you? Say nothing.'

He himself did not feel obligated to report more than the bare facts: 'Sergeant Jaxifer and his well-disciplined detachment of Tenth Cavalry routed the other half of Matark's force, and in doing so, gallantly rescued four white girls who had been held prisoner by the Comanche.'

Matark was taken, as the Peace Policy required, to Camp Hope, where he was turned over to new Quakers who had replaced the unfortunate Earnshaw Rusk. He was then moved to a remote reservation in Florida, from which he launched a barrage of appeals. Two Quaker agents new to the frontier lodged a thoughtful appeal for clemency on the grounds that Chief Matark was at heart a well-intentioned man caught up in the tragedy of a war of extermination.

President Grant was touched by this reasoning, and remembering with what high hopes he had launched his Indian policy, told an aide: 'What does that fellow Rusk from Pennsylvania say about Matark?' and when Earnshaw was invited to make a report, he reflected on all he knew about Matark, and then he prayed. After two days of soul-searching he drafted this response:

I have known Matark for many years. He is a savage striving to find his way in a new civilization governed by new rules which he cannot comprehend. I believe I know every evil thing he has done, and I condemn him for his barbarities. But I assure thee, Mr President, that except for torture, which can never be forgiven, he has committed no act more reprehensible than what the United States Army committed against him and his people. His tragedy was that he was never offered the option of accepting a consistent Peace Policy offered in good faith by the American government, and to punish him now for fighting according to rules established by our side is deplorable.

I have searched my heart to determine what is justice in this affair, and I find I must beg thee to commute his sentence. He is, like thee, an honorable warrior. Allow him to

999

return to his people and to the lands he used to roam.

He was pardoned, with the stern admonition: 'If you ever set foot in Texas, you will be shot on sight,' to which he replied with humility: 'I no want Texas.'

Because the temptation to reinvade Texas might prove irresistible if he was lodged at Camp Hope, from where the traditional hunting grounds would be visible each dawn, he was moved to another section of the Indian Territory, and there a woman reporter for a Texas newspaper found him after peace had been established on the plains:

> Chief Matark can be considered, with much reason, one of the last Indians who warred in Texas. Of all the hundreds of thousands who terrorized our ranches, he was the last, and when I found him sitting peacefully beside an arroyo on his reservation, I asked him what his lasting memories were of our state, and he said: 'Texas, that was the best.'

Two weeks after this interview was published in the Texas papers, Matark quietly disappeared from the reservation, and the Quaker in charge of the area announced: 'He knew he was dying and went, as is the custom of his people, to some lonely spot where he could rejoin the Great Spirit.'

He had actually gone west across the border into New Mexico in response to a smuggled appeal from Amos Peavine, and there he had joined forces with his old comrade, robbing stagecoaches and caravans headed for California. Numerous agitated reports reached Sante Fe and Tucson of this murderous duo who appeared suddenly at the end of a road: 'There was this old man with a withered left arm, this big Indian who said nothing. They took everything.'

There were also reports, more ominous, of what happened when the travelers had tried to resist: 'The white man was so quick on the trigger, he shot two of our men before anyone knew what was happening.'

The depredations became so offensive that posses were organized both in New Mexico and Arizona, and on a blazingly hot August afternoon in the latter state, a gun battle erupted, and when it ended Chief Matark of the Comanche, not yet fifty years old, lay dead on the burning sand. What happened to Amos Peavine was less certain; said the coroner in reporting his inquest: 'He was last seen headed north, trailing blood. Considering the land into which he disappeared, he must be listed as dead.'

Now came one of the curiosities of Texas history. The Comanche threat having been contained, there was no further use for a frontier post like Fort Sam Garner, and so one day in October 1874, George Reed, who had built it out of mud back in 1869 and converted it to stone by 1871, received curt instructions from Lewis Renfro in Washington:

> Capt. George Reed, Co. T, 14th Infantry, Commanding Officer Fort Garner, Texas.
>
> You will proceed immediately to the abandonment of Fort Garner on Bear Creek, dismantling such buildings as can be torn down and returning the land to its civilian owners without any obligation on our part to restore its original condition or make compensation.

Obedient to the orders, Reed assembled his men and informed them that the two companies of the 10th Cavalry would be reassigned to Colonel Mackenzie at Fort Sill, while the two companies of the 14th Infantry under Captain Wetzel would remain at Fort Garner to decommission the post.

On a bright morning the two young officers who had replaced Johnny Minor – 'lost his left leg in the battle at Three Cairns' – and Jim Logan – 'dead from shooting at the tank' – flashed hand signals to John Jaxifer, who blew his whistle and headed his Negro cavalry back toward Jacksborough.

As Jaxifer left the parade ground for the last time, Wetzel stopped him to say, with grudging admiration: 'You were first class, Jaxifer. Your men? They're beginning to learn.' Jaxifer looked back to review his men: saddles polished, boots pipe-clayed, brass gleaming, faces smiling. He was proud of these dark men, for he knew that rarely had a military unit performed more bravely, more consistently, and with so little recognition.

When they vanished in dust, Wetzel's infantrymen began the

task of emptying the buildings, loading the wagons, and demolishing the few wooden structures. The stout stone buildings they did not touch, for these were now the property of an unusual owner who gave every intention of occupying them far into the future.

After careful investigation, Reed had satisfied himself that the legal arrangement which his wife had finally engineered in favor of Emma Larkin still prevailed: 'If I understand you, Judge, the land on which Fort Garner stands reverts to the Larkin girl.'

'It does, and she owns the six thousand other acres we awarded her.'

'Then by Texas law she gets all the buildings we erected?'

'She does. You know that in Texas, the federal government does not own public lands.'

In a quiet ceremony at the fort, which the judge attended, Reed turned the property over to Emma. 'You've been a brave woman. You've earned this land. Occupy it in honor.' He kissed her, as did Wetzel, but the judge whispered to Sanders: 'Small reward. The buildings are worth nothing. The land, maybe ten cents an acre.'

While the men were still dismantling the fort, a general of extraordinary charm sent notice that he intended visiting the fort with the next wagon train, and preparations were made in the diminished quarters to receive him properly. 'What can we do?' Mrs Reed protested. 'Things half packed. He'll think we're slovens.'

When the general arrived, a big, fleshy man with European manners, he put the wives at ease: 'My wife and I were warned that you were closing down. That's why we hurried.' And from his wagon he produced hampers of food, enough for all the troops.

He was General Yancey Quimper, sixty-two years old, hero not only of San Jacinto but now of Monterrey as well, and as always, a soldier whose first thought was for the welfare of his men: 'Feed the troops, Captain Reed, and while they feast let me explain why we've come so far to pay you honor.'

He personally broke open the hampers of beef and duck, arranging a separate table for the four black cavalrymen left behind as guards, and while they toasted him in beer from the two barrels he provided, he told the Reeds and Wetzels: 'This gracious lady who stands at my side is none other than the widow of Captain Sam Garner, for whom your fort was named. And those two fine men slicing the beef were Garner's sons. They're mine now, for I adopted them, and they bear the name of Quimper.' He said this grandiloquently, as if by taking away the honorable name of Garner and bestowing upon them the dubious one of Quimper, he had somehow conferred dignity.

'And that stalwart opening the beer keg is my birth-son James, who merits congratulations, for last week he became a father.'

Mrs Quimper, a gracious lady who said little, leaving explanations to her voluble husband, did slip in a word: 'The general thought it would be proper for us to pay our respects to the fort before it was abandoned,' and her husband broke in: 'I'll wager you've seen a lot of action here.' His lively hands imitated the thrust and parry of cavalry actions.

He made a favorable impression on Wetzel, who said at the conclusion of Quimper's explanation of how his troops had managed the two mountains at Monterrey: 'General, you have a better understanding of uphill attack than anyone I've met in America,' to which Quimper replied: 'It comes from study ... and experience.' He also explained how the Texas troops had managed to hold the lunette at Vicksburg, 'which was a very ugly show, I can tell you.'

Mrs Reed, who followed military conversations closely, realized that Quimper never claimed that he had actually been at either Monterrey or Vicksburg, and she was about to query this point when the general delighted everyone by announcing that he had brought a surprise for 'the commanding officer of our Garner fort,' and after a signal to one of his sons, a large package was brought in and delivered to Reed.

'Open it, sir!' Quimper cried. 'Open it so we can see!' And when Reed did, out came a pair of glistening military boots, fawn-colored and decorated with embossed eagles, swords and the word TEXAS in silver.

'They're genuine Quimpers,' Yancey said. 'Fightin' boots for fightin' men, and it's a privilege to deliver them to the commander of our fort.'

'But how did you get my size?'

'Ah-ha! Did you by chance miss a pair of your old army boots?'

Reed looked at his wife, who shrugged her shoulders. 'Don't stare at her,' Yancey bellowed. 'It was him,' and he pointed at Wetzel, who confessed that five months ago he had purloined the boots in order to make this happy occasion possible.

On the next day Quimper disclosed his purpose in coming so far: he asked to see the girl Emma Larkin, and when she was produced he spoke directly: 'I should like to purchase the land which the courts have awarded you.'

'The courts awarded me nothing,' Emma said, staring at him. 'I've always owned it. My parents patented it in 1869.'

'Yes, but since you were a minor and an orphan, the courts . . .'

'They gave me nothing,' she repeated, and it was obvious that Quimper was not going to have an easy time with this young woman.

'You have six thousand acres, mas o menos as we say in old Mexico, more or less.'

'Why would you wish to buy?'

'We have a saying: "If you acquire enough land in Texas, something good will surely happen." With the money I give you, you can live easily, in town somewhere.' He explained that he was prepared to offer ten cents an acre, slightly above the going rate: 'That would mean six hundred dollars, and you could do wonders with six hundred dollars.'

When she said no, he raised his bid to twelve cents, and when she still refused, he said: 'Because of the heroism of your family, twelve and a half cents. That's seven hundred fifty dollars, a princely sum for a young girl like you.' But as the evening closed, she was still refusing.

When she returned to the Wetzel quarters, the others argued with her, telling her that with $750 she could buy a good house in Jacksborough and learn to sew or help in other ways. It never occurred to them or her that she might one day marry, or even have children. She would always be a homeless waif, and they wished for her own good to see her settled: 'We'll be leaving in a few days, you know. You certainly can't live alone in a great empty fort like this, even if you do own it.' But she would not consent.

In the morning the Quimpers, the Wetzels and the Reeds combined to try to make her see the advisability of accepting the general's offer, but she rebuffed them: 'This is the land my father settled. My whole family paid a terrible price for it. I paid a terrible price. And I will not surrender it, not even if I have to live here with coyotes.'

Nothing could be said to dislodge her, and she was dismissed, as if she were seven instead of seventeen.

When she was gone, Reed asked Quimper if he would like to see the fort as it had functioned in its glory years, and when Yancey said with pomp: 'I would appreciate seeing how our fort operated,' off they went, taking the Quimper sons with them.

Mrs Reed and Mrs Wetzel were left to entertain Mrs Quimper, and this was a pleasing arrangement, for it gave the fort women a chance to clarify certain obscurities. Louise Reed started the questions: 'I wasn't aware that your husband had been at Monterrey, your present husband, that is.'

Bertha Wetzel broke in: 'Of course we knew about your first husband, a great hero. We had a pamphlet to educate the troops about the man for whom their fort was named.'

Mrs Quimper was eager to talk once more with military wives who understood the intricacies of a soldier's life: 'When General Quimper married me, and I was most gratified to find a man so gentle and helpful ... You've seen my first two sons. They were on their way to becoming little ruffians when he stepped in to make men of them. I'll be forever grateful.'

'You were saying that when you married ...' Mrs Reed rarely allowed a visitor to leave a thought unfinished.

'Looking back, I can now see that he was a big, formless man with no character. But when he married me he found himself with a ready-made character, my husband's. He began to dress like him, speak like him. He stood straighter, learned military talk. He took my sons and gave them his name. And soon he was talking incessantly about Sam Garner's exploits at Monterrey. But soon it was "*our* exploits," and before long, "*my* exploits." One night I heard him explain to a group of generals how *he* had charged the Bishop's Palace atop that Monterrey hill. He had also been very brave at Vicksburg. He adopted me, and my sons, and my dead husband's military career.' She held her palms up and smiled: 'So he is now both my first husband and my second.'

'But he did this from a solid foundation,' Mrs Reed suggested. 'San Jacinto and all.'

Mrs Quimper laughed: 'Right after the battle, my first husband told me about Quimper and his capture of Santa Anna. The poor Mexican was hiding in the bushes. His ragged clothing made Yancey think he was a mere peon, but they took him in and only later learned who he was.'

'With such behavior,' Mrs Wetzel asked, 'how did he become a general?'

'Very simply. One day he announced to the world: "I am a general," and Texas was so hungry for heroes, they allowed him to be a general.'

Mrs Reed poured Mrs Quimper a second cup of tea, then said very quietly: 'Have you heard about Lewis Renfro's heroic rescue of that little girl you just saw, the Larkin girl?'

'Everybody's heard. Texas papers were filled with little else.'

'The same.'

Mrs Quimper looked first at Mrs Reed, who was smiling, then at Mrs Wetzel, who was laughing outright, and their humor was so infectious that she had to smile, even though she did not yet understand the reason. 'You mean' – she fumbled for a word that would not be too condemnatory of her husband – 'that he was also a gentle fraud?'

Now Mrs Wetzel could not contain herself: 'This wonderful colored soldier, no neck, could fight anyone. He rescued the little girl from six Comanche.' She collapsed in laughter.

'Yes,' Mrs Reed said. 'Our very brave cavalry sergeant did just that.'

Mrs Wetzel told the rest: 'So then our hero, Lewis Renfro, Commander-in-Chief of Desk Forces, he rides up, recognizes the girl, grabs her, and grabs the glory.'

The three women chuckled at the follies of the self-appointed heroes whose antics they had observed, and when Mrs Wetzel began to gasp for air, the other two broke into very unladylike guffaws.

When the Quimpers departed, with Yancey pleased at having seen his fort but dismayed by his failure to acquire the land, Mrs Reed resumed the task of closing down the post, and as she moved from building to building she saw many things to remind her of the good work she had done in transforming this lonely outpost into a haven of civilization. In this stone building she had organized the social teas for each new wife; in a corner of that building she had arranged for everyone to place his extra books so that a library might be started; in this small garden, fertilized with manure from the stables, she had grown flowers for the hospital; and in the dead-house she had made the disfigured corpses acceptable before their friends or families saw them. In the chapel she had persuaded her husband to conduct prayers when there was no regular chaplain; and on Suds Row she had helped when babies had the croup.

Most important, she had been the guiding spirit in converting this mud outpost into a square-cornered fort of limestone. It had lasted, in its complete form, only three years, but she resolved that if her husband was now assigned to a newly established fort, probably some leagues to the west where the settlers were probing, she would encourage him to build of stone from the start: 'We live in any place only briefly, George. They may laugh and ask us as we depart: "Why did you take the trouble to build of stone?" If they don't understand that this was the home of two hundred soldiers, I'll not be able to explain.' She did not weep as they departed, but she did keep looking backward until Bear Creek disappeared, and the Brazos, and the tops of the buildings at the fort, and she kept doing so until only the vast plain and its endless blue sky were visible.

These eventful days had been difficult for Earnshaw Rusk, for the army despised him as a dreamer who refused to look facts in the face, and his own Quakers deplored him a traitor who in panic had called in the soldiers to settle a temporary difficulty that could have been handled by negotiation.

After his expulsion in disgrace from Camp Hope, he had tried living for a while at Jacksborough, but that robust settlement, where men resolved arguments with guns and fists, provided no place for a man like him. He had also tried the town that had grown up at the edges of Fort Griffin to the south, but that was a true hellhole whose shenanigans terrified him. Then he served as a night nurse in a field hospital at another fort, where his behavior at Camp Hope was not known, and now when he heard that Fort Garner was being disbanded, he came back to the scene of his humiliation.

He went, as he had long planned in his confused imagination, to the house once occupied by Captain Wetzel and his wife, and there he found Emma Larkin working alone as if she were living safely in the heart of some small town. She seemed adjusted to the problem of living without ears or nose, and when, after the first awkward greetings, he asked where she would make her home, she replied in her soft whisper: 'Here at the fort. I like it and it's mine.'

He accepted the tea she offered him in a cup left behind by the Wetzels, and she showed him how she had collected quite a few household items from other departing officers: 'I'll live.'

Sitting in the chair that was once Wetzel's favorite, he began his awkward speech: 'Emma, I've made a terrible mess of my life.' He did not say it, but she knew he intended to say, 'And thee has made a mess of thine. Or, other people made a mess for thee.' Instead he plowed on: 'And I have been wondering . . .'

He stopped. From that first day when he met this pitiful child he had speculated on what might happen to her. How could a human being so abused survive? How could she face the world? It was out of such wonderment that he had been impelled to carve the nose which she now wore: It had not been because of love, for he had no comprehension of that word and little understanding of the complex emotions it represented, but it was out of concern, and caring. And he was caring now.

'I've been wondering what thee would do . . . with thy protectors gone.' By this use of an inappropriate word – for this young woman required no protectors – he betrayed his line of reasoning: 'And I've thought . . .' He could not go on. Nothing in his lonely awkward life had prepared him to speak the words that should be spoken now.

Emma Larkin, damaged and renewed as few humans would ever be, reached out, touched his hand, and used his first name for the first time: 'Earnshaw, I've been given this land, these buildings. I will need someone to help me.'

'Could I be thy helper?' he managed to stammer.

'Thee could, Earnshaw,' she whispered. 'Thee could indeed.'

It was midsummer in Austin, and heat lay over the city like an oppressive blanket which intercepted oxygen and brought blazing discomfort. Day after day the temperature hovered close to a hundred degrees as a cloudless sky glared down like the inside of a superheated bronze bowl. Fish in the lovely lake kept toward the bottom where the sun's incessant beating was lessened if not escaped, and in the countryside torpid cattle sought any vestige of shade. It could be hot in Texas, and all who could afford it fled to New Mexico.

Despite the heat, we were scheduled to hold our July meeting in Beaumont, the famous oil city near the Gulf, where we hoped optimistically there might be breezes. I anticipated a productive meeting, since we were to be addressed by Professor Garvey Jaxifer from Red River State College. My staff assured me that he was not inflammatory, only persistent, and I told them: 'Persistence after truth we can live with,' so the meeting was arranged.

I was therefore disturbed when Rusk and Quimper called me on a conference line to ask that I convene an extraordinary two-day meeting prior to Beaumont. I supposed they were going to protest my invitation to Professor Jaxifer, but they assured me that this was not their concern; Rusk growled: 'I've heard the man twice, here in Fort Worth. If he knew figures, I'd hire him. Solid citizen.'

What the improvised meeting was to discuss I could not guess, but at nine one steamy morning Miss Cobb, Professor Garza and I assembled at Austin's Browning Airport for private planes and watched as two jets landed in swift succession. As they taxied toward us I wondered why two were needed, but when the first opened its doors I saw that Lorenzo Quimper had picked up our three staffers from Dallas, so apparently it was going to be an important session.

The conspirators would not tell us where we were going, but shortly we were flying northwest on a route which would take us, I calculated, over Abilene and Lubbock. 'What's this all about?' I asked Quimper, who rode in my plane, and he winked. I guessed that we were going to hold a preliminary session of some kind in a place like Amarillo, but when we had reached that general area and gave no sign of descending, I knew we must be entering New Mexico.

After Quimper served us a choice of drinks and Danish, we began to descend, and soon one of the young men, a better geographer than I, shouted: 'Hey! Sante Fe!'

Flying low, so that we could see the grandest city of the Southwest, we swung north along the highway to Taos, circled a large ranch, and landed on a private strip, macadamized and six thousand feet long. 'Ransom's hacienda,' Quimper announced, and when we joined the others on the tarmac, Rusk said almost apologetically: 'Il Magnifico and me, we thought Texas was just too damned hot. I want you to enjoy two days of relaxation . . . anything you'd like to do. The helicopter's here . . . riding horses . . . swimming . . . great mountain trails. Taos up that way. Santa Fe down there.'

It was the kind of gesture the very rich in Texas like to make, but I noticed that everything about the place was low key: Ford pickups with gun racks behind the driver's head, not Mercedes; rough bunkhouses with Hudson's Bay blankets for cold nights; and no Olympic-sized swimming pool, just a small, friendly dipping place in which the girl from SMU was going to look just great, because even if she hadn't brought a swimsuit, Rusk's Mexican housekeeper could offer her a choice of six or seven.

It was a splendid break in the heat, for the Rusk ranch was 6,283 feet high, with manificent views of mountains higher than 12,000. But the emotional part of our visit, and I use that word with fondest memories, came at dusk on that first day when Quimper signaled his chief pilot to bring before us, as we sat by the pool drinking juleps, four rather long boxes wrapped in gift paper.

'Working with you characters,' Lorenzo said, 'has been both an education and a privilege. Never knew I could get along so amiably with anarchists.' Bowing to Garza, he said: 'On this happy occasion I cannot refrain from sharing my latest Aggie joke. Seems your aviation experts have invented a new type of parachute. Opens on impact.'

'I'm walking home,' Garza said, whereupon Lorenzo grabbed him: 'I thought you might, so I brought you just the thing for hiking.'

Shuffling the four parcels, he selected one and handed it to

Rusk, who tore off the paper to disclose a long shoebox, inside which rested a pair of incredibly ornate boots. Products of the workmen at the General Quimper Boot Factory, they had been especially orchestrated, with the front showing a bull of the Texas Longhorn breed Rusk was striving to perpetuate on his Larkin County ranch, the side offering one of his oil derricks, and the back of the boot a fine version of his Learjet in blue and gold. The retail cost of such masterpieces I did not care to guess, but I remembered a catalogue that had offered lesser boots at three thousand dollars.

We were still awed by Rusk's gift when Miss Cobb opened hers to reveal a tall, slim pair ideally suited to her grave demeanor. They were silver and gray, with not a bit of ornamentation to detract from the exquisite patterning of the leather itself; it seemed to have been sculpted in eleven subtle shades of gray.

'What kind of leather?' the young woman from SMU cried, and Quimper replied with obvious pride in his men's workmanship: 'Amazon boa constrictor.' They were once-in-a-lifetime boots, and Miss Cobb was so touched by Lorenzo's gesture that she did not allow herself to speak lest she behave in a sentimental manner ill-befitting her Cobb ancestry.

Now it was my turn, and I could not imagine what Lorenzo had deemed proper for a man with few distinguishing characteristics, but when I opened my box it was apparent that he had gone back to my honored ancestor, Moses Barlow of the Alamo, for across the top rims of my boots, in flaming red letters against a pale-blue background, ran the word *Alamo*, and beneath it, in green-and-white leatherwork, stood a depiction of the famous building. Reaching from the sole of the shoe to the top, along the outer flank of each boot, rested a Kentucky long rifle, in black. My boots were pure Texas, and I was glad to have them, for with my own funds I could never have afforded such perfection.

Because of the incipient animosity between Quimper and Garza, rarely overt but never buried, I had to wonder what Lorenzo would do to catch the professor's personality, but when Efrain opened his box we gasped, because for him Quimper had saved his maximum artistry. In a wild flash of red, green and white, the colors of Mexico's flag, he had provided a peon in a big hat sleeping beside an adobe wall, a depiction of the shrine of Our Lady of Guadalupe and an intricate enlargement of the central design of the flag, the famous eagle killing a rattlesnake while perched on a cactus.

Referring proudly to the latter, Quimper said: 'I had my best workman do the vulture eating the worm,' and Garza looked up with a mixture of affection and sheer bewilderment. For more than two hundred years his family had had no permanent affiliation with Mexico; he had traveled within the nation only once, and then not pleasantly, and although he spoke its language and followed its religion, he felt no close association with the country. Yet here he was with boots that proclaimed him loudly to be a Mexican.

'Lorenzo,' he said with obvious gratitude, 'I think I can speak for us all. You are magnificent.'

Our three staff members, who had watched the unveiling of our boots, cheered, but now Quimper signaled his other pilot, who came forward with three boxes. When the young people realized that these must be for them, the two young men clapped hands and the girl from SMU squealed, and the highlight of the ceremony was when she opened her box, for Lorenzo had brought her a pair equal to Miss Cobb's in femininity, but precisely the kind a young woman would appreciate. They were tall and slender, with heels well undercut and uppers made of a soft red leather that seemed to shout: 'I'm twenty-three and unmarried!' The simple decoration was in shining black, and the total effect was one of youthfulness, dancing and an invitation to flirtation. Miss Cobb said: 'Every young woman should know what it's like to own a pair of boots like that,' and the recipient began to cry.

The two men received simple cowboy boots made of valuable leather adorned by big hats, lariats and revolvers, and when the seven pairs were set side by side on the floor, we applauded, but Lorenzo rarely did things partially, for now the chief pilot came in with a box for the boss, and as we cheered, Quimper revealed his own fantastic boots. Basically they were a wild purple, but in their lighter leathers they contained a summary of Texan culture: a saucy roadrunner yakking across the desert, a Colts pistol, an oil well, a coiled rattlesnake. 'I like my boots to make a statement,' Quimper said, and Garza responded: 'Those can be heard on the borders of California.' And that night, when we stepped from the front door of the ranch on our way to dinner at a Santa Fe restaurant, we were what Quimper called 'a splendiferous Task Force.'

As we entered the restaurant I whispered to the SMU girl: 'How much would these eight pairs cost, retail?' and she said: 'I'll call Nieman-Marcus,' and soon she joined our table with a note: 'Twenty-four thousand dollars.' Texans are not afraid of doing things in style.

At dinner, Quimper dominated conversation by expounding in a voice loud enough to be heard at nearby tables his theory that Santa Fe should have been a part of Texas: 'The day will come when Texas patriots will muster an expedition to recapture this town. Then we'll have Texas as it should be, Santa Fe at one end, Houston at the other.'

When we left the restaurant we found our evening somewhat dampened by a sign plastered across our windshield: TEXANS GO HOME, which reminded us that New Mexicans regard the Texans who flood their towns in summer the way Texans regard the visitors from Michigan who invade their state in winter.

Refreshed by this escape from the Texan inferno, we prepared for our forthcoming meeting in Beaumont, where we met Professor Garvey Jaxifer, a sophisticated black scholar. The newspapers usually referred to him as Harvey Jaxifer, unaware that he had been named after the incendiary Jamaican black Marcus Garvey, who had lectured American blacks about their destiny and their rights. That first Garvey had been deported, I believe, but had left behind a sterling reputation as a fighter, and our professor was no less an agitator than his namesake. He presented a short, no-compromise paper, whose highlights follow:

'Throughout their history anglo Texans have despised Indians, Mexicans and blacks. This tradition started with the Spanish conquistadores, who saw their Indians as slaves and treated them abominably. This attitude was intensified by any Mexicans who were not classified as Indians themselves. We have seen how in 1836, General Santa Anna had no compunction about marching his barefoot, thinly clad Yucatecan Indians into the face of a blizzard, losing more than half through freezing to death.

'The early Texians inherited this contempt for the Indian, strengthened by understandable prejudices engendered in frontier states like Kentucky and Tennessee, where warfare with the Indian had been a common experience. But it was fortified in Texas by the fact that many of the Indian tribes encountered by the early settlers were extremely difficult people: the cannibalistic Karankawa, the remorseless Waco and the savage Kiowa. The earliest Americans had to fight such Indians for every foot of ground they occupied, and this blinded them to the positive aspects of the other Indians they encountered, especially the Cherokee.

'Later, of course, the Texians met face-to-face with the fearful Apache and Comanche, and with the most generous intentions in the world it would have been difficult to find any solution to the clash which then occurred. No outsider ignorant of the bloody history of the 1850 and 1875 frontier, with its endless massacres and hideous tortures, has a right to condemn the Texas settlers for the manner in which they responded.

'But Texas lost a great deal when it expelled its Indians, and the debt is only now being collected. For one thing, the state lost a group of people who could have contributed to our wonderful diversity had they remained; but much more important, their expulsion encouraged the Texian to believe that he truly was supreme, lord of all he surveyed, and that he could order lesser peoples around as he wished. The Indian was long gone when the real tragedy of his departure began to be felt, because the Texian diverted his wrath from the Indian to the Mexican and the black, and the scars of this transferral are with us to this day.

'I am assured that previous scholars have spoken of the heavy burden Texas bears because of its refusal to adjust to the Mexican problem, so I shall drop that subject. I shall restrict myself solely to the way in which Texas has handled its black problem, and because my allotted time is short, I shall address you shortly, sharply, and without that body of substantiating material I would normally offer.

'The condition of the black in Texas is one of the great secrets of Texas history, which has been written as if the blacks had never existed. Yet in 1860 blacks constituted thirty-one percent of the population and represented a total tax value of over a hundred and twenty-two million dollars. They vastly outnumbered either the Mexicans or the Indians, and the economy of the state, dominated by cotton, depended largely upon them.

'Despite vast evidence to the contrary, two legends grew up around the blacks, one before the Civil War, one after, and these legends were so persuasive, so consoling to the Texas whites, that they are not only honored today but also believed. They continue to affect all relations between the two races.

'The ante-bellum legend is that the slaves were happy in their servitude, that they did not seek freedom, and that they did not warrant it because they had no skills other than chopping cotton and could not possibly have existed without white supervision. The facts were somewhat different. On most plantations slaves were the master mechanics. They were nurses of extraordinary skill and compassion. They were also custodians of the land, and many saved enough money to buy their own freedom. Properly encouraged and utilized, they could have earned Texas far more as mechanics than they did through cotton.

'But the perplexing part of the legend was that while the slaves were supposed to be happy under the compassionate tutelage of their white masters, Texas newspapers were filled with rumors of slave uprisings, of slaves burning the masters' barns and of general insurrection. Scores of county histories tell of executions of slaves to forestall rebellion, and slave flight to Mexico became so common that from time to time agents were stationed along the border to prevent it. I can speak of this with some authority, because my great-great-grandfather used that route to escape from his slavery on the plantation of your ancestors, Miss Cobb, where, I hasten to add, he told his children that he had been well treated. But once he got the chance – over the Rio Grande into Mexico.'

'What did he do when he got there?' Quimper asked, and Jaxifer replied: 'Made his way to Vera Cruz, caught a ship to New Orleans, where he enlisted in a New York regiment.'

'You mean he fought with the North?' Quimper grumbled, and Jaxifer asked: 'What did you expect?' and Quimper said: 'He could of remained neutral.'

Professor Jaxifer continued: 'The Texians found no difficulty in believing both halves of this ante-bellum legend: that the same slave was deliriously happy, yet thirsting to massacre his master.

'The post-bellum legend was more destructive. The genesis was understandable. The South had been defeated. The North, especially under President Lincoln, wanted to be generous in its treatment, but his assassination opened the way for some radicals in Congress to force upon the South an intolerable Reconstruction. One of the ironies of Texas history is that its newspapers and its people rejoiced when Lincoln was shot, condemning him as one of the supreme tyrants of all time, not realizing that he alone could have enabled their state to avoid the convulsion it was about to suffer. It was 1902 before the first paper was brave enough to print one kind word about Lincoln, and it was abused for having done so.

'The true history of Reconstruction in Texas has not yet been written and probably cannot be in this century; the legend of that tempestuous time is still too virulent. Regarding blacks, it makes three claims: that those blacks elected to office under Northern supervision of the ballot box were incompetent at best, downright thieves at the worst; it claims that blacks who suddenly found themselves with freedom did not know what to do with it; and most important, it claims that the occasional black members of the State Police installed by the carpetbagger government were brutal murderers. Nothing in the history of Texas has damaged the black more than the fact that a few were for a while members of the State Police, that hated and reviled agency.

'Again, the legend is faulty at best, infamous at worst. Black legislators seem to have been no worse than their white contemporaries and successors. Many blacks learned quickly what to do with their freedom, and either established their own homes and small businesses or went back to work on the plantations as sharecroppers. And as for the black policemen, if they did, as charged, kill eight or ten white men without warrant, the Rangers had killed eight or ten hundred Mexicans and Indians, yet the former are reviled and the latter immortalized. It is a disproportion that cannot easily be explained.'

Professor Jaxifer then threw in an obiter dictum which really stunned our Texas landlovers: 'If you suspect I'm overemphasizing the bitterness of Reconstruction, let me cite an incident which you better than most will appreciate. In 1868 a Republican-controlled convention, drawing new laws for peacetime Texas, recalled the hardships under which Texans who had fought on the Union side suffered: "These patriots were mercilessly slandered in their good names and property." In recompense they would be issued free land, but it went unclaimed, because in all of land-hungry Texas no man was brave enough to stand before his neighbors as one who "had been false to the Confederacy and no better than a carpetbagger." '

'You mean,' Quimper asked, 'that all this free land was waiting and no one claimed it?' When Jaxifer nodded, Lorenzo added: 'For a Texan to pass up free land is an act of moral heroism.' Jaxifer smiled and continued with these points:

'The hatreds engendered spawned a curious progeny. Many of the gunslingers of the Old West began by shooting blacks who had given no offense, and such bravado gained them the approbation of their fellows. Billy the Kid started by slaughtering a Negro blacksmith who made a pun upon his name, calling him Billy the Goat. He gained much applause for his quick and deadly response. As one hagiographer has said: "A flick of his wrist, a touch of his finger, and Billy silenced forever those thick, black, insolent lips."

'John Wesley Hardin, a cold-eyed, merciless killer who gunned down twenty-nine men before he was twenty-four, was despised prior to the day when he shot two black policemen; then he found himself a Texas hero. But the prototype of the Texas gunman was Cole Yeager, from Xavier County, who announced one day at the age of eighteen. "I cannot abide a freed nigger." He proved it by shooting in the stomach a young black who had argued with an older black. When asked about this, Yeager muttered: "The Bible says 'Ye shall respect thy elders,' " and no charges were lodged.

'Some time later he saddled up at dusk in the small town of Lexington, not far from the capital, galloped through the street, and slaughtered eight unsuspecting blacks. His high spirits were excused on the ground that "this was the kind of incident that was bound to happen . . . sooner or later."

'Pleased with his reputation as a nigger-killer, he was lounging in Jefferson, up in the Cotton Belt, one Sunday morning when he saw two well-dressed blacks, Trajan Cobb and his wife, Pansy, leaving their cottage and heading for the black church. Enraged that former slaves should be "tryin' to be better than they was," Yeager whipped out his guns and killed them.

'They happened to work as freedmen for Senator Cobb, the one-armed hero of the Confederacy, and when he heard in Washington of what had happened, he returned immediately to Texas, determined to bring Yeager to justice, and with his tiny wife, Petty Prue, he roamed the state, looking for the man who had killed his former slaves.

'Federal marshals, afraid of the scandal which might ensue if Yeager gunned down a one-armed United States senator, tried to dissuade Cobb from stalking his prey, but Cobb would not listen: "When a man has affronted the honor of an entire state, he must be taken care of, and if you gentlemen are afraid to go after him, I must."

'The marshals tried to persuade Mrs Cobb to call off her man, but she snapped: "Trajan Cobb bears our name. He held our plantation together during the war, and if Somerset doesn't shoot the coward who killed him, I will."

'Fortunately, at about this time, Cole Yeager killed a white man, shot him in the back during an argument over fifty cents, and now the law had a viable excuse for arresting him. Under pressure from Senator Cobb, a fearless judge from Victoria County was brought north, and Yeager, who had now killed thirty-seven men, most of them black, was sentenced to be hanged.

'The Cobbs were there when the execution took place, and they groaned as the rope broke, allowing Yeager to fall unscathed. Some in the crowd cited an old English tradition which said that under such circumstances, the condemned man had to be set free, in that God had intervened, and there were murmurs to support this, for many in the audience felt it was unfair to hang a white man primarily because he had killed niggers.

'However, Cobb, with his good right arm, whipped out his revolver and announced: "We are not hanging him according to old English law. We're using new Texas law. String the son-of-a-bitch up" – and it was done.

'One of the more interesting illustrations of how difficult it was for Texans to adjust to the freed Negro came in Robertson County, not far from where we sit. A gifted black, Harriel Geiger, had been elected to the state legislature, and during his tenure in Austin had studied law and become a member of the bar. He excelled in defending black prisoners, but this irritated Judge O. D. Cannon of the Robertson bench, who is described in chronicles as "that hot-tempered segregationist." In any trial involving a black the judge had been in the habit of listening to whatever evidence the white man chose to present – he did not allow any black to testify – then growling, spitting, and sentencing the black to a long term on the prison work force. Naturally, he did not take it kindly when Lawyer Geiger, with the skills he had mastered as a legislator, came into his court arguing points of law.

'One hot afternoon Judge Cannon had suffered enough: "I been warnin' you to watch your step, nigger, but you have insolently ignored my counsel." With that, he whipped out a long revolver, held it three feet from the lawyer's chest, and pulled the trigger five times. The coroner's verdict: Harriel Geiger had been guilty of repeated contempt and had been properly rebuked.

'I agree, there are elements of humor in this incident: the irascible judge, the presumptuous new lawyer, the challenge to old customs, the sullen revenge of the men who had lost a moral crusade in the War Between the States. But I have here in my notes, which you are invited to inspect, a score of other incidents which contain no humor at all, and I shall cite only one more to remind you of the seriousness of the problem we're discussing.

'In 1892 in Paris, Texas, a black man named Henry Smith ravished and killed the three-year-old daughter of one Henry Vance. No doubt of the crime, no doubt of the guilt, no doubt of the sentence of death. But how was he executed? He was driven in a wagon through a crowd of ten thousand, then lashed to a chair perched high upon a cotton sledge, from which Vance, the dead girl's father, asked the horde to be silent while he took his revenge. A small tinner's furnace was brought to Vance, who heated several soldering irons white-hot. Taking one after another, he started at the prisoner's bare feet and slowly working his way up the body, burning off appendages but keeping the torso alive. When he reached the head he burned out the mouth, then extinguished the eyes and punctured the ears. When he felt sated, he offered the irons to anyone else who wanted to share in the revenge, and his fifteen-year-old son took over. Ten thousand cheered.

'The black man deserved to die, but no man ever deserved to die in such a manner. It was made possible only because legend said that the black was not really human.

'It would serve no useful purpose for us to continue to explore the hideous record, for my point is made. Relations between white and black in Texas have been contaminated by legend. I am not asking that you attack the legend, or even make a great fuss about it. But do not prolong it. Don't give it added vitality. Let it die. Speak of your Texas blacks as human beings, no better, no worse than the Czechs, the Poles and the Irish who have helped build this great state.'

When Professor Jaxifer finished, Lorenzo Quimper said: 'Do you expect us to forget how your colored people behaved during Reconstruction? I remember well hearing my father tell how his grandfather, General Yancey Quimper, was accosted by a colored who wanted a pair of boots, free. This colored, six months from chopping cotton, had been elected to the legislature, and he told my grandfather – I can hear my father's words as he told me. This colored, he said: "General, I'm a legislator now and I'm entitled to free boots." And my grandfather said: "Freemont, you are entitled to a swift kick in the ass." And you know what? That colored had my grandfather arrested.'

'Does this old family legend have any relevance?' the professor asked, and I could see Quimper flush, and he said with roiling bitterness: 'A man in my town, big oil man worth millions, was ridin' home the other day in his Cadillac. He sees this poor old colored with broken-down Ford, mendin' a tire by the side of the road while three strappin' young blacks is sittin' by the side of the road laughin' at the old man's efforts. My friend stops his Cadillac, gets out in that hot dusty road, and helps the old man change the tire while the three young bucks sit there laughin' at the both of them. Now what do you think of that?'

'Commissioner Quimper, that story's been circulating through Texas ever since we've had automobiles. Do you really believe it happened . . . this year . . . to your friend?'

'Let me tell you . . .'

'Don't you see, Commissioner? It's today's legend – 1911 version updated.'

We had the makings of a serious confrontation, for Professor Jaxifer showed no signs of backing down; however, Miss Cobb intervened: 'The story you told, Professor, about my grandfather,' and she accented the *my* heavily, 'is true. He grieved over the loss of Trajan Cobb so painfully that he had a monument erected to him at Lammermoor: TO A TRUSTED FRIEND.'

Ransom Rusk delivered a judicious opinion, which I allowed to stand as the judgement of our group: 'Professor, you've honored us with a thoughtful paper. You must be aware, surely, that we cannot revise all of Texas history and correct all imbalances. The best we can do is project an honest course for the future.'

'You could not have stated the case more eloquently,' Professor Jaxifer conceded. 'All we blacks ask is that the legends not be embellished with new additions. The old ones we can never change . . . at least not in this century.'

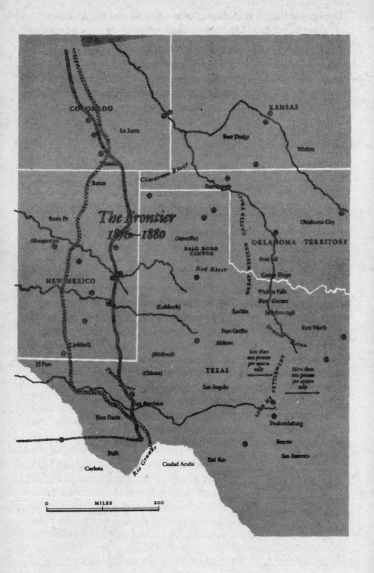

The Frontier 1866–1880

XI

THE FRONTIER

It was paradoxical. After the United States Army abandoned Fort Garner, the real battle for this area began, the contest between the primeval frontier and the settled town. The struggle had a significance greater even than the one between white man and Indian. Its adversaries were marvelously varied: the wild longhorned cattle of the plains versus the ingeniously perfected beef cattle of England; the lone horseman galloping in from the western horizon versus the railroad chugging in from the east; the flash of a vengeful pistol versus the establishment of a courthouse dispensing rational law; the handful of Mexican coins hidden in a sock versus the fledgling bank with its iron safe; the free-ranging cattle drover versus the salesman of barbed wire; and in the bosom of Fort Garner, the nomadic wanderings that Emma Larkin had known with the Comanche versus the steady path toward an ordered life that her husband, Earnshaw Rusk, strove to establish.

In all parts of the American West this homeric battle of conflicting values was fought, but nowhere in more dramatic style than in West Texas. At Fort Garner, in the quarter of a century between 1875 and 1900, it was conducted with particular intensity, and from the struggle emerged many of the lasting characteristics of Texas.

The moment Earnshaw Rusk established his home in the abandoned stone house at Fort Garner, he initiated his fight to bring the civilization he had known in rural Pennsylvania to this untamed frontier. As a pacifistic Quaker he wanted to erase memories of the military post and tried to rename the place in honor of his wife's martyred family; he wanted it to become the village of Larkin. To his dismay, the United States Post Office Department continued to call it Fort Garner, but Rusk corrected people in his high-pitched voice: 'It's really Larkin, you know.'

He was equally adamant about longhorned cattle: 'I want none of those fearful beasts on our land. I'm afraid of them. With those long, savage horns, they seem to come from the devil. And the human beings they attract are a dissolute, ungodly lot.' When his wife asked: 'If you don't want cattle on our land, how will we eat?' he replied: 'I'll think of something,' but it was she who took action. For with the riding skills she had mastered with the Comanche she sped across the plains, driving wild mustangs into corrals and then taming them for sale to various army posts in Texas and Indian Territory. She demonstrated exceptional talent in converting them into fine saddle horses, for where others whipped the mustangs and broke them with punishment, she reasoned with them in soft plains language they seemed to understand: 'Now, my little roan, we change our life for the better. We'll get to know this rope, perhaps to love it. We'll walk about this post, day after day, until it becomes our home.' During the first two weeks, not with force but through the gentleness of her heart, she spoke invariably to the wild horse as *we*, as if she along with the animal were learning a new way, but when the animal's terror had fled, she addressed it always as *you*. 'Now you have the secret!' she would cry joyously as the animal began to respond spontaneously to her commands, and because of her uncanny ability to think like an animal, she would teach the mustang to work with her until human and animal formed a cooperative pair.

Officers began to come from distant forts to buy a Rusk Roamer, as Emma's trainees were called. The mustangs brought good prices, and were treasured for their curious mixture of gentleness and proud spirit, but it soon became obvious that even with Earnshaw's awkward help she could not, in her advancing pregnancy, catch enough or tame them quickly enough to depend upon this for the limited income they needed.

When Emma raised the question as to how they might earn a living, Earnshaw forestalled her with a problem of his own: 'Emma, we must find people to occupy these houses.'

'I don't want a lot of people . . .'

'It's shameful to own good houses like these and see them stand empty. One of the foot soldiers who used to serve here . . .

his wife worked on Suds Row ... they tell me he's rotting in Jacksborough. They want to come back.'

'How would they earn a living?'

'That's the other thing, Emma,' and with his quiet perception of the years ahead and of how this area along the Brazos must develop. he reasoned with her: 'We'll soon be bringing a baby into our empty home. We must bring people into our empty houses.'

'Who has the money for such extravagances?'

'People make money, Emma,' and with the friendly persuasion he had used in trying to bring a vision of peace to the Comanche, he now tried to reveal to his wife the bright future he saw: 'We have the six thousand acres which no plow could break. We have a wonderful stone village which no storm can attack. And we have ourselves, with only thy savings and no prospects of more. This empty land, these empty houses, we shall use them as our money.'

Emma stayed silent, for she could feel the wonder of her plains slipping away; she could feel the press of people invading her lonely acres, her silent houses. She feared change to a different way of life, but she also trusted her husband, who had given such courageous proof of his love. If he had a vision of a new world, she must listen, and when she did she heard the voice of the future: 'Thy empty land, Emma, must produce something. Thy empty houses were made to protect families. A man rode by this morning when thee was out with the mustangs and I told him he was welcome to move into one of thy houses.'

When she started to protest this invasion, he said quietly: 'Emma, if the fort is ever to be a town, we must have people.'

In this unstudied way Frank Yeager, his illiterate Alabama wife and their scrawny son Paul, aged three, moved into the house north of the commander's, and from the moment of their arrival Emma knew the Rusks were going to have trouble, for Yeager was a profane man and his wife a committed Baptist who felt it her duty to bring everyone she met under the moral protection of her church. One evening, after she argued loudly that Quakers were headed for hell because of their unorthodox beliefs, Earnshaw asked his wife: 'She's dead set on converting me, showing mc thc truc way, yet she can't even discipline her own husband?'

Frank Yeager was a violent, difficult man, given to drunkenness and poker, when he could find partners. When his new landlord said austerely: 'I don't gamble,' Yeager said: 'You stay around me long enough, you'll learn.'

The Yeagers had been in residence only a short time when Frank captured Emma's full support: 'A woman as gone pregnant as you ought to stop foolin' around with them wild mustangs. Let's round up all the stray longhorns for fifty miles. Build us a real herd and drive it north to them new railheads in Kansas. Let's earn some real money.' Emma, who loved all animals and especially the wild cattle of the plains, replied with real excitement: 'We'll get the first batch this afternoon.' Two days later Earnshaw rode in to Jacksborough to invite the former soldier and his laundress wife to move into another of the houses at the fort, and the newcomers eagerly helped Yeager at the roundups, the women riding as well as the men, and the Rusk herd grew.

The presence of an extra woman was helpful when Emma had her baby, a chubby boy with a voracious appetite, because Earnshaw was useless both at the birth and during the first difficult days. In fact, he was so much in the way that the former laundress snapped: 'Mr Rusk, this would be a good time for you to ride in to Jacksborough and register your son with the authorities.'

During this trip Earnshaw learned of two Buffalo Soldiers from the 10th Cavalry who were approaching forced retirement, and when he found that one of them was the well-regarded John Jaxifer, he returned to Jacksborough and offered the two men a free house; so as Emma's herd of cattle increased, so did the population of Earnshaw's village.

Fort Garner now consisted of Emma Rusk and her longhorns, Earnshaw and his vision of a community, their son, Floyd, who grew daily, the Yeagers, who could do almost anything, the white soldier and his rough-and-ready wife, the two Negro cavalrymen, and lots of guns. Rusk hated guns; Emma respected their utility on a frontier. The other six were all practiced in arms; make that seven, because the Yeagers were already teaching their three-year-old how to handle a toy revolver. When Earnshaw protested, Yeager said: 'A Texan who can't handle a gun ain't fit to be a Texan.'

When Emma's longhorns were first rounded up at Fort Garner, Earnshaw was contemptuous of them, but when he awakened to the fact that they might provide the economic base not only for his family but also for the community he hoped to establish, he became more attentive. And when he seriously studied those lean Texas beasts with their excessive horns, his Quaker instincts began to operate and he longed to improve them. Very early he conceded that whereas they were admirably adapted to life on the open range, they were never going to produce much saleable meat until they were crossed with the heavier, fatter cattle imported from England. When he proposed to Yeager that they purchase either the Angus or Hereford bulls which agricultural experts were recommending, the lanky herdsman, himself a human longhorn, with all muscle and no fat, protested.

'The longhorn is Texas,' he grumbled. 'Change him, you kill his spirit.'

'Those horns. They're horrible.' When Earnshaw said this he was looking at one of the bulls with horns so wide they were ridiculous, more than six feet tip to tip. 'Look at him. All horns and legs. No meat.'

By ill fortune he was denigrating the longhorn in which Frank Yeager took greatest pride: 'You're speakin' of the best bull we got.'

'Why do you say that?'

'This is Mean Moses. He leads the others to the promised land.' And he explained how this big, ugly creature had nominated himself to be king of this part of the Texas frontier: 'In spring he breeds the cows so they can produce calves big and tough like him. Those horns? He needs 'em to fend off the wolves. Those long legs? He needs 'em to cover the trail north to market without tirin'. Mr Rusk . . . '

'We Quakers don't like titles. I'm Earnshaw.'

'Mr Rusk, a longhorn bull like Mean Moses is one of God's perfect engineerin' feats. You replace him with one of them fancy English breeds . . . He spat. 'Mr Rusk, long ago this frontier was occupied by three powerful things. The Commanche. The buffalo. The longhorn. Only the cattle is left. You replace 'em with fat and blubber, what in hell is Texas goin' to be?

Earnshaw's desire to build a profitable ranching business received a bad jolt when he tried to sell off a few longhorns: 'I can't find buyers, not even at four dollars a head. That's less than it costs us to tend them.' But Yeager had a solution: 'If we can deliver them to the railhead at Dodge City, I know they'll bring forty dollars a head. Eastern markets are so hungry for beef, they'll take even longhorns.'

'How will we get them there?'

'Me and the boys will drove them.'

To this suggestion Rusk responded instantly: 'We'll not have our people making that trek to Kansas,' and when Yeager protested that it could be done easily, Rusk said firmly: 'I've heard about the Chisholm Trail into Abilene, Kansas, and the debauchery that goes with it. No hands from here will ever drove into Kansas.'

He was so adamant about this that Yeager surrendered: 'Tell you the truth, Mr Rusk, it would be better to keep the hands here on the ranch, tendin' to things. We'll find us a reliable cattleman headin' north.'

Upon investigation, Rusk learned that the new cattle trail, called the Great Western, started down near the Rio Grande, swung northwest past San Antonio and Fredericksburg, then across empty land to Fort Griffin, passing not far to the west of Fort Garner. From there it lay due north to the Indian settlement at Camp Hope, then to remote Fort Supply in Indian Territory, followed by a relatively short stint into Dodge City, to which the Eastern railroads had recently penetrated. 'What goes on there,' he told his wife, 'I do not choose to know or dwell upon.'

It was Emma who first heard about R. J. Poteet, from a Mexican trail cook: 'The best. First day he told us: "No gambling in my crew. No fighting." And he meant it.'

The more she heard about R. J. Poteet the more she liked him, and when in June the Mexican rode up to her door with the news: 'Mr Poteet, he's watering at our tank tomorrow,' she saddled up and rode to the northern end of her land to meet him.

She found him in charge of more than two thousand head of longhorns accumulated from various owners during the long trail north. He had with him nine cowboys and the Mexican cook, plus a thirteen-year-old boy to herd the spare horses in the remuda. It was an orderly camp, supervised by an orderly man just turned fifty, tall, thin as a cypress and as dark, with a close-cropped mustache and a wide-brimmed hat. His boots were so pointed at the toe and so elevated at the heel that he walked much like a woman, but he was so rarely away from his horse that this was seldom noticeable. He had a deep, resonant voice, a strong Southern accent, and an elaborate courtesy where women or young boys were concerned. From the manner in which his men went about their duties it was clear that he needed to give few orders, for he respected the men's abilities, including those of two black crew members. He allowed no alcohol in camp except for what he himself carried, and that he used only as medicine for others in times of crisis.

'R. J. Poteet, ma'am,' he said when Emma rode up. 'I've heard of your exploits with the Comanche, and I'm deeply respectful of your courage.'

'My husband and I have some two hundred good animals. Well fed.'

'These grasslands should see to that.'

'And the care we give them.'

'Longhorns tend to care for themselves. Look at the condition of mine. Five hundred miles on the trail, some of them.'

'I've been told you give your animals extra care.'

'I try to, ma'am.' He spoke with an appealing directness, which encouraged her to trust him.

'Would you be able . . .' She hesitated. 'I mean, would you be interested? Looks like you're able to do pretty much as you wish.'

'I've been trail-drivin' north for some years, ma'am. And I judge you want me to carry your cattle to Dodge City?'

'Would you?'

'That's my job,' and before she was out of her saddle she was listening to his clearly defined terms: 'This is the tail end of the journey, ma'am, but the crucial part. I've got to get your cattle across the Red River, through the Indian lands, across the Canadian River and the Cimarron, and into Dodge. Find a buyer for them, make the proper deal, and bring you back your money. That's worth a fee, ma'am.'

1029

'I'm sure it is.'

'I like ten percent now, earnest money, the balance when I sell.'

'You seem reluctant to state your fee, Mr Poteet.'

'I am, ma'am, because some owners, especially the ladies, always think it's too high. But there is much work to do, much responsibility.'

'It's because you're known for reliability that I came.'

'Ma'am, I'd be obliged if you'd get these figures in your head. You owe me one dollar for every animal. I owe you five dollars for every one of your cattle I lose on the way, so I don't intend to lose any. If you want to ride with me to Dodge city to sell your beasts, do so, and I get nothing but my dollar a head. If I act as your agent, and I'm willing, you must rely upon me completely. I'll do my best for you . . .'

'They say so, Mr Poteet.'

'Reputations aren't earned on one drive.' He coughed, then completed his terms: 'If I arrange for the selling, and sometimes it takes three minutes, sometimes three weeks, I get five percent. Some will do it for less, but frankly, I don't recommend them.'

At the noon hour they joined the cowboys at the chuck wagon, that amazing monument to American ingenuity, that contraption on four wheels from which hung all kinds of utilitarian devices: can openers, bone saws, frying pans, crocks with wire handles for sugar, pie plates with holes in their edges so they could be strung on a nail, clotheslines, folding tables, an awning to protect the Mexican cook from the sun, a bin for charcoal, and two dozen other imaginative additions, including drawers of every dimension.

'I took my first chuck wagon from Jacksborough across the Llano in 18 and 68,' Poteet said. 'Through Horsehead Crossing, all the way to Colorado.'

'The Estacado!' Emma said with awe. 'Even the Comanche stayed clear of that. What did you do for water?'

'We suffered. Next year, all the way to Montana. The chuck wagons in those days were simpler affairs. Everything you see on this wagon is in answer to some strong need. It's an invention of sheer intellectual brilliance, you could say.'

'Will your men run into trouble on the way to Dodge?'

'Now there's a misconception, ma'am. We do our very best to stay out of trouble. If Indians are runnin' wild, we head the other way. If a storm threatens, we try to lay low till it passes. Each of my men is armed, save the boy, but in the last five trips, not a shot fired in anger.'

'Why do you keep trailing, Mr Poteet?'

Before he could respond one of his cowboys interrupted: 'You know, ma'am, that some time ago Mr Poteet started a college in South Texas?'

'I can believe it.'

'He makes so much and he pays us so little he had to do somethin' with his money.' The cowboy grinned.

Poteet made a pistol with his right forefinger and shot the cowboy dead, and then turned suddenly to Emma: 'Ma'am, it's bold of me, and maybe it's wrong of me, but these are young men tryin' to learn about Texas. Would you have the courage to show them?' And the forthrightness with which he spoke – indeed, the dignity with which he conducted all his affairs – gave Emma the courage.

Raising her two hands to the sides of her face, she pushed back her hair to reveal the dreadfully scarred ears, and she could hear the cowboys gasp. Then, with her hands still in place, she unloosed the two white strands which controlled her wooden nose, and when it dropped, one of the men cried: 'Oh Jesus!'

'Texas wasn't won easy,' Poteet said.

'I'll have the longhorns gathered and counted this afternoon,' she said, but Poteet interrupted: 'We do the countin' together, ma'am.'

Earnshaw Rusk had always vowed to resist politics, for he had witnessed its lack of principle and its ruthlessness where personal interest was involved. Looking at what politics had done to him in the Indian Territory and to a fine man like Colonel Grierson in Texas, he had concluded: Only a blind man or one whose moral sensibilities were numbed would dabble in it. But when he studied the situation dispassionately, he realized that the goal he sought to attain – the civilization of the West – would be achieved only if Texas had strong representatives in Washington, and as he interrogated various interested persons about whom the Texas legislature might send to the national Senate, the name of Somerset Cobb, the respected gentleman from Jefferson, kept surfacing. And when Cobb felt obligated to run for the U.S. Senate in order to represent the decent parts of the culture of the Old South, Rusk felt obligated to support him, actively.

If any proof was needed to show that this lanky Quaker was a man of principle, this action provided it, because on the surface Cobb represented everything Rusk opposed. Cobb had owned large numbers of slaves in both South Carolina and Texas; Rusk had risked his life to oppose slavery in North Carolina and Virginia. Cobb was a Democrat; Rusk, like most Philadelphia Quakers, was a Republican. Cobb had served in the Confederate army, rising to high rank; Rusk was a pacifist.

What was worse, Cobb had vigorously opposed Northern interference in Texas affairs, calling Reconstruction 'that bastard child of vengeful legislature.' It was, he had preached, 'infamous in conception, cruel in execution, and in its final days a thing of scorn'; Rusk had believed that the South, especially Texas, required stern discipline before it could be allowed free exercise of its powers within the Union.

Finally, Rusk knew that Cobb was a Southerner who refused to apologize for his service to the Confederacy, and had committed treason against the United States. Yet here he was, brazenly offering himself to the Texas legislature as a candidate for the U.S. Senate. Rusk had every reason to reject this man, or even work against him but when it seemed that Cobb's opponent, also a military hero, might win the seat, Earnshaw knew that he must support the one-armed Cobb, so he left his ranch and harangued any members of the legislature he could encounter in the northern areas around Dallas.

Why did he do this quixotic thing? Why did this retiring and painfully bashful man plunge into the centre of a political brawl? Because of what his wife had told him about Cobb's opponent, General Yancey Quimper: 'I was helping Mrs Reed in the big house when General Quimper arrived to inspect what he called his fort. I was in the kitchen, of course ... ' She vaguely indicated her wooden nose. 'But I heard the three women talking.'

'What three?'

'Mrs Reed. Mrs Wetzel. Mrs Quimper.'

'What did they say?'

'That General Quimper had not been the hero of San Jacinto, that he'd been a coward mainly. That he had never dueled Sam Houston or shot wide to spare Houston's life. That he had never been a Ranger at Monterrey or anywhere near the Bishop's Palace. That he had not defended the Texas lunette at Vicksburg. And that he was not entitled to the rank of general, because he simply gave himself that title.'

When Earnshaw heard this litany of deceit, he reacted as a Philadelphia Quaker and not as a Texan inured to such colorful imposture; he deemed it his duty to expose the lifelong fraud practiced by Quimper, and to this end he began pestering the Democratic leaders in Dallas. At first they laughed at him: 'You disqualify liars and frauds, you wouldn't have ten men in the United States Senate, nor six in the Texas.'

But he persisted in his crusade, and by chance he encountered one Texas state senator who was eager to listen. He was Ernst Allerkamp, who represented the German districts around Fredericksburg, and when Rusk approached him regarding General Quimper, he listened: 'Are you sure what you say is true?'

'I've made the most careful inquiries.'

'Didn't you hear about the Nueces River affair?' When Rusk said no, the German sat him down on a tavern bench – Earnshaw had lemonade – and recounted the wretched affair in which General Quimper and his roving force had slain the escaping Germans: 'My father, my brother Emil, so many more. Singing in the night as they left for Mexico. Then they were murdered.'

Rusk was horrified by the brutality this onslaught represented, but he was numbed by what Senator Allerkamp revealed about the infamous hangings at the Red River: 'With no evidence or little, with no justification except supposed patriotism run wild ...' He told of the first hangings, the revulsion, the next surge, the final excesses, and when he was through, Rusk said: 'We must drive this man out of public life.'

Since Rusk had never met Quimper, Allerkamp warned him: 'When you do, you'll like him. Most of the men in the legislature want to send him to the Senate. They say: "He's a real Texan."'

Enraged, Rusk accompanied Allerkamp to Austin, where he continued his politicking among the other state legislators who alone had the right to elect men to serve in the national Senate. He revived so much old rumor detrimental to Quimper that a meeting was arranged with Rusk, Allerkamp, nine of their supporters and General Quimper himself. He appeared in a fine suit, white hair flowing, expensive boots and a big, warm smile that embraced even his enemies. 'Goodness,' Earnshaw whispered to Allerkamp when he first saw the general, 'he looks like a senator!

He talked like one, too, offering bland reassurances that he understood, and understood fully and generously, why certain men might want to oppose him for this august seat. But Rusk cut him short: 'Quimper, if thee continues to solicit votes for the United States Senate, I shall have to publish this memorandum . . . in Texas . . . then carry it to the United States Senate itself. Sir, if this document is circulated, thy life will be ruined.'

And before General Quimper could defend himself, Earnshaw Rusk, standing tall and thin and rumpled, read off the terrible indictment: a lie here, misrepresentation there, an assumed title, a borrowed military record, a claim that he had served at Vicksburg, where real Texas heroes had died at the lunette, the charge up a Mexican hill that he had never seen and, most damaging of all, 'a fraudulent claim that thee had dueled with Sam Houston. Sam Houston? He would have despised thee.'

General Quimper, having insulated himself through the years with a record he had almost convinced himself was his, was not easily goaded into surrendering it and the public accolades to which he felt entitled: 'You blackguard, sir. Publish one word of such blackmail, you die.'

'And what would that accomplish?' Rusk asked. Pointing to Senator Allerkamp, he said: 'Thee must shoot him too, as thee did his father and his brother.'

'What do you mean?'

'At the Nueces River. At dawn. That day of infinite shame.'

As Quimper looked at this circle of unrelenting faces, he had to acknowledge that his charade was over. If he persisted in his pursuit of the Senate seat, his spurious past was going to be assembled and dragged in the mud. He would be excoriated both in Texas and in Washington, and if his anti-Union behavior at the Nueces River, where the pro-Union Germans were slain, and at the Red River, where other Union loyalists were hanged, were dredged up, demagogic Northern senators would bar him from membership in their body, even if the Texas legislature did elect him. How terribly unfair to be destroyed at this late date by a Quaker from Pennsylvania, a man who wasn't even a Texan, and by a German immigrant who had no right being in the state at all.

But in the depths of his tragedy he saw a ray of light: 'If I do withdraw, that paper . . . '

'It becomes thy paper,' Rusk said, and the others nodded.

'You won't . . . '

'This meeting dies here,' Allerkamp promised. 'All we said, all we wrote.'

'You swear?'

Each man gave his word, and as the vows were uttered Yancey Quimper, hero of San Jacinto, Monterrey and Vicksburg, could feel life returning, could visualize himself climbing out of this dreadful pit which had so suddenly entrapped him. He could still be General Quimper. He would still be remembered for his great feats at San Jacinto. He would retain his profitable boot factory, his wife and sons, and high regard of those other politicians who had supported him in his contest for the Senate. He was only sixty-four, with many good years ahead, and he judged that it would be better to spend them holding on to the reputation he had built for himself than to attempt to be a United States senator and run the risk of losing it.

Rising from the chair in which he had slumped, he braced himself, looked at these pitiful little men who had defeated him, and said: 'It's amazin' what some men will do to win an election.' And with that, he stalked from the room, still a general, still a hero, still one of the most impressive Texans of his age.

When Earnshaw Rusk returned to his ranch at Fort Garner he told Emma: 'As thee knows, I've never seen Somerset Cobb. Let's pray he'll prove worthy of our effort.'

* * *

Texans could not be sure whether one-armed Colonel Cobb would prove worthy of the high position to which they promoted him in a special election, but they had no doubt about his spry little wife Petty Prue. When the Cobbs reached Washington they found resentment, for Somerset was not only an unreconstructed Southerner, he was also a military hero of the Confederacy, and his claim to be sworn in as a member of the Senate was a slap in the face for all loyal Union veterans who had fought against him.

Grudgingly he was seated, President Grant encouraging it as a prudent measure to keep Texas and other Southern states in line for the presidential election that would take place in the fall, but certain unrelenting Northern senators prevented him from obtaining any important committee assignments, so for some time the junior senator from Texas remained in outer darkness, and it looked as if he might stay there for the duration of his term.

It was then that Petty Prue swung into action. Fifty-three years old, five feet one, just over a hundred pounds, she began making her persuasive rounds of Washington, starting with the President himself. When she entered his office she stopped, drew back, and said in her lovely drawl: 'I do declare, General Grant, if you'd been twins, the war would've ended two years sooner.' And with her petite hands she indicated one Union army swooping down the Mississippi while the other attacked Richmond.

She exacted from Grant a promise that he would put in a good word with the Republican leaders of the Senate, after which he reminded her: 'You know, Miz Cobb, I carry little weight in that body,' and she assured him: 'General, you carry the weight of the nation on your broad shoulders. Have no fear.'

She did not hesitate to assault the headquarters of the enemy, barging into the offices of Sherman of Ohio and John A. Logan of Illinois. She told the former: 'Just as your brother, William Tecumseh, did his honorable best for the North, so my husband, Senatuh Cobb, did his honorable best for the South, and it's high time all men of honor be reprieved for whatever they did, either at the burnin' of Atlanta or elsewhere. I'm ready to forgive, and I sincerely trust you are too.'

In the evenings she held small dinner parties, flattering her guests with a flow of Southern charm, never mentioning her past in Georgia. She was now a Texas woman, had been since that November day in 1849 when she pulled up stakes in Social Circle and headed west. She was one of the most attractive and clever women Texas had produced, for this state had a saucy trick of borrowing able women from Tennessee and Alabama and Mississippi and making them just a little better than they would otherwise have been.

At the end of four months, every senator knew Mrs Cobb; after five months, Cobb found himself on three major committees, in obedience to the principle stated so often by his wife in her arguments with his colleagues: 'You're goin' to have to admit us Southrons sooner or later. Why not give the good ones like my husband a head start?'

On the night before summer recess started, the Cobbs gave a small dinner to which the President and Senators Sherman and Logan were invited. When cigars were passed, Petty Prue excused herself shyly: 'I know you gentlemen have affairs to discuss which I'd not be able to follow,' and off she traipsed, but not before smiling at each of the national leaders as she passed his chair. When she was gone, Grant said: 'The South could not have sent to Washington a better representative than your wife, Cobb,' and dour Sherman observed: 'Damn shame she didn't bring a Republican with her.' Grant laughed and took Somerset by the arm and said, 'He's even better than a Republican. He's an American.' And in this way the wounds of that fratricidal war between the sections were finally healed.

Sometimes in the early morning when Emma Rusk looked across the plains she loved, she could not escape feeling that the West she had known was dying: *Every move Earnshaw makes to improve his village condemns my wilderness.* She had been sorely perplexed during these past weeks when a Mr Simpson, who had served as sutler to the army when it occupied the fort, came to her husband and said: 'Mr Rusk, I'd like to have that company barracks. Can't pay you anything now, but if the store I plan to open makes money, and I'm sure it will . . .'

Mr Simpson had taken the building, put in a row of shelves and filled them with goods purchased in Jacksborough. He proved to be a congenial man who understood both groceries and housewives, and before that first week was out he had begun to collect customers from a distance, and by the end of the third week he was reordering supplies. Fort Garner had its first store.

But an event which moved Emma most deeply began on 21 June 1879, the longest day, and it caused her abiding grief. At about nine in the morning John Jaxifer galloped in: 'Comanche attacking from the north!'

Since Jaxifer had served in the 10th Cavalry, Emma and Earnshaw had to think that he knew what he was saying, and when they ran out to look, they saw that the warriors were once more on the warpath. In profound consternation Emma cried: 'Have they come for me?'

Rusk, who hated guns and had never learned to use one, felt that he must protect his community, so he ran to the kitchen, grabbed an old washbasin, and started beating it to attract his neighbors. Within a few minutes Frank Yeager arrived, with his wife appearing a few minutes later laden with three rifles. The other black cavalryman had been working on foot, and he ran in with his gun. If the Indians proposed to attack Fort Garner, they were going to face gunfire.

They did not seek war, and when they approached making signs of peace and calling out words of assurance, the Rusks, who knew their language, shouted: 'No firing.' In the pause the Fort Garner people saw that this war party consisted of one old chief attended by fourteen braves, not one of them as much as fourteen years old. Three could not yet be six. The old chief was Wading Bird, named seventy years before for an avocet who visited a pond near his mother's tepee, and when Emma recognized him she whispered his name to instruct her husband.

'Wading bird!' Earnshaw cried in Comanche. 'What news?'

'To see Great Chief Rusk.' Earnshaw had instructed his Indians not to call him by this title, explaining to them that the true Great Chief was in Washington, but they had persisted in calling him so, because it reassured them that he could grant their petitions.

'What does thee seek?' Rusk asked, repeating the phrase he had used so often in his contacts with them, and as he said the familiar words a kind of joy possessed him: he was again the eager young man in command at Camp Hope and these were the wise chiefs and promising young braves he had been certain he could pacify; it was June again and there was hope both in the camp of that name and in his heart; but when he looked away from the old chief he saw that his wife was trembling, and the day returned to the present.

'What does thee seek?' he asked again, this time as a wary trader, not as a poet.

'A buffalo, Great Chief Rusk.'

'We have no buffalo.'

'Yes. Up where the stream ends,' and the old man pointed north toward the tank.

'Have we any buffalo?' Rusk asked, and Yeager said: 'An old one comes wandering in, now and then.'

'He's up there,' Wading Bird said.

'What does thee want with him?' Rusk asked, and the old man gave an anguished explanation which left both Earnshaw and his wife close to tears:

'Not many days are left, not many buffalo roam the plains. All is forgotten. You and I grow older, Great Chief Rusk, and death creeps ever closer to us.

'The young ones of few summers, they have never known our old ways. The hunt. The chase. The look of the buffalo when you are close upon him. The pounding of the hoofs. The cries. The ecstasy. The hot blood on the hands.

'Great Chief Rusk, you have the buffalo. I have the young men who need to remember. Grant us permission to hunt your buffalo as we used to hunt. At Camp Hope you always tried to understand us. Understand us now.'

Rusk looked at the fourteen boys and asked them in Comanche: 'How many have seen a buffalo?' and less than half indicated that they had. He then consulted with Frank Yeager, who grudgingly conceded that with most of the ranch longhorns in the southern reaches, little trouble could ensue if the Indians hunted a buffalo up by the tank, so permission was granted, and the people in the stone houses watched as Chief Wading Bird arranged his braves for the chase.

He placed his two oldest boys in the lead, and he took

position at the rear with the three youngest children, who bestrode their ponies with skill. When the formation was ready, he cried exhortations in Comanche, waved his arms, and pointed north toward the tank. With high-pitched cries the young braves set forth.

The two Rusks, Yeager and Jaxifer followed at a respectable distance, and after about an hour the cavalryman cried: 'They see it!' And there, at a lonely spot where the range tailed off toward the Red River, the Comanche came upon their ancient prey.

With a cry they had learned but had never before used, two boys in the lead urged their companions on, and the chase was joined. Earnshaw, watching this strange performance, had the fleeting thought that perhaps the lone buffalo understood his role in this ancient ritual, understood that this was his last chase, too, for he darted this way and that, over lands which had once contained millions of his fellows, throwing the unskilled riders into gullies from which their old chief had difficulty in extricating them.

But at last their persistent nagging at his heels wore him down, and the great head lowered as if he were preparing to fight off the wolves he had resisted in his earlier days, and his feet grew heavy, and his breath came in painful gasps.

In these climatic moments of the last hunt, Emma felt a wild urge to spur her horse forward and drive the Indian boys away from the old monarch of her plains. 'Let him live!' she shouted to the wind, but no one heard, and she watched with pain as the little lads on their little ponies encircled the buffalo while the old man shouted encouragement from his post of guidance, and at midafternoon on that hot June day the young Comanches killed the last buffalo in the vicinity of Fort Garner. They did it ceremoniously, as in the old days when no rations were issued at the Indian post, those days when the Comanche lived and died with the buffalo, prospering when it prospered, starving when it retreated beyond their grasp.

By no means did that final hunt of 1879 end in solemn ritual, for after the great beast had been slain and his liver cut out for the lads to eat, Chief Wading Bird rode back to the fort, ostensibly to thank his former protector. But when he appeared, Emma suspected that his visit involved not Earnshaw but her, and she was right, because when the boys had tethered their horses he bade them run off, leaving him to talk alone with the Rusks.

'Great Chief, Little Woman who used to live with us, I seek words, important words.'

'Sit with us,' Rusk said, unaware that his wife was trembling.

She had cause, for when the three were seated on the porch of the house which had once been the Wetzels', Wading Bird said: 'I have brought your son.'

At first Earnshaw did not comprehend, but when Wading Bird repeated the word, pointing directly at Emma, he realized that the true purpose of this foray south was not only to hunt buffalo in the old manner, but also to deliver the son of Little Woman to his mother. His impulsive response, the one he could not have stifled had he wished, was one of generous acceptance: 'Wading Bird! He will be welcomed in our home. And he will have a little brother, who now sleeps inside.'

But Emma spoke otherwise: 'I do not want him. Those days are lost. It is all no more.'

The two men stared at her, a mother rejecting her own son. To Wading Bird the experiences which Emma had suffered were an expected part of life, the treatment accorded all prisoners. He could think of a dozen captured women from his warrior days – Mexicans, Apache, many whites – and when, after initial punishments, they had borne chidren, they had loved them as mothers should and helped them to become honorable braves. It was the Comanche way of life, and now Little Woman was being offered her son, and she was refusing him. It passed comprehension.

Nor could her husband understand. He had seen her joy when she was pregnant with their son and daily witnessed her extraordinary love for young Floyd. Because of her own tormented childhood, she had lavished unusual care on Floyd and would presumably continue to do so. As for her Indian son, Earnshaw had often speculated on where the boy was and what he might be doing. Now he learned that the boy was here, at Fort Garner, on a horse, his lips rich with buffalo liver as in the old days, and he believed that if Emma could see him, she would want to keep him.

'Fetch the lad,' he told Wading Bird, but at this suggestion

Emma gave a loud wail: 'No!'

Still believing that the sight of the boy would melt her heart, he dispatched the eager chief, who summoned Emma's son. Blue Cloud was eight years old, a fine-looking fellow, somewhat tall for his age, eager, bright-eyed. 'Does he look like his father?' Earnshaw asked with the Quaker simplicity which stunned those around him.

Coldly, staring right at the boy, she said: 'His father could have been one of twenty.' Then she repeated: 'Those days are lost. Take him away.'

'Emma! For the love of God, this child is thy son.'

'It is ended,' she said.

When the two men tried to dissuade her, she pulled the hair away from her ears and ripped off her wooden nose. Thrusting her face close to her son's, she cried: 'Remember me as your people made me.' And she held her face close to his until he turned away.

Wading Bird took the boy by the hand and led him back to his companions. Sadly he mounted his horse, sadly he waved to the Rusks. Earnshaw, standing at the edge of the parade ground, nodded as the Comanche departed, the last he would ever see. With their broken promises they had broken his heart, and brought him to disgrace because of the love he held for them. He had hoped, during the interview with the boy, that this lad might be the agency through which he could regain contact with the Indians, but it was not to be, for when he sought Emma he found her in a corner, as in the days of her captivity, shivering. If there had been sunlit days on the plains which she wished to remember, there were ugly, dark ones she must forget, and when memories of these came surging back, she felt thankful for the refuge her husband's village now provided.

Earnshaw's struggle to establish Fort Garner as a viable community still hinged upon that problem which assailed all the little Western settlements: 'How can we earn enough income to support a thousand people?' Normal farming was impossible; land even fifty yards back from a stream would be so arid that it could not be tilled. Lumbering was not feasible, for the grassland provided no trees. There were no minerals, and the village could not focus upon transportation, for there was none except for the rickety stage that ran spasmodically to Jacksborough. For the time being it seemed that only the ranging longhorns would provide any cash.

With some humility, Earnshaw confessed: 'It may be thy longhorns, Emma, which will save Larkin,' and once he conceded this, he began to take professional interest in the scientific breeding of his wife's ranch stock, even going so far as to purchase from England two good bulls of a different breed. If numbers alone determined which facts in history would become legendary, the relatively few Texas cowboys who herded their cattle up the Chisholm Trail to Abilene, or up the Great Western to Dodge city, or along the Goodnight-Loving to Colorado, would not qualify. For if you totaled all the cattle these men tended in a decade, you would find that they had accounted for not much more than twenty or twenty-five percent of the cattle produced in America; the vast bulk was bred and marketed east of the Mississippi. But what Texas lacked in quantity it made up for in the dramatic quality of its longhorns and in men like R. J. Poteet who herded them.

Stay-at-homes like Earnshaw Rusk, who never rode a cattle trail, also shared responsibility for the Texas legend, because they saw that if Texas beef was to be competitive with the better beef being produced in the East, a more rewarding breed than the longhorn must be developed. But when these far-seeing men tried to introduce improved bulls onto their ranches, they were greeted with scorn. Even a rational man like Poteet warned: 'The only cattle that can stand those long drives north are Texas cattle, and that will always mean the longhorn.'

Rusk argued: 'If they have railroads in Kansas, won't we have them soon in Texas? Then our cattle won't have to trail hundreds of miles. They'll ride straight through to Chicago.'

Poteet laughed: 'You ever followed the history of railroads in Texas? "Give us five thousand dollars and we'll have a train at your town in seven months." Fifty railroads have been organized that way, and not one of them has seen an engine on its tracks, and most of them haven't seen the tracks.' He studied the bleak land that encompassed Fort Garner and said sardonically: 'You may get trains here about 19 and 81, if then.' And he warned Rusk not to experiment with strange bulls:

'You'll produce an animal that can't trail to market, and I won't try to drove such weaklings north.'

Rusk's own foreman, Frank Yeager, was displeased when Rusk, ignoring all advice, purchased two Hereford bulls from a breeder in Missouri who told him: 'Great idea, Rusk! Your Longhorn from Texas is an authentic breed, just like my Hereford from England. Your strong cows and my fat bulls will produce a majestic animal,' and when Earnshaw received the bill of sale he noticed that it showed the name of his cattle with a L, just as if they had been Black Angus. But when the bulls arrived at Fort Garner, Yeager almost refused to unload them when they arrived by wagon from Jacksborough, but Earnshaw enlisted support from his wife: 'Emma, thy bulls are here and Frank is proving difficult.'

'I didn't order them,' she pointed out, but he pleaded: 'They're thine now. Please help.' So she relented and persuaded Yeager to unload the beasts, but when he saw how fat they were, how listless compared to a rangy Longhorn bull that he preferred called Mean Moses, he refused to deal with them and left that job to the two black cavalrymen and the white infantryman.

But now a problem in ranch management arose, one that was beginning to perplex the entire frontier. Because the imported bulls were so valuable, they had to be grazed in a pasture from which they could not stray. This would have been a simple problem in Missouri, where there were ample oak trees for fence posts and soft soil in which to place them. But in this part of Texas there were almost no trees stout enough to yield wooden posts and split rails, and when they were imported, at prohibitive cost, it was almost impossible to dig post holes in the hard-baked, rocky earth. After many disappointments, Yeager growled: 'If you want to fence in those precious bulls of yours, you've got to buy posts from East Texas.' So a few cartloads were imported at a cost that frightened Earnshaw.

The pastures in which they kept the two bulls were so small that the animals grew fatter and fatter for lack of exercise, and it was Yeager's opinion that if he put half a dozen strong Longhorn cows in with each bull, 'them Longhorn ladies'll chew them dumplin's up.' In this he was wrong; Hereford bull and Longhorn cow mated well, and began to produce stout, reddish-coloured calves of great attractiveness and commercial promise, but this merely aggravated the problem, for now more fences were required to keep the more valuable offspring protected. Every time one of the imported bulls produced another calf – and there were now hundreds of such potent sires on the Western ranches – the Texas frontier was threatened a little more, for when a Longhorn worth only five dollars was replaced by an imported beast worth fifty, procedures had to change, and Rusk was continually saying: 'We must have more fences.'

In the early 1880s one of the most revolutionary forces in American history appeared in West Texas, a brash young man of such explosive enthusiasm that ten minutes' talk with him was bound to produce visions. He was Alonzo Betz, thirty-two years old, out of a place called Eureka, Illinois. He wore a bizarre mixture of clothing, half dude-Chicago, half rural-Texas, and he chattered like a Gatling gun: 'Folks, I bring a solution to your problems. I come like Aaron leading you to the promised land.' None of his listeners could figure out how Aaron got into the picture, but Alonzo gave them scant time for such reflection.

He talked with his hands, drawing vast imaginary pictures, and as he warmed to his subject, he liked to pull his purple tie loose as if its tightness had impeded his words: 'Folks, right here is the answer to your worries. I bring you the future.'

What he brought was one of those inventions like the cotton gin which modify history, and as soon as he revealed it on the former parade ground at Fort Garner, Earnshaw Rusk appreciated its applications: 'This here we call the barbed-wire fence, because at intervals along it, as you can see, our patented machine twists in a very sharp, pointed barb. We also provide you with a post which even this child could hammer into the sod, and when you've strung three strands of this around your fields, your ... cattle ... are ... penned ... in.'

Frank Yeager scoffed: 'My Longhorns'll knock that fence down in one minute.'

Alonzo Betz jumped on the threat. He literally jumped two feet forward, grasped Yeager by the arm, and cried loudly: 'You're right to think that. Everybody does at first. From Illinois to Arkansa, I've been told "My bulls would knock that fence down in one minute," just like you said. So let's get your bulls and you and me build a little pasture right here wired in with my barbed wire, and we'll put a load of fresh hay out here . . . '

He engaged the entire population of Fort Garner, eleven families now, in the erection of a corral, and all were amazed at how easily the thin steel posts could be driven into the hard earth and how deftly the wires could be strung. Several men and one woman scratched their hands on the sharp wire, at which Betz chortled: 'If my wire stops you good people, it'll sure stop your stock.'

When the little area was fenced, he shouted for Yeager to bring in some Longhorns, and he shouted – he never just spoke – for the best available hay to be piled out of reach. For nearly an hour the villagers watched as the powerful animals moved up against the unfamiliar fence and backed off when they came into contact with the barbs.

'It works!' Earnshaw cried, and Emma, too, was pleased, but Yeager would not surrender: 'If we'd of had Mean Moses in there, down goes that fence.'

Once more Alonzo Betz jumped at the challenge: 'Let's fetch this Mean Moses and leave him with the others overnight,' and when this was agreed upon he said: 'I'll stand guard, because one thing I've learned. No honest man from Illinois can match a man from Texas when it comes to sheer devilry. I don't want you goadin' your animals on with no pitchfork.'

So the test was run, with Betz and Yeager enforcing its honesty, and through the long night the two men talked, with Betz proclaiming the glories of the future when every field would be fenced, and Yeager longing for the past when the range from Fort Worth to California remained free. At intervals people from the houses came to watch Mean Moses destroy the fence, but instead they saw the hungry bull start time and again for the succulent hay, only to be turned back by the barbed wire, and when dawn broke over the treeless plains and everyone saw the fence still standing with Moses docile inside, the future of barbed wire in this part of Texas was assured.

But Alonzo Betz was still a showman, one of the best, and when day had well broken he said: 'Now I want to prove to you good people that your Longhorns were really hungry during their vigil. Watch this.' And he produced an instrument they had not seen before, a pair of very long-handled wire cutters. 'The handles have to be long,' he explained, 'so as to apply leverage to these very short, sharp blades. Look what this means, how easy it is to handle barbed wire.'

Going to the fence, he positioned himself halfway between two posts, and with three rapid snips of his cutters, he threw down the fence, and through the opening thus provided, Mean Moses and the hungry Longhorns piled, eager to reach the hay.

'How much will it cost to fence in six thousand acres?' Rusk asked, and Betz replied: 'Show me your configuration,' and when Rusk did, the salesman make a quick calculation: 'Six thousand acres is nine point thirty-eight square miles. If perfectly square, you would need about twelve miles. In your configuration, more like fifteen miles. I can sell you barbed wire and posts for a hundred and fifty dollars a mile, so to do it all, which I would not recommend, would cost you two thousand, two hundred and fifty.'

The figure staggered the Rusks. It was quite beyond their reach, but they could see that the future of ranching was going to be determined by valuable cattle enclosed in relatively small pastures protected by barbed-wire fencing. 'What could we do?' Earnshaw asked, and Betz, eager to get a demonstration ranch started in an area which he felt was bound to prosper, said with great enthusiasm: 'My company, D. K. Rampart Wire and Steel of Eureka, Illinois, we want to establish a chain of ranches exhibiting our product. So everyone can see its application. We can fence in about three thousand of your acres for a special price of one thousand and fifty dollars, and we'd be honored at the opportunity to do so.'

It was agreed. Rusk, Yeager and Betz mounted horses, and accompanied by the two black cavalrymen, surveyed the Larkin lands, and all quickly concluded that they should enclose all fields abutting on Bear Creek and place additional fencing around the tank so that access to this steady supply of water could be controlled: 'This way you protect your water. You protect your valuable bulls. You keep everything neat.' At the end of the ride, even Yeager had to acknowledge that a new day had dawned on the Texas plains, and he began to study the pamphlets that would make him an expert on the handling of barbed wire. But before the deal could be concluded there was the question of money, the perennial problem of the frontier.

* * *

The growth of any village into a town was a subtle procedure. First came the store, for without it there could be no orderly society, and Fort Garner now had a good one run by the former sutler. Next came the school, and third, there had to be a good saloon to serve as social center for the cowhands and such adventurous young women as might want to try their luck in the settlement. Earnshaw, as a good Christian, did not wish to sell one of his barracks buildings to a soldier who had once been stationed at the fort and who proposed to open such an establishment, but he was also a Pennsylvania Quaker, and a cannier lot of businessmen had never been brought across the ocean to America, so a deal was struck, not with Earnshaw, who refused to touch liquor, but with Emma, who said: 'A town needs a little excitement.' The Barracks, as it was named, provided it.

The fourth requisite was a bank, which would lend money, provide stability, and serve as the industrial focus of the surrounding area. Certainly, Fort Garner needed a bank, but it was doubtful that any would regard such a meager economy as a sound basis for taking risks. Where would a bank look for its business? A few stock sales? An exchange of real estate now and then? Money mailed in from stabler societies back east to sons and daughters trying to subdue the plains? It might be decades before a place like Fort Garner could justify a bank, but just as the need became greatest, a man with tremendous vision and steel nerves moved into town, bought one of the better stone houses, imported a big iron safe, and announced himself as the First National Bank of Fort Garner, Texas.

Clyde Weatherby came from Indiana, home of America's shrewdest horse traders, and although he brought with him only limited capital borrowed from his former father-in-law, who wanted to see him, as he said, 'get the hell out of Indiana and stay out,' he did bring a marvelously clear vision of the future, which he confided to no one: Land is the secret. Things have got to happen out here – what, I don't know. Give me some land that touches water, and I'm in business. He had various intricate plans for getting hold of land and using it creatively.

Outstanding because of his well-tailored suits and string ties, he became favorably known as Banker Weatherby, generous in lending, severe in collecting, and when Rusk and young Betz appeared before him to seek a loan for payment on the barbed wire, he was enthusiastic.

'It could prove the making of the West,' he pontificated, and the men agreed. He then asked directly: 'Mr Rusk, what's the total bill to be?' and when Earnshaw explained, he smiled at Betz and said: 'Not excessive. Your price is lower than your competitors',' and Betz said: 'It better be.'

'Now, Mr Rusk, how much of the thousand and fifty dollars can you provide?' When Rusk said: 'Emma and I have five hundred and fifty in cash,' he smiled warmly and said: 'Excellent. So what you wish from me is a mere five hundred dollars.' Both Rusk and Betz were surprised that he should refer to this sum as *mere*; to them it was a fortune.

'How could we arrange this?' Rusk asked, and Weatherby said: 'Simplicity itself! You give me a mortgage, extend it for as many years as it will take you to pay off, and pay only three and three-quarters percent interest each year, no mind to the balance.'

'How much would that be?'

'Less than nineteen dollars a year.'

'That would be easy,' Rusk said, whereupon Weatherby added: 'There is the provision, you know, that if conditions change at the bank, we could demand payment in full, but that never happens.'

'And if I couldn't pay ... in full I mean?'

'It's known as "calling the loan," but it never happens.'

'But what does it mean?'

Very carefully Mr Weatherby explained the legal situation: 'Our Texas Constitution of 18 and 76 forbids me from taking your homestead in fulfillment of an ordinary debt. And it forbids me from issuing you a mortgage simply to acquire funds for idle indulgence. But it does allow me to give you a mortgage on your homestead for its improvement, and that's what we're doing here.'

'So my entire ranch is mortgaged?'

'In this case, yes. If you fail to pay us back our money, we take your ranch, and sell it at auction to get our money, and give you what's left over.'

In one respect, this was not an indecent deal, for the original Larkins had acquired their six thousand acres at an average cost of only four cents an acre, so that its base value was not more than $240, less than half the amount of the loan the bank was making; but in a practical sense the conditions being offered were appalling. The Rusks could pay interest for ten years, and reduce the outstanding balance to $100, but if they ever had a bad year in which they could not come up with the interest to keep the mortgage alive – or if the bank at that bad moment chose to demand payment in full – the Rusks could lose not only their land but also the improvements, which might be extremely valuable. It was one of the cruelest systems ever devised for the conduct of business, but it was sanctified by every court; through this device bankers would gain control of vast reaches of Western land, especially in Texas. When Earnshaw Rusk signed his mortgage of $500 he unwittingly placed his future in jeopardy, but as Banker Weatherby assured him: 'We never foreclose.'

So the deal was made: the Rusks gave Alonzo Betz $300 of their $550 as a down payment; the barbed wire was shipped from Eureka, Illinois; Frank Yeager and his men began building fence; and Banker Weatherby had in his big iron safe a mortgage on the entire Larkin Ranch.

Bob wahr they called it throughout Texas, and when Yeager and his men finished driving their posts and stringing their strands they sounded the death knell of the open range, for they had removed the choicest acres and the best water holes once used by the itinerant cattlemen. With timing that was diabolically unfortunate, they had everything in place just as that year's big cattle drives from the south began, and just as one of the most severe droughts in history started to bake the Texas range.

Emma, watching these restrictive procedures, was not surprised when they caused trouble, for as she had warned: 'Earnshaw, you're chopping this great open land into mean little squares, and the people won't tolerate it.' She wanted to add: 'And my Longhorns won't either.'

The first rumbles of trouble came when school began after

Easter vacation, and they were so trivial that neither Rusk nor Yeager could later recall their beginning. Jaxifer had come to Rusk with a curious protest. The two cavalrymen had met an Indian squaw, a Waco from the eastern regions, and had taken her into their stone house, ostensibly as cook-helper. None of the white families could be sure to whom she belonged, but in due time she had produced a pretty little girl baby, half black, half Indian, and because the cavalrymen had witnessed the advantages children enjoyed if they could read and write – which they themselves could not – they wanted the girl, whosoever daugher she was, to get an education: 'The fence we've put up, Mr Rusk, it makes the teacher walk the long way round instead of across the field, as before.'

'I am sorry about that.'

'And we wondered if there was some way to cut a hole . . . '

'Where the road runs, we've already put in gates. But cut a fence merely to continue an old footpath? Never. That fence cannot be touched.'

'But the teacher . . .

When other parents began to protest the inconvenience to their teacher, Rusk and Yeager went out to study the problem, and they saw immediately that this portion of their fence had been unwisely strung, for it did cut off access to the school, but the fence had been so costly and had required so much effort to construct that it had become a virtue in itself, something that had to be protected. 'What we will do,' Yeager promised, 'is give the people lumber so they can build stiles, but cutting our fences except where roads run through, we cain't allow that.'

The next complaint was more serious. A family not connected with either the ranch or the village rode in to complain bitterly about what the fence had done to them: 'From long before the fort was built, we used the road which runs south from the tank where the soldier and his girl killed their selves. Now your fence cuts it off, and we—'

'The fence is on our land,' Yeager interrupted sternly.

'Yes, but it cuts a public road.'

'The only public road is the one that runs east-west from Three Cairns. And we've put in gates to service that.'

'But we've always used this road.'

'Not any longer. We've fenced our land, and that's that.'

'But if the county seat is going to be at Fort Garner, how can we get—?'

'You'll have to go around and catch the Three Cairns road.'

'Go around! Surely you could add one more gate.'

'The fence stands,' Yeager said, terminating that conversation.

Less than a week later, one of the ranch hands rode in with sickening news: 'Come and see what they done.' And when Rusk and Yeager rode out to where their new fence blocked the disputed road, they found that someone had cut it and knocked down the posts.

'I'll shoot the son-of-a-bitch who did this!' Yeager threatened, but Rusk restrained him: 'There'll be no shooting.'

But there was. When Jaxifer and another hand rode out to rebuild the fence across the road, someone shot at them, and they quickly retreated. Frank Yeager himself went out, well armed, to repair the fence, and when someone fired at him, he coolly waited, watched, fired back, and killed the man.

Thus began one of the ugliest episodes of Texas history, the Great Range War, in which one group of cattlemen who had been utilizing the open range suddenly found that another group with a little more money had fenced off traditional routes and, much worse, traditional water holes. One of the most severe losses of water occurred at the Larkin Ranch, where the Rusks had fenced in their tank north of town, and not with one line of fence, but three, because the outer ring delineated the perimeter of the ranch, while the double strand, with its guarded gate, protected the water from pressures by either the Rusk cattle or strays that might crowd in.

With the first big drive of the summer it became obvious that there would be conflict, because cattle had to have water prior to the long trail up to the Red River. But for some curious reason, Earnshaw Rusk, this peaceable Quaker, refused to see that his action in closing off the water hole was arbitrary, unjustified, and opposed to the public welfare. His recent years of dealing with Texans had indoctrinated him with their fundamental law: 'Private property is sacrosanct, mine in particular.' So he continued to keep other cattle away from his water; he continued to maintain his fences, even if they did cut people off from their accustomed routes. He was neither irrational or obdurate; he had become a Texan.

Almost daily, now, one of the hands reported at dawn: 'They cut more fence,' for if Alonzo Betz had been a genius in selling bob wahr, other salesmen had been equally ingenious in selling long-handled cutters that could lay that wire flat within seconds, so daily Rusk and Yeager were forced to ride out and repair the fences.

The war was not an unequal one, for the cutters, those men who loved freedom and the open range, could in one dark night destroy an immense reach of fence; sometimes every strand for two miles would be cut between each pair of posts, at grievous expense to the rancher. The rancher, on the other hand, could post his trigger-happy ranch hands in dark hiding places among the dips and swerves of his land, and then gunfire exploded, with the newfangled wire-cutters left dangling on the fence beside the corpses.

In this warfare the advantage now began to swing to the fence-cutters, for the hardened men trailing their cattle north hired professional gunslingers to ride along, so that when a battle erupted, the firepower was apt to be on the side of the trail drivers. Frank Yeager learned these facts the hard way when one of his new hands was killed while trying to stop a wire-cutting. He retaliated with fiendish cleverness.

Originally opposed to fencing, he was now its primary defender, for in the act of building a fence he identified with it, and any attack upon it was an attack on him. So when his man was killed he announced: 'No more watching at night. We'll find other ways.' He did. Utilizing his imperfect knowledge of explosives, he devised a number of sensitive bombs which would be placed along the wires and activated if the tension on any wire was released by cutting. Each bomb contained so many fragmentations that the cutter did not have to be close when it went off; the shards would fly a long distance to kill or seriously maim.

Now the hands at Fort Garner slept in their beds, rode out at dawn, and counted the corpses. The trail drivers in retaliation began shooting cattle inside the fences and setting fire to pastures, while settled citizens whose modes of travel had been disrupted by the fences began cutting them with hurtful frequency. So more deaths ensued. On all fronts it was now open warfare.

One hateful aspect of the battle at Fort Garner was that Earnshaw Rusk, contrary to every principle of his upbringing, found himself acting as a kind of general defending his fort. Unwilling to handle a gun himself, he directed the strategies of those who did. Even worse, he also served as leader of those other ranchers in the area who had fenced their properties. He became General Rusk, defender of the bob-wahr fence.

The Range War was resolved in a manner peculiar to this state. No police were sent into the area, no state militia, no army units. In August, when the number of killings became serious, a medium-sized man in his early thirties rode quietly into town, Texas Ranger Clyde Rossiter, slit-eyed and with his hands never far from his holsters. His assigned job was to terminate the Larkin County Range War. He moved soberly, made no arrests, no threats. He was out on the range a good deal, inspecting fences and intercepting herds as they moved north, and wherever he went he made it clear that the fence war was over.

He was successful in halting the carnage, but as the people of the region watched in admiration while he took charge, it became obvious that he always sided with the big ranchers and opposed the little man no matter what the issue, so one night a group of citizens asked if they could meet with him to present what they held to be their just grievances. He refused to listen to their whining, telling them: 'It's my job to establish peace, not to correct old injustices.'

He explained his basic attitude one night when taking supper with the Rusks: 'From what I've seen of Texas, the good things in our society are always done by people with money, the bad things by people without. So I find it practical to work with people who own large ranches, because they know what's best, and against those with nothing, because they never know anything.'

'Do most of the Rangers feel that way?' Earnshaw asked.

'Our experience teaches us.'

'Does thee own a ranch?'

'I do, and I'd not want trespassers cutting my fences.'

'What should I do about the people who protest about our cutting their road?'

'It's your land, isn't it?'

'But how should I respond?'

'I'm not here to pass laws. I'm here to stop the shootin', and I think it's stopped.' But he did, as a careful Ranger, want to inspect all angles of this war, so he left Fort Garner for several days to range the countryside between that town and Jacksborough, and was absent when R. J. Poteet came north with two thousand, seven hundred head bound for Dodge City. When Poteet reached the Larkin Ranch and found to his dismay that the traditional water hole at Bear Creek had been fenced off, he proceeded methodically but with minimum damage to cut the outer fence that his cattle must penetrate before they could approach the tank, whose double fences would also have to be cut if the Longhorns were to drink.

Rusk's watchmen were amazed at the boldness with which this determined stranger was cutting their fence, and when they rode back to inform Rusk, they could find only Yeager, who grabbed a rifle and rode breathlessly to the scene, only to discover that it was Poteet who was doing it.

'Hey there! Poteet! What're you up to?'

'Watering my cattle, as always.'

'That's fenced.'

'It shouldn't be. This is open range, time out of mind.'

'No longer. Times have changed.'

'They shouldn't.'

'Poteet, if your men touch that fence, my men will shoot.'

'They'd be damned fools if they did. I've got some powerful gunmen ridin' with me.'

At this point Earnshaw Rusk rode up, and he was preparing to issue orders to his troops when Poteet spoke: 'Friend Earnshaw, I don't want your men to do any' ing foolish. You see my chuck wagon? Why do you think the sides are up?'

When the Rusk men looked at the ominous wagon, they could see that it had been placed in an advantageous position, with its flexible sides closed. 'Friend Earnshaw, one of my good men in there has his rifle pointed directly at you. Another has you in his sights, Mr Yeager. Now I propose to water my stock as usual, and I shall have to cut your fences to do it.'

Rusk took a deep breath, then said firmly: 'Poteet, my men will shoot if thee touches that fence.'

For a long time no one spoke, no one moved. R. J. Poteet, born in Virginia fifty-six years ago, had acquired certain characteristics in the cattle-herding business which he was powerless to alter, and one was that his animals must be tended daily, honestly and with maximum care. This included regular watering. Since the close of the War Between the States, he had trailed one large consignment north each year and sometimes two, for a total of twenty-one herds, some of huge dimension, and he had never lost even two percent, not to Indians, or bandits, or drought, or stampede, or shifty buyers, and it was unthinkable that he should vary his procedures now. He was going to water his steers.

Earnshaw Rusk believed profoundly in whatever he dedicated himself to. When he saw that a new day was opening upon the once-free range, he spurred its arrival. And perhaps most subtle of all, he had become infected with the Texas doctrine that a man's land was not only his castle, but also his salvation.

In the long wait no one fired, but all stood ready. Then the two leaders spoke. Rusk, still playing the role of general, said: 'Did thee know, Poteet, that Ranger Rossiter is here to end this fighting? If thee shoots me, he'll hound thee to the ends of the earth,' and Poteet snapped: 'Rangers always side with the rich. I'm surprised a man of your principles would want their help. Friend Earnshaw, what would you do if you had twenty-seven hundred head of cattle within smelling distance of water? And none elsewhere to be found?'

There was silence, when life and the values men fought for hung in the balance; it was prolonged, and in it Earnshaw Rusk dropped his pose of being a general and acknowledged that what he and Frank Yeager had been doing was wrong. It might represent the wave of the future, and perhaps it would prevail before the decade faded, but as things stood now, it was wrong. It was wrong to fence in a water hole which had been used, as Poteet said, 'time out of mind.' It was wrong to cut off public roads as if school-teachers and children were of no concern. It was wrong to impose arbitrary new rules merely because one was strong enough to get a loan at the bank, and it was terribly wrong to abolish a neighbor's inherited rights simply because thee had bob-wahr and he didn't.

'What would *you* do if the cattle were yours?' Poteet

repeated, emphasizing the pronoun.

Rusk had been trained to respect the moral implications of any problem, and since he had already conceded that his fencing-in the water hole was wrong, he must now correct that error. In a very low voice, as if speaking philosophically on a matter which did not involve him personally, he said: 'If they were my cattle, I'd have to water them.' And with a motion of his right arm he indicated that Yeager and his men should withdraw.

'We'll replace your fences,' Poteet said as his hands started cutting. 'But if I were you, I'd leave them down.'

Rusk could never turn aside from a moral debate: 'For a few years, Poteet, thee wins. But thee must know the old ways are dead. Soon we'll have fences everywhere.'

'More's the pity.'

'Thee will carry my wife's cattle on to Dodge?'

'As always.'

'I'll go count them.'

'I'll do the countin'.'

Like many a politician, Senator Cobb, abetted by Petty Prue, was an outstanding success in Washington but something less when he returned home to explain his behavior to his constituents. On his latest visit to Jefferson he had barely reached his plantation when a group of irate voters drove up headed by a jut-jawed Mr Colquitt.

'Senator,' the man demanded, 'why did you let 'em blast our Red River Raft?'

While he fumbled for an explanation, they dragged him from the parlor and down to the Lammermoor wharf, and what he saw came close to bringing tears to his eyes, for the stout wharf which he and Cousin Reuben had built with such care back in 1850 now wasted away some fifty feet removed from the sparse water in which no boat of any size could function.

'You allowed 'em to destroy the value of your land,' Colquitt said. 'And in town it's the same way. Our beautiful harbor where the big boats came from New Orleans. All vanished.'

Another man cried in anguished protest: 'Why didn't you stop 'em?'

Seeing the anger of his constituents, Cobb knew that their

questions were vital and that if he wanted to continue as a senator, he must give them a sensible answer, but he was not the man to hide behind platitudes or fatuous promises that could never be kept. He would give them an honest, harsh answer: 'Gentlemen, no one in Jefferson has lost more by the destruction of the Raft than I have. Look at this dry hole. A way of life gone. But on the day that fellow in Sweden made TNT possible, he doomed our Raft. For a hundred years people had been talking about removing the Raft, and they accomplished nothing. TNT comes along and there goes our livelihood.'

'It should have stayed that way,' Colquitt said, and Cobb replied: 'With TNT many valuable things are going to be changed.'

'Well, what are you going to do about it?'

'Do? About the Raft? Nothing. Do you think Louisiana is going to let us rebuild it so that our Jefferson, population eight hundred thirty-one, can have a seaport?'

As soon as he had given this sharp answer he knew he must become conciliatory, so he invited the men back into the parlor, where Petty Prue served tea and molasses cookies: 'Gentlemen, you asked me what I am going to do. Plenty, believe me. First, I'm going to surrender to TNT. It blew our Raft right out of the Red River, and nothing will ever restore it. Second, I will lead the battle to get a railroad into this town, because once we do that, we'll get our cotton to New Orleans faster and better than before. Third, I'm going to make every improvement possible at Lammermoor, because even though we've lost our dock, we'll discover new ways to prosper. In Texas that always happens.'

Mr Colquitt, jaw still out-thrust, growled: 'Cain't you make Washington give us a railroad?'

'I've tried to nudge them, but Washington says: "We have to consider the whole nation, not just little Texas." '

'Senator, I've learned one thing in life,' Colquitt conceded. 'Whenever the United States government meddles in Texas affairs, Texas gets swindled.'

Cobb laughed, as did his wife, who said: 'Our experience has been the same, Mr Colquitt. Texas is so big, it has imperial problems. Congress is used to handling the little troubles of states like Vermont and Iowa. Texas staggers them. They have no comprehension of our needs.'

'But how do you two people feel about the drop in value of your plantation? Who would buy it now, with no dock?' Colquitt asked.

It was Petty Prue who answered, vigorously: 'Of course the value has dropped. And sharply. But you watch! It'll grow back for some reason we can't imagine right now. That's the rule in Texas. Change and adjustment and sorrow. But always the value of our land increases.'

'Why don't we just leave the Union?' Mr Colquitt asked; he had grown up in South Carolina.

'That's been settled.'

'But we can still divide into five separate states, that I'm sure of.' Mr Colquitt had been in Texas only three years but already it was *we*; two more and he would be a passionate devotee of all things Texan.

'We could divide,' Senator Cobb granted, 'but I doubt we ever would.'

'Why not?'

'Which state would get the Alamo?' he asked with a smile.

If Texas had been powerless to halt the dynamiting of the Red River Raft, it did finally end the Great Range War. A number of bills were proposed and enacted, putting an end to the killing; they worked this way, as a small farmer near Fort Garner, where the fighting had been heaviest, saw it:

'Anyone who cuts a fence, anywhere, any time, he's to be arrested, fined, and thrown in jail for a long spell. Anyone found with a pair of cutters – on his person, in his house, in his wagon – he gets similar punishment. Any trail driver like R. J. Poteet who forces his cattle onto lan which had been fenced is sent to jail for one to five.

'But don't you think for one minute that the big owners who have fenced in public land get off scot-free, nosiree. They will be asked politely to unfence land that contains traditional water supplies. they have to provide gates if they've fenced across public roads. And they must not ignore the customary rights of ordinary citizens. But they don't have to do any of these things right away. Government allows them grace periods up to six months, and if they haven't made the alterations by then, they'll be given warnings. When they've ignored such warnings, maybe three years, they'll be severely rebuked . . . in writin'. Fines? Jail? For the big owners? You must be jokin'!

Inexorably the movements launched by Rusk to turn his village into a proper town continued, often in directions he had not anticipated. With the first four keystones in place—store, school, saloon, bank—he was free to turn his attention to the next three: churches, newspaper, railroad. With these he met both success and failure.

Banker Weatherby, also eager to see his town and his bank grow, was instrumental in solving the problem of the churches. 'Earnshaw,' he said one morning when Rusk came in to pay interest on his loan, 'a town does better if it has a core of strong churches.'

'How do we attract them?'

'We have several informal congregations in town right now. They'd be delighted to have free land. Then we'll ask the Fort Worth newspapers to announce that we'll give any recognized religion a free corner lot of its own choosing.'

Weatherby's advice was resoundingly apt, for when this news circulated through Texas eight different churches investigated and six selected their sites and started building. Baptists chose first and nabbed the best spot in the heart of the town; Methodists came second; the Presbyterians chose a quiet spot; and the Episcopalians not only selected on the edge of town but also purchased an adjoining lot because they said they liked lots of space for a generous building. The Church of Christ would be satisfied for the first dozen years with a small wooden building, and a group that called themselves Saviors of the Bible erected only a tent.

This was one of the best trade-offs Rusk would make, because the churches brought stability; they encouraged settlers from older towns to move in; and they deposited their collections in the First National Bank of Fort Garner.

When the bank had been in existence for some time, an official arrived from Washington to inform Weatherby that the title he had invented for his establishment could not be so loosely applied: 'You can't go around calling just any old bank a

National Bank. Take that sign down.' While the official was in town he also listened to Rusk's complaint about the name of the place: 'Can thee please inform the government that we want a better name? Fort Garner existed only a few years. It's a silly, militaristic name. Much more appropriate would be Larkin.'

Earnshaw made no headway with his plea, but it did serve as further inspiration for a campaign he would continue for two decades. Whenever he posted a letter he asked the man in charge: 'When does the name-change take place?' And always the postmaster replied: 'That's in the lap of the gods.' The gods were either opposed to the change or forgetful, because the name stayed the same, and this so irritated Earnshaw that he finally wrote a letter to the President:

> Mr President:
> I have tried constantly to have the name of our post office changed from Fort Garner to Larkin, and have not even received the courtesy of a sensible reply. The state of Texas has so many post offices bearing the word *fort* it seems more like a military establishment than a civilian state. Fort Worth, Fort Davis, Fort Griffin, Fort Stockton and Fort Garner to name only a few. We would appreciate if you would instruct your Postmaster General to rename our town Larkin.
>
> Earnshaw Rusk

He received no reply, but quickly his attention was diverted to a matter of much graver significance than the choice of a name. A bright young man from Massachusetts with a Harvard degree, Charles Fordson, had for some time been moving through the West with two mules, a wagon and a cargo which had since the days of Gutenberg represented real progress. It was a hand-operated printing press with ten trays of movable type, and it was seeking a home.

As soon as Rusk learned of the young man's arrival he cornered him, showed him the five remaining empty buildings, and assured him: 'We need you, and you'll find no better prospect in all of Texas. Larkin! Sure to become a metropolis. Join us and grow!' And so this vital link was added to the tenuous chain of civilization: in 1868, the Larkin brothers had chosen this confluence for the site of their ranch; in 1869, the United States Army confirmed the wisdom of their choice; in 1870 Sutler Simpson thought that if he were to open a grocery here, he could make money, and before long Banker Weatherby thought the same. Now, in 1881 young Charles Fordson with his peripatetic press listens to Earnshaw's blandishments and decides that the newspaper just might succeed, but he names it the *Larkin County Defender*, for he fears that the town alone might not provide enough activity to justify his venture.

During a quiet spell in the winter of 1881, Fordson sought to distract attention from hard times by publishing a series of well-constructed articles combining news and editorial opinion. Random paragraphs indicate the thrust of his argument:

> ... In Larkin County during the past two years there have been four executions by gunfire on the streets of the county seat and ten in the outlying districts.
> ... Certainly, at least half the fourteen victims deserved to die, and we applaud the public-spirited citizens who took charge of their punishment. But it would be difficult to claim that the other half died in accordance with any known principles of justice. They were murdered, and they should not have been.
> ... The only solution to this problem is a stricter code of law enforcement, by our officers, by our juries and by our sentencing judges. This journal calls for an end to the lawlessness in Larkin County and in Texas generally.

The articles evoked a response which Editor Fordson had not anticipated, for although a few citizens, like the Baptist minister and three widows who had lost their husbands to gunfire, applauded the common sense of his arguments, the general consensus was that 'if some popinjay from Massychusetts is afeered of a little gunfire, he should skedaddle back to where he come from.'

The serious consequence of the articles came when the governor directed a fiery blast at the would-be reformer. His defense of Texas was reprinted throughout the state, bringing scorn upon Larkin County:

> Weak-willed, frightened newcomers to our Great State have offered comment in the public press to the effect that Texas is a lawless place. Nothing could be further from the truth. Our lawmen are famed throughout the nation, our judges are models of propriety, and our citizens are noted for their willing obedience to whatever just laws our legislature passes ...

The governor's theories received a test in the case of the Parmenteer brothers, sons of a law-abiding farmer. The boys, as so often happened in families, followed two radically different courses. The elder son, Daniel, did well in school, read for law in an Austin office, passed his bar examination before the local judge, and became one of the leading lights in Larkin County, where he married the daughter of a clergyman and was in the process of raising four fine children.

His younger brother, Cletus, disliked school, hated teachers, and despised law officials. By the age of eighteen he had been widely known as 'a bad 'un,' a reputation that grew as years passed. At first he merely terrorized people his own age, until boys and girls he had known would have nothing to do with him. Then he started stealing things, which his parents replaced, but finally he launched into the perilous business of stealing horses and cattle, and that put him beyond the pale. As an outlaw he participated in two killings, and following a raid into New Mexico, a price was placed on his head in that territory, but as usual, this was ignored in Texas. He became a shifty, quick-triggered idler who brought considerable ignominy to his otherwise respectable family, and he could find no woman willing to risk marriage with him. He consorted only with other petty outlaws, and it was widely predicted throughout the county that sooner or later young Clete would have to be hanged by one sherif's posse or another.

Things were in this condition one bright spring day in 1881 when the growing town of Fort Garner heard the familiar sound of gunfire, and then the shout: 'Parmenteer has killed Judge Bates!' People rushed into the streets to find the alarm correct. At high noon, on the main thoroughfare, a respectable judge – well, not too respectable – had been callously shot in the presence of not less than twenty witnesses, all of whom identified Parmenteer as the killer. But it was not Cletus, the outlaw, who had done the killing; it was Daniel, the law-abiding lawyer.

The judge was dead, of that there could not be the slightest doubt, because four quick bullets had ripped his abdomen apart and he lay bleeding in the middle of the street. Lawyer Parmenteer walked steadily and without emotion to the sheriff's office, where he turned in his gun with the words 'A good deed done on a good day,' a verdict in which the town concurred.

Most towns in Texas had known such incidents, but this particular crime posed extraordinary problems for the editor of the *Larkin County Defender*.

'Jackson,' the young man said to his assistant as they discussed how to handle this case, 'we have a problem.'

'I don't think so. Let me talk with the two dozen people who saw the shooting.'

'The facts? We have no problem with them. The question is, how do we deal with them?'

'We just say "Lawyer Daniel Parmenteer—"'

'Did what?'

'Killed Judge Bates.'

'We dare not say boldly "Lawyer Parmenteer killed Judge Bates." Sounds too blunt, too accusatory.'

'The truth is: "Lawyer Parmenteer, brother of the noted outlaw—"'

'Stop. No mention of the brother. We'd have both of them gunning for us.'

'You may be right. So it's "Lawyer Parmenteer murders—"'

'Impossible to say that, Jackson. Murder implies guilt. How about "Lawyer Parmenteer shoots—"'

'I'm afraid of that on two counts. If we stress that he was a lawyer, it it might be interpreted as our prejudicing the case. And we cannot use the word shoot. Sounds as if he intended to do it.'

'My God! He walked up to him, if what I hear is true, spoke to him once, and pumped him full of lead. If that isn't shooting . . .'

'You don't understand, Jackson. We must not print a single word that in any way impugns either the motives or the actions of two of our leading citizens.'

So Fordson and Jackson agonized over how to handle the biggest story of the year, and they decided that there was almost nothing they could say which would not infuriate either Lawyer Parmenteer on the one hand, or the relatives of Judge Bates on the other. They could not point out that the lawyer had acted because a court case had gone against him, nor could they state what everybody in two counties knew, that Judge Bates was a drunken reprobate who took bribes on the side, as he had flagrantly done in the case which Parmenteer had lost.

In fact, there was almost nothing that the *Defender* could say about this case except that it had happened, and even that simple statement posed the most delicate problems, and when it came time to draft the headline, young Fordson found himself right back at the beginning.

REGRETTABLE KILLING ON MAIN STREET

had to be discarded for three reasons: to stress Main Street would imply that the sheriff had been delinquent; to use the word *killing* was simply too harsh, for as the governor himself had argued in his now-famous letter 'Texans do not go around killing people,' and *regrettable* might prove most troublesome of all, because it implied that the killing was unjustified, and to say this could well bring Lawyer Parmenteer storming into the editorial offices bent on another killing that would be justified.

One by one the two newspapermen discarded the traditional headline words: *deplorable, brutal, savage*. They all had to go, until young Jackson wailed: 'What can we say?' and Fordson remembered: 'There was this case in East Texas last year. They got away with calling it a *fuss*.'

'You mean that Copperthwaite case? Three men dead on Main Street, within five feet of one another? They called that a fuss?'

'In Texas you do,' Fordson said, and then in a stroke of genius he dashed off a headline that might work: UNFORTUNATE RENCONTRE IN FORT GARNER.

'What in hell is a rencontre?' Jackson asked, pronouncing the word in three syllables.

'It's a polite French way of saying that someone got shot in the gut. But I'm not too happy about the word *unfortunate*. The Parmenteer people might take unkindly to that. We don't want to launch a feud.' Fordson sighed, then said resignedly: 'No big headlines at all. No talks with any of the witnesses. Just something that happened on Main Street?' And when that week's edition of the *Defender* appeared, readers scanned the front page in vain for any big handling of the story; on page three buried among notices of meetings and offerings of new goods in the store, appeared the inconspicuous story: RENCONTRE IN FORT GARNER, with no adjectives, no gory details, and certainly no aspersions cast on either side.

The editor was applauded for his good taste and Daniel Parmenteer actually bowed to him as they passed. The lawyer was not apprehended for the killing because no one could be found in Fort Garner who had seen it, and the incoming judge, pleased to have had worthless Judge Bates removed from the bench so he could occupy it, held that because the killing occurred before he assumed jurisdiction, he could ignore it.

Indeed, the Parmenteer-Bates affair would have subsided like a hundred other murders in these frontier areas had not the younger Parmenteer, Cletus the outlaw, suddenly roared back into town, shot the place up, and stolen a horse. The gunfire could be forgiven as an act of high spirits, but the stealing of a horse went so against the grain of Texas morality that a posse had to be organized immediately: 'Men, we can't stand horse theft in this county!' and sixteen amateur lawmen were sworn in prior to setting out to run down the criminal.

By a stroke of poor luck, the leader of the posse – not designated by law but by noisy acclaim – turned out to be the younger brother of dead Judge Bates, and he prosecuted the chase with such a vengeance that by nightfall they had come upon the renegade struggling alone with the stolen horse, which had gone lame. It was quite clear from the stories which circulated afterward that Cletus Parmenteer had remained astride his incapable horse and had tried to surrender, thinking no doubt that his brother could somehow defend him against the charge of theft, but Anson Bates as leader of the posse would have none of that.

'What Anson done,' one of the posse members explained to Daniel Parmenteer later, 'was, he rode up to your brother and said "We don't want none of your kind in jail," and he blasted him six times, right through the chest, him standin' no further away than I am from you.'

When Lawyer Parmenteer heard this, he knew there was no possible response but for him to go shoot Anson Bates, which he did as the latter came out of the barbershop. 'Unarmed, without a call so he could defend hisse'f,' a Bates man explained to his clan, 'this proud son-of-a-bitch kilt our second brother,' and with that a general warfare erupted.

The Bates gang killed four Parmenteers, but were never able to get Lawyer Daniel, who moved quietly about the county, always armed. His people, fatal phrase, gunned down five Bates partisans, and before long the feud had spread, as such feuds always did, to the surrounding counties. For a while Bateses and Parmenteers fell like leaves, but most of the dead did not bear these names; a typical victim was some unimportant man like an Ashton farming in Jack County or a Lawson in Young who happened for some obscure reason to side with one party or the other. By the close of 1881 seventeen people were dead in the Bates-Parmenteer feud, and the former side vowed that the fighting would never stop 'until that sinful bastard Daniel Parmenteer lies punctured from head to toe eatin' dust.'

In December 1881 word of the Larkin County feud reached the Eastern newspapers, one of which pointed out that more white men had already died than had been lost in most of the Indian attacks in the area during the preceding decade. At that point even the governor conceded that he must do something, and what he did was so alien to what an Eastern governor might do that it, too, attracted considerable national attention.

He summoned to his office in Austin a small, wiry sixty-one-year-old man and told him: 'Otto, this could well be the last assignment I'll ever ask you to take. You've earned retirement, but you're the best lawman we have. Go up there and slow those damned fools down.'

So Ranger Otto Macnab returned to his ranch at Fredericksburg, saddled up his best horse, loaded his mule with a tent, rations of food and one small case of ammunition, and prepared to head north toward Larkin County. His wife, Franziska, now fifty-four years old, had often watched him make such preparations, always with apprehension, for she and Otto had attended many funerals of Rangers who had lost their lives on similar lone-wolf missions, but she did not try to dissuade him. 'Take care, Otto, do take care.' He accepted the white linen duster she handed him, the fifth she had made during his years as a Ranger, then kissed her goodbye: 'Take care of the ranch. Be sure the boys watch things.'

He did not follow main roads, but used back trails through the lonely wastes of Llano, San Saba, Comanche and Palo Pinto counties into Jack County, where he made quiet inquiries as to developments in the Larkin County feud. In an eating house where he was not known, a farmer said at table: 'Gonna get worse over there,' but another contradicted him: 'It'll probably settle down. Friend told me the governor's sendin' in some Ranger to stop the killin',' and the first man replied: 'Well, the Bateses is callin' in some reinforcements of their own.'

'What do you mean?' the optimistic man asked, and the farmer explained: 'I'm told that one of the Bates cousins, Vidal, went to New Mexico to hire Rattlesnake Peavine to come east and get Lawyer Parmenteer.'

This ominous news was greeted with silence, and then the second farmer said, professionally: 'That's gonna produce a flock of new killin's,' to which the first man agreed: 'Sure is.'

They turned to Macnab: 'You ever run across Peavine? Left arm a stub. But he only needs his right.'

'Haven't heard of him, but if he's a New Mexico gunman . . .'

'He's a Texas gunman. Ran across the border to escape hangin'.'

'Bad?'

'The worst. The Bateses ain't doin' Texas any favor by bringin' him back. And they ain't doin' Parmenteer any good a-tall.'

In the morning Otto headed due west for Larkin County, knowing that Rattlesnake Peavine was approaching it headed east. Had someone from a superior vantage point been tracking the movements of Macnab on his western heading and Peavine on his eastern, he could have predicted that these two must collide somewhere near the town of Fort Garner, and he would have known that this would produce considerable wreckage, for

Macnab was a man who never turned back or shied away from a difficult confrontation, while Peavine had acquired such mastery of guile and unexpected movement that after twenty years of continuous peril he was still known as one of the two or three most dangerous men in the West.

Otto rode into town late one Thursday afternoon, a small, lone man leading a carefully laden mule that never looked up. He entered by the dusty road from Jacksborough, came slowly, quietly down Main Street, and tied up at the rack in front of the saloon. Watchers noticed that he did not tie the mule, a sign that he had used this beast many times before. No one guessed that he was a Ranger, for he bore not a single sign to indicate that.

Inside the saloon he occasioned little comment, and when he asked in a quiet voice: 'Any place a man could stay?' they willingly told him of a farmer's widow who took in boarders.

'Food any good?'

'Best in town,' the men assured him, but with a shrug which indicated that even that wasn't going to be too palatable. He ordered a beer but drank little of it, then headed out the door, untying his horse, leading it by the bridle, his mule following behind.

He ensconced himself in the home of Widow Holley, where he said his name was Jallow, which caused some discussion among his fellow boarders: 'What kind of name is that?'

'I've often wondered. Mother said it was German, but she was Irish.'

'Where you from?'

'Galveston.'

'Where you headin'?'

'Here.'

'Lookin' for land?' He nodded, and the men offered advice, to which he listened carefully.

He spent the next five days visiting land that might be for sale and listening to accounts of the region. He was much impressed by the Quaker Rusk, and especially by stories of how he had found his bride, but Rusk said firmly: 'No land of mine for sale.'

As he went about, returning regularly to Mrs Holley's for his noon and evening meals so as to catch the gossip, he reached two conclusions: the Bateses were a mean and ugly lot who had indeed sent to New Mexico to import a notorious killer, and Lawyer Parmenteer was one of the most unpleasant men he had encountered in a long time. One night, after a stormy meeting with the man regarding a farm west of town, he muttered to himself: 'If I ever saw a man who invites being killed, Daniel Parmenteer's the one.'

The lawyer was sanctimonious, vengeful, hateful in his personal relations, and mortally afraid of being shot. He apparently felt that his only protection lay in eliminating the Bateses and those associated with them, and to accomplish this he had instituted the worst kind of vigilante community, in which men went in fear of their brothers.

On the sixth day Otto rose as usual, shaved, donned his usual dress, breakfasted with the boarders, then went to the stables, where he mounted his horse, adjusted the two pistols at his waist, and rode to where the Bates brothers lived at the eastern end of town. Dismounting in one quick swing of his leg, he walked quietly but quickly into the Bates house with pistols drawn, and announced: 'Sam and Ed, you're under arrest. Otto Macnab, Texas Ranger.'

Before the startled men could respond in any way, even to the lifting of a cup to throw it, he had shackles about their wrists and a rope uniting them. He walked them quickly to a stout tree at the edge of town, to which he bound them, warning that he would shoot them dead if they tried to escape.

He then rode back into town, where he stalked into the law offices of Daniel Parmenteer, arresting and securing him in the same way. Leading the lawyer into the street, he banged on the door of the sheriff's office and told him to fetch his deputy and follow immediately. When the sheriff started to ask questions, he snapped: 'Otto Macnab, Texas Ranger,' and on foot he led Parmenteer to the east edge of town, where he lashed him also to the big tree.

When the sheriff arrived, Macnab told the prisoners, and the crowd that had gathered: 'Bateses, Parmenteers, people of Larkin County. The feud is over. The killing has ended. My name is Otto Macnab, Texas Ranger, and I am telling you that this town is at rest.' Some cheers greeted this welcome promise.

He then went to stand before the Bates brothers: 'You've had grievances, I know. And you've responded to them. But enough's enough. We will stand for no more.' Taking a long, sharp knife from his belt, he reached out and cut the two men free.

Moving to Parmenteer, he said: 'Daniel, you felt you had to vindicate your brother Cletus, and you have. We all understand, but we can tolerate no more. The feud is over.' And he cut his cords too.

But then Parmenteer asked a sensible question: 'What about Peavine? They've sent to New Mexico to bring him in to kill me and my folks.'

'I've been told that,' Macnab said, never raising his voice, 'and I shall go out now to warn Peavine not to enter this town. He is forbidden.'

With that, he turned to the sheriff: 'Now the job's yours. Watch these men. Keep the peace.' And he walked back to the center of town, where he recovered his horse, packed his mule once again, jammed his felt hat down upon his forehead, and rode out of town to intercept the Rattlesnake.

He rode three days toward the New Mexico border, and toward dusk on the last day, saw figures on the horizon. Neither hurrying nor slowing down, he rode toward them.

They turned out to be three soldiers on patrol from Fort Elliott, and as they camped under the stars, with the soldiers providing much better food than Otto could supply, they told him that they had crossed paths with two men named Bates and Peavine.

'Peavine one-armed?'

'Yep. Left arm just a stump. Said the Indians done it. In the Territory.'

'You say Bates and Peavine are still at Fort Elliot?'

'They helped the captain hunt for deer . . . for the mess.'

In the morning the soldiers continued their patrol. Macnab headed for the distant fort, and at about noon he was rewarded by seeing two men coming eastward, each with two horses. Making sure that they must see him, he rode resolutely right at them, and at hailing distance he called out: 'Peavine! Bates! This is Otto Macnab, Texas Ranger.'

With no guns showing, he went directly up to them and said: 'I've been sent to Larkin County to stop the killing. Four days ago I arrested your two nephews, Sam and Ed, and also Lawyer Parmenteer.'

'He's a killer!' Bates growled.

'I know he is, but so were your people, Bates. And now it's ended.'

Neither of the men responded to this, so Macnab said: 'Rattlesnake, you're not to come into Larkin County. You're to turn around and head back for New Mexico. Bates, you can do as you wish.'

'He's comin' with me,' Bates said, and the one-armed man nodded.

'If he steps foot in town, I shall arrest him. And if he resists, I'll shoot him.'

It was a moment of the most intense anxiety. The two men, watching Macnab's hands, realized that if they made an aggressive move, he could whip out his guns and kill one of them, but they also knew that the survivor could surely kill Macnab. Since it was likely that the Ranger would aim at Peavine, Rattlesnake was careful not to make even the slightest false move.

Showing no emotion, Macnab said: 'You can kill me, but you know the entire force of Rangers will be on your neck tomorrow, and they'll never stop. They'll chase you to California, Peavine, but they'll get you.'

There was a very long silence, after which Macnab said gently: 'Now, why don't you two fellows split up? Rattlesnake, go home. Bates, ride back with me to a new kind of town where you can live in peace.'

He edged his horse away, to give the men a chance to talk between themselves, and for nearly half an hour they did while he waited patiently, not dismounting and never taking his hands far from his guns, but moving close to his mule, whose load he kicked once or twice as if adjusting it.

Finally Peavine rode up to Macnab: 'I'm headin' back.'

Otto nodded approvingly as the notorious killer turned and started west, but before the man had gone even a few paces, he called: 'If you try to come back, I'll kill you.' Rattlesnake said nothing.

By the end of December 1883, Ranger Otto Macnab had every reason to believe that he had quelled the feud, as he had been directed to do, but in the back of his mind he still suspected that the Rattlesnake might slither back into Fort Garner to complete the killing for which he had been hired, so Macnab had the prudent thought of reporting in writing to the governor:

> Fort Garner
> Larkin County
> 27 December 1883

Excellency:

Obedient to your orders I came to this town, arrested the leaders of both parties to the Larkin County feud and pacified them. They proved to be sensible men and tractable, and I expect no more trouble from them.

However, there is a possiblity that the hired killer Rattlesnake Peavine who is hiding in New Mexico might sneak back to resume the killing, as he was at one time hired by the Bateses to do this. I do not know whether to stay here or return to my family and shall await your instructions.

> Otto Macnab

The governor thought it safe to bring the Ranger back, but ten days after Otto rode out of Fort Garner, Peavine rode in. He headed straight for Lawyer Parmenteer's office, where he kicked open a rear door and shot Parmenteer in the back before the latter could reach for his gun.

Macnab was on his way home, well south of Palo Pinto County, riding quietly along his preferred back roads, when he stopped at the growing village of Lampasas and sought lodging with a farmer he had assisted years before when bandits threatened the area. 'They could of used you up north,' the farmer said.

'What happened?'

'Them Larkin County maniacs.'

'What did they do?'

'Rattlesnake Peavine come into town and shot Daniel Parmenteer in the back. All hell broke loose and there must be a dozen dead.'

Macnab said nothing. He ate his evening meal of hard-fried

steak and brown gravy, accepted the bed the farmer provided out of gratitude for past favors, and left early next morning. He rode mournfully south, lost in defeat, heading not for home but for Austin, where he told the governor: 'I've got to go get him.' The governor, who had already accepted full blame for ordering Macnab home, said: 'Shoot that son-of-a-bitch if you have to trail him to Alaska,' and Macnab replied: 'You can depend on it.'

Now he rode west to explain things to his wife, and when she expressed her disappointment about his heading back to trouble, and at his age, he said simply: 'The world is a muddy place, and if good men don't try to clean it up, bad men will make it a swamp.'

Emma Rusk often suspected that she was having so much trouble with her white son, Floyd, because she had rejected her Indian son, Blue Cloud, for although she lavished unwavering love upon Floyd, he refused to reciprocate. At the beginning he had been a normal child, robust and lively, but from the age of six, when he began to realize who his parents were and in what ways they differed from other fathers and mothers, he began to draw away from them, and it pained her to watch the bitterness with which he reacted to life. He was not difficult, he was downright objectionable, and she sometimes thought that it would be better if he moved in with the rough-and-ready Yeagers, who might knock some sense into him.

His principal dislike was his mother, for he saw her as unlike other women, and on those painful occasions when he came upon her without her nose, he would blanch and turn away in horror, but it was when he became vaguely aware of how babies were born that he suffered his greatest revulsion, for he had learned from other children in the stone houses about his mother's long captivity with the Indians and of what they had done to her. He was not sure what rape involved, but he had been told by eager informants who knew no more than he that many Indian men had raped his mother, and from the manner in which this was reported, he knew that something bad had happened.

He thus had two reasons for his antipathy, his mother's physical difference and the fact that she had been abused by

Indians, and it became impossible for him to accept her love. Whatever she did or attempted to do he interpreted as compensation for some massive wrong in which she had participated, and in time he grew to hate the sight of her, as if she reminded him of some terrible flaw in himself.

He grew equally harsh toward his father, for he had learned from the same cruel children, who, like others their age, were eager to believe the worst and report upon it immediately, that his father was a Quaker, 'not like other people.' They said that he was so cowardly he refused to fight: 'At the tank, which he and Mr Yeager had fenced in, this man Poteet forced him to back down. He was scared yellow.' In an area where a gun was the mark of a man, the fact that Earnshaw refused to carry one proved this charge.

There had also been an ugly incident in which a wandering badman of no great fame had stumbled into Fort Garner and tried to hold up the place. He had chosen the Rusk residence for his first strike, and finding Earnshaw with no gun, had terrorized the place for some time before Floyd escaped and ran screaming to the Yeagers: 'Pop's being shot at by a robber!'

Within the minute Frank Yeager had dashed across the open space of the parade ground, burst into the Rusk home, and shot the befuddled gunman dead. As they stood over the corpse, Yeager repeated something he had said before: 'Earnshaw, a Texan without a gun is like a Longhorn without horns. It just ain't natural.'

So now, if Floyd saw his mother as stained because of her experiences with the Indians, he saw his father as emasculated because Frank Yeager had been forced to protect the Rusk household. He was therefore a bewildered, unhappy lad as he approached his teens, and it occurred to him that he must do something about the deficiencies in which he was enmeshed. Concerning his mother, he could do nothing except continue to repel the love she tried to bestow upon him, but the glaring faults in his father's character could be corrected. For one thing, he could behave in a manner totally unlike his rather pathetic father, and he began in a calculated way to make this adjustment.

He went to Jaxifer: 'If I can get the money, will you help me?'

'Maybe.'

'How much must I give you for a pistol?'

'Now what do you need a pistol for?'

'Like when that man came to our house.'

'Yep. Man oughta have a pistol, time like that.'

It was agreed that Jaxifer would provide Floyd with a revolver in fairly good working order, and some shells, for six dollars, and now the problem became how to accumulate so much money.

In these troubled days the United States government did not provide enough currency to enable men to conduct their own businesses. This did not mean that there wasn't enough to pay the men and women who did work. The cause of the trouble was avarice; those fortunate few who already had money, or who worked at jobs whose salaries enabled them to acquire some, saw that it was to their advantage to keep the national supply meager, for then those who lacked funds would have to work doubly hard to earn a portion of what the well-to-do already controlled.

On the Texas frontier cash was in such short supply, thanks to policy decisions formulated by the money-masters in New York and Boston, that hard-working cowboys like the two black cavalrymen rarely saw actual cash, and when they did, it was apt to be Mexican, French or English coins dating from the 1700s, with Spanish coins circulating at a premium. It was a great system for the rich, who could command excessive rates for the money they had acquired, a miserable system for people endeavoring to accumulate enough funds to start a business or keep one going.

Earnshaw Rusk, a man of uncommon insight, saw early the great damage being done by the monetary policy of his nation, for although he and Emma had gained their start through the large land grants obtained by her family and from the free horses and cattle that roamed the prairie in those earlier days, he was aware that others who followed were having a desperate time. Out of regard for them, he wrote frequent letters to the *Defender* explaining his interpretation of the money problem. By imperceptible steps, none consciously taken at the time, he progressed from being merely aware of the problem, to a Free Silver man who argued that silver should be cast into coins at a much greater rate and at a higher value than was now being

1076

done, to an avowed Greenbacker who pleaded for the printing and circulation of more paper money, to an incipient radical Populist who believed that the government ought to protect and not harass its citizens. Long before a much greater orator and thinker than he took up the subject, Earnshaw was warning the people of Larkin County that 'we are slaves to gold,' and people in the growing town began accusing Rusk of being a radical, a socialist and an atheist, giving his son reason for being an opponent of his father's social beliefs, a loud adherent of religion as practiced by Mrs Yeager, and a strong advocate of guns. In one of his letters to the editor, Earnshaw had said:

> I do believe the same family income buys less and less each week, even though the total supply of money diminishes. This is self-contradictory, and I cannot explain it.

The cause was simple. Floyd Rusk was systematically stealing as much as he could from both his mother and his father, and after he had paid the cavalryman more than two and a half dollars for the promised gun, his father caught him taking two Mexican coins.

'What in the world is thee doing in that jar, Floyd?'

'I was looking at the different coins.'

'Thee knows thee is not to touch that jar. Nobody is except thy mother. Not even me.'

'She told me I could.'

It was obvious to Earnshaw that his son was lying, because Emma so treasured the few coins she was able to hoard that she allowed no one to approach them. Rusk knew he ought to have a showdown with his son here and now, but he evaded it because to do so would necessitate involving Emma; he knew that she was already in difficult straits with her headstrong boy and he did not want to exacerbate this. So the moment of significant challenge passed, and Earnshaw said weakly: 'Don't touch that jar. Thy mother wouldn't like it.'

He did not report the affair to his wife, nor could he guess that his son had stolen from his savings too. It would have appalled him to know that the combined thefts totaled nearly six dollars, a considerable amount, and he would have been even more distressed had he known that these thefts had been planned and conducted over an extended period of time. His son was in training to be an accomplished thief, and before the year was out he was a thief with a very good army revolver hidden in an unsuspected corner of the Rusk house.

Fort Garner buzzed with rumors when Ranger Macnab rode back into town. He knocked on the Holley door to ask if he could stay there for a few days, during which it became apparent that he had come to deal with Rattlesnake Peavine if he could flush out that murderous fugitive. Floyd Rusk, possessor of his own gun, was at Macnab's side constantly, asking for pointers on how real gunfighters handled their weapons, and Otto told him a secret the boy chose to ignore: 'Only one, son. Know you're right and keep coming.'

When Floyd asked if it was true that he was after Peavine, Otto said: 'Rangers are always after whoever's done wrong,' and then he disappeared, heading south. But Floyd, a student of shootings, told Molly Yeager, a brash child with her own interest in such matters: 'When a Ranger heads south, you can be sure he's really going in some other direction. Macnab is heading west to see if he can track down the Rattlesnake.'

Floyd's guess was correct, for after a long detour to the south Macnab made easy adjustments in his heading, winding up in the direction of Palo Duro Canyon. As he approached the deep depression he saw signs which tempted him to turn sharply southwest to where a tiny settlement lay across the New Mexico border.

As he rode into town it was like a hundred other episodes on the long frontier: a Ranger comes cautiously into a village, looking this way and that, asking a few questions, nodding and passing on. But this time as Macnab headed toward the western exit, a small wiry man in his late sixties watched him ride past, waited till he was a few feet down the road, then slipped out, threw the stump of his left arm up to serve as a platform, and pumped four quick bullets into the Ranger's back.

With supreme effort Macnab held himself in the saddle, aware that he had been most savagely hit but hoping that the shots might not be fatal. With what strength remained, he turned to face his assailant, who now blasted Otto square in the face and chest. Without a sound, the little Ranger slid from his saddle and fell awkwardly into the New Mexico dust.

Five Texas Rangers set out to kill Amos Peavine, and they tracked him for many weeks, coming upon him one morning at seven in a dirty eating house near Phoenix, Arizona Territory. When the coroner examined the body he found that it had been shot seven times in the back, twice more from the left side and twice more from the right side well to the back. Considering the Rattlesnake's long reign of terror and the relief at his justified death, the coroner saw no reason to publish the fact that the Rangers had killed him with eleven bullets from the rear

When Floyd Rusk, back in Fort Garner, heard the news, he told Molly Yeager: 'I'll bet he died like a man. I'll bet all five of the Rangers was terrified when they came onto the Rattlesnake.'

Floyd, the would-be gunman, had learned the value of money through stealing enough to purchase a revolver; his father would now learn in an equally perilous game. Although he had scrimped on his family's expenditures and paid his savings into the bank to reduce his loan, 1885 found him with $135 still outstanding, and cautious though he was, he could not seem to get ahead by that amount.

Of course, he paid the interest regularly because he knew that if he didn't, Mr Weatherby could declare him in default and take his ranch away from him; the terms of the mortgage were quite clear on this, and the possibility so terrified Rusk that he was usually a day or two early in paying the interest.

But now, when money was tightest, he saw that the banker had another stranglehold on him, for on two occasions recently Mr Weatherby had suddenly and arbitrarily called mortgages on unsuspecting ranchers and farmers; that is, he had demanded full payment at a time when he knew the rancher had no chance of paying it. In each case, according to Texas law, the rancher was judged to have been in default, which meant that if the bank let the man keep his homestead – house and small acreage attached – it could claim title to the rest of the ranch and in this way accumulate vaulable land.

'That was so unfair!' Earnshaw cried when he heard of the second foreclosing. 'A man spends two thousand for his land.

He spends another two thousand improving it. For seven years he meets every mortgage payment, and then because he can't come up with a hundred and seventy-five dollars, he loses everything.'

Rusk often misunderstood business details, and this time he had the situation only partly right, for in the case cited, when the bank foreclosed, it was merely to obtain its outstanding debt, $175. When the ranch was sold at a sheriff's sale, any income beyond that belonged to the former owner, but now the trick was to rig the sale so that either the bank or someone associated with it bought the ranch for a pittance, which meant that there was little or nothing to be returned to the original owner.

When Rusk found that the courts, the newspapers, the churches and the customs of the countryside all supported such moral thievery, he became so enraged that he felt compelled to protest in the *Defender:*

> Surely, the Grange and the Farmer's Alliance are right when they argue that the laws of a nation ought to support the homeowner, the small businessman, the young family trying to get started. No law should allow a bank to deprive a man of his residence and his means of earning a living. If the United States had arranged its affairs so that money was more reasonably available, then the paying off of a mortgage could be done, and people who refused to pay should be punished. But the nation keeps the money supply so constructed that even a prudent man cannot accumulate enough cash to pay his debts, much as he would like to. Something in our society is badly wrong when a good rancher like Nils Bergstrom loses his ranch because he cannot get his hands on a little cash.

No one read Earnshaw's letter with more anger than Banker Weatherby, and when the economy was at its depth, he informed the Rusks that he must demand the balance of his loan, $135, payable as the contract stipulated within thirty days. 'But thee promised me thee'd never do this,' Rusk protested, and Weatherby said: 'Conditions have changed. The bank must have its money, now.'

Then began the month of hell, because in all of Fort Garner, or Larkin County too, there was no one from whom the Rusks could borrow that missing $135. There were ranches worth $6,000 or $7,000, counting land and cattle, which had less than $30 in cash, and these meager funds were so necessary to keep the place operating that to lend them out would have been impossible.

The Rusks themselves, with a ranch now worth nearly $9,000, considering its fencing and cattle, could assemble less than $50, and Mr Weatherby would not consider any partial payment; he was entitled by law to the full amount and he intended to collect it, or take over the ranch.

In despair, Earnshaw laid the prospects before his family: 'Through no fault of our own, we stand to lose our ranch. Emma, thy cattle were never better, but we can't sell them to anybody here. Floyd, we pay only a little for thy schooling, but it can't be continued. We must all try till the last legal day to find this money, and if we fail, well, others better than we have failed before us.'

As he said these word the awfulness of his family's position overwhelmed him, and he wept, an act which sickened his son, who said boldly: 'Someone ought to shoot that Mr Weatherby.'

'Floyd!' his mother and father cried simultaneously, and the force of their words so startled him that he caught his breath. Yet it was he who proposed the one solution which had any chance of saving his family: 'Mr Poteet'll be coming along soon. Why not ride down to meet him?'

As soon as the boy said this, his parents recognized the good sense of his suggestion, and before nightfall Earnshaw Rusk and Frank Yeager were headed south to intercept the cattle drive they knew would be coming north. There were no Comanche now to endanger them, and there was no risk of losing their way, for over the years the thousands of cattle heading north to Dodge City had beaten the plains into a wide, rutted path which a blind man could have followed, and in its dust they spurred their horses.

On the first full day out they came upon one small herd headed for Dodge, and its riders said: 'Poteet can't be far behind. He never is.'

On the third day they saw a huge cloud of dust, like something out of the Old Testament when the Israelites were moving across their desert with the help of God, and they galloped ahead with surging hopes that this might be Poteet. It was, and as soon as he heard their plight he was interested.

'It's criminal for banks to take over so much land, and for the government to protect them in doing it.' He sat astride his horse with only the left foot in the stirrup, as if he intended to dismount, but first he wanted to talk, and the three men kept moving their horses as he did: 'You got yourself into this trouble, Rusk, through buying that fence. It was against reason and against nature. Now comes the dreadful penalty.'

Rusk did not try to defend himself; he was concerned only with the loan he sought, and at this point he could not detect whether Poteet was going to lend him the money or not, but as the talk proceeded, it became clear that the drover sided with the Rusks and not with the bank: 'Course I'll lend you the money, how could I not?' And before night fell, Earnshaw had the funds with which to save his ranch.

'It's not a loan,' Poteet said when the two men tried to thank him. 'It's an appreciation for the business we've done.' He paused to recall those rewarding years. Then: 'You know, Rusk, you mustn't think too harshly about Weatherby. He's just a part of the system.'

'What does thee mean?' Earnshaw asked.

'Life in Texas is like a giant crap game, a perpetual gamble. To succeed, you need grit, courage to take the big chance. Those who succeed, succeed big. A hundred men tried to drive cattle up this trail. They failed. Some of us, like Sanderson and Peters and me, we took great chances and we succeeded, big.' He seemed to be right about Texas; everything was a colossal gamble: 'Years back, Rusk, when I saw you gambling so heavy on that bob wahr, I disliked you for what you were doing to the range, but I had great admiration for what you were doing in your own interest.'

'Why does thee say a money-grubber like Weatherby is necessary?'

'Because he's the agency that punishes us when our gambles turn sour. He's the right hand of God, administering castigation. You escaped him this time, but don't tempt him again, because if Texas is bountiful in rewarding gamblers, it's remorseless in punishing those who stumble.'

When Rusk and Yeager left Poteet next morning, they rode hurriedly back to Fort Garner, where they reported to Emma and Floyd: 'We are, through the grace of God, saved.' They then went to the bank, where with a certain bitterness they counted out the $135. And now a drama which was being enacted in many small Texas towns unfolded. Banker Weatherby, frustrated in his attempt to steal the Larkin Ranch by legal means, surrendered to the fact that the Rusks were going to be the leading citizens in the town. Knowing that he must in the future do business with them, he now displayed no disappointment or ill feelings. With what seemed unfeigned enthusiasm, he cried: 'I'm so pleased you could scrape up your final payment. It's always good to see a successful rancher make his land prosper.' Then he made an offer which staggered the men: 'Now, you don't have to pay in full. If you wish to extend your mortgage, the bank would be most happy . . . '

'We'll pay,' Rusk said.

'Are you two men partners?'

'Yes, in a manner of speaking. When a man serves me as well as Frank Yeager has, I give him part of my profits. He gets the two hundred acres north of the tank.'

'You should enter that gift at the land office,' Weatherby said. 'It's always best to have things in writing.'

In early 1885, Rusk and all forward-looking people in Fort Garner were electrified by the news: 'The Fort Worth & Denver City Railroad is planning to resume!' And men began to dream: 'Now maybe we can get a spur to drop down into our town!'

In 1881 men of great ambition in Fort Worth and Denver had tried to link their two cities by rail and had started bravely to build west from Fort Worth, but had run out of money during the tight times of 1883. Their line had reached only as far as Wichita Falls, north of Fort Garner, where it came to a painful halt. But now, with more prosperous times looming, workmen were being rehired and iron rails ordered.

When the good news was confirmed, Rusk became a cyclone of energy, his tall, awkward figure moving ceaselessly about the town and to ranches outside to learn whether they might join in offering the nascent railway special cash inducements if its engineers agreed to drop a spur to the south.

In this enterprise he was prescient, because the history of Texas written a century later would be filled with doleful entries recording the death of similar communities:

> Pitkin, founded in 1866, flourished for a few decades in the later years of the Nineteenth Century as a center for collecting rural products, but during the railroad boom of the Eighties the town fathers refused to grant the railroads any concessions. The tracks bypassed Pitkin and before the turn of the century the town had died, the last resident leaving in 1909.

Rusk, with his keen sense of how the West was developing, realized that the continued existence of the town depended upon attracting some railroad that would speed its growth. Originally he had dreamed of inducing the main line of the F.W.&D.C. to swing slightly south through Fort Garner, but that plum had been lost to Wichita Falls. However, he could now logically aspire to a spur, and he was determined to get one.

To that end he hectored local citizens to contribute funds with which he could approach the railroad barons in Fort Worth in an effort to convince them that a spur south was in their interests. Grocer Simpson contributed enthusiastically to the fund with which Earnshaw would approach the railroad barons, and the flourishing proprietor of the Barracks Saloon also chipped in, as did Editor Fordson. Ranchers east of town were shown the advantage of having a railroad for their cattle, and ordinary citizens who wanted to be united to the larger world were invited to join the crusade, but Rusk was astounded at the man who volunteered to do the major work.

The campaign had been under way only a few days when Banker Weatherby came voluntarily to the Rusk home, asked to be invited in, and spoke with a warm sincerity which belied the fact that recently he had tried to steal the Rusk lands: 'I am hurt, Earnshaw, that you did not come to me first with your plan to bring a railroad into our town. It's vital that we get one to come our way.' Having said this, he contributed a thousand dollars to the invitation kitty and then proposed that he and

Rusk leave immediately for Fort Worth, where decisions concerning the route were being made.

Rusk had wanted to cry: 'Look here, Weatherby, not long ago thee tried to steal my land. Now thee invites me to travel as thy friend. Why?' But he remained silent because vaguely he understood that Weatherby was merely playing the game of building Texas. In July, Banker A does his best to steal Rancher B's land, but in August, A and B unite to hornswoggle Rancher C. 'Texas poker,' someone called it, because sooner or later, B and C would be certain to gang up on Banker A.

As they rode, Weatherby coached Rusk as to how they must approach the railroad men and how to make them an offer of cash rewards if they could swing the roadway south. By the time they reached the hotel where the F.W.&D.C. directors were meeting, these two rural connivers were prepared to talk sophisticated details with the big-city bankers and engineers.

Alas, they were one of nineteen such delegations, and by the time they reached the decision-makers the route was set. 'Gentlemen,' the directors apologized, 'we're grateful for your coming to see us, and we appreciate the offer you're making, for we know that such sums cannot be collected lightly, but we must allot all our funds to the main line to Denver. There can be no spurs.'

Rusk was crushed, and like a child he showed it, but Clyde Weatherby, an adroit negotiator, masked his disappointment, wished the Colorado and Texas financiers well, and concluded: 'Later on, when you do have enough money to run a spur south, and sooner or later you'll have to, because we're going to amass great riches down our way, I want you to remember us. Fort Garner, Garden city of the New West.' They obviously liked this jovial man and assured him that they would remember, but on the return trip, Weatherby told Rusk in the harshest terms: 'Earnshaw, I like you. But we've got to work in an entirely different way. The future of our town is at stake, and we either get a railroad to come in or we perish.'

Before they reached Fort Garner he had a plan: 'Let me have all the money. I'll spread it around where it'll do the most good. You put up thirty or forty of your acres and I'll do the same with mine.'

'What will thee do with them?'

'Give them to people who will determine where that first spur to the south goes.'

'Why?'

'To buy their support. To be sure of their votes when we need them.'

'But isn't that bribery?'

'It is, and so help me God, it's going to buy us a railroad.'

If Rusk had been tireless in his initial work, Clyde Weatherby was remorseless in his follow-up, yet at the end of six hectic weeks he had to inform Earnshaw: 'I've handed out all the money and accomplished nothing. There's no hope of a spur south.'

'Are we doomed?' Rusk asked, for already he could see in other aspiring towns the dreadful effect of having been by-passed by the railroad.

'We are not,' Weatherby snarled, as if he were furiously mad at some unseen force. 'The people we gave money and land to will remember us. But now I'm asking for one last contribution. From everyone. We'll see if the folks in Abilene have vision,' and off he went to the new Texas town that carried the same name as the famous old railhead in Kansas. Before he left he told Rusk and Simpson: 'If they won't come south to meet us, by God, we'll go north to meet them.' But when he came home, with no money left and no promise of anything, he told his co-conspirators: 'Nothing now, but in this business you plant seeds and pray that something good will spring out of the ground. I have seeds planted everywhere and I give you my word on the Bible, something is going to start growing before another five years pass.' So the men of Fort Garner watched hopefully as the years passed and the railroads inched out to other places but not to theirs.

Three weeks after Franziska Macnab had buried her husband in the family cemetery overlooking the Pedernales, she received word from the capitol at Austin that her younger brother, Ernst, had died at his desk in the Senate chamber. It had happened at nine in the evening, when the Senate was not in session; he had been working late.

So within a month she had to conduct two funerals, and this reminded her of how very much alone she now was. Her mother had died some years ago; her beloved father and her youngest brother, Emil, had been killed in the horrid affair at the Nueces River, and now Ernst and Otto were dead. The sense of passing time, of closing episodes, was oppressive.

Her three children, with her encouragement, were pre-occupied with their own responsibilities, but this left her in sad loneliness. She experienced a strong desire to reestablish contact with her only surviving brother, Theo, who had gained statewide attention in 1875 by his heroic work in rebuilding the town of Indianola after the destructive hurricane of that year. More than forty places of business had been wiped out by the raging waters of Matagorda Bay, more than three hundred lives lost, and when scores of older men announced that they were abandoning the site, Theo had stated to the Galveston and Victoria newspapers: 'I'm going to rebuild my ships' chandlery bigger than before.'

And he had done so. Encouraging other businessmen, he had been responsible for the rejuvenation of the destroyed town and watched with pride as it returned to prosperity. His own store, which serviced the many ships that sailed into Indianola, doubled in size, and his agency for the Gulf, Western Texas and Pacific Railway Company established him as Indianola's leading merchant. He conducted his affairs from an office which stood at the land end of the pier that reached far into the bay; here he greeted captains of the Morgan Line steamers as they docked with cargoes from New Orleans.

Despite the obliteration of so many businesses in that hurricane, Theo continued to envision Indianola, where he had first set foot on Texas soil, as the state's gateway to the West, and his letters to Fredericksburg displayed this optimism:

If you walked with me down our main streets you would think you were in Neu Braunfels, because two names out of three would be German: Seeligson, Eichlitz, Dahme, Remschel, Thielepape, Willemin. This is a real German port, with hundreds like me who saw it first from the deck of their immigrant ship and liked it so much they never left.

We have our own ice machine now and are no longer dependent upon the refrigerated ice ships that used to bring us river ice from New England. We have a new courthouse,

several hotels, at least six good restaurants, shops with the
latest styles from New York and London, our own newspaper and all the appurtenances of a city. You would like it
here, and any of you who tire of farming in the hills ought to
move here quickly, for this is a glimpse of Old Germany
installed in New Texas.

Franziska, welcoming such letters, wondered whether she
should move permanently to Indianola to be with her brother
for the remaining years of their lives, but after several months of
cautious consideration she decided against leaving Fredericksburg, for too many of her cherished memories were
rooted there. And Otto had loved the Pedernales, the wild
turkeys strutting through the oak groves, the deer coming to the
garden, the hurried quail in autumn, the javelinas grubbing for
acorns.

However, in spring of 1886, Theo did send a sensible letter:
'With Otto and Ernst gone, you and I are all that's left. Come
spend the summer with me, for I am lately a widower. Besides,
it's much cooler here with the sea breezes each afternoon.'

Turning the care of the farm over to Emil's children, all of
them married now, she took the stage to San Antonio, where
she boarded the new train connecting that city with Houston,
and at Victoria she dismounted to catch the famous old train
that chugged its way out to Indianola. It left Victoria at nine in
the morning and steamed in to Indianola at half past one in the
afternoon.

She joined her brother on Friday, 13 August 1886, and
shared with him some of the best weeks of her life, for Theo
spoke both of his burgeoning hopes for the future, which
excited her, and of his memories of the Margravate, which
reminded her of how happy she had been as a child. They were
old people now, he sixty-four, she fifty-seven, and the bitter
memories receded as the good ones prevailed.

'Does your tenor voice ... can you still sing so beautifully?'
she asked, and he tried a few notes.

'We have a singing society here, you know,' he told her, 'but
I yield the lead tenor to others.'

On Sunday, when they both attended the German church at
his suggestion, he apologized: 'Father wouldn't approve of our

going to church, but times are different now.' He then took her for a delightful buggy ride in one of his own carriages. They rode out to the great bayous east of town, where he stopped to explain the winds of a hurricane: 'They come in three parts. A fierce storm blows from west to east. Tremendous noise and rain but not much damage. Then a lull like a summer day as the eye passes over. Then a much wilder storm from east to west, and it's the one that blows everything down.'

'Why does one kill and not the other?'

'Neither kills. Oh, a tree falling or some other freak accident.'

'What does?'

'This does,' and he pointed to the flat, empty lands basking in the sun, so quiet and peaceful that they could not be imagined as threatening anyone. 'You see, Franza, tidal waves throw immense quantities of water onto these flat places, so much you wouldn't believe it. And as the storm abates, it has to go somewhere, and with a great rush it finds its way back to sea.'

He dropped his head, recalling that tremendous surge of trapped water that had destroyed so much of Indianola: 'It took thirty hours to build up . . . high tides, rain, hurricane winds. It ran back in two, an irresistible torrent.'

'How did you survive?' They were speaking in German, and he replied: 'Ein wahres Wunder. And prudence. I guessed that the retreating waters would be dangerous, so I took our family to the upper floor of the strongest building in town, not my own, and tied us all to heavy beds, not lying down, of course, just to the heavy iron pieces.'

'And it worked?'

'When the water swirled past, clutching at everything, we could see it sucking people to their deaths. It tried with us, right through that second floor, but we were tied fast.' He chuckled: 'It tore away my wife's clothes, all of them, and she screamed for the rescue party not to save us.' He laughed again: 'Water can do the strangest things.'

'Will it come again?'

'Records show that once a hurricane hits, it never hits that spot again. That's how I've been able to hold the town together. We know we're safe. Only the cowards fled.'

Indianola, under his driving leadership, had restored itself as the premier port in South Texas and many predicted that it must soon outdistance Galveston. It was clear to Franziska, from the respect in which the citizens held her brother, that this revitalization was due primarily to his optimism, and she saw that he was much like his father: 'Remember, Theo, how during the worst days of our Atlantic crossing, he kept spirits high? You're like him.'

On Tuesday, Franza and her brother entertained at John Mathuly's seafood restaurant, and the guests, most with German names, shared an enjoyable evening 'of fine oysters, rich crabs and other succulent viands which could not be surpassed this side of Baltimore,' the menu boasted, 'and equaled in only a handful of the superior establishments in that German city.' After the meal there was singing, and at ten, ice cream, made possible by the new ice machine, was served; it was accompanied by four kinds of cookies baked that afternoon by Franziska. This was followed by more singing and a speech by Theo – 'The Unlimited Progress Possible When Rails Marry Steam' – which alluded to the impending railroad linkage of Indianola, San Antonio and Brownsville.

When they left the restaurant, with some of the men still singing, Franziska became aware of a sharp change in the weather, for while they were dining an excessively humid wind had blown in from the Gulf, and although this disturbed her, it pleased her brother: 'Rain! We've needed it since July.'

But this wind did not bring rain. Instead, when Franziska rose next morning she found Indianola enveloped in billows of dust, and when she accompanied her brother on a visit to Captain Isaac Reed, the United States Signal Service man who now monitored storms in the area, he showed them a telegram he had received from Washington:

WEST INDIAN HURRICANE PASSED SOUTH KEY WEST INTO GULF CAUSING HIGH WINDS SOUTHERN FLORIDA STOP WILL PROBABLY CAUSE GALES ON COAST OF EASTERN GULF STATES TONIGHT

When Franziska asked: 'Isn't that serious?' he assured her: 'Government follows these things carefully, and ninety-nine times out of a hundred, such storms collapse and produce no more than a slight rise in our tide.' But later that morning, when the winds became more intense, Theo and Franza returned to the weather office, and Theo, as the elder statesman, asked: 'Shouldn't you hoist the danger signal?' and Reed said: 'Washington would warn us if such a signal was advisable. Rest easy. This storm will die.'

Later Captain Reed did receive a frantic telegram from Washington, warning of the immediate descent of a full hurricane, but now it was too late. Within minutes the hurricane came roaring in, and before Reed could respond, telegraph lines were whipping in the wind.

Reed was a valiant man, and when it looked as if his Signal Service was going to be blown away, he stayed inside to screw down the anemometer so that the maximum velocity of the wind could be recorded. It hit 102 miles an hour before it and the building were simply blown apart. Reed and a medical man, Dr Rosencranz, were struck by falling timbers as they tried to scramble away, and the incoming waves submerged them. They were seen no more.

When the building fell, a kerosene lamp was thrown to the floor, and its flames were whipped about so violently by the roaring winds, which now gusted to 152 miles an hour, that within an incredible eleven minutes the entire main street was in flames, and residents in panic tried to escape the fire. The Hurricane of 1875, which they said could never be repeated, was now reborn with a fury more terrible than before. Theo Allerkamp, whose ships' chandlery was struck by the first awesome blast of fire, managed to escape the instant conflagration produced when his turpentine and tar exploded into flames, and for one hellish moment he watched as the street he had rebuilt was attacked by flame on its rooftops and flood at is foundations. Buildings spewed sparks hundreds of feet into the storm, then sighed and collapsed as the irresistible flood tore away their walls.

'Mein Gott!' he cried. 'What are You doing to us?'

Mindful of how a hurricane worked, he shouted to those other bewildered men who saw their life's energies destroyed: 'Prepare for the back surge!' To repeat the precautions which had saved his family before, he struggled through the rising waters to his home, where his sister stood pressed against the wall, protecting herself from the tremendous winds and watching the fiery destruction of her brother's handiwork. 'Oh,

Theo!' she cried as he staggered up the three wooden steps which had not yet been washed away by the waters that attacked them. 'How could such punishment come to so good a man?'

He had no time for lamentation, even though flame and flood nearly engulfed him: 'When the calm comes, then's the danger.' And he led her to the highest spot in his house, built to withstand floods such as that of 1875, and fetched ropes with which to bind her to its walls when the waters began to recede.

This time that would not work, for when the tempestuous wind, now gusting occasionally to more than 165 miles, whipped about, it brought with it a summer's sky of flaming meteors. The clouds were filled with embers, thousands of them, and they arched in beauty over the dark space, reaching for the houses not yet aflame.

'We shall burn!' Theo cried, not in desperation or fear, and he ripped away the ropes that bound his sister to the wall and thrust them into her hands. 'To the trees!'

But before they could escape, a hundred blazing embers fell on the Allerkamp house and a like number on those nearby. In one vast, sighing gasp, heard above the howling of the wind, these houses exploded into leaping flame, and those who had not anticipated this likelihood perished.

Waiting for a lull, Theo and his sister headed for the few trees in Indianola, scrawny things barely meriting the name, and she reached them but he did not. A wave wilder than any before came far inland, caught him by the heels, tumbled him about as if he were a wooden toy, then tossed him with terrible force back against one of the newly burning houses. Nothing could have saved him, and he died in the center of the town he had built beside the sea, and then rebuilt.

Franziska, grief-stricken at seeing him perish, did not panic. With studious care she waited for a pause in the wind, then looked back to check where he had disappeared, lest he mysteriously appear still alive. Seeing nothing, she lashed herself as high into a tree as she could, and when the storm abated into that terrible calm which presaged the arrival of the greater danger, she climbed like a squirrel into the highest branches, but as she did so she saw a young mother with two small children, all so frenzied that none could do anything sensible. So she climbed down, all the way, and found the rope which Theo would have used, and then with her hands and knees scarred from the bark, she goaded the three others into the higher branches of the tree, where she tied them fast.

They were there at dawn on Friday morning, when the cruel part of the hurricane struck, and from their high perch they watched the town continue burning, with more homes blazing from time to time, while the great waters of the flood began to recede.

They came first as a slight movement back toward Matagorda Bay, then as a quickening – about the speed of a rill tumbling over a small rock – then as a surge of tremendous power, and finally as a vast sucking up of all things, a swirling, tempestuous, tumultuous rush and rage of water pulling away from the terrible damage it had caused. Now those houses which had missed the flames and withstood the first part of the flood collapsed as if from sheer weariness; they had fought honorably and had lost.

When the raging floods were gone, and the roaring winds had subsided, and the flames had flickered out, Franziska Macnab untied her ropes and helped the others to untie theirs: 'We can climb down now. The storm is past'

The two children would not find their father. Franza would not find her brother's body. Some mesmerized survivors would not even be able to identify where their houses had once stood, for when Friday noon arrived, and the sun was back in its full August brilliance, it looked down upon a town that was totally destroyed. Indianola no longer existed, only the charred streets and the vegetable gardens with no houses to claim them showing where commerce and affection and political brawling and Texas optimism had once reigned. The incessant gamble which R. J. Poteet had said was characteristic of Texas had been attempted once more, and Indianola had lost.

By two in the afternoon people were gasping for water as the sun grew hotter and hotter, but there was none to drink, not any in the entire town, and there were no buildings in which the tormented people could take cover. By four in the afternoon children were screaming, and the collecting of dead bodies had to stop as distraught survivors made makeshift plans for the dreadful night that approached.

Franza, conserving even flecks of spittle to keep her mouth

alive, comforted the children, putting her finger in her own mouth, then rubbing it about the child's, and in this mournful, moaning way the night passed.

At dawn people from another town, less horribly hurt, appeared with water, and Franziska wept: 'The water destroyed us, and the water saves us.' Those first drops, half a cup to each person, she would never forget.

Emma Rusk, safe in her little town four hundred miles northwest of Indianola, heard of the disaster by telegraph one day after it happened, but she paid scant attention, for she was preoccupied with her son, who each year became more difficult. In addition to his other exhibitions intended to demonstrate that he was in no way associated with the parents he despised, he had taken to eating gargantuan amounts of food. At the age of twelve he weighed more than a hundred and sixty pounds, and when his mother tried to control his gorging, he snarled: 'I don't want to be some thin, scared thing like my father.'

She had wanted to slap him when he said such things, but he said them so frequently now and with such venom that she did not know what to do. Dismayed as she was by his behavior toward her – which worsened as he entered puberty and faced its dislocations, for now he identified his mother with the most specific sexual misbehavior during her time with the Indians – she was even more distraught the next year by his relations with eleven-year-old Molly Yeager, the sprouting daughter of their foreman.

'Earnshaw,' she said delicately to her uncomprehending husband, 'I do fear that Floyd is playing dangerous games with little Molly.'

'What kind of games?'

She had to sit her husband down and explain that if Molly was the little minx she appeared to be, Floyd could fall into deep trouble if he continued to disappear with her from time to time, and when she made no headway with Earnshaw, she went directly to Mrs Yeager, a thin, stringy woman with a goiter and a passion for singing hymns loudly and off-key: 'Mrs Yeager, I'm worried about Molly and our Floyd.'

'For why?'

'Because they're alone a good deal. Things can happen, bad things.'

'What happens, happens,' Mrs Yeager said.

'I mean, your daughter could find herself with a baby.'

'What?' Mrs Yeager leaped out of her chair and stormed about her kitchen. 'You mean that hussy ...?'

Before Emma could halt her, Mrs Yeager was on the front porch screaming for Molly, and when the girl appeared, a plump, unkempt child with a very winsome face, her mother began hitting her about the head and shouting: 'Don't you go into no haymows behind my back.' There was not a haymow within a hundred miles of Fort Garner, but since this was the phrase her own mother had drummed into her, it was all she could think of at the moment.

Molly, startled by the ineffectual blows, glowered at Emma as the probable cause of her discomfort and tried to run away, but now Mrs Yeager grabbed her by one arm while the child spun around in a circle like a wobbling top, with both mother and daughter screaming at each other.

It was a lesson in child discipline which Emma could neither understand nor approve, and when she left the Yeager household the two were still at it. Back in her own home, she decided that if her husband would not talk with their son, she must, and when he came straggling in with the snarled inquiry 'When do we eat?' she sat him down and told him that she did not want to see him sneaking off with Molly Yeager any more.

'Why not?' he asked truculently.

'Because it's not proper.'

Her son stared at her, then pointed his pudgy right forefinger: 'Were you proper with the Indians?' And with this, he jumped up and fled from the room, half choking on his own words.

It was this wrenching scene which caused Emma to speak with R. J. Poteet when next he came by on his way to Dodge City: 'R. J., my son is a mess, a sorry mess. Would you please take him to Dodge City with you? Maybe teach him to be a man?'

'I don't like what I've seen of your son, Emma.' At sixty-four, Poteet had lost none of his frankness.

'How have you been able to judge him?'

'I get to know all the boys, all the families we meet on the trail.' He pointed to three of his young cowboys and said: 'A boy unfolds the way a flower unfolds in spring. It's time, and inwardly he knows it. Time to get himself a horse. Time to handle a revolver. Time to court some pretty girl. And in Texas, time to test his manhood on the Chisholm Trail, or on this one to Dodge.'

'What has that to do with Floyd?'

'For the last three years, Emma, I've sort of extended your son an invitation to ride north with me. These other kids, I had only to drop the hint, and they had their horses ready, pestering me. Three years from now they'll all be men.'

'And Floyd did not respond?'

'Your son's a difficult boy, Emma. I don't like him.'

She was tempted to say 'I don't either,' but instead she pleaded: 'Please take him. It may be his last chance.'

'For you, Emma, I'd do anything.' But when she was about to praise him for his generosity, he halted her: 'I'm gettin' to be an old man. Can feel it in my bones. Last winter I decided I'd go north no more. Had no choice, because Kansas has passed a law forbidding the entrance of Texas Longhorns.'

'For heaven's sake, why?'

'They claim we carry ticks. Texas fever. Fatal to their cattle. They've warned me, no more after this year. I didn't want to watch it all come to an end, too mournful, but a lot of families around San Antone had collected steers they had to sell or go broke. So I agreed to one last trail.' He fell silent, looking across the bleak land he had helped tame: 'Never put together a finer team. Look at those boys, the two good men at point. I wanted this to be the best drive I ever made, now you force that no-good boy of yours upon me.' He sank down on his haunches and threw pebbles at his horse's left hoof, and apparently this was a signal of some kind, for the animal moved close and nudged him.

'I'll take him,' he said, rising and shaking her hand. 'And I'll bring him back to you, for better or worse.'

It was a curious trip. Traveling slowly at fifteen miles a day, it took the herd four days to reach the Red River, and in this trial period Floyd Rusk learned a lot about herding cattle: 'Son, the new man always rides drag, back here in the dust. That's why cowhands wear bandanas, and since you got none, I'm going to give you mine. Gift from an old cowhand to a new one.' Poteet had smiled when he said this, but Floyd had not smiled back, nor had he said thank you, but that night when the hands gathered at the chuck wagon, he asked: 'How long do I ride in the dust?' and Poteet said: 'All the way to Dodge. Your second trip, you get a better deal.'

Floyd could not mask his anger, and so livid did he become that his rage showed beneath the dust that caked his face, so Poteet said: 'Same rules for everybody. If you don't like 'em, son, you can always drop out. But make up your mind before we cross the Red River, because gettin' back home from the other side will not be easy.'

Floyd had gritted his teeth and accepted the challenge, and although he was almost grotesquely fat, he did know how to handle a horse, so he did not disgrace himself. In fact, at the fording of the Red he handled himself rather well, remaining on the Texas side and pushing the steers into the water with some skill.

'You know how to ride,' Poteet said with genuine approval, but this did not soften Floyd's attitude, and during the entire crossing of the former Indian Territory he proved to be the surly, unpleasant fellow that Poteet had expected. He was by no means useless, for he knew what cattle were, but he was a decided damper on other young men, and by the time the herd reached the Kansas border, they had pretty well dismissed him.

Poteet did not. In his long years on the range he had watched boys even less promising than Floyd Rusk discover themselves, sometimes through being knocked clear to hell by some fed-up cowboy, sometimes in the thrill of showing that they could ride as well as any of the old hands, often with the mere passage of a year and the rousting about with reasonably clean, straightforward men. Poteet hoped this would happen with Floyd, and he directed his two point men to look after the boy, but when young Rusk repulsed all their good efforts, they told Poteet: 'To hell with him. Herd him into Dodge like the rest of the cattle and ship him home.'

Poteet did not try to argue, for he knew that with three thousand cattle behind them, more than half Longhorns, they had no time to bother with a surly, overweight brat, but he himself could not dismiss his responsibility so easily. If Emma's son could be saved, he would try, and one day when he saw the boy gorging himself at the chuck wagon as they crossed into Kansas, he took him aside and said quietly: 'Son, I really wouldn't eat so much. When you want to find yourself a wife, you know, pretty women don't cotton to young men who are too . . .'

'I don't want to look like my stupid father.'

Poteet drew back his right fist and was going to lay the boy flat when he realized how wrong this would be. Allowing his fist to drop, he said very quietly: 'Son, if you ever again speak of your father or your mother like that in my presence, so help me God, I will give you a thrashing you'll never forget.'

'You wouldn't dare.'

Poteet stepped forward and said, with no anger: 'Son, you don't know it, and maybe there's no way of telling you, but you are in the midst of a great battle. For your soul. For your immortal soul. I think you're going to lose. I think you're going to be a miserable human being for the rest of your life. But for the remainder of this trip, do your best to act like a man.'

He stalked away, profoundly shaken by this ugly experience, for he was frightened by what he might have done. His fist had been inches from that fat, flabby face. His trigger finger had been twitching when the boy scorned his father, for it was obvious that Floyd rejected his mother, too: Dear God, what a burden. He was not sure whether it was he bearing the burden on this last trip to Dodge City, or the older Rusks, who would have to deal with Floyd back in Larkin County.

So now the entire group had turned away from this pathetic boy; even the Mexican cook was unable to hide his disgust at the way Floyd gorged his food. He rode at the right-rear drag, dust in his face, and grumbled constantly about this experience which could have been so rewarding, this conquering of the range which so many boys his age would have given years of their lives to have shared.

As the herd reached the south bank of the Arkansas River, the men could see on the opposite side the low buildings of Dodge City, and their eyes began to sparkle, for citizens of the town themselves had proclaimed it 'The Wickedest Little City in the West.' Here were the famed dance halls, the sheriff's office once occupied by Bat Masterson and Wyatt Earp, the 'entertainment parlor' run by Luke Short, and what was more important to the stability of the town, well-funded agents like J. L. Mitchener who bought the Longhorns and shipped them east.

As the hands prepared to herd their cattle across the toll bridge leading into town, the older men went to Poteet and said: 'Dodge can be a tough town for a young fellow. What'll we do with that miserable skunk Floyd till we head back to Texas?'

'I'll speak to him' Poteet said, and that evening he assembled the first-timers and talked to them as if he were their father: 'Lads, when you cross the toll bridge tomorrow you enter a new world. The Atchison, Topeka and Santa Fe runs through the town. You can see its water tower. North of the railroad the town fathers have cleaned things up. No more gunfights. No more roaring into saloons on horseback. On that far side of the tracks . . . churches, schools, newspapers.'

'Tell 'em what's south,' a point man interrupted.

'On this side of the tracks, it's like the old days. Saloons, dance halls, gambling. You stay north, the better element will protect you. You move south, you're on your own.' He said this directly to Floyd, then added: 'I suppose you'll head south. If you do, don't get killed. I want to take you young fellows back to your mothers.'

When the meeting ended, Floyd asked one of the point men: 'Will Luke Short be in town? He's from Texas and he's killed a lot of men.'

'They ran Luke out years back. And you act up, they'll run you out too.'

During the approach to Dodge, Floyd had spent hours speculating on what he would do when he reached town. Girls figured in his plans, and the hidden pistol, and a gallop down Front Street, and a hot bath and good food. A thousand lads coming north from Texas to the railheads had entertained similar dreams, but few had come with such addled visions as those which attended Floyd Rusk, for he envisioned himself as a reincarnation of Wyatt Earp and Luke Short, though what this might entail he could not have explained.

As soon as the Longhorns, the last batch to enter Kansas

from Texas, had been led to the Mitchener corrals at the railhead, Floyd collected part of his pay and headed to the ramshackle area south of the tracks, and with unerring instinct, found his way to the toughest of all the saloons, The Lady Gay, once owned by Jim Masterson. He was startled when he saw his first dance-hall girls, for they were enticing beyond his hopes, and when he heard the coarse remarks made about them by the cowhands, he became confused and thought the men were somehow casting public aspersions on his mother. When the two rowdy men from another outfit that had started in Del Rio referred to the girls as 'soiled lilies' and 'spattered doves,' he became infuriated and ordered them to shut up.

The men looked at this fat, grotesque boy and unquestionably one of them made a motion as if to push him aside. Anticipating this, Floyd whipped out his gun and shot them dead.

Before the gunsmoke had cleared, Poteet's two point men leaped into action, rushed Floyd out of the saloon, and hid him in a ravine south of the river, for they knew that Poteet, always a man of rectitude, would refuse to cover up for one of his cowboys who committed murder.

When Floyd was safely hidden, the two men rode north of the tracks to where Poteet had rooms in a respectable hotel, and told him: 'Fat Floyd killed two Del Rio cowboys.'

Poteet tensed his jaw, then asked: 'You turn him in to the sheriff?'

'No, we hid him in a gully. We'll pick him up when we ride south.'

'But why? If he murdered someone?'

'Mr Poteet, we give you our word, don't we, Charley? It wasn't cut-and-dried. It looked maybe like they might be goin' for their guns.'

'Where did that boy get a gun?'

'He practiced a lot when you weren't around.'

Suddenly all the fire went out of Poteet. He slumped forward with his hands over his face: 'Oh my God, that poor woman. To have borne such a miserable son-of-a-bitch.' Looking up, he asked the point men: 'Must we take him back to Texas?' Without waiting for an answer, he rose as if nothing worried him and snapped: 'We'll dig him out as soon as we sell the herd.

Keep him in the ravine till we go south.'

When Floyd was dragged before Poteet on the way home, the range boss tried to make him realize the gravity of what had happened: 'Son, on the day a young feller kills his first man, he's in terrible trouble, because it came so easy – a flick of the finger – he may be tempted to do it again. Most gunmen start at your age, killin' somebody. Billy the Kid, and he's dead now. John Wesley Hardin killed his first man at fifteen . . . '

His words had the opposite effect to what he intended: 'They'll never hang John Wesley, never.'

'Son, are you listenin' to me? Hardin is in jail for twenty-five years. Do you realize that if my point men hadn't stepped in to protect you, the people back there would have hanged you?'

'No one will ever hang me.'

Only Poteet's promise to Emma that he would bring her son back home prevented him from thrashing the boy and taking him back to the sheriff in Dodge. Out of respect for Emma, he would tolerate the odious boy, but he would no longer bother with him. The two point men, however, having saved his life, felt a different kind of responsibility, and late one afternoon on the way home they whispered to Poteet: 'We think there'd better be a trial,' and the trail boss agreed.

Just before evening meal, one of the point men rode up to the chuck wagon, where Floyd was first in line, as always: 'Floyd, you're under arrest.'

'What for?' in a whining voice.

'We know you shot them two men in Dodge unjustified.'

'They drew on me.'

'We know what a miserable coward you are, what a skunk, and we're goin' to try you correct, right now.'

Floyd trembled as two other cowhands lashed his wrists and tied his ankles together, and he was terrified when the solemn trial began, with Poteet as judge.

'What charge do you bring against this man?'

'That in Dodge City he willfully gunned down two Texas cowboys.'

'Without provocation?'

'None.'

Floyd tried to raise his hands: 'They were comin' at me.'

'Were they coming at him?' Judge Poteet asked.

'They were not. He done it disgraceful.'

Poteet asked for a vote on Floyd's guilt, and it was unanimous.

'Floyd Rusk,' the judge said solemnly. 'You have been a disgrace on this trail north. You have responded to nothing. You surrendered the respect of your comrades, and in my presence you scorned your father. It is not surprising that in Dodge you murdered two men, and now, by God, you shall hang.'

'Oh no!' the boy cried, for he had certainly not intended to murder anyone in the saloon, and now he pleaded desperately for his life.

The cowboys were obdurate. Perching him sideways on a big roan, they led him to the branches of an oak tree, from which they had suspended a rope. When it was tied about his neck, Poteet stood near and said: 'Floyd Rusk, on the trail north you proved yourself to be a young man without a single saving grace. As a murderer, you deserve to die. Tom, when I drop my hand, whip the horse.'

In terror, the fat boy watched the fatal hand, felt the man slap the horse, and felt the rope tighten about his neck as the beast galloped off. But he also felt R. J. Poteet catch him as he fell, and then he fainted.

'Emma,' Poteet reported to his friend, 'it was my last trail. your check is bigger than ever before.'

'And Floyd?'

'He's no good, Emma. If he continues the way he's headed, you'll be attending his hanging.' He stood aside as she wept, and did not try to console her: 'You've got to hear it sooner or later, but in Dodge City your son murdered two men. Shot them dead with a revolver he got somewheres.'

'Oh my God!'

'My point men spirited him out of town. Saved his life. So on the trail south they held a trial, to show your boy what such actions meant.' He told her about the mock hanging and explained how this sometimes knocked sense into would-be gunmen, but when Emma asked: 'How did Floyd take it?' he had to reply: 'When he came to and realized the trick we'd played on him, he spat in my face and shouted: "Go to hell, you

1102

stupid son-of-a-bitch." '

Emma covered her face, and when her sobbing ended, Poteet said quietly: 'He's alive, Emma, because I promised you I'd bring him back. If he was my son, he'd already be dead.'

When he handed over the last check he would ever bring to the Larkin Ranch, he said with haunting sadness: 'I'd wanted this last drive to be the best of all. An honorable farewell to the great range that you and I knew so well.' When he tried to look across the plains, his view was cut by fences. 'Sometimes things just peter out, like the dripping of a faucet. No parades. No cannon salutes. Just the closing down of all we cherished.'

He said goodbye to this gallant woman with whom he felt so strong an affinity, then turned his horse toward San Antonio. The open range would see him and his breed no more.

It was known among the neighbors around the square as 'the year Earnshaw and Emma had their battle.' There was no open brawling, of course, and bitter words were certainly avoided, but the differences were profound, and pursued vigorously. When the year ended everyone, including the two participants, understood better what values animated these two diverse frontiersmen

The Battle of the Bull, as it was called, was a complicated affair. Back in 1880, when Alonzo Betz, the demon barbed-wire salesman, gave his night-long demonstration of how his wire could discipline the biggest Longhorns, Emma had been surprised that her bull Mean Moses had allowed the fragile wires to restrain him. Indeed, it had been mainly his surrender that had established the reputation of Betz's wire as 'master of the range.' Emma could never explain her bull's cowardly behavior, and several times she voiced her disgust.

When Betz's new fences had surrounded a major portion of the Rusk lands, and when the expensive Hereford and Shorthorn bulls imported from England were safe inside to cross with the Longhorn cows, Earnshaw implored his wife to get rid of her Longhorn bulls so that all the Rusk cattle could be improved, but the use of this word irritated Emma: 'What's improvement? Turning strong range cattle into flabby doughnuts?'

Patiently he had explained that the purpose of raising cattle was to produce as much edible beef as possible, in the shortest time and with a minimum consumption of expensive feed: 'The payoff on thy cattle, Emma, is what they sell for at Dodge City.'

She said: 'I thought the important thing about cattle was that they were just that, cattle as God bred them, not man.'

'It seems blasphemous to bring God into this.'

'No, it seems like common sense. When I look at Mean Moses . . .'

'That's a very unfortunate name for an animal.'

'Well, he is mean, and he does lead the others, and in a way I love him.'

'How can thee say that?' and she replied: 'I just said it.' What she did not say was that she prized her big stubborn bull because he, like her, had survived on the Texas plains. She did not in any sentimental way identify with the bull, nor see him as her surrogate, but she did like him and did not propose to see imported bulls elbow him off her land.

The arguing Rusks had agreed to leave Mean Moses outside the barbed-wire enclosures, free to roam as always, and to range with him a dozen cows and another bull, breeding in the thickets, their calves going unbranded from year to year, with the herd never increasing fabulously the way the tended cattle did, but with a new bull moving in now and then to give renewed vigor. As a result, the Rusk ranch always had out in its barren wastes a solid residue of Longhorns. In the rest of Texas the breed was dying out, upgraded year after year into the fine cattle so highly prized by the Northern markets, but in Larkin County, Mean Moses and his harem had kept it alive.

A great Longhorn was something to behold, for almost alone among the world's cattle it could produce horns of the most prodigious spread, branching straight out from the corners of the head, then taking a thrilling turn forward and a breath-takingly graceful sweep up and out. 'The Texas twist,' this was called, and when it showed in full dignity, men said: 'That one wears a rocking chair on its head.' Men who no longer raised Longhorns were apt to grow maudlin when they encountered on some friend's ranch a beast with really magnificent horns.

The peculiarity of the breed was that only steers and cows produced the great horns, and even then, only occasionally; some unexplained sexual factor caused their horns to grow very large in the first place, and then to take that Texas twist as they matured. A Longhorn bull never showed the twist and only rarely produced horns of maximum size. What horns he did produce were apt to be powerful, straight weapons trained to protect and, if need be, kill, not much different from the horns of a good bull of whatever breed.

So the famed Texas Longhorn of cartoon and poster showing fierce, beautiful-looking horns was always either a castrated male or a cow. Mean Moses, for example, had horns which came out sideways from his head and absolutely parallel to the ground for a distance of about eighteen inches on each side. Then they turned forward, as if controlled by a T-square, ending in very sharp points. Fortunately for the people who had to work him, he had a placid disposition, except when outraged by the misbehavior of some other Longhorn; then he could be ferocious.

In the early years of barbed wire and imported bulls, Mean Moses had stayed off by himself with his Longhorn cows, hiding his yearly calves in forgotten arroyos and testing his saberlike horns on any wolves that tried to attack them. Four or five times he had stood, horns lowered, when wolves attacked, and with deft thrusts had on each occasion impaled some luckless wolf and sent the rest off howling.

Emma sometimes saw her proud bull only three or four times a season, and when she did she was curiously elated to know that he still roamed the range. As she studied the vanishing Longhorns she noticed several things which renewed her determination: The cows never need assistance in giving birth. Sure, Earnshaw's pampered breeds bring in more money, but Earnshaw pays it out for cow doctors at birthing time. And my Longhorns can live on anything. That bad winter when the Herefords died of freezing and starvation, come spring, there my Longhorns were, walking skeletons but alive. Three weeks of good grass, they were ready to breed. And what did they eat during the blizzards? Anything they could chew, just anything they could find in the snow – cactus, wood from old fence posts, sticks. What wonderful animals.

Things might have continued this way had not Earnshaw, always seeking to improve his wife's herd, instructed his Mexican helper González to 'round up that last bunch of cows running wild and bring them within the fence to be properly bred.'

'Okay, boss.' The roundup was not easy, but with the expert help of the two black ranch hands it was accomplished. Mean Moses was deprived of his harem; the cows would be bred to the good bulls; and within three generations even the lesser characteristics of the famed Longhorn would be submerged in the preferred breeds that were developing.

Emma Rusk did not approve of this decision: 'Earnshaw, we don't have to use every cow on the range in your experiments. Let Mean Moses and his Longhorns stay out where they've always been.'

'Emma, thee either breeds cattle properly or thee doesn't breed at all. The utility of the Longhorn is diminishing . . .'

'Those cattle have their own utility, Earnshaw. Play God with your English cattle. Leave mine on the range.'

'Thee will never have first-class cattle . . .'

'I don't want first-class cattle, I want the cattle that grew up here.'

She lost that argument, as did the half-dozen owners in other corners of Texas who struggled to keep the breed alive; like Emma, they were submerged in the sweep of progress. But if Emma was powerless to protect the rights of Mean Moses, the bull was not. During the famous trial of the barbed wire, Moses had been tempted only by a stack of hay, and the pricks of the barbs were sufficiently irritating to fend him off, but now the essence of his being was insulted: his cows had been taken from him, and this he would not tolerate.

Among the two dozen Longhorn cows imprisoned behind barbed wire so that the English bulls could breed them was an extraordinary lady called Bertha, widely known for two virtues: she gave birth to a strong calf each year, and some aberration had allowed her to produce the damnedest pair of horns ever seen in Texas. It must have been a sexual deformity, for her great horns started out flat like a bull's, and when the time came for them to take the Texas twist, they remained flat but turned a wide sweep right back in huge semicircles till they almost met a few inches in front of her eyes. As John Jaxifer said when he drove her inside the barbed wire: 'You could fit one of them new bathtubs inside her horns.' His description was accurate, for the immense sweep of the horns and their smooth curve back to form an ellipse did take the outline of a gigantic bathtub.

It would be preposterous to claim that Mean Moses was in any way attached to Bathtub Bertha; he bred all cows indiscriminately and in a good year he could handle about two dozen, but it did seem, year after year, that he did his best job with Bathtub, for the speckled cow produced an unbroken chain of excellent calves, often twins, and it seemed likely that when Moses died, one of her young bulls would take his place as king of the herd. At any rate, when Moses lost Bathtub and his other cows it was not in the breeding season, so he felt no impetus to join them, but as the season changed he began to feel mighty urges, and when visceral feelings took charge he was impelled to act.

Sniffing the air for scent of his cows, he lowed softly and started in a straight line toward them. Down steep ravines and up their sides he plowed ahead, across arroyos damp from recent rains, and up to the first line of barbed wire he came. Pausing not a moment, he walked right through the three tough strands, pushing them ahead of him till his power pulled loose the post, making them fall useless.

Ignoring the gashes the barbs had inflicted across his chest, he plowed on, and when he reached the second fence, he went through it as easily as the first. Finally he came to where the three concentric fences protected the valuable bulls, and here, close to where his cows were, he simply knocked down the barbed wire, disregarded the wounds that were now pumping blood, and looked for the master bull who had usurped his cows. Head lowered, mighty horns parallel to the earth, he gave a loud bellow and charged.

'Boss! Boss!' González shouted as he ıntered in next morning with the rising sun.

'What is it?' Earnshaw asked, slipping into his trousers.

'Something awful!'

The Mexican deemed it best not to explain during the ride out to the tank, and when Earnshaw reached the fences he had so carefully constructed he stopped aghast. Some titanic beast had simply walked through them, laying barbs and posts alike in the dust. It had then apparently turned around and walked back, leaving a trail of blood but taking all the Longhorn cows with it.

'What happened?'

'Mean Moses.'

And then Earnshaw spotted the real tragedy, for in a corner of the corral, his side ripped open in a bloody mess, lay the wounded Hereford for which Earnshaw had paid $180. Trembling, Rusk hurried back to town, where he informed his wife: 'Thy bull has gored my bull.'

Emma, who appreciated the increase in the herd which her husband had supervised, was distraught at the damage to Earnshaw's prize English bull, but when she saw the leveled fences and realized the power which had thrown them down, that primitive power of the open range of which she had once been a part, she exulted.

'Let Mean Moses go, Earnshaw. He was meant to be free.' So, because of her stubborn defense of her stubborn bull, one corner of Texas was able to keep alive the Longhorn strain. When Mean Moses died, she selected his replacement, a fine young bull sired by Moses out of Bathtub Bertha. This Mean Moses II proved to be almost as good a bull as his father, and in time VII, XII and XIX of other bloodlines would be recognized as the premier bulls of their breed. Emma Larkin's love for the integrity of her animals had ensured that.

On a cold, blustery morning in March, Banker Weatherby sent one of his five clerks to fetch Earnshaw Rusk, and when the summons came, the Quaker had a moment of queasiness. For some time now he had suspected that Clyde Weatherby had taken the railroad funds the Fort Garner nerchants contributed and the acres which he, Rusk, had thrown into the kitty, and had spent them not on opinion-makers in the Wichita Falls-Abilene area but on himself, and he supposed that Weatherby was now either going to confess the malfeasance or ask for more funds. He'll not get another cent from me, Rusk swore as he crossed the area leading to the bank.

But when he walked into Weatherby's office, Rusk found that Simpson was there, the saloon keeper, Fordson and three others, and when all were seated, the banker threw a map before them and shouted: 'We've done it! I promised you a railroad, and we're getting one.'

The details as he explained them were complicated beyond the comprehension of ordinary men, and both Rusk and Simpson lost the trail early, but it was a standard Texas operation: 'Five different railroads are involved. From the F.W.&D.C. in the north, a spur will come south to be built by a new line, the Wichita Standard. From Abilene north will come a second spur, also built by a new line, the Abilene Major. What will unite them? A third spur built by us, the Fort Garner United Railway. President? Your humble servant. Secretary? Earnshaw Rusk.'

The men cheered, then they danced, then some wept and others sent out for beer and champagne. The five clerks were invited in to hear the good news, and they danced too. Rusk sent for his wife, and others did the same, and soon it seemed that an entire town was dancing and shouting and celebrating the fact that it had been saved.

'The railroad's coming!' men shouted, and some set forth on horseback to inform ranchers whose support had helped achieve this miracle. At the height of the festivities, Weatherby was still trying to explain to the directors of Fort Garner United how the complexities would be resolved: 'When we get our line built, we'll sell out to Abilene Major, which will then join with Wichita Standard. Then they'll both sell to F.W.&D.C.,which I'm assured has arranged to sell out completely to a huge new line to be called Colorado and Southern, and I know for a fact that Burlington System will some day buy that. So we'll wind up with baskets full of Burlington stock.'

It was a standard Texas operation, but no one was listening.

Emma had assumed that when her husband finally got his railroad he would relax, but Earnshaw was the kind of Pennsylvania Quaker who had to be engaged in a crusade of some kind or he did not feel alive. Now, in his fifties, with a railroad under his belt, he was determined that Larkin, as the county seat of Larkin County, should have a courthouse of distinction, and he channeled all his considerable efforts to that end.

As secretary of a functioning railroad, he carried a pass which entitled him to ride free across the face of Texas, and he found boyish delight in traipsing from one county to the next inspecting courthouses. On these pilgrimages he began to identify a group of excellent buildings obviously designed by the same daring, poetic architect whose thumbprint was unmistakable, and he wrote to his wife:

> No one can tell me his name, but he builds a courthouse which looks like the embodiment of law. He likes towers and turrets, and so do I. He likes clean, heavy lines, and as a Quaker trained in severity, so do I. And he displays a wonderful sense of color, which is remarkable in that he works in stone. He is the only man in Texas qualified to build our courthouse, which I want to be a memorial to thy heroic family.

At the town of Waxahachie, where the finest courthouse in Texas was under constuction, a marvelous medieval poem in stone and vivid colors, he learned that the architect's name was James Riely Gordon, and he found that this genius was then working at Victoria, the distinguished city in the southern part of the state, so he made the long trip there and met the great man. To his surprise, Gordon was only thirty-one, but so masterful in his courtly manner, for he had been born in Virginia and had acquired a stately style in both speech and appearance, that he dominated any situation of which he was a part. He liked Rusk immediately, for he saw in the serious Quaker the kind of man he respected, straightforward and dependable.

Yes, he would be interested in building his next courthouse in Larkin County because he wanted a real showcase in the West. Yes, he believed he could do it on a reasonable budget. Yes, he would try to preserve the existing stone buildings about the old parade ground. But when he saw the cramped dimensions on the plan Rusk showed him, he protested: 'Sir, I could not fit one of my courthouses into that cramped space. My courthouses need room to display their glories.' And with this, he jabbed at the commander's quarters, the flagpole, and the infantry quarters of Company U on the other side: 'Too constricted. To be effective a courthouse needs space.'

Rusk, not noted for laughing, broke into chuckles of relief: 'Mr Gordon! This is an old diagram, not a map. Merely to show you where the fort buildings are. The parade ground is very wide. Five times wider than this.'

'You mean ... ' With a quick pencil the architect drew a sketch representing Fort Garner as Rusk was describing it, with the splendid parade ground spaciously fitted among the stone buildings, but before he could react to this new vision, Rusk spread before him six photographs showing the handsome stonework in the houses and the infantry quarters.

Gordon was enchanted: 'You mean, I would have all this space and these fine buildings as a background?'

'That's why I've sought you, sir. We have a noble site awaiting your brilliance.'

'I'll do it!' Gordon cried, and he made immediate plans to follow Rusk to meet with the officials of Larkin County, but before Earnshaw departed, Gordon warned him: 'I shall design the courthouse. You shall pay for it. Before I reach Fort Garner, I want all the finances arranged and assured. I refuse to work in the dark.'

'How much will you need?'

'I was working on some ideas last night. Not less than eighty thousand dollars.'

'I don't have it now, but by the time you reach us, it'll be there.'

All the way home, Rusk sweated over how he was going to persuade the authorities of Larkin County to finance his latest dream: 'Goodness, they'll never approve eighty thousand dollars. Bascom County next door built their courthouse for under nine thousand.'

By the time he neared Fort Garner he realized that the only thing to do was to convene the community leaders and confess that in an excess of enthusiasm he had committed them to this large debt, and when he faced them in Editor Fordson's office, he began to tremble, but as soon as he outlined the problem, he received surprising support from Banker Weatherby, who would be expected to find the money: 'The state of Texas, having in mind communities just like ours, has passed a law enabling us to borrow funds for the construction of county courthouses.'

'Oh! I would never want to borrow money again,' Rusk said.

'Not borrow in the old sense. We pass a bond issue. The

entire community borrows. The state provides the funds.'

'Would I have to sign any papers?'

'Damnit, man. This is a new system. The public signs. The public gets a fine new courthouse. And we all prosper.'

Weatherby proved to be the staunchest supporter of the bond drive for the new courthouse and the best explicator of the Texas that was coming: 'Let us build good things now so that our children who follow will have a stronger base from which to do their building.' At one public meeting Frank Yeager, now a rancher with his own land, loudly protested that Larkin County could save money by using one of the old fort buildings as its courthouse, and Weatherby astonished Rusk by whispering: 'Ride herd on that horse's ass,' and Earnshaw rose to do so.

'Frank!' he argued. 'That's a little stable suited to a little town lost on the edge of the plains.'

'What are we?' Yeager asked, and Rusk replied: 'Little today, but not tomorrow. I want a noble building symbolizing our potential greatness. I want to fill the imaginations of our people.' After he had silenced Yeager, he addressed the citizens of Larkin County: 'I want something worthy of the new Texas.'

He had ten days before the architect was due to arrive, and he spent them in tireless persuasion, a tall, gaunt figure moving everywhere, talking with everyone, always with a sheaf of figures in his pocket, always with the bursting enthusiasm necessary to launch any civic enterprise of importance. On the ninth day he and Weatherby had the money guaranteed, and on the tenth day he slept until two in the afternoon.

The visit of James Riely Gordon to the frontier town was almost a disaster, for the austere young architect, one of the most opinionated men in Texas history and its foremost artist, went directly to his room, speaking to no one, not even Rusk. He ate alone and went to bed. In the morning he wished to see no one, and in the afternoon he stalked solemnly about the old parade ground, checking the buildings, satisfying himself that the stone houses were in good repair.

He also ate his evening meal alone, and at seven in the evening he deigned to appear before the local leaders. His appearance created a sensation, for he stepped primly before these hardened frontiersmen dressed in a black frock coat, striped trousers and creamy white vest. He wore a stiff collar three inches high from which appeared almost magically a fawn-colored cravat adorned by a huge diamond stickpin. The lapels of both his coat and vest were piped with silk grosgrain fabric of a slightly different color.

He had a big, square head, a vanishing hairline which he masked by training his forelocks to cover a huge amount of otherwise bare skin, and he wore pince-nez glasses that accentuated his hauteur. He was the most inappropriate person to address a group of frontier ranchers, and had a vote been taken at that moment, Gordon would have been shipped back to San Antonio, where he kept his offices.

But when he began to speak, the tremendous authority he had acquired through travel, study, contemplation and actual building manifested itself, and his audience sat in rapt attention:

'You have a magnificent site here on the plains. This old fort is a treasure, a memorial of heroic days. Its simple stone buildings form a dignified framework for whatever I do, and I would be proud to be a part of your achievement

'I have studied every penny, especially the difficulty of bringing materials here from a distance, and I believe I can build what you will want for seventy-nine thousand dollars, but if you insist on making any wild changes, the cost will be higher. Have you found ways to get the money?'

Satisfied that the funds were available, he astonished the hard-headed county leaders by telling them, not asking them, what the new courthouse was to be:

'It is essential, gentlemen, that we maintain a clear image of what a great courthouse ought to be, and I desire to build none that are not great. It must have four characteristics, and these must be visible to all. To the criminal who is brought here for trial, it must represent the majesty of the law, awesome and unassailable. To the responsible citizen who comes here seeking justice, it must represent stability and fairness and the continuity of life. To the elected officials working here, especially the judges, it must remind them of the heavy responsibility they share for keeping the system honorable and forward-moving; I want every official who enters his office in the morning to think: "I am part of a dignified tradition, reaching back to the time of Hammurabi and Leviticus." And to the town and the county and the state, the courthouse must be a thing of beauty. It must rise high and stand for something. And it must grow better as years and decades and centuries pass.'

And then, as if to prove his point, he asked Earnshaw to fetch the large package from his room, and when an easel was provided, he stunned his audience with a beautifully executed watercolor he had completed earlier. It showed the courthouse he would build at the center of the old fort.

First of all, it was beautiful, a work of recognizable art. Second, it was both magisterially heavy and delicately proportioned. Third, it was a kaleidoscope of color, utilizing three types of stone locally available, but stressing a brilliant red sandstone, alternating with layers of milky-white limestone. Fourth, it had the most fantastic collection of ornamentation an artist could have devised: miniature turrets, balustrades, soaring arches four stories up, Moorish towers at all corners, arched galleries open to the air, fenestrations, clock towers, and perched upon the top, a kind of red-and-white-stone wedding cake, five tiers high and ending in a many-turreted, many-spired tower, from which rose a master spire nineteen feet tall.

Ornate, gaudy, flamboyant, ridiculously overornamented, it was also grand in design and noble in spirit. It was a courthouse ideally suited to the Texas spirit, and it and its fifteen majestic sisters could be built only in Texas. But it was Frank Yeager's comment which best summarized it: 'A building like that, it would show where the seventy-nine thousand dollars were spent. Sort of makes you feel good.'

Each of the officials had changes he wanted made, with Rusk expressing a strong desire for four dominating turrets at the compass points. Gordon listened to each recommendation as if it were coming from Vitruvius, but when the critic stopped speaking and Gordon stopped nodding his head in agreement, the architect patiently explained why the suggestion, excellent though it might be in spirit, could not be accommodated, and as the evening wore on, it became apparent that James Riely Gordon was going to build the courthouse he wanted, for he was convinced that when it was done the citizens would want it, too. At the end of the long evening, with him standing beside his watercolor, his pince-nez still jamming his nose, the ranchers were beginning to speak of 'our courthouse' and 'our architect.'

The construction of the Larkin County Courthouse was the wonder of the age, and one aspect caused nervous comment. To complete the stone work professionally, Gordon had to transfer to the town the team of skilled Italian stonemasons he had brought to Texas to work on his other civic buildings, and these men did not exactly fit into the rugged frontier pattern. For one thing, they were Catholics and insisted upon having a priest visit them regularly. For another, they preferred their traditional food style and could not adjust to the Larkin County diet of greasy steaks smothered in rich gravy. But worst of all, as lonely men working constantly in one small Texas town after another, they clumsily sought female companionship, and this was resented by the local women and men alike.

There was one stonecarver much appreciated by Gordon, who assigned him the more difficult ornamental tasks. His name was Luigi Esposito, but he was called by his Texan co-workers Weegee, and this Weegee, unmarried and twenty-seven, fell in love with a charming and graceful young woman, Mabel Fister, who worked for the county judge, who had his temporary offices in one of the old cavalry barracks. Weegee saw her night and morning, a fine girl, he thought, and soon his day revolved about her appearances. He could anticipate when she would come to work, when she would leave the judge's office and on what errands. Whenever she appeared, he would stop work and stare at her until the last movement of her ankle carried her away.

At this period he was working on the four important carved figures which would decorate the corners on the second tier. Gordon had decided they would be draped female figures representing Justice, Religion, Motherhood and Beauty, and in a moment of infatuation Weegee started with the last-named, carving a really splendid portrait of Mabel Fister. When it was finished, he made bold to stop Mabel one morning as she was going to work; he could speak no English, but he wanted to explain that this statue was his tribute to her.

She was embarrassed and outraged that he should have intruded into her life in this manner, and although she could speak no Italian, and certainly did not wish to learn, she did indicate that she was displeased both with his art and with his having stopped her.

He next carved Motherhood, again in Mabel's likeness, and again he was snubbed when he tried to interest her in it. He then turned to Religion, and this time the beautiful Mabel appeared as a harsh and rather unpleasant type, which he displayed to her one afternoon as she left her work with the judge. She pushed his hand away and spurned his tongue-tied efforts to explain his art and his deep affection for her.

Before he started carving Justice, which he had wanted to be the best of the series, he asked the interpreter provided by Gordon to arrange some way for him to meet with Mabel Fister so that he could explain in sensible words his love for her, so one afternoon Earnshaw Rusk sat with Weegee and listened as the interpreter poured out the sculptor's story. Rusk inspected the three statues and said: 'I should think that any young woman woud be proud to be immortalized so handsomely.'

'Will you speak with her?' Weegee pleaded, and Earnshaw said that he certainly would. Hurrying home, he asked Emma if she would accompany him, and they went together to talk with the attractive secretary: 'Miss Fister, the gifted sculptor Luigi Esposito has asked if we would—'

'I want nothing to do with him. He's a bother.'

'But, Miss Fister, he's working in an alien land.' Emma was speaking, and when Mabel looked at her wooden nose she wanted very little to do with her, either.

'I would not care to speak with a papist,' she said.

'In Rome they claim that Jesus was the first Catholic,' Rusk said.

'We're not in Rome.'

'Very few young women have themselves depicted in marble by young men who love them.'

'That's a foolish word, Mr Rusk. I'm surprised you would use it.'

'No one ever need apologize for the word *love*. I would deeply appreciate it if you . . .'

Miss Fister was adamant. She would not meet with Weegee; she hoped that he would soon finish his carvings and go away: 'He has no place in Texas.' When Justice was finished, Weegee did not try to show it to her, but his mates could see that Mabel Fister had been treated harshly in it. Justice was hard, cruel and remorseless, and not at all what James Riely Gordon had intended. Indeed, he asked Luigi if he would consider trying again on that figure, but the Italian told him, through the interpreter: 'You don't change your plans. I don't change mine.'

Emma Rusk, aware that she too had been rebuffed by Miss Fister, was experiencing an emotional crisis of her own. Her son Floyd, nearly twenty now and as fat and unruly as ever, had made the acquaintance of one of the Italian workmen who had done some building in Brazil, and from him had obtained a most improbable piece of tropical wood. It was called *balsa*, the Italian said, and while it was lighter than an equal bulk of feathers, it was also structurally strong. He had paid the Italian a dollar for a piece three inches square and had then played with it, testing whether it would float and trying to estimate whether it weighed as much as an ounce, which he doubted.

Satisfied with its characteristics and assured that it would accept varnish, he then retired to his room, and after several abortive experiments on fragments of the balsa, came out in great embarrassment, holding out his hands, offering his mother a beautifully carved nose which weighed practically nothing and to which he attached a gossamer thread which he himself had plaited.

He insisted that she try it on, explaining that it had been so thoroughly varnished and rubbed that it would resist water. But when she removed her heavy wooden nose, the one carved in oak by her husband, and Floyd saw her again as she was, the experience was so crushing that he fled from the house, weighed down by the haunting images of his mother in the hands of her Comanche captors.

When he returned two days later, neither he nor his mother mentioned the nose. She wore it, with exceeding comfort; it

1117

looked better than its predecessor and its feathery weight gave her a freedom she had not enjoyed before. She felt younger and so much more acceptable that she went to the judge's office to speak with Mabel Fister: 'Young woman, not long ago you said some very stupid things. Don't interrupt. If God can accept all children as His own, you can be courteous to this gifted man so far from home.'

'I would never marry an Italian.'

'Who's speaking of marriage? I'm speaking of common decency. Of charity.'

'I do not need you to come here—'

'You shied away from me. I understand why. I might have done the same. But do not shy away from humanity, Miss Fister. We need all of it we can get.'

She accomplished nothing, but with a boldness she did not know she had she sought out Luigi Esposito, and with the aid of the interpreter, said: 'Miss Fister has never traveled. She thinks this little town is the universe. Forgive her.'

When these words were translated, Luigi said nothing, but he did bow ceremoniously to Emma as if to thank her for her solicitude. Then he turned abruptly, strode to his workshop, and without orders from Gordon, toiled with passionate concentration on his secret carving for the fifth and last location. When it was completed he asked three of his fellow workers to help him cement it in place, and when it was fixed on the south façade of the courthouse between Beauty and Motherhood, the other Italians laughed until they were weak to think of the joke Luigi had played on the Americans. Covering it with a tarpaulin, they proposed unveiling it at some propitious moment. Then the three masons went to their quarters and got mildly drunk while Luigi searched for a pistol, with which he blew out his brains.

When the courthouse was completed, a thing of flamboyant beauty, the time came for the unveiling of Luigi Esposito's four symbolic sculptures plus the mystery creation, and since they were presented in the order in which he had done them, it was apparent that his model had grown increasingly harsh and ugly, as if Justice in Texas was always going to be a stern and uncertain affair.

Some commented on this, but most were interested in what the fifth mystery sculpture would show, and when the three Italians who had cemented it into place withdrew the tarpaulin, smiling vengefully, a gasp issued from the crowd, for in amazing and intimate detail, Weegee had carved the private parts of a woman, and before nightfall rumor initiated by the workmen was circulating to the effect that Weegee had carved it from life. They vowed they had watched as Mabel Fister posed.

There it stood on the south façade of this magnificent courthouse, immortalized in stone. Two days later Miss Fister left Larkin for Abilene and did not return.

Earnshaw, of course, wanted the lascivious carving removed, but to his surprise Emma did not: 'It's part of the courthouse experience, let it remain.' And she was supported by Clyde Weatherby, who predicted accurately: 'Ten people will come to see the courthouse, but a thousand to see Mabel Fister's unusual pose.'

Surprising news from Jacksborough diverted attention from the statue. Floyd Rusk had disappeared for several days, and his parents feared that he might have gone to old Fort Griffin, where notorious gamblers clustered, but he had gone to Jacksborough, accompanied by Molly Yeager, whom he had married. She was a flighty girl, almost as round and pudgy as her husband, and Emma could find little reason to hope that she would prove a good wife, but as she told Earnshaw: 'If I criticized Miss Fister for not being gracious toward her Italian, I can't be ungracious to Molly.' What she did not tell her husband was that each day she wore her balsa-wood nose she was reminded that in his grudging way Floyd did love her, and that was enough.

As the century ended, a delightful charade occurred. An official from Washington, eager for a paid vacation, had come to Jacksborough just after Floyd's wedding and had fired the postmaster, stating no reasons for his arbitrary act. He had then announced that henceforth the town was to be Jacksboro, whereupon with elaborate ceremony he reemployed the fired man as the new postmaster.

After the celebration, at which he got roaring drunk, he boarded the coach to Fort Garner, where without explanation he fired that postmaster too. When Earnshaw protested such unfairness, the visitor pointed at him: 'Because of your agitation, this town is now named Larkin,' and the postmaster was reappointed by a letter from President McKinley.

During the festivities celebrating the christening, Emma stood well to one side as she heard Weatherby extolling her husband for the good he had accomplished in this town: 'He brought us the wire fence that made our fortunes, he found a way to get us our railroad, he engineered our noble courthouse, and now he has given us a proper name.' The orator pointed out that this was an example to young people of how . . .

Emma stopped listening, for she was staring toward the plains and calculating how costly this so-called improvement had been. 'The buffalo that used to darken these plains,' she whispered, 'the Indians who chased them, the Longhorns who roamed so freely, the unmarked open spaces . . . where are they? Will our children ever see their like?' She expected no answer, for she knew that the glories which had sustained her through the dark years would be no more.

. . . Task Force

I tried to be polite when the governor intruded upon the planning session for our August meeting in Galveston. I explained that we had intended to invite a meteorologist from Wichita Falls to address us on Texas weather: 'You know, things like hurricanes and tornadoes.'

He said: 'Those are the Texas storms aloft. What I'm worried about are the storms here on the ground.'

When I explained that it would be difficult to disinvite Dr Clay, he broke in: 'You mean Lewis Clay? He's one of the best.' A governor, it seemed, was supposed to know everyone in his state, and without consulting me he grabbed a phone, dialed his secretary, and said: 'Get me Lewis Clay, that man who supported me in Wichita Falls,' and within a minute he was speaking to our meteorologist: 'Lewis Clay, your old pal, the governor. I hear you're heading for Galveston with these fine people on our Task Force. Now, Lewis, I'm going to have to preempt the morning session.' There was a long pause, after which I heard: 'Lewis, in running a great state, unexpected things sometimes become imperative. And believe me, this is one of those times.' Another pause: 'Lewis, they'll save you the entire afternoon.'

When he hung up I was more irritated than before, because this really was an unwarranted intrusion, but as things worked out, the split meeting was one of the most instructive we would have, for the day dwelt first on those great tempests of the human soul and then on the tempests of the sky which mirror them, and when we were through, our Task Force understood the spiritual and physical settings of Texas much better.

The impromptu morning session was monopolized by three worried Texans who had worked for the governor's election and who now warned him that unless they were given an opportunity to present their opinions about the spiritual base of Texas history, they were going to lead a statewide campaign against the governor himself for his carelessness in selecting the committee members. When we convened that morning in a beautiful room overlooking the peaceful Gulf of Mexico, we were faced by three determined citizens with a tableful of charts, studies and typed recommendations.

Up to that moment they had not known one another personally, although they had been in correspondence regarding the threatened destruction of their state. The first was a tall, cadaverous man from Corpus Christi, an Old Testament prophet accustomed to dire prediction; he was not an ordained clergyman, but was prepared to advise clergymen as to how they should behave and what they should include in their sermons. He had a sharp, angular face, strong eyebrows and a deep premonitory voice. When he spoke, we paid attention.

The second was a stern housewife from Abilene who sat with sheaves of paper which she had trouble keeping organized. About fifty, she had educated her own three children rather rigorously and was now prepared to do the same with the state's. Her forte was to start talking and to keep going regardless of objections or obstructions thrown in her path. She was a verbal bulldozer, extremely effective in leveling opposition with force if not reason.

The third member was a jovial man from San Angelo, conciliatory, nodding agreeably when introduced, and never offensive in what he said or how he said it. But he was often more effective than his companions because he started each presentation with some phrase like 'It would really be hurtful, wouldn't it, if we taught our children that ... ' And he would follow with some established fact which everyone accepted but him, such as the truth that Texas was composed of some twenty radically different ethnic groups. He and the woman objected to any such statement in our conclusions on the ground that 'it would be divisive, stressing differences in our population, when what we need is a constant reminder that Texas was settled primarily by one master group, the good people from states like Kentucky and Georgia with an Anglo–Saxon, Protestant background.'

The rugged session covered four hours, nine to one, and we Task Force members tired of trying to digest the particularist ideas long before the three protesters tired of presenting them. Indeed, our visitors looked as if they could have continued throughout the evening, and next day too.

The thrust of their argument was simple: 'The essential character of Texas was formed by 1844, and our schoolchildren should be taught only the virtues which dominated at that time.' They were much more interested in what should not be taught than what should, and they had a specific list of forbidden subjects that must be avoided, Each of the three had some personal *bête noire* in which he or she was interested, and I shall summarize the main points of their forceful presentations:

The San Angelo man instructed us to downplay the supposed influence of the Spaniards, the Mexicans, the Germans, the Czechs and the Vietnamese: 'As for the coloreds, there is no real need to mention them at all. They played no significant role in Texas history, and to confuse young minds with the problems of slavery, which rarely existed in Texas and then in a most benevolent form, would be hurtful.' He also advised us to drop excessive coverage of Indians: 'The Texas Indians were cruel murderers, but we don't need to dwell on such unpleasantness. And the fact that we threw them all out of our state proves that they influenced Texas not at all. You needn't be unkind about it. Just ignore it, for they vanished a long time ago.' Most specifically, he warned against adverse comment on the resurgence of the Ku Klux Klan in the 1920s: 'Some people are speaking of this as if it was a blot on our escutcheon, and this has to stop. It really shouldn't be mentioned at all, and if it is, it must be presented as a logical, God-fearing uprising of loyal citizens eager to protect Texas against the radical incursions of coloreds, Catholics, Jews and freethinkers.'

The Abilene woman was gentler in her admonitions: 'The job of the schools is to protect our children from the ugliness of life. We see no reason why you should even mention the Great Depression. It would be a reflection on the American Way. And we're appalled that some textbooks speak of little girls having babies out of wedlock. It's much better not to discuss such things.' She cautioned us against including prominent photographs of Texas women like Barbara Jordan and Oveta Culp Hobby because they made their names in political activity: 'Ma Ferguson is all right, because she was governor and she did stand for old-fashioned virtues, and I suppose you'll have to include Lady Bird Johnson, but feature her as the mother of two daughters. We don't want a lot of manly-looking women in our books. They're not proper role models for our young girls.' She said she supposed we'd have to include Abraham Lincoln and F.D.R., but she hoped we would not praise them, 'for they were worse enemies to Texas than the boll weevil.'

The Corpus Christi man fulminated against secular humanism and what he called the Four Ds: dancing, deviation, drugs and Democrats: 'And when I say *deviation*, I mean it in its broadest sense. There is a wonderful central tendency in Texas history, and when we deviate from it in any respect, we run into danger.' When I asked for an example, he snapped: 'Labor unions. All Texas will be deeply offended if you discuss labor unions. We've striven to keep such un-American operations out of our state and have campaigned to preserve our right-to-work laws. I have four textbooks here which speak of communists like Samuel Gompers and John L. Lewis as if they were respectable citizens, and this will not be tolerated. Organized labor played no part in Texas history and must not be presented as if it did.' Like the Abilene woman, he wanted the roles of the sexes clearly differentiated: 'Boys should play football and there should be no concession to movements blurring the lines between the sexes.' When he preached against dancing, I think all of us listened with condescending respect, but when he came to drugs, we supported him enthusiastically: 'I simply cannot

1123

imagine how this great nation has allowed this curse to threaten its young people. What has gone wrong? What dreadful mistakes have we made?' We nodded when he said in thundering, prophetic tones: 'This plague must be wiped out in Texas.'

At this point Rusk interrupted: 'What positive values are you advocating?' and the man replied: 'Those which made Texas great. Loyalty, religion, patriotism, justice, opportunity, daring.'

As he recited these virtues, most of which I supported, I saw these three earnest visitors in a different light. They were striving to hold back the tides of change which threatened to engulf them. They really did long to recover the simpler life of 1844 and find refuge in its rural patterns, its heroic willingness to defend its principles, its dedication to a more disciplined society. I understood their feelings, for all men in all ages have such yearnings.

When we broke for a belated lunch, Miss Cobb, a descendant of Democratic senators, asked the speakers: 'By what route did you become Republicans? Surely your parents were Democrats.'

The Abilene woman laughed uneasily: 'My father knew only one Republican family. A renegade who joined that party so that the Republican administration in Washington could nominate him postmaster. Father would cross the street to avoid speaking to the scoundrel.' The Corpus Christi man said: 'You mustn't get into that with children. Our families were all Democrats. Nobody thought of being anything else before the 1928 election, when they had to vote Republican to fight Al Smith and his boozing ways.'

Smiling amiably, the San Angelo man said: 'If you do have to explain it, why not use the old joke? Man asked a rancher in the Fort Stockton area: 'Caleb, your six boys are all good Democrats, I hope?" and Caleb said: "Yep, all but Elmer. He learned to read." But I agree with the others. Best to omit the whole question.'

I said: 'You seem to be recommending that we omit a good deal of Texas history,' and the dour Corpus Christi man said: 'A good history is characterized by what's left out.'

I said I'd appreciate an example, and he was more than equal to the occasion: 'In the decades after the great storm of 1900 that destroyed Galveston, loyal citizens rebuilt the city, pretty much as you see it here today. But with their enormous losses and few businesses to take up the slack, how could they earn money? They turned the city into a vast amusement area – houses of ill repute, gambling, gaudy saloons. Men from my city . . . '

'And mine, too,' the San Angelo man chimed in. 'They came here to raise hell in Galveston. Wildest city in America, they boasted.'

'Do we need to include that in a book for children?' the Corpus Christi man asked, and I had to reply 'No,' and he smiled icily: 'There is much that can be profitably omitted.'

At our lunch I wanted to make peace with our vigorous critics and said: 'I'm sure I speak for our entire Task Force when I say that while we must disagree with certain of your positions, we support many of them. Like you, we feel that modern children are pressured to grow up too fast. We deplore drugs. We champion private property. We agree that too often the negative aspects of our society are stressed. And we subscribe to Texas patriotism.'

'What don't you agree with?' the Corpus Christi man challenged, and I answered him as forthrightly as I could: 'We think women have played an important role in all aspects of Texas life. We think Mexicans are here to stay. We think Texas should be proud of its multinational origins. And we are not monolithic. Rusk and Quimper are strong Republicans; Miss Cobb and Garza equally strong Democrats.'

'What about you?' the San Angelo man asked amiably, and I said: 'I'm like the old judge in Texarkana during a heated local election who was asked which candidate he supported: "They're both fine men. Eminently eligible for the big post, they think. Haven't made up my mind yet, but when I do I'm gonna be damned bitter about it." '

Dr Clay started his presentation on Texas weather with three astonishing slides: 'Here you see the Clay residence in Wichita Falls at seven-oh-nine in the evening of the tenth of April 1979. That's me looking up at the sky. This second slide, taken by a neighbor across the street, shows what we were staring at.'

It was an awesome photograph, widely reproduced later, for

it showed in perfect detail the structure of a great tornado just about to strike: 'Note three things. The enormous black cloud aloft, big enough to cover a county. The clearly defined circular tunnel dropping toward the ground. And the snout of the destroying cloud, trailing along behind like the nozzle of a vacuum cleaner.'

When Clay started to move to the next slide, Rusk stopped him: 'Why does the snout trail?'

'Aerodynamics. It lingers upon the ground it's destroying.'

He showed us the most remarkable slide of the three: 'This is the Clay residence one minute after the tornado struck.' No upright part of the former house was visible; it was total destruction, with even the heavy bathtub ripped away and gone.

'How could the man with the camera take such a picture?' Rusk asked, and Miss Cobb wanted to know: 'What happened to you?'

'That's the mystery of a tornado. Its path of destruction is as neatly defined as a line drawn with a pencil. On our side of the street, total wipe-out. Where the photographer was standing . . . merely a big wind.'

'Yes, but where were you?' Miss Cobb persisted.

'Just before it struck, the man with the camera shouted: "Lewis! Over here!" He could see where the pencil line was heading.'

'Remarkable,' Quimper said, but Clay corrected him: 'No, the miracle was that the tornado lifted not only the bathtub from our wreckage but also my mother. Carried her right along with the tub and deposited them both as gently as you please a quarter of a mile away.'

Then, with a series of beautifully drawn meteorological slides, he instructed us on the genesis of the tornadoes which each year struck Texas so violently: 'Four conditions are required before a tornado is spawned. A cold front sweeps in from the Rockies in the west. It hits low-level moist air from the Gulf. Now, this happens maybe ninety times a year and accounts for normal storms of no significance. But sometimes a third factor intrudes. Very dry air rushing north from Mexico. When it hits the front, which is already agitated, severe thunderstorms result, but rarely anything worse. However, if the fourth air mass moves in, a majestic jet stream at thirty thousand feet, it's as if a cap were clamped down over the entire system. Then tornadoes breed and tear loose and do the damage you saw at Wichita Falls.'

'How bad was that damage?' Quimper asked, and Clay said: 'It smashed a path eight miles long, a mile and a half wide. Four hundred million dollars in destruction, forty-two dead, several hundred with major injuries.'

In rapid fire he sped through a series of stunning photographs, throwing statistics at us as he went: 'Most Texas tornadoes strike in May. We get a steady average of a hundred and thirty-two per year, and they produce a yearly average of thirteen deaths. Most tornadoes we ever had in one day, a hundred and fifteen shockers on a September afternoon in 1967. The funnel rotates counterclockwise and can travel over the ground at thirty-five miles an hour, almost always in a southwest-to-northeast direction, and with a funnel wind velocity of up to three hundred miles an hour.'

Numbed by the violent force of the pictures and words, we had no questions, but he added two interesting facts: 'Yes, what you've heard is true. A Texas tornado can have winds powerful enough to drive a straw flying through the air right through a one-inch plank. And there really is such a thing as Tornado Alley. It runs from Abilene northeast through Larkin and Wichita Falls.' Looking directly at Ransom Rusk, who lived in that middle town, he said: 'Statistics are overwhelming. Most dangerous place to be during a tornado is an automobile. The wind picks it up, finds it too heavy, dashes it to the ground. Best place?' He flashed his third slide, the one showing the destruction of his own house: 'Pick your spot. But if you have a tornado cellar, use it.'

The next two hours were compelling, for he gave a similar analysis of the great hurricanes that spawned off the coast of Africa and came whipping across the Atlantic into the Gulf of Mexico, and we sat appalled as he showed us what had happened to Galveston on 8 September 1900: 'Worst natural disaster ever to strike America. Entire city smitten. Whole areas erased by a fearful storm surge that threw twelve feet of water inland. Up to eight thousand lives lost in one night.'

One remarkable series of shots taken by four different

photographers on a single March day in 1983 showed Amarillo in a snow-and-sleet storm at 29° Fahrenheit, Abilene in the middle of a huge dust storm at 48°, Austin at the beginning of a blue norther at 91° and Brownsville in the midst of an intolerable heat wave at 103°. 'From northwest to southeast, a range of seventy-four degrees. I wonder how many mainland states can match that kind of wild variation?'

He spoke also of the famous blue norther, which had amazed Texans since the days of Cabeza de Vaca: 'These phenomenal drops in temperature can occur during any month of the year, but of course they're most spectacular during the summer months, when the sudden drop is conspicuous, but the daddy of all blue northers hit the third of February in 1899. Temperature at noon in many parts of the state, a hundred and one. Temperature not long thereafter, minus three, a preposterous drop of a hundred and four degrees.'

But what interested me even more was his statistics on Texas droughts: 'Every decade we get a major jolt, worst ever in those bad years 1953 to 1957. Much worse than the so-called Dust Bowl years. We really suffered, and the law of probability assures us that one of these days we'll suffer again.'

Clay was a man of great common sense. After decades of studying Texas weather, he had come to see the state as a mammoth battleground over which and on which the elements waged incessant war, with powerful effect upon the people who occupied that ground: 'No human being would settle here, with our incredibly hot summers and our violent storms from the heavens and the sea, if he did not relish the struggle and feel that with courage he could survive. What other state has tornadoes and hurricanes that kill more than sixty people year after year? And blue northers and drought and hundred-degree days for two whole months?' He looked at me, and knowing one of my preoccupations, added: 'And a constant drop in its aquifers? This is a heroic land and it demands heroic people.'

The Larkin Field

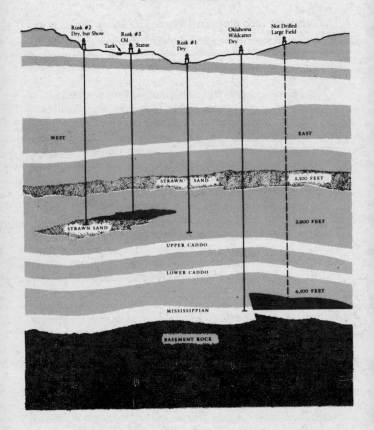

Rusk #2
Dry, but Show

Tank

Rusk #3
Oil

Statue

Rusk #1
Dry

Oklahoma
Wildcatter
Dry

Not Drilled
Large Field

WEST

EAST

STRAWN SAND

2,100 FEET

STRAWN SAND

2,900 FEET

UPPER CADDO

LOWER CADDO

4,600 FEET

MISSISSIPPIAN

BASEMENT ROCK

XII

THE TOWN

The census of 1900 illustrated a basic fact about Texas: it was still a rural state, for out of its population of 3,048,710, only 17.1 percent was classified as urban, and even this was misleading because the scrawniest settlement was rated *urban* if it had more than 2,500.

The biggest city was still San Antonio, with a population of 53,321, much of it German, for the Hispanics who would later give the city its character accounted at this time for not more than 10 percent of the total. Houston was the next largest city, with a population of 44,633, and Dallas was third, with 42,638. Future cities like Amarillo and Lubbock, which would later figure prominently in Texas history, were not cities at all, the former with only 1,442 inhabitants, the later with a mere 112.

But it was essentially in such small towns that the character of the state was developing, and three were of special interest. The first, of course, was the frontier town of Larkin in the west, with a population of 388. The second was that charming agricultural town with the elfin name, Waxahachie, in the north-central area, just south of Dallas; it had a population of 4,215. And the third was the fascinating little hispanic town of Bravo, about as far south as one could go in Texas. It stood on the north bank of the Rio Grande in an area where irrigation would turn what had once been unwieldy brushland into one of the most concentrated farming areas in America. Bravo, with a population of 389, guarded the American end of a small bridge over the river; Escandón, a somewhat larger town, marked the Mexican end.

As the nineteenth century drew to a close, the town of Larkin, the seat of Larkin County, found itself embroiled in an intellectual argument which preoccupied a good many other communities: When did the new century begin?

Tradition, accepted modes of expression and popular opinion all agreed that at midnight 31 December 1899 an old century would die, with a new one beginning a minute later. To any practical mind, even the name of the new year, 1900, indicated that a new system of counting had begun, and to argue otherwise was ridiculous: 'Any man with horse sense can see it's a new century, elsen why would they of given it a new name?'

Yet Earnshaw Rusk, like many thinking men and women across the state, knew that the twentieth century could not possibly begin until 31 December 1900; logic, history and mathematics all proved they were correct, but these zealots had a difficult time persuading their fellow citizens to delay celebrating until the proper date. 'Damn fools like Earnshaw cain't tell their ear from their elbow,' said one zealot. 'Any idiot knows the new century begins like we say, and I'm gonna be ringin' that church bell come New Year's Eve and Jim Bob Loomis is gonna be lightin' the fire.'

Rusk found such plans an insult to intelligence. 'Tell me,' he asked Jim Bob, 'now I want you to just tell me, how many years in a century?' He had stopped using the Quaker *thee* in public.

'A hunnert,' Jim Bob said.

'At the time of Christ, when this all began, was there ever a year zero?'

'Not that I heerd of.'

'So the first century must have begun with the year 1.'

'I think it did.'

'So when we reached the year 99, how many years had the first century had?'

'Sounds like ninety-nine.'

'It was ninety-nine, so the year 100 had nothing special about it. The second century couldn't have begun until the beginning of 101.'

Jim Bob pointed a warning finger at the lanky Quaker: 'You're talkin' atheism, and Reverend Hislop warned us against ideas like yourn.'

For some obscure theological reason that was never spelled out, Reverend Hislop of the Methodist church had taken a strong stand in favor of 1900 as the beginning of the new century, and he had equated opposition to that view as being against the will of God: 'Every man in his right mind knows that the new century begins when it does, and misguided persons who try to argue otherwise are deluded.'

When Rusk asked him: 'All right, how many years were there in the first century?' the clergyman snapped: 'One hundred, like anyone knows.'

'And how could that be?' Rusk pressed. 'How could thy century begin at year 1 and end at year 99 and still have a hundred years?' and the Reverend replied: 'Because God willed it that way.' And that became the general opinion of the community; if God had wanted his first century, when Christianity began, to have only ninety-nine years, it was only a small miracle for Him to make it so.

As December 1899 ended, the wood for the bonfire at the south end of the former parade ground grew higher and higher, with most familes contributing odd pieces to the pile. Jim Bob supervised the throwing on of additional pieces until a ladder was required to reach the top, and then schoolboys took over the task. Ladies from the two major churches, Baptist and Methodist, prepared a nonalcoholic punch, and a band rehearsed a set of marches.

This irritated Earnshaw, who asked his wife: 'Emma, how can people fly into the face of fact?' and she replied: 'Easy. I sort of like 1900 myself. Obviously the beginning of something new.'

Such reasoning disgusted her husband, who withdrew to the companionship of seven other men – no women engaged in such nonsense – who remained convinced that their century, at least, would start at midnight on 31 December 1900 and not before. They remained aloof from the celebrations, so they did not hear Reverend Hislop intone the prayer which welcomed the new century for everyone else:

'Almighty God, we put to rest an old century, one which brought the Republic of Texas victory in war and membership in the Federal Union. It brought us anguish during the War Between the States and sore tribulation when the Indians attacked us and niggers tried to run things. But we have won free. We have settled the wilderness and conquered distance. We have a glorious town where unobstructed winds used to howl, and the prospects ahead are infinite and glorious.

'We cannot foresee what this twentieth century will bring us, but we have good cause to hope that war will be no more, and it is not idle to think that before the century is far gone we shall have a planing mill providing lumber for the many small houses we shall build. Our town is situated so that it must grow, the Boston of the West, with fine churches and perhaps even a college of distinction. I see great accomplishment for this town. Hand in hand with the new century, we shall march to greatness.'

Either the town or the century was laggard, because the year 1900 was one of drought, dying cattle and frustrated hopes about the planing mill. Banker Weatherby, always eager to advance the commercial prospects of his town and willing to risk his own capital, had put together a consortium of interests that had accumulated a purse of thirteen thousand dollars with which to entice a planing mill to start operations on trees hauled in by the railroad, but in July the venture failed, with the Larkin men losing their shirts. Even Weatherby, a perpetual optimist, was heard to say as he closed the books on this latest failure: 'If God had wanted a planing mill in this town, He'd have given us trees instead of rattlesnakes.'

Rusk lost $800 on the deal, which caused him to tell Emma: 'I warned people that 1900 was bound to be a year of ill omen,' at which she snorted: 'You talk as crazy as Reverend Hislop.'

'What do you mean?'

'Well, he says God was in favor of 1900. You argue that nature is against 1900. I don't see much difference.'

Emma Rusk, forty-three now, believed in God and supported the Methodist church in a desultory sort of way, but she avoided theological discussion: 'I think a church is a good thing to have in a town. It civilizes people, especially young people and it deserves our support. But the mysteries it tries to sell . . . some of the things that Reverend Hislop preaches . . . I can do without them.'

She deplored her husband's gambling on the mill: 'We could have given that money to Floyd to help with our two granddaughters. Don't ever mention a planing mill to me again.'

She now thought more kindly of her son than she had in the past, for at twenty-five he was becoming more like a man. He was still grossly overweight, some two hundred and fifty pounds, and his wife, Molly, was much the same at two-twenty. But they had produced two lively girls: Bertha, aged four, and Linda, eleven months. The children looked as if they were going to have their grandfather's ranging height and their grandmother's lively attitude toward the world about them. They showed no signs of being especially intelligent, but Bertha did seem to have her mother's gift of organizing her little world in the way she wanted.

Emma judged that her son had a fighting chance to make something of himself despite his surly temper and his abhorrence of his father, for Floyd could work; the trouble was, as Emma saw it: 'He never sticks at anything. If I had to leave the handling of our cattle to him, heaven knows what would happen.' Fortunately, she could rely on Paul Yeager, two years older than Floyd and two centuries wiser. The Yeagers now occupied a considerable acreage north of the tank, but as the father pointed out to Emma one morning: 'Earnshaw gave us our first two hundred acres, but he's never entered the deed at the courthouse. Would you remind him that my boy and I are putting a lot of work into those acres? We'd feel safer . . .'

'Of course you would! I'll tell him to get jumpin'.'

In mid-December she told her husband: 'Earnshaw, it isn't right to leave those Yeagers dangling without title to their land. Go to the courthouse and fix that up, please.'

'Thee is right!' There was no argument about the propriety of formalizing the gift, and Earnshaw said that he would attend to it as soon as he and his logicians had ushered in the new century properly

The seven men who had sided with Rusk in his defense of reason were now having a high old time preparing to greet the new century; no church would help them celebrate, for it was already acknowledged that God had ordained 1900 to be the year of change, and troublemakers like Rusk and his gang were seen as disrupters of the peace. Their argument that the first century could not possibly have had ninety-nine years had long since been disposed of, and they were largely ignored as they went about the serious business of greeting their new century.

Denied the use of any public building and supported by only one of their eight wives, these stubborn citizens met at eleven on the night of 31 December 1900, with Rusk uttering this prediction:

'Mark my words, and we must get this into the *Defender* as our prediction, in the year 1999 the citizens of this town will relive our debate. Those with no sense of history or responsibility to fact will fire cannon and light bonfires as the last day of that year draws to a close. And I suppose there will be talk of God's preference, too, same as now. But the knowing ones will gather on the last night of the year 2000 to greet the twenty-first century as it really begins on the first day of January 2001.

'I don't drink, but I do propose a toast to those valiant souls a hundred years from now. It is something, in this world of shifting standards, to respect the great traditions, and tonight I can think of none finer than the one which says: "No century can have ninety-nine years." Gentlemen, with my water and your wine, let us toast common sense.'

It was rumored later, after the tragic events of the evening, that Earnshaw Rusk, the Quaker who personified sobriety, had drunk himself silly with wine at his false New Century, but others like Jim Bob Loomis, who had built the bonfire at the real celebration, argued that God had intervened because of Rusk's blasphemy over the false beginning. At any rate, when Rusk left the celebration and started to cross the old parade ground in the shadow of his beloved courthouse, two young cowboys from the Rusk ranch rode hell for leather into the courthouse square, in about the same way their fathers had invaded Dodge City.

Earnshaw saw the first young fellow and managed to sidestep his rearing horse, but he did not see the second, whose horse panicked, knocked Earnshaw to the ground, and trampled him about the head.

The fifty-nine-year-old Quaker was in such strong condition that his heart and lungs kept functioning even though consciousness was lost, never to be regained. For three anguished days he lingered, a man of great rectitude whose body refused to surrender. Emma stayed by his bed, hoping that he would recognize her, and even Floyd came in to pay his grudging respects; he had never liked his father and deemed it appropriate that Earnshaw should die in this ridiculous manner, defending one more preposterous cause.

On the fourth day a massive cerebral hemorrhage induced a general paralysis, but still he held on; it was as if his mortal clock had been wound decades ago and set upon a known course from which it would not deviate. Indeed, as the doctor said: 'It looks like he refused to die. He's dead, but his heart won't admit it.'

On the sixth day his damaged brain deteriorated so badly that Death actually came into the room and said softly: 'Come on, old fellow. I've won.' But even this challenge was ignored. Clenching his hands, Earnshaw held on to the sides of the bed, and his legs tried to grasp the bed too, so that when the end finally came, they had to pry him loose.

On the day of the funeral four Comanche rode into town from the reservation at Camp Hope, and at the graveside they were permitted to chant. Floyd Rusk and his wife were infuriated by this paganism and this hideous reminder of what had happened to Floyd's mother decades ago, and they were further outraged when Emma Rusk, with no ears and a wooden nose, joined the Indians in their chant, using the language with which her ill-starred husband had hoped to tame these avengers of the Texas plains.

The tragedy at Lammermoor, for it could be called nothing less, had begun one morning in 1892 when a field hand ran to the big house, shouting: 'Mastah Cobb, somethin' awful in the cotton bolls.'

Laurel Cobb, the able son of Senator Cobb and Petty Prue and now in charge of the plantation, hurried out to see what minor disaster had struck this time, but he soon found it to be major. 'Half the cotton plants have been invaded by a beetle,' he told his wife, Sue Beth, when he returned.

'Much damage?'

'Total. The heart of the lint has been eaten out.'

'You mean our cotton's gone?'

'Exactly what I mean,' and he took her out to the extensive fields to see the awful damage, this sudden assault upon their way of life.

That was the year when the boll weevil first appeared in the fields of East Texas, and in each succeeding year the scourge became more terrible. Entire plantations were wiped out. and there was no countermeasure to halt this devastation. The weevil laid its eggs in the ripening boll, and as the larvae matured they ate away the choicest part of the lint. When the weevil finished, the plant was worthless.

When times had been good, Cobb was like everyone else in Texas: 'I want no interference from government,' but now when trouble struck he expected immediate help, and he was the first in his district to demand that something be done. A wiry young expert from A&M, a most gloomy man, was sent to share with the local planters what was known:

'Cotton is indigenous to various locations throughout the world. India and Egypt, for example. But our strain comes from Mexico, and a very fine strain it is, one of the best.

'When it jumped north it left behind its major enemies. But now they're beginning to catch up. The boll weevil came across the border into Texas first. Seems to move about two hundred and ten miles a year. Soon it'll be in Mississippi, Alabama. It's sure to move into Georgia and the Carolinas.

'We know of nothing that will halt it, or kill it. All we can do is pray that it will run its course, like a bad cold, or that some other insect will attack it and keep it in bounds. My advice to you? Move to better land, farther west, where it doesn't dominate, because the boll weevil has a built-in compass. It needs moisture and moves always toward the east, seeking it.'

The situation was as bad as he said, and from 1892 to 1900, Cobb watched his once glorious plantation, 'the pride of the bayou' he called it, fall almost into ruin. Fields which had once shipped boatloads and then trainloads of bales to New Orleans could now scarcely put together fifty usable bales.

At the turn of the century, in deep dejection, he went to his wife: 'Sue Beth, we can't fool ourselves any longer. Our fields are doomed.'

'You think Lammermoor is finished?'

'Not if we could find something to kill the weevil. Or some new kind of fertilizer. Or if the government could breed a new strain which could protect itself . . .'

'But you don't expect such miracles?'

He did not answer. Instead he took from his pocket a report from a cotton growers' advisory committee: 'These men say there's wonderful new land near a place called Waxahachie.'

'What a strange name for a town.'

'I haven't seen it, but from what they say, it could prove our salvation.' He took the train to Waxahachie, and returned bubbling with enthusiasm: 'I can get a thousand acres at thirty-one cents an acre.'

'But hasn't the weevil reached there, too?'

'It has, but the rainfall is so much less, the experts have worked out ways to control it . . . more or less.'

'So you've decided to move?'

'I have.'

'Will we be able to sell this plantation?'

'Who would be so crazy as to buy?'

'Does that mean we lose everything?'

'We lose very little. What we do is transfer it to Devereaux. He claims he can operate it at a small profit.'

Devereaux Cobb was a gentle throwback to the eighteenth century. Forty years old and self-trained in the classics, he was the late-born son of that red-headed Reuben Cobb of Georgia who had died at Vicksburg, but he had inherited none of his father's verve and courage. A big, flabby bachelor afraid of women, he had dedicated himself to tending the white-columned plantation home built by his parents; in lassitude he tried vainly to keep alive the cherished traditions of the Deep South, and although he had no cadre of slaves to tend the lawns as in the old days, he did have hired blacks who deferred to his whims by calling him Marse Devvy while he called them Suetonius and Trajan. He was a kindly soul, a remnant of all that was best in that world which the Texas Southrons had striven to preserve.

Since his widowed mother, Petty Prue, had become the

1139

second wife of one-armed Senator Cobb, he had a direct claim to at least half the Jefferson holdings, and now Laurel and his wife were offering him their half: 'You were meant to be the custodian of some grand plantation, Devereaux. We leave this place in good hands.'

'I try,' he said.

On the way home from the lawyer's office where the papers of transmittal were signed, Laurel said to his wife: 'Devereaux's not a citizen of this world. He feels he must hold on to Lammermoor as a gesture, a defense of Southern tradition.' They visualized Devereaux, forty and unmarried, occupying in solemn grandeur the houses which had once counted their inhabitants in the twenties and thirties. He would combine the libraries and sell off some of the pianos and try to get along with four black servants from the town. Some of the fields he would abandon to weevils and weeds, but others he would farm out on shares in hopes of earning enough to support himself. The afternoons would be long and hot, the summer nights filled with insects. Steamers would no longer call at the wharf, for the Red River now flowed freely to join the Mississippi; 'Jefferson's throat been cut,' as the natives said.

There was still a belief in Northern states that everything in Texas prospered, a carryover from the G.T.T. days, and invariably it did, for some years, but failure was as easy to achieve here as it was in Massachusetts or West Virginia. The woods of East Texas displayed the charred roots of what had once been farmhouses and ranch headquarters. Some said: 'The armorial crest of Texas should be an abandoned house whose root stumps barely show.'

'Devereaux will survive,' Laurel said as he and Sue Beth packed their last belongings, 'but I do wish he'd take himself a wife before we leave.'

'I've been brooding about that,' his wife said. She was a practical woman, much like her mother-in-law, Petty Prue, and it bothered her to think that a notable catch like Devereaux was inheriting this mansion without a wife to help him to run it.

She had therefore scoured the town of Jefferson, striving to find a suitable woman to occupy the place, and she told her husband: 'I'd accept any likely woman from age nineteen to fifty. But I find no one in all of Jefferson fitted to the task.'

'Devereaux's the one to do the judging,' her husband said. 'How do you know he wants a wife?'

'He'll do what I tell him,' she responded, and she was soon off to the major town of Marshall, over the line in the next county, and there she heard of an attractive young widow with a baby daughter. The candidate was from an Alabama family of excellent reputation, which cemented her position with Sue Beth: 'Devereaux would never consider a wife who wasn't from the South, but this one is, and she's a charmer.'

She was that, a twenty-nine-year-old of delicate breeding and considerable poise, with a two-year-old daughter named Belle who had been trained to be a prim little lady. The mother spoke in a low voice, held herself very erect when meeting strangers, and was, said a neighbor: 'The perfect picture of Southern womanhood at it best.'

Sue Beth, eager to safeguard Devereaux's future before leaving Jefferson, wanted to approach the problem frontally, but she knew that this would offend the niceties observed by Southern women, so she said tentatively: 'I do wish you could visit Lammermoor one day.'

As if totally ignorant of what was afoot, the widow said quietly: 'I've heard it's delightful.'

'It is, and alas, we're leaving it.'

'Oh, are you?'

'And when we go, Devereaux . . . ' Sue Beth hesitated shyly. 'He'll take over, of course.'

'I've heard of him. People refer to him as the last of the Southern gentlemen.' She knew the names of all the unmarried gentlemen in two counties.

'My husband and I would be so honored if you . . . and your delightful daughter . . . ' Both women hesitated, then Sue Beth took the widow's hands: 'You would honor us if you were to assent . . . '

'It is I who would be honored,' and when the widow and her daughter were seated beside the Cobbs on the new train to Jefferson, the purpose of the visit was clearly understood even though it had not yet been mentioned.

At the station, a painfully embarrassed Devereaux waited with a curtained wagon driven by Suetonius, and after awkward introductions were completed, Sue Beth whispered to her guest: 'You'll find him a crotchety bachelor but delightful,' and Laurel added important reassurance: 'He comes from the finest South Carolina and Georgia blood, and the plantation is all his and paid for.'

It was the kind of meeting that had often happened along the Texas frontier, where death was arbitrary and widowhood commonplace. A farm of eighty acres needed a woman to bake the bread, or a plantation of twenty thousand acres needed a mistress to grace the mansion, so friends scoured the countryside; fumbling introductions were completed; a minister who knew neither bride nor groom was summoned; and the life of Texas went on.

At Lammermoor, such a wedding was arranged.

From Lammermoor to Waxahachie was about one hundred and fifty miles, similar to the distance from New York to Baltimore or Berlin to Hamburg, but in Texas this moved the Cobbs across three radically different types of terrain: pine belt, oak forest, and the rich and rolling blacklands of which Waxahachie was the capital. More significant to the welfare of cotton, the Cobbs had escaped the dank bayou country, where the rainfall neared fifty inches a year, and had come to more manageable lands with about thirty-five inches.

The topsoil was eighteen to thirty inches deep, free of large rocks and often invitingly level; since earlier owners had removed the trees, Cobb could start using the land immediately. The boll weevil had of course reached here in its plundering surge out of Mexico, but by the time the Cobbs took over, the once-gloomy expert from A&M was actually smiling with reassuring news:

'We're a lot brighter now than when I talked with you during those dark days in Jefferson. We've wrestled with the little devil and come out ahead. First thing you have to do, Cobb, is plant a variety of cotton that bolls early. Earlier the better, because then you have a chance of picking it before the weevil starts. Second, plant a trapcrop of corn between the rows. The weevil really loves corn. Let 'em eat that instead of your cotton bolls. Third, and maybe the most important, you have got to burn your stalks in August, September fifteenth latest, because then the stinkers have no place to breed. Fourth, thank whatever god directs your movements that you've come to Waxahachie, because the rainfall is so much less. Weevils love wet, and out here you'll dust them off. Fifth, we aren't sure whether it will work or not, but we've had some promising results from arsenic. Poison the little bastards.'

By following this military advice, Cobb not only got his new cotton plantation started, but by the close of the first year, found himself with such a rich crop that it was reasonable for him to build his own gin, and this made him one of the major farming figures in the area. To his surprise, he found himself following exactly the advice proffered by the intrusive Northern newspaperman Elmer Carmody when he visited the Jefferson plantations in 1850, and which the original Cobbs had resented so strenuously: 'Sue Beth, I burst out laughing when I realized that I was growing the best cotton in the world without the help of slaves, without even one black man working for me. All whites. All working for wages, just as Carmody predicted. I owe him an apology,' and he saluted the place in the bookcase where *Texas Good and Bad* stood.

Carefully calculating his profit, he built a modest house for Sue Beth and the children, and with the money left over he associated himself with other cotton people, all of them pooling their funds to underwrite less well-to-do farmers who wanted to get into the business. To his delight he saw the sale price per pound rise from eight cents in 1901 to twelve in 1903. By 1905, when the price remained high, he was the leading agriculturist in the region and a king of the cotton industry, insofar as the boll weevil allowed anyone to gloat.

'I wish there was another crop we could grow,' Cobb complained one night when he realized how totally dependent he was on cotton, but he could devise none which would produce the safe yields and assured profits that cotton did. As early as 1764 the Cobbs of Edisto Island in South Carolina had wanted to diversify their crops, but the presence of slaves to manage the cotton fields and pick the lint from the seed kept them imprisoned in that economy; the Cobbs had made statistical studies which proved that they were penalized by this adherence to one crop and were prepared to branch out when

Eli Whitney invented his miraculous gin, which revolutionized the industry, and they fell back, entrapped in lint.

In Texas it had been the same. All the Cobbs who settled there had wanted to diversify – 'to break away from our bondage to New Orleans and England,' Senator Cobb had cried in several speeches – but none had done so, and now in their new home, on land which would have welcomed different forms of agriculture, Laurel Cobb and his wife persisted with their cotton.

'We're prisoners of that damned fiber,' Laurel cried one night. 'It binds us to it like the threads of a spider binding its victims.' Then he laughed: 'But it's a glorious bondage. No farmer in the world enjoys a better life than the man who owns a cotton plantation and his own gin.'

Such thinking was making Texas the world's most important cotton-producing area. Strangers thought of the Carolinas and Georgia as the capitals of the Cotton Kingdom, but inexorably the centers were moving west and coming to rest in Texas, and on some mornings in the autumn when Laurel and Sue Beth rode into Waxahachie they were dazzled by the splendor of the scene which greeted them and of which they were a leading part.

'God, this is a fine sight!' Laurel cried one day when bright October sunlight filled the central square, and he was justified in his assessment.

Waxahachie had a town square of most pleasing dimensions, for it was compact and lined on four sides with fine low buildings, some of real distinction, yet it was spacious enough to accommodate the red-and-gray masterpiece of that inspired courthouse builder James Riely Gordon. Here, with a budget more than twice what the less affluent men of Larkin County had been able to put together, Gordon had built a fairy-tale palace ten stories high, replete with battlements and turrets and spires and soaring clock towers and miniature castles high in the air. It was a bejeweled treasure, yet it was also a sturdy, massive court of judgments, one of the finest buildings in Texas.

But it was not the noble courthouse which captivated Laurel Cobb this morning; it was what crowded in upon the building, cramming the copious square that surrounded it, for here the cotton growers of the region had brought cartloads of the best cotton, more than two thousand bales, their brown burlap sacking barely hiding the rich white cotton crop.

Here was the wealth of Texas, these mountains of cotton bales, these pyramids, these piles strewn before the courthouse where buyers would come to make their choice; trains would carry the bales to all parts of the nation and to Europe, and even to Asia or wherever else cloth was needed.

'Look at it!' Laurel shouted to his wife as he reined in their horses. 'This will go on forever.'

When he compared this vital, robust scene to the tentative, cautious way they had been living previously on their plantation in the dark woods at Jefferson, he impulsively kissed his wife and exclaimed: 'My God, am I glad we came to Waxahachie!'

In the chain of Spanish-speaking counties which lined the Texas side of the Rio Grande, three types of elections were held, each with its highly distinctive character. There were, of course, the general statewide elections in November in which Democrats contested with Republicans for the governorship of Texas or the presidency of the United States, but because of the lingering animosities growing out of the Reconstruction years, when Black Republicans tormented the state, no Republican would be elected to major office in Texas for nearly a century. So these November elections were a formality.

The statewide election which counted came in the summer, when Democrats, often of the most lethal persuasion, fought for victory in their primary, for then tempers rose so high that sometimes gunfire resulted. Prior to 1906, the Democrats had nominated their contenders in convention, which encouraged chicanery, but in that year a reform act was passed requiring nomination by public election, with a lot of frills thrown in so that the professionals could still dominate. Now statewide brawls took place, and nowhere were these new primaries more corrupt than along the Rio Grande, where some county would have a precinct with a total population of 356, counting women, who were not eligible to vote, and their babies, and report late on election night that its favorite Democrat had won by a vote of 343 to 14. Quite often two Texas Democrats of great probity, one a judge from along the Red River in the north, the other a distinguished state senator from the Dallas area, would conduct high-level campaigns across the state, only to see their fate determined in the so-called Mexican Counties of the Rio Grande, where elections were conducted with the grossest fraud.

But it was the third type of Rio Grande election which displayed Texas politics at its rawest. This was the strictly local election, town or county, in which Republicans and Democrats vied evenly, victory going first to one, then the other. A local election in these counties could be horrendous.

How, if Texas never voted Republican statewide, could that party expect to win local elections along the river? The answer was threefold: legal citizens of Texas who could not speak English could be manipulated by bosses; citizens of Mexico could be handed fake poll-tax certificates and enrolled as Republicans or Democrats; and the presence of the international bridges that gave employment to political henchmen. These bridges were sorry affairs, often wooden and sometimes one-lane, but they were staffed by customs officials appointed in Washington, and since these were years when Republican presidents like McKinley, Roosevelt and Taft ran the country, it was their Republican appointees who ran the bridges. Republicans hired local toll collectors and customs inspectors. Republicans controlled the flow of federal funds, and Republican functionaries, often newcomers from Republican states in the North, were told by Washington: 'Forget the statewide offices but vote your county Republican, or else.'

Sixty miles upstream from where the Rio Grande debouches into the Gulf of Mexico, a rickety wooden bridge connected Mexico and the United States, and on each bank of the river a small town of little consequence had grown up; the bridge was more important than either of the towns.

As was to be the rule along the entire reach of the Rio Grande, and along the land border as well in New Mexico, Arizona and California, whenever two such towns faced each other in the two countries, it was invariably the Mexican one which came to be the larger. Thus, Matamoros with its advantageous Zona Libre (free customs zone) was larger than Brownsville; Reynosa, much larger than Hidalgo; Nuevo Laredo, substantially bigger than the Texas Laredo; and, to the surprise of many, Ciudad Juárez, bigger than El Paso.

The reasons for this were clear. No Texan town bordering Mexico constituted an irresistible magnet drawing Texas citizens wishing to settle there permanently – Dallas was always a much more promising town than Laredo – but the contrary was not true. Mexican citizens caught in the poverty-stricken parts of northern Mexico were lured to the border town, where jobs across the river might become available and where American stores stocked with bargains were a temptation. There were a hundred reasons why Mexicans sought to crowd the Rio Grande, and they did.

At this particular bridge the rule prevailed. At the Mexican end the town of Escandón, named after the excellent man who had explored this region, contained about two thousand citizens; on the Texan end the little town of Bravo had less than half that number. The bridge was important, and sometimes it seemed as if the history of the county was identical with that of the bridge.

In these early years of the century the Bravo Customs Office was occupied by a ruthless gentleman of great ability and considerable charm. He was a big, brawling, red-headed Irishman named Tim Coke, imported from New York, forty years old and a graduate of that corrupt school of Republicanism which existed only to fight the worse corruption of Tammany Democrats. With the brazen assistance of three others like him from Eastern cities and nine tough local men, Tim Coke had long ago declared war on the Saldaña Democrats, and saw this year of 1908 as a real chance for victory: 'Time has come to turn this county Republican, once and for all. Last two local elections we won one, lost one. This year we nail it down.'

In Saldaña County, as elsewhere along the Rio Grande, it was the custom to smuggle across the river large numbers of Mexican nationals, pay each one a small fee, vote him illegally, and send him back to the jacales south of the river. Since the legal population of the county tended to be Democratic, the Republicans were required to sneak in a good many more transient voters than the Democrats, and no one was more adept at this than tough-minded, inventive Tim Coke. A newspaperman from Austin, summarizing Texas politics, wrote: 'When loyal Democrats along the Rio Grande see redheaded Tim Coke manipulationg the patronage at his bridge, they tremble.'

'The sumbitch has one big advantage over us,' the Democrats whined. 'He controls the bridge. He can march his voters across bold as you please. Ours we have to swim.'

When Coke heard such complaints he cursed: 'We may have the bridge, but they have that damned Precinct 37.' It was a legitimate protest, because the wily Democrats kept sequestered deep in the heartland of Saldaña County a rural precinct which had the habit of waiting till four or five in the morning to report its tally. By then the leaders of the party in Bravo would know how many Precinct 37 votes they needed to win the election, and the call would go forth: 'Elizondo, you've got to turn in figures which give us a three hundred and three majority,' and half an hour later Elizondo would report: 'Democrats, three forty-three; Republicans, fourteen.' There was always a howl, charges of fraud, and threats of federal action, but alway Elizondo explained: 'We were a little late, but up here everyone votes Blue.'

It was the rule along the Rio Grande, where vast numbers of voters could not read English, to identify the two major parties by color, which varied from county to county. In Saldaña the Republicans had always been the Reds, Democrats the Blues, so that when a vote was held, each party devised some trick to help its imported constituents know how to cast the votes for which they had been paid. The color scheme was also helpful to those Hispanics who lived in Texas and were legally entitled to vote but had not yet mastered English: 'Pablo, when they hand you your ballot, you'll find a little red mark at the right place. You scratch your big X there and you get your dollar.' Before the ballot was deposited, Republican workers would erase the telltale red mark, aware that the Democratic workers would be doing something similar with their blue marks.

Any election in Saldaña County was apt to be a lively affair, and for two good reasons. First, after voting booths closed and the counting began, both the Reds and Blues threw parties for their imported voters, with tequila, hot Mexican dishes and whiskey, and if the Reds won, their partisans were apt to grow rambunctious, with the losing Blues growing resentful. Gunfire was so customary at Saldaña elections that some thoughtful anglo residents said: 'It would be better if one side was clearly superior. Let them celebrate and leave the rest of us alone.'

The second reason for unrest was that Democrats, denied the patronage associated with the Customs Office, had to work extra hard, and for some years they had placed their fortunes in the hands of one of the most competent political leaders Texas had so far produced. Horace Vigil was an anglo, of that there could be no doubt, for he was somewhat taller than an ordinary Mexican; more robust, whiter of skin and more confident in manner, yet the pronunciation of his name Vee-HEEL, indicated that at some time long past he must have had Mexican or Spanish ancestors. Much of his genial manner seemed to have stemmed from them, for he was a markedly courteous man, and when he used his fluent Spanish he sounded like a born hidalgo.

When people first saw Vigil standing beside Tim Coke they were apt to think: What an unfair competition! – for the big Irishman, with his forthright and engaging ways, was in the full force of his vigorous manhood and seemed to dominate all about him; at the bridge he was unquestionably in charge, while Vigil, twelve years older and slightly stooped, was obviously a retiring man seeking to avoid notice. He accomplished this in two ways: by twisting his torso slightly to the left, creating the impression that through diffidence or even cowardice he was going to avoid any impending unpleasantness; and by speaking in public in a voice so soft that it seemed a whisper. Women especially thought of him as 'that dear Señor Vigil.'

But if in public he gave the appearance of a somewhat bumbling and well-intentioned grandfather, in private, when surrounded only by his Spanish-speaking subordinates he could rasp out orders in a voice that was completely domineering. In protecting his personal interests and in furthering those of the Democratic party he could be ruthless, and observers of of the system warned: 'Don't touch his beer business or the way he buys his Democratic majorities.'

He had for many years operated a lumber and ice establishment, and in developing the latter he had eased over into the lucrative trade of distributing beer, so that now he controlled how men built their houses, how they stayed cool in summer, and how they relaxed when the brutally hot Rio Grande days turned into those very hot Rio Grande nights. He was not a scholarly man and he lacked formal instruction in politics, but he understood the two essentials required for governing his county: he hated customs officials – 'They prey off the public, they contribute nothing to the community, they're all Northerners and damnit, they're Republicans' – and he loved Mexicans, holding them to be 'God's children, warm-hearted, kind to their parents, and loyal up to a point.'

He was an American patrón, one of those fiercely independent rural leaders so common in Mexico. They were self-appointed dictators who paid lip service to the central authority but continued to rule their regions according to their own vision. Horace Vigil decided who would be judge and what decisions that judge would hand down when he reached the bench; he did not collect taxes but he certainly spent them, rarely on himself but with joyous liberality among his Mexican supporters; it was he who determined which daughters of which friends got jobs in the school system; it was he to whom the people came when they needed money for a wedding or a funeral.

In return, Vigil demanded only two things: 'Vote Blue and buy my beer.' Any who voted Red found themselves ostracized; those who tried to buy their beer direct from the breweries in San Antonio awakened some morning to find their establishment afire or their beer spouts running wide open, with no thirsty patrons to catch the flowing brew.

In the 1908 local election the great showdown between Coke and Vigil occurred. Prior to the balloting, Customs Officer Coke had so many Mexican nationals in compounds just north of the river that Vigil had to become alarmed. Twice at the end of the last century Coke had stolen elections in this manner, and with rambunctious Teddy Roosevelt still in the White House, he could depend upon vigorous support from the federal courts. Indeed, word had come down from the Justice Department in Washington: 'You must break Vigil's stranglehold,' and Coke was determined to do so.

On the Friday morning prior to the election, Vigil received disturbing news: 'Señor Vigil, Señor Coke he is bringing a hundred and fifty more Reds from Mexico.' The report was true; about half these men had voted in previous elections, each receiving his dollar plus a couple of good meals for doing so, but the other half had never before stepped foot in Texas. Like the Mexicans imported earlier by Democrats, they were herded into adobe-walled compounds, and there they whiled away the time until the customs people arrived with instructions as to how they must vote.

'Héctor!' a worried Vigil called to his principal assistant, a smiling young man of eighteen, 'you've got to cross into Mexico and round up at least a hundred more votes.'

'Yes, sir!' He had spent his last three years doing little but saying 'Yes, sir' to Señor Vigil, so as soon as the orders were given he knew what to do. Reporting to the campaign treasurer, he asked for twenty dollars to entertain his voters while they were still on the Mexican side, knowing that if he could swim them across and slip them into the Blue compound, additional payoff money would be awaiting him there. With the coins secured in his belt he entered Mexico, but not via the bridge, because there the Republicans would be on watch, and if they spotted him entering Mexico they would deduce that he was going there to import more Blues, and he would hear Coke bellowing: 'Hilario, bring us a hundred more Reds.' So Héctor rode his horse west about two miles, swam it across the river, and doubled back to Escandón, where he picked up a group of congenial men who could use a dollar.

This enterprising young fellow was Héctor Garza, descendant of those Garzas who had immigrated to these parts from San Antonio in the 1790s and grandson of the outlaw Benito Garza, who had caused such consternation among the Texans in the 1850s. Héctor and his immediate forebears had been good United States citizens; he loved Texas and wanted to see it enjoy good government, which was why he sociated himself with Horace Vigil.

Like the vast majority of Hispanics, he had received only spasmodic education, partly because Texas did not consider it necessary to educate Hispanic peasants and partly because he was, like Benito Garza, a free wandering spirit who would not be trapped in any schoolroom. His real education had come from watching Vigil, and he was confident that if he continued to work for the beer distributor, he would learn all that was necessary about Saldaña County.

Had the election of 1908 gone according to schedule, the Democrats, with Garza's last-minute voters, would have won by a comfortable margin, but a Mexican storekeeper who acted as spy for the Customs Office alerted Tim Coke to the hidden influx of Blue voters, and Coke summoned his aides: 'Round up every Mexican in Escandón who can walk,' and this was done.

On Saturday, Vigil, having learned of this, called a meeting of his war cabinet and told them: 'We face a major crisis. Coke and his Yankees are tryin' to steal this election. If we can win it, we can hold this county for the next fifty years. Teddy Roosevelt will be out of the White House and the pressure from Washington will end. So whatever can be done must be done. If Precinct 37 has to give us five-hundred to seven, it must.'

'But the precinct only has a hundred and seventy-nine registered voters.'

'Come voting day, it'll have more.'

But even so, Vigil knew that he needed some additional miracle to win, and next morning it arrived, for at about noon a man came shouting: 'Dead girl! In the bushes by the river!' And when the town officials, Republicans and Democrats alike, ran to verify the report, most of Bravo forgot the election, but Horace Vigil did not. Assembling his precinct workers, he asked them: 'How can we use this sad affair to our advantage?' and much thought was given. When the meeting ended, Héctor Garza performed his part of the strategy which had been agreed upon; he moved through the town whispering to citizens: 'The Rangers have uncovered mysterious facts, but they won't say what.'

The morning before election the voters of Saldaña County read the startling details: TIM COKE, REPUBLICAN LEADER, ARRESTED FOR HIDEOUS MURDER.

Under the lash of Horace Vigil's demand that justice be done, detectives under his control had uncovered clues, not very substantial, which led to Tim Coke, so the police, also in Vigil's pay, had arrested the Republican leader. The local judge, a reliable Vigil man, had refused to issue a writ of habeas corpus, so that when the voting started, Coke was still in jail.

The Republicans did their best to preserve their slight lead; they voted their Mexicans, stole ballots when they could, and put into practice the tricks Tim Coke had mastered while fighting Tammany Hall in New York. But the awful charge that their leader had committed a murder, and of a girl, sickened the voters, and many who had intended voting Republican found themselves unable to do so.

Vigil and Garza, meanwhile, were whipping up enormous enthusiasm for the unsullied Blue cause, and even before Precinct 37 reported its traditional count – 343 to 14 in favor of the Democrats – it was known that the Blues had won.

On Wednesday, when Coke was released from jail, Vigil personally apologized: 'Deplorable mistake. The Mexican informant couldn't speak English, and the Rangers misinterpreted his information.' He also drafted a statement for the press: 'Every right-thinking citizen feels how wrong it is when a respected member of our community is subject to unwarranted indignities. All Saldaña County sends Tim Coke, custodian of our Bravo-Escandón Bridge, an apology and a solemn promise that nothing like this will ever happen again.'

With crusading Teddy Roosevelt about to leave the White House and with Precinct 37 sticking to its habit of not reporting its count till dawn, the Democrats of Saldaña County appeared to be safe for the coming decades.

Laurel Cobb had never considered running for the seat in the United States Senate once held by his father, but in 1919 a surprising chain of events forced him to change his mind. To begin with, a revival tent was pitched on his farm, and as a consequence he began to teach a Sunday School class, which led to the excommunication proceedings with the Jordan Baptist congregation.

The little towns of North Texas never seemed more exciting and attractive than in those hot summers when some wandering evangelist pitched his tent in a country grove and conducted a revival. If the man was noted for either his piety or his eloquence, people streamed in from forty or fifty miles, pitching their tents or boarding with strangers. Family reunions were held; courtships were launched; choirs came from distant churches; food abounded; and for fifteen joyous days the celebration continued. But the basic attraction was the fiery religious oratory, allowing people whose lives were otherwise drab a glimpse of a more promising existence.

The revival was an important aspect of Texas culture, some thought it the major aspect, for it determined that Texas would become largely a dry state, it reinforced the power of the local churches, it kept stores closed on Sundays, and it defined in fundamentalist terms what religion was. But it was also a social celebration, and the family that did not participate found itself in limbo.

Some of the wandering evangelists ranted, some threatened, while others were little more than vaudeville performers with an overlay of Old Testament religiosity. All had their loyal patrons, but there was one who excelled in all aspects of the calling. He was Elder Fry, not associated with any specific Protestant denomination but equally at home with all – Methodist, Baptist, Presbyterian, Campbellite – and a servant to all. He did not, like some others, come into a community to denigrate the local clergymen, claiming that only he had the truth while they were straying; he came to help, to ignite the fires of faith so that when he left, the resident pastors could do a better job. It was said of Fry: 'He sometimes roars but he never rants. He warns of punishment in afterlife but he does not terrify. And he never tears down, he builds up.' If the phrase 'a man of God' had any meaning, Elder Fry tried to be such a man.

In the summer of 1919 he drove his buggy south from Waxahachie to the Cobb plantation, as they called their acreage, where he met with Laurel and his wife: 'I know that a revival tent causes problems to the landowner, but if you let me use that far field, I'll keep our visitors to only one road and we'll do little damage.'

'Elder Fry,' Sue Beth interrupted, 'we think of the good life we enjoy as a gift from God, and the least we can do in return is to thank Him. Will it be for fifteen days, as usual?'

'The older I get the more I think that I ought to cut back to one week. Half as much work for everyone, but to tell you the truth, Mrs Cobb, I need a week to instruct, a week to inspire, and that final glorious day for rejoicing and salvation. I'll need the fifteen days.'

His manner was deceptive, for he was sixty-six years old, white-haired, almost childlike with only a modest voice incapable of filling a tent, and during the first week of a revival some had difficulty hearing him, but in the second, as he became inspired, he seemed to change: he was taller, more fiercely dedicated, and possessed of a voice which thundered its impassioned message that Jesus Christ had come down to earth to rescue human beings otherwise condemned to darkness. He never tried to force conversion, nor did he promise cures; he simply offered the testimony of a man who had lived a long life in the service of God and who believed without question that heaven awaited such faithfulness.

Laurel instructed his servants to help the old man pitch his tent and personally worked at arranging the chairs. Sue Beth helped organize the picnic tables that would be so important a part of the two-week festival, and workmen from the farm repaired the road that would give access. As a consequence, the Waxahachie revival of 1919 was one of the best; the weather was clement and the crowds tremendous. Although the recent world war had barely touched daily life in the state, it had claimed many sons of Texas, and now people wanted to celebrate the coming of peace and were ready to accept Fry's thesis that God himself had been responsible for the victory. Cobb, listening to the long sermons, gained the impression that Fry thought that God watched over the United States with special attention and the state of Texas with deep personal concern: 'He loves Texas, and it grieves Him when a community votes to sell liquor. Do not cause Him remorse! Halt any evil behavior which might offend him!'

During the second week Fry lodged with the Cobbs, at their insistence, and they enjoyed several long talks: 'Dear friends, I find in North Texas a degree of spiritual concern unmatched anywhere else. God has chosen your territory for some special commission. He holds Texas close to the bosom, for here He sees the working-out of His Holy Bible.'

On Wednesday of the final week he launched into that steady ascendancy of voice and manner which brought his revivals to such triumphant conclusions, and on Friday he preached so compellingly, Cobb got the feeling that the words were directed specifically at him. Laurel was not an overly religious person – his wife was – but he did believe that society improved when it stayed close to the Bible, so on the last Saturday night he was spiritually prepared to be touched by Fry's farewell sermon; it dealt with the Faithful Servant, and as Cobb listened to the majestic voice of this good and kindly man, he felt that he, Cobb, was undergoing what could only be termed a rebirth.

Certainly it was a rededication, for when his local Baptist minister came out to the plantation on Monday to ask a favor, Cobb greeted him warmly: 'Come in, Reverend Teeder. Wasn't that a splendid two weeks?' Teeder, a much different man from Fry, admitted grudgingly that it had been: 'But Elder Fry seems to lack the fire that marks a true man of God.' Cobb, not wishing to argue at a time when his heart was filled with new understandings, said merely: 'But he wins a lot of souls,' and Teeder said: 'For the moment, yes, but permanently, no. I believe a sterner message is required than the one he delivers.'

Teeder and the Cobbs belonged to the Jordan Baptist Church, situated in a pretty village just south of Waxahachie, and because it dominated a large rural population, it enjoyed a membership rather greater than one might have expected and a minister of more than ordinary fervor. In 1919, Simon Teeder stood at the midpoint of his religious career; he had started in a devout community in Mississippi, had been promoted to this good job in Texas, and would soon be moving on to a really important church in the new state of Oklahoma. He was an intense man, convinced that he understood God's will and driven by a determination to see it prevail.

He had been surprisingly effective in making the members of his Texas congregation feel that he, Teeder, had a personal interest in each one's welfare, and as soon as he had settled in he established two groups to help him with the work of the church. After studying carefully the character of his parishioners, he nominated seven devout men for election to the church Council; they would advise on doctrine. He then selected a quite different group of men, respected for their business acumen, to serve as his Board of Deacons; they would look after the financial and household affairs of the congregation.

When he had his structure completed – seven devout council members, nineteen prosperous deacons – he pretty well controlled his area of rural Texas, and he exercised his control sternly:

'Jordan Baptist is founded on sturdy principles, and if all live up to them and glorify them in our hearts, we shall never have a rumble of trouble in this church, nor a confusion of scandal among its membership.

'First, we believe in the Bible as the revealed Word of God, and we accept every single passage in that Holy Book. We admit no popular modern questioning, no cheapening of that Sublime Word. If you cannot accept the Bible as written, this church cannot accept you.

'Second, we believe that every man who aspires to membership in our church must take it upon himself to live a Christian life, in the fullest sense of that commitment.

'Third, we condemn all forms of loose and licentious living which have crept upon us since the end of the Great War, and anyone who aspires to fellowship of this church must take a solemn oath to avoid drinking, gambling, horse racing, prize fighting, licentiousness with women, and other immoral behaviors. Particularly, young and old must reject dancing, which is the principal agency by which the devil seduces us.'

When these stricter rules had been circulated and understood, Reverend Teeder began visiting various members of his congregation, pleading with them to assume additional responsibilities for the success of Jordan Baptist, and it was largely due to his imagination and drive that his church improved yearly.

Up to now he had not visited the Cobbs, for he had good reason to suspect that Laurel did not accept the stern fundamentalism that he preached, and he wanted no dissidents or infected liberals in his congregation, but word of Cobb's strong support for Elder Fry's revival had caused Teeder to change his mind, and when he discussed the matter with the seven members of his Council, they agreed that Laurel was a man worth keeping within the body of the church; it was in pursuit of this decision that he drove out to see the Cobbs.

'Brother Laurel,' he said when discussion of the Fry revival ended, 'God has an important mission for you, and I pray you will accept.'

'I already tithe. Have for years.'

'It's not money, although God notices and appreciates your

generosity. It's you He wants.'

'I have no calling to the ministry,' Laurel said.

'No, that comes to few, and it's as much a burden as it is a glory. I'm speaking of something much simpler.'

'What?'

'I want you to teach Sunday School. Every Sunday. To a group of young boys that I shall assemble.'

'I'd be no good at that.'

'Ah, but you would. Boys fear their minister. They see him only on the pulpit. But if you, a man like themselves, only older, a plantation owner who wrestles with his fields the way their fathers wrestle with theirs ... That could make a great deal of difference.'

The two men talked for more than an hour, with Cobb reminding himself of how lucky their congregation had been to find this devoted minister. He had been on the search committee back in 1918 and had traveled to Mississippi to hear Teeder preach: 'He's a little too intense for my taste, but in the pulpit he glows like a burning ember. I'll vote for him.'

At the end of the hour Cobb found himself ensnared by Teeder's persuasiveness, but the manner of Cobb's submission startled the minister: 'Reverend, if you have a weakness, it's that you always speak of our church as if it were composed only of men. You ignore women.'

'I follow Jesus and St Paul. They placed their church in the hands of men. There were no women disciples, no women preachers, no women in command of the manifold churches of Asia. A woman's responsibility is to find herself a Christian man, to support him, and to rear children who will follow Christian ways.'

'Well, I won't teach a class of boys. If you want me to help, you must arrange for a class of girls, because I want them to be a part of our church, too.'

'That's quite impossible.'

'Then my participation becomes impossible.' At this point Laurel called for his wife to join the discussion, and when Sue Beth understood what her husband was saying, she approved: 'Reverend Teeder, it's really time women were brought more closely into your church.'

'They could not serve on the Council or the Board of

Deacons. That's man's work.'

'But—'

'Our church provides joyous opportunities for women. You women are too delicate to make decisions. Yet there's still much important work to be done. Our little church seems twice as holy since you good women have been decorating it with flowers.'

'We're entitled to do much more,' Sue Beth argued, but Reverend Teeder put a stop to such complaint: 'Jesus and St Paul have decided the character of the church, and you must find your spiritual happiness within the rules they established.'

So the first meeting ended in a stalemate, but as he was leaving, Teeder did make one concession: 'About that girls' Sunday School class, you could be right. Let's both ponder it,' and Cobb knew that what Teeder really meant was: I must discuss this with my councillors and my deacons.

Laurel belonged to neither group, for he was not stern enough to serve on the Council, nor had he the spare time to tend the household chores of a deacon. He was merely another silent member of one of the two major religions in North Texas: Methodist, the majority; Baptists, the more vigorous. But Cobb did take his religion seriously, as he had recently demonstrated during the revival, and he believed that God was a reality who governed the significant parts of his life.

There was nothing spurious in this Texan preoccupation with religion. Citizens like the Cobbs believed in the Bible; they tithed; and they strove to lead lives of Christian observance, if they were allowed to define what that meant. Specifically they sought a society founded on a universal brotherhood in Christ, so long as the brotherhood did not have to include Indians, blacks or Mexicans.

On Saturday, Cobb told his wife: 'I have a feeling the men are going to approve the class for girls. They must know it's long overdue.' And on Sunday, at the conclusion of the worship services, Reverend Teeder, accompanied by Willis Wilbarger, the dour head of the Council, stopped him at the exit from the church: 'Cobb, the men have approved your idea of a class for girls, and from their group alone they've enrolled eleven girls for next Sunday.'

The class became a great success – eleven at the first session, then nineteen, then more than thirty. Cobb was a stern taskmaster, requiring his girls to memorize crucial verses and to study entire chapters for later discussion. Always he drew the moral of the assignment back to life in Waxahachie, and especially to the region contiguous to Jordan Baptist. This caused Jane Ellen Wilbarger to complain to her father that 'Mr Cobb always talks about Waxahachie and never about heaven,' a complaint which the sour-visaged man reported to the other members of the Council.

A deputation led by Reverend Teeder and Councillor Wilbarger visited Cobb, advising him that the Baptist religion concerned itself principally with spiritual matters, not temporal, and Laurel became aware that young Miss Jane Ellen Wilbarger was taking careful note of every word he said.

The real trouble arose that spring when the Waxahachie newspaper, goaded by Councillor Wilbarger, who used reports provided by his daughter, printed a list of forty-two boys and girls from Jordan Baptist who had brazenly attended a dance at the country club, where they were seen by many reliable witnesses to be doing the 'bunny hug, the foxtrot, the grizzly bear, the tango and other immoral African extravaganzas.' Of the nineteen girls listed, fifteen were members of Laurel Cobb's Sunday School class, a fact that was noted in the report.

The newspaper appeared on Wednesday afternoon, and long before the prayer meeting convened that night, outraged members of the church were telephoning one another and scurrying about the countryside in their new Fords and old buggies. During the service, attended by almost every member of Jordan Baptist, no allusion was made to the scandal, but during the long prayer Reverend Teeder's voice broke several times when he sought guidance for the perilous tasks which lay ahead, and at the conclusion of the prayer meeting he asked both the deacons and the councillors to remain behind to face the infamy which had stained their community and which threatened the foundations of their church.

Cobb, of course, was not allowed to attend this somber meeting, but by Thursday noon he was aware of what had transpired: 'Laurel, they're going to throw all your girls who attended that dance out of the church, and they're going to censure you as the cause of their sin.'

'That's downright preposterous. Those girls . . . '

On Friday a general meeting was held, and he was powerless to prevent it from passing a resolution ousting the girls from the church, but before a confirming vote could be taken, he demanded the floor. This was denied, but he ignored the rebuke, rose to his feet, and in quiet, forceful words defended his girls:

> 'They danced! Did not the guests attending at Cana dance? Do little children not dance with joy when they receive a goody? Does your heart not dance at the coming of spring?
>
> 'To throw these Christian girls out of their church for such a trivial offense would be an error of enormous magnitude. Do not make either the church or the men who command it appear ridiculous by inflicting such a harsh penalty.
>
> 'I oppose your verdict for three reasons. Dancing is not a mortal sin. Young children of high spirit must not be denied the rights of their church because of an infraction of a man-made rule. And as their teacher, I know the goodness in their hearts. You must not do this wrong thing.'

Reverend Teeder did not want a public debate over what was essentially a matter of church discipline, but he could not allow a layman to question his authority. 'Dancing is forbidden by church law,' he thundered, whereupon Cobb thundered back: 'It shouldn't be.' From his place in the congregation Councillor Wilbarger shouted: 'That's apostasy! Repent! Repent!' What had begun as a sedate meeting ended in wild recrimination.

On Sunday, Reverend Teeder preached for ninety minutes, a passionate, well-reasoned defense of church discipline. Never raising his voice, never condemning any individual, but always defending the right of the church to set its own rules, he took as his text that powerful proclamation of St Paul as delivered in Second Thessalonians, Chapter 3, Verse 6:

> 'Now we command you, brethren, in the name of our Lord Jesus Christ, that ye withdraw yourselves from every brother that walketh disorderly, and not after the tradition which he received of us.'

At the eighty-fifth minute of his exhortation he entered upon a most remarkable display, for without warning he stepped aside from the pulpit and extended his left leg toward the audience, and holding his extremity in this position, he concluded his sermon:

'Nine years ago when my church in Mississippi faced a scandal far less severe than the one we face here in Texas, I preached for ninety minutes with my leg upraised like this, where none could see it because it was so inflamed by an abscess that I almost fainted with the pain. But I carried on because it was my duty to explain to my congregation why we must expel one of our deacons who had transgressed our law. And tonight I charge this congregation with the task of expelling one of its members. Let God's will be done.'

After the elders met in secret on Monday night, it became common knowledge that Laurel Cobb was to be hauled before a public meeting, where he would be tried for 'destroying the morals of the young women of this congregation in that he encouraged them in the lewd and lascivious exhibition of dancing, and that he further defended them against the due strictures of this church.'

The trial would be Thursday night, which meant that Cobb had only two days for preparation, and this distressed him, for as he told his wife: 'I love the church, but I cannot stand silent if it makes a horrendous mistake. Have you seen the law they propose passing the minute I've been expelled?' He showed her the startling document which Councillor Wilbarger and his fellows, in their Monday night meeting, had concocted as the basis for Baptist faith:

We, as Christians and brethren in full fellowship with one another, pledge ourselves not to drink, play cards, gamble, dance or look at others dancing, or attend card parties, theaters, music halls, moving picture shows or any other worldly and debasing amusement. And we shall expel from church membership any who do participate in the behavior we have forbidden.

The Cobbs agreed that this was extremism of the worst sort; they had seen certain theater performances, especially by

Walter Hampden and Fritz Leiber, which were ennobling, and they could not agree that all moving picture shows entailed damnation, although some might, but when they tried to enlist support for Laurel's defense and for a more sensible church discipline, they were met with silence, and on Tuesday night it looked as if Cobb would be expelled at the huge public assembly.

However, early Wednesday they were awakened by an extraordinary member of their church, a man to whom they had never spoken. He was five feet two, about a hundred and fifteen pounds, with a lower jaw that protruded inches as if its owner were constantly seeking a fight. His snow-white hair was cropped close, and his beady blue eyes challenged anyone to whom he spoke to refute even one comma on pain of getting his head bashed. He was Adolf Lakarz, son of Czech emigrés, and he made his living caning chairs and doing odd jobs of carpentry. He was not an easy man to do business with, for when a job was proposed, he studied it, made calculations on a note pad, and quoted a price, with his jaw so far forward that the customer was terrified to comment.

This was deceiving, for one day when he told a church member, an elderly lady, that it would cost her three dollars and twenty-five cents for him to rebuild her favorite rocker, she snapped: 'Far too much,' so he recalculated and said: 'You're right. Two dollars and twenty-five cents,' and she said: 'That's more like it.' She said later: 'Mr Lakarz always looks at you as if you were evil and about to do him in, and I suppose that in politics he's right.'

His visit to the Cobb plantation had a clear purpose: 'Cobb, what they're doing to you is wrong. My parents came to Texas to escape that kind of tyranny. We've got to stop them.'

'How?'

The two men, with the sun coming up behind them, stood by an old pump and discussed strategies, and the more Lakarz talked the more Cobb realized that he now had a supporter who was going to fight this battle through, even though the end might be bloody: 'You know, Lakarz, if you do this, it could hurt your business.'

'This is why we came to America.'

When nine struck in the kitchen, they had still decided upon nothing, but then Sue Beth happened to show the carpenter the proposals for the new discipline, and as he read its prohibitions against theater and motion pictures and entertainment generally, he became furious, but in his rage he kept a cool head, and Mrs Cobb saw his eyes flash when he studied more carefully the other details of the new regime.

'By God, Cobb, we've got them!' And without explaining his intentions, he dashed to his third-hand car and sped toward the county courthouse in Waxahachie.

At two o'clock that afternoon the community was staggered by a scandal much worse than the dancing of Laurel Cobb's girl students. Two policemen strode into the office of Councillor Willis Wilbarger and arrested him for playing high-stakes poker in a shebang north of town.

Adolf Lakarz had never played in the games, which met regularly in a hidden spot, but he had heard several times from men who had, and for some archane reason of his own – 'I'll throw it at them in some election' – he had kept a diary of dates, participants and amounts wagered. When the local judge saw his evidence, and listened to the testimony of four or five of the players summoned to his chambers, a bench warrant was issued; the players had never liked Wilbarger, who pouted when he lost and gloated when he won. 'Besides,' as one man told the judge, 'he was so damned sanctimonious. Never allowed us to drink while we were playin'. Claimed it was against the law of God.'

Now the whole crusade fell apart. Reverend Teeder, outraged that the criminal element should have attacked a member of his Council, was more determined than ever to expel Cobb. But he further insisted that Adolf Lakarz be thrown out too, so on a hot August day in a large tent usually reserved for revivals, the good farmers from the area south of Waxahachie convened to try the two men in the same spirit that had animated such trials in southern France in 1188, Spain in 1488, England in 1688.

Three members of the Council recited the charges against Cobb, and two others outlined the misdeeds of Lakarz; Wibarger himself was unable to lead the attack, for he was still in jail. Cobb refused to speak in his own d fense, for he judged accurately that the affair had become s ridiculous that he would be aquitted, but Lakarz, having joined a defense of moral freedom, could not remain silent. Great issues were at stake, and he knew it; in Central Europe his forefathers had fought these battles for centuries:

'Dear Brothers in God of Jordon Baptist. The dearest thing in my life is my wife, brought here under vast difficulties from Moravia. Second dearest is my membership in this church, which I love as a bastion of freedom and God's love.

'It is wrong to condemn young girls for dancing. Our greatest musicians have composed gigues and gavottes and waltzes so that the younger ones can dance.

'It is equally wrong to condemn Laurel Cobb for teaching his girls the joy of life, the joy of Christ's message. I am not wise enough to tell you how to love, and you are not wise enough to pass this kind of foolishness . . .

Here he waved the proposed new laws, and with biting scorn read out the interdictions against Shakespeare and Mendelssohn and Sarah Bernhardt. When he was through, no one spoke.

But now came the vote, and white with anger, Reverend Teeder called for those who loved God and righteousness and an orderly church to stand up and show that they wanted Cobb and Lakarz expelled. The voting process was somewhat demoralized, because only twenty-six out of that entire multitude stood up, and when they saw how few they were, they tried to sit down. But at this moment of victory, Adolf Lakarz shouted in a powerful voice: 'Keep 'em standin'. I want the name and look of every man who voted against me.'

And with pencil and note pad he moved through the crowd, chin thrust out, blue eyes flashing as he stood before each man, taking his name and address. For the remainder of his life in Waxahachie he would never again speak to one of those twenty-six.

The scandal in Waxahachie over the dancing Sunday School girls was an amusing diversion which might have happened in any Texas town of this period and which could be forgiven as misguided religiosity. But the much more serious madness that gripped Larkin at about the same time was an aberration which could not be laughed away, for it came closer to threatening the stability of the entire state.

Precisely when it started no one could recall. One man said: 'It was patriotism, nothing more. I saw them boys come marchin' home from war and I asked myself: "What can I do to preserve our freedoms?" That's how it started, best motives in the world.'

Others argued that it had been triggered by that rip-roaring revival staged in Larkin by the ranting Fort Worth evangelist J. Frank Norris, a type much different from the spiritual Elder Fry. Norris was an aggressive man who thundered sulphurous diatribes against saloon keepers, race-track addicts, liberal professors, and women who wore bobbed hair or skirts above the ankle. He was especially opposed to dancing, which, he claimed, 'scarlet women use to tempt men.'

His anathema, however, was the Roman Catholic church, which he lambasted in wild and colorful accusation: 'It's the darkest, bloodiest ecclesiastical machine that has ever been known in the annals of time. It's the enemy of home, of marriage and of every decent human emotion. The Pope has a plan for capturing Texas, and I have a plan for defeating him.'

He was most effective when he moved nervously from one side of the pulpit to the other, extending his hands and crying: 'I speak for all you humble, God-fearing folks from the forks of the creek. You know what's right and wrong, better than any professors at Baylor or SMU. It's on you that God relies for the salvation of our state.'

One man, not especially religious, testified: 'When J. Frank Norris shouted "I need the help of you little folks from the forks of the creek," I knowed he was speakin' direct to me, and that's when I got all fired up. I saw myself as the right arm of God holdin' a sword ready to strike.'

A University of Texas historian later published documents proving that in Larkin, at least, it had originated not with Norris but with the arrival of three quite different outsiders who had not known one another but who did later act in concert. The earliest newcomer was a man from Georgia who told exciting yarns of what his group had accomplished. The next was a man from Mississippi who assured the Larkin people

1166

that his state was taking things in hand. But the greatest influence seemed to have been with the third man, a salesman of farm machinery who drifted in from Indiana with startling news: 'Up there our boys are pretty well takin' over the state.'

From such evidence it would be difficult to assess the role played by religion, for while very few ministers actually participated, almost every man who did become involved was a devout member of one Protestant church or another, and the movement strenuously supported religion, with the popular symbols of Christianity featured in the group's rituals.

Whatever the cause, by early December 1919 men began appearing throughout Larkin County dressed in long white robes, masks and, sometimes, tall conical hats. The Ku Klux Klan, born after the Civil War, had begun its tempestuous resurrection.

In Larkin it was not a general reign of terror, and nobody ever claimed it was. The local Klan conducted no hangings, no burnings at the stake and only a few necessary floggings. It was best understood as a group of unquestioned patriots, all of them believing Christians, who yearned to see the historic virtues of 1836 and 1861 restored. It was a movement of men who resented industrial change, shifting moral values and disturbed allegiances; they were determined to preserve and restore what they identified as the best features of American life, and in their meetings and their publications they reassured one another that these were their only aims.

Nor was the Larkin Klan simply a rebellion against blacks, for after the first few days there were no blacks left in town. At the beginning there had been two families, offspring of those black cavalrymen who had stayed behind when the 10th Cavalry rode out of Fort Garner for the last time. At first these two men had kept an Indian woman between them, but later on they had acquired a wandering white woman, so that the present generation was pretty well mixed.

They were one of the first problems addressed by the Ku Kluxers after the organization was securely launched. A committee of four, in full regalia, moved through the town one December night and met with the black families. There was no violence, simply the statement: 'We don't cotton to havin' your type in this town.' It was suggested that the blacks move on to

1167

Fort Griffin, where anybody was accepted, and a purse of twenty-six dollars was given them to help with the expense of moving.

One family left town the next morning; the other, named Jaxifer, decided to stay, but when a midnight cross blazed at the front door, the Jaxifers lit out for Fort Griffin, and there was no more of that kind of trouble in Larkin. The Klan did, however, commission four big well-lettered signs, which were posted at the entrances to the town:

NIGGER!
DO NOT LET THE SETTING SUN
FIND YOU IN THIS TOWN.
WARNING!

Thereafter it was the boast of Larkin that 'no goddamned nigger ever slept overnight in this town.'

Nor did the Klan stress its opposition to Jews. Banker Weatherby, an old man now who had been among the first to join the Klan, simply informed three Jewish storekeepers in town that 'our loan committee no longer wishes to finance your business, and we all think it would be better if you moved along.' They did.

The strong opposition to Catholicism presented more complex problems, because the county did contain a rather substantial scattering of this proscribed sect, and whereas some of the more vocal Klansmen wanted to 'throw ever' goddamned mackerel-snatcher out of Texas,' others pointed out that even in as well-organized a town as Larkin, more had drifted in than they thought. They had not been welcomed and their mysterious behavior was carefully watched, but at least they weren't black, or Indian, or Jewish, so they were partially acceptable.

The Larkin Klan never made a public announcement that Catholics would be allowed to stay, and at even the slightest infraction of the Klan's self-formulated rules, anyone with an Irish-sounding name was visited, and warned he would be beaten up if he persisted in any un-Christian deportment.

When the town was finally cleaned up and inhabited by only white members of the major Protestant religions, plus the well-behaved Catholics, it was conceded that Larkin was one of the finest towns in Texas. Its men had a commitment to economic prosperity. Its women attended church faithfully. And its crime rate was so low that it barely merited mention. There was some truth to the next signs the Klansmen erected in 1920:

LARKIN

BEST LITTLE TOWN IN TEXAS

WATCH US GROW

If the Klan avoided violence against blacks or Jews or Catholics, who were its targets? An event in the spring of 1921 best illustrates its preoccupations, for then it confronted a rather worthless man of fifty who had been working in the town's livery stable when Larkin still had horses. He now served as janitor and polishing man at the Chevrolet garage, but he had also been living for many years with a shiftless woman named Nora as his housekeeper; few titles in town were less deserved than hers, for she was totally incapable of keeping even a dog kennel, let alone a house. Jake and Nora lived in chaos and in sin, and the upright men of the Klan felt it was high time this ungodly conduct be stopped.

In orderly fashion, which marked all their actions, they appeared at Jake's cabin one Tuesday night carrying a lighted torch, which all could see, and in their clean white robes, their faces hidden by masks, they handed down the law: 'All this immoral sort of thing is gonna stop in Larkin. Marry this woman by Friday sundown or suffer the consequences.'

Jake and Nora had no need of marriage or any understanding of how to participate in one had they wanted to. By hit and miss they had worked out a pattern of living which suited them and which produced far fewer family brawls than some of the more traditional arrangements in town. The Klansmen were right that no one would want a lot of such establishments in a community, but Jake felt there ought to be a leeway for the accommodation of one or two, especially if they worked well and produced neither scandal nor a horde of unruly children.

On Wednesday the Klansmen who handed Jake and Nora their ultimatum watched to see what corrective steps the couple proposed taking, and when nothing seemed to have been done, two of the more responsible Klansmen decided to visit the couple again on Thursday night, and this they did in friendly fashion: 'Jake, you don't seem to understand. If you don't marry this woman ... '

'Who are y'all? Behind them masks? What right ... ?'

'We're the conscience of this community. We're determined to wipe out immoral behavior.'

'Leave us alone. What about Mr Henderson and his secretary?'

The boldness of this question stunned the two Klansmen, each of whom knew about Mr Henderson and his secretary. But it was not people like Henderson whom the Klan policed, and for someone like Jake to bring such a name into discussion was abhorrent. Now the tenor of the conversation grew more ominous: 'Jake, Nora, you get married by tomorrow night or suffer the consequences.'

Jake was prepared to brazen the thing out, but Nora asked in real confusion: 'How could we get married?' and the two hooded visitors turned their attention to her: 'We'll take you to the justice of the peace tomorrow morning, or if you prefer a church wedding, Reverend Hislop has said he'd do it for us.'

'Get out of here!' Jake shouted, and the two men withdrew.

The next day passed, with Jake sweeping at the Chevrolet garage and showing no sign of remorse for his immoral persistence. Those Klansmen in the know watched his house – or was it Nora's house? – and saw that nothing was happening there, either, so at eight that Friday evening seven Ku Kluxers met with the salesman from Indiana, and after praying that they might act with justice, charity and restraint, marched with a burning cross to Jake's place. Planting the cross before the front door, they summoned the two miscreants.

As soon as Jake appeared he was grabbed, not hurtfully, and stripped of his shirt. Tar was applied liberally across his back, and then a Klansman with a bag of feathers slapped handfuls onto the tar. He was then hoisted onto a stout beam, which four other Klansmen carried, and there he was held, feet tied together beneath the beam, while the moral custodians tended to the slut Nora.

Around the world, in all times and in all places, whenever men go on an ethical rampage they feel that they must discpline women: 'Your dresses are too short.' 'You tempt men.' 'Your behavior is salacious.' 'You must be put in your proper place.' This stems, of course, from the inherent mystery of women, their capacity to survive, their ability to bear children, the universal suspicion that they possess some archane knowledge not available to men. Women are dangerous, and men pass laws to keep them under restraint. All religions, which also deal in mysteries, know this, and that is why the Muslim, the Jewish, the Catholic and the Mormon faiths proscribed women so severely and why other churches ran into trouble when they tried belatedly to ordain women as ministers.

The men of the Ku Klux Klan were as bewildered by sex as any of their reforming predecessors, and on this dark night they had to look upon Nora-with-three-teeth-missing-in-front as a temptress who had seduced Jake into his immoral life. But what to do with her? There was no inclination at all to strip her, but there was a burning desire to punish her, so two men dragged her out beside the flaming cross and tarred her whole dress, fore and aft, scattering feathers liberally upon her.

She then was lifted onto the rail, behind her man, whereupon two additional men supported it, and in this formation the hooded Klansmen paraded through the streets of Larkin behind a sign which proclaimed:

EMORALITY IN LARKIN
WILL STOP

Jake and Nora did not respond as the Klansmen had hoped. They did not marry, and when the long parade was over they returned home, scraped off the tar, and said 'nothin' to nobody.' Early Saturday morning Jake was at the garage, sweeping as usual and saying hello to any who passed. He had no idea who had disciplined him, and at noon he walked home as usual for his lunch. Nora went to the store late Saturday for her weekend supplies, and on Sunday, Jake finished as always, up at the tank, which contained some good-sized bass, while Nora sat on her front lawn where scars from the burned cross still showed.

Such behavior infuriated the Klansmen, who convened after church on Sunday a special meeting at which it was discussed with some heat as to whether the two should be flogged. The

Indiana man was all for a public whipping in the courthouse square, but the Georgia man argued against it: 'We found it does no good. Creates sympathy. And it scares the womenfolk.'

Instead, the men found an old wagon and a worthless horse, and there they drove to Jake's place on Monday evening. Throwing the two adulterers into the back, they piled the wagon with as many of their household goods as possible, then drove west of town till they were beyond sight of the beautiful courthouse tower which bespoke order and justice for this part of texas. There the Klansmen plopped Jake onto the driver's bench and gave him the reins: 'Straight down this road is Fort Griffin. They'll accept anybody.'

The hooded posse returned to Larkin after sunset, and two hours later Jake and Nora, driving the old horse that Jake had often tended in the livery stable, came back to town. With no fanfare they rode down familiar streets to their home, unpacked their belongings, and went to bed.

That was Monday. On Wednesday night Jake was found behind the garage shot to death.

No charges were ever filed against the Klansmen, and for the very good reason that no one knew for sure who they were, or even if they had done it. At least, that was the legal contention. Of course, everyone knew that Floyd Rusk – who could not hide his size even under a bedsheet – was one of the leaders, perhaps *the* leader, because he was obvious at all the marches and the cross burnings, but no one could be found who could swear that yes, he had seen Floyd Rusk tarring Jake.

It was also known that Clyde Weatherby was an active member, as were the hardware merchant, the doctor, the schoolteacher and the druggist. Some four dozen other men, the best in the community, joined later. With an equal mix of patriotism and religion, these men of good intention began to inspect all aspects of life in Larkin, for they were determined to keep their little town in the mainstream of American life as they perceived it.

They forced six men to marry their housekeepers. They lectured, in an almost fatherly manner, two teen-aged girls who seemed likely to become promiscuous, and they positively shut down a grocer against whom several housewives had complained. They did not tar-and-feather him, nor did they horsewhip him; those punishments were reserved for sexual infractions, but they did ride him out of town, telling him to transfer his shop to Fort Griffin, where honesty of trade was not so severely supervised.

By the beginning of 1922 these men had Larkin in the shape they wanted; even some of the Catholics, fearing that reprisals would next be directed at them, had moved away, making the town about as homogeneous as one could have found in all of Texas. It was a community of Protestant Christians in which the rules were understood and in which infractions were severely punished. Almost none of the excesses connected with the Klan in other parts of the nation were condoned here, and after two years of intense effort the Klansmen, when they met at night, could justifiably claim that they had cleaned up Larkin. With this victory under their belt, they intended moving against Texas as a whole, and then, all of the United States.

In 1922 they got well started by electing their man, Earle B. Mayfield, a Tyler grocer, to the United States Senate, but this triumph had a bitter aftermath, because for two years that august body refused to seat a man accused of Klan membership, and when it did finally accept him, he was denied reelection. The local members assuaged their disappointment by achieving a notorious victory in the local high school, where the principal, an enthusiastic Klansman, inserted in the school yearbook a well-drawn full-page depiction of a nightrider in his regalia of bedsheet, mask and pointed hat astride a white stallion under a halo composed of the words GOD, COUNTRY, PROTESTANTISM, SUPREMACY. At the bottom of the page, in a neatly lettered panel, stood the exhortation LIKE THE KLAN, LARKIN HIGH WILL TRIUMPH IN FOOTBALL.

In the growing town, however, the Klan suffered other frustrations. The editor of the *Defender*, an effeminate young man from Arkansas, had the temerity to editorialize against them, and in a series of articles he explained why he opposed what he called 'midnight terrorism.' This unlucky phrase infuriated the Klansmen: 'We have to guard the morals of Larkin at night because during the day we have to run our businesses. Terrorism is shooting innocent people, and no man can claim we ever done that, and live.'

They handled the newspaper with restraint. First they approached the editor, in masks, and explained their lofty motives, pointing out the many good things they had done for Larkin, like eliminating vice and increasing church membership, but they made little impression on the young man.

Next they threatened him. Three Klansmen, including one of enormous bulk, visited him at his home at two in the morning, warning him that he must halt all comment on the Klan 'or our next visit is gonna be more serious.'

The young editor, despite his appearance, was apparently cut from a robust Arkansas stock, because he ignored the threats, whereupon the governing committee of the Klan met to discuss what next to try. The meeting was held in the bank, after hours and without masks. Nine men, clean-shaven, well-dressed, giving every evidence of prosperity and right living, met solemnly to discuss their options: 'We can tar-and-feather him. We can whip him publicly. Or we can shoot him. But one way or another, we are going to silence that bastard.'

There was support for each of these choices, but after additional discussion, the majority seemed to settle upon a good horsewhipping on the courthouse steps, but then Floyd Rusk, huffing and puffing, introduced a note of reason: 'Men, in this country you learn never to bust the nose of the press. If you flog that editor publicly, or even privately, the entire press of Texas and the United States is goin' to descend upon this town. And if you shoot him, the federal government will have the marshals in here.'

'What can we do?' the banker asked.

'You have the solution,' Rusk said.

'Which is what?'

'Buy the paper. Throw him out.' When this evoked discussion, Rusk listened, judged the weight of various opinions, and said: 'It's quick, it's effective, and it's legal.'

So without even donning their hooded costumes, the leading members of the Klan accumulated a fund and bought the paper, then avoiding scandal, quietly drove the young editor out of town. That source of criticism was silenced, because before hiring a new editor, also a young man but this time from Dallas, the leading Klansmen satisfied themselves that he was a

1174

supporter of their movement and had been a member in the larger city.

The second problem was not so easily handled. Reverend Hislop was no irritating liberal like the editor from Arkansas, for he was against everything the Klan was against – immorality, adultery, drunkenness, shady business practice, the excesses of youth, such as blatant dancing – but he taught that these evils could best be opposed through an orderly church; he suspected that Jesus would not have approved of nightriders or flaming crosses, for the latter symbol was too precious to be so abused. Hislop was not a social hero; he kept his suspicions to himself, but as in all such situations wherein a man of good intention tries to hide, the facts had a tendency to uncover him, and that is what happened.

The Klansmen, eager to adopt a procedure which had proved effective in many small towns across the state, initiated the policy of having a committee of six members dress in full regalia each Sunday morning and march as a unit to either the Baptist or Methodist church, timing their arrival to coincide with the collection. Silently, and with impressive dignity, they entered at the rear, strode up the middle aisle in formation, and placed upon the altar an envelope containing a substantial cash contribution. 'For God's work,' the leader would cry in a loud voice, whereupon the six would turn on their heels and march out.

Such pageantry impressed the citizens, gaining the Klan much popular support, especially when the amount of the contribution was magnified in the telling: 'They give two hunnerd big ones for the poor and needy of this community.' Many believed that God had selected them as His right arm, and the moral intention of most of their public acts supported this view. Some thoughtful men came to believe that soon the Klan would assume responsibility for all of Texas, and that when that happened, a new day of justice and honest living would result.

Reverend Hislop did not see it this way. As a devout Southerner and a strong defender of the Confederacy, he understood the emotions which had called forth the original Klan back in the dark days after 1865, and supposed that had he lived then, he would have been a Klansman, because, as he said, 'some kind of corrective action was needed.' But he was not so sure about the motives of this revived Klan of the 1920s: 'They stand for all that's good, I confess. And they also support the programs of the church. They're against sin, and that puts them on my side. But decisions of punishment should be made by courts of law. In the long range of human history, there is no alternative to that. When the church dispensed justice in Spain and New England, it did a bad job. When these good men dispense their midnight justice at the country crossroads, they do an equally imperfect job. Martha, I cannot accept their Sunday contributions any longer.'

The decision had been reached painfully, but it was set in rock. However, Hislop was not the kind of man to create a public scandal; that would have been most repugnant. So on Sunday, when the six hooded Klansmen marched into his church, their polished boots clicking, he accepted their offering, but that very afternoon he summoned Floyd Rusk and the Indiana salesman to his parsonage, where he told them: 'It is improper for you to assume the duties of the church.'

'Why do you tell me this?' Rusk asked, and Reverend Hislop pointed a finger at the rancher's enormous belly: 'Do you think you can hide that behind a costume?'

'But why do you oppose the Klan?' Rusk asked. 'Surely it supports God's will.'

'I am sometimes confused as to what God's will really is.'

'Are you talkin' atheism?' Rusk demanded.

'I'm saying that I'm not sure what is accomplished by tarring a silly woman like Nora.'

'Surely she was an evil influence.'

'They thought that in Salem, when old women muttered. They hanged them. What are you going to do to Nora now?'

'Nora has nothing to do with this. We're turning Larkin into a Christian town.'

'In some things, yes. Mr Rusk, don't you realize that for every wayward person you correct, there are six others in our town who cheat their customers, who misappropriate funds . . . Life goes on here much as it does in Chicago or Atlanta, but you focus only on the little sinners.'

'You do talk atheism, Reverend Hislop. You better be careful.'

'I am being careful, Mr Rusk, and I'm asking you politely, as a fellow Christian who approves of much that you do, not to enter my church any more with your offerings. The money I need, and it can be delivered in the plate like the other offerings, but the display I do not need.'

On Sunday the six Klansmen in full regalia entered the church as usual. Led by a portly figure, they marched to the altar, where the large one said in a loud voice: 'For God's work.'

Before they could click their heels and retreat, Reverend Hislop said quietly: 'Gentlemen, God thanks you for your offering. His work needs all the support it can get. But you must not enter His church in disguise. You must not associate God with your endeavors, worthy though they sometimes are. Please take your offering out with you.'

No Klansman spoke. At the big man's signal they tramped down the aisle and out the door, leaving their money where they had placed it.

On previous Sundays the deacons who passed the collection plates and then marched to the altar, where the offerings were blessed, had rather grandiloquently lifted the Klan donation and placed it atop the lesser offerings, but on this day Reverend Hislop asked them not to do this. To his astonishment, one of the deacons who was a member of the Klan ostentatiously took the envelope from where Rusk had left it and placed it once more atop all the offerings, as if it took precedence because of the Klan's power in that town and in that church.

The battle lines were drawn, with a good eighty percent of the church members siding with the Klan rather than with their pastor. On the next Sunday the same three characters played the same charade. Floyd Rusk in his bedsheet made the donation; Reverend Hislop rejected it; and the deacon accepted it.

On the following Tuesday the church elders met with Reverend Hislop, a quiet-mannered man who deplored controversy, and informed him that his services were no longer required in Larkin. 'You've lost the confidence of your people,' the banker explained. 'And when that happens, the minister has to go.'

'You're the elders,' Hislop said.

'But we want to make it easy for you,' the man from Indiana said. 'There's a Methodist church in Waynesboro, Pennsylvania, lovely town among the hills. It needs a pastor, and the bishop in those parts has indicated that he would look kindly upon your removal there.'

Like the purchase of the newspaper and the elimination of its editor, the Larkin Methodist Church was purified without public scandal. Reverend Hislop preached on Sunday; he rejected the Klan offering; the deacons accepted it; and on Thursday he quietly disappeared.

The Klan now ruled the little town. All blacks were gone; all Jews were gone; no Mexicans were allowed within the town limits; and the lower class of Catholics had been eased out. It was a town of order, limited prosperity, and Christian decency. All voices of protest had been effectively silenced. Of course, as Reverend Hislop had pointed out, the same amount of acceptable crime prevailed as in any American town: some lawyers diverted public moneys into their own pockets; some doctors performed abortions; some politicians contrived election results to suit their purposes; and a good many deacons from all the churches drank moderately and played an occasional game of poker. There was a fair amount of adultery and not a little juggling of account books, but the conspicuous social crimes which offended the middle-class morality of the district, like open cohabitation or lascivious dancing, had been brought under control.

Then, just as the Ku Kluxers were congratulating themselves, a small, dirty, sharp-eyed man named Dewey Kimbro slipped into town, bringing an irresistible alternative to the Klan, and everything blew apart.

He first appeared as a man of mystery, under thirty, with sandy red hair and a slight stoop even though he was short. He would often ride his horse far into the countryside and tell nobody anything about it. He spoke little, in fact, and when he did his words fell into two sharply defined patterns, for sometimes he sounded like a college professor, at other times like the roughest cowboy, and what his inherited vocabulary had been no one could guess.

He attracted the attention of the Klansmen, who were not happy with strangers moving about their domain, and several extended discussions were held concerning him, with Floyd

Rusk leading the attack: 'I don't want him prowling my ranchland.' To Rusk's surprise, the banker said: 'When he transferred his funds to us, he asked about you, Floyd.'

'He did? He better lay off.'

Things remained in this uncertain state, with Kimbro attracting increased attention by his excursions, now here, now there, until the day when Rusk demanded that his Klansmen take action: 'I say we run him out of town. No place here for a man like him.' But the others pointed out that he had transferred into the Larkin bank nearly a thousand dollars, and that amount of money commanded respect.

'What do we know about him?' Rusk asked with that canny rural capacity for identifying trouble.

'He boards with Nora.'

'The woman we tarred-and-feathered?'

'The same.'

'Well,' announced a third man, 'he sure as hell ain't havin' sex with someone like her.'

'But it don't look good,' Rusk said. 'We got to keep watchin'.'

Then Kimbro made his big mistake. From Jacksboro he imported on the Reo bus, which ran between the two towns, a twenty-year-old beauty named Esther, with painted cheeks and a flowery outfit she could not have paid for with her clerk's wages. Kimbro moved her right into Nora's place, and on her third night of residence the couple was visited by the hooded Klan.

'Are you two married?'

'Whose business?' Kimbro asked the question, but it could just as well have come from Esther.

'It's our business. We don't allow your kind in this town.'

'I'm here. And so is she.'

'And do you think you'll be allowed to stay here?'

'I sure intend to. Till I get my work done.'

'And what is your work?' a masked figure asked.

'That's my business.'

'Enough of this,' a very fat Klansman broke in. 'Kimbro, if that's your real name, you got till Thursday night to get out of town. And, miss, you by God better be goin' with him.'

On Tuesday and Wednesday, Dewey Kimbro, named after the Hero of Manila and just as taciturn, rode out of town on his speckled horse. Spies followed him for a while, but could only report that he rode awhile, stopped awhile, dismounted occasionally, then rode on. He met no one, did nothing conspicuous, and toward dusk rode back into town, where Esther and Nora had supper waiting.

The three had gone to bed – Kimbro and the girl in one room – when four hooded figures bearing whips appeared, banging on the door and calling for Kimbro to come out. Under the hoods were Lew and Les Tumlinson, twin brothers who ran the coal and lumber business, Ed Boatright, who had the Chevrolet agency where the dead Jake had worked, and Floyd Rusk, the big rancher.

When Kimbro refused to appear, the Tumlinson twins kicked in the door, stormed into Nora's small house, and rampaged through the rooms till they found Kimbro and his whore in bed. Pulling him from under the covers they dragged his small body along the hallway and through the front door. On the lawn, in about the same position as when Jake and Nora were tarred, Rusk and Boatright had erected a cross, and were in the process of igniting it when the twins shouted: 'We got him!' When the cross lit up the sky, a horde of onlookers ran up, and there was so much calling back and forth among the hooded figures that the crowd knew who the four avengers were: 'That's Lew Tumlinson for sure, and if he's here, so's his brother. The fat one we know, and I think the other has got to be Ed Boatright.'

Dewey Kimbro, who never missed anything, even when he was about to be thrashed, heard the names. He also heard the fat man say: 'Strip him!' and when the nightshirt was torn away and he stood naked, he heard the same man shout: 'Lay it on. Good.'

He refused to faint. He refused to cry out. In the glare of the flaming cross, he bore the first twenty-odd lashes of the three whips, but then he lost count, and finally he did faint.

At nine o'clock next morning he barged into Floyd Rusk's kitchen, and the fat man, who was an expert with revolvers from an early age, anticipated trouble and whipped out one of his big six-shooters, but before he could get it into position, he glared into the barrel of a small yet deadly German pistol pointed straight at a spot between his eyes.

For a long, tense moment the two men retained their positions, Rusk almost ready to fire his huge revolver, Kimbro prepared to fire first with his smaller gun. Finally Rusk dropped his, at which Kimbro said: 'Place it right here where I can watch it,' and Floyd did, sweating heavily.

'Now let's sit down here, Mr Rusk, and talk sense.' When the big man took his place at the kitchen table, with his gun in reach not of himself but of Kimbro, a conversation began which modified the history of Larkin County.

'Mr Rusk, you whipped me last night—'

'Now wait!'

'You're right. You never laid a rawhide on me. But you ordered the Tumlinson twins and Ed Boatright ...' Rusk's glistening of sweat became a small torrent. 'I ought to kill you for that, and maybe later on I will. But right now you and I need each other, and you're far more valuable to me alive than dead.'

'Why?'

'I have a secret, Mr Rusk. I've had it since I was eleven years old. Do you remember Mrs Jackson who ran the little store?'

'Yes, I believe I do.'

'You wouldn't remember a boy from East Texas who spent one summer with her?'

'Are you that boy?'

'I am.'

'And what secret did you discover?'

'On your land ... out by the tank ... '

'That's not my land. My father gave it to the Yeagers.'

'I know. Your father promised it in the 1870s. You formalized it in 1909.'

'So it's not my land.'

Kimbro shifted in his chair, for the pain from his whipping was intense. He had a most important statement to make, and he wanted to be in complete control when he made it, but just as he was prepared to disclose the purpose of his visit, Molly Rusk came into the kitchen, a big blowzy woman who, against all the rules of nature, was pregnant. She had a round, happy face made even more placid by the miracle of her condition, and with the simplicity that marked most of her actions, she took one look at Kimbro and asked: 'Aren't you the man they whipped last night?' and he said: 'I am.'

She was about to ask why he was sitting in her kitchen this morning when Rusk said respectfully: 'You better leave us alone, Molly,' and she retired with apologies, but she had barely closed the door when she returned: 'There's coffee on the stove.' Then she added: 'Floyd, don't do anything brutal with that gun.'

'True, the land is no longer yours. Mr Rusk,' Kimbro said quietly. 'Your daddy promised it to Yeager, but when you transferred it legally, you were clever enough to retain the mineral rights.'

Rusk leaned far back in his chair. Then placed his pudgy hands on the edge of the table, and from this position he sat staring at the little stranger. Finally, in an awed voice he asked: 'You mean . . . '

Kimbro nodded, and after readjusting his painful back, he said: 'When I stayed here that summer I did a lot of tramping about. Always have.'

'And what did you find at the tank?'

'A small rise that everyone else had overlooked. When I kicked rocks aside, I came upon . . . guess what?'

'Gold?'

'Much better. Coal.'

'Coal?'

'Yep. Sneaked some home and it burned a glowing red. Kept on burning. So I kept on exploring . . . '

'And you located a coal mine?'

'Nope. The strain was trivial, played out fast. But I covered the spot, piled rocks over it, and if you and I go out there this morning, we'll find a slight trace of coal hiding where it's always been.'

'And what does this mean?'

'You don't know? I knew when I was ten. Read it in a book.' He shifted again. 'I read a lot, Mr Rusk.'

'And what did you read, at ten?'

Kimbro hesitated, then changed the subject entirely: 'Mr Rusk, I want you to enter into a deal with me, right now. Word of a gentleman. We're partners, seventy-five to you, twenty-five to me.'

'What the hell kind of offer is that? I don't even know what we're talkin' about.'

'You will. In two minutes, if you make the deal.'

'You'd trust me, after last night?'

'I have to.' Kimbro banged the table. 'And by God, you have to trust me, too.'

'Is it worth my while? I have a lot of cattle, you know.'

'And you're losing your ass on them, aren't you?'

'Well, the market ... '

'Seventy-five, twenty-five for my secret and the know-how to develop it.'

Again Rusk leaned back: 'What do you know about me, personally I mean?'

'That you're a bastard, through and through. But once you give your word, you stick to it.'

'I do. You know, Kimbro, when I was fourteen or thereabouts I rode to Dodge City with a—'

'You went to Dodge City?'

'I did, with the greatest trail driver Texas ever produced, R. J. Poteet. He tried to make a man of me, but I wouldn't allow it. At Dodge, I killed two men, yep, age fifteen I think I was. Poteet's two point men spirited me out of town. Just ahead of the sheriff. But on the ride back to Texas he and his men held a kangaroo court because they knew damned well I hadn't shot in self-defense. Found me guilty and strung me up. I thought sure as hell ... ' He was sweating so profusely that he asked: 'Can I get that towel?'

'Stay away from the gun.'

'They slapped the horse I was sitting on. I fell, I felt the rope bite into my neck. And then Poteet caught me. He lectured me about my wrong ways, and I spat in his face.' He laughed nervously. 'I was scared to death, really petrified, but I wouldn't show it. Poteet went for his gun, then brushed me aside.'

He rocked back and forth on the kitchen chair, an immensely fat man of forty-seven. Replacing his hands on the table, he said: 'That hanging was the making of me, Kimbro. Taught me two things. You've uncovered one of them. I am a man of my word, hell or high water. And I have never since then been afraid to use my gun when it had to be used. If you're partners with me, be damned careful'

'That's why I brought this,' Kimbro said, indicating the gun

1183

which he had kept trained on the fat man during their discussion.

'So what did you learn?' Rusk asked.

'Partners?' Kimbro asked, and the two shook hands, after which the little fellow delivered his momentous information: 'At ten I knew that coal and petroleum are the same substance, in different form.'

Rusk gasped: 'You mean oil?' The word echoed through the quiet kitchen as if a bomb had exploded, for the wild discoveries in East Texas had alerted the entire state to the possibilities of this fantastic substance which made farmers multimillionaires.

'At fourteen,' Kimbro continued, 'I studied all the chemistry and physics our little school allowed, and at seventeen I enrolled at Texas A&M.'

'You a college graduate?'

'Three years only. By that time I knew more about petroleum than the professors. Got a job with Humble, then Gulf. Field man. Sort of an informal geologist. Worked the rigs too, so I know what drilling is. Mr Rusk, I'm a complete oilman, but what I really am is maybe the world's greatest creekologist.'

'What's that?'

'A contemptuous name the professors give practical men like me. We study the way creeks run, the rise and fall of land forms, and we guess like hell.' He slammed the table. 'But by God, we find oil. It's downright infuriating to the college people how we find oil.'

'And you think you've found some on my land?'

'From the run of the creeks and the rise in your field, I'm satisfied that we're sitting near the middle of a substantial field.'

'You mean real oil?'

'I do. Not a bunch of spectacular gushers like Spindletop. But good, dependable oil trapped in the rocks below us.'

'If you're right, could we make some real money?'

'A fortune, if we handle it right.'

'And what would right be?'

'How much of this land around here do you own?'

'I'm sure you've checked at the courthouse. Well over seven thousand acres.'

'Where does it lie, relation to the tank?'

'South and some across Bear Creek to the west.'

'I'm glad you can tell the truth. But if I'm right, the field runs north and east of the tank. Could you buy any of that land?'

'Look, I don't have much ready cash.'

'Could you lease the mineral rights? I mean right now. Not tomorrow, now.'

'Is speed so necessary?'

'The minute anyone suspects what we're up to ... if they even guess that I'm a creekologist ... then it's too late.'

'How does an oil lease work?'

Kimbro had to rise, adjust his scarred back, and sit gingerly on the edge of the chair: 'There can be three conditions of ownership. First, you own your seven thousand acres and all mineral rights under them. Second, Yeager owns the good land we want, the surface, that is, but he owns nothing underneath. Tough on him, good for us.'

'Yes, but do we have the right to invade his property in order to sink our well?'

'We do, if we don't ruin his surface. And if we do ruin it, we pay him damages, and he can't do a damned thing about it.'

'He won't like it.'

'They never do, but that's the law. Now, the third situation is the one that operates mostly. Farmer Kline owns a big chunk of land, say three thousand acres. He also owns the mineral rights. So we go to him and say: "Mr Kline, we want to lease the mineral rights to your land. For ten years. And we'll give you fifty cents an acre year after year for ten years. A lot of money."'

'What rights do we get?'

'The right to drill, any place on the farm, as many holes as we want, for ten years.'

'And what does he get?'

'Fifteen hundred dollars a year, hard cash, year after year, even if we do nothing.'

'And if we strike oil?'

'He gets a solid one-eighth of everything we make, for as long as that well produces. To eternity, if he and it last that long.'

'Who gets the other seven-eighths?'

'We do.'

'Is it a good deal ... for all of us, I mean?'

'For Farmer Kline, it's a very fair deal. He gets an oil well without taking any risk. For you and me, the deal with Kline is about the best we can do, fair to both sides. It's his oil but we take all the risks.'

'And between you and me – seventy-five, twenty-five?'

'Tell you the truth, Rusk, with some men like me you could get an eighty, twenty deal, but nine out of ten such men would never find a bucket of oil. I know where the oil is. For you, it's a very good deal. As for me, if I had the land or the money, I wouldn't say hello to you. But I don't have either.'

'So what should we do?' Rusk asked permission to pour coffee, whereupon Kimbro pushed the big revolver across the table to him.

'I trust you, Rusk. I have to. We're partners.'

When reports of the notorious Sunday School trial at Waxa-hachie circulated through Texas, accompanied by sardonic laughter, the voters began to realize that in Laurel Cobb, son of the famous post-Reconstruction senator, they had a man of common sense and uncommon courage, and a movement was launched to send him to Washington to assume the seat once held by his father. Said one editorial, recalling the older man's dignified performance in the chaotic 1870s: 'He restored honor to the fair name of Texas.'

Prior to 1913, Laurel would have had little chance to win the seat, for in those years United States senators were elected by their respective state legislatures and he would have enlisted only minor support, for he was more liberal than the Demo-cratic leadership. In fact, his father had been acceptable in 1874 only because Texas wanted to show the rest of the nation that it was not ashamed of how it had conducted itself during the War Between the States: 'Damnit, we want a man who held high rank in the army of the Confederacy, and if the rest of the nation don't like it, the rest of the nation can go to hell.' However, the men who sent him to Congress on those terms were often embarrassed by how he acted when he got there, and it would have been impossible for their sons to accept Laurel.

But with adoption of the Seventeenth Amendment, senators were elected by popular ballot, and the general public wanted Cobb, so a serious campaign was launched on his behalf. It was Adolf Lakarz, the fighting little fellow who defended him in the

Sunday School trial, who persuaded Cobb to run, using this argument: 'If you fight for justice in a church, you can do the same in a nation.' As soon as Cobb accepted this challenge, he began contesting the Democratic primary in earnest, and this took him to Saldaña County and the machinations of Horace Vigil and his dexterous assistant Héctor Garza.

Cobb, aware of Vigil's unsavory reputation, had balked at paying court to the old patrón, but Lakarz had quickly put an end to such revolt: 'Laurel, you're one of four good Democrats who want this Senate seat, and the other three will do anything short of murder to grab it from you. The competition will be especially tough for those easy votes that Vigil keeps in his pocket. We need them, and if you have to kiss ass to get them, start bending down.'

'How does one man control so much?'

'Because he still has that good old Precinct 37.'

'I should think the government would take it away.'

Lakarz laughed: 'Texas tried to, many times. Federals try to every time there's a Republican administration, but old Horace holds on.'

'Sounds illegal,' Cobb said, but Lakarz corrected him: 'Sounds Texan.'

So Cobb and Lakarz drove from Waxahachie along what might be called the spine of settled Texas: Waco on the Brazos, with its rich agricultural land; Temple, with its proud high school football team; Austin, with its handsome buildings and growing university; Luling and Beeville, in the sun; Falfurrias, with its multitude of flowers; and then that shocking emptiness which had been the stalking ground of Ranger Macnab and the bandit Benito Garza.

'It can be hot down here,' Cobb groaned as the temperature rose to a hundred and stayed there.

'Oooooh, Mr Candidate, never say that! Down here they call a day like this bracing, and if you want their votes, you better call it bracing, too.'

'I imagine it could be glorious in winter.'

'Say that to everyone you meet, and you'll win.'

When Cobb thought he could begin to smell the river, Lakarz told him: 'This land up here used to be attached to Saldaña County, but about 1911 huge chunks were lopped off

1187

the old counties to form new ones. But what's left is still big enough to carry a lot of weight.'

'What advice on handling Horace Vigil?'

'Easy. Let him know you're a loyal Democrat. If you're thinking of opening a saloon, buy your beer from him. And always speak well of his Mexicans. For without their support, you will never go to Washington.'

As they approached the outskirts of Bravo, Cobb saw an astonishing sight: 'Are those palm trees?' For mile after mile the tall swaying trees baked in the sun, as if standing on the banks of the Nile, and sometimes in their shade would rest acres of experimental orange and grapefruit trees. In the blazing heat a new industry was quietly expanding into Texas, and some of the farmers who had pioneered it were becoming richer than their neighbors in other parts of the state who had oil wells.

'Vigil doesn't need to bother with votes. He has a paradise here,' Cobb said, but Lakarz warned: 'Horace always bothers with votes.'

They found Vigil in the adobe-walled building from which he ran his beer distributorship. He was an old man now, white-haired and in his late sixties. He was markedly stooped, but no one could doubt that he was still the shrewd dictator of his county; as always when meeting strangers he spoke in near-whispers: 'Never met your daddy, but they tell me he was first rate. I heard about him trackin' down that gunman who shot his two niggers. In those days that took courage.'

He sat surrounded by his usual cadre of young men, sons of the functionaries who had served him in the past; they fetched his cigarettes, instructed the judge as to the cases in which Mr Vigil had a special interest, supervised the counting of ballots, and distributed alms to the needy. Little had changed politically. Vigil was still the patrón, dispensing his rude justice, and to the citizens of Saldaña County he was still Señor Vee-heel.

The old man coughed: 'Mr Cobb, of the four Democrats running' for the Senate, I prefer you. Now tell me, what can I do to help you win?'

Cobb liked this old dictator; he felt the man's warmth and respected his authority: 'No, you tell me.'

'That's reasonable, because I know this territory. Not as big as it once was, but more voters, more leverage.' He turned away from Cobb and called to his principal assistant: 'Héctor, I want you to meet the man we're sendin' to Washington to take his daddy's place.' And the four laid plans for nailing down the primary.

But as Cobb toured other sections of the state he became aware that one of his opponents was taking his own bold steps to steal the election, and this embittered Adolf Larkarz, who reminded Cobb: 'We've got to get a huge majority in Saldaña County, because, as the papers keep saying, "In Texas winning the Democratic primary is tantamount to election." '

'You ever think about that word, Adolf? It's one of those curious cases in which a perfectly good word had been restricted to only one use. You never hear "A hot dog is tantamount to a sausage." ' Lakarz, irritated that his candidate was wasting his time on such nonpolitical reflection, warned: 'You better hope this primary is tantamount to your election.'

The campaign in Saldaña had only begun when one of those political events which perplexed outsiders took place. Horace Vigil, who had fought the Republican customs officer Tim Coke for decades, learned that his old nemesis was leaving the Bravo-Escandón Bridge for a better job in New York, so he organized a gala farewell to which he contributed a new Chevrolet in which the Cokes could drive to their new post. In his speech of thanks, Coke said: 'I hate to leave Saldaña just as the Democrats are preparing to tear themselves apart in their primary. I'd like to see my old friend Horace get his nose busted. But I say this here and now. I want all my Republicans to cross party lines and get into the polling booths one way or another. And you're to vote for Vigil's man, Laurel Cobb, and vote three or four times, like you always did for me. Because in thirty years of fighting that sumbitch Vigil, I always had respect for him. I never knew what infamous or criminal thing he was going to hit me with next, but the battles were fun. I look forward with relief to fighting those Democratic hoodlums in Tammany Hall. They're the worst snakes ever thrown out of Ireland. But these Democrats in Texas, they're rattlesnakes.'

Three days before the election Lakarz slipped back into Bravo for a strategy meeting, and what he learned was ominous. Vigil himself outlined the sorry details: 'Reformers in Washington, bunch of Republicans, they're comin' down to take control of Precinct 37.'

'We've got to have those votes.'

'We'll be allowed to count them and report whatever totals we need. Texas law demands that, but as soon as the countin' ends, we have to deliver the ballot boxes to the federals.'

'What do you think they'll do?'

'Send me to jail, if they can prove anything.' Lakarz could see that this possibility frightened the old man, who said quietly: 'Jail I do not seek, but if it's the only way we can win this election, jail it will have to be.'

'Our friends will never let that happen.'

The old warrior was not so confident, but he did not lament his problems; he had one more election to win, and he would speak only of it: 'When the boxes reach Bravo, they'll recount the votes in the presence of a federal judge. We could be in a lot of trouble.'

'Have you a plan for getting out of this?'

'Normally we'd bribe the judge, but this time he's a federal. I'll think of somethin'.'

A council of war occupied Saturday afternoon, and it was Héctor Garza, a little taller, a little bolder than his predecessors, who devised the winning strategy: 'We must have absolute secrecy. So that when the federals come after us, we can honestly swear: "We don't know." '

'You think they will come?' Vigil asked in a whisper, and Garza said: 'For sure. The Republicans will see to that. But I know a way to hold them off.'

Sharing his intricate plan with no one, not even Vigil, he orchestrated a strategy in which no one except he and the person performing one small part of the job knew what anyone else was doing. On the eve of the election he said to Vigil and Lakarz with confidence: 'As soon as the votes have been counted across the state, tell me how many votes we'll need to win.'

Late on election night Vigil telephoned Garza, standing watch at Precinct 37: 'We've got to have more than four hundred and ten,' and an hour later the three officials at the precinct certified the vote to have been 422 to 7.

When the men from Washington, waiting in Bravo, heard this, they exulted: 'Now we have them! Impossible for a vote to be so lopsided.' And almost hungrily they waited to get their hands on the incriminating box: 'This time Vigil goes behind bars, and not some half-baked county jail. The federal pen.'

But now a singular thing happened. The ballot box disappeared. Yes, on its way down F.M. 117 it disappeared, and since the election officials had legally reported their results, those results had to stand. The preposterous 422 to 7 stood, enabling Laurel Cobb to win the election by a twenty-seven-vote margin.

How could an object as big as a ballot box disappear? It was never fully explained. It had been handed by the judges to a Mr Hernández, who passed it along to a Mr Robles, who gave a receipt for it, and he gave it to a Mr Solórzano, and that was where it disappeared, because Mr Solórzano could prove that he had been in San Antonio when all this happened.

Texas newspapers, which had supported one or another of Cobb's opponents, screamed for an investigation, while the more impartial journals in New York and Washington editorialized that the time had come to cleanse American politics of the stigma of Saldaña County. However, the case became somewhat more complicated when it was revealed that the mysterious Mr Solórzano had been in the employ of the Washington men.

Héctor Garza revealed to no one his role in this legerdemain, but Horace Vigil, in a show of righteous morality, did issue a pious statement deploring the carelessness of the men, whose ineptness had allowed aspersions to be cast upon fine officials of Precinct 37: 'I personally regret the loss of that box because had its contents been counted by the federal judge, the results would have proved what I have always claimed. The election officials of Precinct 37 are honest. They're just a mite slow.'

This time their tardiness enabled a good man to go to Washington.

On a gray morning in October 1922 schoolboys sitting near the window cried: 'Look at what's comin'!' and their classmates ran to see three large trucks moving down the Jacksboro road. They carried long lengths of timber, piles of pipe, and ten of the toughest-looking men Larkin County had seen in a long time. Two lads who had been reading science magazines shouted:

'Oil rig!' and in that joyous frenzied cry the Larkin boom was born.

The trucks rolled into Courthouse Square, pulled up before the sheriff's office, and asked where Larkin Tank was. Then, consulting the maps they had been given, they headed north toward the land whose surface was owned by the Yeagers but whose mineral rights were still controlled by Floyd Rusk.

No sooner had the three trucks left town than Rusk appeared in his pickup, accompanied by Dewey Kimbro, and when the new newspaper editor shouted: 'What's up?' Rusk cried back: 'We're spudding in an oil well.'

Much of the town followed the trucks out to a marked depression east of the tank where Rusk #1 was to be dug, and what they saw became the topic of conversation for many days, because when Paul Yeager, forty-nine years old and soft-spoken, saw the three men on the lead truck preparing to open his gate and drive onto his land, he ran forward to protest: 'This is Yeager land. Keep off.'

'We know it's Yeager land. We've been lookin' for it,' and the truck started to roll toward the open gate.

'I warned you to stop!' Yeager cried, his voice rising.

'Mister, it ain't for you to say.' And in the next frantic moments, with Yeager trying to halt the trucks, the people of Larkin learned a lot about Texas law.

'Mr Yeager,' the man in charge of the drilling rig explained, 'the mineral rights to this here land reside with Mr Floyd Rusk, and he's asked us . . . '

'Here's Rusk now. Floyd, what in hell . . . ?'

'Drillin' rig, Paul. We think there may be oil under this land.'

'You can't come in here.'

'Yes, we can. The law says so.'

'I don't believe it.'

'You better check, because we're comin' in.'

'You can't bring those big trucks through my crops.'

'Yes we can, Paul, so long as we compensate you for the damage. The law says so.' And with that, huge Floyd Rusk gently pushed his brother-in-law aside, so that the three trucks could drive in, make a rocky path through the field, and come to a halt at the site decided upon intuitively by the creekologist Dewey Kimbro.

A lawyer hired by Yeager did come out to contest Rusk's right to invade another man's property and destroy some of its crop, but reference to Texas law quickly satisfied him that Rusk had every right to do just what he was doing: 'He's protected, Paul. Law's clear on that.'

So the town watched as Rusk #1 was started in the hollow, and the efficiency of the crew dazzled the watchers, for the men, using an old-style system popular in the 1910s, set to work like a colony of purposeful ants, digging the foundations for the rig, lining the tanks into which the spill would be conserved for analysis, and erecting the pyramidal wooden derrick which would rise seventy feet in the air, that consoling feature of the Texas landscape which proclaimed: 'There may be oil here.'

When the pulley sheaves were fixed atop the derrick and the cables drove through them, the men were ready to affix one end of the cable to the huge drum that raised and lowered it, the other end to the cutting bit that would be dropped downward with considerable force to dig the hole. The rig, when set, would not drill into the earth in any rotary fashion; by the sheer force of falling weight the bit would pulverize its way through rock.

And how was this repetitive fall of the two-ton bit assembly controlled? 'See that heavy wooden beam that's fixed at one end, free at the end over the hole? We call it the *walking beam*, and every time it lifts up, it raises all the heavy tools in the hole. When it releases – Bam! Down they crash, smashing the rock to bits.'

The townspeople could not visualize the force exerted at the end of that drop, nor the effectiveness of the tools used to crush the rock, but after the walking beam had operated for about two hours, the man in charge of the rig signaled for the cutting bit to be withdrawn from the hole, and now the ponderous process was reversed, with the cables pulling the heavy tools up out of the hole, so that the worn bit at the end which had done the smashing could be removed to be resharpened while a replacement, keen as a heavy knife, was sent down to resume the smashing.

'What do they do with the old one?' a garage mechanic asked, and he was shown a kind of blacksmith's shed in which two strong men with eighteen-pound sledges heated the worn bit and hammered it back into cutting shape.

And that was the basic process which the people of Larkin studied with such awe: sharpen the bit, attach it to the string of tools, raise it high on the cable, lower it into the hole, then work the walking beam and allow the sharp edge to smash down on the rock until something gave; then undo the whole package, fit on a new bit, resharpen the old, and hammer away again.

To the newspaper editor who wanted to share with his readers the complexity of the process, the rig boss said: 'One bit can drill thirty feet, more if it encounters shale. But when it hits really hard sandstone or compacted limestone . . . three feet, we have to take it out and resharpen.'

'Where does the water come from that I see going into the tank?'

'If we're lucky, the hole lubricates itself. If not, we pump water in. The bottom has to be kept wet so that the bit can bite in. Besides, we have to bring up samples.' And he showed the newsman how a clever tool called the *bailer* was let down into the hole from which the drilling bit had been removed: 'It has this trick at the bottom. Push it against the bottom, and water swirls inside. Let it rise, it closes off the tube. Then pull it up on the cable and dump it into the slush pit.' When the newsman looked at the big square hole the crew had prepared, thirty feet on a side, ten inches deep, he thought that the waste water was being discarded.

'Oh, no! Look at that fellow. One of the most important men we have. He samples every load of water. What kind of rock? What consistency? What kind of sand?'

'Why?'

'It's his job to paint a picture of the inside of our well. Every different layer, if he can do it. Because only then do we know what we have.'

The operation of the rig, twenty-four hours a day, was so compelling, with men delving into the secrets of earth, lining the hole with casing to keep it open, cementing sections of the hole, fishing like schoolboys for parts which had broken and lodged at the bottom, calculating the tilt of the rocks and their composition – that it became a fascinating game which preoccupied all of Larkin and much of Texas, for it was known throughout the oil industry that 'Rusk #1 west of Jacksboro is down to eighteen hundred feet, stone-dry.' Spectators learned new words, which they bandied deftly: 'They're underreaming at two thousand,' 'They've cemented-in at two thousand two.' And always there was the hope that on this bright morning the word would flash: 'Rusk # 1 has come in!'

But the town was also involved in something equally colorful, for the ten roughnecks who had come with the rig were proving themselves to be a special breed, the likes of which Larkin had never before seen. Rugged, powerful of arm, incredibly dirty with the drilling business, they were among the ablest professionals in the country. The three top experts had come down from the oil fields of Pennsylvania, where their forebears had been drilling for oil since 1859, when Colonel Drake brought in that first American well at Titusville; he had struck his bonanza at a mere sixty-nine feet. The next echelon were Texas men who had worked in Arkansas and Louisiana in years when activity focused there. But the men who gave the crew character were Texans who had worked only in this state. They were violent, catlike men who knew they could lose a finger or an arm if they dallied with the flashing cable or did not jump quickly enough if something went wrong with the walking beam.

On the job they were self-disciplined, for if even one man failed to perform, the safety of all might be imperiled, but off the job they wanted things their way, and what they wanted most was booze, women and a good poker game. This brought them into conflict with the Ku Klux Klan, which had disciplined Larkin along somewhat divergent lines, and the trouble started when three of the men imported high-flying ladies from Fort Griffin and set them up at Nora's place, where the creekologist Dewey Kimbro and his girl Esther still maintained quarters.

Within two nights the Klansmen learned of the goings-on, and in their hoods three of them marched out to Nora's to put a stop to this frivolity, but they were met by the three roughnecks, who said: 'What is this shit? Take off your nightshirts.'

'We're warning you, get those girls out of town by Thursday night or face the consequences.'

'You come out here again in those nightshirts, you're gonna

get your ass blown off. Now get the hell out of here.'

The Klansmen returned on Thursday night, as promised, but the three sponsors of the girls were on the night shift, so the protectors of morality satisfied themselves by having the three girls arrested and hauling them off to jail. When the oilmen reached Nora's after a hard night on the rig, they expected a little companionship, but instead found Nora weeping: 'They warned me that if the girls ever came back, and that included Esther, they was gonna burn the place down.'

The oilmen, collecting the other two from their shift, marched boldly to the jail and informed the custodian there, not the sheriff, that if he didn't deliver those girls in three minutes, they were going to blow the place apart. He turned them loose, and with considerable squealing and running, the eight rioters – three girls, five oilmen – roared back to Nora's, where they organized a morning party with Esther.

The Klan met that night to decide what to do about the invaders, and many of the men looked to Floyd Rusk for guidance: 'What I say is, let's get the well dug. If we find oil like Kimbro assures me we will, we'll all have enough money to settle other questions later.' When there was grumbling at such temporizing, he said: 'You know me. I'm a law-and-order man.'

'There ain't much law and order when a gang of roughnecks can raid our jail and turn loose our prisoners.'

'Oilmen are different,' Rusk said, and there the matter rested, for in Texas, when morality was confronted by the possibility of oil, it was the former which had to give ... for a while.

Dewey Kimbro had guessed wrong on Rusk #1. It went to three thousand feet, and was still stone-dry. So the great Larkin oil boom went bust, but it was not a wasted effort, for at two thousand feet Dewey had spotted in the slush pond indications of the Strawn Sand formation, which excited him enormously. Sharing the information only with Rusk, he said: 'Let them think we missed. Then buy up as many leases as we can west of our dry Number One, because Strawn is promising.'

So, wearing his poor mouth, Rusk went to one landowner after another, saying: 'Looks like the signs deceived us. But maybe over the long haul ... ' He offered to take their mineral leases off their hands at twenty-five cents an acre, and when he had vast areas locked up, he asked Kimbro: 'Now what?'

'I'm dead certain we have a major concentration down there. I see evidences of it wherever I look. It's got to be there, Mr Rusk.'

'But where?'

'That's the problem. East of Number One or west? I can't be sure which.'

'Your famous gut feeling? What's it say?'

Kimbro drove Rusk out to the area and showed him how Rusk #1 had lain at the bottom of a dip: 'It's the land formations west of here that set my bells ringing. Damn, I do believe our field is hiding down there, below the first concentration of Strawn sand, like maybe three thousand feet.'

'We have money for only one more try. Where should it be?'

'I am much inclined toward the tank,' and he indicated a spot close to the statue which sentimentalists had erected to mark the spot where the lovers Nellie Minor and Jim Logan had committed suicide by drowning – that was the legend now – but Rusk objected to digging there: 'The women in town would raise hell if we touched that place.' So they moved farther west, and finally, on a slight rise, Dewey scraped his heel in the dust: 'Rusk Number Two. And I know it'll be good.' When he said this, Rusk asked: 'If you know so much, why don't the big boys? They have their spies here, you know.'

'The big companies depend on little men like me to find oil for them. Then they move in, fast. We get our small profit. They get their big haul.'

'I want the big haul, Kimbro.'

'So do I. So let's drill over here where I've marked Rusk Number Two.'

'That's on Yeager's land.'

'But it's in your mineral rights.'

'We'll have trouble if we go back again.'

'Law's on our side.'

So Rusk #2 was started, with the same drilling team and the same girls staying at Nora's; when there was still a good chance for oil, even the Klan had to adjust.

With scouts from nine large companies watching every move Dewey Kimbro made, Floyd Rusk drilled a second dry hole at

3,100 feet, and now his money began to run out. He had invested most of his ready cash in hiring the drilling crew, and a good portion of his savings in buying up leases.

But when the crunch came, Dewey Kimbro, like a true wildcatter, wanted to risk more money; 'Mr Rusk, so help me God, what we must do is acquire more leases. If you have to pawn your wife's wedding ring, do it and get those leases. They'll be dirt cheap now. People are laughing at us. But they don't know what we know.'

'And what's that?'

'More signs of oil, I saw them myself when I took the samples at twenty-nine hundred feet.'

'Was that significant?'

'Significant? My God, don't you realize what I'm saying? On Rusk Number One we found indications at twenty-three hundred feet. Now, over here, at Rusk Number Two, we find it at both twenty-three hundred and twenty-nine hundred. Means that oil is down there somewhere. My judgment is our next well has got to hit. I know the field must lie between Number One and Number Two, and we've got to get those leases.'

'You find the money. I don't have any more.'

So Dewey Kimbro set out to con the entire state of Texas into supporting his wild dream of an oil field north of Larkin, in an area which had never produced a cup of oil. He hectored his friends from his student days at A&M, and young men who specialized in the practical courses offered there often did well, so they had money, but they refused to risk it. He badgered his oil acquaintances from the eastern fields, but they knew from their own studies that Larkin held no promise. And he buttonholed any gambler who had ever taken a chance of Texas oil, traveling as far as Nevada and Alabama to trace them.

He was, of course, only one of several hundred visionaries who were flogging the Texas dream that year. Some crazies were trying to convince their friends that there had to be oil in unlikely places like Longview, Borger and Mentone. Others claimed that the area north of Fort Stockton had to have oil, and a hundred others lobbied for places of their choice, where oil would never be found. It was a time of oil fever, and no one had the malady more virulently than Dewey Kimbro.

Except, perhaps, Floyd Rusk, for when the fat man realized that all his savings and even his ranch were committed to this adventure, he became monomaniacal about bringing in the field that Dewey kept assuring him existed under the leases which he already controlled. He was determined to see this exploration through, for he had convinced himself that he could recognize the formations when Kimbro pointed them out. Millions upon millions of years ago a lake of oil had been trapped down there among the sandstone and the limestone tilts, and he wanted it.

But he had no money. Digging the two dry holes had exhausted his funds, and with Kimbro finding little success in borrowing replacements, he did not know where to turn, but one morning when the drillers said they wanted to haul their rig back east to more promising sites, and would do so unless paid promptly, he went to the one person in whom he did not wish to confide.

Emma Larkin Rusk, the onetime prisoner of the Comanche, was sixty-six that year, a frail shadow weighing not much over a hundred pounds. The stubs of her ears showed beneath the wisps of hair that no longer masked her deformity, and her balsa-wood nose seemed to fit less properly, now that she had lost so much weight. But she was alert and already knew that her difficult son was in trouble.

'My first two wells were dry,' he said.

'I know.'

'But we're sure the next one will hit.'

'Why don't you drill it!'

'No money.'

'None?'

'Not a dime.'

'And you want me to lend you some?'

'Yes.'

She sat with her hands folded, staring at her unlovely son, this glutton who had never done anything right. When she had hoped to make a man of him, through R. J. Poteet, he had fumbled the opportunity, and when in 1901 after her husband's death she had turned over the operation of the ranch to him, he had bungled it so badly that she had to step back in and save it. Now he wanted to borrow her life savings, the funds which allowed her to live in her own house rather than impose on him and Molly.

There was no sensible reason why she should lend this grotesque man the money he wanted, but there was an overpowering sentimental one. He had carved the nose she wore and which had made such a difference to her life, and although their relationship had been a miserable one, she loved him for that one gesture. She had known great terror in her life, and little love apart from that which her daydreaming husband had given so freely, so she cherished every manifestation made in her behalf. Floyd was her son, and at one accidental point in his miserable life he had loved her. She would lend the money.

But life had made her a wily woman, so before she relinquished her funds she drove a bargain. When he asked her 'What interest?' she said 'None,' and he thanked her.

Then she added: 'But I do want five thousand more acres for my Longhorns,' and since he was in the perilous position of having to accept any terms in order to get his gambling money, he said: 'Promised,' and she asked: 'Fenced in?' and he had to reply: 'Yes.'

However, when they went out to inspect the land she had thus acquired for her chosen animals, she saw that the proposed rig was going to stand very close to the statue commemorating the two lovers, and Floyd expected her to raise the devil.

Instead she stood quietly and looked at the unassembled derrick. 'How appropriate,' she said. 'They lived in turbulence. Better than most, they'll adjust to an oil boom . . . if we get one. I'm sure they hope you hit, Floyd. I do.'

And so with his mother's money, Rusk kept his gamble alive.

Then began the days of anxiety. Even with Emma's contribution the partnership lacked enough funds to start drilling its third well, the one that seemed likely to produce, and this meant that the ill-assorted team – gross, surly Floyd and tenacious, ratlike Dewey – faced double disasters. The leases on the very promising land, which they had taken for only one year, were about to run out, and the drilling crew was eager to move east. The partners knew they had less than two months to resolve these problems.

The nature of a Texas oil lease was this: if a lease expired on 30 June 1923, as these did, the holder had a right to start drilling at his choice of time up to one minute before midnight on the thirtieth. If he did not or could not start, the lease lapsed and could be resold to some other wildcatter. But if the holder did start his drilling within his time allowance, the full provisions of the lease came into effect and prevailed for centuries to come. So each of the partners, in his own way, began to scrounge around for additional funds.

Rusk stayed in Larkin, badgering everyone, begging them to lend him money, and he was embittered when his Ku Klux Klan compatriots turned him down. Some did so out of conviction, because they felt it was his greed that had brought the ten oil-field roughnecks, with their devil-driven ways, into Larkin. But most rejected him because they saw him to be a burly, aggressive, overbearing man who deserved to get his comeuppance.

Kimbro, on the other hand, traveled widely, still hoping to find the speculator who would grubstake him for the big attack on the hidden field. He would go anywhere, consult with anyone, and offer almost any kind of inducement: 'Let me have the money, less than a year, ten-percent interest, and I'll give you one-thirty-second of my participation.' He offered one-sixteenth, even one-eighth, but found no takers.

When he returned to Larkin in April 1923, he was almost a defeated man, but because he was a born wildcatter he could not let anyone see his despair. Each morning when he was in town he repaired to the greasy café where the oilmen who had begun to infiltrate the area assembled to make their big boasts, and he knew it was essential that they see him at the height of his confidence: 'We expect to start Number Three any day now. Big investors from Tulsa, you know.' But each day that passed brought the partnership closer to collapse.

Now the serious gambling started, the reckless dealing away of percentages. One morning Floyd rushed to the café, took Dewey into the men's room, and almost wept: 'The drilling crew is hauling their rig back to Jacksboro.'

'We can't let them do that. Once they get off our land, we'll never get them back,' so the partners, smiling broadly as if they had concluded some big deal in the toilet, walked casually through the café, nodding to the oilmen, then dashed out to the rig.

Rusk had been right, the men were starting to dismantle it prior to mounting it on trucks, but when Dewey cried: 'Wait! We'll give you one-sixteenth of our seven-eighths,' they agreed to take the chance, for they, too, had seen the Strawn signs.

Later Rusk asked: 'Could we afford to give so much?' and Dewey explained the wildcatter's philosophy: 'If the well proves dry, who gives a damn what percentage they have? And if it comes in big, like I know it will, who cares if they have their share?'

A week before the termination of the leases the partners still had insufficient funds to drill their well, but now Kimbro heard from two of his A&M gamblers who wanted to get in on the action, but to get their money he had to give away one-eighth of his share to the first friend, one-sixteenth to the other – and the final ownership of the well became so fractionized that the partners could scarcely untangle the proportions.

Three days before the lease expired, scandal struck the operation, for the two A&M men, always a canny lot, heard the rumor that their old buddy Dewey Kimbro had pulled an oil-field sting on them, and they rode into town ready to tear him apart.

'He sold two hundred percent of his well. Peddled it all over East Texas.'

'What's that mean?' the Larkin men asked.

'Don't you see? If he drills dry, and he's already done so twice, he owes us nothing. He's collected twice, spends about one-quarter of the total, and goes off laughing with our dough.'

They drove out to the proposed drilling site at the tank to challenge Kimbro, but when they found him hiking back and forth over the rolling terrain, trying to settle upon the exact spot for his final well, they found him honestly engaged in trying to find oil. He had not sold two hundred percent of what he knew was going to be a dry well; he was gambling his entire resources upon one lucky strike, and as Texas gamblers, they were satisfied to be sharing in his risk.

Two days before the lapse of their leases, Rusk and Kimbro finally got a break. An Oklahoma wildcatting outfit had figured that if Dewey Kimbro, once of Humble and Gulf, thought there was oil in the Larkin area, it was a good location in which to take a flier. They had drilled a well just to the east of Rusk #1, gambling that the suspected oil lay in that direction and not toward the tank. These men, of course, could not know that Dewey had struck indications to the west, so down they went to five thousand feet, missing the field entirely and producing nothing but a very dry well, whose failure they announced on June 28.

This helped Kimbro in two ways: it verified his hunch that the field did not lie to the east of Rusk #1, and it so disheartened the Larkin landowners – three test holes, three buckets of dust – that they became determined to offload their worthless leases throughout the entire area. In a paroxysm of energy, Dewey shouted at Rusk and his two A&M buddies: 'Now's the time to pick up every damned lease in the district. My God, won't somebody lend me ten thousand dollars?' Faced by total disaster if his Rusk #3 did not come in, he spent two days committing his last penny to his belief that he would strike it rich this time. By dint of telegrams, telephone calls and the most ardent personal appeals to speculators in the Larkin-Jacksboro-Fort Griffin area, he put together a substantial kitty, which he spent on leases that encapsulated the field.

At six in the morning of 30 June 1923, Dewey Kimbro appeared at the oilmen's café with a smile so confident and casual that a stranger might think he was about to start a well with the full weight of Gulf Oil behind him, and when Floyd Rusk came in, sweating like a pig, Dewey caught him by the wrist and whispered: 'Dry your face,' for he, Dewey, had been in such perilous situations before; Rusk had not.

When they rode out to the field, with Dewey commenting on the brightness of this summer's day, Rusk v s vaguely aware that if Rusk #3 did strike oil, profits would be divided in this typically Texan way, the intricate details of which had been worked out by lawyers and filed in long legal documents: See table on page 1204.

On an August afternoon in 1923 a hanger-on who had watched the drilling of Rusk #3 as he would a baseball game, came riding back to Larkin in his Ford screaming: 'They got oil!'

Participants		Legal Division	Actual Split of all Income
Owner of mineral rights, standard lease	$\frac{1}{8}$	0.125000	0.125000
Rusk and Kimbro for their enterprise	$\frac{7}{8}$	0.87500	
		1.000000	
But Rusk and Kimbro split their $\frac{7}{8}$:			
Drilling team for staying on job	$\frac{1}{16}$	0.054688	0.054688
Rusk and Kimbro will share	$\frac{15}{16}$	0.820313	
		0.875001	
Rusk and Kimbro split their 0.820313:			
Rusk	$\frac{3}{4}$	0.615235	
Kimbro	$\frac{1}{4}$	0.205078	
		0.820313	
But Rusk must split his 0.615235:			
Emma Rusk	$\frac{1}{4}$	0.153809	0.153809
Floyd Rusk	$\frac{3}{4}$	0.461426	0.461426
		0.615235	
And Kimbro must split his 0.205078:			
A&M first investor	$\frac{1}{8}$	0.025635	0.025635
A&M second investor	$\frac{1}{16}$	0.012817	0.012817
Kimbro	$\frac{13}{16}$	0.166626	0.166626
		0.205078	1.000001

Thus, the second A&M investor was entitled to $\frac{7}{8} \times \frac{15}{16} \times \frac{1}{4} \times \frac{1}{16}$ of the whole, or $\frac{105}{8192}$ (.012817), which meant that every time the well produced $100,000, he received $1281.74 for as long as the well operated.

The citizens, hoping to see a great gusher sprouting from the plains, sped out to the tank, where, on its flank, hardened men were dancing and crying and slapping each other with oil-spattered hands. They did not have a gusher; the famous field at Larkin did not contain either the magnitude or the sub-terranean pressure to provide that kind of spectacular exhibition, but Dewey Kimbro, seeing the oil appear and making such guesses as he could on fragmentary evidence, said: 'Could be a hundred and ten barrels a day, for years to come.'

He was right. The Larkin Field, as it came to be known, was going to be a slow, steady producer. Spacious in extent but not very deep, it was the kind of field that would allow wells to be dug almost anywhere inside its limits with the sober assurance that at around three thousand feet in the Strawn sand a modest amount of oil would be forthcoming, year after year after year.

'And the glory of it is,' Kimbro told Rusk when they were back home at midnight, 'we know pretty well the definition of the field. Our first dry well to the east plus the dry Oklahoma wildcatter showed us where it ends in that direction. Our dry Number Two proved where it ends in the west. What we don't know is how far north and south.'

'Forever,' Rusk said, ' and by God, we control it all.' For one glorious moment these two men who had once wanted to kill each other danced in the darkened kitchen.

In the early fall of 1923, Larkin became the hottest boom town in Texas, with oilmen from all parts of America streaming in to try their luck at the far perimeters of the undefined field. To a stranger, the Larkin Field did not look like a typical oil site, because as soon as a well was dug, the towering pyramidal structure that meant oil to the layman was quickly moved to some other location for more drilling. The actual pumping of oil from deep below the surface was turned over to an unromantic donkey engine, a small, low-slung affair which could barely be seen from a distance. The donkey, powered by gasoline, worked its relatively short arm up and down incessantly, and from it poured the oil which was turning Larkin gamblers into millionaires.

Companies big and little rushed in their landmen to acquire leases, and wherever they turned they found themselves confronted by Floyd Rusk, who either owned the land, controlled the leases, or had power of attorney for handling the leases owned by his partner, Dewey Kimbro.

It was now that Rusk demonstrated both his devious managerial skill and his untamed voraciousness, for he saw quickly that he and Kimbro controlled far more land than they could ever drill. And if they didn't act quickly, they would lose certain of their short-term leases outright and then watch as other men's wells sucked out the oil from under their long-term ones. As if he had been in the business for generations, Rusk dealt out his leases to the major companies, scattering them so they would do his own holdings the most good, and using the money he obtained from them for the drilling of his own additional wells.

'A man could make a good livin',' he told Kimbro, 'just buyin' and sellin' leases and never drillin' an inch into the ground. Let some other dumb bastard do the hard work.'

Now a fundamental difference between the two partners surfaced. Kimbro loved oil itself, the endless search, even the heartbreaking failures, the lucky hit, the bringing of oil to the surface, while Rusk's interest blossomed only when the bubbling oil came into his actual possession. He reveled in the tricky deals, the exploitation, the pyramiding of the wealth that oil provided.

If left alone, Kimbro would have ranged over all of Texas, identifying new fields, bringing them to fruition, and then turning them over to the managerial care of Floyd Rusk; his only interest in the money which his wells produced was that it enabled him to search for others. However, under Rusk's canny leadership, Kimbro was kept close to the Larkin Field, which the partners manipulated as if it were some giant poker game, and more than one major company entered into its files a recommendation that Floyd Rusk be either shot or placed on the board of directors: 'That son-of-a-bitch knows oil.'

They were only partly right, for if Rusk quickly mastered the intricacies of dealing in leases, he never could visualize the lake of oil which lay hidden under his ranch and under the leases he controlled. Kimbro was powerless to explain that an oil field was one of the most delicately balanced marvels of nature: 'Floyd, goddamnit, our field has a limited life. The pressure which delivers the oil to us must be maintained.'

Kimbro drew maps of the underground reservoir, showing Floyd how the entrapment by rocks kept the lake of oil in position, and how water and gas provided the pressure which enabled the drillers to bring it to the surface: 'Destroy that pressure, or dissipate it, and you can lose your field.'

He astounded Rusk by predicting that if wells continued to be dug so promiscuously at Larkin, the pressure would be drawn off at so many random sites that only about ten percent of the oil locked underground would ever be recovered, and when Rusk did finally understand this, it had exactly the opposite result from what Kimbro had intended.

'By God, if it's limited, let's get ours now.'

So he dug numerous wells on his own property, producing vastly more raw petroleum than could be marketed, and on his better leases he encouraged everyone else to do the same, until Larkin fairly groaned with oil. When all the fuel lines were jammed and the open earthen pits were rotting with the dark stuff, whose volatile oils were thus dissipated, he watched as the price dropped from a dollar a barrel to the appalling figure of ten cents, and even then he could not comprehend the need for more disciplined measures. Like a true Texan he bellowed: 'We don't want no government interference. We found this field. We developed it, and by God, we'll work it our way.'

His wasteful procedure was not preposterous, so far as he was concerned, because he had varied ways to multiply his wealth. He owned thirty-three wells outright; he shared a seventy-five-percent interest in nineteen others; and he received huge yearly rentals for leases which the big companies held on the acreage he could not himself develop. By the close of that first year he was a millionaire four times over, with every prospect of doubling and then redoubling and then quadrupling.

His tremendous good luck had little effect upon him personally, for he rarely spent money on himself beyond the sheerest necessities. He still moved his huge bulk about the oil fields in a Ford truck; he wore the same rancher's oufit, the same battered Stetson, the same cheapest-line General Quimper boots. At the morning breakfasts in the café, which now had thirty tables filled with oilmen, he never picked up the checks at his corner unless he had specifically invited someone to eat with him, which he did infrequently. He gave no money to the Baptist church, none to the school, none to the hospital. In fact, he attended only spasmodically to his income and would have been unable to tell anyone how much he had accumulated.

He did buy three good bulls, for in Texas, oil and ranching enjoyed a symbiotic relationship which no Northern oilman ever understood. If you took a thousand Texas oil wells, you could be sure that nine hundred were drilled so that some dreaming man without a dime could buy himself a ranch, for it was said in the business: 'Ain't nothin' makes a steer grow better than good pasturage, a pinch of phosphorus in the soil, and freedom to scratch hisself on an oil derrick.'

With his first big check from Gulf for his leases, he purchased an additional five thousand acres for his ranch, and with his second check, he drove north to meet with Paul Yeager: 'I think my father made a mistake promisin' you this land, and I made a bigger mistake transferrin' it to you legal. Paul, I want to buy it back. Name your price.'

'I'm not selling.'

'Paul, you got no mineral rights. You got no leasin' rights. To you this is just so much rock and grama grass. You'll never do anything with it. I need it.'

'I told you, it's not for sale.'

You know, we're goin' to put six, seven more wells on your place.'

'I don't think you are.'

'Now, Paul! Law's the law. Name your price – sixty dollars an acre? Eighty dollars?'

Rusk was unable to swing a deal, and some days after he had sent his men up to the tank to start a new well on the Yeager land, they came roaring back with a horrendous story: 'Like you ordered, we was headed for the north end of the Yeager lease, but he met us at the gate with a shotgun. We said "We got legal right" and he said "No more laws. You come on my land, I shoot." So we drove right in, as you said to do, and by God, he shot.'

'Kill anybody?'

'Elmer's hurt bad. Doctor's tendin' him.'

In gargantuan fury Floyd Rusk rampaged around town looking for the sheriff, and after he found him, a posse drove north to handle Paul Yeager. They found him standing at the gate to his ranch, shotgun still in hand.

'Don't come in here!' he warned.

'Paul, the law says—'

'Stand back, Fat Belly. No more of your trucks on my land.'

'Yeager!' the sheriff shouted. 'Put down that gun and—'

Yeager fired, not at the sheriff but at Rusk, who with extraordinary nimbleness dropped to the ground, whipped out his Colts, and drilled his brother-in-law through the head.

There were seventeen witnesses, of course, to testify that Paul Yeager had aimed a shotgun at the sheriff and had nearly killed Floyd Rusk, who had fired back in self-defense. No trial was ever held, and after the burial Rusk asked the sheriff to ride out to the Yeager ranch and offer Mrs Yeager a good price for her lands without saying who the bidder was. Before the month was out, Rusk had regained the land his father should never have given away, and the Rusk rigs were free to move about it as they wished.

If Floyd Rusk was little moved by his sudden wealth, this was not the case with Molly, for when that first check from Gulf Oil proved that prosperity was real, she went to Ed Boatright at the Chevy garage, rented a car and a driver, and posted in to Neiman-Marcus in Dallas. There she went to the most expensive salon in the store and announced, in a loud voice, that she wanted the head saleslady and a very large wastebasket.

When she was shown into a discreet area where only the best clothing was sold – fabrics from England, styling from France – she started undressing, throwing each of her old and long-worn garments into the wastebasket, and when it was filled with every item except her panties, she announced: 'I want them burned.'

'We'll take them to the basement.'

'I want them burned here. I never want to see those damned rags again.'

'But madam—'

'Don't madam me, burn them.'

The manager was called, but since Molly was nearly naked, he could not speak with her directly; he did, however, give strict orders that there would be no burning of anything on that floor, but Molly was so vociferous that he asked: 'Who is this crazy dame?' and Molly heard the saleswoman explain: 'She's the wife of that fellow who hit the big oil field at Larkin,' and the manager said: 'Burn them.'

Firemen were alerted, but before they could appear, Molly was covered with an expensive lounging robe, of which she said: 'I'll take it.' And so draped, she watched as men with fire extinguishers supervised the burning of her old wardrobe. When the fire went out, and her applause died down, she proceeded to spend $5,600 on replacements and left an order for $3,800 worth of other items to be sent to Larkin as soon as they arrived from New York and London.

She sent Ed Boatright's driver home alone, carrying in the back of his Chevy many of her purchases. For herself she bought a large new Packard from a Dallas dealer recommended by Neiman-Marcus and hired one of the firm's drivers to chauffeur her back to Larkin.

In four months the population of Larkin jumped from 2,329 to more than 19,700, and this resulted in revolutionary change. Take housing, for example. The little town obviously could not accommodate such a tremendous influx in existing structures, so extraordinary solutions had to be sought, and old-time residents gaped when they saw a convoy of sixty mules on the road from Jacksboro, each four hauling on a farm flatbed a house lifted from its foundations farther east. Tents were at a premium, and any householder with a spare room could rent it at three dollars a day to each of four occupants. Many beds were used three times a day, in eight-hour shifts, and food was grabbed wherever it was provided and in whatever condition.

Every businessman saw his turnover quadrupled within the month, and by the end of the year, men who sold what the oil crews needed found themselves enormously wealthy. The Tumlinson twins maintained six trucks to haul in the long lengths of lumber required for building derricks and the associated small buildings at a site. They also imported huge supplies of coal for the winter months and almost any hardware they could find in places like Fort Worth and Dallas. One twin said: 'All we are, really, is a turnover point. We rarely keep anything past the weekend.'

And Ed Boatright sold absolutely any car he could get his hands on and employed six new mechanics to keep the cars he had sold running: 'The roads to an oil field are murder on cars, but my men are geniuses.'

The sudden inflow of money altered many things, because it was the very type of man who had played a major role in the reactionary Ku Klux Klan who found himself in position to make the most profit from the exploding trade, and one-time leaders like the Tumlinson twins and Boatright became so preoccupied with their expanding businesses that they no longer had time to monitor community morals. An older man who had taken the Klan quite seriously tried to summon his cohorts back to the continuing task of policing, but some of the younger men told him: 'Let's get this oil thing settled ... the buildings we need and everything ... and then we'll take care of the riffraff that's wandered in.' The Klan did not intend closing shop; its impulses were too deep and strong for that, but it did propose to make a dollar while the chance existed.

Some activities of the boom did eventually occasion real soul-searching on the part of Larkin citizens, whether they were members of the Klan or not. The woman Nora, whom the Klan had once punished, now ran a house which contained eleven young women who had flocked in from as far away as Denver, and no one could ignore what business the young ladies were conducting. The founder of the town's good fortune, Dewey Kimbro, still lived in the house with his girl Esther, but he had to be indulged because he was now well on his way to becoming a millionaire, and that excused a lot.

As a matter of fact, the former puritans would have been happy if the seamier side of their town had been as quietly run as Nora's place, but Larkin received a black eye when a reporter for *The New York Times* came to town to verify the rumor that 'Larkin was the most sinful little town in America.' He probed about for nine or ten days, picking up the usual colorful stories about 'a saloon called The Bucket of Blood, and a gambling hall named The Missionary's Downfall,' but such accounts could have applied to almost any oil-boom town or any temporary railhead in the West. What made this man's story provocative was his detailed account of how the town fathers were profiting from the boom:

Each Sunday morning, just after dawn, the sheriff and his enthusiastic men prowl the dives and the haunts, arresting any ladies of the night found therein and carting them off to jail in the Ford paddy wagon belonging to the police. This happens in any frontier town and is not remarkable.

What is remarkable is that on Monday morning these ladies, some of them extremely beautiful, are lined up on a public balcony of the fine red-and-white courthouse in the public square, and while the oilmen and the young fellows of town gather enthusiastically below, a judge of some kind steps onto the balcony, lifts the left arm of one of the young women, and announces the amount of her fine.

The men below then bid vigorously for the right to pay her fine, but the first bid must be the fine itself. Thus, if Mary Belle has been fined three dollars, the bidding must start there, but it can rise as high as the young woman's charms justify, and calls from all parts make the bidding quite exciting.

When a winner has been determined, he pays the amount bid and then receives all rights to the young lady for the next twenty-four hours. On Tuesday through Saturday, of course, she works at her regular stand, but on Sunday she will be arrested and on Monday the auction will resume.

When this reporter asked a Larkin official how such behavior could be justified, he explained: 'We have to pay for the extra police somehow.'

When this story reached New York, the editors of the *Times* felt, with some justice, that here was a case where the legend of the paper ought to be respected – 'All the News That's Fit to Print' – and they decided that such a yarn, with its many implications, would have to be excluded if the legend were to be honored. They killed the story, which so angered the young reporter that he gave it lock-stock-and-barrel to a reporter from Chicago, whose paper not only refrained from censoring it, but telegraphed for pictures. A professional photographer took a series of graphic shots and provided a caption explaining that the rowdy ladies had on this Monday morning fetched an average price of $9.80, which figured to be $6.80 above their basic fines.

Such affairs were amusing, but another aspect of the boom was more ominous. Any town which found itself the center of an oil strike, and especially one which expanded horizons with each new well that struck oil, was bound to attract the really criminal elements of society, and as the winter of 1924 started,

Larkin had a plethora of gamblers, holdup men, con artists, thieves, escaped murderers, and every other kind of human refuse imaginable.

'This town is becoming ungovernable,' Floyd Rusk cried one January morning when two corpses were found in an alley near the courthouse, but when he spoke he did not yet know who one of the dead men was.

'My God, Floyd! It's Lew Tumlinson!'

It was. There was no record of his having been involved with any of the hoodlums, and he was not robbed. True, he was some distance from his coal and lumber business, but he was in a respectable part of town and no one recalled his having been mixed up with any of the imported girls. His death was a mystery, but was soon forgotten.

The shootings in Larkin produced an average of one murder every two and a half weeks, by no means a record for an oil town. Usually the deaths occurred as a result of gambling or fighting over women; there was almost no murder for profit, as in the old days when Rattlesnake Peavine prowled these parts. Opined the editor of the *Defender:* 'It is understandable that men who have been too long restrained in less adventurous occupations will find release for their spirits in an oil town.'

But then Ed Boatright was found shot dead, and people began to ask: 'Is the lawlessness going to attack all of us? Have things gotten out of hand?' Some of the old Ku Kluxers felt that maybe they would have to reconstitute the vigilantes and bring the town back under control. Affairs drifted along in this way, with a gambler or a roughneck being shot now and then, until one day in early March when the town echoed with gunfire and the other Tumlinson twin was found dead.

Now terror gripped the area, and men working in oil began employing armed guards. Chief among those frightened by the spate of killings was Floyd Rusk, who, because of his preeminence and his new fortune, would seem to be an attractive target, and when associates suggested that he hire himself a bodyguard, he listened. But one night as he sat alone in his kitchen – he did not yet have an office – contemplating the dismal condition into which his oil town had fallen, a terrible thought attacked him: My God! Boatright! The Tumlinsons! They were with me when we whipped Dewey Kimbro.

He began to sweat. Desperately he tried to recall anything that Dewey had said either during the flogging or next day when they made their pact about the oil field: I'm sure he didn't speak during the flogging. Nothing. He deserved it and he knew it. But then his assurance left him, for he could remember bits of the conversation in the kitchen that next remarkable morning. He knew I hadn't touched him. He said so. Yes, he did say that, I remember clearly. Taking hope from the fact that he had not actually whipped his future partner, he was beginning to breathe more easily, when an appalling recollection gagged him: My God, I'm sure he mentioned the names of the other three. I can hear him now: 'But you ordered the Tumlinson twins and Ed Boatright . . . '

Jesus! He discovered all our names and he's killed three of us. As soon as he thought this, he corrected himself, eagerly, nervously: Not *us*. I had no part in that affair. I never touched him. He's killed the three who did. Then he rose and paddled about the kitchen, a huge, sweating man: He's my partner. We bought leases together, surely . . .

He fell back onto his chair and stared bleakly at the wall. Three dead and one to go. Deceiving himself no longer, he reflected on the cleverness of this wiry little man with the sandy red hair: He waited till the town was filled with drifters. He waits till there's action in the streets. Remember the little pistol he had that morning when we talked? God, the man's a determined killer.

Taking a pen from the fruit jar in which he and Molly had always kept one, he drafted a letter to the Governor of Texas, whose campaign he had supported:

> The town of Larkin, in Larkin county, is no longer governable. Please send militia.
>
> FLOYD RUSK

He came into town on a horse, as his grandfather had done in 1883. Like him, he announced himself to no one, sharing a bed with the oilmen and quietly patronizing the saloons and the gambling halls. He visited the cribs in which the prostitutes lived their rowdy lives and studied the bank which had already been held up once. He walked out to the cemetery and checked the rude tombstones for any names which tallied with his printed list of desperadoes to be apprehended on sight, and at the end of five careful days, during which he alerted no one as to his identity, he gained a clear impression of how the town of Larkin functioned.

He was twenty-five years old, about five-seven, not much over a hundred and fifty pounds, and he had the blue eyes so common among both the lawless and the lawmen on the frontier. He was quick with a gun and more prone to use it than his grandfather had been, and like him, he was fearless. He did not consider it unusual to be dispatched alone to clean up a rioting boom town, for that was his business, and on the sixth day he began.

Presenting himself unostentatiously at the café where the oilmen met with town leaders at six each morning, he banged a glass with a spoon to attract attention, and announced: 'I'm Oscar Macnab, Texas Ranger, sent by the governor to bring order to this town.' Before anyone could respond he moved like a cat, gun drawn, and arrested three men well known to be dealing in stolen oil gear. Rounding them up in a corner, he turned them over to the frightened sheriff, with the warning: 'When I get to your place I want to see these men in jail.'

Deputizing three well-regarded citizens, which he had no legal right to do, he asked: 'Are you armed?' and when one said no, an extraordinary admission in Larkin, he asked for the loan of a gun, and with his aides he left the café and started through the town.

Fortunately, most of the desperate characters, the worst troublemakers, were in bed at that hour, so he had little trouble finding them, and in nightshirts or trousers hastily climbed into, the gamblers, the thieves and the pimps were moved to the courthouse, in whose basement he crowded some three dozen malefactors. This was not a jail, but it was reasonably secure, and he posted at the door two men with shotguns, giving them orders that chilled the captives: 'If anybody tries to escape, don't hesitate. Fire into the mob.'

He then went to the sheriff's office and demanded that he summon the town's policemen, and when representatives of these two agencies stood before him and his new deputies, he asked scornfully: 'Why have you let this town run so wild?' and they said truthfully: 'Because everybody wanted it that way.'

Oscar Macnab, despite his youth and his bravado, was no fool, and after pumping some self-respect into the local officers he went to the telegraph station and wired Rangers headquarters, asking for a famous lawman who had faced similar situations in the boom towns back east: NEED HELP SEND LONE WOLF. Then he quietly proceeded to consolidate his position before the rabble discovered that he was alone.

He went to the home of Floyd Rusk and sat with him in the kitchen, no gun visible, no scowl on his face: 'I understand it was you who wrote the governor. Tell me about it.'

Rusk was more than eager to; in fact, he blurted out such a lava-flow of information and complaint that Macnab had frequently to direct it: 'But you *were* among the men who flogged Dewey Kimbro that night?'

Later he asked: 'Let me be sure I understand. Dewey Kimbro is now your partner? And as a partner you like him just fine?'

Finally he bore in: 'Have you any possible clue, any proof at all that Kimbro shot your three companions?'

'They were never companions of mine, Ranger Macnab. They just happened to be assigned that job by the Klan.'

'You were, I'm told, the leader of the Klan?' He did not accuse Rusk of this; he merely asked the question, which Floyd rebutted vehemently: 'I was never the Kleagle. We didn't have one, really.'

'But you made the decisions?' Again it was a question, not an accusation, and again Rusk denied that he had held any position of leadership: 'I was just another member.'

'I believe you. Speaking as just another member, why did your group decide to horsewhip Dewey Kimbro?'

'Well now, he was behavin' immorally. He was livin' with this woman . . . You've met her, Esther, and we told him he had to quit that or get out of town.'

'You didn't tell him. You flogged him.'

'But we had warned him. We warned everybody. We would not tolerate immoral livin'.'

Macnab smiled as much as he ever smiled: 'You seem to tolerate a good deal of it right now. All those women, those cribs.'

'Times have changed, Ranger Macnab.'

Just how much they had changed, Macnab was still to learn, because he had not yet been in Larkin on a Monday morning to see the auction of the whores, and when the legal officials who had not yet adjusted to his presence proceeded with the Monday bidding, Macnab did not interrupt. He stood in the background, appalled by what he saw, and decided to take no further steps until help arrived.

It came in the presence of a legendary member of the Texas Rangers, Lone Wolf Gonzaullas, an extremely handsome man in his thirties noted for his meticulous dress and Deep South courtesy. His greater fame, however, derived from his ever-ready willingness to use the pearl-handled revolvers given him by citizens who had profited from the law and order he had brought to their ravaged towns, and from the fact that he would be the only Ranger captain of partly Spanish descent.

Like Oscar, he came into Larkin on a horse, and like Otto, he did not announce himself to anyone but his fellow Ranger. When he had studied the situation, checking the jail and the cellar of the courthouse, he told Oscar: 'You've handled this right so far, but now we need something that will attract their attention.'

'What did you have in mind?' Macnab asked, and he said: 'I've had good luck in spots like this with a snortin' pole.'

'What's that?'

'Find me two shovels,' and when he had them, he and Oscar rode to the edge of town, where they dug a deep hole, lining it with rocks. Then the two Rangers mounted their horses and dragged in a twelve-foot telephone pole, which they placed in the hole, tamping it with more rocks.

Then, in a series of lightning-swift moves, the two Rangers stormed into one saloon after another and into all the gambling areas, grabbing unlovely characters at random, dragging them out to the edge of town and handcuffing them to chains circling the pole. 'Now snort,' Gonzaullas said, 'while the decent people of this town laugh at you.'

While he stood guard, Macnab hurried to the basement of the courthouse, where he brought forth his original three dozen prisoners. Marching them with his revolvers drawn, he drove them to the snortin' pole, where Gonzaullas bound them to the chains.

When the pole was surrounded by milling outlaws, he issued his orders: 'Think things over till four this afternoon. Then we'll reach decisions.'

As they sweated in the blazing sun, one of the men who had been drinking beer whimpered: 'I have to go to the toilet,' and Lone Wolf said: 'No one's stopping you,' and it was this humiliation which broke the spirit of these culprits.

At four, Gonzaullas revealed his plan: 'If you men are out of town by sunset, no further trouble. If you're in town after dark, beware. Ranger Macnab, start releasing them.' And as the handcuffs were unlocked and the ropes loosened, the prisoners started making plans to flee.

When the field was fairly well cleared, Lone Wolf addressed the citizens: 'People of Larkin, it's all over.' Turning on his heel, pearl-handled revolvers riding on his hips, he went to his horse, signaled Macnab, and rode back to town, where he wanted to meet with Floyd Rusk.

When the two Rangers sat in Floyd's kitchen with him, reviewing the case against Dewey Kimbro, Gonzaullas did the questioning: 'In the period when the Tumlinson twins and Boatright were murdered, how many other men were shot in this town?'

'About nine.'

'What makes you think their case was something special?'

'The others were drifters . . . no-goods.'

This impressed Gonzaullas, and he spent two days interrogating townspeople, especially Nora and Esther, whom he met together: 'You say, Nora, that you and Jake were tarred and feathered and later he was shot?'

'Yes.'

'Do you know who did it?'

'I can guess.'

'And you, Miss Esther, you saw your man Kimbro horse-whipped? Did you know who did it?'

'I heard names.'

'What names?'

'Lew Tumlinsion.'

'Who else?'

'His brother Les.'

'Anybody else?'

'Ed Boatright.'

'And all three are dead?'

'They deserved to be.'

'Did Kimbro know those names?'

'He told me to remember them. After they let him go.' She hesitated, suspecting that she was doing her man no good by these admissions: 'He was all cut up, you know. His back . . .'

'Do you think he shot those three men? Getting even?'

'I'm glad somebody did. They came back, you know, and threatened to whip me, too, if I stayed around.'

'Why did you stay?'

'Dewey made a deal with Mr Rusk. Me stayin' was part of the deal, Dewey said.'

'But if Dewey, as you call him, if he's Mr Rusk's partner, he must've made a lot of money. Why does he still live in a house like this? Why do you live here?'

'We live simple.'

It was clear to Gonzaullas and Macnab that Dewey Kimbro had probably shot his three assailants, but there could never be any proof, so one morning when the town was pretty well subdued, and permanently, Lone Wolf suggested to Macnab: 'I think we better deal with the principals,' and they summoned Kimbro to Rusk's kitchen.

In ice-cold terms they spelled out the situation, with Macnab doing the talking, since although Gonzaullas was eight years senior, he was the man officially in charge: 'Rusk, you led the posse that night on your partner Kimbro. Kimbro, we know that you learned the names of the men who flogged you, and we have very solid reasons to suspect that you shot those men, one by one, in revenge. But we can't prove it.

'We know something else. If you, Kimbro, have killed three men, so have you, Mr Rusk, two in Dodge City and Paul Yeager at his ranch gate. And Ranger Gonzaullas and I have had to kill men in our day, in line of duty. So all of us in this room are equal, in a manner of speaking. Ranger Gonzaullas, will you tell them what we recommend?'

'It's simple. The flogging happened a long time ago. If you forget it, we'll forget it. You've been partners for some time now, good partners we're told, reliable. Now, Mr Rusk, you told us that you were afraid you were going to be shot, by Mr Kimbro, of course, although you didn't say so in your letter to the governor. I have a surprise for you, Mr Rusk. Did you know that Mr Kimbro told us he was afraid *you* were going to shoot *him*? To get his share of the partnership, the way you got Yeager's land? And we think he had good reason to be afraid.'

Rusk looked at his partner in dismay: 'Dewey, my God, I'd never shoot you.'

'So here it is,' Lone Wolf said, hands on the table. 'You two are partners, for better or worse, like they say at the wedding. Make the best of it, because when we leave, if we hear that either of you has been shot, we're comin' back to swear out a warrant for the survivor.'

'No court in the land—' Rusk began, but Gonzaullas cut him short: 'Tell him, Macnab.'

'It won't go to court. Because you will be shot, by him or me, resisting arrest.'

In this rough-and-ready way the oil town of Larkin, after eighteen months of flaming hell, was cleaned up. It was a Texas solution to a Texas problem, and it worked.

The little town of Larkin, population reduced to a sane 3,673, now boasted seven millionaires: the richest was Floyd Rusk, whose fortune from his main wells and leases was becoming immense; he was followed by his partner, Dewey Kimbro, who shared in some of Rusk's wells and owned others outright. The Larkin Field was proving out as shrewd Kimbro had predicted, a large, shallow field with an apparently unlimited supply of oil that seemed to dribble out of the ground, not gush. No single well now producing much over a hundred barrels a day, but 100 barrels × 365 days × 40 wells meant a lot of oil.

Some of the new millionaires spent their money conspicuously, and Dewey often spoke of one who had never fully appreciated the intricacies of the oil game: 'When I went to talk him into leasing us his land, I offered him the standard one-eighth royalty, but he said: 'I know you city slickers. I want one-tenth," so after considerable pressure I surrendered. Some time later he came to me, all infuriated: "You dirty scoundrel, you cheated me." I said: "Hold on a minute. You set the royalty, not me," and he said: "I know that. But Gulf offered me one-twelfth." '

Rusk and Kimbro built no big houses and bought no extra cars, but they did almost desperately long for some way to express their wealth, and it was in this uneasy mood that they discovered football; not Texas A&M football or University of Texas football, but Larkin High School football, and in those years, once an oilman or a well-to-do rancher became alerted to the grandeur of Texas high school football, he was lost, for he developed a mania which lasted forever, growing each year more obsessive.

It started because such men worked hard all week – Dewey Kimbro never ceased looking for oil – and longed for some vigorous relaxation on the weekends. There was hunting, and fishing, and breeding cattle and breaking horses, but in time these palled, and it was then that these men plunged into the Friday afternoon madness.

In those days Texas had no worthy professional football teams, or basketball, either, and good baseball teams played far to the north in St Louis. Even the universities were far to the east, but there was always the local high school football team, and in time its partisans became as madly concerned with its fortunes as men elsewhere became involved emotionally with the New York Yankees or the Detroit Tigers. Competing area teams, like Wichita Falls, Jacksboro, Abilene and Brecken-ridge, became monsters who had to be subdued, by fair means or foul, and the glorious days of autumn in Texas became heroic.

The mania started casually, with Rusk and Kimbro attending a Friday game in which Larkin's small high school was playing Jacksboro, which had a slightly larger student body. It was a good game, nothing special, with scattered scoring in the first half and Larkin holding on to a 19–14 lead as the game drew to a close. Jacksboro had the ball and it looked as if they might score, for they had mounted a determined drive down the field, but as the seconds ticked away, both Rusk and Kimbro started shouting: 'Hold that line! Get them!' and the roar of the little hometown crowd must have taken effect, for the Larkin men – average age sixteen – did muster courage from somewhere and they did hold.

It was fourth down and nine, twenty seconds to go, with the

crowd roaring encouragement, when the Jacksboro coach signaled his captain to call for time-out. Always alert in such situations, Rusk noticed that the coach was wigwagging frantically from the lines, and he whispered to Kimbro: 'I don't like this. Something's up.'

It was a play which would be discussed for years on the oil fields, because just before the whistle blew to resume, Jacksboro made a last-second substitution. A tall end was taken out of the game, and a much shorter boy was inserted, a fact which caused Rusk to tell Kimbro: 'Now that's crazy. They have to pass. You'd think they'd keep the tall fellow in there.'

However, the tall end did not quite come off the field. With the attention of the Larkin team and most of the spectators focused on the kneeling linemen as they prepared for the last play, Rusk saw to his horror that the tall end had not left the field. He had run purposefully to the sidelines but had stopped one foot from the chalk, remaining legally in bounds. At that moment, on the far side, another player calmly stepped off the field, leaving the required eleven players eligible for the final play.

Rusk was one of few who saw the evil thing the Jacksboro coach was doing, and he began punching his seatmate in the arm and screaming 'Pick him up,' and Dewey bellowed: 'Hey, he's eligible!' But no one could hear the two oilmen, and when the ball was snapped, the Jacksboro quarterback coolly dropped back and lifted the ball easily across the field to his tall end, who caught it and ran untouched into the end zone: final score, Jacksboro 20, Larkin 19.

Rusk and Kimbro went berserk. Roaring out of the stands, they shouted that someone ought to shoot any sumbitch who would pull such a trick. They wanted the referee banned for life. And they shouted loudly that never again should a team from Jacksboro be allowed on that field. When Kimbro finally cooled Rusk down they sought some other oil-men, with the proposition: 'Let's waylay their bus before it gets out of town and give that coach a thrashing.' and they went in search of it, but the Jacksboro team, fearing just such action, had scuttled out before sunset.

In the angered days that followed, Rusk gave orders that no employee of his should ever purchase anything, no matter how small, from any outfit in Jacksboro, and when he was forced to go there on business, he spat on the sidewalks when no one was looking.

Of course, when Wichita Falls came down and administered a 31–7 drubbing, he gave the same orders about that infamous town, charging it with having brought in ringers who had never set foot in a Wichita Falls classroom, and Kimbro joined him in condemnation. In their new-found hatred for Jacksboro and Wichita Falls, the two former adversaries buried their suspicions of each other.

It was Dewey who had the bright idea: 'Floyd, if Wichita Falls hired outsiders, why can't we?' Assembling the Larkin millionaires, they proposed that 'we do something to restore the honor of this town.' and Rusk threw himself into this project with all the energy he had once given to the Ku Klux Klan. He and his men gave the coach, a mild-mannered fellow, a hundred dollars a month in cash to spend as he deemed best. Rusk himself built a dressing room at the edge of the field so that, as he was fond of saying, 'Larkin can go first class.' The oilmen scouted the region for big, tough boys and moved their families into Larkin so that the lads could play on the local team, and when the next autumn came around, it was obvious that Larkin High had a fighting chance to become a football power.

One morning, when Rusk delivered his mother's royalty check to her – more money than she and Earnshaw had spent in a dozen years – he found her playing with his son Ransom, a big-boned child, and he cried impulsively: 'Damn, I wish he was old enough to play for Larkin!' Catching the boy and throwing him high in the air, he caught him and started running through the room like a halfback. Dropping the child back in his crib, he shook his finger at him: 'Son, you're gonna see real greatness in this town. And maybe you'll even be on the team yourself, some day.'

He then turned his attention to the serious problem of finding an appropriate name for what he now called 'my team,' and he found that the desirable names had been preempted: Lions, Tigers, Bears, Bearcats, Panthers, Pirates, Rebels, Gunslingers, Hawks. Any animal whose behavior was terrifying had been used, any role requiring violent or even murderous deportment had been adopted by some small school in the area. One town famous for its hunting called its team the Turkeys, an unfortunate name, but Larkin did little better. By a process of painful elimination it came up with the name of the beast once common in those parts, the antelope, and when this was reluctantly adopted, a more difficult problem arose, because every Texas team had to be the Fighting This or That: the Fighting Tigers, the Fighting Buffalo, the Fighting Wildcats. So it had to be the Fighting Antelopes, even though, as Rusk said: 'There's no man in Texas ever saw an antelope fight anything.'

Under their new leadership, and with a level of support from the oilmen that they had never known before, Larkin's Fighting Antelopes had an autumn of glory, up to a point. The team played nine regular games, and won them all. As Rusk boasted at the morning breakfasts in the café: 'We really crucified Jacksboro, thirty-seven to six.' They manhandled Brecken-ridge, too, 41–3, and they even took much bigger Wichita Falls to the cleaners, 24–7. When they won the regional champion-ship in a tight game against Abilene, 9–7, it became clear to Rusk and his associates that 'our team can go all the way,' and the heady prospect of state championship began to be discussed seriously.

'By God, if we can win our next game,' Rusk bellowed in the café, 'we'll get a crack at Waco,' but his enthusiasm for such a game distressed the coach of the Fighting Antelopes, for he knew the facts, which he tried to explain to Rusk and Kimbro: 'We've played some good teams, yes. But Waco, they're much different.'

'Are you chicken?' Rusk demanded, and the coach surprised him by saying: 'Yes. Our little team would have no chance against Waco.'

'You oughta be fired!' Rusk bellowed. 'What kind of talk is this, welshing on your own team?'

'Mr Rusk, Waco is coached by Paul Tyson. Does that mean anything?'

'He puts his pants on one leg at a time, don't he?'

'Yes, but when he gets them on, he's something special.' Almost in awe the coach recited the fearsome accomplish-ments of that Waco powerhouse: 'One year the Waco Tigers scored a total of seven hundred eighty-four points;

opponents had thirty-three.'

'Who did they play?' Rusk asked. 'The Sisters of Mercy?'

'The best. Of course, there was one game with the Corsicana Orphans Home, one hundred nineteen to nothing.'

'Did the Orphans have eleven men?'

'Only thirteen, but they were a real team.'

'No real team loses by a hundred points.'

'Against Waco they do,' the worried coach said, and he continued: 'They brought down a team from Cleveland, Ohio. National championship. Waco, forty-four, Cleveland, twelve. And in their best year, Waco, five hundred sixty-seven, opponents, zero, with no opposing team ever moving the ball inside the Waco thirty-five-yard line. And you ask me if I'm scared.'

But Rusk and his optimistic oilmen were not, and when the Fighting Antelopes won their thirteenth straight game – for high schools played barbarous schedules – the big showdown with Waco for the state championship became inevitable. Most of Larkin and all of Waco found ways to get to Panther Park in Fort Worth that memorable Saturday afternoon. For a mere high school game, more than twenty thousand showed up; the newspapers had skillfully promulgated the myth that in this age of miracles, Antelopes had an outside chance of defeating Tigers.

It was a day Floyd Rusk would never forget; it eclipsed in significance even that wonderful morning when Rusk # 3 came in with its verification of the Larkin Field, because this game would be remembered as one of the extraordinary events in the annals of Texas sporting history, but not in a way that Rusk would have wished: Waco Tigers 83, Larkin Antelopes 0.

Before the excursion train left Fort Worth, copies of a Dallas newspaper with mocking headlines were available: IT REALLY WAS TIGERS EATING ANTELOPES, and during the train ride home, Rusk took an oath. Brandishing the offensive paper in the faces of his friends, he swore: 'This will never happen again. If we have to chew mountains into sand, it will never happen again.'

Assembling any oilmen who had gone to the game, he extracted promises that Larkin would regain its honor, regardless of cost, and Dewey Kimbro supported him: 'Whatever you need, Floyd. The dignity of our town must be restored.'

Prowling the train to locate the unfortunate coach whose prophecy of Waco invincibility had proved correct, the fat man snarled: 'You're fired. No team of mine loses by more than eighty points. Tomorrow we start searching for a real coach.'

Revenge for the dreadful humiliation in Panther Park became Rusk's obsession, and as he roamed the state looking for what he called 'my kind of coach,' he kept hearing of a man in a small school near Austin, and men who knew football assured him: 'This here Cotton Hamey, he's a no-nonsense coach, knocks a kid on his as if he don't perform,' so Rusk telegraphed three of his oilmen to come down from Larkin to look the young genius over.

As soon as the committee met Hamey they knew they had their man. He had gone to A&M to learn animal husbandry, but had been so good at football that he switched to coaching, with the not unreasonable hope that one day he might return to his alma mater in some capacity or other, line coach perhaps, or even head coach, for he had the intelligence to handle either job.

They met a man who stood only five feet eight but who was still a crop-headed bundle of muscle and aggression. In college he had been such a relentless opponent that sportswriters had started a legend, which still clung to him: 'At the training table they feed him only raw meat, two pounds with lots of gristle at each sitting.' Nicknamed Tiger, he told one sportswriter: 'I like to play in the other team's backfield,' and this imaginative reporter produced a great line: 'Tiger Hamey invades the opposition backfield, grabs three running backs, and sorts them out till he finds who has the ball.'

The oilmen got right down to cases: 'Did you see the state championship?' and Hamey said: 'That's my job,' and Rusk asked: 'What did you think?' and Hamey said: 'Your team had no right being on that field.'

'If you had unlimited power, and I mean unlimited, could you build us a championship team for next December?'

Hamey rose and walked about the meeting room, flexing his muscles. He was an attractive young man, quick in his movements, intelligent in his responses to questions, and compact both physically and mentally. He wasted little time on nonessentials: 'I can get you into the play-offs, and Waco is losing many of its best players. But I don't think I could beat

Paul Tyson next year.'

'Could you beat him year after next?' Rusk asked, and Hamey said: 'You get me the horses, I'll get you the championship.'

'You're hired,' Rusk said. He had no authority to hire or fire anyone, for that was the prerogative of the school board, but when a Texas town set its heart on a state fooball championship, everything else had to give, and when the oilmen returned to Larkin the board quickly confirmed the appointment of Cotton Hamey as teacher of Texas history. On the side he would also do some coaching.

Now it became the responsibility of the wealthy oilmen to provide the horses, and as soon as Hamey was relieved of his duties at the small school near Austin, he moved to Larkin. On his first day in town he gave Rusk a list of nine boys living in various parts of Texas whom he would like to see in Antelopes uniforms when the season opened in September. When Rusk visited these boys he found they all had certain characteristics: 'They seem to have no neck. Their legs aren't all that big, but their shoulders ... carved in granite. And they all look about twenty-two years old.' Rusk said on one return to Larkin: 'Coach Hamey, I don't think any of those boys can run,' and Hamey explained a fact of life: 'To produce a really good team, you have to have linemen. That's where the battles are determined, in the trenches.'

'But you will get some runners?'

'I have a second list, almost as important.' And when the oilmen went to scout these boys, they found quite a different set of characteristics: 'None of them much over a hundred and sixty. But they are quick. And only half of them seem to be in their twenties.'

When they reported back to Hamey, Rusk asked: 'Aren't some of these boys a trifle old?' and he said: 'you move them in here. I'll worry about their ages.'

So now the oilmen began prowling the country, visiting with the parents of these young fellows and offering the fathers good jobs in the oil field, the mothers employment in the local hospital or stores. One widowed mother said she taught piano lessons, and Rusk said: 'You get two pianos. One for you, one for your students.'

In some twenty visits the question of grades was never raised, for it was supposed that if a boy was good enough to play for Cotton Hamey, some way would be found to keep him eligible, and as July came, Rusk could boast: 'Not one player on that pitiful team last year will even make the squad this time.' He was wrong. Part of the greatness of Hamey as a coach was that he could take whatever material was available and forge it into something good, so he found a place for more than a dozen of last year's Antelopes; but he also knew that if he wanted a championship team, he had better have an equal number of real horses, and when August practice started, he had them, brawny young men from various parts of Texas, practiced hands of twenty and twenty-one who had already played full terms at other schools, and two massive linemen who must have been at least twenty-two, with college experience. In this frontier period the rules governing eligibility in Texas high school football were somewhat flexible.

On the eve of the first game, Coach Hamey convened a meeting of his backers: 'We have a unique problem. We must not win any of these early games by too big a score. I don't want to alert teams like Abilene or Amarillo. And I certainly don't want to let Waco know we're gunning for them.'

'What are we goin' to do?' Rusk asked.

'Fumble a lot. When we get the ball, we'll run three, four powerhouse plays to see what our men can do.' He never used the word *boys*. 'And when we're satisfied that we can run the ball pretty much as we wish, we'll fumble and start over. I don't want any Waco-type scores, eighty-three nothing.'

'I want to win,' Rusk said, and Hamey snapped: 'So do I. But in an orderly way. When we go into Fort Worth this year to face Waco, I want them to spend the entire first half catching their breath and asking: What hit us?'

So in the first seven games against the smaller teams of the area, Coach Hamey kept his Fighting Antelopes under wraps; 19-6 was a typical score, but as the Jacksboro game approached, at Jacksboro, Rusk begged for his team to be unshackled; 'Erase them. Leave grease spots on the field. I believe we could hammer them something like seventy to seven and I'd like to see it.'

Hamey would not permit this, and the game ended 21-7,

enough to keep the record unblemished, but not enough to alert the public that Cotton Hamey had a powerhouse. However, in the Wichita Falls game, everything clicked magically, and at the end of nine minutes the Antelopes led 27–0, and the first team was yanked. 'It could of been a hundred and seven to nothing,' Rusk said.

The Antelopes won their division, undefeated, and then swept the regionals, which placed them once more in the big finals against the supermen from Waco.

The big newspapers ridiculed the match-up, pointing out that something was wrong with a system which allowed, in two successive years, a team as poorly qualified as Larkin to reach the finals against a superteam like Waco, and all papers had long articles about the disaster of the previous year, with speculation as to whether or not the Antelopes could keep Waco from once again scoring over eighty.

There were a few cautions: 'We must remember that Cotton Hamey does not bring any team into a stadium expecting to lose. This game is not going to be any eighty-three-to-nothing runaway. I predict Waco by forty.'

Because the Larkin Antelopes appeared to be so weak, the crowd in Fort Worth was not so large as the previous year, but those who stayed home missed one of the epic games of Texas football, because when Waco received the opening kickoff and started confidently down the field, they were suddenly struck by a front line which tore their orderly plays apart, and before the startled champions could punt, a huge Antelope with no neck had tackled a running back so hard that he fumbled. Larkin recovered, and in four plays had its first touchdown.

On the next kickoff almost the same thing happened. Larkin linemen simply devoured the Waco backfield, again there was a fumble on the third down, and once more the rampaging Antelopes carried the ball into the end zone: Larkin 13, Waco 0.

But Paul Tyson, considered by many to be the best high school coach ever, was not one to accept such a verdict, and before the next kickoff he made several adjustments, the principal one being that against that awesome Antelope line, his men would pass more, depending upon the speed of their backs to outwit the slower Larkin men.

Now the game developed into a mighty test of contrasting skills, and for the remainder of this half the Waco men predominated, so that when the whistle blew to end the second quarter, the score was Larkin 13, Waco 7.

But the power of the new Larkin team was obvious to everyone in the stands, and people who had tired of Waco's domination during the Tyson years began to cheer in the third period for the Antelopes to score again, and this they did: Larkin 19, Waco 7.

That was the last of the Antelope scoring, for now the superb coaching of the Waco Tigers began to tell: pound at the line and get nowhere; a quick pass for nineteen yards, deceptive hand-off, a deft run for seventeen yards. Three times in that quarter the Tigers approached the Larkin goal line, and three times the Fighting Antelopes turned them back in last-inch stands, but at the start of the fourth quarter the Waco quarterback pulled a daring play. Faking passes to his ends and hand-offs to his running backs, he spun around twice and literally walked into the end zone: Larkin 19, Waco 13.

The fourth quarter would often be referred to as 'the greatest last quarter in high school history,' because the Waco team, smelling a chance for victory, came down the field four glorious times, bedazzling the Antelopes with fancy running and lightning passes, but always near the goal, the Antelope line would stiffen and the drive fail. After a few futile rushes, the Larkin kicker would send long punts zooming down the field, and the inexorable Waco drive would restart. Four times Coach Tyson's men come close to scoring, four times they were denied, and from the stands a leather-lunged spectator cried: 'They sure are Fightin' Antelopes.' But on the fifth try, with only minutes on the clock, the Waco team could not be stopped, and the score became Larkin 19, Waco 19.

Then one of those beautiful-tragic episodes unfolded which make football such a marvelous sport, beautiful to the victors, tragic to the losers. With little more than a minute to play, Waco fielded a punt deep in its own territory, and instead of playing out the clock, unleashed three swift plays that carried the ball to the Larkin eleven. Time-out was called, with only seconds left, and Waco prepared for a field-goal attempt. 'Dear God, let it fail!' Rusk prayed and he could see around him other oilmen voicing the same supplication: 'Just this once, God, let it fail.'

The stadium was hushed. The teams lined up. The ball was snapped. The kicker dropped the ball perfectly, swung his foot, and sent the pigskin on its way. With never a waver, the ball sped through the middle of the uprights: Waco 22, Larkin 19.

On the train trip home, Floyd Rusk surprised himself, for he could feel no bitterness over the loss; passing back and forth through the train, he embraced everyone, spectators, team members, his fellow oilmen, and to all he said: 'This is the proudest day in my life.' Then he would begin to blubber: 'Who said our Antelopes couldn't fight.'

But when he reached Coach Hamey, who also had tears in his eyes, he said, 'I want the names of fifteen more men we could use next autumn. I want to crush Waco. I want to tear 'em apart, shred by shred.'

'So do I,' Hamey said grimly, and within a week of their return home he had given Rusk eighteen names of high school players whose presence in Larkin would reinforce the already good team. Before the first of January, Rusk and his oilmen had more than a dozen of these fellows transferred into the Larkin district, where parents were given jobs in the local businesses. Score that following year: Larkin 26, Waco 6.

These were the years when the Fighting Antelopes met in homeric struggle with teams from much larger towns like Abilene, Amarillo, Lubbock and Fort Worth. With one winning streak of thirty-one regular games and two additional state championships, the team attracted national attention, and when a Chicago sportswriter asked Cotton how he accounted for the record, the coach replied: 'Two things. Attention to detail. And character building.'

While Floyd Rusk was enjoying his victories with the imaginary Antelopes, and they were his victories because he had purchased most of the players, his mother was having her own victories with her real Longhorns.

In 1927 the federal government became aware that on its Western plains the Longhorn breed was about to become extinct, like the passenger pigeon and the buffalo. When agitation by lovers of nature awakened national attention, a bill sponsored by Wyoming Senator John B. Kendrick was passed, allocating $3,000 to be used in an attempt to save the breed.

A large buffalo refuge in the Wichita Mountains of Oklahoma, not far from the Texas border, was set aside for such pure stock as could be found, but then it was discovered that in all the United States there seemed to be less than three dozen verified Longhorn cows and no good bull. Even when these were located, most were found to be of a degenerate quality, untended for generations and bred only by chance. Loss of horn was especially noted, for the famous rocking chairs were being produced no more.

Often the federal research team would hear of 'them real Longhorns down to the Tucker place,' only to find six miserable beasts not qualified to serve as breeding stock. Better luck was found in the rural ranches of Old Mexico, where unspoiled cattle that retained the characteristcs of the Texas Longhorn could occasionally be found. Some objected to basing the revived strain for what was essentially a Texas breed on imports from Mexico, but the US experts stifled that complaint with two sharp observations: 'Mexico is where they came from in the first place' and 'When you Texas people did have them, you didn't take care of them.' So the famous Texas cattle were saved in Oklahoma by a senator from Wyoming importing cattle from Mexico.

However, late in their search the federal men heard of a magical enclave near the town of Larkin, Texas, where a feisty old woman with no nose had been rearing Longhorns for as long as anyone could remember. In great excitement they hurried down from the Wichita Refuge to see what Emma Rusk had stashed away in her own little refuge, and when they first saw Mean Moses VI grazing peacefully among his cows, his horns big and heavy and with never a twist, they actually shouted with joy: 'We've found a real Longhorn!' And what made this bull additionally attractive were the cows and steers sired by him, their horns showing the Texas twist, some to such an exaggerated degree that they were museum pieces.

'Can we buy your entire herd?' the federal men asked ten minutes after they saw Emma Rusk's Longhorns.

'You cannot,' she snapped.

'Can we have that great bull you call Mean Moses VI?'

'Not if you came at me with guns.'

'What can we have? For a national project? To save the breed?'

When she sat with them and heard the admirable thing they were trying to do, and when she saw the photographs of the terrain at the Wildlife Refuge, she became interested, but when they showed her the scrawny animals they had been able to collect so far, she became disgusted: 'You can't restore a breed with that stock.'

'We know,' the men said, allowing the logical conclusion to formulate in her mind.

She said nothing, just sat rocking back and forth, a little old woman whose mind was filled with visions of the vast plains she had loved. She saw her father and his brothers probing into the Larkin area and deciding to establish their homestead on the Brazos. She saw scenes from her life with the Comanche, when she and they galloped over terrain from Kansas to Chihuahua. But most of all she saw R. J. Poteet droving his immense herds of Longhorns to market at Dodge City and from that herd of swirling animals emerged the creatures she had identified as worth saving. Lovingly she recalled the morning when Earnshaw cried: 'Thy bull has gored my bull!' And then she visualized that first Mean Moses striding through strands of barbed wire. The wire had kept him away from the hay when he wasn't really hungry, but when he knew his cows needed him, he had pushed it aside as if it were cobwebs on a frosty morning.

She knew what she must do: 'I'll let you have Mean Moses VI and any four of his bull calves you prefer. But of greater importance, I suspect, will be the cows in direct line from Bathtub Bertha. I've always thought that the spectacular horns we find in our Longhorns can be traced to Bathtub. Have you ever seen a photograph of her?'

From her mementos she produced two photographs of the extraordinary cow, and when the visitors saw those incredible horns, the tips almost touching the cow's eyes, they realized that they had found something spectacular, something Texan. At Wichita the Larkin strain would become known as MM/BB, and wherever in the United States men attentive to history sought to reinstitute the Longhorn breed, they would start first with a good MM/BB bull from the Wichita surplus and a score of cows descended from Bathtub.

Emma was not content to have the federal people load her animals into trucks and haul them into Oklahoma; she wanted to deliver them personally, and when she saw Moses fight his way down the ramp and make a series of lunges at everything around him, she felt assured that in the dozen good years he still had ahead of him, he would get his line firmly established. As she watched her animals disperse into the grasslands of their new home, one of the federal men asked: 'Are you sorry to lose your great bull?' and she snapped: 'What you didn't see at Larkin was his son, the one I hid aside to be Mean Moses VII. That one's going to be twice the bull his father was.'

She was not allowed to see this prediction come true, for on the trip home she began to feel a heavy constriction across her chest. 'Would you drive a little faster?' she asked, and each time the pain became greater she called for greater speed.

The car was now near the Texas border. Ahead lay the Red River, that shallow, wandering stream which had always protected Texas on the north, and she was eager to cross it. 'Could you please drive a little faster?' she pleaded in her customary whisper, and only later did the occupants of the car realize she had been determined to get back to Texas before she died.

... Task Force

Because our members were always striving to identify which special agencies produced the uniqueness of Texas, we invited the dean of writers on high school football to address us at our October meeting in Waco, and although he said he had no time to prepare a formal paper, since this was the height of the football season, he would be honored to join us on any Monday or Tuesday when the high schools were not holding important practices. We informed him that we could adjust our schedule to his and that he had things backward: we were the ones who would be honored.

He was Pepper Hatfield of the *Larkin Defender*, and when Miss Cobb and I met him at the airport we saw a man of seventy-three who retained the same lively joy in things he'd had at forty: 'They gave me the best job in the world. Still love it. Still amazed by what young boys can accomplish.' His eyes sparkled; his marine haircut was a clean iron-grey; and his voice had a lively crackle.

He launched our three-hour discussion on a high philosophical note: 'The essential character of Texas, at least in this century, has been formed by three experiences, but before I say what they are, let me remind you of this essential truth about things Texan. The significant ones have never been determined by the big cities. Houston, Dallas, San Antone, they've never defined what a Texan is. That insight comes only from the small towns. Always has and I'm convived always will. The good old boy with his pickup, his six-pack and his rifle slung in the rack behind his head, he's a small-town creation. Limited to places of under eight thousand, I'd say.'

Miss Cobb would not accept this: 'Do you mean to say the pickup and the six-pack define Texans?'

'I do not. What I intended to point out was that *even* these modern characteristics are predominantly small-town.'

'What are the essentials?' she asked.

'I was about to say,' Hatfield said, with just the slightest irritation at having been interrupted on the subject of football by a woman, 'that my significant characteristics derived from the small town, and I think you'll agree that they account for most of the Texas legend as it exists today: the ranch, the oil well, Friday night football.

'Now, it's curious and I think particularly Texan that books and plays and movies and television shows galore have idealized the first two. How many cowboy films have we had? How many television shows about Texas oil people? You ever see that great Clark Gable, Spencer Tracy, Claudette Colbert picture *Boom Town*? Or the best Texas picture made so far, *Red River*, or the second best, *Giant*? All oil and ranching, and I could name a dozen other goodies.

'That's because outsiders made the pictures. That's because outsiders were defining how we should look at ourselves. But there's never been a really first-rate book or play or dramatic presentation of Friday night football. And why not? Because people outside of Texas don't appreciate the total grandeur of that tradition.

'I never met a single stranger to Texas who had any appreciation of what high school football means to a Texan.

Closest were those clowns in the Pennsylvania coal regions. They started boasting that they were the hotbed of high school football, and I do admit they sent a lot of their graduates to colleges all over America, like Joe Namath to Alabama, but I started a movement to send an All-Texas high school team north to play the All-Pennsylvanians. You know what happened. A slaughter. Texas won every game – twenty-six to ten, thirty-four to two, forty-five to fourteen.' He rattled off the scores as if the games had occurred yesterday, and he could do this with all the statistics of his chosen field. He needed no notes.

'So after we'd clobbered Pennsylvania three times, they called off the game. Too humiliating. And if we'd played any other state on the same basis, our scores would have been higher. Texas high school football is unbelievable. We have about a thousand schools playing each weekend. Five hundred fascinating games. In a year, maybe half a million spectators will see the eight Dallas Cowboys' home games. Eight million will see their favorite high school teams.'

He now dropped his voice to that whispered, seriotragic level which clergymen use when conducting funeral services for people they had never known while living: 'As you know, an all-Oklahoma high school team beat an All-Texas the last two years. We didn't send our best players, but you just can't explain it,' and he sighed.

'But let's get back to fundamentals of the Texas character. The ranch gives us the cowboy, and now that there are hardly any of them left, what's more important, the cowboy clothes. You ever see that great picture of Bum Phillips walking across the football field in his Stetson hat and his General Quimper boots? That's Texas. Or the Marlboro man herding his steers in a Panhandle blizzard? That's Texas.'

'I thought the Marlboro man was from Wyoming,' Garza said, and Pepper dismissed him: 'They shoot all the photos out on the 6666 Ranch in Guthrie, King County. Keep the Marlboro store right on the ranch.

'And the same goes for the oilman. He may no longer be the dominant economic factor, what with OPEC misbehavior and the rise of Silicon Valley over in Dallas, but emotionally he is still emperor of the Texas plains. Best thing ever happened to oil, it moved from being a monopoly of East Texas out to Central Texas, where I grew up, and then on to the Permian Basin, real out west. Made it universal Texan the way cattle never were, and gave us some powerful imagery, not only in the production of the oil well itself, that wonderful gusher blackening the sky, but in the oilman, too. Best cartoon on Texas I ever saw showed a typical West Texas wildcatter, living in this shack with his bedraggled wife. Behind them you see a gusher coming in on their pasture, and the old woman is yelling to her husband: "Call Neiman-Marcus and see how late they stay open on Thursdays!" '

'You seem to incline always toward the cheapest view of our state, Mr Hatfield,' Miss Cobb protested, and Pepper replied, with never a pause: 'I don't do the choosing, ma'am, the people do, and one of the best things I ever heard about any state came from Hawaii. Group of local politicians there, about 1960, awoke to the fact that their new state was no longer a bunch of hoolie-hoolie girls waving their hips. It was a modern state, with a sugar industry and pineapple and a good university. So they started advertising such things in mainland magazines, and tourism dropped forty percent. Right quick they went back to the hoolie-hoolies, and there they stay, with tourism way up. Texas, ma'am, is ranches and oil and Friday night football, and you people in command better not try to sell anything else.'

Pepper was at his best when reminiscing about the great high school teams and players he had known: 'I started as a boy, watching Coach Cotton Hamey's immortal teams at Larkin: they won three state championships. As some of you may remember, I got my big break as a sportswriter by a romantic piece I submitted to a Dallas newspaper about the five awesome linemen Coach Hamey brought with him to Larkin. I called them the five Oil Derricks, and the name caught on.'

He smiled, recalling that lucky shot: 'Three papers spoke to me about jobs, so I prepared a second article about my Five Derricks, because they awed me. They all seemed older than my pop, because eligibility rules were a little looser then. Well, my second article proved that when those five men enrolled as freshmen at Larkin, they'd already played a total of twenty-three years in high school or beyond.

'Do you know what that means? Four years of high school in

some place far distant for each man, with three of them having one year beyond that. The oldest man was married, had two children and had played for an Oklahoma college. Now he had four more years with us. Ten years in all and still in high school.'

'I never read that story,' Rusk said, ' and as you know, my father was crazy about Larkin football.'

'There was good reason you didn't read it. Someone warned your father about my story before I finished it, and he came to me one night: "Son, you're not going to print that pack of lies, are you?" I showed him my documentation, and he brushed it aside: "Son, would you pee on your mother's grave? To befoul Texas football is the same thing." He grabbed my story and tore it up, my notes too. And next day the editor of the *Larkin Defender* called and said: "Mr Rusk has recommended you highly for a job on our paper." I've never left.'

He smiled at Ransom Rusk, then said: 'Other sportswriters didn't have the same high regard for the welfare of the game. During the years of our second championship, maybe the best high school team Texas ever produced, a cynical writer on a Dallas newspaper did a famous column in which he wrote: 'My All-Texas high school team for this year is the Larkin Fighting Antelopes, because each player on that team comes from a different town in Texas and is the state's best in his position." I never stooped to cheap shots like that.'

'But certain fundamental facts must be remembered if you're searching for the true Texas character. The population of Larkin in those days after the oil boom had retreated to its natural level, leaving just a little boost, thirty-six hundred. But when the Antelopes played at home in the golden years, forty-two hundred attended each game, and when they played at some nearby bitter rival like Ranger, Cisco, Breckenridge or Jacksboro, nineteen hundred of our thirty-six would travel to the other town.

'It was mass mania. Nothing in life was bigger than Friday football, and when lights made it possible to play at night, even more people could attend and the field became a kind of cathedral under the stars. Now it was Friday Night Football, as grand an invention as man has made, with the entire community meeting for spiritual warmth.

'A storekeeper who wasn't a hundred percent behind the team, his business would go bust. A bank would have to close shop if its manager wasn't at every game, and putting up money on the side to pay for uniforms, and paying for training tables and other goodies. Every man in town had to root for the Antelopes, or else. And that still applies throughout this state.'

'It sounds to me,' said Miss Cobb, 'like the birth of the macho image. A lot of grown men playing like boys and no women allowed.'

'Ah, now there's where you make your great mistake, ma'am! Because the genius of Texas football was that, early on, it realized it must involve the girls. So in Larkin we started the cheerleader tradition, and the drill team, and the rifle exhibition, and the baton twirlers, and the marchers in their fluffy uniforms. On a good Friday night now a big high school may have two hundred boys doing something, what with the squad and the band, but it'll have two hundred and ten pretty girls in one guise or another. So girls play almost as important a role as the boys. Otherwise, the spectacle might have lost its grip on the public.'

Like all Texas fooball coaches and sportswriters, Pepper aspired to be the perfect gentleman, and now he smiled at Miss Cobb: 'You were right on one thing, though, ma'am. Football does carry a strong macho image. One of the reasons why Texans distrust Mexicans or even despise them at times, they can't play football. Quite pitiful, really. Put them on a horse, they can swagger. But the one game that matters, they can't play.'

'Aren't you stressing the values rather strongly, Mr Hatfield?'

'Not at all! Texans identify honest values quickly. They can't be fooled, not for long. That's why seventy-eight percent of our high school administrators are ex-football coaches.'

'That may account for the sad condition of Texas education,' Miss Cobb said.

'Wait a minute! Back up! School boards hire football coaches to be their administrators because they know that anyone connected with football has his head screwed on right. He understands the important priorities, and he isn't going to be befuddled by poetry and algebra and all that. He knows that if he can get his students involved in a good football program, girls and boys alike, the other things will take care of themselves.'

Miss Cobb had a penetrating question: 'I read that last year Texas colleges graduated five hundred football coaches and only two people qualified to teach calculus. Is that the balance you recommend?'

'For many Texas boys high school football will be the biggest, noblest thing they'll ever experience. Calculus teachers you can hire from those colleges in Massachusetts.'

He was especially ingenious in outlining the symbiotic relationship between oil and football: 'Never underestimate the importance of oil. That's where the extra money came from. Great teams like Breckenridge and Larkin and Ranger were bought outright by oilmen. Odessa Permian, too, in a way. You see, each stresses the big gamble. If you're in oil, you wildcat and lose everything. If you're that first Larkin team, you go up against Waco and lose eighty-three nothing. You don't give a damn. You came back with another try. Oilmen and football heroes were made for each other.

'But there was another aspect, equally strong. An oil millionaire in a place like Larkin had damned little to spend his money on. No opera, no theater, no museums, no interest in books, and when you've had one Cadillac you've had them all. What was left? The high school football team. You cannot imagine how possessive the oilmen of Ranger and Breckenridge and Larkin became over their football teams. Most of them hadn't gone to college, so they didn't become agitated over SMU or A&M. The high school team was all they had. And they supported it – boy, did they support it! I know high school teams right now that have a head coach and ten assistants. Yes, a coach for tight ends, one for wide ends. Two coaches for interior linemen, offensive and defensive. Quarterback, running backs, linebacker, defensive backs, a coach for each. Special-teams coach, kicking coach. The four top Texas high school teams could lick the bottom fifty percent of college teams up north.'

The highlight of his comments came toward the end of the afternoon, when he said, with his eyes half closed: 'I can see them now, those legions of immortal boys who got their lives started on the right track through Friday night football. They were enabled to go on to college, and some to big money in the pros, and there wasn't a hophead or a drunk or a bum among them: Sammy Baugh, Davey O'Brien, Big John Kimbrough, Doak Walker, Don Meredith, Kyle Rote, Earl Campbell. And add the two who were famed only in high school, they may have been the best of the bunch – Boody Johnston of Waco, and Kenny Hall, the Sugar Land Express.'

His eyes misted over. He was an old man now, but he could recall each critical game he had attended, each golden boy whose exploits he had described as if they had been fighting not on the football fields of Texas but at the gates of Troy or on the plains of Megiddo.

'Thank you, Mr Hatfield,' Miss Cobb said in closing. 'We needed to be reminded of the values you represent. You see, I was sent north to school.'

'Ma'am, you missed the heart of Texas.'

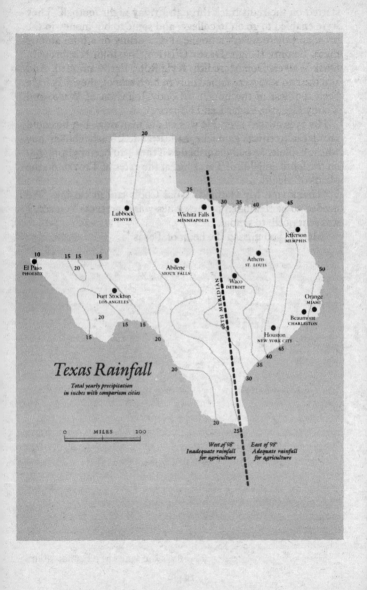

Texas Rainfall

Total yearly precipitation
in inches with comparison cities

20

25

30 35 40 45

Lubbock
DENVER

Wichita Falls
MINNEAPOLIS

Jefferson
MEMPHIS

10

15 15 15

20

El Paso
PHOENIX

Abilene
SIOUX FALLS

Athens
ST. LOUIS

50

Fort Stockton
LOS ANGELES

Waco
DETROIT

20

15 15

Orange
MIAMI

98TH MERIDIAN

18

20

Beaumont
CHARLESTON

Houston
NEW YORK CITY

45

20

40

35

30

0   MILES   100

20 25

West of 98°
Inadequate rainfall
for agriculture

East of 98°
Adequate rainfall
for agriculture

XIII

THE INVADERS

In the four decades following the Larkin Antelopes' last
football championship, 1928–1968, that little oil town witnessed many changes, as did the state. In World War II, Texas
fighting men performed with customary valor: one native son,
Dwight D. Eisenhower, was leading the Allied armies to victory
in Europe while another, Chester W. Nimitz, was doing the
same with the fleet in the Pacific; and still another, Ira Eaker,
was sending his Eighth Air Force planes to devastate Nazi
military production. One tough little Texas G.I., Audie
Murphy, was so eager to get into combat that he lied about his
age, and won so many medals that he leaned forward when he
walked.

Equally important was the emergence of Texas politicians as
powers in Washington, because previous Texans with leadership possibilities had usually seen Texas politics as more
important than national. For example, John Reagan, Postmaster General of the Confederacy and one of the very greatest
Texans, had served in the national Congress for many years and
was a United States senator when an appointment to the Texas
Railroad Commission opened in 1891. Without hesitation he
surrendered his Senate seat to help regulate this important
aspect of Texas life, apparently in the belief that what happened
in Texas was what really mattered. Under the principles laid
down by his prudent leadership, this commission became the
arbiter not only of railroads so essential to the state's development, but eventually, also of trucks, utilities and particularly
the oil business, including the transport in pipe lines of
petroleum products to the rest of the country. Insofar as his
career was concerned, Texas was more important than the
nation.

This provincialism denied Texas the voice in national affairs

1243

to which it was entitled. But now a trio of ornery, capable, arm-twisting Democratic politicians came on the scene, to become three of the most capable public servants our nation has had. In 1931, Cactus Jack Garner became Speaker of the House of Representatives in Washington, and soon after, a powerful Vice-President. In 1940, Sam Rayburn became one of the most effective Speakers of the House, a job he held, with two short breaks, till his death in 1961. And tall, gregarious and able Lyndon Johnson became a congressman, later majority leader of the Senate, then Vice-President and, finally, on 22 November 1963, in an airplane standing on Love Field in Dallas, the thirty-sixth president of the United States.

Coincident with these accomplishments in war and politics, Texas surged to the fore in another aspect of American life, which sometimes seemed to have equal importance. Motion pictures of striking originality and power began to depict life in Texas in such a compelling way that the grandeur and the power of the state had to be recognized. Audiences by the millions swarmed to see movies like *Giant*, *The Alamo*, and the various John Wayne cowboy epics, especially the excellent *Red River*. Other good westerns involved Texas in no specific way but did help keep alive the legend: *Cimarron* (1931), *Stagecoach* (1939), *The Ox-Bow Incident* (1943), *High Noon* (1952), *Shane* (1953), and the film of his which Wayne preferred above all others, *The Searchers* (1956). Even in faraway Italy, the 'spaghetti western' created an alluring vision of the West, and Texas reaped the benefit. The state was seen as heroic, colorful and authentic. Its men were tall, its women beautiful, its Longhorns compelling. Even its Mexican villains displayed uniqueness, if not charm, and each year the legend grew.

Of course, there were disadvantages. Many thoughtful people in other parts of the nation began to resent this emphasis on Texas and saw the state as a haven for broken-down cowboys, rustlers and prairie misfits, men who treated Indians, Mexicans and women with contempt. Jokes about Texas braggadocio became popular, one of the most imaginative concerning the Connecticut river expert who was hired by Dallas to determine whether the Trinity River could be deepened so as to give the city shipping access to the sea. 'Very simple,' the engineer said. 'Dig a canal from Dallas to the Gulf, and if you characters can suck half as hard as you blow, you'll have a river here in no time.'

Thousands of Americans developed a love-hate relationship with the state, with the love predominating, and starting in the mid-sixties, citizens in what Texans called 'the less favored parts of our nation' began to drift toward Texas, attracted by the myth, the availability of good jobs, the pleasant winter climate and the relaxed pattern of life. Men wrote to friends back in Minnesota: 'Down here I can wear the same outfit winter and summer.'

To appreciate the various ways in which the magnetic attraction of Texas could be exerted, it is necessary to understand the related cases of Ben Talbot and Eloy Músquiz. Neither was born in Texas, yet each came to treasure it as a home he did not wish to leave.

Talbot was tall and thin, a reticent man born in northern Vermont close to the Canadian border, and since his father had served for many years as a US Border Patrol officer checking the movement of Canadians south from Montreal, he, too, decided to apply to the service after graduating from the University of Vermont in 1944. Instead, the son was tapped by Selective Service for the army and sent to the South Pacific, where on steaming Bougainville up the Slot from Guadalcanal he vowed that if he got out alive, he would never again live in a hot climate – 'Vermont for me!' – and on sweltering nights, lying beneath his mosquito net bathed in sweat, he thought of his father's cold assignment along the Canadian border.

When he returned to the States he found that his military duty in a hardship post had given him so many credits that the Immigration and Naturalization Service was almost forced to accept him, but after he had been sworn in, with his father watching in approval, Talbot Senior told his son: 'Ben, work hard in the Spanish school, master the language, and serve your obligatory stretch along the Mexican border. We all had to learn Spanish and do our tour down there. But do everything you can, pull every trick in the book to get assigned back here for your permanent duty.'

'I intend to.'

The Spanish teacher in the academy despaired of ever teaching Talbot a word of that mellifluous language, for his flat

Vermont drawl caused him to pronounce every word in a high, nasal wail, with equal emphasis on each syllable; *mañana* came out *mah-nah-nah* – no tilde – as if each group of letters was personally repugnant, and he pronounced longer words like *fortaleza* as if the syllables were a chain of connected boxcars bumping slowly down a track.

'Candidate Talbot,' the instructor pleaded, 'don't you ever sing words, when your heart is joyous?' and he replied: 'I sing hymns. Words I speak.' But because of his studious mastery of vocabulary and his skill in putting these words together in proper sentences, his teacher had to concede: 'Talbot, you speak Spanish perfectly, but it isn't Spanish.'

'They'll understand,' Ben countered, and when he reached his indoctrination assignment at El Paso and began apprehending illegal Mexican aliens trying to sneak into the country, the wetbacks did understand when he interrogated them, for he spoke very slowly, like a machine running down, and enunciated each of his Vermont-style syllables clearly. Older officers would listen in amazement to the sounds which came from his lips and watch with sly grins as the Mexican listening to them gazed in wonder. But slowly, after about his third question, a light would suffuse the Mexican face as the alien realized that the tall man with the severe frown was speaking Spanish. Often the captive would gush out answers in relief at having solved the mystery, so that Talbot proved quite effective. At the end of his training his superior reported: 'Ben looks so stiff and forbidding and speaks such horrible Spanish that he starts by terrifying the men he interrogates. But when they see the sympathy in his eyes and listen to the slow, careful way he pronounces each syllable, I think they feel sorry for him. At any rate, he gets better results than most.'

His avowed plan of doing well along the border so that he might return to the more pleasant duty along the Canadian frontier received its first slight tremor when he was assigned to the duty station at Las Cruces, up the line in New Mexico. He had been there only a few weeks when he realized that he wanted rather strongly to be back in El Paso: That's where the real work goes on. He was not homesick for the place, and certainly not for the food or the heat, but he did miss the teeming vitality of that bilingual town, with Ciudad Juárez across the river, and he must have conveyed his feelings to his superiors, because after six months of chasing illegals through the brush of New Mexico he was reassigned to El Paso, and there began the long years of his service.

His childhood days in the Vermont woods had enabled him to master the tricks of tracking, and to him the traces of all animals, including man, told a clear story. He could look at a dry riverbank around El Paso and determine how many Mexicans had made it across during the night, their approximate ages by the patterns of their shoes, whether he was seeing the signs of a group or merely an accumulation of many singles, and where they were probably heading. He was uncanny in predicting, or as he said, 'making a wishbone guess' as to where these fugitives would intersect some main road, and often when they appeared he would be there awaiting them.

He never abused a Mexican he captured. Calling them all *Juan*, which he pronounced as if it were *Jew-wahn*, he talked with them patiently, offered them coffee or a drink of cold water and shared his sandwiches, explaining in his oxlike Spanish that they would not be mistreated but that they must be sent back home. Of course, once they were back across the Rio Grande, they would probably turn around and come north again. That was understood by all.

Nothing deterred them, not the clever detective work of Border Patrol Officer Talbot, nor the formal checkpoints along the highways, nor the surveillance airplanes that flew overhead, nor the dangers involved in running across a rocky yard and jumping onto a moving Southern Pacific freight train headed east. They came alone, in pairs, in well-organized groups of eighteen or twenty and in casual hundreds. They were part of that endless chain of Mexican peasants who left their homeland in search of employment in a more affluent country. How many crossed the river illegally? Thousands upon thousands. How many were caught? Perhaps only ten or fifteen percent. But if dedicated men like Ben Talbot had not been working diligently since the Border Patrol was first established in 1924, the flood northward would have been three times as great.

In early 1960, Talbot sent a well-reasoned report to his superiors stating that in his opinion more than two million illegal Mexican aliens had crept into the United States in the preceding decade and that there appeared to be no diminution of the flood: 'The pressures which send them north – poverty, the cruel indifference of their government, the mal-distribution of wealth in a wealthy country, and the awful pressures of population growth which both church and government encourage – show no signs of being brought under control, so we must expect an unending continuation of the present inflow and must begin to study what it will mean when the southern part of Texas becomes a de facto Hispanic enclave.' He ended his report with two revealing paragraphs:

The gravity of the situation is exemplified by the case of one Eloy Músquiz, citizen of Zacatecas, 850 miles to the south. Thirty-one years old, perpetually smiling, and apparently a good citizen whether in Mexico or the United States, he leaves his home in Zacatecas every winter about the tenth of February, travels by bus to Ciudad Juárez, crosses the Rio Grande illegally, either evades me or is captured by me. If I catch him, I send him back to Mexico, and that afternoon he recrosses the river and eludes me. He hops a freight, heads east to where I do not know, works in Texas till the fifteenth of December, when he reappears in El Paso heading south. Since he is then leaving the States, we let him go. He returns by bus to his home in Zacatecas, plays with his sons, gets his wife pregnant once more, and on the twelfth of February is back in Ciudad Juárez trying to break through our lines. He always succeeds, and just before Christmas we see him with that perpetual smile, walking briskly along and wishing us a Merry Christmas as he heads home. Eloy Músquiz is our perpetual problem.

One other thing. I should like to withdraw my application for reassignment to the Vermont-Canada border. I have now learned colloquial Spanish and feel a growing affection for El Paso and its problems. I would like to continue my duty on the Texas–Mexico border.

He was accurate in every statement he made about Músquiz, but there were a few crucial facts which the persistent Mexican worker had succeeded in keeping hidden. He did smile all the time, even when captured at the railway yards, and he was a good citizen in both his countries. He did go home each Christmas to be with his wife and children, and he judged his visit successful if he left her pregnant; his daughter and two sons were each born in September. He did invariably move east by hopping a Southern Pacific freight, and he did reappear in El Paso about the fifteenth of December, each year with a somewhat larger roll of American fifty-dollar bills, which he would deliver to his wife in Zacatecas. It was the long period from 12 February to 15 December that remained a blank in Ben Talbot's records.

In 1961, for example, Músquiz came north to Ciudad Juárez on schedule, and as always he went to a Mexican grocery, where he filled his small canvas backpack with the staples required for the trip northeast: two small cans of sardines, six limes, four cans of apricots with lots of juice, two very important cans of refried beans, and a large bag of the one essential for an excursion into the United States, pinole, a mixture of parched corn, roasted peanuts and brown sugar, all ground to the finest possible texture. When mixed with water it produced a life-sustaining beverage, but it could also be eaten dry, and then it was more tasty than candy. As Eloy told the woman shop-keeper: 'Four pinches of pinole keeps you moving for a whole day. A bag like this? It could carry me to Canada.'

With all items packed according to what he had learned on seven previous trips, he left the store casually at about one in the afternoon, walked down to the dry riverbed, watched for an appropriate time when the immigration officers were occupied with three Mexicans they had caught, and slipped into the United States. Working his way cautiously eastward, he came upon the familiar freight yards of the Southern Pacific, where he hid beside a line of stationary boxcars, peeking out to watch the freight engines shunt long lines of laden boxcars before they started on the cross-Texas trip to San Antonio and on to Houston.

That was the train he would be catching within a few hours, and during the waiting period he reminded himself of safety precautions he had accumulated on various trips: Remember, if it should rain in the next hour, don't try. Let the train ride off without you. That was how Elizondo lost his legs, slipping on mud. Remember, if it should be rocky where you make your jump, let the train go. That's how Gutiérrez died, tripping and falling under the wheels. Remember, keep your hands clear of the coupling. That's how Cortinas lost his left hand, when the engines stopped suddenly. And remember, if the car you land in has cargo that can shift, get out, even if you have to jump. When the marble blocks shifted sideways they crushed Alarcón, didn't they? And when that cargo of grain broke loose it smothered Salcedo, didn't it?

On the freight trains east, death was a constant companion, and it was prudent to wedge a block in the sliding doors to keep them from slamming irrevocably shut; once forty were trapped in a freight car which had to lay over in a blinding Texas blizzard; all froze to death. In another instance, thirty-seven died from the stifling heat, which reached one hundred and forty degrees.

At two-ten on this February day, Eloy Músquiz watched the freight forming with the greatest concentration, calculating his line of approach and trying to identify some car in which it would be relatively safe to ride. At two-twenty he adjusted his bundle, grasping the strings at the bottom and securing them about his waist so that his groceries would not bounce about as he ran. At two-twenty-five the engineer sounded his whistle, and the first straining of the heavy wheels occurred.

As long as the train remained stationary, the wetbacks dared not board, since the Border Patrol would pick them off, but once the boxcars started forward, there would be a general rush in which so many Mexicans dashed for the train, the guards had no chance to intercept everyone. Now as the train lurched forward in sudden jolts, Eloy and some seventy other men – looking like a horde of ants rushing toward some fallen morsel – made a wild dash for the boxcars and the metal framework under them. Músquiz, easily in the lead, was about to reach the cars when the tall, thin figure of Ben Talbot stepped out from behind his own hiding place to intercept him and two others.

There were two rules in the El Paso game: it was widely known that American officers would not treat their captives brutally, and it was understood that no Mexican fugitive would strike or fire at an immigration officer. It was a relentless struggle, carried on through all the hours of a day, but it was honorable, and now when Talbot grabbed the three Mexicans, it was as if they had been playing a friendly game of touch football. They stopped trying to run, Talbot said: 'Okay, compadres,' and Eloy looked up at him, smiled as if they were brothers, and walked calmly into captivity.

He was led to a clearing station, documented for the eighth time, and returned once more to Ciudad Juárez, where without even changing stride he walked to the river, crept across when no one was patrolling, made his way to the railroad yards, and headed for the next freight, which hauled more than a hundred and fifty boxcars. With customary skill, his bundle tied close to his back, he sped across the yard, calculated his leap, and made his way into a boxcar filled with freight that was safely lashed down.

The Border Patrol in El Paso always assumed that Músquiz remained aboard the train to San Antonio, losing himself in that growing metropolis where Spanish-speaking citizens were commonplace, and Officer Talbot had sent inquiries to that city, asking immigration people there to be on the lookout for Eloy, but Músquiz was too clever to act in so predictable a manner.

When the freight train stopped for water in Fort Stockton, 245 miles to the east, he remained hidden for twenty minutes, knowing that La Migra – the immigration people – would be chasing the men who jumped off right away. When this did happen, with him watching the frantic game from a peephole, he casually dropped down from the boxcar and sauntered across the yard to a rusted Ford station wagon that had stood beside a deserted road for years. Opening the creaking door carefully lest it fall off, he crept inside, pulled the door shut behind him, and went to sleep, the fourth time in four years he had done this.

At dusk, with the train long gone for its destination in Houston, Eloy started walking up the familiar road to Monohans, Odessa, Midland and Lubbock. He covered many of the two hundred and twenty-three miles on foot, caught a few hitches, turned down job offers from two different ranchers, and paid American dollars for the bus ticket which carried him from Midland to Lubbock; at the station in the former city a well-dressed woman asked if he needed work and was obviously disappointed when he said no.

As he neared Lubbock on its unbelievably flat plain his heart expanded, for now he was on land he knew and loved. Nodding to several acquaintances in the bus station, he assured them that when summer came he would again tend their lawns, but then he started walking west on Highway 114, and before long a rancher who recognized him carried him on to Levelland, where, with his usual broad smile, he bade the man goodbye and headed for the customary cotton gin, where he reported to the foreman of the idle plant; 'I'm back.'

'Where you working till we start our run?'

'Mr Hockaday, he asked.'

'Good man. But come August first, we want you here.'

'I'll be here.'

That year he had fourteen different jobs. Everyone he met sought his help, for he was known throughout the community as reliable, congenial and the father of three children down in Zacatecas to whom he sent nine-tenths of his wages. He did yard work; one woman of considerable wealth arranged for him to get a driver's license, strictly illegal, so that he could chauffeur her about; he worked at stores cleaning up after midnight; and he did occasional baby-sitting for young couples.

By 1968, Músquiz had become a fixture at a local cotton gin, supervising the machinery, and as December approached he went to see the owner of the installation. Before he had spoken six words he broke into tears. When the owner asked in Spanish what the matter was, Eloy handed him a letter from his oldest boy: Señora Músquiz, Eloy's stalwart wife who had run their family without a man, had died, leaving the three children motherless.

'Dear trusted friend, this is a tragedy. My heart goes out to you.'

'Señor, if I bring my children north with me, could you find them work?'

'How would you get them here?'

'I get here, don't I? Señor, I love Lubbock. I love Texas. This is my home now.'

'Any rancher in Texas would want a man like you. If they're good children . . .'

'They are. Their mother saw to that.'

Suddenly it was the owner who was sniffling: 'We'll find a

place. Here's some money for your trip.'

As Eloy stepped off the bus in El Paso he found Ben Talbot waiting for him and he supposed that he was going to be arrested, and the tall officer who spoke the peculiar Spanish took him by the arm, led him to a bar, and said, over Dr Peppers: 'Eloy, the big man has given me hell. Says I let you come in and out of the country as if you owned it. He wants you arrested.'

'General Talbot' – Músquiz called every officer General, in either Mexico or Texas, for he had learned that such an error produced few reprisals – 'you must not arrest me! My wife has died.'

After Talbot studied the sweat-stained letter, he blew his nose and delivered his warning: 'Eloy, go back to Zacatecas. Take care of your children. And don't come up this way again. Because next time I catch you, the big boss insists, you go to jail.'

'But I must come back, General Talbot. And I must bring my children.'

'Damnit, Eloy. There's no way you can sneak past us with three kids. You'll be caught, and into the calaboose you go. Then what will happen to your children?'

'General Talbot, we must come back. We are needed.'

That was the haunting phrase which put this border problem into perspective. The Mexicans who were streaming across in such uncounted numbers were mostly illiterate and they showed no inclination toward becoming Americanized, as immigrants from Europe had done in the early 1900s; instead, they clung to their Spanish language and their Mexican ways, and there were fifty other things wrong with them, but they were needed. They were needed by ranchers who could not otherwise find cowboys and by young mothers who could not find helpers. They were needed in restaurants and hotels and shops and in almost every service activity engaged in by the people of Texas. They were desperately needed, and as long as this was true, they would be enticed over the border by the millions.

As 12 February 1969 approached, Border Patrol Officer Talbot, who now wore cowboy boots, a large hat and a bolo tie when off duty, and could scarcely remember when he had been a Vermonter, realized that his old friend and nemesis Eloy Músquiz was due to make his appearance in Ciudad Juárez in preparation for his dash to paradise, this time with three children in tow, so he telephoned a Mexican officer in Juárez with whom he had established good relations, and asked: 'You see a man about forty years old with three kids buying groceries for a dash across?'

'No, but I'll keep watch,' and after a while the Mexican called back: 'Yep. Buying sardines, canned refried beans, canned fruit juices and a big bag of pinole.'

'Let me know when he crosses.'

As if obedient to some inner schedule, one which had worked in the past, at about one in the afternoon Eloy led his three children across the dry river and eastward toward the freight yards. From a distance Talbot, marking their progress through field glasses, saw the father instruct his children as to how they must run to leap aboard the moving freight. He saw the engine getting up steam, the surreptitious movement of illegals edging toward the still motionless boxcars, and he could feel the tension. Then, to his dismay – almost his horror – he saw that his fellow officer Dan Carlisle had spotted Eloy and his children and was placing himself in position to nab them within the next few minutes. Without hesitation he activated his walkie-talkie: 'Three-oh-three! Three-oh-two calling. I'm on to a crowd that might prove difficult.'

'Three-oh-three speaking. Cannot help. Following my own crowd.'

'Could be I'll need help.'

'You want me to come over?'

'You'd better.' With relief he saw Carlisle stop his tracking of the Músquiz family and start west: When he reaches here I'll think of some explanation.

With his glasses he watched the engineer climb aboard the diesel, saw the trainmen wigwag their signals, and studied carefully the long line of boxcars as it strained to get started. Wheels spun; the engines coughed; the cars started to inch forward. Another spin, then all the wheels seemed to catch at the same instant, and the long train began to pick up speed.

Almost trembling, he watched as Músquiz started his three children for the boxcars, urging them forward. Christ in heaven, Talbot prayed, don't let them slip. And he watched with strange satisfaction as the two boys leaped for the train, grasping the proper handholds.

Now the little girl, twelve years old, had to make the flying leap, and Talbot watched, teeth clenched, as her father spurred her on, her long dress flapping in the February sunlight. 'Faster, kid!' Talbot cried under his breath, and then he sighed with relief when he saw Eloy lift her and almost throw her toward the train, where her brothers dragged her to safety. 'Okay, Músquiz!'

He gasped, for at this moment one of the many scrambling wetbacks slipped and fell toward the implacable wheels, which had destroyed so many in such situations. Was it Músquiz? Talbot saw the sliding man frantically clutch at rocks, until with bleeding fingers, he caught one that saved him, and there he lay as the train moved past, its wheels turning always faster.

Eloy, leaping over the fallen man, grabbed the handholds, swung himself into the boxcar, and disappeared.

At the Fort Stockton stop Músquiz explained to his children why they must wait till the first frenzied action dissipated, then quietly he led them to the rusted Ford station wagon that still stood beside the road. In it they slept for some hours, side by side, waking when it was time to head cautiously for Midland, where they caught the bus to Lubbock.

When they reached Levelland they were greeted with warmth and even embraces, for many families needed their help. When they were safe in the two-room shack which the plantation owner provided, Músquiz told his children: 'This is our home now. We will never leave.'

If Ben Talbot developed a feeling of brotherhood toward Eloy Músquiz because of the latter's decency and courage, he knew another Mexican for whom he felt only loathing, and this slimy operator preoccupied his attention, both when Talbot was on the job or resting beside the swimming pool at the house he and his wife, María Luz, had built at the edge of El Paso. His notes on this infamous man explained why he despised him:

El Lobo, real name unknown. Birthplace unknown. Frequents the cantina El Azteca. About thirty-two, slight, neatly trimmed mustache, toothpick in corner of mouth. Always present when some deal is being engineered. Never present when trouble starts. Stays in Ciudad Juárez mostly, but is willing to come boldly into El Paso when business requires it. Occupation: coyote. Smuggles groups of wetbacks to rendezvous in the desert. Collects his fee and often deserts them.

1. Locked 63 wetbacks into a closed truck with space for 16 at most. Drove across desert to Van Horn in blazing heat. More than 20 died.

2. Dropped 17 wetbacks into the small opening of a tank car that had been carrying gasoline, closed the hatch at El Paso yards. All dead when hatch opened at Fort Stockton.

3. Packed 22 into a Chevrolet, plus two locked in the trunk. In order to protect springs on car, wedged wooden posts between them and body. Friction from driving set wood on fire. He ran from car, but did not stop to open trunk. Two men incinerated.

4. On at least two occasions led groups of girls who wanted to be waitresses across the desert and sold them to men from Oklahoma City.

Talbot vowed that he would catch this evil man during some foray north of the river, but El Lobo was so clever and self-protective that he could not be trapped, and often Talbot had to watch with disgust as the slim, tricky fellow came boldly into El Paso on the maternity gambit, leading some pregnant peasant girl to Thomason General Hospital, and charging her a fee for the service. Since El Lobo broke no law during such missions, and since the deaths listed on his dossier could not be proved against him, he moved with impunity, but events were about to unfold in a dusty little town well south of the border which would place him in real jeopardy.

On the bleak and sandy plains of northern Mexico, midway between the cities of Chihuahua and Ciudad Juárez, stood the adobe village of Moctezuma, seven small huts, one of which served as a roadside shop dispensing allegedly cold drinks to American motorists. The place was called by the grandiloquent name of La Tienda del Norte and was operated by the Guzmáns, a widowed woman with two daughters and a son.

The older girl was married to the man who ran the nearby Pemex station, and it was her responsibility to wash the windshields of any cars that stopped, and to send orders to the national gasoline monopoly for such additional supplies as her husband thought he might sell to motorists who found themselves short of gas on this rather frightening road. If one did not fill up at Moctezuma, one could well be stranded before reaching Chihuahua.

It was this constant flow of big cars passing south that caused discontent in the little village, for when one stopped for either gas or a cold drink, the Mexicans could see the wealth the owners possessed: 'They are all richer than the archbishop. It must be fun to live in Los Estados Unidos where money is so easy!'

The young wife, Eufemia, had often thought of this as she tended the rich travelers, but more so now that she was pregnant. Her condition occasioned great discussion among the residents of Moctezuma, for what a young woman did when she was pregnant made a universe of difference, as two of the older women reminded the mother, Encarnación: 'It is important. It is life and death, really, that you get her to El Paso.'

'True, but neither her husband nor any of his friends have done this thing, and they have no way of instructing her.'

'What you must do,' one of the women said, 'is to get her to Juárez and put her in touch with my cousin. El Lobo, that's his name, and his job is to slip people into the States.'

The other woman had a simpler plan: 'To get into El Paso is nothing, you just walk across the bridge. But to leave El Paso for the rest of the States, that's when you need El Lobo.'

'You think that Eufemia can just go to Juárez, cross over and reach Thomason General without getting caught?'

'Others have done it, haven't they?'

And that was the nagging fact: other pregnant women from villages far off the main road had somehow reached Juárez, got across the river and entered the hospital, had their babies and come home with that precious piece of paper, more valuable than gold, which certified that this child, male or female and of such-and-such a name, had been born within the United States.

Such a paper meant that for as long as he or she lived, that child could enter the States, assume his citizenship, get a free education, and build a good life. Without such a certificate, life would almost certainly be one of unending poverty in northern Mexico; therefore, women like Eufemia were willing to undergo any hardships to ensure that their unborn children received a fair start in life, and that was why even the poorest, even the least-educated, headed for El Paso in their ninth month.

But these benefits did not fully explain why so many citizens of Moctezuma yearned to live in the States. Nothing differentiated their land from that of New Mexico or Arizona, and it was actually better than many parts of West Texas; the strain of people was no different from that of people who prospered in those American states; and the climate was the same. But the sad fact was that in Mexico no way had been devised whereby the unquestioned wealth of the land, almost unequaled in the Americas, could be justly distributed. The wealthy grew immensely wealthy; the Guzmáns could see the great cars sweeping north to the shops across the Rio Grande and then come roaring back loaded with goods purchased in American stores. But in the Mexican system none of that wealth filtered down to the peasants who did most of the work. Indeed, it would be difficult to find a more cynical system than that which trapped Encarnación and her three children, for the national leaders had been preaching since the 1920s the triumph of La Revolución, and each succeeding administration had cried at election time: 'Let us march forward with La Revolución!' but the same reactionary cadre had remained in power, cynically stealing the nation's wealth and allowing the great masses of the people to plod along, sometimes at the starvation level.

Any young person living in Moctezuma would try to get to the States, and if a pregnant woman wanted to ensure that her baby was born with rights to that superior economic system, she was entitled to try every known device to accomplish it. The flood of people streaming north never seemed to diminish.

The plan that the Guzmáns worked out was this: brother Cándido, a clever seventeen-year-old, would take his sister Eufemia to Juárez, where he would make contact with El Lobo, and for a small fee, which Cándido would carry in his shoe, Eufemia would be taken across the bridge two or three days before her labor was supposed to begin. She would be kept in a house run by El Lobo's friends, and on the morning when birth seemed imminent, she would be taken to a place close to the hospital. At the proper time, and this would be crucial but women in the area could help determine it, she would be rushed as an emergency patient to the hospital, where she would give birth, she hoped, to a son. Then her friends would show her how to acquire a birth certificate and purchase three or four photographed copies. She would then recross the bridge, rejoin her brother, and return to Moctezuma – and eighteen years later she would bid her son goodbye when he left to take up residence in the States.

The awful price exacted by this system was the inevitable breakup of the family, for the time would come when this child with his precious documents would leave Mexico forever; but the good part was that when as a young man he established his American citizenship, he could send down to Moctezuma and bring in his entire family under 'the compassion rule'. So once Eufemia gained entrance to Thomason General, she was guaranteeing future American citizenship for herself and, perhaps, as many as a dozen family members. 'Make no mistake,' warned an older man who had worked as an illegal in Texas, 'many things happen up there that no one in his right mind would wish, but it's better than here. It's worth the risk.'

Cándido and his sister caught a ride north with one of the Pemex trucks, and as they neared Juárez the driver said: 'You understand, it's easy to cross over into El Paso. Anyone can do that. But it's hell to slip out of the city and move north. Guards and stops everywhere.'

'I don't intend to stay,' Cándido said, and the driver said: 'They all say that. When you see it, you'll want to.'

Although Juárez was a large city, they had no difficulty in finding El Lobo: 'I'll get your sister to the hospital at the right time. I can also take you to fine cities in Texas, Cándido. Lots of work.'

'I'm not staying.'

'For fifteen dollars, all the way to Fort Stockton and a good job.'

'Just my sister.'

It was agreed that Cándido would accompany her to the first

stopping house and would at the appropriate time move her close to the hospital, and he did this effectively, so that Eufemia had a minimum of worry. At the stopping place six other pregnant women counseled with her, and she watched as they moved on to the American hospital; she saw two of them when they returned with their babies, both girls, and displayed the precious birth certificates. 'You are so lucky,' she said, and they replied: 'We know you'll be lucky, too.'

She was. With the skill of an expert, Cándido moved her nearer the hospital, and when her labor pains became intense, he led her to the emergency entrance, where a young intern with a mustache cried: 'Here's another Aztec princess!' and before Cándido could ask even one question, his sister was whisked away.

It cost the city of El Paso about twelve hundred dollars to deliver a Mexican baby and care for the mother prior to release, but the most Thomason General could extract from the constant stream of pregnant women was seventy-five dollars each, and most, like Eufemia, could pay nothing. Why did Texas allow this preposterous system? 'I'll tell you,' Officer Talbot explained to a newspaperman from Chicago. 'We're a compassionate people down here. We do not turn away pregnant women. But we also like the cheap labor the Mexicans provide. Mercy and profit, one of the most rewarding combinations in world history.'

The Pemex driver had been right. Once Cándido saw the riches of El Paso and the good life available to even poor Mexicans, he wanted to stay, not in that crowded city but in the hinterland, where he heard that jobs were plentiful, and this desire tempted him to come back across the international bridge as soon as he placed his sister and her baby on the Pemex truck heading south.

Since he did not purchase the services of El Lobo, he was able to penetrate only a few miles past the immigration blockades when a tall Border Patrol officer named Talbot detected him on the road and sent him back to Mexico.

On his next try he did use El Lobo, who put him well inland, but again he had the bad luck of running into Officer Talbot, a misfortune that was repeated on his third attempt. 'Haven't I seen you before?' Talbot asked, and this time when he shoved the boy across the border he warned: 'Next time, jail.'

So Cándido, with his burning memories of riches in the United States, returned to Moctezuma, but in June of the following year, when he was eighteen and working at his brother-in-law's garage, his younger sister, Manuela, informed her family that she wanted to try to get into the States, and again the women of Moctezuma decided that Cándido should take her to Juárez, where, for fifteen dollars, El Lobo would lead her not into El Paso, where she would be apprehended if she tried to sneak past Officer Talbot, but to a safe crossing he had developed some seventy miles to the east. Said a man who had used that route under El Lobo's guidance: 'It's not easy. You cross the Rio Grande, walk inland about a mile, and a truck picks you up. Costs another fifteen dollars, but you can't make it alone. Cándido, warn your sister that she cannot make it alone.'

For Cándido the next days were agonizing, because the old longing to get into the United States revived, but he knew that if he went, he would leave his mother alone: Eufemia married. Manuela gone. If I go, who's left to help? But then he began to think of his sister: I can't leave her in a truck at the edge of the desert. By the time he and his sister were ready to board the Pemex truck he had not made up his mind, but as he said farewell to his mother he embraced her with unusual ardor and burst into tears. She must have known what tormented him, for she said: 'Do whatever's right.'

When they reached Ciudad Juárez and Cándido actually saw El Lobo again, he knew he must not leave Manuela in that man's corrupt hands. So without having made a major decision himself, he eased into the Lobo operation, reserving the right to back out at the last moment.

The truck carrying the would-be emigrants left Juárez at five in the afternoon with seventeen passengers, eleven men and six women at fifteen dollars a head, and drove southeast along a bumpy road traveled by other trucks returning empty from the trip to the crossing. At dusk the emigrants pulled up at a lonely spot east of Banderas, and there Cándido had to make up his mind: 'Well, are you joining them or not? Fifteen dollars if you do.' And on the spot the boy said: 'I'll stay with my sister.'

At this place the Rio Grande was so shallow that the Mexicans could walk almost completely across, needing to swim only the last few yards to the American side, and there the American guides had stationed two Mexican men, who helped the women. When all were safely ashore, El Lobo blinked his lights and was gone.

They had come to some of the loneliest land in Texas, that stretch along the river which not even the hardiest settlers had attempted to tame. Rocky in parts, steeply graded, bereft of trees, with only dirt trails leading inland, it was a terrain so forbidding that Cándido was glad he had stayed with his sister: 'This is dangerous. Stay close to me.'

The eighteen wetbacks were led to a miserable truck, which had bounced over these roads many times, but before they were allowed to climb in, a man named Hanson growled: 'Fifteen bucks, and I put you on a back road to Fort Stockton.' He stood in the shaded glare of the headlights, verifying the payments, and when all were accounted for, he piled the Mexicans in and started north, but as he drove, a cohort rode atop the cab of the truck, keeping a shotgun aimed at the passengers.

'Don't no one try to jump off,' he warned. 'We don't want to show La Migra how we move about.'

There was a moon, rising at about nine and throwing only modified light, but it was enough to permit the Mexicans to see the wild terrain they were traversing. 'Oh, this can't be Los Estados Unidos!' a woman cried, and the gunman replied in Spanish: 'It sure is. Three hundred miles of it.'

At four in the morning, when they were far from the river, the driver, seeing a chance to earn a lot of money with no responsibility, made the engine cough and then conk out. 'Damnit,' he cried, 'we've got to fix this,' and he ordered the Mexicans to leave the truck and stand well back while he worked on it. To their delight the engine began to sputter, caught, and then purred nicely. At these welcome sounds the Mexicans started toward the truck, when, to their horror, the two anglos revved the motor and took off across the desert, leaving the wetbacks stranded, with no guide, no food and, worst of all, no water.

It was a trip into hell. At ten in the morning of the second day when the sun was blazing high, the first Mexican died, a man in his forties whose swollen tongue filled his mouth. By ten, six others were dead, but the two Guzmáns still survived. 'Manuela,' Cándido whispered, 'we must look for plants, anything.'

They found nothing, none of the big cacti which often saved lives in such circumstances, and by noon, three more were dead. Overhead, the sky was an arch of blue; not a blemish obscured the sun, which beat mercilessly on the hapless Mexicans. Two o'clock passed, with more than half the wetbacks, ironic name, dead, and in the late afternoon, in that dreadful heat, Manuela gasped one last plea for water, stared madly at her brother, and died.

Three men made it to US 80, a hundred and forty miles west of Fort Stockton. In despair they tried to flag down motorists; none stopped. Cándido finally threw himself in front of an approaching car while his companions waved frantically, but they did not need to do this, for the man driving the car was Officer Talbot, who had been searching for them.

'Poor sons-a-bitches,' he said to his partner, 'let's get them something to drink.' They drove eastwards to Van Horn, where Talbot tossed the three in jail, but not before providing them with all the liquid they could drink.

They were returned to Mexico, of course, and since Cándido was too ashamed to go back to Moctezuma to inform his family of Manuela's death and of how it had occurred, he slipped back into El Paso, found a job, saved his money, bought a gun, grew a mustache so as to alter his appearance, and went back to El Lobo as if he had never seen him before: 'Is it true, you take people into Los Estados Unidos?'

'Fifteen dollars to me, fifteen to the men on the other side.'

'I'll go.'

'I'll take you through the barriers in north El Paso.'

'I was told there was a better crossing at Banderas.'

'You want to go that way, all right.'

This time a party of nineteen illegals drove beside the Rio Grande to the little town, where the emigrants paid their fee and swam the river. On the far side Hanson was waiting with his same rickety truck, the same shotgun assistant. They left the river at dusk, rode through the night, and at about three in the morning, the truck broke down again.

'Move over here while we fix it,' Hanson said, but as he spoke, Cándido and two other wetbacks whom he had recruited en route shot him and the assistant dead. Commandeering the truck, they sped toward where US 80 would have to be, and long before dawn they were at the outskirts of Fort Stockton. Disposing of the truck in a gully, they shook hands and made their way variously into the town and into the fabric of American life.

Cándido, moving alone along the highway, started back west, to give the impression, if questioned by police regarding the desert murders, that he had been in the States for some time. But he had walked only a few miles when he was met by a pickup roaring eastward from El Paso. As soon as the driver spotted Cándido, whom he identified as a wetback, he screeched to a halt: 'What you lookin' for, son?'

The driver was a big, florid man in his late thirties, dressed like a sheriff, and he terrified Cándido, who whispered: 'Solamente español, señor,' whereupon the man surprised him by saying in easy Spanish: 'Amigo, if you seek work, you've met the right man.'

He invited Cándido to sit beside him, and together they rode to Fort Stockton and a short distance to the north, where they came upon a frontier ranch with an ornate stone gate and a sign which said:

EL RANCHO ESTUPENDO
LORENZO QUIMPER
PROPRIETOR

'Come in and grab yourself some grub,' the rancher said, and in this way Cándido Guzmán became a permanent resident of the United States, and a lifelong employee of Lorenzo Quimper, who owned some nine ranches for which he needed reliable workmen. Few immigrants had ever dared so much to find a haven in Texas, few would serve it more faithfully.

In the city of Detroit things were not going well for the Morrisons. Todd, the father, could see that within a few more months his branch of the Chrysler Corporation might have to shut down. The ax had already fallen on his wife, Maggie, for one Friday morning three weeks earlier the principal of her school had handed her the gray-toned sheet of paper teachers dreaded:

> The Cascade Public Schools District Board of Education, meeting in regular session, voted last night to take certain actions necessary for its survival. It is my duty to inform you that your teaching contract will not be renewed upon its expiration at the close of the 1968 spring term, and both your job and your salary will end at that time.

The Morrisons were aware that even with the loss of Maggie's income, they could survive if Todd kept his job, but there was an additional aggravation: their two children – Beth, an extremely bright thirteen, and Lonnie, aged eleven – had already stated that under no circumstances did they want to leave the Cascade schools, which they had grown to love and which enrolled all their friends.

The Morrisons had long practiced the art of family democracy, with ample discussion of most problems, and they did not back off from this unpleasant one: 'Kids, if things get worse at Chrysler, I'm going to get laid off. What then?'

'That would be horribly unfair,' Beth cried.

'They fired your mother, didn't they?'

'Yes, but the school board's a bunch of cruds.'

'We must consider the possibilities if I do lose my job,' Todd said.

'You could become a policeman,' Lonnie suggested. 'The *News* had an article about needing more cops.'

'Not my age, and not my salary,' his father replied. He was thirty-seven, his wife thirty-three, at the exact time in their lives when they needed every penny to enjoy the amenities they treasured – a good movie now and then, books – and to afford careful attention to health, orthodontics, a sensible diet, durable clothes. And these cost money. Their house carried only a six-thousand-dollar mortgage, and they had never been extravagant with cars or socializing; they drove one new Plymouth and one very old Ford.

Normally they should have been at the cresting point in their careers, with Todd looking forward to rapid promotion and

Maggie being considered for a principalship. Now the bottom was falling out of their world, and they could not even guess where the terrifying drop would end.

'Well, what shall we do if I'm fired?' Todd asked again, and his three advisers sat silent, so he explored the subject: 'Ford and GM won't take me on, that's for sure. Stated frankly, my type of work is ended unless I can find a job in Japan.'

The Morrisons laughed at this suggestion, but then Beth asked: 'Transfer? What's a practical possibility?'

'I don't really know. For your mother, no school jobs in these parts, nor in places like New York, but I hear there are openings in California and boom towns like Atlanta.'

'I'm attracted to neither,' Beth said bluntly in her surprisingly adult manner, whereupon her mother said: 'You'll like whatever we have to do, Miss Beth, and remember that,' and the girl said: 'I know. I don't want to leave Cascade, but if we have to, we have to.'

'I vote for California,' Lonnie said. 'Surfing.'

Todd ignored this suggestion: 'I really think I'll have to start looking for a new job.'

'What could you do?' Beth asked.

'I'm good at what I do . . .'

'Yes, you are, dear,' Maggie said quickly.

'I can keep an organization on its toes. Maybe labor relations. Maybe selling something.'

'*Death of a Salesman*!' Beth cried. 'Willie Loman of the auto trade.'

'You'd be awfully good at labor relations,' Maggie said as she cleared the table. 'But where?'

The next three weeks passed in growing apprehension as Maggie Morrison applied to one school district after another; the results were not depressing, they were terrifying. At night she told her family: 'Enrollments dropping everywhere in the city. Everyone suggests we move to some new area. We may have to.'

In the month that followed, the spate of news from Chrysler was so depressing that Todd could barely discuss it with his family, and it was at one of these doleful meetings that the word *Texas* was first voiced. Todd said: 'I hear that electronics is real big in the Dallas area. If they're expanding . . .' Beth said she did not want to go to Texas, too big, too noisy, but Lonnie could hardly wait to get started: 'Cowboys! Wow!'

On the next Friday night Todd was fired.

In their despair, the Morrisons organized as a team: Todd studied the want ads; Maggie continued to seek work as a teacher, or even as a teacher's helper; Beth, with remarkable maturity, took charge of the housework; and Lonnie volunteered for extra chores; but each week the family savings declined, and the children knew it.

Todd applied for three dozen different jobs, and was rejected each time: 'I'm too old for this, too young for that. I know both the assembly line and sales, but can't land a job in either. This is one hell of a time to be out of work.'

It was Maggie who found him a job, and she did it in a most peculiar way. She was in the industrial section of the city interviewing at a school for children with special problems, when she met a woman whose husband worked for a firm that had developed a new line of business: 'What they do, Todd, they overhaul automobile engines. They have new diagnostic machines to spot weaknesses, other machines to fix them. They've had real success in Detroit and Cleveland, and they want to franchise widely. This woman said there were real opportunities.'

Early next morning Todd was at the new company's office, and he learned that what his wife had reported was true. Engine Experts had hit upon a system for adding years to the life of the average automobile engine and its subordinate parts; intricate new machines diagnosed trouble spots and instructed the workmen how to repair them. The initial cost of the system was rather high, but the cash return of the four installations that Todd was allowed to inspect was reassuring, and he entered into serious discussion with the owners.

'What we want to do,' the energetic men said, 'is break into the Dallas, Houston market. Go where the cars are, that's our motto.'

'I don't have the funds to buy in,' Todd said truthfully, but the men said: 'We don't want you to. You know cars. You have common sense. We want you to go to Texas, scout out the good locations, what we call the inevitables, and buy us an option on the corner where the most cars pass, but where an industrial shop would be allowed. Would you be interested?'

'What are the chances I'd fall on my ass?'

'We'd carry you for one year, sink or swim. But we think you'd swim, especially in Texas, where they have poor public transportation and people are nuts about their cars.'

They offered Todd a year's assignment in Texas – Dallas or Houston, as he wished – during which he was to identify eight locations and arrange for the purchase of real estate and the issuance of licenses to open Engine Experts shops. That night he handed his wife and children pencils and paper and asked them to take notes as he lined out their situation: 'Six months ago this family had income as follows. Father, twenty-six thousand dollars; mother, eight thousand dollars. Total how much, Lonnie?'

'Thirty-four thousand dollars.'

'Well, we both lost our jobs. Salary right now, zero. We can get something for the house. Our savings go steadily down, but still nineteen thousand dollars. Should have been a lot more, but we didn't anticipate.'

'We can cut back,' Beth said. 'I don't need special lessons.'

'We can all cut back, or starve. Now, I've been offered a job in Texas ...'

'Hooray!' Lonnie cried. 'Can I have a horse?'

'The salary will be eighteen thousand, with promise of a bonus if I do well.'

'You'll do well,'' Maggie said.

It was agreed. The Todd Morrisons of Michigan, a family deeply embedded in that state, would move to Houston, Texas. On a morning in July 1968, with tears marking all their faces, they left Michigan forever and headed south. They did not paint on their truck the ancient sign G.T.T., but they could have, for the social disruptions which were forcing them south were almost identical with those which had spurred the migrations to Texas in 1820 and 1850. They, too, were in search of a better life.

In that summer of 1968 a different family of immigrants – mother, father, four daughters – moved quietly into the oil town of Larkin, and within three weeks had the owners of better-class homes in a rage. They were such a rowdy lot, especially the mother, that an observer might have thought: The rip-roaring boom days of 1922 are back!

They were night people, always a bad sign, who seemed to do most of their hell-raising after dark, with mother and daughters off on a toot marked by noise, vandalism and other furtive acts. They operated as a gang, with their weak and ineffective father along at times, and what infuriated the townsfolk particularly was that they seemed to take positive joy in their depredations.

Despite their unfavorable reputation – and many sins were charged against them which they did not commit – they really did more good than harm; they were an asset to the community, and they had about them elements of extraordinary beauty, which their enemies refused to admit.

They were armadillos, never known in this area before, a group of invaders who had moved up from Mexico, bringing irritation and joy wherever they appeared. Opponents of the fascinating little creatures, which were no bigger than small dogs, accused them of eating quail eggs, a rotten lie; of raiding chicken coops, false as could be; and of tearing up fine lawns, a just charge and a serious one. Ranchers also said: 'They dig so many holes that my cattle stumble into them and break their legs. There goes four hundred bucks.'

The indictment involving the digging up of lawns and the making of other deep holes was justified, for no animal could dig faster than an armadillo, and when this mother and her four daughters turned themselves loose on a new lawn or a nicely tilled vegetable garden, their destruction could be awesome. The armadillo had a long, probing snout, backed up by two forefeet, each with four three-inch claws, and two hind feet with five shovel-like claws, and the speed with which it could work those excavators was unbelievable.

'Straight down,' Mr Kramer said, 'they can dig faster than I can with a shovel. The nose feels out the soft spots and those forelegs drive like pistons, but it's the back legs that amaze, because they catch the loose earth and throw it four, five feet backwards.'

Mr Kramer was one of those odd men, found in all communities, who measured rainfall on a regular basis – phoning the information to the Weather Service – and who recorded the depth of snowfall, the time of the first frost, the strength and direction of the wind during storms, and the fact that in the last blue norther 'the temperature on a fine March day dropped, in the space of three hours, from 26.9 to 9.7 degrees Celsius.' He was the type who always gave the temperature in Celsius, which he expected his friends to translate into Fahrenheit, if they wished. He was, in short, a sixty-two-year-old former member of an oil crew who had always loved nature and who had poked his bullet-cropped sandy-haired head into all sorts of corners.

The first armadillos to reach Larkin were identified on a Tuesday, and by Friday, Mr Kramer had written away for three research studies on the creatures. The more he read, the more he grew to like them, and before long he was defending them against their detractors, especially those whose lawns had been excavated: 'A little damage here and here, I grant you. But did you hear about what they did for my rose bushes? Laden down with beetles, they were. Couldn't produce one good flower even with toxic sprays. Then one night I look out to check the moon, three-quarters full, and I see these pairs of beady eyes shining in the gloom, and across my lawn come these five armadillos, and I say to myself: "Oh, oh! There goes the lawn!" but that wasn't the case at all. Those armadillos were after those beetles, and when I woke up in the morning to check the rain gauge, what do you suppose? Not one beetle to be found.'

Mr Kramer defended the little creatures to anyone who would listen, but not many cared: 'You ever see his tongue? Darts out about six inches, long, very sticky. Zoom! There goes another ant, another beetle. He was made to police the garden and knock off the pests.'

Once when a Mrs Cole was complaining with a bleeding heart about what the armadillos had done to her lawn, he stopped her with a rather revolting question: 'Mrs Cole, have you ever inspected an armadillo's stomach? Well, I have, many times. Dissected bodies I've found along the highway. And what does the stomach contain? Bugs, beetles, delicate roots, flies, all the crawling things you don't like. And you can tell Mr Cole that in seventeen autopsies, I've never found even the trace of a bird's egg, and certainly no quail eggs.' By the time he was through with his report on the belly of an armadillo, Mrs Cole was more than ever opposed to the destructive little beasts.

But it was when he extolled the beauty of the armadillo that he lost the support of even the most sympathetic Larkin citizens, for they saw the little animal as an awkward, low-slung relic of some past geologic age that had mysteriously survived into the present; one look at the creature convinced them that it should have died out with the dinosaurs, and its survival into the twentieth century somehow offended them. To Mr Kramer, this heroic persistence was one of the armadillo's great assets, but he was even more impressed by the beauty of its design.

'Armadillo? What does it mean? "The little armored one." And if you look at him dispassionately, what you see is a beautifully designed animal much like one of the armored horses they used to have in the Middle Ages. The back, the body, the legs are all protected by this amazing armor, beautifully fashioned to flow across the body of the beast. And look at the engineering!' When he said this he liked to display one of the three armadillos he had tamed when their parents were killed by hunters and point to the miracle of which he was speaking: 'This is real armor, fore and aft. Punch it. Harder than your fingernail and made of the same substance. Protects the shoulders and the hips. But here in the middle, nine flexible bands of armor, much like an accordion. Always nine, never seven or ten, and without these inserts, the beast couldn't move about as he does. Quite wonderful, really. Nothing like it in the rest of the animal kingdom. Real relic of the dinosaur age.'

But he would never let it end at that, and it was what he said next that did win some converts to the armadillo's defense: 'What awes me is not the armor, nor the nine flexible plates. They're just good engineering. But the beauty of the design goes beyond engineering. It's art, and only a designer who took infinite care could have devised these patterns. Leonardo da Vinci, maybe, or Michelangelo, or even God.' And then he would show how fore and aft the armor was composed of the most beautiful hexagons and pentagons arranged like golden coins upon a field of exquisite gray cloth, while the nine bands were entirely different: 'Look at the curious structures! Elongated capital "*A*"s. Go ahead, tell me what they look like.

A field of endless oil derricks, aren't they? Can't you see, he's the good-luck symbol of the whole oil industry. His coming to Larkin was no mistake. He was sent here to serve as our mascot.'

How beautiful, how mysterious the armadillos were when one took the trouble to inspect them seriously, as Mr Kramer did. They bespoke past ages, the death of great systems, the miracle of creation and survival; they were walking reminders of a time when volcanoes peppered the earth and vast lakes covered continents. They were hallowed creatures, for they had seen the earth before man arrived, and they had survived to remind him of how things once had been. They should have died out with Tyrannosaurus Rex and Diplodocus, but they had stubbornly persisted so that they could bear testimony, and for the value of that testimony, they were precious and worthy of defense. 'They must continue into the future,' Mr Kramer said, 'so that future generations can see how things once were.'

'What amazes me,' Mr Kramer told the women he tried to persuade, 'is their system of giving birth. Invariably four pups, and invariably all four identicals of the same sex. There is no case of a mother armadillo giving birth to boys and girls at the same time. Impossible. And do you know why? Because one fertilized egg is split into four parts, rarely more, rarely less. Therefore, the resulting babies have to be of the same sex.

'But would you believe this? The mother can hold that fertilized four-part egg in her womb for the normal eight weeks, or, if things don't seem propitious, for as long as twenty-two months, same as the elephant. She gives birth in response to some perceived need, and what that is, no one can say.'

As he brooded about this mystery of birth, wondering how the armadillo community ensured that enough males and females would be provided to keep the race going, he visualized what he called 'The Great Computer in the Sky,' which kept track of how many four-girl births were building up in a given community: 'And some morning it clicks out a message. "Hey, we need a couple of four-boy births in the Larkin area," so the next females to become pregnant have four male babies, and the grand balance is maintained.'

Mr Kramer could find no one who wished to share his speculation on this mystery, but as he pursued it he began to think about human beings, too. 'What grand computer ensures that we have a balance between male and female babies? And how does it make the adjustments it does? Like after a war, when a lot of men have died in battle. Normal births in peacetime, a thousand and four males to a thousand females, because males are more delicate in the early years and have to be protected numerically. But after a war, when The Great Computer knows that there's a deficiency in males, the balance swings as high as one thousand and nine to one thousand.'

So when he looked at an armadillo on its way to dig in his lawn, he saw not a destructive little tank with incredibly powerful digging devices, but a symbol of the grandeur of creation, the passing of time, the mystery of birth, the great beauty that exists in the world in so many different manifestations: An armadillo is not one whit more beautiful or mysterious than a butterfly or a pine cone, but it's more fun. And what gave him the warmest satisfaction: All other sizable animals of the world seem to be having their living areas reduced. Only the armadillo is stubbornly enlarging his. Sometimes when he watched this mother and her four daughters heading forth for some new devastation, he chuckled with delight: There they go! The Five Horsewomen of the Apocalypse!

Another Larkin man had a much different name for the little excavators. Ransom Rusk, principal heir and sole operator of the Rusk holdings in the Larkin Field, had a fierce desire to obliterate memories of his unfortunate ancestry: the grand fool Earnshaw Rusk; the wife with the wooden nose; his own obscenely obese father; his fat, foolish mother. He wanted to forget them all. He was a tall, lean man, quite handsome, totally unlike his father, and at forty-five he was at the height of his powers. He had married a Wellesley graduate from New England, and it was amusing that her mother, wishing to dissociate herself from her cotton-mill ancestry, had named her daughter Fleurette, trusting that something of French gentility would brush off.

Fleurette and Ransom Rusk, fed up with the modest house in whose kitchen Floyd had maintained his oil office till he died, had employed an architect from Boston to build them a mansion, and he had suggested an innovation which would distinguish their place from others in the region: 'It is very fashionable, in the better estates of England, to have a bowling green. It could also be used for croquet, should you prefer,' and Fleurette had applauded the idea.

It was now her pleasure to entertain at what she called 'a pleasant afternoon of bowls,' and she did indeed make it pleasant. Not many of the local millionaires — and there were now some two dozen in the Larkin district, thanks to those reliable wells which never produced much more than a hundred barrels a day, rarely less — knew how to play bowls, but they had fun at the variations they devised.

Ransom Rusk, as the man who dominated the Larkin Field, was not spectacularly rich by Texas standards, whose categories were popularly defined: one to twenty million, comfortable; twenty to fifty million, well-to-do; fifty to five hundred million, rich; five hundred million to one billion, big rich; one to five billion, Texas rich. By virtue of his other oil holdings in various parts of the state, and his prudent investments in Fort Worth ventures, he was now rich, but in the lowest ranks of that middle division. His attitudes toward wealth were contradictory, for obviously he had a driving ambition to acquire and exercise power in its various manifestations, and in pursuit of this, he strove to multiply his wealth. But he remained indifferent to its mathematical level, often spending an entire year without knowing his balances or even an approximation of them. Impelled by an urge to control billions, he did not care to count them. On the other hand, he had inherited his father's shrewd judgment regarding oil and had extended it to the field of general financing, and he always sought new opportunities and knew how to apply leverage when he found them.

He was brooding about his Fort Worth adventures one morning when he heard Fleurette scream: 'Oh my God!' Thinking that she had fallen, he rushed into the bedroom to find her standing by the window, pointing wordlessly at the havoc which had been wreaked upon her bowling green.

'Looks like an atomic bomb!' Ransom said. 'It's those damned armadillos,' but Fleurette did not hear his explanation, for she was wailing as if she had lost three children.

'Shut up!' Ransom cried. 'I'll take care of those little bastards.'

He slammed out of the house, inspected the chopped-up bowling lawn, and summoned the gardeners: 'Can this be fixed?'

'We can resod it like new, Mr Rusk,' they assured him, 'but you'll have to keep them armadillos out.'

'I'll take care of them. I'll shoot them.' In pursuit of this plan, he went to the hardware store to buy a stack of ammo for his .22 rifle, but while there, he happened to stand beside Mr Kramer at the check-out counter, and the retired oilman, who had worked for Rusk, asked: 'What are the bullets for?' and unfortunately, Ransom said: 'Armadillos.'

'Oh, you mustn't do that! Those are precious creatures. You should be protecting them, not killing them.'

'They tore up my wife's lawn last night.'

'Her bowling green? I've heard it's beautiful.'

'Cost God knows how much, and it's in shreds.'

'A minor difficulty,' Kramer said lightly, since he did not have to pay for the repairs. And before Ransom could get away, the enthusiastic nature-lover had drawn him to the drugstore, where they shared Dr Peppers.

'Did you know, Ransom, that we have highly accurate maps showing the progress north of the armadillo? Maybe the only record of its kind?'

'I wish they'd stayed where they came from.'

'They came from Mexico.'

'One hell of a lot comes from Mexico – wetbacks, boll weevils . . .'

'A follower of the great Audubon first recorded them in Texas, down along the Rio Grande, in 1854. They had reached San Antonio by 1880, Austin by 1914, Jefferson in the east by 1945. They were slower reaching our dryer area. They were reported in Dallas in 1953, but they didn't reach us till this year. Remarkable march.'

'Should have kept them in Mexico,' Rusk said, fingering his box of shells.

'They're in Florida too. Three pairs escaped from a zoo in 1922. And people transported them as pets. They liked Florida, so now they move east from Texas and west from Florida.

They'll occupy the entire Gulf area before this century is out.'

'They aren't going to occupy my place much longer,' Ransom said, and that was the beginning of the hilarious adventure, because Mr Kramer persuaded him, almost tearfully, not to shoot the armadillos but to keep them away from the bowling green by building protection around it: 'These are unique creatures, relics of the past, and they do an infinite amount of good.'

The first thing Rusk did was to enclose his wife's resodded bowling green with a stout tennis-court-type fence, but two nights after it was in place, at considerable expense, the bowling green was chewed up again, and when Mr Kramer was consulted he showed the Rusks how the world's foremost excavators had simply burrowed under the fence to get at the succulent roots.

'What you have to do is dig a footing around your green, six feet deep, and fill it with concrete. Sink your fence poles in that.'

'Do you know how much that would cost?'

'They tell me you have the money,' Kramer said easily, and so the fence was taken down, backhoes were brought in, and the deep trench was dug, enclosing the green. Then trucks dumped a huge amount of cement into the gaping holes, and the fence was reerected. Eight feet into the air, six feet underground, and the armadillos were boxed off.

But four days after the job was finished, Fleurette Rusk let out another wail, and when Ransom ran to her room he bellowed: 'Is it those damned armadillos again?' It was, and when he and Mr Kramer studied the new disaster the situation became clear, as the enthusiastic naturalist explained: 'Look at that hole! Ransom, they dug right under the concrete barrier and up the other side. Probably took them half an hour, no more.'

The scientific manner in which Kramer diagnosed the case, and the obvious pleasure he took in the engineering skill of his armadillos, infuriated Rusk, and once more he threatened to shoot his tormentors, but Kramer prevailed upon him to try one more experiment: 'What we must do, Ransom, is drive a palisade below the concrete footing.'

'And how do we do that?'

'Simple, you get a hydraulic ram and it drives down metal stakes. Twenty feet deep. But they'll have to be close together.'

When this job was completed, Rusk calculated that he had $218,000 invested in that bowling green, but to his grim satisfaction, the sunken palisade did stop the predators he had named 'Lady Macbeth and Her Four Witches.' The spikes of the palisade went too deep for her to risk a hole so far below the surface.

But she was not stopped for long, because one morning Rusk was summoned by a new scream: 'Ransom, look at those scoundrels!' and when he looked, he saw that the mother, frustrated by the palisade but still hungry for the tender grass roots, had succeeded in climbing her side of the fence, straight up, and then descending straight down, and she was in the process of teaching her daughters to do the same.

For some minutes Rusk stood at the window, watching the odd procession of armadillos climbing up his expensive fence, and when one daughter repeatedly fell back, unable to learn, he broke into laughter.

'I don't see what's so funny,' his wife cried, and he explained: 'Look at the dumb little creature. She can't use her front claws to hold on to the cross wires,' and his wife exploded: 'You seem to be cheering her on,' and it suddenly became clear to Rusk that he was doing just that. He was responding to his wife's constant nagging: 'Don't wear that big cowboy hat in winter, makes you look like a real hick.' 'Don't wear those boots to a dance, makes you look real Texan.' She had a score of other don'ts, and now Ransom realised that in this fight of Fleurette versus the lady armadillos, he was cheering for the animals.

But as a good sport he did telephone Mr Kramer and asked: 'Those crazy armadillos can climb the fence. What do we do?' Mr Kramer noted the significant difference; always before it had been 'those damned armadillos,' or worse. When a man started calling them crazy, he was beginning to fall in love with them.

'Tell you what, Ransom. We call in the fence people and have them add a projection around the upper edge, so that when the armadillos reach the top of the fence, they'll run into this screen curving back at them and fall off.'

'Will it hurt them?'

'Six weeks ago you wanted to shoot them. Now you ask if it'll hurt them. Ransom, you're learning.'

'You know, Kramer, everything you advise me to do costs money.'

'You have it to spend.'

So the fence builders were brought in, and yes, they could bring a flange out parallel to the ground that no armadillo could negotiate, and when this was done Rusk would sit on his perch at night with a powerful beam flashlight and watch as the mother tried to climb the fence, with her daughters trailing, and he would break into audible laughter as the determined little creatures clawed their way to the top, encountered the barrier, and tumbled back to earth. Again and again they tried, and always they fell back. Ransom Rusk had defeated the armadillos, at a cost of \$238,000 total.

'What are you guffawing at in the dark?' Fleurette demanded, and he said: 'At the armadillos trying to get into your bowling green.'

'You should have shot them months ago,' she snapped, and he replied: 'They're trying so hard, I was thinking about going down and letting them in.'

'You do,' she said, 'and I'm walking out.'

That was the beginning of the sensational Rusk divorce case, though of course many problems more serious than armadillos were involved, and most of them centered upon the husband. He had wanted the social cachet of an Eastern bride, but he had also wanted to remain a Texan. He had wanted to forget his noseless grandmother, his strange Quaker grandfather and especially his obese and ridiculous parents, but Fleurette often dragged them into conversation, especially when strangers were present. And although he had wanted a wife and had courted Fleurette arduously, he also wanted to be left alone with his multitude of projects. Had he married a woman of divine patience and sublime understanding, he might have made a success of his marriage, but Fleurette had proved increasingly giddy and insubstantial. A wiser woman would never have inflated armadillos into a cause célèbre, but once it reached that status, there was no turning back.

She charged him with numerous cruelties and more

insensitivities. She swore, in her affidavit, that life with such a brute had become quite impossible, and when the case was well launched, she did the one thing that was calculated to ensure her victory: she hired Fleabait Moomer from Dallas to press her claim for a financial settlement in the Larkin County court.

Ransom's lawyer almost shuddered when he learned that Fleabait was coming into the case: 'Ransom, we're in deep trouble.'

'Why?'

'Fleabait tears a case apart. When he's in the courtroom anything can happen. Do you really want to go ahead with this?' And when Rusk replied: 'I sure as hell do, I want to get rid of that millstone,' the lawyer felt he had better explain Fleabait Moomer:

'He's a country genius. Very bright, no morals at all. He'll do anything to win, and I warn you right now that with a case like this, he'll probably win.

He gets his name from his habit of scratching himself like a yokel while he's pleading. Scratch here. Scratch there. But twice in each case he stops, looks at the jury, crosses his arms, and scratches with both hands. The jury expects this, and they lean forward with special attention because they know he's going to make an important point. And God help you when he scratches with both hands, because that's when you're going to be crucified.

'He'll charge you with sodomy, with theft of public funds, with the corruption of juveniles, with murder, with surreptitious dealing with the enemy, anything to make you the hideous focus of the case and not your poor, wronged wife. Are you strong enough to go up against Fleabait?'

Ransom said he thought he was, and the notorious trial began. It was held in that majestic room designed seventy years earlier by James Riely Gordon, and when the disputants began their inflamed accusations, an observer might have wished that the dignified hall of justice had been reserved for worthier cases.

The judge was a serious jurist, aware of the sensational nature of the trial he was conducting, but he was powerless against the antics of Fleabait Moomer, who told the jury: 'My client, that beautiful and distressed woman you see over there, all she claims in this divorce proceeding is twenty-two million dollars. Now, that might seem a lot to you, especially if you have to work as hard for your money as I do.' And here he wiped his brow, his wrists, and his fingers. 'But it will be my duty to prove that the defendant, that slinkin' man over there –'

'I object, your Honor!'

'Objection sustained. Mr Moomer, do not cast aspersions on the defendant.'

'That unfeeling, ungentlemanly, ungenerous and –'

'I object, your Honor!'

'Objection sustained. You must not attack the defendant, Counselor Moomer.'

'It will be my task to show you good people of the jury that Ransom Rusk, who inherited all his money from his father and never did a day's lick of work in his life –'

'I object, your Honor!'

'Objection sustained. The jury will disregard everything Counselor Moomer has said regarding the defendant.'

Fleabait, who wore a string tie, suspenders, a belt, and his hair combed forward in the Julius Caesar style, scratched and mumbled and fumbled his way along, playing the role of the poor country boy doing his best to defend the interests of a wronged wife, but on the third day he stopped abruptly, crossed his arms, and scratched himself vigorously while the jury, having expected him to do this, smiled knowingly. When he finished scratching, he asked ominously: 'Have you members of the jury considered the possibility that Ransom Rusk might have been involved with a gentleman in the neighborhood, whose name I refuse to divulge because of my innate sense of decency?' There was a flurry of objections, stampedes to the telephones and general noise, after which the trial continued.

The second time Fleabait scratched with both hands, the jury leaned forward with almost visible delight to hear what scandalous thing was about to be revealed, and this time the lawyer said: 'You might well ask "How did Ransom Rusk acquire his wealth?" Did he do it by ignoring every decency in the book, every law of orderly business relations between men of honor?'

The judge properly ordered this to be stricken, but the jury were as powerless to forget what had been said as they were to ensure Rusk the impartial justice to which he was entitled. Their recommendation was for the full $22,000,000, which the judge would later scale down to $15,000,000. Fleabait had told Fleurette: 'We'll go for twenty-two and be happy if we get twelve.' Of the award, he would take forty percent, or $6,000,000.

On the evening of the adverse verdict, and while it still stood at twenty-two million, Ransom returned to his big house overlooking Bear Creek and watched with satisfaction as the sun went down. In the darkness, Mr Kramer stopped by to check on the new fence, and Ransom told him: 'I'm happier tonight than I have been in years. Free of that terrible millstone.'

'How did you happen to marry her?' The men of Larkin had long known her to be quite impossible.

'Worst reasons in the world. Reasons I'm ashamed of, believe me. Like a lot of Texas boys, I went north to Lawrenceville School, in New Jersey. One of the best. Strong teachers and all that. Well, they had this Father's Day or something, and my parents came up. Filthy rich. My father weighing three hundred, my mother the cartoon version of a Texas oilman's wife. He a slob, she ridiculous in her jewels and oil-field flamboyance. The worst three days of my life, because all the boys knew they were super-Texas, but out of decency no one said anything unkind. They just looked and laughed behind my back. When, by the grace of God, my parents finally left, I overheard one of the boys on my hall say: "She was a walking oil derrick, with the dollar bills dripping off. Poor Ransom." '

In the darkness he shuddered at that searing memory: 'Right then I decided that I would never be oil Texas. I dated the most refined girls from Vassar and Wellesley. I talked art, philosophy, anything to be unlike my father and mother. That's how I met Fleurette. I think the French name had a lot to do with it. And her determination to be so refined . . . so Eastern.'

'To tell you the truth, Ransom, you picked one hell of a lemon. You're well off, especially if you can afford the settlement.'

'Kramer, do you have a pair of wire cutters?'

'In the back of my truck.' When he returned with the long-handled instrument, which had once been outlawed in these parts, he was surprised when Rusk grabbed it and marched to the wire fence protecting his former wife's bowling green. With powerful clicks he cut a vertical path from ground to bending tip, then moved to a spot three feet away and cut another. When this was done he called for Mr Kramer to help him knock the panel flat, trampling it on the ground.

Moving farther along to where he thought the armadillos nested, he cut down two more panels, and then the fence-busters, who would have been shot for such action eighty years earlier, returned to the porch, where they sat with flashlights, and when the moon was up, Ransom cried with sheer delight: 'Here they come!'

By morning the armored destroyers would have that green looking as if it had been run over by careless bulldozers, and Ransom Rusk, $22,000,000 poorer, plus $238,000 for the fence, was happier than he had been in a long time.

As soon as Todd Morrison started digging into Houston he liked what he found. 'This town has room for a stepper,' he told his wife, 'and I think I can step.' With the funds provided by the men in Detroit, he began looking around for likely spots at which to locate his franchises, and he became excited about the possibilities.

'This place is incredible!' he told the family one night. 'A population this large and absolutely no zoning. A man can build anything he pleases, and no one can say him nay.' He pointed out that this remarkable freedom did not result in hodgepodge: 'Some kind of rational good sense seems to prevail. Builders don't go wild. They just do what they damned well please, but they sort of hold things together.'

As with many operations in a democracy, cost seemed to enforce common sense, for no builder would erect his monumental new set of condominiums next to some hovel. What he did was buy up four hundred shacks, level them, and on this cleared land erect his Taj Mahal. Some other builder would place his huge Shangri-La half a mile away, and then, out of self-respect, all the property in between would be subtly cleaned up. Houston was not a city; it was an agglomeration of stunningly beautiful spots connected by strips that would be beautiful later on. 'Zoning on the measles principle,' Todd called it. 'A red splotch here, one over there, and finally, all bound together in interrelated patterns.' Houston was the last bastion of free, private enterprise, laissez-faire at its best, and Todd relished it.

As he worked he found that a good many of the locations he preferred were controlled by a hard-working real estate agent named Gabe Klinowitz, sixty-three years old and hardened in the Houston way of doing things. He was a small, round man, smoked a cigar and wore conservative business suits when the rest of Houston preferred less formal dress. And he was bright, as the success of his firm proved.

During his first meeting with Todd he revealed one of his guiding principles: 'I look for the bright young man just entering the field. Help him get started right. Then expect to do profitable business with him for the next thirty years.'

When Todd said he'd appreciate guidance, Gabe suggested: 'What you must do is master the wraparound.'

'Which is what?'

Taking a piece of paper, Klinowitz showed Todd the secret of buying real estate for a large corporation like a gasoline company: 'You find a good spot, on the corner of two busy roads. The owner has two acres, won't break it up into smaller lots. The company, say Mobil or Humble in the old days, they can use a quarter of an acre, only. That leaves you with an acre and three-quarters wrapping around the corner in a kind of capital L. Your job as a buyer is to buy the entire piece, but not before you've found someone like me who'll take the wrap-around off your hands. Do you see the economics?'

When Todd said that he did not, Klinowitz asked him to write down the figures: 'You personally buy the whole two acres from the farmer for sixty thousand dollars. You've already arranged to sell the choice corner to Mobil for seventy-five thousand dollars. And you sell me the wraparound, all that good land next to the corner, for fifty-thousand dollars. Your profit on the deal, a cool sixty-five thousand dollars.'

Morrison studied this for a while, then pointed to the flaw: 'But I'm buying this for the company, not for myself,' and Klinowitz said: 'Before long, I suspect you'll be buying it for yourself.'

The more Todd worked with Klinowitz, the more he liked him. The man was forthright, quick and impeccably honest. He was constantly making sharp deals, but he insisted that all participants understand the intricacies, and he would go to great lengths to explain to a farmer whose land he was trying to buy what the good and bad points of the proposed deal were. Often Todd heard him say: 'You wait eight, ten years, undoubtedly you'll get a better buy. But why wait? I promise you, you'll not get a better deal right now than I'm offering.'

From watching many sales, Morrison learned one secret of Gabe's remarkable success in Houston real estate: 'Todd, you must go to bed each night reassuring yourself: "This is going to go on forever." I think it is. Houston is going to grow and grow and grow. You told me the other day that compared to Detroit prices, these are outrageous. Todd, I give you my solemn word, the two acres you buy today for sixty thousand, you'll live to see them resell for six hundred thousand. You must tell yourself that every night, and you must believe. This can go on forever.'

Once when he gave this sermon he grabbed Todd by the arm: 'So you warn me: "Gabe, the bottom can fall out of this dream," and I'm the first to confess: "Yes, it can. But only temporarily. Two, three bad years, then we come zooming back." Todd, this really can go on forever.'

Having confessed that the bottom might drop out, temporarily, he gave Todd his first piece of long-range advice: 'Always keep yourself in a position to weather a few bad years. Fire three-fourths of your staff. Put your wife and kids on severe allowance. Draw in your horns. Bring the wagons into a circle. But never lose faith. Houston real estate will always bounce back.'

And then he reached the operative part of his counsel: 'Do you see the logical consequences of this situation? If real estate is bound to zoom, it does not really matter how much you pay for a good site today. If you think the corner is worth no more than forty thousand and the farmer wants sixty thousand, give him the sixty, but he must allow you to write the terms.'

'What terms?'

'Smallest possible down payment, longest possible payout, lowest possible interest.' And he shared with Todd the details

1284

of one of his latest deals: 'This big corner, prime shopping area in the future, worth, I'd say, a hundred thousand dollars. Farmer thought he'd make a killing and ask a hundred and twenty-five thousand. Without blinking an eye I agreed, but then I insisted on an eleven-year payout, and a six-and-a-half-percent interest. He was glad to sign.'

'What's the point?'

'Don't you see? Suppose I was able to buy it at my price, but had to pay eight-percent interest for eleven years. Total interest, eighty-eight thousand dollars. If I pay his price with interest at six and a half percent, my interest bill for eleven years is eighty-nine thousand, three hundred and seventy-five, only about a thousand dollars higher. Add that to the extra twenty-five thousand he chiseled me out of, I spent only twenty-six thousand extra dollars to make him very, very happy. He can boast to all his friends: "I certainly handled that sharp Jew real estate fellow."'

'But it still cost you twenty-six thousand extra bucks.'

'Todd, you miss the whole point! If Houston real estate is going to climb like I think, eleven years from now that corner will bring me not the hundred and twenty-five thousand I paid, but more than a million. You give a little today, you make a million tomorrow.'

And when Todd still deemed it imprudent to pay more now than one had to, Gabe revealed his last principle: 'Always leave a little something on the table for the other guy. Six years from now, when the rest of the man's property is for sale, he'll come to me because he'll remember that I treated him square in 1969. I left a little on the table.'

It was strange, but perhaps inevitable, that of all the advice Gabe Klinowitz shared with his new friend, the one thing Todd remembered longest was a chance remark: 'You may be buying for the company now, but before long you'll be buying for yourself.' And the more he contemplated this prediction the mose sensible it became. One night he told his wife: 'With a little cash and a lot of gumption, a man could make a killing in this market.'

He began riding tirelessly about the highways and country roads, looking not for franchise sites, because he had that end of his business rather well in hand, thanks to leads provided by

Klinowitz, but for any stray properties which he might one day purchase for himself, and as he rode he found himself drawn northward, almost as if by magnet, to a peculiarity of the Texas scene: FM-1960.

Up to about 1950, Texas had been predominantly an agricultural state, with its laws, banking procedures and business habits attuned to the rancher and the farmer. Not even oil had exceeded in general and financial interest the importance of the land, and a generation of Texas politicians had invented and supported a creative idea of high quality, the farmer-to-market road, which ignored the through highways in favor of the small rural roads that wound here and there, enabling the farmer to bring the produce of his fields to the marketplace in the big towns. Forget the fact that if the quiet farmer-to-market road was not well planned, it quite promptly became a jammed thoroughfare; the end result of this commendable system was a network of rural roads equaled in few states.

So far to the north of central Houston that it seemed construction could never reach it, a modest farm-to-market had been established in the 1950s, called FM-1960. It was a narrow, bumpy road, well suited to a farmer's slow-moving trucks, but Morrison could see that with a little impetus from a growing population, it had a strong chance of becoming a major thoroughfare. He was so enthusiastic about its possibilities that he took options on two corners, well separated, believing that automobiles must soon be careening past, but when one of the owners of Engine Experts flew down from Detroit, the man decided instantly that these two corners were too far out to be of any use to his company, and Todd was ordered to unload.

'We have eight thousand dollars tied up in option money,' he protested, and the man said: 'That's why you pay out option money, so you gain time to correct mistakes.' In no way did he rebuke Todd, for he appreciated what a good job the latter had done in Houston, but long after he had flown back to Detroit, his decision rankled, and it was what happened as a consequence that launched Morrison on his unexpected career.

Without telling Klinowitz that he had been forced to unload the options, he went to him and said: 'I think I'd better stay closer to town. The kind of market I'm in. I have eight thousand dollars tied up in these two options on FM-1960. Must I lose the down payments, or is there some way I could unload?'

When Klinowitz saw the excellent sites he said immediately: 'I'll give you twelve thousand for your options right now. They're choice.'

'Why would you give me twelve when you know I'd be glad to get back my eight?' Todd asked and Klinowitz said: 'Always leave a little something on the table.'

Now Morrison faced a grave moral problem: Should he inform the Detroit men of the $4,000 profit he had made on the deal, or should he pocket the windfall? He consulted with no one, not Gabe, not his wife, and certainly not the big men in Detroit, but he did argue with himself: First, I was acting as their agent. Second, they laughed at the deal. Third, what are the chances they'll find out? In the end he decided to keep the money, and that, along with the $3,000 bonus he received at Christmas, plus the money his wife was earning as receptionist in another big real estate firm, enabled him to enter the new year with a nest egg of more than $11,000 and some tantalizing ideas.

In January, as he was exploring further possibilities along FM-1960, he came upon a wedge of farmland owned by an elderly Mr Hooker, and while Todd was more or less jousting with him over the possibility of buying a corner lot, a white Ford pickup screeched onto the gravel and came to a dusty stop. Apparently the driver was in the oil business, for big letters along the side proclaimed ROY BUB HOOKER, DRILLING. From the cab, which had a two-gun rack behind the driver's head, stepped a big, jovial, twenty-four-year-old wearing overalls, cheap cowboy boots and a checkered bandanna. He was your typical Texas redneck, of that there could be no doubt, but when he spoke, it was obvious that he had received a good education. It came not from his teachers, for he had despised school, but from his mother, who had taught him both a proper vocabulary and acceptable manners, neither of which he felt much inclination to use.

As soon as he stepped up to Morrison and stuck out his hand, grunting: 'Hi, I'm Roy Bub Hooker, his son,' it was obvious that details of any sale would be in Roy Bub's hands, and during one of the early meetings he explained: 'My older sister couldn't say *brother*, so she stuck me with *Bubba*, and it became Roy Bub.'

He was so shrewd a bargainer, quoting what prices corner lots had brought along FM-1960, that Todd had to warn him: 'Hey, look, Roy Bub, two things. I'm not a millionaire and I'm not even sure I want to buy' and Roy Bub snapped back: 'Who said my old man wanted to sell?'

Since he was almost offensive in the brusque manner in which he dismissed Morrison, Todd felt he must strike back to maintain balance in the bargaining: 'They warned me I could never do business with a redneck.'

'Hey, wait!' Roy Bub cried as if he were sorely wounded. 'I'm no redneck. I'm a good ol' boy.'

'What's the difference?'

'Hey! A redneck drives a Ford pickup. He has a gun rack behind his ears. He has funny little signs painted on his tailgate. He drives down the highway drinking Lone Star out of a can, which he tosses into the middle of the road.'

'I don't see the difference. You have a Ford. You have that gun rack. Look at the signs on your tailgate.' And there they were, revealing the emotional confusions that activated Roy Bub and his compadres.

HONK IF YOU LOVE JESUS
THE WEST WASN'T WON WITH A REGISTERED GUN
NATIVE BORN TEXAN AND PROUD OF IT
SECESSION NOW
SURE I'M DRUNK. — DO YOU THINK I DRIVE THIS WAY ALL THE TIME?

And off to one side, a little dustier than the others: IMPEACH EARL WARREN.

'And,' Todd added, 'I see you have one of those holders for your Lone Star. So what's the difference?'

'Old buddy!' Roy Bub cried. 'A redneck throws his empties in the middle of the road. A good ol' boy tosses his'n in the ditch.'

No sale could be agreed upon at this time, and the uncertainty gave Morrison sleepless nights in the darkness as he

1288

lay beside Maggie, exhausted after her long hours at work and housekeeping; he could never discern whether she liked Houston or not, but she certainly worked at making a good home from whatever Houston provided, and this he appreciated.

His nervousness sprang from real causes. The Hooker corner could be bought, he felt sure, for $71,000, two and three-quarter acres at a location any expert would classify as superb. He would have to make the deal on his own, because he already knew that Engine Experts would not be interested, but if he could locate a big gasoline company that wanted a prime spot for a filling station, one that would dominate the market, he might sell off the corner for $60,000, leaving him with two and a half acres for a cost of only $11,000, which would exhaust his savings.

However, if he could sell off even a small portion of his wraparound, he could discharge his debt and have two acres or even more scot-free. Then, if he was energetic, he could sell off more segments of the wraparound and come out a big winner. Also, if he could interest Gabe in some of the land he acquired in this way, he could have his profit in hand before July. And then he could take that profit . . .

During the entire month of January he slept only fitfully, for the temptations of the deal were so alluring that he spent the first half of each night calculating his possible winnings and the second half staring in the darkness at the possible catastrophes. In early February he took his wife, but not his children, into his confidence: 'Maggie, I face the chance of a lifetime. This young fellow Roy Bub Hooker has power of attorney to sell a corner lot on FM-1960. We could swing it if, and I repeat if, we could find an oil company to take the corner bit off our hands. We'd wind up with two and a half choice acres practically free, and then if, and again I repeat if . . .'

'Are you trying to convince me, or yourself?' she asked.

'You know what Houston real estate is doing. I don't have to prove anything.'

'I know what it's doing for others. Who have the land or the money. I'm not sure what it could do for us.'

'Would you be willing for us to take the risk? All our savings?'

She said a curious thing: 'You'd have to tell Detroit, of course.'

'Why?'

'Dealing in property on the side. The temptation would always be to give them the poor deal, keep the good one for yourself.'

'I don't see why they'd have to know anything.'

'I do. Business ethics. The sanctity of the arm's-length deal.'

'Now what do you mean by that?'

'It's something they drummed into me when I got my license. An honest deal involves two people who shake hands across a carefully protected distance. No internal hanky-panky. No secret brother-in-law shakedown.' Something in the recent behavior of her fast-moving husband caused her to warn: 'Todd, any deal you engage in must be at arm's length.'

On Sunday she rode out to FM-1960, and as soon as she saw the corner, she wanted to buy it, and after they had supper with Roy Bub, she liked him even more than she had his land: 'You're an original, Roy Bub, don't ever change.'

'Minute we sell that land, I'm gettin' me a Cadillac.'

'That'll be the day,' she said, and he confided: 'But I will tell you this, your husband buys that corner, I am gettin' me a first-class stereo for my truck.'

She shuddered: 'The new Texas. Roy Bub roaring down the highway at ninety with his stereo full blast. Won't even hear the siren when the cops chase him,' and he said: 'Ma'am, that's exactly what I have in mind.'

So on the fourth of February she gave permission for the deal, if Todd thought he could swing it, and on the fifth, adhering to Gabe's strategy, he agreed to Roy Bub's price if he could dictate the terms: 'Nine thousand cash on signing, so's you can get that stereo. Eleven-year payout. Six-percent interest.' Roy Bub, who had studied so hard to determine the fair price for his land, had paid no attention to the going rates of interest and did not realize that he might have got seven and a half percent on the unpaid balance.

But now the sweating in the rented house in Quitman Street really began, for when Todd inquired casually among the men who bought land for the big oil companies, he found they were not eager to locate their filling stations so far north of the city, and although he praised FM-1960 rather fulsomely, they tended to say: 'Sure it's good, but we can wait till traffic picks up, if it does.'

He went through March, April and May without a nibble, and one night as he tossed sleeplessly he faced the fact that come next January, only seven months away, he would be required to pay Roy Bub the first instalment of interest plus a reduction of the balance, and he could not imagine where he could find that kind of money. Nor had he located anyone interested in his remainder of the wraparound. The future seemed extremely bleak, and he joined that endless procession of Texan gamblers who had risked mightily on the chance of winning big. Mattie Quimper had tried to claim both banks of the river in the 1820s, and Floyd Rusk had pulled his own tricks a hundred years later when trying to sew up the Larkin Field. It was the Texas game, and all who played it to the hilt sweated in the dark night hours, but like Todd Morrison in 1969, they gritted their teeth: 'Something will turn up.'

His savior, as he might have anticipated, was Gabe Klinowitz: 'Todd, I believe you're on the pointy end of a long stick.'

'I am. But I put myself there.'

'Have you told the people in Detroit what you're doing?'

'No.'

'You should. Fiduciary responsibility. When lawyers forget about this, they go to jail. You forget, you could be fired.' He spoke from the widest possible experience in oil, insurance, real estate and the legal profession; men who cut too many corners ran the risk of jail.

'I'll tell them when I get sorted out.'

'I hope that won't be too late.' He changed his tone: 'I've heard that an independent is looking for a choice site on FM-1960.'

'Independents pay bottom dollar, don't they?'

'But they pay.' When Todd said nothing, Gabe said: 'Always remember the advice J. P. Morgan gave a young assistant. Young fellow said: "Mr Morgan, how much should a man my age buy on margin?" and Morgan said: "That depends," and the young fellow said: "I've borrowed so much I can hardly sleep at night," and Morgan said: "Simple. Sell to the sleeping point."'

'Meaning?'

'Your prime responsibility, Todd, is to get some cash back in your hand. If I offered you forty thousand dollars today, grab it. Pay off your obligations. Make a little less on the deal, but remain in condition to hold on to the rest of your wraparound.'

'Could you get me forty thousand?'

'I'm sure I can do better. Fifty-one thousand, maybe as much as fifty-three.'

'My God! That would get me off the hook.' He grasped Gabe's hand, then asked: 'But why would you do this for me? You know you could take it off my hands at whatever price you set, and make yourself a bundle.'

'Todd, I have sixteen deals cooking. I think you're going to be in this business for the rest of my life. In years to come we'll arrange a hundred deals. I can wait for my big profits. You need your fragile profits right now.' They shook hands formally, and Todd said: 'A man like you is worth a million.'

And then, just as Todd was about to sign the papers Gabe had sent him, Gulf Oil decided that, after all, they would experiment with an FM-1960 location, and they heard that Todd had the inside track on a fine corner. With his knees shaking, Todd told them: 'I think I could put you on the inside track for seventy-one thousand dollars.' The Gulf representative, eager to close a deal once the decision had been made by his head office, agreed, and the sale was closed, with Todd and the Gulf man shaking hands.

Elated but nervous, Todd now had to inform Klinowitz that the deal with the independent had to be canceled, even though a gentleman's agreement had been reached: 'Nothing was signed, you know, Gabe, and Gulf was so hungry to get the land, they demanded an answer right away. I tried to call you, but you were out.' And although each man knew that a handshake had sanctified the sale to the independent, Gabe merely said: 'I'll find them something, but, Todd, I hope you inform Detroit that you've been dealing on your own. There are rules to this game, you know,' and Todd said: 'Absolutely!' but the letter he had drafted in his head, aware that it ought to be sent, was never written.

The Morrisons as a family ran into their first serious Texas decision when daughter Beth entered Miss Barlow's

1292

junior-high class in Texas history. Each child in the Texas system studied state history at two different levels, first as a legend when young, then as simplified glorification at Beth's age. The scholarly could also take it as an elective in high school and as an optional course in college. The goal of this intense concentration was, as one curriculum stated, 'to make children aware of their glorious heritage and to ensure that they become loyal Texas citizens.'

Few teachers, at any of the four levels, taught with the single-minded ferocity exhibited daily by Flora Barlow. She was in her sixties, a cultured quiet woman whose ancestors had played major roles in the periods she talked about, and while she was not family-proud, as some teachers of her subject tended to be, she was inwardly gratified that her family had helped to shape what she was convinced was the finest single political entity in the world, the semi-nation of Texas.

Standing before a massive map of Texas that showed all the counties in outline only, she said softly: 'Your Texas has two hundred and fifty-four counties, many times more than less fortunate states, and one day when I was just starting to teach, a young fellow teacher, educated in the North, looked at our map with its scatter of counties and said, rather boldly I thought: "Looks as if Texas had freckles."'

When her children laughed, she said: 'It would be quite silly of me, wouldn't it, if I required you to memorize the names of all the counties?' When the children groaned, she said solemnly: 'But I can name them. With their county seats.'

She called to the front of the room one of her pupils, and it chanced to be Beth Morrison: "Here is the pointer, Beth. Point as you will at any county on that map, and I shall give you its name and the name of its county seat.'

Stabbing blindly at the center of the map, Beth's pointer struck a large, oddly shaped county: 'That's Comanche County, named after our raiding Indians; county seat, Comanche.'

When Beth tried the northeast corner, Miss Barlow said promptly: 'You've chosen Upshur County, named after a United States Secretary of State, Abel P. Upshur; county seat, Gilmer.'

Now Beth indicated one of the many squared-off western counties, a score of them almost identical in size and shape, but without hesitation Miss Barlow said: 'You're on Hale County, named for our great hero Lieutenant J. C. Hale, who died gallantly defeating General Santa Anna at San Jacinto; county seat, the important city of Plainview. If you're going to live and prosper in Texas, it's prudent to know where things are.'

When Beth reported this amazing performance to her parents, they at first laughed, for they had undergone an amusing embarrassment over one of the Texas counties, Bexar, which contained the attractive city of San Antonio. 'It's spelled B-e-x-a-r,' Mrs Morrison said, 'and for the longest time your father and I pronounced it Bex-ar, the way any sensible person would. But then we kept hearing on the radio when we drove to work "Bare County this and Bare County that," and one day we asked: "Where is this Bare County?" and the old-timers: "That's how we say Bexar." So now your father and I know where Bare County is.'

But as the family studied this matter – Beth in school, her parents in the daily life – they discovered that Miss Barlow was not being arbitrary in insisting that her pupils know something about the multiple counties of Texas, because unlike any other state, Texas wrote its history in relationship to its counties. This was partly because the state was so enormous that it had to be broken down into manageable regions, but more because the towns within the regions were often so small and relatively unimportant that few people could locate them. A man or a family did not come from some trivial county seat containing only sixty persons; that man or family came from an entire county, and once the name of that county was voiced, every knowing listener knew what kind of man he was.

The statement "We moved from Tyler County to Polk,' told the entire story of a farmer who had sought better land to the west. 'My grandfather raised cotton in Cherokee County, but when the crop failed three times running, he tried cattle in Palo Pinto.' That summarized three decades of Texas agricultural history.

One either knew the basic counties or remained ignorant of Texas history, and Miss Barlow did not intend that any of her students should have such a handicap. To help them master the outlines, she had devised an imaginative exercise, and it was in the execution of this that Beth, and indeed the entire Morrison family, fell foul of the Deaf Smith school system: 'My former students have found it helpful to identify five counties ... Choose any five you wish, but they must be in five widely separated parts of the state. After you select your counties, memorize them and their county seats. Then you will always have a kind of framework onto which you can attach the other counties in that district.'

Most of the students, eager to escape extra work, chose easy picks whose important county seat bore the same name as the county, such as Dallas in the north, El Paso in the far west, Lubbock in the west, and Galveston on the Gulf of Mexico. Boys usually picked popular names like Deaf Smith along the New Mexico border, Maverick on the Rio Grande, or Red River on the boundary stream of that name. And of course, there were always some smart alecks who chose 'Floyd County; county seat, Floydada' or 'Bee County; county seat, Beeville.' Miss Barlow indulged such choices because she had learned that any student who nailed down his five counties, wherever they were, could build upon them the relationships required in Texas history.

'I'll start with Kenedy,' Beth told her mother that night, 'because even though it's a different spelling, it's practically your maiden name.' This took care of the southeast corner of the state, and she was about to move on to four other regions when she happened to jot down in her notebook the salient facts about Kenedy County, and as soon as she had done so, a naughty idea flashed into her mind, and for about an hour she pored over the data in an old copy of the *Texas Almanac*, checking this county and that. Somewhat irritated by Miss Barlow's constant hammering on the size of Texas, she was seeking the five most insignificant counties, a d in the end she came up with a startling collection, as the extremely neat page in her notebook proved: see table on p. 1296.

As soon as Beth's parents saw the cynical heading, they realized that if she submitted it in that form, she was going to get into trouble not only with her teacher but with her xenophobic classmates as well, and her mother asked tentatively: 'Don't you think, Beth, that your heading is ... well ... couldn't it be considered inflammatory?'

NAME	POP.	DERIVATION OF NAME	COUNTY SEAT	POP.
Kenedy	678	Cattle baron, helped start King Ranch	Armstrong	20
King	464	Great hero, member Gonzales Immortal 32	Guthrie	140
Loving	163	Cattle driver, corpse hauled in lead box	Mentone	41
McMullen	998	Famous Irish immigrant, found murdered	Tilden	420
Robert	967	Chief Justice and Governor of Texas	Miami	746
	3,270			1,367

'I'm sick and tired of being teased because I wasn't born in Texas.'

'But don't you think this is rather arrogant? I mean . . . Aren't you rubbing their noses in it?'

Beth considered this carefully, and although she refused to alter her choice of counties on the grounds that Miss Barlow had said she could choose any she wished, so long as they were well scattered, she did have to agree that her title was combative, so she changed it to MY FIVE FAVORITE COUNTIES OF TEXAS. And without complaining she redid her chart, making it even more attractive than before.

Unfortunately, on Saturday night, several of Beth's classmates dropped by the Morrisons' for an after-the-movie snack, and the matter of county choices came up. Todd, overhearing a discussion in which minor counties were accorded the deference usually reserved for continents, cried: 'Hey! Don't you kids have things slightly out of proportion?' When they asked what he meant, he questioned them: 'Where is Korea? Can you identify Belgium on the map? Where do you think Rumania is? Where's Thailand?'

He learned to his astonishment that whereas Beth's friends could identify Borden County – population 907; named after the man who invented condensed milk; county seat, Gail, population 178 – few of them could accurately place Argentina – population 22,000,000; name derived from the Latin word for silver; capital city, Buenos Aires, population 3,768,000 – and none of them had heard of places like Mongolia, Albania or Paraguay.

In school on Monday these students would remember that Mr Morrison had laughed at the counties of Texas, remarking that he considered Malaysia, with a population of more than eleven million and occupying a strategic point on the world's trade routes, was at least as important as his daughter's King County, Texas, with its population of 464 and its roads leading nowhere.

Even this ungenerous comparison would have led to nothing had not Miss Barlow, hoping to get this important lesson properly launched, called on Beth to recite her five, and with the sureness of a trained cartographer, Beth rattled off name, population and county seat, jabbing accurately with her pointer at Kenedy to the southeast, King hidden among the central squares, Loving far out west, McMullen, the Irish county due south of San Antonio, and Roberts up in the northwest.

It was, as Miss Barlow had anticipated, a sterling performance, but then the teacher spoiled it by asking: 'What was your principle of selection, Beth?' and the latter replied honestly: 'I looked for the five with the smallest population.' At this the class began to giggle, and one of the boys who had been present Saturday night reported: 'Mr Morrison said that Malaysia, or somewhere, with eleven million people was a damned sight more important than King County, Texas, with four hundred and sixty-four.'

'What word did you use?' Miss Barlow said sternly.

'I didn't use it. He did.'

At this, Miss Barlow held out her hand for Beth's notebook and looked at the mocking table. Her face flushed, and after school she telephoned the senior Morrisons, informing them that she must see them.

When she sat, prim and defiant, in their living-room, she launched her complaint against a girl who should by every indication have been her prize pupil: 'Your daughter is talented, to be sure, but she lacks a proper respect for subject matter.'

'Where is she deficient?' Mrs Morrison asked.

'She laughs at Texas history,' Miss Barlow said primly.

'I believe she studies very hard,' Mrs Morrison said

defensively.

'Studies, yes. But she does like to make fun of things.'

'Whatever do you mean?'

'Wait a minute,' Mr Morrison interrupted. 'Was it her list of counties, Miss Barlow?'

'Indeed it was, Mr Morrison. But that's only part of my complaint.'

'Look, Beth is a bright child, an imaginative one. If you ask me, her choice showed industry, wit, a sense of . . .'

'Mr Morrison, no child will get far living in Texas if she makes fun of Texas history.'

'Well, you must admit that a county like What's-its-name, with a population of a hundred and sixty plus or minus and county seat of forty people, by normal standards . . .'

'Texas is not judged by normal standards. Did you know, Mr Morrison, that when nine-tenths of our counties were first authorized by the legislature, each contained less than fifty white people? We were subduing a wild, empty land, and we did it very cleverly, I believe, by first establishing the counties and hoping that people would come along to fill them. The county you refer to so inaccurately is Loving, I believe. It hasn't received its people yet, but it will be waiting there, and in good order, when the people finally arrive.'

'I'm sure Beth meant no disrespect,' Mrs Morrison said.

'Well, she showed it.'

'Miss Barlow, Beth identified five counties with a total population, if I remember correctly, of less than three thousand three hundred persons. Crossroads villages in Michigan have more than . . .'

What an unfortunate comparison! Miss Barlow stiffened and said: 'Texas is not to be judged by the standards you would use for Vermont or Indiana,' and the scorn she poured into those two names indicated her opinion of the backward states referred to. 'Texas was its own sovereign nation, and it still forms an empire off to itself. Neither you nor your daughter will be happy here if you fail to acknowledge that.'

Mrs Morrison said mildly: 'I'm sure that if Beth has offended either you or your class, she will apologize.'

'Your daughter has not misbehaved in any overt way, but her attitude has been almost frivolous. One must take Texas history

1298

seriously, and sometimes children unlucky enough to have been born in other ...' She dropped that sentence, for although she used it often inside her classroom, she realized that outside, it did sound rather chauvinistic. She was emotionally and morally sorry for those children who had not been born in Texas, but she realized that blazoning her condescension was not always fruitful.

'Beth is a bright child,' she conceded. 'And if she acquires the right attitudes she can go far ... perhaps even the university at Austin.'

'We're thinking of Michigan,' Mr Morrison said coldly.

'I'm sure it's respectable,' she said, and then, with the honest warmth which made her a successful teacher, she added: 'No one in our grade writes more beautifully than your Beth. In her mature use of words she's exceptional. Don't encourage her to waste such marked talent by being what the children call "a smart ass."'

No more was said about the counties, either in class or out, until one blustery day at the end of February, when Miss Barlow said quietly: 'Beth, in your list of counties, if I remember, you had King County. Could you locate it now if I hand you the ruler?' And it was remarkable, but almost every child in that class could now go to the big outline map and point unerringly to his or her five counties; Miss Barlow's exercise had imprinted these locations forever, and as she predicted, her students were now beginning to relate the other two hundred and forty-nine counties to those already learned.

Without hesitation Beth pointed to four-square King, almost identical in shape to another twenty clustered about it. 'Now, Beth, do you remember whom that county was named after?'

'William P. King of the Immortal ʿ ʾhirty-two from Gonzales.'

'And do you know who the Immortal Thirty-two were?'

Frantically Beth scoured her mind, and only the vaguest data came forth, so that finally she was forced to confess: 'I don't know, Miss Barlow, but somehow I think they had to do with the Alamo.'

'You are right, and you may sit down.'

Then, in a low voice which none of the children who heard it that day would ever forget, Miss Barlow began a quiet recitation of the facts surrounding one of the overwhelming incidents of Texas history, and as she spoke, time shifted backward and her listeners were in the small town of Gonzales, east of San Antonio:

'It was on this very day, one hundred and thirty-three years ago, that a messenger galloped into Gonzales with the dreadful news that the Alamo was surrounded by General Santa Anna's troops and that the brave defenders inside were doomed to death, all of them, unless they received help. "They must have reinforcements," was all the messenger said. As he uttered these words the men of Gonzales knew that even if they did march to the rescue, the Alamo was doomed. There was no way that so few Texans, however brave, could hold off so many Mexicans, however cowardly. Whoever entered the Alamo was certain to die.

'So what did they do? Thirty-two of the bravest men Texas would ever produce shouldered their muskets, kissed their women goodbye, and marched resolutely into the sunset. And I want you to remember this, young people. The men of Gonzales didn't just go up to the gates of the Alamo and cry "Let us in!" No, they had to fight their way in, cutting a path through the Mexican army. At any point they'd have been justified in turning back, but none did. They fought to enter, and in doing so, found death and immortality.

'As sure as the sun rises, every one of you in this classroom, boys and girls alike, will some day find yourself in the town of Gonzales, listening to your messenger cry "Help us or we perish!" It may happen to you in El Paso or Lubbock or Galveston.' (Miss Barlow was incapable of visualizing her graduates as living outside Texas.) 'And each of you will be called upon to make a decision of the most vital importance: right or wrong . . . life or death. And the manner in which you respond will determine whether you will be known as immortal or craven.

'If I tell you about the glories of Texas history with pride and deep feelings it's because one of the Thirty-two Immortals was my great-grandfather Moses Barlow, and the woman he kissed goodbye as he marched off to the Alamo

1300

was my grandmother Rachel, who was four years old at the time but who remembered that day until she died in 1930 in Milam County at the age of ninety-eight. So I heard of Gonzales personally from a woman who was there that day, and when you are an old person in San Antonio or Fort Worth, you can tell your grandchildren in the year 2036 that you yourself heard me speak of a woman who was present when the heroes of Gonzales marched voluntarily to death and immortality.'

On no student did the impact of that lesson fall more heavily than on Beth Morrison. For two days she went directly to her room after supper, preferring to speak to no one and refusing even to answer her telephone when it rang. On the third day she asked wanly: 'What parts of Texas did we like best when we saw those slides?' and she joined her family in analyzing the virtues of the forested northeast, the blazing sands of the Rio Grande and the mountains of the west. Her brother said he liked best the sign in the park which said BEWARE RATTLESNAKES. She ignored this, and on the fourth morning she appeared at breakfast with a single sheet of paper, which she hesitantly showed her mother, who cried: 'Beth, this is really good. This is much better than I could have done.' When her father asked to see it, Beth grabbed it nervously and said: 'Later.'

She went to school early, slipped into her classroom and deposited on Miss Barlow's desk a brown envelope that showed no indication of its source, and when class began Miss Barlow coughed and said: 'Today we have a most wonderful surprise. One of our members has written a beautiful poem, which I want to share with you. It's called "A Song of Texas."'

'Bluebonnets, paintbrush on trails through the pine,
Sweep of the meadow that climbs to the hill,
My hungry heart makes this loveliness mine.
Sleep or awake I shall cherish you still—
O Texas, your beauty enchants me forever.

Cactus and mesquite, the bold Rio Grande
Cuts a deep swath through your perilous waste,
Marks me a path through the treacherous sand,
Leads me to wonders that I have embraced—
O Texas, your harshness invites me forever.

Blue mountains, brush on wild plains of the west,
Challenging eagles to soar to new heights,
Offering refuge to only the best,
You dazzle us all with your wondrous delights—
O Texas, your greatness rewards me forever.'

The room was very quiet as Miss Barlow folded the paper and returned it to its brown envelope: 'I think we can guess who wrote this lovely poem, can't we?' and with no exception, all in the class turned to look at Beth, for only she ever used such words or framed them into such images.

That evening Miss Barlow telephoned the Morrisons to reassure them: 'I think your little Beth is coming around. She's developing a proper attitude toward things that matter.' And the next morning at breakfast Beth startled her parents, almost to the point of making them choke on their coffee, by saying with great fervor: 'Gosh, wouldn't it be awful to marry a man who wasn't from Texas?'

In the Rio Grande Valley things were not going well for Héctor Garza. Seventy-eight years old and far less agile than he had been in the days when he helped Horace Vigil run the Valley, he had been forced to watch his Mexican community fall into sad disarray, for the dictatorship had been taken over by Horace's nephew, an austere, grasping man named Norman Vigil, who considered the area to be his fiefdom but did not accord peasants like Héctor the courtesies due them.

'He derives his power from us,' Héctor complained to younger men, 'but he shows us no thanks. Worst of all, he shows us no respect.'

Héctor could have made his protest much stronger, for Norman Vigil, displaying none of that classic grandeur of the typical Mexican patrón who robbed and ruled with style, was a mean-spirited man who grabbed everything and shared nothing. 'He sends his beer trucks over three counties but never gives the Little League a dime.' He also never gave hospitals or schools a dime, either, and Héctor sometimes thought that the slim strand of inheritance that had once kept Horace Vigil so strong a member of the Hispanic community had vanished in the case of Norman.

'He's not Mexican at all,' Héctor said, 'He's pure gringo, and in this Valley that's a bad thing to be.'

To explain how Vigil managed to keep his power was rather difficult, for the anglos with whom he associated exclusively represented only twelve percent of the population, while the Hispanics made up eighty-eight. Yet Vigil saw to it that the anglos controlled the school board, the police department, all the banks and most of the retail establishments. He did this by dominating the politics and determining who should run for what office; obviously, he could not himself cast all the ballots for his candidates, but because of his economic power he could terrorize the local Mexicans, forcing them to vote for his men, and he did still control that vital Precinct 37, and from it, late on election night, he extracted whatever number of votes he required to keep his preferred Democrat in power. He was also protected by state officials, who appreciated his votes, and in the wild Senate primary of 1948, when the upstart Democrat Lyndon Johnson defeated the established Democrat, ex-Governor Coke Stevenson, by eighty-seven votes out of nearly a million cast, Norman Vigil had provided from Precinct 37 a vote of Stevenson 13, Johnson 344, and such a reliable man was not going to be treated roughly by state investigators so long as the Democratic party stayed in power.

But the principal reason why Vigil continued his dictatorship was one which would have applied in no other state, even though its police could be as rough as those in Texas: for several decades the captain of the Texas Rangers along the border had been Oscar Macnab, now sixty-nine years old and retired from active duty, but still a dominant figure in Saldaña County politics and one of Norman Vigil's chief supporters.

Macnab had made his reputation as a young Ranger in the oil fields of Larkin County when he tamed a boom-town frenzy almost single-handedly. Cool in temperament, determined when he got started, and severely just according to his own definitions, he had transferred about 1940 to the Rio Grande, where, during the years of World War II, he ran the territory pretty much as he wished. Since he had acquired the Ranger's traditional distrust of Indians, blacks and what he called 'Meskins,' and the traditional respect for anyone who had

acquired an unusual amount of money, he had found it easy to
fit into Rio Grande life; white American men of importance,
like Norman Vigil, were to be protected; brown Hispanics, like
Héctor Garza, were to be kept in their place; and outright
Mexicans, like those who swam across the river to vote Norman
Vigil in elections, were to be eliminated if they stepped out of
line.

In his nearly thirty years of control in Saldaña County,
Macnab had served as the right arm of Norman Vigil, arresting
those Vigil wanted arrested, frightening those Vigil wanted to
chase out of his county. At election time he policed the polls,
keeping away troublemakers and suspected liberals. After the
votes were counted, he saw to it that any complaints were
muffled, and if the protester pursued his objections, Macnab
helped muscle him out of the area.

The captain never thought of himself as the colleague and
protector of the local dictator, but that's what he was. Nor
would he admit that he was prejudiced against Mexicans or
Hispanics: 'I don't like Meskins. Don't trust them. And I
expect to give them an order only once. But I am certainly not
prejudiced against them. I have solved many murders involving
only Meskins and will do so again if called upon. But you
cannot force me to like them.'

He had had in his company from time to time Rangers who
had blazed away at Mexicans with almost no provocation, and
there were, he would admit privately, 'a few scoundrels on my
team that could have been tried for murder, but this is a frontier
area and I must insist that by and large, justice was done. I saw
to that.'

Justice for Macnab consisted of identifying the interests of
those in command, Norman Vigil, for example, or the big
landowners, and then seeing that those interests were protected
and if necessary furthered; in an orderly society that was the
only thing to do. For example, when field workers on the big
citrus plantations, now the principal source of wealth in the
Valley, sought to form a labor union, an un-Texas thing to do,
Captain Macnab found every excuse for hampering their
efforts, including arresting them, threatening them, and keeping them from holding public meetings. He never opposed
them as union agitators, which they were, but only as people

threatening the peace of an otherwise quiet and pleasant valley: 'If their hearts are set on a union, let them move to New Jersey, where anything goes.' He was equally stern when teachers agitated for higher wages in the Saldaña school system: 'To strike or even talk about striking is un-American and will not be tolerated in my district.'

It was the custom, in the Spanish-speaking community, to refer to Rangers as Rinches, and Captain Macnab became the premier Rinche of his district. It was he who enforced the laws on the Hispanics, who kept their children in line the way the anglos preferred, and who dictated the terms of general behavior. If a Hispanic behaved himself and made no move to strike the citrus growers for higher wages, he encountered no trouble from Captain Machab.

During his first twenty years of duty along the Rio Grande he arrested two white men. One had holed himself up in a shack with his estranged wife, threatening to kill her if anyone moved toward the place. Macnab never hesitated. Gun at the ready, he walked in and saved the distraught woman, who then refused to bring charges against her man. The other was a persistent drunk who tried to deliver the Sunday sermon at the Baptist church; he was easily removed.

But he found it necessary to arrest hundreds of Mexicans who seemed not to fit into Texas life. They either stole things, or beat their wives, or refused to send their children to school, or ran off with cars belonging to white men. If one had talked with Macnab during these years, he would never have heard of the countless law-abiding Hispanics. Like the Swedes of Minnesota or the Czechs of Iowa, the Hispanics of Texas were good and bad. Macnab dealt only with the bad, and in this group he placed anyone of Mexican heritage who endeavored, by even the slightest move, to alter any aspect of Valley life from the way he believed it had always been, and should remain. He was therefore alerted when Norman Vigil, who now lived in a spacious house far removed from the beer-distribution office, summoned him to an unscheduled meeting.

'Captain, I can see trouble, real trouble, coming at us down the road.'

'Like what?'

'This Héctor Garza, used to work for my uncle, reliable sort normally, he wants to run a damned Meskin for mayor.'

'You already have a mayor, don't you?'

'Good man. Selected him myself. Used to work on one of the big citrus plantations.'

'Then why should Héctor . . . ?'

'He says it's time the Meskins had their own mayor.'

'Hell, how old is he?'

'You won't believe it, but he must be past seventy-five.'

'Why don't he roll over and quit makin' trouble?'

'How old are you, Captain?'

'I'm sixty-nine, but I'm not tryin' to run the Ranger office. Tell him to knock it off.'

'He won't do it. I think he sees this as his last battle.'

'It *will* be his last if he tries to mess up this county. Things are in good shape here. Let's keep them as they are.'

'I don't think he sees it that way. One of my men heard him speak to a group. He told them: "The time has come to exert our numbers," or some damned nonsense like that.'

'He certainly doesn't want the office himself, does he? At his age?'

'No! He's been coaching his grandson.'

'Simón? The one who went to college up in Kansas?'

'Yep. You give one of those Meskins a book, he thinks he's Charlemagne.'

'We should of slowed Simón down years ago.'

'Once they go to college, they should never be allowed back.'

And that was how the Bravo Incident, which commanded the national press for several months, began. Héctor Garza, in the waning years of his life, thought that if his Hispanics constituted over eighty-five percent of the Valley population, they should have some say in how the Valley was run, but once he publicly voiced this belief, he put himself athwart the political power of Norman Vigil and the police power of Oscar Macnab.

The confrontation started on a low key, with Macnab utilizing every political trick to keep the Hispanics off balance. Wearing his fawn-gray whipcord suit, his big hat and his boots, he appeared suddenly wherever they were proposing to hold a rally, and quietly but forcefully informed them that this was illegal without permission from the local judge. He would also dominate hearings convened by the judge and guide the decisions handed down. He was tough in breaking up political meetings, citing possible subversion or endangerment to the community, and whenever the two Garzas devised some way to neutralize his quiet tyranny, he would come up with a new trick to harass them.

He refrained from ever touching either the elder Garza or his grandson, but he did have them arrested twice, for blocking the highway, and he did see to it that they spent three nights in jail. But with the lesser Hispanics he could be extremely rough, knocking them about and threatening them with greater harm if they persisted in their attempt to elect a Mexican mayor in opposition to the perfectly good man who had been running the town, with Norman Vigil's help, for the past dozen years.

One morning, in frustration, Macnab marched in to the Hispanic political headquarters and demanded to see Héctor Garza: 'What in hell are you Meskins tryin' to do?'

'We're trying to govern this town, as our numbers entitle us to do.'

'Your numbers, as you call them, have no right to trespass on the rights of those good folks who have given us good government for all the years of this century.'

'That's not good enough any more, Captain.'

'It'll be good enough if I say so. You stop this nonsense, Héctor, and get back to your patio. These are things that don't concern you.'

'They concern us very much. Mr Vigil can't run this town any longer the way he wants to.'

The meeting ended in an impasse, with Ranger Macnab, a little heavier now, handing out the orders as in decades past, and Héctor Garza, a little thinner, resisting them. As Macnab left the headquarters, frustrated by this sudden emergence of a power he could not suppress, he warned: 'Héctor, if you go ahead with this, you're goin' to get hurt, bad hurt.' To him, Bravo and its resurgent Mexicans were exactly like Larkin and its rioting roughnecks: you subdued each by the application of steady force, and he was prepared to import all the force required to put down this insurgency.

But then Héctor Garza sent a telegram to Washington, and a Mr Henderson appeared in town, a tall man in a blue-serge suit.

Summoning Norman Vigil and Oscar Macnab to his hotel room, he informed them: 'Thomas Henderson, Justice Department. I'm here to see that the civil rights of your Hispanic citizens are protected in the coming election. I'm bringing in two deputies, so you men keep your noses clean.'

The Vigils of Saldaña County had been fending off Washington since 1880, and never had they allowed its representatives to penetrate the power structure of the Rio Grande. Norman assumed that he could resist them again, but Mr Henderson sought his injunctions not in Bravo but in the federal court in Corpus Christi, and he opposed every connivance put forward by Vigil and the Rangers. Finally, in irritation because these men continued acting as if the twentieth century had never dawned, he went to see Oscar Macnab, for whom he had considerable respect: 'Captain, why does a man of your apparent good sense always side with a man like Norman Vigil?'

'Because he represents the law.'

'You ever heard of justice?'

'I've noticed, sir, that whenever somebody starts talkin' about justice, everybody else runs into a lot of trouble. Law I can understand, it's specific. Norman Vigil has represented the law in this community since I can remember. Justice is something people make parades about.'

'Why do you always side with the few whites against the many Mexicans?'

'This is a white man's country, Mr Henderson, and when you fellows in Washington forget that, you're headin' into deep trouble. We don't want that trouble down here. We seek to avoid it as long as possible.'

'You seem to classify all Mexicans as crooks and rioters.'

'In my experience, that's what most of them are.'

'Captain Macnab, it's two weeks before election. If you don't change your attitude, right now, when the election is over I'm going to hale you into federal court with a list of charges this long.'

In a dozen similar situations Mr Henderson had been able to strike fear into the hearts of the local tyrants, but he had never before tried to interfere in a Texas county filled with many Hispanics and a few determined whites. He was startled by the brazen defiance Vigil and Macnab threw at him, and when election day arrived he was unprepared for the open violence with which these two men threw back the Hispanics who wanted to vote, the repressions, the animosities, and he was shocked to find that Vigil had imported from south of the Rio Grande more than a hundred peons who had been paid two dollars each to vote against the interests of their Hispanic cousins north to the river.

The Garza challenge lost, for Precinct 37, with more than ninety percent Hispanic voters, reported an overwhelming majority for the Vigil slate, which meant that Norman would remain patrón for four more years.

Héctor and his grandson vowed to resume the fight in the next election, but this was not to be, for shortly after the failed election Héctor fell ill, passed into a coma, and died without regaining consciousness. From the time of his youth in the early 1900s, and during the violent years of Horace Vigil, ending with the old man's death in the 1920s, he had been a loyal foot soldier for the dictator. He had then served Norman Vigil faithfully, but in his seventies he had begun to see what a fearfully heavy price the Hispanics paid for this allegiance. He had tried to break it and had failed, but he had inspired his grandson Simón to launch an effort, and he died trusting that Simón would carry on this crusade.

In the meantime, law and order, Rio Grande style, remained in effect.

With a little money in their pockets, the Morrisons of Detroit were having an exciting time in Texas. When the big bosses in the home office discovered that Todd had been buying and selling real estate on his own without informing them, they summarily fired him. Loss of the salaried job meant that Todd had to work more diligently at his deals, but with continued advice from Gabe Klinowitz he accumulated commissions and outright deals in his own name. Also, Maggie, having obtained her own real estate license, was now selling rather effectively for a large central-city firm. She wrote to her friends in Detroit:

Each week we like it more. Todd is doing amazingly well as what the Texans call a wheeler-dealer, and with my own license I am becoming Madam Real Estate.

What has been most difficult to adjust to? You'd never guess! The size of the cockroaches. I mean, as big as sparrows and terribly aggressive. The other evening I heard Lonnie screaming in the kitchen, and there he stood with a broom. 'Mummy!' he cried 'Two of them were trying to drag me outside.' I gave him a real swipe.

You would be unprepared for the noise and bustle of Houston. Where Detroit was dying, this place springs to a more abundant life each morning. Whew! Life in the fast lane! Dips and darts on the roller-coaster! And you'd also never guess the little things that we like so much.

Beth and Lonnie both excel in school, claiming that Texas schools are about two years behind the ones they attended in Detroit. I doubt this. Just a different approach.

The city is a joy, and half you kids ought to pack up right now and move down here, for this is tomorrow. I'm sure I wouldn't have advised this fifteen years ago, because the temperature in summer can be ugh! But air conditioning has remade the city, and they should erect a monument to Westinghouse or whoever invented it. A step forward in civilization.

The barbecue, about which we heard so much, has been a disappointment. Not that delicious stuff we bought on Woodward Avenue, bits of beef with that tangy sauce. Here it's great slabs of beef, well roasted I'll grant, but no sauce, no taste unless you like the smell of charred mesquite, which I don't.

What do I miss most? You'd never guess. *The New York Times* crossword puzzles. Remember how we used to wait for the one o'clock arrival of the Sunday *Times*, and then we'd call one another about five in the afternoon: 'Did you get 43 across? Sweet idea, eh?' It sort of made the week legitimate, a test of whether the old cranium was still functioning. Well, I doubt there's a person in Houston does that puzzle, and we're all the worse for it.

Todd was entering the most rewarding span of his life, for in Roy Bub Hooker he had discovered a man who loved the outdoors as much as he did, and after the sale of the Hooker corner was completed and Roy Bub did buy the expensive stereo for his truck, they drove about the suburbs of Houston, talking real estate, listening to country and western music, and sharing their attitudes on wildlife.

'Todd, they ain't nothin' on this earth more fun than stalkin' a brood of wild turkey. Man, them birds has radar, they can outsmart you ever' time. Only thing saves the hunter is that they are also some of the dumbest birds God ever made. They escape you, run in a circle, then double right back to where you're waitin'.'

'Best I ever experienced,' Todd said, 'was hunting whitetail deer in northern Michigan when snow was on the ground. Icicles in the trees. Brown grass crackling. And all of a sudden, whoosh, out of a hollow darts this buck. Temptation is to shoot him in the rear, but that always loses you your buck. You cannot kill him from the rear. So you wait. He turns. Wham, in that instant you got to let fly.'

They continued to differ on turkey, which Todd had never hunted, and whitetail, which Roy Bub scorned, but they did agree on quail, and that was how their long and intense friendship began: 'Todd, I got me these two partners, sort of. A young oilman who may be goin' places, and this dentist who loves dogs. We've been rentin' a place, week by week, and if you cared to come along . . .'

It startled Todd to learn that in Texas one leased a place to hunt, for he was familiar with Michigan and Pennsylvania: 'A man wants to hunt, say he lives in Detroit or Philadelphia, he just buys himself a gun and a license, and he can go out in the country almost anywhere and shoot his heart out. Millions of acres, thousands of deer just waiting for him.'

'That ain't the way in Texas. Someone owns ever' inch of our land, and if you trespass without payin' a prior fee, the owner'll shoot your ass off.'

'Prehistoric,' Todd said. 'Where is your place?'

'Close to Falfurrias.'

'Never heard of it. How far – fifty miles?'

'Two hundred and forty.'

'I wouldn't drive two-forty to shoot a polar bear.'

'This is Texas, son. You drive two-forty to go to a good football game . . . and some not so good.'

When Todd met the oilman and the dentist, both in their early thirties, he liked them, for they were true outdoorsmen, and like most men of that type, each had his strong preferences. 'I like to hunt on foot, without dogs,' the oilman said. 'I got me this fabulous A.Y.A. copy of a Purdy with a Beasley action . . .'

'What's that?' Todd asked.

'A Purdy is the best shotgun made. English. Sells for about eleven thousand dollars. Who can afford that?'

'You can,' Roy Bub said.

'Maybe later. But there's this amazing outfit in a little town in Spain. They make fabulous copies. Aguirre y Arranzabel. They made me a Purdy, special order, my name engraved on it and all – forty-six hundred bucks.'

'You paid that for a gun?' Todd asked, and the oilman said: 'Not just for a gun. For an A.Y.A.'

The dentist did not take any gun with him to the hunts; he loved dogs and had rigged up the back of his Chevrolet hunting wagon with six separate wire pens, three atop of the others, in which he kept six prize dogs: two English pointers, two English setters, and the two he liked best, a pair of Brittany spaniels. He had trained them to a fine point, each a champion in some special attribute, and when they reached the fields he liked to carry the men and dogs in his wagon, with Roy Bub driving, till Todd, keeping watch from an armchair bolted to the metal top of the wagon, spotted quail and gave the cry 'Left, left,' or wherever the covey nestled.

Then as the car stopped, the dentist would dash out, release the dog chosen for this chase, and dispatch him in the direction Todd had indicated. In the meantime, the three men with their guns would have descended, Todd scrambling down from his perch and Roy Bub from behind the wheel, and all would leave the car and proceed on foot after the dog, who would flush the quail and follow them deftly as they ran along the ground.

It was not light exercise to follow the birds and the dog, heavy gun at the ready, but at some unexpected moment the covey of ten or fifteen quail would explode into the air and fly off in all directions, seeking escape by the speed and wild variety of their flight. Then the guns would bang, each hunter firing as many shots in rapid succession as his guns allowed. Fifteen birds in fifteen heights and directions, maybe a dozen shots, maybe three birds downed.

Then came the excitement of trying to locate the fallen quail, and now the dog became a major partner, for he scoured the terrain this way and that, in what seemed like frantic circles but with the knowing purpose of vectoring the land until he smelled the blood of the dead bird.

'It could be the best spot in the world,' Todd said one day after the team of three guns and six dogs had knocked down forty-seven quail, each a delicious morsel relished by the families of the three married hunters – Roy Bub had no wife yet, but did have four likely prospects whom he took out at various times and to various honky-tonks. Maggie Morrison roasted hers with a special marinade made of tarragon vinegar and three or four tangy spices.

In September one year the oilman presented a stunning offer to his three buddies: 'I've located forty-eight hundred acres of the best quail land in Texas. Just north of Falfurrias. Owner wants four dollars and twenty cents an acre just for quail; five dollars for quail and deer and one turkey each; six for twelve months, including javelina and all the deer and turkey we can take legally.'

On Tuesday the four men took off from their obligations in Houston, thundered south to Victoria, then down US 77 to Kingsville and across to the proposed land. They covered the two hundred and forty miles in just under three hours, thanks to an electronic fuzz-buster that Roy Bub had installed in the dentist's car; it alerted him to the presence of lurking Highway Patrol radars. The four arrived at the acreage about an hour before dusk and spent those sixty minutes in a dream world, because this land was obviously superior. 'Look at that huisache and mesquite,' Roy Bub cried, for he was the expert. 'No tall trees, but those gorgeous low shrubs providing plenty of cover. And the mesquite aren't too close together, so the quail will have to strike open ground.' He pointed out that the fence rows had not been cut, which meant there would be plenty of protection for the quail during the nesting seasons, and he was specially struck by the richness of the weed cover.

'Look at that seed supply. All the right weeds, all properly spaced. This place, to tell you the truth, is worth double what they're asking.'

The owner, eager to get top dollar but not hurting for the money, was a rancher who said frankly: 'I'd like to rent it for the full six dollars, but you're working men. If you want it during a trial period just for quail in the autumn, I'll be more than happy to rent it for the four-twenty I said. Feel it out. See if it seems like home. If so, we might have ourselves a longtime deal.'

'Have you other prospects?' the oilman asked, for the $20,160 involved was a little steep and the $28,800 for twelve months, all rights, was forbidding.

'I do, but people tell me you're four responsible men. They say you'll help keep the hunting good. For the long haul, I'd prefer someone like you.'

That night the four Houstonians held a planning session, and it was clear that the oilman and the dentist could afford rather more of the total fee than could Roy Bub and Morrison, so a deal was arranged whereby Roy Bub would continue to drive the dentist's wagon while Todd would occupy the armchair topside and also care for the land. This meant that in the off season he would lay out roadways through the mesquite, drag the earth so that weeds would prosper, and look after the quail and turkeys in general.

'We promise you this,' Roy Bub told the owner, 'when we leave, your land will be in better shape than when we came.'

'One important thing,' the oilman said, for he was an expert in leases. 'We have the right to shoot October to January?' The owner agreed. 'But we have the right to visit all year long. Picnics, families?' The owner said of course. 'And we have the right, as of now, to build ourselves a little shack?'

'You certainly do,' the man said. 'But you understand, anything you erect on my land remains my property.'

'Now wait!' the oilman said. 'If we affix it to your land, dig cellars and all that, it's yours. But if it remains movable, we can take it with us if you close us out.'

'Of course!' There was a moment of hesitation, after which he said impulsively: 'I like your approach to the land. Twenty thousand even.'

So the four young men obtained the right to hunt this magnificent land – flat as a table, few trees, no lake, no river – during the legal quail season, and permission to roam it during the other months. The elaborate division of labor they had

1314

worked out to protect the oilman and dentist who were paying more than their share of the cost was unnecessary, because those two worked as hard as anyone. They built the lean-to; they planted seeds along the trails so that weeds would grow; they tended the hedgerows where the quail would nest; and they cared for the dogs.

The team's first autumn on their lease was gratifying. With the dentist running his dogs and Todd spotting from his perch atop the wagon, they uncovered quail almost every day, and with the practice they were getting, the three gunners became experts. From time to time the oilman allowed one of the other two to use his A.Y.A., and one day toward Christmas, when they were huddling in the lean-to after dark, he asked quietly: 'Either of you two want to buy the Spanish gun? Real bargain.'

'What about you?' Roy Bub asked.

The oilman went almost shyly to the wagon, and as if he were a young girl showing off her first prom dress, produced an item he had sequestered when they packed in Houston. Unwrapping it, he revealed one of those perfect English guns, a Purdy with a Beasley action which he had purchased for $24,000. When it stood revealed in the lantern light, it was not handsome, nor garishly decorated, nor laden with insets of any kind. It was merely a cold, sleek, marvelously tooled gun which fitted in the shoulder like a perfectly tailored suit. 'There it is,' he said proudly.

'How much for the Spanish job?' Todd asked.

'It cost me forty-six hundred, like I said. I'd like to keep it in the crowd, maybe use it now and then for old times' sake. I'll let you have it for twenty-six.'

'Time payment?'

'Why not?'

So at the end of the season, and a very fine season it had been, the quartet had both a genuine Purdy and an A.Y.A. copy, and Roy Bub also had a very good gun, because Morrison sold him the good weapon he'd been using at a comparable discount.

They were a congenial crowd that winter, for at least twice a month, when no hunting was allowed at their lease, they left Houston at dusk on a Friday, roared down to Falfurrias, and worked on their place. They turned the lean-to into a real house, with eight bunks, two temporary privies and a portable shower, and they improved the roadways through the far edges of the fields. In March everyone but Roy Bub brought wife and children down for a festival, kids in sleeping bags, older ones in blankets under the cold stars, and Maggie said to one of the other wives: 'I wouldn't want to cook like this four Saturdays a month, but it's worth every cent the men spend on it.'

In June, after a serious meeting in the bunkhouse, Roy Bub drove to the owner's house and invited him to join them. When he appeared, the oilman said: 'Mr Cossiter, you know we like your place. We'd like to take it all year, at six dollars an acres unrestricted. That would be twenty-eight thousand eight hundred. And we were wondering if you could shade that a little?'

'Men, you care for this place better than I do. Twenty-six thousand for as many years as you care to hold it.'

'A deal,' the oilman said, but Roy Bub cried: 'Hell, we could of got him down to twenty,' and the owner said: 'Blacktop me a four-lane road north and south through the middle so I can subdivide later on, and you can have it for twenty.'

Maggie Morrison analyzed it this way: 'I'm sure Roy Bub felt totally left out during our family stay at the hunting lease. Everyone else with a wife and kids.' At any rate, shortly after their return home, Roy Bub informed his team that they and their wives were invited to his wedding, which was to be solemnized at midnight Tuesday in Davy Crockett's, a famous Houston honky-tonk on the road to the oil fields near Beaumont.

'Do we really want to attend such a rowdy affair?' Maggie asked, for Crockett's was hardly a traditional wedding chapel, but Todd said: 'Not only are we going, so are the kids.' Maggie did not like this, not at all, and went to speak with Roy Bub: 'It's not proper to hold a wedding at Crockett's, you being in oil and all that.'

He looked at her in a funny way and said: 'I'm not in oil,' and she said: 'But I remember your white truck that first day. ROY BUB HOOKER, DRILLING.'

'That was my truck. But I don't drill for oil. I put that on so that people would *think* I did.'

'What do you drill?'

'Septic tanks. When your toilet clogs up, you call me. I wouldn't feel happy bein' married anywhere but Crockett's.' And when she told the others, the oilman and the dentist agreed, so at ten in the evening, the six adults and seven children drove out to the huge unpaved parking lot that was already crowded with pickups whose owners were hacking it up inside.

The oilman, who had been here once before, assembled his crowd outside the door and warned: 'Nobody is to hit anybody, no matter what happens,' and he led the way into the massive one-story honky-tonk.

Wide-eyed, they found Davy Crockett's, the workingman's Copacabana, a riotous affair, with more than a thousand would-be cowboys in boots and Stetsons, neither of which they ever took off, dancing the Cotton-Eyed Joe and the two-step with an abandon that would have horrified any choreographer. The place had numerous bars, dance bands which came and went, and an atmosphere of riotous joy.

It was a gala place, and the Morrisons had not been inside ten minutes before a cowboy approached Beth, bowed politely, and asked her to dance. Maggie tried to object, but the girl was gone, and once on the floor, she did not wish to return to her family, because one attractive young fellow after another whisked her away.

Roy Bub, rosily drunk, welcomed everyone enthusiastically. The bride appeared at about eleven-fifteen, twenty-two years old, peroxide-blonde hair, very high heels, low-cut silk blouse, extremely tight double-knit jeans, and a smile that could melt icebergs. When Roy Bub saw her, he rushed over, took her hand, and announced in a bellow: 'Karleen Wyspianski, but don't let the name scare you. She's changin' it tonight.' She was, he explained, a waitress in a high-class diner: 'Honcho of the place, and I grabbed her before the boss did.'

She had grown up in one of those little foreign enclaves so numerous in Texas and so little known outside the state. In her case it was Panna Maria, a Polish settlement dating back to the 1850s whose inhabitants still spoke the native language. She had quit school after the eleventh grade and come immediately to Houston, where she had progressed from one job to another, always improving her take-home pay. Her present employment, because of the large tips she promoted, paid more than a hundred and fifty a week, and had she married the boss, as he wished, she would have shared in a prosperous business.

But she had fallen in love with Roy Bub and his white pickup, and the fact that he went hunting almost every weekend did not distress her, for those were her busiest days, and she was content to join him on Tuesdays, Wednesdays and Thursdays as a 'Crocketteer.' They were good dancers, liberal spenders, and never loath to join in any moderate fracas that was developing.

Karleen had for some time been aware that Roy Bub intended sooner or later proposing marriage, but she was not overly eager for this to happen, for she had an enjoyable life and did not expect marriage to improve it substantially. But she did love the energetic well-driller, and when he returned from the family outing at the Falfurrias ranch with the blunt statement: 'Karleen, I think we better get married,' she said: 'Sure.'

Neither partner considered, even briefly, getting married anywhere but Crockett's. Karleen was Catholic and intended staying so, but she cared little about church affairs. Roy Bub was Baptist, but he was willing to let others worship as they pleased, so long as he was not required to attend his own church. But each was resolved to rear their children, when they came along, as devout Christians in some faith or other.

At quarter to twelve the minister who would conduct the marriage arrived, Reverend Fassbender, an immensely fat fellow of over three hundred pounds who served no specific church but who did much good work as a kind of floating clergyman. One of his specialties was weddings at Crockett's, where the cowboys revered him. Dressed in black, with a cleric's collar size twenty, he exuded both sanctity and sweat as he passed through the crowd bestowing grace: 'Blessings on you, sister. Glad to see you, brother, may Christ go with you.'

The wedding was an emotional affair, for when a space was cleared beneath one of the bandstands, Reverend Fassbender put an end to the frivolity and began to act as if he were in a cathedral, which in a sense he was, for this honky-tonk was where the young working people of Houston's refineries worshipped, and when two bands struck up Mendelssohn's 'Wedding March' Maggie Morrison and other women in the audience began to sniffle.

Karleen, in her tight jeans, and Roy Bub, in his tight collar, the only one he had worn in a year, formed a pair of authentic Crocketteers, and cheers broke out as they took their place before the minister, who quickly halted that nonsense: 'Dearly Beloved, we are gathered here in the presence of God ...' Maggie whispered to Beth: 'Jesus attended a wedding like this at that big honky-tonk in Cana.'

When the ceremony ended, and an honor guard of cowboys fired salutes in the parking lot, Roy Bub's hunting partners watched with approval as the white pickup was delivered at the door to serve as the honeymoon car. While the wedding was under way it had been decorated with leagues of streaming toilet paper, Mexican decorations, and a broom lashed to the cab. But what Maggie liked best, as the pickup drove off, was the new sign Roy Bub had added to his tailgate, for its emotion and the design of the heart seemed appropriate to this night:

IF YOU ♥ NEW YORK
GO TO HELL HOME

When the *Rusk v. Rusk* divorce proceedings revealed just how much money Ransom Rusk had, a score of beautiful women, and Texas had far more than its share, began plotting as to how each might become the next Mrs Rusk, but the austere man directed most of his attention to multiplying by big factors the wealth he already had. He did not become a recluse, but his divorce did make him gun-shy, so he focused on the main problem, never voicing it publicly or even to himself. Intuitively he thought that if he retained, after paying off Fleurette, nearly $50,000,000, there was no reason why he could not run that figure up to $500,000,000, which would move him into the big-rich category.

His first decision in pursuit of this goal was to shift his operations from the pleasant little town of Larkin, population 3,934, and into the heart of Fort Worth, population 393,476. He chose Fort Worth rather than Dallas because the former city was a Western town, with its focus on ranching, oil and fearless speculation in both, while Dallas was more a Texas version of New York or Boston, with huge financial and real estate operations but little touch with the older traditions that had made Texas great. In brief, an oil wildcatter and a Longhorn man like Ransom Rusk felt at home in Fort Worth; he did not in Dallas: 'Those barracuda are too sharp for me. I feel safer paddling around with the minnows.'

In Fort Worth he associated himself with many others who were risking ventures in oil, and especially servicing of the oil industry. With his strong basic knowledge of how petroleum was found and delivered to the market, he was an asset to the men who financed those operations, and before long he was in the middle of that exciting game. The joy his father had found in Texas high school football he found in Texas big-time finance.

He was a major partner in a company which built and sold drilling rigs; the wooden one that had spudded in Rusk No 3 back in 1923 had cost $19,000; the ones he now built were well over a million each. He had also bought into a mud concern, that clever process whereby a viscous liquid, whose properties were modified according to the depth and character of the hole, was pumped into a hole while it was being drilled to correct faults and ensure production if oil was present. But mostly he toured Texas, like a hound dog chasing possums, looking for promising land that could be leased, and this took him to the Austin Chalk, the petroliferous formation around Victoria, where he made a killing, and to the Spraberry Field, where he bought up seventy leases which produced dust and seven which were bonanzas.

At the end of one of the most aggressive campaigns in recent oil history, the value of Rusk's holdings had tripled, and he felt with some justification that 'I'm really just at the beginning. What I need now is to find that big new field.'

He was in this pattern of thought when into his modest Fort Worth office came an old man whose vision had never faded but whose capacity to capitalize upon it had. The years since 1923 had not been kind to Dewey Kimbro, now a seedy seventy-one with no front teeth and very little of the millions he had made on the Larkin Field. When he stood before the son of his former partner, he was a small, wizened man who had been married three times, each with increasing disaster: 'Mr Rusk, my job is to find oil. I've found three of the good fields, you know that. I want you to grubstake me, because I have my eye on a real possibility north of Fort Stockton.'

'Wouldn't that put you in the Permian Basin?'

'On the edge, yes.'

'But everyone knows the good fields in the Permian have been developed.'

The men were speaking of one of the major oil fields in the world, a late discovery that had occurred in the middle of a vast, arid flatland of which it was once said: 'Any living thing in this godforsaken land has thorns, or fangs, or stingers, or claws, and that includes the human beings.' It was a land of cactus, scorpions, mesquite and rattlesnakes. Some intrepid heroes had tried running cattle on it; in a cynical deal the University of Texas had been given vast amounts of the barren land instead of real money, and an occasional oil well had been tried, with more dust at two thousand feet than at the surface.

Then on 28 May 1923, when the latest dry well had sunk beyond three thousand feet, workers were eating breakfast when they heard a monstrous rumble and felt the ground shake. Down in the depths of the earth, an accumulation of oil under intense pressure, broke through the thin rock which had kept it imprisoned for 230,000,000 years and roared up through the well casing, exploding hundreds of feet into the air. Santa Rita No 1 had come in, signaling a vast subterranean lake of oil in the Permian Basin. The first wells were on university lands, and hundreds of the subsequent wells would be too, providing that school with a potential revenue exceeding that of any other university in the world.

Later, when the Yates Field came in with its Permian oil, one well produced nearly three thousand barrels an hour from a depth of only eleven hundred and fifty feet: 'Drilling in the Yates, you just stick a pole in the ground and jump back.'

With its incredible millions from the Permian, the university would leverage itself into becoming a first-class school, and a thousand dry-soil farmers would find themselves to be millionaires, with a ranch in the country – the old homestead dotted with oil rigs – and a bright new home in Midland, identified by the Census Bureau as 'the wealthiest town per capita in the States,' with more Rolls-Royces than New York.

But by 1969 those days of explosive wealth were over; the

Permian had died down to a respectable field that still produced more oil than most, but did not throw up those soaring gushers whose free-flowing oil had once darkened the sky. Midland now served as husbandman to wells already in operation and was no longer in the exciting business of drilling new ones. As Ransom Rusk told his father's favorite wildcatter: 'Dewey, the Permian Basin is a discovered field.'

'Don't you believe it, Mr Rusk. Petroleum products come in at a dozen different levels. Maybe the easy oil is finished, but how about the deep gas?'

'Dewey, stands to reason, if there was oil or gas out there, the big boys would have found it.'

'No, Mr Rusk,' Dewey pleaded, still standing, for Ransom had not invited him to sit and he knew he must not appear presumptuous. 'Big boys only find what little boys like me take them to. I know where there's oil, but I need your money to buy the leases and sink a well. This time it'll be a deep well.'

'Dewey, you've been peddling that story across Texas. What I will do, because you were a good partner to my father, here's four hundred dollars. Get yourself some teeth.'

'I was going to do that, Mr Rusk, but what I really need is your support on this new prospect.'

He was given no money beyond the four hundred dollars, which he did not use for teeth; he spent it traveling to other oil centers in search of funds which would enable him to pursue his latest dream, and in the meantime Ransom was visited by someone who wanted a contribution for a much different enterprise. It was Mr Kramer, the old-time oilman who was now interested only in wind velocities and armadillos.

'Mr Rusk, to put it bluntly, I'm asking you for four thousand dollars to trap armadillos and deliver them to this leprosy institute in Louisiana.'

'What are you talking about?'

'You may not know it, few people do, but the armadillo seems to be the only living thing besides man that can contract leprosy. Their low body temperature, twenty-nine point seven to thirty-five degrees Celsius, encourages the bacillus.'

'You mean those critters in my front lawn . . .'

'Don't get excited. It's not transferrable to humans, the kind they develop. But it is the only way that our scientists and medical people can experiment on what causes and cures this dreaded disease.'

'Of course you can have the money, but you mean that our little bulldozers have some utility in the world?'

'That's just what I mean. You see, with nature, you can never tell. The armadillo has been preserved through these millions of years, so we must suppose that it can host a particular disease which has also existed for millions of years.'

'Now wait a minute, I don't want you trapping Lady Macbeth and her Four Witches.'

'Make that eight witches. She just had four more pups, all female again.'

'Where do the males come from?'

'It balances out. Don't ask me how.'

It was a hundred miles from Fort Worth to Larkin, but with Rusk driving, it would require only an hour and twenty minutes, so the men decided to dash out to inspect the armadillo problem, and as they sped along the broad and well-engineered roads Ransom asked Mr Kramer what he thought of Dewey Kimbro, who had haunted the oil fields during the period that Kramer had worked them.

'Standard Texan. Always going to hit it big. Wastes his money on women. You'll have to bury him some day, two hundred dollars for the funeral, because he'll wind up without a cent.'

'He brought in a lot of wells.'

'You're not thinking of bankrolling him, are you?'

'Most of the big finds in Texas, even the real gushers, have been found by crazy geologists like Dewey. He says he knows something ...'

'I'll admit this, Mr Rusk. Men like me, we work the fields, it's a living. We get paid well, we save our money, we retire to a decent life. A man like Dewey, he never retires. Four days before he dies, not a cent to his name, he'll be promoting the next well. I was an oil worker. He's an oil dreamer.'

In Larkin, after Rusk noticed with some satisfaction that Lady Macbeth and her eight helpers had by now pretty well chopped the one-time bowling lawn to shreds, he asked: 'Now, where do you propose to trap these armadillos for the hospital in Louisiana?' Kramer took him a few hundred yards to the banks of Bear Creek where a family of about fifty of the armored animals centred and to a spot farther along the creek where another settlement of about forty maintained its headquarters: 'They like moist ground. Two things that can kill the armadillo, very cold winters and a prolonged drought.'

'Do they need so much water?'

'Like camels, they can exist on practically none, but when the sun bakes the earth during a drought, they can't dig easily. And that means they can't eat.'

The part of any visit to Mr Kramer's place that Rusk liked best came when he was allowed to play with the three tame creatures that Kramer still kept in his kitchen and out in the yard, and it was difficult for Ransom to explain why he found so much pleasure in them: 'They aren't cuddly, and they aren't very responsive, but they are endlessly fascinating.'

'I think you like them because of the oil derricks on their backs.'

'Now that makes sense.' But what really pleased him was the way they rousted about like oil-field workers, bruising and brawling, one over another, then scampering like a team to the latest noise or the newest adventure. They were social animals, accustomed to working together, and when holes were to be dug, they were formidable.

'It just occurred to me, Kramer. If we could train those little devils, we could dig oil wells in half the time.' The armadillos seemed to sense that Rusk was their friend, for when he sat in a chair they enjoyed romping with his feet, or sitting in his lap. They had no teeth that could bite a person, and when at ease, kept their eighteen formidable, lancelike toes under control.

But in the long run, it was the extraordinary beauty of their armor and the ever-present sense that these were creatures from a most distant past that allured. Sometimes Rusk would sit with one in his hands, staring at its preposterous face – all nose, beady eyes that could barely see – and he would ask Kramer: 'In what bog did this one hide for twenty million years?'

He provided the funds for leprosy research, but was pleased when his gardener informed him that more than twenty armadillos now resided in the Rusk fields. None of them was tame, but they made a noble procession when they set out at dusk to excavate some neighbor's lawn.

When he returned to Fort Worth he found Dewey Kimbro, still with no teeth, perched outside his office, talking excitedly with his secretary. As soon as the old wildcatter spotted him, he jumped up, took his arm, and accompanied him into the inner office: 'Mr Rusk, I don't want to talk if or how or even how much. Just when.'

'What do you mean?'

'I've spotted a field you have to put under lease. And then you have to pay for the exploration well.'

'Now look, Kimbro . . .'

'No, you look. Where do you suppose you got the money you now have? They say in the papers more than a hundred and fifty million. Because I found a field for your daddy. I'm an oilman, Mr Rusk. You owe me one last shot, because I know where oil can be found.'

The plea was irresistible. In an average year Rusk had been spending three million dollars on the hunches of men with far dimmer track records than Dewey Kimbro and with far less dedication to the oil business. He did owe the old man one last shot: 'I'll do it.'

'No tricks. I'm too old for tricks.'

'My father warned me that you were completely honest, Dewey, but if anyone crossed you, you bided your time, then shot him in the back . . . dead of night.'

'Your father ever tell you how we got the Yeager land back under our control? He had me goad the poor devil till he lifted his shotgun, then your father drilled him.'

'It's a deal. Now where is this precious land that's going to make us both rich?'

'You richer, me rich.' And he drove Rusk to a big ranch, El Estupendo, tucked away among the mesas north of Fort Stockton.

'This land couldn't produce goats,' Rusk complained, but Dewey's enthusiasm could not be quenched, and in their secret explorations he showed the financier faults whose edges protruded and domes half hidden by mesquite.

'There could be oil down there,' Rusk conceded, and Dewey cried: 'There has to be!'

The ranch was one of the nine accumulated by Lorenzo Quimper in obedience to the principle laid down by his famous ancestor Yancey: 'If you grab enough Texas land, somethin' good is bound to happen.' Quimper was not in residence, and in his absence the place was run by a young Mexican in whom he apparently placed much confidence. 'I am Cándido Guzmán,' the manager said in carefully enunciated English. 'Mr Quimper's the man in charge.'

'Where is he?'

'Who knows? Maybe at the Polk ranch, down on the Rio Grande.'

They made a series of phone calls and located Quimper, not at any of his western ranches but in his newly built ranch on the shores of Lake Travis near Austin, and as soon as he heard the name Rusk he told Guzmán: 'Keep him there. I'll fly right out.' Climbing into his Beechcraft, he directed his pilot to drop him off at the improvised runway at El Estupendo, where Cándido was waiting, as always, with his pickup. 'What's the focus?' he asked, using a phrase he liked, and Guzmán replied: 'Oil, I think. I went in to Fort Stockton to ask about Kimbro and they told me "Oil." '

'Well, if a man has nine Texas ranches, one of them ought to have oil,' Quimper said, and Cándido replied: 'Mr Quimper, the papers say you already have two with oil,' and Quimper said: 'You can never have too many.'

When Rusk and Quimper met in a tin-roofed shack on the ranch, they formed a powerful pair, Rusk older and more cautious in Texas gambling, Quimper more eager to leap at a promising chance. In personal appearance, too, they were contrasting, Rusk leaner and more sharklike, Quimper fleshier and more prosperous-looking. Ransom said little, and Quimper could hardly be stopped, indulging in such Texas phrases as 'Wiser'n a tree full of owls' and 'We'll dig the damned well and nail the coonskin to the barn door.' He also uttered a great truth about oil in Texas: 'My pappy told me: "Lorenzo, in an oil deal always be satisfied with the overriding royalty of one-eighth. Let the other dumb bastards do the drillin' and grab their seven-eighths. You'll always come out ahead." And time has proved him right. Gentlemen, you can have your lease, but in some ways I'm a lot wiser than my pappy. Not ten years, like the early ones. Two years. Not fifty cents an acre, like he did. Three dollars, because this is prime land. And not one-eighth, three-sixteenths.'

'They told me you were a miserable bastard, Quimper,' Rusk said, 'but you have the land, you've been to law school, even though you flunked out, and they say they're putting you on the Board of Regents at the university, so you must know something. It's a deal.' They shook hands, and that's how the exploration of those barren wastes north of Fort Stockton began.

They left the positioning of the first well to Kimbro, but from a distance they hovered, watching him. 'Vultures waiting for the old man to die,' Dewey said of them one day as his drilling probed deeper and deeper, with no results. 'They'll wait in vain.'

This enforced waiting had one productive consequence; it became an opportunity for Rusk to renew acquaintance with a gifted gentleman who worked the oil fields. He was Pierre Soult, collateral descendant of one of Napoleon's better marshals, and another of the engineering geniuses France was producing in these years.

Pierre Soult, latest of this enterprising breed, had worked with Rusk before; it was his genius that prodded development of the procedure of digging a deep hole in the earth, filling it with dynamite, and then placing a dozen sensitive detectors at varied distances and exploding the charge. His detectors recorded how long it took for the reverberation to penetrate the earth below, strike a granite base, and come bouncing back. Exquisite timing and even more exquisite analysis revealed secrets of the substructure, and from these Soult could advise his clients as to what lay beneath the ground and where best to dig for it.

'Seismographic exploration,' Soult called his process. 'We are like the scientists who detect and record earthquakes thousands of miles away. With our dynamite we make the little earthquake and record it half a mile away.'

Of course, his procedures were now much advanced over those primitive ones Rusk had employed in his early days of oil exploration, and when Rusk complimented him on this, Soult said: 'I've about run my course with seismography. I'm thinking seriously about a new device to solve mathematical problems, useful in all fields, very daring. A hand-held computer.'

'What?'

'Given the proper technical advances, and I think I know a way to ensure them, you can carry in your hand, Mr Rusk, more mathematics than Newton and Einstein together ever mastered.'

'Come and see me when this is over. That is, if we strike oil.'

'If there is any around here, you'll find it. My little earthquake ensures that.'

One very hot afternoon, temperature 104 degrees, humidity seven percent, when the log at 22,000 feet had shown not a sign of carbon, a mighty roar from below signaled an upsurge of oil and gas so powerful that it tore away the superstructure as it struck the air, ignited from a spark thrown by crashing steel girders, and flamed into a beacon visible for seventy miles across the flat and arid land.

Five crew members were incinerated. A hundred thousand dollars' worth of petroleum products burned for days, then a million dollars' worth. Dewey Kimbro's men tried every trick to control the wild flames of Estupendo No 1; they poured in tons of mud to seal off the flow of oil, they tried dynamiting the hole to exhaust its oxygen, but nothing worked. The flames roared into the midnight sky and helped the sun illuminate the day.

Red Adair, the Texan who specialized in the dangerous task of subduing oil-well fires, was summoned, and after three weeks he brought this tremendous conflagration under control. Rusk, bleary-eyed from watching the flames, told his new partner: 'Quimper, it hurts to see so much wealth vanishing in smoke. But when you know that a million times as much is still down there . . .'

With his royalty from the Estupendo field, Quimper more than doubled his wealth and was promoted into the rich category. Dewey Kimbro's share was more than two million, with which he purchased some new teeth, but within two years he was back prowling marginal fields, listening for leads at the morning breakfasts, searching for some new source of exploration capital; his wealth had vanished in divorce settlements, the acquisition of a fourth wife, and extensive lawyers' fees for getting rid of her after seven months.

The knowledge that his assets now totaled just under $400,000,000 altered Ransom Rusk very little. He retained four Mexican servants at his Larkin home, but because he still tried to avoid entanglement with women, the mansion saw little social life. He spent most of his time in Fort Worth, where his frugal office had to be enlarged, for he now required a full-time accountant to keep track of his intricate participations in the various wells he supervised.

But he was never satiated; always he looked for that next big field, that lucky wildcatter who was going to lead to the next gusher, and it was in pursuit of what he called 'the significant multiplier,' that he sought out Pierre Soult, the oil seismographer: 'Is what you told me that day while we were waiting for Estupendo Number One true?'

'You mean about the radical new system for calculators?'

'Yes. How much would you need?'

'We must invent a new way to form silicon chips, and I believe I have it.'

'How much?'

'I'll have to hire real brains, you know. The best the Sorbonne and Cambridge and MIT produce.'

'How much, damnit?'

'Real brains cost real money. Maybe twenty million.'

'If we're going to do it, let's do it Texas style. You can count on fifty.' They shook hands, and because of the way the world was developing, this investment would turn out to be the wisest he would make.

Spending so much time in Midland, a city ninety-eight-percent Republican, produced a significant change in Ransom Rusk. Already conservative, like most oilmen who took great risks but did not want others to do so, he moved steadily right to become a reactionary, dedicated to the principle that all government was bad and that enterprising men should be allowed to write their own rules. But at the same time he defended the depletion allowance, which enabled him to retain a huge percentage of the income he gathered, and he sought to drive from public life any political leader who spoke or acted against this preferential treatment enjoyed by oilmen. Government was all bad except that which furthered his interests.

He was partly justified in this stand: 'I gamble fantastic sums trying to find oil. Fifty, sixty million and three-fourths of it can go down the drain. I deserve protection.'

Of course, on the one-fourth of his venture capital which was not lost he made gigantic profits, and these he spent freely in trying to defeat candidates who were not supportive of the oil industry: 'A basic rule of self-defense. The man who attacks my interests is my enemy.' It so happened that only Republicans could be seen as protecting his interests, so he was forced to oppose most Democrats, which he did with huge sums of money.

He had never liked Lyndon Johnson personally, but Johnson had been one of the staunchest defenders of big oil, so with his left hand Rusk slipped him generous contributions while with his right he continued to pull the straight Republican lever. He was quietly pleased when Johnson decided not to run in 1968, but when Hubert Humphrey was nominated to succeed him, he sprang into furious action: 'The man's an ass, a bumbling ass. The Republic will fall if he's elected.' And in his sour, sharply focused way, Rusk spent millions to defeat him, all the Democratic senators running that year, and sixteen selected Democratic congressmen whose votes had offended him.

He was delighted when the Republicans nominated Richard Nixon, for here was a man who had proved over a long period in public service that he knew what was good for the nation. Ransom invited Nixon to Texas, spent lavishly to influence his fellow oilmen, and literally bit his fingernails on election night when it looked as if Humphrey and George Wallace might, because of the inane electoral college, succeed in throwing the election into the House of Representatives. He did not go to bed all that night, and when morning came, with Nixon the victor by a precarious margin, he cried to the empty rooms at Larkin: 'The Republic has been saved!'

* * *

While these developments were taking place, another aspect of Texas life was undergoing a radical change, which might, in the long run, prove more important to the state than either oil or financing. Sherwood Cobb, grandson of the late United States senator from Waxahachie, had decided regretfully that the splendid plantation his family owned just south of that engaging town was so beset by the boll weevil, the declining bale-per acre ratio and the inflated value of land that the only sensible thing to do was to leapfrog his entire cotton operation out to the far western part of the state, where land was still cheap, flat and so high in altitude that the boll weevil could not survive the winters.

Nancy Nell Cobb, raised on a farm, asked about the extreme dryness of the region in which her husband proposed to grow his cotton, a crop which needed a lot of water, and he assured her: 'Aridity makes it impossible for boll weevils to breed.' But she countered: 'If weevils can't grow, neither can cotton. Jefferson had forty-six inches of rain a year, and cotton thrived, Waxahachie has thirty-six inches, and cotton did well till the weevils took over. But Lubbock had only sixteen inches last year, and I can't see how your plants can prosper.'

It was then that he revealed to her one of the miracles of the United States, and of how Texas profited from it. Spreading before her a map which the Department of Agriculture had provided cotton growers in the Waxahachie area in a commendable effort to make them quit trying to grow cotton there and move out to the high plains, where production was booming, he indicated the eight Western states – South Dakota to Texas – under which lay hidden the nation's greatest water resource, barring the Mississippi: 'Think of it as a vast underground lake. Bigger than most European countries. Dig deep and you invariably find water. It's called the Ogallala Aquifer, after this little town in Nebraska where it was discovered. Fingers probe out everywhere to collect immense runoffs, and the aquifer delivers it right to our farm.'

'How can you know all this? If it's hidden, like you say?'

'They've been studying it, in all the states. Seems to be an interrelated unit. And its inexhaustible.'

'You mean it's down there and anyone can use it?'

'That's how we're going to grow cotton in Lubbock. You pay for your well once, and you have water for the rest of your life.'

Nancy Nell had trouble in believing that an area which gathered only sixteen inches of rainfall a year could grow a crop which required thirty-six or more, and she told Sherwood: 'Seems like an enormous risk to me. I really think we ought to stay where we are and fight the weevil with field-dusting, like the Andersons are doing.'

'Nancy Nell,' he said, sighing her name as if it were one unbroken syllable, 'hundreds of farmers out in that dryland are getting the best cotton crop in Texas, and with the know-how they're accumulating, it's bound to be the best in the world within a decade. We're going to make them try.'

To show her the land where her home was to be, he roused his family one morning at four, packed them into the big Buick, and headed west at sunrise, displaying the same excitement that his grandfather had shown in the early 1900s when shepherding his family from the closed-in Old South atmosphere of Jefferson to the black earth and open spaces of Waxahachie.

They angled across to Fort Worth, avoiding the breakfast traffic about Dallas, and as they drove west, Sherwood became sensitive to one of the miracles of Texas, operative for the past five thousand years. With each fifteen miles of travel, east to west, the yearly rainfall dropped by one inch, and through one of the coincidences of nature, the ninety-eighth parallel of longitude coincided roughly with the line that demarcated thirty inches of rainfall. East of that line the standard agriculture of planting and harvesting crops was possible; to the west it was not. There settlers had to rely not upon farming but upon ranching and perhaps mining.

'It's as if a mighty wall had been erected along this line,' Cobb told his family as they approached the imaginary ninety-eighth, 'to warn farmers "Halt here!" Each mile we go from here on, not enough rain to grow a crop.' After his passengers had digested his unpleasant fact, he laughed: 'What saves us is hiding down below. Because it's also true that each mile we travel, we get closer to the Ogallala. And that means cotton.'

Once past the ninety-eighth, they were into the real West: Jacksboro, past Three Cairns, where the state had erected a monument recalling the 10th Cavalry stand against the Comanche, and on to Larkin, where they stopped to see the famous courthouse with the portraits of Mabel Fister; they did not allow their children to find the notorious fifth sculpture.

West of Larkin the rolling plains began, sometimes not even a tree visible in any direction, but with softly dipping hills, and far beyond that they entered upon the high plains, as flat as earth could be and twice as empty. Awed by the immensity of the land they proposed to occupy, they drove past Lubbock and west to locate their six thousand acres which, in their pristine state without irrigation, could feed only one cow and calf to every sixty acres.

They had come three hundred and forty-nine miles in one day, touching neither the eastern border of the state nor the western, and had traversed four different terrains as distinct from one another as Italy and Portugal: the Black Prairies of Waxahachie, the Cross Timbers of Larkin, the Lower Plains marked only by little towns, and the High Plains of Lubbock. As they pulled into the little town of Levelland, where they would spend the night, population 10,445, Sherwood said: 'Our farm will lie north of here. Properly handled, it's going to be a gold mine. All the land we'll ever need, and all the water.' That night, ravenously hungry after their long ride, they had some of the best chicken-fried steak and grits they'd had in a long time, while the restaurant jukebox ground out a song which had gained recent popularity: 'It takes a lot of squares to make the world go round.'

When they inspected their land next morning, Nancy Nell and the children gasped, for it was flatter by far than any seen on the previous day and it contained not one tree or shrub of noticeable size. The horizon was so endless that Nancy Nell asked: 'How many other farms can we see from here?' and her husband quipped: 'Sixteen in Montana and seven in Canada.'

He showed the children where the house would stand and assured them that it was going to be first class: 'With the money we get for the old place, we can build a little paradise here.'

'Will you plant a windbreak to the northwest?' Nancy Nell asked, and he said: 'That goes in tomorrow.' But like his ancestors when they occupied their new lands in Texas, the first thing he erected was a cotton gin, because like them he expected to be the leading cotton grower in his region.

Even before the house was started he entered into a contract with the Erickson brothers, the deep-well people, and they took pleasure in teaching him about the water situation: 'Two hundred feet below us as we stand, a thick, impermeable rock formation, the Red Bed. The Ogallala rests on it. Water level rises to within thirty feet of the surface, but to play it safe, so that not even the severest drought can affect you, we're going to

1333

drill your wells down to one hundred feet.'

'How many?'

'We calculate that to work the good center areas of your land, you'll need six wells.'

'I thought five would handle the job,' Cobb said, and they agreed: 'Sure, you can do it with five, but you might be puttin' a mite of strain on them. Take our advice, go with six.'

'How much?'

'We give you the best well ever drilled, thirty-five hundred dollars a well, and that includes a converted Chevy 1952 engine set in a concrete box three feet down to protect it from rain and dust.'

'What's it run on?'

'We provide a butane tank, two hundred gallons, they fill it for you from town.'

The Ericksons also showed him how to rent a tractor before he bought his own, throw a fourteen-inch ridge around his entire cotton area, and box it in: 'That way, you trap every drop of water that falls on your land.'

'We get sixteen inches a year,' the second man said, 'steady as God's patience with a sinful man, and you ought to be here the afternoon it falls.'

After Cobb had consulted with the experts at Texas Tech in Lubbock to learn which strains of cotton were appropriate for his new land, and when his first fields were planted by tractor, broad and open and requiring no stoop work by imported Mexicans, he heard from the college expert the best news of all: 'This year Lubbock cotton is bringing top dollar.'

'Sounds like we're home safe,' Cobb said as he studied his fields with the banked-up ridges hemming them in.

'There's one small cloud on the horizon,' the expert warned. 'Each year from South Dakota to Lubbock, the Ogallala seems to drop an inch or two.'

'You mean the level could go down, permanently?'

'Unless we use it properly,' the man said.

Maggie Morrison's life in Houston was made more pleasant when she located a drugstore that received an airplane shipment of *The New York Times* each Sunday afternoon at two. Since her husband was usually down at the quail camp with his three buddies – grown men playing at games – she put on her bathrobe and slippers, made herself comfortable in a big chair, and wrestled with the crossword puzzle, her chief intellectual enticement of the week.

As in Michigan, she had found several other wives who enjoyed the puzzle, men apparently not having adequate intellect for this teaser, and when she had completed filling in her little white squares, she delighted in calling these other women to compare notes and gloat if she had found all the answers and they had not. She recalled with keen pleasure one Sunday evening when she had unraveled one of the more tantalizing puzzles. At the start, the clues for the five long lines were of little help:

17 across.	Precious metal things.
33 across.	Chief metal things.
54 across.	Alloy metal things.
79 across.	Soft metal things.
89 across.	Valuable metal things.

Not until she had solved many of the difficult *down* words could she assemble enough letters to provide clues, but even when she had a goodly selection she could not fathom the secret of the word fragments thus revealed. Finally, on the 'Alloy metal things' line she had the letters *kn* and this encouraged her to decipher the word *knuckles*, and like the sudden flashing of a light in a darkened room, she perceived that the alloy had to be brass, and the precious metal, gold:

Precious metal.	BUGDUSTFOILLEAFANDSTANDARD
Cheap metal.	EARGODTYPEPAHATHORNANDCAN
Alloy metal.	BANDKNUCKLESANDCANDLESTICK
Soft metal.	PENCILPIPESHOTANDPOISONING
Valuable metal.	CHLORIDEFISHFOXWAREANDSTAR

When she made her nightly calls that Sunday she found that only one of her team had solved the five lines, and the two congratulated themselves on having superior intellects, but some weeks later both were rebuffed by what all the players agreed was one of the most ingenious of the puzzles.

As before the four *across* lines gave only bewildering clues; they were not intelligible at first, nor even after some serious speculation, and she surrendered: 'I'm ignorant about the military. I give up.' She failed to solve it, but that night one of her friends gloated: 'Maggie! I got it quicker than usual,' and Maggie said: 'Yes, but your husband was an officer. You know about battles and stuff.' And then her friend cried: 'Maggie! It's not about war. It's about automobiles.' And with that simple clue Maggie was able to fill in the squares, chuckling at her stupidity in not having discovered that the lines referred to a car at a stoplight:

19 across.	March!	BACKBERETSWARDGAGEHOUSEHORN
42 across.	Halt!	HANDEDLETTERINKSHIRTHERRING
63 across.	Mark time!	GRISJACKIFEROUSBEADSFOREVER
89 across.	Retreat!	BENCHERGAMMONLASHSLIDEWATER

With her husband prospering in his business, her children adjusting to their schools, and her small circle of friends sharing crossword-puzzle results on Sunday evenings, Maggie, without being aware of the change in her life, was becoming a Texan. She revealed this in a letter to a friend in Detroit:

Tonight I feel joy being in Texas. It's so big, so alive, so filled with a sense of the future. In fact, I'm so kindly disposed that I even want to apologize for the unkind things I said about our Texas cockroaches. I told you they were as big as sparrows. Well, I had one this morning as big as a robin. But an oilman who bought some land from me told me that roaches may be the oldest continuing form of life on earth, and he showed me a fossil his geologists dredged up from the Pennsylvanian Level. That's 330,000,000 million years ago, he said, and anything that can survive this Texas heat for that long has earned my respect.

She was congratulating herself on defending the cultural life in Houston – 'We're candles blowing in the wind,' she had once said to one of her friends – when she received a stupefying counterblow which stunned. Daughter Beth, a willowy fifteen now, came shyly into the room where her mother was tangled in her big chair, and said: 'Mummy, I'm going to be a cheerleader.'

'You're what?'

'All the girls, it's the very best thing you can be, they vote for you.'

'What are you saying?'

'That I'm reporting for cheerleader practice tomorrow. I have to be at school an hour early.'

'Beth, are you out of your mind?'

'No, Mummy. It's what I want most.'

'Well, you can't have it. A cheerleader! Beth, cheerleaders are pretty little fluffs who can't do anything else. You can do math. You can write poetry. You can do anything you put your mind to, but not cheerleading, for heaven's sake!'

'But all the girls . . .'

'Sit down, Beth. You must understand one thing and keep it always in mind. You are not "all the girls." You have an extraordinary mind, inherited it from your grandmother, I think. God knows it skipped me. Beth, you're special. You could win top honors at Michigan. You're not a cheerleader . . .'

'I don't want to go to Michigan.'

'Where do you want to go?'

'Texas, where all the good kids go. Or A&M, it's real neat.'

'For God's sake, stop saying "real neat." A&M is not real neat and neither is cheerleading.

Beth was so persistent in her desire to have what every Texas high school girl was supposed to want that Maggie finally said: 'We'll talk to your father about this when he gets back from Falfurrias,' and when Roy Bub Hooker pulled the hunting wagon up to the Morrison residence at eleven-thirty that night, Maggie called upstairs: 'Beth, come down and let's talk about this.'

To her joy, her father sided with her: 'I don't see anything wrong with a little cheerleading, if that's what her school features.'

'But, Todd, it's a step backward. It surrenders all the gains women are beginning to make. Next you'll be entering her in a beauty contest, bathing suits yet.'

'Nothing wrong with bathing suits, properly filled out.'

Beth allowed her parents to fight the thing out and was gratified when her father won, but next morning she found that

1337

it had only appeared that way, because her mother blocked the door at seven-thirty when Beth prepared to run out and join the kids in the car for first-day practice of the cheerleading squad. 'Hey, Killer!' they called. 'Time's wastin'.'

'Beth cannot join you,' Mrs Morrison informed them. 'I'm so sorry.'

Inside the door, Beth stood white and trembling. 'Mom!' she cried, dropping the customary *Mummy*. 'If I can't be a cheerleader, I'll die.'

'If you can't be a contributor, a brain at whatever level you're capable of, you'll really die. Now eat your cereal and be off to school like a proper scholar, which you are.'

For three unhappy days the sparring continued – Mr Morrison siding with his daughter, and Mrs Morrison standing like Horatius at the bridge table, as he said, refusing to allow her daughter to take what she called 'this first step down to mediocrity.' It then looked as if Beth was going to solve the problem by refusing to eat until she starved; poetry, math, her designs for a new fabric, all were forgotten in her determination to be one of the gang and to gain the plaudits of her fellow students.

The impasse was resolved in a manner which Maggie Morrison, trained in Michigan and with Michigan values, could never have anticipated, but on the Friday of that first awful week she was summoned from her real estate desk to the office of Mr Sanderson, principal of Deaf Smith High in north Houston: 'Mrs Morrison, I'm sure you know you have a most superior daughter.'

'I want to keep her that way.'

'But you cannot do it by opposing her natural desire to be one of our cheerleaders.'

'I doubt that cheerleading is natural.'

'At any serious Texas high school it is.'

'It oughtn't to be.' She was startled by her willingness to fight but was convinced that she was fighting for the preservation of her daughter's integrity and intelligence.

'Mrs Morrison, I think we'd better have a serious talk. Please sit down.' When she was seated, her legs fiercely crossed, her jaw forward, he charmed her by saying: 'I wish we had more mothers concerned about the welfare of their daughters. Feel free to come here and visit with me about these things at any time.'

'I'm visiting now, and I don't like what you're doing to Beth.'

'Mrs Morrison, she is no longer in Michigan. She's in Texas, and there's a world of difference. No girl in Houston can achieve a higher accolade than to be chosen for our cheerleading team, unless maybe it's to be the baton twirler. To have the approval of the whole student body. To stand before her peers, the prettiest, the most popular. Mrs Morrison, that is something.'

'Is it true, Mr Sanderson, that your high school has eleven football coaches?'

'We need them. In this state, competition is tough.'

'And is it true that four out of five of Beth's teachers this year are not prepared in their academic subjects, because their first responsibility is coaching?'

'Our coaches are the finest young men the state of Texas produces. Your daughter is lucky to share them in the classroom.'

'But can a coach of tight ends teach a girl poetry?'

'At Deaf Smith we don't hit poetry very heavy.'

'What do you hit?'

'Mrs Morrison, I run one of the best high schools in Texas, everybody says so. Beth will tell you the same. These aren't easy years, drugs and all that, new social pressures. Negroes and Hispanics knocking at the door. Holding a big school like this together is a full-time job, and one of the strongest binders we have is football. I want every child in this school to be involved in our team, one way or another.'

'Even the girls?'

'Especially the girls. Football at Deaf Smith is not a boy's empire.' He pointed to the stunning photographs that decorated his office. 'The girls' marching squad, best in the state. The cheerleaders, runners-up last year. The rifle-drill squad, have you ever seen a nattier bunch of kids? And look at the number of girl musicians we have in our band, and their spiffy uniforms.'

There were also girl baton twirlers, three of them, the pompon squad and the marshals. Maggie was startled by the overflowing abundance of girls, smiling, stepping, preening, twirling their wooden rifles, tossing their batons in the air.

'And I've saved the good news till last, Mrs Morrison. Here's a report I received from Mrs Crane the week before you startled us by your refusal to let Beth take her logical place in the system,' and he handed her a typed report from the woman who directed the girls' activities and who taught world history on the side:

> I have been watching Beth Morrison closely, and she gives every indication of having the hands, the necessary skills and the innate sense of balance which are required to make a great baton twirler.
>
> Let's keep her on the cheerleading squad for the time being, but let's also watch her very closely, because I think she has the ability to become a twirler of university class.

Mr Sanderson rocked back and forth on his heels as Maggie read the heartwarming report, and he reflected on how many mothers in his district would be overjoyed to learn that their daughter might one day be chief twirler at a major college. He waited till she had digested the report, then smiled and lifted his hands, as if to indicate that this had resolved all problems.

'Mrs Morrison, your daughter has a chance to achieve what every girl dreams of.'

Maggie felt beaten, but she still wanted to protect her daughter: 'I don't think Beth would find much happiness being a baton twirler,' to which Mr Sanderson said, with some asperity: 'If she's going to make her life in Texas, she will.' Quickly he modified that harsh statement: 'You and your husband are happy here, aren't you? I've heard he's doing famously. Syndications and all.'

'We're increasingly happy.'

'Then look to the future, Mrs Morrison, that's all I'm asking of you.'

So Beth Morrison appeared one day with pompons and what she called 'a really cool uniform,' and apparently Mrs Crane liked what she saw of Beth's coordination because two weeks later Beth came home with a silver baton and the exciting news that 'Mrs Holliday, who's trained all the real cool kids, is willing to give me special lessons, Saturday and Sunday. Fifty dollars for the first course.'

She did not immediately drop her interest in words and colorful images, for she had become addicted to a silly game called 'The White House.' It consisted of asking a partner: 'What do you call the White House?' and when the other person said: 'I don't know. What do you call the White House?' you said: 'The President's residence.'

For several weeks she pestered her parents and her brother with her questions, and one night she crushed them with what she called 'a four-alarm sizzler': 'What do you call a Canadian Mountie who works undercover?' and the answer was: 'A super-duper-tooper-snooper.'

About this time Maggie came upon that remarkable study of child genius and music in which it was pointed out that from a society much like America's between 1750–1830, Europe produced hundreds of gifted musicians because that was the thrust of the society; that was what counted in Germany and Austria and Italy. 'Today in America,' reasoned the study, 'we have the same amount of innate talent, we must have because the genetic pool assures that, but we concentrate on games, not music or the arts. So we produce a plethora of great athletes and no musicians, because parents and schools do not want Mozarts or Haydns. They want Babe Ruths and Red Granges, and so that's what they get.'

She was about to discuss this with Beth when her daughter appeared one evening after school dressed in one of the sauciest, sexiest costumes the older Morrisons had ever seen – certainly they had not expected to see their daughter in anything like it – the uniform of a baton twirler, with padded bosom, padded rump and tightly drawn waist. She was totally fetching as she pirouetted before her family: 'What would you call me tonight?' When each had guessed wrong, she said: 'A sassy lassie with a classy chassis.'

Beth Morrison, once headed for English honors at the University of Michigan, had changed her plans.

In these exciting days her father was playing a game much more daring than twirling or football. He had learned from his mentor, Gabe Klinowitz, how to put together a real estate syndicate, and he had already launched three, with outstanding success. 'What you do,' he explained to his wife, 'is find a group of people with money to invest, doctors and dentists primarily, because they often have ready cash, and oilmen if you can get to them. You have to keep it less than thirty-six, because beyond that level Internal Revenue says: "Hey, look, that's not a syndicate, that's an ordinary stock offering," and you fall under much stiffer rules. But suppose you find seven partners, twenty thousand dollars each. There's a lot of people around Houston who have twenty thousand dollars they'd like to play with.'

As he said this he stopped: 'God, Maggie, doesn't Detroit seem a far distance? Nobody up there had even two thousand dollars.'

He went on: 'Now, everybody knows that seven people cannot run a business, so they agree that you, who have the time, will be the general partner in charge, and they will be the limited partners. Very careful legal papers spell this out. You are to make the decisions. So with the hundred and forty thousand from the seven of them ... You put in no money of your own, you're the manager. So with their dough as down payment, you buy this great piece of property worth three million dollars. Immense future. You get ten percent of the action as your fee, plus another five percent as broker if and when you arrange to sell it.

'With your hundred and forty thousand dollars you've sewed up a hundred acres of choice land, worth millions later on, but you've paid only a down payment, long-term payout, everybody happy. Now, here comes the tricky part, and you have to have nerves of steel. The day comes when you sell that gorgeous piece of land so that your investors can get their money out plus a reasonable profit. And who do you sell it to? To yourself. You wave around a little money of your own as if you were putting it up, a new set of investors who pay for everything, and under the legal document determining what you can do as general partner, you sell it to the new group, not informing your earlier partners of your participation in the new syndicate.

'You already own ten percent of the sale price, and there's that five percent for acting as broker, and here's the clever part. You leave on the table—'

'What do you mean *leave on the table*?'

'Gabe taught me. Always leave on the table a reasonable

1342

profit for the other man. You see to it that your original partners each make a nice profit. Not spectacular, respectable. Everybody's happy, presto-changeo a lot of action, and you wind up with forty per cent of the new syndicate, which now owns one hundred extremely valuable acres, and you started without a cent in the kitty.' He chuckled: 'And of course, you pay yourself a nice brokerage fee, which gives you even more ready cash.'

'Sounds illegal to me.'

'As legal as the Bank of England. All you have to do is keep your group of investors so happy that they won't try to oust you as general partner.'

It was legal, but it was not honorable, and after a second syndicate had been sold by its original owners, to another consortium controlled by Morrison, at a price far below real value, Gabe Klinowitz, one of his partners, came to see him: 'Todd, this is an unhappy day. I'm pulling out of your deals.'

'You've made money on them.'

'You've seen to that. But nowhere near what I should have made. I'm like your other partners. You trickle down just enough to keep us from suing you. I can't afford scandals, neither can they. But we know what you've been doing.'

'But wait a minute, Gabe. You and I . . .'

'That's the sad part, Todd. If you would do this to me . . . Do you realize how much you owe to me?'

'It's in my mind constantly. I told Maggie just the other day . . .'

'If you would do this to friend, Todd, some day you'll do it to a stranger, and he'll throw you in jail . . . or into a coffin.'

'Now wait . . .'

'We play hard in Texas. In Houston we p y very hard and very rough. But we play honest. A handshake is a handshake, and by God, you better not forget it. Twice with me you've abused a handshake, Todd, that Gulf Oil deal and now this. Sooner or later when you do that around here, somebody blows a very loud whistle, and either the sheriff or the undertaker comes running. Goodbye, Todd. Keep your nose clean. Right now it's very dirty.'

As if he were intuitively aware that what he was doing was immoral if not illegal, Todd would not permit his quail-hunting friends to participate in his first syndicates, but when they heard of the considerable profits being made in such deals, they wanted in. Now, when he had a firm grasp of the intricacies, he told them on a ride south to their lease: 'All right, you clowns, you wanted to share in the action. I have a lead on a swell chunk of property north of FM-1960 but well south of Route 2920, place near Tomball, two hundred choice acres, about ten thousand an acre.'

'Hey,' the oilman said, 'that's two million bucks.'

'But we don't put it up. Most we have to contribute, maybe ten thousand each. The rest, a mortgage, long payout, whatever interest the seller demands, because the rate of growth on this property is going to be sensational. Let time take care of the mortgage and the interest.'

They were approaching Victoria when he made this proposal, and Roy Bub, who was driving as usual, slowed down and stared at him: 'You sneaky sumbitch! When you bought my place you didn't have a nickel to your name, did you? All hokey-pokey and fancy dance steps.'

'Did you lose a penny on the deal, cowboy?'

'No, and I've been tryin' to figure out who did.'

'Nobody, that's who. We were playing the Texas game, all of us, and that time it worked. It can work this time too.' His final talk with Gabe Klinowitz had scared him, and he had vowed that on this deal with his three friends, he would play it completely honest; they would share totally in any growth this land achieved, and if there was a sale, it would be at arm's length to some complete stranger, with all the papers visible to the partners.

He was so determined to avoid the traps that Gabe had warned about that he even called on Gabe in the latter's grubby office: 'You scared me, Gabe. I can see what you were warning me about, been brooding over it. Three of my close friends and I are organizing this syndicate for some choice land up by Tomball. I want you to come in, open books and a final sale to some third party. Clean.' But Gabe said: 'I never double back.' And when the time came to liquidate the Quail Hunters' Syndicate, as they termed it, Todd could not resist putting together a secret syndicate in which he had an unannounced share and of which he would be the sub rosa general partner, and he sold the Tomball acreage to this syndicate for about half its real value.

In addition to his share of the Quail Hunters' profit, he took a ten percent brokerage fee for handling the sale, and a huge percentage of the new syndicate. Todd Morrison was now a multimillionaire.

When Maggie Morrison made out the family's income tax she discovered that in liquidating the Quail Hunters' Syndicate, her husband had inadvertently failed to distribute to his three hunting partners profits to which they were legally entitled, and she drew his attention to this oversight. Todd, not wishing to reveal that his retention of those profits had been far from accidental, said with ill-feigned astonishment: 'Maggie, you're right. There's forty thousand dollars they should split among them,' and she replied: 'At least.'

So on the next drive down to Falfurrias he told the men, as if bringing good news which he had uncovered: 'Hey, you junior J. P. Morgans! Final figures on our syndicate show that we have an unexpected forty-eight thousand to split up,' but when the cheering stopped and time came to tell them it would be split three ways, for it was their money, he found himself saying: 'So that means an extra twelve thousand dollars for each of us. Come Monday, we can all buy new Cadillacs.'

When the Cobbs settled into their home north of Levelland, Sherwood started immediately to make his gin the premier one in the area, and he began in the traditional way. He became a vociferous supporter of the Levelland Lobos, who consistently seemed to wind up their seasons three and seven, if they got the breaks. The countryside appreciated his enthusiasm and entered the judgment that 'this here Cobb is dependable.' From this solid foundation he could build.

At the end of the third year, Sherwood gathered Nancy and their children in the kitchen and spread the figures before them: 'At our old place at Lammermoor, a hundred nineteen pounds of lint to the acre, bringing nine cents a pound. In Waxahachie, two hundred thirty-nine pounds at twenty-eight cents a pound. Here in Levelland, three hundred ninety-one pounds at forty-two cents a pound. Year's profit from our cotton, our gin and our other operations – one hundred forty-nine thousand dollars.'

In view of these figures he advised his family not to complain about the disadvantages of living atop the Cap Rock: 'This is the cotton capital of the world, and no gin in the United States processed more of it last year than we did. I'm putting every cent we earned into more land and more wells. This can go on forever.'

It was a sultry afternoon in May when Ransom Rusk and Mr Kramer were on Rusk's patio discussing the latter's work in providing armadillos for the leprosy research in Louisiana. It was going well, Kramer said, and new discoveries were being made every month, it seemed, toward an ultimate cure for Hansen's Disease: 'They don't like to call it leprosy any more. The Bible gave what's an ordinary disease a bad name.'

To the surprise of the two experts, Lady Macbeth and her eight witches were moving about, long before sunset, and this was so unusual that Rusk commented on it, and Kramer said: 'Something's afoot,' and they watched the little insect-eaters for some minutes as they darted here and there, their armor reflecting in the sun.

Then, suddenly, the mother began rounding up the four youngest pups and nudging them toward their burrow in the middle of the former bowling lawn, and as she herself headed for the hole, the four older pups galloped across the lawn and beat her to the entrance.

'They must know something,' Kramer said, and before he could begin to speculate on what it was, a maid came onto the patio: 'Radio says tornado watch!' and Kramer dashed inside. Telephoning a friend who helped him maintain a close guard on the weather, he spoke only a few words, then ran back to Rusk: 'Not a watch. A real warning. Tornado touch down at the southern end of Tornado Alley.' The words were ominous.

'I must get to my anemometers,' Kramer cried, running toward his car.

'Stay here!' Rusk bellowed, and so imperative was his voice that the expert on weather obeyed.

From a vantage point on the second floor of the mansion, they studied the southwestern sky, supposing that the tornado, if it sustained its forward motion, would move north along its customary corridor, and they had been in position only briefly

1346

when they saw a sight that meant horror to anyone who had ever experienced a tornado. As if some giant scene shifter were rearranging the sky, the desultory clouds which had been filtering the heat were moved aside, their place taken by a massive black formation.

'It's a real one,' Kramer said quietly. He started below, seeking some sturdy archway under which to hide, but Rusk grabbed his arm: 'We have a cellar.' So for some minutes the two stayed aloft to watch the frightening cloud.

It came directly at Larkin on its way to Wichita Falls, and Kramer spotted the twister first, a terrible, brutal finger reaching down, a black funnel twisting and turning and tearing apart anything unlucky enough to lie within its path. It was going to hit, and hard.

'One of the big ones,' Kramer said.

But still Rusk held fast, mesmerized by the awesome power of that churning finger as it uprooted trees, tossed automobiles in the air and disintegrated houses. His final view, before Kramer dragged him to the first floor, was of the upper cloud moving much faster than the lower spout, with the latter trailing behind and trying to catch up, destroying everything in its way as it did so.

Rusk showed remarkable control, checking rooms, as he ran: 'Everybody to the cellar!' On the ground floor he led the way to the heavy door that opened upon a flight of steel stairs, at the bottom of which waited a small, dark room lined with bottles of water, dehydrated foods, medical supplies and blankets. With that door closed, the household members were as safe as anyone could be with the needle of a tornado passing overhead.

Walls shook, windows shattered as suction pulled them outward from their frames. A roar like that 〔 a train passing echoed through the heavy door, and even this strongly built house trembled as if made of the frailest adobe. For one sickening moment it seemed as if the rooms above were being torn apart, and a Mexican maid began to sob quietly, but Rusk reassured her in an effective way: 'Magdalena, when the storm ends, the people out there will need your help,' and he issued directions: 'As soon as I open the door, fan out and collect the wounded. If you find any dead bodies, put them on the lawn out front.'

When Rusk gingerly opened the door, the servants scrambled up the steel stairway to view the desolation. No windows were left along the south and west faces of the mansion. Large chunks of the roof had been torn away. In the garden, trees had been uprooted, and to demonstrate the grotesque power of the storm, a small bungalow had been carried two hundred feet through the air and deposited upside down in the middle of the bowling lawn, its structure intact.

After a brief survey, the servants began to search the streets and alleys, and the tragic task of finding bodies in the rubble began. Some were miraculously pulled free minutes before they would have suffocated; others would not be found for two days. Mr Kramer saved four men by piping oxygen to them through metal tubes which he forced through the debris that could not at the moment be moved. One woman was distraught, for her five-year-old son had been torn from her arms and sucked high into the air, to be thrown down she could not guess where. Frantically she searched for him through the mass of damaged buildings, and she was trying to tear boards away to look for him when a neighbor found him four hundred yards away, unscathed.

Fourteen people died in Larkin, ten of them in automobiles, a heavy toll for such a small town. 'Remember, damnit,' Mr Kramer muttered as men helped him pull a body out of one of the crushed cars, 'worst place to hide in a tornado, your car. Wind must have lifted this one three hundred feet in the air and smashed it down. We'll need torches to get him out.'

The dead man inside was Dewey Kimbro. For seventy years he had roamed Texas, looking for carboniferous signals. Four times his discoveries had made him a millionaire; four times he had allowed the money to slip away. His will distributing his final fortune displayed his customary gallantry, for it awarded two hundred thousand dollars each to the five women with whom he had been entangled, and that included the girl Esther, whom he had brought to Larkin with him that first time but had never married. When the citizens heard of his generosity to the women who had given him so much trouble, they forgot how they had censured him, and said at his funeral: 'Good old Dewey, he was a character.'

Of course, when his will was probated the court found that it had less than three thousand dollars to distribute; all the wealth Dewey had accumulated in those last wonderful years in the Permian Basin had been dissipated. The tombstone, which Ransom Rusk erected, said: A REAL TEXAS WILDCATTER.

... Task Force

For the past twenty-eight years Lorenzo Quimper had participated in the Texas Olympics, that is Man *versus* Mesquite, and the score stood Mesquite 126, Quimper 5, which was better than many Texans did.

Whenever Lorenzo had acquired a new ranch he started the same way, as if following the score of a ritual ballet: 'Cándido, we've got to clear these fields of mesquite!' In 1969 he had tackled his first field: 'Cándido, we'll chop it down.'

He and his Mexican work force did just that, using power saws instead of axes, and they did a respectable job: 'Meadow's completely clean.' But since the pesky mesquite had one very deep taproot plus innumerable laterals for every branch that showed above, this laborious cutting was nothing more than a helpful pruning. Nearly two years later: 'Good God, Cándido! There's more out there than when we started!'

So in 1970 he and his workers burned off the mesquite, but this was a dreadful mistake, because the ashes served as a perfect fertilizer for the roots; a year later the fields were positively luxuriant, not with grass but with new mesquite.

In 1972, following the advice of experts at A&M, he once more cut down the trees and then used acid on the visible roots, and this did kill them, definitely. But his acid reached only some six percent of the roots, whereupon the survivors leaped into action to take up the slack. 'You'd think there were devils down there, proddin' them to spring up through the soil,' he groaned one day, and Cándido said: 'You may have something there, boss.'

In 1974 a new group of experts, including men from the great King Ranch in South Texas who had fought mesquite for half a century, visited the Quimper ranches to demonstrate a new technique: 'What we do, Lorenzo, is cut the tree off at the base of the trunk, then use these two huge tractors to drag a chain which cuts deep beneath the soil. We don't just pull up the main roots, we root prune the entire plant, get all the little trailers.'

For three years the Quimper ranches looked fairly good, with a minimum of mesquite, but by 1977 the savage trees were back in redoubled force: 'They been sleepin', Mr Quimper, jess conservin' their strength.' They had a lot of it when they reappeared, so that in 1978, Lorenzo said: 'To hell with it,' and his costly fields grew a little grass for his cattle, a lot of mesquite in which his quail, his deer and his wild turkeys could hide.

Of course, Il Magnifico did not lose completely; as the score indicated, he did win five times, but only because he poured into selected fields a modest fortune in dynamite, tractors, chains, acid and muscle. He calculated that for a mere $6,000 an acre any man could effectively drive mesquite off land which had cost $320 an acre to begin with. His victories were Pyrrhic, and he did have a limited revenge.

Since our June meeting was to be held in the nearby German community of Fredericksburg, Quimper invited us to spend the preceding evening at what he called 'my home ranch,' on Lake Travis, west of Austin. When we entered his living-room we saw that he had finally triumphed over his mesquite. He had directed Cándido to cut down two hundred of their biggest mesquites – most of them not over ten feet tall or eight inches across – and from the cores of these trunks his men had cut a wealth of squares, three inches on the side, half an inch thick. Using them as parquetry, he had fitted them into a heavy cement base and then burnished the surface with heavy buffers usually reserved for marble.

When the floor was leveled and smoothed, and after a thin silicone paste had been applied and polished to a gleaming finish, the result was a most handsome floor. The jagged patterns of the mesquite thus laid bare formed an intricate work of art: predominantly purple but with red, green, yellow and brown flecks or scars. 'It's a floor of jewels!' said one delighted visitor. And it was, the neat squares of wood showing a thousand different patterns, a hundred variations in color.

Lorenzo had triumphed, but it had not been easy: 'Come out here to the workshed. Look at that pile of burned-out saw blades. Cutting that floor was hell.' He looked at the stack of blades, nearly three feet high, and said: 'Of course, doin' the library was even worse. The blocks were smaller.'

Our session the next day was memorable, for it consisted of three unique stages. When we convened for breakfast in Fredericksburg, one of the finest small towns of Texas, with an immensely wide main street, good German restaurants, European music and citizens eager to make visitors welcome, we were met by representatives of six of the state's minorities: Germans, Czechs, Italians, Poles, Scots and Wends, and we could have talked with twenty other such groups had we had the time, for Texas is truly a state built from minorities.

When the speaking ended, the groups brought in dance teams in native costume and regional orchestras playing unfamiliar instruments, and as we applauded, older people served ethnic dishes of wondrous complexity. This was a Texas which not many outsiders imagined, and among the scores who entertained us, there was not an oilman or a cowboy.

After lunch we drove fourteen miles east to adjacent rural parks, one national, one state, honoring Lyndon Baines Johnson. At the heart of the parks, overlooking the Pedernales, stood an unpretentious one-room house which had been converted into a recreation center. Here we held our afternoon session, at which three scholars from New York and Boston addressed us on the significance of Johnson's occupancy of the White House. As we met there in a meeting to which the public had been invited, we could see the Hill Country which L.B.J. had loved, we could feel his tall, gangling presence, a sensation that was enhanced when Lady Bird herself came unannounced to invite us to refreshments at her ranch across the river. Texas history seemed very real that day.

When we ended our meeting at six-thirty, we were handed another surprise by Il Magnifico: 'The missus and me are throwin' a little do back at our ranch in favor of our daughter, Sue Dene, her sixteenth birthday, and we want y'all to come. Spend the night.' So we piled into the limousines which Rusk and Miss Cobb provided for the occasion and drove the forty-odd miles back to the Quimper ranch. As we saw that splendid rolling country of scattered oak, mesquite and huisache, Efraín said to Miss Cobb: 'I imagine a newcomer from the wooded hills of New Hampshire or from the real mountains of Montana would find this rather ordinary. But when you've worked all day in steaming Houston and fly up here in your own plane on

Friday night, this must seem like heaven.'

'It is,' she said.

As we approached Lake Travis, which came into being in 1934 when the Colorado River was dammed, I commented on the incredible good luck that seemed to crown any Quimper real estate venture: 'Do you have a crystal ball?' and he replied apologetically in country style: 'I swear to you on a stack of Bibles, my pappy was just ridin' along here one sunny day in 1930 and said to hisself: "Some day they'll build a dam here and make theirselves a lake." So he bought seven thousand acres at sixty-three dollars each, and now it's worth six thousand an acre, five times that much if it fronts the lake.'

'How was he clever enough to foresee that?' I asked, and Lorenzo said: 'He had no privileged warnin'. Just believed that whenever you grab onto Texas land, somethin' good is likely to happen.'

At the entrance to his ranch a massive stone gateway had been erected in a style borrowed from ancient Assyria, monstrous blocks of granite piled helter-skelter but with dramatic effect; as we passed through these stones uniformed police hired for the evening directed us to an assembly area – ten or fifteen acres kept cleared by a flock of sheep – where several hundred people awaited instructions.

After our cars were unloaded, a whistle blew, policemen waved, and a make-believe train of nine cars dragged by a tractor-locomotive pulled up to carry us to wherever the girl's birthday party was to be held. The train took us along a country lane, through a stand of oak trees and onto another empty field. Traversing this at slow speed, it brought us into an area which caused us to gasp.

To prove to his daughter that he loved her, Quimper had hired a complete circus: there stood the Ferris wheel, the two merry-go-rounds, the Bump-a-Car enclosure, the Krazy Kwilt Palace of Delights with its distorting mirrors, the barkers luring people into the free sideshows, and the line of cages with lions, tigers and bears. Six clowns did impossible things and the high-wire act was enthralling.

At the height of the show the lead clown came roaring across the field in a Mercedes 450SL, vanity license plates Q-SUE, which he presented to the Quimper girl as her birthday present.

Miss Cobb whispered: 'Doesn't every lassie get a Mercedes?' But my attention was diverted to a scene that was taking place between Quimper and his wife. I heard him tell her: 'Honey, we're in trouble! We're runnin' out of food.'

'Impossible,' she said. 'I baked the cookies myself. Thousands of them. And we have more than enough barbecue.'

'That's not the problem. About a hundred of our neighbours have seen the lights and they've come over to join in the fun.'

It was a warm-hearted party, and by Texas-rich standards, not preposterous or even ostentatious. The Quimpers had the ranch, they had the money, and they enjoyed entertaining their neighbors. Above all, they wanted to be sure their daughter and her friends met the right kind of young people against the day when they must choose their marriage partners, for as Mrs Quimper said; 'If they don't meet people from the right schools and the right families, they might marry just anybody.'

We were sitting in Quimper's living room and congratulating ourselves on one of the best days our Task Force had spent when the whole façade collapsed, for Mrs Quimper brought into the room one of the men who had addressed us that afternoon, a Professor Steer from Harvard, forty-eight years old, suave and sure of himself in his gray-touched hair, bow tie and London tailoring. 'What a coincidence,' he said as he reached for a drink, and settled down. 'My son, who's doing graduate work at SMU, is one of the young men out there dancing with the young ladies, especially a Miss Grady, and he dragged me along. I never dreamed you were the people I'd been addressing this afternoon.

'We're mighty glad to have you,' Quimper said, bringing him a plate of barbecue.

The conversation started well, with Steer asking our two older men: 'In Texas, are you considered oilmen or ranchers?' to which Quimper replied: 'In this state a man can have thirty oil wells and a little ol' nothin' ranch with a thousand acres and six steers, but he calls hisself a rancher.'

Rusk, trying to be amiable, said: 'I have many friends who never wear a cowboy Stetson in Texas but always when they go to New York or Boston.'

Miss Cobb said: 'You'll find, Professor Steer, that Texas ranchers like to brag about their prize bull, the pilot of their airplane and their unmarried daughter, in that order.'

Tricked by the apparent warmth of this greeting, Steer said: 'I'm so glad to find you here. I sort of held back on certain fundamentals this afternoon. Too many of the public listening.'

'Like what?' Quimper asked, and the professor startled me by the frankness with which he responded.

'I should have pointed out that Lyndon Johnson suffered bad luck in ascending to the presidency in the way he did.'

'How so?' Quimper probed.

'Well, John Kennedy, for whom I worked, was a charismatic type, handsome, well groomed, educated, able in leadership, and gifted with a beautiful sophisticated wife.'

As this was said I happened to be looking at Rusk, a Republican leader who had contributed to Johnson's campaigns but voted against him. He was studying his knuckles, not looking up, so I could not ascertain how he might be receiving this attack upon a fellow Texan.

Steer continued: 'A regrettable aspect of Johnson's ascendancy was that he came, in our interpretation . . .' Here I noticed that Steer had subtly changed from referring, as he had in his speech, to the Eastern Establishment as *them*, and was now including himself in the ruling group.

'We saw Vice-President Johnson as a prototypical citizen of Dallas, the city which had killed the real President.'

Miss Cobb interrupted: 'Dallas didn't kill anybody. A crazy drifter from New Orleans and Moscow did.'

'But the nation perceived it as a Dallas crime, and I must say, so did I.'

'Why?' Miss Cobb asked.

'I was working for President Kennedy in those delicate days . . . twenty-one years ago this week. I'd accompanied Adlai Stevenson to Dallas when the women leaders of your society spat upon him.'

'It was not my society,' Miss Cobb protested. 'They were right-wing extremists. You find them everywhere.'

'But especially in Dallas.'

Since no one could reasonably contest this, Steer plunged ahead. 'I was in the advance party that bleak November day in 1963 when Kennedy made his fatal visit. I was not near him . . .

far off to the side when the motorcade came swinging into Dealey Plaza. But at breakfast I had presented him with the *Dallas Morning News* and its deadful, irrational attack. You know what the last words he said to me were: "We're heading into Nut Country today." And a short time later he was dead. In my interpretation, and it remains very firm this November, Dallas killed him.'

There was with Texans like the five of us a residual shame for what had happened back in 1963, and we were sophisticated enough to realize that some of what Professor Steer was so arrogantly reconstructing was true. The climate of Texas at that time, especially in Dallas, had been antithetical to much of what Kennedy as president stood for, even though the state had voted for him in 1960, and even though our own L.B.J., had been instrumental in squeaking him into the White House by the slimmest margin ever. We were not disposed to argue vehemently in defense of Dallas.

But now Steer, obviously pleased with the progress he was making in hacking Texas down to size, continued his impetuous drive: 'What happened was that Johnson came to impersonate the worst of Texas as opposed to the best of New England. Texas was anti-labor, we were pro. Texas was fundamentalist in religion, we were enlightened. Texas was deficient in education, we stressed it. Texas was uncouth, the voice of the barbarian, New England was gently trained, the voice of academe. Texas was cowboys and oil, the North was libraries and theater and symphony orchestras. Texas was the raw frontier, Boston was the long-established bulwark of inherited values. And what was especially difficult for us to accept, Texas was flamboyantly nouveau riche, and the Northeast had long since disciplined such ostentation.'

I saw that Quimper was about to explode, but what Steer said next delayed the fuse: 'I grant you that in those days Texas had energy and wealth and sometimes valuable imagination. But it was not a likeable place, and few in the Establishment liked it.'

For the first time Rusk spoke, deep in his chest: 'How exactly do you define the Establishment?'

This was the kind of question Steer liked, for it provided an excuse to parade his skill at summarization: 'I suppose I mean the opinion makers. The agencies that give us our mind-sets.

Two newspapers, *New York Times* and *Washington Post*. Three magazines, *Time*, *Newsweek*, the London *Economist* and three networks, and one special publication, *The Wall Street Journal*, plus the faculties of the better universities and colleges.'

'And what are those better schools?' Rusk asked as if he were ignorant, and Steer obliged: 'Yale, Harvard, Princeton and maybe Chicago. Brown, yes, and maybe Dartmouth. A few of the smaller colleges like Amherst and Williams. A smattering of the old girls' schools, Vassar, Smith, perhaps Bryn Mawr.'

'They're the ones who passed judgment on Lyndon Johnson?' Rusk asked.

'We found him quite unacceptable.' Again I watched Rusk carefully, and he said no more, just kept studying his knuckles, which were now white. He was not under pressure, but he was listening intently.

Steer, unaware of how close he was to a live volcano, proceeded with what was for him a fascinating bit of social phenomenon: 'I think Texas is destined to play Rome to our Greece.'

'What do you mean?' Quimper asked, and Steer responded: 'When Greece lost world leadership to Rome, she fell back on the perfectly honorable role of providing Rome with intellectual leadership – art, history, philosophy, logic, world view. Rome had none of these, could create none from her own resources. But she could borrow from Greece . . . import Greek tutors, Greek managers. And the symbiosis proved a fruitful one.'

'What's *symbiosis* mean?' Quimper asked naïvely, even though I'd heard him use the word at our last meeting.

'Interlocking relationship, each part depends on the other.'

'Could the Texas-Massachusetts symbiosis be fruitful?' Quimper asked, and Steer said he thought that perhaps it could: 'You'll continue to inherit our representation in Congress, and you'll provide the money, the energy and, yes, the vitality I suppose, all very necessary if an organism is to survive.'

'What will you give us in return?' Lorenzo asked sweetly, and Steer said: 'The intellectual analysis, the philosophical guidance, the historical memory. Believe me, a raw state like Texas will not be able to go it alone. Rome couldn't.'

'Will Texas ever be accepted? By your Eastern

Establishment, I mean?' Quimper asked.

'Oh, when time softens your raw edges. When the television show *Dallas* slinks off the tube, if it ever does. When your petroleum reserves deplete and you can no longer terrorize us with your oil money.' Up to this point neither Rusk nor Quimper showed any inclination to dispute our visitor's analysis, but Steer stumbled ahead and triggered a bear trap. 'The real test will be whether any of your colleges or universities can become first class. If they do, maybe the rest of America will be able to tolerate your extravagances.'

Now came an ominous pause, during which I looked at Professor Garza, who was smiling quietly and shrugging his shoulders as if to ask me: 'Why should we two sane people get mixed up in this?'

So I was not watching when Rusk rose from his chair and straightened his drooping shoulders to their full height, but I did turn quickly when I heard him say in his deep, rumbling voice: 'Get out of here!'

When Steer mumbled 'What? What?' Rusk lost control and fairly bellowed: 'Get the hell out of here!' and I saw with horror that he was trying to grab our visitor by the neck.

'You can't do this!' I cried, interposing myself between the two men, but then Quimper lunged forward, as if he too wanted to throw the Harvard man out, and I looked to Miss Cobb for help, but to my dismay, she was encouraging the men.

Before either Rusk or Quimper could reach Steer, I engineered our tactless visitor out of the door and put him on the path to where his son would be. When I returned, I looked in dismay at my associates, but they showed no remorse. They had been mortally offended by the Establishment's renewal of its assault on the dignity of Texas and had absorbed all the abuse they could tolerate. They were pleased at having ejected him.

'Why did you become so enraged?' I asked, and Rusk said: 'When a Yankee denigrates L.B.J., he denigrates Texas. And when he insults Texas, he insults me.'

'You never supported Johnson,' I said and he agreed: 'Voted against him every time he ran. But he was a Texan, and I cannot abide—'

I broke in to ask Quimper if he'd ever voted for Johnson, and he said: 'I've voted in various ways at various times.'

At this point Mrs Quimper appeared with a plate of fresh barbecue, and I was privileged to witness Quimper's face-saving victory in his war with mesquite. When Garza asked: 'How do you make your barbecue so delicious?' Lorenzo took him by the arm: 'I'll show you!' and he led us to a huge woodpile back of the house where rows of mesquite logs, twenty-one inches long, lay stacked.

'On each of my ranches I have crews doin' nothin' but harvestin' mesquite. We grow it now as a cash crop.'

'What for?' Garza asked, and Quimper said: 'We ship it to topflight restaurants all over America. "Twenty-One" in New York, the Plaza, that type. Everyone with money to spare orders Texas-style beef.' He kicked at the pile affectionately: 'I'm known as The Mesquite King of Texas. I'm makin' more on mesquite than I am on my boots. Like I always said, don't ever think Texas is licked till the fat lady sings.' Then he stared at us and snapped his fingers: 'Tomorrow mornin' I'm stoppin' all shipments to Boston. Those Ivy Leaguers don't deserve mesquite.'

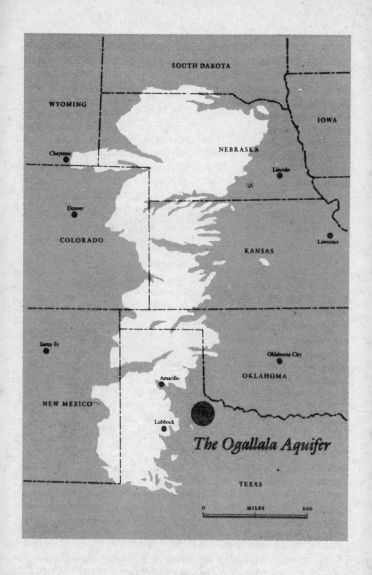

The Ogallala Aquifer

XIV

POWER AND CHANGE

During most of its history the citizens of Texas were poor.

When the Garzas trekked north from Zacatecas in 1724 they were virtual slaves, with pitiful housing, inadequate food and never a second set of clothing. The early Quimpers lived in an earthen cave without knowing bread for almost a year. The Macnabs did through a ruse get land, but they were always land-poor, and when young Otto finally became a Texas Ranger he served for miserable pay, if any, and was expected to provide his own horse, gun and clothing. Because the supply of money was so rigidly controlled, he rarely had any.

The Allerkamps labored like lackeys, all of them, and it was a long time before they had enough to live with any sense of ease. The two Cobb families from Carolina and Georgia had real slaves, a thriving gin and a lumber mill, but their Jefferson neighbors did not. Of a hundred Cobb slaves, the ninety field hands lived in only poverty; they enjoyed enough food but not a decent house or proper clothes. And during the Civil War and the Reconstruction, even the white folks in the plantation mansions knew real deprivation.

When Fort Garner folded, Emma Larkin and her husband, Earnshaw Rusk, owned a fine set of stone buildings and thousands of acres, but they had no money with which to operate; they spent carefully, but because they could not save up even a few dollars in ready cash, they almost lost their holdings.

That was the condition of Texas: plenty of land, a niggardly existence, a dream of better days. However, with the 1901 discovery of limitless petroleum deposits at Spindletop near Beaumont, some Texans began to accumulate tremendous riches, and by the 1920s even families as far west as the Rusks in Larkin County shared in the bonanza. In Texas one could leap from land-poor to oil-rich in one generation ... or one weekend.

Now the perpetual poverty of Texas was obscured by the conspicuous display of wealth, and the history of the state began to be told in dollar signs followed by big numbers, and some could be very big, because here and there certain lucky Texans became billionaires. To the rest of the nation it sometimes looked as if the dollar sign governed the state.

For example, as the decade of the 1980s opened, the whole state seemed to be on what gamblers called a roll, with each throw of the dice producing a winning seven or eleven. Everything looked so promising that enthusiasts started voicing the old boast: 'This can go on forever.'

There was solid reason for believing that Texas was certain to achieve national leadership, for the census then under way would show that the state had gained so much population – 3,009,728 in ten years – it would gain three new seats in Congress, while the less fortunate states in the cold Northeast would lose twice that number.

As always, oil was the harbinger of good fortune and when, with help from the Arab states, it soared to thirty-six dollars a barrel, Ransom Rusk's bank in Midland told its depositors: 'Oil has got to go to sixty, expand now,' and funds were provided for this next round of extraordinary gambling.

Airlines with a strong Texas base, like Braniff and Continental, freed at last from the petty regulations of the Civil Aeronautics Board, were flying into scores of new cities and picking up astronomical profits, while TexTek, the computer sensation based in Dallas was, as its shareholders boasted, 'soaring right off the top of that Big Board they run in Wall Street.' More than two dozen millionaires had been created through ownership of this stock, with three or four early investors, like Rusk, garnering nearly five hundred million each.

The sensation of the Texas scene, however, was Houston real estate, for it had no discernible upward limit. Farmers who owned land to the north and west of the city could demand almost any price an acre – $50,000, $100,000 – and there were many takers who knew that with just a little break, they could peddle it off at a million an acre. Investors from West Germany and Saudi Arabia were hungry for Houston real estate, but the major profits came from those Mexican politicians who had stolen their country blind and were now stashing their fortunes in the security provided by Houston hotels and condominiums. Anyone who could build anything in Houston could sell it: office space, hotels, condominiums, private homes. And if real estate ever did lag, the city could rely upon its oil industry. 'Houston is the hottest ticket in the world,' its boosters said.

The aspect of Texas life which seemed to give its noisier citizens the greatest boost was the Dallas Cowboys football team. Dubbed by an enthusiastic publicist 'America's Team,' it caught the nation's fancy, and year after year its stalwarts appeared in the play-offs and Bowl games. At the same time, in obedience to the sage precepts established by Friday night high school football, young women were enrolled in the madness, the Dallas Cowboy Cheerleaders becoming famous for the skimpiest costumes and the sexiest routines. A Cowboy's home game became a ritual at which devout Texans worshipped, for the players on the field were heroic and the cheerleaders along the sidelines irresistible. Boasted one partisan: 'Our football girls make those in New York and Denver look like dogs.' Just as the Larkin Fighting Antelopes had consolidated public enthusiasm in that small Texas town, so the Dallas Cowboys solidified enthusiasm and loyalty across Texas and in many other parts of the nation.

Nowhere was Texas optimism more obvious than in Larkin, where Ransom Rusk judged the week beginning 2 November 1980 to be the finest he had ever known. He was fifty-seven years old and resigned to the fact that the rest of his days would be spent in convenient bachelorhood; his mansion in Larkin was now staffed exclusively by illegal Mexican immigrants who performed well and taught him Spanish. The bowling lawn, which had dominated his life during his married years, was now a pleasant grassland, kept reasonably neat by a gang mower that shaved it twice a month.

One could say that he spent Sunday of this week with his beasts, for as his relations with other human beings, starting with his divorce from Fleurette, diminished, his reliance upon animal friends increased. Early morning was dedicated to his armadillos, a mother, father and four males this time; they had dug themselves into both his garden and his heart and had learned to come for vegetable roots when he whistled, their golden bodies shimmering in the dawn.

At about ten in the morning he rode out to his ranch, also run exclusively by Mexicans, none legal residents, and a more pleasant day he could not recall. Some seven years back he had gotten rid of his white-face Herefords, the breed introduced by his grandfather Earnshaw, and had started raising Texas Longhorns, whose strain had been kept alive by his grandmother, Emma Larkin Rusk. He had purified his herd until it contained only the MM/BB strain, animals descended from Mean Moses and Bathtub Bertha.

On Sunday mornings he liked to observe a ritual that re-created the grandeur of the vanishing Texas frontier: throwing a heavy paper sack in his Jeep, he would drive down the lane leading away from his ranch house and into a large fenced-in field at whose far end stood a beautifully scattered grove of trees. There, on a rise, he would halt his Jeep, blow the horn three times, and stand in the open, rustling his stiff paper bag.

On this Sunday, he did so for at least ten minutes, accomplishing nothing, and then slowly from distant trees shadowy forms began to emerge, hesitant, cautious, for they were wily animals. But as the sound of possible feed reached them they became more daring, and big Longhorn steers, handsomely mottled in gray and brown and white, began walking tentatively toward Rusk.

Another appeared and then another, until more than thirty had left the trees, and when they were in the open, reassured that no danger awaited them, they broke into a quiet lope that soon turned into a run. On they came, these wonderful animals out of the past whose survival had been made possible only because some Texans loved them, and as they drew closer, Rusk could see once more the tremendous horns these selected steers carried, great rocking chairs set on their heads. When they were nearly upon him, hungry for the food he promised, he studied them as if they were his children, and jumbled thoughts raced through his head:

No plotting man framed your character. Nature built you, alone on the prairies. Storms killed off your weaklings. Drought slaughtered those that had no will to survive. In years of hunger, you learned to eat almost anything, to forage off the moss of rocks. Through merciless selection, you learned to produce very small calves with a fantastic determination to grow into big adults. I don't waste money on veterinarians when I raise you Longhorns. You animals raise yourselves, just like us Texans.

When the first steers were eating all about him, so close that he could reach out and touch them, a huge old animal emerged from the woods and started walking in stately steps toward the feast, and when he approached, the others moved aside. He was Montezuma, self-appointed lord of the herd, and he maintained his noble advance until he stood nose-to-nose with Rusk, demanding to be fed by hand. For a moment these two survivors, gamblers of the plain, stood together, the great horns of Montezuma practically encircling Rusk.

Of all the cattle in the world, only you Longhorns produce a steer worth saving. Steers of all other strains are sent off to the butcher at age two, but you live on because men prize you, and want to see you sharing their land, for you remind them of the cleaner days. It's good to see you, Montezuma.

As he stood there surrounded by these incredible beasts, he could not escape, as a businessman, making a calculation: 'After the War Between the States, when Texas hadn't a nickel, our grandfathers herded ten million Longhorns to cowtowns like Dodge. At forty dollars a head, that meant four hundred million dollars pumped into the Texas economy when scarcely a dime was reaching it from other sources ... Montezuma, you Longhorns rebuilt this state.

Saluting his treasures, he drove back to a remarkable new building adjoined to his mansion, and there, as his Mexican butler served cold drinks, he watched his favorites, the Dallas Cowboys, play at St Louis. Had the game been in Dallas, he would have occupied his private box, entertaining, as usual, twelve or fourteen business acquaintances. He cheered when Wolfgang Macnab, a linebacker he had sent to the University of Texas on a football scholarship, mowed down St Louis like an avenging scythe: 'Tear 'em apart, Wolf Man. I knew back then you were headed for greatness.'

The building in which he sat was named the African Hall, for it resembled a stone lodge he had seen in South Africa's famed

Kruger park. He had built the place in his loneliness after his divorce when he had associated himself with a group of bachelors in similar circumstances who took safaris to Kenya, where in the splendor of its animal parks they shot kudu and giraffe and lion, bringing the heads home to be displayed on Texas walls. Rusk's hall was one of the best, and to sit surrounded by his handsome trophies while his Cowboys rampaged on the TV screen was a delight.

On Monday, when he drove to his office in Fort Worth, his two accountants asked if they might see him, and he expected trouble, for they rarely approached with good news, but this time was different: 'Mr Rusk, a singular development in Mid-Continent Gas has produced a situation in which you may be interested.'

At the mention of this name, Rusk had to smile, one of his thin, sardonic smiles, because he was thinking of the time when the Carpenter Field roared in with an almost unlimited supply of natural gas: 'Remember how my stupidity made me miss that bonanza completely?'

But the field had been operating only briefly when he saw an opportunity for a gamble of staggering dimension: 'The owners had no way of getting their gas to market. So I organized Mid-Continent and guaranteed them thirty-two cents a thousand cubic feet for all they could produce for the next forty years. They jumped, thinking they'd stuck me with gas I wouldn't be able to market, either.'

'I worked on that pipeline you bulldogged through the hills,' the chief accountant recalled. 'Nobody believed you could do it, including me. That was one hell of a job, Mr Rusk.'

Against professional advice, against prodigious odds, Rusk had driven his pipeline across sixty-seven miles of rolling hell, and when he was through he found an insatiable market for his gas: 'I bought it at thirty-two cents, sold it for a dollar ten and thought I was making a fortune. But when it went to three dollars and twenty-two cents, I did make a fortune. A thousand percent profit. And for the past two years, we've sold it for nine dollars and eighteen cents. That's a nearly three-thousand percent profit, and all because we took those insurmountable chances.'

'That's what we wanted to show you,' the accountants said,

and on a pristine sheet as neat as a tennis court they presented
him with two figures:

New estimated value Mid-Continent Gas at present prices
$448,000,000
New estimated value your total holdings $1,060,000,000

When Rusk looked briefly at the figures, he realized that he was
now officially Texas Rich. It was in large part due to the antics
of the Organization of Petroleum Exporting Countries, which
had so increased the value of his oil holdings that he had
accumulated some ninety million dollars which he had not
known about.

Rusk had never been heard to say a bad word about OPEC,
his standard comment among his friends being: 'Maybe those
Arabs are extortionists, but they do our work for us.' If oil still
brought ten dollars a barrel, he would not be a billionaire, but
when the price soared to nearly forty, he became one.

'It will go to sixty,' he predicted, and based on this hope, he
doubled his stable of rigs and drilling crews. He also believed
that the northeast section of the United States must accustom
itself to much higher prices for Texas gas, of which he was now
a major supplier: 'For too long they've had a free ride at our
expense. I don't want to gouge them, but I do want them to pay
their share of the freight.'

To arguments, advanced by some, that such talk represented
an economic holdup and a conscious drive to steal the
leadership of the United States away from New York and
Boston and into the so-called Sun Belt, he replied: 'The
leadership of this nation rests with those of us who see its future
clearly and who use creatively whatever leverage God has given
us. The future must lie with those parts of the nation which
have our remarkable mix. Oil, brains and courage.'

He was never arrogant about his beliefs, advancing them
quietly but with irresistible force. When truckdrivers employed
by his companies to move oil pasted insulting bumper stickers
on their vehicles – LET THOSE BASTARDS UP THERE FREEZE – he
made them scrape them off, but he did allow them to keep
others that came close to representing his thoughts – YANKEES
OUT OF GOD'S COUNTRY – and he positively chuckled over the

brilliance of the beer advertising which proclaimed that Lone Star was THE NATIONAL BEER OF TEXAS.

'We are our own nation,' he told his friends, 'and it's our duty to see that our ideas prevail throughout the friendly nation which lies to the north.' He was not speaking of Canada.

It would be a mistake to visualize Rusk as some wizened gnome, evil in purpose, huddling in his vault at night, counting his wealth. He was tall, straight, beetle-browed, good-looking, and easily able to smile when not furiously pursuing some special interest. But more than a year could pass without his being more than vaguely aware of the value of his holdings; he certainly never brooded about it. He knew it was tremendous and he intended keeping it that way, as his daring support of Pierre Soult's Texas Technologies proved. TexTek had not merely been a good idea; it had been stupendous, and under the inspired leadership of the Frenchman, had often swept the field before competitors even guessed what the company had in its long-range plans. Office-sized computers, word processors, software, superb merchandising, TexTek had pioneered them all, and in doing so, had multipled Rusk's impulsive investment many times.

This enabled him to operate rather boldly in fields which concerned him, such as the the disciplining of labor and the expulsion from public life of woolly-headed liberals like many of the Northern senators, but he never thought of himself as reactionary: 'I represent the Texas experience. The land, always the land. My grandmother had no nose, no ears, but she did have this glorious land we sit on. My grandfather, that crazy Quaker, was a dreamer who stocked their land with those great bulls from England. My father probed the land for oil. And because I was working the land with seismology, I stumbled into TexTek. We never had any nefarious designs, no special tricks. We stayed close to the land and accumulated power, which I am obligated to use sagaciously.'

But it was not the placid Sunday in the country or the startling financial news on Monday which made this week so memorable. Tuesday was Election Day, the culmination of Rusk's effort to bring this nation back to its senses, and he rose early in his frugal Fort Worth apartment and drove out to Larkin to cast his vote. He rarely used one of his Mexicans as a chauffeur, because he loved the feel of a big car eating up the superb Texas highways, and on this exciting day, when he had lots of time, he opted for a road that was only slightly longer than the direct route through Jacksboro. He preferred this more southerly road, for it took him through Mineral Wells, where he liked to stop at the edge of town and contemplate an enormous building that dominated the skyline. Fifty years ago it was one of the supreme hotels in America. Hollywood stars, New York bankers, everybody came here to take the waters. How many rooms? How much glory? And now a rotting shell. On three different occasions excited investors had come to him with plans for revitalizing the great spa, and always he had told them: 'It was a fine idea in its day. Well, that day has gone. Look at it standing there empty, a ghost of Texas grandeur. And look at the little motel at its feet, filled all the time. You change with the times, or the times steamroller you.'

From Mineral Wells he headed for Graham, where he controlled a dozen wells, and then on to Larkin, where the ten o'clock crowd of women voters filled the polling places. He cast his ballot in the basement of the handsome courthouse, then went to his home to make and receive telephone calls.

Six years earlier he and a handful of other Texas oilmen had quietly assembled to discuss the future of their state and their nation, in that order, and he had warned them: 'God and the American way have allowed us to accumulate tremendous power in this Republic and we would be craven if we did not apply it intelligently. That means we must defeat communists in office, regardless of what state they operate from, and replace them with decent Americans.'

'Have we the right to interfere in other states?' a timid man from Dallas asked, and he snapped: 'When McGovern casts his South Dakota vote in the Senate against our interests, he becomes a Texas senator, and I say: "Kick him the hell out of South Dakota." We've got to protect South Dakota from its own errors.'

'You're saying that we'll enter campaigns in all the states?'

'Wherever there's a man who votes against the interests of Texas. To accomplish this cleansing of public life we must spend money . . . and I mean a great deal. We're fighting for the future of this great nation.'

In the present election he had, by various intricate devices, poured contributions into different campaigns across the country. The bulk of it went to support Ronald Reagan, a most attractive man who had often lectured to Texas business groups on the dangers of communism, the need to muzzle our central bureaucracy and the absolute necessity of eliminating the national debt, but Rusk had also pinpointed various Democratic senators, real crazy liberals, who had to be defeated, plus a variety of notorious congressmen who had spoken against what he called Big Oil.

All of them were to be expunged, and as the long day wore on, he spoke with various allies around the nation: 'Rance! Looks like we might oust them all. Glorious day for the Republic!'

Before the sun had set in Texas he was assured, as he sat alone in his Larkin mansion before the two television sets, that Reagan had won, but he was startled by the ineptness of Jimmy Carter in handling the situation: My God! He's conceding while the Western polls are still open! That must damage his people in tight races out there. He threw down the newspaper whose tabulations he was checking off: That poor peanut grower never had a clue. How did we ever allow him to be president?

Still the resplendent night rolled on, and during an exulting phone call to friends in Houston, he shouted: 'By damn, we showed them how to win an election. We cleaned house on the whole damned bunch.'

He did not go to bed, for he wanted to hear the final Alaska returns, and when he learned that candidates he had backed so heavily retained a slight lead, with prospects of a much larger one when the rural districts came in, he leaned back, stared at the ceiling and reflected: A man works diligently for what he believes in, and when the fight grows hot, he'd better throw in all his reserves. What did we contribute, one way and another? Eleven million dollars, more or less. Small price to pay for the defeat of known enemies of the people. Small price to ensure good government.

Toward morning he learned that the Democrats had held on to their seat in Hawaii, but he dismissed this with a growl: 'They're all Japs, anyway. They'd bear some looking into.

Maybe next time we can fix that.' Of nine Democratic incumbents that his team had targeted, seven had been defeated, and as the sun rose on Wednesday morning he told his fellow conspirators on the conference call: 'We're going to rebuild this nation to make it more like Texas.' When an oilman in Midland asked what that meant, he said: 'Religion, patriotism, the old-fashioned virtues, and willingness to stand up and fight anybody. The things that make any nation great.' His father, Fat Floyd, had voiced exactly those sentiments sixty years earlier.

But then, when Texas seemed impregnable, changes began to take place in all aspects of Texas life, subtly at first, like a wisp of harmless smoke at the edge of a prairie, then turning into a firestorm which threatened all the assumed values.

The Sherwood Cobbs, at their cotton farm west of Lubbock, were one of the first families to detect the shift. One afternoon an event occurred which seemed a replay of that day in 1892, when a former slave ran to the plantation house at Jefferson with the startling news that boll weevils had eaten away the heart of the cotton crop. That information had altered life in Texas, and now another virtual slave, brown this time instead of black, Eloy Múzquiz, the illegal Mexican field hand, came running to the Cobb kitchen with news of equal import: 'Mister Cobb! Deep Well Number Nine, no water!'

'Electricity fail?' 1952 Chevy engines were no longer used.

'No, we tested. Plenty spark.'

'Maybe the pump's gone.' Cobb said this with a sick feeling, because for some months he had been aware that the water table upon which the Lubbock area depended had dropped toward the danger point. Could the failure of #9, a strong well, be a warning that the mighty Ogallala Aquifer was failing? He did not hazard a guess.

During the first ten years on their cotton farm in Levelland, the Sherwood Cobbs realized that they had, by some fortunate chance, stumbled upon a paradise. Of course, it had required a special aptitude for anyone to appreciate that it was a paradise, for their land was so flat that even when the slightest haze intervened, no horizon could be identified; it started level and went on forever. Also, it contained not a tree, and what locally passed for a hedgerow was apt to be six inches high and covered with dust. Distances to stores and towns were forbidding, and when the sun went seriously to work in June, the average temperature stayed above ninety, day and night, for nearly four months. In 1980 there had been twenty days, almost in succession, when it soared above one hundred.

But with air conditioning it was bearable, and during the winter months there were about a dozen inches of snow; 'white gold,' the farmers called it, because it lingered and seeped into the ground. Of course, extreme cold sometimes accompanied the snow, with the thermometer dropping to minus seventeen on one historic occasion.

Only rarely did the year's total rainfall exceed sixteen inches, but with deep pumps working, water from the aquifer was poured out in a stream so reliable that the cotton really seemed to jump out of the ground. 'The part I appreciate,' Cobb said, 'is that you can lay the water exactly where you want it, when you want it.' He also mixed fertilizer and needed minerals in the flow, so that while he irrigated he also nourished.

'You might call it farming by computer,' he told his sons. 'We calculate what we've taken from the soil and then put it back. Same amounts. Properly handled, fields like ours could go on forever.'

The results were more than gratifying. Back east, a bale of lint to an acre; here, two bales, and of a superior quality. This area around Lubbock was the dominant producer in America and one of the best in the world. A gin like Cobb's on the road from Levelland to Shallowater produced five-hundred-pound bales of pure silver, so consistent was the quality and so assured the value. Brokers in Lubbock often dominated the world's markets, for what they supplied and in what quantity determined standards and prices.

'Imagine!' Cobb exulted one night after finishing a long run with his gin. 'Finding land where there's always enough water and a boll weevil can't live.' It was a cotton grower's dream, which explained why so many of the plantation owners in East Texas had made the long jump west.

But now, as he jumped in his pickup to inspect #9, he had a suspicion that the great years might be ending, and he inspected the silent well only a few minutes before telling Múzquiz: 'Go get the Ericksons.'

When the brothers drove up to the well, Cobb clenched his teeth as they delivered the fatal news: 'Same everywhere. The Ogallala has dropped so fast ... these dry spells ... the extra wells you fellows have put in.'

'What can I do?'

'For the present, we can chase the water.'

'Meaning?'

'Deepen all your wells.'

'How much deeper?'

'The Red Bed, on which our part of the Ogallala rests, is two hundred feet down. The wells we dug for you back in 1968 go down only one hundred feet.'

'What did they cost?'

'Thirty-five hundred dollars per well.'

'How many must I deepen?'

'Twenty,' and the estimates they placed before him showed that the cost of merely deepening an existing well was going to be more than twice the cost of one of the original five: 'To do the digging, fifteen hundred dollars. To install the submersible pump, five thousand. To wire for electricity and protect the system, one thousand. Total per well, seventy-five hundred. Total cost per twenty wells, a hundred and fifty thousand dollars.'

'Have I any alternative?' Cobb asked, and the brothers agreed: 'None.' Then the younger added: 'Each year the aquifer drops only slightly. But the rate of fall is steady, and soon it'll fall below your present pumps. But if we go down to Red Bed, you ought to be safe for the rest of this century.'

The older brother summed it up: 'Stands to reason, Cobb, you wouldn't want to call us back to redig your wells two or three times, just to keep pace with the drop. Dig 'em once. Dig 'em right. Dig 'em deep.' So Cobb chased the aquifer downward.

Even those farms which used windmills to work their pumps, and many did, had to deepen their wells, but when the pipes were safely down, these farms had assured water, because the winds on the plains could be relied upon: 'And sometimes they can be trusted to blow the whole mill flat as a freshly plowed field.'

Weather in the Lubbock area was rugged, no doubt about it, with the blazing summers, the frigid winters and now and then a tornado to keep people attentive, but the challenges could be rewarding, and the warm social life of the area diverted attention from the hardships. The Cobbs were especially appreciative of the local university. Texas Technological College it had been called when they arrived, but with the hard practicality which governed so much of Texas life the legislature had listened to the complaint of a West Texas representative: 'Hell, ever'body calls it Texas Tech, and that's how those who love it name it. I propose that the name be officially changed to Texas Tech, and while we're about it, let's make it a full university.'

So there it was, Texas Tech University, with a curriculum of agricultural, mechanical and modest liberal arts programs. Its students were sought after in the oil fields and in Silicon Valley, but what residents like the Cobbs especially appreciated were the cultural programs it sponsored: a string quartet now and then, a choral presentation of an opera – no sets, no costumes – or a series of three Shakespearean plays. Challenging lectures were available, with notable conservatives like William Buckley applauded, and farmers like the Cobbs could easily arrange casual meetings with the professors.

But what gratified Nancy Cobb, and attracted her most often to the university, was the unequaled ranch museum it had put together: a collection of houses and buildings assembled from all over the state, showing how ranchers had lived in the various periods. Thirty minutes among these simple structures, with their rifle ports for holding off the Comanche, taught more of Texas history than a dozen books.

One hot afternoon in 1981 when Nancy had taken a group of visitors from the North to see the open-air museum – it covered many acres – she was standing before one of the box-and-strip houses built by the 1910 pioneers and explaining how the settlers, deprived of any local timber, had imported it precariously from hundreds of miles to the east, and had then used it like strips of gold to shore up their mud-walled huts, and as she talked she began to choke: 'It must have been so hellish for the women.'

One symposium series gave the Cobbs a lot of trouble, for a

lecturer predicted that the day would come, and possibly within this century, when the rising cost of electricity and the constant lowering of the water table would make agriculture on the Western plains uneconomic:

'And I do not mean marginally uneconomic. I mean that you will have to close down your wells, abandon your cotton fields, and sell off your gins to California, where their farmers, because of sensible planning, will have water. We would then see towns like Levelland and Shallowater revert to the way they were when the Indians roamed, except that here and there the traveler would find the roots of houses which had once existed and the remnants of towns and villages.

'We could avoid this catastrophe if all the states dependent upon the Ogallala Aquifer united in some vast plan to protect that resource, but all would have to obey the decisions, because any one state, following its own selfish rules and depleting the aquifer, could defeat the strategy.'

Cobb, extremely sensitive to the problem of which he was a vital part, and interested in possible solutions, raised enough donations from local farmers and ranchers to offer Texas Tech funds for conducting a symposium on 'Ogallala and the West,' which attracted serious students from across Texas and representatives of the governments of all the Ogallala states.

It was a gala affair, with Governor Clements giving the keynote address and with two lectures each morning and afternoon on the crises confronting the Western states. As the talks progressed, especially those informal ones late at night, several harsh and inescapable conclusions began to emerge:

... The Ogallala was not inexhaustible, and at its present rate of depletion, might cease to function effectively sometime after the year 2010.

... Diversion of rivers and especially the snow-melt from the eastern face of the Rockies could be let into it to revitalize it, but such water was already spoken for.

... Strict apportionment at levels far below today's usage would prolong its life.

... State departments of agriculture were prepared to

1375

recommend more than a dozen ways in which farmers and ranchers could use less water.

... Texas would soon see the day when it would be profitable to purchase from surrounding states like Oklahoma, Arkansas and Louisiana, and perhaps from those as far away as Colorado, entire rivers and streams whose water would be piped onto its thirsty fields. (Delegates from the named states hooted this proposal.)

... Commercial desalinization of Gulf waters plus great pipelines west might well be the answer, if nuclear energy were to become available at low rates.

... Every state, right now, must organize itself on a statewide basis to ensure the most prudent use of every drop of water that fell thereon.

It was in the working out of this last recommendation, which the conference adopted unanimously, that Cobb learned how divisive a subject this was insofar as Texas water users were concerned, because when the Texas delegation met, these points were stressed by the more active participants:

Ransom Rusk, Longhorn breeder: 'Every word said makes sense. But what we must take steps to ensure is that cattle raisers be allowed to retain the water rights on which they've built their herds, often at great expense.'

Lorenzo Quimper, operator of nine large ranches, some with serious water deficiencies: 'Regulation and apportionment are inescapable, but we must protect the backbone industries of the state, and in them I include ranchin'. Cattle cannot live without water, and from time immemorial their rights have been predominant and must remain so, if Texas is to continue the traditions which made it great, and I must say, unique.'

Charles Rampart, cotton grower, north of Lubbock: 'You need only look at the level of the aquifer year by year to know that something must be done, but the prior rights of our wells in this agricultural area, and I drilled mine in the 1950s, they've got to be respected. All the wells in this region will have to be grandfathered. If they're in, they stay in.'

Sam Quiller, farmer, Xavier County: 'The irrigation ditches that lead off the Brazos River to water my fields date back to 1818. Any court of law would support my claim that those rights, and in the amounts stated, are irreversible. Read *Mittle v. Boyd* and you'll find you cannot impede the flow of the Brazos.'

Tom and Fred Bartleson, fishermen, mouth of the Brazos: 'Water must be regulated, we all know that. But I would ask you to keep in mind that Texas courts have said repeatedly and confirmed repeatedly that a constant flow from rivers like the Brazos must be maintained so that a proper salinity in the waters just offshore be protected. That's where we catch our fish. Those are the waters our restaurants and supermarkets depend upon.'

At the end of the conference it was pathetically clear that Nebraska, Colorado and all the other aquifer states would repel even the slightest attack upon their sovereignty, and that every user in Texas appreciated the need for others to conserve water so long as his inherited rights were not infringed. Almost every drop of water inland from the Gulf Coast had been spoken for, usually in the nineteenth century, and to reapportion it or even control it was going to be impossible. Since the Ogallala Aquifer was a resource which could not be seen, the general public had no incentive to protect it; the Brazos and the Colorado and the Trinity were already allocated and could not be touched. Arkansas and Lousiana needed the water they had, and would repel with bayonets anyone who attempted to lead away even a trickle. So all that could be done was to continue exactly as things were, and then sometime in the decade starting in 2010, when disaster struck, take emergency measures.

'No!' Cobb cried when the insanity of this solution hit him. 'What we should do right now is build a huge channel from the Mississippi into Wichita Falls, and pipelines from there to the various Texas regions.' The idea was not fatuous, for millions of acre-feet of wasted water ran off each year past New Orleans, but when he seriously proposed such a ditch as a solution, experts pointed out: 'Such a channel would have to run through Arkansas and Oklahoma, and that would not be permitted.'

When Cobb checked the water level at the new pumps the Erickson Brothers had installed, he found that it had fallen by an inch and a quarter, and it was then that he decided to seek nomination as a member of the Water Commission.

A second Texan to become personally aware of the big shifts

under way lived at the opposite end of the state. Gabe Klinowitz, the real estate operator who had sponsored Todd Morrison when the latter drifted down from Detroit, was immensely informed concerning land values. His last big venture had been with a group of seven Mexican political figures to invest the massive funds they controlled.

They had stunned him with the magnitude of what they wanted to do, but in obedience to their orders, he had quietly assembled the costly land and then watched as they spent $170,000,000 on The Ramparts, an interlocking series of the finest condominiums in Houston. Irritated by this brazen display of wealth by citizens of a nation which sent a constant stream of near-starving peasants into Texas for food and jobs, Gabe consulted with a University of Houston professor who specialized in Latin-American finances: 'Tell me, Dr Shagrin, how do these people get hold of so much money?'

'Quite simple. They've learned how to outsmart our New York bankers.'

'You lose me.'

'Don't apologize. Took me two years to unravel the intricacies.' And with that, he spread upon his desk a series of figures so improbable that they perplexed even Klinowitz, who was accustomed to the chicaneries of mankind: 'From impeccable United States government sources I find that our big banks have loaned the Latin countries to the south three hundred billion dollars. And from equally reliable sources in the recipient countries, I find that clever politicians and business magicians have diverted one hundred billion dollars into either secret Swiss accounts or business ventures here in the US.'

'Would you care to give me a synonym for that word *diverted*?'

'How about *legally embezzled* or *cleverly sequestered* or good old-fashioned *stole*?' He laughed: 'Whichever you elect, the result's the same. The money we loaned them is no longer in the country where we hoped it would serve a constructive purpose.'

'The original loans, will they ever be repaid?'

'I don't see how they can be, with the money vanished from the countries. I see no way that the Mexican government can recover the money your group has wasted here in Houston.'

'Have you the figures for Mexico?'

'I haven't assembled the accurate figure for the total loans, but I can prove that in 1980 they borrowed sixteen billion from us and allowed their manipulators to siphon off more than seven billion of our dollars into their private accounts.'

'As an American taxpayer,' Gabe said, 'I'd like to know what happens if the original loans go sour.'

'You guessed it. One way or another, you'll pay.'

Gabe frowned: 'If the American money had been kept in Mexico, could it have forestalled the poverty we see?'

'Now you touch a very sore point, Mr Klinowitz. From the very beginning, Mexico was always much richer than Texas. Anything we did for our people, they could have done for theirs.'

'What went wrong?'

'I use the word *diverted*. It avoids moral judgment.'

So Klinowitz was not surprised when the peso, its backup funds having been so callously diverted, began to stagger: 36 to the dollar one day, 93 the next, 147 later, then 193, with a threat of further plunging. He was prepared and almost gleeful when the Mexican politicians flashed the distress signal: 'For the time being, halt all construction.'

But he was a professional real estate man and was actually relieved when the Mexicans rounded up some additional capital and resumed building, for as he told Maggie Morrison: 'I have pains in my stomach when a client of mine runs into trouble.' However, he was shrewd enough to add: 'If I were you, Maggie, I'd keep my eye on those three towers of The Ramparts.'

'I'm no rental agency,' she protested. 'That's a heartache business.'

'I don't mean rentals. I've learned that if a building falls into trouble once, it'll do so again.'

'What could I do for the Ramparts people?'

'Maggie! How I wish I was thirty years old, with a small nest egg. In a fluctuating market like this, a daring trader can perform miracles.'

'I don't depend on miracles,' she said cautiously.

'Real money is made in a falling market. Look at the unrented space in this city.'

1379

And when she did she perceived two startling facts. The sharp decline in oil values had caused the bankruptcy of many smaller firms servicing that industry, and this meant that space which should have been rented for offices stood idle. When she totted up the appalling figures she found that 32,000,000 square feet of the finest office space in America stood vacant in Houston.

But what alarmed her more, with the rich Mexicans unable to visit the United States because of the disastrous devaluation of their peso, some twelve or thirteen major Houston hotels were suffering from lack of business. Fine establishments accustomed to seventy- and eighty-percent occupancy were getting no more than twenty or thirty, so that those which had depended on the Mexican trade were shutting down for the time being while others were going onto a five-day week to stanch the hemorrhaging.

Every intuition she had acquired in Michigan warned Maggie to retrench; every lesson she had learned from wise old Texans like Gabe Klinowitz urged her to make bold moves. In this impasse she would have liked to consult with her husband, but he was preoccupied with other ventures, so taking counsel only with herself, she monitored the chaos that seemed to have struck Houston business, but always at the end of the day she drove past The Ramparts to check on what the seven Mexican politicians were doing with their beautiful chain of buildings, and every sign she saw whispered confidentially: 'Gabe was right, these Mexicans are in deep trouble.'

The precipitous fall in the peso endangered more than the Mexican politicians, because all along the border, from Brownsville to El Paso, the Rio Grande bridges that once had brought thousands of brown-skinned people into American shops, where cameras, fine clothes, stereos and perfume were sold at bargain prices unattainable in Mexico itself, were strangely empty. The devalued peso bought nothing. For three painful days the Bravo-Escandón bridge, so long the scene of Mexican inflow, had no visitors from the south, and then the activity resumed, but in an ugly way that brought shame to the United States.

American citizens streamed into Mexico to buy at bargain

prices all the gasoline, baby food, vegetables and beef the Mexican markets provided, for if the peso was down, the dollar had to be up. The drain of essentials continued. 'The norteamericanos are stealing us into starvation!' came the justified cry from south of the border, and it was in this crisis period that feisty Simón Garza, now the mayor of Bravo as a result of the revolution in voting patterns following the disturbances in the 1960s, projected himself into prominence. By the simple, illegal device of stationing his policemen at the Bravo end of the international bridge and forbidding its citizens from going into Mexico to buy what were bargains for them but subsistence for the Mexicans, he attracted statewide approval.

'We do not profit from the despair of others,' he announced repeatedly, and he said this with such force that even those who had been depriving Mexico of its foodstuffs and means of movement applauded. Belatedly, the Mexican government placed an embargo on its dwindling supplies of food, and the situation righted itself, with the peso at the shocking black-market rate of 193 to the dollar.

But now Mayor Garza was confronted by his own problems, for with the absolute cessation of Mexican traffic into the town, the Bravo stores began to close down, as they were doing all along the Rio Grande. Seeking guidance as to what he must do to halt the strangulation of his community, he attended a meeting of the Valley mayors in Laredo, and in that city he saw real panic, because fully forty percent of the luxurious emporiums were boarded up. Their business had not declined, it had vanished; there was no escape but the immediate firing of all employees and the barring of doors.

If one had ever needed proof of the symbiotic relationship between northern Mexico and southern Texas, it was provided now, because each side of the river, deprived in its own way, staggered toward economic breakdown. Unemployment on the American side rose to twenty, then to forty, percent, and a movement was started to have the region declared a disaster area.

Among all the leaders on both sides of the river, one man stood out for the coolness with which he handled the catastrophe and the steps he took to alleviate it. Simón Garza had been reared in a rugged school, fighting the remnants of the

Horace Vigil dynasty, combatting the Texas Rangers who had been determined to keep that dynasty in operation, and insisting that his fellow Hispanics go to college and learn the tricks of American life. 'Eat tortillas at home. Speak Spanish in your games. But learn who Adam Smith and Milton Friedman are.' In this drive toward educating his constituents he was assisted by his brother Efraín, the professor at A&M, who uncovered scholarships at all the Texas universities to which bright girls and boys from Bravo could apply. 'The revolution of the mind,' the Garza brothers cried repeatedly, 'that's what we must engineer.'

It was Simón who persuaded President Reagan, by means of a hard, nonhysterical telegram to the White House, to come down to the Valley to see for himself the devastation wrought by the drop in the peso, and as he led the well-intentioned President past the empty bridge and the boarded-up stores he was photographed with Regan time and again, so that when the summary meeting was held in Laredo, the Northern reporters, to whom conditions along the Rio Grande were a mystery, suddenly discovered that in Simón Garza, Texas had a Hispanic politician who made sense and who used most cleverly the perquisites of his office. Considerable attention was paid to the grateful statement of the Escandón mayor, who told the reporters in Spanish: 'Garza, he knew what to do. He closed the bridge to keep us from starving.' People would remember this.

In his modest offices in Fort Worth, Ransom Rusk was facing such an assault from all sides that he groaned: 'God must be mad at Texas!' And while he was trying to sort things out, he received a preemptive call from his bank in Midland: 'Better come down here and give us help.' So in his private plane he flew to the Midland-Odessa airport, linchpin in the Texas oil complex, where he was met by the three managers of his service companies, who reported unanimous ruination for anything connected with oil.

'Mr Rusk, Activated Mud can find no customers at all. I think we'll have to fire everybody.' Electronic Logging was little better, for it showed a ninety-two-percent decline. But it was when he drove to the vast parking area between the two oil towns that he found visual proof of what had happened to the bonanza region, for there, stacked neatly in rows like dinosaurs whose time had passed, stood rusting in the bright sunlight nineteen of the twenty-three giant drilling rigs that would normally have been standing proudly erect in fields scattered across the landscape from the Gulf to New Mexico. Now their towers lay prostrate, their drilling engines silent and gathering dust.

'What did we pay for that last batch?' Rusk asked, and when his drilling manager said: 'Special electronics, special everything, thirteen million each.' Instantly calculating thirteen times nineteen, Rusk said quietly: 'That's two hundred forty-seven million dollars down the drain.' He had multiplied thirteen by twenty and subtracted thirteen.

'Not completely lost,' the manager assured him. 'If oil comes back, which it will have to . . .'

'What could you get for this, right now?' Rusk asked, kicking one of the rigs.

'Maybe a hundred and fifty thousand . . . if we could find a buyer.'

'That's one percent of its value. I call that loss.'

And in that sickening moment by the fallen rigs, there among the dinosaurs whose days of rampaging were gone, Rusk had to make his decision. A powerfully organized man just entering his sixties, he should have been free to enjoy his favorable position in the world, his power and his billion dollars; instead, he found himself attacked on all sides, with foundations crumbling. But he did not propose to go down whimpering. He would fight back with all the energy he had been acquiring through past decades. He would ride out this storm, husband his resources, and prepare to fight back when conditions were more favorable.

'Close down Activated Mud. Just close it down. We'll find something for the top people to do till oil recovers. Electronic Logging, it's got to be of permanent value. What do you suggest?'

It was agreed that logging services would always be required, so long as one man wildcatted anywhere in Texas: 'Mr Rusk, I think we should retain a core of the real experts, no matter . . .'

'I think so, too. Cut to the bone and hunker down. And these?' Almost lovingly he touched with the toe of his cowboy

1383

boot the nearest prostrate rig. 'What in the world do we do with these?'

The question was almost academic, for it had no sensible solution. There lay the mighty rigs, their towering super-structures humbled, and unless prospecting for oil resumed, they would not rise again. They would be valueless.

When none of his advisers offered a sensible solution, Rusk cut the Gordian knot: 'Fan out across Texas. Find young men who are willing to take a risk. Sell off these nineteen idle rigs for whatever they'll bring. But get rid of them. We'll keep the four that are working. For when things start up again.'

'You mean, sell them regardless of what we can get?'

'Exactly what I mean. The gamble for oil passes into younger hands.'

'Mr Rusk, I want your firm order on this. You're willing to sell this thirteen-million-dollar rig for a hundred and fifty thousand dollars?'

'For a hundred thousand, if that's what it brings.'

With that harsh decision behind him he drove into Midland, where the managers of the bank in which he was heavily invested were in quiet panic: 'Ransom, the bottom is dropping out. It's all quicksand.'

'Just how bad?' And they explained what he had already suspected: 'If you drove in from the airport, you saw the service fields lying idle, your own among them. Did you notice the string of motels? Two years ago they had to limit guests to three nights in a row. Everybody wanted to come to Odessa to get in on the action.'

'I noticed the few cars parked outside.'

'Paul here owns three of them. Eight-percent occupancy. Foreclosures everywhere.'

Rusk looked at Paul Mesmer, the distressed motel owner, and swore that under no circumstances would he, Rusk, allow himself to look like that. Firmly he asked: 'What's the worst aspect of our situation?' and he listened in a shock he did not betray as these good men, who had expected oil to go to sixty dollars a barrel, explained what they faced when it dropped to twenty-seven.

'Bluntly . . .'

'That's the way I want it, bluntly.'

'We may have to close our doors.'

'How much?'

'A billion and a quarter dollars.'

'That's a manly sum.'

'Depositors protected?'

'In part.'

'Us investors?'

'A complete wipe-out.'

Rusk heard this doleful news without wincing. He had $16,000,000 in bank shares, and to lose it on top of his heavy losses in the oil business would be inconvenient but not disabling. Still, he hated to admit that his business judgment had been faulty, so he asked: 'Any way we can prevent the Feds from moving in?'

'If we all chipped in more of our own money . . .'

'How much you want from me?'

'If you could see your way clear . . . five million.'

'Done.'

'Before you sign anything, Ransom, you realize that whatever you give will be in jeopardy?'

He did not answer the question. Instead, he looked at the embattled directors, these sturdy men of the plains who had gambled fantastically, making it big when things went their way, now willing to put up small fortunes when things turned sour. They were Texas gamblers and they did not whimper.

'I like the way you're handling things,' and he flew back to Fort Worth.

But on the way east he had a vision, you could term it nothing else: The action has got to swing to Dallas. With Houston in trouble on its real estate, and Midland in shock over oil, and the Rio Grande with up to forty-five percent unemployed, leadership passes to Dallas. That's where the big fight for the soul of Texas is going to be conducted. That's where I want to be.

So he directed his pilot to land not at Meacham Field, the city airport for Fort Worth, but at Love Field in Dallas. Radioing ahead for his driver to meet him at the new destination, he sped, immediately upon landing, toward that imposing complex of new construction in North Dallas, some fourteen miles out from the traditional center of the city, and in one of the many rental offices peddling space in the bright new buildings, he rented what would become a major center of Dallas power: Ransom Rusk Enterprises.

He had been in position only a few weeks when the wisdom of this move was proved, because as a major stockholder in TexTek, he was summoned up to their board room when that huge conglomerate stumbled into trouble. Pierre Soult, founding genius of the electronics end of the business, had died, throwing his pioneering but fragile company into such temporary disarray that the new management had to inform Rusk: 'Due to increased competition from Japan and an unforeseen collapse in electronic games and home computers, we've experienced a loss in the first quarter of a hundred million dollars and can expect a repeat or worse next quarter.'

'When do we inform the public?' Rusk asked as he calculated the effect on his huge holdings.

'Tomorrow.'

So Rusk was on hand when the devastating losses were announced to Wall Street, and he sat grim-lipped as the ticker reported the sensational drop in TexTek. Within one trading day in New York, the paper value of TexTek stock dropped by one billion dollars.

He was also on the scene, as a major investor, when Braniff Airlines, once the pride of Dallas, stumbled and fumbled, striving vainly to stay alive but missing every tenuous opportunity. In the panic meeting, he gave Braniff management counsel he had given his oil-field managers in Odessa: 'Cut back. Decide ruthlessly what must be done. And do it now.'

He supervised the cutting away of the once-profitable South American routes. He tried to halt the tremendous losses on the new routes the company had unwisely pioneered in recent months, and he did his best to find new funds, but in the end he had to admit: 'We gave it a good try. It's bankrupt.' And Texas travelers through the massive new Dallas-Fort Worth Airport looked shamefacedly at the varicolored Braniff planes stowed aimlessly on the parking lots and tried to calculate the loss in money and pride which their clipped wings represented.

One New York banking expert, dispatched to Dallas to investigate the mood in Texas, reported confidentially to his superiors:

People outside Texas, especially those in less-favored states like Michigan, Ohio and Pennsylvania, had begun to look upon Dallas and Houston as places where the figures could only go up. Now they are learning with the rest of us that they can also come down. Houston, Midland, Abilene, El Paso, Laredo and the so-called Golden Triangle are disaster areas, and in certain hard-struck industries unemployment reaches past fifty percent.

Friends in the know advise me that Ransom Rusk, heavily involved in all the fields which have been hit, has suffered staggering losses. I have verified the following: his commanding position in TexTek, loss $125,000,000; sharp drop in the value of his oil holdings, loss $85,000,000; bankruptcy of his mud company and idleness of his nineteen drilling rigs, loss $35,000,000 now, with more to come later; his position in Braniff Airlines, loss $45,000,000; Houston real estate reversal due to peso, loss $14,000,000. Collapse of the Midland Bank, loss maybe $21,000,000. Total Rusk loss in one calendar year: $325,000,000 minimum.

How did Rusk react to these losses, which were much greater than the visitor had estimated? He sat in his new office, surveyed the Dallas skyline with its multitude of soaring new construction, and said only to himself: Now is when I dig in. I have more work to do than ever before. His shoulders did not slump, nor did he try to avoid inquisitors who wanted to ferret out the effect of these stupendous reversals. Instead, he showed his icy smile, stuck out his lower jaw, and predicted: 'Every item in Texas will revive. The Mexican peso will stabilize. Oil will come back. We'll see the rigs operating again. Braniff will fly, we'll see to that. TexTek has a dozen new inventions ready to astound the market. And the Dallas Cowboys will win the Super bowl.'

'Then you're not pessimistic?'

'I don't know that word.'

When the bad years ended and his accountants showed him the final figures on his losses, much worse than those in the New Yorker's confidential report, he laughed and asked: 'How many of your friends can say they lost nearly half a billion dollars in one year?' and they said: 'Not many.'

But even his aplomb was shaken by a series of those family tragedies which so often enmeshed the very rich in Texas. His famous father, Fat Floyd, had produced two daughters, Bertha and Linda, born almost a full generation before Ransom. Each had had four children, so that Ransom had eight nieces and nephews for whose fiscal welfare he was responsible.

Just as his father had seen ownership of his first well split into minute fragments, so Ransom and the courts supervised the various allocations of ownership of the Rusk Estate. Insofar as the offspring of Bertha and Linda were concerned, the pattern was this:

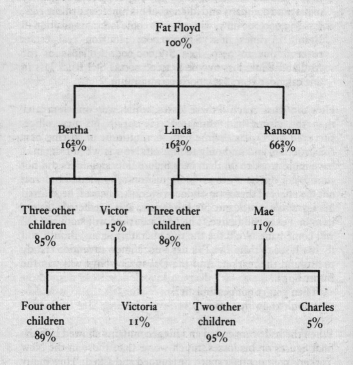

To take only the case of the two fourth-generation children, Victoria and Charles, if one multiplied out the percentages, one found that Victoria owned 0.002750 of the Rusk Estate and Charles 0.000917. Since the estate, which participated only in the oil portion of Ransom's total holding, was now worth some $700,000,000, this meant that Victoria's share at an early age, was worth $1,925,000 and Charles' $641,900. And since Ransom's adroit handling of the oil reserves produced a yearly income of about sixteen percent on investments, young Victoria received some $308,000 each year, and Charles $102,700. Various young Texans had comparable holdings.

But these two, and their six siblings, were not enjoying their money these days, because their parents had become involved in shattering tragedies. Mae, of the third generation, had married a worthless young man who had angled for her shamefully, caught her, and then found himself unable to maintain pace with her lively interest in Texas life. He had escaped his deficiency by committing suicide.

Victor, Mae's cousin and a most likable fellow, had fared little better. His wife, a beautiful girl but lacking in both character and will, had taken to the bottle early and with great vigor, deteriorating so totally that she had to be placed in an institution. It was one of the finest drying-out establishments in Texas, but it had an inadequate fire-alarm system, and when an inebriated gentleman on the ground floor fell asleep while smoking a cigarette, the entire wing burst into flame, and only the heroic efforts of two Mexican caretakers saved Mrs Rusk. She was horribly burned, but did survive; however, any chance of escaping her addiction to alcohol vanished, and both she and her family could look ahead only to a lifelong hospitalization.

In this dual impasse, the cousins Victor and Mae started seeing each other, at first out of mutual commiseration and eventually because of a deep and passionate love, despite the fact that they were cousins. When Victor felt that it would be shameful to divorce his stricken wife, he and Mae loaded the latter's Mercedes-Benz with cans of gasoline, roared down a Fort Worth freeway at ninety miles an hour, and plunged head-on into a concrete abutment.

Ransom was left to answer the inquiries of the media and to care for his nieces and nephews, and the pitiful experiences resulting from these two obligations deepened his understanding. Summoning the children, he told them: 'You've all known what was happening. You understand better than anyone else. So what's to do? Pull up your socks. Grit your teeth. And take an oath: "It's not going to happen to me."' And as he spoke he visualized those intrepid Rusks who had preceded them, and he began to see his ancestors in a kindlier light. His mother had been dowdy, but she had kept the family together when her husband was striving to locate an oil well, and Emma Larkin may have had no nose or ears, but he now realized that she'd had incredible fortitude. 'Never forget,' he continued, 'that your great grandmother Emma suffered far worse tragedies then you'll ever be required to face.' And now he wanted to exorcise the guilt he felt for the ugly manner in which he had once dismissed his parents: 'Don't forget that your ancestor, the one they called Fat Floyd, was willing to gamble his last penny on the oil well that got our family started. He had courage, and so must you.' As he watched the effect of his words upon these young people, he thought: This generation isn't going to be defeated. But then he realized that something more fundamental than fighting spirit was required to build a satisfactory life, so with much embarrassment he stood before them and said softly: 'I love you very much. I will be here to help no matter what happens. Let's stick together.'

Back in his new office, after the accountants had his family's affairs straightened out, he said: 'Well, we can be sure of one thing – 1984 has to be better.' And then his old fire returned: 'Reagan'll be reelected, best president we've had in more than sixty years, but a mite long in the tooth. We'll eliminate more of those communists in the Senate. And we'll see oil bounce back. Maybe even Braniff will fly again.' On the phone to Houston he said cheerfully: 'Good and bad, I'd rather be working in Texas than anywhere else in the world.' Then, supremely confident that he would recover his lost dollars within two years, he flew to Kenya for a safari with his friends.

If Ransom Rusk was finding new challenges in North Dallas, a small, sparkling, dark-eyed young woman of twenty-five named Enriqueta Múzquiz was having an even more exciting adventure in South Dallas.

Dallas consisted of three separate cities, really, and it was possible to live in any one and scarcely be aware of the other two. There was downtown Dallas, the historic city on the Trinity River which had boasted two log cabins in 1844 and not much more by 1860. An unpublished diary tells what happened in that year:

On Sunday, 8 July 1860, the citizens of this town awoke to find every store and rooming house ablaze. When the terrible conflagration was finally brought under control a jury of 52 leading citizens was impaneled and upon their finding that the fire must surely have been part of a slave plot, three Negroes were promptly hanged.

Despite its slow start, downtown Dallas had prospered, and now contained the business heart of a metropolis with more than a million inhabitants and of a metropolitan area with more than three million.

North Dallas, where Rusk had his new office, was a golden ghetto of palatial homes, resplendent new skyscrapers, luxurious shopping centers and a way of life that was, said one critic, 'both appealing and appalling.' It was appealing because of its brazen flaunting of wealth. But the true secret of North Dallas was that it was a world to itself; residents could live there quite happily and rarely bother about venturing into the clutter of Central Dallas. Boasted the average North Dallas housewife: 'I go into that maelstrom only when there's a meeting of the Art Museum board.'

And almost no one from North Dallas ever crossed the Trinity River to enter South Dallas, where blacks and Hispanics lived, and rarely did anyone from Central Dallas go there. It was a city to itself, impoverished, poorly cared for, and constantly embattled with its wealthier neighbors to the north. Those residents of Northern states who had imbibed from television and newspapers the illusion that Texas, and Dallas in particular, was populated only by millionaires received a shock if they ventured into South Dallas.

There were many reasons for the impoverishment of this area. Texas, perhaps the wealthiest of the states, was among the most niggardly in its services for the poor, and in certain criteria like unemployment benefits, it stood at the bottom of the fifty states. It was not good to be a poor person in Texas, and downright miserable to be one in South Dallas.

But this was where Enriqueta Múzquiz was having her exhilarating experience. Following that February afternoon in 1969 when she leaped aboard the Southern Pacific freight train in El Paso, she spent her first years in Texas in Lubbock, where she had suffered the full force of West Texas discrimination, which in many ways was worse than anything known along the Rio Grande, since the northern region held so few Hispanics and disregarded them with such insolence.

'When I was young,' she told her fourth-grade pupils, 'no Hispanic was allowed in the better restaurants, and we were not welcomed in the movie theaters. We were expected to quit school at the eighth grade. Boys could not get haircuts in the regular barbershops. And we were held in contempt.' When she gave such lectures, which she did repeatedly and to all her classes, she invariably ended with a refrain which summarized the major triumph of her life:

'In 1974 the Supreme Court of the United States handed down a decision called *Lau v. Nichols*, which you must remember, because it is your Declaration of Independence. It did not deal directly with us but with a Chinese boy named Lau, and it said: "Even if he is Chinese, and even if he cannot speak a word of English, the United States of America must provide him with an education, and since he cannot speak English, this education must be in Chinese." Don't you see? The Supreme Court is saying the same to you children. If you cannot speak English, you must be educated in Spanish, and that's why I'm here.'

Señorita Múzquiz, as she wanted her students to call her, even though she, along with her father and two brothers, had attained United States citizenship, spoke to her thirty children in Grade Four and her thirty-three in Grade Three only in Spanish, and in this language, which she was supposed to use only temporarily as a bridge to English, she spent about half her time haranguing them about the injustices of American life, with special emphasis on the inequities they suffered in Dallas.

1392

She did this because she visualized herself as an agency of revenge for all the suffering she and her people had undergone in West Texas, and as she labored to create in her students a burning appreciation of their Spanish heritage and the glories of Mexican culture, she foresaw the day when the Spanish-speaking people along the Rio Grande, south and north, would form a kind of ipso facto republic, half Mexican, half American, in which pesos and dollars would both be used. A common currency and a common outlook on life would prevail, and a common language, Spanish, would be spoken: 'Of course, it will be an advantage if you have English as a second language – to work in stores and such – but the effective language will be Spanish. And the mode of life will be Mexican, with large families closely bound together and with priests who give their sermons in Spanish.'

'What citizenship will we have?' her older children sometimes asked, and she said: 'It won't really matter, because Mexico will not rule the area, nor will the United States. It will be a union of the two, with free passage across the river.'

'How big will it be?' the children asked, and on the map of Mexico that she kept in her room – a map in Spanish, so cut across at the top that it included Texas as far north as Lubbock – she used her pointer to indicate a swath which encompassed San Antonio, San Angelo and El Paso on the north, and Monterrey, Saltillo and Chihuahua on the south: 'The new nation of our dreams already exists. Spanish is spoken up here, and English is understood down there. Trade between the two halves is already flowing and will grow as years pass. Brownsville and Matamoros at the eastern end of the river, who can tell which is which?'

'Will the nation reach all the way to California?' a child asked one day, and she said: 'It already does,' but another child said: 'Señorita Múzquiz, I grew up in San Angelo and they don't speak much Spanish there,' and she said: 'They will, when enough of us come north and fill the places.'

Her dream was not an idle one. There were many living along that protracted border who were already effecting the change which she promulgated with her students during the day and with her adult friends at night. Experts, and even those with only a casual interest, could see that the unstoppable flow of

Mexican nationals into the United States must inevitably create a new society with new attitudes and, perhaps, new political affiliations.

Señorita Múzquiz's early appreciation of this fact was intensified when in the summer of 1982 she enrolled in a special seminar in Los Angeles, and when she returned she carried exciting news to her Texas friends:

'Los Angeles is already the second largest Spanish-speaking city in the world, larger even than Madrid, smaller only than Mexico City. The food, the culture, the manner of thought are totally Mexican, and our newspaper, *La Opinión*, prints sixty thousand copies a day. More than ten theaters show movies only in Spanish, and the schools are filled with dedicated teachers like me, keeping our beautiful language alive and reminding our children of their Mexican heritage.

'What is happening is simple in process, glorious in effect. We are quietly reclaiming the land which Santa Anna lost through his insane vanity. Vast areas which are rightfully Mexican are coming back to us. No battles ... no gunfire ... no animosities, simply the inexorable movement of people north. The anglos still control the banks, the newspapers, the courts, but we have the power which always triumphs in the end, the power of people.'

Proof of her contention came dramatically when Immigration agents raided a big ranch south of Dallas and arrested some twenty illegal immigrants who had evaded the Border Patrol. From Dallas came a general cry of approval, but when officials looked more deeply into the matter, they found that Lorenzo Quimper, owner of the ranch, had arranged for his traveling factotum, Cándido Guzmán, to obtain citizenship, and Cándido, in turn, had imported from his small home town of Moctezuma six young nephews who, he claimed, had proof of having been born in that hospital in El Paso. So instead of having nearly two dozen wetbacks to deport, the agents had fewer than fifteen, and the affair caused much amusement in Dallas.

Señorita Múzquiz jumped on this unfortunate affair as a major topic for her two classes to analyze, and with her careful

1394

guidance, the young Hispanics learned of the government's brutality and of the heroism of the Mexicans, legal or otherwise, who had worked their way so far north without having been detected: 'They are the heroes of our conquest. And like my father, they will stay.' Studiously she avoided uttering the word *revolución*, and even when she voiced it silently to herself she always followed it with *pacifico*; she did not visualize gunfire or rebellion, because there was no need. Everything she desired was attainable through slow but persistent penetration. For the present she did not include Texas cities as far north as Dallas in her looming confederacy: 'At least not for the remainder of this century. The anglos are too strong. But I can see it happening sometime after 2030.' When she assured personal friends that it must happen, she called it: 'The inevitable triumph of the marriage bed. Mexican women have many children. Anglos don't.'

In her general activity Señorita Múzquiz conducted herself with strict legality, but without advising her superiors, she operated against the rules as they were intended. The Supreme Court decision *Lau v. Nichols*, and the subsequent orders which implemented it, known as Lau Relief, had as their purpose the education of very young children in America, whether citizens or not, in their native tongue so that an easier transition into English could be made. Thus, certain large cities throughout the nation – and many with no Spanish-speaking minority at all – were required to teach elementary-school classes in many different tongues, and to accomplish this, they had to find qualified young persons who could teach arithmetic, geography, music and science in Chinese, Portuguese, French, Russian, Polish and some fifty other languages.

As a consequence, the teaching of Chinese flourished, but that of science and arithmetic did not, for there were few of the hastily enlisted teachers who had the solid competence in their subject areas that Señorita Múzquiz had in hers. 'She's one of the best teachers in Dallas,' her supervisor said. 'Her only fault is that she is slow in getting her pupils to switch over into English.'

This tardiness was not accidental, for after these new teachers of Spanish had been on the job only a little while, they promoted the theory called *maintenance*, which meant that even after their pupils had reached a stage at which they could switch over to English, instruction in Spanish continued on the principle that the mastery of a second language was so valuable to the United States that proficiency in that language became a goal in itself.

Thus, Señorita Múzquiz's students came to school at age six knowing almost no English, and at seven or eight they were supposed to swing to the English-speaking classes, but under the new theory of maintenance, they were kept in Spanish right through elementary school, until learning in Spanish, with inadequate mastery of subject matter, became the rule. And in Spanish they learned from certain teachers like the Señorita that they were an oppressed group, discriminated against and obligated to lead the great social changes which would transform their portion of America into a reclaimed Mexican homeland.

Señorita Múzquiz did not have clear sailing in her program, for SMU had a charismatic professor of history who had worked for five years in the Peace Corps in various South American countries, and he had come home with a few hard-won conclusions about life in that world. His name was Roy Aspen – University of Texas, Stanford, University of Hawaii – thirty-seven years old and iron-tough. He had first attracted Señorita Múzquiz's attention in 1983 when he gave a widely discussed lecture, 'The Error of Bilingualism,' in which he pointed out with scholarly precision the dangers inherent in establishing even accidentally a two-language nation.

Had he kept to the main point his lecture might have gone unnoticed, but at the end he added two unfortunate paragraphs, which aroused unnecessary antagonism:

'A major corollary to this problem can be expressed in a question which we consistently avoid: "Why did those parts of the Western Hemisphere which fell under Spanish control fail to develop rational systems of self-government? And why did those regions falling under English control succeed?" The facts are overwhelming. No American nation deriving from a Spanish heritage, except possibly Costa Rica, has learned to govern itself in an orderly and just manner. Those with a different heritage have.

'Now, you may not want to admit that the non-Spanish nations have achieved responsible government and a just distribution of wealth, while the Spanish-speaking nations never have, but those are the facts. So to encourage a bilingualism which might bring into Texas the corrupt governmental systems of our neighbors to the south would be folly, if not suicide.'

When she left the lecture hall, Señorita Múzquiz was trembling, and to the fellow Hispanics she met that night, she said: 'We must declare war on this racist pig. He's reviving The Black Legend that was discredited a century ago.' And she drafted a letter to the editor, which surprised readers with its daring argument:

I am sick and tired of hearing that Spanish-speaking nations cannot govern themselves. Since Lázaro Cárdenas was elected President of Mexico in 1934, our well-governed nation to the south has had an unbroken sequence of brilliant leaders, each of whom has served his full six years without incident. In that same period the United States has had Roosevelt die in office, Truman, Ford and Reagan attacked by would-be assassins, Kennedy murdered, Nixon expelled, and Johnson, Ford and Carter denied reelection.

Mexico is the stable, well-governed nation. The United States terrifies its neighbors by its reactionary irresponsibility.

And as for the vaunted American system of distributing income fairly, we who live in South Dallas see precious little of either generosity or reward.

Her assault was so bold and her data so relevant that she was encouraged by her Hispanic friends to keep fighting, and when Dr Aspen ended the session with the acerbic comment that Señorita Múzquiz should remember that a return passage to Mexico was always easier than an infiltration of our border, her infuriated sympathizers urged her to initiate what developed into the notorious Múzquiz-Aspen Debates of 1984. They focused on bilingual education – and generated intense partisanship.

The protagonists were evenly matched: this dedicated, attractive young woman of Mexican derivation opposing an able professor of Swedish heritage who knew the Latin countries better than she. Each spoke from the most sincere conviction, and neither was reluctant to lunge for the jugular.

She made two points which gave thoughtful Texans something to chew on, and she did so with enough insolence to command attention and enough validity to command respect:

'Let's look at this anglo charge of cultural impoverishment in Mexico. Where in the United States is there a museum one-tenth as glorious as the new archaeological one in Mexico City? It celebrates with explosive joy the glories of Mexico. And where can I go in the United States to see the grandeur of your Indian heritage? Are you ashamed of your history?

'Don't tell me about the Metropolitan Museum in New York or the Mellon in Washington. They're fine buildings, but they're filled with the work of Europeans, not Americans. Impoverished intellectually? Who is impoverished?'

Her second bit of evidence received wide circulation and verification from various social agencies:

'If you check with social services here in Dallas, you will find that they carry on their books three hundred and sixteen otherwise responsible anglo men who ignore court orders directing them to help support children whom they have abandoned, while your post office reports that Mexican workers in this metropolitan area, poorest of the poor and under no compulsion other than human decency, send home to their families south of the border more than four hundred thousand dollars monthly. Which society is more civilized?'

Dr Aspen, realizing that he could not best Señorita Múzquiz in the disorderly brawling at which she excelled, sought to bring the debate to a higher level by convincing SMU to organize a powerful staff symposium entitled 'Bicultural Education, Fiction and Fact.' From the moment the brochures were printed, everyone could see that this was going to be an explosive affair, and experts from many states crowded into

1398

SMU, filling the university dormitories and occasionally standing at the rear of conference halls in which every seat was taken.

The United States as a whole had a profound interest in this subject, and national newspapers carried summaries of the opening address, in which a United States senator said:

'I voted for the legislation which spurred the initiation of bilingual education, and of course I applauded the Supreme Court decision of *Lau v. Nichols*. I did so because I believed that all young people in this country, whether citizens or not, deserved the best education possible, the soundest introduction to our system of values.

'I now realize that I made a dreadful mistake and that the Supreme Court decision, *Lau v. Nichols*, is one of the worst it has made in a hundred years. Together we have invited our beloved nation to stagger down a road which will ultimately lead to separatism, animosity and the deprivation of the very children we sought to help. I hereby call for the revocation of the system we so erroneously installed and the abolishment of the legislation sponsoring it.'

There was an outcry from the floor, and a man from Arizona who supported Señorita Múzquiz's theories demanded the podium for an immediate rebuttal, but with a calm which infuriated, Professor Aspen ignored the clamor and called for the second speaker, an elderly Jewish professor from Oregon, who gave a most thoughtful analysis of past American experience:

'I will be forgiven, I hope, if I draw upon my family's experience, but my grandfather came to New York in 1903 from the Galician region of what was then Austria but which had through most of history been Poland. He landed knowing not a word of English, and when in 1906 he was able to send to Galicia for the rest of his family, his wife and three children, including my father, landed at Ellis Island, again with no English.

'My grandfather spoke abominable English, my grandmother never learned. But the three children were thrown into the American school system and within four months were jabbering away. Both my father and my Aunt Elizabeta were writing their homework in English by the end of that first year, and both graduated from grade school with honors.

'That was the grand tradition which produced a melting pot from which poured an unending stream of Italian, German, Polish, Slavic and Jewish young people prepared to grapple on equal terms with the best that Harvard, Yale and Chicago were producing. In fact, my father went to Yale, and others from the various ghettos went to Stanford and Michigan and North Carolina.

'To change a system which has worked so well and with such honorable results is a grave error and one which, having been made, requires immediate reversal.'

Again there was an outcry from those whose careers had been enhanced by the introduction of bilingualism, but once again Professor Aspen ignored the hullabaloo, taking the podium himself to speak of his experiences:

'If one looks at the linguistic tragedy that impends in Canada, where French-speakers want to fracture the nation in defense of their language, or in Belgium, where French-speakers fight with Walloons who speak Flemish, or in the Isle of Cyprus, where Turk and Greek quarrel over languages, or in South Africa, where a nation is rent by language differences, or in India, where thousands are slain in language riots, or anywhere else where language is a divisive force, one can only weep for the antagonisms thus inherited.

'These countries bear a terrible burden, the lack of a common tongue, and more fortunate nations ought to sympathize with them and give them assistance in seeking solutions to what appear to be insoluble problems. Charity is obligatory.

'But for a nation like the United States, which has a workable central tongue used by many countries around the world, consciously to introduce a linguistic separatism and to encourage it by the expenditure of public funds is to create and encourage a danger which could in time destroy this nation, as the others I spoke of may one day be destroyed.

'India inherited its linguistic jungle; it did not create it willfully. History gave South Africa its divisive bilingualism; it did not seek it. Such nations are stuck with what accident and history gave them, and they cannot justly be accused of having made foolish errors, but if the United States consciously invents a linguistic dualism, it deserves the castigation of history.

'Let us focus on the main problem. If we continue to educate our Spanish-speaking immigrants and native-born in Spanish for the first six years of their education, and if we teach the vital subjects of literature and history in that language, we will see before the end of this century exactly the kind of separatism which now plagues Canada, but our example will be much worse than theirs, because our sample of the disaffected will be larger and will have on its southern border a nation, a Central America and an entire continent speaking that language and sponsoring that separatism. Let us face these ominous facts and see what we can do to counteract and forestall them.'

At the close of his address, reporters immediately crowded about Aspen: 'Do you oppose Señorita Múzquiz personally?' and he replied amiably: 'Not at all. She serves a most useful purpose in providing Mexican immigrants with leadership. Texas profits from its Mexican workers, and they're entitled to her guidance, But when her ideas are so erroneous that they might lead our entire nation into irreversible error, they must be corrected.'

'What did you think of her statement that if history had been just, Los Angeles and Houston would now be Mexican cities?'

He considered this for a moment: 'Interesting speculation. The cities might be Mexican but they would not be Los Angeles and Houston. Under traditional Mexican misman-agement, they'd be more like Guaymas and Tampico.'

When Miss Múzquiz gained the floor to counteract the strong points made by Professor Aspen, she controlled her seething fury and gave one of the better presentations of the symposium. She denied that teachers like her kept their students imprisoned in Spanish when they must lead their adult lives in English; she denied that she ever taught Mexican imperialism; she denied that the Supreme Court case infringed in any way on American rights. Since she really believed that she acted only in the best interests of her pupils, she had no hesitancy in denying that she or teachers like her kept their students from learning English.

Then, in sober terms, she reminded her audience of the grave disadvantages Mexican immigrants had suffered in Texas, the cruel way in which their culture had been abused, the remorseless way they had been handled by Rangers along the border, and the thoughtless contempt with which they were so often treated:

'We have lived side by side with the North Americans since 1810, and we have made every concession to their superior power. They had the votes, the guns, the law courts and the banks on their side, and we bowed low in the gutters and allowed them to usurp the sidewalks. But when they now demand that we surrender our language and our patterns of life, we say "No." '

She gave a stirring defense of bicultural life, which she refrained from equating with bilingual education paid for by the host state, and in the end, in a peroration that brought tears to some, she shared her vision of a de facto state along the border, from Brownsville to San Diego, in which the two cultures, the two economic systems and the two languages would exist in a mixed harmony.

As the symposium wound to a close, argument over the Simpson-Mazzoli Bill erupted, shattering her carefully nurtured impression of reasonableness. Simpson-Mazzoli was an effort by a Republican senator and a Democratic representative to stanch the hemorrhaging along the Mexican border and to bring order among the estimated ten million illegal immigrants who had drifted north and who existed in a kind of judicial no-man's-land. The bill offered three solutions: halt further illegal entry, grant generous amnesty to those well-intentioned and well-behaved Mexicans already here, and penalize American employers who hired illegals. It was a good bill, basically, but Hispanic leaders like Señorita Múzquiz opposed it vehemently on the dubious grounds that it would require immigrants like her who had later obtained legal status to carry identification cards. 'Am I to wear a yellow star, like Hitler's Jews?' she shouted. 'Must I carry proof that I'm a legal resident? What anglo employer will run the risk of hiring me when he can hire a fellow anglo with no danger of breaking the law?'

Professor Aspen dismissed such reasoning with one compelling question: 'Can a sovereign democracy control its borders or can't it?' Without waiting for an answer, he added: 'The incessant flow of illegals from Mexico and Central America must be halted, or the United States will be engulfed by hordes of uneducated persons who will try to convert it into just another Hispanic dictatorship.'

Señorita Múzquiz opposed the bill for defensible reasons, but there were other Hispanic leaders who fought it for personal gain: they wanted either an assured supply of cheap labor or a constant inflow of potential voters to bolster Hispanic claims. To all opponents of the bill, Dr Aspen asked: 'Are you recommending a completely open border across which anyone in Mexico can come as he or she wishes?' and the Señorita replied: 'You'd better keep the border open, because Texas and California prosper only because of the profit they make on this guaranteed supply of cheap labor. Stop the flow, and Texas will collapse in depression.'

A television newsman, overhearing the argument, asked: 'But Señorita, if the Mexicans and Central Americans keep pressing in, won't this mean that eventually most of Texas will become Mexican?' and she said, looking defiantly into the camera: 'If Hispanic mothers in Central America have many babies and anglo mothers in Texas have few, I suppose there will have to be an irresistible sweep of immigrants to the north. Yes, Texas will become Spanish.'

And even as she spoke, the American Congress, debating in Washington, refused to pass the reasonable Simpson-Mazzoli Bill, thus destroying any attempt by the United States to control the influx of illegals across its borders. For the most venal reasons the citizens of Texas were in the forefront of this cynical rejection of common sense; they were willing to accept immediate profits while ignoring future consequences. As a result, the Immigration authorities along the Rio Grande stopped trying to stem the unceasing inflow of illegals, turning their attention rather to keeping them out of the larger cities like Dallas and Amarillo; the creation of the ipso facto Mexican-American nation along the Rio Grande was under way. So the embittered Múzquiz-Aspen debate ended with a rousing victory for the Señorita. And the well-intentioned peasants from Mexico, Guatemala, Nicaragua and El Salvador, yearning for freedom and a decent life, continued to stream across the Rio Grande.

When Señorita Múzquiz heard on the evening news that Simpson-Mazzoli was dead, she cried in Spanish to those who were listening with her: 'Hooray! We'll win back every bit of land Santa Anna gave away. And we won't have to fire one shot.'

Professor Aspen, when he heard the same news, told his students: 'Before the end of this century Texas will start contemplating her privilege of breaking into smaller states. There'll be a movement to create along the Rio Grande a Hispanic state.'

'Are you serious?' they asked.

'Doesn't matter whether I am or not. The unquenchable flood of immigration will determine it.'

Sociologists called them 'rites of passage,' and this theory enabled them to predict certain inevitables which had to occur in any society, no matter how primitive or advanced. At age two, babies would begin to assert their own personalities, often with reverberations that altered family relationships; at fifteen, young males would begin to concentrate on girls, who had been concentrating on boys since thirteen; and at about twenty-seven, men would begin thinking about challenging the older leaders of the tribe, with similar inevitables trailing a man to his grave.

In Houston comparable rules dictated behavior. Among society's more fortunate few, men in their early thirties, like Roy Bub Hooker, Todd Morrison and their two friends, the oilman and the dentist, would want to find themselves a quail lease somewhere to the south along the borders of the great King Ranch; in their late thirties they'd want an airplane to fly them quickly to their preserve; in their early forties they'd begin to do what all sensible Texans did, aspire to take their vacations, summer or winter, in Colorado; and in their late forties, sure as thunder after a lightning stab, they'd want to find themselves a ranch in that glorious Hill Country west of Austin; and when this happy day occurred they would almost certainly switch to the Republican party.

On schedule, these urges hit the four members of Roy Bub's hunting team, with results that could have been anticipated: in their occupations the men had prospered unevenly, with the oilman finding headline success, and Todd Morrison, once of Detroit, approaching the well-to-do category of a real estate millionaire with close to twenty million. But the dentist was mired in the lower levels with only one or two million, and Roy Bub still dug sewers with no millions at all.

So Morrison and the oilman bought the plane, a four-seater Beechcraft, but it was Roy Bub who learned to fly it, and for three memorable years they flew almost each weekend during the hunting season and at least twice a month therafter down to Falfurrias to their lease, which was now a minor Shangri-La, but they had not been doing this for long when the greatest of the Houston urges trapped them, and they began to think about purchasing a ranch west of Austin.

In Houston a young man of ambition and talent was allowed so much elbowroom that he could progress pretty much at his own speed, but if he passed into his forties without owning a ranch, he betrayed himself as one who had left the fast track to find refuge in mediocre success along the more relaxed detours.

Although Morrison and the oilman had the money, they still looked to Roy Bub as the outdoor expert, so that when they started searching seriously for their ranch, they placed in his hands the responsibility for finding it. Often in the late 1970s Roy Bub and one or two of the others would fly out for scouting trips through the lovely hills and valleys beyond the Balcones Fault.

Few visitors from the North ever saw this wonderland of Central Texas, this marvelously rich congregation of small streams winding down valleys, of sudden meadowlands encompassed by hills, of a hundred acres of bluebonnets in the spring, and of the probing fingers of the man-made lakes, creeping deep into the rolling corners of the land. To see it from the highways that wandered through was delectable, but to see it as the four hunters now did, from low altitude in their plane, was a privilege of which they never tired. This was the golden heart of Texas, and a man was entitled to a share after he had brought in his third oil well or built his fourth skyscraper.

It was Roy Bub who first spotted their dreamland. He had flown west from Austin and was keeping to the south shore of the huge lake which had appeared one day among the hills, when he saw a small feeder river winding here and there, aimlessly and with many bends, as if reluctant to lose its identity in the larger body of water. He told Morrison, who had accompanied him this time: 'That's got to be the Pedernales,' and he pronounced the name as Texans did: Per-dnal-iss.

As he followed the little stream westward he suddenly twisted the Beechcraft about, doubled back, and shouted: 'There it is!' They were over the magnificent ranch put together by Lyndon Johnson, and for some minutes they circled this Texas monument to a prototypical Texas man. Morrison, looking down at the airstrip built with federal taxes, the roadways paved by the state, the fences built by friends, and the pastures stocked by other friends, thought: Who really cares if he was a wheeler-dealer? He was a damned good president and one day this will all seep back to public ownership. I'd like to be president . . . just for one term.

And then, after they passed the Johnson ranch, Roy Bub saw it, a stretch of handsome land on the north bank of the Pedernales. It contained everything the four hunters sought: a long stretch fronting the river, good ground cover for grouse and turkey, ample trees for deer to browse, plus a kind of park along the river and bleak empty spaces for wildlife to roam. It was the original Allerkamp ranch of five thousand acres, to which had been added the Macnab holdings of equal size, and when Roy Bub landed his plane at Fredericksburg, he and Morrison discovered to their delight that it was for sale. Once they satisfied themselves that it suited their purposes, neither man ever turned back, Roy Bub assuring his partners that it was the best available ranch in Texas, and Morrison convincing the oilman that it was a bargain, regardless of what the German owners wanted, and a deal was struck, with Todd and the oilman putting up most of the money and Roy Bub and the dentist doing most of the work.

On a sad November Friday in 1980 they flew down to Falfurrias to inform the owner of their present lease that they would be terminating it on March first, and he was genuinely unhappy to see them go: 'You lived up to every promise you ever made. I'll miss you.' The oilman said: 'Now, if this causes you to lose any money—' but he interrupted: 'I'll be able to arrange a new lease by tomorrow noon. Must be two hundred young tigers in Houston panting for a lease like this.'

On one point the old contract was clear: any building which they had erected belonged to him ... if it was fastened to the ground; any that remained movable belonged to them, and Roy Bub surprised the owner by saying: 'We'll want to take all the buildings with us.'

'They're yours, but I was hopin' you'd want to sell them ... at an attractive price ... save you a lot of trouble,' but Roy Bub said: 'No, we can use them at the new place,' and the owner looked in amazement as the oilman moved in three of his crews, who sawed the six small houses apart, mounted them on great trucks, and headed them two hundred and forty-one miles northwest to their new home, where they would be reassembled to form an attractive hunting lodge in a far corner of the Allerkamp land.

The four hunters and their families had occupied the new ranch only two years when once more the inevitable pressures exerted by the rites of passage attacked them. The dentist discovered that he was now strong enough financially to abandon his practice and devote himself full-time to the propagation and sale of his hunting dogs; he withdrew from the consortium and opened a master kennel on the outskirts of Houston. At the same time, the oilman was struck by an insidious disease which affected many Texas oilmen: 'All my life I've dreamed of shooting in England and Scotland. The moors. The hunt breakfasts with kippers under the silver covers. The faithful ghillies. The long weekends. Gentlemen, I've leased a stretch of good salmon river near Inverness and you're invited to come over in season.'

His Scottish adventure so absorbed him, what with the purchase of another Purdy gun and the making of arrangements for his Highland headquarters, that one night he informed

Morrison and Roy Bub that he wanted to sell off his portion of the Allerkamp ranch, but when Todd said, almost eagerly: 'I think I could swing it,' he surprised both men by saying: 'I'd want to cut Roy Bub in. Let him get a grubstake.' And he persisted in this decision, arranging for Hooker a long-term payment with no interest: 'I owe that to you, Roy Bub. You taught me what the outdoors was.'

Six months later the Houston social pages diplayed photographs of the oilman at his lodge in the Scottish Highlands, where he had been entertaining a British executive of Shell Oil, a Lord Duncraven, and a financier involved with the big oil operation in the North Sea, a Sir Hilary Cobham. It was an engaging shot, with the Houston man looking more like a Scottish laird than the locals.

So now Todd Morrison and Roy Bub Hooker owned a ranch on the Pedernales and half a Beechcraft airplane, but the latter awkwardness was resolved when the oilman, totally pre-occupied with his holdings in Scotland, offered to sell his part of the plane at a tremendous bargain, which Todd and Roy Bub gladly accepted. When the deal was closed with this remarkably generous old friend, they saw him no more. He had leaped five steps up the social ladder.

But Morrison was generating enough income from his manifold real estate deals to permit him to absorb most of the cost of the ranch, and after an airstrip had been installed well away from the river, the private planes of many Houston real estate managers appeared at Allerkamp, and the place became known as a site where developers and their wives could enjoy a good time.

Despite this concentration on business, and Morrison was never far removed from a deal of some kind, his love for the land never diminished, and he was therefore in a receptive mood when Roy Bub came to him one weekend with a challenging proposition: 'Ol' buddy, I think we got ourself a gold mine here. My recommendation, we fence it in . . .'

'It's already fenced in.'

'I mean gameproof fence.'

These were startling words, and Todd remained silent for some time, simply staring at the driller of septic tanks. Finally he asked, very slowly: 'You mean those fences eight and a half feet high?' And before Roy Bub could respond, he asked: 'You thinking of exotics?' Then Roy Bub said: 'I sure am. Todd, with your money and my management and my feel for animals, we could have us a ball on this ranch.'

'Do you know what gameproof fencing costs?'

'I do,' and from his wallet he produced a study of costs: 'Very best, guaranteed to hold ever'thin' but an armadillo, around nine thousand dollars a mile.' Rapidly he analyzed this situation: 'Ten thousand acres, divide by six hundred forty acres to the mile, that's about sixteen square miles. If it was a perfect square, which it isn't, that would be a perimeter of twelve miles we'd have to fence. But we'd need cross fencing to break it into pastures, so add eight miles. Twenty miles of fencing at nine thousand a mile. Jesus, Roy Bub! That's a hundred and eighty thousand, just for the fences, without the stock, which doesn't come cheap.'

'Todd, I got me a lead on some of the best exotics in the United States. Everybody wants to deal with me. The basic stock I can pick up for a hundred and thirty thousand, believe me.'

They sat in the evening darkness reviewing these notes, and when Karleen and Maggie came in to see if they wanted drinks, the men asked their wives to stay. 'The land isn't square,' Todd explained, 'so the fencing might be even more than we've calculated.'

'But I'll bet I can get us a lot better bargain than nine thousand a mile.' Roy Bub said.

'What do you ladies think?' Todd asked, and Maggie responded quickly: 'I believe we could swing it. So long as real estate stays up,' and Karleen said: 'Roy Bub's always liked animals. I suppose we'd want to move up here to get things organized,' and Roy Bub said: 'We sure would.'

He did manipulate a much better price than $9,000 a mile, and when the fences were erected, nearly eighteen miles of the best, he fulfilled the rest of his promise, for he knew where to locate real bargains in aoudad sheep, sika deer, mouflon rams and eight American elk. He astonished Morrison by also acquiring nine ostriches and six giraffes. 'We won't allow anyone to shoot them, but they do add color to the place.'

When the animals began to arrive, often by air, Roy Bub

greeted each one as if it were a member of his family, showing it personally to the large, almost free fields in which it would roam: 'Madam Eland, you never had it better in Africa than you're gonna have it right here.'

From the start it had been intended that when the exotics were well established, and this would come soon, for the Allerkamp ranch was much like the more interesting parts of South Africa from which the elands and other antelopes came, big-game hunters would be invited to come and test their skill against animals in the wild. 'Year after next,' Roy Bub said, 'when we have the lodge fixed up and my wife has hired some cooks and I've got guides, we're in business.'

They would charge substantially for the privilege of killing one of their exotics, but as the pamphlet which Roy Bub composed pointed out: 'It's a danged sight cheaper coming to Allerkamp for your eland than going to Nairobi.' Extremely practical where his own money was concerned, he established a rather high rate for the Texas hunters:

Animal	Source	Our cost pair yearlings	Our cost mature male	Hunter pays trophy size
Axis deer	India	$500	$850	$1,800
Sika deer	China	500	850	1,200
Blackbuck	India	250	850	1,100
Fallow deer	Germany	250	450	1,000
Whitetail	USA	450	800	2,500
Red stag	Scotland	2,400	3,800	6,650
Elk	USA	3,500	4,500	7,000
Aoudad ram	Africa	360	850	1,500
Corsican ram	Corsica	75	100	250
Mouflon ram	Sardinia	380	500	1,000
Eland	Africa	1,750	1,500	3,000
Ibex	Africa	3,500	2,400	4,500
Sable antelope	Africa	10,000	8,000	***
Horned oryx	Africa	3,500	2,000	4,000
Gemsbok	Africa	5,000	2,750	3,750
Zebra, Grant's	Africa	4,500	2,800	4,000
Turkey, wild	USA	100	150	250

*** No hunting allowed

But when they were in place, with Morrison paying one bill after another for their purchase and their transportation, Roy Bub introduced a stunning addition, which he paid for out of his own pocket. One morning he called Houston with exciting news: 'Todd, Maggie! Fly right up. It's unique.'

When they reached the ranch they found that a large trailer had moved in with animals of some kind. 'You'll never guess,' Roy Bub cried.

The van was maneuvered to one of the smaller fields where hunting was forbidden, and when the gate was opened and men stationed so that the animals, when released, could not scamper back toward the trailer, ramps were placed, the door swung out – and down came a quiet, noble procession. The watchers gasped, for Roy Bub had acquired from an overstocked zoo four of nature's loveliest creations: sable antelope, big creatures as large as a horse, but a soft purplish brown, a majestic way of walking and the finest horns in the animal kingdom.

When they felt themselves free, they sniffed the unfamiliar air, pawed at the rocky soil so like their own in South Africa, then raised their stately heads and began moving away. When they did this, the observers could see the full sweep of their horns, those tremendous lyrelike curves that started at the forehead and turned backward in an imperial arch till the tips nearly touched their flanks. Almost as if they appreciated how grand and eloquent they were, they posed at the edge of a tree cluster, then leaped in different directions and lost themselves in the woodlands of their new home.

Sometimes a whole month would pass without anyone seeing one of the sables; then a visitor would be driving aimlessly along the ranch roads and suddenly before him would appear that stately animal, purplish gold in the afternoon sun, with sweeping horns unlike any the traveler would have seen before, and he would come scrambling back to the lodge, shouting: 'What was that extraordinary creature I saw?' and Roy Bub would ask: 'Sort of purple? Huge horns?' and when the man nodded, he would say proudly: 'That was one of our sables, glory of the Allerkamp.'

'What would it cost me to shoot one?'

'They ain't for shootin'.'

* * *

During the early years of the Houston crises, no real estate people escaped the adverse effects, but since Maggie Morrison had always avoided the rental business, she did not see at first hand the damage done to hotels and condominiums by the weakened peso. Nor did she suffer immediately from the collapse of petroleum prices. Associated with one of the solid firms, she continued to specialize in finding expensive homes for Northern executives whose corporations had moved them into the Houston area: 'I sometimes wonder who's running the store up there. All the bright vice-presidents seem to be moving down here.'

She did not yet have the courage to do what her husband did so easily: put together a really big operation with outside financing from Canada or Saudi Arabia, but she was doing well and could have supported herself had she been required to do so. She had fallen into a Texas pattern of thought in which any gamble, if it had even a forty-percent chance of success, was worth the taking: 'And anyway, Todd, if it all did collapse, we could start over as clerks in somebody's office and within six months own the place.'

That she was now a complete Texan manifested itself in two ways. In her letters home to her friends in Detroit she no longer even spoke of returning:

Something in Houston catches the imagination and sets it aflame. Last week I found a home for one of the most famous of the astronauts out at NASA east of here. For years he'd been saying: 'One of these days I'll go back to Nebraska.' Last week he bit the bullet and will be staying here, even after retirement from the program. He has a little business going on the side.

The thing that catches you, I think, is the dynamism of the place. It's like watching some great flywheel whirring about. In the first moments you marvel at its speed, and then suddenly you find yourself wanting to be a part of it, and you're sorely tempted to jump in. Well, I've jumped. Would you believe it, Pearl, I've put together a deal for three Arabs involving some of the finer houses, $14,000,000, of which I hold on to a small part. Until I close, I'll be so nervous I won't sleep.

*   *   *

That turned out to be a frightening one-week nightmare, which, when disposed of, she swore never to repeat. She took this oath because she had become aware that her husband frequently found himself in rather delicate positions from which he extricated himself by moves which she supposed she would not have approved had she known the details. For example, when the oilman who had been their partner shifted from the ranch on the Pedernales to the hunting lodge in Scotland, he confided: 'Maggie, I don't like to say this, but I'm very fond of you, and so is Rachel. Protect yourself. I've been in four financial deals with your husband, and damn it all, in every case he pulled some swiftly. The Lambert Development, the ranch at Falfurrias, the airplane, out at Allerkamp. He cuts corners. He gigs his friends. He's always looking for that little extra edge. And that's one of the reasons why I'm switching my hunting to Scotland.'

'Have his actions . . . I mean . . . have they been . . . ?'

'Illegal?' He intertwined his fingers until they formed a little cathedral. 'The line is tenuous . . . shady. When you deal with big numbers you face big problems. But you must never gig your own associates.'

'Certainly he's treated Roy Bub fairly?' The fact that she asked this as a question indicated that doubt had been sown.

'Roy Bub's the best man in Texas. Everybody treats him fair. But even Roy Bub had better watch out, because some day he's going to find he owns no part of that ranch. "So long, Roy Bub, nice to have known you." '

'I can't believe that.'

'And you better watch out, Lady Meg, or you're going to be out on your keester with the rest of us.'

He did not see her again, and to her surprise, the dentist with the big kennel ignored her too, so one day while she was surveying corner lots that might be converted into modest wraparounds, she stopped by the kennels and asked bluntly: 'Did my husband have anything to do with your pulling out of the Allerkamp deal?' and he said frankly: 'After a while, Maggie, men get fed up with dealing with your husband. Watch out.'

The second way in which Maggie indicated that Texas had

captured her was the manner in which she adjusted to her daughter's strange behavior. Beth, a spectacular beauty in her late teens, had refused to attend the University of Michigan: 'The only place I want to go is UT.'

'Stop using that nonsensical phrase! If you mean Texas, say so.'

'That's certainly what I mean,' and at UT she had become chief baton twirler.

In disgust, Maggie had refused to attend any games, but one Saturday afternoon when Texas was playing SMU she chanced to see on the half-time television show a most remarkable young woman from the other university, a real genius at twirling. The SMU girl wore a skimpy costume that revealed her lovely grace and she threw the baton much higher than Maggie would have believed possible, catching it deftly, now in front, now behind.

'Extraordinary,' Maggie said. As a girl she had seen circus performers who were no better than this young artist, so she stayed by the television as her own daughter appeared for Texas, and what she saw made her catch her breath.

When the SMU band and performers left the field, the mighty Texas band swung into action, more than three hundred strong, dressed in burnt-orange. In front came the six-foot-seven drum master, followed by sixteen cheerleaders, men and women. After them came the three baton twirlers, with Beth Morrison in the middle. Behind her came the endless files of the musicians, all stepping alike, all inclining their cowboy hats in rhythm.

At the rear came a couple of dozen drummers, cymbalists, glockenspiel players and whatnots, followed by the sensation of the Texas campus: a drum so huge that three men were needed to keep it secured to its carriage and moving forward. It was taller than two men and was clubbed by a player whose arm muscles were huge; its deep, booming sound filled the stadium.

And then Beth stood forth alone, this poet manqué, and with a skill that staggered Maggie, she sent first one, then two batons into the air, catching them unfailingly and creating a kind of mystic spell for this important autumn afternoon.

'Who in his right mind,' Maggie asked aloud as she switched off the television, 'would invent something like that spectacle and call it education?' But later, when she was forced to reconsider all aspects of the situation, she conceded that Mr Sutherland, principal at Deaf Smith High, had been right when he predicted that Beth would find her life within the Texas syndrome and be very happy in it. Beth had been pledged by one of the premier sororities, the Kappas, whose senior members arranged for her to meet one of the more attractive BMOCs. Wolfgang Macnab, descendant of two famous Texas Rangers, was indeed a Big Man on Campus, for he stood well over six feet, weighed about two hundred and twenty lean pounds, and played linebacker on the Longhorn football team.

He was five years older than Beth and should have graduated before she entered the university, but in the Texas tradition he had been red-shirted in both junior high school and college – that, is, held back arbitrarily so that he would be bigger and stronger when he did play. He was a bright young fellow, conspicuous among the other football giants, in that he took substantial classes in which he did well. After their meeting in the Kappa lounge, he and Beth studied together for an art-appreciation seminar, in which he excelled, and before long they were being referred to as 'that ideal Texas couple.' What happened next was explained by Beth's mother in one of her periodic letters to Detroit:

What you Northerners never appreciate, Pearl, is that Texas is so big that you can live your life within its limits and never give a damn about what anybody in Boston or San Francisco thinks. A girl like our daughter Beth can enjoy a stunning life at the university here without giving a hoot what the social leaders at Vassar or Stanford think. Matrons here do not have to consider Philadelphia or Richmond. They're their own bosses. All that matters is how they're perceived in Dallas and Houston.

A writer can build a perfectly satisfactory reputation in Texas and he doesn't give a damn what critics in Kalamazoo think. His universe is big enough to gratify any ambition. Same with businessmen. Same with newspapers. Same with everything.

I share these reflections because I've been thinking of Beth. She could have had a noble career at Michigan or

Vassar, of that I'm sure. The kid's a near-genius, and was a wonderful poet at fourteen, when the real poets start. But at her local high school she was brainwashed into becoming a baton twirler . . . pompons . . . the bit, and when I challenged this, she said: 'Let's face it, Mom, how could Texas produce a poet when its favorite food is chicken-fried steak smothered in white library paste?' She went her way, and damned if she didn't become the best baton twirler of the lot. Also a puffy-pretty sorority girl without a brain in her head, you know the type.

So what happens to my adorable little nitwit? She marries one of the handsomest football players God ever made, and at their wedding his brother Cletus appears, six feet six, a full-fledged Texas Ranger with big hat and hidden gun holster. When the three of them stood before the minister, Baptist naturally, with little Beth in the middle and those two gorgeous hunks on either side, all I could do was hide my tears and recall the biblical quotation 'Male and female created He them.'

And then I got two real surprises. What do you suppose they did with the wedding purse her sorority and his fraternity contributed? They bought a Picasso print. Yep, those redneck hillbillies bought a Picasso. And this evening's news announces that Wolfgang has been drafted by the Dallas Cowboys, said to be the best football team in America. Surely it's better than Detroit. So I'm not to be the mother of a poetess but the mother-in-law of a football hero, and I find myself shouting with the rest of Texas: 'So who gives a damn about Vassar? The real world is down here.'

Of course, when the recession grew acute in 1982, and oil dropped to twenty-nine dollars a barrel, and the fall of the Mexican peso prostrated Houston real estate, threatening many of the big hotels with bankruptcy because those spectacular ten-room suites were no longer being rented to Mexican millionaires, even fortunately situated couples like the Morrisons began to feel pinches. Todd had only a vague awareness of the economic slump until he saw at the commuter airport the number of private planes that were suddenly for sale. This struck home, and he quickly convened a strategy session with his wife: 'Now, now's the time to make our big moves.'

'You must be crazy! The bottom's falling out.'

'That's exactly when opportunities appear. A good real estate agent, and you're one of the best, Maggie, can make a bundle when the market is going up. But he can make even more when it's going down. Because people have to sell, and there's damned few buyers around.'

'How can we buy?'

'Credit. We hock everything we have. We look for distress bargains, and we buy it to the hilt.'

When they had done this, and exhausted their own funds, Todd said: 'The luscious plums, the real big ones, are beginning to ripen. Go up to Dallas and line up some real money.'

It was in this manner that Maggie Morrison, a one-time schoolteacher in a suburb of Detriot, fired during retrenchment, walked into the office of Ransom Rusk in Dallas, trying to interest him in a Houston real estate speculation requiring $143,000,000. In the first eight minutes of their meeting she learned much about Texas financing: 'I apologize, Mr Rusk, for coming at you like this when the papers say you've suffered reverses,' and he laughed: 'My dear Mrs Morrison, it's precisely at such times that a man like me is looking for new ventures. Some of the old ones have worn thin.'

'Then you'll consider the deal?' and he said: 'I've always been willing to consider any deal ... if there's enough leverage. That's how I landed with TexTek.'

She next asked: 'How much would you expect my husband and me to throw in?' and he said: 'Every nickel you have. I want you to be as concerned about this as I would be.'

Finally he said: 'You want a hundred and forty-three million dollars. I'll put up twenty-five million if you put up four,' and she said: 'But that leaves us more than a hundred million short. Where do we get it?' and he said: 'The banks. You'll be amazed at how eager they are to lend money to anyone with a hot idea, and yours is hot.'

She asked: 'Why are you doing this?' and he said: 'Winning, losing, I care little about either. But I do like to be in the game.'

If one kept focusing attention on big ranchers like Lorenzo

Quimper, or big oilmen like Ransom Rusk, or big cotton growers like Sherwood Cobb, or real estate honchos like Todd Morrison, one might conclude that power in Texas was exerted only by those who controlled large sums of money, but this would be wrong. In many aspects of Texas life it was 'the little folks from the fork in the creek' who cast the deciding ballots. They kept racetrack gambling out of Texas. They allowed no state lotteries. And with refreshing frequency they bullheadedly voted in a way that surprised the big cities. An excellent example of this strong-mindedness came in Larkin in 1980 when some misguided liberals reminded the town that one of its first occupants had been a respectable saloon keeper and that alcohol had been outlawed only by the ill-conceived Prohibition movement. 'It's high time our town had stores that sold liquor and saloons in which law-abiding citizens could enjoy a sociable drink.' Eager to put their money where their mouth was, these energetic people collected a huge war chest, hired Kraft and Killeen, the public relations firm from Dallas, and petitioned for a referendum. The war was on.

Under Texas law a county had the right to vote itself dry if a majority so desired, and out of 254 counties, 74 did, but there were so many ramifications that newcomers rarely understood what was happening. One county would outlaw everything – wine, beer, whiskey – another would allow beer but not wine or whiskey; and a third, fourth and fifth would create their own mixes. As a result, only 36 counties were totally wet.

After the wild years of the oil boom, Larkin had voted itself dry, and in both the sixties and seventies, had repulsed efforts to rescind that law. 'This town,' boasted Reverend Craig, pastor of the First Baptist Church of Larkin, 'is a haven of decency and sobriety in a state which has too many examples of the opposite character.' Craig was a good clergyman, especially revered for his fatherly interest in orphans and his loving attention to elderly people without families. Much of the good that occurred in Larkin could be attributed to his acts, and wealthy oilmen like Ransom Rusk kept him in funds sufficient to cover the numerous little charities he performed. He preached well, did not rant, was ecumenical toward the lesser churches that had crowded into Larkin, and had goaded his congregation into welcoming even Mexicans and blacks into the church, if they were passing through.

'Craig adds a touch of humanity and decency to our town,' one of the oilmen said when making his annual contribution, and this was the general opinion. Young people appreciated him because in a willing effort to keep up with the times, he had encouraged his elders to allow dancing at church socials, a radical move when one recalled the old days.

Craig was not a fanatic where morals were concerned, and he had several times helped prostitutes stranded by their pimps, for he suspected that Jesus would have done the same, and he served as a surrogate father for children who fell into trouble; but he could be remarkably forceful when discharging two of his Baptist obligations: he believed in a literal interpretation of the Bible, and he abhorred demon rum: 'I have been forced to witness so much human tragedy resulting from alcohol that I stand in wonderment that any man would willingly allow this evil substance to pass his lips, and as for women who do so, they are anathema.'

He was, in many respects, the most powerful force in Larkin, and when one particularly offensive oil tycoon flouted all the implicit laws of North Texas, Craig preached such a powerful pair of sermons against him that he was in effect ex-communicated, not only from the Baptist church but from the community as well. The miscreant moved to Dallas, where he was quite happy.

It was largely due to Craig that Larkin remained dry, for it had been his vigorous leadership which had repelled the last two attempts to turn it wet, and he was now girding his loins to fight again. He chose to ignore the fact that a large majority of his flock enjoyed a short snifter now and then, but he did frequently praise his congregation for hiding no outright drunks in its membership. He was contemptuous of those Rio Grande counties which, because of their heavily Hispanic population, refused to outlaw alcohol, and in his more inflammatory prohibition sermons he sometimes referred to them as 'our southern cousins to whom drunkenness is a way of life,' refusing to acknowledge that their orderly use of beverages produced less actual drunkenness than did Larkin's severe code.

Of course, under the complex Texas system anyone who

wanted a drink could find one, and each dry county contained its quota of enthusiastic topers, because the law contained a built-in weakness which drinkers were quick to take advantage of. A respectable county like Larkin could vote itself dry while its more disreputable neighbor remained stubbornly wet, and since most counties, especially in the west, were small and square – something like thirty miles to a side, with the county seat dead center – it was possible for a town at the heart of a dry county to be only fifteen miles from a flowing source of liquor. In Larkin's case, the distance from bone-dry to sopping-wet was twelve miles down Highway 23 to Bascomb County, 'that notorious and nauseous sink of sin,' as Reverend Craig like to describe it in his sermons.

When officials at the Larkin County Courthouse announced that a referendum had been authorized for the spring of 1980, Craig looked with awe at the forces arrayed against him, and told his deacons: 'Brethren, this is the fight that will determine the character of our county for the rest of this century. Look at those who assault us! All the distilleries of America. All the breweries of Texas. All the saloon keepers of those wet Red River counties. Kraft and Killeen of Dallas. Brother Carnwath, please tell the gentlemen the size of the war chest we face.'

A tall, thin man, with deep-set eyes and a lock of hair that fell across his brow, rose: 'We have good reason to believe that they have amassed more than seven hundred thousand dollars to crush us, for they know that if they can bring their whiskey in here, they can lug their barrels into any county.'

'Gentlemen,' Craig said, 'the battle lines are drawn. Once more it is David against Goliath, and once more God will favor the pure in heart, puny though we may seem at the start.'

It really was little David against the forces of darkness, but the shepherd boy was by no means powerless, for Craig organized groups on three levels: The Sages of the Community, Children for a Decent Texas, and in the middle, a large and forceful group, The Watchdogs of the Fort. With all the skills remembered from former battles he brought pressure to bear on the editor of the *Larkin Defender*, who if left alone might have sided with the liquor people on three solid grounds, which he espoused privately to his friends: 'Orderly sale would be good for trade. Keeping our kids at home would stop those car crashes when they go seeking booze. And I hate the hypocrisy of drinking wet and voting dry.' But when he found that his larger advertisers ardently supported Reverend Craig, even though they were themselves heavy drinkers, he found himself compelled to write a series of hard-hitting editorials favoring retention of the ban.

To one outsider, the situation in Larkin seemed paradoxical: 'Everyone in this crazy town drinks but wants to stop anyone else from doing so.' An explanation of this curious Texas trait was spelled out in a letter written by a Baptist woman to a friend in New Mexico:

It is true that Albert takes a small drink now and then, but only socially when we are in the homes of those who favor alcohol. Even I am not above a congenial nip on holidays, and I'm told that boys in school, and especially the older ones who work in town, drink somewhat. Yet all of us who have the vote prefer to keep alcohol out of the stores, and saloons off our quiet streets.

We do this, I think, because we know that to restrain evil in even the smallest degree is good, in that it sends a signal through the community that we shall not allow it to run rampant. On the three nights prior to the vote Reverend Craig will hold prayer meetings in which we will commit ourselves to fighting the devil, for we are convinced that unrestricted use of alcohol is a principal agency through which he attacks individuals and their communities.

The crusade against alcohol, which had to be fought repeatedly in what Reverend Craig called 'our Christian counties of the north,' produced one grave weakness, which the people of Larkin did not like to discuss. Highway 23 leading to Bascomb became a well-traveled route, and when young men and women roared south to get liquored up, often drinking out of their bottles as they weaved their way back, there was apt to be accidents, more coming north than going south, and there were many involving some solitary drunk heading north who smashed head-on into some innocent car coming south with its four sober passengers. TRAGEDY IN SUICIDE GULCH became the headline, and often it was the four sober travelers who were killed, while the solitary drunk survived because he had sped into the accident completely relaxed.

Rarely did a year pass without some horrendous accident along Highway 23, and occasional protests appeared in the press about this nasty habit of young people driving down to Bascomb to buy their liquor and then guzzling it on their way home, but no one seemed to blame the carnage in Suicide Gulch on Larkin's lack of orderly places in which to buy a drink.

So as the critical vote approached, the lines were drawn in typical North Texas fashion: outside forces pouring in huge sums in hopes of being allowed to peddle their product, the Baptists fighting valiantly to maintain the status quo they had inherited from their God-fearing parents. Partisans on each side were sensible, and patriotic, and driven by respectable motives, but there was such enmity between them that no meeting ground could ever be established.

Watchers of the campaign refused to predict how this one was going to result: 'Can't never tell the effect of all that money on their side or prayers on ours.'

A peculiarity of the Texas system was that any plebiscite on booze was effective for only a few years, after which the other side could try again; ordinarily, the losers licked their wounds for about six years before storming back, but regardless of the outcome, it was never final. As Reverend Craig said five days before the vote: 'In this world of sin the forces of evil never rest.'

This year it looked as if evil would triumph, for its Dallas managers, Kraft and Killeen, had run a masterful campaign focused not on alcohol but on human rights and the advantages of a free society, but at almost the last moment the drys received help from an unexpected quarter. In the oil town of San Angelo, a hundred and seventy miles to the southwest, a Catholic priest named Father Uecker awoke to the fact that during the past twelve months he had been required to conduct burial services for five impetuous young men of his congregation who had been shot and killed during five different drunken brawls on church property. In anguish over such mayhem he had, with considerable publicity, announced that he would no longer rent his parish hall for any dance or entertainment at which liquor was consumed.

He said that this would cost his church more than three thousand dollars in lost fees, but he felt that this would be a small price to pay if it would halt or even slow down the carnage. Father Uecker ended his announcement with a paragraph which somewhat dampened its effect among the Larkin Baptists, but even so, they clutched at the support his action provided:

> We are fairly certain that Jesus himself enjoyed the wedding feast at Cana, which certainly included wine and dancing. We believe that wine is also part of God's creation and, therefore, it is good. We believe that dancing can be very wholesome recreation. We categorically deny that drinking and dancing are evil of themselves, but it seems to be impossible at this time and in this place to conduct public dances with the abuse that alcohol brings.

This tragic news from San Angelo, that five young men in one small parish had died of gunshot wounds, plus Reverend Craig's imaginative use of the report, neatly ignoring the priest's reminder that he was not a prohibitionist, swung just enough votes to the drys to ensure that once again Larkin County had obeyed the voice of its religious leader. When the vote was announced church bells rang and some members of the various congregations, including the pastor's sixteen-year-old son, rode through the county seat, tooting their horns in celebration of the victory.

The other three youngsters in the car containing young Craig were so jubilant that when the informal parade in town ended, they rode joyously down Suicide Gulch to the grogshops of Bascomb County, drank immoderately, and then came zigzagging homeward with two bottles of Old Alamo, one for the front seat, one for the back.

As they approached the intersection of Highway 23 and FM-578 the driver became confused by the lights coming at him from dead ahead and by those angling in from 578. In a moment of supreme confidence he decided to thread his way through the middle; instead, he smashed broadside into the car coming from the right. The driver, young Craig, the other two passengers and the husband and wife in the other car were killed, not instantly but in the flames which engulfed them.

The changes which assaulted Texas affected everyone. On the day before the regents' meeting the new governor called the Quimper ranch: 'Lorenzo, the new regent I appointed is flying up from the Valley. You've been a regent for two terms. Would you please meet him at the airport and more or less explain how things work?'

The new man was Simón Garza, the thoughtful mayor of Bravo and the first Hispanic to be appointed to the university's Board of Regents. Quimper, who had always employed Mexican wetbacks on his nine ranches and who had promoted one of them, Cándido Guzmán, to general foreman, found no difficulty in talking with Mayor Garza, brother of the A&M member of the Task Force with whom he had argued so congenially.

It was a thoughtful conversation because Garza immediately showed his desire to learn, and faced with that sincerity, Il Magnifico realized that he must not clown around with his redneck humor: 'You do us honor joining the regents, Mayor Garza. You've built a fine reputation throughout Texas.' When Garza looked down at his hands to avoid having to respond to this formal flattery, Quimper said: 'Being a regent is a privilege. One of the most important assignments in Texas.'

'And I'm honored to be the first Mexican-American. Although I do think it's about time, seeing how many of our people attend the place.'

'I'm glad to have you aboard,' Quimper said, and when Garza asked: 'Wasn't your father the famous regent?' Lorenzo was encouraged to speak with him as a serious equal.

'He had the job for years, and people either exalted or despised him, depending on whether or not they could read.' When Garza smiled at the joke, Lorenzo grew more specific.

'My father did everything practical to promote the university football team, and everything possible to annihilate any influences he felt were not in harmony with the spirit of the gridiron. On the positive side, he created generous scholarships for football players, initiated the plan of having wealthy ranchers contribute steers to feed his athletes at their training table, and organized a fleet of private planes, some of them jets, which the dozen coaches could use when recruiting in the fall and winter months. He also provided, out of his own oil money, two different sets of uniforms for the 334 members of the university's show band of the Southwest, "biggest and best in the nation and twice as big as anything in Europe or Asia," he said. On crisp October days when the Texas football team ran onto the field in the enlarged stadium he had helped provide, and the band marched out to greet them, he could sit back in his special box and think: I'm responsible for a hell of a lot of that, and when boys he had recruited swept to national championships, he could say truthfully: "I brought most of that backfield to Texas. What a bargain." '

'Why is your father's name so familiar?' Garza asked, and Quimper said frankly: 'Bad publicity,' and he explained.

'There was a negative side. My father practically destroyed the faculty, disciplining anyone he disliked and firing those he distrusted. At the height of his reign of terror he told me: 'Runnin' a university is like runnin' a ranch. The man with money owns it, and he hires a manager and assistants. He gives them wide latitude in day-to-day operations, but he never lets them forget who's really in charge." He had an interesting theory about professors: "I like to have colorful men on my staff. Fellows who wear old-fashioned clothes, or who go to northern Sweden in their summers, or who wear string ties. Makes the campus distinctive. But I do not want them meddling in the running of the place or speaking out on politics." Teachers who ignored his rules or openly contested them did not last long on my father's academic ranch.'

'What was that famous fracas about Frank Dobie?'

Quimper seemed to ignore the question, for he launched instead into a philosophical discussion about the arts in Texas. 'Compared to the other Southern states, Texas has not produced its quota of artists, musicians, novelists or philosophers, and my old man was one of the reasons. If we did not have world-class intellectuals, we did have, in my early days, two men who were building a foundation, and my father scorned them. Walter Prescott Webb had a fine, clear vision of the West and wrote about it with skill and passion, but he favored liberal causes, and for my father that was forbidden.

1425

Frank Dobie! What a man! Traipsed about the campfires gathering cowboy yarns and tall stories about coyotes, Longhorns and rattlesnakes. I knew him and loved him. He could be as gentle as a hummingbird, as mean as a scorpion. He defined our state in terms of its rural heritage and made us proud of what we had accomplished.'

'Did Dobie ever write anything of national importance?' Garza asked, and Quimper snapped: 'He did a damned sight better. Carried the culture of Texas overseas to Cambridge University, where he was a star. But he also had strong feelings about the long-term welfare of the state. And that infuriated my father. I remember him roaring one night: 'Until we get rid of that communist sumbitch Frank Dobie we'll never have a safe university." As a fellow regent, let me advise you on one thing. The phrase *a safe university*'s a contradiction, because a real university must question everything, but with my old man ridin' herd, few professors dared.'

He laughed and suggested that perhaps Garza might like a fire, so big mesquite logs were dragged in by two Mexican workers, and soon the unique aroma that made mesquite barbecue so flavorful permeated the room, and talk grew more casual: 'The things my old man said! At the height of his battle with Dobie he told me: "The faculty should accept the buildings we give them and keep their mouths shut." And how about the time he told the reporters: "The University of Texas has one overriding obligation. To turn out football teams of which the state can be proud." '

'Your father fire Dobie?'

'Yep. And muzzled Webb, two of the most original performers our university ever produced.' He leaned far back in his chair, studied the mesquite flames, and reflected on a problem which had agitated him of late: 'If our Southern sisters to the east have produced this outpouring of fine writers – Eudora Welty, William Faulkner, Robert Penn Warrn, Truman Capote, Tennessee Williams, Thomas Wolfe, Flannery O'Connor, I can never remember whether she's a woman or he's a man – why have we produced only one? Katherine Anne Porter?'

He knew part of the answer: 'Texas was a true frontier, right down to 1920. We were far removed from east-west routes of travel, and we offered damn little to the north-south travelers. When a man in 1840 or a woman in 1860 crossed the plains up north, what did they find? Thriving places like California and Oregon. You cross Texas and what do you face? The deserts of New Mexico and Arizona. The empty cactus lands of northern Mexico. Also, the railroads reached us pathetically late. In those years when European artists were crossing Wyoming as a matter of course on powerful continental trains, Texas had a couple of rural stations.'

Pouring Garza a drink, he asked: 'You know much about Austin? You'll love it. Marvelous town. But it's failed to produce the artists and thinkers it should have. Somehow we were cheated.' He thought about this for some moments, then growled: 'But damnit, with your help we can catch up.'

Mayor Garza took from his pocket a confidential report supplied him by the university, and as he studied it by the light of the mesquite fire, he thought: How strange that Lorenzo Quimper should be telling me about the devastation his father had wrought!

And it was strange, because the secret report told how Lorenzo, this redneck who played the loudmouth buffoon, had, when he became a regent in 1978, initiated at his own expense a study comparing salaries at Texas with those at first-class state universities like North Carolina, Wisconsin and California, and what he learned disgusted him: 'We pay twenty thousand dollars, thirty thousand less than they pay their top chairs. What in hell is wrong with Texas?'

With guidance from a thoughtful administration, he had visited many graduates of the university who had profited from the education it had provided them: 'Herman, the great power that the state of Texas is accumulatin', and the wealth our university commands means nothin' if we don't use that power constructively.' All agreed with this, for the clever application of power was a Texas tradition. 'So what I'm recommendin', and I'll need your help, fellows like you who've struck it rich. Give us five hundred thousand dollars to endow a chair in your name. The Herman Kallheimer Chair in Jurisprudence. And if you have an associate who can't handle that amount, he can give us a hundred thousand to provide extra funds for some good professor at the lower levels.' All across the state he had moved, appealing to what he called 'The National Pride of Loyal Texans,' and he succeeded in amassing funds for seventy-six full endowments and for five hundred twenty lesser supports.

Garza looked across the top of his paper at the inscrutable man staring into the fire: the big hat beside the chair, the expensive whipcord suit, the wide leather belt with brass buckle in front showing the state of Texas and the bold engraving Garza had seen on the back, IL MAGNIFICO. The man conformed in no way to the data on the paper, and Garza raised the question: 'This report says that in a relatively short period you provided the administration with an unexpected forty-two million dollars for upgrading teachers' salaries. With that kind of money, we can have one of the best faculties in America.'

Quimper downplayed his contribution: 'In my principal mission I've failed.'

'I don't call a sum like that failure.'

'It's those damned clowns out on the prairie. They'll give unlimited endowments for the Law School. Same for the School of Business and Science. Or the geology of oil. But not a thin dime for poetry, or drama, or fine arts, or English, or philosophy, or history. That young professor who came to see me after our last meeting was right. We've established a university for the trainin' of technicians. The work of the spirit, to hell with that.'

As soon as he said these words he realized that he was condemning himself and, especially, his father: 'It was us Quimpers who set the style. Frank Dobie asked questions about ultimate values, so kick him to hell out. Walter Webb asked about the sources of Texas power, so move him gently to one side. I bear a heavy burden.'

As they talked an ember fell from the fire, and since Quimper was at the portable bar pouring a drink, Garza grabbed the poker to push back the flaming mesquite, but as he did so he noticed the curious shape of the poker. It was, to his surprise, a branding iron such as cattlemen used to mark their cattle, and when he brought the business end forward to study it, he found that it consisted of a four-inch letter U, inside which rested a neatly forged T.

He was about to ask what this meant when Quimper reached for the brand, waved it about in his left hand, and said, with impressive emotion: 'This represents one of the highlights of my life.'

'Your first cattle brand? What do the letters signify?'

'Mayor Garza! That's the University of Texas.' And he proceeded to unfold a story so improbable that Garza sat riveted: 'When my father enrolled at the university, there was a kind of secret society – all the important men on campus, those judged to be winners. There were arcane rites, secret handgrips . . . all that stuff. Father was a member, of course. One of the proudest achievements of his life.'

'What did the society do?'

'Defend the honor of the university. And they had a unique initiation rite, which the university made them abandon in 1944 when a student's life was endangered. By the time I entered in 1949 that special deal was long gone.'

'What was it?'

Quimper ignored the question, laid aside the brand, and gazed intently at Garza: 'I was a sophomore when they took me in. Paddling . . . a little drinking . . . you know, the usual. And I'll confess I was very proud. But when I'd been a member about six months my father and three big wheels here in Austin, judges, banker, you know, all graduates of the university, they invited me to a posh dinner, then drove me out to a lonely spot on the shores of Lake Travis, a rather wild spot, where they built quite a large fire.'

He stopped talking, took a swallow of his drink, and stared once more at Garza: 'When the fire was extremely hot, they placed this brand, this one here, in it. Then they spread-eagled me on the ground, tied my arms and legs to stakes they'd driven in the earth, ripped off my shirt, and branded me on the chest with that brand over there.'

Garza gasped: 'You're kiddin'.'

Slowly, as if he were a priest conducting a ritual, Quimper opened his shirt revealing a powerful chest on which was a deeply imbedded T.

'Is that a tattoo?' Garza asked, to which Quimper replied forcefully: 'No! It's a brand, like you brand cattle. And when it was burned in, my father rubbed it with salt so as to make a real scar, like they do after those duels in Heidelberg, and he told me in awed tones: "Now you're really one of us. Each of us carries the same brand." ' He reached for the brand, placed it against his chest, and allowed Garza to satisfy himself that the conformance was perfect.

Rebuttoning his shirt, he said: 'As you move about Texas you'll come upon many men in their sixties who carry this secret brand under their vested suits. Leaders of the state. We never speak of it. Never reveal who else carries it. But I will tell you this. At the regents' meeting tomorrow, I won't be the only one hiding it.' He paused: 'My father told me that night by the lake as he rubbed in the salt: "I'd not want to have a son who didn't carry over his heart the badge of the university." He loved the place you're about to help govern. And so do I.'

The night grew late, and he told Mayor Garza: 'We've needed you on our board for some years. Talk sense to us. Support the good proposals.' He sounded like a philosopher.

But next morning, when he drove Garza onto the campus and saw the poster announcing that next week the university baseball team would play A&M, he reverted to type. Once more he became the florid, beefy, extroverted Texas rancher whom the undergraduates would noisily toast as the fifth inning came to a close: 'Il Magnifico ... the Bottom of the Fifth,' with the leader finishing off a bottle of whiskey. He hoped they would smother A&M.

Chuckling, he asked Garza: 'You ever hear about the time some years back when the state decided to make A&M a full-fledged university? Dreadful mistake. Ambitious A&M alumni wanted to upgrade the name of their town, College Station, to something more exalted. So I offered a hundred-dollar prize for the most appropriate suggestion. The winner? Malfunction Junction. A&M officials were not amused.'

Then he confided: 'Actually, I think it's a fine school. I help it whenever I can. But our board expects me to turn up at every meeting with a new Aggie joke, and this time I have a zinger.'

So after Mayor Garza had been introduced to warm applause, for the regents were relieved to have the Hispanic barrier broken, Quimper said:

'This Aggie was infuriated by the way people in Texas downgraded him and he consulted a counselor, who advised: "Best way in the world to demonstrate intellectual superiority is to salt and pepper your conversation with French phrases." So off he goes to Paris to a tutoring school, and on the day of his return he marches boldly into the best store in Austin and says: "Garcon, I would like some paté de fois gras avec poivre, four croissants, a coq-au-vin, and a bottle of champagne trés, trés sec."

'The clerk looks up and asks: "When did you go to A&M?" and the former Aggie sobs: "How did you know?" and the clerk says: "Son, this is a hardware store." ' '

He had barely stopped receiving congratulations on his latest masterpiece when a folded note was passed along the table to him:

> I don't think Aggie jokes are funny. My brother teaches there and says it's a fine school. Next you'll be telling Mexican jokes, and I won't like that, either.
>
> Your new friend,
> Simón Garza

Quimper flushed, recognized the propriety of this complaint, and concluded that the new regent was not going to be anybody's pushover. Bringing his palms together under his chin in the Buddhist gesture of deference, he nodded to his friend of the previous evening, then, using his right thumb in a gesture of cutting his throat, he indicated that there would be no more Aggie jokes.

Then he submitted his report as chairman of the finance committee, informing his colleagues that with the unexpected increase in oil prices, Texas now had a much higher return on its endowment than places like Harvard and Stanford: 'This has enabled us to bring onto our faculty winners of the Nobel Prize, outstanding figures in science like John Wheeler of Princeton, and a whole bevy of notable experts in law and business. We're headin' for the very top ranks of academia and will not be denied.'

As for the other financial aspects, he said: 'Like the comedian, I have good news and bad news. The good news is that the program we launched to underwrite our professors has enjoyed amazin' success. As of today we have no room to accept any more five-hundred-thousand-dollar endowments in law, business or science, because all the chairs have been funded.' This brought applause from the board, some of whose members had funded endowments.

'The bad news is that we have not received one endowment in the liberal arts such as English, poetry and philosophy.' Allowing time for this striking news to percolate, he added: 'I've argued fruitlessly with successful lawyers and business-men, till my tongue has cleaved to the roof of my mouth, remindin' them that they are able to succeed in life not because of the technical trainin' they received at our university but because of the solid instruction they had in the meanin' of life ... in their basic courses in the liberal arts. They haven't understood a word I said.

'Gentlemen and ladies, if this continues, the great univer-sities of Texas are goin' to become trade schools, places to train mechanics, centers for the crunchin' of numbers on computers. The ideas which will govern our society will be delivered to us from Harvard and Oxford and the Sorbonne.'

He became eloquent, Texas-ranch style, in defending those values which his father had outlawed, and after prolonged discussion he said: 'I'll tell you what I'm goin' to do. I'm goin' to accept ever' one of the proposed contributions for additional endowments in law and business and divert 'em to the humanities.'

'But, Lorenzo,' a cautious regent asked, 'what will you tell the donors?' and without hesitation he snapped: 'I'll lie.'

'I think we'd better consider this,' a lawyer said, and the others laughed, but Quimper silenced them: 'I feel so strong about this that I am herewith establishin' full endowments, half a million each, for two chairs, one in philosophy, one in poetry.'

It was in this spirit that Regent Quimper, Il Magnifico, started to reverse the damage done by his father, that inspired builder of the university campus.

When Maggie Morrison, forty-seven years old, discovered how easy it was to borrow large sums of money in Texas, especially from big oilmen, she studied the real estate market in Houston with special care and learned that after the savage devaluation of the Mexican peso many fine buildings were near bankruptcy, so that remarkable bargains were available, but only if one had faith that the market would rebound. She had that faith.

Her fourteen years in what Houstonians like to call 'our go-go town' had almost obliterated memories of Detroit. She no longer made comparisons between Michigan and Texas, being content to accept her new home as *sui generis*, obedient only to its own rules. She had grown to like Western dress, the informality of social life, the Texas brag, and she positively adored Mexican food, especially the tang of fresh chile relleno or a really well-made enchilada. And her affection for Houston itself had grown solidly, so that when the figures for the 1980 census were extrapolated to 1981, she found positive joy in learning that Houston was now the fourth largest city in the United States, having displaced Philadelphia, with every prospect of surpassing Chicago before the century ended.

But as she studied the economy, deluding herself on nothing, she learned that as of now Houston was in sad shape: The oil business, kerplunk! The hotel business, what with the Mexican millionaires staying home, likewise kerplunk! She conducted one survey which indicated that some of those huge new splashy hotels could produce only a twenty-percent occupancy, which meant that if help did not arrive from somewhere and soon, they too would go bankrupt.

Even more depressing was the fact that Houston's unoccupied office space had now grown to 43,000,000 square feet: 'The builders have built too much, too fast, with funds that carried too high a rate of interest. With mortgages at seventeen percent, somebody must go broke.'

Wherever she looked she found telltale signs of the city's perilous position. The big oil companies were cutting back on personnel; the little ones were solving that problem more simply: they were in bankruptcy. And this sent echoes throughout the business community, as leasing experts closed shop, drilling rigs were sold for ten cents on the dollar, and banks foreclosed loans. Registration at local colleges dropped because parents could not scrape together the tuition, and retail stores began to lay off salespeople.

But the crunch that interested Maggie was the one in real

estate, and in the late afternoons when she sat in the fifteenth-floor condominium overlooking Buffalo Bayou, her attention focused on that splendid set of tall buildings erected by Gabe Klinowitz's Mexican politicians – The Ramparts. Their wraparound glass facing shone in the sunset, but they were only fifteen percent occupied; had rentals continued at the spectacular levels of 1980 the Mexicans would have made a killing, but now they faced disaster. 'I'm sure they have at least a hundred and seventy million dollars in the three towers,' Maggie had told her husband, but he was so involved with Roy Bub Hooker in their exotic-game ranch that he could not pay full attention to the interesting proposal she was making, so she sat alone and stared at the mesmerizing target.

One night as the moon shone on the shimmering glass she made up her mind, and early next morning she dressed in her best business suit and flew up to Dallas: 'The poor Mexicans have this enormous investment, Mr Rusk . . . '

'Never feel sorry for the other guy. If he's made an ass of himself, gig him while he's bent over.'

'There's no way they can diminish their debt, and they may be paying as high as nineteen-percent interest.'

'You're sure they have a hundred and seventy million in it? What would they listen to? If we bailed them out?'

'I have a gut feeling we could get it for fifty million, maybe even forty.'

'See what you can do.'

She returned to Houston with a tentative deal much like the one before, for Rusk had said: 'Maggie, I'll chip in as much as thirteen million if you add your two. But you must convince the Houston banks to lend us the rest at a decent interest.'

Her first job was to confront the Mexicans with their perilous situation and convince them that in bankruptcy they might lose everything. Wearing her gentlest and most feminine clothes, she minimized the staggering difference between the $170,000,000 they had obligated themselves to pay and the mere $40,000,000 she was offering, and quietly she assured them that they had no reasonable alternative: 'Besides, gentlemen, as you and I well know, a great deal of what you call your loss is paper money only. This is a drying out of the market, and if you'd had your funds in oil, you'd have lost even more.'

With the banks she was soft-spoken but relentless: 'What alternative have you? Your loans are bust, but so are the ones you have in oil. Help my partner and me to refinance this disaster and you'll get back more than you had a right to expect.'

Just when she had everyone on the edge of the chair, each ready to jump forward if the others did, Beth announced that she was going to have a baby, and so Maggie dropped her negotiations for about a week, leaving Mexicans, Houston bankers and Ransom Rusk dangling; she had not planned it this way, but it was the cleverest move she could have made, for by the time she returned to the bargaining table, all the players would be nervously eager to reach a decision. Said one banker: 'Trust a woman to play a trick like this. We could use her on our board.'

But Maggie did not engage in tricks. For several years now, she had been aware that she was a much stronger person than her husband, much more attuned to the pressures and responsibilities of Houston finance; although she would never express it in this arrogant manner, she had character and he did not. If these delicate negotiations regarding The Ramparts evolved as she hoped, she would back them with every penny of her small fortune, every minute of her working life. Her deal would be meticulously honest and as fair to each participant as the exigencies of the economic situation allowed. She wanted a just share of the profits, but was prepared to suffer her share of the loss if her calculations were in error. A Michigan schoolteacher who believed in George Eliot had become a Texas manipulator who believed in Adam Smith.

In growing into this status, she was conscious of how far behind she had left her breezy, glib-speaking husband: he played at games; she juggled with empires. He had been a good husband and a better father, but she could not escape realizing that under pressure he had revealed himself as a shifty, small-caliber man. She hoped he would stay out of trouble and hold on to some of the easy money he had made, but on neither point was she confident.

And finally the tears came. Toughened in the brutal world of Houston real estate, she had not allowed herself this indulgence since weeping with joy at Beth's wedding to Wolfgang Macnab, but now that she reviewed her own life with Todd, remembering how it had started with such love and mutuality, she could not ignore the sad loss she had suffered: Oh, Todd! We should have done much better! And in this lament she generously took upon herself, improperly, half the blame.

While the Mexican politicians and the Texas businessmen fretted, she spent her days with her daughter, talking about marriage, and children, and responsibility, and one afternoon when Beth was visiting her mother, Maggie called her attention to The Ramparts: 'The buildings are not only beautiful, Beth. They're in excellent physical condition. But they're only fifteen-percent occupied. Frozen tears. Monuments to dreams gone wrong.'

'Mummy, why would you want to get mixed up with such a failure?'

'Because I'm convinced that Houston is the liveliest spot in America. Because I know it's bound to snap back.'

'But if you know this, don't you think they know it, too?'

'Yes, but I'm the one that has faith.'

'Are you gambling all your money on these towers?'

The two women looked at the shimmering beauty of The Ramparts, admiring the subtle manner in which the three spires formed a unit, with the curve of one iridescent expanse linking with the other two and complementing them. They formed a work of art, Houston modern, and Maggie would be proud to be its owner if she could acquire it, as seemed likely, at twenty-four cents on the dollar.

'Are you doing this out of vanity, Mummy?'

Maggie pondered this. It was exciting to operate in what had been considered a man's field and to perform rather better than most of the men; of course she felt proud of her achievements. And it was breathtaking to gamble with such large funds, hers and other people's, and she was prepared to acknowledge this to her daughter, but at this critical time in both their lives she felt it improper to operate from such trivial and almost degrading impulses.

'Beth, you really do like Texas, don't you?'

'I'm in love with it. I can't even remember Detroit.'

'Do you want to remember?'

'No! This is freedom, excitement, the future. Wolfgang and I see unlimited possibilities. I don't mean life in the fast lane, or any of that nonsense. But a man like Wolfgang, with me beside him, he can do anything from a Texas base. Anything.'

'I feel the same way, Beth.'

'But Daddy isn't at your side.'

'No, he isn't.'

They dropped that subject, and after a while Maggie confided: 'I'm gambling most of my savings.' Before Beth could reprimand her, she took her daughter's hands: 'But do you think your mother . . . you know me . . . how cautious I am. Do you think I'd take such a gamble blind?'

'I'm not sure I know you any more.'

'Look at yourself. The way you were when we came down here. Lady poet and all that. Then lady baton twirler. Now lady socialite. I don't know you.' Quickly she added: 'But I'm very proud of you just as you are. Resplendent transformation.'

'What safeguards have you, Mother?'

'Mr Rusk is in this with me, and we'd be out of our minds to buy that turkey.' She flipped a thumb contemptuously at the towers: 'We could never make it pay . . . all that unrented space.'

'My conclusion too. All that glass with nothing behind it.'

'However!' And here Maggie smiled. 'I've found a group of potential buyers. Canadians. They have a hotel chain behind them. They believe that if they can get title at a low enough figure, they can install an operation that will pay out.'

'Why don't they buy it themselves?'

'Because they need someone like me to honcho the details.'

'If the second tier of deals works, do you make a bundle?'

'You always phrased things delicately, Beth. Yes.'

'And if you can't unload to the unknown buyers and the hotel chain . . .'

'Now wait. The hotel chain puts up no money. Just a managerial contract, but a very enticing one, I must say.'

'How do you know about the contract?'

Maggie Morrison smiled softly: 'Oftentimes, Beth, a dumb-looking peasant from Detroit can learn things a billionaire like Ransom Rusk could never learn.'

'But if your clever plan falls flat? If your secret buyers drop out?'

'I lose everything.' In the silence Beth looked across to the glorious towers; they seemed almost to sway with the wind, and she understood why her mother would find exhilaration in this game of Houston roulette, and she understood her gambling everything on such a precarious toss, but then her mother said: 'I wouldn't lose everything. We'll be buying this for twenty-four cents on the dollar. If we did have to bail out, we could probably get back eighteen cents.'

When Maggie turned her attention from her pregnant daughter to the long-pregnant purchase of The Ramparts, she found the other players almost thirsting to conclude the deal, so she finished things off with a flourish. For $42,000,000 she acquired buildings worth $170,000,000, and she and Rusk had had to ante up only $12,000,000 between them, the banks being happy to carry the rest. Even the Mexican politicians showed relief: 'Only paper money, as you said. We feared we might lose it all.'

In July 1983, when things were looking slightly better in Houston, she sold The Ramparts to the well-heeled Canadians who would convert the top floors of the buildings into superpenthouses for their wives. The price that Maggie was able to swing for this part of the deal was $62,000,000, which meant that she and Rusk had picked up $20,000,000 for about a year's work. Generously, he split this fifty-fifty with Maggie, telling her that it was the traditional finder's fee.

When the sale was completed – *finalized*, in Houston jargon – Maggie took Beth to a victory lunch: 'Why did I risk so much? I wanted to give you and Lonnie the best start possible in Texas life. I'm afraid your father will lose everything with his exotic ranch.'

'Mummy! Wolfgang and I earn a good living. Far beyond what I dreamed.'

'For the time being. Linebackers don't last forever.'

This meeting occurred in August of 1983 and as it ended, the television in the posh restaurant was broadcasting continuous alerts regarding the first hurricane of the season, Alicia, which stormed about in the Gulf, with winds exceeding a hundred and twenty miles an hour, presumably heading toward Galveston. The two women stopped to listen, and Maggie, who studied such storms because they could influence real estate values, said:

'Poor Galveston. In 1900 it was wiped out by a storm like this.'

'I've heard about it. Was it bad?'

'Are you kidding? Six thousand drowned. Worst natural disaster in American history.' When Beth gasped, she added, professionally: 'But they built a seawall afterward, and it's been impregnable.'

'I would hope so,' Beth said.

During the next two days Maggie followed the tropical storm, but only casually, for the winds dropped to a relatively safe eighty miles an hour, which the Texas coast had learned to cope with. She had almost forgotten the threat when the storm stopped dead, about fifty miles offshore, and whirled about upon itself, as if uncertain where to land.

Now those who understood the rudiments of tropical storms became apprehensive, for this stationary whirling meant that the eye of the storm was picking up terrible velocities, perhaps as much as a hundred and sixty miles an hour, and with such accumulated force the hurricane could be a killer wherever it crashed ashore . . . and it did head for Galveston.

By the grace of a compassionate nature, the wild storm veered off during the final moments of its approach to land and struck a relatively unpopulated area of the beach, so that instead of killing thousands as it might have done, it killed only twenty. With a sigh, Galveston went to its churches and gave thanks for yet another salvation. The great storm of 1983 with its violent winds had passed inland.

Through a curious trick of the winds aloft, when it was well past the coast it turned back on itself and struck Houston, not from the east as might have been anticipated, but from the southwest, and as it came roaring in at velocities no architect or builder had foreseen, it began to whip around the tall buildings, creating powerful currents not experienced before.

Now the lovely architecture of Houston, those spires challenging the sky, those castles of glass so brilliant in the rising or setting sun, were subjected to a tremendous battering, and one by one the window panes began to shatter. Glass from one building would somersault through the air and smash into the glass of an adjacent building, which would in turn throw its panes toward another.

Maggie Morrison, hearing of the savage effects of the storm, went outside, against the advice of everyone, to see at close hand what was happening to The Ramparts, for which she felt a custodian's responsibility even though the buildings were no longer hers. Finding partial refuge behind a concrete abutment, she watched in anguish as the fantastic winds struck at the towers.

'Pray God they hold!' she whispered as the climax of the hurricane struck, and she drew breath again when she saw that although they swayed, as Beth had imagined them to do that afternoon, they behaved with grace and dignity, bending slightly but not surrendering. 'Thank God,' she sighed.

However, when the winds at this great velocity passed around the curved expanse of the three buildings, it acquired that capacity which lifts an airplane – a kind of venturi effect as when material of any kind is constricted and flows faster – and on the far side of the buildings, away from the frontal force of the gale, the wind began to suck out the windows, popping them outward from their frames, and as they fell to the streets below, they formed a delicate, deadly shower of glass, millions of shards, little and big, clattering to the asphalt streets and the cement pavements, maiming any who stood in the way, covering the passageways with icicles that would never melt.

Oh God! Look at my buildings! She stood behind her refuge, her fingers across her face in such a manner as to allow her to see the devastation, and as the glass showered down around her, missing her miraculously with its lethal chunks, she wept for the tragedy of which she was not really a part but for which she felt a personal responsibility.

Standing in the howling wind and the falling glass, she wept for the broken dreams of the oilmen she knew whose world had collapsed; she cried for all the recently unemployed, many of whom had given up everything in the North to move to the lure of steady work in Houston; she sobbed for the Mexicans who had gambled so heavily and seen the ground swept from under them; and she felt particular sorrow for the Canadians who had purchased these buildings three weeks ago. The Ramparts, with their empty rooms and shattered façade, were the responsibility of the new buyers – of that there was not the slightest doubt – but she had escaped this disaster by only twenty days, and had she been dilatory in her manipulations, she would have borne the full weight of this catastrophe.

In the storm she wept for all those in Texas whose great gambles came crashing down.

'This could be the most dangerous road in America,' Ranger Cletus Macnab said to his tall, hefty brother as they sped southwest from Fort Stockton toward the pair of little border towns which faced each other across the Rio Grande, Polk in Texas, Carlota across the rickety bridge in Chihuahua.

'Doesn't look too bad to me,' Wolfgang said, nor did it: a solid macadam roadway no narrower than most secondaries, bleak plains east and west, with cautionary white flood gauges at the dips where a bridge would have been too costly for the relatively little use it would have gotten. Looking at the black warning marks, foot by foot, Wolfgang asked: 'Can a flood really rise thirteen feet through this land? Looks bone-dry.'

'When it flashes up in those hills, fifteen feet in ten minutes, and if you're caught in this hollow, farewell.'

'Is that what you mean, "the most dangerous in America"?'

'No! Sensible travelers learn to beware when they see rising water. Those warning poles are for tourists . . . like you.'

'Then why the danger?'

The Ranger, a very tall, thin man in his mid-thirties, wearing Texas boots, a fawn-gray whipcord ranch suit and the inevitable Stetson, pointed to a car speeding south ahead of them: 'On this road I would stop that car only with the greatest caution, Wolfgang. And if I saw it stalled over on the shoulder, I'd approach it only with drawn gun, expecting trouble.'

'Why that particular car?'

'On this road, any car, watch out. Chances are it's been stolen up north. That one's from Minnesota, so what in hell is it doing on this road? I'll tell you what. Some goon has stolen it up there, late-model Buick, and is high-tailing it to Mexico to sell it for a million.'

'Is there a market?'

'Are you kidding? They caught the head of a Mexican police agency, fronting for an organization of hundreds, buying stolen American cars all along the border, changing numbers, repainting, selling them all over Mexico at outrageous prices.

So if I try to stop them, they shoot.'

'If it's known, why don't they . . . ? Did they throw the police chief in jail?'

'What do you think? We're approaching northern Mexico, a world unto itself, a law unto itself.'

'So you steer clear of cars heading south?'

'And on this road, cars heading north, too.' He indicated a low-slung, modified Pontiac roaring north with Kansas plates. 'Probably loaded with marijuana or cocaine.' He studied the car as it whizzed past. 'If they are running the stuff, they'll give me a gun battle.'

'So what do you do?'

'I notify Narcotics farther along the line. They intercept them with machine guns.' And he cranked up his police radio: 'Vic, Macnab. Nineteen eighty-two Pontiac four-door. Kansas plates ending seven two one. Heading north on US Sixty-nine.'

'And I suppose many of the northbound cars carry wetbacks?'

'We don't bother with them.'

'Why not? If they're illegal?'

'Border Patrol has charge of that. So we let them handle it.' He hesitated: 'Of course, if a wetback commits any kind of crime . . .'

'They give you much trouble?'

'In the old days, almost never. Today, a more vicious element moving in. They rob. Now and then a murder. But we can track them pretty easy.'

Wolfgang, four years younger than his brother, a mite taller at six-seven and much heavier, reflected on this strange state of affairs, then said: 'Grampop Oscar would go out of his mind if he heard how you were running the show. Remember how he hated Meskins, how he ordered them around?'

'All that's changed, Wolfgang. I work very closely with Mexican officials on the other side of the river.' Before his brother could reply, the Ranger added: 'Couldn't do my job without their help.'

When they approached the dip that would carry them down to the Rio Grande, Cletus slowed the car and said gravely: 'Wolfgang, you sure you want to go the rest of the way? This isn't for fun, you know.'

'I asked you to come, didn't I?'

'True, but once across that bridge . . .'

'That's the part I want to see.'

'So be it, little brother. Here we go.'

They dropped in to the American town of Polk, named after the Tennessee president who had fought so valiantly to bring Texas into the Union; it was a miserable testimony to a great leader, a town of sixteen hundred persons living for the most part in crumbling Mexican-style adobe huts. The town's chief fame derived from summer weather reports: 'And once again the hottest spot in these United States – Polk, Texas, down on the Rio Grande, a hundred and nine degrees.'

But to those who appreciated the Southwest, and the Macnab brothers did, this town, like its sisters along the river, had a persuasive charm: 'Reminds me of how it must have been in 1840. I love these dusty streets, the Mexican women peerin' at me through the shutters, the dogs chasin' their fleas.'

'I wouldn't be able to tell this was the US of A,' Wolfgang said.

'It isn't,' the Ranger said. 'It's something new. Maybe one day we'll call it Texico.'

'That's a gasoline.'

'No more flammable than this.'

Cletus did not stop in Polk, for he wanted as few people as possible to know he was on the prowl, and at the international bridge, a sorry affair, the customs people, American and Mexican alike, waved him through without an inspection or a question. This confidence in his trustworthiness was a tribute to the years of patient work he had performed along the border: 'I have never failed to accept the word of one of my counterparts here in Mexico. If they say a ma I've arrested is a good citizen, in momentary trouble across the river, I drive him down here and kick his ass back into Mexico. They do the same with me if some college yahoo gets into big trouble down in Chihuahua. We live and let live, and they've never gigged me on a heroin shipment or anything like that, so I let their cattle cross, if there aren't too many and if they pick some spot well hidden and away from the bridges.'

Once safely within Carlota, named for the tragic young bride of the Emperor Maximilian, who had been executed by firing squad in 1867, he drove by circuitous back streets to the office of the chief of police. As was so often the case, the Mexican town was much prettier than the American, and bigger too, with a sense of going forward while the American seemed to be slipping backward.

'Officer Macnab,' the Mexican jefe said in Spanish, 'we have not seen the plane ...' He stopped, gaped, pointed at the Ranger's brother, and cried: 'Wolfman Macnab! Linebacker! Dallas Cowboys!' When his discovery was confirmed, all work in the office halted, as men and women gathered around to question the rocklike man they had seen so often on the American television shows transmitted into Mexico. They wanted to know what he thought of the Pittsburgh and Miami and Oakland teams, and they especially wanted to hear about that covey of wild linebackers which the press had labeled 'The Dallas Zoo.'

'Well,' he explained, always delighted to talk football with real aficionados, 'we are three pretty tough guys, but the league is full of men like us. What makes us different, our names. They call me Wolfman, Rumsey they call the Gorilla, then Joe Polar, you can guess his name.' Many of the Mexicans could speak English and they translated this jargon to those who couldn't, after which one woman asked in Spanish: 'Is it true, you take the Gorilla to away-games in a cage?' and he assured her: 'He could break your arm like this,' and for three days she would feel the pressure of his hands.

'All-American at Texas?' one of the officers asked, and he replied truthfully: 'One evening newspaper – Wichita Falls, I think it was – they nominated me for All-American. Nobody else, because in my junior year I weighed only two-twenty and opposing offensive tackles ate me up. But in my biography, circulated by the Cowboys, it says clear as day "Consensus All-American," like as if all the papers in the country hailed me.'

'But in the pros? You have been All-Pro five times?'

'Six, and if I make it this year, maybe my last season.'

'Oh, no!' the men protested, but a woman clerk said in great admiration: 'You want to get on with your art, don't you?' and he nodded to her as if she were a duchess.

The men now asked: 'Is it true? You're an artist?' The Dallas management had made so much of this that his skill was known

1444

even in distant Carlota, and on the spur of the moment he reached for a pencil and a sheet of paper and completed a good likeness of the woman who had asked the question. As the men applauded the speed and dexterity with which he drew, he asked in English: 'How do you say "To a Beautiful Lady"?' and a would-be poet in the group said: 'A una princesa bellisima,' and as they spelled the words for him he wrote them down and handed the portrait to the woman, who began to sniffle.

'Shall we proceed?' the jefe asked, and when Cletus nodded, the Mexican indicated two assistants, who procured a veritable battery of guns and a load of ammunition, which they piled into a battered Land Rover.

Since it was some hours before darkness, they drove far south of Carlota to a small cantina, where they had a delicious meal of hot chili and freshly made tamales. As they ate, Cletus explained the situation: 'We got word two nights ago. Thieves in La Junta, Colorado, we have reason to think they're part of a cocaine ring, stole a Beechcraft, two-engine job, flew right down the New Mexico-Texas border, well west of detectors at Fort Stockton, and into Mexico, south and east of here to that field they've used before.'

'The one on the high plateau south of the canyons?'

'The same. From clues we picked up, they've got to be there, because their gas supply won't permit them to go any farther south. And we believe they'll try to make their return flight after dark tonight.'

'Do you want them, or the cocaine, or the plane?'

'Reverse order. Plane first, the drugs, whatever they are, next, them last.'

'So if we have to shoot?'

'We shoot. We do not let them lift that plane off the ground. My brother and I fly that plane north. This hijacking has got to stop.'

'Understood,' the jefe said. Then he asked a curious question: 'Macnab, can you assure me? I mean, these are American citizens, not Mexicans?'

'I give you my word, the three airplane men are Americans. Anglo-Saxons, not even Spanish names. The ground men, supplying them, of course they're your turkeys.'

'We'll take care of them, the bastards. But we must not have

Rinches killing Mexicans, not any more.'

'Compade,' Macnab said, placing his arms about the jefe, 'my usefulness along this border is destroyed if I kill even one Mexican chicken, let alone a smuggler.'

'I know that, Macnab. So you promise not to shoot at the ground crew?'

'Promise.'

They drove slowly away from the setting sun, trying not to throw dust, and at about nine they dismounted, crept through the low grass, and came to a secluded field on which sat the stolen Beechcraft, shimmering, loading doors open in the moonlight. The three American smugglers, easily identified, were directing the loading of their plane, and it was apparently going to carry a maximum cargo of two types: large bales, probably of marijuana, and smaller packages, most likely of heroin or cocaine. Cletus, watching the care with which they stowed the stuff, whispered to his brother: 'Like they always say, "with a street value of millions." This batch will not hit the street.'

When the plane was fully loaded, the jefe gave the signal and his men ran toward the field, firing high so that the Mexican suppliers could escape, but Cletus ran right for the plane, guns blazing but with no intent to kill. The American smugglers, frightened by the thunder of gunfire from what seemed all sides, started to fire back, then turned, dodged, and ran to a truck, which whisked them into the night.

As soon as they were gone – no one dead – the Mexican policemen ringed the plane to prevent counterattack while the Macnab brothers scrambled into the pilots' seats. The Mexican officer closed the door and waved, whereupon Cletus opened his window and shouted : 'Send my car to Alpine, like before,' and the officer saluted.

With a skill that amazed Wolfgang, his brother wheeled the plane about, revved the engines to a roar, checked the brakes, and took off into the night: 'Clean operation, kiddo. I could have killed one or two of those bastards, but I shot late. It would mean a lot of paperwork for the jefe. We'll catch them up north one of these nights.'

'Are you disappointed?'

'We got the plane. We got the cargo. "Who could ask for

anything more? " ' "

Their course back to the American airfield at Alpine required them to fly directly across those hidden, unknown canyons of the Rio Grande east of Polk-Carlota, and in the silvery night Wolfgang saw that marvelous display of deep rifts in the earth, tortuous river passages and sheer-walled cliffs that seemed to drop a thousand feet. This was the unknown Texas, the wild frontier unchanged in ten thousand years.

'That is something!' Wolfgang shouted, and his brother replied: 'I recapture about seven hijacked planes a year . . .'

'My God, why don't the police . . . ?'

'Who can protect all the American airfields? This plane came from La Junta, God forbid. It's the new rustling on the old frontier.' He flew in circles so that Wolfgang could catch an even better view of the great canyons: 'I like to check them out after each capture.'

When he landed the stolen plane at Alpine in the early dawn the Narcotics boys were on hand to confiscate the drugs and an insurance man was there to take possession of the plane, but Cletus was diverted from such matters by an urgent telephone call from the Ranger at Monahans, north of Fort Stockton: 'Cletus, woman clerk at the convenience store murdered. About eleven last night. Almost certain it was a wetback, headin' south.'

'Now take it easy. Before midnight? Get much cash? Peanuts, eh? But the woman's dead? Mack, my guess is he'll hitchhike to Stockton, catch that morning bus to Fort Davis, drop down to Marfa, then try to make it back to Carlota, like they all do. I'll intercept the bus.'

'We've got to catch this bastard, 'cause she was a fine kid.'

'We'll trail him to see if he made it to Stockton. We'll alert Marfa and the folks on the bridge at Polk. I think we can close in on this paisano.'

At great speed the Macnabs headed for Marfa, where they reached the bus stop fifteen minutes before the arrival of the Fort Davis special. As they waited, Cletus asked: 'You want to go aboard with me? In case he tries to run?'

'Why are you so sure he's coming this way?'

'Averages. We play the averages.'

It was agreed that the huge linebacker would accompany his

brother onto the bus, but behind, in hopes that his sheer size would cow the murderer. Cletus would keep his gun at the ready, but every precaution would be taken to avoid shooting.

'Here she comes!' Quietly, purposefully, the two Macnabs pushed aside those waiting for the bus, and as soon as the brakes took effect, sprang aboard like cats and moved immediately to the rear, where a very frightened wetback cowered in a corner of the back seat. Without touching his gun, Cletus said in good Spanish: 'All right, paisano. Game's up.' And when they frisked the man they found the murder weapon, the small amount of money from the store and two candy bars.

They were with the Marfa police for about three hours, making telephone calls back to Monahans and Fort Stockton, and as Macnab worked, rabid supporters of the Dallas Cowboys crowded about, and one man asked: 'It's confusin'. Sometimes they call you Wolfman, and other times it's the One-Man Gang.'

'Don't you see?' the star explained. 'They used both halves of my name. Wolf and Gang. Two for the price of one.'

It was obvious that the capture of a Mexican murderer on the main street was an event of some importance in Marfa, but to have a linebacker for the Dallas Cowboys in town, so close you could touch him, that was something to be remembered.

The sleepy brothers returned to Alpine to recover their car, and found that the Mexican driver from Carlota had delivered it safely; however, when Wolfgang inspected it he was appalled by its condition: 'Looks like a chain gang of sixty slaves had been ferried north,' and Cletus explained: 'The jefe down in Carlota, he probably loaded twenty wetbacks into that car. Cigarettes, sandwiches, tortillas.'

'For what?'

'To bring them up near the big road. The jefe probably got ten dollars a head, the driver five.'

'You allow that? Isn't that criminal?'

'Little brother, it's how we operate down here. Do you think I could go into Mexico, a Texas Ranger, and bring out a stolen airplane – no permission, no papers, no clearances – unless I gave them something in return?'

'But . . .'

'Little brother, you play a tough game, football. I play a

1448

tougher one, life and death, and when I go down there next time, it'll be the same. The jefe will shoot high so he doesn't kill any Mexicans. I'll shoot late so I don't muddy up the place with any American corpses. I'll get the plane, and the jefe will get twenty safe passages into the United States for his wetbacks on which he will pick up his usual *mordida*.'

'What's that?'

'The most useful word on the border. Means *little bite*. And sometimes not so little. It's the oil that makes Mexico run. Payola. Graft.'

'Isn't this entire scenario illegal?'

'Sure is, and if I spot my car coming north with those wetbacks, I'm supposed to arrest the lot and call the Border Patrol. But when the car comes through I arrange to be far distant. Never spotted it once.'

'That's a hell of a way to run a border.'

'It's the only way. Grampops would understand, and so would Old Otto. In fact, it's how they ran their border. And it's how my grandson will handle Polk and Carlota in his day. Because there will never be any other way.'

'To hell with Burma!' The speaker was Ransom Rusk sitting in his mansion in Larkin with a world atlas in his lap. He had been trying to determine what foreign country was a few square miles smaller than Texas, so that he could say in his next address to the Booster's Club: 'Texas is a country in itself, bigger than ... ' He had hoped it would be some prominent land like France, but that comparison would belittle Texas, which had 267,338 square miles, while France had a meager 211,207 and Spain a miserable 194,884. No, the true comparison was with Burma, which had 261,789. But who had heard of it?

Rechecking his figures, he slammed the atlas shut: Hell, the men in our club would think it was in Africa!

Africa was much on his mind these days, for he had spent his last three vacations in Kenya collecting trophies for his distinguished African Hall: elephant, eland, zebra. Of course he knew that Burma was not in Africa, but it pleased him to dismiss it in that insulting way: Who could imagine Burma giving Texas competition! Kills my whole point.

Fortunately, he had devised another way of making it, and now he took out the mimeographed sheets his secretary had prepared, one page for each man who would attend, and this study pleased him. It was an outline map of Texas, with five extreme points marked. El Paso, for example, stood at the farthest west, Brownsville farthest south, and radiating from each point in Texas thus identified were dotted lines to cities in the other fifty states and Mexico.

His figures were startling. The longest distance between two points in Texas was 801 miles, northwest Panhandle catty-corner to Brownsville at the southeast, and if you applied this dimension to the rest of the nation, you came up with some surprises:

If you stand at El Paso, you are much closer to Los Angeles than you are to the other side of Texas.

If you stand at the eastern side of Texas, you are much closer to Tampa than you are to El Paso.

If you stand in the Panhandle, you are closer to Bismarck, North Dakota, than you are to Brownsville.

And always remember, if you stand on the bridge at Brownsville, you are 801 miles to the edge of the Panhandle, but only 475 miles to Mexico City and 690 to Yucatán.

As he finished these comparisons, which showed certain Texas points closer to Chicago than to El Paso, he received an urgent phone call from Todd Morrison at the Allerkamp Exotic Game Ranch: 'If you fly down right away, I might have something rather interesting.' Accepting the challenge, he called for his Larkin pilot and within the hour was on his way to the Pedernales.

During the flight he tried to recall whether he had met Todd Morrison through Maggie or the other way around. All he knew was that he liked them both, him for his custodianship of the large game ranch, her for her aptitude in handling big real estate deals: The way she masterminded that Ramparts affair! Remarkable. She got us in at just the right time, then out three weeks before the hurricane. I don't know whether she's bright or lucky, but she's better than most men in handling money. He could think of half a dozen situations in which he could profitably use a woman with her skills.

But he was more interested in Todd Morrison, for the man had shown determination in putting together the ranch and in stocking it with some of the best animals in Texas: 'I've never known how much that other fellow, Roy Bub Hooker, has contributed, and I don't care, because I don't feel easy with him. You pay big money to shoot one of his animals, and he looks at you as if you'd shot his cousin.'

He thought that Todd had been wise in shifting his attention from real estate to ranch management: Anyone can make a buck in Houston, but it takes a real man to raise a buck in Fredericksburg. He chuckled: I like that. I'll use it sometime when I introduce him.

When the plane landed at the long paved strip which Morrison had built at the edge of the ranch, Rusk hurried out, called for his guns to be handed down, and joined the handsome graying fifty-two-year-old rancher: 'Hiya, good buddy. What's the big news?'

'Which animal – and maybe the best of all – have you consistently missed?'

'You mean the sable?'

'That's exactly what I mean.'

'You have one in the wild?'

'I do.'

'Your Mr Hooker told me the sables would never be turned loose.'

'He doesn't run the place. I do.'

'And you've decided that your herd . . . ? How many have you?'

'We have eight now. And we can certainly spare one of the bucks.'

'Where is he?'

'In the big field. With the rocks. You may search two days without finding him.'

'That's the challenge.'

They did not go out that first afternoon, because the guides warned that the light would fade so fast that no shots would be possible, and at supper in the old house that the German Allerkamps had built during the middle years of the last century, Rusk noticed that Roy Bub Hooker was not present.

Rusk decided not to ask about this, for the partners might have suffered a break, or maybe Morrison had bought the lesser man's shares.

Early in the morning Rusk, Morrison and two guides carefully opened the high iron gates protecting one of the pastures, then fastened it behind them. They were now in an area of about four thousand acres, completely fenced, in which a variety of African game animals existed in about the life style they would have followed on the veldt: the land was the same, the low trees were quite similar and similarly spaced, the occasional rocky tor was much like the kopje of South Africa, and the availability of water was identical. It was a splendid habitat, and splendid creatures roamed it, but to find them was extremely difficult.

'Believe me,' Ransom said, 'this isn't shooting fish in a rain barrel. This is work.' He looked askance when Morrison told him how many animals were in that huge enclosure: 'Sixty eland, I promise you. Big as horses, and we haven't seen one. And maybe we won't.' In fact, during the entire morning they saw only a few native Texas deer, and they were does protected from hunters except for a few days in late autumn.

At noon Morrison said: 'They'll be resting during the heat. You couldn't find a sable now with a magnet and a spyglass,' so the men went to the ranch house for chow, and in the afternoon they did see oryx and a couple of zebra, but no sign of the sable.

'You promise me he's in here?' Rusk asked, and Morrison said: 'On my oath. We checked him out before you came, helicopter. He's here.'

They did not find him that afternoon, even though they stayed within the high fencing till dusk, and when night fell they gathered at the lodge to swap yarns about hunting experiences in various parts of the world; it was the opinion of those who had been to the notable safari areas of Africa that the two big enclosures at Allerkamp provided both a terrain and a spirit almost identical with the best of the Dark Continent: 'Soil, hills, everything comparable. The fact that animals transported directly here from Kenya or the Kruger adjust with never a day's illness proves that.'

Rusk was especially interested in what one guide said: 'I wish

Roy Bub was here to explain his idea, because I agree with him. It'd work and would teach us a whale of a lot about animal behavior.'

'Where is Roy Bub?' Rusk asked.

The guide ignored the question, preferring to continue with his description of the co-owner's plan: 'Roy Bub, he says: "Let's fix a field for our native white-tail deer. Less than a mile wide, five miles long. Good cover. Lots of rocky places." And we'll put a hundred deer in there, guaranteed, and we'll start you off, Mr Rusk, with another gun at this end and let you two prowl that field from sunup to sundown, and challenge you to get one of those deer.'

'From today's experience with that sable, we'd have a hard time finding them.'

'That you would. Mr Morrison, how about settin' up such a long narrow field?'

'Could be done. Take a lot of expensive fencing for a little area.'

'Let's talk about it, maybe,' Rusk said, and both Morrison and the guide glowed, for when an enthusiastic man with a billion dollars uttered that reassuring phrase, it meant that something might happen.

In the morning, Rusk, Morrison and the two guides stalked the big enclosure and just as the noonday heat was becoming excessive, so that all animals but man would be taking cover, the guide who had spoken of the proposed deer test whispered: 'Movement, two o'clock!' and when Rusk looked dead ahead, then slightly to the right, he saw shadowy evidence that an animal of some size was moving there. The other three men froze as Rusk carefully worked his way into a more favorable position, and when he had done so he saw in the direction from which the wind was blowing one of nature's grandest creations, a large bull sable antelope, splendidly colored in the body, with a white-and-black-masked face and the majestic back-curved horns which were the animal's hallmark.

The sable was so perfect in both manner and appearance, that even an avid hunter like Rusk, lusting for his prize, had to watch in awe as it moved toward a patch of fresh grass: How did God fashion such a beast? Why spend so much effort to make it perfect? The horns? Who could have thought up such horns?

1453

He was sweating so copiously that if the wind had shifted only a fraction, the sable would have dodged and darted back among the deeper shadows.

'When's he gonna shoot?' the lead guide whispered to Morrison, for occasionally some Texas hunter would come onto the ranch and stalk an eland or a zebra for two days and then refuse to kill the animal when it was in full sight: 'He was too handsome. I don't want a head that bad.' Always the man would pay the fee, as if he had killed the animal – $3,000 for an eland, $4,000 for a zebra – and would return home exalted.

'Trust Rusk,' Morrison whispered back. 'In everything, he's a killer.'

And then the explosive shot, shattering the noontime air, and the swift rush of the three watchers to where the great sable lay dead. There was much backslapping, many congratulations, and then the guide calling on his walkie-talkie: 'Clarence, Mr Rusk just got his sable. Field Three, by the small rocky outcrop. Bring in the large truck with the rack in front. No, the Jeep won't be big enough.'

In due course, after the animal had been disemboweled on the spot, the truck rolled up and four men muscled the splendid beast onto its rack, but as they left the enclosure, and the guide ran back to lock the high wire fence, they had the bad luck to run into Roy Bub Hooker as he returned unexpectedly from his trip to Austin, where he had arranged with Wildlife officers for the importation of two planeloads of animals from Kenya.

When he saw the dead sable coming at him, he recognized it as the specific male he had been cultivating to be master of the herd and whose semen he had been distributing to other American ranches and zoos that were endeavoring to keep the species from extinction. This was not some casual animal; this was a precious heritage worth enormous effort to keep it alive.

Roy Bub did not cry out; he screamed at the top of his voice as if he had been mortally lacerated, a beefy, thirty-seven-year-old man, shrieking as if he were a wounded child: 'What in hell have you done?'

When he saw that the murderer was Ransom Rusk, he leaped at him and began pounding at him with his fist: 'You-son-of-a-bitch! You murderin' son-of-a-bitch! Comin' onto this land . . .'

Rusk was more than able to defend himself, and with strong

arms pushed the enraged Roy Bub back, but this did not stop the game specialist: 'Off of this land, you murderin' bastard! Off! Off!'

Morrison and the guides were appalled when they saw Roy Bub reach for his gun, which he carried regularly, for they could visualize a terrible tragedy. But it was Rusk, cool as a blue norther, who stopped him: 'Roy Bub! You horse's ass, put up that gun.'

The harshness of the words, their authority and the correct use of profanity stopped the big gamekeeper. Lowering his gun, he said quietly and with quivering force: 'Take your sable, God damn you, and get off this land. And don't never come back, because if you do, I'll kill you, for certain.'

Shaken, Rusk started toward the car that would take him to his plane, but Roy Bub would not allow this: 'Take your sable with you.' When Rusk ignored him, the hefty man screamed: 'Take him. You killed him. Get him out of here.'

And when Rusk turned back to supervise the delivery of his sable to the taxidermist, he could hear Roy Bub shouting at Todd Morrison, his partner: 'You slimy son-of-a-bitch, I ought to shoot you,' and then Morrison's hesitant voice: 'Roy Bub, we're running a business, not some toy zoo.'

They did not meet at Allerkamp, because Rusk was afraid to return there, and besides, he did not want to discuss this important affair in Todd Morrison's presence. They met in a private suite at the Driskill Hotel in Austin, where Rusk had spread maps and real estate plans on a table. He was there first, and when Roy Bub arrived Rusk hurried forward to shake his hands, both hands at the same time, as if they were old friends: 'Roy Bub, I apologize,' and before the younger man could say anything, Rusk added, in a rush of words: 'You have haunted me. All my life I've admired men who stood for something, who were willing to fight. Roy Bub, you're my kind of people, and I apologize.'

They opened cold beers taken from the refrigerator in the suite, after which Roy Bub asked: 'So what?' and Rusk said: 'I love animals as much as you do,' and Roy Bub replied: 'You have a strange way of showin' it.'

'I think I was hypnotized. At Gorongosa once, that's in

Mozambique, I saw a group of sables, and right there I vowed ... ' He stopped, bowed his head, and said: 'Shit, I pressured Morrison. But he did call me down when he knew you wouldn't be there. I should have suspected.'

'It was a very precious animal, Mr Rusk. He was on all the zoo computers, father of the revived herd. He was ... ' His voice broke, and he lifted the empty beer bottle to drain the last few drops.

'I know. The man from San Diego called and tore me apart. So what I want to do, Roy Bub, and maybe this is what I've always wanted to do, I want to buy out Morrison, give him a hefty profit, and I want you and me ...'

'I doubt he would sell his share.'

'Share? He owns it all.'

'Now wait, we bought this place ... I found it. I did the deed search.'

'But it was bought in his name, Roy Bub. He owns it. You do have certain rights.'

'He owns it?' The big man's voice began to rise, so Rusk placed the documents before him, and there was a lot of gobbledegook about this and that, but it was painfully clear that where the actual ownership of the land was concerned, Todd Morrison had it all.

When Rob Bub finished reading the incriminating documents and listened as Rusk explained each twisting labyrinth, he did not shout or even swear: 'Mr Rusk, in everything I've ever done with that S.O.B. he's gigged me. Buy him out and let's wash our hands.'

'In his real estate deals, I now find, he operates the same way. And I cannot understand it, because his wife is so completely honest. I've see her turn back commissions when she's loused up some deal. She did it with me, voluntarily.'

'Todd Morrison!' Roy Bub repeated as he handed back the mournful papers. 'With land as important as ours, with him dependin' on me to keep it goin', you'd think ... '

'How many acres do you two have? I mean how many does he have?'

'About ten thousand. The Allerkamp ranch plus the Macnab, dating back to the 1840s, I believe.'

'If you and I were to do something, we'd do it Texas style,' and he asked Roy Bub to study the plans he had brought along: 'I've had my men looking into the land situation out there along the Pedernales, and they think they could get us an additional thirty thousand acres, not all of it contiguous but we might make some trades.'

'There isn't that much money in the world,' Roy Bub said. 'We paid very heavy for the Allerkamp acres.'

'I think it could be managed,' Rusk said. 'If it could be, would you run the place? I mean really first class, everything.'

'I wouldn't be interested in no chrome motel, Mr Rusk, like some of them others.'

'To hell with the customers. I mean the animals.'

Roy Bub thought a long time as to how he should reply, and then decided to share his vision of Allerkamp: 'Mr Rusk, if you have the money, and they tell me you do, one of the best things in this world you could do with it is put together a real game refuge on the Pedernales. Sure, we'll rent out fields for hunters and charge 'em like hell for the shootin' of game that can easily be replaced ... eland, elk, zebra. But in the back fields, where you only go with cameras, we could hide the animals that are in danger.' He stopped, walked about the room, then said: 'Helpin' to preserve an animal that might disappear from this earth, that would be a good thing to do, Mr Rusk.' And before Ransom could respond, Roy Bub added: 'I thought that's what Morrison and I would be doin', not shootin' sables for a few lousy bucks.'

They spent the next two days in the Driskill, drawing maps and meeting surreptitiously with Rusk's lawyers and real estate men, and when they were through they found themselves with an imaginative design for a master exotic-game ranch covering 44,000 acres along the Pedernales, with a small contributory stream running in from the north. It was divided into seven major fields, each of which would be defined by game fencing eight and a half feet high. It would contain the old Allerkamp and Macnab buildings as lodges for guests, but a central administrative building just inside the gates would also be required. 'Low key,' Rusk said, 'like the best buildings in Africa.'

'How do you know Morrison will sell?' he asked Mr Rusk, and the latter said: 'For money he'll do anything. Don't worry about his acres. We'll have them.' And he added: 'When the deal goes through, Roy Bub, I'll insist that he give you a share of the purchase price,' and Roy Bub said: 'You can try, but he never surrenders a nickel, especially if it's an Indian head worth nine cents.'

It was Roy Bub's job to figure the cost of the fencing, which Rusk proposed erecting right away, and when Roy Bub placed the figures before Rusk, he was apologetic; 'You see, we'll have to rebuild that fence along the Pedernales. Morrison wanted to use every inch of our land and he put the posts too close to the river. Floods wash them out. And we have to fence both sides of the creek. To do the job right, and I'm ashamed of these figures, almost eighty miles of fencing at about ninety-five hundred per mile, that means well over seven hundred fifty thousand dollars just for fences, let alone animals.'

Rusk turned to his real estate men: 'Let the contracts right away, but get a much lower price than that ninety-five hundred.'

When the second day ended, Rusk and Roy Bub shook hands, after which Rusk's Austin lawyer said: 'Mr Hooker, you'll have ten million dollars for the purchase of animals. Scour the dealers and management areas, but get the best prices possible.'

'Ten million?' He gasped, but Rusk placed his arm about him and said: 'Let's do it Texas style.'

Two nights later, as Rusk was at his Larkin estate watching the armadillos, his Austin lawyer called: 'Mr Rusk! Have you heard?'

'What?'

'Roy Bub Hooker has just shot Todd Morrison. Three shots. Stone-dead.'

There was silence, then Rusk's quiet voice: 'Have Fleabait Moomer call me . . . immediately.'

In his historic defense of Roy Bub Hooker, Fleabait made several prudent moves. Claiming local prejudice, he had the venue changed from Gillespie County, in which the Allerkamp Ranch stood, to Bascomb, a more rough-and-ready county just south of Larkin where juries were more accustomed to a good murder now and then. Also, he employed two private detectives to trace every business deal in which Todd Morrison of Detroit – which was how the dead man would be invariably described during the trial – had ever been engaged, whether in Michigan or Texas.

The county prosecutor in Bascomb, having heard of these investigations, summoned his first assistant and gave him the stirring news: 'Welton, I'm not going to prosecute the Roy Bub Hooker case. You get the assignment. Now, don't thank me. Frankly, I'm running out because I have no desire to face Fleabait Moomer with the local press looking on. You're young. You can absorb the punishment.'

'What do you mean?' the Yale Law School graduate asked.

'You've never seen Fleabait in action? Suspenders and belt, both. Snaps the suspenders when he throws off some rural expression like "Of course bulls are interested in cows, but only at the right time."'

'I'm sure I can handle that. Besides, the case is cement-proof. Hooker did it before five witnesses, three of whom heard him utter threats at the killing of the sable antelope.'

'Welton, you miss the point. Fleabait is not going to defend Roy Bub. He's going to convict Morrison.'

'Not if I—'

'Welton, it doesn't matter what you do, or what the judge does. Fleabait is going to conduct this trial, and he is going to condemn Todd Morrison of crimes so hideous that your jury is going to commend Roy Bub Hooker for having removed him from the sacred soil of Texas.'

'But that won't be allowed.'

'Allowed? Fleabait determines what is allowed. Two bits of advice. Study up on Michigan and Detroit, because they're going to be on trial, not Roy Bub. And when Fleabait stops, sticks both hands under his coat and begins to scratch, hold your breath, because what he says next will blow your case right out of court.'

'I've handled exhibitionists before,' Welton said, whereupon the older man warned: 'But Fleabait Moomer is not an exhibitionist. He believes everything he does. He's protecting Texas against the Twentieth Century.'

Mr Welton of Dartmouth and Yale Law required only one morning to nail down his case, and an irrefutable one it was:

'Ladies and gentlemen of the jury, I shall show you that Robert Burling Hooker, known as Roy Bub, threatened his trusting partner Todd Morrison with shooting, and I will bring three witnesses who heard the threat. I shall show you that two persons of excellent repute heard the argument between the two men on the day of the shooting, and I shall put five men on the stand who actually saw the shooting. Furthermore, I will bring you the gun that did the shooting, and an expert to prove that it was this gun that fired the bullet which killed Todd Morrison. Never will you sit on any jury where the evidence makes your vote so automatic. Roy Bub Hooker killed his partner Todd Morrison, and you will be present at the murder.'

Fleabait, scowling at his table, challenged none of this evidence, but he did go out of his way to show extreme courtesy to Todd Morrison's widow, who would sit every day of the trial in somber dignity, accompanied by her daughter, the famous baton twirler from the University of Texas, and her son-in-law, Wolfgang Macnab, the giant linebacker of the Dallas Cowboys; cautious members of the Cowboys' staff had deplored his association with a murder trial and had even hinted that he might wish to take a hunting trip to Alaska, but he said: 'If Beth's family is in trouble, I'm in trouble,' and sat stone-faced as Fleabait's plodding defense paraded before the court unsavory details of his father-in-law's life.

Mrs Morrison's son, Lonnie, the electronics expert, also attended each day with his wife, to whom Fleabait was also unctuously courteous. Said one watcher: 'You'd think he was defendin' the Morrisons, not Roy Bub,'

Ransom Rusk did not attend the trial, even though he was paying for the defense; the state did not know that Roy Bub had also threatened to shoot him, and Fleabait was certainly not going to introduce such incidental evidence. But when the trial recessed for a long lunch on the morning of the third day, Fleabait jumped in his car and drove not to the restaurant where lawyers ate, but twenty-two miles up the road to Larkin, where he consulted with Rusk in the latter's mansion: 'It's possible I could be wrong, Rance, but from watchin' Mrs Morrison closely, I'm convinced that if we could get her to testify, she'd support everythin' I've been tryin' to prove. She knows her husband was a jerk. She knows he hornswoggled everybody he ever did business with.'

'Leave her alone. She has a heavy enough burden.'

'Her son-in-law would testify the same way. He's a clever lad. He must know.'

'Fleabait! Don't touch the family!'

'I'm pretty sure we can win without their evidence. But it would be neat to startle the court with a request for a surprise witness.'

'You old fraud, you know you can't use a wife to testify against her own husband.'

'That's what the layman always thinks. There are a dozen ways—'

'Fleabait!'

'You want that boy to walk out of that courtroom free, don't you?' With Fleabait, an accused client was always a boy; his nefarious opponent, whether living or dead, a corrupt, evil man.

'I certainly do. And you're the man to do it.' At the door, as the lawyer started back to the courthouse, Rusk said: 'In my divorce trial, when you accused me of sodomy, sort of, that was just good clean fun. This case is real. Haul in your biggest guns, Fleabait, but leave the Morrisons out of it.'

On the fourth day of what should have been a simple trial, Fleabait spent the entire morning interrogating the other two members of the original Morrison-Hooker hunting quartet, the oilman who had transferred his affections to Scotland, and the dentist who loved dogs, and rarely did he have two witnesses who supported a case more handsomely. Each man in his own way proved that he was a dedicated sportsman, and each disclosed secrets of Todd Morrison's behavior which proved that he had never been. 'He was not a true sportsman,' the oilman said with a decided English accent. 'He never gave the game a fair chance.'

'You mean he would fire at a quail sitting on the ground?,' Fleabait asked in horror.

As soon as the oilman replied 'He would,' the county prosecutor leaped up: 'Objection! Distinguished defense counsel is leading the witness.'

'Objection sustained. The jury will ignore that last reply.'

Fleabait stood apart, as if detached from the proceedings, and shook his head as if in pain. At the same time he muttered to himself, but loud enough to be heard throughout the courtroom: 'Shot a sittin' bird. I can't believe it.'

He then sighed, returned to the trial, and asked the oilman: 'And he shot a doe out of season, with no license to shoot one even in season?'

Again the charade was repeated: 'Objection!' 'Sustained.' And Fleabait brooding aloud: 'A doe out of season. I can't believe it.'

And then, patiently: 'Did Mr Hooker, the man you call Roy Bub, did he ever do such things?'

'Oh, no! Roy Bub taught us all what sportsmanship was.'

'Now, as to the financial arrangements covering your lease at Falfurrias, I understand that when you pulled out, some rather harsh words were spoken.'

'I believe that was the dentist . . . about his dogs.'

'Yes, yes. Very harsh words indeed. We'll get to that. But in your case it dealt with money matters, did it not?' And in this patient way the sleazy shifts and dodges of Morrison's operations were unraveled.

The dentist was an admirable witness.

'You say you never fired a gun at the Falfurrias lease. What in the world did you do?'

'I trained my dogs.'

'You brought your dogs along so that the other three could profit from their skill, which I am told was extraordinary.'

'Yes.'

'You surrendered all your free time so that others could enjoy the hunt? I call that true sportsmanship. Was Todd Morrison a sportsman?'

'Didn't know the meaning of the word.'

'When you quit the foursome, I believe you had words with Morrison. About his financial dealings.'

District Attorney Welton objected to this line of questioning, charging that without any kind of substantiation, it was mere hearsay, but the judge overruled the objection.

'In my dealings with Morrison, he invariably tried to chisel me. He was not a likable man.'

'But you were his partner, so to say – in the lease, I mean?'

'At first I thought he had no money, so I sort of carried him. Later I discovered that he had more than I did. He was not a pleasant person.'

On the fifth day Fleabait practically destroyed Todd Morrison, proving much, intimating more, and then, after a dramatic pause, thrusting both hands under his armpits and scratching. The jury, having been alerted to watch out for this, smiled knowingly.

'Now, you know and I know, that people from Michigan do not adhere to the same high moral principles that govern behavior in Texas. They can be fine people by their own lights, and they can get along fairly well in the more relaxed moral climate of Detroit and Pontiac. But when they move to Texas, as so many do, they find themselves confronted by a much stricter moral code. Here a man is supposed to behave like a man. A sportsman has certain clearly defined patterns of acceptable behavior, which the newcomer from Michigan has a difficult time honoring. I have nothing against Michigan. I'm sure there are fine people in Michigan, many of them. But when they come into Texas they are held to a nobler code of behavior, and to tell you the truth, many of them fail to meet the mark. They are not ready for Texas. They are not prepared to face our more demanding standards.

'Todd Morrison was such a man. I do not want you to judge him harshly, because he knew no better. He had not been raised with the clean wind of the prairie blowing away the cobwebs that entangle human beings. He never rode a horse across the plains. He was not trained in the harsh lessons of honor and trust and sportsmanship. I do not want you to condemn this poor dead man who lost his way in a new and more exacting land. I want you to forgive him.' (Here he scratched again.) 'And I want you to understand why an honest, God-fearing Texan, born in the heart of good sportsmanship, felt that he had to shoot him. You surely know by now that Todd Morrison, this pathetic stranger who never fitted in, who could not obey our strict code of honor, deserved to die.'

*   *   *

The foreman of the jury asked the judge if it was obligatory for them to leave the jury box before handing in their verdict, and he said: 'It would look better,' so they marched out and marched right back in.

During Sherwood Cobb's first two years as a member of the Water Commission he could make no headway in his campaign for a sensible water plan for Texas, but now two natural disasters struck which awakened the state to the fact that it lived in peril, like all other areas of the world, where the perils might be different, but all stemmed from the inherent limitations imposed by nature.

Drought hit some portion of Texas about every ten years, but the state was so large that other areas did not suffer; however, about once each quarter of a century great portions of the state were hit at the same time. Farms were wiped out, ranches were decimated, and land-gamblers were reminded that there were definite limits beyond which they dare not go. In 1932 the Great Drought had struck in Oklahoma, reaching Texas in 1933 and converting large areas of both states into dust bowls, and 1950 had delivered a savage drought which lasted seven years. Now another crushing dry spell gripped the western half of the state. Waterholes went dry, rivers that were supposed to be perpetual failed, and even a supposedly safe coastal city like Corpus Christi was forced to institute water rationing.

Now when Cobb moved about the state, seeking to generate support for his plans, people listened, and he told his wife: 'I used to say we'd have no serious approach to our water problems till the year 2010. A few more years of this drought and you can advance that to about 1995. But I want to see it happen in 1985.'

He went to all parts of Texas, pleading with farmers, ranchers and businessmen to devise a water system for their state, but in addition to talking, he acted, sometimes twenty hours a day, to rescue ranchers who were about to lose their cattle. He urged grassland farmers in the unaffected eastern half to truck in cattle from the arid areas and water them without cost till the emergency waned. He organized auctions at which ranchers with no water at all could sell their animals to buyers from other states whose fields did have water, for as one rancher who had to sell at distress said: 'I'd rather see my cattle live and make a profit for someone else than stand here and watch them perish.' And Cobb persuaded other Texas cattlemen to adopt the same attitude.

In short, Sherwood Cobb acted in this emergency the way his ancestor Senator Somerset Cobb had responded to the disasters of the Civil War and Reconstruction, and as another ancestor, Senator Laurel Cobb, had acted when great changes were under way in the 1920s: he rolled up his sleeves and went to work. Like Ransom Rusk gritting his teeth and bearing his enormous financial setbacks, Cobb accepted the challenge of the natural ones, but in the midst of his constructive work Texas was struck with a final assault of such magnitude that even Cobb reeled.

Folk legend said that once every hundred years snow fell in Brownsville, the southernmost city in Texas and a land of palm trees and bougainvillea. On Christmas Day in 1983 the thermometer along the Rio Grande dropped far, far below freezing, and the results were staggering.

When Cobb arrived two days after Christmas on emergency assignment from the Department of Agriculture, he found entire grapefruit orchards wiped out by the excessive cold. Avocado trees were no more. Orange groves were obviously destroyed. And the famous palm trees of Corpus Christi and other southern towns were dead in the bitter winds. Hundreds of millions of dollars were lost in this one terrible freeze, so that communities who had watched their stores close because of the fall of the peso now saw their agriculture destroyed by a fall in the thermometer. The Valley, staggered before, now lay desolated.

Cobb found in the distraught area one local leader who seemed to have as firm a grasp of reality as he, Cobb, had. It was Mayor Simón Garza of Bravo, who toured the Valley ceaselessly, organizing relief operations, and as the two men worked together, Cobb ten years the older, they formed a pact that would endure through the years ahead: 'Garza, you make more sense than anyone else I've met. People live on the land, the rancher out west, the citrus grower down here, the farmer up the coast. We're restricted by what the land will allow us to do, and when we forget that, we're in trouble.'

1465

Garza said: 'I read an editorial the other day. It said "God has gone out of His way to remind us that even Texans are mortal." These are devastating years, but we can build upon them.' And the two men, optimists as all Texans are required by law to be, went quietly ahead with their plans, however fragmentary, to save the citrus industry in the Valley, ranching on the high plains and water supplies everywhere.

But Cobb, like his valiant ancestors and like his aunt Lorena up in Waxahachie, was an ebullient man, and as he toured his state, proud of its ability to fight back, he savored the many hilarious behaviors that made Texas different from any other state he knew. And as he witnessed these crazy things he jotted down brief notes, which he mailed back to his wife so that she, too, could laugh.

... In Jefferson, I attended in the schoolhouse a lecture entitled 'The Heritage of Robert E. Lee,' and at the end the chairlady said, voice throbbing with emotion: 'Now if we will all stand, please,' and with her hand over her heart she led the singing:

> 'I wish I was in de land ub cotton
> Old times dar am not forgotten ... '

Fervently we sang of a glory none of us had ever known but whose legends were etched on our hearts, and when we reached that marvelous chorus, one of the most powerful ever written, I was shouting with the others:

> 'In Dixie Land I'll take my stand
> To lib and die in Dixie.
> Away, away, away down South in Dixie.'

When the song ended, with some of us wiping our eyes, I said to the man next to me: 'If a bugle sounded now, half this crowd would march north,' and he said: 'Yep, and this time we'd whup 'em.'

... You and I have often talked about what our favorite town in Texas was. North Zulch always stood high. Oatmeal was good. You liked Muleshoe. The other day I drove through my favorite, Megargel, population 381, with a sign that says WATCH US GROW. As I drove through I saw a pickup with the bumper sticker SUPPORT JESUS AND YOUR LOCAL SHERIFF. Carry on, Megargel!

... At Larkin, where they have that famous statue you wouldn't let me photograph, I saw something I hadn't noticed before. On the courthouse lawn were two bold bronze plaques, one proclaiming that for three glorious years during the 1920s the Larkin Fighting Antelopes had been state champions in football, the other that one night in 1881 the notorious one-armed gunman, Amos Peavine, had slept in Larkin prior to his gunning down of Daniel Parmenteer, respected lawyer of the place, and as I studied the two memorials I had to reflect upon the mores of the small Texas town.

I'm sure Larkin must have produced dedicated women who taught their students with love and constructive influence. It surely had bright boys who went on to become state and national leaders. It must have had brave judges who tamed the western range, and men who built fortunes which they spent wisely. And there must have been citizens of no wide repute who held the town together, perhaps a barber or a seamstress on whom the weak depended. I can think of a hundred citizens of Larkin that I would like to memorialize, but what do we do?

We erect monuments to a murderous gunman who slept here one night and to a football team whose coach and most of whose players came from somewhere else. Just once I would like to drive into a Texas town and see a bronze plaque to a man who wrote a peom or to a woman who composed a lasting song.

... Returning from the session on catchment dams, I had the radio on and heard the song I'm going to recommend as the official state song of Texas, because it honors the two noblest aspects of our culture, football and religion: 'Drop-Kick me, Jesus, Through the Goal Posts of Life.'

... I grow mournful when I hold a water meeting in some little town that used to flourish but is now dying. There must be hundreds of such places doomed to disappear before the end of the century, and I've constructed Cobb's Law to cover the situation: 'If a town has less than four hundred population and stands within twenty miles of a big shopping center, it's got to vanish.' The automobile determines that and there's not a damned thing we can do about it. Texas, always dying, always arising in some new location with some new mission.

. . . I love the redneck songs of Texas, 'San Antonio Rose,' 'El Paso,' and the new one I've memorized so I can sing it to you when we're traveling:

> Blue flies lazin' in the noon-day sun,
> Dogies grazin' at their rest,
> Old steers drinkin' at the salty run . . .
> This is Texas at its best.
> Sleep on, Jim, I'll watch the herd,
> Doze on, Slim, fly northward bird.
> All the range is peaceful.

He had a chance to sing this ballad to his wife when she accompanied him to two water meetings held by chance in two of the truly bizarre places in Texas. The first was the schoolhouse in the little oil town of Sundown, southwest of Levelland. The feisty town fathers, discovering that the oil companies would have to pay for whatever the board legally decided, opted to have the finest school in America. So for a total school enrolment of only a hundred and forty pupils they built a seven-million-dollar Taj Mahal, featuring a gymnasium fit for the Boston Celtics, an auditorium finer than most New York theaters and an Olympic-sized swimming-pool under glass.

'What staggers me,' Cobb told his wife, 'is that in the pool they teach canoeing. Yep, look at those two aluminum canoes, and there isn't any water within miles. When I asked about this, a member of the school board said: "Well some of our kids may emigrate to Maine, where canoeing is real big." ' Mrs Cobb preferred the miniature condominium built into the center of the school: 'What's it for?' And an official explained: 'We want to teach our home-ec girls how to make beds.' The superintendent's office was special: directly under it at a depth of thousands of feet, rested an oil well, drilled at an angle. 'It's how we get our petty cash,' an official said.

But what gave the Cobbs renewed hope for Texas every time they saw it was an amazing structure in the roughneck oil town of Odessa, where the oil rigs Ransom Rusk had been unable to sell at a heavy loss rusted in the sun. There, years ago, a young woman schoolteacher without a cent had fallen in love with William Shakespeare. Driven by a vision that never faltered, she had begged and borrowed and scrounged until she had accumulated enough money to build an accurate replica of Shakespeare's Globe Theatre. There it stood in the sandy desert, full scale, and to it came Shakespearean actors from many different theaters and countries to orate the soaring lines of the master.

'We don't do many of his historical plays,' the director told Cobb. 'Our customers prefer the love stories and the tragedies.'

'I'll be sending you a check one of these days,' Mrs Cobb said, for the Globe was kept alive by families like the Cobbs who felt that Shakespeare added a touch of grace to the drylands.

As Cobb left the meeting at which, speaking from the Shakespearean stage, he had pleaded for water legislation, he stopped and looked back at this preposterous building: 'I love the craziness of Texas. It's still the biggest state in the Union . . . without Eskimos.'

Maggie Morrison had been shocked by the murder of her husband, not by the fact that his shady behavior had resulted in the shooting, for she had anticipated something like this, but by the fact that it was Roy Bub who had done it. She knew him to be a man of intense integrity, and for him to have pulled the trigger added extra pain.

After the verdict was returned, a proper one she thought, she learned that she stood to inherit all of Allerkamp, a fair portion of which morally belonged to Roy Bub. With the honesty which characterized her, she flew to Dallas to consult with Rusk: 'I cannot keep Allerkamp. Much of it is Roy Bub's, but I can't offer him an adjustment because it would look as if we had conspired to have my husband eliminated.'

'Allow the will to be probated. Take Allerkamp and keep your mouth shut.'

'To do that would strangle me.'

'Maggie, I wasn't going to tell you this, but I've taken care of Roy Bub. What we call a finder's fee.'

'What did he find?'

'Allerkamp. Before Todd died, the scoundrel was preparing to sell me Allerkamp. He was going to quit the exotic business.'

'What about Roy Bub?'

'Your husband never gave a damn about him.'

'I'm not surprised. Houston ruined Todd. When we first came down we held family meetings: "Kids, Maggie, we're going into this deal and we could lose our shirts." We shared everything. Then, when he began to shave corners, we knew only the honest parts. Finally we knew nothing.'

'Your husband and I agreed on a fair price for the place. I'll show you the papers. His lawyer, mine, will confirm their authenticity. You should allow the deal to go through.'

'What will it mean to me?'

'Four million dollars.'

The deal did go through, and on the day it was settled Maggie initiated three moves which symbolized her changed attitudes. She drove out to Allerkamp to inspect the manner in which Roy Bub Hooker had laid out the seven main areas that would make it one of the best exotic ranches in Texas, and when Rusk explained how it would be used, she told the partners: 'You're putting the place to good use. May it succeed beyond your dreams.'

The second thing of importance she did was surrender the family's fancy condominium along Buffalo Bayou. As she confided to her children: 'I feel uneasy sitting here and looking across the way at those three towers of The Ramparts, thinking how I bought them at distress from the Mexicans and sold them to the Canadians three weeks before the hurricane. It haunts me . . . seems immoral.'

She moved instead to a beautiful, dignified condominium well west of the center of town, the St James, where she bought one of the smaller units on the twenty-third floor for $538,000 and spent another $92,000 decorating it. There, overlooking a park, she did the brainwork for her real estate business, driving to her office early each morning.

When real estate acquaintances in other cities called to ask: 'Did Hurricane Alicia destroy values in Houston?' she felt so defensive about her city that she drafted a thoughtful form letter:

I know you saw the horrendous scenes on television, our beautiful buildings with their windows knocked out like old women with no front teeth. I assure you with my hand on the Bible that only a few buildings were so hit and not one of them suffered any structural damage.

Houston has snapped back stronger than before. I am buying and selling as if there had never been a hurricane, for I know that if we survived Alicia, we can survive anything. If you crave action, come aboard.

But it was her third change that represented the most significant modification, because when she moved to the St James she found herself conveniently close to Highway 610, that magic loop which encircled the central Houston she loved. Now, two or three nights a week after dinner when the intolerable traffic abated, she went down to her garage, climbed into her Mercedes, and drove thoughtfully eastward till she hit a ramp leading to 610. There she weaved her way onto the striking thoroughfare, one of the busiest in America, and started the thirty-eight-mile circuit of the city, ticking off her position on an imaginary clock.

Where she entered was nine o'clock, due west. Up where the airport waited, with its enormous flow of plane and auto traffic, was twelve. Three o'clock on the extreme east carried her into the smoke-filled, bustling commercial district that huddled about the Houston Ship Channel with its hundreds of plants affiliated with the oil industry; this area interested her immensely, for in it she saw many prospects for growth. Six o'clock was due south where the immense Medical Center and the handsome Astrodome predominated, and at the end of fifty minutes she was back at Westheimer, taking a last look at the city she had grown to love: What a glorious town! Spires everywhere glinting in the moonlight! God smiled at me when He brought me here. To help build and sell those splendid buildings!

Two nights a week, sometimes three, she made this circuit of her city, checking upon current building, predicting its future growth; sometimes male dinner companions accompanied her: 'Maggie, you mustn't do this alone. Six-ten is a jungle, worst highway in America. You know that during the rush hour the police won't even enter it to check on ordinary fender-benders. They got beat up too often by enraged motorists, sometimes shot and killed.'

'But I stay clear during the rush hours.'

'And for God's sake, don't drive with your window down.'

'This is my town. I love it and I want to check on it.'

One night as she was driving, with her eye on lands outside the circle, a full moon illuminated a section of the city she had never before studied seriously; it stood at ten o'clock, to the northwest, and it comprised about fifteen blocks of housing which could be torn down at no great loss, and she eased into an outer lane so that she could slow down and inspect the place. With imaginary bulldozers and wrecking balls, she leveled the houses, then erected a pair of soaring towers with all attendant shopping areas: Forty-eight floors to each tower, right? Six condominiums per floor? But save the first four levels for office space. We could get five hundred units easily, plus six gorgeous penthouses at $3,500,000 each.

Futura she dubbed her imaginary towers, and now when she circled the city at night she waited breathlessly for the approach of Futura, analyzing it from all angles. In the daytime, after work, she drove through the area and found that seventeen blocks would provide the necessary land area. Then she began to consult secretly with Gabe Klinowitz as to prices in the district, and with his figures in her head she started sketching plans for a major development. When she costed them, as the phrase in her industry went, she found that for $210,000,000 she could probably acquire the land, raze the buildings on it, and erect her twin-towered masterpiece.

As soon as she had a working budget in mind, she realized that there was only one source available to her for such a vast amount, so she flew to Dallas and placed her design before Ransom Rusk, who was recovering nicely from the shocks of the preceding years when he saw his net worth drop by nearly half a billion. He was deeply engaged in the election, sweating over whether or not Reagan would be reelected: 'So many damned blacks and Mexicans registering, a man can't make predictions.' He was also contributing vast sums toward the defeat of eight or nine Democratic senators around the country, because he felt, as he told Maggie: 'This is one of the crucial elections of our national history. If Reagan's coat-tails are long enough, we'll even regain control of the House, and then we can turn this sloppy nation around permanently. Reagan, a great patriot in the White House. His nominees filling the Supreme Court. A Republican Congress. And we'll start taking over the state houses.' With each potential triumph he became more excited: 'Maggie, we can put some backbone into this nation. Clean up things in Central America. End the disgrace of public welfare, and see America tall in the saddle again. We'll wipe out the stain of Franklin Roosevelt once and for all.'

As a lifelong Democrat whose parents had come from the working class, she was amused when Rusk fulminated in this way and did not take him seriously, but gradually he said things which astonished her: 'It's criminal for the Democrats to go around making Mexicans register, when they understand none of the issues. The vote should be reserved for the people who own the nation and pay the taxes.'

'Do you mean that?' she had asked, and his thoughtful reply surprised her: 'I calculated the other day that my efforts ensure the employment of nearly four thousand people. Counting four to a family, that's sixteen thousand citizens I support. Am I to be outvoted by two unemployed Mexican hangers-on who can't read English?'

When she pursued the matter, he confessed: 'Yes, I'd like to see a means test for the vote. Only people who have a real stake in society can know what's best for that society.'

She was not yet ready to accept this new philosophy which was sweeping the nation, but in August when Rusk invited her to join him at the Republican National Convention in Dallas, she had an opportunity to observe him as he moved among people of his own kind, and she was impressed to find that he knew all the leaders and was welcomed in the suites of both President Reagan, delightful man, and Vice-President Bush, a reassuring fellow Texan from Midland. She noticed that Rusk was warmly greeted by the famous clergymen who had swarmed into Dallas to prove God was a Republican and America a Christian nation.

It was an exciting week, and once when she sat in a privileged seat she felt a surge of pride as she looked down upon the delegates, that endless parade of fine, clean-cut people from all parts of the nation: the bankers, the managers, the store owners, the elderly women with blue-tinted hair. And not too often a black or a Hispanic to confuse the pattern. It was at this euphoric moment that Maggie first began to consider seriously her partner's philosophy that the men who own a nation ought to govern it. The idea was crudely expressed and she knew that if the newspapers got hold of it, they would make sport of Rusk, but it did summarize a fundamental truth about America, and it was worth further study.

On the morning after the convention ended on a note of high triumph, Maggie placed before Rusk the plans for her master development, and was distressed when he seemed to back off, as if the project was too big for him to finance at this time.

'Ransom, are you turning me down?'

'No. But I am turning down Houston. Now is not the time to start new building in that town.'

She gasped, then said defensively: 'I love Houston. It gave me life ... maturity ... even happiness of a sort.'

'Time to be realistic. New buildings are standing empty.'

'But, Ransom, I've been mailing brochures assuring real estate customers that Houston is not finished.' She hesitated, looked pleadingly, saw the obdurate scowl, and asked softly: 'Are you suggesting Dallas?'

'I haven't mentioned Dallas. It's overbuilt too.'

'What do you have in mind?'

'Austin.'

She had never contemplated shifting her operations from a city with more than two million to one about one-fifth that size, but Rusk was adamant: 'Houston twenty years ago is Austin today.'

'Can it absorb something like Futura?'

He avoided a direct answer: 'That's a dreadful name. Sounds like a bath soap.'

'What would you propose?'

'Something classy. English. Like the Bristol or Warwick Towers. But they've been overdone.' Then he snapped his fingers: 'I have it. The Nottingham. Our logo? Robin Hood in outline wearing that crazy peaked hat. We'll make it the most fashionable address in Texas.'

Maggie, trying not to smile at the picture of Ransom Rusk offering himself as a Robin Hood stealing from the poor to aid the rich, kept her mind on the main problem: 'Where do we get the two hundred million?'

Without hesitation he replied: 'West Germany or the Arabs. They're itching to invest in Texas.' And while she waited, he called his bankers in Frankfurt and asked: 'Karl Philip, do your boys still have those funds you talked about last month? Good. I'm putting you down for two hundred and ten million.' There was a pause which Maggie interpreted as shock on the other end, but it was not: 'No, not Houston, it's marking time at present. And not Dallas, either, it's overbuilt. Austin.' Another pause: 'State capital, America's new silicon valley, our fastest growing city. Hotter than an oil-boom town.'

When he hung up he gave Maggie a simple directive: 'Fly right down to Austin, locate the perfect spot, and get someone to buy the real estate in secret.'

With the design for her two luxury towers firmly in mind, she rode to the airport in Rusk's car, which delivered her to the door of the Rusk plane. In less than forty minutes she was landing at the Austin airport, and the next four days were hectic.

In a rented car she explored the unfamiliar beauties of this lovely little city, and by noon she had counted a dozen giant cranes busy at the job of erecting very tall buildings. 'My God,' she cried. 'This really is the new Houston,' and that afternoon she chanced on a young man, Paul Sampson, recently down from Indianapolis, who could have been Todd Morrison in 1969. He had the same brash approach, the same nervous eagerness, the same indication that he was going to be adroit in arranging deals. He worked for a large real estate firm but gave every promise of owning the outfit within two years, and by nightfall he had shown Maggie sixteen sites which could accommodate new buildings.

That night she called Rusk: 'Ransom, real estate is so hot down here that the place simply has to go bust.'

Very quietly he assured her: 'Of course it'll go bust. Everything does sooner or later. Our job is to get in fast and out first.'

'Then you want me to go ahead?'

'With German money, how can we go wrong?'

So early next morning she was at Paul Sampson's office with

the kind of proposition cagey operators had brought her husband in the early 1970s: 'Could you quietly assemble about six city blocks for me? Standard commission?'

'I can do anything you require, madam,' he said, and she could see that his palms were sweating. 'Where do you want them? In the heart of the city?'

'Show me the possibilities,' and when he kept stressing an area which she distrusted, she said: 'You own a parcel in there, don't you?' and he protested: 'Look, madam, if you don't trust me, we can't do business,' and she said: 'If you try to sell me that junk you're stuck with, we'll never do business.'

Startled by her shrewd understanding, he stopped trying to peddle his third-rate property and started driving her to the eligible areas, and by the end of the fourth day she had found something farther out than he had expected her to go. It was a grand area west of Route 360 and atop a rise which gave a splendid view of both Lake Travis and the famed Hill Country.

'Will people buy this far out?' Sampson asked, and she said: 'When they see what we're going to build,' and with that, she gave him a commission to acquire four parcels of about ten acres each, and when the agreement was signed, in great secrecy, he said: 'Can I ask what you're going to build out there?' and she said: 'A hunting range for Robin Hood.'

When she saw the excitement in his eyes and his eagerness to get started, she thought of her former husband, and wished the young man good luck. She hoped he would handle himself better than Todd had done, but she had a strong premonition that he was going to go the same way, because three weeks later, after he had delivered the forty acres to her at a price that was gratifying, she learned that he had mortgaged himself to the hilt in order to buy for his own account two small choice plots that would dominate any roads into or out of the Nottingham.

'You'll do well, Sampson,' she said as she ended negotiations. 'Stay clean,' and he startled her by saying with great assurance: 'Mrs Morrison, you'll bless the day you met me. That land will be worth millions, because this Austin thing can go on forever.'

That night she flew back to Larkin, and when she informed Rusk of her proposed land purchase in Austin, he congratulated her. Then, ignoring the two-hundred-million-dollar deal as if it were an ordinary day's work, he took his seat before two television sets as the first Reagan–Mondale debate started.

The next ninety minutes were a nightmare for Ransom, because he had to watch the man who was supposed to save the Republic fumble and stumble and show himself to be uninformed on basic problems. At one point Rusk growled: 'Maggie, how in hell did he ever allow himself to get tangled in a debate? He looks ninety years old.'

But soon his anger was directed at the three newspeople asking the questions: 'They shouldn't speak to him like that! He's President!' And then, as Maggie had anticipated, his ire fell on Mondale: 'Reagan ought to walk over and belt him in the mouth.' Toward the end, when Reagan confessed 'I'm confused,' Rusk shouted at the television: 'They didn't ask that question fair. They're trying to mix him up.'

The next weeks were agonizing, for the press, very unjustly Rusk thought, kept bringing up the question of Reagan's age and his capacity to govern. 'He doesn't have to govern like other people,' Rusk told Maggie. 'He has good men around him who look after details. What he does is inspire the nation.' Calling his friends in the administration, he advised: 'Keep him on the big picture. Patriotism . . . the Olympics . . . standing tall in the saddle.' And when Reagan did just this, smothering Mondale in the final debate, Rusk said: 'The incumbent must never allow upstarts to get on the same platform with him.'

On Election Day, Rusk would drive out to Larkin to vote while Maggie would have to remain in Houston to cast hers, but it was agreed that then Rusk's jet would ferry her to his place, where they would watch the returns together. As she approached the polling place she was still undecided as to how she would vote: 'I can't turn my back on eighty years of family history. I don't think a Svenholm has voted Republican since Teddy Roosevelt ran in 1904. But then she recalled the persuasive logic with which Rusk had defended his thesis that those who own a nation ought to be allowed to govern it, and she suspected that the time had come when dependable Americans like him should be handed the reins, since they had the most to win or lose. Also, like many women, she had some misgivings about Geraldine Ferraro.

Realizing that what she was about to do would have pained

her hard-working parents, whose lives had been rescued by Democratic legislation in the 1930s, she willingly took the step that transformed her from a Michigan liberal into a Texas conservative. Stepping boldly into the voting booth, she looked toward heaven, crossed herself, and said with a chuckle: 'Pop, forgive me for what I'm about to do.' Then closing the curtain behind her, she did what hundreds of thousands of other Democratic refugees from wintry states like Ohio, Michigan and Minnesota were doing that day: she voted the straight Republican ticket.

That night as she sat with Rusk, watching as the early victories rolled in, she agreed when he cried: 'Maggie, we're going to put some iron in this nation's backbone.' Toward nine o'clock, when the magnitude of the swing was obvious, he said with fierce determination: 'We have the White House, the Supreme Court, the Senate and enough right-thinking Democrats on our side to control the House. Maggie, we've captured the nation! For as long as you and I live, things are going to be handled our way.'

At a point when it was clear in the returns that all areas reporting so far, except the nation's capital, had chosen Reagan, Rusk growled: 'If that city full of niggers is so out of tune with national thinking, it shouldn't have the vote,' and Maggie said sharply: 'Ransom! You're never to use that word again,' and he grumbled: 'I'll watch myself when I'm in your hearing,' but she said: 'Never! And I mean it! A man in your position cheapens himself with such a word.' He turned from the television, stared at her as if he had never seen her before – or had not appreciated her if he had seen her – and then returned to his victorious watching.

When it was certain that all states except Minnesota had cast their votes for Reagan and proper American values, he said: 'That entire state should be sent to a psychiatrist. To be offered a choice between Reagan and Mondale and to choose Phinicky Phfritz . . . the whole place must be sick.'

In triumph, a man who had helped save a nation, he drove her primly to one of the Larkin motels, promising as he left her: 'Tomorrow I'll close the financing,' and she realized that all his life he had been able to throw his full attention into something like the election of a president, then start afresh the next morning on a new assignment that bore no relationship to the preceding one. In this regard he was a lot like Texas: the first settlers lived off cattle, the next off cotton and slaves, then came the big empty ranches, then oil, then computers, and what would come next, only God knew. She hoped she and Rusk would be able to unload their share of The Nottingham before Austin went bust.

. . . Task Force

During the two-year existence of our Task Force we had often suffered snide attacks that were launched upon Texas, and always they seemed to focus on its wealth. Outsiders either envied our possession of it or resented the way we spent it. As our deliberations drew to a close in December 1984, I had the opportunity to witness and even participate in three typical explosions of Texas wealth, and I report them without venturing a judgment.

When it came time to draft our report, we encountered little difficulty, although Ransom Rusk did insist upon a minority statement, signed only by him, decrying emphasis on multicultural aspects of Texas history and calling for a return to the simple Anglo-Saxon Protestant virtues which had made the state great; Professor Garza submitted his own nonhysterical minority report defending Señorita Múzquiz's interpretation of bilingual education and recommending that it continue through at least the sixth grade.

When none of us would co-sign either document, Garza taunted us amiably for what he called our 'ostrichlike capacity for hiding from reality.' When Miss Cobb asked: 'What do you mean, Efraín?' he said: 'I want each of you to answer honestly, "How many illegal Mexican immigrants do you employ?"' Rusk said: 'That's a fair question. Various projects, maybe forty.' Quimper said: 'I have about six each on my nine ranches. Four extra at the home ranch.' Miss Cobb said she employed two maids and two men, and I surprised them by saying: 'Lucky for me, I have a maid who comes in three days.'

But it was Garza who startled us: 'I have a husband and wife. Invaluable.' Then he smiled: 'And this committee, which depends upon Mexicans, thinks that the problem is going to fade away? So be it.'

On all other content we agreed easily; we recommended more careful structuring of the two levels of teaching in Texas history: 'The primary level, where the child first encounters the glories of Texas history, should depend less on fable and more on historical reality, which is miraculous enough to ignite young minds. And in the junior-high obligatory course, educators must remember that because of heavy immigration from the North, classrooms will be filled with young people who have never before studied the glories of Texas history and who will not be familiar with its unique and heroic nature. A most careful effort must be made to inform them properly before it is too late.'

Philosophically I supported Miss Cobb in a statement she proposed: 'We recommend strongly that in both primary and junior-high, Texas history be taught only by teachers trained in the subject.' But to our surprise, Rusk, Quimper and Garza refused to vote in favor, for, as Quimper pointed out: 'We have to have somewhere to stack our football coaches in the off season.' Miss Cobb wanted me to join her in signing a minority report, but I told her I would not, since I felt that it would be improper for the chairman to reveal that he could not hold his horses together. My real reason was that I did not want to stir up the football fanatics, for if I did, there was little chance that our report would be accepted. Texas history might be revered, but Texas football was sacred.

I was involved in the first money explosion. On the December day our report was to be signed, I announced that my temporary duty in Texas had proved so congenial that I was surrendering my job at Boulder in order to accept an appointment to the Department of Texas Studies at the university. My colleagues and our staff applauded my action, and when I was asked why I had made what must have been a difficult decision, I said: 'It was easy. Consider the things that have happened here since I took this chairmanship. The Mexican peso has collapsed, turning the Rio Grande Valley into a disaster area. Then Hurricane Alicia struck, threatening to wreck Houston, which had already been suffering from forty-three million square feet of unrented business space. Next the Great Freeze of 1983 destroyed the citrus crop, completing the wreckage of the Valley. The west didn't escape, either, what with that Midland bank going under for a billion and a quarter and the Ogallala Aquifer dropping precipitously, so that farmers out there are beginning to cry panic. The Dallas area got its share, with Braniff going bankrupt and TexTek dropping a billion dollars in one day. Farmers everywhere were hit with a drought. And to top it all, the Dallas Cowboys folded three straight years. Hell, the blows this state has had to absorb in one brief spell would collapse the ordinary nation.'

'What's your point?' asked Rusk, who had been rocked by many of the disasters.

'Point is, I respect a state that can spring back, pull up its socks, and forge ahead as if nothing had happened. And I like the way Lorena's nephew out in Lubbock is fighting for sensible water legislation.'

But Miss Cobb had a much simpler statement, and one that came closer to the truth: 'Texas seduced him to come back home, as it has a way of doing.' And I agreed.

But then Rusk released his bombshell: 'Barlow, even though you are a liberal and a near-communist, the three of us, Miss Lorena, Lorenzo and I, have put together a little kitty to endow your chair in Texas Studies at the university.'

'One million clams,' Quimper said as the research staff gasped.

Miss Cobb explained: 'Under the terms of the grant, Barlow can't spend a penny on himself, but he can apply the yearly interest to the purchase of books for the library and fellowships for his graduate students – not generous, but enough to live on. So why don't you assistants enroll with him for your Ph.D.s?'

This unexpected bonanza had an interesting effect on our staff. I had been aware, as our work drew to a close, that they were growing apprehensive about their futures, and to have this sudden manna descend upon them was a boon. The young woman from SMU, seeing herself reprieved from a life of writing publicity releases, showed tears. The young man from El Paso sat stunned. But the young fellow from Texas Tech acted sensibly: he kissed Miss Cobb. What did I do? I remained gratefully silent, thinking of the tenured years ahead and of the endless chain of young scholars who would work with me and of the good we would accomplish together.

After mutual congratulations, we attacked the final agenda, and Garza, Miss Cobb and I suggested that we conclude our report with two vital paragraphs. Knowing that they would occasion sharp comment from the public, we wanted them to say exactly what we intended, and no more:

Any state which acquires great power is obligated to provide outstanding moral and intellectual leadership. Although we believe that Texas has the capacity for such leadership, we cannot identify in what significant fields it will be exerted. When Massachusetts led the nation, its power was manifested in its religious and intellectual leadership. When Virginia gained preeminence, it was because of the learning, the philosophy and the style of her citizens. When New York undertook the burden, it excelled in publishing, theater and art. When California led, it was through Hollywood, television and attractive life styles.

In what fields is Texas qualified to lead? It has no major publishing house, no art except cowboy illustration, no philosophical preeminence. Obviously, it has other valuable assets, but not ones that society prizes highly. It leads the nation in consuming popular music; it has bravado, and is wildly devoted to football. It runs the risk of becoming America's Sparta rather than its Athens. And history does not deal kindly with its Spartas.

When Rusk saw our draft he exploded: 'You sound like a bunch of commies, and frankly, Lorena, I'm amazed you would put your signature to such a document.'

'You have it wrong, Ransom. I didn't agree to it. I wrote it. the other two support it.'

'The Cobb senators will be turning in their graves. They loved Texas.'

'And so do I. I will not stand by and see it converted into a Sparta.'

'Quimper,' Rusk cried, 'help me kill this thing!' But to everyone's surprise, Lorenzo sided with us: 'Ransom, it's a proper warning. Hand it over, I'll sign it.'

'Is everyone going crazy?' Rusk bellowed, and Quimper said: 'I've been looking into the real Il Magnifico, that Medici fellow.

And what do I find? In his day he led the Florentine Mafia, like my father led the Texas Mafia. But he's remembered for his patronage of the arts. He tried to make Florence think. I feel the same about Texas.'

'If you people insert that statement,' Rusk threatened, 'I'll blast hell out of it in a minority disclaimer.'

'You won't,' Miss Cobb said quietly, 'because if you did, you'd look foolish, and you can't afford that.' When he continued to bristle, she soothed him until he surrendered; he'd refrain from public dissent if we'd allow him to alter a few phrases. He changed *Although we believe that Texas has the capacity* . . . to *We know that Texas has the capacity* . . . He also changed *In what fields is Texas qualified to lead?* to *In what fields will Texas lead?* And he changed *it has bravado* to something which we all preferred: *it still has the courage to take great risks*.

Then Quimper made his own good change, knocking out the condescending part about popular music and substituting *It has four universities which will soon be among the best in the land, Texas, Rice, A&M, SMU* . . .

When all was done, Rusk asked Miss Cobb: 'Was Sparta so bad?' and she replied: 'It was a flaming bore, and we must avoid that in Texas,' whereupon he growled: 'Only an ass would call Texas boring.'

The million dollars for my chair was the first display of obscene Texas wealth. Now to the other two. They focused on Ransom Rusk and came well after our December report had been submitted. The first was initiated by Lorenzo Quimper, the second by Miss Cobb, and each was quite wonderful in its own Texas way.

At the amicable year-end dinner which ended our final session, Quimper said, as the wine was being passed: 'Ransom, you sit on all that money of yours, and you don't do a single constructive thing with it. You're a disgrace to the state of Texas.'

'What should I do?' Rusk asked, and this was a mistake, because Quimper had a proposal worked out in detail. He needed several months of telephone calls to flesh it out, but when he was done and all parts were in place, he produced a Lorenzo Quimper extravaganza which would be talked about for years to come.

'What we're going to do,' he explained in my Austin office, 'is introduce Ransom Rusk, secretive Texas billionaire, to the general public, who will be allowed to see him as the lovable and generous man we Task Force members have discovered him to be.'

'What will you offer,' I asked, 'a mass execution of Democrats?'

'No, we're going to put on a masterful Texas bull auction. Ransom is proud of his Texas Longhorns, some of the best in America, but few people get a chance to see them. What we'll do is sell off eighty-three of the choicest range animals you ever saw.'

'That could involve a lot of people, maybe three, four hundred.'

Lorenzo looked at me as if I had lost my mind: 'Son, we're talkin' about five, six thousand.'

'Why would that many come to a . . . ?'

Quimper put his arm about my shoulder in his confidential style, and said in a low, persuasive voice: 'Son, half of Texas will be fightin' to get in.'

Excited by the prospects of a really slam-bang cattle sale, he involved me in the wild festivities he had planned on Rusk's behalf, and I was staggered by what a Texas multimillionaire would recommend to a friend who was a Texas billionaire.

By sunset on the Friday before the auction eleven Learjets were lined up on the grassy field beside the Larkin runway, and next morning at least eighty smaller planes flew in, including six helicopters that ferried important guests to the ranch, eleven miles away. On Saturday eighteen huge blue-and-white Trailways buses, each with uniformed driver, moved endlessly around the motels, hostels and guest houses, stopping finally at the airport to finish loading before heading for the Rusk ranch.

At four different barricades on the way armed security men in uniform halted us to inspect our credentials, and when we were cleared, the buses delivered us to a huge field prepared for the occasion. It was lined by thirty-six green-and-white portable toilets. 'Experience has taught,' Quimper said as he showed me around, 'that proper division is twenty-one for women, fifteen for men, because women take longer.'

More than a hundred Rusk employees and high school students hired for the day were scattered through the vast crowd, each dressed in the distinctive colors of the ranch, gold and blue, and twenty of the more attractive young girls, in skimpy costume, manned that number of drink stands, serving endless quantities of beer, Coke, Dr Pepper and a tangy orange drink, all well iced. What gave me great pleasure, a mariachi band of seven musicians – two blaring trumpets, two guitars, two violins, one double bass guitar – strolled amiably through the grounds, playing 'Guadalajara' and 'Cu-cu-ru-cu-cu Paloma.'

At noon four open-air kitchens operated, serving a delicious barbecue with pinto beans, salad, wholewheat buns, cheese, pickles and coconut cake, and at one o'clock we all gathered in the huge tent, where a large stand had been erected behind a sturdily fenced-in area in which the Longhorns would be exhibited one by one as the sale progressed. Eighteen hundred interested men and women filled the tent as the two auctioneers appeared to considerable applause. They were a fine-looking pair of men in their early forties, prematurely silver-haired and possessed of leather lungs. 'The Reyes brothers,' Quimper said as they bowed, acknowledging the applause of spectators who were proud of them. 'Their father was born a penniless peasant in Durango, northern Mexico,' Quimper said. 'Walked to the Rio Grande, that muddy highway to salvation, swam across, and found a job at a dollar a day. He sired fourteen children and sent them all to college. The six girls became teachers, medical assistants, what have you. The eight boys all went to A&M, doctors, accountants and these two skilled auctioneers. Shows what can be done.'

The Reyes would be assisted, I learned, by four energetic young men who made themselves the highlight of the sale, for they remained at ground level, each wearing a big cowboy hat, and it was their job to excite the crowd, encourage the bidding, and wave frantically, shouting at the top of their voices: 'Twenty-three thousand here!' or 'Twenty-four in the back!' I asked Quimper who they were, and he smiled proudly: 'What I do, we establish a generous budget for advertising. Maybe a dozen major cattle publications. But before I give any magazine a bundle of cash, I make a deal: 'I'll give you the advertising,

Bert, but you must send me one of your editors to help." These are the men the magazines have sent.' They were an active screaming lot.

The Reyes brothers were verbal machine-guns, rattling off a jargon of which I understood not one word until they slammed a piece of oak wood against a reverberating board: 'Once, twice, sold to Big L Ranch of Okmulgee, Oklahoma.'

Since there were eighty-three animals to be sold, each one groomed and perfect, and since the average price seemed to be about $29,000, it was obvious that the sale was going to fetch more than $2,000,000, which explained why no bidder ever sat for fifteen minutes before one of the costumed Rusk girls appeared with a tray of iced drinks. 'We want to keep them happy,' Quimper said, but I pointed out a curiosity of the sale: 'Lorenzo, if you sell only eighty-three animals, and if the same bidders keep buying two and three each, there's only thirty or forty people in this tent who are seriously participating.'

'You're right. The rest are like you. They come for the freebies ... food, drinks and entertainment.' He indicated the huge crowd of watchers, then added: 'And to see what Ransom Rusk looks like.'

He looked great. Tall, thin, dressed in complete cowboy garb, smiling wanly, nodding occasionally when a particularly fine animal was sold, he stood at the far side of the auctioneer's stand, saying nothing unless the manager of the sale halted the bidding to ask him: 'Mr Rusk, this bull brought top dollar at the Ferguson Dispersal, did it not?' and then Rusk would say, with the microphone in his face: 'It did. A hundred and nine thousand dollars,' and the rapid-fire chatter of the Reyes would resume.

Quimper had a dozen surprises for the crowd. After the second bull had been sold, a roar went up, and when I looked about I saw that a remarkable man had taken his place in the middle of the screaming helpers. He was in his sixties and weighed about two hundred and sixty pounds. 'It's Hoss Shaw,' Quimper informed me. 'Imported him from Mississippi. Enthusiastic aide, best in the business.'

If the four young men were active, Hoss was volcanic. Chewing on a long black cigar, he leaped about, roared in a bullfrog voice, wheedled shamelessly, and when he elicited a bid he went into paroxysms. Throwing both arms aloft, he kicked one leg so high, he looked as if he were a crow about to take off. Watching Hoss Shaw report a bid could be exhausting.

'He adds two, three thousand dollars to each animal,' Quimper whispered. 'Worth every penny of his commission.'

With his arrival the serious part of the auction began, and I was perplexed by the confusing variety of cattle items for sale. An expert beside me explained: 'We call it a bull sale, and as you can see, we do sell bulls. In various ways. You can buy a bull outright and take him home to your ranch. Or you can buy part of a bull – breeding rights and profits from the sale of frozen semen – but the bull stays here. Or you can buy a straw of frozen semen and impregnate your cow on your own ranch.'

But it was when the cows came up for sale that I really became bewildered. The expert again explained: 'First you have a cow, pure and simple, like this one being sold now. Then you have a cow, but she's certified pregnant by a known bull. Then you have a pregnant cow, with a calf suckling at her side . . . that's a three-fer, and you buy enough three-fers, you've got yourself a big start.'

'That sounds simple enough,' I said, but he laughed: 'Son, I'm only beginning. In the old days a great Longhorn cow like Measles, best in forty years, could produce a calf a year . . . maybe sixteen in her lifetime, each one more valuable than gold. But now we can feed her hormones, collect her eggs as she produces them in her ovaries, inseminate them artificially, and encourage her to give us not one calf a year, but maybe thirty or forty.'

'Sounds indecent!' Then I asked: 'But how does she give birth to them all?' and the expert laughed: 'That's where genius comes in. We place each fertilized egg, one b one, in the uterus of any healthy cow . . .'

'Another Longhorn?'

'Any breed, so long as the cow is big and healthy and capable of giving good milk to her young.'

'And that nothing cow produces a Longhorn calf?'

'She does. But it's the next step that tickles me. Experts can slice a fertilized egg in half, implant each half in a different recipient cow, and produce identical twins, three times out of ten.'

'Aren't you fellows playing God?'

'Son, we're doin' with Texas Longhorns today what scientists are gonna do with people tomorrow.'

But I was most interested in the next items, for into the auction ring came, one by one, six animals with the longest, wildest horns I had ever seen. They were steers, so in normal husbandry they would have been good only for the meat market if young or the dog-food industry if aged, but here, because of their tremendous horns, they were remarkable assets, eagerly sought by Texas ranchers. 'We call them "walkin'-around Longhorns,"' the man said. 'We buy them to adorn our ranches so women can "Oh!" and "Ah!" when they come out to see us from Houston or Dallas. They're also very effective if you're trying to borrow money from a visiting Boston banker.'

How grand those horns were! 'Real rocking chairs,' my informant said admiringly, and when a huge, rangy beast stalked in with horns seventy-seven inches from tip to tip, he started bidding wildly, and I cheered him on, for this was a remarkable animal. Finally I winked at Hoss Shaw, as if to say; 'You got a live one here,' and Hoss put on his act until my man bought the magnificent steer for $11,000. 'You got some real walkin'-around stock that time,' I whispered, and he said: 'Thanks for your encouragement. I might have dropped out.'

At one point I got the impression that more than half the bidders were medical doctors, and when I asked Quimper about this, he said: 'In Texas, never get sick during a cattle sale. Most of the doctors will be at the auction.'

It was a dreamlike day – the dust of the great buses, the noise of the helicopters, the aromatic smoke from the mesquite logs toasting the barbecue, the soft singing of the mariachis, the whirling about of the pretty girls in their short skirts as they passed out drinks, the rapid-fire cries of the Reyes brothers: 'Hoody-hoody-hoody-harkle-harle-krimshaw-krimshaw twenty-six thousand,' the figure repeated eleven times before Hoss Shaw screamed, arms waving, one foot in the air: 'Twenty-seven thousand.'

But when the noise was greatest, there was a solemn moment, forcing even the rowdiest participants to come to attention as a splendid Longhorn bull was brought into the pen. An expert from Wichita Refuge in Oklahoma took the microphone and said: 'Ladies and gentlemen! As you may remember, in 1927 the United States woke up to the fact that the famed Texas Longhorn was about to vanish from this earth. Fortunately, the thoughtful men and women of that period took action, and my predecessors at the Refuge scoured the West and Mexico looking for authentic animals with which to rebuild the breed. It was here in Larkin, at the ranch of our host's grandmother, Emma Larkin Rusk, that they found that core of great Longhorns on which we rebuilt.

'No name was prouder, no animal meant more to the recovery of the Longhorn than Mean Moses VI, the perfect bull that Emma Rusk sent up to the Refuge. Along with the sensational cow Bathtub Bertha, these animals launched the famous MM/BB line, and right now we're going to bring before you the living epitome of the breed – Mean Moses XIX.' As we cheered, the left-hand flanking gate opened and up the ramp came the stately bull, long, mean, rangy, not too fat but tremendously prepotent.

'Ladies and gentlemen,' intoned the auctioneer. 'Mean Moses XIX, top animal in his breed, is owned by a consortium. He lives on this ranch, but he belongs to the industry. Today we are selling one-tenth interest in this greatest of the Longhorns. One-tenth only, ladies and gentlemen, and the bull stays here. But you participate fully in the nationwide sale of his semen. Do I hear a bid of fifty thousand?'

I gasped, for if Reyes could get a starting bid of that amount, it meant that Mean Moses was valued at $500,000. The bid was immediately forthcoming, and before I could catch my breath it stood at $80,000, at which Hoss Shaw sprang into action, dancing and wheedling the bidders until the hammer fell at $110,000. Mean Moses, whose line had been kept extant only by the affection of Emma Larkin Rusk, was verifiably worth $1,100,000.

As night fell, six thousand bowls of chili were served with Mexican sweets on the side, and the visitors found seats about the place, facing the large stage which Quimper had erected for the occasion and onto which now came the first of three orchestras that would entertain till two in the morning.

It was a beautiful night, as fine as this region of Texas

provided, and the music was noisy and country. People wandered about freely, locating old friends, making appointments and closing deals. Men running for office circulated, shaking hands, and some of the most beautiful women in America moved about, lending grace to the night.

I should have suspected that something was up when I saw among these beauties one who was especially attractive, a girl I had cheered with the graduate assistant at the University of Texas. She had been Beth Morrison then, premier baton twirler of the South West Conference and everybody's sweetheart. Now she was Beth Macnab, wife of the Dallas Cowboys' linebacker. She and her husband went to New York a good deal, the gossip columns said, where they were friends with various painters, who stayed with them when the artists had one-man exhibitions in Texas.

I could not imagine why Beth, who was now regarded as one of our Texas intellectuals, had bothered to attend a bull auction in Larkin, but I gave the matter no further thought, because Quimper took the stage to make an announcement which stunned the crowd: 'Our brochure said we'd have four bands. The mariachis, the dance band you've been hearing, and the Nashville Brass, who were so sensational. What the brochure did not say was that the fourth band which we'll now hear brings with it the immortal Willie Nelson!'

The crowd went berserk, because many of its members had known Willie when he was a voice wailing in the wilderness, adhering to a simple statement which seemed to lack the ingredients of popular acceptance. I used to listen to him in the small Austin bars and tell my friends: 'This cat can sing. He has a statement to make.' And then in the 1970s the world discovered that people like me had been right, and he became not only a roaring success, but also a symbol of that stubborn Texas type which clings to a belief, ignores snubs, and survives into a kind of immortality. Willie Nelson was basic Texas, and when he came on stage in tennis shoes, beat-up jeans, ragged shirt and red bandanna about his head, some of us old-timers had tears in our eyes. What a voice! What a presence! By damn, when Lorenzo Quimper threw a bull sale, he threw it just short of Montana.

But even Willie was not the highlight of the evening, for after he had given us a masterful rendition of 'Blue Eyes Cryin' in the Rain' Quimper took the stage, drums rolled, and Willie stepped aside. 'Friends,' Quimper said, 'my dear associate Ransom Rusk, who has arranged this celebration, has been just what the cartoonist pictured, a lonely, self-motivated Texas oilman of untold wealth. He was afraid of people, so I prevailed upon him to invite six thousand of his most intimate friends here tonight to share with him a moment of transcendant joy. Friends!' – Lorenzo's voice elevated to a bellow – 'Ransom Rusk, that mean-spirited, lonely son-of-a-gun, sittin' in his office at midnight countin' his billions, he's gonna get married!'

As we cheered and whistled, Rusk, in a freshly pressed blue whipcord rancher's outfit featuring a pair of special gold boots provided by Quimper, came on stage and bowed. Taking the microphone, he said, pointing to Quimper: 'Loudmouth is right. I'm getting married. And I want you to be the first to meet the bride.' From the wings he brought in Maggie Morrison, forty-nine years old, one hundred and twenty-one pounds, and the portrait of a successful Houston real estate magnate. She wore, to her own surprise but at the insistence of Quimper, the Mexican China Poblana costume, complete with Quimper boots and topped by a delightful straw hat from whose brim dangled twenty-four little silver bells. She was a warm-hearted, smiling woman of maximum charm, and I thought: Rusk is lucky to land that one.

But Quimper was not finished – indeed, he was never satisfied with anything he did, so far as I could recall, for there was always a little something he wanted to add – and this time he added a stunner: 'Good Ol' Rance is not only gettin' hisse'f a stunnin' wife, but he also gets one of the most beautiful daughters in Texas, Beth Macnab!' When B h came onstage, Lorenzo signaled to the wings and a pretty girl of fourteen ran out with a silver baton.

'This is a surprise, folks, and I haven't warned Beth, but how about some of those All-American twirls?'

It had been some years since Beth had performed at the various half-times throughout the state – Dallas Cowboys, Cotton Bowl and the rest – and she could properly have begged off, but this was her mother's big night, so she kicked off her high heels and said: 'A girl doesn't usually twirl in an outfit like this, but if Mom is brave enough to marry Ransom Rusk after what the papers say about him, I'm brave enough to make a fool of myself.'

She threw the baton high in the air, waited with her lovely face upturned, and was lucky enough to catch it. Bowing to the crowd, she returned the baton to the girl, then blew kisses fore and aft: 'Never press your luck. Mom, this is wonderful. Pop, welcome to the family.' And she parked a big kiss on Ransom's cheek.

When the couple returned to Texas in August after a hurried honeymoon in Rome, Paris and London, Miss Cobb called me on the phone and asked me to rush immediately to Dallas, where our disbanded Task Force was to meet with Ransom Rusk and his new wife, and when we filed into the room to meet him, she spoke bluntly: 'Ransom, my work with you on our committee and my attendance at your bull sale made me appreciate you as a real human being. And the fact that you were brave enough to marry this delightful woman from Houston confirms my feelings.'

'Sounds like an ominous preamble,' he said, and she replied: 'It is.'

None of us knew what she had in mind and we were startled when she disclosed it: 'I think your good friend Lorenzo did you a great service when he prevailed upon you to throw that bash. Best thing you ever did, Ransom. Made you human. But it's not enough.'

'What else did you have in mind?' he asked gruffly.

'You're one of the richest men in our state, maybe the richest. But you've never done one damned thing for Texas. And I think that's scandalous.'

'Now wait . . .'

'Oh, I know, a football scholarship here and there, your fund for leprosy research. But I mean something commensurate with your stature.'

'Like what?'

'Have you ever, in your pinched-in little life, visited the great museum complex in Fort Worth?'

'Not really. A reception now and then, but I don't like receptions.'

'Are you aware that Fort Worth, which people in Dallas like to call a cowtown ... do you know that it has one of the world's noblest museum complexes? A perfect gem?'

'I don't know much about museums.'

'You're going to find our right now.' And she dragooned all of us, plus Mrs Rusk, whom she insisted upon, and we drove over to that elegant assembly of buildings which formed one of the most graceful parts of Texas: the delicate Kimbell museum, with its splendid European paintings; the heavy museum of modern art, with its bold contemporary painting; and the enticing Amon Carter Museum of Western Art, with its unmatched collection of Charley Russell, Frederick Remington and other cowboy artists. Few cities offered such a compact variety of enticing art.

'What did you want me to do?' Rusk asked when the whirlwind trip ended, and Miss Cobb said boldly: 'Rance, there's an excellent piece of land in that complex still open. I want you to place your own museum there. Build the best and stock it with the best.'

'Well, I ...'

'Rance, in due course you'll be dead. Remembered for what? A gaggle of oil wells? Who gives a damn? Really, Rance, ask yourself that question, and let's meet here two weeks from today.'

'Now wait ...'

She would not wait. Standing boldly before him, she said: 'Rance, I'm talking about your soul. Ask Maggie, she'll know what I mean.' And she started for the door, but when she reached it she reminded him: 'Two weeks from today. And I shall want to hear your plans, because in my own way, Rance, I love you, and I cannot see you go down to your grave unremembered and uncherished.'

No one spoke. Of course it was Quimper who finally broke the silence, for he did not like vacant air: 'She's right, Rance. It would be a notable gesture.'

Rusk turned harshly on his friend: 'What the hell have you ever done with your money, Quimper?' and Lorenzo said: 'Get your spies to uncover how much I've given to the university. Did you know that it now has a chair of poetry in my name?'

'And forty baseball scholarships,' Garza said, and Quimper laughed: 'Each man to his own specialization.'

When the meeting broke, Rusk asked me to remain behind, and this started one of the wildest periods of my life, for he wanted me to discuss with him in the most intricate detail what would be involved if he donated a fourth museum to the Fort Worth complex, but first we had to decide what the museum would cover. He arranged with the university for me to take a six-month leave, paid for by him, and patiently we went over the options. When he suggested a cowboy museum, I reminded him that the Amon Carter had preempted that specialty, and then he proposed an oil museum but I reminded him that what we were talking about was an art museum: 'Besides, both Midland and Kilgore already have excellent oil museums. And what's worse, oil has never produced much art.'

He asked me if a man like him could buy enough European art to compete with the Kimbell, and I had to tell him no: 'Besides, that's already been done.'

I shall never forget the long day we spent at the Kimbell, with him trying to discover what it was that justified such a magnificent building, a poem, really, for he wanted to know everything. I remember especially his comments on several of the paintings. The chef-d'oeuvre of the collection was the marvelous Giovanni Bellini 'Mother and Child,' and when he finished studying it he said: 'That's real art. Reverent.' He dismissed the great Duccio, which showed Italian watchers hiding their noses as the corpse of Lazarus was raised from the dead: 'That's a disgrace to the Bible.'

He paid his longest visit to a beautiful Gainsborough, a languid young woman in a blue gown seated beneath a tree. 'Miss Lloyd' the picture was titled, and I thought that she had awakened some arcane memory, for he returned to the portrait numerous times, in obvious perplexity. Finally he took out a ball-point pen, not to make notes but to hold it to his right eye as he made comparisons. After about twenty minutes of such study he said: 'She'd have to be eleven feet nine inches tall,' and when I restudied the delightful painting, I saw that he was right, for Gainsborough had elongated Miss Lloyd preposterously.

'Whoever painted it should be fired,' he growled, and I said:

'Too late. He died in 1788.'

But he did not miss the glory of this museum, its excellent structure and the way it fitted into its landscape: 'What would a building to match this one cost?' I told him that with current prices it could run to eighteen or twenty million, minimum, and even then, with far less square footage. He nodded.

At three A.M., three days before our scheduled meeting with Miss Cobb, my phone rang insistently, and Rusk cried: 'Come right over. I've sent my driver.' And when I reached his modest Dallas quarters in which the new Mrs Rusk shared the lone bedroom and bath, I found both of them in nightrobes, in the bedroom, surrounded by a blizzard of newspapers.

'I've got my museum! I was reading in bed, running options through my mind, and I asked myself: "What is the biggest thing in Texas?" And this newspaper here gave me the answer.' It was a Thursday edition of the *Dallas Morning News* and I looked for the headlines to provide a clue, but I could not find any. Instead, Rusk had about him eight special sections which the paper had added that day, making it one of the biggest weekday papers I'd seen. He grabbed my arm and asked: 'What *is* the biggest thing in Texas?' and I said: 'Religion, but the cathedrals take care of that.'

'Guess again!' and I said: 'Oil, but Midland and Kilgore handle that.'

'And again?' and I said: 'Ranching, but the Amon Carter Museum covers that.' So he slapped the eight special sections of the newspaper and said: 'Look for yourself. The *Dallas News* knows what really counts,' and when I picked up the sections I found that the paper, in response to an insatiable hunger among its Texas readers, had published one hundred and twelve pages of extra football news: Professional, with the accent on Dallas. Professional, other teams. Colleges, with the accent on Texas teams. Colleges, the others. High Schools, very thick. High Schools, how star players should handle recruiting. Sixteen full pages on the latter, plus, of course, the customary sixteen pages of current fooball news, or one hundred and twenty-eight pages in all.

Rusk, having made his great discovery, beamed like a boy who has seen the light regarding the Pythagorean theorem: 'Sport!' And as soon as he uttered that almost sacred word, I could see an outstanding museum added to those in the park.

Neither he nor I, and certainly not Maggie Rusk, visualized it as a Sports Hall of Fame filled with old uniforms and used boxing gloves. Every state tried that, often disastrously. No, what we saw was a real art museum, a legitimate hall of beauty filled with notable examples of how sport had so often inspired artists to produce work of the first category: 'No junk. No baseball cards. No old uniforms.' Rusk was speaking at four in the morning: 'Just great paintings, like that Madonna we saw.'

I warned him that the art salesrooms were not filled with Bellini studies of football players, but he dismissed the objection: 'It will be American art depicting American sports.' And when dawn broke we three went out to an all-night truck stop and had scrambled eggs.

By the time Miss Cobb and the others reached Dallas that weekend, the Rusks had a full prospectus roughed out, but before they were allowed to present it, Miss Cobb distributed a glossy pamphlet that had been printed in high style by the Smithsonian in Washington: 'Before we mention specific plans, I want to upgrade your horizons. I want us to do something significant, and to do that we must entertain significant thoughts.'

Holding the pamphlet in her hand, she looked directly at Rusk and Quimper: 'You two clowns thought very big with your bull sale. Glorious. Real Texas. My two Cobb senators would have applauded. They said it was important to keep alive the old traditions, and I must confess, Rance and Lorenzo, you not only kept them alive, you added a few touches. Now look at someone else who has thought big.'

I was perplexed when I looked at my copy of the pamphlet, for it apparently recounted a gala affair at the Smithsonian in which a Texas oil and technology man, Pierre Soult, had been honored by the President, the Chief Justice and some hundred dignitaries from American and European universities. It was a rather thick pamphlet and three-fourths of it was taken up by photographs; before I could inspect them, Rusk said: 'I worked with Soult. One of the best. Died far too soon.'

What the rear two-thirds of the pamphlet showed were the twenty-seven colleges and universities to which Pierre Soult, the seismographer and founder of TexTek, had given either magnificent solo buildings or entire complexes. Any one would have been the gesture of a lifetime – a tower at MIT, a quadrangle at the University of Vancouver in Canada, a School of Geology at Sydney in Australia – but when I saw the two entire colleges, and I mean all the buildings, which he had given to Cambridge in England and the Sorbonne in France, I was staggered.

Twenty-seven tremendous monuments dug from the soil of the most barren fields in Texas, twenty-seven halls of learning paid for by the exalted profits of TexTek. The total cost? Incalculable. But there they stood, in nine unconnected corners of the world, more than half in the United States, and more than half of those in Texas, centers of learning and light.

'I want us all to think in those terms,' Miss Cobb said, and Rusk snapped: 'It's my money we're talking about,' and she said: 'My father always told us "Rich people need guidance." We're here to help you, Rance, because we love you and we don't want to see you miss the big parade. Now what bright idea did you and Barlow come up with?'

'Sport,' Rusk said, and Miss Cobb asked: 'You mean one of those pathetic Halls of Fame? Old jockstraps cast in bronze? Old men recalling the lost days of their youth?'

'I do not,' Rusk snapped. 'I mean an art museum. As legitimate as any in the world. Fine art, like the Kimbell, but glorifying sport.'

Miss Cobb pondered this, and then said enthusiastically: 'That could be most effective, Ransom, but don't keep it parochially American. Be universal, the way Pierre Soult was with his gifts.'

'You mean art from all over the world?' he asked, and she replied: 'I do. We Americans forget that our three big sports – football, baseball, basketball – are focused here. If you do this, don't be parochial.'

If there was one thing the new Texan, of whom Rusk was a prototype, did not want to be, it was parochial: 'You make sense, Lorena.' Then, turning to me, he issued an imperial ukase: 'Barlow, we'll make it universal.'

At the end of that long day she kissed Ransom: 'I have a feeling, Rance, you'll do it right. Make Quimper your treasurer. He likes to spend other people's money. And keep Barlow at your side. He'll know what art is.'

Early next morning Rusk summoned me to his office: 'Hire the man who built the Kimbell and tell him to get started.'

'Louis J. Kahn is dead. That was his masterpiece.'

'Get me the next man . . . just as good.'

'They don't come "just as good," but there are several around who design buildings of great beauty.'

'Get me the best and have him start his drawings this weekend.'

'Architects don't work that way,' I warned him, and he growled: 'This time they will,' and within a month, an architect from Chicago, noted for buildings of great style which caught the spirit of the West, was making provisional designs for a new kind of museum ideally suited to the Fort Worth site, and two months later, ground was broken, with no announcement having been made to the public.

In the meantime I had opened an office in New York to which all the dealers in America, it seemed, traipsed in with samples of their wares, and I was astonished at how many fine American artists had created works based on sport. With a budget larger than any I had ever played with even in my imagination, I put together a guiding committee of seven, three art experts, two artists and two businessmen unfamiliar with Texas or Ransom Rusk, and with the most meticulous care we began reserving a few pieces we would probably want to buy when we started our actual accumulations. Rusk flew in from Dallas to see if we were prepared to fill his fine new museum when the scores of builders and landscape architects working overtime had it ready. For when a Texas billionaire cried 'Let us have a museum!' . . . zingo! he wanted it right now.

Loath to accept personal responsibility for what he termed 'this disgraceful delay,' I assembled my committee and seven major curators and experts for a day's meeting at the Pierre, and there we thrashed out our problems. Rusk listened as a curator from the Metropolitan explained that in the case of a wonderful Thomas Eakins painting, 'Charles Rogers Fishing,' negotiations with the present owners could require as much as a year: 'The Sturdevant family is divided. Half want to sell, the other half don't. A matter of settling the old man's estate.'

'Then we'll forget that one,' Rusk snapped, but the Met man counseled patience: 'Were you fortunate enough to get that Eakins, it alone would set the style for your whole museum. Men like me, and Charles here, we'd have to come to Fort Worth to see what other good things you have.'

'You're satisfied there's enough out there to build a topnotch museum?'

'Unquestionably!' and these fourteen experts grew rhapsodic over the possibilities.

One man from Cleveland summarized the situation: 'Even we were uninformed as to the magnificent possibilities. In the short time we've worked we've come up with a dazzling list of how artists have portrayed men engaged in sports. Ancient Greek statues, Roman athletes, Degas jockeys, Stubbs' unmatched portraits of racehorses.'

'Never heard of that one. Who was he?'

'George Stubbs of England – 1724 to 1806. No one ever painted horses better than Stubbs.'

'Can we buy one of his works? I mean, one of his recognized masterpieces?'

And that was the question which led to the explosive idea which got the Fort Worth Museum of Sports Art launched with a bang that no one like me could have engineered, because when these experts explained that to find a Stubbs or a Degas that might be coming onto the market took infinite patience and a high degree of skill to negotiate the sale, Rusk saw that his building was going to be finished long before he had much to put in it.

'The things you've been talking about are European. I understand why they might be difficult to find and deal for. But how about American art? Have we produced any good things?'

It was here that the experts became poetic: 'Wonderful things! But again, Mr Rusk, all requiring many months of bargaining and cajoling.'

'Why can't we just find a good painting and say "I'll take that"?' and the man from Cleveland laughed: 'Mr Rusk, if it were that easy, experts like us would lose our jobs.'

I now set up a screen, and with slides I'd been accumulating, gave a preview of the Rusk museum, with the experts gasping at the beauty of some of the artwork we'd located but not yet

1499

purchased, and several times some museum curator would sigh: 'I'd like to get that one!' at which a member of our staff would warn: 'Remember, we promised that Fort Worth would get first crack.'

I showed a marvelous Winslow Homer, one of the finest George Bellows prizefight canvases, cattle-roping scenes by Tom Lea, Charley Russell and Frederick Remington, a masterful George Bingham which someone said we might get for $800,000 and a wonderful semi-hunting scene by Georgia O'Keeffe. But the one which brought cheers was a football scene by Wayne Thebaud entitled 'Running Guard 77,' in which an exhausted lineman sat dejected on the bench, his huge numbers filling the canvas.

Nineteen fine paintings in all flashed across that screen, and at the end the man from the Met said: Mr Rusk, if you can land those nineteen beauties, you're in business. Add nineteen like them, and you have a museum.'

And then Rusk returned to his penetrating question: 'How long to buy them? Assuming we can find the money?' and the men agreed: 'Maybe three years. If you're lucky.'

'I can't wait three years,' Rusk said. 'Why don't we borrow them? Let people see the kind of stuff we're after?'

A hush fell over the darkened room as these wise men, who had assembled so many enlightening and enriching shows of borrowed art, contemplated this perceptive question, and finally the man from Boston said, with guarded enthusiasm: 'Mr Rusk, if it were done right, and if you could establish a committee of sufficient gravity to give the thing credibility with the foreign museums ... goodness!'

His confreres were less inhibited: 'It's never been done!' 'It's a capital idea!' 'I can think right now of forty items you'll have to have ... and probably can get!' I had rarely seen a workable idea catch such immediate fire, and within the hour we had put together recommendations for a prestigious group of financial and publicity sponsors. Reaching for the list, Rusk began telephoning the well-known men and women and received the consent of most. At the same time the rest of us were drawing up a list of great works of art from various museums in the world, and plans were launched to request loans for a huge show to open the Fort Worth Sports Museum. When Texans dream, they do so in technicolor.

Then something happened which brought our meeting back to an equally exciting reality. A New York dealer who had sat outside waiting to present seven good canvases for my inspection, asked if he could now come in, and I was pleased to see that these world-famous experts were always eager to see whatever the art world was putting forth.

He was a modest man, as were his seven canvases, but after we had been soaring in the empyrean it was good to come back to earth: 'These are fine works of museum quality and condition. I wanted you to see what is immediately available.' And he showed us a perfectly splendid painting by a man I had not heard of, Jon Corbino, of athletes posturing on a beach, and then an exhilarating oil by Fletcher Martin titled 'Out at Second.' It presented a baseball ballet, showing the runner coming in from first with a hook slide to the right, the shortstop sweeping down with a tag from the left, and the energetic umpire throwing his arm up in the hooking 'Out' signal.

When the man completed his presentation, Rusk said: 'Would you please step outside for a moment?' and when he was gone, Ransom asked his advisers: 'I liked them. But were they good enough for a museum?' and the experts agreed they were.

'Call him in,' Rusk told me, and when the dealer returned, Rusk said: 'We'll take them all.'

'But we haven't talked price, sir.'

'Barlow will do that, and I've already warned him to offer no more than half what you ask.'

'With your permission, I've brought along a European painting I thought you might want to consider. It's certainly not American and the sport it presents isn't the way we play it today. But please take a look.' And he placed on the easel a rather small canvas painted by the Dutch painter Hendrick Avercamp, 1585–1634, showing a frozen canal near Amsterdam with lively little men in ancient costume playing ice hockey.

It was the epitome of sport – timeless, set in nature, animated, real – and in addition, it was a significant work of art. The curators and experts applauded so noisily that I cried: 'Accession Number One.'

But Rusk forestalled me: 'We want it, surely. That's just the kind of thing we do want. So old. So beautiful. But not as our first acquisition. I've already bought that, and it ought to be in Fort Worth ready for installation when we get back.'

This man Rusk never ceased to surprise me, for when I returned to Fort Worth two weeks later, I found that he had installed in the rotunda of his emerging museum a splendid antique Italian copy of perhaps the most famous sport-art item in the world, the dazzling Discobolus of Myron, dating back to the original Olympic games.

'Where'd you get it?' I asked, and he said: 'Old Italian palace. Saw it on our honeymoon and remembered it ever since.'

An art dealer from New York had come to Dallas with color slides of eight canvases relating to sport, including a Thomas Hart Benton of a rodeo cowboy trying to rope a steer, and I was concluding arrangements for their purchase when Ransom Rusk phoned urgently from Larkin: 'Come right over! Catastrophe!'

Since Rusk rarely pushed the panic button, I excused myself, hopped in the car Rusk provided when I worked in Dallas, and sped out to the mansion, where in the African Hall, I met Rusk and Mr Kramer, the armadillo expert, in mournful discussion with a Dr Philippe L'Heureux of Louisiana, a very thin man with a beard and piercing eyes. When I looked at his card and fumbled with his name, he said: 'Pronounce it Larue. Half my family changed it to that when they reached America.'

'Tell him the bad news,' Rusk said, slumping into a chair made from the tusks of elephants he and his partners had shot on safari, and L'Heureux, standing straight as if giving a laboratory lecture to a class of pre-meds, revealed a shocking situation.

'We have solid reason for believing that the armadillo not only serves as a laboratory host for the study of human leprosy but can also infect people with the disease.'

There was a painful silence as we four stared at one another. L'Heureux stood rigid, prepared to defend his accusation. Mr Kramer, whose years in retirement had focused on Texas storms and the armadillo, looked mutely from one of us to the other, unable to speak. Rusk, whose walls bespoke his constant interest in animals, was confused, and I, whose only contact with the armadillo had been chuckling at the beer advertisements which featured them, did not know what to think.

Finally L'Heureux spoke: 'We're recommending that since the threat of leprosy is real, and since we have identified five documented cases in Texas in which persons handling the animals have contracted it, all armadillos that might come into contact with humans be eradicated.'

'You mean we're to poison them?' Rusk asked.

'Or shoot them.'

Mr Kramer rose, moved about for some moments, then looked out toward the former bowling lawn: 'I could not shoot an armadillo. I suspect your evidence is nothing but rumors.'

'I wish it were,' L'Heureux said. 'But I assure you, the danger is real.'

'Actual cases?' Kramer asked, his white hair glowing in the morning sunlight.

'Yes.'

'And you're recommending extermination?' Rusk asked.

'We are. And so are the experts in Florida. And the epidemiologists in Atlanta.' And hearing this verdict delivered with such solemn authority, Rusk said: 'As responsible citizens we must do something, but what?'

'You have two choices. You can shoot them all . . .'

'I'd never do that,' Rusk snapped. 'They're my friends.'

'Or you can trap the lot and ship them to our research station in Carville, Louisiana.' While Rusk considered this, L'Heureux added: 'You'd be doing us a considerable favor. Leprosy is a terrible disease if left unchecked, only minor if treated quickly. Your armadillos could help us to solve some of the mysteries.'

'We'll let you have them,' Rusk said, and I remained in Larkin with L'Heureux for the remainder of that week while Rusk supervised a team of his illegal Mexican workmen in placing traps about the lawn. When the young armadillos there had been captured and caged for shipment, the Mexicans were loaned to Mr Kramer, who was busy trapping other animals known to be at various spots around Larkin, and when that task was completed, L'Heureux told us: 'I feel better, and assure you that you are much safer than you were a week ago.' He returned to Louisiana that afternoon, so that only Rusk, Kramer and I were present when the improvised lights came on and we saw the old mother armadillo come out alone, for her eight children were gone, and stand in perplexity in the middle of the bowling green.

Mr Kramer said: 'Don't trap her, Mr Rusk. She knows she belongs here.'

Years back, when I studied geography, a professor drummed into us the fact that we must never stumble into the pathetic fallacy, and I remember asking him what it was: 'The sentimental attributing of human motivations to inanimate objects like *angry clouds* or *the vengeful tornado*. It's particularly offensive to confer on animals such human reactions as *the mother buffalo was eager to fight off the wolves* or *the collie obviously preferred the runt of her litter*. Things are things and animals are not humans. Treat them dispassionately.'

Now, when Mr Kramer was presuming to explain what the mother armadillo was thinking, I rejected his assumptions. She was not *mourning the loss of her children*, nor was she *recalling the good times she'd had on this lawn*. My scientific training forced me to think of her as a dumb animal that might be carrying leprosy, and I felt no other emotion as I watched the workmen close in on her when Rusk signaled: 'Edge her toward the trap.'

But she had always been a canny creature, and now some instinct warned her that with the disappearance of her children, she also was in peril, so evading the trap, she scurried toward the entrance to her underground sanctuary. Normally a nimble man can run down an armadillo, and since there were three Mexicans ready to chase her, they should have nabbed her, but she made a dive between their legs and escaped.

'You'll have to shoot that one,' someone said, 'I've seen old-timers like her fool the best trappers.' So Rusk asked a servant to fetch from the African Hall a high-powered rifle used normally on elephants or Cape buffalo. Handing it to Mr Kramer, he said: 'Take care of her,' but Kramer refused to do so. Rejecting the gun, he told Rusk: 'She's your responsibility, not mine.'

I thought it appropriate that Ransom, who had in a sense sponsored the armadillos in Larkin, should eliminate the colony, and when the mother of them all came out of her hole to investigate the ominous silence, he drew a bead on her.

But he could not pull the trigger. Looking at me pleadingly,

he said: 'I can't do it,' and I found myself with the rifle . . .
   Pinnnggg!
   The armadillos of Larkin were no more.

The next months were some of the most exciting I have ever
spent, because into our temporary offices in Fort Worth came a
sequence of cables which caused us to rejoice:

> THE LOUVRE IS PLEASED TO INFORM YOU THAT WE
> SHALL BE SENDING THE DEGAS 'HORSE RACE AT AUTEUIL'
> THE CEZANNE 'WRESTLERS AT THE BEACH' AND
> THE LA TOUR 'DUEL AT MIDNIGHT.'

From Tokyo came word that a museum would ship nine
Japanese prints of the most glowing quality depicting the
greatest of the ancient sumo wrestlers, one Tanikaze, who
flourished in the late eighteenth century. When they arrived I
decided that they must have a small room of their own, for they
were bound to be one of the hits of the opening show: this
massive human figure, more than three hundred and fifty
pounds, with its sense of controlled power, all shown in high
style by four different artists of world class.

   The cable from the Prado in Madrid caused both jubilation
and fracas, because we were being sent a precious first printing
of Goya's remarkable series of etchings on bullfighting, plus a
glowing canvas of same, and our Mexican population showered
encomiums upon us for paying this tribute to Hispanic art, but
a dedicated women's group opposed to bullfighting warned that
they would picket our opening if it included the Goyas, and a
wild brouhaha erupted in the press.

   Less provocative was the cable from Scotland promising a
rare series of prints depicting the development of golf; Rusk
appreciated that. But another cable from London pitched us
into serious trouble:

> WE SHALL BE SENDING YOU A NOTABLE COLLECTION
> OF RARE PRINTS AND CANVASES BIG ENOUGH TO FILL
> TWO ROOMS, SHOWING THE WORLD'S MOST POPULAR SPORT,
> IF ATTENDANCE ALONE IS THE CRITERION,
> HORSE RACING.

I was delighted with the prospect of hanging that part of the show, because I like horses, but an anonymous group of Irish patriots warned that if this English display was shown, the new museum would be bombed.

It was now apparent that this opening show was going to be not only a spectacular success, with art of the highest quality from unexpected corners of the world, but also the first-ever of its kind, and as I studied photographs of the three hundred items that would comprise the exhibition and began to allot each to its probable location in the building which was being rushed to conclusion, I became aware that I was making decisions that ought to be the prerogative of whoever was going to direct the museum over the long run, but we had no director, and I took steps to correct this deficiency.

'Mr Rusk, you really must get your top man in position . . . and soon.'

'I have that in hand, Barlow,' he assured me, and the next day as I sat in his office I overheard two of the strangest phone calls of my life. My close contact with Rusk over the past years had made me appreciate the man; I had watched him grow in courage during the disasters and in wisdom as he reached out to embrace a larger world. Before my eyes he had matured, as I hoped I would mature in my new position; I not only liked him now, I respected him. However, he could at times do the damnedest things, and these two calls ranked high on the roster of Rusk improbables.

'Get me Tom Landry,' he told his secretary, and shortly he was speaking to the coach of the Dallas Cowboys: 'Tom, this is Ransom. Yes. Tom, I need your confidential advice. Is Wolfgang Macnab what you would call manly?'

I could hear Landry sputter as he defended his linebacker, after which Rusk said: 'I know all that, Tom, but you must have heard the stories that are surfacing. Defensive tackles kissing each other at the end of the game.' Again Landry sputtered, so Rusk put it to him straight: 'Tom, can you assure me that Wolfgang is manly? You know what I mean . . . not queer?'

Apparently Landry wanted to know what in hell Rusk was talking about, and he must have given Ransom a dressing down, because Rusk said: 'Of course he's my son-in-law, but a lot's riding on this and I have to be sure. Any man who studies art, you've got to suspect him.' Landry made some comment, and Rusk continued: 'You ought to see some of the so-called experts up in New York who've been spending my money. Yes, for my new museum. If you ever left Dallas and came over to God's country in Fort Worth you'd know about it.'

Assured by Landry that Wolfgang Macnab was a macho terror, Rusk now called his trusted friend Joe Robbie of the Miami Dolphins and asked me to listen in:

RUSK: Hiya, Joe. Your old buddy Rance Rusk.

ROBBIE: You fellows showing anything this year?

RUSK: Always enough to beat you bums. Joe, I want to ask a very personal question. Most important to me.

ROBBIE: Shoot. I owe you one for your help on our boy Martínez.

RUSK: In your opinion, is Wolfgang Macnab manly?

ROBBIE: Hell, Don Shula's been trying to get him for three years. Shula doesn't fool around.

RUSK: I know he's a good player, the One-Man Gang they call him. But is he ... you know what I mean?

ROBBIE: How would I know anything like that? All my players are Democrats.

RUSK: You know those rumors about football professionals. That bit about defensive tackles.

ROBBIE: Forget it. Macnab's the best.

That afternoon Rusk summoned Wolfgang Macnab to his office, and when the All-Pro was seated, Rance said out of the blue: 'Son, I want you to be the director of my sports museum. Don't speak. You've got one, two more years of professional ball. Good, stay with it. But at our big press conference Friday, I want to announce you as our director.'

'I love art, Mr Rusk. I know something about it ... but director? A major museum?'

'If you can handle those Pittsburgh running backs, you can handle a bunch of paintings.'

'You know, sir, I take art far more seriously than I do football. I'm not kidding around.'

'I wouldn't want you if you were.'

They discussed salary, and Macnab almost fell out of his chair at its proposed size. So did I.

And then the young man showed his maturity by asking a penetrating question: 'As director, would I have a small budget for acquisition of new works?'

'You sure would. As of today, assuming you take the job, you have thirty-two million dollars on deposit.'

When Macnab blanched, no more stunned than I, Rusk rose and put his arm about his shoulders: 'Never forget, son, when you represent Texas always go first class.'

THE END

TO FIND OUT ABOUT A
FANTASTIC HOLIDAY OFFER
PLEASE TURN THE PAGE

£100

TEXAS TOURS
£100

⊙ per person discount ⊙

on the special Texas Tours featured on the inside back cover of this book.

This voucher is redeemable only when used against the price of the tours departing 20 October 1987 and 10 November 1987. No cash refund or alternative payment will be given. Valid only in conjunction with the completed Booking Form and deposit.

£100

£100

£100